Patterns of global terrorism 1985-2005 :
REF 303.6 PAT   28425

Antioch Community High School

D1689363

Antioch Community High School
Library
1133 S. Main Street
Antioch, IL 60002

DEMCO

PATTERNS of GLOBAL TERRORISM 1985–2005

U.S. DEPARTMENT OF STATE REPORTS WITH SUPPLEMENTARY DOCUMENTS AND STATISTICS

PATTERNS of GLOBAL TERRORISM 1985–2005

U.S. DEPARTMENT OF STATE REPORTS WITH SUPPLEMENTARY DOCUMENTS AND STATISTICS

Anna Sabasteanski, Editor

www.PatternsofGlobalTerrorism.com

Volume Two

BERKSHIRE PUBLISHING GROUP

Great Barrington, Massachusetts U.S.A.

Copyright © 2005 by Berkshire Publishing Group LLC

All rights reserved. No part of this book may be reproduced or utilized in any form or by any means, electronic or mechanical, including photocopying, recording, or by any information storage and retrieval system, without permission in writing from the publisher.

Most of the material included in this collection was obtained from the U.S. government. Some of the data has been retrieved from the MIPT Terrorism Knowledge Base, accessed between July and September of 2005, from the website at http://www.tkb.org. The Terrorism Knowledge Base is the property of the National Memorial Institute for the Prevention of Terrorism (MIPT) (http://www.mipt.org) and incorporates information from MIPT and third parties, which is the property of the respective copyright holders. In some cases, quotations and other material have been incorporated under "fair use" provisions of the Copyright Act.

This collection contains information compiled from sources we believe to be reliable, and we have used our best efforts to ensure accuracy of the material. However, errors may be present. Berkshire Publishing Group and its partners disclaim any liability for direct, indirect, secondary or any other damages resulting from use of this material.

Adverse mention of individuals associated with any political, social, ethnic, religious, or national group does not imply that all members of that group are terrorists.

Inclusion of web links (URLs) does not imply endorsement, nor are we responsible in any way for the content of third-party websites.

For information:
Berkshire Publishing Group LLC
314 Main Street
Great Barrington, Massachusetts 01230
www.berkshirepublishing.com

Printed in the United States of America

Library of Congress Cataloging-in-Publication Data
Patterns of global terrorism 1985–2005: U.S. Department of State reports with supplementary documents and statistics/Anna Sabasteanski, editor.
    p. cm.
  Summary: "A comprehensive reference—designed for military, government, and security professionals as well as students of politics, international relations, history, public policy, homeland security, foreign policy, emergency management, and military science—that collates the U.S. Department of State reports on terrorism, Patterns of Global Terrorism, with additional analytical and statistical material"—Provided by publisher.
  Includes index.
  ISBN 0-9743091-3-3 (alk. paper)
  1. Terrorism—Sources. 2. Terrorism—Statistics. I. Sabasteanski, Anna, 1958–
  HV6431.P3773 2005
  303.6'2509049—dc22   2005026976

Contents

Reader's Guide ix

Publisher's Preface xiii

Introduction xv

Acknowledgments xxvii

About the Editors xxviii

Part 1 Counterterrorism 1

U.S. Policies in Combating Terrorism *4*
U.S. Legal Response *27*
Sanctions *35*
State Sponsors of Terrorism *52*
Terrorist Financing *111*
U.S. Military Response *135*
International Response *142*

Part 2 International Terrorist Groups 151

Part 3 Country Reports 1985–2004 203

Part 4 Chronology of Significant Terrorist Incidents 1961–2005 725

v

Part 5 Terrorist Incidents by Country and Group 1985–2004 859

Tables of Terrorist Incidents by Country 1985–2004   *861*

Maps of Terrorist Incidents by Country 1985–2004   *883*

Tables of Terrorist Incidents by Group 1985–2005   *924*

Part 6 Trends over Time: Graphs on Terrorism 971

Incidents   *974*

Casualties   *979*

Targets   *986*

Tactics   *1009*

Index   1021

Reader's Guide

The Reader's Guide below serves as an expanded table of contents, allowing you to see in the space of four pages all the elements of Patterns of Global Terrorism *grouped by topic or, in the case of the* Country Reports *and collateral documents, by chronology.*

Introduction to *Patterns of Global Terrorism 1985–2005: U.S. Department of State Reports with Supplementary Documents and Statistics*

Part 1 Counterterrorism

Overview of Counterterrorism *Anna Sabasteanski*

U.S. Policies in Combating Terrorism
Overview of U.S. Policies in Combating Terrorism *Anna Sabasteanski*
Policy Developments After September 11 *Patterns of Global Terrorism 2002*
Present U.S. Policy *George W. Bush Speech*
Foreign Terrorist Organization Designations *Anna Sabasteanski*
Combating Terrorism: Department of State Programs to Combat Terrorism Abroad *GAO Report*
Terrorism and National Security: Issues and Trends *CRS Report*

U.S. Legal Response
Overview of U.S. Legal Response *Anna Sabasteanski*
Selections from *Patterns of Global Terrorism 1987 and 1996–2003*

Sanctions
Overview of Sanctions *Anna Sabasteanski*
Sanctions Lists

Economic Sanctions to Achieve U.S. Foreign Policy Goals *CRS Report*

State Sponsors of Terrorism
Overview of State Sponsors of Terrorism *Anna Sabasteanski*
Collated Reports on State Sponsors of Terrorism *Patterns of Global Terrorism*
  Afghanistan, Cuba, Iran, Iraq, Libya, Nicaragua, North Korea, South Yemen, Soviet Union and Eastern Europe, Sudan, and Syria

Terrorist Financing
Overview of Terrorist Financing *Anna Sabasteanski*
Countering Terrorism on the Economic Front *Patterns of Global Terrorism 2002 and 2003*
U.S. Measures Implementing the 2004 U.S.-EU Declaration on Combating Terrorism *U.S. Department of State*
Narcoterrorism *Patterns of Global Terrorism 1989*
Money Laundering and Terrorist Financing in the Middle East and South Asia *U.S. Department of State*
Terrorist Financing: The 9/11 Commission Recommendation *CRS Report*
The Financial Action Task Force: An Overview *CRS Report*

U.S. Military Response
Overview of U.S. Military Response *Anna Sabasteanski*
The Military Campaign in Afghanistan, 2001 *Patterns of Global Terrorism 2001*
The Military Counterterrorism Campaign in 2002 *Patterns of Global Terrorism 2002*

The Military Counterterrorism Campaign in 2003 *Patterns of Global Terrorism 2003*

Iraq and Terrorism *Patterns of Global Terrorism 2003*

The Evolving Terrorist Threat *Patterns of Global Terrorism* 2004

International Response

Overview of International Response *Anna Sabasteanski*

International Response to September 11 *Patterns of Global Terrorism 2001*

U.N. Actions Against Terrorism *Patterns of Global Terrorism 2001*

International Counterterrorism Laws *Anna Sabasteanski*

Part 2 International Terrorist Groups

Overview of International Terrorist Groups *Anna Sabasteanski*

The "FTO List" and Congress: Sanctioning Designated Foreign Terrorist Organizations *CRS Report*

Profiles of International Terrorist Groups Collated from *Patterns of Global Terrorism 1985–2004*

Part 3 Country Reports 1985–2004

Overview of Country Reports *Anna Sabasteanski*

Terrorism in the 1980s

Overview of Terrorism in the 1980s *Anna Sabasteanski*

Patterns of Global Terrorism 1985
Patterns of Global Terrorism 1986
Patterns of Global Terrorism 1987
Patterns of Global Terrorism 1988
Patterns of Global Terrorism 1989

Terrorism in the 1990s

Overview of Terrorism in the 1990s *Anna Sabasteanski*

Patterns of Global Terrorism 1990
Patterns of Global Terrorism 1991
Patterns of Global Terrorism 1992
Patterns of Global Terrorism 1993
Patterns of Global Terrorism 1994
Patterns of Global Terrorism 1995
Patterns of Global Terrorism 1996
Patterns of Global Terrorism 1997
Patterns of Global Terrorism 1998
Patterns of Global Terrorism 1999

Terrorism in the New Millennium

Overview of Terrorism in the New Millennium *Anna Sabasteanski*

Patterns of Global Terrorism 2000
Patterns of Global Terrorism 2001
Patterns of Global Terrorism 2002
Patterns of Global Terrorism 2003

Rollout of Patterns of Global Terrorism 2003 *Department of State Transcripts*

The Department of State's Patterns of Global Terrorism Report: Trends, State Sponsors, and Related Issues *CRS Report*

Review of the Department of State's Patterns of Global Terrorism Report 2003 *Office of the Inspector General's Report*

Proposals for Intelligence Reorganization, 1949–2004 *CRS Report*

Terrorism: Key Recommendations of the 9/11 Commission and Recent Major Commissions and Inquiries *CRS Report*

Country Reports on Terrorism 2004

Global Jihad: Evolving and Adapting *Country Reports on Terrorism 2004*

Release of Country Reports on Terrorism for 2004 *U.S. Department of State Transcripts*

Reviewing the Department of State's Annual Report on Terrorism *U.S. House of Representatives Hearing*

The National Counterterrorism Center: Implementation Challenges and Issues for Congress *CRS Report*

Part 4 Chronology of Significant Terrorist Incidents 1961–2005

Overview of Chronology of Significant Terrorist Incidents 1961–2005 *Anna Sabasteanski*

Chronology of Significant Terrorist Incidents 1961–2005

Part 5 Terrorist Incidents by Country and Group 1985–2004

Overview of Terrorist Incidents by Country 1985–2004 *Anna Sabasteanski*

Tables of Terrorist Incidents by Country 1985–2004
  Overview of Tables of Terrorist Incidents by Country 1985–2004 *Anna Sabasteanski*

Maps of Terrorist Incidents by Country 1985–2004
  Overview of Maps of Terrorist Incidents by Country 1985–2004 *Anna Sabasteanski*

Tables of Terrorist Incidents by Group 1985–2005
  Overview of Tables of Terrorist Incidents by Group 1985–2005 *Anna Sabasteanski*

Part 6 Trends over Time: Graphs on Terrorism

Overview of Trends over Time: Graphs on Terrorism *Anna Sabasteanski*

Incidents
  Overview of Incidents *Anna Sabasteanski*
  Terrorist Incidents and Incidents by Region (1981–2004)
  Anti-United States Attacks and Non-United States Attacks (1981–2004)
  Anti-United States Attacks and Non-United States Attacks as Percentages of Total Attacks (1981–2004)
  Anti-United States Attacks by Region (1981–2004)

Casualties
  Overview of Casualties *Anna Sabasteanski*
  Number of People Killed and Injured by Region (1968–2004)
  Number of Deaths by Region (1968–2004)
  Number of Injuries by Region (1968–2004)
  International Casualties by Region (1988–2004)
  Anti-United States Casualties (1988–2004)
  Anti-United States and Non-United States Casualties as Percentages of Total Casualties (1988–2004)

Targets
  Overview of Targets *Anna Sabasteanski*
  Abortion-Related—Incidents, Injuries, and Fatalities (1968–2005)
  Airports and Airlines—Incidents, Injuries, and Fatalities (1968–2005)
  Businesses—Incidents, Injuries, and Fatalities (1968–2005)
  Diplomatic—Incidents, Injuries, and Fatalities (1968–2005)
  Educational Institutions—Incidents, Injuries, and Fatalities (1968–2005)
  Food Water Supply—Incidents, Injuries, and Fatalities (1968–2005)
  Government—Incidents, Injuries, and Fatalities (1968–2005)
  Journalists and Media—Incidents, Injuries, and Fatalities (1968–2005)
  Maritime—Incidents, Injuries, and Fatalities (1968–2005)
  Military—Incidents, Injuries, and Fatalities (1968–2005)
  Non-Governmental Organizations—Incidents, Injuries, and Fatalities (1968–2005)
  Other Targets—Incidents, Injuries, and Fatalities (1968–2005)

Police-Related—Incidents, Injuries, and
  Fatalities (1968–2005)
Private Citizens and Property—Incidents,
  Injuries, and Fatalities (1968–2005)
Religious Figures or Institutions—Incidents,
  Injuries, and Fatalities (1968–2005)
Telecommunications—Incidents, Injuries, and
  Fatalities (1968–2005)
Terrorists—Incidents, Injuries, and Fatalities
  (1968–2005)
Tourists—Incidents, Injuries, and Fatalities
  (1968–2005)
Transportation—Incidents, Injuries, and
  Fatalities (1968–2005)
Unknown—Incidents, Injuries, and Fatalities
  (1968–2005)
Utilities—Incidents, Injuries, and Fatalities
  (1968–2005)
Number of Attacks on Business, Diplomatic,
  Government, Military, Other Facilities
  (1989–2003)

Tactics
Overview of Tactics *Anna Sabasteanski*
Armed Attacks—Incidents, Injuries, and
  Fatalities (1968–2005)

Arson—Incidents, Injuries, and Fatalities
  (1968–2005)
Assassination—Incidents, Injuries, and
  Fatalities (1968–2005)
Barricade/Hostage—Incidents, Injuries, and
  Fatalities (1968–2005)
Bombing—Incidents, Injuries, and Fatalities
  (1968–2005)
Hijacking—Incidents, Injuries, and Fatalities
  (1968–2005)
Kidnapping—Incidents, Injuries, and Fatalities
  (1968–2005)
Other—Incidents, Injuries, and Fatalities
  (1968–2005)
Unconventional Attack—Incidents, Injuries,
  and Fatalities (1968–2005)
Unknown Tactics—Incidents, Injuries, and
  Fatalities (1968–2005)

Index

Notes

Spelling conventions have varied through the years and between organizations within and outside the government. For example, within these volumes a reader will see "al-Qaeda" in one government document and "al-Qaida" in another. When possible, however, we have standardized inconsistent spellings within particular reports so that they would not appear to be typographic errors. We have listed alternate spellings in our index.

Also, the footnotes in the *Country Reports* are from the reports themselves; the pronouns "we" and "our" referred to in them relate to the State Department. However, in the early footnotes Berkshire Publishing does interject the information that the State Department's definitions of terrorist incidents can be found in Berkshire's own Introduction to this work.

PATTERNS of GLOBAL TERRORISM 1985–2005

U.S. DEPARTMENT OF STATE REPORTS WITH
SUPPLEMENTARY DOCUMENTS AND STATISTICS

Patterns of Global Terrorism 2002/Western Hemisphere/Canada, continued from Volume 1, page 535.

In the autumn, Canada also became the first country to ratify the Inter-American Convention Against Terrorism, which was opened for signature in June. Canadian armed forces participated in Operation Enduring Freedom with the largest deployment of Canadian troops overseas since the Korean War. Canada also maintained a naval task force group engaged in interdiction operations in the Arabian Sea. On 5 December 2002, the United States and Canada established a binational planning group at North American Aerospace Defense Command (NORAD) to prepare contingency plans to respond to threats and attacks and other major emergencies in Canada or the United States.

Mexico

Mexico remained a strong supporter of the global war on terrorism during 2002. The Mexican Senate ratified three international conventions on counterterrorism. The UN International Convention for the Suppression of Terrorist Bombing and the UN International Convention for the Suppression of the Financing of Terrorism were ratified on 29 October, and the Inter-American Counterterrorism Convention was signed in June and ratified in November. Mexico's military has been on high alert since the September 11 attacks, with increased military checkpoints throughout the country. Mexico has cooperated fully with the United States in implementing a 22-point border-action plan signed in March that aims to improve border infrastructure, expedite the secure flow of people, and facilitate the secure flow of goods across the United States-Mexico border.

There were no international acts of terrorism in Mexico within the past five years, but during times of demonstrations outside the US Embassy, the Mexican Government routinely cooperated by providing extra security to the Embassy. Notably, Mexico closed the offices of the Revolutionary Armed Forces of Colombia in Mexico City in April 2002, after a presence of 10 years.

Patterns of Global Terrorism 2003

The Year in Review

There were 190 acts of international terrorism in 2003, a slight decrease from the 198 attacks that occurred in 2002, and a drop of 45 percent from the level in 2001 of 346 attacks. The figure in 2003 represents the lowest annual total of international terrorist attacks since 1969.

A total of 307 persons were killed in the attacks of 2003, far fewer than the 725 killed during 2002. A total of 1,593 persons were wounded in the attacks that occurred in 2003, down from 2,013 persons wounded the year before.

In 2003, the highest number of attacks (70) and the highest casualty count (159 persons dead and 951 wounded) occurred in Asia.

There were 82 anti-US attacks in 2003, which is up slightly from the 77 attacks the previous year, and represents a 62-percent decrease from the 219 attacks recorded in 2001. Thirty-five American citizens died in 15 international terrorist attacks in 2003:

- Michael Rene Pouliot was killed on 21 January in Kuwait when a gunman fired at his vehicle that had halted at a stoplight.
- Thomas Janis was murdered by Revolutionary Armed Forces of Colombia terrorists on 13 February in Colombia. Mr. Janis was the pilot of a plane owned by Southern Command that crashed in the jungle. He and a Colombian army officer were wounded in the crash and shot when the terrorists discovered them. Three American passengers on the plane—Keith Stansell, Marc D. Gonsalves, and Thomas R. Howes—were kidnapped and are still being held hostage.
- William Hyde was killed on 4 March in Davao, Philippines, when a bomb hidden in a backpack exploded in a crowded airline terminal. Twenty other persons died, and 146 were wounded. The Moro Islamic Liberation Front (MILF) denies any connection to the suspected bomber who claimed he was an MILF member.
- Abigail Elizabeth Litle was killed on 5 March when a suicide bomber boarded a bus in Haifa, Israel, and detonated an explosive device.
- Rabbi Elnatan Eli Horowitz and his wife Debra Ruth Horowitz were killed on 7 March when a Palestinian gunman opened fire on them as they were eating dinner in the settlement of Kiryat Arba.
- The deadliest anti-US attack occurred in Riyadh, Saudi Arabia, on 12 May when suicide bombers in booby-trapped cars filled with explosives drove into the Vinnell Jadewel and Al-Hamra housing compounds, killing nine US citizens. Killed at the Vinnell compound were: Obaidah Yusuf Abdullah, Todd Michael Blair, Jason Eric Bentley, James Lee Carpenter II, Herman Diaz, Alex Jackson, Quincy Lee Knox, and Clifford J. Lawson. Mohammed Atef Al Kayyaly was killed at the Al-Hamra compound.
- Alan Beer and Bertin Joseph Tita were killed on 11 June in a bus bombing near Klal Center on Jaffa Road near Jerusalem.
- Howard Craig Goldstein was killed in a shooting attack near the West Bank settlement of Ofra on 20 June.
- Fred Bryant, a civilian contractor, was killed on 5 August in Tikrit, Iraq, when his car ran over an improvised explosive device.
- Three Americans were among the victims of a deadly truck bombing of the UN headquarters in Baghdad's Canal Hotel on 19 August. They were Arthur Helton, Richard Hooper, and Martha Teas. UN Special Representative Sergio Vieira de Mello was also among the 23 fatalities.
- Five Americans were killed in Jerusalem on 19 August when a suicide bomber riding on a bus detonated explo-

sives attached to his body. They were Goldy Zarkowsky, Eli Zarkowsky, Mordechai Reinitz, Yessucher Dov Reinitz, and Tehilla Nathansen. Fifteen other persons were killed and 140 wounded in the attack.

- Dr. David Applebaum and his daughter Naava Applebaum were killed on 9 September in a bombing at the Cafe Hillel in Jerusalem.
- Three Americans were killed on 15 October in Gaza Strip as their US Embassy Tel Aviv motorcade was struck by an apparent roadside blast. They were John Branchizio, Mark T. Parson, and John Martin Linde, Jr. All three were security contractors.
- Lt. Col. Charles H. Buehring was killed on 26 October in Baghdad during a rocket-propelled grenade attack on the Al-Rasheed Hotel. Deputy Secretary of Defense Paul D. Wolfowitz was staying at the hotel at the time of the attack.
- Two Americans, William Carlson and Christopher Glenn Mueller, were killed in an ambush by armed militants in Shkin, Afghanistan, on 27 October. Both were US Government contract workers.

Note: Most of the attacks that have occurred during Operation Iraqi Freedom and Operation Enduring Freedom do not meet the longstanding US definition of international terrorism because they were directed at combatants, that is, US and Coalition forces on duty. Attacks against noncombatants, that is, civilians and military personnel who at the time of the incident were unarmed and/or not on duty, are judged as terrorist attacks.

Africa Overview

Westerners and Africans alike continued to be the victims of terrorism in Africa during 2003. Nevertheless, the cooperation of African governments in the war on terrorism improved and strengthened during the year.

East Africa, particularly Somalia, continued to pose the most serious threat to American interests due to the presence of active al-Qaida elements.

In nearby Kenya, a policeman was killed in August when a terrorist suspect detonated a hand grenade, killing the suspect and the policeman, but permitting a confederate of the suspect to escape. As a result of this and other events, Kenyan authorities reevaluated their views of terrorism. They appear to have concluded that terrorism in Kenya is not just a foreign problem and that terrorism has put down roots in Kenya too.

The US East Africa Counterterrorism Initiative (EACTI) has dedicated sizeable resources to improving police and judicial counterterrorist capabilities in the East African countries of Kenya, Uganda, Tanzania, Djibouti, Eritrea, and Ethiopia. The EACTI also provides training and some equipment for special counterterrorism units for senior-level decisionmakers and for legislators who are concerned with drafting legislation on terrorist financing and money laundering. EACTI also includes a strong public diplomacy and outreach component.

During February and March, an Algerian terrorist group, the Salafist Group for Call and Combat (GSPC), kidnapped some 30 European tourists in Algeria. They took their captives to Mali, whose government was instrumental in securing their release in August. Members of the GSPC continued to hide in the Sahel region, crossing difficult-to-patrol borders between Mali, Mauritania, Niger, and Algeria.

The United States continued to work with the Governments of Mali, Mauritania, Niger, and Chad on the implementation of the Pan-Sahel Initiative, a program designed to assist those nations in protecting their borders, combating terrorism, and enhancing regional stability. Components of the program are intended to encourage the participating countries to cooperate with each other against smuggling and trafficking in persons, as well as in the sharing of information.

Africans themselves have taken cooperative action against terrorism. Many nations made real efforts to sign and ratify the 12 international conventions and protocols relating to terrorism. Botswana, Ghana, Kenya, Mali, and Sudan have signed all 12 protocols. The African Union (AU) has designated Algiers as the location of an AU counterterrorism center. Several nations have formed national counterterrorism centers.

The Revolutionary United Front of Sierra Leone no longer exists as a terrorist organization, although some former members have organized a political party that has a small following. The Allied Democratic Front terrorist organization in Uganda has lost the ability to function as a group. However, the Lord's Resistance Army (LRA) continues to kill and plunder Ugandan civilians and villages, even though the Ugandan Government has offered amnesty (though not for all) and negotiations with the group. Sudan appears to have cut off the supplies for the LRA in large part. Sudan itself remains one of seven state sponsors of terrorism, however, and is discussed in the state sponsorship section of this report.

Angola

With a year having passed since the final peace agreement ending the Angolan civil war, Angola has made limited progress in reconstruction and national reconciliation. As a nonpermanent member of the United Nations Security Council, Angola actively supported UN antiterrorism efforts. It has publicly condemned acts of international terrorism and has worked domestically to strengthen immigration and border controls. In the past, Cabindan separatists have kidnapped Westerners, including an American citizen in 1990; however, there were no reports of terrorist incidents in Angola this year.

Djibouti

Djibouti, a staunch supporter in the global war on terrorism and a member of the Arab League, has taken a strong stand against international terrorist organizations and individuals. Djibouti hosts the only US military base in Sub-Saharan Africa. In addition to US forces, it hosts Coalition forces from four other countries including France, Germany, Spain, and

Italy. There were no confirmed acts of domestic or transnational terrorism in Djibouti in 2003, but the Government took extraordinary measures from its limited resources to try and ensure the safety and security of Westerners posted in Djibouti. The Government also began an aggressive immigration campaign to remove illegal aliens from Djibouti in an attempt to weed out potential terrorists. The Government also has closed down terrorist-linked financial institutions and shared security information on possible terrorist activity in the region. The counterterrorism committee under President Guelleh moved to enhance coordination and action on information concerning terrorist organizations.

In October 2002, the United States established the Combined Joint Task Force–Horn of Africa (CJTF–HOA). Based in Djibouti, CJTF–HOA coordinates Coalition counterterrorism operations in six East African countries and Yemen.

Djibouti is a party to three of the 12 international conventions and protocols relating to terrorism and signed the Convention for the Suppression of the Financing of Terrorism on 15 November 2001.

Ethiopia

Ethiopia has been consistently helpful in its cooperation in the global war on terrorism. Significant counterterrorism activities included political, financial, media, military, and law-enforcement actions. To counter the threat from the Somalia-based Al-Ittihad al-Islami (AIAI), Ethiopia has undertaken increased military efforts to control its lengthy and porous border with Somalia. The Government also has enhanced counterterrorism coordination with the United States.

Ethiopia is a party to seven of the 12 international conventions and protocols relating to terrorism.

Kenya

Kenya remains a responsive and active partner in the war on terrorism, providing assistance with ongoing terrorist investigations and stepping up efforts to target terrorist groups operating within Kenya. In 2003, Kenya began to more vigorously address institutional weaknesses that impede its ability to pursue terrorists and respond to threats. In April of 2003, Kenya published a draft "Suppression of Terrorism" bill and is in the process of redrafting the bill to incorporate concerns from civil society leaders who fear the bill may violate human rights.

Kenya and the United States continue to share information on suspected terrorists, including those associated with or supportive of al-Qaida. It has taken the initiative in arresting terrorist suspects and disrupting terrorist operations. Kenya, for example, is an active participant in the Terrorist Interdiction Program. As one of the nations affected by the East Africa bombings in 1998, Kenya remains fully cooperative in assisting the US investigations of those attacks.

The Kenyan Government has been more outspoken on the domestic nature of Kenya's terrorist threat and the involvement of Kenyan nationals in terrorist activity, particularly after a policeman was killed while attempting to apprehend suspected terrorists in August 2003. Kenyan Cabinet ministers, some of whom had earlier downplayed the terrorist presence in Kenya, have called for communities to be vigilant in looking for terrorists working in their midst. Courageous leadership combined with success in revealing and disrupting terrorist activity has contributed to a nationwide change of attitude toward terrorism in 2003.

Kenya has ratified all 12 international counterterrorism conventions and protocols.

Mali

Mali has taken consistent and active steps to combat terrorism and has been particularly responsive on terrorist financing issues. The Government, for example, regularly distributes terrorist finance watch lists to the banking system.

The Malian Government has been receptive to the idea of strengthening its borders and is the key recipient of the Pan-Sahel Initiative, which is primarily focused on common border-security issues with Chad, Niger, Mali, and Mauritania. There were no acts of terrorism against US interests in Mali during 2003. However, the Government was actively involved in the freeing of European tourists in northern Mali who had been kidnapped in Algeria by the Algeria-based terrorist group the Salafist Group for Preaching and Combat.

Mali has ratified all 12 UN conventions and protocols relating to terrorism.

Nigeria

Nigeria remained committed to the global war against terrorism and has continued diplomatic efforts in both global and regional forums concerning counterterrorism issues. The President and other African heads of state founded the New Partnership for African Development—geared toward sustainable development in Africa—which has helped African countries combat terrorism.

Nigeria has been helping to monitor threats to US citizens living in Nigeria and has cooperated with the United States on tracking and freezing terrorists' assets. Nigeria's relatively large and complex banking sector, combined with widespread corruption, makes combating terrorism financing more difficult, however. The Government has actively shared information about the rise of radical Islam in Nigeria—home of Africa's largest Muslim population.

Nigeria is a party to six of the 12 international conventions and protocols relating to terrorism, including the Convention for the Suppression of the Financing of Terrorism.

Rwanda

The Rwandan Government has continued to give full support to US-led efforts to combat terrorism. The Government has been responsive to US requests to eradicate terrorism financing and has increased surveillance of airports, border controls, and hotel registrations in an effort to identify potential terrorists. Rwanda established an intergovernmental counterterrorism committee and has an antiterrorism section in its police intelligence unit.

During 2003, the Government aggressively pursued the Democratic Forces for the Liberation of Rwanda, formerly known as the Army for the Liberation of Rwanda (ALIR), an armed rebel force composed of former soldiers and supporters of the previous government that orchestrated the genocide in 1994. The group, which operates in the Democratic Republic of the Congo, employs terrorist tactics. In 1999, ALIR was responsible for the kidnapping and murder of nine persons, including two US tourists in Bwindi Park. With the assistance of Rwandan authorities in 2003, three suspects in the attack were transferred to the United States for prosecution, and other evidence was obtained through interviews with witnesses.

Rwanda is a party to eight of the 12 international counterterrorism conventions and protocols.

Sierra Leone

The Government of Sierra Leone has cooperated in the struggle against terrorism. The Revolutionary United Front, essentially dismantled by the imprisonment of its leader Foday Sankoh in 2001, has disappeared as a terrorist organization, although some of its former members have organized into a political party that has attracted a small following. Allegations of West African and particularly Sierra Leonean diamonds being used by al-Qaida to finance terrorism have not been proven.

The government of Sierra Leone is a party to seven of the 12 international conventions and protocols relating to terrorism.

Somalia

Somalia's lack of a functioning central government; protracted state of violent instability; and long coastline, porous borders, and proximity to the Arabian Peninsula make it a potential location for international terrorists seeking a transit or launching point to conduct operations elsewhere. Regional efforts to bring about a national reconciliation and establish peace and stability in Somalia were ongoing in 2003. The US Government does not have official relations with any entity in Somalia. Although the ability of Somali entities to carry out counterterrorism activities is constrained, some have taken limited actions in this direction.

Members of the Somali-based AIAI have committed terrorist acts in the past, primarily in Ethiopia. AIAI was originally formed in the early 1990s with a goal of creating an Islamic state in Somalia. In recent years, AIAI has become highly factionalized, and its membership is difficult to define. Some elements of AIAI continue to pose a regional domestic threat, other factions may be targeting Western interests in the region, while still other elements are concerned with humanitarian issues. At least one faction is sympathetic to al-Qaida and has provided assistance to its members.

Somalia has signed, but has yet to become a party to, the Convention for the Suppression of the Financing of Terrorism.

South Africa

South Africa has taken a number of actions in 2003 as part of the global war on terrorism. It has declared its support for the antiterrorism Coalition and has shared financial, law-enforcement, and intelligence information with the United States. Approximately one year after President Mbeki signed into law the Financial Intelligence Center legislation, the center is focusing on suspicious transaction reports and plans to broaden its services in the coming year.

Parliament's National Assembly adopted broad antiterrorism legislation entitled Protection of Constitutional Democracy Against Terrorists and Related Activities Bill. The measure is expected to pass the bicameral legislature in early 2004. Despite initial opposition to previous versions of the bill, all South African political parties supported the final version.

Public and private statements by South Africa have been supportive of US counterterrorism efforts. President Mbeki has, on several occasions, voiced his opinion that there is no justification for terrorism.

In the past year, South Africa acceded to four United Nations antiterrorism conventions, making South Africa a party to nine of the 12 UN antiterrorism conventions.

Tanzania

Tanzania continues to be a supportive partner in the global war against terrorism. It has cooperated on several multiyear programs to build law-enforcement capacity, enhance border security, improve civil aviation security, and combat money laundering and terrorist finance.

Tanzanian and US authorities established a close working relationship after the bombing in 1998 of the US Embassy in Dar es Salaam and have cooperated in bringing bombing suspects to trial in New York and Dar es Salaam; one suspect stood trial in Tanzania in 2003. Although cooperative, Tanzanian law enforcement authorities still have a limited capacity to investigate terrorist suspects and bring them to justice. A comprehensive Prevention of Terrorism Act—approved in late 2002—has yet to be enforced, and implementing regulations for the law have not been drafted.

Tanzania is a party to seven of the 12 international conventions and protocols relating to terrorism.

Uganda

Uganda continued its firm stance against local and international terrorism in 2003. A new anti-money laundering bill is slated to go before Parliament for adoption in early 2004. In 2002, the Government enacted the Suppression of Terrorism Act, which imposes a mandatory death penalty for terrorists and potential death penalty for their sponsors and supporters. The Act's list of terrorist organizations includes al-Qaida, the LRA, and the Allied Democratic Front (ADF).

The Ugandan military continued its successful operations against the ADF, resulting in a decrease in ADF activities in western Uganda. There were no bombings by the ADF in 2003, although there were numerous fatal attacks by the LRA against civilian targets in northern Uganda.

Uganda is a party to 10 of the 12 international conventions and protocols relating to terrorism.

South Asia Overview

In 2003, South Asia continued to be a central theater of the global war on terrorism. The Afghan Transitional Authority convened a *Loya Jirga*, and representatives debated and approved a new national constitution. The first units of the Afghan National Army joined in US and Coalition operations against antigovernment forces in the south and east of the country. The national police force continued to grow as government institutions prepared for elections in 2004.

Despite this progress, security remained a concern; the Taliban, al-Qaida, and Hizb-I Islami Gulbuddin (HIG) continued to target the Coalition, noncombatant reconstruction civilians, and the Afghan Government. The NATO-led International Security Assistance Force (ISAF) announced its intention to expand its operations outside of Kabul.

Pakistan remained a key partner in the war on terror and continued its close cooperation with the United States in law enforcement, border security, and counterterrorism training. In 2003, the Musharraf government began to increase pressure on terrorists seeking refuge along the border with Afghanistan, conducting antiterrorist operations in the Federally Administered Tribal Areas for the first time. As in the previous year, Pakistani security authorities made numerous arrests of suspected terrorists, including important members of the al-Qaida leadership.

India continued to be the object of attacks by foreign-based and Kashmiri groups operating in Jammu and Kashmir. Nevertheless, Indian counterterrorist authorities could point to significant progress in the areas of legislation, finance, and investigations. India remained an important US partner in the global war on terror, and the United States hopes to continue to strengthen this relationship.

The cease-fire in Sri Lanka between the Liberation Tigers of Tamil Eelam (LTTE) and the Sri Lankan Government held throughout 2003, despite a political crisis within the government that has delayed the resumption of direct talks between the two sides. International aid has begun to reach Sri Lankans living in LTTE-controlled territory, addressing one of the obstacles to a negotiated settlement. In contrast, the Maoists in Nepal abrogated an eight-month cease-fire and resumed their campaign of armed attacks, bombings, assassination, and extortion against the Government and citizens of Nepal. The Maoists have also extorted money from Western tourists and threatened US citizens and interests, as well as nongovernmental organizations (NGO) and businesses connected with the United States.

Afghanistan

Afghanistan made progress toward rebuilding the government and the country in 2003. In December, Afghanistan successfully held the Constitutional *Loya Jirga* or Grand Assembly, with delegates from around the country assembling in Kabul and approving a national constitution. Other achievements include: continued development of the Afghan National Army (ANA) and expanded training of the Afghan National Police, preliminary efforts to demobilize militia forces, and initial voter registration. In the coming year, Afghans will face challenges as they prepare for elections—scheduled for June 2004—with a precarious security environment in parts of the country.

President Karzai and the Afghan Government remained committed to the war on terrorism. The ANA began combat operations against antigovernment elements, including the Taliban, al-Qaida, and HIG, largely in Afghanistan's south and east in support of the US-led international Coalition and the ISAF.

The Taliban, al-Qaida, and HIG targeted Afghan Transitional Administration (ATA), US, Coalition, and ISAF assets in Kabul and in eastern and southern Afghanistan in an effort to destabilize the country. These groups also hampered reconstruction efforts with attacks on nongovernmental organizations and United Nation facilities and personnel.

Al-Qaida regards Afghanistan as an important base of operations and continues its armed opposition to US presence. Al-Qaida fighters remain along the rough eastern border between Afghanistan and Pakistan's tribal areas. Afghan troops conduct joint operations against antigovernment elements with US military and Coalition forces. Through a series of tripartite commission meetings, Afghanistan and Pakistan have also made significant progress in sharing information and coordinating their efforts to improve security along the border.

Afghanistan is a party to 11 of the international conventions and protocols relating to terrorism.

India

The Indian Government remained steadfast in its desire to combat terrorism in 2003 and has worked closely with the United States in this regard. For example, several hundred Indian law enforcement officials participated in training as part of the Antiterrorism Assistance program. During the year, the Indian Government also moved to strengthen its international cooperation in curbing terrorism financing. In January, the Parliament enacted an anti-money laundering law that provides the legal basis for establishing a financial intelligence unit to monitor suspect transactions.

In March, the Indian Government announced that 32 terrorist organizations had been listed under the Prevention of Terrorism Act and, in July, informed Parliament that 702 persons had been arrested under the Act.

The Indian Government stepped up its efforts to counter the activities of various groups. In the states of Jammu and Kashmir, killings of civilians by foreign-based and Kashmiri militant groups continued and included the murder of numerous political leaders and party workers. The Indian Government asserted that Lashkar-i-Tayyiba and Jaish-e-Mohammed were behind a number of high-profile attacks in the state, which included the massacre of 24 Hindu civilians in southern Kashmir in March and an attack on 17 October outside the Chief Minister's residence compound in Srinagar.

Attacks took place in other parts of the country as well. Indian police said they had captured or killed all of the individuals responsible for the twin bombings on 25 August in Mumbai that left 53 dead and 160 injured. The Indian Government asserted that the responsible individuals were associated with Lashkar-i-Tayyiba. The People's War Group—a Maoist "Naxalite" organization—claimed responsibility for a car-bomb attack in October that seriously injured Chandrababu Naidu, chief minister of Andhra Pradesh.

India is a party to all 12 of the international conventions and protocols relating to terrorism.

Nepal

The Government of Nepal in 2003 strongly supported US counterterrorism activities and was responsive to multilateral efforts to police international terrorism. On 25 April 2003, Nepal signed an agreement with the US Government to establish an antiterrorism assistance program. Nepal's primary focus, however, remained the Maoist insurgency, active in Nepal since February 1996.

The Maoist insurgency poses a continuing threat to US citizens and property in Nepal. Repeated anti-US rhetoric and actions suggest the Maoists view US support for Kathmandu as a key obstacle to their goal of establishing a doctrinaire communist dictatorship. After they unilaterally withdrew from a seven-month cease-fire on 27 August, the Maoists resumed full-scale hostilities. Since then, the Maoists have been responsible for the deaths of an estimated 259 civilians and 305 government security forces. The Government says that Nepalese security forces have arrested thousands of suspected Maoists and killed more than 1,000 during the year. As part of their program, the Maoists have threatened attacks against US-sponsored NGOs and have sought to extort money from Westerners to raise funds for their insurgency. The Maoists' public statements have criticized the United States, the United Kingdom, and India for providing security assistance to Nepal.

Limited government finances, weak border controls, and poor security infrastructure have made Nepal a convenient logistic and transit point for some outside militants and international terrorists. The country also possesses a number of relatively soft targets that make it a potentially attractive site for terrorist operations. Security remains weak at many public facilities, including the Tribhuvan International Airport in Kathmandu, but the United States and others are actively working with the Government to improve this situation.

Nepal is a party to five of the 12 international conventions and protocols relating to terrorism and is a signatory to the Convention for the Suppression of Terrorist Bombings.

Pakistan

Pakistan continues to be one of the United States' most important partners in the global coalition against terrorism. President Musharraf has himself been the target of terrorist violence, narrowly escaping two assassination attempts in late 2003. US assistance supported Pakistan's efforts to establish a government presence along the Pakistan-Afghanistan border and eliminate terrorist safehavens. Pakistan continued operations in the autonomous Federally Administered Tribal Areas, capturing and killing a number of terrorist operatives.

Pakistan's military, intelligence, and law-enforcement agencies are cooperating closely with the United States and other nations to identify, interdict, and eliminate terrorism both within Pakistan and abroad. To date, hundreds of suspected operatives of these groups have been successfully apprehended with the cooperation of Pakistani authorities. Among those captured in 2003 were Khalid Shaykh Muhammad—the mastermind of the 9/11 attacks—and Walid Bin Attash—a prime suspect in the attack on the USS Cole in October 2002. When several militant and sectarian groups that had been banned in 2002 began operating under new aliases, the Pakistani Government banned them as well.

Pursuant to its obligations under UN Security Council Resolutions 1267, 1333, 1390, and 1455, Pakistan continues to work with the UN 1267 Sanctions Committee to freeze the assets of individuals and groups identified as terrorist entities linked to al-Qaida or the Taliban.

Pakistan's Anti-Terrorism Courts continue to respond to both international and domestic cases of terrorism. In April 2003, an Anti-Terrorism Court in Karachi convicted four defendants charged with organizing the bombing of the US Consulate in June 2002 in Karachi and, in June 2003, convicted three men charged with the bombing in May 2002 that killed 11 French naval technicians. In November 2003, the same court handed down death sentences for three members of the banned extremist groups Lashkar-i-Jhangvi for planning and committing sectarian murders.

US-Pakistan joint counterterrorism efforts have been extensive. They include cooperative efforts in border security and criminal investigations, as well as several long-term training projects. In 2002, the United States and Pakistan established the Working Group on Counterterrorism and Law-Enforcement Cooperation. The meetings provide a forum for discussing ongoing US-Pakistani efforts, as well as a means for improving capabilities and cooperation. Pakistan provides significant assistance in the investigation of international terrorism, acting on leads provided to its counterterrorism and law enforcement agencies by the United States and other nations.

Pakistan has signed 11 of the 12 international conventions and protocols relating to terrorism and is a party to 10.

Sri Lanka

Sri Lanka continues to support our global efforts to combat terrorism as well as undertaking their own efforts to combat terrorism domestically. Sri Lanka has actively supported international regimes to combat terrorist financing as well.

There were no incidents of international terrorism in Sri Lanka in 2003, as the cease-fire signed between the Government of Sri Lanka and the LTTE held, despite a halt in face-to-face negotiations and a serious political crisis within the Sri Lankan Government. There were no LTTE suicide bomb attacks throughout 2003, and the group continues to pursue ways to further peace talks. The LTTE has publicly accepted the concept of internal autonomy within a federal Sri Lankan state, conceding its longstanding demand for a separate Tamil Eelam state. In support of the peace process, the US Government has made limited, working-level contact with LTTE authorities to facilitate delivery of humanitarian aid.

Despite this progress, the LTTE, one of the world's deadliest terror groups, did not renounce terrorism or disband its "Black Tiger" suicide squads. It continues to smuggle weaponry into Sri Lanka and to forcibly recruit children into its ranks.

It is too early to tell whether the Sri Lankan peace process will ultimately bear fruit or whether the LTTE will actually reform itself. Although guarded optimism continued to surround the peace process, the United States will maintain the designation of the LTTE as a Foreign Terrorist Organization until it unequivocally renounces terrorism in both word and deed.

Sri Lanka is a party to 10 of the 12 international conventions and protocols relating to terrorism.

East Asia Overview

The capture by Thai authorities in August of top Jemaah Islamiya (JI) leader and al-Qaida's representative in Southeast Asia, Nurjaman Riduan bin Isomuddin (a.k.a. Hambali) was a significant victory in the global war on terrorism. Hambali, an Indonesian, was captured at an apartment complex in Ayutthaya, Thailand, and is suspected of masterminding numerous terrorist attacks in Southeast Asia, including the Christmas Eve church bombings in 2000 in Indonesia (19 dead, 47 wounded); the bombings on 30 December 2000 in metro Manila, Philippines (22 dead); the Bali attacks on 12 October 2002 (202 dead, more than 330 wounded); and possibly the J.W. Marriott Hotel bombing on 5 August 2003 in Jakarta (12 dead, over 150 wounded). Furthermore, Hambali was key in planning terrorist attacks with multiple targets in Singapore, disrupted in December 2001, and in planning Thailand attacks that were disrupted in May 2003. Hambali's capture and detention serves as a major blow to both JI and al-Qaida.

In 2003, as Hambali's capture illustrates, it became clearer that the Asia-Pacific region, primarily Southeast Asia, is an attractive theater of support and logistics for al-Qaida and a theater of operations for the regional terrorist group Jemaah Islamiya, acting alone or in collaboration with indigenous extremist groups. Hambali's case—an Indonesian national perpetrating attacks in Indonesia and the Philippines and planning attacks in Singapore and Thailand—serves as a case in point and accurately reflects the transnational nature of the terrorist threat in Southeast Asia.

Overall, counterterrorism cooperation with Asian governments was good in 2003, and solid progress was made to close seams between jurisdictions and share information on terrorist groups and their activities. As governments in the region continued their efforts to arrest and interdict terrorists by building and improving their counterterrorism capabilities, JI and other terrorists adapted by focusing on softer Western targets in Southeast Asia. The bombing on 5 August 2003 of the J.W. Marriott Hotel in Jakarta that killed 12 marks a continuation of this trend. This attack galvanized the Indonesian Government's will to take action.

Although most indigenous terrorist and Muslim separatist groups in Indonesia, Malaysia, the southern Philippines, and Thailand share an ideology and general rejection of Western influence held by international Islamic terrorists, they are focused primarily on effecting change within their home countries. Many leaders of Southeast Asian groups fought or claim to have fought in Afghanistan in the "Jihad" and brought back critical skills and contacts—along with burnished extremist credentials. The relationships formed in Afghanistan developed into a widening network in which local extremists were able to tap into international terrorist networks for operational support, training and/or funds, and vice versa. The net effect of the influence of such groups is to decrease the likelihood of peaceful and long-term solutions to separatist movements/ethnic conflicts, to exacerbate current regional terrorism, and to foster an environment conducive to terrorism's continued growth.

Extremists have been able to win supporters by financially supporting schools and mosques that espouse their brand of Islam and exploiting religious sympathies or discontent among Muslim populations. Muslim populations in the Philippines, Indonesia, Malaysia, Thailand, Singapore, and Cambodia are vulnerable to such radical influences.

Partners such as Australia, Japan, the United Kingdom, Canada, New Zealand, and others are working with the United States to assist governments in the region to overcome these challenges by providing training and assistance. The primary tools to build such capacity remain bilateral engagement programs, but much progress was made in working multilaterally to promote regional and transnational approaches to the challenges of counterterrorism. Building upon the Association of Southeast Asian Nations Regional Forum (ARF) for Counterterrorism Workplan, the Asia-Pacific Economic Cooperation (APEC) Counterterrorism Task Force, and other mechanisms, the region as a whole made advances in areas such as law enforcement, border control, transportation security, information sharing, antiterrorist financing, and the development of legal regimes.

Australia and Japan maintained their strong counterterrorism stance in 2003, both domestically and abroad. Senior officials from both countries publicly declared their firm commitment to work with the United States to combat terrorism over the long term in a meeting of the three counterterrorism ambassadors in November in Canberra. Australia and Japan continue to contribute to the war on terrorism in Afghanistan. Australia made strong contributions to the US-led Coalition in Iraq, while Japan's October passage of the Iraq Reconstruction Assistance Law, which includes provision for dispatching the Japan Self-Defense Forces to Iraq, reflects its strong commitment to assist in reconstruction and humanitarian efforts (deployment, in fact, took place in early 2004).

Australia and Japan are active in helping Asia-Pacific countries build their capacity in various international and regional forums to combat terrorism. Australia, for example, has broadened its network of bilateral counterterrorism arrangements in Southeast Asia to eight nations. The APEC Leaders' Summit in 2003 endorsed two Australian counterterrorism-related initiatives: advancement of passenger information systems and development of a regional movement-alert system. Japanese officials led seminars on immigration control, aviation security, customs cooperation, export control, law enforcement, and terrorist financing.

In May, Cambodian authorities arrested one Egyptian, two Thais, and one Cambodian suspected of being members of JI. The cell was plotting to conduct terrorist attacks in Cambodia and had been operating out of an Islamic school on the outskirts of Phnom Penh run by the Saudi Arabia–based nongovernmental organization, Umm al-Qura.

China continues to take a clear stand against international terrorism and is broadly supportive of the global war on terror. China actively participated in the Shanghai Cooperation Organization (SCO) and engaged in SCO joint counterterrorism exercises in Kazakhstan and Xinjiang Province in August. The People's Bank of China is in the process of establishing an Anti-Money Laundering Bureau, which will include a Terrorist Finance Investigative Department. Beijing displays a general willingness to cooperate with international terrorism investigations and continues to assert that terrorists—primarily based in Xinjiang Province—operate on Chinese territory.

Indonesia continued its firm public stance against terrorism in 2003. The government, led by the Indonesian National Police, has taken effective steps to counter the threat posed by JI, arresting 109 suspected JI members—most in 2003—including suspects in the Bali attacks, the Marriott attack, and other criminal acts linked to terrorism. Indonesia has adopted a comprehensive terrorism law defining various acts of terror and providing police and prosecutors with broader powers to combat terrorism—such as extended pretrial detention periods and the use of electronic evidence in court.

Nevertheless, persistent Indonesian domestic sensitivities, political pressures, and institutional weaknesses limit the Government's effectiveness. The Government, for example, made little effort to investigate the activities and affiliations of six students suspected of terrorist involvement who were deported from Pakistan in early December 2003; two were released within days of their repatriation to Indonesia.

On 1 July, Malaysia established a Southeast Asia Regional Center for Counterterrorism (SEARCCT). SEARCCT is expected to focus on regional training, information sharing, and public awareness campaigns. In August, SEARCCT hosted a training program sponsored by the US Treasury's financial intelligence unit and Malaysia's Central Bank on combating terrorist financing. Other nations, including the United Kingdom, Germany, and Australia, are also expected to provide trainers and training materials to the center.

Malaysia has detained more than 100 suspected terrorists under the Internal Security Act (ISA) since May 2001 and assisted Indonesian efforts to prosecute terrorist suspects by making video testimony from suspects in Malaysian custody available to Indonesian prosecutors. Malaysia has responded quickly to UN Security Council requirements to prohibit terrorist financing and freeze the assets of named entities. In September, Malaysia deposited the instruments of ratification for two international antiterrorism conventions: the International Convention for the Suppression of Terrorist Bombings and the Convention on the Prevention and Punishment of Crimes against Internationally Protected Persons. It has not yet become a party, however, to the critical International Convention for the Suppression of the Financing of Terrorism.

New Zealand appointed its first Ambassador for Counterterrorism in September to build upon the measures taken since the attacks of September 11 in the United States and to ensure that New Zealand has a stronger capacity to develop and implement policies on global terrorism and related security issues. New Zealand continues to support Operation Enduring Freedom. It deployed troops to Iraq and Afghanistan to participate in the reconstruction efforts and pledged to provide humanitarian aid, as well as keeping its previous commitment of sending military forces to the region.

The Philippines was the victim of a number of terrorist attacks in 2003, including the car-bomb attack adjacent to a military airfield in Cotobato, on the southern island of Mindanao on 21 February; the bombing on 4 March at the International Airport in Davao, Mindanao that killed 17 (including one US citizen); the Sasa Wharf bombing on 2 April also in Davao that killed 15; a series of bombings in Koronadal City, Mindanao, that took more than 15 civilian lives; as well as a number of kidnappings-for-ransom operations.

President Gloria Macapagal-Arroyo and other Philippine officials continue to be outspoken supporters of the global Coalition against terrorism and have been swift and direct in condemnation of terrorist acts, both domestic and international. The Government of the Philippines created a multiagency counterterrorism task force chaired by the National Security Advisor and consisting of officials from 34 Philippine Government agencies representing the security, economic, and social components essential for an effective counterterrorism strategy. In October, the Philippine Government ratified the remaining six of the 12 United Nations counterterrorism conventions.

Philippine authorities made several significant arrests of suspected terrorists in 2003. In May, security forces arrested a sub-commander of the separatist Moro Islamic Liberation

Front (MILF) involved in the explosion of 30 December on a Manila commuter train that killed 22 people. In October, a JI operative was arrested at a JI safehouse in Cotabato City, on the southern island of Mindanao. In December, Philippine Armed Forces captured Abu Sayyaf Group (ASG) leader "Commander Robot," a leader of one of the main ASG factions responsible for numerous kidnappings and bombings during the last decade, including the kidnapping in April 2000 of Western tourists from the Malaysian resort of Sipadan.

Despite its overall positive record, Manila continues to face setbacks and challenges on the counterterrorism front. In July, a senior Indonesian JI operative escaped from Philippine National Police headquarters in Manila along with two suspected ASG members. All three were eventually killed or recaptured.

Singapore continued its strong public and private opposition to terrorism and maintained vigorous counterterrorism action in bilateral and multilateral contexts. There were no acts of international or domestic terrorism in Singapore in 2003, although authorities continued investigation and detentions of members of JI, which plotted to carry out attacks in Singapore in the past.

During 2003, Singapore continued its cooperation with a variety of governments, including the United States, to investigate terrorist groups, especially JI, through both intelligence and law-enforcement channels. Singapore provided Thailand information that ultimately led to the arrest in May of a Singaporean JI member in Thailand. As a result of that investigation, Thai authorities also arrested several Thai citizens believed to be members of a JI cell plotting to blow up five embassies in Bangkok, including the US Embassy. Singapore provided key information that helped Thailand track down and arrest top JI leader Hambali in August and also facilitated video testimony of three of its ISA detainees in the Indonesian trial of JI spiritual leader Abu Bakar Bashir in August.

Thailand's domestic and international counterterrorism efforts, which were bolstered in the wake of the deadly bombing in Bali, Indonesia, in October 2002, intensified during 2003. Prime Minster Thaksin Shinawatra publicly expressed the will of the Royal Thai Government to cooperate closely with the United States and other nations in fighting the global war on terror. In August, Thai authorities captured top JI leader with close ties to al-Qaida, Nurjaman Riduan bin Isomuddin (a.k.a. Hambali) in Ayutthaya, Thailand. In June and July, Thai authorities in southern Thailand arrested four men suspected of being either JI supporters or operatives. The four are implicated in a conspiracy to bomb a number of high-profile targets and tourist venues in Thailand including the embassies of the United States, United Kingdom, Israel, Singapore, and Australia.

In August, the King signed an emergency antiterrorist decree, giving the government powerful new legal tools to fight terrorism. There were no significant acts of terrorism in Thailand during 2003. The Thai Government's effectiveness in precluding a terrorist incident during the APEC Summit in October was considered a major success both domestically and internationally.

Australia

Australia continued its strong counterterrorism stance in 2003, both domestically and abroad. Australia continues to contribute to the global war on terror in Afghanistan. Between September 2001 and June 2004, Australia expects to have contributed more than US $46 million in humanitarian and reconstruction assistance to Afghanistan. Australia has also made strong contributions to the US-led Coalition in Iraq, with more than 800 Australian Defence Force personnel in Iraq. Its commitment to Iraq's stabilization and development continues across humanitarian, agricultural, and other economic sectors.

Canberra further improved its domestic counterterrorism arrangements and consultative mechanisms in 2003. The National Counterterrorism Committee completed a National Counterterrorism Plan in June. The Government also created a National Security Hotline, conducted a public campaign to ensure that Australians remain alert to the possible threat of terrorism, and formed the Business-Government Task Force on Critical Infrastructure. A National Security Division was established in the Department of Prime Minister and Cabinet to ensure a continued high level of coordination and reinforce a government-wide approach to terrorism and national security issues. Canberra also established the National Threat Assessment Centre to provide integrated assessment capability across the government.

In March, the Government created a position of Ambassador for Counterterrorism. Similar to the Coordinator for Counterterrorism in the United States, the Ambassador provides a focal point for coordinating, promoting, and intensifying Australia's international counterterrorism efforts.

Underpinning Australia's commitment to fighting terrorism is a detailed legislative response. In 2002, the Commonwealth Parliament created specific offenses for involvement in terrorist activities and terrorist organizations and designated 16 such terrorist groups as of December 2003. Parliament also provided additional powers to the Australian Security Intelligence Organisation in 2003.

The Parliament passed new measures in 2002 to deny terrorists the funds on which they rely, and during 2002 and 2003 specifically listed more than 400 terrorist-related individuals, entities, and organizations, including HAMAS and Hizballah. Australia has taken action to block transactions, accounts, and assets relating to persons or organizations identified as terrorists or the sponsors of terrorism, including those listed under US Executive Order 13224. Australia has a highly developed legal regime in place to combat terrorist financing. The Australian financial intelligence unit AUSTRAC has strengthened its network by signing a further ten Memoranda of Understanding (MOU) with other Financial Intelligence Units throughout the world in 2003, bringing the total to 24. AUSTRAC is also cooperating with the US counterpart, FinCEN, on financial intelligence.

Australia is helping countries in the Asia-Pacific region build their capacity to combat terrorism in areas such as law enforcement, border management, transportation security, intelligence, antiterrorist financing, and the development of legal regimes. In July, Prime Minister Howard announced a three-year $3.6 million package with the Philippines to support the building of counterterrorism capacity. Australia's $7.2 million counterterrorism package to Indonesia is in the second of its four years. Australia spent $5.38 million specifically on building counterterrorism capacity throughout the entire Asia-Pacific region and expects to spend an additional $6.12 million this year.

Australia has broadened its network of bilateral counterterrorism arrangements in Southeast Asia, signing MOUs on cooperation to combat international terrorism with the Philippines, Fiji, Cambodia, East Timor, and India during 2003, bringing Australia's network of MOUs to eight. These MOUs are umbrella arrangements that set out a framework for bilateral cooperation in law enforcement, defense, intelligence, customs, and immigration.

The MOU with the Philippines facilitated cooperation between the Australian Federal Police and the Philippine National Police, including in the investigation of the bombing in Davao City in the southern Philippines in March 2003, in which 17 were killed, including one US citizen. In Indonesia, the joint Australian and Indonesian police investigation into the Bali bombings in October 2002 that killed 202, including 88 Australians, is testimony to the successful combination of Australian and Indonesian investigative and forensic techniques—and a model for successful international cooperation to bring perpetrators of terrorism to justice. By November 2003, 36 suspects were in Indonesian custody. Among these, 29 had been convicted and an additional four were before the courts.

In the Pacific Islands, Australia has continued working with the region's key political body—the Pacific Islands Forum—and with other regional entities such as the South Pacific Chiefs of Police Conference, the Oceania Customs Organization, and the Pacific Immigration Directors Conference, to reduce the possibility of countries in the region being exploited by terrorists and to combat organized crime.

The APEC Leaders' Summit in 2003 endorsed two Australian counterterrorism-related initiatives: advance passenger information systems and development of a regional alert system. Australia is working hard in the Association of Southeast Asian Nations (ASEAN) Regional Forum to focus on the very real danger of terrorism and ways to counter it. In June 2003, Australia and Singapore co-hosted a seminar on managing the consequences of a major terrorist attack, which focused on practical measures that governments can take to recover from such an incident.

Australia is a party to 11 of the 12 international conventions and protocols relating to terrorism.

Burma

Burma maintained its solid position against international terrorism in 2003. The regime previously enacted, but has not yet implemented, an anti-money laundering law that could help block terrorist assets. The military government is fighting several low-intensity conflicts against ethnic insurgents. At least one of these groups is alleged to have ties to South Asian terrorist networks.

The junta has occasionally sought to portray insurgent attacks against infrastructure such as bridges and pipelines as terrorism, but there were no known acts of international terrorism during 2003. Dozens of improvised explosive devices exploded or were discovered in various locations throughout Burma in 2003. With the exception of two bombings of an oil pipeline claimed by the insurgent Karen National Union, there were no claims of responsibility for these acts. In March, two improvised explosive devices were found in Rangoon, one of which exploded and killed two municipal workers. The perpetrators' identities and motives are unclear, but the junta arrested a number of anti-regime activists.

Burma is a party to seven of the 12 international conventions and protocols relating to terrorism and is a signatory to the International Convention for the Suppression of the Financing of Terrorism.

Cambodia

In May, Cambodian authorities arrested one Egyptian, two Thais, and one Cambodian suspected of being members of JI. The Government stated publicly that the group was plotting to conduct terrorist attacks in Cambodia. The group had been operating out of an Islamic school run by the Saudi Arabia–based NGO, Umm al-Qura, on the outskirts of Phnom Penh. The school was allegedly being used as a front for channeling al-Qaida money into Cambodia from Saudi Arabia. In addition to the arrests of the four, who remain in custody awaiting trial, the Cambodian Government shut down two branches of the Umm al-Qura Islamic School and deported 28 foreign teachers and their dependents.

In November, Cambodian authorities arrested seven members of the Cambodian Freedom Fighters, an antigovernment group, which was reportedly planning a terrorist attack in the southwestern town of Koh Kong. The suspects remain in custody while the government completes its investigation.

Although there were no acts of international terrorism on Cambodian soil in 2003, Cambodia recognizes that it is not immune from the problem of international terrorism and understands that it needs to work actively to counter the threat. The information leading to the arrest of the suspected JI members in the Umm al-Qura Islamic School and subsequent knowledge that Indonesian JI terrorist leader Hambali resided temporarily in Cambodia have hardened Cambodia's attitude.

Cambodia's ability to independently investigate potential terrorist activities is limited by a lack of training and resources. In addition, Cambodia's lack of comprehensive and effective domestic legislation to combat terrorism is a serious constraint on the Government's ability to arrest and prosecute terrorists. To address these deficiencies, the Cambodian Government has requested international assistance to upgrade its counterterrorism capabilities. Beginning in 2003, the government made significant headway in instituting computerized border control systems at Phnom Penh's international airport. The Cambodian Government has also cooperated fully with US requests to monitor terrorists and terrorists entities listed as supporters of terrorist financing.

Phnom Penh has been vocal in condemning terrorist acts. Foreign Minister Hor Namhong, for example, issued a strongly worded statement condemning the bombing attack in October 2002 in Bali, Indonesia. Cambodia has actively participated in international counterterrorism forums. As ASEAN Chair from July 2002 to June 2003, Cambodia took the lead in coordinating ASEAN statements on terrorism, such as the Joint ASEAN-EU Declaration on Cooperation to Combat Terrorism and the relevant text in the Chairman's Statement of the Tenth ASEAN Regional Forum released in June.

Cambodia is a party to four of the 12 international conventions and protocols relating to terrorism and is a signatory to the International Convention for the Suppression of the Financing of Terrorism.

China

China continues to take a clear stand against international terrorism and is broadly supportive of the global war on terror. Chinese officials at all levels regularly denounce terrorism, and China regularly participates in discussions of counterterrorism in both international and regional forums. For example, China actively participated in the SCO, assisting in the establishment of an SCO Counterterrorism Center in Tashkent, Uzbekistan, scheduled to begin operation in 2004, and engaging in SCO joint counterterrorism exercises in Kazakhstan and Xinjiang Province in August 2003.

China is supportive of diplomatic actions and efforts to block and freeze terrorist assets. China treats designations of terrorists under US Executive Order 13224 on an equal basis with those designated by the United Nations UNSCR 1267 Sanctions Committee. The United States and China hold regular counterterrorism consultations and expert-level consultations on curbing terrorist financing. The People's Bank of China is in the process of establishing an Anti-Money Laundering Bureau, which will include a Terrorist Finance Investigative Department.

China displays a general willingness to cooperate with international terrorism investigations. Chinese authorities actively participated in the investigation of the case of the "Portland Six"—a group in Portland, Oregon, indicted on terrorism charges in October 2002—providing hotel records and other information that proved instrumental in obtaining guilty pleas from the defendants.

There were no acts of international terrorism committed in China in 2003. There were several reports, however, of bombings and bomb threats in various parts of China, although it is unclear whether these were politically motivated acts of terrorism or criminal attacks. Chinese authorities assert that terrorists, primarily based in Xinjiang Province, continue to operate on Chinese territory. On 15 December, for example, China's Ministry of Public Security (MPS) issued a list of "East Turkestan" groups and individuals that the Chinese Government considers to be terrorist entities. The list includes four groups: the East Turkestan Islamic Movement (ETIM), the East Turkestan Liberation Organization (better known as SHAT), the World Uighur Youth Congress, and the East Turkestan Information Center.

The list also specifically names 11 individuals as terrorists, including the leaders of each of the above groups. The MPS stated that it has incontrovertible evidence that each listed group has organized and executed specific terrorist acts in Xinjiang and that these groups are all linked to each other and the al-Qaida network. Following the release of the list, the Chinese Government called for international assistance in China's fight against these organizations and individuals, requesting that the assets of the groups be frozen, that the organizations be outlawed, and that countries stop supporting and financing them. Beijing also asked the international community to assist in the investigation, apprehension, and repatriation of the designated individuals. The US Department of State has designated the ETIM as part of the Department of State's Terrorist Exclusion List and under Executive Order 13224 but has not designated the other three groups under US law.

China is a party to 11 of the 12 international conventions and protocols relating to terrorism and is a signatory to the International Convention for the Suppression of the Financing of Terrorism.

Indonesia

Indonesia continued its firm public stance against terrorism in 2003. The terrorist bombings in Bali on 12 October 2002 that killed 202—mostly foreign tourists—and the bombing of the J.W. Marriott Hotel in Jakarta on 5 August 2003 that killed 12 forced the Indonesian Government into action. The Government, led by the Indonesian National Police, has taken effective steps to counter the threat posed by the regional terrorist organization Jemaah Islamiya (JI), which has ties to al-Qaida. Indonesian police have arrested 109 suspected JI members—most in 2003—including suspects in the Bali attacks, the Marriott attack, and other criminal acts linked to terrorism. Those arrested included numerous senior JI leaders, a number of regional and subregional commanders, most of the masterminds of the Bali attack, several key planners of the Marriott bombing, former instructors at JI training camps, and financiers of terrorist attacks.

In a case symptomatic of persistent Indonesian domestic sensitivities, political pressures, and institutional weaknesses, however, the Government made little effort to investigate the activities and affiliations of six students suspected of terrorist involvement, who were deported from Pakistan in early December 2003 and released two within days of their repatriation.

Indonesia, hampered by weak rule of law, a poorly regulated financial system, and serious internal coordination problems, has not yet frozen any terrorist assets. The Government, however, did enhance its legal framework in September by passing amendments to its anti-money laundering law, which strengthened the government's legal authority to combat terrorist finance. Indonesia has also created a financial intelligence unit with US assistance.

In March, Indonesia adopted a comprehensive antiterrorism law, defining various acts of terror and providing police and prosecutors with broader powers to combat terrorism such as extended pretrial detention periods and the use of electronic evidence in court. The Government, however, has been unwilling to ban JI, saying the organization never formally applied for recognition and thus cannot be prohibited. The absence of such a prohibition has impeded police and prosecutors in arresting and trying suspected terrorists and will most likely further hamper prosecutors' efforts to put JI leaders behind bars.

On 2 September, the Central Jakarta District Court convicted the spiritual leader of JI, Abu Bakar Bashir, on treason and immigration charges. The panel of judges stated in its decision that the prosecutors had presented sufficient evidence to convince them of JI's existence, its goal of overthrowing the Government of Indonesia, and Bashir's involvement with the group. However, despite video-conference testimony from Bali bombers naming Bashir as the head of JI, judges were not convinced of his leadership role and sentenced him to only four years in prison. Both Bashir and the prosecution appealed the decision. In November, the court reduced Bashir's sentence to three years, reversing the treason charge but upholding his conviction for document fraud and immigration violations.

The Indonesian judicial system undertook the trials of approximately 63 terror suspects in 2003, including 17 for involvement in the bombing of a McDonald's restaurant and a car showroom in Makassar, South Sulawesi, in December 2002; as well as 46 members of JI for involvement in the church bombings on Christmas Eve 2000, the bombing of the Philippine Ambassador's residence in Jakarta in August 2000, and the Bali and Marriott Hotel bombings. As of 1 December 2003, Indonesian courts had convicted a total of 50 terror suspects and acquitted two. Thirty-nine of these convictions were of suspects involved in the Bali bombings on 12 October 2002. Three key planners—Amrozi bin Nurhasyim, Abdul Ghoni (a.k.a. Mukhlas), and Abdul Aziz (a.k.a. Imam Samudra)—were all sentenced to death. Many others were given life in prison.

The numerous convictions and tough sentences handed down by the courts are a reflection of the Government's seriousness in combating terrorism and its commitment to bring to justice those implicated in terrorist attacks in Indonesia. Fifteen terrorist trials remain under way, and many suspects await trial. At year's end, Indonesian Police continued steadily to arrest suspected JI members and were devoting considerable resources to hunting JI bombmakers Azahari Hussein and Noordin Mat Top, as well as several other known fugitives.

Indonesia is a party to four of the 12 international conventions and protocols relating to terrorism and is a signatory to two additional conventions, including the International Convention for the Suppression of the Financing of Terrorism.

Japan

Japan continued its strong counterterrorism stance in 2003. Prime Minister Koizumi and numerous other senior officials have publicly declared their firm commitment to stand by the United States to combat terrorism over the long term. Japan's significant rear-area support to Operation Enduring Freedom (OEF) in Afghanistan and strong statement of support for US-led military action in Iraq bear out this commitment. In July 2003, the Japanese Diet passed the Iraq Reconstruction Assistance Law, which includes provision for dispatching the Japan Self-Defense Forces to Iraq to assist in reconstruction and humanitarian efforts. In October 2003, the Japanese Diet approved a two-year extension of the Anti-Terrorism Special Measures Law and another six-month basic plan, which stipulate the activities that the Japan Self-Defense Forces may perform in support of OEF. Japan provides approximately 40 percent of the fuel used by US naval forces engaged in OEF. Japan Air Self-Defense Force planes continued to provide transportation for US forces.

Japan actively participates in strengthening counterterrorism measures in various international and regional forums. In August 2003, Japan signed a mutual legal assistance treaty with the United States and plans to submit the treaty to the Diet for ratification in 2004. Once ratified, it will make cooperation in investigations and prosecution of terrorists easier. To help stem the flow of terrorist financing to al-Qaida and the Taliban, Japan designated under its asset-freezing program all entities and individuals included on the UN 1267 Sanctions Committee's consolidated list. Tokyo announced in October 2003 that Japan will join the Advanced Passenger Information System, obliging Japanese officials to share information about departing international passengers with other participating countries, including the United States, Canada, Australia, and New Zealand.

Japan continues to make valuable contributions to building counterterrorism capacity among Asian countries. Japanese officials have led seminars on immigration control, aviation security, customs cooperation, export control, law enforcement, and terrorist financing. Japanese National Police Agency officials were dispatched to assist the Indonesian Police investigation following the Marriott Hotel bombing in Jakarta in August 2003. Japan had also dispatched criminal investigators to Indonesia in the wake of the terrorist attacks in Bali in October 2002. In addition, Japan is providing technical assistance to Southeast Asian countries working to create a system for monitoring terrorist financing. For example, Japan sponsored a seminar on establishing financial intelligence units for Southeast Asian countries in October 2003.

There were no incidents of international terrorism in Japan during 2003. Trials continue of members of the Aum Shinrikyo Group, a US-designated foreign terrorist organization, accused of perpetrating the sarin gas attack on the Tokyo subway system in 1995. The prosecution has requested the death penalty for Aum Shrinrikyo leader Matsumoto, and a ruling is expected in early 2004. Three suspects in the incident in 1995 remain at large. The Public Security Intelligence Agency is continuing its surveillance of the group through 2005, as authorized by the Public Security Commission in December 2002.

Japan is a party to all 12 international terrorism conventions and protocols relating to terrorism.

Laos

The Government of Laos has continued to support the global war on terrorism. Although the Government's intentions regarding counterterrorism are positive, implementation of multilateral agreements is hampered by weak enforcement procedures and lack of control of areas outside the capital. The Government cooperated bilaterally on counterterrorism issues with the United States and other nations and multilaterally with the United Nations and the Association of Southeast Asian Nations.

Since Laos lacks distinct counterterrorism laws, the Office of the Prosecutor General plans to introduce amendments to existing criminal law, under which acts of terrorism fall, to make more explicit the descriptions of and punishments for terrorism-related crimes. In September, Lao courts sentenced two active-duty soldiers to life imprisonment for orchestrating a series of bombings in Vientiane in 2000 and 2002. Laos has continued to seek the extradition of 17 Lao citizens from Thailand suspected of involvement in an armed attack against a Lao customs checkpoint in the southern part of the country in July 2000.

Laos suffered many incidents of domestic terrorism in 2003, carried out by groups of unknown identity opposed to the Lao Government. Some of these terrorist incidents were ambush-style attacks against buses and private vehicles, resulting in the deaths of 34 civilians, and others targeted government officials, killing three Lao officials. A group calling itself the Free Democratic People's Government of Laos claimed credit for at least one in a series of bombings in the latter half of the year that killed one person and injured several more.

The Bank of Laos continued to search government and commercial bank holdings for possible terrorist assets, as identified by US-provided lists of terrorist organizations and individuals, and has issued freeze orders for assets of organizations and individuals named on these lists. The Bank, however, had yet to take steps to report on Government compliance with UNSCR 1373 or to require the freezing of the assets of individuals and entities associated with Usama Bin Ladin, members of al-Qaida, and members of the Taliban as included on the UNSCR 1267 Sanctions Committee's consolidated list, as required by mandatory provisions of UN Security Council resolutions.

Laos is a party to seven of the 12 international conventions and protocols relating to terrorism but has not yet become a party to the International Convention for the Suppression of the Financing of Terrorism.

Malaysia

On 1 July, Malaysia established a Southeast Asia Regional Center for Counterterrorism (SEARCCT). SEARCCT is expected to focus on regional training, information sharing, and public awareness campaigns. In August, SEARCCT hosted a training program sponsored by the US Treasury's financial intelligence unit, FinCEN, and Malaysia's Central Bank (Bank Negara) on combating terrorist financing. Other nations, including the United Kingdom, Germany, and Australia, are also expected to provide trainers and training materials to the center. Malaysia assisted Indonesian efforts to prosecute terrorist suspects by making video testimony from suspects in Malaysian custody available to Indonesian prosecutors.

Malaysia has detained more than 100 suspected terrorists under the Internal Security Act (ISA) since May 2001. Malaysia issued 10 and renewed 11 two-year detention orders for terrorist suspects in 2003. On 10 November, 13 Malaysian terrorist suspects were held under 60-day detention orders upon their return from Pakistani custody. Eight of these suspects have been released. In August, the Malaysian Government chose not to renew a detention order for Muhammad Iqbal (a.k.a. Abu Jibril) an Indonesian national and terrorist suspect, seeking instead to deport him to Indonesia. At year's end, Iqbal remained in Malaysian custody.

Malaysia has responded quickly to UN Security Council requirements to prohibit terrorist financing and freeze the accounts of named entities. In November, Malaysia's Parliament amended its anti-money laundering legislation of 2001 to include terrorist activity as a predicate offense. Parliament also amended the penal and criminal procedure codes to increase penalties for terrorist acts, allow for the prosecution of individuals who provide material support for terrorists, expand the use of wiretaps and other surveillance of terrorist suspects, and permit video testimony in terrorist cases.

On 24 September, Malaysia deposited the instruments of ratification for two international antiterrorism conventions: the International Convention for the Suppression of Terrorist Bombings and the Convention on the Prevention and Punishment of Crimes against Internationally Protected Persons. Malaysia is a party to three additional international conventions and protocols relating to terrorism and is a signatory to the Protocol for the Suppression of Unlawful Acts of Violence at Airports Serving International Civil Aviation. It has not yet become a party to the International Convention for the Suppression of the Financing of Terrorism.

In March, Malaysian police announced the discovery of four tons of explosive ammonium nitrate fertilizer often used in truck bombs. According to press reports, the ammonium nitrate had been purchased in September 2000 by ex-Army captain and scientist, Yazid Sufaat, who is currently under ISA detention for allegedly being involved in JI activities. The chemicals were to have been used by JI in Singapore to make truck bombs to attack foreign embassies and other Western targets.

New Zealand

New Zealand appointed its first Ambassador for Counterterrorism in September to consolidate and build upon the measures taken since the attacks of September 11 and to ensure New Zealand has a stronger capacity to develop and implement policies on global terrorism and related security issues. In October, the New Zealand Parliament passed new antiterrorism laws that will allow the Government to investigate, detect, and prosecute terrorist activities more effectively. The laws create new offenses to address terrorist threats, empower the New Zealand Police and Customs Officials to investigate and prosecute those offenses, and bring New Zealand into full compliance with its UN obligations.

New Zealand continues to support Operation Enduring Freedom. It deployed troops to Iraq and Afghanistan to participate in the reconstruction efforts and pledged to provide humanitarian aid, as well as keeping its previous commitment of sending a frigate and a P-3 Orion to the region.

New Zealand is a party to 11 of the 12 international conventions and protocols relating to terrorism and is a signatory to the Convention on the Physical Protection of Nuclear Materials.

Philippines

The Philippines continues to be an outspoken supporter of the global Coalition against terrorism and has been swift and direct in condemnation of terrorist acts, both domestic and international.

The Philippines was the victim of a number of terrorist attacks in 2003, including the car-bomb attack on 21 February adjacent to a military airfield in Cotobato, on the southern island of Mindanao; the bombing on 4 March at the International Airport in Davao, Mindanao, that killed 17 (including one US citizen); the Sasa Wharf bombing on 2 April also in Davao that killed 15; a series of bombings in Koronadal City, Mindanao, which took more than 15 civilian lives; as well as a number of kidnappings-for-ransom operations.

The Philippines faces threats from internal terrorism on several fronts. The United States, for example, has listed four indigenous groups as Foreign Terrorist Organizations—the Abu Sayyaf Group (ASG), the Communist Party of the Philippines/New People's Army, Alex Boncayo Brigade, and the Pentagon Gang.

In her speech to the UN General Assembly in September, Philippine President Gloria Macapagal-Arroyo noted that growing international coordination and cooperation is countering the global threat of terrorism. She further emphasized that the Philippines is working with other heads of state to ensure continued cooperation in the battle to rid Southeast Asia of the terrorist threat. During the ASEAN post-ministerial conference held in Phnom Penh, Cambodia, in June, Philippine Foreign Secretary Ople expressed the desire of ASEAN to reinforce collaboration with its dialogue partners, highlighting the area's capacity building and training in law enforcement.

The Government of the Philippines created a multiagency counterterrorism task force chaired by the National Security Advisor and consisting of officials from 34 Philippine Government agencies representing the security, economic, and social components essential for an effective counterterrorism strategy. In October, President Arroyo appointed former Defense Secretary Angelo Reyes to a newly created cabinet-level position, Ambassador-at-Large for Counterterrorism. The Philippines also established a task force on protection of critical infrastructure chaired by the Undersecretary of the Presidential Office of Special Concerns.

Philippine authorities made several significant arrests of suspected terrorists in 2003. In May, security forces arrested Saifullah Yunos (a.k.a. Muklis Yunos), a subcommander of the separatist MILF. During his arraignment in July, Yunos entered a guilty plea for his involvement in the explosion on a Manila commuter train on 30 December 2000 that killed 22 people. In October, JI operative Taufek Refke was arrested at a JI safehouse in Cotabato City, on the southern island of Mindanao. Police reportedly recovered manuals on bomb-making and chemical-biological warfare. In December, Philippine Armed Forces captured ASG commander Ghalib Andang (a.k.a. "Commander Robot") on the southern island of Jolo. Andang was the leader of one of the main ASG factions and is responsible for numerous kidnappings and bombings during the last decade, including the kidnapping in April 2000 of Western tourists from the Malaysian resort of Sipadan.

In February, the Philippine Armed Forces overran a base area of the separatist MILF near the town of Pikit on the southern island of Mindanao. Manila claimed that criminals, including the notorious Pentagon Gang, found refuge and protection in the area. Thousands of civilians were displaced as a result of the ensuing days of fighting.

In August, the Philippines sent 96 members of the Philippine Humanitarian Contingent to Iraq to assist in Coalition reconstruction efforts. Philippine officials remained steadfast in word and deed to contribute troops—even in the wake of the terrorist bombing of the UN compound in Baghdad that same week that killed two of their countrymen. If additional funding is available, Manila plans to send 79 additional members and extend the contingent's stay longer than the planned six months.

Despite its overall positive record, the Philippines continues to face setbacks and challenges on the counterterrorism front. In July, senior Indonesian JI operative Fathur Rahman al-Ghozi escaped from Philippine National Police headquarters in Manila along with two suspected ASG members, Omar Opik Lasal and Abdulmukim "Mukim" Idris. Originally detained in the Philippines in January 2002, al-Ghozi was serving a 17-year prison sentence. Al-Ghozi was eventually killed in a shootout with Philippine security forces in North

Cotabato Province on Mindanao on 12 October. Philippine Armed Forces shot and killed Idris on 7 August in Lanao del Norte Province on Mindanao and captured Lasal on 7 October in North Cotabato Province in Mindanao.

For the second straight year, the Philippines failed to enact new antiterrorism legislation in 2003. Major evidentiary and procedural obstacles in the Philippines hinder the building of effective terrorism cases, such as the absence of a law defining and codifying terrorist acts and restrictions on gathering of evidence. Generic problems in the law enforcement and criminal justice systems also hamper bringing terrorists to justice in the Philippines. Among them: low morale, inadequate salaries, recruitment and retention difficulties, and lack of cooperation between police and prosecutors.

Tracking terrorist financing continues to pose a problem to prosecuting cases. Poor communication between Philippine law enforcement agencies and the Anti-Money Laundering Council (AMLC) remains an impediment to effective implementation of the Anti-Money Laundering Act amended in March 2003. The amendments to the Act granted Central Bank personnel unfettered access to deposit accounts. However, the Central Bank and the AMLC face logistic challenges due to the lack of information technology platforms to collect and process covered transaction reports. Although the amendments addressed international Financial Action Task Force (FATF) concerns about the Philippines legal and regulatory framework, the Philippines remains on the FATF's list of noncooperating countries and territories (NCCT). Removal from the NCCT list awaits the adoption of an anti-money laundering implementation plan and corresponding actions.

In October, the Philippine Government ratified the remaining six of the 12 international conventions and protocols relating to terrorism.

Singapore

Singapore continued its strong public and private opposition to terrorism and maintained vigorous counterterrorism action in bilateral and multilateral contexts. There were no acts of international or domestic terrorism in Singapore in 2003, although authorities continued their investigation and detentions of members of the JI Southeast Asian regional terrorist network, which had plotted to carry out attacks in Singapore in the past.

Singapore did not announce any new domestic terrorist arrests in 2003, although four of its citizens who are terrorist suspects—believed to be members of JI—were repatriated. All four men are being held under the Internal Security Act, bringing the total number of JI-related detainees to 35. Singapore officials stated publicly that while JI continues to pose a threat in the rest of the region, in Singapore, the JI threat has been significantly minimized since Singapore is believed to have been successful in identifying and breaking up the JI operational cells that had been active in the city-state.

During 2003, Singapore continued its cooperation with a variety of governments, including the United States, to investigate terrorist groups, especially JI, through both intelligence and law enforcement channels. Singapore provided Thailand information that ultimately led to the arrest in May of a Singaporean JI member in Thailand, Arifin bin Ali. As a result of that investigation, Thai authorities also arrested several Thai citizens believed to be members of JI. Singapore authorities later stated that they had conveyed to Thailand information from Arifin that the JI group intended to blow up five embassies in Bangkok, including the US Embassy.

Singapore also provided key information that helped Thailand track down and arrest top JI leader Hambali in August. In February, a tipoff from Singapore led to the arrest of Singapore citizen and alleged leader of JI in Singapore, Mas Selamat Kastari, on the Indonesian island of Batam, near Singapore. Kasteri is alleged to have planned to hijack a plane and crash it into Singapore's Changi Airport. Singapore also facilitated video testimony of three of its ISA detainees in the Indonesian trial of JI spiritual leader Abu Bakar Bashir in August. Singapore designated both the United States and the United Kingdom in May as "prescribed" countries under the terrorist financing law of 2002. This step allows Singapore to respond to requests for information on terrorist financing.

Singapore's new export-control law, which went into effect on 1 January, represents a major step forward. Though largely aimed at preventing proliferation of weapons-of-mass-destruction (WMD) goods to governments, the new framework may also assist in preventing such materials from fallings into the hands of terrorists. In March, Singapore became the first port in Asia to begin operations under the US Container Security Initiative. Singapore officials have expressed strong concern about maritime security in nearby waters, especially the Strait of Malacca. These concerns include terrorist threats as well as pirate and other criminal attacks. Singapore has stepped up security within its own waters and also its efforts to work with other countries.

Singapore actively participated in counterterrorism efforts through various international forums, including the ASEAN Regional Forum in June, the APEC Leaders Summit in October, and the Commonwealth Heads of Government Meeting in December. In addition, Singapore hosted and co-sponsored with the United States a January workshop on measures to cut off terrorist financing. Attendees at the workshop included representatives of ASEAN states and Pacific Island Forum members, the UN Counterterrorism Committee, the FATF, and the Asia-Pacific Group on Money Laundering. During 2003, Singapore ratified the International Convention for the Suppression of the Financing of Terrorism and the Convention on the Marking of Plastic Explosives for the Purpose of Detection. In November, Singapore passed legislation to enable it to implement the Convention for the Suppression of Unlawful Acts against the Safety of Maritime Navigation; at year's end, it had not signed the convention.

Singapore's port and air bases continued to be available to transiting military forces engaged in the global war on terrorism, including those of the United States. In November, a Singapore Landing Ship Tank began a deployment to assist Coalition efforts in Iraq; Singapore has also pledged a C-130.

During President Bush's October visit, Singapore and the United States announced plans to conclude a "Strategic Framework Agreement" on defense and security. In addition to military-to-military cooperation, the statement noted that the agreement was expected to increase cooperation against terrorism and proliferation.

Singapore is a party to six of the 12 international conventions and protocols relating to terrorism.

Taiwan

Taiwan has supported the global war on terrorism and continues to take steps to improve its counterterrorism laws and regulations, port and container security, and terrorist finance legislation. At a ministerial meeting in June 2003 of the Asia-Pacific Economic Cooperation Forum, Taiwan's Economic Minister voiced Taiwan's strong support for counterterrorism efforts in the Asia-Pacific region, which focused on plans to enhance security measures in airplanes, airports, ships, and harbors.

In October, the Cabinet approved a draft law that would mandate the formation of a task force to coordinate terrorism prevention measures and provide an integrated legal framework for counterterrorism efforts. The proposed legislation also would grant special powers for telecommunication surveillance, provide measures to check the identity of terrorists, inspect transportation equipment, and confiscate the property or assets of suspected terrorists.

The United States and Taiwan continued negotiations on the Department of Homeland Security's Container Security Initiative, which aims to protect containerized shipping from exploitation by terrorists. Taiwan operates one of the busiest container ports in the world and has been identified by Homeland Security as one of the top 20 foreign ports for implementation of the initiative.

Taiwan also has been working to identify financial assets controlled or utilized by international terrorists, but to date, no terrorist assets have been located in Taiwan.

Thailand

Thailand's domestic and international counterterrorism efforts, which were bolstered in the wake of the deadly bombing in Bali, Indonesia, in October 2002, intensified during 2003. Prime Minster Thaksin Shinawatra publicly expressed the will of the Royal Thai Government to cooperate closely with the United States and other nations in fighting the global war on terror. In August, Thai authorities captured top JI leader with close ties to al-Qaida, Nurjaman Riduan bin Isomuddin (a.k.a. Hambali) in Ayutthaya, Thailand. Hambali's capture serves as a major blow to both JI and al-Qaida and represents a significant victory in the war on global terror.

In June and July, Thai authorities in southern Thailand arrested four men suspected of being either JI supporters or operatives. The four are implicated in a conspiracy to bomb a number of high-profile targets and tourist venues in Thailand, including the Embassies of Australia, Israel, Singapore, the United Kingdom, and the United States. Court hearings for the four began in November, although a decision is not expected until 2004.

In August, the King signed an emergency antiterrorist decree, giving the Government powerful new legal tools to fight terrorism. These measures establish the criminal offense of terrorism in the penal code and make that offense a predicate under the Anti-Money Laundering Act. The executive decree was approved after nearly two years of parliamentary consideration. Although existing legislation does not cover terrorist financing, Thailand is planning to expand its Anti-Money Laundering Act to include terrorism. The Government and Thailand's central bank continued to cooperate closely with the United States on reviewing and disseminating lists of persons blocked under US Executive Order 13224. To date, Thailand has not identified any entities on the list, and no assets have been blocked or frozen.

As Thailand continues to expand its government-to-government cooperation with other ASEAN states, it is becoming more difficult for members of regional terrorist organizations to move from country to country while evading national law enforcement agencies. Thailand is a participant in the new Southeast Asia Center for Counterterrorism based in Malaysia. As host of the APEC Leader's Summit in October 2003, Thailand was instrumental in persuading APEC members to adopt the "Bangkok Goals," which place security concerns on an equal footing with the economic objectives that previously dominated this forum.

Throughout most of 2003, Thailand provided 130 military engineers and medical personnel to Bagram, Afghanistan, in support of Operation Enduring Freedom. Thailand has also dispatched engineers to Iraq to help with reconstruction tasks there.

Thailand is a major recipient of the US Anti-Terrorism Assistance program, with numerous Thai police and security officials participating in US-sponsored training courses since 1995. Thailand is also working closely with the United States to enhance the security of its borders by upgrading to more effective, state-of-the-art controls.

There were no significant acts of terrorism in Thailand during 2003. The Thai Government's effectiveness in precluding a terrorist incident during the APEC Summit in October was considered a major success both domestically and internationally.

Thailand is a party to four of the 12 international conventions and protocols relating to terrorism and is a signatory to the Convention for the Suppression of the Financing of Terrorism.

Eurasia Overview

Central Asia, which for years had suffered attacks from Afghanistan-based guerilla and terrorist groups, saw no mass-casualty terrorist attacks in 2003. The operations of the Islamic Movement of Uzbekistan (IMU), a group on the US Foreign Terrorist Organization list that seeks to overthrow the Government of Uzbekistan and create an Islamic state, were seriously disrupted when some of its leaders and many of its members were killed in Afghanistan fighting with the Taliban against Coalition forces in 2001 and 2002. The IMU has been incapable of significant military operations since the beginning of Operation Enduring Freedom (OEF), and, with the help of outside training and financing, has switched primarily to terrorism. Law enforcement and counterterrorism actions by Kazakhstan, Kyrgyzstan, Tajikistan, and Uzbekistan disrupted IMU operations, led to arrests and prosecutions, and prevented planned attacks on US interests.

Russia, however, continued to be the target of terrorist attacks in 2003 carried out by Chechen terror groups that have adopted suicide/homicide bombing techniques, including the use of young women as bombers. The three largest such attacks resulted in more than 40 deaths each. In addition, venues in Moscow were attacked, including Red Square and a rock concert six miles from the Kremlin. The Moscow attacks killed 22 and injured several dozen as the perpetrators sought to sow terror in the capital.

States in the region continued to provide overflight and temporary basing rights; share law-enforcement and intelligence information; and identify, monitor, and apprehend al-Qaida members and other terrorists. Countries in the region also took diplomatic and political steps to contribute to the international struggle against terrorism, such as becoming party to some or all of the 12 United Nations international conventions and protocols relating to terrorism.

Enhancing regional counterterrorism cooperation has been a priority for the United States. Toward that end, the US Department of State's Coordinator for Counterterrorism, working closely with the Bureau of European and Eurasian Affairs, hosted the Fifth Counterterrorism Conference for Eurasian states in Vienna, Austria, in June 2003. Participants included most of the countries of Eurasia, Turkey, and the Organization for Security and Cooperation in Europe (OSCE). Delegations consisted of officials from the ministries of Foreign Affairs, Health, Defense, and Interior and the intelligence services. The conference consisted of a tabletop exercise based on a bioterrorism incident (the intentional release of pneumonic plague at a major international soccer match). Exercise groups concentrated on the broad range of public health, law enforcement, political-military, socioeconomic, and human rights issues, emphasizing the need for interdisciplinary communication, cooperation, and advance planning. The basic structure of the conference provided participants an opportunity to describe and identify components of their national programs to respond to a bioterrorism attack and make recommendations to their head of state to deal with the situation presented in the exercise scenario.

The United States also participated in the OSCE's first Annual Security Review Conference in June 2003, bringing in Ambassador Cofer Black as a keynote speaker. Also in the context of the OSCE, the United States led the drive to adopt a Ministerial decision committing OSCE-participating states to adopt International Civil Aviation Organization travel document standards by December 2005 or as soon as technologically and financially feasible.

Armenia

Armenia was a full and active participant in the global Coalition against terrorism in 2003 and is in the process of strengthening its domestic antiterror legislation. Armenian officials, including the president, issued repeated statements condemning terrorism and supporting the United States and the global Coalition against terrorism. Armenia provides no support for international terrorism or for any international terrorist group and has made no statements in support of terrorism or of a terrorism-supporting country. Armenia maintains diplomatic and economic relations with two countries on the US State Sponsors of Terrorism List—Iran and Syria. Iran and Syria have large ethnic Armenian populations.

Armenia was very cautious in public statements regarding the war with Iraq, due primarily to a substantial ethnic Armenian population in that country, but has since volunteered military units for postwar reconstruction. The Government also offered engineering and medical forces to stability operations in Iraq.

There were no actions before the Armenian judicial system in 2003 regarding international terrorism or acts of terror against US citizens or interests nor were there any new actions initiated regarding domestic terrorism. A new Armenian criminal law more clearly defining terrorist acts replaced Soviet-era legislation in 2003. Other legislation on terrorism and terrorist finance currently pending in the National Assembly should strengthen the ability of the Government to prosecute terrorist-related offenses. Five participants in the terrorist attack against the Armenian Parliament that killed Prime Minister Vazgen Sargsian, Speaker Karen Demirchian, and six other Government officials on 27 October 1999 were sentenced to life imprisonment in December 2003. They will be denied amnesty under a new law signed by President Robert Kocharyan on 26 November.

The Armenian National Assembly is also considering laws establishing an intergovernmental antiterrorism center and combating terrorist financing and money laundering. The Government strongly supports the legislation. The antiterrorism center will serve as a central government body to develop a national antiterror strategy and to coordinate the antiterrorism efforts of government ministries. The National Assembly also passed an export-control law in October 2003, which could assist efforts to monitor the export of dual-use goods. The Armenian Central Bank has acted under the authority of the new criminal code to freeze the assets of designated terrorist entities.

The Armenian Government did not extradite or request the extradition of any suspected terrorists during the year. Armenia does not have mutual legal assistance treaties with most nations, including the United States, although criminal suspects have been sent to the United States for trial on a case-by-case basis.

Armenia is a party to six of the 12 international conventions and protocols relating to terrorism and has signed a seventh.

Azerbaijan

Cooperation between Azerbaijan and the United States on counterterrorism is longstanding and has intensified since the September 11 attacks. Azerbaijan has turned over approximately 32 foreign citizens with suspected ties to terrorists, including eight to Egypt and three to Saudi Arabia, and has aggressively prosecuted members of suspected terrorist groups. It has also joined 10 European conventions on combating terrorism, and President Heydar Aliyev instructed his Government to implement UN Security Council Resolutions 1368, 1373, and 1377.

In August 2003, 150 Azerbaijani soldiers joined the peacekeeping contingent in Iraq. A platoon of Azerbaijani soldiers has been working with the Turkish peacekeeping contingent in Afghanistan since November 2002. Azerbaijan maintains diplomatic relations with Iran, which is on the US State Sponsors of Terrorism List.

During the past two years, the Azerbaijan Government has stepped up its effort to combat terrorist financing, including distribution of lists of suspected terrorist groups and individuals to local banks. In May 2003, the Government created an interministerial task force on money laundering and financial crimes, which will develop a government-wide strategy to combat financial crimes, including the financing of terrorism. It will also establish a financial intelligence unit. In January 2003, Azerbaijan revoked the registration of the Benevolence International Foundation, a designated financier of terrorism, after having frozen the organization's bank accounts. The Justice Ministry also revoked the registration of two other Islamic charities—the Kuwait Fund for the Sick and the Qatar Humanitarian Organization—for activities against the national interests of Azerbaijan.

The government also approved changes to the criminal code that increased the maximum penalty for acts of terrorism from 15 years to life imprisonment and added a provision making the financing of terrorist activities a crime under Azerbaijani law. Azerbaijan has deported numerous terrorists and persons suspected of having ties to terrorists and closed three Islamic organizations that were suspected of supporting terrorist groups. Members of Jayshullah, an indigenous terrorist group, who were arrested in 2000 and tried in 2001 for plotting to attack the US Embassy in Baku, remain in prison.

While Azerbaijan has served as a route for international mujahidin with ties to terrorist organizations seeking to move men, money, and materiel throughout the Caucasus, it has had some success in reducing their presence and hampering their activities. In May 2002, the Government convicted seven Azerbaijani citizens who, intending to fight in Chechnya, received military training in the Pankisi Gorge in Georgia. Four received suspended sentences, and the others were sentenced to four-to-five years in prison. Throughout 2003, Azerbaijan made successful and significant efforts to prevent international terrorists from transiting Azerbaijani territory.

Azerbaijan is a party to eight of the 12 international conventions and protocols relating to terrorism.

Georgia

The Georgian Government remained deeply committed to combating international and domestic terrorism and has consistently and publicly condemned acts of terror. Georgia has not engaged in any form of support for international terrorism, terrorists, or terrorist groups and has not made any public statement in support of any terrorist-supporting country. The Government frequently expresses full support for the global war on terror and expresses sympathy and support to those individuals and countries victimized by terrorist attacks. Georgia maintains diplomatic relations with Iran, which is on the US State Sponsors of Terrorism List.

Although Georgia prosecuted no acts of international or domestic terrorism in 2003, the Georgian Government is fully committed to prosecuting individuals who engage in terrorist activities. In 2003, Georgia extradited several Chechen fighters arrested in Georgia to Russia.

Throughout 2003, the Georgian Government took significant strides to support US-led efforts in the war against terrorism. Specifically, the Government demonstrated its willingness to provide the United States with information related to possible terrorist activities in Georgia. In support of Georgia's counterterrorism efforts, the United States continued to fully fund and support the Georgia Train and Equip Program (GTEP). GTEP supports the training of four Georgian army battalions and a mechanized company, plus training in tactics for operations against terrorists for smaller numbers of Interior Ministry troops and border guards. Georgia is still used to a limited degree as a terrorist transit state, although much less so since the Georgian crackdown on the Pankisi Gorge in late 2002.

In August 2003, the Georgian Government sent 70 military personnel for a six-month deployment to Iraq in support of Coalition operations. In February 2004, 200 GTEP-trained servicemen will replace these personnel. Georgian law-enforcement and security authorities continued to maintain a presence in the Pankisi Gorge throughout 2003.

Georgia is a party to six of the 12 international conventions and protocols relating to terrorism.

Kazakhstan

The Government of Kazakhstan has been publicly outspoken in support for the fight against terrorism and categorically denounces acts of terrorism. Kazakhstan is a member of the Shanghai Cooperation Organization along with China, Russia, Tajikistan, Uzbekistan, and Kyrgystan. Kazakhstan maintains diplomatic relations with Cuba, North Korea, Libya, the Palestinian Authority, Sudan, and Iran.

Under the terms of a Memorandum of Understanding of

2002, Kazakhstan allows Coalition forces the use of Almaty International Airport for emergency flight diversion in support of OEF. Since December 2001, Kazakhstan has also allowed more than 1,100 overflights in support of OEF at no cost. In the summer of 2003, Kazakhstan sent a 27-member military engineering and ordnance-disposal contingent to Iraq. In 2003, representatives of Kazakhstan successfully completed an introductory two-year program consisting of 14 courses offered by the antiterrorism training assistance office of the State Department's Bureau of Diplomatic Security.

Kazakhstan is a party to 11 of the 12 international conventions and protocols relating to terrorism.

Kyrgyzstan

Kyrgyzstan in 2003 remained a dependable and outspoken ally in the global war on terrorism, hosting Coalition forces engaged in OEF and taking political, legislative, and law enforcement initiatives to disrupt and deter terrorism. President Akayev has staunchly defended the US presence within Kyrgyzstani borders. In 2001, the Kyrgyzstani Government authorized the construction of a Coalition base adjacent to the existing Manas airport near the nation's capital of Bishkek, in support of OEF. The base currently hosts approximately 1,100 Coalition forces. In 2003, this included soldiers from the United States, Denmark, Italy, the Netherlands, South Korea, and Spain. The base is used for combat support, transport, refueling, tanker and cargo shipments, and ground operations in Afghanistan.

President Akayev proclaims that antiterrorism efforts are of extremely high priority for Kyrgyzstan and noted that terrorism is not only a threat to Kyrgyzstan but to regional and international security as well. In September 2003, a Russian airbase was opened near the village of Kant, approximately 20 miles from Bishkek. The base was constructed under the auspices of the Collective Security Treaty Organization (CSTO) and is used for security and antiterrorism efforts for CSTO members Russia, Armenia, Belarus, Tajikistan, Kazakhstan, and Kyrgyzstan.

Kyrgyzstan is a member of the Shanghai Cooperation Organization (SCO) with China, Russia, Kazakhstan, Tajikistan, and Uzbekistan. The SCO voted to create an antiterrorism center in Bishkek in 2003. Although the location of this center was later changed to Tashkent, Uzbekistan, Kyrgyzstan has provided logistic support for its creation.

Kyrgyzstan suffered one deadly act of terrorism in 2003. In May, militants from the IMU bombed a currency exchange in Osh, killing one man.

An attack in March on a bus traveling between Kyrgyzstan and China killed 21 people, including 19 Chinese citizens. This incident is still under investigation and may have been terrorism or crime related.

Kyrgyzstan's courts in February sentenced Sherali Akbotoyev, a captured Kyrgyzstani member of the IMU, to 25 years in prison for violating six articles of the Kyrgyzstani criminal code, including his involvement in armed attacks against Kyrgyzstani military forces during the IMU incursions of 1999 and 2000. In November, the Kyrgyzstani Supreme Court banned four groups, including the East Turkestan Islamic Movement, enabling the state to lawfully seize its property.

Security forces in Kyrgyzstan played a major role in combating terrorism in 2003, successfully disrupting terrorist operations reportedly aimed at US interests. Security authorities in May detained five IMU operatives whom they later determined had conducted the terrorist bombing in December 2002 at the Oberon Market in Bishkek that killed seven people and the Osh currency-exchange bombing in May 2003. Kyrgyzstani authorities worked closely with Uzbekistani authorities to disrupt the cell and provided information that helped Uzbekistan capture one of the cell's members in Andijan, Uzbekistan. In November, Kyrgyzstani authorities announced that they had detained three suspects who had been planning an attack on US interests.

Kyrgyzstan's military and internal forces worked to improve their counterterrorism capabilities and to expand their cooperation with regional partners in 2003. In March, Kyrgyzstan's Interior Ministry conducted counterterrorism exercises in the southern part of the country and, in July, seized a cache of hidden weapons in the Batken region. Bishkek also moved to bolster the security of the nation's borders from terrorists, announcing in March it would increase the number of border checkpoints and in September that border troops, working jointly with border forces from neighboring Tajikistan, would operate together to identify mountain paths used by terrorists. Kyrgyzstan is party to nine of the 12 international conventions and protocols relating to terrorism.

Russia

Russia pursued several major domestic and global counterterrorism initiatives in 2003, sustaining its key role in the global war on terrorism. Russian political, legislative, and law enforcement efforts supported international cooperative efforts and a number of successful domestic terrorist prosecutions. Russian attitudes toward terrorism, however, continue to be influenced by the ongoing war in Chechnya. Local insurgents in the North Caucasus remained the greatest terrorist threat to Russia and were responsible for the murder of hundreds of Russian citizens, civilians as well as military. There is evidence of a foreign terrorist presence in Chechnya, although much of the actual terrorist activity there is homegrown and linked to the Chechen separatist movement.

Russia passed several new antiterrorism laws, began implementing previously passed legislation, and facilitated effective interdiction of terrorist finance flows by becoming a full member of the Financial Action Task Force (FATF). In February, the Russian Supreme Court issued an official Government list of 15 terrorist organizations, the first of its kind in Russia and an important step toward implementation of counterterrorism statutes. Following the promulgation of the list, the 15 organizations were prohibited from engaging in any financial activities.

Some proposed Russian counterterrorism legislation has

stirred controversy. Duma-drafted amendments to the 1991 "Law on Mass Media," designed to restrict the dissemination of information that could be useful to terrorists, were vetoed by President Putin in November 2002 following criticisms that they unduly restricted freedom of the press. A long-promised redrafting of the media law, prompted by Kremlin criticism of the role played by some media outlets during the Dubrovka Theater hostage crisis of October 2002, has yet to occur.

Examples of noteworthy law enforcement and judicial actions undertaken by Russia in 2003 include:

- Zaurbek Talkhigov was sentenced to eight and a half years incarceration in June for tipping off terrorists about police attempts to rescue hostages during the siege of the Dubrovka Theater in 2002.
- Failed suicide bomber Zarema Muzhikhoyeva was arrested after attempting to detonate a bomb in a Moscow cafe. An explosives ordnance disposal officer was killed trying to disarm the explosives she had been carrying.
- Ayyub Katayev and Magomed Gakayev were convicted of banditry and possession of illegal weapons in connection with their participation in a terrorist attack in January 2001 on a Doctors Without Borders convoy in Chechnya. The two were also charged with kidnapping US citizen Kenneth Gluck, the head of Doctors Without Borders, but were later acquitted.
- Sergei Chochiyev was convicted and sentenced to 15 years incarceration in October for kidnapping a United Nations aid worker in 1998 on behalf of Chechen insurgents.

Russia's international efforts have focused on building multilateral support for counterterrorist actions and strengthening the international legal basis for such cooperation.

At the United Nations, Russia cosponsored a draft General Assembly resolution on human rights and terrorism in November 2003. Russia also submitted the names of Chechen rebels Zelimkhan Yandarbiyev and Shamil Basayev, in June and August respectively, for inclusion on the UNSC Resolution 1267 Sanctions Committee list of designated terrorists for their links to al-Qaida. The United States joined Russia in submitting Basayev's name to the sanctions committee, and Secretary Powell designated both as foreign terrorists under Executive Order 13224.

After Secretary of State Powell designated The Islamic International Brigade, the Special Purpose Islamic Regiment, and the Riyadus-Salikhin Reconnaissance and Sabotage Battalion of Chechen Martyrs as terrorist organizations in February 2003, the five permanent members of the UN Security Council, along with Spain and Germany, jointly submitted the names of the three Chechen groups to the 1267 Sanctions Committee—the first time that the permanent members made such a joint submission on a terrorist designation.

Russia used its leadership in the Commonwealth of Independent States (CIS) and the CSTO to push for expanded counterterrorist operations. It also sought the establishment of a counterterrorism center in Central Asia. Russia also worked through the SCO to support creation of a joint antiterrorism center in Tashkent in 2004.

Russian policymakers continue to believe that the NATO-Russia Council can play a role in counterterrorism cooperation and the prevention of the proliferation of weapons of mass destruction. Russia hosted the first-ever Moscow meeting of the NATO-Russia Council in May 2003, which focused on developing concrete joint antiterrorism training projects and operations.

Russia maintains diplomatic relations and historically good ties with all the states on the US State Sponsors of Terrorism List. For example, Russian Foreign Minister Igor Ivanov paid a working visit to Syria in July 2003, and Hassan Rohani, secretary of the Supreme National Security Council of Iran, visited Moscow in November 2003. Although Russia has never condoned Palestinian terrorist acts, Russian officials do not necessarily view all Palestinian actions as inherently terrorist in nature and sometimes argue that armed resistance is justified against an Israeli occupation of Palestinian territory. Nevertheless, the Government of Russia firmly opposes state-sponsored terrorism and supports international initiatives to combat it. The Russian Government maintains that its relationships with states on the US terrorism list serve as a positive influence that has—or may have—moderated or diminished these governments' support for terrorist groups.

Cooperative effort in the global war on terrorism remains a key pillar of Russia's strategic partnership with the United States. Regular meetings of the Working Group on Counterterrorism, cochaired by US Deputy Secretary of State Richard Armitage and Russian First Deputy Foreign Minister Vyacheslav Trubnikov, continue to facilitate counterterrorism cooperation between the two nations. The Working Group has encouraged expanded direct agency-to-agency contacts and specific antiterrorism projects. Russia has established similar bilateral working groups on terrorism with a number of other countries, including the United Kingdom, India, France, and Germany.

The Russian Federal Security Service (FSB) and the US Federal Bureau of Investigation (FBI) regularly exchanged operational counterterrorism information in 2003. Russian authorities provided the United States Department of Homeland Security and FBI with evidence leading to the prosecution of an individual in the United States for fundraising activities associated with terrorism. The FSB also assisted the FBI in several important international terrorism investigations during 2003. Unprecedented cooperation between the FBI and FSB was essential to the FBI's arrest in New Jersey in August 2003 of Hermant Lahkani for attempting to sell a shoulder-fired missile to an undercover operative posing as an al-Qaida terrorist. Lahkani was indicted on 18 December 2003.

A mutual legal assistance treaty is in force and has been used effectively in some cases.

According to the Russian General Procuracy, 90 percent of terrorist acts in Russia during 2003 were committed within Chechnya and its surrounding areas. Some were directed against military or internal security forces, while others targeted specific civilians. The terrorists' strategic use of women to conduct increasingly random, indiscriminate, and sensational suicide attacks emerged as a key development in 2003. Major terrorist acts perpetrated against Russia during 2003, in chronological order:

- 15 April: Sixteen civilians die when a bomb explodes on a bus near Khankala.
- 9 May: Victory Day bombing at the Dynamo Stadium in Groznyy, the Chechen capital, injures three.
- 12 May: Two women and a man detonated an explosive-laden truck inside an administrative complex in Znamenskoye in northern Chechnya, killing 60 and wounding more than 250.
- 14 May: Groznyy resident Larisa Musalayeva detonated an explosive belt at a crowded Muslim religious festival east of Groznyy, killing herself and 18 others and wounding 46, in a probable attempt to assassinate Chechen administrator Akhmad Kadyrov.
- 5 June: Samara resident Lidiya Khaldykhoroyeva detonated an explosive belt beside a bus filled with federal air force personnel near Mozdok, a major staging area for Russian troops serving in Chechnya, killing herself and 18 others.
- 20 June: A man and a woman detonated a truck bomb in the vicinity of an Internal Ministry building in Groznyy, killing themselves and wounding 36.
- 5 July: Twenty-year-old Kurchaloy resident Zulikhan Alikhadzhiyeva and a female accomplice each detonated explosive belts at a crowded rock concert in the Moscow suburbs, killing themselves and 16 others and wounding more than 50.
- 9 July: Twenty-three-year-old Bamut resident Zarema Muzhikhoyeva was apprehended after trying unsuccessfully to detonate an explosive within her handbag while seated at a table in the Mon cafe on Moscow's Tverskaya street.
- 1 August: A suicide truck bomber completely destroyed a military hospital in Mozdok near Chechnya, killing himself and 52 others and injuring more than 80.
- 3 September: Six people are killed in an explosion onboard a commuter train near the Northern Caucasus spa town of Pyatigorsk.
- 16 September: Two suicide bombers drive a truck laden with explosives into a government security services building near Chechnya, killing three and wounding 25.
- 5 December: A suicide bomber detonated a bomb on a morning commuter train near Yessentuki in the Stavropol region north of Chechnya, killing 44 and wounding more than 150.
- 9 December: A female suicide bomber detonated a bomb near Moscow's Red Square, killing herself, five others, and wounding 14. The woman and an accomplice had asked passersby for directions to the state Duma moments before the detonation.

Russia is a party to 11 of the 12 international conventions and protocols relating to terrorism. Ratification of the Convention on the Marking of Plastic Explosives for the Purpose of Detection is expected in 2004.

Tajikistan

The Government of Tajikistan continues to be a staunch supporter of the United States in the global war on terrorism. Tajikistan does not support any terrorist groups or activities and allows its territory and air space to be used for counterterrorist actions. President Emomali Rahmonov reiterated Tajikistan's adamant opposition to terrorism and terrorist activities to the United Nations General Assembly in 2003.

On the national level, the Government continues to develop national counterterrorism legislation to supplement the Antiterrorist Law of the Republic of Tajikistan of 1999, the State Program on Strengthening the Fight against Terrorism of 2000, and the Tajik criminal code, which allows harsh punishments for acts of terrorism, including the death penalty. The Tajikistani Government closely monitors terrorist groups operating within its borders such as the Islamic Movement of Uzbekistan. In addition, Tajikistan has taken steps to combat terrorist financing by distributing lists of designated terrorist groups and individuals to local banks and other financial institutions.

On the international level, Tajikistan participates in antiterrorist initiatives advanced by the SCO and the CIS Antiterrorist Center. On 14 November 2003, Tajikistan and India created a bilateral counterterrorist working group and agreed to create an antiterrorist framework. In his address to the UN General Assembly in 2003, President Rahmonov focused on issues related to the struggle against international terrorism and ways to eradicate it. He expressed an interest in the role of narcotics trafficking in financing terrorism and called for establishing a global partnership for countering the dangers of drugs.

The United States currently provides technical aid to the antiterrorist units of the Tajikistani Government. With the assistance of the United States and other foreign countries, Tajikistan's law enforcement personnel receive training in such areas as crisis management, bomb detection, and post-blast investigation. Tajikistan and Russia are joined in a bilateral effort that employs the Russian 201st Motorized Rifle Division and the Russian Border Guard Service in a counterterrorism role.

Tajikistan has not had a domestic terrorist incident since 2001. The Tajikistani Government made no requests for extradition nor extradited any suspected terrorists in 2003.

Tajikistan is a party to eight and signatory to nine of the 12 international conventions and protocols relating to terrorism.

Turkmenistan

The Government of Turkmenistan has been a member of the international Coalition against terrorism, taking action to seal its border with Afghanistan, identifying and freezing any financial assets used to support terrorism, and instituting new airport security measures. Turkmenistan is officially a neutral country and assists the Coalition in nonmilitary initiatives such as allowing the overflight of US aircraft and small "gas and go" operations in support of humanitarian relief missions in Afghanistan. The Government also participated in "Six plus Two" meetings on forming a new Afghan Government and in international donor meetings on Afghan reconstruction. Turkmen officials have made no statements in support of a terrorist-supporting country on a terrorism issue.

Turkmenistan courts carried out no prosecutions on charges of international terrorism in 2003. On 25 November 2002, an armed attack was carried out on President Niyazov's motorcade. This attack is considered by the Government to have been a case of domestic terrorism. Trials of those implicated in the plot were held in January and February 2003; international observers were not allowed to attend, and there were serious concerns about the due process accorded to defendants. All of those convicted for the attack received lengthy jail sentences.

There has been a significant change in the Government's attitude toward terrorism, specifically domestic terrorism, following the attack on President Niyazov. Measures adopted in the wake of the attack in November 2002 are ostensibly designed to "strengthen" Turkmenistan's security; however, in its implementation of the new strictures, the Government has further infringed on civil liberties and violated human rights.

Turkmenistan is a party to nine of the 12 international conventions and protocols relating to terrorism.

Ukraine

The fight against terrorism is a priority for the Government of Ukraine. The president, cabinet of ministers, and foreign ministry publicly condemned acts of international terrorism on several occasions. Ukraine supported both Operation Iraqi Freedom and Operation Enduring Freedom in 2003. Ukraine is one of the largest Coalition troop providers in Iraq. Kiev does, however, maintain trade relations with several countries listed by the United States as State Sponsors of Terrorism.

Ukraine supported the Coalition in Iraq by sending a 450-member Nuclear, Biological, and Chemical remediation unit to Kuwait; elements of this group later joined the current deployment to Iraq. A 1,650-member Ukrainian brigade is now serving in the Polish-led Multinational Division. Ukraine also grants overflight rights to support counterterrorist efforts in Afghanistan, allowing approximately 2,000 overflights in 2003. Air bases in Ukraine have also been identified for emergency use by the OEF Coalition.

Significant Ukrainian legislative developments during 2003 in the fight against terrorism included adoption by the Parliament of an omnibus "Law on Combating Terrorism," adoption of a new criminal code containing Article 258 that explicitly defines terrorism, and adoption of the "Program of National Antiterrorist Measures for 2003–2005." The Parliament also passed additional legislation, including amendments that bring the law on money laundering into line with FATF requirements.

In 2003, the Government reports that Ukrainian courts carried out no prosecutions on charges of international terrorism and prosecuted only two domestic cases in which terrorism charges were filed. Ukrainian law enforcement agencies exchanged information with the Anti-Terrorism Center of the CIS and law enforcement agencies of the United States, France, Israel, Turkey, Portugal, Germany, Malaysia, Czech Republic, Slovakia, Latvia, Lithuania, Russia, Kazakhstan, Azerbaijan, Belarus, and others.

Although Article 25 of the Ukrainian constitution prohibits the extradition of Ukrainian citizens, the criminal code provides for extradition of foreigners and persons without citizenship who are not permanent residents of Ukraine. Ukrainian authorities deported several persons with suspected or alleged ties to terrorism in 2003, including several transient Chechens.

Control over the procedures for entry, departure, and stay in Ukraine for representatives of Islamic organizations and centers, including those from the Caucasus region, has been tightened. These measures include shortening the period of stay in Ukraine, expelling individuals from the country, and banning entry. The Interior Ministry is developing a database to document and register (including automated fingerprinting) persons detained for illegally crossing Ukraine's state border and/or staying illegally in Ukraine.

Pursuant to UN Security Council resolutions 1333, 1390, and 1455, Ukraine is taking measures to block the funds and other financial resources of Usama Bin Ladin and his supporters. Thus far, none have been identified. The Ministry of Finance is charged with collecting, processing, and analyzing financial transactions subject to obligatory financial monitoring. There have been problems with implementation of these provisions.

Ukraine is a full party to all 12 international conventions and protocols relating to terrorism.

Uzbekistan

Uzbekistan was among the first states to support US efforts in the global war on terrorism. President Islom Karimov consistently stresses the importance of Uzbekistani counterterrorism cooperation in both public and private venues. Uzbekistan continues to host US military forces within its borders and views the US base at Karshi-Khanabad as fundamental to Uzbekistan's support for the war on terror and central to stability in Central Asia.

Uzbekistan has played an important role in multilateral regional efforts to combat terrorism. Uzbekistan has recently engaged with Kazakhstan and Kyrgyzstan on antiterrorist issues, especially those related to the IMU. In August 2003, Tashkent was designated as the location for a Shanghai Cooperation Organization Regional Anti-Terrorism Center. Uzbekistan publicly condemns state sponsors of terrorism, despite the presence of Iranian and North Korean diplomatic missions in Tashkent.

The Karimov regime is concerned with the threat posed by the IMU, presently operating primarily outside its borders.

The Government of Kazakhstan recently extradited two IMU members to Uzbekistan.

Uzbekistan continues to make countering terrorism and antiregime threats a high priority. Tashkent mounted robust efforts in 2003 to limit the destabilizing effects of militant Islam by further securing its borders, identifying extremists, and conducting arrests of suspected radicals and terrorists. Uzbekistani prosecutors obtained more than 100 convictions in 2003 for actions that fell under the Uzbekistani criminal code for terrorist or extremist activity, as well as more than 600 other prosecutions under a less stringent Uzbekistani administrative code that, nevertheless, allows for detention of up to three years. The Government of Uzbekistan did not adopt any new antiterrorism laws in 2003. One high-profile prosecution is the recent sentencing of IMU member Azizbek Karimov, who admitted to planning attacks against the US Embassy in neighboring Kyrgyzstan.

Uzbekistan is signatory to all 12 international conventions and protocols relating to terrorism.

Europe Overview

European nations worked in close partnership with the United States in the global counterterrorism campaign and have continued to strengthen their legal and administrative ability to take action against terrorists and their supporters, including freezing their assets. The contributions of European countries in sharing intelligence, arresting members of terrorist cells, and interdicting terrorist financing and logistics continued to be vital elements in the war on terrorism. Allies such as France and the United Kingdom were particularly responsive during periods of heightened security, cooperating with United States officials to monitor airline flights of concern.

The European Union (EU) has been a reliable partner in the war on terrorism and has significantly strengthened its legal and administrative ability, and that of EU member states, to take action against terrorists and their supporters—including freezing their assets—in the past several years. International judicial cooperation advanced in 2003, as EU members changed domestic legislation to incorporate provision of the European Arrest Warrant, which was scheduled to come into effect in early 2004. The EU and United States signed new Extradition and Mutual Legal Assistance Treaties at the G-8 Summit in June 2003 that will expand law enforcement and judicial cooperation. Significant deficiencies remained, however, and some countries have legal impediments to taking firm judicial action against known terrorists, often stemming from asylum laws, inadequate counterterrorism legislation, or high standards of evidence that afford loopholes and limit the ability of authorities to hold suspects. The EU as a whole was reluctant to take steps to block the assets of charities associated with HAMAS and Hizballah.

The United Kingdom continued its longstanding close partnership with the United States, providing the second-largest contingent of forces for the liberation of Iraq, arresting extremists in the United Kingdom on terrorism-related charges, and stepping up efforts to disrupt and prosecute terrorists. The United Kingdom aggressively moved to freeze the assets of organizations and persons with terrorist links and to proscribe terrorist groups. UK overseas interests were attacked in November when suicide bombers struck the British Consulate and a British bank in Istanbul, killing 25 people. The United Kingdom provided significant counterterrorism assistance and training to foreign governments around the world.

Italy continued its exemplary work against terrorism, deploying forces to Afghanistan and Iraq. Nineteen Italian citizens were killed in a terrorist attack on Italian Carabinieri in Iraq. Italian authorities continued to disrupt suspected terrorist cells linked to al-Qaida and, for the first time, expelled suspects believed to pose a terrorist threat. Members of the Red Brigades–Communist Combatant Party staged a shootout with police, leading to the arrest of the group's leader and subsequent significant progress in dismantling it.

Spain's vigorous investigation of extremist groups continued, with Spanish authorities indicting Usama Bin Ladin and 34 others for complicity in the September 11 attacks. Substantial progress was made against the Basque Fatherland and Liberty (ETA) terrorist organization; more than 100 persons connected to ETA were arrested, and several operational ETA cells were dismantled.

France made many significant terrorism-related arrests, including suspects linked to persons who assisted the September 11 hijackers. Investigations continued into the activities of terrorist cells connected to plots against the US Embassy in Paris. French authorities, working with their Spanish counterparts, put intensive pressure on ETA, arresting top leaders of the Basque terrorist group's military wing in December. France continued to engage numerous non-EU countries in dialogue on counterterrorism issues.

Cooperation among European law-enforcement authorities was a feature of many successes during the past year. For example, France and Spain became the first countries to create "multi-national police investigation teams" under the terms of an EU agreement of 2002.

Germany contributed significantly to international forces in Afghanistan and took a lead role in that country's reconstruction. In February, a German court became the first to convict a terrorist linked to the September 11 attacks. German authorities continued extensive investigations into Islamic extremist–based terrorism and arrested a number of suspects. In November, Germany extradited suspected al-Qaida financier Sheik Mohammed ali Hasan al Moayad and an associate to the United States.

In Turkey, two separate—but probably coordinated—attacks by suicide bombers on British and Jewish targets in Istanbul in November killed 61 people. Turkey and the United States continued to discuss cooperation against Kongra-Gel (KADEK—the former Kurdistan Workers Party), which, for its part, continued to launch attacks against Turkish targets. Despite progress by Turkish police against the Revolutionary People's Liberation Party (DHKP/C), that group continued its attacks as well.

In December 2003, a Greek court convicted 15 members of Revolutionary Organization 17 November (17N) of hundreds of crimes, sentencing five 17N leaders to multiple life terms and imposing sentences of up to 244 years on others. Four suspects were acquitted.

Estonia, Latvia, Lithuania, Denmark, and Norway contributed forces and reconstruction assistance to Afghanistan and Iraq. Sweden and Finland also have peacekeepers in Afghanistan and are active in reconstruction in both nations. Norwegian authorities continued to investigate suspected Ansar al-Islam leader (and Norway resident) Mullah Krekar and froze an account linked to that organization.

Despite limited resources, the countries of southeast Europe have actively supported the international Coalition against terrorism. Albania, Serbia-Montenegro, Bosnia and Herzegovina, Croatia, and Bulgaria cooperated to combat organized crime and various forms of trafficking, enhance border security, and improve training for border security personnel.

The United States and the EU signed extradition and mutual legal assistance agreements in June that, as US Attorney General John Ashcroft noted, will provide "additional tools to combat terrorism, organized crime, and other serious forms of criminality." The EU and its member states have made significant contributions to the reconstruction of Afghanistan.

Albania

Despite limited resources, Albania has provided considerable support to US and international counterterrorism initiatives. Albania continues to implement its National Action Plan against Terrorism, originally approved in 2002.

The government has frozen the assets of a notorious terrorist financier, curtailed the activities of suspect Islamic NGOs, and detained or expelled individuals suspected of having links to terrorism or attempting to foment religious intolerance. In June 2003, Parliament passed a strong money-laundering law that included antiterrorist financing provisions, bringing Albania's legislation into compliance with international standards. The Bank of Albania has also established a task force to monitor all financial activities of secondary banks and their compliance with client verification. Legislation is pending that would define what constitutes a terrorist act, identify the antiterrorism responsibilities of specific Government agencies, and create an interministerial National Coordinating Committee for the Fight Against Terrorist Acts. Albania continues to cooperate extremely closely with the United States and other governments in sharing information and investigating terrorist-related groups and activities. Albania has also started cracking down on ethnic Albanian extremists, recently convicting a key leader of the ultranationalist Albanian National Army on charges of inciting national and religious hatred and using falsified documents.

Albania has ratified all 12 UN international conventions and protocols relating to terrorism.

Belgium

The Belgian Government continues to participate in the global war on terrorism and cooperates with its European neighbors and the US Government on multiple levels. Brussels remains active in sharing information with the United States regarding terrorist threats to US interests or persons.

The Belgian judicial system effectively applied the rule of law to terrorist conspirators in 2003 when it prosecuted Europe's largest terrorism trial since 11 September 2001. Among the 23 defendants was Nizar Trabelsi, a Tunisian national and al-Qaida associate arrested by Belgian authorities in September 2001 for plotting against various targets, including an Antwerp synagogue, the Kleine Brogel military air base, and the US Embassy in Paris. Trabelsi was sentenced to 10 years in prison—the maximum permitted under Belgian law at the time of trial. Also sentenced was Tarek Maaroufi, a Tunisian-born Belgian national arrested in December 2001 for providing forged travel documents to the two assassins of Afghan Northern Alliance leader Ahmad Shah Massoud. Maaroufi was sentenced to six years in prison. Despite the absence of terrorism-specific legislation at the time of trial, the Belgian court was able to convict 18 of the other 21 defendants with sentences ranging from two to five years in jail.

In January 2003, Belgium enacted a bill granting law enforcement authorities the power to take "special investigative measures" such as wiretapping and infiltration for the investigation of terrorism and other serious crimes. In December 2003, the Belgian Parliament passed legislation implementing the EU's Framework Decision of June 2002 on combating terrorism, as well as the European Arrest Warrant. (The King was to sign the legislation into law in January 2004.) The legislation implementing the EU Framework Decision criminalized terrorism and financial contributions to those who commit terrorist acts. The European Arrest Warrant should streamline the process of arresting and extraditing terrorists within the EU.

Belgium has participated in the International Security Assistance Force (ISAF) in Afghanistan since early 2003; 250 Belgian troops under ISAF currently provide security at Kabul International Airport. Belgium sent 5.5 million euros of humanitarian aid to Afghanistan in 2003.

Belgium has signed 11 of the 12 international conventions and protocols relating to terrorism but has ratified only six. In December 2003, two more conventions appeared on the way to ratification in early 2004. The Belgian Senate approved a bill providing for ratification of the UN Convention on the Suppression of the Financing of Terrorism, and the lower house of Parliament—the Chamber of Deputies—was expected to pass it quickly as well. The Convention on the Punishment and Prevention of Crime against Internationally Protected Persons was presented to Parliament on 8 December. Its signature and ratification was also expected in early 2004.

Bosnia and Herzegovina

The Government of Bosnia and Herzegovina (BiH) has continued to condemn acts of international terrorism. Combating terrorism in BiH remains difficult because of the country's ethnic divisions and the lack of strong central institutions, such as a state-level intelligence agency and law-enforcement authorities with both executive powers and national jurisdiction. BiH also lacks established procedures for dealing with such issues as denaturalization, extradition, deportation, and preventive detention.

The Bosnian Government introduced measures to address some of the administrative and legal challenges it faces in combating terrorism. A state-level intelligence and security agency, as well as an internal security service with significant counterterrorism responsibilities, are planned for 2004. In 2002, the Parliament passed a law creating the State Information and Protection Agency whose mission includes combating terrorism, illegal trafficking, organized crime, and smuggling of weapons of mass destruction. To shore up this agency's authority and resources, an amended law will be submitted for Parliament's approval in 2004. Although BiH lacks a financial intelligence unit, comprehensive money-laundering and terrorist-financing laws, and legislation dealing with forfeiture of assets, this amended law is designed to address these weaknesses.

The BiH Government's commitment to the fight against terrorism and its decisive action in apprehending suspects and shutting down NGOs and bank accounts tied to terrorist organizations slowed with the change of government in October 2002, which brought nationalist parties to power. Moreover, foreign Islamic extremists, who entered Bosnia during the war in 1992-95, remain in the country. Nonetheless, the Federation Financial Police continued to shut down NGOs with terrorist links, and Federation banking authorities continued to freeze accounts of suspected terrorist supporters. In particular, the Government disrupted the operations of the Benevolence International Foundation (BIF), Al-Haramain Islamic Foundation (including its successor, Vazir), and the Global Relief Fund, which have direct links to al-Qaida and Usama Bin Ladin. Documents seized from the offices of the BIF link its leader directly to Usama Bin Ladin. BIF leader Enaam Arnaout, who—among other things—was charged in US courts with concealing his relationship to al-Qaida, received a 15-year prison sentence.

The Government's investigative proceedings into the role of six former Bosnian Federation officials suspected of operating a terrorist-training camp in BiH with Iran in the mid-1990s concluded at the end of 2003, and indictments—if issued—are expected in 2004.

Bosnia and Herzegovina is a party to 11 of the 12 international conventions and protocols relating to terrorism, ratifying five in 2003.

Bulgaria

To aid in the fight against terrorist financing, the Government of Bulgaria enacted in February 2003 the Law on Measures Against the Financing of Terrorism, which links existing laws against terrorism with the financing of those crimes. The law was drafted in accordance with the Financial Action Task Force's Eight Special Recommendations Against the Financing of Terrorism. The Bulgarian Financial Intelligence Agency has full authority to obtain information without a court order, to share information freely with law-enforcement agencies, and to process and act on allegations of terrorist financing.

In the past year, Bulgarian Ministry of Interior and Customs training has begun to include nuclear, biological, and chemical detection and handling. Customs officers have begun using the TRACKER licensing system as their primary permit-screening tool.

In December 2003, Bulgaria joined the United Nations Convention Against Corruption. Sofia is a party to all 12 international conventions and protocols relating to terrorism.

Czech Republic

The Czech Republic is a stalwart ally in the war against terror and is providing assistance both domestically and abroad. In support of Operation Iraqi Freedom, the Czechs posted a nuclear-biological-chemical (NBC) unit to Camp Doha and a military field hospital to Basra, where it treated more than 10,000 civilians and military personnel. Although both returned home at the end of 2003, a Czech Civilian-Military Cooperation Team, 80 military police, and 13 Czech experts serving in the Coalition Provisional Authority are still in the theater. Per commitments made in Madrid, the Czech Republic provided 10 experts to train Iraqi police in Jordan.

In Afghanistan, the Government of the Czech Republic provided its NBC unit and military hospital before sending them to Iraq. The Government is considering a deployment of up to 150 special forces troops to Afghanistan.

There were no cases of international terrorism within the Czech Republic in 2003, but Czech authorities addressed several domestic cases of extortion involving the use of explosives or poison. Neither bombs nor poison were ever found, but the Czech police made arrests and are prosecuting the cases appropriately.

The Czech Republic is a party to nine of 12 conventions and protocols relating to terrorism. Its main goal in combating terrorism is to ratify the UN Convention on the Suppression of Financing of Terrorism and the amendment of the Measures against Legalization of Proceeds of Criminal Activity. The latter is currently before Parliament.

Denmark

Denmark has actively supported the global war on terrorism. In 2003, the Danish Government froze the assets of the Danish branch of al-Aqsa and arrested a Danish citizen originally from Morocco with alleged ties to al-Qaida and pressed still-pending weapons charges against him.

The Danish Government contributed naval assets to Operation Iraqi Freedom and has more than 500 military personnel deployed in southern Iraq assisting with security and reconstruction efforts. Denmark contributed 50 military personnel to the ISAF in Afghanistan in 2003, in addition to Danish officers deployed with NATO. In December 2003, the Parliament authorized deployment of 40 additional personnel to provide communications and information support to ISAF.

Denmark is a party to all 12 international conventions and protocols relating to terrorism.

Estonia

Estonia has been fully supportive of the war against terrorism. Estonia contributed a demining team in support of the ISAF in Afghanistan. In Iraq, Estonia is contributing a cargo-handling team and 24-man infantry platoon under US command, as well as providing humanitarian assistance.

Estonia is a party to 11 of the 12 international conventions and protocols relating to terrorism.

Finland

In 2003, Finland implemented regulations that allow it to freeze terrorist assets without EU or UN approval in cases when another government presents a legal request for action or the individual or organization is suspected of having committed an offense within Finland's borders. Finland also amended its criminal code to make it possible to sentence leaders of terrorist groups to 15 years in jail, although the group has to have actually committed acts of terrorism in Finland before investigation and prosecution can begin. If the charge also includes murder, the maximum sentence could be life imprisonment. In January 2004, the Finnish Security Police also created a special unit concentrating solely on fighting terrorism, the first of its kind in Finland.

Approximately 50 Finnish Civil-Military Cooperation troops are currently deployed in Afghanistan in support of ISAF. In 2003, Afghanistan was the single-largest country recipient of Finland's foreign aid (10 million euros each year), which included support for the Afghan army and police force.

Finland is a party to all 12 international conventions and protocols relating to terrorism and implemented EU legislation against terrorism.

France

France remains an active and engaged participant in the war against terrorism, exemplified by an aggressive police force and judiciary. French authorities work closely with US and other foreign counterparts to investigate and prosecute terrorist operatives. France is currently changing its domestic legislation to incorporate the provisions of the European Arrest Warrant and to strengthen its procedures for international judicial cooperation. (The Arrest Warrant is expected to enter into force on 1 January 2004 in France and the other 14 EU member states.)

Throughout 2003, France continued to take rapid action in support of US requests under Executive Order 13224 to freeze Taliban, al-Qaida, and other terrorist financial assets. The Ministry of Finance's terrorism financing coordination cell, FINTER, maintains direct coordination with the US Treasury Department's Financial Terrorism Task Force and Office of Foreign Asset Controls.

The year 2003 saw many significant terrorism-related arrests in France. In June, French authorities arrested Moroccan national Karim Mehdi at Paris's Charles de Gaulle airport. Mehdi is suspected of having ties to the al-Qaida cell in Hamburg whose members aided the hijackers of September 11 and for plotting against tourist facilities on Reunion Island. Arrested at the airport several days later was a German convert to extremist Islam, Christian Ganczarski, implicated in the al-Qaida attack on the synagogue in Djerba, Tunisia, and closely associated with al-Qaida in Germany. Both arrested extremists are residents of Germany.

French judicial authorities continued their investigation into the activities of suspected terrorist Djamal Beghal, the leader of an al-Qaida–associated cell in France, for plotting to attack the US Embassy in Paris. Several additional suspects remain in custody in France on charges relating to this conspiracy. One member of Beghal's cell, Algerian national Kamel Daoudi, was sentenced on 4 November to six months in prison for his criminal association with a terrorist network plotting attacks in France.

France has also made significant progress against non-Islamic indigenous terrorist groups, including ETA, the Real IRA, and the Corsican Separatists. In October 2003, a Paris court sentenced presumed ETA militant Alberto Rey-Domecq to six and a half years in prison for participating in a criminal association with terrorist aims. On 4 November 2003, French authorities arrested five French nationals who were suspected of providing support to the Real IRA, a dissident faction of the Irish Republican Army. In late June, French judicial authorities convicted eight Corsican nationalists for the assassination in 1998 of the Corsican Prefect Claude Erignac. Four of the conspirators were given life in prison, and the remaining four received lesser sentences.

France continues to cooperate with its neighbors to combat terrorism, for example, building upon last year's protocol with Spain to include new provisions such as joint investigation teams. This agreement provides the teams with authority to conduct police investigations in each other's countries, subject to the judicial authorities of the country in which they act.

In addition, France has joined numerous other non-EU countries in dialogue on counterterrorism issues, including Turkey, Pakistan, Singapore, and India. France has engaged other European, Mediterranean, and North African countries in dialogue to create an area of security in the Western Mediterranean that will focus on combating Islamic terrorism. US and French authorities enjoyed exemplary cooperation in providing enhanced security for airline flights of concern during a period of heightened threat around the Christmas holidays and beyond.

France has designated as terrorist groups those that appear on the EU list of terrorist organizations. In 2002, France designated HAMAS as a terrorist organization but has yet to designate the related charities. France, along with its EU partners, has not yet designated Lebanese Hizballah as a terrorist organization.

The plot to attack tourist facilities of French overseas department Reunion Island in a manner similar to the Bali nightclub bombings of October 2002 best signifies the continued threat to French citizens or interests posed by Islamic extremist terrorists in 2003, reinforcing the notion that France is both a short- and medium-term target for al-Qaida and associated groups.

This year, France became a party to all 12 international conventions and protocols relating to terrorism by ratifying the UN Convention on the Prevention and Punishment of Internationally Protected Persons.

Germany

Germany continues to be a prominent participant in the global Coalition against terrorism, reflecting many German security officials' assessments that Germany is a terrorist target and an important al-Qaida logistic hub. Germany also is an active supporter of the counterterrorism campaign in international forums, including the EU, UN, NATO, OSCE, and the G-8.

Germany continues to contribute significantly to international forces in Afghanistan with approximately 2,700 soldiers deployed on missions in support of the ISAF, Operation Enduring Freedom, and Operation Active Endeavor in the Mediterranean. Germany and the Netherlands were lead nations for ISAF from February until August, when NATO assumed command. In October, the German Parliament extended authorization for Germany's participation in ISAF for another year. German naval forces continue to be a major participant in the antiterrorism naval task forces off the Horn of Africa and in the Mediterranean that are tasked with ensuring the security of shipping routes and cutting off the supply and escape routes used by terrorists.

Germany has taken a lead role in Afghanistan's reconstruction through humanitarian and development assistance. German personnel continue to train and equip a new Afghan police force, and Germany has committed to spend approximately 320 million euros in Afghanistan by 2006.

German bilateral assistance with Iraq's reconstruction has been modest, with aid largely limited to humanitarian assistance, demining, and restoration of the water system, as well as offers to help in training the country's reestablished police force. Berlin's multilateral assistance for Iraq includes 25 percent of the European Commission's 200 million euro pledge for reconstruction.

Germany was the first country to convict a terrorist linked to the attacks of September 11. In February, the Hamburg Higher Regional Court sentenced Moroccan national Mounir el Motassadeq to 15 years in prison—the maximum sentence allowable under German law—for accessory to murder and membership in a terrorist organization. A trial on similar charges against a second suspected terrorist of September 11, Moroccan Abdelghani Mzoudi, took place in Hamburg and ended with his acquittal in February 2004. Germany is still seeking Hamburg cell suspects Said Bahaji, Ramzi Binalshibh, and Zakariya Essabar under international arrest warrants.

German federal and state criminal offices are conducting 177 preindictment investigations into Islamic extremist–based terrorism, and several terrorists have been sentenced to prison. Four members of the Meliani Group were sentenced to 10-to-12 years in prison for plotting an attack on the Strasbourg Christmas market in December 2000. A member of the German "al-Tawhid" cell, which has close ties with al-Qaida, was sentenced to serve four years for passport forgery and membership in a terrorist organization, and charges have been brought against four other al-Tawhid members. A Turkish citizen was sentenced to 18 months in prison for illegal possession of explosives and drug charges, but the prosecution failed in its attempt to convict him of charges of planning a terrorist attack on the US Army's European Headquarters in Heidelberg.

Notable arrests and indictments include the arrest of several extremists affiliated with Berlin's al-Nur Mosque, who were plotting to carry out a suicide operation during anti-Iraq war demonstrations in Berlin, and a suspected former leader in the DHKP-C—a Turkish left extremist organization with cells in Germany that was banned in August 1998.

Germany also agreed in November to extradite to the United States two Yemeni nationals who were wanted for material support to terrorism, after receiving assurances that they would not be tried before a US military commission.

German authorities, however, have failed in some efforts to bring indictments against several prominent al-Qaida suspects, including German national Christian Ganczarski—a contact of the hijackers of September 11 and a suspect in the Djerba bombing in April 2002 in which several German citizens were killed. He and his associate Karim Medhi—who confessed to helping plan a terrorist attack in Reunion Island last spring—were arrested by French authorities in June and are being held in France for prosecution.

Germany has adopted antiterrorism reforms that should enhance its ability to fight terrorism. New and stronger provisions in the German law on associations have been used to ban several foreign extremist organizations in Germany. The Interior Ministry has banned the extremist Islamic association Hizb ut-Tahrir—based outside Germany—from any activity within the country and has seized the association's assets in Germany. The Federal Constitutional Court in October upheld the ban against the Islamic extremist group "Caliphate State," which has now exhausted all appeals. The court has temporarily lifted the ban against the Al-Aqsa Foundation, which is accused of providing financial support to HAMAS, pending a final ruling, but authorities continue to monitor the members' activities.

Germany signed in October a bilateral Mutual Legal Assistance Treaty with the United States in criminal matters—the result of nine rounds of negotiations conducted during the past 20 years. This treaty should streamline and expedite the process of mutual legal assistance between the United States and Germany.

Of the 12 existing UN conventions and protocols relating to combating terrorism, Germany has signed all—and ratified eleven—of the conventions. The UN Convention for the

Suppression of the Financing of Terrorism is still in the process of ratification.

Greece

Greece continues to make progress in the fight against terrorism, particularly against domestic groups. The Greek Ministry of Justice announced in November that it would seek to enact new counterterrorism legislation to comply with a decision made by the European Council in 2002. This law will for the first time in Greek jurisprudence define terrorism as a crime. The law also increases the statute of limitations on terrorist-related killings from 20 to 30 years and increases prison terms for terrorist leaders.

Greece has participated in the ISAF in Afghanistan since 2002. Currently, more than 130 individuals from the Greek Corps of Engineers and other support elements are deployed in Kabul. A Greek navy frigate was stationed in the Arabian Sea until July, and two Greek C-130 aircraft are operating in the Afghan theater.

In December, a Greek court concluded a nine-month trial of 19 accused members of the 17N terrorist group, which was responsible for the deaths of 23 individuals, including five US Embassy employees. A special three-member judiciary panel convicted 15 of the 17N terrorists of hundreds of crimes—five of the terrorists were given multiple life terms, and four were acquitted because of a lack of evidence. The Greek Chief of Police has stated that additional members of the group are at large, and investigations are continuing.

Greek authorities in the spring arrested five members of the Revolutionary People's Struggle (ELA)—the country's oldest, although lesser-known terrorist group—marking Athens's first-ever arrests against the group. The five members were charged with killing a police officer and other crimes, and the trial against them began in February 2004 and is ongoing. ELA has not conducted an attack since 1995, but Revolutionary Nuclei (RN)—widely believed to be the successor to or offshoot of ELA—may be responsible for attacks in July against an insurance company and bank in Athens, on the basis of forensic evidence. RN's few communiques show strong similarities in rhetoric, tone, and theme to ELA proclamations. RN's last confirmed attack was in November 2000.

Anarchists and leftwing terrorists continued to conduct arson attacks and some low-level bombings against an array of perceived establishment and so-called imperialist targets, such as banks, courts, and personal vehicles. Between September and late December, more than 50 anarchist attacks took place—mainly conducted in solidarity with imprisoned anarchists and 17N trial defendants. Overall, there were 10 low-level attacks against US businesses and vehicles in 2003, compared to a total of eight such attacks the previous year. Anarchists also were responsible for a "barrage" of low-level bombings of banks in November on the eve of the visit of FBI Director Mueller and claimed them as a "warm welcome" to the US official. These attacks only caused property damage but underscore the lingering nature of leftwing terrorism in Greece.

Athens is enhancing security preparations for the 2004 Olympic Games. The Olympic Security Advisory Group—a seven-state group—is a key forum for assisting this effort. Greece plans to spend $750 million to counter potential terrorist and other security threats during the Games.

Greece has signed all—and ratified 11—of the UN conventions and protocols relating to terrorism.

Hungary

Hungary has been fully supportive of the war against terrorism and US initiatives against al-Qaida and other terrorist organizations both within its borders and abroad. Throughout 2003, Hungary maintained consistent political support for the war on terror, actively promoting the US position in NATO and the UN and giving high-level endorsement to US policies.

In support of Operation Enduring Freedom, Hungary developed a package of excess weapons, ammunition, and equipment for the Georgia Train and Equip Program and the Afghan National Army training project.

The total amount donated for Afghanistan was 437 tons, valued at $3.7 million. The Georgia program comprised 8 tons, valued at $25,000. In 2003, the Hungarian Parliament approved the sending of up to 50 troops to the ISAF in Afghanistan. Also in 2003, Hungary contributed a military medical unit as part of the ISAF. The medical unit was deployed there from March to September. The Government delivered $1 million in humanitarian aid to Afghanistan in 2003.

Hungary passed a law in December 2001 on money laundering and terrorist financing that brought it into full compliance with EU and Financial Action Task Force norms. Now, however, the Government has put before its Parliament additional legislation that would go well beyond that of most countries in reporting requirements for financial transactions.

Cooperation with US and regional officials on export and border controls continues to be outstanding. In several cases, Hungarian officials have aggressively pursued and developed leads and provided extensive cooperation to US officers that have stopped the transshipment of hazardous goods. Hungary is actively improving its technical ability to track and control dangerous materials, and its imminent accession into the EU is accelerating this process.

Hungary is a party to all 12 international conventions and protocols relating to terrorism.

Iceland

Despite having no indigenous military forces, Iceland has contributed to the war on terrorism efforts in Afghanistan and Iraq. Building on its experience from running Pristina airport in Kosovo on behalf of the Alliance, Iceland is due to take sole responsibility for the operation of the Kabul airport on 1 June 2004. The Government decided in February 2004 to provide chartered airlift for Dutch military assets en route to Afghanistan. Other supportive actions include the deployment during 2003-04 of two bomb disposal experts with Danish forces in southern Iraq and earlier airlift contributions for Operation Enduring Freedom.

Iceland is a party to all 12 international conventions and protocols relating to terrorism.

Italy

Italy has been a staunch ally in the war against terror and has made significant contributions in Afghanistan and Iraq. Italy deployed a 1,000-troop task force in Afghanistan, its first major combat deployment since World War II. The Italian Government also maintains approximately 3,000 troops, civilian personnel, and paramilitary Carabinieri in Iraq. Despite the terrorist bombing of 2 November of the Italian Carabinieri headquarters in Nasiriyah, Iraq, which killed 19 Italian citizens, Italy remains one of the four largest contributors of troops and personnel to ongoing stabilization operations in Iraq.

Italy's law enforcement authorities maintained an ongoing and largely effective initiative against Italy-based terrorist suspects, including investigation, detentions, prosecutions, and expulsions. According to Ministry of Interior data, Italian authorities in 2003 arrested 71 individuals suspected of planning or providing support to terrorist activity. Many of those arrested were suspected al-Qaida operatives and recruiters or facilitators for Ansar al-Islam and other al-Qaida–linked extremist organizations.

In November, Italy's Minister of Interior for the first time exercised ministerial authority to expel seven terrorist suspects who he assessed posed a serious terrorist threat to Italy's national security. The Italian Government declared that, while there may have been insufficient evidence to arrest the suspects, lengthy investigation had compiled compelling evidence that the seven were Islamic extremists who posed a threat to the national security.

Preventing terrorism financing has also been a key goal of the Italian Government as a part of its war against terrorism. To date, Italy has fully complied with the asset-freezing requirements imposed by UN Security Council Resolutions and EU mechanisms. In January, Italy ratified and brought into effect the International Convention for the Suppression of the Financing of Terrorism and adopted a number of provisions to adjust Italian legislation accordingly. Under the ratification law, penalties for the crimes of money laundering—if committed during banking or professional activities—are now extended to terrorism financing crimes. The Government of Italy in 2003 also submitted 30 names of individuals suspected of links to al-Qaida to the UN 1267 Sanctions Committee for listing on its consolidated list of individuals and/or entities associated with al-Qaida, the Taliban, or Usama Bin Ladin, making them subject to sanctions. The Italian Government froze their assets in Italy.

The domestic leftwing terrorist group, the new Red Brigades–Communist Combatant Party (BRCCP), also presents an ongoing terrorist threat to Italian national security. Italian authorities continue their efforts to dismantle and prevent terrorist acts by the BR-CCP, which has used assassination of government officials as a tool of terror during the last several years. In March, two BR-CCP activists engaged police officers in a shootout on a train. One of the group's leaders was arrested and remains in detention; another member was killed. Subsequently, Italian authorities in October arrested several suspected BR-CCP activists using evidence seized from the detained leader, and they assess that they have made significant progress in dismantling the terrorist group.

Italy is a party to all 12 international conventions and protocols relating to terrorism.

Latvia

Latvia has been fully supportive of the war against terrorism. Latvia contributed a medical team in support of the ISAF in Afghanistan. In Iraq, Latvia contributed a 103-man infantry company under Polish command, undertaking patrols, assisting in maintaining public order, and helping efforts to rebuild and reconstruct Iraq; it also deployed cargo-handling and bomb disposal specialists. The Government has offered technical assistance for the reconstruction of Iraq.

The Government takes its terrorist financing responsibilities seriously and has been very responsive in those instances when the United States has shared information on terrorist financing. Drawing on US and other sources, Latvia has compiled a terrorist-financing database that it shares with local banks.

Latvia is a party to all 12 international conventions and protocols relating to terrorism.

Lithuania

Lithuania has been fully supportive of the war against terrorism. Lithuania is implementing the National Security Strategy of May 2002 and the National Counter Terrorism Program of January 2002. These plans include: participation in the international fight against terrorism; expanding and sharing resources; defending possible targets and infrastructure; identifying terrorists, their groups, and supporters; identifying and cutting off sources of terrorist finances; clarifying the procedures for investigating terrorist cases; strengthening rapid reaction and crisis management capabilities; strengthening of counterterrorist intelligence; and strengthening of internal economic and social security in general.

Lithuania has also sent troops and other military personnel to Afghanistan and Iraq. Since November 2002, Lithuanian Special Operation Forces have participated in Operation Enduring Freedom in Afghanistan. About 100 Lithuanian troops and logistic specialists are operating in Iraq. In October, Parliament voted to extend the missions to Afghanistan and Iraq until the end of 2004. The Government also pledged modest financial assistance to Iraqi reconstruction.

In September, Lithuania and the US Government cooperated in moving 140 kg of irradiated beryllium—a strategic material—to a safe storage facility. Lithuania is a party to 11 of the 12 international conventions and protocols relating to terrorism, including the International Convention for the Suppression of the Financing of Terrorism. The Government has been very cooperative in investigating and detecting potential terrorist finances.

Netherlands

The Dutch have responded to the global terrorist threat with leadership and energy in the areas of border and shipping security, terrorist financing, and Alliance efforts in Afghanistan and Iraq. However, the Dutch continue to struggle with successfully prosecuting terrorists.

In 2003, the Netherlands assumed joint command over the ISAF with Germany and pledged $15 million during three years to the Afghan Reconstruction Trust Fund. The Netherlands contributed a frigate, fighter aircraft, and reconnaissance planes to Operation Enduring Freedom in Afghanistan but drew down these forces on 1 October. The Netherlands continues to participate with two frigates and one maritime patrol aircraft in the NATO-led naval antiterrorism campaign, Operation Active Endeavor, in the Mediterranean. The Dutch have had a contingent of 1,100 troops in Iraq since summer 2003 (scheduled to remain until summer 2004) and have pledged 21 million euros for reconstruction. In addition, the Netherlands has pledged 300,000 euros to establish the Iraqi Bureau of Missing Persons.

The Dutch have not successfully prosecuted a terrorist case since September 11, 2001. Recent unsuccessful prosecutorial efforts against suspected terrorists, including four men suspected of plotting to bomb the US Embassy in Paris and 12 alleged Muslim extremists suspected of recruiting for jihad, have highlighted weaknesses in the Dutch legal infrastructure.

Pending changes to Dutch counterterrorism laws from July 2002 would address some of these deficiencies and bring the Netherlands in line with EU-mandated sentences for leading and participating in a terrorist group—and even go beyond EU minimums when a crime was committed with "terrorist intent." In August 2003, amendments were proposed to the counterterrorism legislation criminalizing recruitment for jihad violence and also conspiracy to commit terrorist crimes. The Second Chamber of Parliament on 9 December approved the Government's bill of July 2002 on terrorist crimes and the amendments of August 2003. The bill will be considered by the First Chamber and is expected to come into force in mid-2004.

In April 2003, The Second Chamber also authorized the use of "criminal civilian" infiltrators in exceptional situations in terrorism cases. For national security purposes, the Dutch Government agreed in October 2003 to investigate the feasibility of introducing a systemized file comparison between the information from the immigration department and the security agencies.

Dutch officials remain committed to establishing financial protocols to combat terrorism and have cooperated with the United States in freezing the assets of known terrorist organizations. Using national sanctions authority, the Dutch blocked the accounts and financial transactions of a HAMAS fundraiser, the al-Aqsa Foundation, and al-Qaida–affiliated Benevolence International Nederland. Neither the Dutch nor their EU partners, however, have designated Lebanese Hizballah as a terrorist group.

In 2003, the Netherlands continued its commitment to shipping and port security by increasing cooperation with the United States. The first meeting of the bilateral Aviation Security Working Group was held in April, and the inaugural meeting of the Port and Maritime Security Working Group was held in May. In addition, radiological monitors in the port of Rotterdam were expected to be installed and operational by 2004.

There were no international terrorist attacks in the Netherlands in 2003.

The Netherlands has signed and ratified all 12 international conventions and protocols relating to terrorism.

Norway

Norway has been a solid ally in the war on terrorism. Norwegian authorities continue to investigate suspected Ansar al-Islam leader (and Norway resident) Mullah Krekar and have frozen an account linked to that organization. The Norwegian Government has provided Special Operations Forces and Explosive Ordinance Disposal units on a rotating basis to Operation Enduring Freedom and ISAF in Afghanistan since October 2001. Elements of a Mechanized Infantry Company of 180 personnel, the Telemark Task Force, deployed to Afghanistan in December 2003. The unit provided security for the *Loya Jirga* proceedings and is now conducting security missions in and around Kabul as part of the ISAF. Norway contributed more than $46 million to Afghan reconstruction in 2002 and $53 million in 2003. In 2003, Norway designated Afghanistan a priority-assistance country, making a long-term commitment to development and reconstruction there. The Royal Norwegian Navy has maintained a near-continuous presence in Operation Active Endeavor with frigates, submarines, or torpedo boats.

Although Norway did not participate in the Coalition to liberate Iraq, they have contributed a 150-man engineering contingent operating with the United Kingdom and six staff officers operating with the Poles to the reconstruction effort in southern Iraq. In 2003, Norway contributed $42 million to the reconstruction and stabilization effort in Iraq, and at Madrid it pledged more than $11 million per year through 2006 for this effort.

Norway is a party to all 12 international conventions and protocols relating to terrorism.

Poland

Poland continues to play an important regional role in advancing the war against terrorism, both as a NATO ally and in the broader coalition against terrorism. Members of Poland's special forces took part in Operation Iraqi Freedom, and on 3 September a Polish-led multinational division assumed control of the Central-South security zone in Iraq. More than 2,000 Polish soldiers currently are serving in Iraq, and the Government of Poland has also offered to assist in training the new Iraqi police force. In Afghanistan, some 100 Polish military personnel are involved in mineclearing operations at Bagram Air Base, and the Polish Government recently conveyed $100,000 worth of weapons and ammunition to the new Afghan National Army. Poland is providing most humanitarian assistance on an as-available basis.

Poland agreed to a Memorandum of Understanding (MOU) with the US Treasury Department's Financial Crimes Enforcement Network (FinCEN) to facilitate information sharing on terrorist financing. The Government of Poland implemented stopgap measures to freeze terrorist assets. In September, Polish law enforcement officials arrested an Algerian citizen wanted in Algeria on terrorist charges, and Polish officials cooperated with US law enforcement in the investigation of other terrorist cases.

Poland is a party to 9 of the 12 conventions and protocols relating to terrorism. The Polish Government has actively promoted the war on terrorism in bilateral and multilateral forums, and Poland continued to make progress in ratifying outstanding antiterrorism conventions. It ratified the Convention on the Suppression of Terrorist Financing, passed legislation authorizing signature of the Convention on the Suppression of Terrorist Bombing, and approved measures to attack the sources of terrorist finances, including amendments to broaden an anti-money laundering law.

Romania

Romania is a staunch ally of the United States in the global war against terrorism, providing full public and diplomatic support for US goals to counter terrorism. In 2003, about 1,200 Romanian troops served at the same time in Iraq and Afghanistan, and Romania has promised to maintain its commitment of troops in 2004. Romania suffered its first casualties in the war against terror in November 2003 when two Romanians were fatally shot in an ambush in Afghanistan. Romania has made its airspace, ground infrastructure, and naval facilities available to US and NATO forces engaged in the global war against terrorism. Throughout 2003, Romania consistently supported US-led initiatives in the UN and NATO against terrorism.

The Romanian Government has established internal mechanisms to combat terrorism, including adoption of a "National Anti-Terrorism Strategy" and guidelines to prevent the use of the Romanian financial and banking system for the purpose of financing terrorist acts. In 2003, Romania adopted a law establishing a new regime for the control of dual-use items and technologies. Bucharest is the site of the Southeast European Cooperation Initiative, a regional center that provides law-enforcement training and intelligence sharing on transborder criminal activities, including terrorism, for 12 member countries in Southeastern and Central Europe.

Romania has signed all 12 counterterrorism conventions and ratified all but the Convention for the Suppression of Terrorist Bombings.

Slovakia

Slovakia has acted as a staunch ally in the global war against terrorism and has made significant contributions in Afghanistan and Iraq, as well as in peacekeeping missions in the Balkans and elsewhere. The Slovaks sent a 75-person NBC contingent to Iraq, integrated into the Czech NBC unit. The Slovak unit was later replaced by an 82-person military engineering unit deployed to the Polish sector. The Parliament in February 2004 approved sending an additional 23 troops to Iraq. Slovakia sent a 40-person engineering unit to Afghanistan, which they have extended twice at the request of the United States. There is a proposal expected to pass Parliament to send an additional 16-person demining unit to Afghanistan to serve under the ISAF.

Slovakia has one of the largest per capita peacekeeping contingents, with more than 800 troops deployed worldwide. Approximately 100 Slovaks are deployed in the joint Czech-Slovak mechanized battalion assigned to the NATO Kosovo Force. Since 1998, the Slovak military has had five officers operating within the command structures of the NATO Stabilization Force in Bosnia and Herzegovina. Slovak troops also participate in UN peacekeeping missions in the Golan Heights, Ethiopia and Eritrea, Cyprus, and East Timor.

Shortly after September 11, 2001, terrorism was criminalized in Slovakia. Officials regularly make public statements denouncing terrorism after international events and on anniversaries such as September 11. There is an antiterror police unit within the Organized Crime Bureau, and the expulsion of a group of Real IRA members from Slovakia two years ago is a promising precedent for future cooperation if more such cases arise. Slovakia cooperates fully with US requests to freeze terrorist assets, and joint US-Slovak projects on export and border controls have been extremely successful.

Slovakia is a party to all 12 international conventions and protocols relating to terrorism.

Slovenia

There were no terrorist acts in Slovenia in 2003. Slovenia is planning to deploy special forces to Afghanistan in March 2004 and has made modest humanitarian contributions to Iraq. Slovenia has stepped up its efforts to mentor its non-EU neighbors on border security and enforcement against financial crimes. A very active Slovene NGO, the TOGETHER Center, is working to bring hope to children in the Balkans and in Iraq to prevent them from becoming a disaffected youth, and thus targets for recruitment by terrorists.

Slovenia is a party to 11 of the 12 international conventions and protocols relating to terrorism.

Spain

Spain is a firm ally in the global war against terrorism. Spain has authorized the use of Spanish military bases at Rota and Moron in support of military operations in Afghanistan, provided materiel support to Operation Enduring Freedom, and supported the reconstruction of Afghanistan with humanitarian and developmental assistance. In August, Spain deployed 1,300 troops to southern Iraq.

Spain has arrested and indicted dozens of individuals with possible links to al-Qaida since September 11. In January, a Spanish judge indicted Usama Bin Ladin and 34 others for complicity in the attacks of September 11; 15 of these individuals are now in Spanish custody. Spain has had some success in prosecuting terrorism cases. Sixteen North African nationals with suspected ties to al-Qaida operatives in the United Kingdom and France were released after their arrest in January. On 7 March, Spanish national police in Valencia arrested four Spaniards and one Pakistani. They were accused of belonging to a financial network involved in laundering money that was then sent to al-Qaida operatives. The Spanish Ministry of Interior also linked these suspects to a terrorist attack that took place in April 2002 in Yerba, Tunisia, in which 19 people were killed. On 12 March 2003, a Spanish judge ordered two of these suspects remanded to prison pending further investigation of the case. The other three suspects were released. In October, a judge cited health reasons for releasing on bail an Al-Jazeera television network journalist with alleged ties to the Spain-based al-Qaida network of Eddin Barakat Yarkas.

Spain made extensive progress in its decades-old campaign to eliminate domestic terrorist groups, including the Basque Fatherland and Liberty (ETA) organization—a radical terrorist group. Spanish police arrested 126 individuals in 2003 for association with or membership in ETA and dismantled several ETA operational terrorist cells, dealing a blow to ETA's logistic, recruitment, and operational capabilities. In December, French police arrested top leaders of ETA's military wing, who were allegedly planning attacks in Spain to coincide with the Christmas season. There are now more than 500 ETA members in Spanish jails and another 100 imprisoned in France.

In March, Spain's Supreme Court upheld a ban passed in 2002 on Batasuna, the political wing of ETA. The ban freezes Batasuna's funds and prohibits ETA supporters from serving on local and regional government seats. These steps have dampened the group's political clout and cut off a major source of financing by depriving ETA members of the benefits of being able to channel funds from local government into pro-ETA activities. The number of ETA attacks and casualties also remained low.

Spanish and French authorities also made joint advances against the domestic terrorist group First of October Anti-Fascist Resistance Group, all but eliminating the group.

Spain is one of the primary advocates within the EU for enhancing mechanisms to fight terrorism. Spain led the effort in the EU to approve the EU-wide common arrest and detention order, which the EU approved in late 2001.

Spain and France are the first two countries to create "multi-national police investigation teams" under terms of the EU agreement reached in 2002. The agreement allows Spanish and French police forces to work in each other's country investigating cases related to the ETA, Islamic terrorism, and other crimes.

Spain is a party to all 12 international conventions and protocols relating to terrorism and currently chairs the UN Counterterrorism Committee and co-chairs with the United States the Financial Action Task Force (FATF) Terrorism Finance Working Group. Spain is pressing to become a standing member of the G-8's Counterterrorism Action Group on the basis of its high level of technical counterterrorism assistance to third countries.

Sweden

Sweden has provided good cooperation and support in the fight against terrorism in 2003. In July, it adopted legislation implementing the EU framework decision on terrorism. The new legislation defines acts of terrorism and imposes penalties beyond those for traditional criminal acts. The Swedish Government has been responsive to US requests for security measures to protect diplomatic and official installations and personnel in response to heightened threats. Sweden has participated in ISAF since its inception with a 45-person rotating unit that has included Special Forces and engineering personnel. In 2004, Sweden assumed chairmanship of the Financial Action Task Force. Sweden also decided on 19 February 2004 to contribute 16 persons to the ISAF in Kabul. This group will consist of staff officers and one domestic logistic unit. Sweden is studying the possibility of contributing to a Provincial Reconstruction Team in Afghanistan.

Sweden is a party to 11 of the 12 international conventions and protocols relating to terrorism.

Turkey

The Turkish Government is a strong, long-term counterterrorism partner. In addition to dealing with major terrorist attacks on its soil this year, Turkey also combated several domestic terrorist groups that continue to threaten Turkish and US interests.

In November, four suicide bombers attacked Jewish and British targets in Istanbul in two separate but probably coordinated attacks that killed at least 61 people, including the British Consul General. On 15 November, Turkish operatives exploded truck bombs outside the Beth Israel and Neve Shalom synagogues, followed on 20 November by a second wave of attacks against the British Consulate and HSBC Bank.

Turkey maintained support for Operation Enduring Freedom in 2003. From June 2002 through February 2003, Turkey assumed leadership of the ISAF in Afghanistan. As part of this effort, Turkey provided approximately 1,400 peacekeepers to the mission and continues to have a military contingent in Afghanistan of 140 troops. Turkey also continued to permit Incirlik Airbase to be used for refueling for planes flying into Afghanistan.

The United States and Turkey met several times to discuss cooperation against the Kurdistan Freedom and Democracy Congress (KADEK), and in October, Secretary Powell reiterated the US commitment to assist Turkey in eliminating this threat. In October, KADEK—formerly known as the Kurdistan Workers' Party (PKK)—made yet another name change to the Kurdistan People's Congress (KHK or Kongra-Gel) in an effort to masquerade as a political party. KHK launched several attacks, which it claimed were in retaliation for losses the group suffered from Turkish counterinsurgency operations, and periodically threatened to increase its attacks against Turkish targets.

Turkish police arrested several members of the Revolutionary People's Liberation Party (DHKP/C) during the course of the year. The DHKP/C—a virulently anti-US group that killed two US defense contractors and wounded a US Air Force officer during the Gulf war—continued to launch attacks in Turkey. In May, a DHKP/C female suicide bomber prematurely detonated her explosive belt in Istanbul, killing herself and wounding another. The group struck in June, attacking a bus carrying Turkish prosecutors in Istanbul with a remote-controlled bomb, and it launched several other bombings against official Turkish interests in August.

Turkey has signed and ratified all 12 international conventions and protocols concerning terrorism.

United Kingdom

The United Kingdom has been and remains one of the United States' strongest allies in the global fight against terrorism. It continues to take important political, financial, and law enforcement steps to advance international counterterrorism efforts. The British Government was also a staunch ally in the international effort to enforce UN Security Council Resolution 1441 in Iraq. The British contributed more than 40,000 troops to the Iraqi conflict and continue to play a critical role in the Coalition's efforts to construct a democratic, market-oriented Iraq that is a model for the region rather than a threat to its neighbors and global security.

Islamist terrorism poses a significant threat to the United Kingdom at home and to its interests overseas. The most dramatic and tragic evidence of this in 2003 came on 20 November when suicide bombers attacked the British Consulate and the offices of the British bank HSBC in Istanbul, Turkey, killing 33 people, including the British Consul General. A UK citizen was also killed in the suicide bomb attacks on 12 May on three residential compounds in Saudi Arabia.

In February, the British Government stepped up security in and around London in response to a terrorist threat. Her Majesty's Government increased police presence around government buildings and London's financial district, but security changes were most visible at Heathrow Airport where the British Government deployed soldiers and additional policemen. Security returned to normal after the threat window passed. British Airways briefly suspended all flights to Kenya in May and to Saudi Arabia in August due to other reports of terrorist threats in those regions. UK authorities cooperated closely with the United States to provide enhanced security for airline flights of concern during a period of heightened threat around the Christmas holidays.

In June, the British Government established the Joint Terrorism Analysis Center (JTAC), which is responsible for assessing and disseminating information about the terrorist threat to UK domestic and overseas interests. JTAC, an interagency body that includes both intelligence producers and consumers, works closely with the US Terrorist Threat Integration Center. The United States and United Kingdom are also planning to conduct a major joint counterterrorism exercise in 2005.

Since the attacks of September 11, British authorities have stepped up their investigative and intelligence collection efforts against Islamic extremists in the United Kingdom. A key objective is to reduce the threat of terrorism by stopping and disrupting it. Between September 11 and the end of 2003, the police have arrested 537 individuals under the Terrorism Act of 2000. Of these, 94 were charged with terrorism-related offenses under the act, 71 were charged with offenses under other legislation, and 263 were released without charge.

In January 2003, the British Government uncovered a North African network involved in the production and importation of toxins, including ricin, in the United Kingdom. Nine individuals associated with the ricin threat were charged with conspiracy to murder and other related charges, and their trials are slated to begin in May and September 2004.

Between October 2002 and October 2003, more than 50 new terrorism-related cases have been brought to the Crown Prosecution Service. British prosecutors also enjoyed some successful terrorism-related convictions, including 11-year sentences for two al-Qaida fundraisers—the latter marking the first conviction of an al-Qaida member in the United Kingdom. In addition, Islamic extremist Abdullah e-Faisal was convicted for "inciting racial hatred and incitement to murder" and sentenced to a nine-year jail term.

The United Kingdom and United States completed negotiations on a new extradition treaty in 2003 that will streamline the extradition process, but neither country has ratified the new treaty. The United Kingdom continues to assist in extraditing four individuals charged with terrorist acts in the United States or against US citizens, including a key suspect in the African bombings of 1998 and an Algerian suspected of involvement in the "Millennium Conspiracy" to blow up Los Angeles airport in 2000. Although all four individuals have lost appeals with Britain's highest court, they have all exercised their right to make representations against their surrender to the United States to the Home Secretary, who has the final decision over their extradition. The Home Office is still awaiting a response to some of the queries on these cases it has since sent to the United States.

Training and financial assistance have been in the forefront of the United Kingdom's bilateral counterterrorism relationships. The United Kingdom launched a new assistance program in 2003 aimed at increasing international capacity to counter terrorism and other threats in support of its bilateral and multilateral counterterrorism policy objectives. The United Kingdom anticipated spending £3.24 million in UK fiscal year 2003/04 on operational counterterrorism assistance aimed at counterterrorism experts in foreign governments, assistance to support the UN's counterterrorism committee, and wider capacity-building initiatives.

The United Kingdom continued its vigorous efforts against terrorism in Northern Ireland in 2003. Security officials disrupted terrorist planning for attacks, defusing numerous bombs—including one in June larger than the explosive that went off in the Omagh bombing in 1998. During the course of the year, one suspect was arrested and charged in connection with Omagh. UK officials assisted with the Dublin prosecution of Real IRA (RIRA) leader Michael McKevitt, who was convicted of directing terrorism, and the Blair government decided to help fund a civil case brought by the families of the victims of Omagh. In April, five RIRA members were sentenced to a total of 100 years for a series of car-bombings in 2001. Sectarian violence persists, but marching season in 2003 was one of the quietest in decades, with only a few reports of violence.

The United Kingdom is a party to all 12 international conventions and protocols relating to terrorism. The United Kingdom actively campaigned in the EU, G-8, NATO, and UN for coordinated counterterrorism efforts and routinely lobbied UN members to become parties to the 12 antiterrorism conventions and protocols. It supported the G-8's initiative in 2003 to create the Counter Terrorism Action Group (CTAG) and is an active CTAG participant.

Middle East Overview

The Middle East continued to be the region of greatest concern in the global war on terrorism. Major terrorist attacks occurred in Morocco, Saudi Arabia, Iraq, and Israel during 2003, highlighting the damage that terrorism can wreak on innocent people. Terrorist groups and their state sponsors continued terrorist activities and planning throughout 2003. Active groups included al-Qaida, Islamic Resistance Movement (HAMAS), Hizballah, Palestine Islamic Jihad (PIJ), Ansar al-Islam (AI), and the remnants of the Zarqawi network, among others. Despite these discouraging indicators, significant counterterrorism cooperation continued on the part of almost all countries in the region. Furthermore, the regime of Iraqi tyrant Saddam Hussein was ousted from power by a US-led Coalition conducting Operation Iraqi Freedom, marking an important advance for the global war on terrorism.

Across the region, governments demonstrated the political will to tackle the threat of terrorism on their soil and lent their weight to bilateral and multilateral efforts to fight terror. Terrorist assets were targeted, as most Middle East governments froze al-Qaida financial assets pursuant to UN Security Council Resolutions 1373, 1267, 1333, 1390, and 1455. Many countries provided essential support to Coalition military activities in the liberation of Iraq and have continued vital support to ongoing operations in Afghanistan. Several countries signed or became parties to the international conventions and protocols relating to terrorism. Every country hosting an American diplomatic and/or military presence responded to US requests to provide enhanced security, particularly during Operation Iraqi Freedom. The United States provided training throughout the region to augment the capacity of our allies in the fight against terrorism.

Saudi Arabia suffered two major, horrific terrorist attacks during 2003 and responded with an aggressive campaign against the al-Qaida network in the Kingdom. Saudi cooperation with the United States improved markedly in 2003, particularly in the sharing of threat information and well-publicized steps to combat terrorist financing. Using its unique position in the Muslim world, Saudi Arabia also initiated an ideological campaign against Islamist terrorist organizations with the objective of denying extremists the use of Islam to justify terrorism. The Saudi Government has also widely publicized a rewards program for the capture of the Kingdom's most-wanted terrorist suspects. Saudi security forces arrested more than 600 individuals on counterterrorism charges following the attacks on 12 May. In addition, Saudi and Yemeni officials have met to develop joint approaches to better secure their shared land border to check the influx of weapons into Saudi Arabia from Yemen.

There were no reported terrorist attacks against Western targets in Yemen in 2003. The Government of Yemen made a number of key al-Qaida–related arrests in 2003, but it raised concerns with its release of extremists without full disclosure of information and its inability to recapture escaped USS Cole suspects. The United States and Yemen continue joint counterterrorism training and cooperation, and there has been significant progress on standing up the Yemen Coast Guard.

The other states of the Arabian Peninsula also made important progress, particularly in locating and blocking terrorist finances, sharing information and intelligence on terrorists and terrorist groups, and strengthening law enforcement cooperation.

Morocco stepped-up its already robust counterterrorism actions following the tragic suicide bombings in Casablanca on 16 May. Taking swift action to identify the culprits, Moroccan authorities uncovered the involvement of several deadly terrorist groups and took decisive legal actions to address the threat. Egypt continued to be a leader in the counterterrorism fight and increased its dialogue with the United States on this issue. Algeria also remained at the forefront of regional counterterrorism cooperation, supporting Coalition efforts against al-Qaida while acting decisively against indigenous terror groups. Tunisia ratified the International Convention on the Suppression of the Financing of Terrorism in February 2003, making Tunisia a party to all 12 international conventions and protocols relating to terrorism.

Jordan took decisive legal steps against terror, indicting 11 individuals for the murder of USAID officer Laurence Foley, and also brought charges against possible al-Qaida and Ansar al-Islam members suspected of planning attacks against tourists and foreigners. Israel maintained its resolute stand against terrorism, weathering numerous casualties in terrorist attacks against civilians. Unfortunately, the Palestinian Authority (PA) continued to take insufficient steps to stop terrorist operations. Lebanon also remained problematic, as it continued to host numerous terrorist groups and refused to take actions against certain terrorist elements in the country.

[*Eds. Note:* Iran, Iraq, Libya, and Syria—which have been designated as state sponsors of terrorism—are discussed in Part 1 in the section on "State Sponsorship of Terrorism."]

Algeria

Algeria continued to be a proactive and aggressive regional leader in the global Coalition against terrorism. Algeria's support of US counterterrorism efforts on a case-by-case basis demonstrated its strong overall support of Coalition efforts against al-Qaida. In May 2003, Algerian security forces secured the release of 17 of the 32 European hostages kidnapped by a faction of the Salafist Group for Call and Combat (GSPC) in February and March. The GSPC is believed to be under the new leadership of Nabil Sahraoui (a.k.a. Abu Ibrahim Mustapha). On 11 September 2003, the GSPC issued a statement declaring allegiance to several jihadist causes and leaders, including al-Qaida and Usama Bin Ladin. Algerian law enforcement and security forces continued to pursue GSPC terrorist operatives, disrupting their activities and capturing or killing several of them. Algeria participated in a pan-Sahel regional counterterrorism seminar in Bamako, Mali, in October.

Algerian officials have stated that the number of active terrorists within the country has fallen from more than 25,000 in 1992 down to a few hundred today, due in large part to a series of successful offensives undertaken by Algerian security forces. Algeria has, in fact, made great strides toward eliminating terrorism in most parts of the country.

The Algerian Government has focused much of its counterterrorism efforts on the international level toward creating international consensus for an international convention against terrorism. This would include defining what constitutes an act of terror as distinct from an act of "national liberation." To this end, Algeria hosted a summit in September 2002 of the African Union (formerly the Organization of African Unity—OAU) aimed at ensuring the implementation of the OAU's 1999 Convention on the Prevention and Combating Terrorism. Algeria has strongly condemned acts of international terrorism.

With regard to enforcement and international agreements, Algeria has ratified all but one of the international conventions and protocols relating to terrorism. Algeria is gradually implementing, in its domestic legislative and regulatory systems, the requirements of these instruments, which may result—among other changes—in the extradition of wanted terrorists.

Algeria was among the first states to criminalize the financing of terrorism. The Finance Act of 2003 expanded these efforts by lifting banking secrecy regulations and formalizing procedures that banks and insurance companies must follow in reporting suspicious transactions to the Government's Financial Information Processing Unit—which turns over actionable information to the courts. In addition, Algeria is seeking an extradition treaty with the United States, and President Bouteflika has proposed an international treaty, under UN auspices, that would replace the need for individual bilateral extradition treaties.

Algeria is a party to 11 of the 12 international conventions and protocols relating to terrorism.

Bahrain

Bahrain is providing important support to our counterterrorism efforts, particularly efforts to block the financing of terror groups. Bahrain has continued to respond positively to requests for assistance to combat terror financing; it has frozen about $18 million in terrorist-linked funds. Bahrain also continued to provide intelligence cooperation and made some significant arrests.

- In February, the Government of Bahrain arrested five Bahrainis suspected of plotting terrorist attacks in Bahrain. In May, the Government released three of the five, claiming to have insufficient evidence to support a trial. In June and July, the other two were convicted—one by a civilian criminal court and one by court martial, for illegal gun possession. In December, the King reduced the sentence of the civilian from three years to two.
- In April, Bahrain expelled an Iraqi diplomat for involvement in setting off an explosive device near the entrance of the headquarters of the US Navy Fifth Fleet on 24 March. The Government also arrested the bomber—an Iraqi Intelligence Service major—tried him in open court, and sentenced him to three years in prison.

Bahrain's lack of a domestic conspiracy law hampers its ability to intervene against suspected extremist plots. This could encourage terrorists to value Bahrain as a potential logistic haven.

Bahrain is a party to five of the 12 international conventions and protocols relating to terrorism and is a signatory to the Convention for the Suppression of the Financing of Terrorism.

Egypt

The Egyptian and US Governments continued to deepen their already close cooperation on a broad range of counterterrorism and law-enforcement issues in 2003. The first US-

Egypt Counterterrorism Joint Working Group meeting was held in Washington in July 2003. The United States continues to closely coordinate with Egyptian authorities on law enforcement and judicial matters involving terrorism. The Egyptian Government has agreed to provide assistance in an important terrorist trial scheduled to take place in New York in May 2004. Egyptian authorities, particularly the Central Bank, have tightened their assets-freezing regime, consistent with requirements under UNSC Resolutions 1373, 1267, 1333, 1390, and 1455 and E.O. 13224. Demonstrating Egypt's commitment to stanch the flow of funds to terrorist organizations, Egypt passed strong anti-money laundering legislation in 2002, enabling it to establish an anti-money laundering financial intelligence unit in March 2003. Egypt has significant antiterrorism legislation in place and did not see the need to enact new laws this year.

The Egyptian Government continued to place high priority on protecting US persons, facilities, and interests before and continuing after the Iraq war.

There is a high state of security for Americans and facilities and for American forces both stationed in Egypt and transiting the country to the Gulf, by air or through the Suez Canal. Both government and religious officials continued to make statements supporting the war on terrorism and condemning terrorist actions around the world. Egypt has maintained its strengthened airport security measures and has instituted more stringent port security measures.

Itself a victim of terrorism in the past, Egypt is actively monitoring and rooting out old and new cells of groups with violent tendencies. In January 2003, 43 members of a jihad group known as Gund Allah (Soldiers of God) were arrested for planning attacks against US and Israeli interests. They will be tried in the Military Tribunal in 2004. The "zero tolerance" policy toward extremism has resulted in the arrest in October 2003 of 12 alleged members of Al-Takfir wa Al-Hijrah, in the continuing arrests of Al-Gama'at Al-Islamiyya (IG) members who do not agree with the historic leadership's new policy of nonviolence, and in the discovery and arrest of extremist cells and nascent groups. A verdict is due in the spring of 2004 in the trial of 26 members (including three Britons) of the Islamic Liberation Party (Hizb Al Tahrir Al Islami), begun in October 2002. The prosecution has requested 25-year sentences for the defendants, charged with reviving an illegal, violent organization.

In October 2003, Egypt completed the release from prison of the historic leadership and as many as 1,000 members and supporters of the IG. This release, begun a year before, was based on what the Government considered to be a conversion in thought and religious values by the IG leadership, who authored several books and gave lengthy public interviews on their new nonviolent philosophy. This conversion has not been accepted by all IG members in Egypt and elsewhere and has given rise to reports in Egyptian media of new IG splinter cells who refuse to accept nonviolence.

The Egyptian judiciary is tough on terrorism. There is no plea bargaining in the Egyptian judicial system, and terrorists have historically been prosecuted to the full extent of the law.

They are tried in Military Tribunals or in Emergency Courts, neither of which affords a right of appeal. There have been no terrorist cases tried in these courts this year. Press reports indicate that Egypt is actively involved with other nations to extradite Egyptian extremists from abroad. Egypt actively participates in a variety of bilateral counterterrorism and law-enforcement training opportunities. Egypt is also preparing to become a regional counterterrorism training hub for other Middle Eastern and North African nations.

Egypt is a party to nine of the international conventions and protocols relating to terrorism and is a signatory to an additional two, including the International Convention for the Suppression of the Financing of Terrorism.

Israel, the West Bank, and Gaza

Israel maintained staunch support for US-led counterterrorism operations as Palestinian terrorist groups conducted a large number of attacks in Israel, the West Bank, and Gaza Strip in 2003. HAMAS, the PIJ, and the al-Aqsa Martyrs Brigades—all of which the United States has designated as Foreign Terrorist Organizations pursuant to Executive Order 13224—were responsible for most of the attacks, which included suicide bombings, shootings, and mortar firings against civilian and military targets. Terrorist attacks in 2003 killed almost 200 people (mostly Israelis, as well as a number of foreigners, including 16 US citizens), a decrease from the more than 350 people killed in 2002.

On 15 October, Palestinian militants attacked a US diplomatic convoy in Gaza with an improvised explosive device, killing three Americans. To date, this was the most lethal attack ever to directly target US interests in Israel, the West Bank, or Gaza. The Popular Resistance Committee (PRC), a loose association of Palestinians with ties to various Palestinian militant organizations such as HAMAS, PIJ, and Fatah, claimed responsibility. Although that claim was later rescinded, and official investigations continue, the PRC remains the primary suspect in the attacks. At the end of the year, the Palestinian Authority (PA) had yet to identify the perpetrators and bring them to justice.

Israeli authorities arrested individuals claiming allegiance to al-Qaida, although the group does not appear to have an operational presence in Israel, the West Bank, or Gaza. Palestinian terrorist groups in these areas continue to focus their attention on attacking Israel and Israeli interests within Israel and the Palestinian territories, rather than engaging in operations worldwide.

Israel employed a variety of military operations in its counterterror efforts. Israeli forces launched frequent raids throughout the West Bank and Gaza, conducted targeted killings of suspected Palestinian terrorists, destroyed homes—including those of families of suicide bombers—imposed strict and widespread closures and curfews in Palestinian areas, and continued construction of an extensive security barrier. Israel expelled more than 12 alleged terrorists from the West Bank to Gaza in the fall of 2003. Israeli counterterrorism measures appear to have reduced the frequency of attacks;

continuing attacks, however, show that the groups remained potent.

HAMAS was particularly active, carrying out more than 150 attacks, including shootings, suicide bombings, and standoff mortar-and-rocket attacks against civilian and military targets. The group was responsible for one of the deadliest attacks of the year—the suicide bombing in June on a Jerusalem bus that killed 17 people and wounded 84. Although HAMAS continues to focus on conducting anti-Israeli attacks, it also claimed responsibility for the suicide bombing at a restaurant adjacent to the US Embassy in Tel Aviv, demonstrating its willingness to attack targets in areas frequented by foreigners.

The PIJ remained active in 2003, conducting several deadly attacks against Israeli targets, and began using women as suicide bombers. The PIJ claimed responsibility for one of the deadliest suicide bombings of 2003—a suicide bombing in October at a Haifa restaurant that killed 21 people and wounded at least 50. The PIJ also claimed responsibility for the joint attack in January with the al-Aqsa Martyrs Brigade for a double-suicide bombing in Tel Aviv, which killed 23 people and wounded more than 100—the deadliest suicide bombing of the year.

The al-Aqsa Martyrs Brigade conducted numerous shooting attacks and suicide bombings in 2003. In August, a suicide bombing claimed by al-Aqsa in Rosh Ha'ayin killed two people and wounded at least 10. Al-Aqsa used at least three female suicide bombers in operations.

Hizballah remained a serious threat to the security of the region, continuing its call for the destruction of Israel and using Lebanese territory as a staging ground for terrorist operations. Hizballah was also involved in providing material support to Palestinian terrorist groups to augment their capacity and lethality in conducting attacks against Israel.

Israel arrested several Jewish extremists in 2003 who were planning terrorist attacks against various Palestinian targets. Several prominent Jewish extremists were sentenced to prison for planning to detonate a bomb near a girls' school in East Jerusalem in 2002.

The PA's efforts to thwart terrorist operations were minimal in 2003. The PA security services remained fragmented and ineffective. The services were also hobbled by corruption, infighting, and poor leadership. There are indications that some personnel in the security services, including several senior officers, have continued to assist terrorist operations.

Israel has signed all 12 international conventions and protocols relating to terrorism and is a party to eight, including the International Convention for the Suppression of the Financing of Terrorism.

Jordan

The Jordanian Government continued to strongly support global counterterrorism efforts while remaining vigilant against the threat of terrorism at home. Jordan was highly responsive to the security needs of US citizens in the country.

In 2003, Jordan pursued several terrorism-related cases, some of which involved attempts at weapons smuggling and border infiltration. Jordan indicted 11 individuals in May 2003 for the murder in 2002 of USAID officer Laurence Foley, and several are currently standing trial for his murder. In September, the State Security Court charged 13 Jordanians—allegedly affiliated with al-Qaida and Ansar al-Islam—with conspiring to carry out attacks against tourists and foreigners. Jordanian authorities requested that Norway extradite Mullah Krekar—the spiritual leader of Ansar al-Islam—for involvement in a terrorist plot.

Suspected terrorists continued attempts to exploit Jordanian territory to transport weapons to and from groups in neighboring states or to use Jordanian territory to facilitate terrorist attacks. Jordanian authorities have successfully intercepted weapons shipments and personnel transiting the country at virtually all of its borders. Although largely responsive to US requests on terrorist-related issues, the Jordanian Government has shied away from measures that would be unpopular with Jordan's pro-Palestinian population. The Central Bank of Jordan rescinded instructions to commercial banks to freeze assets belonging to HAMAS-affiliated individuals in the face of harsh criticism from the public and Parliament, although the organization has not been active in Jordan since its leaders were expelled in 1999.

Jordan has signed 10 of the 12 international conventions and protocols relating to terrorism and is a party to eight, including the International Convention for the Suppression of the Financing of Terrorism.

Kuwait

Kuwait continued to act in concert with the US Government and with its neighbors against a number of domestic threats to Kuwaiti and foreign interests and also provided significant support to US efforts to stem terror financing. During Operation Iraqi Freedom, Usama Bin Ladin and a previously unknown domestic group, the Kuwaiti HAMAS movement, threatened to continue carrying out attacks against Kuwait for aiding Coalition forces. The four terror attacks carried out against Coalition forces between October 2002 and December 2003—which resulted in the death of one US Marine and a US defense contractor—have mobilized domestic counterterrorism efforts, but the potential for further attacks remains a concern. The Kuwaiti Government has taken significant measures to bolster force protection, and it also reacted swiftly and forcefully to detain and prosecute the perpetrators. However, some judges released suspects on bail pending trial and also commuted the sentences of others convicted in the attacks of 2002–03.

Kuwaiti officials and clerics also implemented preventative measures in the wake of terrorist bombings of Western housing compounds in Saudi Arabia in May and November. Soon after the May attacks, Kuwaiti security forces heightened alert levels. Kuwaiti officials and clerics also launched a vocal public campaign to denounce terrorism. In November, Kuwaiti clerics publicly applauded the recantation by extremist Saudi clerics of *fatwas* that encouraged violence and also discouraged their countrymen from engaging in jihad or harming Coalition forces based in Kuwait.

Kuwaiti officials have also heightened security along their border with Iraq to prevent militant infiltration and have also worked with Syria and Iran to develop procedures to increase intelligence sharing and enhance customs and border-monitoring cooperation.

Kuwait also continued to implement every US-ordered terrorist-fund freeze. In August, the Government froze the assets of HAMAS over the objections of conservative elements of the Kuwaiti population.

Kuwait is a party to nine of the 12 international conventions and protocols relating to terrorism.

Lebanon

Despite a decrease from the previous year in anti-US terror attacks in Lebanon and the introduction of counterterrorism legislation, Lebanon remains host to numerous US-designated terrorist groups. At the same time, a number of legislative, legal, and operational initiatives showed some promise in Lebanon's counterterrorism efforts. However, Beirut continues to demonstrate an unwillingness to take steps against Lebanese Hizballah, the PIJ, the Popular Front for the Liberation of Palestine–General Command (PFLP-GC), the Abu Nidal organization (ANO), and HAMAS.

The Lebanese Government recognizes as legitimate resistance groups those organizations that target Israel and permits them to maintain offices in Beirut. Beirut goes further by exempting what it terms "legal resistance" groups—including Hizballah—from money-laundering and terrorism-financing laws. Lebanese leaders, including President Emile Lahud, reject assessments of Hizballah's global reach, instead concentrating on the group's political wing and asserting that it is an integral part of Lebanese society and politics. In addition, Syrian and Iranian support for Hizballah activities in southern Lebanon, as well as training and assistance to Palestinian rejectionist groups, help promote an environment where terrorist elements flourish. Hizballah conducted multiple attacks in the Shab'a Farms region during 2003, including firing antitank rockets.

The Lebanese security forces remain unable or unwilling to enter Palestinian refugee camps—the operational nodes of terrorist groups such as 'Asbat al-Ansar and the Palestinian rejectionists—and to deploy forces to much of the Beka'a Valley, southern Beirut, and the south of the country bordering Israel. Furthermore, Syria's predominant role in Lebanon facilitates the Hizballah and Palestinian rejectionist presence in portions of Lebanon.

The Lebanese Government acknowledges the UN 1267 Sanctions Committee's consolidated list but does not acknowledge groups identified by only the US Government: Beirut will not take action against groups designated solely by the United States. In addition, constitutional provisions prohibit the extradition of Lebanese nationals to a third country. Lebanese authorities further maintain that the Government's provision of amnesty to Lebanese individuals involved in acts of violence during the civil war prevents Beirut from prosecuting many cases of concern to the United States—including the hijacking in 1985 of TWA 847 and the murder of a US Navy diver on the flight—and the abduction, torture, and murder of US hostages from 1984 to 1991. US courts have brought indictments against Hizballah operatives responsible for a number of those crimes, and some of these defendants remain prominent terrorist figures.

The Lebanese Government has insisted that "Imad Mugniyah"—wanted in connection with the TWA hijacking and other terrorist acts, who was placed on the FBI's list of most-wanted terrorists in 2001—is no longer in Lebanon. The Government's legal system also has failed to hold a hearing on the prosecutor's appeal in the case of Tawfiz Muhammad Farroukh, who—despite the evidence against him—was found not guilty of murder for his role in the killings of US Ambassador Francis Meloy and two others in 1976.

In October, the Lebanese National Assembly passed two bills strengthening existing legislation against money laundering and terrorist financing. Law 547—while differentiating between terrorism and what Lebanon calls the "legal resistance" of Hizballah and Palestinian rejectionists—expands existing legislation on money laundering, making illicit any funds resulting from terrorism. Law 553 stipulates penalties for persons who financially support terrorist acts or organizations. A Special Investigations Commission in 2003 investigated 245 cases involving allegations of money laundering, including 22 related to terrorist financing. No accounts used for financing terrorism—as defined by Beirut—were discovered in Lebanese financial institutions. Signifying the difficulty Lebanon will have in enforcing the new legislation, the Central Bank in September asked Lebanese financial institutions to identify accounts held by six HAMAS leaders whose assets are the target of a US freeze. The inquiry sparked a public uproar and caused the Central Bank to end the investigation.

Lebanon has taken other counterterrorism measures in 2003, primarily directed against Sunni extremists, including those affiliated with al-Qaida. For instance:

- In May, a military tribunal convicted eight individuals of attempting to establish an al-Qaida cell in Lebanon.
- In July, Lebanese security forces began a series of arrests in connection with the bombing in April of a McDonald's, part of a series of bombings of Western food outlets during 2002–03.
- In September, military tribunals commenced hearing the cases of more than 40 individuals charged with planning or executing the series of restaurant attacks and planning to assassinate the US Ambassador to Lebanon and bomb the US Embassy in Beirut.
- In October, the Lebanese Government arrested three men and indicted 18 others in absentia on charges of preparing to carry out terrorist attacks and forging documents and passports.
- The Lebanese Government continued to cooperate with US officials in the investigation of the murder in November 2002 of a US citizen in Sidon.

- In December, Lebanese forces personnel cooperated with US Embassy security when a Lebanese man approached the Embassy carrying a bag containing TNT, nitroglycerin, and a detonator.
- In late December, a military tribunal sentenced 25 members of a terrorist group accused of targeting US official and commercial targets to prison terms ranging from six months to life.
- Lebanon is a party to 10 of the 12 international conventions and protocols relating to terrorism.

Morocco

The Government of Morocco has remained a steadfast ally in the war on terror in the face of unprecedented terrorist activity in the Kingdom in 2003. King Muhammad VI has unambiguously condemned those who espouse or conduct terrorism, has been a consistent voice for tolerance and moderation, and has worked to keep Rabat firmly on the side of the United States against extremists. Domestically, Morocco's historical record of vigilance against terrorist activity remained uninterrupted in 2003.

Despite these efforts, on 16 May, suicide bombers simultaneously detonated bombs at restaurants, hotels, and a Jewish cultural center in the seaside city of Casablanca, killing 42 —including many of the bombers—and wounding approximately 100 others. Moroccan authorities quickly identified the bombers as local adherents of the "Salafiya Jihadiya" movement. In the following months, investigators learned that many of those involved in orchestrating the attacks were Moroccan extremists who had trained in Afghanistan and had links to North African extremist groups—mainly the Moroccan Islamic Combatant Group, the Libyan Islamic Fighting Group, and al-Qaida.

The attacks underscored the danger of terrorism from domestic extremists and their international allies, and Moroccan authorities reacted swiftly to reduce the threat. Days after the attacks, the Moroccan legislature passed a law that broadened the definition of terrorism, proposed heavy sentences for inciting terrorism, expanded the power of authorities to investigate suspected terrorists, and facilitated prosecution of terrorist cases. Throughout the summer and fall, authorities arrested hundreds of terrorist suspects and sentenced dozens to lengthy prison terms and, in some cases, execution. Courts tried in absentia extremists located overseas who were suspected of facilitating the attacks in Casablanca and issued warrants for their arrest. The King also took measures to facilitate greater information sharing between the country's security services and national police force. FP

Morocco is a party to 10 of the 12 international conventions and protocols relating to terrorism, including the International Convention for the Suppression of the Financing of Terrorism.

Oman

Oman continued to provide public statements of support for the global war on terrorism and has been responsive to requests for Coalition military and civilian support. During the last two years, the Government has implemented a tight anti-money laundering regime, including surveillance systems designed to identify unusual transactions. Omani financial authorities have committed to freezing the assets of any UN-listed individual found in Oman. There were no incidents of terrorist activity in Oman in 2003.

Oman has become a party to 10 of the 12 international conventions and protocols relating to terrorism but has not yet acceded to the other two, including the International Convention for the Suppression of the Financing of Terrorism.

Qatar

The Government of Qatar provided the United States with significant counterterrorism support during 2003, building on the bilateral cooperation it has maintained since September 11. Qatar provides ongoing support for Operation Enduring Freedom in Afghanistan and is a key regional ally. Amir Hamad bin Khalifa al-Thani has pledged his Government's full support to the global war on terrorism. When requested, Doha has provided additional security for US installations and facilities.

Doha has had some success in disrupting terrorist activity, although the security services traditionally have monitored extremists passively rather than attempting to penetrate or pursue them. Members of transnational terrorist groups and state sponsors of terrorism are present in Qatar. The security services' limited capabilities make it difficult for them to warn against or disrupt a terrorist attack by al-Qaida or affiliated groups.

Qatar remains cautious about taking any action that would cause embarrassment or public scrutiny when Gulf Cooperation Council nationals are involved.

Doha acceded to a number of international agreements during 2003. It also promulgated a revised version of its anti-money laundering law and drafted a criminal law to address terrorist-financing crimes. This law broadened the definition of money laundering to include any activities related to terrorist financing. It authorizes the Central Bank to freeze suspicious accounts. Doha participated in three anti-money laundering training courses organized by the US Government. Legislation provides for a financial intelligence unit, although it has not yet been effectively established.

Qatar is a party to seven of the 12 international conventions and protocols relating to terrorism.

Saudi Arabia

The terrorist attacks in Saudi Arabia on 12 May and 9 November galvanized Riyadh into launching a sustained crackdown against al-Qaida's presence in the Kingdom and spurred an unprecedented level of cooperation with the United States. Riyadh has aggressively attacked al-Qaida's operational and support network in Saudi Arabia and detained or killed a number of prominent operatives and financial facilitators.

The attack of 9 November, which resulted in the deaths of

a number of Muslims and Arabs during the holy month of Ramadan, transformed Saudi public acceptance of the widespread nature of the threat in the Kingdom. This acceptance has facilitated increased security and counterterrorism efforts by the Saudi Government, including stepped up security at a variety of locations throughout the country, such as residential facilities.

The attacks also led Riyadh to implement a variety of programs aimed at directly combating terrorist activity. In early May 2003, the Saudis began to publicize their counterterrorist efforts, including naming 19 individuals most wanted by the security services for involvement in terrorist activities. In early December, Riyadh announced the names of 26 individuals—including the seven remaining fugitives from the list of 19—wanted for terrorist-related activities and provided background information on the suspects to help the public to identify them. Soon thereafter, Saudi security forces killed operative Ibrahim bin Muhammad bin Abdallah al-Rayyis, a terrorist named on the list. Also in early December, Saudi authorities announced a rewards program—ranging from $270,000 to $1.87 million—for information leading to the arrest of suspects or the disruption of terrorist attacks and have used local newspapers to publish pleas from operatives' family members to turn themselves in to authorities.

Since May, Riyadh has arrested more than 600 individuals during counterterrorism operations and continues investigating the Riyadh attacks. Saudi security forces have suffered significant casualties while conducting counterterrorism operations and raids. Raids in Mecca, Riyadh, and Medina led to arrests and document seizures and netted large quantities of explosives and a variety of weapons. In July alone, security services seized more than 20 tons of explosive-making materials in Qassim. In November, the authorities seized a truck bomb at a reported al-Qaida safehouse in Riyadh. Meanwhile, Saudi officials met several times with their Yemeni counterparts in an effort to stanch the flow of weapons into Saudi Arabia from Yemen.

During the past year, Riyadh expanded its cooperation with the United States in combating terrorist financing. The Government prohibited the collection of cash donations at mosques or commercial establishments, and in May the central bank issued a banking circular prohibiting charities from depositing or withdrawing cash or transferring funds abroad. In August 2003, Saudi Arabia adopted a new anti-money laundering and antiterrorist financing law, which criminalized money laundering and terrorist financing. The law also established a single financial intelligence unit, as required by the Financial Action Task Force, to collect against and analyze suspicious financial transactions and placed stringent "know your customer" requirements in the banking system. The Kingdom also established with the United States a Joint Task Force on Terrorist Financing to facilitate law-enforcement cooperation at the operational level. On 22 December, the United States and Saudi Arabia publicly announced their request to the UN 1267 Sanctions Committee to add the names of two organizations and one individual to its consolidated list.

On both the domestic and international fronts, Saudi Arabia initiated an ideological campaign against Islamist terrorist organizations, using its unique credentials as the custodian of Islam's two holiest shrines. Senior Saudi Government and religious officials espouse a consistent message of moderation and tolerance, explaining that Islam and terrorism are incompatible. Notably, in October speeches at the Organization of Islamic Conference Summit in Malaysia and later in Pakistan, Crown Prince Abdullah recommended to a broader audience concrete steps to counter extremism and improve relations between Muslims and non-Muslims.

For its part, Saudi Arabia has expressed its commitment to undertake internal political, social, and economic reforms aimed at combating the underlying causes of terrorism, and authorities have worked to delegitimize or correct those who would use Islam to justify terrorist acts. In early December, jailed cleric Ahmed al-Khalidi renounced his previous endorsement of violent jihad. Khalidi's statement followed similar public renunciations by extremist clerics Shaykh Ali bin Ali al-Khudayr and Nasir al-Fahd.

Saudi Arabia provided essential support to Operation Iraqi Freedom and continues to support Operation Enduring Freedom in Afghanistan.

Saudi Arabia has signed nine of the 12 international conventions and protocols relating to terrorism and is a party to six.

Tunisia

The Government of Tunisia has publicly supported the international Coalition against terrorism and has responded to US requests for information and assistance in blocking financial assets. Tunis's active stance against terrorism has been reinforced by its own recent experience with international terrorism. In April 2002, a suicide truck bomb detonated outside the el-Ghriba synagogue on the island of Djerba, killing more than 20.

In response to terrorism, the Government of Tunisia has taken steps to strengthen its laws and international agreements. The Tunisian legislature in December 2003 passed a comprehensive law to "support the international effort to combat terrorism and money laundering."

On the enforcement front, in March, Tunis issued a warrant for the arrest of Khalid Sheikh Mohammed for his role in the suicide truck bombing of the el-Ghriba synagogue in 2002. In addition, Belgacem Nawar, an uncle of Djerba suicide bomber Nizar Nawar, remains in Tunisian custody and is charged with complicity in the attack.

Tunis has consistently emphasized the threat that terrorism poses to security and stability in the region. Further, it has encouraged Libya to abandon terrorism and, in particular, to reach an agreement with France on additional compensation for the UTA airliner bombing of 1989. Domestically, the Tunisian Government has prohibited the formation of Islamist groups, which it believes pose a terrorist threat.

After the terrorist bombing of the UN compound in Baghdad, Tunis expressed its deep concern over the bombing and stated that it "firmly rejects any action aimed at undermining UN efforts to help Iraq and its brotherly people to recover security and stability and to complete the country's reconstruction process."

Since September 11, 2001, Tunis has each year called for an international conference to address the root causes of terrorism.

Tunisia ratified the International Convention on the Suppression of the Financing of Terrorism in February 2003, making it a party to 11 of the 12 international conventions and protocols relating to terrorism.

United Arab Emirates

In 2003, the United Arab Emirates continued to provide outstanding counterterrorism assistance and cooperation. The UAE Government publicly condemned acts of terrorism, including the attack in August against UN headquarters in Baghdad and the attack in November against a housing compound in Riyadh. In September, the UAE successfully hosted the annual International Monetary Fund/World Bank meetings, an event marked by close cooperation between the Dubai police and UAE armed forces.

In suppressing terrorist financing, the UAE Central Bank continued to aggressively enforce anti-money laundering regulations. Tightened oversight and reporting requirements for domestic financial markets resulted in a stronger legal and regulatory framework to deter abuse of the UAE financial system. The Central Bank has provided training programs to financial institutions on money laundering and terrorist financing.

It has also investigated financial transactions and frozen accounts in response to UN resolutions and internal investigations, as well as begun registering hawala dealers. The UAE has frozen the accounts of terrorist entities designated by the UN, and the US Government has provided the UAE with antiterrorism and anti-money laundering training, as well as technical assistance for bankers, prosecutors, judges, and police.

The UAE has provided assistance in several terrorist investigations. In early 2003, the UAE became a party to the 1973 Convention on the Prevention and Punishment of Crimes against Internationally Protected Persons.

The UAE is a party to eight of the 12 international conventions and protocols relating to terrorism.

Yemen

There were no reported terrorist attacks against or kidnappings of Westerners in Yemen in 2003. The Republic of Yemen Government continued to cooperate with US law enforcement and to take action against al-Qaida and local extremists in 2003, including arresting several al-Qaida–associated individuals, disrupting an al-Qaida–affiliated cell targeting Western interests, and prosecuting and convicting the perpetrators of the shootings of three Americans in Jibla on 30 December 2002. Abed Abdulrazak al-Kamel, the shooter, and Ali Ahmed Mohamed Jarallah, the planner, were tried, convicted, and sentenced to death in separate trials in 2003. On 1 December 2003, a three-judge panel affirmed the death sentence of al-Kamel, who will appeal the decision to the Yemen Supreme Court. Court officials expect that the conviction will be upheld and passed to President Saleh, who is likely to sign off on the order to carry out the sentence. Post representatives attended al-Kamel's trial and appeal proceedings, which were relatively transparent and openly reported in the local media.

Yemen publicly expressed its support for the global war on terrorism. In meetings with senior US officials, President Saleh underscored Yemen's determination to be an active counterterrorism partner.

However, there is still more work to be done to improve counterterrorism capabilities, including implementing a Maritime Security Strategy and increasing border security. Ongoing US-Yemeni cooperation includes counterterrorism training for Yemeni military forces, establishment of Yemeni Coast Guard capabilities (including seven 44-foot US-manufactured patrol boats arriving February 2004), and equipment and training for Yemen's Terrorist Interdiction Program.

Yemeni authorities arrested several high-profile al-Qaida associates in 2003. In late November, authorities arrested Muhammad Hamdi al-Ahdal (a.k.a. Abu Asim al-Makki)—the senior-most extremist in Yemen—who has supported mujahedin and terrorist operations throughout the Middle East and in Chechnya. In late September, Yemeni authorities arrested several members of an al-Qaida–affiliated cell planning attacks against a variety of targets in the country. Following the attack in mid-June on a medical assistance convoy in the Abyan Governorate, US- and UK-trained Yemeni Central Security Forces (CSF) raided a facility used by the Aden-Abyan Islamic Army (AAIA)—the local extremist group suspected of orchestrating and conducting the attack—and made a number of arrests. Consistent, but unconfirmed, reports from the press and other sources put the number of extremists killed or captured at between 20 and 30. CSF also indicated that a large amount of explosives and weapons were seized.

In October 2003, despite repeated statements that AAIA leader Khalid Abd-al-Nabi was dead, Yemeni officials revealed that he was not killed in the confrontations between the hardline Islamic group and a Yemeni army antiterrorism unit. Instead, al-Nabi surrendered to the Yemeni authorities, was released from custody, and is not facing charges for any of his activities. Earlier in 2003, authorities arrested al-Qaida operative Fawaz al-Rabi'I (a.k.a. Furqan) and al-Qaida associate Hadi Dulqum.

Land border security, particularly the long frontier with Saudi Arabia, is a major concern for Yemen. In the aftermath of the Riyadh bomb attacks in May 2003, the Government has improved cooperation with its Saudi neighbors. Representatives of both countries met several times in 2003 to discuss border security and ways to impede the flow of weapons from Yemen to Saudi Arabia. The Ministry of the Interior has an ambitious plan to establish 18 districts along the Yemeni-Saudi border to provide antismuggling defenses. In keeping with a bilateral security agreement, Sanaa and Riyadh have exchanged prisoners and terror suspects, including an operative from the Saudis most-wanted list.

The escape of 10 prisoners—including several suspects in the USS Cole bombing of October 2000—from an Aden jail in April was a setback to bilateral counterterrorism efforts. Although Sanaa responded quickly, dismissing two senior security officers and several prison guards, eight of the escapees have not yet been apprehended.

Following the model of other Arab countries, including Egypt, an Islamic scholarly commission formed in August 2002 continued its dialogue with detainees arrested in connection with extremism and/or terrorist attacks, which reportedly include Yemeni returnees from Afghanistan and members of the Al Jihad organization. Before being released, the detainees are screened by Yemen's Political Security Organization and commit to uphold the Yemeni constitution and laws, the rights of non-Muslims, and the inviolability of foreign interests. Ninety-two detainees were released post-Ramadan in 2003.

In the latter part of 2003, senior government officials, including President Saleh, publicly announced the detainees' release—some of whom may have ties to al-Qaida and other extremist groups—because they reportedly had renounced violence. The public announcement of the releases preceded the sharing of information with the US Government, which has now identified specific concerns with several of the individuals released and is working with the Government on the issue.

Several terrorist organizations continued to maintain a presence in Yemen throughout 2003. HAMAS and PIJ are recognized as legal organizations—and HAMAS maintains offices in Yemen—but neither has engaged in terrorist activities, and PIJ does not have any known actual or operational presence. Al-Qaida is attempting to reconstitute an operational presence in Yemen. Other international terrorist groups with a presence in Yemen include remnants of the Egyptian Islamic Jihad and al-Gama'a al-Islamiyya.

Yemen is a party to eight of the 12 international conventions and protocols relating to terrorism.

Western Hemisphere Overview

The international terrorism threat in the Western Hemisphere remained low during 2003 compared to other world regions. Even so, the region is by no means exempt from exploitation by groups that would use it to seek safehaven, financing, illegal travel documentation, or access to the United States via long-established narcotics and migrant-smuggling routes. The domestic terrorist threat remained high in Colombia and to a lesser extent in Peru.

Political will to combat terrorism remained steady in the Western Hemisphere during 2003, although efforts to update essential counterterrorism legislation were uneven. In addition, operational counterterrorism capacity and expertise remains lacking in many states in the hemisphere. Nevertheless, countries in the region actively continued efforts to fortify hemispheric border and financial controls to prevent or disrupt terrorism-related activities on their territories to the greatest extent possible.

The Organization of American States (OAS) Inter-American Committee Against Terrorism (CICTE, Spanish-language acronym)—a body under the Organization of American States—continues to set the standard among regional institutions through its effort to institutionalize the long-term international campaign against terrorism, according to the chair of the United Nations Counterterrorism Committee in March 2003. During a very active year under strong Salvadoran leadership, CICTE convened the first meeting of its National Points of Contact in Washington in July with the aim of fostering working-level contact and information sharing throughout the year. In July 2003, the Inter-American Convention Against Terrorism entered into force after six countries deposited their instruments of ratification (Antigua and Barbuda, Canada, El Salvador, Mexico, Nicaragua, and Peru). As 2004 commenced, another two states—Panama and Venezuela—ratified the convention. During its successful Fourth Regular Session in Montevideo, OAS member states agreed to enhance CICTE's mandate to effectively address threats to seaport and aviation security, as well as cybersecurity.

Money flowing to Islamic terrorist organizations continued to be a primary counterterrorism focus. To strengthen the efforts of friends in the region to disrupt potential terrorism fundraising activity, the United States continued to actively support the development of the "Three Plus One" (3+1) Counterterrorism Dialogue with partners Argentina, Brazil, and Paraguay. Meetings in Brasilia and Asuncion during 2003 led to new agreements on mutual capacity building in the areas of border security and financial controls. The United States looks forward to participating in 3+1–sponsored programs during 2004 and to hosting the next senior-level meeting in Washington in the fall.

Governments throughout the Southern Cone were active on the legal front against suspected terrorist activity. Uruguay, Paraguay, and Brazil took action to convict or extradite suspected international terrorists, either on terrorism or on criminal charges. The Argentine investigating judge in the suspected Hizballah bombing of the Argentine-Jewish cultural center in 1994, which killed 86 people, issued international arrest warrants for several Iranian Government officials who were assigned to Buenos Aires at the time, as well as the head of Hizballah's terrorist wing. Efforts to extradite the former Iranian ambassador to Argentina failed for a lack of evidence, and by the end of the year, the investigating judge had been replaced by order of an Argentine court. The trial, which began in 2001 against 20 Argentines believed to form the local connection in the bombing, continued into 2004.

Colombia continued to experience terrorist violence as the Revolutionary Armed Forces of Colombia (FARC) and other narcoterrorist groups sought to respond to an increasingly aggressive Colombian military posture with wanton terrorist attacks against civilians in Colombia's urban areas. The

El Nogal Club car bomb in February that killed 36 innocent civilians drew a swift condemnation from the OAS. Also in February, the FARC murdered American civilian contractor Thomas Janis and Colombian soldier Luis Alcides Cruz, whose plane had made an emergency crash landing in southern Colombia while conducting a counter-drug mission. Three other American aircraft crew members were taken hostage by FARC elements in the incident and at publication press time remained in FARC hands, along with many others, mostly Colombian hostages.

Under President Uribe, the Colombian military, police, and intelligence forces scored significant victories in 2003 against the FARC, National Liberation Army (ELN), and United Self-Defense Forces of Colombia (AUC) terrorist groups. They began to strike hard at the FARC's leadership ranks with targeted operations, spurred a sharp increase in desertions from the terrorist ranks, initiated peace talks and a pilot demobilization program with large elements of the AUC, invigorated anti-kidnapping efforts, and eradicated record levels of coca and poppy cultivation to cut off sources of funding for narcoterrorists.

The United States continued a long-term cooperative relationship with Canada by hosting another session of the Bilateral Consultative Group on Terrorism. Canada also was an active participant in the second Top Officials terrorist incident response exercise in May, and both countries are committed to supporting the capacity-building work of the Counterterrorism Action Group assistance donor countries, created by the G-8 countries in 2003.

The United States worked closely with several countries in the region, particularly Mexico, to respond in a coordinated, prudent fashion to emerging aviation security threats affecting American and foreign citizens. The US Government also has worked cooperatively with Mexico to implement a security program on its border with the United States.

Cuba, one of the seven state sponsors of terrorism, is discussed in the state sponsorship portion of this report.

Bolivia

There were no significant acts of international terrorism in Bolivia in 2003. The Government signed the Inter-American Convention Against Terrorism in 2002, but it has not yet been ratified. Bolivia's financial investigations unit actively collaborated with the US Embassy to share information about possible terrorist-linked financial transactions, prevent the abuse of Bolivian financial institutions by terrorists, and enhance the monitoring and enforcement of financial networks.

Despite many resource constraints, corruption, political tampering, and lack of expertise in handling sophisticated international investigations, the Government made progress in several—mostly domestic—terrorist-related cases. Most significantly, suspected National Liberation Army–Bolivia organizer Colombian Francisco Cortes and two Bolivian radical members of the Movement Towards Socialism party were arrested in 2003 and charged with espionage, terrorism, and subversion after they were found with weapons and organizational materials about guerrilla networks and plans to instigate violent revolution in Bolivia.

On 15 August, the Government of Bolivia signed the Asuncion Declaration in which several South American nations committed themselves to support Colombia in its ongoing struggle against terrorism and drug trafficking.

Bolivia's Government maintained the policy of forcibly eradicating illegal coca plants to help ensure that Bolivia does not revert to its former status as a major source of cocaine, which is the major economic underpinning of terrorism in the Andes. Militant illegal coca growers (*cocaleros*) are thought to be responsible for various domestic terrorism events, and there is concern that they may have foreign help to make their attacks more deadly. On 12 November, eight counternarcotics agents were kidnapped and beaten in the Yungas region. Similarly, in the Chapare region five members of the security forces were killed and 25 wounded through November by improvised explosive devices (IEDs) that exploded during coca eradication operations. *Cocaleros* are suspected of planting devices that have become increasingly sophisticated and may indicate outside technical assistance. Three *cocaleros* have been indicted for planting IEDs; others are suspected of sniper ambushes of security forces. Likewise, in the Chapare, in 2003 prosecutors made progress in the case of torture, rape, and murder of policeman David Andrade and his wife in 2000, and several *cocaleros* have been indicted or implicated in the crimes.

Bolivia is party to all 12 United Nations conventions and protocols related to terrorism and to one OAS counterterrorism convention.

Chile

The Government of Chile is a consistent and active supporter of US counterterrorism efforts and has taken an active interest in the activities of Islamic extremists connected to the Triborder area of Argentina, Brazil, and Paraguay and their potential links to the Free Trade Zone in Iquique, Chile. Chile continued its active support of US counterterrorism efforts in various international forums. Chile holds the chair of the UN's al-Qaida and Taliban sanctions committee and worked to improve the effectiveness of the sanctions. With Chile hosting the Asia-Pacific Economic Cooperation in 2004, President Ricardo Lagos listed security as the first of four points on which Chile would focus—in particular, security of trade and travel. In the Asuncion Declaration signed 15 August, President Lagos joined other South American leaders in condemning terrorism and drug trafficking. The declaration also expressed solidarity with Colombia in its domestic fight against terrorism. Similarly, Chile's UN Ambassador noted current UN sanctions were only partially enforced in many countries, and some were reluctant to submit terrorists' names to the UN. The Foreign Minister added that Chile was "a country willing to assume challenges and responsibilities."

Chilean law enforcement agencies were consistently cooperative in investigating links to international terrorism. The ability to conduct counterterrorist activities is hampered by a requirement that any investigation be directly related to prosecutable criminal offenses. The plainclothes investigations police (PICH—roughly equivalent to the FBI) continued to investigate several terrorism-related cases, but no prosecutions were developed.

The Chilean Congress passed a new money-laundering statute in September 2003 to cover terrorist finances and expand the Government's ability to freeze and seize assets. The new provisions have yet to be applied in a criminal case, and it remains unclear how the statute will operate in practice or how swiftly Chile will be able to react against terrorist assets identified by other governments or international institutions. The same legislation created a Financial Analysis Unit (UAF) to investigate suspicious transactions reported by financial institutions, but the Constitutional Tribunal ruled some of the UAF provisions to be unconstitutional. The Government is working to restore the UAF's ability to operate effectively and constitutionally. The current extradition treaty between Chile and the United States is more than 100 years old and has never been updated. Efforts are under way to explore negotiation of a new and viable extradition treaty.

Although no incidents of explicit terrorism occurred in Chile in 2003, terrorist-like tactics were employed in several cases, particularly in protest to the US-led invasion of Iraq. For example, a protester threw a Molotov cocktail at the US Embassy perimeter wall in March to protest policy on Iraq. *Carabineros* (uniformed police) guarding the embassy quickly arrested the perpetrator. Although two suspicious letters containing white powder delivered to the embassy and a telephonic bomb threat were all determined to be hoaxes, the *Carabineros* supplied HAZMAT teams and bomb-sniffing dogs in short order. In March, small bombs targeted Bank of Boston branches in Santiago and a BellSouth office in Concepcion. A similar bomb exploded at the Court of Appeals in Temuco. There were no injuries, no claim of responsibility, and no arrests made in any of the blasts. In March and April, the Chilean-American Binational Centers were subject to violent protests, some vandalism, and bomb threats by Chileans opposed to US policy in Iraq.

In August 2002, Chile requested the extradition from Brazil of former Manuel Rodriguez Patriotic Front leader Mauricio Hernandez Norambuena to finish his sentence for the murder of rightwing Chilean Senator Jaime Guzman in 1991. Hernandez escaped prison in 1996. The Brazilian Attorney General ruled that Hernandez should be extradited to Chile, but the Brazilian Supreme Court must approve the decision—a process said to be in the final stages and likely to result in extradition in the near term.

Chile is a party to all of the 12 international conventions and protocols relating to terrorism.

Colombia

Colombia fully comprehends the devastation caused by terrorism as it has faced large-scale domestic terrorism for several decades. From the day the Uribe Administration assumed office in August 2002, it has demonstrated a firm resolve to combat terrorists of all stripes. The Government of Colombia is supportive of US Government efforts to combat terrorist acts, target terrorist finances, and cooperate with extradition requests. Colombia continued to speak out forcefully and often against terrorist organizations throughout the year.

Colombia continued its struggle against the country's three main terrorist groups—the Revolutionary Armed Forces of Colombia (FARC), the National Liberation Army (ELN), and the United Self-Defense Forces of Colombia (AUC)—all of which were redesignated by the United States as Foreign Terrorist Organizations in 2003. In June, the United States also designated the FARC and the AUC as significant foreign narcotics traffickers under the Kingpin Act.

Colombia suffered many large and small domestic terrorist attacks throughout 2003. Car bombs, kidnapping, political murders, the indiscriminant use of landmines, and economic sabotage were common occurrences. Some of the more noteworthy examples included the FARC's car bombing in February of Bogota's El Nogal Club killing 34 and wounding more than 160; the FARC hostage taking of three US contractors and killing of another American and a Colombian when their plane crashed near Florencia, Caqueta Department (the three Americans remain hostages) in February; a "house bomb" in February in Neiva that killed 16 and wounded more than 40; an ELN kidnapping in September of eight foreign tourists visiting archaeological ruins (one escaped, two were released in November, and five were freed in December); a grenade attack in November by the FARC that wounded Americans in Bogota's restaurant district; and attacks in November and December utilizing antitank rockets. Both FARC and the ELN continued attacks against the country's infrastructure and oil pipelines in 2003, albeit at reduced levels. Many more attacks were thwarted nationwide through excellent intelligence and security work.

In 2003, President Uribe increased military pressure on illegal armed groups and implemented an ambitious national security strategy including securing passage of antiterrorism legislation, promoting the desertion and reintegration of former illegal armed militants, and engaging the AUC in demobilization negotiations. President Uribe submitted to Congress two important draft laws with significant public security implications—the Antiterrorism Bill and a Conditional Parole Bill. The Anti-Terrorism Bill was approved by Congress on 10 December and allows the Government to conduct wiretaps, search residences, and detain suspects more easily. The conditional parole legislation is connected to the broader peace process and would provide the Government the means to waive prison sentences in exchange for demobilization. Through legislation and with possible US assistance, the Government of Colombia expected the voluntary surrender of more than 4,000 illegal armed militants in 2003 (an increase of 84 percent over 2002) and the demobilization in December of some 1,000 paramilitaries with more planned for 2004.

Overall, Colombia's ambitious security strategy produced substantial achievements in 2003. Murders decreased by 16 percent, assassinations of trade unionists were down 68 percent, and kidnappings were 30 percent lower in 2003. The military completed the early phases of its national defense plan with significant successes, including the killing of at least five midlevel FARC commanders in Cundinamarca Department near Bogota. In January 2004, the most senior FARC official ever to be captured was detained by Ecuadorian National Police in Quito and deported to Colombia. Another major accomplishment was the restoration of a Government presence in every one of the country's 1,098 municipalities (county seats) by the end of 2003.

Colombia cooperated fully in blocking terrorist assets. A Colombian Financial Information and Analysis Unit, created in 2001 following the model of the US Financial Crimes Enforcement Unit (FinCEN), collaborated closely with the US Treasury's Office of Foreign Assets Control. US Anti-Terrorist Assistance in August inaugurated a school for Colombian military and police who specialize in anti-kidnapping. Kidnappings are sources of revenue for the FARC and the ELN and a means to influence the political process. The Government also took steps at self-improvement by expanding an antiterrorism unit in the Prosecutor General's Office. Lessons learned in the counternarcotics fight have led to better prosecutions of those who attack the nation's infrastructure, particularly in oil-producing areas.

Colombia made significant strides in combating narcotrafficking, a primary source of revenue for terrorist organizations. The UN Office on Drugs and Crime estimated that coca cultivation could be reduced by aerial eradication as much as 50 percent in 2003. Eradication programs targeting coca and opium poppies continued throughout the year. In August, the United States resumed the air Bridge Denial Program that assists Colombia in intercepting aircraft trafficking in narcotics and illegal weapons.

Colombia was particularly cooperative in cases and investigations involving Americans, such as the hostage taking of Defense Department civilian contractors in February and the grenade attack in Bogota in December. The US-Colombia extradition relationship continues to be one of the most successful in the world; Colombia extradited 67 persons to the United States in 2003. In May 2003, Colombia extradited Nelson Vargas Rueda, the first FARC member to be extradited to the United States. Vargas is accused of the kidnapping and murder of three American NGO activists working with Colombian indigenous groups in northern Colombia in 1999. Colombia also extradited Gerardo Herrera Iles, accused of kidnapping foreign and US oil workers, to the United States in 2003.

Colombia has signed eight of the international conventions and protocols relating to terrorism and is a party to six.

Ecuador

The Government of Ecuador supports the war on terrorism in all international and bilateral forums. Quito signed the Inter-American Convention Against Terrorism but has not yet ratified it. President Gutierrez, during a visit in February to the United States, expressed his intent to make Ecuador a solid ally in the war on terrorism. Nevertheless, resource constraints, a lack of training, and sometimes-corrupt governmental organizations impede progress in the battle against both international and regional terrorism. Ecuador's judicial system, which is susceptible to outside pressure and corruption, adjudicated no terrorist cases in 2003.

At the working level, the National Police (ENP) supported US counterterrorism initiatives throughout 2003 and into 2004. In January 2004, the most senior FARC official ever to be captured was detained by Ecuadorian National Police in Quito and deported to Colombia in a concrete example of Ecuador's will to defeat the narcoterrorist threat in the region. In March, the ENP arrested an Ecuadorian citizen who detonated two bombs at a Government office in Guayaquil. A string of weapons seizures in Ecuador demonstrated the arms trade in Ecuador supporting Colombian narcoterrorists. In August 2003, the police broke up an arms smuggling operation supplying Colombian narcoterrorists. In September, an Army captain was arrested and accused of providing operational information to the Colombian FARC. In addition, a DEA-trained counter-drug policeman apprehended an Italian citizen trying to board Continental Airlines in Quito with explosives and a firearm in November.

Although no terrorist-related incidents were launched from Ecuador, its porous borders, endemic corruption, and well-established illegal migrant networks make it an attractive entry point for would-be terrorists. Ecuador has been historically lax in securing the northern border from Colombian illegal armed groups. Only in recent years has the Government recognized the threat from Colombia and undertaken serious efforts to impose control along the border. Ecuador's security forces disrupted several Colombian narcoterrorist encampments in Ecuador from late 2002 through October 2003. Although the FARC still operates in the area, it realizes now that Ecuador is less hospitable than before.

The Government of Ecuador banking superintendency acts swiftly to include suspect individuals and groups into bank lookout databases upon receipt of terrorism finance information. In 2003, Ecuador ordered two pharmacies closed because of information from the United States that proved ties to Colombian drug-trafficking organizations. Unfortunately, due to ineffective enforcement, the companies were still operating at the end of the year.

Ecuador is party to 10 of the 12 international conventions and protocols relating to terrorism.

Peru

Peru continued to take many actions against both international and domestic terrorism in 2003. President Toledo made combating terrorism one of the keynotes in his annual state-of-the-nation speech in July, pledging increased funding for security forces and social development projects in areas where the domestic Shining Path (Sendero Luminoso-SL) operates. The Foreign and Defense Ministers consistently condemned terrorism and implemented counterterrorism actions.

On 15 August, the Government of Peru signed the Asuncion Declaration in which several South American nations committed themselves to support the Government of Colombia in its ongoing struggle against terrorism and drug trafficking. Peru ratified the Inter-American Convention against Terrorism in June 2003.

A director for the Financial Intelligence Unit (FIU), established in 2002, was named in April 2003. He expanded the staff and began receiving reports of suspicious activity from banks. The US Embassy worked closely with the FIU to provide a technical advisor and funding for the acquisition of hardware and software.

The Peruvian Congress created a national security system designed to improve intergovernmental cooperation and strengthen prosecutors. Meanwhile, the National Police (PNP) Directorate of Counterterrorism continued its strong cooperation with the Embassy in counterterrorism activities. The United States did not make any extradition requests to Peru for terrorists in 2003.

Peru has aggressively prosecuted terrorist suspects. In January, the Constitutional Tribunal overturned numerous provisions in Fujimori-era decree laws on terrorism, in conformance with decisions of the Inter-American Court of Human Rights. Military court convictions in approximately 2,000 cases were vacated and reviewed for retrial. President Toledo issued decree legislation revising Peru's antiterrorism legislation in line with the Constitutional Tribunal decision and established the procedures for reviewing and retrying terrorism cases. Some were dropped because sentences are nearing completion, and some 750 cases are sufficiently strong to be retried beginning in 2004.

In September, four Chilean defendants were retried and convicted of membership in the Tupac Amaru Revolutionary Movement and participation in an attack on the Peru-North American Cultural Institute and a kidnapping-murder in 1993.

Eight members of SL remain in custody awaiting trial. They were arrested for complicity in the bombing in March 2002 across the street from the US Embassy that killed 10 people. Peru successfully sought the extradition from Spain of Adolfo Hector Olaechea, a suspected SL official, in 2003. He was released from custody but ordered to remain in Peru while the public prosecutor prepares the case for trial.

The most serious SL event in 2003 was the kidnapping of 68 workers and three police guards in June at a Camisea gas pipeline project in Toccate, Ayacucho Department. The SL abandoned the hostages two days after the kidnapping and a rapid military response; a ransom may or may not have been paid to the SL. The PNP also broke up many SL camps and captured many members and leaders in 2003. More than 200 indigenous people held in virtual slavery by the SL were released in the process. Terrorist incidents fell to 96 by late October, projecting an annual rate of 115 or a 15-percent drop from the 134 kidnappings and armed attacks in 2002. Six military and three self-defense personnel were killed in 2003, while six SL militants were killed and 209 captured.

Peru is a party to all 12 of the conventions and protocols relating to terrorism.

Triborder Area (Argentina, Brazil, and Paraguay)

The Triborder area (TBA)—where Argentina, Brazil, and Paraguay converge—has long been characterized as a regional hub for Hizballah and HAMAS fundraising activities, but it is also used for arms and drug trafficking, contraband smuggling, document and currency fraud, money laundering, and the manufacture and movement of pirated goods. Although there continued to be reports in 2003 of an al-Qaida presence in the TBA, these reports remained uncorroborated by intelligence and law-enforcement officials.

In December, a high-level interagency delegation from the United States attended a special meeting in Asuncion, Paraguay, of the Tripartite Commission of the Triple Frontier, a security mechanism established by the three TBA countries in 1998. This "Three Plus One" meeting (the three TBA countries plus the United States) serves as a continuing forum for counterterrorism cooperation and prevention among all four countries. At the December talks, the four countries exchanged current views on terrorism prevention in the region and on measures to enhance cooperation, including proposals to establish a joint regional intelligence center, convene a conference of "Three Plus One" partner financial intelligence units in the first half of 2004, deepen border security cooperation, and increase dialogue among national prosecutors responsible for counterterrorism cases. The parties concluded that available information did not substantiate reports of operational activities by terrorists in the TBA. However, international terrorist financing and money laundering in the area remained an area of primary concern. A concerted effort will be made to develop legitimate economic activity in the TBA.

Argentina continued to express strong support for the global war on terrorism and worked closely with the United Nations, the OAS, the Southern Common Market (MERCOSUR—Brazil, Uruguay, Paraguay, and associate members Bolivia and Chile), and the United States to ensure full implementation of existing agreements. The Argentine Government, executive branch officials, and the Central Bank were extremely cooperative and responded quickly and effectively to ensure the assets of terrorist groups identified by the United States or UN would be blocked if detected in Argentine financial institutions. Though no leads were found in 2003, the Government of Argentina continually expressed its willingness to freeze assets in compliance with international agreements.

Diplomatically, Argentina cooperated fully in 2003 with all significant international counterterrorism efforts in the UN, the OAS, and the "Three Plus One" Counterterrorism Dialogue to strengthen security and search for terrorist support networks, especially in the Triborder area. Argentina worked within existing regional and international forums to elicit strong condemnations of terrorism and support to organizations combating terror. Argentina maintains an active role in the OAS CICTE, established in response to an Argentine initiative in the 1990s. Multilateral meetings—including high-level US officials with counterterrorism responsibilities—were held in Brasilia in May 2003 and Asuncion in December to focus on the Triborder.

On 15 August, the Government of Argentina signed the Asuncion Declaration in which several South American nations committed themselves to support the Government of Colombia in its ongoing struggle against terrorism and drug trafficking.

Although there were no acts of international terrorism in Argentina in 2003, investigations into the bombing of the Israeli Embassy in 1992, in which 29 persons were killed, and the bombing in 1994 of the Argentina-Israeli Community Center (AMIA), in which 86 persons were killed, continued. The trials of 20 suspects in the AMIA bombing—of whom 15 are former police officers—continued throughout 2003 and appeared to be nearing a close. The judge in the AMIA case indicted 12 Iranian officials, including diplomats stationed in Buenos Aires in 1994 and one Lebanese official believed to head Hizballah's terrorist wing. Although no countries requested terror-related extraditions from Argentina, Argentina requested the extradition of the former Iranian ambassador to Argentina from the United Kingdom, indicted in the AMIA case.

The request was denied due to a lack of evidence presented by Argentina.

Proposed antiterrorism legislation has long provoked an active debate over the balance between civil rights and the need to address potential terrorism. As a result, there has been little progress toward the passage of new comprehensive antiterrorism legislation. Nevertheless, the Government strongly and consistently deplored terrorist acts when they occurred. In 2003, both ex-President Duhalde and his successor, Nestor Kirchner, publicly condemned terrorism and reiterated Argentina's support for the war on terrorism. Despite the lack of new legislation, Argentina continued to improve intragovernmental coordination on counterterrorism to enhance the framework within which better international cooperation can occur.

Argentina has signed all of the 12 conventions and protocols relating to terrorism and is a party to 10.

Brazil has extended practical, effective support to US counterterrorism actions. The Government of Brazil has been cooperative in checking records provided by US intelligence, law enforcement, and financial agencies regarding hundreds of terrorist suspects. For example, Brazilian authorities actively followed up on press reports in March 2003 that al-Qaida operative Khalid Sheikh Mohammed visited the Triborder area in 1995.

Although the Government of Brazil is politically committed to the fight against terrorism, lack of resources and training sometimes hamper its response. The United States continues to work with Brazil in several bilateral, multilateral, and international forums to identify groups and individuals suspected of possible ties to terrorist activity. Brazil hosted a working group meeting under the 3+1 Counterterrorism Dialogue in May, which focused on technical cooperation related to the fight against terrorism financing. Technical specialists from the United States are fully engaged with elements of the Brazilian Government responsible for combating terrorism, including the Federal Police. Brazil is willing and increasingly capable of monitoring domestic financial operations and has effectively utilized its Financial Activities Oversight Council (COAF). Bilateral assistance and training of the COAF began in 1998 and emphasized upgrades to its database in 2003.

Since taking office in January 2003, President Lula da Silva has vigorously condemned terrorism and called the attack on the UN building in Baghdad "the insanity of perpetrators of terrorism." In January, Brazil backed the CICTE with a financial contribution. In July 2003, Brazil approved legislation criminalizing the financing of terrorist activities. On 15 August, the Government of Brazil signed the Asuncion Declaration in which several South American nations committed themselves to support Colombia in its ongoing struggle against terrorism and drug trafficking.

In addition, the Brazilian Chamber of Deputies passed a bill on cybercrime—to prevent terrorist hack attacks—that awaits Senate consideration.

There are no significant impediments to the prosecution or extradition of suspected terrorists by Brazil. The Brazilian extradition law prohibits the extradition of Brazilian citizens but allows very measured and careful consideration for the extradition of naturalized citizens (for previous crimes and drug trafficking only) and foreigners (not for ideological or political crimes). In November 2003, Brazil extradited Assad Ahmad Barakat to Paraguay. Barakat was arrested in June 2002 by Brazilian authorities in Foz do Iguacu, Parana, in the TBA acting on a Paraguayan extradition request related to criminal charges. Barakat is a naturalized Paraguayan of Lebanese origin who lived in the TBA for approximately seven years and was known to have been involved in political and financial activities supporting Hizballah organizations.

In February 2003, Brazil declined a request from Colombia to designate the FARC as a terrorist organization. Brazil stated it did not maintain a formal list of terrorist groups but condemns specific terrorist actions taken by the FARC and other groups. Brazilian security forces continued to investigate possible links between domestic criminal groups—especially drug traffickers and those with no discernible political agenda—that sometimes employed terrorist tactics. In 2003, organized crime groups at times shut down Rio de Janeiro tourist and business areas and systematically attacked police stations in Sao Paulo to weaken Government resolve to combat them. At the end of 2003, Brazil had increased it readiness to confront domestic groups and reinforce against FARC incursions in northwestern Brazil. The Brazilian Army augmented its Special Forces capabilities—including counterterrorism—and began compiling data on global terrorist threats to enhance its ability to respond.

Brazil signed all of the 12 UN conventions on terrorism and is a party to nine.

Paraguay has aided the global Coalition against terrorism by ratifying a number of international treaties and conventions and actively supporting counterterrorism at the UN and the OAS. On 15 August, Paraguay signed the Asuncion Declaration in which several South American nations committed themselves to support the Government of Colombia in its ongoing struggle against terrorism and drug trafficking.

On 30 October, Congress ratified the CICTE. Paraguay is also strengthening its domestic legal framework to deal more effectively with terrorism and ancillary support activities. Paraguay hosted the successful third meeting of the 3+1 Counterterrorism Dialogue in December 2003.

Paraguay has determined that there is a domestic problem with fundraising that might support terrorist causes. It looks to assistance from other governments—including the United States—to help it fight the problem. The primary impediment to the prosecution of suspected terrorists is the absence of an antiterrorist law. Without such a law, the Government is forced to prosecute suspected terrorist fundraisers for tax evasion or illegal financial activities. Paraguay is drafting new legislation to strengthen its anti-money laundering regime, as well as a specific antiterrorism bill. Both bills are fully backed by the Duarte Administration and expected to go before Congress in 2004.

Despite the lack of specific antiterrorist statutes, Paraguay actively prosecuted known terrorist fundraisers. Two prominent Hizballah fundraisers, Sobhi Fayad and Ali Nizar Dahroug, were sentenced to lengthy prison terms in November 2002 and August 2003, respectively. Paraguay's antiterrorist police continued to provide excellent support for the arrest and prosecution of terrorists. A major accomplishment in 2003 was the successful extradition request for Hizballah fundraiser Assad Ahmad Barakat from Brazil on charges of tax evasion. Additional charges of bank fraud are being considered but will require Brazil's acquiescence under the terms for extradition.

Paraguay is a party to six of the international conventions and protocols relating to terrorism and is a signatory to an additional five.

Uruguay

The Government of Uruguay is supportive of international terrorist measures undertaken in a variety of international forums and cooperates fully with the United States. Uruguayan officials routinely condemned terrorism and specific terrorist acts. Although Uruguay is supportive of the global Coalition against terrorism, it lacks the resources to play a significant role. However, it does provide troops to international peacekeeping forces in Africa and the Middle East.

Uruguay is active in the OAS CICTE and has seconded personnel to its Executive Secretariat. Uruguay hosted the annual CICTE meeting in Montevideo in January 2004 and assumed the CICTE chairmanship through 2004. Uruguay is a member of a MERCOSUR permanent working group on terrorism along with Argentina, Brazil, Chile, Paraguay, and Bolivia. The group facilitates cooperation and information sharing among countries fighting terrorism and places special emphasis on the Triborder area and the Uruguay-Brazil border. Uruguay is, likewise, active in counterterrorism groups in the Rio Group and in the OAS.

On 15 August, the Government of Uruguay signed the Asuncion Declaration in which several South American nations committed themselves to support the Government of Colombia in its ongoing struggle against terrorism and drug trafficking.

In 2003, Uruguay ratified the International Conventions for Suppression of the Financing of Terrorism and the Physical Protection of Nuclear Material. The Government of Uruguay faces some challenges in fully implementing UN Security Council Resolutions 1373 and 1456, especially in curtailing terrorist financing activities. This might have more to do with the Government's uncertainty about its ability to effectively track money laundering and terrorist financing—in spite of the creation of a unit for financial analysis in the central bank.

Uruguayan law enforcement authorities assisted with international investigations of the movement and activities of suspected terrorists in 2003, but Uruguay was not directly involved in terrorist events. At present, there are no known terrorist operatives in Uruguay, and Uruguayan banking and law enforcement officials have discovered no terrorist assets in Uruguayan financial institutions. Banking and law enforcement agencies cooperated with US counterterrorism efforts by pledging to search for bank accounts, individuals, and groups with links to terrorism. Uruguay is assisting in the investigation of potential terrorist support emanating from the Triborder area and along Uruguay's northern frontier with Brazil.

Uruguay has no significant impediments to the prosecution or extradition of suspected terrorists. The judicial system is independent of external influences, but, as elsewhere, the judges' personal political leanings can influence the outcome of some cases.

In July 2003, Uruguay extradited Al Said Hassan Mokhles to Egypt. Egypt requested the extradition of the member of al-Gama'a al-Islamiyya, possible associate of al-Qaida, in 2002. Egyptian authorities tied Mokhles to a terrorist attack in Luxor, Egypt, that killed 58 foreign tourists in 1997. He was arrested in Uruguay on charges of document fraud in 1999 after attempting to enter the country with a false passport. Uruguayan authorities released him to Egypt under the conditions that he not be subjected to the death penalty, permanent imprisonment, or charged for document fraud (for which he already served four years).

Uruguay has signed and ratified all 12 UN terrorism conventions and protocols.

Venezuela

Venezuelan cooperation in the international campaign against terrorism was inconsistent in 2003. Public recriminations against US counterterrorism policies by President Chavez and his close supporters continued to overshadow and detract from the limited cooperation that exists between specialists and technicians of the two nations.

President Chavez's stated ideological affinity with the Revolutionary Armed Forces of Colombia (FARC) and the Colombian National Liberation Army (ELN) limits Venezuelan cooperation with Colombia in combating terrorism. Venezuela is unwilling or unable to systematically police the Venezuela-Colombia 1,400-mile border. The FARC and the ELN often use the area for cross-border incursions and regard Venezuelan territory near the border as a safehaven. In addition, weapons and ammunition—some from official Venezuelan stocks and facilities—continued flowing from Venezuelan suppliers into the hands of Colombian terrorist organizations. It is unclear to what extent the Government of Venezuela approves of or condones material support to Colombian terrorists and at what level. Efforts by Venezuelan security forces to control their sides of the border and to interdict arms flows to these groups are ineffective.

Current Venezuelan law does not specifically mention crimes of terrorism, although the UN Convention on Terrorist Bombings of 1997 and the UN Convention on Terrorism Financing of 1999 became law in Venezuela on 8 July 2003. An organized crime bill pending in the National Assembly would define terrorist activities, establish punishments, and facilitate the prosecution and asset forfeiture of terrorism financiers. Venezuela signed the OAS Inter-American Convention Against Terrorism in June 2002 and ratified it in January 2004.

Terrorist tactics were employed throughout 2003 by unidentified domestic groups attempting to influence the tenuous political situation, particularly in Caracas. A series of small bombs and threats throughout the year were variously blamed on supporters of President Chavez or the Government's political opponents.

Venezuela extradited one member of the terrorist organization Basque Fatherland and Liberty to Spain and arrested another. Unconfirmed press accounts continued to allege the presence of radical Islamic operatives in Venezuela—especially on Margarita Island. In February 2003, a Venezuelan national managed to fly from Venezuela to London with a hand grenade in his checked luggage, but his intent remains unclear.

Venezuela is a party to six of the 12 international conventions and protocols relating to terrorism.

North America (Canada and Mexico)

The Government of **Canada** remained steadfast in its condemnation of international and domestic terrorism and has been a helpful and strong supporter of the United States in the fight against international terror. Though there have been differences, overall antiterrorism cooperation with Canada remains excellent and serves as a model for bilateral cooperation. Day-to-day cooperation between US and Canadian law-enforcement agencies is close and continuous. Canadian Armed Forces participated in Operation Enduring Freedom in 2001, and Canada currently has some 1,900 soldiers in Afghanistan where they will lead the International Security Assistance Force in 2004. Canada has pledged $230 million to reconstruction efforts; participated in a Justice Department–led international assessment of Iraq's police, prisons, and court sectors; and is currently involved in training the Iraqi police force.

Canada's 2001 Anti-Terrorism Act created measures to identify, deter, disable, prosecute, convict, and punish terrorist groups. It also provides investigative tools for Canadian law enforcement agencies while providing substantial safeguards to privacy and due process. As of November 2003, there were 34 organizations listed under the statute as entities engaging in terrorist activities. Although they are subject to prosecution under the Criminal Code of Canada, the law is untested since no prosecutions have taken place. Canada cooperates closely with the United States on investigations, and there is a heavy volume of extradition requests between the two countries. Canadian privacy laws, limited resources, and criminal procedures more favorable to the defendant than in the United States sometimes inhibit a more full and timely exchange of information and exclude some potential supporters of terrorism.

Canada was the first country to ratify the Inter-American Convention Against Terrorism in December 2002. Canada implements terrorist finance listings in compliance with UN requirements and coordinates closely with the United States on plans to freeze assets. Efforts to counter terrorist financing include implementing UNSCR 1373, promoting the Special Recommendations on Terrorist Financing of the Financial Action Task Force, and actively participating in the G-7, G-8, and G-20.

Canada and the United States take part in a number of joint counterterrorism forums. In October 2003, they participated in a new round of talks under the auspices of the Bilateral Consultative Group on Counterterrorism Cooperation (BCG, established in 1988). The BCG is tasked to review international terrorist trends and to plan ways to intensify joint counterterrorism efforts. Canada will host the next BCG meetings in 2004. In May 2003, Canada and the United States participated in the second Top Officials simulation to test local, state/province, and federal disaster responses to a terrorist attack against civilian populations. The US Attorney General and Canadian Solicitor General coordinated policy at the US-Canada Cross-Border Crime Forum. The forum met in West Virginia in 2003 and established a counterterrorism subgroup to enhance cooperation in law enforcement and prosecutions. Future efforts include continued implementation of provisions of the Smart Border Accord and the further integration of border enforcement teams that are operating in 12 regions.

Canada has signed and ratified all 12 UN conventions and protocols relating to terrorism, including the International Convention for the Suppression of the Financing of Terrorism, under which Canada has listed and frozen the assets of more than 420 entities.

The Government of **Mexico** remained a strong international and bilateral partner in counterterrorism efforts throughout 2003. Mexico accepted a new methodology of evaluating and regulating money laundering and terrorism financing adopted by the IMF, the World Bank, and the FATF.

Among the many bilateral initiatives undertaken, Mexico cooperated fully with the United States in continuing to implement the US-Mexico Smart Border Accord—a 22-point border action plan signed in 2002 that aims to improve border infrastructure, expedite the secure flow of people, and facilitate the secure flow of goods across the US-Mexico border. Exchanges such as the Senior Law Enforcement Plenary, the Binational Commission, and the Mexico-US Committee on Transborder Critical Infrastructure Protection helped improve cooperation, trust, and confidence. Routine training, education, and technical assistance at various levels took place throughout 2003.

Mexico's Federal Investigative Agency arrested six Spanish citizens and three Mexicans at locations throughout Mexico on 18 July and alleged they had ties to the Basque Fatherland and Liberty (ETA). In public statements, Mexican officials said the suspects were laundering money to fund ETA terrorism and forging documents to support ETA members.

A continuing issue of strategic concern to US-Mexico counterterrorism efforts is the existence and continued exploitation of longstanding smuggling channels traversing the US-Mexico border. These routes have existed for many years to facilitate movement across the border while avoiding US and Mexican authorities. Despite active and prolonged cooperation by the Mexican Government to address these smuggling routes, many smugglers have avoided prosecution.

Mexico has ratified all 12 international conventions and protocols against terrorism.

Rollout of Patterns of Global Terrorism 2003

U.S. Department of State Transcripts

The Original Report

The text below consists of the remarks made by Ambassador-at-Large Cofer Black, coordinator for counterterrorism, and a subsequent question-and-answer session that took place on 29 April 2004, with the release of Patterns of Global Terrorism 2003.

Ambassador Black: Good afternoon. [In] the terrorist attacks that took place throughout 2003 in every region of the world, but there is some good news as well. Last year, we saw unprecedented collaboration between the United States and foreign partners to defeat terrorism. We also saw the lowest number of international terrorist attacks since 1969, and that's a 34-year low.

There were 190 acts of international terrorism in 2003. That's a slight decrease from 198 attacks that occurred the previous year, and a drop of 45 percent from the 2001 level of 346 attacks.

There were also fewer casualties caused by terrorists last year. A total of 307 persons were killed in last year's attack[s], far fewer than the 725 killed during 2002. A total of 1,593 persons were wounded in the attacks that occurred in 2003, down from 2,013 persons wounded the year before.

There were 82 anti-U.S. attacks last year, which is up slightly from the 77 attacks the previous year.

I'd like to clarify one point for you. Most of the attacks that have occurred during Operation Iraqi Freedom in Iraq and Operation Enduring Freedom do not meet the longstanding U.S. definition of international terrorism because they were directed at noncombatants, essentially American and coalition forces on duty.

Question: At combatants?

Ambassador Black: Excuse me?

Question: At combatants?

Ambassador Black: Yes, at combatants. Excuse me. Thank you.

Attacks against noncombatants, essentially civilians and military personnel, who, at the time of the incident, were unarmed and/or not on duty, are judged as terrorist attacks. The very low level of terrorist attacks last year certainly does not mean that the problem is fading away; indeed, we're currently at war with terrorists, with major fronts in Iraq and Afghanistan, where terrorists are working with other elements to launch attacks against coalition targets.

Whether they target combatants or civilians, terrorists must know that we and our partner nations around the world will not relent in our global effort to defeat them. Moreover, numbers do not tell the whole story. Terrorists, last year, carried out attacks that were indiscriminate and intended to cause mass casualties. They went after soft targets such as: places of worship, commuter trains, hotels, police stations and crowded markets.

There is every indication that al-Qaida continues to plan mass casualty attacks against American and other targets worldwide. Although the group poses as a defender of a great faith, they have hijacked Islam as a cover for their violence. Numerous Muslims have died in al-Qaida attacks. Much of the Islamic world stands with the United States in fighting this great evil.

In 2003, we saw less state sponsorship of terrorism: Saddam Hussein no longer presides over a regime that served as a lifeline and sanctuary for the terrorists; Libya has renounced terrorism. Sudan has taken significant steps to be a cooperative partner in the global war on terrorism; and Afghanistan is no longer a breeding ground for terrorism as a result of Operation Enduring Freedom.

Despite this progress, state sponsorship remains an unprecedented advantage for terrorists that enables them to acquire the weapons, training and logistical support they need to commit terrorist atrocities and afterwards to enjoy safe haven and freedom from the prosecution of their crimes.

Iran and Syria, especially, are culpable in this regard. They should immediately cease their sponsorship of terrorist murderers. Along with our likeminded foreign partners, the United States continues to pursue the global campaign against terrorism on five fronts: diplomatic, military, economic, intelligence and law enforcement. On that score, it's important to recognize that the record clearly shows America's most effective counterterrorism strategy is building the will and skill of indigenous forces to fight terrorism on their own turf and in their own self-interest.

This report discusses what nations are doing in all these areas, and in some cases what more they should be doing. It is vital that nations sustain the political will to wage this war as effectively as possible for as long as is necessary. Many nations have greatly improved their capabilities to fight terror and the United States will help wherever possible to build and further expand international counterterrorism capacities.

With the international counterterrorism coalition's enhanced intelligence sharing and law enforcement cooperation, we're seeing more terrorist plots thwarted, more terrorists identified, tracked and arrested, and more perpetrators brought to justice for their crimes.

It's a pleasure to be here today and I'll try and answer some of your questions.

Question: Can I ask you two very, very technical questions that you probably—you may not be the right person to answer? And they have to do with the designations, the state sponsor designations. And I realize that this report is not the, you know, the be all and end all, that the list can change at any time, but I'm just wondering, are you—the fact that Iraq remains on that list, when sovereignty is transferred on June 30/July 1st, do you know if the interim government there, the interim government that comes in, will have enough authority to be able to do the things it needs to do to get off the list?

Ambassador Black: Okay. It's an important question. Let me try and encapsulate an answer for you. Essentially, on May the 7th, 2003, the President exercised his authorities to suspend the Iraq Sanctions Act. The President effectively waived all sanctions on Iraq as a state sponsor.

What we have here essentially is that we need to assure ourselves that a new government in Baghdad renounces terrorism as well as proves, by fact and deed, that they have renounced and they are taking every action to renounce terrorism as well as be an effective partner in the international community to do this.

So for us to be able to remove them from the list, we need a government in power. Sovereignty will be transferred on the 30th of June, and at that point we can go through with the assumption that the government takes power, that renounces terrorism and shows every indication, we then begin the process of validating that and moving forward.

Question: Yeah, but the discussion for the last couple of weeks has been that this government is not going to be entirely sovereign. And I'm just asking, and maybe you don't know the answer to this, but will they, because they are not going to have complete control of their security forces, for example, be able to do what they need to do to your satisfaction to get off the list?

And secondly, if you—as you say, Libya has renounced terrorism, which you did in your opening remarks, and that is a condition for Iraq to get off, Libya has a sovereign government. Why are they still on?

Ambassador Black: Well, in the first instance, what I've relayed to you is the rules and regulations, how we see this issue. We will have to see what we have after 30th of June, and we'll have to make a determination. It is likely that it will be viewed favorably. I can't assure you that would be the case.

In the case of the Libyans, indeed, they have—they've come a long way. They have clearly renounced terrorism. They have established themselves as no longer supporting international terrorism. There are some outstanding issues with the Libyans that we're in contact with them now that we will need to resolve with them, and that is to make sure that they have no continued association with terrorist groups in any form. That will be a key determinant for consideration to recommend to remove them from the list.

Yes, sir.

Question: Two things. One, on Libya, in the report you say you believe that they may have residual contacts with terrorist groups. Secretary Powell, in an interview earlier this week, was specifically asked if he believed that they have residual contacts with terrorists, and he said, "Not that I'm aware of."

I realize the report deals with 2003, but do you now believe that they have residual contacts, or not?

Ambassador Black: I certainly would never be in the position to reflect negatively on anything the Secretary of State would say, so what he says is absolutely true. However, we need to assure ourselves, I have to be in a position that I can recommend to the Secretary of State that, indeed, that they continue to have renounced terrorism, they're no longer supporting international terrorism, and I have to be able to assure him that they have no residual contacts with terrorist groups, and I need to do that.

Question: Okay. The second question. Simply stated, why do you think there was the small reduction in the number of terrorist attacks last year and the dramatic reduction in the number of people who died? Why?

Ambassador Black: It is a direct result of the enhanced relationships among the community of nations that are addressing this common scourge. The fact of the matter is that the world is a far better place now in terms of how we interact with each other. Communication is enhanced. The law enforcement agencies of the respective participant countries, as well as the security services, as well as most recently the financial departments of these countries, are communicating more efficiently and effectively. There is increased transparency.

It is truly what it should have been all along: a team sport.

We're in this together. We have a commonality of interests. We're in the business of saving each other's people and citizens. The accepted objective is to protect innocent men, women and children. We're just doing a better job of it, and I think that's reflected in these numbers. And I think at the rate we're keeping at it, we will be more efficient and effective. Whether we're able to keep these numbers down or to reduce them further, only time will tell, but we're getting a lot better at this.

I should probably ask somebody else. Here, in the back there. Yes, sir.

Question: On North Korea, do you have anything else to say on that? And what sort of substantial steps do they need to take in order to combat international terrorism, to get themselves off the list?

Ambassador Black: Yeah. The Koreans have been on this list something longstanding. They remain on the state sponsored list following the 1987 bombing of the Korean Air Boeing 707, as well as in light of the 1983 bombing in Rangoon.

The standards for removal are high. We have to make absolutely sure that they are no longer in the business of supporting international terrorism, that they do not have contacts with international terrorists. We're also deeply concerned about the issue of the Japanese abductees. You know, we have great sympathy for Japan and the Japanese people on this issue. The United States has raised this issue repeatedly with North Korean officials, and we also discussed this in this issue of *Patterns*.

I think a point that I should underscore is essentially that the United States has a long memory, and we will not expunge a terrorist sponsor's record simply because time has passed. It is the North Koreans that need to assure us. We'd be happy to work with them. They need to assure us that they are no longer sponsoring international terrorism, that they no longer have any contacts with international terrorists, and we'll be happy to review this issue with them when they feel clear to do so.

In the back, yes, sir.

Question: How long before you can determine if Libya has no longer any residual contacts with terrorists?

Ambassador Black: This is an ongoing issue that we're exploring with the Libyans, and I don't want to specify a timeframe. The burden of proof is upon the Libyan Government. We are dealing with them, and once we have—we're confident we have the assurances that we need, then we would make a recommendation to the Secretary. And there's essentially a process of recommending to Congress that is likely to cover a period of approximately six months before they can be removed from the list if they meet all the criteria.

Question: Thank you.

Ambassador Black: Yes, sir.

Question: Looking at your list, this being the lowest number of terrorist attacks since 1969, what happens to that number if you do include the attacks on military targets in Iraq, which, after all, the President routinely calls terrorist attacks? I know they're not, for the definition's report, terrorist attacks, but they're often called by senior officials, including the President, terrorist attacks. What happens to the numbers if you include them?

And also, you talk about al-Qaida having their operations seriously, their capabilities seriously downgraded. But by my account in here, and tell me if I'm wrong, there were about a dozen attacks that are either al-Qaida or seemingly al-Qaida, which seems to me a big increase from the previous year.

So do we have an increase in the number of attacks from al-Qaida, or supposedly al-Qaida, despite the fact that it's—they're downgraded?

Ambassador Black: Yeah. I think it's important to stick—I do counterterrorism, so I kind of stick with the basics of that.

Truly, I don't know what the figure would be if you included combatants. Certainly in Afghanistan or Iraq, you'd have to ask the Department of Defense. According to our definition, the way we view this issue, it is not terrorism if these people engaged—engaged coalition or U.S. military forces that are armed and in a combat situation. That's conflict and combat. We don't consider that to be terrorism. If one were to include all these numbers, it would obviously be a lot higher. I don't know what that number would be, nor am I particularly responsible for it.

In terms of al-Qaida, you'd have to talk about al-Qaida and al-Qaida-associated. The way I would characterize this is to refer to statistics I think that you're pretty comfortable with, and have heard before. Seventy percent of their leadership of the period of 9/11 have been arrested, detained or killed, but more than 3,400 of their supporters and associates have also been arrested or detained.

The capability of al-Qaida has been significantly degraded as an organization of the 9/11 period. They are truly under catastrophic stress. They're very defensive. That's the good news.

The bad news is that, nevertheless, a sufficient percentage of their personnel are out there and are operating and are planning to execute attacks against U.S. interests and the United States. So the threat is very real and credible, and every day we use the full spectrum of law enforcement, security service to identify these people and to protect innocents from them.

Question: Just a quick definitional question. On your definition then, would the attack on the Cole not be a terrorist attack?

Ambassador Black: Well, the Cole was essentially a force at rest. It was in harbor, with the crew not on alert. I think the way I personally, from my perspective, would characterize it would be they were not in a combat situation, would be analogous to the Marines that were killed in the barracks in Beirut. That was also an act of terrorism.

These are, you know, the finest, most capable troops in

the world. They were not in a combat situation. They were off duty. They were at rest. That would be considered terrorism.

Yes, ma'am, right here.

Question: Could I have a follow up on that (inaudible)?

Ambassador Black: Why don't I just talk with both? We'll get around to you in a minute, sir.

Yes, ma'am.

Question: I have a two-part question. They're kind of related. If you can talk a little bit about how—many officials have talked about how al-Qaida, it's not necessarily a group anymore, but it's a mentality that's kind of following the al-Qaida philosophy.

And then some of your counterparts in some of the allied countries in Europe have said that, for instance, with the Madrid bombing, some of the suspects, you know, weren't crossing borders, weren't using a lot of money transfers, and some of the ways of sharing equipment, information, money have been much more undercover and it's presenting a challenge for counterterrorism officials as they go forward, that, you know, your traditional means of combatting terror might not apply in some of these attacks.

Ambassador Black: Well, I think you've asked several things there. Classically, the al-Qaida organization of 9/11 was—had an established hierarchy, had a chain of command, had pretty established lines of communication, and orders were issued, received and moved along and validated. That organization and those people, I think, have been, to a significant degree, effectively countered and we are engaged in following up the remnants, the survivors of that organization.

I think what you're referring to are localized groups that have been vulnerable to incitement, what they see in the news media, what they hear, also influenced by very extreme radicalized preaching. And yes, many of these have limited or greatly reduced contacts with people outside of their cells.

So this represents challenges for law enforcement and security services to identify them and counter them. The good news to that is that, in general, their training, their operational experience and their ability to securely move from essentially independent localized groups through the spectrum of having the wherewithal and the equipment to conduct terrorist attacks, to do secure casings of potential targets, to bring all these things together, is not as great, and in that are significant advantages for local law enforcement and security services.

What is it dependent upon is the will of the leadership of these respective countries to support and empower the people that catch terrorists to make sure that they're funded, they have the right equipment and resources to be able to move effectively to identify these people and effectively move against them.

Question: Can I—if I could follow up. To what extent do you think al-Qaida is kind of indirectly, or even directly, supporting some of these groups? A lot of times when there's a terrorist attack, you hear it's a local group with ties to al-Qaida. But it seems like that doesn't mean what it used to mean.

Ambassador Black: Yeah, I think you're right. It doesn't mean what it used to. And I think it's—there is no longer a hard relationship. These relationships tend to be increasingly tenuous and based upon contacts and associations of the past, particularly that were anchored in the terrorist safe haven of Afghanistan, where large amounts of trainees went through, their contacts were made.

This, currently, the follow-on sets of threats are more diverse, but we do have the advantage, as long as we go about it in a systematic way, communicate among countries, use leads, pass information, do it quickly and take action when you identify them, the advantage is certainly with us.

Yes, sir.

Question: The United States has promised Turkey to eliminate PKK-KADEK or Kongra-Gel terrorist organization in northern Iraq. So what's going to be done to eliminate this threat?

Ambassador Black: Right. We have made it very clear to our Turkish friends that we share a common issue. There is no place in Iraq for KADEK. It cannot be allowed to represent a threat to the good people of Iraq or to the people in neighboring countries. There is no place for it, and as a threat it is our position that it needs to be taken care of.

As a result of working with Turkish officials, the Turkish Government, we have developed what has been referred to in Ankara as a "Plan of Action," where we are using the various elements of statecraft, which cover the entire spectrum. This is—the American view, it's very important. Counterterrorism not only is not only exclusively the use of military force, military force is a last resort.

The most efficient and effective way to address this is using elements of diplomacy, to get the community of nations to assist us in this, to use law enforcement, to use financial means. So we are moving—in our plan of action, we are moving through the spectrum of tools that we use against this target. We consider them a terrorist group. We consider them a threat. We're going to deal with them. And if we are unable to reach our objective using the—this spectrum of elements of statecraft, we will use military force when that is appropriate.

Yes, sir, in the back. You've been very patient. Thank you.

Question: Sir, by saying that the United States has a long memory, is it safe to assume that the United States is also poised to mete out some severe punishment to Hezbollah and other perpetrators of those accused of bombing the Marine barracks in 1983?

Ambassador Black: We have never forgotten our Marines. We are determined to bring to justice the individuals that planned and committed that action. We do have a long memory and we plan to render these individuals to justice.

We do consider Hezbollah a terrorist group. We do monitor them and we do counter, up to our ability, their actions to kill innocent men, women and children. And that's what this is about, and there should be no doubt about it. We keep a close watch on them, and they should be very mindful of that. We are against killing in all its forms, and we encourage them to utilize other avenues to meet their needs.

Let's see, where—yes, sir.

Question: Thank you. Regarding North Korea, first case, this is the first time that you mentioned the abductee—Japanese abductee case in the report, and also you say that you are deeply concerned on this issue. So is it safe to say that the United States put a new condition to—for North Korea to lift the sanction based on the terrorist designation? That's my first question.

Ambassador Black: I'm sorry. Could you repeat that one more time?

Question: Yes, sorry about that.

Ambassador Black: I think you're rephrasing what I said. I'm not too sure. Either I or you got it right, I just want to make sure.

Question: Yes. You mentioned the abductee cases—

Ambassador Black: Yes.

Question:—the first time. So that means are you putting new conditions for North Korea for—I mean, to lift the sanction, or whatever, based on the U.S. state sponsors designations? That's my first question, sir.

Ambassador Black: Why don't I answer that one—

Question: Thank you.

Ambassador Black:—so I can keep track of them.

Question: Yes.

Ambassador Black: For North Korea to be considered to be taken off the list, we have to be absolutely sure that they are no longer supporting any terrorist group—is the first thing—and that they have no contacts with terrorist groups.

We are very mindful of the abductee issue, and we are pressing the North Korean Government to resolve this and to present all the information that they know. And I understand this is a little bit outside the counterterrorism, but also the repatriation of the families of abductees needs also to be resolved. So it's very important to us, and I think it is a part of our concern of North Korea being on the state sponsor list.

Did you have one other question?

Question: Yes. Can I follow up on that?

Ambassador Black: Mm-hmm.

Question: Also, compared to last year's report, a little bit positive about the hijacking case and the (inaudible), the North Korean, the giving a safe haven to the hijackers at the—

Ambassador Black: Right.

Question:—with the Japanese airplanes. And that I just want to quote what the report says, "DPRK also has been trying to resolve the issue of harboring Japanese Red Army members."

You used to writing also. [*sic*] So that sounds like North Korea is trying to solve the problem of abductees also. Is that right understanding? And even North Korea is refusing to—

Ambassador Black: Yeah. Well, whenever you talk about North Korea, it gets very complicated. Let me just say that a key element of North Korean support remains Pyongyang's provision of safe haven to the Japanese Red Army hijackers of a JAL airliner to North Korea in 1970. So we want to work with them to resolve this.

Yes, sir, in the back.

Question: I have, basically, three straightforward questions. One of them is just a follow-up to some of the other questions being asked so I'll get to that first.

Understanding this, how you're distinguishing people in Iraq, do you consider a foreigner, non-Iraqi, who crosses a border into Iraq and participating in an attack on American forces a terrorist, regardless? Would you still distinguish that if our forces are at rest this foreigner who crossed the border is not a terrorist?

Ambassador Black: I, from a counterterrorism perspective, would consider this individual a foreign fighter, and depending on the target that this fighter engages and how he engages would bring into question whether this is a terrorist or not.

As an example, if this individual were to harm innocent people, whether it's Iraqis associated with the coalition, were to harm someone like that, someone who is not a combatant, that would be terrorism. Someone who plants a weapon, a bomb, kills innocent people would be a terrorist. So that's how we would view it.

Question: Okay. My two questions.

Ambassador Black: Yes.

Question: If you go—a specific case. If you have an Israeli soldier, whether it be a reservist or active duty, in uniform, getting on a bus to go to their place, their duty station, and that bus is bombed, is that an act of terrorism perpetrated against the Israeli in uniform?

And my other question—

Ambassador Black: If I can—let me just answer that one.

Question: Sure.

Ambassador Black: I think that would be similar to—I'm not a lawyer. I do counterterrorism. That would be similar to the engagement of uniformed military personnel at rest. Someone, you know, who is on home leave, you know, walking down a road with a rucksack, you know, to get on a bus would seem akin, to me, to our Marines, as an example, that were killed in Beirut.

Question: Okay.

Ambassador Black: They're not on alert. They're not in formation. They're not engaged in action.

Question: And in your section on Lebanon, you say the Lebanese Government will not recognize as a terrorist group a group solely identified by the United States. So my question is, do you have any indication from the Lebanese Government what they would be looking for, for example, regarding Hezbollah? Would they be looking for the EU to designate it as a terrorist organization or the UN? What is Lebanon—

Ambassador Black: Well, I think the issue with Lebanon is that they don't seem to be solely acting in their own prerogative. They're heavily influenced by Syria, as an example, which is one of the leading state sponsors of terrorism, so I think their definition and their view of this issue is skewed, certainly against the position that we would encourage them to take.

Question: Thank you.

Ambassador Black: Any other questions? Let's see. Who have I missed?

Yes, ma'am.

Question: Can I ask about al-Qaida's infrastructure in Iraq, and is this principally Abu Musab al Zarqawi? And if you could talk a little bit about Zarqawi, he's described as an al-Qaida associate, and he's also been linked to Ansar al-Islam, so if you can shed any light on, on where he fits.

Ambassador Black: Yeah, I think you've almost answered the question of another colleague. I mean, I think one needs to choose words carefully.

Zarqawi has been associated with al-Qaida for a considerable period of time. We have been watching him and watching his movements and been very interesting—interested in him, certainly not only as a classical terrorist, but also as a purveyor of what we would describe as weapons of mass destruction.

He is a little bit of an independent actor in that he does not require the guidance and orders issued by the classical al-Qaida organization of 9/11, but he does conduct his operations sympathetically with al-Qaida's objectives. He has personnel that have been trained by al-Qaida. There are associations there. And we consider him, essentially, to be a part of the al-Qaida organization and the al-Qaida threat.

Although he is not integrated within it, he is associated with al-Qaida and its objectives, and he—he is representative of a very real and credible threat. His operatives are planning and attempting, now, to attack American targets; and we are after them with a vengeance.

Any other questions? Yes, sir.

Question: Two questions. One is you—there was some discussion before about how the Iraq situation is not included in international terrorism in the context of this report. Also, there are some major domestic terrorism attacks. Secretary Armitage referred before to the Bogotá bombing, nightclub bombing, where I think 34 people were killed. That wouldn't be included in the statistics either.

Does that take away from the significance of this drop in —reduction in—

Ambassador Black: Well, I think the attack in Bogotá, the Nogal nightclub—is that what you're talking about?

Question: Yeah.

Ambassador Black: That would be.

Question: But, for example, in Latin America, your statistics —you've only three dead for all of Latin America for 2003, but you had 34 dead in the Bogotá attack.

Ambassador Black: Well, I'll have to check. That would seem like an inconsistency to me, so I'll have to check.

Question: Well—the explanation I was given to that before was that was considered a domestic attack because there probably weren't any non—it was perpetuated by Colombians against Colombians.

Ambassador Black: Okay, I'm going to have to check. I'll take that and I'll get back to you for the record, there.

Question: Just one quick, one quick follow up question on that. Not related to that. But you talked before about the difficulty of nations getting off the list of state sponsored terrorists. How about getting onto the list? Are there any nations that have become increasingly problematic over the course of the last year and may be considered candidates to be added to the list?

Ambassador Black: We are constantly looking at all the countries of the world to see which ones have the potential to be put on the list, on this list. But we would not discuss that until we actually were to recommend that action.

Question: Are there any in particular—

Ambassador Black: I wouldn't talk about that. That's not how we do it.

Question: Ambassador Black, you note a slight positive trend, a reduction in the number of attacks and a less than slight, a more dramatic trend, in the reduction of number of people killed. As is usual with these reports, we're a little bit into the following year now.

Ambassador Black: Yes.

Question: And I'm wondering what—whether you think this trend line is going to continue.

And throwing the second question in at the same time, can you tell us anything about why the President has expressed to Members of Congress concern about the possibility of terrorism in the lead-up to the election?

Ambassador Black: Well, I think, David, I don't know what this year will look like. The situations in Afghanistan and Iraq have not been completely resolved. We'll need to see where it is.

I think internationally, if one were to remove from the equation what is essentially a combat zone in Afghanistan and Iraq, I would speculate, it's my view, that the trend line would continue, would still be positive. The combat situations, I think, sort of change the picture and make estimates harder to make.

In terms of your last question was the President's reporting to the American people that—I think he validated their concern, I think, about the potential of a terrorist threat against U.S. actions before the November elections. And I think, as I recall, the President commented that he thought there was—there was reason to be concerned.

I think that the terrorists have concluded that in the wake of Madrid, whereas they may not have had the intent going in, I think those, those terrorist groups that saw the terrible attack on Madrid have concluded, with the help of many others, that there may be a relationship between a terrorist action and an election in a democracy, and that these groups may decide that this is a good target date to look towards among all democracies, not only the United States, but others.

And so as long as they have the intent, we have to be, you know, mindful this is something to counter with that in mind.

Question: But that's just a hypothesis. It's not that there's specific intelligence suggesting a group is targeting the United States in, say, October at the moment.

Ambassador Black: Well, there are groups targeting the United States, clearly. It's our job to identify them and stop them from launching these attacks. As I tried to convey, I think terrorist groups have noted the relationship between a terrorist attack and the upcoming elections in Madrid and I think they are likely to factor this into their calculations when they conduct operations.

On the other hand, I would say that, you know, they seek to have operations that work, which means they have to overcome all of the defenses that we have, all our offensive collection activities, as well as the activities of the Department of Homeland Security. So there are hurdles and firebreaks, a concentric ring of defenses that becomes stronger with every day that they have to overcome. So it's not—it's not easy for them.

Yes, sir.

Question: I have a question on Saudi Arabia, which you praised rather strongly for its work, particularly since May.

You say Saudi Arabia has expressed its commitment to undertake internal political, social and economic reforms aimed at combatting the underlying causes of terrorism. What do you think are the underlying causes of terrorism in Saudi Arabia?

Ambassador Black: I think there has been an inordinate amount of radicalized teaching in the Kingdom. I think this has been recognized by the Kingdom's leadership. They have validated it. They are addressing it. As an example, they will not stand for incitement. They will not stand for anti-Semitism. They have established procedures to vet religious leaders, and those that are unable to conform to the common-held view that renounces anti-Semitism and violence, they are no longer allowed to preach.

They are looking at ways to enhance the strength of their society, and they have the issue of counterterrorism on one hand, which is basically the business of identifying terrorists and capturing them so that they can't hurt innocent people. On the other hand, they are looking at ways to reduce funding for terrorism, as well as to reduce incitement in their society.

Question: What about the political and economic dimension, which you cite here? I mean, do you think that the absence of democracy, for example, in Saudi Arabia, the absence of economic opportunities for native Saudis, is part of the underlying causes of terrorism?

Ambassador Black: I think the leadership is looking to ways to liberalize, to make more equitable their society. They're also very mindful of the numbers of graduates that leave school and need to find jobs. They are mindful of the high unemployment rate among youth, and they are looking at ways to—to resolve, if not improve, that.

Let's see, in the back, standing in front.

Yes, sir. Did you have a question for you—

Question: I did on Colombia. In the Colombia section, there is a lot of emphasis on the narcotrafficking, narcoterrorist groups, the three groups; and then in the Venezuelan section, it mentions the affinity and ideology from President Chavez and the FARC.

This morning, Senator, U.S. Senator [name missing] mentioned that President of Colombia has specific information about a connection between Chavez and the FARC. Do you have any information, or do you have that information that will help fight narco-terrorism in that particular area, Colombia and Venezuela?

Ambassador Black: Well I just—I would answer the question that I'm not going to address the specific contacts aspect. I will say that we are concerned about the movement of people and materiel across the border. The border is not as effectively patrolled as we would like, and I think both the Colombians and the Venezuelans should like to have. We would like to see improvements in that area, and we think that the government in Caracas can do, you know, a better job in terms of what moves across the border and to keep these groups from being as effective as they are.

A Participant: Ambassador Black, we're almost out of time if we could—

Ambassador Black: Okay, great.

Let's see. One last—who hasn't asked a question? In the back. Yes, ma'am.

Question: Regarding Venezuela, how do you feel about problems such civilians, air-, ground-, and waterborne illicit traffic? The Venezuela participation in the Caribbean (inaudible) network, and an interception of illicit traffic seize operations—has seize—Venezuela has seize operation close to 26 million kilogram of illegal drugs as a way of cooperating with—against terrorism? And how can we improve—can Venezuela improve the—its way of cooperation against terrorism?

Ambassador Black: I think, certainly it can interact more efficiently and more effective with the United States as well as the CICTE members of the Organization of American States.

We'd like to see greater cooperation in the border area between Bogotá and Caracas. We think a lot more can be done. There's not enough communication, there's not enough mutual support, and we think there is a lot of room for improvement.

Question: Could I just ask about your (inaudible) in 1969? Were there simply more attacks in 1968, or was that the year that you guys began keeping these statistics, and so that's how you got—because, I mean, I was three in 1968, but I don't—a study of history. I mean, I don't even know if there were more terrorist—

Ambassador Black: Well, I was 18. So I'll take the same defense on that. I don't know what the answer is. I'll have to get back to you.

Thank you very much.

Revised Patterns of Global Terrorism 2003

The text below consists of the remarks made by Ambassador-at-Large Cofer Black, coordinator for counterterrorism, and John Brennan, director of the Terrorism Threat Integration Center (TTIC), and a subsequent question-and-answer session that took place on 22 June 2004, with the release of the revised edition of Patterns of Global Terrorism 2003.

Ambassador Black: Thank you, Mr. Secretary. The way I would like to start, I'll make some introductory remarks. I'll make some introductory remarks about a chart, which is an aid to describe a picture, and then I'll turn it over to my colleague for some remarks, John Brennan, from the Terrorist Threat Integration Center. And then we'll take your questions, if that's all right

The 2003 *Patterns of Global Terrorism* was marred by significant errors. Over the past few weeks in particular, the past several days and nights, my staff here and John's at TTIC, and others in the U.S. Government counterterrorism community have conducted a comprehensive review of the figures in the 2003 *Patterns* report. We've revisited both the numbers themselves and the way we arrived at them. From the reexamination, we have concluded there were obvious problems with some of the numbers themselves. Events were left out. Some were mislabeled and counted in the wrong categories. Some events were counted twice and some portions of the year were omitted entirely.

I hope it goes without saying that we've already begun the process of improving the way we arrive at these numbers for future reports. The revised figures indicate that our earlier assessment was overly positive in some respects. Overall, the new numbers show that in 2003, total terrorist incidents were higher than last year, but still comparatively lower than 2001. There were 37 more Significant Incidents in the last year. There were 27 fewer Non-Significant events than 2002. The number of fatalities is slightly lower than last year, but the sharp increase in the number of the injured reflects the comparative increase in the proportion of significant attacks.

We have 18 more total events, five more significant events and 13 more Non-Significant events, than originally reported. These new figures are accompanied by a dramatic increase in the numbers of casualties originally calculated.

I want to be very clear: We here in the Counterterrorism Office, and I personally, should have caught any errors that marred the *Patterns* draft before we published it. But I assure you and the American people that the errors in the *Patterns* report were honest mistakes, and certainly not deliberate deceptions as some have speculated, as I said, when the *Patterns* was released.

However, numbers do not tell the whole story. The most important things in the report continue to be valid. We saw less state sponsorship of terrorism. Libya has renounced terrorism. Sudan has taken significant steps towards being a cooperative partner in the global war on terrorism. Afghanistan is no longer a breeding ground for terrorism.

I noted that terrorism showed no sign of fading away. Regardless of the number of attacks reported, we continue to be at war with terrorists, with the major fronts in Iraq and Afghanistan, where terrorists are working with other elements to launch attacks against coalition targets.

I noted that with enhanced intelligence sharing and law enforcement cooperation, we are seeing more plots thwarted, more terrorists identified and more perpetrators brought to justice. While great progress has been made in the war on terror, and we have killed or captured a significant portion of the leadership of al-Qaida and its affiliates, the number of significant terrorist attacks, and particularly of casualties, underscores the seriousness of the remaining threat. The unprecedented cooperation between the United States and its foreign partners which are cited in the report continues and will empower us to prevail.

I have a chart here to my left and I would just make a couple of remarks about it before we bring on Mr. Brennan. You need to appreciate, as I'm sure you will, historians and others will look at these figures and pore over them with calculators. The attempt here, at least initially, will be to give you the essence of the situation. The numbers developed and the methodology has remained constant over the various patterns. There have been inconsistencies and we will go over these a little bit.

What I've tried to do, if you look at the top two rows— and, again, the essence here is to convey something that is imminently understandable and help you to phrase your questions. In the top row across you have the 2003 corrected, we have a number of 208. These are total events and they are essentially a combination of significant events, the 175, and Non-Significant events, 33; essentially the combination of these two together, significant events being premeditated, politically motivated, conducted by subnational actors or clandestine agents against noncombatants with the intent to influence. The Non-Significant essentially meets the criteria of being international involving individuals of at least two different countries but does not meet the criteria for significant.

I think it is very important to note the injuries here, the dead and the injured. And I think, again, when reviewing the figures and looking at it, we find that to be certainly of significance.

Right below that line is the published. This is what we put out in the *Patterns* and you see the statistics of the year before. One thing I want to point out in that in *Patterns,* if you look, whatever you look at, essentially it will refer to the previous year or perhaps even to years before where there is an adjustment. This is very much a dynamic process. It is one of accuracy in reporting. It is one of compilation, recordkeeping and the like.

So, as an example, to give you a sense of how dynamic it is, you take 2002: 198 is what we carry in the *Patterns*; with a revision over time we think that it is 205. You look at 1998, 273. We think that that has gone to 274. Invariably, this has to do with examples such as there was an attack and six people allegedly were killed and it turned out to be perhaps seven. Someone that was wounded we found subsequently had died, and so the number can fluctuate.

So what we had said before and we want to—you know, the numbers are what essentially drive patterns. Historically when we speak of what goes first, historically over the years what we have reported to you all is the figure here, "Total Events." And when you look at this, there are a lot of different things one can count. There are a lot of different views one can approach this. Essentially, in the past, we've always gone with the total events.

It has been pointed out to us, and I want to underscore this and this is correct, the significant events are extremely important. And when you see, "Significant Events," you see the numbers essentially increasing. So, as an example, you get 119 here in 1998, you have a significant event corrected at 175, which is the highest and has significance, remember. This is the significance in terms of hostage taking, kidnapping, people have been killed, wounded. It can also do with economic attacks, terrorist attacks, if it is assessed the value is over [$]10,000. So "significant" is important. It has gone up to 175 and it is in the realm, essentially, to what we had in 1999. So the total events, combination of significant and Non-Significant.

The dead and the injured, I think it's very important with the horrific news of the execution of the South Korean citizen, I think it's very important to emphasize the thrust of this report is the patterns of global terrorism. Yes, numbers are crucially important. We have to pay certainly a lot more attention than we have in this report to the general trend. Where are we? The global war on terrorism. A lot of people losing their lives. The lives that have been saved have been a result of international cooperation, increased effectiveness among law enforcement agencies around the world, intelligence services, financial operations and the like.

But in this, a lot of people are being hurt, a lot of people are dying. And, as an example, in 2003, approximately 1.5 percent of all the fatalities, the dead and the injured, are American; the other percentage at 98.5 percent are non-U.S. citizens, which I think is a real indicator—this is a global war.

These attacks have been significant. In 2003, an important statistic, which Mr. Brennan can talk about a little bit more, I think, is that almost as much as 50 percent of the casualties have taken place in 11 incidents in 7 countries and they have all been the result of Islamic extremist terrorists.

So I will stop here just for a minute, if you can hold you rquestions. I'll turn it over to Mr. Brennan, who will give you the piece from the intelligence side, and then we'll try and answer your questions.

John.

Mr. Brennan: Thank you, Cofer.

Good afternoon. My name is John Brennan. I'm the Director of the Terrorist Threat Integration Center known by its acronym TTIC. TTIC is a multi-agency entity that is composed of analysts from the major federal departments and agencies involved in the fight against terrorism. TTIC reports to the Director of Central Intelligence, George Tenet. Although I am a CIA officer, TTIC is not part of the CIA.

Numerous factors contributed to the inaccurate information contained in the 2003 *Patterns of Global Terrorism* publication. TTIC provided incomplete statistics to CIA, which incorporated those statistics into material passed to the Department of State. The statistics were generated by a long-standing interagency review process and database over which TTIC assumed administrative control in May 2003. No changes were made to that process by TTIC and the same database was used to compile the statistics for the 2003 *Patterns* publication that was used in previous years.

I must point out that this database is retrospective in focus and is not used to monitor, track or analyze current terrorist threats.

There was insufficient review and quality control throughout the entire data compilation, drafting and publication process, including the inaccurate and incomplete database numbers provided by TTIC. I assume personal responsibility for any shortcomings in TTIC's performance and I regret any embarrassment this issue has caused the Department or the Secretary.

Anyone who might assert that the numbers were intentionally skewed is mistaken. Over the past several weeks, TTIC personnel have conducted rigorous review of the database, computer technology, procedures, interagency process, methodology, criteria and definitions that have been used to compile international terrorism statistics over the past 20 years. This review has exposed serious deficiencies and ambiguities that need to be addressed immediately. As a result, I have directed that the interagency process that has been used to compile statistics and to support the Department in its annual *Patterns* publication be overhauled and that changes be made in the staffing, database and computer technology involved in this effort.

To date, TTIC's technical and analytic focus has been on how we, as a government, can more effectively identify, integrate and correlate intelligence, law enforcement, homeland security and other terrorism-related information to prevent future terrorist attacks. While this focus will remain our number one priority, and we will allocate analytic and budget resources accordingly, we will put in place a system in conjunction with our partner agencies that will provide accurate and meaningful metrics on international terrorist events. The Department must have confidence that whatever information it receives from TTIC is accurate.

I would now like to say a few words about the revised statistics, charts and chronologies that are being made available today. When it was brought to our attention that the information in *Patterns* was incorrect, TTIC staff conducted a thorough review of all reported terrorist incidents that took place in 2003. On the basis of that review, a total of 208 incidents were determined to meet the definition of international terrorism as articulated in Section 2656f of Title 22 of the U.S. Code. One hundred and seventy-five of these incidents met the threshold for Significant Incidents as defined by the Incident Review Panel, known as the IRP, which is an interagency panel established in the early 1980s consisting of representatives of CIA, the Defense Intelligence Agency, the National Security Agency and the Bureau of Intelligence and Research of the Department of State.

Since May of 2003, a member of TTIC has chaired this panel and has voted in cases of tie. The interagency Incident Review Panel is the body that makes the decisions on international terrorist incidents. In addition to the 176 Significant Incidents, TTIC staff identified another 33 incidents that were deemed Non-Significant, according to the definition established by the Incident Review Panel many years ago.

The definitions for Significant and Non-Significant International Terrorist Incidents are included in the material that is being provided today. These 208 total incidents, including the breakdown between Significant and Non-Significant, were then reviewed and validated at a special session of the Incident Review Panel that was convened last week.

One final point. Frequently, there is incomplete and often contradictory information available on reported terrorist events. Thus, it is up to the Incident Review Panel to make the best possible decisions on whether incidents meet the established definitions and thresholds, as well as to make informed judgments on the number of casualties involved. The materials being made available today reflect those decisions and judgments.

Ambassador Black: Yes, ma'am.

Question: I wonder if you gentlemen can tell me—you've accepted responsibility now—is anybody going to be fired or disciplined or has anybody resigned as a result of this very embarrassing mistake that seems to have involved several people in systems and layers?

Ambassador Black: Well, I think that we've got a lot of hardworking people doing a lot of different things. And we have been looking at the architecture, the process involved with this. We're going to look at the entire spectrum of how the information is stored, how it's put together both here at the State Department and particularly at the Terrorist Threat Integration Center.

In terms of your question, certainly the Secretary of State will determine what is and what is not appropriate. As I tried to indicate, you've got some fine people working very hard doing a lot of things. And this was an error of commission, but it was one developed over a significant period of time. We're dealing with old equipment and how we store it, being able to extract information out of the computers. We've got to update our equipment. And I think we will be able to develop a product that's more meaningful.

What I have learned in this, and, you know, hopefully, there are good things that come out of something like this. Obviously, no one would want this to happen. I want to leave you with the sense that these are very hardworking, well-intentioned people that do make mistakes. There is the omission in the chronology—but not in the narrative, but in the chronology, there is an omission from about the 11th of November onwards. And the vote of the Incident Review Panel was—in the process of December—should have been caught clearly. And we're still amazed it was not, but it was not. And not to make excuses, but the people in our shop as well as John's and in other agencies at that time were working around the clock, were not on holiday. We all missed Christmas and the holidays. We were looking at saving lives—as you remember, the aviation threat—we were addressing that and other issues.

So this is not in the realm of excuse-making. Please don't get me wrong. But it is in the realm of everyone has a lot to do and we should have caught this. But I think that we need to support our people a lot better in terms of the technology support that we give them so that we can more readily keep track of this information and codify it and put it one system. Mr. Brennan is looking at that. And then the objective will be, you know, what do we want *Patterns* to do? I think Mr. Brennan would state the fact that, you know, essentially what it was asked to do was provide a narrative on countries of particular significance in terrorism. It was initially not to provide statistics and chronologies. We sort of added this on over time. We need to look at and we need to make proposals to the Secretary. Working with others is exactly what we would like the *Patterns* to be able to indicate to our customers. This example of the horrific reported beheading of the South Korean citizen. You know, there are ways, I think, that we can look at developing a new *Patterns* that can be more useful to our superiors and our customers and you than what, on occasion, has been a compilation of new numbers. But we need to do a better job to keep track of that.

Yes, ma'am.

Question: Can you—just to follow up on the questions posed by Secretary Powell, can you talk about how the new numbers reflect your assessment of the pattern, of the trend, of the threat of terrorism, and how you feel this affects—these new numbers reflect how you're doing in the war on terrorism?

Ambassador Black: Sure. I will give you one answer and, if I may, also turn to Mr. Brennan, who makes his living doing specifically that. The key points, I think, that one has to walk away with when looking at this, there is truly a global war on terrorism underway. There continue to be unacceptably high loss of life and injured. We and Americans take this very personally and we—and our highest priority here in the States is to defend the homeland. We've established procedures to do this and mechanisms. We're getting stronger and stronger every day as a function of effort.

But I think what these numbers will tell you, or suggest to me anyway, is that the considerable loss of life, only a little bit more than 1.5 percent of the killed and wounded are American, that the vast majority of these incidents have been perpetrated by Islamic extremist terrorists on non-Americans around the world.

There is an international partnership. It is that partnership that will save lives. We're truly in this all together. This is not American focused, and I think the numbers reflect that. Tremendous progress has been made tactically in how we do counterterrorism. And I keep coming back to this theme with you always, and even if the numbers had fluctuated even more than that, this is what I would be telling you: The practitioners of this type of work are growing increasingly effective. They're doing a great job.

What we don't have—I'd love to have a chart of this—is, you know, the incidents that we stop and the lives that we save. And that number would certainly be going up. But it is bloody, significant loss of life, and there it seems to be a lot of it al-Qaida-associated or -related, and it's something that we are dealing with more efficiently. And the bottom line is we have to do a better job to protect people, get the wounded and the killed down.

Yes, sir.

Question: Can I just—two very quick things: One, the explanation from TTIC as to the omissions post—mid-November, but I guess also the November 8th Saudi Arabia attack, is simply that they were forgotten about and just passed over? I mean we're talking about, in addition to the Saudi attack, four extremely huge car bombings in Istanbul, which were neglected.

And, secondly, I just want to—when you go back in the previous years, 2002 and the revisions, say, the 198 to 205, has that been—were there any additional casualties that—or have the casualty figures for those years been—been altered to include those?

Ambassador Black: Yeah. As I said, this is a dynamic thing, and there is associated with these a range that we're still looking at. We're going to still be, you know, working on this and refine that more.

Question: Because while you may have revised the 198 to 205, the published versions has those same—

Ambassador Black: That's correct.

Question: And, presumably, those seven additional attacks did cause some death and injury.

Ambassador Black: Yes.

Question: So those figures are, basically, all incorrect.

Ambassador Black: Well, no, they can—as I say, they are subject to being updated. We are working on that. The majority of these have to do with individuals, in hindsight, where the numbers have changed. But we will continue to work on this and we'll continue to have updated figures.

Question: Just to follow up on that. Do you think the 725—

Question: Well, wait a second. Answer the first—

Question: Do you think the 725 and 2,013 are wrong?

Ambassador Black: Excuse me?

Question: Do you think the 725 dead in 2002 and the 2,013 injured in 2002 are undercounted because now you've added some events?

Ambassador Black: Yeah. I do not believe so. I believe there is accuracy to this. As we say at the bottom, you know, there continues to be research associated with this. This is the best snapshot that we can give you at this time.

Question: And the first—the first one? They were just—all these major incidents in the second half of November and December were just forgotten about? Is that—

Ambassador Black: No, they were not forgotten about.

Question: Well, I mean, by your people who were putting this together.

Ambassador Black: No.

Question: Why were they not counted?

Ambassador Black: A couple of issues here. One is that the initial request that came in, came in at the end of December and early January of the statistics. The Incident Review Panel did not meet until the middle of January in order to review those incidents in the latter half of November and in the month of December. When those incidents were determined to be Significant or Non-Significant, they were input into the database. Now, this database is an exceptionally antiquated database. It has been in use for more than 10 years, one that TTIC inherited and one that we now understand exactly its flaws and its deficiencies.

When they were input and it was input through only two parts of this database, they didn't spill over then to the other side that would actually generate the statistics. They were still captured in the database. Therefore, when the statistics and the chronologies that were built from those statistics were provided to CIA, it only stopped—it only provided those—that information up to the 11th of November. And, therefore, when that information went forward, as I said, there was inattention as far as the quality control and reviewing and seeing whether or not there was a complete statistical run at that time.

Question: That doesn't explain the 8th of November attack in Saudi.

Ambassador Black: Well, what I said was then we also—TTIC staff did a thorough review of all the terrorist incidents that were reported in 2003. Some of those incidents were deemed to be not international terrorist incidents. When our staff went back and took a look at them, in fact, they did meet the threshold for international terrorism. So you will see many changes throughout the course of the year as far as incidents that were included in *Patterns* that had been taken out and new incidents that have been put in prior to November 11th. This is a result of a thorough and constant review over the last two weeks and the analysts involved have scrubbed all of this information and that is why the special Incident Review Panel was convened last week in order to validate that.

Question: But, in plainer English, isn't the answer to that question that this was a computer error?

Ambassador Black: It is a combination of things. There was a transition from CIA to TTIC. There was the individual who was responsible for this unit left the position in December and was not replaced, has not yet been replaced. It's a CIA officer who left. There were individual contractors who actually had the inputting responsibilities for the database. Contractors rotated. And so the individual who was in charge of those contractors who left and the contractors then mis-input the new information into the database. So it was a combination of things: inattention, personnel shortages and database that is awkward and is antiquated and needs to have very proficient input be made in order for to be sure that the numbers will spill then to the different categories that are being captured.

Question: Excuse me, if I could follow up? Then the failure, apparently, was that once this flawed information went to the CIA, it was not properly vetted there? And, similarly, it then went to the State Department where it was also not properly, if at all, vetted? Is that what happened?

Ambassador Black: I will leave it to CIA and State Department to talk about the review that was provided to that information.

Question: Well, we don't have them or we don't have the CIA here. What's your understanding?

Ambassador Black: My understanding is that the incomplete and inaccurate statistics that TTIC provided to CIA was then passed on to State Department in its same form.

Question: Mr. Black, the Kerry Campaign is critical of you today, I mean of the report process, and at least a couple of members of the House Democrats are critical. They see a pattern, not just here but elsewhere. The Terrorism Office has been looked at pretty much as a politically neutral, you know, people who are serious about analysis.

Wasn't it a mistake as you look back just a couple of months for administration officials—wasn't it poor form for administration officials to be using analytical material as examples of the President's success in a political—in a politically charged campaign to say that this shows that he's doing a great job? Was that right? Didn't you sort of bring this on yourself—not you necessarily, but by being a little exuberant? The man who was most exuberant is on vacation now so we can't ask him.

Ambassador Black: Well, the numbers are developed. TTIC provided those numbers to us and we analyzed those and we have tried to figure out what this meant, what the trends were.

Question: Right.

Ambassador Black: And I think as we've gone over this today, I guess one of the themes I'm trying to describe to you is the constancy: what was true then, what is true now. And there are a lot of ways to tell a story and I think the bottom line of the story remains constant: There is a global war; the terrorists need to be engaged and they are effectively being engaged; lives are being saved in this process; there has been unacceptably high loss of life and injury.

And as I pointed out, I think it is very important to look at the significant numbers of events, 175. That's a high. That's where most of your casualties are. And that is essentially in the realm—if you look down the chart, we have the numbers here—to 168. It's kind of in that range. Yet if you look at the total events, you know, you can choose and you may have to decide what to weigh.

We, historically, with the patterns, the State Department has put forward, you know, the patterns of terrorism, the overall number, the composite of the Significant and the Non-Significant. I think what we need to do is take this as an opportunity to figure out, you know, what the thrust is. And I think a good argument that can be made is that we should essentially go back to an emphasis of the narrative, and to develop what is a trend that is of use to our customer, to the Secretary of State and to all of you. And if it were me, whereas, you know, we are going to work very hard to get new technology and put enough people on this problem, I think it is the trend that is important, and perhaps get a little bit away from the minutiae of the, you know, determination between a Non-Significant event and something that's not even counted and stick with the fundamental charts.

Question: Ambassador Black—

Question: Ambassador, can I follow up—

Question: Ambassador Black, could you explain to us, give us an example of what a Non-Significant event is? I know you've said that before. But one more time. What is a—what constitutes a Non-Significant event?

Ambassador Black: Well, sure. If you look—I think we've provided you a handout and there's a list of them and you can see for yourself what they are. But, essentially, the Non-

Significant would be international. In other words, they involve the personnel of two countries or more, or the territories of two countries or more, and that are international but don't—do not—meet the criteria for being Significant.

And this goes back to, you know, the definition that we work with in Title 22, you know, a premeditated, politically motivated and the like. And as Mr. Brennan pointed out, these are all things that we are looking forward to working on. But it is assessed, analyzed and adjudicated by the interagency panel.

Question: Ambassador Black—

Question: Also, sir, did you measure—

Ambassador Black: Yes, sir.

Question: Also, sir, did you measure how—

Question: Ambassador Black—

Ambassador Black: Please. Yes, sir.

Question: Going back to your storyline, one of the reasons that this has attracted so much interest, of course, is the trend that was drawn from those earlier remarks. And you had Deputy Secretary Armitage saying, "Indeed, you will find in these pages clear evidence that we are prevailing in the fight." And what we're wondering is whether you would make the same statement today, based on numbers that show that the number of dead has increased from 307 to 625, more than doubled; the injured have gone up from 1,500 to 3,600, almost 150 percent. Secretary Powell said that, well, Rich Armitage was saying something based on a report that was, in fact, wrong.

Now that we know these numbers, would you say that the Bush Administration, in fact, and the report shows and that there is clear evidence that you're prevailing in the war on terrorism?

Ambassador Black: Well, I mean, I think we have to look at the numbers and consider them. I think it is important to emphasize, as you pointed out, the general thrust of the pattern of global terrorism. I mean, just as an aside, you know, the figure that you're pointing out in terms of injured, too, if you look in 1998, there were 5,952, and that's larger than the ones up above.

I think the way I would characterize it is that, and as the President has stated, this is a war of uncertain duration. It is global. You have Islamic extremist terrorists, primarily, that are focusing on the United States and leading nations in the global war on terrorism, and that the significant loss of life so far has been non-American. I think the fight is underway and it is the international relationships that we have with foreign countries that will allow us to prevail. We are determined to prevail. And I think as time goes by, we increasingly make improved progress in counterterrorism efficiency.

Question: You're not prepared to—

Ambassador Black: I'm not—

Question: You're not prepared to repeat what he said?

Ambassador Black: Yeah, I'm going to—

Question: You don't see the same evidence in this report that he did in that one?

Ambassador Black: Well, I don't think there is—I don't think there is a difference. I'll let Mr. Armitage speak for himself. I'm giving you my view.

Yes, sir, in the back. Yes, sir.

Question: Yes. Ambassador Black, aren't you even now, with the corrected numbers, understating the problem? You said that terrorism—terrorist incidents are down from where they were in 2001. In fact, if you look at Significant events, which are the ones, by definition, that we care about—this is where there are casualties—

Ambassador Black: Have gone up.

Question:—have gone up and are at a 20-year high. Is it not right—they're at a 20-year high with these new numbers?

Ambassador Black: That is correct, in terms of the 175 figure.

Question: A 20-year high. Why didn't you mention that? I mean, it's not in the report. You have this—the spin seems to be here that we're in a situation where, yeah, it's up a little bit from last year but it's not as high as it was in 2001. But what matters, the Significant events, a 20-year high. That's a different story.

Ambassador Black: I think you need—well, what I'm trying to get to is, you know, one can emphasize various things. I think in my statement I've repeatedly said Significant events, and I pointed out 175, I said it is a high, that is true. You know, it is a high statistically. There are other, you know, there are other—168 is a reasonably close figure. You know, you can look at this and I guess it's like a Rorschach test. You know, you can see what you want.

What I'm trying to do is stick with the aspects of counterterrorism. I think this gives an opportunity to make a product, a publication, that is increasingly useful to people. You are—if you're looking for me to say it—which I have said repeatedly, 175 is a high—

Question: A 20-year high.

Ambassador Black: The significance of that, I think, is right there, 175. It is close to 168. And, you know, I think that the significant change is in terms of the casualties in a very small number of attacks. You know, you've got basically last year almost 50 percent. You know, it depends. What we're trying to do is count in a meaningful way, and if you look at last year, 2003, almost 50 percent of the casualties, the killed and wounded, come from 11 attacks. And included—I should get—

Question: This was last year?

Ambassador Black: Yeah, this was last year. But over—I mean, it is significant. Please don't misunderstand me, I'm not arguing. I'm just trying to give some perspective of that. What would be considered as a major attack—and I have to find a piece of paper here just to jog my memory—as an example. This was determined by the interagency panel, but terrorism, whether it's Significant or Insignificant, is a function of this interagency panel of experts that come together and validate. And as an example of a low-end, what I would consider a low-end incident, would be: In Spain, on 8 September of 2003, Madrid, Spain, authorities safely defused a partial bomb hidden in a book that was sent to the Greek consulate. According to press reports, authorities suspected an anarchist group is responsible.

Okay. Now that would be carried as an incident. Okay? And what is the—when you weigh these things, what is the value of that incident in terms of the 11 incidents that produce 50 percent of the casualties?

I'm not trying to argue. I'm just trying to say that there is, I think, a better way of looking at this, a lot better way to present it, perhaps, than we have with these kinds of numbers.

Question: But, if I could, let me follow up on that point. Your first report said that the number of terrorist incidents, it didn't give us Significant or "Insignificant" terrorists incidents, was at a 34-year low.

Ambassador Black: Correct.

Question: Now this report says "Significant events," those that we care about, those that cause death, serious injury, and more than $10,000 in damage, are at a 20-year high. Doesn't that not only mean a difference in the charts here, but also in the first sentence of your conclusion that we have made significant progress in the two and a half years in the global war?

Ambassador Black: We have made significant progress. We have presented, historically, the overall total of Significant and Non-Significant combined. And this is what we originally published, the 190, This is what's been updated and adjudicated, 208. And if you see that, that statistically is true. The 175 is high. You can choose that statistic. You can choose another one, you know. It's what we're trying to do is to present, I think, the essence of it.

I think it has significance that the numbers of incidents, you know, the Significant and "Insignificant" were, I think, it was like at a 34-year low. I do think it is also very important, as I have pointed out, the 175 figure, it's just previously, historically, that's not what we presented. And, in fact, you know, the presentation of a chronology is also an option that we put in. We, historically, also have not published the Non-Significant events which we have presented to you today.

Yes, sir.

Question: Mr. Black, in your calculus, is there any calculation for those who are killed in the government or any government in the world war on terrorism of civilians who are killed by mistake, like in Iraq and Israel and anywhere when the government tries to counter terrorism, civilians are killed. Is there any calculation for these people, as well?

Ambassador Black: Yeah. I'll probably ask Mr. Brennan to jump in on this. I mean, again, the way that *Patterns* has come about, this is through our definitions of what is Significant, what is Non-Significant. And, essentially, to sort of essentially answer your story, if it is a domestic action, if a national of a country is killed by an individual of the same country, the same national in the same country, that's domestic and we don't count it.

Question: But if it was killed by other forces, like the American forces in Iraq or Israeli forces in Palestine?

Ambassador Black: Well, I mean, these kinds of things go —the—it has to be against a noncombatant to be a terrorist incident, not against a combatant. It has to be involved individuals who are subnational, in other words, don't belong to a country, or be a clandestine agent for us to count them. Otherwise, outside of that, according to our definitions that are passed to us, we don't count it.

Yes, ma'am.

Question: Can I just say one quick question to follow up?

Ambassador Black: Yes, ma'am. Yeah.

Question: You were talking before about Islamic—Islamic terrorism actually rising. The war in Iraq was supposed to be to change the dynamic in the Middle East and decrease that. I wonder if you—what can you tell us about the impact of Iraq on the patterns of terrorism?

Ambassador Black: Well, I think the approach is to when there is a threat against civilization, it is probably prudent to confront it, to face it in an effective manner, and I think that's the approach that the President has taken and that's what we are doing.

And in the course of war, there are losses. And, unfortunately, whereas, our effectiveness in this type of activity is increasing because of the global nature of it and the viciousness of it, as we have seen today with the execution of the South Korean, you know, the numbers are unacceptably high.

Question: If I could follow up on that. The International Institute for Strategic Studies, which is a fairly prestigious think tank in London, two weeks ago said in a report that the main effect of the U.S. invasion of Iraq was "accelerated recruitment" of terrorism.

Will you respond to that? I mean some people say the war in Iraq has made it worse not better.

Ambassador Black: I don't think so. I think when you, when you reduce the areas in which terrorists can be trained, from which they can be facilitated and sent against targets, this is a good thing.

And I will tell you, my friend, I've heard that type of argument for years and that was the same justification that I had heard in similar quarters of, you know, why we did not defend ourselves in terms of against al-Qaida in Afghanistan. When there is a threat, a mortal threat of terrorists, those that facilitate this process have to be encouraged not to continue to provide that support.

Question: Can we just ask Mr. Brennan a technical question?

Ambassador Black: Sure, you can ask. If you want to ask Mr. Brennan, I certainly would permit you to do it.

Question: No, no, you were deferring to him on a similar question.

Ambassador Black: Please. So do you want to talk to—

Question: I want to know how the Arab-Israeli or the Israeli-Palestinian attacks and counterattacks were dealt with here. In other words, when a café is blown up those are victims of terror, correct?

Mr. Brennan: As long as it meets the established definition of international terrorism which means that it's politically motivated violence perpetrated by subnational groups or clandestine agents involving the citizens or territory of more than one country—again, politically motivated violence perpetrated by subnational groups involving the citizens or territory of more than one country.

Now, as I look back over the years and the criteria that—established by the IRP, it involves more than just citizens and property—citizens and territory. It also seems to include property as well as symbols of another country.

Question: Did we get hung up on one country? The question being, of course, that most of the terror groups operate out of the West Bank. Some operate out of Lebanon. Hezbollah is moving more—getting a bigger presence in Gaza, and in all, but it's essentially been a Lebanon operation. Do you know what I'm talking about?

When cafes are blown up by Palestinian terrorists, the victims are listed here as victims of terrorism, no?

Mr. Brennan: Frequently, if they involve citizens of other countries.

Question: Well, is Palestine another country? It's not a country.

Mr. Brennan: I'm sorry?

Question: Palestine isn't a country.

Mr. Brennan: That's correct.

Question: So, but—so are they victims—are they victims of something going on within the country?

Mr. Brennan: If it's politically—

Question: And I want to know about the Israeli counterattacks. What do you do with that?

Mr. Brennan: If it's politically motivated violence and there are many instances here, in Significant attacks, as well as the Non-significant attacks, for example, bus bombings in Jerusalem, attacks on the West Bank and other places that are included here.

Question: Right.

Mr. Brennan: And it is based on the IRP's determination about whether or not the type of attack meets the established legal definition of international terrorism and whether it meets the criteria for Significant or Non-significant. That's what they do.

Question: When the Israelis attack searching for terrorists, they say a refugee camp and civilians are killed. Are they victims of terrorism?

Mr. Brennan: Again, going back to the definition, subnational group or clandestine agents. So, that type of attack would not constitute that.

Question: How do you take into account the Israeli soldiers that were killed in the West Bank? Just to follow up on Barry's point, how did you account for Israeli soldiers that were killed in the West Bank which is an occupied territory?

Mr. Brennan: If they were deemed to be combatants, they do not—it has to be noncombatant target. I should have included that as well.

Question: They were still in uniform?

Mr. Brennan: I'm sorry?

Question: If they were in uniform, they were not clandestine agents.

Mr. Brennan: Well, there are individuals that are included in here, such as peacekeepers and others, who are, just because they are in uniform does not make them a combatant. So a determination is made by the IRP about whether or not they fit that combatant status. If they do, then that's deemed to be not international terrorism.

Question: Can we go back to the—

Question: Pardon me, sir. That's—

Question: —which would seem to be the genesis of the errors? It seemed to me that you initially said that the information was correctly inputted into your antiquated database, then for some reason it was not totaled, and then later you said that it was incorrectly inputted.

Mr. Brennan: No, I did not say it was correctly inputted. I said that there was information that was subsequently inputted into the database that was not generated then when the database was pulsed. So some of the information from November and December was, in fact, input. But, in fact, looking back over the entire year, including that period, there were some incidents that should have been deemed to be international terrorist events.

Question: Okay. So it was put in, but it just wasn't counted right, then, once it was put in?

Mr. Brennan: Once it goes into the database, it's another step, in fact, several steps based on this database system that requires the individuals to generate the statistics based on incidents and whether they are Significant, Non-Significant, and casualties, whatever. That extraction process did not work for a combination of database problems, individuals who were not sufficiently trained on that, apparently, and also that there was lack of management oversight there because of the individual who was in charge of that unit left.

Question: One question for Mr. Black. Can you tell us, the Significant event of 175 last year, that is the highest since when exactly, since what year?

Ambassador Black: It's '82? I think it's 1982.

Question: Thank you.

Question: Mr. Ambassador, can I ask one question with two semicolons to it, if I may? Okay? All right. And here goes my question. Talking about your definition of international terrorism, as applied to coalition forces in Iraq, if a Syrian or any non-Iraqi were to attack coalition forces that would not be a terrorist incident?

Ambassador Black: Do you want to take that?

Question: And I still have two other parts to this question.

Ambassador Black: I'll turn it over to Mr. Brennan, since it's his people that chair the—

Mr. Brennan: A determination would have to be made by the Incident Review Panel to determine whether those individuals in uniform, as part of the coalition, were combatant forces.

Question: And the same would hold true, then, if Hezbollah attacked Israel Defense Forces within Israel? Would Israeli forces be considered combatants?

Mr. Brennan: It would all depend on the situation, the individuals involved and what their position was. Again, the Incident Review Panel, which is this multi-agency element, makes that determination.

Question: So I guess then, in context of a war on terrorism, in your professional opinions, if you're free to respond to this, do you think the definition of international terrorism needs to be revised, given the realities of 2004? Is it—does it tell the whole story?

Mr. Brennan: I think the definition, as included in the law, is exceptionally broad, and is, in fact, quite inclusive, and therefore we need to take a look at whether or not that definition is as clear and unambiguous as possible in order to take into account the realities of 2003 and 2004.

In addition, the criteria that was developed by the Incident Review Panel many years ago to determine Significance or Non-Significance, I think is in need of immediate overhaul, as I mentioned, because a Significant incident will be determined if, in fact, there is serious bodily injury, death, major property damage of $10,000 or more, or the intent to do any of those.

So, therefore, a Molotov cocktail against an ATM machine, which is outside the Citibank, let's say, in some foreign country, and it was done, it was perpetrated by a group in order to show opposition against, let's say, a U.S. presence there, that is deemed then to be significant because it exceeds the $10,000 threshold.

Now I think one of the issues that we have to look at here is over the past 20 years, the Incident Review Panel consists of different representatives. There have been many different people there and there's a certain degree of subjectivity that is required as far as determining whether or not it meets the threshold, and then the application of that criteria.

And so I think Ambassador Black was exactly correct in terms of what type of metrics, what type of statistics, what type of lessons do we really want to learn from international terrorist events?

And so I think what we're going to be doing over the next several weeks is working very closely with the Department to determine exactly what needs to be done in order to fulfill the statutory intent of having an annual publication from the State Department that gives the government and the American people a true and fair assessment of the status of international terrorism. And I think over the years this has been on autopilot, and there are a number of issues here I think need to be addressed. And I think it needs to get on the right track so that we really come away with this type of information, so we learn from those lessons.

As far as TTIC is concerned, we are focusing, as I said in my remarks, on trying to stop the next attacks. We're putting our resources, we're trying to improve and enhance the technology on the different databases that we have access to, so we can bring it together in some type of integrated architecture.

We need to get this right. But this is looking back, as far as statistics. We need to understand this, that it's a stand-alone system. But if we're going to continue to do this, we have to make sure it's done well and it satisfies the need of Ambassador Black, Deputy Secretary Armitage, and Secretary Powell to give them what they need in order to really understand and then to comment on the status of international terrorism.

Question: One more question.

Question: Just a quick one on Iraq. If—I understand your reasons for not counting attacks by terrorists, even Zarqawi, on-duty military personnel in Iraq, doesn't fit in your definition. But do you have any idea, either one of you, if you did include those? After all, the President continually refers to those as terrorist attacks; Zarqawi is a terrorist. If you did include those attacks, what would happen to your numbers?

Mr. Brennan: They are terrorist attacks. The question is whether or not they meet the statutory language of international terrorist attacks. There are many incidents included in the material passed out today of events in Iraq. There were a number of attacks against hotels and other places.

Again, it's based on a determination. If it's an attack inside Iraq, by Iraqis, against an Iraqi target, that is domestic violence—domestic terrorism. It doesn't meet the definitions as established for international terrorism. But if, in fact, it involves other types of citizens, noncombatants, or other features that are called for here in the international terrorism definition, then it would make it. Again, there are individual case-by-case decisions that need to be made on these incidents.

Question: No, but I'm just asking, do you have any idea if you did count the attacks of Zarqawi and others on U.S. on-duty personnel, what would happen to those numbers?

Mr. Brennan: When attacks take place and by the Zarqawi network or others, many of those have involved deaths of American soldiers, as well as noncombatants, and those deaths are included in the statistics and those events included in the statistics.

Ambassador Black: That's why I think it's very important. You know, we're going to look forward to the opportunity to make this a better product and we'll go back to those that are the ones that come up with the definitions that we work with and look at a way to refine this to make it more useful, and hopefully, you know, begin to answer some questions like that.

Thank you very much.

Question: One last question. Mr. Black?

Ambassador Black: Yes, sir.

Question: Just to clarify, the initial failure was the computer and programming input problem that was described by Mr. Brennan, then there was an apparent lack of vetting by the CIA, although you have not said so explicitly. And then, was there also a failure at the State Department to vet the material as received from those sources before you put it out? And has that now changed? Can you describe—can you just clarify that?

Ambassador Black: We are in the process of changing that and looking at it. Clearly, since I am the one that recommend[s] to the Secretary that this document be published, it is my responsibility that it be error-free. It was not.

We do rely upon the TTIC and the CIA to provide us accurate information. And you've heard from Mr. Brennan about the plans he is making, both in terms of technology and personnel, to do that. But we, in my office, have to do a better job of proofreading what we get, and we obviously didn't do a good enough job of that and we're going to make corrections to do that.

Question: Thank you.

CRS Report for Congress

The Department of State's Patterns of Global Terrorism Report: Trends, State Sponsors, and Related Issues

Raphael Perl
Specialist in International Affairs Foreign Affairs, Defense, and Trade Division

Summary

This report highlights trends and data found in the State Department's annual *Patterns of Global Terrorism* report, *(Patterns 2003)* and addresses selected issues relating to its content. This report will not be updated.

On April 29, 2004, the Department of State released its annual *Patterns of Global Terrorism* report. Data at release showed minimal change in the number of terrorist attacks *worldwide* in 2003 over 2002 levels—a decrease from 198 attacks to 190. In 2003, the overall number of reported *anti-U.S.* attacks remained more or less constant as well, 82 anti-U.S. attacks in 2003 as opposed to 77 attacks in the previous year. In 2003, the number of *persons killed* in international terrorist attacks was 307, down from 725 in 2002. In 2003, *persons wounded* numbered 1,593, down from 2013 the previous year. In 2003, as in 2002, both the highest number of attacks (70) and highest number of casualties (159 dead and 951 wounded) continued to occur in Asia. Notably, the report defines terrorist acts as incidents directed against noncombatants. Thus, attacks in Iraq on military targets are not included.

Patterns, a work widely perceived as a standard, authoritative reference tool on terrorist activity, trends, and groups, has been subject to periodic criticism that it is unduly influenced by domestic, other foreign policy, political and economic considerations.

This year for the first time, data contained in *Patterns* —which some critics in Congress view as incomplete if not flawed—was provided by the newly operational Terrorist Threat Integration Center (TTIC). TTIC is providing an errata sheet, which will include, among other information, data on terrorist attacks after November 11, 2003.

It has been some fifteen years since Congress mandated the first *Patterns* report. At the time when the report was originally conceived as a reference document, the primary threat from terrorism was state sponsored. Since then, the threat has evolved with Al Qaeda affiliated groups and non-state sponsors increasingly posing a major threat. Given the increased complexity and danger posed by the terrorist threat, one option available to Congress and the executive branch is to take a fresh look at *Patterns*, its structure and content.

Overview of 2003 Terrorist Trends

On April 29, 2004, the Department of State released its *Patterns of Global Terrorism* report (hereafter referred to as *Patterns 2003*).[1] Data, as originally published, show minimal change in the number of terrorist attacks *worldwide* in 2003 over 2002 levels—a decrease from 199 attacks to 190. In 2003, the overall number of reported *anti-U.S.* attacks remained more or less constant as well, 82 anti-US attacks in 2003 as opposed to 77 attacks in the previous year. The report indicates that *worldwide deaths* from international terrorist activity were down roughly 58% in 2003 (from 725 to 307) and the *number of wounded* was down roughly 21% from 2,013 to 1,593. In 2003, as in 2002, both the highest number of attacks (70) and highest number of casualties (159 dead and 951 wounded) continued to occur in Asia where the number of attacks declined roughly by one-third, and the number of casualties declined roughly 13%. The report emphasizes that most of the attacks in Iraq that occurred during Operation Iraqi Freedom do not meet the U.S. definition of international terrorism employed by *Patterns* because they were directed at combatants, that is, "American and coalition forces on duty."[2]

In additional to statistical charts, *Patterns*, includes in its Appendixes a summary chronology of significant terrorist incidents and background information on U.S designated foreign terrorist organizations and other terrorist groups.[3]

---

[1] *Patterns* is an annual report to Congress required by Title 22 of the United States Code, Section 2656f(a).

[2] See 22 United States Code, Section 2656f(d) which defines acts of *international* terrorism as meaning "involving citizens or the territory of more than one country." Thus, excluded here would be major *domestic* terrorist acts in a country which might have major national or international impact. "Terrorism" is defined as "premeditated, politically motivated violence perpetrated against noncombatant targets by subnational groups or clandestine agents, usually intended to influence an audience." N.B., *Patterns* includes in this definition attacks on military personnel who are unarmed, or not on duty, and attacks on military installations, or unarmed military personnel, when a state of military hostilities does not exist at the site.

[3] For a detailed and authoritative discussion of Foreign Terrorist Organizations and the criteria for their designation, see CRS Report RL32223, *Foreign Terrorist Organizations* by Audrey Kurth Cronin

State Sponsors of Terrorism

In addition to data on terrorist trends, groups, and activities worldwide, the report provides a description as to why countries are on the U.S. list of state sponsors of terrorism that are subject to U.S. sanctions. Thus, included in *Patterns* are detailed data on the seven countries currently on the "terrorism list": Cuba, Iran, Iraq, Libya, North Korea, Sudan and Syria. U.S. Administration officials maintain that the practice of designating and reporting on the activities of the state sponsors of terrorism list and concomitant sanctions policy has contributed significantly to a reduction in the overt—and apparently overall—activity level of states supporting terrorism in the past decade. Libya and Sudan are frequently cited as examples of such success.

Countries designated as state sponsors of terrorism are subject to severe U.S. export controls—particularly of dual use technology. The Anti-Terrorism and Arms Export Amendments Act of 1989 (P.L. 101-222) prohibits export of dual use items, as well sales of military items and foreign economic assistance to countries on the terrorism list. Also, the Foreign Assistance Act prohibits providing foreign aid to these designated countries. Section 6(j) of the 1979 Export Administration Act stipulates that Congress must be notified at least 30 days in advance before any licenses are issued for exporting equipment or services that could be used for terrorist or military purposes. Other sanctions include denying foreign tax credits on income earned in those countries.

The degree of support for, or involvement in, terrorist activities typically varies dramatically from nation to nation. In 2003, of the seven on the U.S. terrorism list, Iran continued to be characterized on one extreme as an active supporter of terrorism: a nation that uses terrorism as an instrument of policy or warfare beyond its borders. Closer to the middle of the spectrum is Syria. Although not formally detected in an active role since 1986, *Patterns* reports that the Assad regime reportedly uses groups in Syria and Lebanon to export terror into Israel and allows groups to train in territory under its control. On the less active end of the spectrum, one might place countries such as Cuba or North Korea, which at the height of the Cold War were more active, but in recent years have seemed to settle for a more passive role of granting ongoing safe haven to previously admitted terrorists. Also at the less active end of the spectrum, and arguably falling off it, are Libya and notably Sudan, which reportedly has stepped up counter-terrorism cooperation with U.S. law enforcement and intelligence agencies after the attacks of September 11, 2001.

Country Highlights
Terrorism List Nations

Iran. *Patterns 2003* again designates Iran as the "most active" state sponsor of international terrorism. The report, which incorporates data from U.S. and allied intelligence services, notes that Iran's Islamic Revolutionary Guard and Ministry of Intelligence and Security were "involved in the planning of and support for terrorist acts and continued to exhort a variety of groups that use terrorism to pursue their goals."[4] Actions cited include (1) providing safe haven to members of Al Qaeda; (2) providing money, weapons and training to HAMAS, Hizballah, and Arab Palestinian rejectionist groups; and (3) helping members of the Ansar al Islam group in Iraq transit and find safe haven in Iran. The report notes that Iranian officials have acknowledged detaining Al Qaeda operatives during 2003, but have resisted calls to transfer them to their countries of origin. On December 19, 2003, Iran announced it will sign an agreement allowing international inspections of nuclear sites. Iran is not considered to be a likely candidate for removal from the Department of State's Terrorism Sponsors List in the coming year.

North Korea. North Korea, designated a member of the "axis of evil" by President Bush in his 2003 State of the Union Address, is not known to have sponsored any terrorist acts since 1987 according to the report. However, it continued to give sanctuary to hijackers affiliated with the Japanese Red Army. *Patterns 2003* stresses that North Korea announced it planned to sign several antiterrorism conventions, but did not take any substantive steps to cooperate in efforts to combat terrorism. Although *Patterns* notes that North Korea's support for international terrorism appears limited at present, its efforts to restart its nuclear program and its role in proliferation of ballistic missiles and missile technology suggest that its removal from the terrorism list will not occur anytime soon.

Iraq. Iraq, under Saddam Hussein, had been cited in the 2002 *Patterns* report for a longstanding policy of providing safe haven and bases for terrorist groups and as having laid the groundwork for possible attacks against civilian and military targets in the United States and other Western nations throughout 2002. However, in the event of a substantive regime change, a nation may be removed from the terrorism list. Under U.S. law, (Paragraph 6 (j) (4) of the Export Administration Act, the President must first report to Congress that the government of the country concerned: (1) does not support terrorism and (2) has provided assurances that it will not support terrorism in the future. On May 7, 2003, President Bush suspended all sanctions against Iraq applicable to state sponsors of terrorism, which had the practical effect of putting Iraq on a par with non terrorist states. Iraq is expected to be removed from the terrorism list as soon as it has its own government in place that pledges not to support terrorist acts in the future, a requirement expected to be met shortly after June 30, 2004. The report notes that the line between insurgency and terrorism has become "increasingly blurred" in Iraq, as attacks on civilian targets have become more common. By the

---

et al. and CRS Report RL32120, *The FTO List and Congress: Sanctioning Designated Terrorist Organizations* by Audrey Kurth Cronin.

4 *Patterns 2003*, p. 88

end of 2003, coalition forces had detained more than 300 suspected foreign fighters in Iraq.[5]

Libya. In 2003 Libya reiterated assurances to the U.N. Security Council that it had renounced terrorism, had shared intelligence with Western intelligence agencies, had taken steps to resolve matters related to its past support of terrorism, and on December 19, 2003 announced it would rid itself of weapons of mass destruction and allow inspections of its nuclear facilities.[6] The report states that in 2003, Libya held to its pattern in recent years of curtailing support for international terrorists, although Tripoli continued in 2003 to maintain contact with "some past terrorist clients." President Bush lifted sanctions against Libya on April 23, 2004, after successful intelligence cooperation on WMD issues and efforts by Libya to resolve compensation for Pam Am flight 103 survivors.

Syria. Syria, according to *Patterns 2003*, continued to provide political and material support to Palestinian rejectionist groups and continued to permit Iran to use Damascus as a transhipment point for resupplying Hizballah in Lebanon. On a positive note, the report notes that Damascus has cooperated with other governments "against al Qaeda, the Taliban, and other terrorist organizations and individuals," has discouraged signs of public support for Al Qaeda, including in the media and mosques, and has made efforts to tighten its borders with Iraq to limit the movement of anti-Coalition foreign fighters. On May 11, 2004, President Bush imposed economic and trade sanctions against Syria under the Syrian Accountability Act,[7] but also waived some of the provisions, notably provisions applying to the export of select items.[8]

Cuba. Cuba, a terrorism list carryover from the cold war has, according to *Patterns 2003*, "remained opposed to the U.S.-led Coalition prosecuting the global war on terrorism"[9] and continued to provide support to designated terrorist organizations. It is considered unlikely that Cuba will be removed from the terrorism list, absent a regime change.[10]

Sudan. Sudan is generally considered by observers to be a strong candidate for removal from the terrorism list. *Patterns 2003* claims that the nation has "deepened its cooperation with the U.S. Government," producing significant progress in combating terrorist activity, but "areas of concern" remain, notably the active presence in Sudan of Hamas and the Palestine Islamic Jihad (PIJ). In 2004, Sudan was removed from the list of countries designated by the Secretary of State as not fully cooperating with the United States in the war on terrorism.

Report Issues

Politicization of Report

Some critics of *Patterns* and its designation of state sponsors of terrorism charge that the *Patterns 2003* report generally, and specifically its reporting of activities of nations, is unduly influenced by a complex web of overlapping and sometimes competing political and economic agendas and concerns. As cases in point, they refer to activity cited in *Patterns* reports used to justify retaining Cuba and North Korea on the state sponsors list.[11] Others suggest that *Patterns'* heavy focus on state sponsors of terror make such reports less useful in a world where terrorist activity is increasingly neither state supported nor state countenanced. Still others ask whether, and to what degree, *Patterns* supports a sanctions policy that is unrealistically achievable and too unilateral when imposing sanctions on nations in which U.S. and allied economic and strategic geopolitical interests run high.

However, *Patterns* in its current form is not intended to set policy. Thus, one potential shortcoming of the criticisms cited above is that they are either policy oriented or revolve around disagreement with policy issues instead of centering on disagreement with the data and analysis presented in *Patterns* reports. Moreover, such criticisms, they maintain, arguably place too much emphasis on the state sponsors section of *Patterns*, with little or no emphasis on the plethora of useful data provided in the report on trends in terrorist activity and background on terrorist organizations.

Over- or Under-Emphasizing Levels of Cooperation

Particularly strong have been suggestions by some that *Patterns* plays down undesirable levels of counter-terrorism cooperation and progress in the case of nations seen as vital to the global campaign against terror. *Patterns 2003*, in contrast to pre "9/11" report versions, is silent about Pakistan's alleged ongoing support for Kashmiri militants and their attacks against the population of India. Some critics argue that *Patterns 2003* also falls far short of criticizing Saudi Arabia, perceived by many analysts as a slow, unwilling, or halfhearted ally in curbing or cracking down on activities which support or spawn terrorism activities outside its borders. In contrast, *Patterns 2003* cites Saudi Arabia as "an excellent example of a nation increasingly focusing its political will to fight terrorism." Some suggest, however, that often at play here is simply a desire to put the best face on terrorist related relationships in the hopes of obtaining better cooperation in the future.

On the flip side of the coin is an issue, yet to be resolved, of how to inform Congress and give countries credit in *Pat-*

---

5 See generally CRS Report RL32217, *Iraq and Al Qaeda: Allies or Not?*, by Kenneth Katzman.

6 See generally CRS Report IB93109, *Libya*, by Clyde R. Mark.

7 P.L. 108-175.

8 See CRS Report IB92075, *Syria: US Relations and Bilateral Issues* by Alfred B. Prados.

9 See *Patterns 2003*, p. 86.

10 See generally, CRS Report RL32251, *Cuba and the State Sponsors of Terrorism List*, by Mark Sullivan.

11 See CRS Report RL32251, *Cuba and the State Sponsors of Terrorism List* by Mark Sullivan.

terns for cooperation in such matters as intelligence or renditions when, for domestic political concerns, they do not want this made public. One option might be to produce more frequently a classified annex to the *Patterns* report which has been done in the past. A downside, however, is that preparation of a classified version is much more time consuming for those tasked with simultaneously preparing the public document.

Review and Restructuring of Patterns

Some also suggest that *Patterns* reports could be stronger in their coverage of the ideological and economic impact of terrorism on individual nations and the global economy. One issue here, as raised by some observers, is whether *Patterns* places too much emphasis on quantifying and measuring terrorist success in terms of physical damage to persons and property when terror groups may increasingly be measuring mid- and long-term success by economic and political criteria.

Going beyond the question, raised by some, of any perceived shortcomings in data, which may or may not be found in *Patterns 2003*, is the question of the quality of strategic analysis of the data provided. To what degree might such analysis be enhanced? Some observers suggest the issue here is the degree to which *Patterns* is designed to reflect, or might be construed to reflect, a "body count" reporting mentality.[12] Would there be benefits to Congress and the counterterrorism policy community if the focus of *Patterns* reports was less on presenting statistics and facts, and more on gaining meaning from the data? And if so, how might Congress effect such a change in policy focus? Admittedly, overall numbers by themselves may not always present a complete picture. For example, each small pipeline bombing in Colombia is cited as one incident in *Patterns* as would be a major terrorist incident as the multiple train bombings in Madrid in March 2004. Another possible shortcoming, some note, is that *Patterns* sometimes may not include, or adequately note, incidents that are not international in nature but which may have a major political or economic impact on the target nation and well beyond it.

Indeed, *Patterns 2003* has been subject to criticism on the issue of data completeness or accuracy, as well as on the issue of data relevance.[13] In a May 17, 2004 letter to Secretary of State Colin L. Powell, Henry A. Waxman, Ranking Minority Member of the House Committee on Government Reform,

---

12 Note that this is part of a much broader policy debate, in which CRS takes no position, regarding the place in U.S. anti-terror strategy of short-term measures designed to produce physical security versus long-term strategic measures designed to win "hearts and minds." Arguably, some suggest the course of wisdom is a mix of policies designed to win "both the battle and the war", policies which require reporting, data, and analysis supportive of both tactical and strategic objectives.

13 See "Faulty Terror Report Card," by Alan B. Krueger and David Laitin, *Washington Post* guest editorial, May 17, 2002, p. A21.

suggests that data in *Patterns 2003* which indicate that non-significant terrorist attacks have declined in the last two years is in sharp contrast to independent analysis of the same data which concludes that significant terrorist attacks (acts causing, or reasonably expected to cause: death, serious personal injury or major property damage) actually reached a

Table 1 Patterns of Global Terrorism Data, 2002–2003

	2002	2003	% Change
Worldwide Overview			
No. of attacks[a]	198	190	−4.04
No. of deaths	725	307	−57.66
No. of injured	2,013	1,593	−20.86
No. of anti-American acts[b]	77	82	+6.49
No. of American casualties[c]			
Dead	27	35	+29.63
Wounded	35	17	−51.43
Attacks by Region			
Africa	5	4	−20.0
Asia	101	70	−30.69
Eurasia	8	2	−75.0
Latin America	46	53	+28.26
Middle East	29	37	+27.59
North America	0	0	0
Western Europe	9	24	+166.67
Casualties by Region			
Africa	12	11	−8.33
Asia	1,283	1,110	−13.48
Eurasia[d]	615	5	−99.12
Latin America	54	12	−77.78
Middle East	772	760	−1.55
North America	0	0	0
Western Europe	6	2	−66.67
Attacks by Target Category			
Business	122	93	−23.77
Diplomat	14	15	+7.74
Government	17	13	−23.53
Military	1	2	+100.0
Other	83	84	+1.20

Note: Based on data originally published in *Patterns 2003*. Traditionally, this data had been provided to the State Department by the Central Intelligence Agency. More recently this function has been transferred to the newly operational Terrorist Threat Integration Center (TTIC). Periodic requests from analysts at the Department of State and from analysts at the Congressional Research Service in April 2004 for quarterly access to an unclassified version of the data base of terrorist incidents have, to date, not resulted in access to the data desired.

a Compared with 487 attacks in 1982.

b In 2003 the highest percent of targets were businesses (67%); the most common method of attack was bombing (71%).

c Casualties include dead and wounded.

d 2002 figures include relatively high casualties in a number of anti-Russian attacks, such as the October 2002 Moscow theater attack.

20-year high in 2003.[14] Also questioned is completeness, if not factual accuracy, of the data relied upon in the *Patterns 2003* report. The list of significant incidents in *Patterns 2003*, as originally disseminated, concludes abruptly on November 11, 2003, presumably therefore, not counting major multiple terrorists attacks that occurred later in the year.[15]

The statistical data which forms the basis for *Patterns* have traditionally been provided to the State Department by the CIA. More recently this function has been transferred to the newly operational Terrorist Threat Integration Center (TTIC).[16] TTIC is providing an errata sheet to correct incomplete data.[17]

Conclusion

It has been some fifteen years since Congress mandated the first *Patterns* report. At the time the report was originally conceived as a reference document, the primary threat from terrorism was state sponsored. Since then, the threat has evolved, with Al Qaeda affiliated groups and non-state sponsors increasingly posing a major threat. Over the years, the report has increased in length and expanded in scope. It has been disseminated on the internet, translated into five additional languages, and is widely recognized as a primary resource on terrorist activities and groups. However, in view of the earlier-noted data issues, the report may be subject to increased criticism and scrutiny. In light of the high level of international attention attached to the report and the increased complexity and danger posed by the terrorist threat, some observers have suggested that a thorough Executive/Congressional review of *Patterns*, its structure and content, may be timely and warranted.

Order Code RL32417, June 1, 2004

---

14 See note 13, *supra*.

15 [www/house.gov/reform/min/pdfs_108_2/pdfs_inves/pdf_admin_global_terror_report_may_17_let.pdf] Note that conversations between a CRS analyst and State Department and TTIC staff in May 2004 produced suggestions that the end of year data omission may have been to some degree the result of a desire to meet the publication deadline for the printed version of the report. Note also that data and analysis provided CRS by Larry Johnson, a former Officer in the State Department's Office of Counter Terrorism and now Director of Berg Associates, indicates that the ratio of significant terrorist incidents to total terrorist actions rose fairly steadily from 10% in 1981 to 90% in 2003. See [http://www.berg-associates.com].

16 For information on TTIC, see CRS Report RS21283, *Homeland Security: Intelligence Support* by Richard Best. President Bush, in his State of the Union address delivered on January 28, 2003, called for the establishment of a new Terrorist Threat Integration Center (TTIC) that would merge and analyze all threat information in a single location under the direction of the Director of Central Intelligence [DCI]. Included in TTIC are representatives of the CIA's Counterterrorist Center (CTC) and the FBI's Counterterrorism Division, along with elements of other agencies, including DOD and DHS. TTIC began operations on May 1, 2004.

17 Some observers suggest that TTIC's omissions of data may well give rise to questions about the overall ability and effectiveness of TTIC in assuming and performing newly assigned tasks.

United States Department of State and
the Broadcasting Board of Governors

Review of the Department's Patterns of Global Terrorism— 2003 Report

Office of Inspector General

Executive Summary

In a June 18, 2004 letter to Secretary of State Colin Powell, six members of the U.S. Senate requested that the Office of Inspector General (OIG) review how inaccurate and incomplete data and statements came to be included in the *Patterns of Global Terrorism—2003* report. *Patterns—2003*, released on April 29, 2004, asserted that acts of international terrorism had declined slightly in the past several years and that 2003 had the "lowest annual total of international terrorist attacks since 1969," suggesting that the Administration was winning the global war on terrorism. Shortly thereafter, an op-ed piece in the *Washington Post* alleged that there were statistical errors in the report. Subsequent articles in various periodicals claimed terrorist acts had been left out, mislabeled, and counted incorrectly. On June 22, 2004, the Department of State (the Department) issued a revised version of the *Patterns—2003* report that identified an increase in the number of significant terrorist events.

Before Congress mandated that the Department report on terrorism in 1987,[1] the Central Intelligence Agency (CIA) produced a report on terrorism, which was viewed largely as the reference on significant trends in international terrorism. With the 1987 legislation, *Patterns* began its transition to serving as a "report card" on how well the U.S. government was responding to the threat of terrorism. Although the Department has overall responsibility for producing the annual report on international terrorism, the Terrorist Threat Integration Center (TTIC) produces the data that form the basis of the report's Appendix A— Chronology of Significant Terrorist Incidents. An Incident Review Panel (IRP), which includes members of the Intelligence Community, reviews a monthly listing of terrorist incidents provided by TIC and determines which events are "significant."

OIG's review has found that the inaccurate statements in the report were based on omissions of IRP-adjudicated decisions and apparent inconsistencies in the database of terrorist events maintained by TTIC. The database formed the basis for Appendix A, as well as for the charts and graphs in the report's Appendix G—Statistical Review, and for the statistics used in the report's Year in Review section. The reasons for the omissions and inconsistencies in the TTIC database were:

- Data entry lagged toward the end of 2003, and IRP decisions of adjudicated terrorist incidents between November 11 and the end of December were not entered into TTIC's database until April 2004, after the report had been printed.
- No one questioned the omissions before the report was printed.
- It appears that there was no consistent, replicable methodology that IRP used for selecting events to be included in Appendix A.

OIG was also asked to look at whether the process for assembling the report and the participants involved in the process differed significantly from previous reports. The major difference in the process between the 2003 report and previous reports was the transfer to TTIC from the CIA's Counterterrorist Center (CTC) of maintenance of the database. The TTIC unit manager, who was formerly from CTC and who was responsible for updating the database, left TTIC in December 2003 and was not replaced. According to TTIC officials, data entry for the events adjudicated by the IRP in January 2004[2] did not begin until April 2004, well after Appendix A was first sent to the Department in February 2004.

The office and procedures involved in the preparation of *Patterns* within the Department were the same in 2003 as in prior years. However, a personnel change and staffing shortages within the office of the Coordinator for Counterterrorism (S/CT) likely affected oversight of the report. A Foreign Service public affairs officer who previously helped produce the report left in the spring of 2003, and the position was reassigned elsewhere within S/CT. The S/CT associate coordinator, whose office was responsible for producing the report began working in that office in June 2003 and had no previous experience in preparing the *Patterns* report.

In summary, OIG found that the omissions and apparent inconsistencies were due to a number of factors. The shift from CTC to TTIC of responsibility for maintenance of the database of terrorist events, along with the lack of trained,

---

[1] Title 22 of the United States Code (USC), Section 2656f, requires that the Department of State produce an annual report of terrorism.

[2] The IRP met on January 23, 2004, to adjudicate events for the rest of November and December 2003.

long-term personnel working in that office, also probably contributed to the lack of supervision of the database. In addition, the process for assembling the report at the Department, while differing little from that of previous years, lacked sufficient oversight and coordination.

Both S/CT and TTIC personnel greatly regretted the errors in the 2003 report, and both have begun to formulate more rigorous methodologies for the compilation of data. OIG's recommendations, along with the innovations and remedial action already undertaken by S/CT and TTIC, should provide future *Patterns* reports a more useful and accurate analysis of terrorist and anti-terrorist activities.

Objectives, Scope, and Methodology

The objectives for OIG's review were to determine: 1) how "inaccurate" statements came to be included in the Department's *Patterns of Global Terrorism—2003*, 2) whether there was a significantly different process used in assembling the report, and 3) whether there were different participants involved in the process, compared to previous years.

OIG performed fieldwork in Washington, D.C., from July to August 2004. The team conducted interviews with Department management officials from S/CT, the Bureau of Intelligence and Research (INR), and the Bureau of Diplomatic Security. The Team also met with the Director of TTIC and other relevant TTIC officials. TTIC also conducted an internal review of its support to the Department's preparation of *Patterns,* and OIG met with TTIC's review team on several occasions throughout the review process. Both teams shared their findings and recommendations. OIG's team consisted of Ambassador Fernando Rondon, team leader, and Anita Schroeder, Margaret Ann Linn and Stephanie Hwang. This evaluation was conducted in accordance with the *Quality Standards for Inspections* issued by the President's Council on Integrity and Efficiency. OIG discussed its findings and recommendations with S/CT officials at the conclusion of the review. Their comments are addressed within the report.

Background

In a June 18, 2004, letter to Secretary Powell, six members[3] of the U.S. Senate requested that OIG identify how inaccurate and incomplete data and statements came to be included in the *Patterns of Global Terrorism—2003* report. The Senators referred to a need for clearer accounting in the war on terrorism as a reason why Congress mandated the annual *Patterns* report in 1987. Hence, they said they "were very disturbed" to learn of the inaccuracies in the report and of the incomplete picture of global terrorism that it offered. Furthermore, the Senators found the Administration's use of the report in press conferences and press releases to be "especially troubling." (For the full text of the Senators' letter, see Appendix A.)

Patterns—2003, released on April 29, 2004, indicated that acts of international terrorism had declined slightly in the past several years and that 2003 had the "lowest annual total of international terrorist attacks since 1969," which was used to bolster the assertion that the Administration was winning the global war on terrorism. Shortly thereafter, an op-ed article in the *Washington Post* alleged that there were statistical errors in the report. Subsequent articles in various periodicals claimed events were left out, mislabeled, and counted incorrectly. On June 22, 2004, the Department issued a revised *Patterns—2003* report that said there was an increase in the number of significant international terrorist events over the period.

History of Patterns of Global Terrorism

The CIA issued the U.S. government's first annual report on international terrorism in 1976 as a research paper. The goal of that report, *International and Transnational Terrorism: Diagnosis and Prognosis,* was to provide a framework for understanding international terrorism. In 1978, the CIA began to issue the report annually and added coverage on significant trends in terrorist activities, including foreign-government support for terrorist groups and international efforts to deter terrorism.

In 1982, the role of producing a report on international terrorism shifted from CIA to the Department when the first publication under the Department's purview, *Patterns of International Terrorism: 1981,* was published. The first "Chronology of Significant Terrorist Events" (Appendix A) appeared in the following year's report.

In December 1987, the Foreign Relations Authorization Act, Fiscal Years 1988 and 1989 (P.L. 100-204, Section 104, as amended), required that the Department provide Congress a full and complete annual report on terrorism for those countries and groups meeting the criteria for international terrorism. The reporting requirement changed in 1996 to include the extent to which other countries cooperate with the United States in apprehending, convicting, and punishing terrorists responsible for attacking U.S. citizens or interests. A more complete history of the *Patterns* reports may be found in Appendix B.

As now designed, *Patterns* serves as a unique, comprehensive accounting of significant acts of global terror and of the diplomatic record of the United States and its partners in cooperatively countering such terror. Its unclassified nature facilitates wide distribution and contributes to greater public understanding of the global war on terrorism.

Criteria

Title 22, Section 2656f, of the U.S. Code requires that the Department, by April 30 of the following year, produce an

---

[3] Senators Tom Daschle, Joseph R. Biden Jr., Carl Levin, Harry Reid, Patrick Leahy, and John D. Rockefeller IV.

annual report on terrorism that includes "detailed assessments" for each country in which there were significant acts of international terrorism. The law defines an international terrorist event as premeditated, politically motivated violence that is perpetrated against noncombatant targets by subnational groups or clandestine agents to influence people and which involves citizens of two or more countries. The definition of "significant" is left to the Secretary. In November 1996, with further modifications in later years, criteria were developed to define which international terrorist attacks were "significant." An incident is now considered significant if there was loss of life or serious injury to people, major property damage of $10,000 or more, or the abduction or kidnapping of people.

In 1996, the congressional reporting requirements were amended to require the Department to report on the extent to which other countries cooperate with the United States in apprehending, convicting, and punishing terrorists responsible for attacking U.S. citizens or interests.

Organizational Responsibilities

Although the Department has the overall responsibility for producing the annual report on international terrorism, other U.S. government entities (primarily TTIC) assist in writing portions of the report and in producing the statistics used for the report's Appendix A.

S/CT is the Department's program office responsible for coordinating and producing *Patterns*. The responsibility for preparing *Patterns* has belonged to S/CT since the Department began issuing the report annually in 1982. S/CT gets input from various sources (overseas posts, functional and regional bureaus) to prepare the report, drafts the Coordinator's Year in Review section, which discusses trends and numbers of events and writes introductions to the regional overview. S/CT also takes the lead on drafting Appendix D —U.S. Programs and Policy, with the assistance of the Department's Bureau of Diplomatic Security.

The Department's INR draft[s] individual country reports within the regional overviews. The drafts are then sent to S/CT, which sends them to the regional bureaus for review and comment.

TTIC[4] reviews information on terrorist events and maintains this information in a database, which is inherited from the CIA's CTC.[5] The database is used to compile Appendix A—Chronology of Significant Terrorist Incidents at the end of each year. TTIC also provides data for the charts and graphs that are used in the report.

The IRP,[6] which was made up of representatives from INR, CIA, Defense Intelligence Agency, and the National Security Agency, reviewed terrorist incidents and determined which events met the established definition of significant international terrorism. A representative from TTIC, a non-voting member of the IRP, chaired the panel. The results of the IRP's meetings are contained in TTIC's database.

[*Eds. Note:* Appendixes B and C of *Patterns* contained descriptions of "designated foreign terrorist organization" and "other terrorist groups." These descriptions are compiled in Part 2, Terrorist Groups.]

The Process

TTIC tracks worldwide acts of terror and maintains this information in a database. On a daily basis, TTIC analysts reviewed reporting of events for possible inclusion in the database. If an analyst determined that a terrorist incident should be considered by the IRP, a description of the incident was entered into the database and summary information, such as the date of the incident, the country, type of event (e.g., kidnapping), was also entered. Monthly, TTIC sent terrorist incident summaries[7] to the members of the IRP for their consideration. IRP members could study and share the information with staff from their respective agencies before they met, on the first Wednesday of each month, to determine (adjudicate) which of the previous month's events were significant international terrorist events. TTIC, in turn, updated the database with a record of the IRP's decision.

The Department began drafting portions of the *Patterns —2003* report in November 2003, but the chronology of significant international terrorist events was not received by the Department until February of 2004. The draft version of *Patterns*, without Appendix A, was also circulated to regional and functional bureaus for review and comment. Because of the short timeframe in which S/CT has to coordinate the report, Appendix A was never circulated for review or comment within S/CT or with other Department offices, accompanied by the draft version of the report. In March 2004, the report was forwarded for production, to meet the April 30 congressional deadline.

Addressing Congressional Concerns

Congress requested that OIG determine: 1) how "inaccurate" statements came to be included in the Department's *Patterns*

---

4 TTIC's mission and organizational responsibilities are described in the Director of Central Intelligence Directive 2/4, *Terrorist Threat Integration Center*, dated 1 May 2003. These responsibilities include integration and analysis of terrorist-related information collected domestically and from abroad.

5 Previously, CIA's CTC maintained the database, which produces data on Terrorism, Report Number SIO-S-04-18, September 2004.

6 TTIC informed OIG at the conclusion of this review that the IRP had been disbanded. A new group made up of individuals from TTIC's partners, with assignees to TTIC, will review and adjudicate terrorist events.

7 The TTIC database summaries provided to the IRP included information on the date, arena (international or not), type of event (e.g. bombing), and country of occurrence. The summaries gave a short description of the event. For example, the summaries might have noted that "extremists bombed two restaurants, partially collapsing a wall, which injured a pedestrian."

of Global Terrorism—2003 report, 2) whether there were significantly different processes used in assembling the report than in previous years, and 3) whether the participants involved differed significantly from those who produced previous reports. The answers to these questions are summarized here briefly and are discussed in more detail in the Findings and Recommendations section of this report.

OIG found that the inaccurate statements were due to omissions and apparent inconsistencies in the database of terrorist events maintained by TTIC. These include:

- Even though the IRP had in January 2004 adjudicated terrorist events for the remainder of the previous calendar year, data entry lagged toward the end of 2003, and information on terrorist incidents between November 11 and the end of December 2003 was not entered into the database until April 2004.
- No one questioned the omissions before the report was printed.
- It appears that there was no consistent, replicable methodology used by the IRP for selecting events to be included in the chronology in Appendix A.

Given the above circumstances, Appendix A and the statistics used as a basis for official Department briefings cannot be viewed as reliable.

OIG was also asked to look at whether the process and the participants involved in producing the report were significantly different from those of previous reports. OIG found that the process remained the same, but that the major difference between the 2003 report and previous reports was the involvement of TTIC in the maintenance of the database used to prepare Appendix A. Prior to the formation of TTIC, responsibility for maintenance of the database rested with CTC. The TTIC unit manager, who was formerly from CTC and who was responsible for updating the database, left TTIC in December 2003 and was not replaced. Efforts to fill the position were unsuccessful until after the report was published. According to TTIC officials, data entry for the events adjudicated by the IRP in January 2004[8] did not begin until April 2004, well after Appendix A data was first sent to the Department, in February 2004.

The offices involved in the preparation of *Patterns* within the Department were the same in 2003 as in prior years. However, a personnel change and staffing shortages within S/CT likely affected oversight of the report. A Foreign Service public affairs officer who previously helped produce the report left in the spring 2003, and the position was reassigned elsewhere within S/CT. The associate coordinator whose office was responsible for producing the report began working in that office in June 2003 and had no previous experience in preparing the *Patterns* report.

In summary, OIG found that the omissions and apparent inconsistencies were due to a number of factors. The shift of responsibility from CTC to TTIC for maintenance of the database of terrorist events, along with the lack of trained long-term personnel working in that office, probably contributed to the lack of supervision of the database. The process for assembling the report at the Department, while differing little form that of previous years, lacked sufficient oversight and coordination. Recommendations to correct these problems are presented in the following section.

OIG found that both S/CT and TTIC personnel greatly regretted the errors in the 2003 report and have already begun formulating more rigorous methodologies for the compilation of data. The recommendations discussed in the next section, along with innovations and remedial action already undertaken by S/CT and TTIC should provide future *Patterns* reports a more useful and accurate analysis of terrorist and anti-terrorist activities.

Findings and Recommendations

The Department's *Patterns of Global Terrorism—2003* report contained erroneous information largely because of gaps in data entry, inconsistently applied methodology, and lack of oversight. In this section, OIG presents its findings and recommendations regarding these issues.

Data Inconsistencies and the Compilation of Appendix A

The omission from the report of terrorist attacks occurring after November 11, 2003, was perhaps the most egregious error, but OIG also found that this omission highlighted other weaknesses in the compilation of Appendix A. What appear to be inconsistencies in the application of the definitions, as described in the criteria and the adjudication by the IRP, also affected the quality of the data. Finally, Appendix A was never circulated within the Department nor was it made available to the analysts responsible for writing regional overviews and country specific narratives, individuals who could have identified the omissions and inconsistencies.

Appendix A Methodology

OIG reviewed a sample of significant international terrorist events that were identified in Appendix A in both the original and revised *Patterns—2003* reports and found that the definitions and criteria for identifying and classifying international terrorist events appear to have been applied inconsistently. Some incidents were removed from the original version of Appendix A, but other incidents, similar to those that were deleted, were then added. For example:

- On March 31, IBM employees in Italy found an explosive device and notified police, who described it as a dangerous, though rudimentary, bomb. This incident was deleted from the revised Appendix A.

---

8 The IRP met on January 23, 2004, to adjudicate events for the balance of November 2003 and December 2003.

- On September 8, authorities in Madrid, Spain, safely defused a parcel bomb hidden in a book that was sent to the Greek Consulate. This incident was not included in the original version of Appendix A but was included in the revised version.
- On February 1, a time bomb was discovered and defused in a McDonald's restaurant in Turkey. There were no injuries and no one claimed responsibility. This incident was deleted from the revised report.
- On February 25, an incendiary bomb was thrown at a McDonald's restaurant in Saudi Arabia. There were no injuries and no one claimed responsibility. This incident was included in both reports.

TTIC explained that there are several reasons for what appear to be inconsistencies in the application of the criteria. In some cases, details were not available when the IRP first considered an event. Over time, as more information became available, the IRP would reconsider the event, and this may have changed how the event was categorized. Since the IRP did not keep records or minutes of how determinations were made, TTIC could only speculate on why some events were included or not included. TTIC also opined that the criteria are complex and decisions can be subjective. For example, when the IRP reconsidered the February 1 event, it may have deleted it because the panel determined that there was not enough firepower involved to cause significant damage. In contrast, the February 25 event may have been included because incendiary bombs cause significant property damage.

There also appear to be inconsistencies in how events are counted. Multiple similar events offering more or less simultaneously or in succession in one area are sometimes counted as one incident and at other times are counted individually. For example:

- On February 25, two bombs that exploded in Caracas, Venezuela, and damaged the Spanish and Colombian embassies, were listed as one incident, as were four bomb attacks on March 25 in Pristina, Serbia, against police stations of the United Nations Interim Administration Mission in Kosovo.
- On April 12, grenade attacks at two different targets in Anantnag District, Kashmir, one at a bus station and another at an army patrol, were listed as separate events.
- On November 15 in Istanbul, Turkey, vehicle-bomb attacks at the Beth Israel and Neve Shalom synagogues were listed as separate events.

TTIC and S/CT explained that the IRP had analyzed these events and that the panel had a basis for determining that some events should be considered as one incident and other events should be listed as separate incidents. Unless a rationale is explained, it is difficult for the reader to understand why some multiple events are counted as only one incident and why others are counted individually.

TTIC and S/CT are developing an algorithm that explains how multiple events are counted. OIG encourages S/CT to include this supporting material in the report to assist the reader in understanding the methodology. OIG also believes that, for purposes of transparency, S/CT should include an explanatory footnote for each event that may not obviously fit the criteria and methodology.

Accepted standards of data collection and analysis require that there be a reliable and complete database (the universe of events under consideration) and that classification of events from the database be performed in a consistent, replicable manner. This means that a separate determination of events as significant or non-significant, using the same database, should yield the same results. When terrorist events do not fit established criteria or definitions, this circumstance should be flagged, allowing classification criteria to be adjusted periodically. The definitions for classifying events from the database (the criteria for determining if an event is significant, international or domestic, etc.) should be based on hard data. If hard data are not available, then a thorough explanation of how decisions are made must be provided.

The accuracy of the report is dependent on accurate and complete data and a comprehensive adjudication process. The role of TTIC in the preparation of the terrorism database is also vital to the accuracy of the data. Although S/CT does not have a direct role in the preparation of Appendix A, it is in the Department's best interest to ensure that a reliable methodology is used in determining the data for the *Patterns* report. Therefore, OIG recommends that S/CT and TTIC formalize the roles and responsibilities of the two agencies.

The following recommendation calls on S/CT to conclude a memorandum of understanding (MOU) with TTIC. This MOU should ensure that:

- Specific, replicable criteria for classifying terrorist events for *Patterns* are established and applied consistently;
- In cases where terrorist events do not fit the established criteria, an explanation is recorded as to how the event was classified; and
- The classification criteria are periodically adjusted to include or exclude certain types of events, as needed.

OIG also recommends that TTIC keep complete minutes of meetings and notes on how decisions were made, and that they make this information available to the Department and other users upon request, as appropriate.

Recommendation 1: The Department should conclude a memorandum of understanding (MOU) with the Director of the Terrorist Threat Integration Center, specifying the information needed to meet the Department's congressional reporting requirements. The MOU should include an agreed upon methodology for classifying and adjudicating terrorist events, including documentation for how determinations are made. (Action: S/CT)

OIG also found that the *Patterns—2003* report contained internal inconsistencies, particularly between the chronology and the geographic overview sections and between the charts and graphs and other sections. For example, the Year in Review section refers to "190 acts of international terrorism." However, Appendix A lists 169 "significant terrorist incidents." Country-specific portions of the geographic portions of the geographic overviews, meanwhile, often include references to domestic terrorist events and to international terrorist events.

In general, OIG found that the commingling of discussions of domestic and international terrorism and of significant and non-significant terrorism led to confusion and difficulty in interpreting the numbers cited. OIG suggests that S/CT include in the report's introduction an explanation of the report's methodology for classifying significant international terrorist events, preventing readers from becoming confused about which types of events are being discussed. OIG notes that previous early editions of Patterns included such a reference. S/CT has agreed and intends to include a section on methodology in future reports. That section would define international and domestic incidents and significant and non-significant incidents and state the procedures used to make these determinations. References to major incidents in future reports will make clear whether the incident is domestic or international.

Frequency and Review of Appendix A
In the past, the annual list of significant international terrorist events was forwarded to S/CT in February of the subsequent year. However, S/CT analysts who prepare the regional overviews did not have access to Appendix A. Moreover, the chronology has not traditionally been vetted throughout the Department by such bureaus as INR,[9] the Bureau of Consular Affairs, and the Bureau of Diplomatic Security, all of which have independent sources of information on terrorist events. S/CT said there was insufficient time in the publishing schedule for it to circulate Appendix A to other Department offices for comment. It also stated that the chronology represented the vote of the IRP, and S/CT did not question the decisions made by the IRP. However, had Appendix A been circulated to other analysts at S/CT or elsewhere in the Department, these analysts would likely have identified the omissions and inconsistencies contained in Patterns—2003.

Analyzing patterns of terrorism requires a reliable, periodic chronology of significant events that can be compared and examined in context, along with information from other sources. The chronology is more likely to be complete and accurate if it is vetted by a number of offices dealing in antiterrorist activities and terrorism reporting. The final arbiter of the chronology must, however, be TTIC.

TTIC agrees that the chronology can be produced more frequently and has suggested that it will, in the future, produce a quarterly chronology.

---

9 INR received a list of terrorist events before IRP meetings, but IRP members did not get the annual cumulative listing for review.

Recommendation 2: The Coordinator for Counterterrorism (S/CT) should request that the Terrorist Threat Integration Center prepare and submit a chronology of significant international terrorism events (Appendix A) to S/CT for review and circulation within the Department. This chronology should be prepared at a minimum on a quarterly basis. S/CT should compile adjustments, corrections, and amendments to the chronology and return these to TTIC for consideration and updating of the database, if appropriate. (Action: S/CT)

Oversight and Staffing

OIG found that the process for assembling the *Patterns—2003* report lacked oversight and adequate review. Statistics presented in the Year in Review section were not examined for appropriateness before being finalized. An experienced analyst might have questioned the inconsistencies and data abnormalities in the chronology while preparing the Year in Review figures; however, an individual experienced in data analysis and reporting did not draft that portion of the report. Data collection and analysis requires that analysts verify the suitability and completeness of the data and double-check their calculations against historical patterns and other existing information.

An S/CT Civil service public affairs specialist, who had handled production of the report since 1986, directed general coordination of the report. S/CT previously had a second public affairs position, a Foreign Service officer who helped produce *Patterns*. When this individual left, in the spring 2003, the position was transferred to other functions within S/CT.

Management of the preparation of a report as important as *Patterns* should include oversight of the entire publication by a knowledgeable person who has responsibility for the accuracy of the data analysis presented, the consistency of data presented in different sections of the report, and the cohesiveness of the entire report. Given the importance of the global war on terrorism to U.S. national interests and foreign policy, *Patterns* should have the support and staff needed to produce a world-class product.

Recommendation 3: The Coordinator for Counterterrorism should re-establish a second public affairs officer position with analytic reporting skills and assign to this position responsibility for drafting and oversight of the analytical positions of the Patterns of Global Terrorism. (Action: S/CT)

Recommendation 4: The Coordinator for Counterterrorism should establish and fill a Public Diplomacy unit chief position that will be responsible for providing oversight to the Patterns of Global Terrorism report. This individual should be responsible for ensuring that the entire report is consistent, that portions of the report do not contradict or disagree with each other, and that terrorist incidents are presented and described uniformly throughout the report. (Action: S/CT)

Attribution

When the errors in the data were first brought to the public's attention the Department was presumed to be entirely responsible. With responsibility for maintaining the database comes acknowledgement of authorship and accountability for the charts, graphs, and lists of events generated from that information. This attribution is not acknowledged in the *Patterns* report, but OIG believes that it is an important factor in ensuring that the information presented in the report is accurate, transparent, and verifiable.

Recommendation 5: The Coordinator for Counterterrorism should identify the Terrorist Threat Integration Center as the source of the data in Appendix A of the Patterns of Global Terrorism report and for the report's charts and graphs. This acknowledgement should be included where appropriate in the report. (Action: S/CT)

Progress to Date

As it conducted its review, OIG found that S/CT and TTIC had already begun to review the steps involved in the preparation of *Patterns* and to discuss changes. S/CT is proposing to include more information in the report on the membership of the IRP and on how possible incidents are identified, processed, and adjudicated. Future reports will also discuss international versus domestic terrorism and significant versus non-significant events. In addition, *Patterns* reports will clarify the adjudication of incidents in Kashmir, Israel, and Chechnya, since all of these incidents involve cross-border support for terrorist groups.

S/CT has informed OIG that it has prepared a draft MOU with TTIC outlining the responsibilities of each office or agency. S/CT has also reviewed the clearance and approval procedures for *Patterns* and is improving the process. Finally, S/CT plans to add two positions having direct responsibility for *Patterns*, a Public Diplomacy unit chief and a Public Diplomacy analytic officer.

TTIC, meanwhile, has also conducted an internal review of the *Patterns* process. One of its key findings was the need to restructure and expand the scope of responsibilities of the incident adjudicative body that replaces the IRP. The new panel will include a more diverse representation from across the counterterrorism community and will include TTIC assignees from each of the original agencies whose members originally comprised the IRP, as well as TTIC assignees form the Department of Homeland Security and Federal Bureau of Investigation. TTIC is also requesting that a representative from S/CT, as a non-voting member, attend each session to provide insight into incidents that will be included in *Patterns*. TTIC is providing guidelines to address complex issues such as multiple events, disputed borders, timing of incidents, and the maintenance of record of the rationale behind these decisions, should questions arise in the future. TTIC agrees that there is a need to distribute the list of significant international terrorist incidents more frequently.

OIG believes that all parties involved in the preparation of *Patterns* are taking effective steps to ensure that future reports contain the most complete and accurate depiction possible of international terrorism.

Appendix A: Request Letter from Congress

The letter below was sent to Secretary of State Colin I. Powell on 18 June by Senators Tom Daschle, Harry Reid, Joseph R. Biden Jr., Patrick Leahy, Carl Levin, John D. Rockefeller IV.

Dear Mr. Secretary:

We are writing to express out deep concern with the latest edition of the Department of State's *Patterns of Global Terrorism 2003* report.

Defeating global terrorism is a goal we all share. Yet, over the course of the last several months, Defense Secretary Rumsfeld has repeatedly indicated that the Administration lacks the "metrics" to determine whether the United States is winning the war on international terrorism. Given that this effort is likely to take considerable time and resources, we agree with Secretary Rumsfeld that success requires that the American people be provided a clearer accounting from their leaders of how we are fighting and faring in the war on terrorism.

The desire for clearer accounting of our efforts against terrorism was part of the rationale that led Congress in 1987 to pass legislation mandating an annual *Patterns of Global Terrorism* report. Congress believed this report could help ensure that our government's decisions to defeat terrorism are informed by the latest and most accurate data.

Because defeating terrorism will require accurate data, we were very disturbed to learn that the State Department's *Patterns of Global Terrorism* annual report for 2003 presented an inaccurate and incomplete picture. As you know, the *Patterns of Global Terrorism 2003* report indicated a decline in global terrorism when, in fact, the number of terrorist incidents increased—to the highest level in more than 20 years. Especially troubling is the fact that senior Administration officials used this erroneous data in a series of press conferences and press releases to claim that the United States is winning the war on international terrorism.

We are pleased that you committed to address this problem and urge you to aggressively follow through on these pledges. We submit a series of additional recommended steps for you to consider while you are editing the earlier report.

1. immediately remove from the State Department's website the inaccurate and incomplete version of the report as well as any public testimony, speeches or transcripts based on that report;
2. upon completion of the revised report, forward the new report to any Congressional Committee that heard testimony based on the faulty report;

3. in order to clear up any misimpression that the earlier report may have left with the American public or with Congress, particularly as Congress begins deliberation on FY2005 appropriations measures, hold a public press conference to describe the corrections made to the original report and the implications of the new conclusions for our government's success in the war on terror;
4. initiate an investigation by the State Department's Inspector General into how the inaccurate statements found their way into the latest version of this report and whether the process for assembling this report and the participants involved differed significantly from previous years.

Prevailing in the war on terrorism will require the long-term cooperation of the American people and the world. Our government's credibility is essential to these efforts. By releasing an inaccurate report, the Administration has undermined out nation's credibility at a critical moment in the war on terrorism. We believe the best thing you can do to restore some of this lost credibility is to pursue the initiatives described above.

Thank you for your consideration.
Sincerely,

Tom Daschle	Harry Reid
Joseph R. Biden Jr.	Patrick Leahy
Carl Levin	John D. Rockefeller IV

Appendix B History of Patterns Report (1975–2003)

Year	Report Title	Issued by	Reporting
1975	International and Transnational Terrorism: Diagnosis and Prognosis[1]	CIA	Research study on trends in international terrorism. Data based on new "data bank" called International Terrorism: Attributes of Terrorist Events.
1976	International Terrorism in 1976[2]	CIA	Research paper
1977–1979	International Terrorism	National Foreign Assessment Center, CIA	Research papers
1981	Patterns of International Terrorism: 1981	Department of State (DOS)	Report issuance shifts from CIA to the Department
1982	Patterns of International Terrorism: 1982	DOS	First time Chronology of Significant Events appears in Patterns Report as Appendix A.
1983	Patterns of Global Terrorism: 1983	DOS	The report title changed to "Patterns of Global Terrorism."
1987	Patterns of Global Terrorism: 1987	DOS	Public Law 100-204 (Foreign Relations Authorization Act, FYs 1988–1989) required Department to provide Congress a full and complete annual report on terrorism.
1996	Patterns of Global Terrorism: 1996	DOS	Congress amends reporting requirements to include a requirement that the Department report on the extent to which other countries cooperate with the US in apprehending, convicting, and punishing terrorists responsible for attacking US citizens or interests and the extent to which foreign governments are cooperating in preventing future acts of terrorism.
2003 (revised)	Patterns of Global Terrorism	DOS	Appendix B, Chronology of Non-significant International Terrorist Incidents, was added.

1 Report contains caveat that study does not represent a CIA position, but that judgments are those of the author.
2 Ibid.

CRS Report for Congress

Proposals for Intelligence Reorganization, 1949–2004

Richard A. Best, Jr.
Specialist in National Defense, Foreign Affairs,
Defense, and Trade Division

Summary

Proposals for the reorganization of the United States Intelligence Community have repeatedly emerged from commissions and committees created by either the executive or legislative branches. The heretofore limited authority of Directors of Central Intelligence and the great influence of the Departments of State and Defense have inhibited the emergence of major reorganization plans from within the Intelligence Community itself.

Proposals to reorganize the Intelligence Community emerged in the period immediately following passage of the National Security Act of 1947 (P.L. 80-253) that established the position of Director of Central Intelligence (DCI) and the Central Intelligence Agency (CIA). Recommendations have ranged from adjustments in the DCI's budgetary responsibilities to the actual dissolution of the CIA and returning its functions to other departments. The goals underlying such proposals have reflected trends in American foreign policy and the international environment as well as domestic concerns about governmental accountability.

In the face of a hostile Soviet Union, early intelligence reorganization proposals were more concerned with questions of efficiency. In the Cold War context of the 1950s, a number of recommendations sought aggressively to enhance U.S. covert action and counterintelligence capabilities. The chairman of one committee charged with investigating the nation's intelligence capabilities, Army General James H. Doolittle, argued that sacrificing America's sense of "fair play" was wholly justified in the struggle to prevent Soviet world domination.

Following the failed invasion of Cuba at the Bay of Pigs, the unsuccessful results of intervention in Vietnam, and the Watergate scandal, investigations by congressional committees focused on the propriety of a wide range of heretofore accepted intelligence activities that included assassinations and some domestic surveillance of U.S. citizens. Some forcefully questioned the viability of secret intelligence agencies within a democratic society. These investigations resulted in much closer congressional oversight and a more exacting legal framework for intelligence activities. At the same time, the growth in technical intelligence capabilities led to an enhanced—but by no means predominant—leadership role for the DCI in determining community-wide budgets and priorities.

With the end of the Cold War, emerging security concerns, including transnational terrorism, narcotics trafficking, and proliferation of weapons of mass destruction, faced the United States. Some statutory changes were made in the mid-1990s, but their results were not far-reaching. In the aftermath of the September 11, 2001 attacks and the Iraq War, some observers urge reconsidering the intelligence organization. The 9/11 Commission has specifically recommended the establishment of a National Intelligence Director to manage the national intelligence program. Current intelligence organization issues can be usefully addressed with an awareness of arguments pro and con that were raised by earlier investigators; this recommendation has been incorporated in a number of bills, including S. 2845. This report will be updated as circumstances warrant.

Major portions of this report previously appeared as a separate section of the 1996 Staff Study published by the House Permanent Select Committee on Intelligence, *IC21: Intelligence Community in the 21st Century*. That report was prepared by Richard A. Best, Jr. and Herbert Andrew Boerstling.

Introduction

The National Security Act of 1947 (P.L. 80-253) established the statutory framework for the managerial structure of the United States Intelligence Community, including the Central Intelligence Agency (CIA) and the position of Director of Central Intelligence (DCI). A fundamental intent of this legislation was to coordinate, and to a certain extent centralize, the nascent intelligence efforts of the United States as an emergent superpower in the face of a hostile Soviet Union. In addition, the act provided the CIA with the ability to assume an operational role by charging it with:

> Perform[ing] such other functions and duties related to intelligence affecting the national security as the National Security Council may from time to time direct.[1]

In 1947, the foundation of the present-day Intelligence Community consisted only of the relatively small intelligence components in the Armed Services, the Departments of State and the Treasury, the Federal Bureau of Investigation (FBI), and the fledgling CIA. Since 1947, however, the Intelligence

---

1 Section 102(D)5, National Security Act of 1947, P.L. 80–253; hereafter cited as National Security Act of 1947.

Community "has greatly expanded in size and acquired a much broader range of responsibilities in the collection, analysis, and dissemination of foreign intelligence."[2]

The U.S. Intelligence Community is defined in the National Security Act as amended. It currently includes the following:

- Central Intelligence Agency;
- National Security Agency;
- Defense Intelligence Agency;
- National Geospatial-Intelligence Agency;
- National Reconnaissance Office;
- Intelligence elements of the Army, Navy, Air Force, Marine Corps, the Federal Bureau of Investigation, the Department of the Treasury, the Department of Energy, and the Coast Guard;
- Bureau of Intelligence and Research, Department of State;
- Elements of the Department of Homeland Security concerned with analyses of foreign intelligence information; and
- Coast Guard.[3]

Beginning in January 1948, numerous independent commissions, individual experts, and legislative initiatives have examined the growth and evolving mission of the Intelligence Community. Proposals by these groups have sought to address perceived shortcomings in the Intelligence Community's structure, management, role, and mission. These proposals have ranged in scope from basic organizational restructuring to the dissolution of the CIA.

In 1948 and 1949, two executive branch commissions examined the intelligence and operational missions of the CIA, and identified fundamental administrative and organizational loopholes in P.L. 80-253. By the 1950s, however, the physical growth and evolving mission of the Intelligence Community led subsequent commissions to broaden the scope of their proposals to include the enhancement of the DCI's community-wide authority, and the establishment of executive and legislative branch intelligence oversight committees. Unlike the intelligence investigations of the 1970s and 1980s, these early studies were primarily concerned with questions of efficiency and effectiveness rather than with issues of legality and propriety.

Following the Vietnam War and "Watergate," investigatory bodies became increasingly critical of the national intelligence effort. Beginning in the mid-1970s, the impetus shifted to the legislative branch where investigatory committees led by Senator Frank Church and Representative Otis G. Pike issued a broad range of proposals, including the separation of the DCI and CIA Director positions, dividing the CIA's analytical and operational responsibilities into two separate agencies, and the establishment of congressional oversight committees. In 1976 and 1977, respectively, recommendations by the these committees led to the establishment of the Senate Select Committee on Intelligence (SSCI) and the House Permanent Select Committee on Intelligence (HPSCI). These committees were heavily involved in the investigations into the Iran-Contra affair of the mid-1980s.

With the end of the Cold War, and in the wake of the Aldrich Ames espionage case, both the executive and legislative branches undertook studies to determine the future roles, capabilities, management, and structure of the Intelligence Community. These studies include such issues as the need to maintain the CIA as a separate entity, the extent and competence of U.S. counterintelligence (CI) efforts, and the managerial structure of intelligence components in the armed services and the Department of Defense (DOD). A comprehensive examination of the DCI's roles, responsibilities, authorities, and status was also undertaken. In an era of budgetary constraints and shifting policy concerns, these studies also examined personnel issues, allocation of resources, duplication of services, expanded use of open source Intelligence (OSCINT), and the need for maintaining a covert action (CA) capability. The results of this effort were reflected in organizational adjustments made by the Intelligence Authorization Act for FY1997 (P.L. 104-293), but some observers have subsequently concluded that this legislation did not go far enough and that, in the light of the events of September 11, 2001 and the Iraq War, intelligence organization questions need to be reevaluated.

The history of these investigations has witnessed the gradual transformation of intelligence from a White House asset to one that is shared between the executive and legislative branches. Congress not only has access to intelligence judgments but to most information that intelligence agencies acquire as well as to the details of intelligence activities. Congress has accepted some responsibility as a participant in the planning and conduct of covert actions. In significant measure, this process has been encouraged by these external intelligence investigations.

This report provides a chronological overview and examination of the major executive and legislative branch intelligence investigations made from January 1949 to date. Major proposals are listed in chronological order with a brief discussion of their respective results. Proposals specifically relating to congressional oversight of the Intelligence Community are not included in this report.

Intelligence Reform Proposals Made by Commissions and Major Legislative Initiatives

The Truman Administration, 1945–1953

Following the Second World War, the United States emerged as a global political, military, and economic leader. In the face of Soviet aggressiveness, the U.S. sought to enhance its national defense capabilities to curb the international spread of communism and to provide security for the nation itself.

The National Security Act (P.L. 80-253), signed July 26,

---

2 CRS Report 89–414 F, *Intelligence Community Leadership: Development and Debate since 1947*, by Alfred P. Prados, June 27, 1989, p. 1; hereafter cited as Prados, 89–414 F. (Out of print report; available upon request from the author.)

3 50 USC 401a(4)

1947, established the statutory framework for the managerial structure of the United States Intelligence Community, including the Central Intelligence Agency (CIA) and the position of Director of Central Intelligence (DCI). The act also created a semi-unified military command structure under a Secretary of Defense, and a National Security Council (NSC) to advise the President "with respect to the integration of domestic, foreign, and military policies relating to the national security."[4] The fundamental intent of this legislation was to coordinate U.S. national defense efforts, including intelligence activities, in the face of a Soviet Union intent upon expanding and leading a system of communist states.

In response to the rapid growth and changing role of the Federal government following the Second World War, several studies were conducted to examine the structure and efficiency of the executive branch, including the intelligence agencies.[5] Between 1948 and 1949, two important investigations of the national intelligence effort were conducted. The first, the Task Force on National Security Organization of the First Hoover Commission, was established by a unanimous vote in Congress. The second, known as the Dulles-Jackson-Correa Report, was initiated by the NSC at the request of President Harry S. Truman.

The First Hoover Commission, 1949

The Commission on Organization of the Executive Branch of the government was established pursuant to P.L. 80-162 of July 27, 1947.[6] Under the chairmanship of former President Herbert Hoover, the twelve member bipartisan commission conducted a comprehensive review of the federal bureaucracy, including the intelligence agencies. The commission's Task Force on National Security Organization was headed by Ferdinand Eberstadt, a strong advocate of a centralized intelligence capability who had been instrumental in drafting the National Security Act of 1947.[7]

Hearings conducted by the task force began in June 1948. On January 13, 1949, the Hoover Commission submitted the task force's 121 page unclassified report to Congress.[8] Known as the Eberstadt Report, it found the "National Security Organization, established by the National Security Act of 1947, [to be] soundly constructed, but not yet working well."[9] The report identified fundamental organizational and qualitative shortcomings in the national intelligence effort and the newly created CIA.

A principal concern of the task force was the adversarial relationship and lack of coordination between the CIA, the military, and the State Department. It suggested that this resulted in unnecessary duplication and the issuance of departmental intelligence estimates that "have often been subjective and biased."[10] In large measure, the military and State Department were blamed for their failure to consult and share pertinent information with the CIA. The task force recommended "that positive efforts be made to foster relations of mutual confidence between the [CIA] and the several departments and agencies that it serves."[11]

In short, the report stressed that the CIA "must be the central organization of the national intelligence system."[12] To facilitate community coordination in the production of national estimates, a founding intent of CIA, the task force recommended the creation within CIA "at the top echelon an evaluation board or section composed of competent and experienced personnel who would have no administrative responsibilities and whose duties would be confined solely to intelligence evaluation."[13] To foster professionalism and continuity of service, the report also favored a civilian DCI with a long term in office.[14]

In the arena of covert operations and clandestine intelligence, the Eberstadt Report supported the integration of all clandestine operations into one office within CIA, under NSC supervision. To alleviate concerns expressed by the military who viewed this proposal as encroaching upon their prerogatives, the report stated that clandestine operations should be the responsibility of the Joint Chiefs of Staff (JCS) in time of war.[15]

In examining the daily workings of the CIA, the task force found the agency's internal structure and personnel system "not now properly organized."[16] This led to recommendations for the adoption of clearer lines of departmental responsibilities, and the establishment of proper personnel selection and training systems.[17] In response to legislative concerns regarding intelligence budgets, the report supported establishing a legal framework for budgetary procedures and authorities, and in maintaining the secrecy of the CIA budget in

---

4 Section 101(a), National Security Act of 1947.

5 For a comprehensive examination of similar Commissions see CRS Report RL31446, *Reorganizing the Executive Branch in the Twentieth Century: Landmark Commissions,* by Ronald C. Moe, June 10, 2002.

6 The Report was reprinted as *The Hoover Commission Report on Organization of the Executive Branch of the Government* (Westport, CT: Greenwood Press, 1970.)

7 For background on Eberstadt, see Jeffrey M. Dorwart, *Eberstadt and Forrestal: A National Security Partnership: 1909–1949* (College Station, TX: Texas A & M University Press 1991.)

8 The Commission on Organization of the Executive Branch of the Government, *Task Force Report on National Security Organization,* Appendix G, January 1949; hereafter cited as the Eberstadt Report.

9 Eberstadt Report, p. 3.

10 Eberstadt Report, p. 76.

11 Eberstadt Report, p. 16, paragraph d.

12 Arthur B. Darling, *The Central Intelligence Agency: An Instrument of Government to 1950* (University Park, PA: Pennsylvania State University Press, 1990), p. 293. This is a reprint of an official CIA history prepared

13 Eberstadt Report, p. 76.

14 Darling, introduction to Chapter VIII.

15 Darling, introduction to Chapter VIII.

16 Eberstadt Report, p. 76.

17 Darling, pp. 295–298.

order to provide the "administrative flexibility and anonymity that are essential to satisfactory intelligence."[18] The report also addressed, and rejected, the possibility of placing the FBI's counterintelligence responsibilities in the CIA.[19]

Of particular concern was the level of professionalism in military intelligence, and the glaring inadequacies of medical and scientific intelligence, including biological and chemical warfare, electronics, aerodynamics, guided missiles, atomic weapons, and nuclear energy.[20] The report declared that the failure to appraise scientific advances in hostile countries (i.e., the Soviet Union) might have more immediate and catastrophic consequences than failure in any other field of intelligence. Accordingly, the report stressed that the U.S. should establish a central authority "to collect, collate, and evaluate scientific and medical intelligence."[21]

Intelligence Survey Group (Dulles-Jackson-Correa Report), 1949

On January 8, 1948, the National Security Council established the Intelligence Survey Group (ISG) to "evaluate the CIA's effort and its relationship with other agencies."[22] Commissioned at the request of President Truman, the group was composed of Allen W. Dulles, who had served in the Office of Strategic Services (OSS) during the Second World War and would become DCI in 1953, William Jackson, a future Deputy DCI, and Matthias Correa, a former assistant to Secretary of Defense James V. Forrestal when the latter had served as Secretary of the Navy during the war. Under the chairmanship of Dulles, the ISG presented its findings, known as the Dulles-Jackson-Correa Report, to the National Security Council on January 1, 1949.

The 193-page report, partially declassified in 1976, contained fifty-six recommendations, many highly critical of the CIA and DCI.[23] In particular, the report revealed problems in the agency's execution of both its intelligence and operational missions. It also criticized the quality of national intelligence estimates by highlighting the CIA's—and, by implication, the DCI's—"failure to take charge of the production of coordinated national estimates."[24] The report went on to argue that the CIA's current trend in secret intelligence activities should be reversed in favor of its mandated role as coordinator of intelligence.[25]

The Dulles Report was particularly concerned about the personnel situation at CIA, including internal security, the high turnover of employees, and the excessive number of military personnel assigned to the agency.[26] To add "continuity of service" and the "greatest assurance of independence of action," the report argued that the DCI should be a civilian and that military appointees be required to resign their commissions.[27]

As with the Eberstadt Report, the Dulles Report also expressed concern about the inadequacies in scientific intelligence and the professionalism of the service intelligence organizations, and urged that the CIA provide greater coordination.[28] This led to a recommendation for increased coordination between the DCI and the Director of the Federal Bureau of Investigation (FBI) in the arena of counterespionage. In turn, the report recommended that the Director of FBI be elevated to membership in the Intelligence Advisory Committee (IAC), whose function was to help the DCI coordinate intelligence and set intelligence requirements.[29]

The principal thrust of the report was a proposed large-scale reorganization of the CIA to end overlapping and duplication of functions. Similar to the Eberstadt Report, the Dulles study suggested incorporating covert operations and clandestine intelligence into one office within CIA. In particular, the report recommended that the Office of Special Operations (OSO), responsible for the clandestine collection of intelligence, and the Office of Policy Coordination (OPC), responsible for covert actions, be integrated into a single division within CIA.[30]

Accordingly, the report recommended replacing existing offices with four new divisions for coordination, estimates, research and reports, and operations. The heads of the new offices would be included in the immediate staff of the DCI so that he would have "intimate contact with the day-to-day operations of his agency and be able to give policy guidance to them."[31] These recommendations would become the blueprint for the future organization and operation of the present-day CIA.

---

18 Darling, p. 297.

19 Darling, p. 289.

20 Eberstadt Report, p. 77; Darling, p. 296.

21 Eberstadt Report, p. 20.

22 Mark M. Lowenthal, *U.S. Intelligence: Evolution and Anatomy* (Westport, CT: Praeger, 1992), p. 20.

23 "The Central Intelligence Agency and National Organization for Intelligence: A Report to the National Security Council," January 1, 1949. Hereafter cited as the Dulles-Jackson-Correa Report; the declassified report remains highly sanitized. A version was reprinted William M. Leary, ed., *The Central Intelligent Agency: History and Documents* (University, AL: University of Alabama Press, 1984).

24 Lowenthal, p. 20; Dulles-Jackson-Correa Report, p. 5, 11.

25 Dulles-Jackson-Correa Report, p. 39.

26 DCI Hillenkoetter disputed these findings by producing evidence that CIA's employee turnover was no different than in other government agencies and that only two percent of CIA personnel were active duty military. Darling, p. 327.

27 Dulles-Jackson-Correa Report, p. 138.

28 Dulles-Jackson-Correa Report, pp. 3–3, 149.

29 Dulles-Jackson-Correa Report, p. 58. Although the DCI served as chairman of the IAC, he was not given budgetary or administrative authority over the other intelligence agencies.

30 Dulles-Jackson-Correa Report, p. 129, 134.

31 Dulles-Jackson-Correa Report, p. 11.

Summary of the Truman Administration Intelligence Investigations

The Task Force on National Security Organization was almost immediately eclipsed by the Dulles-Jackson-Correa Report, that found a sympathetic ear in the White House. On July 7, 1949, the NSC adopted a modified version of the Dulles Report, and directed DCI Roscoe H. Hillenkoetter to begin implementing its recommendations, including the establishment of a single operations division at CIA. In 1953, the OSO and OPC were merged within the CIA to form the Directorate of Plans (DP). (DP was designated the Directorate of Operations (DO) in 1973.)

Although the Eberstadt Report was not as widely read among policymakers as the Dulles study, it did play a principal role in reorganization efforts initiated by DCI Walter Bedell Smith in 1950. The two reports, and the lessons learned from [the] fall of China to the Communists and the unexpected North Korean invasion of South Korea in June 1950, prompted Smith to create an intelligence evaluation board called the Board of National Estimates (BNE). Designed to review and produce National Intelligence Estimates (NIEs), the BNE was assisted by an Office of National Estimates (ONE) that drew upon the resources of the entire community.[32]

The Eisenhower Administration, 1953–1961

The Eisenhower Administration witnessed the Soviet Union solidify its hold over Eastern Europe, crushing the Hungarian revolution, and the rise of Communist insurgencies in Southeast Asia and Africa. This was a period in which extensive covert psychological, political, and paramilitary operations were initiated in the context of the threat posed by Soviet-led Communist expansion. However, between 1948, when a covert action program was first authorized through NSC Directive 10/2, and 1955 there was no formally established procedure for approval.

Between 1954 and 1956, this prompted three investigations into U.S. intelligence activities, including the CIA. The first, the Task Force on Intelligence Activities of the Second Hoover Commission on Organization of the Executive Branch of the Government, was sponsored by Congress. The second, the Doolittle Report, was commissioned at the request of President Dwight D. Eisenhower in response to the Second Hoover Commission. The third, the Bruce-Lovett Report was initiated by the President's Board of Consultants on Foreign Intelligence Activities (PBCFIA), and reported to President Eisenhower.

Second Hoover Commission, 1955

The Commission on Organization of the Executive Branch of the Government, also chaired by former President Hoover, was created pursuant to P.L. 83-108 of July 10, 1953. Known as the Second Hoover Commission, it contained a Task Force on Intelligence Activities under the chairmanship of General Mark W. Clark. In May 1955, the task force submitted both classified and unclassified reports. The classified version was sent directly to President Eisenhower, and has not been declassified according to available information. The unclassified version was sent to Congress.

The unclassified report's seventy-six pages contained nine recommendations and briefly described the evolution of the Intelligence Community and its then current functioning. The report initiated the official use of the term "Intelligence Community."[33] Until that time, the U.S. had sought to apply increasing coordination to departmental intelligence efforts, without the concept of a "community" of departments and agencies.

The task force began by expressing the need to reform the CIA's internal organization, including the recommendation that the DCI concentrate on intelligence issues facing the entire community by leaving the day-to-day administration of the CIA to an executive officer or chief of staff.[34] It foresaw the need for better oversight of intelligence activities and proposed a small, permanent, bipartisan commission, including Members of Congress and other "public-spirited citizens," to provide independent oversight of intelligence activities that were normally kept secret from other parts of the government.[35] The full commission's report elaborated on this by recommending the establishment of both a congressional oversight committee and a presidential advisory panel. The task force also expressed concern about counterintelligence and recommended systematic rechecking of all personnel every five years "to make sure that the passage of time has not altered the trustworthiness of any employee, and to make certain that none has succumbed to some weakness of intoxicants or sexual perversion."[36]

In addition, the task force recommended that the CIA replace the State Department in the "procurement of foreign publications and for collection of scientific intelligence."[37] Finally, there were a number of "housekeeping" recommendations

---

32 The work of BNE is described in Donald P. Steury, ed., *Sherman Kent and the Board of National Estimates: Collected Essays* (Washington: Center for the Study of Intelligence, 1994).

33 Commission on Organization of the Executive Branch of Government, A Report to Congress, *Intelligence Activities,* June 1955, p. 13, hereafter cited as Clark Task Force Report.

34 Clark Task Force Report, pp. 70–71. For a more detailed account of the evolution of the DCI's roles and responsibilities, see Herbert Andrew Boerstling, "The establishment of a Director of National Intelligence," unpublished Master of Arts Paper, Boston University, August 1995.

35 Clark Task Force Report, p. 71.

36 Clark Task Force Report, p. 74.

37 Clark Task Force Report, p. 74.

such as the need to construct an adequate CIA headquarters, to improve linguistic training, and to raise the salary of the DCI to $20,000 annually.[38]

The Doolittle Report, 1954

In response to the establishment of the Second Hoover Commission's Task Force on Intelligence Activities, President Eisenhower sought and secured an agreement for a separate report to be presented to him personally on the CIA's Directorate of Plans, that now had responsibility for both clandestine intelligence collection and covert operations. Accordingly, in July 1954, Eisenhower commissioned Lieutenant General James Doolittle (USAF) to report on the CIA's covert activities and to "make any recommendations calculated to improve the conduct of these operations."[39]

On September 30, 1954, Doolittle submitted his 69-page classified report directly to Eisenhower. Declassified in 1976, the Doolittle Report contained forty-two recommendations. The report began by summarizing contemporary American Cold War attitudes following the Korean War:

> It is now clear that we are facing an implacable enemy whose avowed objective is world domination by whatever means and at whatever cost. There are no rules in such a game... If the United States is to survive, long-standing American concepts of "fair play" must be reconsidered. We must develop effective espionage and counterespionage services and must learn to subvert, sabotage and destroy our enemies by more clever, more sophisticated and more effective methods than those used against us. It may become necessary that the American people be made acquainted with, understand and support this fundamentally repugnant philosophy.[40]

The report went on to recommend that "every possible scientific and technical approach to the intelligence problem" be explored since the closed society of the Eastern Bloc made human espionage "prohibitive" in terms of "dollars and human lives."[41]

In examining the CIA, Doolittle found it to be properly placed in the organization of the government. Furthermore, the report found the laws relating to the CIA's functions were sufficient for the agency to meet its operational needs, i.e. penetration of the Soviet Bloc.[42] The report went on to issue several recommendations calling for more efficient internal administration, including recruitment and training procedures, background checks of personnel, and the need to "correct the natural tendency to over classify documents originating in the agency."[43] It also called for increased cooperation between the clandestine and analytical sides of the agency, and recommended that the "Inspector General... operate on an Agency-wide basis with authority and responsibility to investigate and report on all activities of the Agency."[44] Finally, the report mentioned the need to provide CIA with accommodations tailored to its specific needs, and to exercise better control (accountability) of expenditures in covert projects.

Shortly after submitting the written report, General Doolittle voiced his concern to President Eisenhower over the potential difficulties that could arise from the fact that the DCI, Allen Dulles, and the Secretary of State, John Foster Dulles, were brothers and might implement policies without adequate consultation with other administration officials.[45]

Bruce-Lovett Report, 1956

In 1956, PBCFIA's chairman, James Killian, president of the Massachusetts Institute of Technology, directed David Bruce, a widely experienced diplomat, and Robert Lovett, a prominent attorney, to prepare a report for President Eisenhower on the CIA's covert action programs as implemented by NSC Directive 10/2. The report itself has not been located by either the CIA's Center for the Study of Intelligence or by private researchers. Presumably, it remains classified. However, Peter Grose, biographer of Allen Dulles, was able to use notes of the report prepared years earlier by historian Arthur M. Schlesinger, Jr.[46]

According to Grose's account of the Schlesinger notes, the report criticized the CIA for being too heavily involved in Third-World intrigues while neglecting the collection of hard intelligence on the Soviet Union. Reportedly, Bruce and Lovett went on to express concern about the lack of coordination and accountability of the government's psychological and political warfare program. Stating that "no charge is made for failure," the report claimed that "No one, other than those in CIA immediately concerned with their day-to-day operation, has any detailed knowledge of what is going on."[47] These operations, asserted Bruce and Lovett, were in the hands of a "horde of CIA representatives (largely under State or Defense cover),... bright, highly graded young men who

---

38 Clark Task Force Report, pp. 72–76.

39 The Report on the Covert Activities of the Central Intelligence Agency, September 30, 1954, Appendix A, p. 54; hereafter cited as the Doolittle Report.

40 Doolittle Report, pp. 6–7.

41 Doolittle Report, pp. 7–8.

42 Doolittle Report, p. 10.

43 Doolittle Report, p. 14.

44 Doolittle Report, p. 17.

45 John Ranelagh, *The Agency: The Rise and Decline of the CIA* (New York: Simon and Schuster, 1987), p. 278.

46 Peter Grose, *Gentleman Spy: The Life of Allen Dulles*, (Boston: Houghton Mifflin, 1994), pp. 445–448; also the CIA's Center for the Study of Intelligence *Newsletter*, Spring 1995, Issue No. 3, pp. 3–4. In writing this book, Grose reported using notes Arthur M. Schlesinger, Jr. discovered in the Robert Kennedy Papers before they were deposited in the John F. Kennedy Library, p. 598, n. 33 and n. 34. Reportedly, the JFK Presidential Library has unsuccessfully searched for the RFK papers for the report.

47 Grose, p. 446; from excepts of the Schlesinger notes.

must be doing something all the time to justify their reason for being."[48]

As had Doolittle, Bruce and Lovett criticized the close relationship between Secretary of State John Foster Dulles and his brother DCI Allen W. Dulles. Due to the unique position of each brother, the report apparently expressed concern that they could unduly influence U.S. foreign policy according to their own perceptions.[49]

The report concluded by suggesting that the U.S. reassess its approach to covert action programs, and that a permanent authoritative position be created to assess the viability and impact of covert action programs.[50]

Summary of the Eisenhower Administration Intelligence Investigations

As a result of the Second Hoover Commission's Report and General Doolittle's findings, two new NSC Directives, 5412/1 and 5412/2, were issued pertaining to covert activities in March and November 1955, respectively. Together, these directives instituted control procedures for covert action and clandestine activities. They remained in effect until 1970, providing basic policy guidelines for the CIA's covert action operations.

In 1956, in response to the Clark Task Force, and to preempt closer congressional scrutiny of intelligence gathering, President Eisenhower created the President's Board of Consultants on Foreign Intelligence Activities (PBCFIA) to conduct independent evaluations of the U.S. intelligence program. PBCFIA became the President's Foreign Intelligence Advisory Board (PFIAB) in 1961. Permanent intelligence oversight committees were not established in Congress until the mid-1970s.

When the Bruce-Lovett Report was first issued in the autumn of 1956, its immediate impact was muted due to the contemporaneous Suez Canal crisis and the Soviet invasion of Hungary. However, it did establish a precedent for future PBCFIA investigations into intelligence activities.

The Kennedy Administration, 1961–1963

In the 1950s, the Eisenhower Administration had supported covert CIA initiatives in Iran (1953) and Guatemala (1954) to overthrow governments unfriendly to the United States. These operations were planned to provide the United States with a reasonable degree of plausible deniability. During the last Eisenhower years, revolution in Cuba resulted in a Communist government under Fidel Castro. In the context of the Cold War, a communist Cuba appeared to justify covert U.S. action to secure a change in that nation's government. In April 1961 an ill-fated U.S. backed invasion of Cuba led to a new chapter in the history of the Intelligence Community.

On April 17, 1961, some 1,400 Cuban exiles of the Cuban Expeditionary Force (CEF), trained and supported by the CIA, landed at the Bay of Pigs in Cuba with the hope of overthrowing the communist regime of Fidel Castro. Known as Operation Zapata, the invasion was a complete disaster. Over the first two days, Castro succeeded in defeating the invasion force and exposing direct U.S. involvement.

The fiasco led to two official examinations of U.S. involvement and conduct in Operation Zapata. The first, the Taylor Commission, was initiated by President John F. Kennedy in an attempt to ascertain the overall cause of the operation's failure. The second, the Kirkpatrick Report, was an internal CIA investigation to determine what had been done wrong.

The Taylor Commission

On April 22, President Kennedy asked General Maxwell Taylor, former Army Chief of Staff, to chair a high-level body composed of Attorney General Robert Kennedy, former Chief of Naval Operations Admiral Arleigh Burke, and DCI Allen Dulles to ascertain the reasons for the invasion's failure. Known as the Taylor Commission, the study group's 53-page classified report was submitted to President Kennedy on June 13, 1961.

Declassified in 1977, the report examined the conception, development, and implementation of Operation Zapata. The commission's final report focused on administrative rather than operational matters, and evenly leveled criticism at the White House, the CIA, the State Department, and the Joint Chiefs of Staff.[51]

The report found that the CIA, at White House direction, had organized and trained Cuban exiles to enter Cuba, foment anti-Castro sentiment, and ultimately overthrow the Cuban government. Originally intended by the Eisenhower Administration as a guerrilla operation, Zapata was supposed to operate within the parameters of NSC Directive 5412/2, that called in part for plausible U.S. deniability. However, in the Kennedy Administration, the operation grew in size and scope to include a full-scale military invasion involving "sheep-dipped" B-26 bombers, supply ships and landing craft.[52] The report found that "the magnitude of Zapata could not be prepared and conducted in such a way that all U.S. support of it and connection with it could be plausibly disclaimed."[53]

---

48 Grose, p. 446; this observation is also taken from excerpts of the Schlesinger notes.

49 Grose, p. 447.

50 Grose, pp. 447–448; from excerpts of the Schlesinger notes.

51 Grose, p. 532.

52 "Sheep-dipped" is a colloquial intelligence term used for administrative arrangements designed to ensure that the origin of a person or object is non-traceable.

53 The report was published as *Operation Zapata: The "Ultrasensitive" Report and Testimony of the Board of Inquiry on the Bay of Pigs* (Fredrick, MD: University Publications of America, Inc., 1981), p. 40; hereafter referred cited as the Taylor Report.

In large measure, the report blamed the operation's planners at the CIA's Directorate of Plans for not keeping the President fully informed as to the exact nature of the operation. However, the report also criticized the State Department, JCS, and the White House for acquiescing in the Zapata Plan, that "gave the impression to others of approving it" and for reviewing "successive changes of the plan piecemeal and only within a limited context, a procedure that was inadequate for a proper examination of all the military ramifications."[54]

The Taylor Commission found the operation to be ill-conceived with little chance for ultimate success. Once underway, however, the report cited President Kennedy's decision to limit overt U.S. air support as a factor in the CEF's defeat.[55] This decision was apparently reached in order to protect the covert character of the operation. The report criticized this decision by stating that when an operation had been approved, "restrictions designed to protect its covert character should have been accepted only if they did not impair the chance of success."[56]

The failure in communication, breakdown in coordination, and lack of overall planning led the Taylor Commission to conclude that:

> The Executive Branch of government was not organizationally prepared to cope with this kind of paramilitary operation. There was no single authority short of the President capable of coordinating the actions of CIA, State, Defense and USIA [U.S. Information Agency]. Top level direction was given through *ad hoc* meetings of senior officials without consideration of operational plans in writing and with no arrangement for recording conclusions reached.[57]

The lessons of Operation Zapata led the report to recommend six courses of action in the fields of planning, coordination, effectiveness, and responsibility in overall Cold War strategy. The report recommended the creation of a Strategic Resources Group (SRG) composed of representatives of under-secretarial rank from the CIA and the Departments of State and Defense. With direct access to the President, the SRG would act as a mechanism for the planning and coordination of overall Cold War strategy, including paramilitary operations. The report recommended including the opinions of the JCS in the planning and implementation of such paramilitary operations. In the context of the Cold War, the report also recommended a review of restraints placed upon the United States in order to make the most effective use of the nation's assets, without concern for international popularity. The report concluded by reaffirming America's commitment to forcing Castro from power.[58]

The Kirkpatrick Report

Concurrent with the Taylor Commission, DCI Dulles instructed the CIA's Inspector General, Lyman B. Kirkpatrick, Jr., to conduct an internal investigation to determine what the CIA had done wrong in the Cuban operation. Completed in five months, the report was viewed by the few within CIA who read it as professionally shabby.[59] Whereas the Taylor Report had more of the detached perspective of a management-consultant, the Kirkpatrick Report was viewed as a personal attack against the CIA and DCI Dulles.

The 170-page report remains classified. However, in 1972, Kirkpatrick published an article in the *Naval War College Review* that apparently reflected the findings of his report.[60] In particular, Kirkpatrick criticized the Zapata planners at the Directorate of Plans for not having fully consulted the CIA's Cuban analysts before the invasion. The article also criticized the operation's internal security, that Kirkpatrick claimed was virtually nonexistent. Calling the operation frenzied, Kirkpatrick accused the CIA of "playing it by ear" and misleading the President by failing to inform him that "success had become dubious."[61] In Kirkpatrick's view, the CIA bore most of the blame, and the Kennedy Administration could be forgiven for having trusted the advice of the operation's planners at the Agency.

Summary of the Kennedy Administration Intelligence Investigations

On May 4, 1961, following the Bay of Pigs, President Kennedy reconstituted the PBCFIA as the President's Foreign Intelligence Advisory Board (PFIAB). Although little is known of the Kirkpatrick Report's impact, the Taylor Report influenced Kennedy's desire to improve the overall management of the intelligence process. In 1962, this prompted the President to instruct the new DCI, John McCone, to concentrate on his community-wide coordination role:

> As [DCI], while you will continue to have overall responsibility for the Agency, I shall expect you to delegate to your principal deputy, as you may deem necessary, so much of the detailed operation of the Agency as may be required to permit you to carry out your primary task as [DCI].[62]

---

54 Taylor Report, p. 43.

55 Taylor Report, p. 38.

56 Taylor Report, p. 40.

57 Taylor Report, p. 39.

58 Taylor Report, pp. 44–53.

59 Ranelagh, p. 380.

60 Lyman B. Kirkpatrick, Jr., "Paramilitary Case Study—Bay of Pigs," *Naval War College Review*, (November-December 1972). By the same author, see *The U.S. Intelligence Community: Foreign Policy and Domestic Activities* (New York: Hill and Wang, 1973).

61 Evan Thomas, *The Very Best Man, Four Who Dared: The Early Years of the CIA* (New York: Simon and Schuster, 1995), p. 268. Thomas was given special permission to review the report for use in his book even though it remains classified.

62 Memorandum for the Director of Central Intelligence, January 16, 1962; quoted in Prados, 89–414F, p. 45.

The Johnson Administration, 1963–1969

No major investigations of the Intelligence Community were conducted under President Lyndon B. Johnson. In large measure, this was due to America's growing preoccupation with the Vietnam conflict and the strain that this placed on the community's resources. The only major investigation during the Johnson Administration was the Warren Commission on the assassination of President Kennedy. Former DCI Allen Dulles served on the commission.

The Nixon Administration, 1969–1974

During the Vietnam War, the Intelligence Community devoted enormous attention in both manpower and resources towards achieving U.S. policy objectives in Southeast Asia. As the U.S. effort in Vietnam and Laos wound down, and attention turned towards strategic weapons concerns with the Soviet Union, some members of the Nixon Administration believed that the community was performing less than adequately. In 1970, President Richard M. Nixon and National Security Advisor Henry A. Kissinger undertook a review of the Intelligence Community's organization.

The Schlesinger Report, 1971

In December 1970, President Nixon commissioned the Office of Management and Budget (OMB) to examine the Intelligence Community's organization and recommend improvements, short of legislation. In March 1971, the report, "A Review of the Intelligence Community," was submitted by Deputy OMB Director James R. Schlesinger, a future DCI.

Known as the Schlesinger Report, the study's forty-seven pages noted the community's "impressive rise in . . . size and cost" with the "apparent inability to achieve a commensurate improvement in the scope and overall quality of intelligence products."[63] The report sought to uncover the causes of this problem and identify areas in which constructive change could take place.

In examining the Intelligence Community, Schlesinger criticized "unproductively duplicative" collection systems and the failure in forward planning to coordinate the allocation of resources.[64] In part, the report cited the failure of policymakers to specify their product needs to the intelligence producers.[65] However, the report identified the primary cause of these problems as the lack of a strong, central Intelligence Community leadership that could "consider the relationship between cost and substantive output from a national perspective."[66] Schlesinger found that this had engendered a fragmented, departmental intelligence effort.

To correct these problems, Schlesinger considered the creation of a Director of National Intelligence (DNI), enhancing the DCI's authority, and establishing a Coordinator of National Intelligence (CNI) who would act as the White House-level overseer of the Intelligence Community to provide more direct representation of presidential interest in intelligence issues.[67] In the end, the report recommended "a strong DCI who could bring intelligence costs under control and intelligence production to an adequate level of quality and responsiveness."[68]

Summary of the Nixon Administration Intelligence Investigation

The Schlesinger Report led to a limited reorganization of the Intelligence Community under a Presidential directive dated November 5, 1971. In part, the directive called for:

> An enhanced leadership role for the [DCI] in planning, reviewing, and evaluating all intelligence programs and activities, and in the production of national intelligence.[69]

Consequently, two boards were established to assist the DCI in preparing a consolidated intelligence budget and to supervise community-wide intelligence production. The first, was the ill-fated Intelligence Resources Advisory Committee (IRAC), that replaced the National Intelligence Resources Board (NIRB) established in 1968 under DCI Richard Helms. The IRAC was designed to advise the DCI on the preparation of a consolidated budget for the community's intelligence programs. However, IRAC was not afforded the statutory authority necessary to bring the intelligence budget firmly under DCI control. The second, and the only long lasting result of the Nixon directive, was the establishment of the Intelligence Community Staff (ICS) in 1972. Created by DCI Helms, the ICS was meant to assist the DCI in guiding the community's collection and production of intelligence. However, the ICS did not provide the DCI with the statutory basis necessary for an expanded community-wide role[70] In 1992, DCI Robert Gates replaced the ICS with the Community Management Staff (CMS).

---

63 *A Review of the Intelligence Community*, March 10, 1971, p. 1; hereafter cited as the Schlesinger Report.

64 Schlesinger Report, pp. 8–9.

65 Schlesinger Report, p. 9.

66 Schlesinger Report, p. 13.

67 Schlesinger Report, pp. 25–33.

68 U.S. Congress, Senate, 94th Congress, 2nd session, Select Committee to Study Governmental Operations with Respect to Intelligence Activities Intelligence, *Final Report*, 1976, Book I, p. 66; hereafter cited as the Church Committee Report.

69 Recognition of the U.S. Intelligence Community," *Weekly Compilation of Presidential Documents*, November 4, 1971, pp. 1467–1491, 1482.

70 Prados, 89–414F, p. 46.

The Era of Public Investigations, 1974–1981

In the late 1940s and throughout the 1950s, there had been widespread public agreement on the need for an effective national security structure to confront Soviet-led Communist expansion. However, by the late 1960s, the war in Vietnam had begun to erode public consensus and support for U.S. foreign policy. The controversy surrounding the Watergate Investigations after 1972, and subsequent revelations of questionable CIA activities involving domestic surveillance, provided a backdrop for increasing scrutiny of government policies, particularly in such fields as national security and intelligence.

Between 1975 and 1976, this led the Ford Administration and Congress to conduct three separate investigations that examined the propriety of intelligence operations, assessed the adequacy of intelligence organizations and functions, and recommended corrective measures. A fourth panel, convened earlier to look more broadly at foreign policy, also submitted recommendations for intelligence reform.

Murphy Commission (Commission on the Organization of the Government for the Conduct of Foreign Policy), 1975

The Commission on the Organization of the Government for the Conduct of Foreign Policy, created pursuant to the Foreign Relations Authorization Act for FY1973 (P.L. 92-352) of July 13, 1972, was headed by former Deputy Secretary of State Robert D. Murphy. It looked at national security formulation and implementation processes rather than the government as a whole. As such, the Murphy Commission was more focused than either of the two Hoover Commissions and devoted greater attention to intelligence issues. Although it made reference to the need to correct "occasional failures to observe those standards of conduct that should distinguish the behavior of agencies of the U.S. Government,"[71] the commission's approach was marked by an emphasis of the value of intelligence to national security policymaking and was, on the whole, supportive of the Intelligence Community.

Many of the Murphy Commission's recommendations addressed problems that have continued to concern successive intelligence managers. The commission noted the fundamental difficulty that DCIs have line authority over the CIA but "only limited influence" over other intelligence agencies.[72] Unlike other observers, the Murphy Commission did not believe that this situation should be changed fundamentally: "[It] is neither possible nor desirable to give the DCI line authority over that very large fraction of the intelligence community that lies outside the CIA." At the same time, it recommended that the DCI have an office in close proximity to the White House and be accorded regular and direct contact with the President. The commission envisioned a DCI delegating considerable authority for managing the CIA to a deputy while he devoted more time to community-wide responsibilities. The commission also recommended that the DCI's title be changed to Director of Foreign Intelligence.[73]

The commission provided for other oversight mechanisms, *viz.*, a strengthened PFIAB and more extensive review (prior to their initiation and on a continuing basis thereafter) of covert actions by a high-level interagency committee. It argued that although Congress should be notified of covert actions, the President should not sign such notifications since it is harmful to associate "the head of State so formally with such activities."[74] It was further recommended that intelligence requirements and capabilities be established at the NSC-level to remedy a situation in which "the work of the intelligence community becomes largely responsive to its own perceptions of what is important, and irrelevant information is collected, sometimes drowning out the important."[75] It also recommended that this process be formalized in an officially approved five-year plan. A consolidated foreign intelligence budget should also be prepared, approved by an inter-agency committee and OMB and submitted to Congress.

Although the importance of economic intelligence was recognized, the commission did not see a need for intelligence agencies to seek to expand in this area; rather, it suggested that the analytical capabilities of the Departments of State, Treasury, Commerce, Agriculture, and the Council of Economic Advisers should be significantly strengthened.

The commission noted the replacement of the Board of National Estimates by some eleven National Intelligence Officers (NIOs) who were to draw upon analysts in various agencies to draft National Intelligence Estimates (NIEs). This practice was criticized because it laid excessive burdens on chosen analysts and because NIEs had in recent years been largely ignored by senior officials (presumably Secretary of State Kissinger) who made their own assessments of future developments based on competing sources of information and analysis. Thus, the commission recommended a small staff of analysts from various agencies assigned to work with NIOs in drafting NIEs and ensure that differences of view were clearly presented for the policymakers.

Rockefeller Commission (Commission on CIA Activities within the United States), 1975

Prior to the mid-1960s, the organization and activities of the Intelligence Community were primarily the concern of specialists in national security and governmental organization. The Murphy Commission, although working during a subsequent and more politically turbulent period, had approached

---

71 U.S. Commission on the Organization of the Government for the Conduct of Foreign Policy, *Report*, June 1975, p. 92.

72 Commission on Organization of the Government, p. 98.

73 Commission on Organization of the Government, pp. 98–99.

74 Commission on Organization of the Government, pp. 100–101.

75 Commission on Organization of the Government, pp. 101.

intelligence reorganization from this perspective as well. The political terrain had, however, been shifting dramatically and the Intelligence Community would not escape searching criticism. During the era of the Vietnam War and Watergate, disputes over national security policy focused attention on intelligence activities. In 1975, media accounts of alleged intelligence abuses, some stretching back over decades led to a series of highly publicized congressional hearings.

Revelations of assassination plots and other alleged abuses spurred three separate investigations and sets of recommendations. The first was undertaken within the Executive Branch and was headed by Vice President Nelson A. Rockefeller. Other investigations were conducted by select committees in both houses of Congress. The Senate effort was led by Senator Frank Church and the House committee was chaired by Representative Otis Pike. These investigations led to the creation of the two permanent intelligence committees and much closer oversight by the Congress. In addition, they also produced a number of recommendations for reorganization and realignment within the Intelligence Community.

Established by Executive Order 11828 on January 4, 1975, the Commission on CIA Activities within the United States was chaired by Vice President Rockefeller and included seven others appointed by President Ford (including then-former Governor Ronald Reagan). The commission's mandate was to investigate whether the CIA had violated provisions of the National Security Act of 1947, precluding the CIA from exercising internal security functions.

The Rockefeller Commission's 30 recommendations[76] included a number of proposals designed to delimit CIA's authority to collect foreign intelligence within the United States (from "willing sources") and proscribe collection of information about the domestic activities of U.S. citizens, to strengthen PFIAB, to establish a congressional joint intelligence committee, and to establish guidelines for cooperation with the Justice Department regarding the prosecution of criminal violations by CIA employees. There was another recommendation to consider the question of whether the CIA budget should be made public, if not in full at least in part.

The commission recommended that consideration should be given to appointing DCIs from outside the career service of the CIA and that no DCI serve longer than 10 years. Two deputies should be appointed; one to serve as an administrative officer to free the DCI from day-to-day management duties; the other a military officer to foster relations with the military and provide technical expertise on military intelligence requirements.

The CIA position of Inspector General should be upgraded and his responsibilities expanded along with those of the General Counsel. Guidelines should be developed to advise agency personnel as to what activities are permitted and what are forbidden by law and executive orders.

The President should instruct the DCI that domestic mail openings should not be undertaken except in time of war and that mail cover operations (examining and copying of envelopes only) are to be undertaken only on a limited basis "clearly involving matters of national security."

The commission was specifically concerned with CIA infiltration of domestic organizations and submitted a number of recommendations in this area. Presidents should refrain from directing the CIA to perform what are essentially internal security tasks and the CIA should resist any effort to involve itself in improper activities. The CIA "should guard against allowing any component...to become so self-contained and isolated from top leadership that regular supervision and review are lost." Files of previous improper investigations should be destroyed. The agency should not infiltrate American organizations without a written determination by the DCI that there is a threat to agency operations, facilities, or personnel that cannot be met by law enforcement agencies. Other recommendations were directed at CIA investigations of its personnel or former personnel, including provisions relating to physical surveillance, wire or oral communications, and access to income tax information.

As a result of efforts by some White House staff during the Nixon Administration to use CIA resources improperly, a number of recommendations dealt with the need to establish appropriate channels between the agency and the Executive Office of the President.

Reacting to evidence that drugs had been tested on unsuspecting persons, the commission recommended that the practice should not be renewed. Also, equipment for monitoring communications should not be tested on unsuspecting persons within the United States. An independent agency should be established to oversee civilian uses of aerial photography to avoid any concerns over the improper domestic use of a CIA-developed system.

Concerned with distinguishing the separate responsibilities of the CIA and the Federal Bureau of Investigation (FBI), the commission urged that the DCI and the Director of the FBI prepare and submit to the National Security Council a detailed agreement setting forth the jurisdictions of each agency and providing for effective liaison between them.

The commission also recommended that all intelligence agencies review their holdings of classified information and declassify as much as possible.

Church Committee (Senate Select Committee to Study Governmental Operations with Respect to Intelligence Activities), 1976

Established in the wake of sensational revelations about assassination plots organized by the CIA, the Church Committee had a much wider mandate than the Rockefeller Commission, extending beyond the CIA to all intelligence agencies.[77]

---

76 *Report to the President by the Commission on CIA Activities Within the United States*, June 1975.

77 An informed account of the Church Committee's work is Loch K. Johnson, *A Season of Inquiry: Congress and Intelligence*, 2nd ed. (Chicago: Dorsey Press, 1988).

It too, however, concentrated on illegalities and improprieties rather than organizational or managerial questions *per se.* After extensive and highly publicized hearings, the committee made some 183 recommendations in its final report, issued April 26, 1976.[78]

The principal recommendation was that omnibus legislation be enacted to set forth the basic purposes of national intelligence activities and defining the relationship between intelligence activities and the Congress. Criticizing vagueness in the National Security Act of 1947, the committee urged charters for the several intelligence agencies to set forth general organizational structures and procedures, and delineate roles and responsibilities. There should also be specific and clearly defined prohibitions or limitations on intelligence activities. The effort to pass such legislation would consume considerable attention over a number of years, following the completion of the work of the Church Committee.

A number of recommendations reflected the committee's views on the appropriate role of the National Security Council in directing and monitoring the work of the intelligence agencies. The apparent goal was to encourage a more formal process, with accountability assigned to cabinet-level officials. The committee concluded that covert actions should be conducted only upon presidential authorization with notification to appropriate congressional committees.

Attention was given to the role of the DCI within the entire Intelligence Community. The committee recommended that the DCI be recognized by statute as the President's principal foreign intelligence advisor and that he should be responsible for establishing national intelligence requirements, preparing the national intelligence budget, and for providing guidance for intelligence operations.

The DCI should have specific responsibility for choosing among the programs of the different collection and production agencies and departments and to insure against waste and unnecessary duplication. The DCI should also have responsibility for issuing fiscal guidance for the allocation of all national intelligence resources. The authority of the DCI to reprogram funds within the intelligence budget should be defined by statute.[79]

Monies for the national intelligence budget would be appropriated to the DCI rather than to the directors of the various agencies. The committee also recommended that the DCI be authorized to establish an intelligence community staff to assist him in carrying out his managerial responsibilities. The staff should be drawn "from the best available talent within and outside the intelligence community."[80] Further, the position of Deputy DCI for the Intelligence Community should be established by statute (in addition to the existing DDCI who would have responsibility primarily for the CIA itself). It also urged consideration of separating the DCI from direct responsibility over the CIA.

The DCI, it was urged, should serve at the pleasure of the President, but for no more than ten years.

The committee also looked at intelligence analysis. It recommended a more flexible and less hierarchical personnel system with more established analysts being brought in at middle and upper grades. Senior positions should be established on the basis of analytical ability rather than administrative responsibilities. Analysts should be encouraged to accept temporary assignments at other agencies or on the NSC staff to give them an appreciation for policymakers' use of intelligence information. A system should be in place to ensure that analysts are more promptly informed about U.S. policies and programs affecting their areas of responsibility.

In addressing covert actions, the committee recommended barring political assassinations, efforts to subvert democratic governments, and support for police and other internal security forces engaged in systematic violations of human rights.

The committee addressed the questions of separating CIA's analysis and production functions from clandestine collection and covert action functions. It listed the pros and cons of this approach, but ultimately recommended only that the intelligence committees should give it consideration.

Reflecting concerns about abuses of the rights of U.S. citizens, the committee made a series of recommendations regarding CIA involvement with the academic community, members of religious organizations, journalists, recipients of government grants, and the covert use of books and publishing houses. A particular concern was limiting any influence on domestic politics of materials published by the CIA overseas. Attention was also given to proprietary organizations CIA creates to conduct operations abroad; the committee believed them necessary, but advocated stricter regulation and congressional oversight.

The committee recommended enhanced positions for CIA's Inspector General (IG) and General Counsel (GC), urging that the latter be made a presidential appointee requiring Senate confirmation.

In looking at intelligence agencies other than the CIA, the committee recommended that the Defense Intelligence Agency (DIA) be made part of the civilian Office of the Secretary of Defense and that a small J-2 staff provide intelligence support to the Joint Chiefs of Staff. It was urged that the directors of both DIA and the National Security Agency (NSA) should be appointed by the President and confirmed by the Senate. The committee believe that either the director or deputy director of DIA and of NSA should be civilians. Turning to the State Department, the committee urged the Administration to issue instructions to implement legislation that authorized ambassadors to be provided information about activities conducted by intelligence agencies in their assigned countries. It also stated that State Department efforts to collect foreign political and economic information overtly should be improved.

---

78 U.S. Congress, Senate, 94th Congress, 2nd session, Select Committee to Study Governmental Operations with respect to Intelligence Activities, Foreign and Military Intelligence, *Final Report*, Book I, S.Rept. 94–775, April 26, 1976; hereafter cited as the Church Committee Report.

79 Church Committee Report, pp. 434–435.

80 Church Committee Report, p. 435.

Funding for intelligence activities has been included in Defense Department authorization and appropriations legislation since the end of World War II. The Church Commission advocated making public, at least, total amounts and suggested consideration be given as to whether more detailed information should also be released. The General Accounting Office (GAO) should be empowered to conduct audits at the request of congressional oversight committees.

Tests by intelligence agencies on human subjects of drugs or devices that could cause physical or mental harm should not occur except under stringent conditions.

The committee made a number of recommendations regarding procedures for granting security clearances and for handling classified information. It also recommended consideration of new legislative initiatives to deal with other existing problems. Finally, the Committee recommended the creation of a registry of all classified executive orders, including NSC directives, with access provided to congressional oversight committees.

Pike Committee (House Select Committee on Intelligence), 1976

The House Select Committee on Intelligence, chaired by Representative Otis G. Pike, also conducted a wide-ranging survey of intelligence activities. In the conduct of its hearings, the Pike Committee was far more adversarial to the intelligence agencies than the Senate Committee. Publication of its final report was not authorized by the House, although a version was published in a New York tabloid. The Pike Committee's recommendations, however, were published on February 11, 1976.[81] There were some twenty recommendations, some dealing with congressional oversight, with one dealing, anomalously, with the status of the Assistant to the President for National Security Affairs.

The Pike Committee recommended that covert actions not include, except in time of war, any activities involving direct or indirect attempts to assassinate any individual. The prohibition was extended to all paramilitary operations. A National Security Council subcommittee would review all proposals for covert actions and copies of each subcommittee member's comments would be provided to congressional committees. The committee further recommended that congressional oversight committees be notified of presidential approval of covert actions within 48 hours. According to the proposal, all covert actions would have to be terminated no later than 12 months from the date of approval or reconsidered.

The committee recommended that specific legislation be enacted to establish NSA and define its role in monitoring communications of Americans and placed under civilian control.

The Pike Committee further recommended that all "intelligence related items" be included as intelligence expenditures in the President's budget and that the total sum budgeted for intelligence be disclosed.

The committee recommended that transfers of funds be prohibited between agencies or departments involved in intelligence activities. Reprogramming of funds within agencies would be dependent upon the specific approval of congressional oversight and appropriations committees. The same procedures would be required for expenditures from reserve or contingency funds.

The Pike Committee also looked at the role of the DCI. Like many others who have studied the question, it recommended that the DCI should be separate from managing any agency and should focus on coordinating and overseeing the entire intelligence effort with a view towards eliminating duplication of effort and promoting competition in analysis. It advocated that he should be a member of the National Security Council. Under this proposal the DCI would have a separate staff and would prepare national intelligence estimates and daily briefings for the President. He would receive budget proposals from agencies involved in intelligence activities. (The recommendations did not indicate the extent of his authority to approve or disapprove these recommendations.) The DCI would be charged with coordinating intelligence agencies under his jurisdiction, eliminating duplication, and evaluating performance and efficiency.

The committee recommended that the GAO conduct a full and complete management and financial audit of all intelligence agencies and that the CIA internal audit staff be given complete access to CIA financial records.

The committee recommended that a permanent foreign operations subcommittee of the NSC, composed of cabinet-rank officials, be established. This subcommittee would have jurisdiction over all authorized activities of intelligence agencies (except those solely related to intelligence gathering) and review all covert actions, clandestine activities, and hazardous collecting activities.

It was recommended that DIA be abolished and its functions divided between the Office of the Secretary of Defense and the CIA. The intelligence components of the military services would be prohibited from undertaking covert actions within the U.S. or clandestine activities against U.S. citizens abroad.

Relations between intelligence and law enforcement organizations were to be limited. Intelligence agencies would be barred from providing funds to religious or educational institutions or to those media with general circulation in the United States.

The committee recommended that specific legislation be considered to deal with the classification and regular declassification of information.

It was also recommended that an Inspector General for Intelligence be nominated by the President and confirmed by the Senate with authority to investigate potential misconduct of any intelligence agency or personnel. He would make annual reports to the Congress.

---

81 U.S. Congress, House of Representatives, 94th Congress, 2nd session, Select Committee on Intelligence, *Recommendations of the Final Report of the House Select Committee on Intelligence*, H.Rept. 94–833, February 11, 1976.

The committee also made recommendations regarding the organization and operations of the FBI and its role in investigating domestic groups.

In an additional recommendation, Representative Les Aspin, a member of the committee, urged that the CIA be divided into two separate agencies, one for analysis and the other for clandestine collection and covert operations. A similar recommendation was made by Representative Ron Dellums, who also served on the committee.

Clifford and Cline Proposals, 1976

In 1976 hearings by the Senate Committee on Government Operations, Clark Clifford (who had served as President Johnson's final Secretary of Defense and, in an earlier position in the Truman Administration, had been involved in legislation creating the CIA) proposed the creation of a post of Director General of Intelligence to serve as the President's chief adviser on intelligence matters and as principal point of contact with the congressional intelligence committees. There would be a separate director of the CIA whose duties would be restricted to day-to-day operations.[82]

In the same year, Ray Cline, a former Deputy Director of the CIA, made a number of recommendations.[83] He recommended that the DCI exert broad supervisory powers over the entire intelligence community and the CIA be divided into two agencies, one to undertake analytical work and the other for clandestine services. He also proposed that the DCI be given cabinet rank, a practice that would find support in both the Reagan and Clinton administrations.

Proposed Charter Legislation, 1978-1980

Subsequent to the establishment of permanent intelligence oversight committees in the Senate in 1976 and the House of Representatives in 1977, attention in Congress shifted to consideration of charter legislation for intelligence agencies.[84] It was envisioned that the charter legislation would include many of the recommendations made earlier by the Church and Pike Committees. Introduced by Senator Walter Huddleston and Representative Edward Boland, the draft National Intelligence Reorganization and Reform Act of 1978

---

82 U.S.Congress, Senate, 94th Congress, 2nd session, Committee on Government Operations, *Oversight of U.S. Government Intelligence Functions*, Hearings, Jan. 21-Feb. 6, 1976; pp. 203-204.

83 In his book *Secrets, Spices, and Scholars* (Washington: Acropolis Books, 1976).

84 The effort to pass intelligence charter legislation is described in John M. Oseth *Regulating U.S. Intelligence Operations: A Study in Definition of the National Interest* (Lexington, KY: University Press of Kentucky, 1985); also, Frank J. Smist, Jr., *Congress Oversees the United States Intelligence Community*, Second Edition, 1947–1994 (Knoxville, TN: University of Tennessee Press, 1994).

(S. 2525/H.R. 11245, 95th Congress) would have provided statutory charters to all intelligence agencies and created a Director of National Intelligence (DNI) to serve as head of the entire Intelligence Community. Day-to-day leadership of CIA could be delegated to a deputy at presidential discretion. The draft legislation contained numerous reporting requirements (regarding covert actions in particular) to Congress and an extensive list of banned or restricted activities. The draft legislation of more that 170 pages was strongly criticized from all sides in hearings; some arguing that it would legitimize covert actions inconsistent with American ideals and others suggesting that its complex restrictions would unduly hamper the protection of vital American interests. The bills were never reported out of either intelligence committee, although the Foreign Intelligence Surveillance Act of 1978 (P.L. 95-511) provided a statutory base for electronic surveillance within the United States.

Charter legislation was also introduced in the 96th Congress. It contained many of the provisions introduced in the earlier version, but also loosened freedom of information regulations for intelligence agencies and the requirements of the Hughes-Ryan amendments of 1974 requiring that some eight committees be notified of covert actions. This legislation (S. 2284, 96th Congress) came under even heavier criticism from all sides than its predecessor. It was not reported by the Senate Intelligence Committee, but other stand-alone legislation did pass and a shorter bill reducing the number of committees receiving notification of covert actions—and "significant anticipated intelligence activities"—was introduced and eventually became law in October 1980 as part of the FY1981 Intelligence Authorization Act (P.L. 96-450).

The Executive Branch Response, 1976–1981

Concurrent with, and subsequent to, these legislative initiatives, the Executive Branch, in part to head off further congressional action, implemented some of the more limited recommendations contained in their respective proposals. Presidents Gerald Ford, Jimmy Carter, and Ronald Reagan each issued detailed Executive Orders (E.O.) setting guidelines for the organization and management of the U.S. Intelligence Community.

Issued by President Ford on February 18, 1976, prior to the release of the Church and Pike Committee findings, Executive Order 11905 undertook to implement some of the more limited recommendations of the Rockefeller and Murphy Commissions. In particular, E.O. 11905 identified the DCI as the President's primary intelligence advisor and the principal spokesman for the Intelligence Community and gave him responsibilities for developing the National Foreign Intelligence Program (NFIP). It also delineated responsibilities of each intelligence agency, provided two NSC-level committees for internal review of intelligence operations, and established a separate three-member Intelligence Oversight Board to review the legality and propriety of intelligence activities. It placed restrictions on the physical and electronic surveillance of American citizens by intelligence agencies.[85]

On January 24, 1978, President Carter issued Executive Order 12036, that superseded E.O. 11905.[86] Carter's Executive Order sought to define more clearly the DCI's community-wide authority in areas relating to the "budget, tasking, intelligence review, coordination and dissemination, and foreign liaison."[87] In particular, it formally recognized the establishment of the National Foreign Intelligence Program budget and the short-lived National Intelligence Tasking Center (NTIC), that was supposed to assist the DCI in "translating intelligence requirements and priorities into collection objectives."[88] E.O. 11905 also restricted medical experimentation and prohibited political assassinations.

President Reagan continued the trend towards enhancing the DCI's community-wide budgetary, tasking, and managerial authority. On December 4, 1981, he issued Executive Order 12333, detailing the roles, responsibilities, missions, and activities of the Intelligence Community. It supplanted the previous orders issued by Presidents Ford and Carter. E.O. 12333 remains the governing executive branch mandate concerning the managerial structure of the Intelligence Community.

E.O. 12333 designates the DCI "as the primary intelligence advisor to the President and NSC on national foreign intelligence."[89] In this capacity, the DCI's duties include the implementation of special activities (covert actions), liaison to the nation's foreign intelligence and counterintelligence components, and the overall protection of the community's sources, methods, and analytical procedures.[90] It grants the DCI "full responsibility for [the] production and dissemination of national foreign intelligence," including the authority to task non-CIA intelligence agencies, and the ability to decide on community tasking conflicts.[91] The order also sought to grant the DCI more explicit authority over the development, implementation, and evaluation of NFIP.[92]

To a certain extent, E.O. 12333 represented a relaxation of the restrictions placed upon the community by Carter. Although it maintained the prohibition on assassination, the focus was on "authorizations" rather than "restrictions." "Propriety" was removed as a criterion for approving operations. Arguably, the Reagan Administration established a presumption in favor of government needs over individual rights.[93] However, in the absence of legislation, the DCI continued to lack statutory authority over all aspects of the Intelligence Community, including budgetary issues.

The Turner Proposal, 1985

In 1985, Admiral Stansfield Turner, DCI in the Carter Administration, expressed his views on the need for intelligence reform.[94] In part, Turner recommended reducing the emphasis on covert action and implementing a charter for the Intelligence Community. The most important recommendation involved the future of the DCI of which Turner maintained:

The two jobs, head of the CIA and head of the Intelligence Community, conflict. One person cannot do justice to both and fulfill the DCI's responsibilities to the President, the Congress, and the public as well.[95]

Turner went on to propose the separation of the two jobs of DCI and head of the CIA with the creation of a Director of National Intelligence, separate and superior to the CIA. Turner also recommended placing less emphasis on the use of covert action than the Reagan Administration.

Iran-Contra Investigation, 1987

During highly publicized investigations of the Reagan Administration's covert support to Iran and the Nicaraguan Resistance, the role of the Intelligence Community, the CIA, and DCI Casey were foci of attention. Much of the involvement of National Security Council staff was undertaken precisely because legislation had been enacted severely limiting the role of intelligence agencies in Central America and because efforts to free the hostages through cooperation with Iranian officials had been strongly opposed by CIA officials. The executive branch's review, chaired by former Senator John Tower, expressed concern that precise procedures be established for restricted consideration of covert actions and that NSC policy officials had been too closely involved in the preparation of intelligence estimates.[96] The investigation of the affair by two congressional select committees resulted in a number of recommendations for changes in laws and regulations governing intelligence activities.

Specifically the majority report of the two congressional select committees that investigated the affair made a number

---

85 Executive Order 11905, February 18, 1976, United States Foreign Intelligence Activities, as summarized in Alfred B. Prados, *Intelligence Reform: Recent History and Proposals*, CRS Report 88–562F, August 18, 1988, p. 18; hereafter cited as Prados, 88–562F. (Out of print report; available upon request from the author.)

86 Executive Order 12036, January 24, 1978, United States Intelligence Activities; hereafter cited as Executive Order 12036.

87 Lowenthal, p. 107.

88 Bruce W. Watson, Susan M. Watson, and Gerald W. Hopple, *United States Intelligence: An Encyclopedia* (New York, Garland Publishing, 1990), p.231.

89 Section 1.5(a), Executive Order 12333, December 4, 1981, United States Intelligence Agency.

90 Executive Order 12333, Section 1.5(d,e,h).

91 Executive Order 12333, Section 1.5(k,h).

92 Lowenthal, p. 107.

93 See Oseth, *Regulating U.S. Intelligence Operations*, especially p. 155.

94 In his book *Secrecy and Democracy: The CIA in Transition* (Boston: Houghton Mifflin, 1985).

95 *Secrecy and Democracy*, p. 273.

96 U.S., President's Special Review Board, Report, 1987, pp. V-5–V-6.

of recommendations regarding presidential findings concerning the need to initiative covert actions. Findings should be made prior to the initiation of a covert action, they should be in writing, and they should be made known to appropriate Members of Congress in no event later than forty-eight hours after approval. Further, the majority of the committees urged that findings be far more specific than some had been in the Reagan Administration. Statutory inspector general and general counsels, confirmed by the Senate, for the CIA were also recommended.[97] Minority members of the two committees made several recommendations regarding congressional oversight, urging that on extremely sensitive matters that notifications of covert actions be made to only four Members of Congress instead of the existing requirement for eight to be notified.[98]

These recommendations were subsequently considered by the two intelligence committees. A number of provisions was enacted dealing with covert action findings in the Intelligence Authorization Act for FY1991 (P.L. 102-88).

Boren-McCurdy, 1992

A major legislative initiative, reflecting the changed situation of the post-Cold War world, began in February 1992, when Senator David Boren, the Chairman of the Senate Select Committee on Intelligence, and Representative Dave McCurdy, the Chairman of the House Permanent Select Committee on Intelligence, announced separate plans for an omnibus restructuring of the U.S. Intelligence Community, to serve as an intelligence counterpart to the Goldwater-Nichols Department of Defense Reorganization Act of 1986. The two versions of the initiative (S. 2198 and H.R. 4165, 102nd Congress) differed in several respects, but the overall thrust of the two bills was similar. Both proposals called for the following:

- Creating a Director of National Intelligence (DNI) with authority to program and reprogram intelligence funds throughout the Intelligence Community, including the Defense Department, and to direct their expenditure; and to task intelligence agencies and transfer personnel temporarily from one agency to another to support new requirements;
- Creating two Deputy Directors of National Intelligence (DDNIs); one of whom would be responsible for analysis and estimates, the other for Intelligence Community affairs;

- Creating a separate Director of the CIA, subordinate to the new DNI, to manage the agency's collection and covert action capabilities on a day-to-day basis;
- Consolidating analytical and estimative efforts of the Intelligence Community (including analysts from CIA, and some from DIA, the Bureau of Intelligence and Research (INR) at the State Department, and other agencies) into a separate office under one of the Deputy DNIs (this aspect of the proposal would effectively separate CIA's analytical elements from its collection and covert action offices);
- Creating a National Imagery Agency within the Department of Defense (DOD) to collect, exploit, and analyze imagery (these tasks had been spread among several entities; the House version would divide these efforts into two new separate agencies); and
- Authorizing the Director of DIA to task defense intelligence agencies (DIA, NSA, the new Imagery Agency) with collection requirements; and to shift functions, funding, and personnel from one DOD intelligence agency to another.

This major restructuring effort would have provided statutory mandates for agencies where operational authority was created by executive branch directives. Both statutes and executive branch directives provided the DCI authority to task intelligence agencies outside the CIA and to approve budgets and reprogramming efforts; in practice, however, this authority had never been fully exercised. This legislation would have provided a statutory basis for the DCI (or DNI) to direct collection and analytical efforts throughout the Intelligence Community.

The Boren-McCurdy legislation was not adopted, although provisions were added to the FY1994 Intelligence Authorization Act (P.L. 102-496) that provided basic charters for intelligence agencies within the National Security Act and set forth in law the DCI's coordinative responsibilities *vis-à-vis* intelligence agencies other than the CIA. Observers credited strong opposition from the Defense Department and concerns of the Armed Services Committees with inhibiting passage of the original legislation.

Commission on the Roles and Capabilities of the U.S. Intelligence Community (Aspin/Brown Commission), 1995–1996

Established pursuant to the Intelligence Authorization Act for FY1995 (P.L. 103-359) of September 27, 1994, the Commission on the Roles and Capabilities of the U.S. Intelligence Community was formed to assess the future direction, priorities, and structure of the Intelligence Community in the post-Cold War environment. Originally under the chairmanship of Les Aspin, after his sudden death the commission was headed by former Secretary of Defense Harold Brown. Nine members were appointed by the president and eight nominated by the congressional leadership.

---

97 U.S. Congress, 100th Congress, 1st session, Senate Select Committee on Secret Military Assistance to Iran and the Nicaraguan Opposition and U.S. House of Representatives Select Committee to Investigate Covert Arms Transactions with Iran, *Report of the Congressional Committees Investigating the Iran-Contra Affair with Supplemental, Minority, and Additional Views,* S.Rept. 100–216/H.Rept. 100–433, November 17, 1987, pp. 243–427; hereafter cited as the Iran-Contra Report.

98 Iran-Contra Report, pp. 583–586.

The Report of the Aspin/Brown Commission[99] made a number of recommendations regarding the organization of the Intelligence Community. Structural changes in the NSC staff were proposed to enhance the guidance provided to intelligence agencies. Global crime—terrorism, international drug trafficking, proliferation of weapons of mass destruction, and international organized crime—was given special attention with recommendations for an NSC Committee on Global Crime. The Commission also recommended designating the Attorney General to coordinate the "nation's law enforcement response to global crime," and clarifying the authority of intelligence agencies to collect information concerning foreign persons abroad for law enforcement purposes. It urged that the sharing of relevant information between the law enforcement and intelligence communities be expanded, and their activities overseas be better coordinated.[100]

The Commission noted that it considered many options for dealing with limitations in the DCI's ability to coordinate the activities of all intelligence agencies. The Aspin/Brown Commission recommended the establishment of two new deputies to the DCI—one for the Intelligence Community and one for day-to-day management of the CIA. Both would be Senate-confirmed positions and the latter for a fixed six-year term. The DCI would concur in the appointment of the heads of "national" intelligence elements within DOD and would evaluate their performance in their positions as part of their ratings by the Secretary of Defense. "In addition, the DCI would be given new tools to carry out his responsibilities with respect to the intelligence budget and new authority over the intelligence personnel systems."

The Aspin/Brown Commission recommended the realignment of intelligence budgeting procedures with "discipline" (i.e. sigint, imagery, humint, *etc.*) managers having responsibilities for managing similar efforts in all intelligence agencies. "The DCI should be provided a sufficient staff capability to enable him to assess tradeoffs between programs or program elements and should establish a uniform, community-wide resource data base to serve as the principal information tool for resource management across the Intelligence Community."[101]

Responding to a longstanding criticism of intelligence budget processes, the Commission recommended that the total amounts appropriated for intelligence activities be disclosed—a recommendation that was implemented by the Clinton Administration for Fiscal Years 1997 and 1998. Subsequently, however, figures were not made public.

In regard to congressional oversight, the Aspin/Brown Commission recommended that appointments to intelligence committees not be made for limited numbers of years but treated like appointments to other congressional committees.

IC21: Intelligence Community in the 21st Century, 1996

In addition to the Aspin/Brown Commission, in 1995–1996 the House Intelligence Committee undertook its own extensive review of intelligence issues. Many of the conclusions of the resultant IC21 Staff Study were consistent with those of the Commission.[102] The "overarching concept" was a need for a more "corporate" intelligence community, i.e. a collection of agencies that recognize that they are parts of "a larger coherent process aiming at a single goal: the delivery of timely intelligence to policy makers at various levels." Accordingly, "central management should be strengthened, core competencies (collection, analysis, operations) should be reinforced and infrastructure should be consolidated wherever possible."[103]

Specific IC21 recommendations provided for a radically restructured community and included

- the DCI should have a stronger voice in the appointment of the directors of NFIP defense agencies;
- the DCI should have greater programmatic control of intelligence budgets and intelligence personnel;
- a Committee on Foreign Intelligence should be established within the National Security Council;
- two DDCIs should be established; one to direct the CIA and managing analysis and production throughout the Community and the other responsible for IC-wide budgeting, requirements and collection management and tasking, infrastructure management and system acquisition;
- establishment of a Community Management Staff with IC-wide authority over, and coordination of, requirements, resources and collection;
- there should be a uniformed officer serving as Director of Military Intelligence with authority to manage/coordinate defense intelligence programs (JMIP and TIARA);
- the Clandestine Service, responsible for all humint, should be separated from the CIA, reporting directly to the DCI;
- a Technical Collection Agency should be established to create an IC-wide management organization responsible for directing all collection tasking by all agencies and ensuring a coherent, multidiscipline approach to all collection issues;
- there should be common standards and protocols for technical collection systems, from collection through processing, exploitation and dissemination;
- a Technology Development Office should be established to perform community research and development functions; and

---

99 Report of the Commission of the Roles and Capabilities of the United States Intelligence Community, *Preparing for the 21st Century: An Appraisal of U.S. Intelligence* (Washington Government Printing Office, 1996).
100 Ibid., p. xix.
101 Ibid., p. xxi.

102 U.S. Congress, 104th Congress, House of Representatives, Permanent Select Committee on Intelligence, Staff Study, *IC21: Intelligence Community in the 21st Century*, April 9, 1996.
103 Ibid., p. 9.

- congressional oversight should be strengthened by the establishment of a joint intelligence committee; alternatively the House intelligence committee should be made a standing committee without tenure limits.

The Response to Aspin/Brown and IC21: The Intelligence Authorization Act for FY1997

Congressional Response

The recommendations of the Aspin/Brown Commission and the IC21 Study led to extensive congressional consideration of intelligence organization issues. The House Intelligence Committee considered separate legislation on intelligence organization (H.R. 3237, 104th Congress); the Senate included extensive organizational provisions as part of the intelligence authorization bill for FY1997 (S. 1718, 104th Congress). In addition, the Defense Authorization Act for FY1997 (P.L. 104-201) included provisions establishing the National Imagery and Mapping Agency (NIMA)[104] that combined elements from intelligence agencies as well as the Defense Mapping Agency which had not been part of the Intelligence Community.[105]

The conference version of the FY1997 intelligence authorization legislation, eventually enacted as P.L. 104-293, included as its Title VIII, the "Intelligence Renewal and Reform Act of 1996." The act established within the NSC two committees, one on foreign intelligence and another on transnational threats. The former was to identify intelligence priorities and establish policies. The latter was to identify transnational threats and develop strategies to enable the U.S. to respond and to "develop policies and procedures to ensure the effective sharing of information about transnational threats among Federal departments and agencies, including law enforcement agencies and the elements of the intelligence community...."[106]

Two deputy DCI positions were established, one for Deputy DCI and the other for a Deputy DCI for Community Management, both Senate-confirmed positions. While the Deputy DCI would have responsibilities coterminous with those of the DCI, the Deputy DCI for Community Management would focus on the coordination of all intelligence agencies. Congress did not attempt to establish a position for a head of the CIA separate from that of the DCI.

In addition to the two deputy DCIs, the legislation provided for three assistant DCIs—for Collection, for Analysis and Production of Intelligence, and for Administration. The statute calls for all three assistant DCI positions to be filled by, and with, the advice and consent of the Senate. The statute is clear that the positions were envisioned as being designed to enhance intelligence capabilities and coordination of the efforts of all intelligence agencies. In addition, the legislation required that the DCI concur in the appointment of three major defense intelligence agencies—NSA, the NRO, and NIMA (later renamed the National Geospatial-Intelligence Agency). If the DCI failed to concur, the nominations could still be forwarded to the President, but the DCI's non-concurrence had to be noted. The act required that the DCI be consulted in the appointment of the DIA director, the Assistant Secretary of State for Intelligence and Research, and the director of the Office of Nonproliferation and National Security of the Energy Department.[107] The FBI director is required to give the DCI timely notice of an intention to fill the position of assistant director of the FBI's National Security Division.

The act gave the DCI authority to develop and present to the President an annual budget for the National Foreign Intelligence Program and to participate in the development by the Secretary of Defense of the Joint Military Intelligence Program (JMIP) and the Tactical Intelligence and Related Activities Program (TIARA). Moreover, the DCI gained authority to "approve collection requirements, determine collection priorities, and resolve conflicts in collection priorities levied on national collection assets, except as otherwise agreed with the Secretary of Defense pursuant to the direction of the President."[108]

Presidential Statement.

President Clinton signed the legislation on October 11, 1996, but in so doing he stated concerns about provisions that "purport to direct" the creation of two new NSC committees. "Such efforts to dictate the President's policy process unduly intrude upon Executive prerogatives and responsibilities. I would note that under my Executive authority, I have already asked the NSC to examine these issues." Furthermore, he criticized provisions requiring the DCI to concur or be consulted before the appointment of certain intelligence officials. This requirement, he argued, "is constitutionally questionable in two areas: regarding limitations on the President's ability to receive the advice of cabinet officers; and regarding circumscription of the President's appointment authority."

---

104 In 2003 NIMA was renamed the National Geospatial-Intelligence Agency (NGA).

105 For the creation of NIMA, see Anne Daugherty Miles, "The Creation of the National Imagery and Mapping Agency: Congress's Role as Overseer," Occasional Page Number Nine, Joint Military Intelligence College, April 2001.

106 Codified at 50 USC 402(i)(4)(F); transnational threats were defined as "any transnational activity (including international terrorism, narcotics trafficking, the proliferation of weapons of mass destruction and the delivery systems for such weapons, and organized crime) that threatens the national security of the United States," 50USC 402(i)(5)(A).

107 Subsequently modified in 2001 by P.L. 107–108 to substitute the Director of the Office of Counterintelligence of the Department of Energy. More recently, legislation signed in 2003 added the Assistant Secretary of Intelligence and Analysis of the Department of Treasury (P.L. 108–381).

108 50 USC 403-3(c)(1)(3).

The statement also noted the "strong opposition" by DCI John Deutch to provisions establishing three new assistant DCIs, each requiring Senate confirmation. President Clinton added: "I share his concerns that these provisions will add another layer of positions requiring Senate confirmation without a corresponding gain in the DCI's authority or ability to manage the Intelligence Community. I understand that the DCI intends to seek repeal or significant modification of these provisions in the 105th Congress. I will support such efforts."[109]

Implementation

George Tenet, nominated to succeed John Deutch, responded to a question from Senator Robert Kerrey during his Senate confirmation hearing in May 1997, that "I may have some changes in the law in my own mind, if I'm confirmed, that allows us to meet your objectives. And I want to come work with you on it." Tenet also indicated that he believed that the DCI's statutory responsibilities for coordinating the work of all intelligence agencies was adequate.[110]

In May 1998, the Senate Intelligence Committee held a hearing on the nomination of Joan A. Dempsey as the first Deputy DCI for Community Management. In opening remarks, Chairman Shelby noted discussions with the executive branch regarding the positions established by P.L. 104-293:

> we have reached an accommodation with the Director of Central Intelligence on these positions, and we expect that the President to put forward a nominee for the position of Assistant Director of Central Intelligence for Administration, or ADCI, soon. We have agreed to allow the DCI to fill the positions of ADCI for Collection and ADCI for Analysis and Production without exercising the Senate's right for advice and consent for up to one year while we assess the new management structure.[111]

Dempsey in her testimony succinctly set forth the fundamental problem of intelligence organization:

> It's somewhat amusing to me—and I've spent most of my career in the Department of Defense... and when I was in DOD there was always this fear that a very powerful DCI with a full-time emphasis on intelligence and managing the community would fail to support the DOD the way it needed to be supported with intelligence. Since I've come over to the Central Intelligence Agency side of the intelligence community, I've found the same fear, but this time directed at what DOD is going to do to subvert the role of the DCI.

She noted, however, the establishment of coordinative mechanisms such as the Defense Resources Board and the Intelligence Program Review Group and "constant accommodations made by Secretaries of Defense and DCIs to work together to find solutions to problems." In general, she argued, "the relations have been good."[112]

The following February, the Senate Intelligence Committee met to consider the nomination of James Simon as Assistant DCI for Administration. At the hearing, the Vice Chairman, Senator Robert Kerrey, noted that the DCI had taken the interim steps of appointing Acting Assistant Directors for collection and for analysis. He added: "I expect Presidential nominations for these positions will be forthcoming soon."[113] He noted, however, that "Once the 1997 Authorization Act was passed, the Community resisted mightily the appointment of Assistant Directors of Central Intelligence for collection and analysis."[114]

Simon testified that he would be responsible for "the creation of a process to ensure that the needs of all customers—strategic and tactical, intelligence and battlefield surveillance, traditional and novel—are articulated, validated, and made manifest in our programs.[115] Simon noted in passing the importance of a highly capable staff to perform coordination missions; he referred to the former Intelligence Community Staff as having had "a certain percentage of people there who, frankly, had retired in place or were considered to be brain dead and wanted a quiet place where they could make it to retirement without being bothered. A greater proportion were those that their agencies either didn't want or that they felt were not progressing acceptably within their own agency...."[116]

Both Dempsey and Simon were confirmed by the Senate and served for several years in their respective positions. In July 2003 Dempsey, having left the DDCI position, was appointed Executive Director of the President's Foreign Intelligence Advisory Board; Simon retired in 2003. Only in July 2004 was Larry Kindsvater confirmed by the Senate as DDCI for Community Management; nominations for assistant DCI positions have not been submitted. The statutory provisions remain in place, however.

Despite the effort that went into the FY1997 legislation, the efforts intended to enhance the DCI's community-wide

---

109 Statement on Signing the Intelligence Authorization Act for Fiscal Year 1997, October 11, 1996, *Weekly Compilation of Presidential Documents,* October 14, 1996, p. 2039.

110 U.S. Congress, 105th Congress, 1st session, Senate, Select Committee on Intelligence, *Nomination of George J. Tenet to be Director of Central Intelligence,* S. Hearing 105–314, May 6, 1997, pp. 64, 89.

111 U.S. Congress, 105th Congress, 2nd session, Senate, Select Committee on Intelligence, Hearing, *Nomination of Joan M. Dempsey to be Deputy Director of Intelligence for Community Management,* Senate Hearing.

112 Ibid., p. 40.

113 U.S. Congress, 106 Congress, 1st session, Senate, Select Committee on Intelligence, Hearing, *Nomination of James M. Simon, Jr., to be Assistant Director of Central Intelligence for Administration,* Senate Hearing 106–394, February 4, 1999, p.3.

114 Ibid., p. 4.

115 Ibid., p.41.

116 Ibid., p.43.

role have not been fully implemented.¹¹⁷ The FY1997 Act established four new Senate-confirmed positions having responsibilities that extend across all intelligence agencies. Since enactment, the Senate has received nominations for only two individuals to these positions (both were duly confirmed and sworn in) but both left office in 2003 and replacements have not yet been nominated. Some observers also believe that the DCI's authorities in the preparation of budgets for all intelligence agencies have not been fully exercised.¹¹⁸ Observers suggest that there is little likelihood that serious efforts will be made, however, to seek repeal of the provisions at a time when intelligence agencies are under scrutiny for their abilities to "connect the dots" on international threats.

Joint Inquiry on the Terrorist Attacks of September 11, 2001; Additional Views of Senator Shelby, 2002

In the aftermath of the September 11, 2001 attacks on the World Trade Center and the Pentagon, the two congressional intelligence committees agreed to conduct a Joint Inquiry into the activities of the Intelligence Community in connection with the attacks. The Joint Inquiry undertook an extensive investigation and conducted a number of public and closed hearings. The two Committees' recommendations were published in December 2002 some of which addressed issues of Intelligence Community organization. The unclassified version of the Inquiry's report was published in mid-2003.

Principally, the two committees urged that the National Security Act be amended to create a statutory Director of National Intelligence, separate from the head of the CIA. This DNI would have the "full range of management, budgetary and personnel responsibilities needed to make the entire U.S. Intelligence Community operate as a coherent whole." These would include "establishment and enforcement" of collection, analysis, and dissemination priorities; authority to move personnel between Intelligence Community elements; and "primary management and oversight of the execution of Intelligence Community budgets."

The committees also recommended that Congress consider legislation, similar to the Goldwater-Nichols Act of 1986 which reorganized the Defense Department, to instill a sense of jointness throughout the Intelligence Community, including joint education, joint career specialties, and more "joint tours" in other agencies that would be designated as "career-enhancing."

The then-Vice Chairman of the Senate Intelligence Committee, Senator Richard Shelby, submitted additional views that also advocated organizational changes in the Intelligence Community.¹¹⁹ Shelby argued that "The fragmented nature of the DCI's authority has exacerbated the centrifugal tendencies of bureaucratic politics and has helped ensure that the IC responds too slowly and too disjointedly to shifting threats." Accordingly, the "office of the DCI should be given more management and budgetary authority over IC organs and be separated from the job of the CIA Director."¹²⁰

Further, Shelby argued that the basic structure of the National Security Act needs to be re-examined to separate "central" analytical functions from "resource-hungry collection responsibilities that make agencies into self-interested bureaucratic 'players.'" Shelby acknowledged that, "Creating a *true* DCI would entail removing dozens of billions of dollars of annual budgets from the Defense Department, and depriving it of 'ownership' over 'its' 'combat support organizations.' In contemporary Washington bureaucratic politics, this would be a daunting challenge; DOD and its congressional allies would make such centralization an uphill battle, to say the least."¹²¹ Shelby also recalls the Goldwater-Nichols precedent in urging that the Intelligence Community be restructured, but cautions that the Intelligence Community should not be reformed solely to meet the terrorist threat: "*we need an Intelligence Community agile enough to evolve as threats evolve, on a continuing basis.* Hard-wiring the IC in order to fight terrorists, I should emphasize, is precisely the *wrong* answer, because such an approach would surely leave us unprepared for the next major threat, whatever it turns out to be."¹²²

National Commission on Terrorist Attacks Upon the United States (The 9/11 Commission), 2004

Established by the Intelligence Authorization Act for FY2003 (P.L. 107-306), the 9/11 Commission, chaired by former New Jersey Governor Thomas H. Kean, undertook a lengthy investigation of the "facts and circumstances relating to the terrorist attacks of September 11, 2001." Although the Commission's mandate extended beyond intelligence and law en-

---

117 A somewhat pessimistic academic assessment of the effects of the IC21 study can be found in Abraham H. Miller and Brian Alexander, "Structural Quintessence in the failure of IC21 and Intelligence Reform," *International Journal of Intelligence and Counterintelligence*, Summer 2001. Management of ISR programs is discussed in CRS Report RL32508, *Intelligence, Surveillance, and Reconnaissance, (ISR) Programs: Congressional Oversight Issues*.

118 See U.S. Congress, 107th Congress, 2nd session, Senate Committee on Intelligence and House Permanent Select Committee on Intelligence, *Joint Inquiry into Intelligence Community Activities Before and After the Terrorist Attacks on September 11, 2001*, S.Rept., 107–351, H.Rept. 107–792, December 2002, pp.347–348.

119 "September 11 and the Imperative Reform in the U.S. Intelligence Community," Additional Views of Senator Richard C. Shelby, Vice Chairman, Senate Select Committee on Intelligence, December 10, 2002.

120 Ibid., p. 3.

121 Ibid., p. 16.

122 Ibid., p. 18 (italics in original).

forcement issues, a number of principal recommendations, made public on July 22, 2004 address the organization of the Intelligence Community. The Commission argues that with current authorities the DCI is:

> responsible for community performance but lacks the three authorities critical for any agency head or chief executive officer: (1) control over purse strings, (2) the ability to hire or fire senior managers, and (3) the ability to set standards for the information infrastructure and personnel.[123]

The 9/11 Commission recommends the establishment of a National Counterterrorism Center (NCTC), responsible for both joint operational planning and joint intelligence, and the position of a Director of National Intelligence. In addition to overseeing various intelligence centers, the DNI would manage the National Foreign Intelligence Program and oversee the agencies that contribute to it. The Community Management Staff would report to the DNI. The DNI would manage the agencies with the help of three deputies, each of whom would also hold a key position in one of the component agencies. A deputy for foreign intelligence would be the now-separate head of the CIA, a deputy for defense intelligence would be the Under Secretary of Defense for Intelligence, and the deputy for homeland intelligence would be either an FBI or Department of Homeland Security (DHS) official. The DNI would not have responsibilities for intelligence programs affecting only Defense Department consumers. The report does not describe how the person serving simultaneously as the DNI's assistant for defense intelligence and as an Under Secretary of Defense would resolve any differing guidance from the DNI and the Secretary of Defense. The 9/11 Commission also recommends a separate intelligence appropriation act the total of which would be made public.[124]

Conclusion

The efforts of committees, commissions and individuals to encourage restructuring of the U.S. Intelligence Community have led to numerous changes through internal agency direction, presidential directives and executive orders, and new statutes. The general trend has been towards more thorough oversight both by the executive branch and by congressional committees. The position of the DCI has been considerably strengthened and DCIs have been given greater staff and authority to exert influence on all parts of the Community. They have not, however, been given "line" authority over agencies other than the CIA, and the influence of the Defense Department remains pervasive. Some have argued that, in the light of the Intelligence Community's inability to provide warning of the September 2001 attacks on the World Trade Center and the Pentagon and inaccurate intelligence estimates about Iraqi weapons of mass destruction, the need for reorganizing the Intelligence Community has become self-evident. Others argue that many of the reforms that have been proposed could make matters worse. The issue appears to be moving higher on the congressional agenda. Specific legislation to reorganize the nation's intelligence effort, including S. 2845, is currently under consideration and the 9/11 Commission's recommendations are receiving widespread interest.

Order Code RL32500; Updated September 24, 2004

---

[123] U.S. National Commission on Terrorist Attacks Upon the United States, *The 9/11 Commission Report*, July 2004, p. 410.

[124] For further background on the 9/11 Commission proposals, see CRS Report RL32506, *The Position of Director of National Intelligence: Issues for Congress.*

CRS Report for Congress

Terrorism: Key Recommendations of the 9/11 Commission and Recent Major Commissions and Inquiries

Richard F. Grimmett
Specialist in National Defense; Foreign Affairs, Defense, and Trade Division

Summary

This report highlights key recommendations set out in the report of the 9/11 Commission organized by the following major thematic areas: (1) Focus of U.S. International Anti-Terrorism Policy; (2) Institutional Steps to Protect Against and Prepare for Terrorist Attacks; (3) Intelligence Issues; and (4) Congress and Oversight Issues. A bulleted summary is made, under each of these major thematic headings, of the key recommendations of the 9/11 Commission, the Gilmore Commission, the Bremer Commission, the Joint Inquiry of the House and Senate Intelligence Committees, and the Hart-Rudman Commission.

What is provided here is a structured road map to the most important recommendations of the 9/11 Commission, to those recommendations of the three other Commissions, and to those of the Joint Inquiry of the House and Senate Intelligence Committees that are *directly related* to the recommendations made by the 9/11 Commission set out within each the stipulated four thematic areas. Links are also provided to the texts of the original reports prepared by these entities. This will facilitate access to the detailed commentaries of each of these entities, providing direct access to the rationales for each of the respective recommendations. Background details on the formation and mandates of the Commissions reviewed are set out in Appendix 1 of this report, as are the links to the pertinent websites where the full texts of the individual reports may be found.

This report will not be updated.

Introduction

This report highlights key recommendations set out in the report of the 9/11 Commission organized by the following major thematic areas: (1) Focus of U.S. International Anti-Terrorism Policy; (2) Institutional Steps to Protect Against and Prepare for Terrorist Attacks; (3) Intelligence Issues; (4) Congress and Oversight Issues. Key recommendations made by other major commissions sponsored by the United States Government since 1999, and those of the Joint Inquiry by the House and Senate Select Committees on Intelligence, are also set out within each of the above four thematic areas. A bulleted summary is made, under each of these major headings, of the key recommendations of the 9/11 Commission, followed by bulleted summaries of key recommendations made by the Gilmore Commission, the Bremer Commission, the Joint Inquiry of the House and Senate Intelligence Committees, and the Hart-Rudman Commission. What is provided here is a structured road map to the most important recommendations of the 9/11 Commission, and to those recommendations of the three other Commissions, and to those of the Joint Inquiry of the House and Senate Intelligence Committees that are *directly related* to those made by the 9/11 Commission.[1] Background details on the origins and mandates of the Commissions whose recommendations are discussed are set out in Appendix 1 of this report, as are links to the pertinent websites where the full texts of the reports of these entities may be found.

Focus of United States International Anti-Terrorism Policy

Key 9/11 Commission Recommendations

- The U.S. government must attack terrorists and their organizations by identifying and prioritizing actual or potential sanctuaries for terrorists, and have a realistic strategy to keep possible terrorists insecure and on the

---

1 The National Commission on Terrorist Attacks Upon the United States (known as the 9/11 Commission was established by Title VI of P.L. 107-306, 107th Cong., 2nd Sess., November 27, 2002. It made its report public on July 22, 2004. Its charter (Sec. 602 of P.L 107-306) called for it, among other things, to: examine and report on the facts and causes relating to the terrorist attacks of September 11, 2001 on the United States, evaluate and report on the evidence developed by all relevant governmental agencies regarding the facts and circumstances surrounding the attacks; to build upon the investigations of other entities, and avoid unnecessary duplication, by reviewing the findings, conclusions, and recommendations of the Joint Inquiry of the Select Intelligence Committees of the House and Senate, and other executive branch, congressional or independent commission investigations into the terrorist attacks of September 11, 2001, other terrorist attacks, and terrorism generally; to make a full and complete accounting of the circumstances surrounding the attacks, and the extent of the United States' preparedness for, and the immediate response to, the attacks; and to investigate and report to the President and Congress on its findings, conclusions, and recommendations for corrective measures that can be taken to prevent acts of terrorism.

run, using all elements of national power. The U.S. should reach out, listen to, and work with other countries that can help in this regard.
- The United States should be willing to make the difficult long-term commitment to the future of Pakistan. Sustaining the current scale of aid to Pakistan, the United States should support Pakistan's government in its struggle against extremists with a comprehensive effort that extends from military aid to support for better education, so long as Pakistan's leaders remain willing to make difficult choices of their own.
- The United States and the international community should make a long-term commitment to a secure and stable Afghanistan, in order to give the government a reasonable opportunity to improve the life of the Afghan people. Afghanistan must not again become a sanctuary for international crime and terrorism. The United States and the international community should help the Afghan government extend its authority over the country, with a strategy and nation-by-nation commitments to achieve their objectives.
- The problems in the U.S.-Saudi relationship must be confronted, openly. The United States and Saudi Arabia must determine if they can build a relationship that political leaders on both sides are prepared to publicly defend — a relationship about more than oil. It should include a shared commitment to political and economic reform, as Saudis make common cause with the outside world. It should include a shared interest in greater tolerance and cultural respect, translating into a commitment to fight the violent extremists who foment hatred.
- We should offer an example of moral leadership in the world, [be] committed to treat people humanely, abide by the rule of law, and be generous and caring to our neighbors. America and Muslim friends can agree on respect for human dignity and opportunity. Where Muslim governments, even those who are friends, do not respect these principles, the United States must stand for a better future.
- Just as we did in the Cold War, we need to defend our ideals abroad vigorously. America does stand up for its values. The United States defended, and still defends, Muslims against tyrants and criminals in Somalia, Bosnia, Kosovo, Afghanistan, and Iraq. If the United States does not act aggressively to define itself in the Islamic world, the extremists will gladly do the job for us.
- The U.S. government should offer to join with other nations in generously supporting a new International Youth Opportunity Fund. Funds will be spent directly for building and operating primary and secondary schools in those Muslim states that commit to sensibly investing their own money in public education.
- A comprehensive U.S. strategy to counter terrorism should include economic policies that encourage development, more open societies, and opportunities for people to improve the lives of their families and to enhance prospects for their children's future.
- The U.S. should counter the continued growth of Islamist terrorism by engaging other nations in developing a comprehensive coalition strategy against Islamist terrorism. There are several multilateral institutions in which such issues should be addressed. But the most important policies should be discussed and coordinated in a flexible contact group of leading coalition governments.
- The United States should engage its friends to develop a common coalition approach toward the detention and humane treatment of captured terrorists. New principles might draw upon Article 3 of the Geneva Conventions on the law of armed conflict.
- The U.S. should make a maximum effort to strengthen counterproliferation efforts against weapons of mass destruction by expanding the Proliferation Security Initiative and the Cooperative Threat Reduction program.
- The U.S. should engage in vigorous efforts to track terrorist financing. This should be a central part of U.S. counterterrorism efforts.

Key Gilmore Commission Recommendations

- The President should develop a national strategy for combating terrorism.
- The United States should negotiate more comprehensive treaties and agreements for combating terrorism with Canada and Mexico.

Key Bremer Commission Recommendations

- The President should not make further concessions toward Iran and should keep Iran on the list of state sponsors of terrorism until Tehran demonstrates it has stopped supporting terrorism and cooperates fully in the Khobar Towers investigation.
- The President should actively seek support from U.S. allies to compel Iran to cooperate in the Khobar Towers bombing investigation.
- The President should make clear to Syria that it will remain on the list of state sponsors of terrorism until it shuts down training camps and other facilities in Syria and the Bekaa Valley and prohibits the resupply of terrorist groups through Syrian-controlled territory.
- The Secretary of State should designate Afghanistan as a sponsor of terrorism and impose all the sanctions that apply to state sponsor.
- The President should make more effective use of authority to designate foreign governments as "Not Cooperating Fully" with U.S. counterterrorism efforts to deter all state support for terrorism. Specifically, the President should direct the Secretary of State to: Consider Greece and Pakistan, among others, as candidates for this designation.
- Review the current list of state sponsors and recommend that certain states be moved to the "Not Cooperating Fully" designation after they have undertaken specified measures to cease sponsorship of terrorism.

- Increase publicity of the activities of state sponsors and countries designated as "Not Cooperating Fully" through special reports, making extensive use of the Internet.
- The Secretary of State should ensure the list of Foreign Terrorist Organizations (FTO) designations is credible and frequently updated.
- The Secretary of State, in concert with other departments and agencies, should take the lead in developing an international convention aimed at harmonizing national laws, sharing information, providing early warning, and establishing accepted procedures for conducting international investigations of cyber crime.

Key Recommendations of the Joint Inquiry of House and Senate Intelligence Committees

- The National Security Council, in conjunction with the Director of National Intelligence, and in consultation with the Secretary of the Department of Homeland Security, the Secretary of State and Secretary of Defense, should prepare, for the President's approval, a U.S. government-wide strategy for combating terrorism, both at home and abroad, including the growing terrorism threat posed by the proliferation of weapons of mass destruction and associated technologies. This strategy should identify and fully engage those foreign policy, economic, military, intelligence, and law enforcement elements that are critical to a comprehensive blueprint for success in the war against terrorism. As part of that effort, the Director of National Intelligence shall develop the Intelligence Community component of the strategy, identifying specific programs and budgets an[d] including plans to address the threats posed by Osama Bin Laden and al Qa'ida, Hezbollah, Hamas, and other significant terrorist groups. Consistent with applicable law, the strategy should effectively employ and integrate all capabilities available to the Intelligence Community against those threats and should encompass specific efforts to:
  - —develop human sources to penetrate terrorist organizations and networks both overseas and within the United States; fully utilize existing and future technologies to better exploit terrorist communications; to improve and expand the use of data mining and other cutting edge analytical tools; and to develop a multi-level security capability to facilitate the timely and complete sharing of relevant intelligence information both within the Intelligence Community and with other appropriate federal, state, and local authorities;
  - —maximize the effective use of covert action in counterterrorist efforts;
  - —develop programs to deal with financial support for international terrorism;
  - —facilitate the ability of CIA paramilitary units and military special operations forces to conduct joint operations against terrorist targets.
- The State Department, in consultation with the Department of Justice, should review and report to the President and the Congress by June 30, 2003 on the extent to which revisions in bilateral and multilateral agreements, including extradition and mutual assistance treaties, would strengthen U.S. counterterrorism efforts. The review should address the degree to which current categories of extraditable offenses should be expanded to cover offenses, such as visa and immigration fraud, which may be particularly useful against terrorists and those who support them.
- The Intelligence Community, and particularly the FBI and the CIA, should aggressively address the possibility that foreign governments are providing support to or are involved in terrorist activity targeting the United States and U.S. interests. State-sponsored terrorism substantially increases the likelihood of successful and more lethal attacks within the United States. This issue must be addressed from a national standpoint and should not be limited in focus by the geographical and factual boundaries of individual cases. The FBI and CIA should aggressively and thoroughly pursue related matters developed through this Joint Inquiry that have been referred to them for further investigation by these Committees.

Key Hart-Rudman Commission Recommendations

- The President should develop a comprehensive strategy to heighten America's ability to prevent and protect against all forms of attack on the homeland, and to respond to such attacks if prevention and protection fail.

Institutional Steps to Protect Against and Prepare for Terrorist Attacks

Key 9/11 Commission Recommendations

- The United States should combine terrorist travel intelligence, operations, and law enforcement in a strategy to intercept terrorists, find terrorist travel facilitators, and constrain terrorist mobility.
- The U. S. border security system should be integrated into a larger network of screening points that includes our transportation system and access to vital facilities, such as nuclear reactors. The President should direct the Department of Homeland Security [DHS] to lead the effort to design a comprehensive screening system, addressing common problems and setting common standards with systemwide goals in mind. Extending those standards

among other governments could dramatically strengthen America and the world's collective ability to intercept individuals who pose catastrophic threats.
- The Department of Homeland Security, properly supported by the Congress, should complete, as quickly as possible, a biometric entry-exit screening system, including a single system for speeding qualified travelers. It should be integrated with the system that provides benefits to foreigners seeking to stay in the United States. Linking biometric passports to good data systems and decision making is a fundamental goal.
- We should do more to exchange terrorist information with trusted allies, and raise U.S. and global border security standards for travel and border crossing over the medium and long term through extensive international cooperation.
- Secure identification should begin in the United States. The federal government should set standards for the issuance of birth certificates and sources of identification, such as drivers licenses.
- The U.S. government should identify and evaluate the transportation assets that need to be protected, set risk-based priorities for defending them, select the most practical and cost-effective ways of doing so, and then develop a plan, budget, and funding to implement the effort. The plan should assign roles and missions to the relevant authorities (federal, state, regional, and local) and to private stakeholders.
- Improved use of "no-fly" and "automatic selectee" lists should not be delayed while the argument about a successor to CAPPS continues. This screening function should be performed by the TSA [Transportation Security Administration], and it should utilize the larger set of watch lists maintained by the federal government. Air carriers should be required to supply the information needed to test and implement this new system.
- The TSA and the Congress must give priority attention to improving the ability of screening checkpoints to detect explosives on passengers. As a start, each individual selected for special screening should be screened for explosives. Further, the TSA should conduct a human factors study, a method often used in the private sector, to understand problems in screener performance and set attainable objectives for individual screeners and for the checkpoints where screening takes place.
- As the President determines the guidelines for information sharing among government agencies and by those agencies with the private sector, he should safeguard the privacy of individuals about whom information is shared.
- The burden of proof for retaining a particular governmental power should be on the executive, to explain (a) that the power actually materially enhances security and (b) that there is adequate supervision of the executive's use of the powers to ensure protection of civil liberties. If the power is granted, there must be adequate guidelines and oversight to properly confine its use.

- At this time of increased and consolidated government authority, there should be a board within the executive branch to oversee adherence to the guidelines we recommend and the commitment the government makes to defend our civil liberties.
- Homeland security assistance should be based strictly on an assessment of risks and vulnerabilities. Now, in 2004, Washington, D.C., and New York City are certainly at the top of any such list. We understand the contention that every state and city needs to have some minimum infrastructure for emergency response. But federal homeland security assistance should not remain a program for general revenue sharing. It should supplement state and local resources based on the risks or vulnerabilities that merit additional support.
- Emergency response agencies nationwide should adopt the Incident Command System (ICS). When multiple agencies or multiple jurisdictions are involved, they should adopt a unified command. Both are proven frameworks for emergency response. We strongly support the decision that federal homeland security funding will be contingent, as of October 1, 2004, upon the adoption and regular use of ICS and unified command procedures. In the future, the Department of Homeland Security should consider making funding contingent on aggressive and realistic training in accordance with ICS and unified command procedures.
- Congress should support pending legislation which provides for the expedited and increased assignment of radio spectrum for public safety purposes. Furthermore, high-risk urban areas such as New York City and Washington, D.C., should establish signal corps units to ensure communications connectivity between and among civilian authorities, local first responders, and the National Guard. Federal funding of such units should be given high priority by Congress.
- We endorse the American National Standards Institute's [ANSI] recommended standard for private preparedness. We were encouraged by Secretary Tom Ridge's praise of the standard, and urge the Department of Homeland Security to promote its adoption. We also encourage the insurance and credit-rating industries to look closely at a company's compliance with the ANSI standard in assessing its insurability and creditworthiness. We believe that compliance with the standard should define the standard of care owed by a company to its employees and the public for legal purposes.
- We recommend the establishment of a National Counterterrorism Center (NCTC), built on the foundation of the existing Terrorist Threat Integration Center (TTIC). Breaking the older mold of national government organization, this NCTC should be a center for joint operational planning and joint intelligence, staffed by personnel from the various agencies. The head of the NCTC should have authority to evaluate the performance of the people assigned to the Center.

Key Gilmore Commission Recommendations

- There should be a national level strategy on combating terrorism that clearly delineates and distinguishes Federal, state, and local roles and responsibilities and articulates clear direction for Federal priorities and programs to support local responders; and a comprehensive, parallel public education effort.
- More needs to be done and can be done to obtain and share information on potential terrorist threats at all levels of government, to provide more effective deterrence, prevention, interdiction or response, using modern information technology. Efforts should be accelerated to develop and to test agreed-on templates for command and control under a wide variety of terrorist threat scenarios.
- Create a "National Office for Combating Terrorism" with the Director appointed by the President, confirmed by the Senate, located in the Executive Office of the President. To have no operational control, but specified control of Federal programs and budgets. To have responsibility for strategy formulation and review of plans. To have Assistants for Domestic Preparedness, Intelligence, Health and Medical, RDT&E/National Standards, and Management and Budget. To serve as the point of contact for the Congress.
- Enhance Intelligence/Threat Assessments/Information Sharing. (Note: the entity/person indicated in parentheses is expected to take the lead in carrying out the given recommendation.)
  - Improve human intelligence by rescinding CIA guidelines on certain foreign informants (DCI).
  - Improve measurement and signature intelligence through enhanced RDT&E (Intelligence Community).
  - Review/modify guidelines and procedures for domestic investigations (Review Panel/Attorney General).
  - Review/modify authorities on certain CBRN [Chemical, Biological, Radiological, Nuclear] precursors and equipment (Executive and Congress).
  - Improve forensics technology/analysis, and enhance indications and warnings systems (National Office for Combating Terrorism—hereafter National Office).
  - Provide security clearances and more information to designated State and local entities (National Office).
  - Develop single-source, protected, web-based, integrated information system (National Office).
  - Develop a training program for State, local, and private sector for interpreting intelligence products (DHS).
  - Establish comprehensive procedures for sharing information with relevant State and local officials (DHS).
- Foster Better Planning/Coordination/Operations
  - Designate Federal Response Plan as single-source "all hazards" planning document (National Office).
  - Develop "model" State plan (NEMA [National Emergency Management Association] and FEMA [Federal Emergency Management Agency]).
  - Conduct inventories of State and local programs for nationwide application (National Office).
  - Promote/facilitate the adoption of multi-jurisdiction/multi-state mutual aid compacts (National Office).
  - Promote/facilitate adoption of standard ICS [Incident Command System], UCS [Unified Command System], and EOC [Emergency Operations Center] (National Office).
  - Designate agency other than DoD as "Lead Federal Agency" (President).
- Enhance Training, Equipping, and Exercising
  - Develop input to strategy and plans in close coordination with State and local entities (National Office).
  - Restructure education and training opportunities to account for volunteers in critical response disciplines.
  - Develop realistic exercise scenarios that meet State and local needs (National Office).
- Improve Health and Medical Capabilities
  - Obtain strategy input/program advice from public health/medical care representatives (National Office).
  - Promote certification programs for training and facilities (National Office).
  - Clarify authorities and procedures for health and medical response (All jurisdictions).
  - Improve surge capacity and stockpiles (All jurisdictions).
  - Evaluate and test response capabilities (All public health and medical entities).
  - Establish standards for communications/mandatory reporting (All public health/medical entities).
  - Establish laboratory standards and protocols (All public health/medical entities).
- Promote Better Research and Development and Developing National Standards
  - Develop, with OSTP [Office of Science and Technology Policy], equipment testing protocols and long-range research plan (National Office).
  - Establish national standards program with NIST [National Institute of Standards and Technology] and NIOSH [National Institute for Occupational Safety and Health] as co-leads (National Office).
- Civil Liberties
  - Establish a civil liberties oversight board to provide advice on any statutory, regulatory, or procedural change that may have civil liberties implications.
- State and Local Response Capabilities
  - Increase and accelerate the sharing of terrorism-related intelligence and threat assessments.
  - Design training and equipment programs for all-hazards preparedness.
  - Redesign Federal training and equipment grant programs to include sustainment components.
  - Increase funding to States and localities for combating terrorism.

—Consolidate Federal grant program information and application procedures.
—Design Federal preparedness programs to ensure first responder participation, especially volunteers.
—Establish an information clearinghouse on Federal programs, assets, and agencies.
—Configure Federal military response assets to support and reinforce existing structures and systems.
—Combine all departmental grant making programs into a single entity in DHS (DHS).
—Establish an interagency mechanism for homeland security grants (President).
—Develop a comprehensive process for establishing training and exercise standards for responders (DHS).
—Revise the Homeland Security Advisory System to include (1) a regional alert system (2) training to emergency responders about preventive actions; and (3) specific guidance to potentially affected regions (DHS).
—Establish sustained funding to enhance EMS [Emergency Medical Services] response capacity for acts of terrorism (Congress).
—Reestablish a Federal office specifically to support EMS operational and systems issues (Congress).
—Establish a "Matrix" of Mutual Aid in coordination with local, State, and other Federal agencies, for a nationwide system of mutually supporting capabilities (DHS).
—Adopt the Business Roundtable's Principles of Corporate Governance security component (DHS and private sector).

- Improving Health and Medical Capabilities

    —Implement the AMA [American Medical Association] Recommendations on Medical Preparedness for Terrorism.
    —Implement the JCAHO [Joint Commission on Accreditation of Healthcare Organizations] Revised Emergency Standards.
    —Fully resource the CDC [Centers for Disease Control and Prevention] Biological and Chemical Terrorism Strategic Plan.
    —Fully resource the CDC Laboratory Response Network for Bioterrorism.
    —Fully resource the CDC Secure and Rapid Communications Networks.
    —Develop standard medical response models for Federal, State, and local levels.
    —Reestablish a pre-hospital Emergency Medical Service Program Office.
    —Revise current EMT [Emergency Medical Technician] and PNST [Paramedic National Standardized Training] training and refresher curricula.
    —Increase Federal resources for exercises for State and local health and medical entities.
    —Establish a government-owned, contractor-operated national vaccine and therapeutics facility.
    —Review and recommend changes to plans for vaccine stockpiles and critical supplies.
    —Develop a comprehensive plan for research on terrorism-related health and medical issues.
    —Review MMRS [Metropolitan Medical Response System] and NDMS [National Disaster Medical System] authorities, structures, and capabilities.
    —Develop an education plan on the legal and procedural issues for health and medical response to terrorism.
    —Develop on-going public education programs on terrorism causes and effects.
    —Strengthen the public health system with support on the order of $1 billion per year for five years.
    —Coordinate and centralize funding information from various agencies and simplify the application process.
    —Implement a formal process for evaluating the effectiveness of investments in preparedness.
    —Fund studies on health care and public health workforce requirements.
    —Assess the resources required by the nation's hospital system to respond to terrorism.
    —Strengthen the Health Alert Network and other secure and rapid communications systems.
    —Increase resources for public health and medical emergencies.
    —Articulate and integrate the roles, missions, capabilities and limitations of, and effectively train special response teams.
    —Improve system for providing required technical assistance to States and localities.
    —Develop an electronic, continuously updated handbook on best terrorism response practices.
    —Strengthen and prioritize basic medical and applied public health research.
    —Adopt the Model Health Powers Emergency Act or develop and adopt an alternative.
    —Clarify the special conditions under which HIPAA [Health Insurance Portability and Accountability Act] information can be shared; and require State plans for enhanced cooperation between law enforcement and public health, EMS and hospital officials.
    —Educate the public on health and medical information before, during and after an event.
    —Enhance research into the short and long-term psychological consequences of terrorist attacks.

- Immigration and Border Control

    —Create an intergovernmental border advisory group.
    —Fully integrate all affected entities into local or regional "port security committees."
    —Ensure that all border agencies are partners in intelligence collection, analysis, and dissemination.
    —Create, provide resources for, and mandate participation in a "Border Security Awareness" database system.
    —Require shippers to submit cargo manifest information simultaneously with shipments transiting U.S. borders.
    —Establish "Trusted Shipper" programs.
    —Expand Coast Guard search authority to include U.S. owned—not just "flagged"—vessels.

- —Expand and consolidate research, development, and integration of sensor, detection, and warning systems.
- —Increase resources for the U.S. Coast Guard for homeland security missions.
- —Negotiate more comprehensive treaties and agreements for combating terrorism with Canada and Mexico.

■ Improving Cyber Security Against Terrorism

- —Include private and State and local representatives on the interagency critical infrastructure advisory panel.
- —Create a commission to assess and make recommendations on programs for cyber security.
- —Establish a government funded, not-for-profit entity for cyber detection, alert, and warning functions.
- —Convene a "summit" to address Federal statutory changes that would enhance cyber assurance.
- —Create a special "Cyber Court" patterned after the court established in FISA [Federal Intelligence Surveillance Act].
- —Develop and implement a comprehensive plan for cyber security research, development, test, and evaluation.

■ Use of the Military in Homeland Security

- —Establish a homeland security Under Secretary position in the Department of Defense.
- —Establish a single unified command and control structure to execute all military support to civil authorities.
- —Develop detailed plans for the use of the military domestically across the spectrum of potential activities.
- —Expand training and exercises in relevant military units and with Federal, State, and local responders.
- —Direct new mission areas for the National Guard to provide support to civil authorities.
- —Publish a compendium of statutory authorities for using the military domestically to combat terrorism.
- —Improve the military full-time liaison elements in the ten Federal Emergency Management Agency regions.

■ Organizing the National Effort

- —Produce continuing, comprehensive "strategic" assessments of threats inside the United States.
- —Ensure DHS authority to levy direct intelligence requirements, and robust DHS capability for combining threat and vulnerability information.
- —Clearly define DHS and other Federal agency responsibilities before, during, and after an attack.
- —Designate DHS as lead, and DHHS [Department of Health and Human Services] as principal supporting agency, for bioterrorism attack.
- —Perform a comprehensive National Intelligence Estimate on the threats to infrastructure.
- —Restructure interagency mechanisms for better coordination.
- —Thoroughly review applicable law and regulations; propose legislative changes.
- —Establish separate Congressional authorizing committee and appropriation subcommittee for homeland security.
- —Establish a Federal Interagency Homeland Security Research and Development Council (President).
- —Improve capacity in the Intelligence Community for health and medical analysis.
- —Enhance technical assistance to states to develop plans and procedures for distributing the NPS [National Pharmaceutical Stockpile].
- —Establish a national strategy for vaccine development.
- —Implement the smallpox vaccination plan incrementally; and raise the priority on research for a safer smallpox vaccine.
- —Implement IOM [Institute of Medicine] Committee's recommendations on psychological preparedness (DHS and DHHS).
- —Provide increased funding and DHS and DHHS monitor State and local compliance of incorporating in plans an appropriate focus on psychological and behavioral consequence preparedness and management (Congress, DHS and DHHS).
- —Create a Federal task force on psychological issues, jointly led by DHHS and DHS (President).

■ Defending Against Agricultural Terrorism

- —Designate DHS as the lead and USDA [United States Department of Agriculture] as the technical advisor on food safety and agriculture and emergency preparedness (President).
- —Include an Emergency Support Function for Agriculture and Food in the Federal Response Plan and the National Incident Response Plan.
- —Allow specially designated laboratories to perform tests for foreign agricultural diseases.
- —Institute a standard system for fair compensation for agriculture and food losses.
- —Improve and provide incentives for veterinary medicine education in foreign animal diseases; and improve education, training, and exercises between government and the agricultural private sector.

Key Bremer Commission Recommendations

■ Neither the Department of Justice [DoJ] nor the FBI has attempted to clarify the FI [Foreign Intelligence Collection and Foreign Counterintelligence Investigations] guidelines for international terrorism investigations, and the Attorney General guidelines on General Crimes Racketeering Enterprise and Domestic Security/Terrorism Investigations [which govern domestic terrorism], the Attorney General and the Director of the Federal Bureau of Investigation should develop guidance to clarify the application of both sets of guidelines. This guidance should specify what facts and circumstances merit the opening of a preliminary inquiry or full investigation and should direct agents in the field to investigate terrorist activity vigorously, using the full extent of their authority.

- During the period leading up to the millennium, the FISA [Foreign Intelligence Surveillance Act] application process was streamlined. Without lowering the FISA standards, applications were submitted to the FISA Court by DoJ promptly and with enough information to establish probable cause. The Attorney General should direct that the Office of Intelligence Policy and Review not require information in excess of that actually mandated by the probable cause standard in the Foreign Intelligence Surveillance Act statute.
- To ensure timely review of the Foreign Intelligence Surveillance Act applications, the Attorney General should substantially expand the Office of Intelligence Policy and Review staff and direct it to cooperate with the Federal Bureau of Investigation. The Director of the Federal Bureau of Investigation should establish and equip a dedicated staff of reports officers to develop terrorism and foreign intelligence information obtained at field offices and headquarters for prompt dissemination to other agencies, especially those within the intelligence community, while protecting privacy and pending criminal cases.
- The Attorney General should clarify what information can be shared and direct maximum dissemination of terrorist-related information to policymakers and intelligence analysts consistent with the law.
- The President should direct the creation of a joint task force consisting of all the agencies in the U.S. Government that possess information or authority relevant to terrorist fundraising. The task force should develop and implement a broad approach toward disrupting the financial activities of terrorists. This approach should use all available criminal, civil, and administrative sanctions, including those for money laundering, tax and fraud violations, or conspiracy charges.
- The Secretary of the Treasury should create a unit within the Office of Foreign Assets Control dedicated to the issue of terrorist fundraising.
- The President and Congress should work together to create an effective system for monitoring the status of foreign students nationwide.
- The Attorney General should direct the Department of Justice to pursue vigorously the criminal prosecution of terrorists in an open court whenever possible.
- The Attorney General should further direct that where national security requires the use of secret evidence in administrative immigration cases, procedures for cleared counsel and unclassified summaries, such as those provided in the Alien Terrorist Removal Court (ATRC), should be used.
- The President should require the Director of the Office of Management and Budget and the national counterterrorism coordinator to agree on all budget guidance to the agencies, including the response to initial budget submissions, and both officials should be involved in presenting agencies' counterterrorism budget appeals to the President.
- The President should direct the preparation of a manual on the implementation of existing legal authority necessary to address effectively a catastrophic terrorist threat or attack. The manual should be distributed to the appropriate federal, state, and local officials and be used in training, exercises, and educational programs.
- The President should determine whether any additional legal authority is needed to deal with catastrophic terrorism and make recommendations to Congress if necessary.
- The President should direct the Assistant to the President for National Security Affairs, in coordination with the Secretary of Defense and the Attorney General, to develop and adopt detailed contingency plans that would transfer lead federal agency authority to the Department of Defense if necessary during a catastrophic terrorist attack or prior to an imminent attack.
- The Secretary of Defense should establish a unified command structure that would integrate all catastrophic terrorism capabilities and conduct detailed planning and exercises with relevant federal, state, and local authorities.
- The President should direct (1) the Exercise Subgroup, under the direction of the national coordinator for counterterrorism, to exercise annually the government's response to a catastrophic terrorism crisis, including consequence management; and (2) all relevant federal agencies to plan, budget and participate in counterterrorism and consequence management exercises coordinated by the Exercise Subgroup and ensure senior officer level participation, particularly in the annual exercises.
- The President should establish a comprehensive and coordinated long-term Research and Development program to counter catastrophic terrorism.
- The Secretary of Health and Human Services should strengthen physical security standards applicable to the storage, creation, and transport of pathogens in research laboratories and other certified facilities in order to protect against theft or diversion. These standards should be as rigorous as the physical protection and security measures applicable to critical nuclear materials.
- The Secretary of Health and Human Services, working with the Department of State, should develop an international monitoring program to provide early warning of infectious disease outbreaks and possible terrorist experimentation with biological substances.

Key Recommendations of the Joint Inquiry of House and Senate Intelligence Committees

- Enhance the depth and quality of domestic intelligence collection and analysis by, for example, modernizing current intelligence reporting formats through the use of existing information technology to emphasize the existence and the significance of links between new and previously acquired information.
- Congress and the Administration should ensure the full development within the Department of Homeland Security of an effective allsource terrorism information fusion

center that will dramatically improve the focus and quality of counterterrorism analysis and facilitate the timely dissemination of relevant intelligence information, both within and beyond the boundaries of the Intelligence Community. Congress and the Administration should ensure that this fusion center has all the authority and the resources needed to:

—have full and timely access to all counterterrorism-related intelligence information, including "raw" supporting data as needed;

—have the ability to participate fully in the existing requirements process for tasking the Intelligence Community to gather information on foreign individuals, entities and threats;

—integrate such information in order to identify and assess the nature and scope of terrorist threats to the United States in light of actual and potential vulnerabilities;

—implement and fully utilize data mining and other advanced analytical tools, consistent with applicable law;

—retain a permanent staff of experienced and highly skilled analysts, supplemented on a regular basis by personnel on "joint tours" from the various Intelligence Community agencies;

—institute a reporting mechanism that enables analysts at all the intelligence and law enforcement agencies to post lead information for use by analysts at other agencies without waiting for dissemination of a formal report;

—maintain excellence and creativity in staff analytic skills through regular use of analysis and language training programs; and

—establish and sustain effective channels for the exchange of counterterrorism related information with federal agencies outside the Intelligence Community as well as with state and local authorities.

■ Given the FBI's history of repeated shortcomings within its current responsibility for domestic intelligence, and in the face of grave and immediate threats to our homeland, the FBI should strengthen and improve its domestic capability as fully and expeditiously as possible by immediately instituting measures to:

—strengthen counterterrorism as a national FBI program by clearly designating national counterterrorism priorities and enforcing field office adherence to those priorities;

—establish and sustain independent career tracks within the FBI that recognize and provide incentives for demonstrated skills and performance of counterterrorism agents and analysts;

—significantly improve strategic analytical capabilities by assuring the qualification, training, and independence of analysts, coupled with sufficient access to necessary information and resources;

—establish a strong reports officer cadre at FBI Headquarters and field offices to facilitate timely dissemination of intelligence from agents to analysts within the FBI and other agencies within the Intelligence Community;

—implement training for agents in the effective use of analysts and analysis in their work;

—expand and sustain the recruitment of agents and analysts with the linguistic skills needed in counterterrorism efforts;

—increase substantially efforts to penetrate terrorist organizations operating in the United States through all available means of collection;

—improve the national security law training of FBI personnel;

—implement mechanisms to maximize the exchange of counterterrorism-related information between the FBI and other federal, state and local agencies; and

—finally solve the FBI's persistent and incapacitating information technology problems.

■ The Attorney General and the Director of the FBI should take action necessary to ensure that:

—the Office of Intelligence Policy and Review and other Department of Justice components provide in-depth training to the FBI and other members of the Intelligence Community regarding the use of the Foreign Intelligence Surveillance Act (FISA) to address terrorist threats to the United States;

—the FBI disseminates results of searches and surveillances authorized under FISA to appropriate personnel within the FBI and the Intelligence Community on a timely basis so they may be used for analysis and operations that address terrorist threats to the United States; and

—the FBI develops and implements a plan to use authorities provided by FISA to assess the threat of international terrorist groups within the United States fully, including the extent to which such groups are funded or otherwise supported by foreign governments.

■ The President should review and consider amendments to the Executive Orders, policies and procedures that govern the national security classification of intelligence information, in an effort to expand access to relevant information for federal agencies outside the Intelligence Community, for state and local authorities, which are critical to the fight against terrorism, and for the American public. In addition, the President and the heads of federal agencies should ensure that the policies and procedures to protect against the unauthorized disclosure of classified intelligence information are well understood, fully implemented and vigorously enforced.

■ Congress and the Administration should ensure the full development of a national watchlist center that will be responsible for coordinating and integrating all terrorist related watchlist systems; promoting awareness and use of the center by all relevant government agencies and elements of the private sector; and ensuring a consistent and comprehensive flow of terrorist names into the center from all relevant points of collection.

Key Hart-Rudman Commission Recommendations

- The President should propose, and Congress should agree to create, a National Homeland Security Agency (NHSA) with responsibility for planning, coordinating, and integrating various U.S. government activities involved in homeland security. The Federal Emergency Management Agency (FEMA) should be a key building block in this effort.
- The President should propose to Congress the transfer of the Customs Service, the Border Patrol, and Coast Guard to the National Homeland Security Agency, while preserving them as distinct entities.
- The President should propose to Congress the establishment of an Assistant Secretary of Defense for Homeland Security within the Office of the Secretary of Defense, reporting directly to the Secretary.
- The Secretary of Defense, at the President's direction, should make homeland security a primary mission of the National Guard, and the Guard should be organized, properly trained, and adequately equipped to undertake that mission.
- The National Security Council (NSC) should be responsible for advising the President and for coordinating the multiplicity of national security activities, broadly defined to include economic and domestic law enforcement activities as well as the traditional national security agenda. The NSC Advisor and staff should resist the temptation to assume a central policymaking and operational role.
- The President should create an implementing mechanism to ensure that the major recommendations of this Commission result in the critical reforms necessary to ensure American national security and global leadership over the next quarter century.

Intelligence Issues

Key 9/11 Commission Recommendations

- The current position of Director of Central Intelligence should be replaced by a National Intelligence Director with two main areas of responsibility: (1) to oversee national intelligence centers on specific subjects of interest across the U.S. government and (2) to manage the national intelligence program and oversee the agencies that contribute to it.
- The CIA Director should emphasize (a) rebuilding the CIA's analytic capabilities; (b) transforming the clandestine service by building its human intelligence capabilities; (c) developing a stronger language program, with high standards and sufficient financial incentives; (d) renewing emphasis on recruiting diversity among operations officers so they can blend more easily in foreign cities; (e) ensuring a seamless relationship between human source collection and signals collection at the operational level; and (f) stressing a better balance between unilateral and liaison operations.
- Lead responsibility for directing and executing paramilitary operations, whether clandestine or covert, should shift to the Defense Department. There it should be consolidated with the capabilities for training, direction, and execution of such operations already being developed in the Special Operations Command.
- The overall amounts of money being appropriated for national intelligence and to its component agencies should no longer be kept secret. Congress should pass a separate appropriations act for intelligence, defending the broad allocation of how these tens of billions of dollars have been assigned among the varieties of intelligence work.
- Information procedures should provide incentives for sharing, to restore a better balance between security and shared knowledge.
- The president should lead the government-wide effort to bring the major national security institutions into the information revolution. He should coordinate the resolution of the legal, policy, and technical issues across agencies to create a "trusted information network."
- A specialized and integrated national security workforce should be established at the FBI consisting of agents, analysts, linguists, and surveillance specialists who are recruited, trained, rewarded, and retained to ensure the development of an institutional culture imbued with a deep expertise in intelligence and national security.

Key Gilmore Commission Recommendations

- Establish a National Counter Terrorism Center (NCTC).
- Transfer the collection of terrorism related intelligence inside the United States to the NCTC.
- Establish the Terrorist Threat Integration Center as an independent agency and require TTIC to have permanent staff from representative State and local entities (Congress).
- Produce continuing, comprehensive "strategic" assessments of threats inside the United States.
- Develop and disseminate continuing comprehensive strategic threat assessments (Intelligence Community and DHS).
- Ensure DHS authority to levy direct intelligence requirements, and robust DHS capability for combining threat and vulnerability information.
- Perform a comprehensive National Intelligence Estimate on the threats to infrastructure.
- Perform a National Intelligence Estimate on the threat to agriculture and food.

Key Bremer Commission Recommendations

- The Director of Central Intelligence should make it clear to the Central Intelligence Agency that the aggressive recruitment of human intelligence sources on terrorism is one of the intelligence community's highest priorities.
- The Director of Central Intelligence should issue a directive that the 1995 guidelines will no longer apply to recruiting terrorist informants. That directive should notify officers in the field that the pre-existing process of assessing such informants will apply.
- The President should direct the Director of Central Intelligence, the Secretary of Defense, and the Director of the Federal Bureau of Investigation to work with Congress to ensure that adequate resources are devoted to meet essential technology requirements of the National Security Agency and the Federal Bureau of Investigation and to expand and accelerate the DCI's Counterterrorist Center's activities.
- The Director of Central Intelligence should authorize the Foreign Language Executive Committee to develop a larger pool of linguists and an interagency strategy for employing them, including flexible approaches to reduce problems related to handling of classified material.

Key Recommendations of the Joint Inquiry of House and Senate Intelligence Committees

- The National Security Act of 1947 should be amended to create and sufficiently staff a statutory Director of National Intelligence who shall be the President's principal advisor on intelligence and shall have the full range of management, budgetary and personnel responsibilities needed to make the entire U.S. Intelligence Community operate as a coherent whole. These responsibilities should include:

  —establishment and enforcement of consistent priorities for the collection, analysis, and dissemination of intelligence throughout the Intelligence Community;
  —setting of policy and the ability to move personnel between elements of the Intelligence Community;
  —review, approval, modification, and primary management and oversight of the execution of Intelligence Community budgets;
  —review, approval, modification, and primary management and oversight of the execution of Intelligence Community personnel and resource allocations;
  —review, approval, modification, and primary management and oversight of the execution of Intelligence Community research and development efforts;
  —review, approval, and coordination of relationships between the Intelligence Community agencies and foreign intelligence and law enforcement services; and
  —exercise of statutory authority to insure that Intelligence Community agencies and components fully comply with Communitywide policy, management, spending, and administrative guidance and priorities.

- The Director of National Intelligence should be a Cabinet level position, appointed by the President and subject to Senate confirmation. Congress and the President should also work to insure that the Director of National Intelligence effectively exercises these authorities.
- To insure focused and consistent Intelligence Community leadership, Congress should require that no person may simultaneously serve as both the Director of National Intelligence and the Director of the Central Intelligence Agency, or as the director of any other specific intelligence agency.
- Current efforts by the National Security Council to examine and revamp existing intelligence priorities should be expedited, given the immediate need for clear guidance in intelligence and counterterrorism efforts. The President should take action to ensure that clear, consistent, and current priorities are established and enforced throughout the Intelligence Community. Once established, these priorities should be reviewed and updated on at least an annual basis to ensure that the allocation of Intelligence Community resources reflects and effectively addresses the continually evolving threat environment.
- The position of National Intelligence Officer for Terrorism should be created on the National Intelligence Council and a highly qualified individual appointed to prepare intelligence estimates on terrorism for the use of Congress and policymakers in the Executive Branch and to assist the Intelligence Community in developing a program for strategic analysis and assessments.
- Recognizing that the Intelligence Community's employees remain its greatest resource, the Director of National Intelligence should require that measures be implemented to greatly enhance the recruitment and development of a workforce with the intelligence skills and expertise needed for success in counterterrorist efforts, including:

  —the agencies of the Intelligence Community should act promptly to expand and improve counterterrorism training programs within the Community, insuring coverage of such critical areas as information sharing among law enforcement and intelligence personnel; language capabilities; the use of the Foreign Intelligence Surveillance Act; and watchlisting;
  —the Intelligence Community should build on the provisions of the Intelligence Authorization Act for Fiscal Year 2003 regarding the development of language capabilities, including the Act's requirement for a report on the feasibility of establishing a Civilian Linguist Reserve Corps, and implement expeditiously measures to identify and recruit linguists outside the Community whose abilities are relevant to the needs of counterterrorism;
  —the existing Intelligence Community Reserve Corps should be expanded to ensure the use of relevant per-

sonnel and expertise from outside the Community as special needs arise;
- The Director of National Intelligence should require more extensive use of "joint tours" for intelligence and appropriate law enforcement personnel to broaden their experience and help bridge existing organizational and cultural divides through service in other agencies. These joint tours should include not only service at Intelligence Community agencies, but also service in those agencies that are users or consumers of intelligence products. Serious incentives for joint service should be established throughout the Intelligence Community and personnel should be rewarded for joint service with career advancement credit at individual agencies. The Director of National Intelligence should also require Intelligence Community agencies to participate in joint exercises.
- The Intelligence Community should enhance recruitment of a more ethnically and culturally diverse workforce and devise a strategy to capitalize upon the unique cultural and linguistic capabilities of first-generation Americans, a strategy designed to utilize their skills to the greatest practical effect while recognizing the potential counterintelligence challenges such hiring decisions might pose.
- Steps should be taken to increase and ensure the greatest return on this nation's substantial investment in intelligence, including:
  — the President should submit budget recommendations, and Congress should enact budget authority, for sustained, long-term investment in counterterrorism capabilities that avoid dependence on repeated stop-gap supplemental appropriations;
  — in making such budget recommendations, the President should provide for the consideration of a separate classified Intelligence Community budget;
  — long-term counterterrorism investment should be accompanied by sufficient flexibility, subject to congressional oversight, to enable the Intelligence Community to rapidly respond to altered or unanticipated needs;
  — the Director of National Intelligence should insure that Intelligence Community budgeting practices and procedures are revised to better identify the levels and nature of counterterrorism funding within the Community;
  — counterterrorism funding should be allocated in accordance with the program requirements of the national counterterrorism strategy; and
  — due consideration should be given to directing an outside agency or entity to conduct a thorough and rigorous cost-benefit analysis of the resources spent on intelligence.
- Assured standards of accountability are critical to developing the personal responsibility, urgency, and diligence which our counterterrorism responsibility requires. Given the absence of any substantial efforts within the Intelligence Community to impose accountability in relation to the events of September 11, 2001, the Director of Central Intelligence and the heads of Intelligence Community agencies should require that measures designed to ensure accountability are implemented throughout the Community. To underscore the need for accountability:
  —The Director of Central Intelligence should report to the House and Senate Intelligence Committees no later than June 30, 2003 as to the steps taken to implement a system of accountability throughout the Intelligence Community, to include processes for identifying poor performance and affixing responsibility for it, and for recognizing and rewarding excellence in performance;
- As part of the confirmation process for Intelligence Community officials, Congress should require from those officials an affirmative commitment to the implementation and use of strong accountability mechanisms throughout the Intelligence Community;
- The Inspectors General at the Central Intelligence Agency, the Department of Defense, the Department of Justice, and the Department of State should review the factual findings and the record of this Inquiry and conduct investigations and reviews as necessary to determine whether and to what extent personnel at all levels should be held accountable for any omission, commission, or failure to meet professional standards in regard to the identification, prevention, or disruption of terrorist attacks, including the events of September 11, 2001. These reviews should also address those individuals who performed in a stellar or exceptional manner, and the degree to which the quality of their performance was rewarded or otherwise impacted their careers. Based on those investigations and reviews, agency heads should take appropriate disciplinary and other action and the President and the House and Senate Intelligence Committees should be advised of such action.
- The Administration should review and report to the House and Senate Intelligence Committees by June 30, 2003 regarding what progress has been made in reducing the inappropriate and obsolete barriers among intelligence and law enforcement agencies engaged in counterterrorism, what remains to be done to reduce those barriers, and what legislative actions may be advisable in that regard. In particular, this report should address what steps are being taken to insure that perceptions within the Intelligence Community about the scope and limits of current law and policy with respect to restrictions on collection and information sharing are, in fact, accurate and well-founded.

Key Hart-Rudman Commission Recommendations

- The President should ensure that the National Intelligence Council: include homeland security and asymmetric threats as an area of analysis; assign that portfolio to a National Intelligence Officer; and produce National Intelligence Estimates on these threats.

- The President should order the setting of national intelligence priorities through National Security Council guidance to the Director of Central Intelligence.
- The Director of Central Intelligence should emphasize the recruitment of human intelligence sources on terrorism as one of the intelligence community's highest priorities, and ensure that operational guidelines are balanced between security needs and respect for American values and principles.
- The intelligence community should place new emphasis on collection and analysis of economic and science/technology security concerns, and incorporate more open source intelligence into analytical products. Congress should support this new emphasis by increasing significantly the National Foreign Intelligence Program (NFIP) budget for collection and analysis.

Congress and Oversight Issues

Key 9/11 Commission Recommendations

- Congressional oversight for intelligence and counterterrorism is now dysfunctional. Congress should address this problem. We have considered various alternatives: A joint committee on the old model of the Joint Committee on Atomic Energy is one. A single committee in each house of Congress, combining authorizing and appropriating authorities, is another.
- Congress should create a single, principal point of oversight and review for homeland security. Congressional leaders are best able to judge what committee should have jurisdiction over this department and its duties. But we believe that Congress does have the obligation to choose one in the House and one in the Senate, and that this committee should be a permanent standing committee with a nonpartisan staff.
- Since a catastrophic attack could occur with little or no notice, we should minimize as much as possible the disruption of national security policymaking during the change of administrations by accelerating the process for national security appointments. We think the process could be improved significantly so transitions can work more effectively and allow new officials to assume their new responsibilities as quickly as possible. The Department of Defense and its oversight committees should regularly assess the adequacy of Northern Command's strategies and planning to defend the United States against military threats to the homeland. The Department of Homeland Security and its oversight committees should regularly assess the types of threats the country faces to determine (a) the adequacy of the government's plans—and the progress against those plans—to protect America's critical infrastructure and (b) the readiness of the government to respond to the threats that the United States might face.

Key Gilmore Commission Recommendations

- Concentrate oversight of the NCTC [National Counter Terrorism Center] in the intelligence committee in each House.
- Establish separate Congressional authorizing committee and appropriation subcommittee for homeland security.

Key Bremer Commission Recommendations

- Congress should promptly ratify the International Convention for the Suppression of the Financing of Terrorism and pass any legislation necessary for full implementation.
- Congress should enact legislation to make countries designated as "Not Cooperating Fully" ineligible for the Visa Waiver Program.
- Congress should review the status of the Foreign Terrorist Organizations (FTO) statute within five years to determine whether changes are appropriate.
- Congress should develop a mechanism for reviewing the President's counterterrorism policy and budget as a whole. The executive branch should commit to full consultation with Congress on counterterrorism issues.
- House and Senate Appropriations Committees should immediately direct full-committee staff to conduct a cross-subcommittee review of counterterrorism budgets.
- The Congress should:
  —Make possession of designated critical pathogens illegal for anyone who is not properly certified.
  —Control domestic sale and transfer of equipment critical to the development or use of biological agents by certifying legitimate users of critical equipment and prohibiting sales of such equipment to noncertified entities.
  —Require tagging of critical equipment to enable law enforcement to identify its location.
  —By recent statute, federal agencies must reimburse up to one half of the cost of personal liability insurance to law enforcement officers and managers or supervisors. Congress should amend the statute to mandate full reimbursement of the costs of personal liability insurance for Federal Bureau of Investigation special agents and Central Intelligence Agency officers in the field who are combating terrorism.

Key Recommendations of the Joint Inquiry of House and Senate Intelligence Committees

- The establishment of Intelligence Community priorities, and the justification for such priorities, should be reported to both the House and Senate Intelligence Committees on an annual basis.

- The Intelligence Community should fully inform the House and Senate Intelligence Committees of significant developments in these efforts, through regular reports and additional communications as necessary, and the Committees should, in turn, exercise vigorous and continuing oversight of the Community's work in this critically important area.
- Congress and the Administration should carefully consider how best to structure and manage U.S. domestic intelligence responsibilities. Congress should review the scope of domestic intelligence authorities to determine their adequacy in pursuing counterterrorism at home and ensuring the protection of privacy and other rights guaranteed under the Constitution. This review should include, for example, such questions as whether the range of persons subject to searches and surveillances authorized under the Foreign Intelligence Surveillance Act (FISA) should be expanded.
- Based on their oversight responsibilities, the Intelligence and Judiciary Committees of the Congress, as appropriate, should consider promptly, in consultation with the Administration, whether the FBI should continue to perform the domestic intelligence functions of the United States Government or whether legislation is necessary to remedy this problem, including the possibility of creating a new agency to perform those functions.
- Congress should require that the new Director of National Intelligence, the Attorney General, and the Secretary of the Department of Homeland Security report to the President and the Congress on a date certain concerning:
    - the FBI's progress since September 11, 2001 in implementing the reforms required to conduct an effective domestic intelligence program, including the measures recommended above;
    - the experience of other democratic nations in organizing the conduct of domestic intelligence;
    - the specific manner in which a new domestic intelligence service could be established in the United States, recognizing the need to enhance national security while fully protecting civil liberties; and
    - their recommendations on how to best fulfill the nation's need for an effective domestic intelligence capability, including necessary legislation.
- The House and Senate Intelligence and Judiciary Committees should continue to examine the Foreign Intelligence Surveillance Act and its implementation thoroughly, particularly with respect to changes made as a result of the USA PATRIOT Act and the subsequent decision of the United States Foreign Intelligence Court of Review, to determine whether its provisions adequately address present and emerging terrorist threats to the United States. Legislation should be proposed by those Committees to remedy any deficiencies identified as a result of that review.
- The Director of the National Security Agency should present to the Director of National Intelligence and the Secretary of Defense by June 30, 2003, and report to the House and Senate Intelligence Committees, a detailed plan that:
    - describes solutions for the technological challenges for signals intelligence;
    - requires a review, on a quarterly basis, of the goals, products to be delivered, funding levels and schedules for every technology development program;
    - ensures strict accounting for program expenditures;
    - within their jurisdiction as established by current law, makes NSA a full collaborating partner with the Central Intelligence Agency and the Federal Bureau of Investigation in the war on terrorism, including fully integrating the collection and analytic capabilities of NSA, CIA, and the FBI; and makes recommendations for legislation needed to facilitate these goals.
- In evaluating the plan, the Committees should also consider issues pertaining to whether civilians should be appointed to the position of Director of the National Security Agency and whether the term of service for the position should be longer than it has been in the recent past.
- Congress should consider enacting legislation, modeled on the Goldwater-Nichols Act of 1986, to instill the concept of "jointness" throughout the Intelligence Community. By emphasizing such things as joint education, a joint career specialty, increased authority for regional commanders, and joint exercises, that act greatly enhanced the joint warfighting capabilities of the individual military services. Legislation to instill similar concepts throughout the Intelligence Community could help improve management of Community resources and priorities and insure a far more effective "team" effort by all the intelligence agencies.
- Congress should expand and improve existing educational grant programs focused on intelligence-related fields, similar to military scholarship programs and others that provide financial assistance in return for a commitment to serve in the Intelligence Community.
- Recognizing the importance of intelligence in this nation's struggle against terrorism, Congress should maintain vigorous, informed, and constructive oversight of the Intelligence Community. To best achieve that goal, the National Commission on Terrorist Attacks Upon the United States should study and make recommendations concerning how Congress may improve its oversight of the Intelligence Community, including consideration of such areas as:
    - changes in the budgetary process;
    - changes in the rules regarding membership on the oversight committees;
    - whether oversight responsibility should be vested in a joint House-Senate Committee or, as currently exists, in separate Committees in each house; the extent to which classification decisions impair congressional oversight; and how Congressional oversight can best contribute

to the continuing need of the Intelligence Community to evolve and adapt to changes in the subject matter of intelligence and the needs of policy makers.

- Congress should also review the statutes, policies and procedures that govern the national security classification of intelligence information and its protection from unauthorized disclosure. Among other matters, Congress should consider the degree to which excessive classification has been used in the past and the extent to which the emerging threat environment has greatly increased the need for real-time sharing of sensitive information.
- The Director of National Intelligence, in consultation with the Secretary of Defense, the Secretary of State, the Secretary of Homeland Security, and the Attorney General, should review and report to the House and Senate Intelligence Committees on proposals for a new and more realistic approach to the processes and structures that have governed the designation of sensitive and classified information. The report should include proposals to protect against the use of the classification process as a shield to protect agency self-interest.
- The Director of Central Intelligence should report to the House and Senate Intelligence Committees no later than June 30, 2003 as to the steps taken to implement a system of accountability throughout the Intelligence Community, to include processes for identifying poor performance and affixing responsibility for it, and for recognizing and rewarding excellence in performance.
- As part of the confirmation process for Intelligence Community officials, Congress should require from those officials an affirmative commitment to the implementation and use of strong accountability mechanisms throughout the Intelligence Community.

Key Hart-Rudman Commission Recommendations

- Congress should establish a special body to deal with homeland security issues, as has been done with intelligence oversight. Members should be chosen for their expertise in foreign policy, defense, intelligence, law enforcement, and appropriations. This body should also include members of all relevant Congressional committees as well as ex-officio members from the leadership of both Houses of Congress.
- Congress should rationalize its current committee structure so that it best serves U.S. national security objectives; specifically, it should merge the current authorizing committees with the relevant appropriations subcommittees.
- The Executive Branch must ensure a sustained focus on foreign policy and national security consultation with Congress and devote resources to it. For its part, Congress must make consultation a higher priority and form a permanent consultative group of Congressional leaders as part of this effort.

- The Congressional leadership should conduct a thorough bicameral, bipartisan review of the Legislative Branch relationship to national security and foreign policy.

Appendix: Origins and Mandates of Commissions Reviewed in this Report

The National Commission on Terrorist Attacks Upon the United States (9/11 Commission)

Its website is [http://www.9-11commission.gov/].

Popularly referred to as the "9/11 Commission" it was established by Title VI of P.L. 107-306, 107th Congress, 2nd session (November 27, 2002). It released its report on July 22, 2004. This Commission was charged with:

— examining and reporting on the facts and causes relating to the terrorist attacks of September 11, 2001 on the United States;
— evaluating and reporting on the evidence developed by all relevant governmental agencies regarding the facts and circumstances surrounding the attacks;
— to build upon the investigations of other entities, and avoid unnecessary duplication, by reviewing the findings, conclusions, and recommendations of the Joint Inquiry of the Select Intelligence Committees of the House and Senate, and other executive branch, congressional or independent commission investigations into the terrorist attacks of September 11, 2001, other terrorist attacks, and terrorism generally;
— to make a full and complete accounting of the circumstances surrounding the attacks, and the extent of the United States' preparedness for, and the immediate response to, the attacks; and
— to investigate and report to the President and Congress on its findings, conclusions, and recommendations for corrective measures that can be taken to prevent acts of terrorism.

The Advisory Panel to Assess Domestic Response Capabilities for Terrorism Involving Weapons of Mass Destruction (Gilmore Commission)

Its reports can be found at this website: [http://www.rand.org/nsrd/terrpanel/].

Popularly known as the Gilmore Commission it was created pursuant to section 1405 of P.L. 105-241 105th Congress, 2nd session (October 17, 1998), and whose authorities were extended for two additional years by section 1514 of

P.L. 107-107, 107th Congress, 1st session (December 28, 2001). Produced an annual report each year from 1999-2003 in December of every year. Its final report was released December 15, 2003. This Commission was charged with:

- —assessing Federal agency efforts to enhance domestic preparedness for incidents involving weapons of mass destruction;
- —assessing the progress of Federal training programs for local emergency responses to incidents involving weapons of mass destruction;
- assessing deficiencies in programs for response to incidents involving weapons of mass destruction, including a review of unfunded communications, equipment, and planning requirements, and the needs of maritime regions;
- —recommending strategies for ensuring effective coordination with respect to Federal agency weapons of mass destruction response efforts, and for ensuring fully effective local response capabilities for weapons of mass destruction incidents; and
- —assessing the appropriate roles of State and local governments in funding effective local response capabilities.

Each of the annual reports of the Commission, submitted to the President and to Congress, was to set forth the Commission's findings, conclusions and recommendations for improving Federal, State, and local domestic emergency preparedness to respond to incidents involving weapons of mass destruction.

The National Commission on Terrorism (Bremer Commission)

Its report is at this website: [http://w3.access.gpo.gov/nct/].

Popularly known at the Bremer Commission it was created pursuant to section 591 of P.L. 105-277, 105th Congress, 2nd Session (October 21, 1998). Its final report was released on June 5, 2000. This Commission was charged with:

- reviewing the laws, regulations, policies, directives, and practices relating to counter-terrorism in the prevention and punishment of international terrorism directed towards the United States;
- assessing the extent to which, laws, regulations, policies, directives, and practices relating to counter-terrorism have been effective in preventing or punishing international terrorism directed towards the United States. This assessment was to include a review of:

  (1) Evidence that terrorist organizations have established an infrastructure in the western hemisphere for the support and conduct of terrorist activities;
  (2) Executive branch efforts to coordinate counterterrorism activities among Federal, State, and local agencies and with other nations to determine the effectiveness of such coordination efforts;
  (3) Executive branch efforts to prevent the use of nuclear, biological, and chemical weapons by terrorists.

The Commission was to recommend changes to counterterrorism policy in preventing and punishing international terrorism directed toward the United States not later than six months after the date the Commission first met, providing a final report to the President and the Congress.

The U.S. Commission on National Security/21st Century (Hart-Rudman Commission)

The final report is found at this website: [http://www.crs.gov/staff/911/pdf/rmap_ns1.pdf].

Popularly known as the Hart-Rudman Commission it was authorized by Secretary of Defense William S. Cohen on September 2, 1999. It produced and submitted three separate reports. The first: New World Coming: American Security in the 21st Century on September 15, 1999; the second: Seeking A National Strategy: A Concert for Preserving Security and Promoting Freedom on April 15, 2000; the third: Road Map for National Security: Imperative for Change was submitted on March 15, 2001. This Commission was charged with:

- conducting a comprehensive review of the early 21st Century global security environment;
- developing a comprehensive overview of American strategic interests and objectives for the security environment likely to be encountered in the 21st Century;
- delineating a national security strategy appropriate to that environment and the nation's character;
- identifying a range of alternatives to implement the national security strategy, by defining the security goals for American society, and by describing the internal and external policy instruments required to apply American resources in the 21st Century;
- developing a detailed plan to implement the range of alternatives by describing the sequence of measures necessary to attain the national security strategy, to include recommending concomitant changes to the national security apparatus as necessary.

The Joint Inquiry of the House Permanent Select Committee on Intelligence and the Senate Select Committee on Intelligence

The report can be found at the following website, which includes the report and the recommendations and findings which are printed separately as an errata compilation as noted on the homepage: [http://www.gpoaccess.gov/serialset/creports/911.html].

The two Congressional Committees responsible for oversight of the U.S. intelligence community agreed in February

2002 during the 2nd session of the 107th Congress to conduct a "Joint Inquiry" into a range of issues related to the terrorist attacks on the United States on September 11, 2001 with the focus on the activities of the U.S. Intelligence Community. The committees issued a final report on December 15, 2002, entitled "Intelligence Community Activities Before and After the Terrorist Attacks on September 11, 2001," H.Rept. 107-792 and S.Rept. 107-351, printed jointly, 107th Congress, 2nd session. The goals of the Joint Inquiry were to:

- conduct a factual review of what the Intelligence Community knew or should have known prior to September 11, 2001, regarding the international terrorist threat to the United States, include the scope and nature of any possible international terrorist attacks against the United States and its interests;
- identify and examine any systemic problems that may have impeded the Intelligence Community in learning of or preventing these attacks in advance; and
- make recommendations to improve the Intelligence Community's ability to identify and prevent future international terrorist attacks.

Order Code RL32519, August 11, 2004

Country Reports on Terrorism 2004

Africa Overview

A small number of al-Qaida operatives in East Africa, particularly Somalia, continued to pose the most serious threat to American interests in the region. It is unclear to what extent terrorist groups are present in South Africa, however, the activity of al-Qaida and affiliated persons or groups in South Africa and Nigeria, home to Africa's largest Muslim population, is of growing concern. Hizballah continues to engage in fundraising activities in Africa, particularly in West Africa.

Though civil conflict and ethnic violence continued in a number of African countries in 2004, there were few significant international terrorist incidents in Africa during the year. An increase in anti-American and anti-Western rhetoric from a number of Islamic radicals is of growing concern. Many African governments improved their cooperation and strengthened their efforts in the war on terrorism. Both the African Union (AU) and other African regional organizations undertook initiatives to improve counterterrorism cooperation and information sharing.

In October, the Government of Chad helped negotiate the turnover of captured Salafist Group for Call and Combat (GSPC) factional leader Amari Saifi (aka Abderazak al-Para) from a Chadian rebel group to the Algerian Government. Chadian military forces had routed the GSPC element led by al-Para in northern Chad in March, and he was subsequently captured by the rebel group. Al-Para headed a GSPC faction responsible for the kidnapping of 32 European tourists in Algeria in the summer of 2003. Al-Para took the captives to Mali, where the government was instrumental in securing their release. Members of the GSPC continue to operate in the Sahel region, crossing difficult-to-patrol borders between Mali, Mauritania, Niger, Algeria and Chad. With the help of US-funded training, those countries have increasingly cooperated against the GSPC. At year's end, al-Para was in Algerian custody.

Sahel countries Mauritania, Mali, Niger, and Chad are devoting more resources to improve their counterterrorism capabilities. These countries also participate in the US-sponsored Pan-Sahel Initiative (PSI), a program designed to assist those nations in protecting their borders, combating terrorism, and enhancing regional stability. Components of the program are intended to encourage the participating countries to cooperate with each other against smuggling and trafficking in persons, as well as in the sharing of information. The State Department funded and currently supervises the program, which has included providing equipment and training by US European Command (EUCOM) trainers to Sahel country military units. The United States has also provided counterterrorism training for senior police and other officials from eastern and southern Africa at the International Law Enforcement Academy in Gaborone, Botswana. A continuation of the PSI program, called the Trans Sahara Counterterrorism Initiative, is now under consideration.

Many African nations have taken cooperative action against terrorism, including making real efforts to sign and ratify the 12 international conventions and protocols relating to terrorism. Botswana, Burkina Faso, Ghana, Kenya, Madagascar, Mali, Niger, the Seychelles, and Sudan have signed all 12 protocols. In October, the African Union (AU) opened the new African Center for Study and Research on Terrorism in Algiers. Several nations have formed national counterterrorism centers, including Nigeria, Kenya, and South Africa.

Djibouti

Djibouti has taken a strong stand against international terrorist organizations and individuals. Djibouti hosts the only US military base in Sub-Saharan Africa, the Combined Joint Task Force-Horn of Africa, as well as Combined Task Force 150 which operates offshore and is headquartered in Bahrain.

The Djiboutian Government has increased its efforts to train security forces, secure borders, and expand its capacity for maritime interdiction. Djibouti also joined the ranks of countries participating in the US Government's Safe Skies for Africa program in late 2004. Through this program, Djibouti is scheduled to receive assistance to improve its airport security and infrastructure. The Government has also closed down terrorist-linked financial institutions and shared information on possible terrorist activity in the region. The counterterrorism committee under President Guelleh moved to enhance coordination and action on information concerning terrorist organizations.

Ethiopia

Ethiopia's support in the global war on terrorism has been consistently solid and unwavering. The Government of Ethiopia has conducted investigations regarding regional rebel and possibly transnational terrorist threats to Westerners and US military officials in the Ogaden region of Ethiopia. Ethiopia has also been cooperative in sharing information with the United States on terrorist activities. To counter the threat from these groups and from elements of the Somalia-based Al-Ittihad al-Islami (AIAI), Ethiopia has undertaken increased military efforts to control its lengthy and porous border with Somalia. Its draft penal code includes provisions that criminalize terrorism, money-laundering, and providing financial support for terrorism. The Government also has developed and installed new security systems for Addis Ababa's international airport that allow the tracking of terrorists and terrorist supporters, and introduced a new, more secure passport that includes anti-tampering features.

Kenya

Kenya remains an active and critical partner in the war on terrorism. The Government established the National Counter Terrorism Center in January 2004 as well as the National Security Advisory Committee to oversee its operations. However, Kenya registered only slow progress towards the overall strengthening of its capabilities to combat terrorism, prosecute terror suspects, or respond to emergency situations. In April 2003, Kenya published a draft "Suppression of Terrorism" bill, but withdrew it in 2004 due to broad human rights concerns. At year's end, the Kenyan Government had not submitted to parliament a revised draft to address these concerns.

The Kenyan Government has taken the initiative in arresting terrorist suspects and disrupting terrorist operations. The trials of seven terror suspects—arrested in November 2003 on charges related to the Kikambala hotel bombing and attempted shoot-down of an Israeli airliner in November 2002, the 1998 Embassy bombings and a subsequent plot to attack the US Embassy in 2003—continued but were not concluded by year's end. Kenya made many security improvements at airports and hotels in 2004, particularly in Mombasa. The Government's uncoordinated response to an explosion at Nairobi's Wilson Airport in October, however, indicates the need for better coordination and continued improvement of security measures.

Nigeria

In 2004, Nigeria remained committed to the global war against terrorism and has stepped up diplomatic efforts in both global and regional forums concerning counterterrorism issues. Nigerian President Olusegun Obasanjo and other African heads of state founded the New Partnership for African Development—geared toward sustainable development in Africa—that has helped African countries combat terrorism. Nigeria initiated and sponsored the first-ever regional conference of security and intelligence service chiefs during 2004 under the auspices of the Economic Community of West African States (ECOWAS). A central theme during this conference was the need to share information and cooperate more fully on a host of transnational issues, particularly terrorism. This effort was followed by an African Union conference, chaired by President Obasanjo, which specifically addressed the need for broader cooperation within the intelligence and security service communities of AU member countries on the issue of terrorism.

Nigeria has participated actively in international efforts to track and freeze terrorists' assets. However, Nigeria's relatively large and complex banking sector, combined with widespread corruption, makes combating terrorism financing more difficult. There are growing concerns about the rise of radical Islam in Nigeria—home of Africa's largest Muslim population. Links were also uncovered connecting Nigerians to al-Qaida in 2004.

In late December 2003, early January and again in September 2004, a group calling itself the "Taleban" raided police stations in the northeastern states of Yobe and Borno, reportedly taking several police officers hostage, stealing weapons, and killing at least seven civilians. Nigerian security services quickly responded to both attacks and claim to have killed or captured dozens of the "Taleban" members in the aftermath of the attacks.

Rwanda

The Rwandan Government has continued to give full support to international efforts to combat terrorism. The Government has been responsive on efforts to combat terrorism financing and has increased its border control measures to identify potential terrorists. Rwanda established an intergovernmental counterterrorism committee and has an antiterrorism section in its police intelligence unit. Despite lack of training and resources, Rwanda's Central Bank and Ministry of Finance officials have provided outstanding cooperation on terrorist financing issues. Rwanda has participated in regional initiatives on international counterterrorism cooperation with other African countries.

During 2004, the Democratic Forces for the Liberation of Rwanda (FDLR), known as the Army for the Liberation of Rwanda (ALIR) until 2001, an armed rebel force including former soldiers and supporters of the previous government that orchestrated the genocide in 1994, continued to operate in Rwanda and the Democratic Republic of the Congo. Rwanda continues to pursue the rebels. An ALIR unit was responsible for the kidnapping and murder of nine persons, including two US tourists, in Bwindi Park in 1999. In 2004, the Rwandan Government assisted US law enforcement officials seeking to prosecute three suspects in the attack who were transferred to the United States for prosecution in 2003. At year's end, the suspects were in US custody awaiting trial.

Somalia

Somalia's lack of a functioning central government, protracted state of violent instability, long unguarded coastline, porous borders, and proximity to the Arabian Peninsula make it a potential location for international terrorists seeking a transit or launching point to conduct operations elsewhere. Regional efforts to bring about a national reconciliation and establish peace and stability in Somalia are ongoing. Although the ability of Somali local and regional authorities to carry out counterterrorism activities is constrained, some have taken limited actions in this direction.

Members of the Somalia-based al-Ittihad al-Islami (AIAI) have committed terrorist acts in the past, primarily in Ethiopia. AIAI rose to power in the early 1990s with a goal of creating an Islamic state in Somalia. In recent years, AIAI has become highly factionalized and diffuse, and its membership is difficult to define. Some elements of AIAI continue to pose a threat to countries in the region, other factions may be targeting Western interests in the region, while still other elements are concerned with humanitarian issues. Some members are sympathetic to and maintain ties with al-Qaida.

South Africa

South Africa publicly supports global efforts against terrorism and has shared financial, law enforcement, and intelligence information with the United States. South Africa took several strong steps forward in combating terror in 2004, particularly in the legislative arena. The South African Parliament in November adopted the thorough "Protection of Constitutional Democracy Against Terrorist and Related Activities Bill," which has been sent to the President's office for signature into law. The act clearly defines terrorism and specifically criminalizes terrorist activities in application of its international obligations. It prescribes prison sentences of up to 15 years or large fines for those convicted.

Two South Africans were arrested in Pakistan in July as part of the Pakistani Government's efforts against al-Qaida. South African officials were satisfied they were not planning to conduct attacks in South Africa. This incident, however, brought to international attention the possibility of South Africans participating in terrorist activities. Some weaknesses of the South African passport were identified, and the Home Affairs Department is taking initial steps to improve the security of both the passport and national identity document.

The South African Government in March organized a four-week multinational Anti-Terrorism Training Program in Pretoria, which brought together police from South Africa and eleven other African countries to teach methods for combating terrorism. In early October, the Government released a report on the first full year's activities of the Financial Intelligence Unit. The Unit received almost 7,500 reports of suspicious financial transactions. Though the quality of the reports was uneven, this is expected to improve during the Unit's next year of operation. Also in October, the Government announced the establishment of an anti-terrorism "nerve center," to bring together several police and intelligence agencies. A specialized rapid response anti-terrorism unit also is planned for the future.

Tanzania

Tanzania continues to be a supportive partner in the global war on terrorism. It has cooperated on several multi-year programs to build law enforcement capacity, enhance border security, improve civil aviation security, and combat money laundering and terrorist finance. It also hosts the East and Southern Africa Anti-Money Laundering Group (ESAAMLG), an international group whose aim is to develop a comprehensive anti-money laundering regime on a regional scale.

Tanzanian and US authorities established a close working relationship after the bombing in 1998 of the US Embassy in Dar Es Salaam and have cooperated in bringing bombing suspects to trial in New York and Dar Es Salaam. Rashid Sweleh Hemed, on trial in Tanzania in late 2003 for his role in the 1998 Embassy attacks, was acquitted in late December by the High Court following the government's appeal of his initial acquittal earlier in the year. A Tanzanian suspected of involvement in the 1998 bombing, Ahmed Khalfan Ghailani, was arrested in July in Pakistan. Although cooperative, Tanzanian law enforcement authorities still have a limited capacity to investigate terrorist suspects and bring them to justice. A comprehensive Prevention of Terrorism Act, approved in late 2002, has yet to be enforced, and implementing regulations for the law have not been drafted.

Uganda

Uganda continued its firm stance against local and international terrorism. Uganda enacted the Anti-Terrorism Act in 2002, which provides a legal basis for bringing suspected terrorists to court and freezing assets of certain terrorist entities.

The Government of Uganda has fought the Lord's Resistance Army (LRA) since the 1980s. This group has carried out acts of extreme brutality against innocent civilians (kidnapping children for use as soldiers and sex slaves) and operates in northern and eastern Uganda and southern Sudan. In February, the LRA attacked the Barlonyo refugee camp near Lira, Uganda, killing nearly 200 people. In previous years, the LRA received assistance from the Government of Sudan. During 2004, the Sudanese Government cooperated with the Ugandan Government to cut off supplies to the LRA, and to allow the Ugandan military to operate on Sudanese territory. The Ugandan Government inflicted severe setbacks to the LRA. It also continued an amnesty program for senior LRA combatants, many of whom opted to come out of the bush and accept the offer. In an attempt to hold a direct dialogue with the LRA, the Government announced a limited ceasefire in mid-November and extended it through December 31, 2004. At year's end, however, no peace had been agreed, and fighting resumed on January 1, 2005, when the LRA ambushed a government vehicle.

East Asia and Pacific Overview

East Asian countries made significant progress in 2004 in preventing terrorist attacks and creating an international environment inhospitable to terrorists. Despite this progress, Southeast Asia continues to be an attractive theater of operations for terrorist groups such as Jemaah Islamiya (JI) and the Abu Sayyaf Group (ASG). The region faced continuing terrorist threats on several fronts, and in 2004 several terrorist assaults occurred. In February, the Philippines suffered the worst terrorist attack in its history when a bomb planted by the ASG sunk SuperFerry 14, killing approximately 130 passengers. In September, a car bomb was detonated in front of the Australian Embassy in Indonesia, reportedly killing 10 and wounding nearly 200. JI claimed responsibility for the attack.

Because terrorism in Asia is a transnational problem, capacity building in a regional context has emerged as a priority alongside national capacity building efforts. In an important development, centers like the Southeast Asia Regional Center for Counterterrorism (SEARCCT) in Malaysia and the US-Thailand International Law Enforcement Academy (ILEA) in Bangkok expanded their activities to provide counterterrorism training to law enforcement officers throughout the region. Likewise, the Australian-Indonesian Jakarta

Center for Law Enforcement Cooperation (JCLEC) is a promising additional regional center for capacity building. Multilateral fora, including the United Nations Security Council's Counterterrorism Committee (UNCTC), G8's Roma-Lyon and Counterterrorism Action Groups (CTAG), Asia-Pacific Economic Cooperation (APEC), the Association of Southeast Asian Nations (ASEAN) and the ASEAN Regional Forum (ARF), also emerged as important organizations for regional and transnational counterterrorism cooperation.

Australia deserves special recognition for its continuing robust counterterrorism posture in 2004, as the Government undertook strong measures not only to improve domestic counterterrorism capacities, but also to strengthen cooperation and capabilities throughout the region. Japan also made valuable contributions to regional counterterrorism capacity building efforts.

Measures to strengthen law enforcement efforts supportive of the global war on terror accelerated in 2004, and several economies in the region developed new institutions to address gaps in their current counterterrorism efforts. The People's Bank of China established an anti-money laundering bureau, which created a terrorist finance investigative unit, and in November Beijing joined the Eurasia Group, a regional anti-money laundering group. In the Philippines, President Arroyo created a multi-agency Anti-Terrorism Task Force (ATTF), which captured over 60 suspected terrorists in its first five months of existence. New Zealand further enhanced its capacity by allocating funds for the creation of National Security Teams specially designated to combat terrorism. Taiwan authorities announced the creation of a counterterrorism policy committee chaired by the Premier of the Executive Yuan and composed of seven multi-agency task forces.

Several countries achieved successes in bringing terrorists to justice, as the fight against terrorism in East Asia matured to move beyond arrests towards prosecutions. The Indonesian police arrested approximately two dozen terrorist suspects, including suspected senior JI leaders, former instructors at JI training camps, financiers of attacks, and members of splinter networks who joined with JI to carry out attacks. When JI Emir Abu Bakar Ba'asyir completed a sentence for document fraud and immigration violations, Indonesian police rearrested and charged him with conspiracy to commit terrorist acts, linking him to the Bali and Jakarta Marriott bombings as well as to a cache of arms and explosives found in central Java. Ba'asyir's trial on these charges was underway at year's end. Following up on 2003 arrests for channeling terrorist money into Cambodia through the Umm al-Qura Islamic school, a Cambodian court convicted three suspects of supporting JI and sentenced them to life imprisonment. The Philippines arrested numerous ASG members, including a senior ASG leader wanted by the United States for his role in the kidnappings of Americans in 2001, and a Philippines court sentenced 17 ASG members to death, although four were convicted in absentia after having escaped from jail. Lack of specific anti-terrorism legislation continues to be a challenge to comprehensive law enforcement efforts in several countries in the region.

Although governments in Southeast Asia made progress in the fight against terrorism in 2004, they face tremendous challenges as they continue to deal with the terrorist threat. Separatist insurgencies, currently ongoing in the Philippines, Indonesia, and southern Thailand, also contribute to an environment of lawlessness, which terrorist groups may attempt to exploit for their own purposes.

Australia

Australia maintained its robust support for domestic and international counterterrorism efforts in 2004, adding to already significant commitments of personnel and resources. Demonstrating a clearer appreciation than most for the scope and nature of the terrorist threat, the Australian Government worked to advance practical proposals for regional cooperation to deter attacks, disrupt terrorist cells, mitigate the effects of any attacks that did occur, and bring terrorists and their supporters to justice.

In 2004, Australia committed significant resources to strengthen its own national security capabilities in areas such as intelligence collection, protective security, and border protection. In May, the National Threat Assessment Center located within the Australian Security Intelligence Organization (ASIO) began operating 24 hours a day, seven days a week. The Australian Transaction Reports and Analysis Center also assisted regional financial intelligence units by building investigation skills and by helping officers throughout the region detect patterns of financial transactions that could be used in terrorist financing.

The Australian Government also introduced legislation to give ASIO new powers to fight terrorism. By the close of 2004, Australia had designated 17 groups as terrorist organizations under legislation creating offenses for membership in, or other specified links to, such groups. Australia also extended measures to freeze terrorist assets of an additional 55 individuals and entities pursuant to Australia's obligations under UN Security Council Resolutions 1267 and 1390 (and their successor resolutions) and 1373.

The Australian Government conducted a national review of the regulations, reporting requirements, and security for the storage, sale, and handling of hazardous materials, with ammonium nitrate a particular priority because of its ready availability and history of terrorist use. The Council of Australian Governments agreed to ban access to ammonium nitrate for other than specifically authorized users. The agreement mandated establishing in each state a licensing regime for the use, manufacture, storage, transport, supply, import, and export of ammonium nitrate.

The Australian Ambassador for Counterterrorism continued to serve as a focal point for coordinating, promoting, and intensifying Australia's international counterterrorism efforts throughout 2004. In continuation of a major diplomatic initiative, Australia broadened its network of bilateral counterterrorism arrangements in Southeast Asia. By the end of 2004, the Australian Government had signed nine bilateral memoranda of understanding (MOUs) on cooperation to combat international terrorism with Indonesia, Malaysia, Thailand, Papua New Guinea, the Philippines, Fiji, Cambodia, East Timor, and India.

Australia launched a number of multi-year plans to help countries in the Asia-Pacific region build capacity to combat terrorism in areas such as law enforcement, border management, transportation security, intelligence, anti-terrorist financing, and the development of legal regimes. Australia's support for the Jakarta Center for Law Enforcement Cooperation (JCLEC) in Semarang, Indonesia is a particularly noteworthy development, as JCLEC will serve as a counterterrorism training resource for regional law enforcement agencies. Australia also funded the establishment in 2004 of the Transnational Crime Center (TNCC) in Jakarta, which will provide a focal point within the Indonesian police for prevention, identification and dismantling all forms of transnational crime, including terrorism.

In February, Australia and Indonesia convened a regional meeting of Justice and Interior ministers to strengthen law enforcement efforts on counterterrorism information sharing and cooperative legal frameworks. Australian law enforcement agencies continued to build working-level relationships with their regional counterparts in 2004. The Australians also provided legal drafting assistance to Pacific Island Forum (PIF) states seeking to adopt UN conventions against terrorism and to bring their domestic laws into conformity with the conventions.

In partnership with the United States, Australia played a leading role in continuing development of a Regional Movement Alert List (RMAL) system. A fully functional RMAL should strengthen the ability of participating countries to fight terrorism by monitoring the movement of people across borders. Following completion of a feasibility study undertaken by Australia and the United States, APEC ministers agreed in November to pilot the RMAL in 2005.

Cambodia

Despite legislative and investigative limitations, Cambodia took several important measures to counter the threat of terrorism. On March 31, 2004, Cambodia, with the assistance of the United States, destroyed its entire stock of man-portable air defense systems (MANPADS) in part to ensure these weapons would never fall into the hands of terrorists.

In April, a bomb detonated at a ferry in the southwestern town of Koh Kong, slightly injuring several people. Five persons allegedly belonging to the Cambodian Freedom Fighters (CFF), an anti-government group, were subsequently arrested. Cambodian authorities had previously arrested seven members of the CFF in November 2003 for allegedly planning a terrorist attack in Koh Kong. However, in October 2004 the court dropped all charges in these cases. Some of the accused claimed they were coerced into confessions.

In December, a Cambodian court convicted three suspects (one Cambodian and two Thai) of supporting Jemaah Islamiya (JI), sentencing them to mandatory life imprisonment. The court acquitted an Egyptian defendant. The case began in May 2003 when the four were arrested by Cambodian authorities for using an Islamic school run by the Saudi Arabia-based non-government organization (NGO) Umm al-Qura as a front for channeling terrorist money into Cambodia from Saudi Arabia. In addition to the arrests of the four, the Government shut down two branches of the Umm al-Qura Islamic School and deported 28 foreign teachers and their dependents. During the trial, the court also convicted in absentia JI operations chief Hambali and two others of attempted murder for terrorist purposes. According to evidence presented in court, Hambali and the others convicted were involved in the planning of terrorist attacks on the US and UK embassies in Phnom Penh.

The Cambodian Government's ability to investigate potential terrorist activities is limited by a lack of training and resources, and it has requested international assistance to upgrade its law enforcement/security capabilities, particularly in border security. The Government has installed with US assistance computerized border control systems at Cambodia's international airports in Phnom Penh and Siem Reap, and land border crossing points at Poipet and Koh Kong. The Cambodian Government has also cooperated fully with US requests to monitor terrorists and terrorist entities listed as supporters of terrorist financing.

China

China continues to take a clear stand against international terrorism and is broadly supportive of the global war on terror. China holds regular counterterrorism consultations with the United States, and is supportive of international efforts to block and freeze terrorist assets. The Chinese Government treats designations of terrorists under US Executive Order 13224 on an equal basis with those designated by the United Nations UNSCR 1267 Sanctions Committee. In 2004, the Bank of China established a financial intelligence unit (FIU) to track suspicious transactions. China joined with Belarus, Kazakhstan, Kyrgyzstan, Tajikistan, and Russia to form the Eurasia Group, a newly created regional anti-money laundering organization or Financial Action Task Force-style regional body, and is in the process of becoming an observer in the Financial Action Task Force (FATF).

In 2004, China agreed to grant permanent status to the FBI Legal Attaché Office in Beijing, thus providing for long-term stability and expansion of US-Chinese law enforcement and counterterrorism cooperation. Although US authorities have sought more timely Chinese responses to terrorist investigation requests, substantive intelligence has been exchanged in some cases. Lack of training and counterterrorism expertise remains an issue for Chinese law enforcement officials, but some received training in combating terrorist financing at the International Law Enforcement Academy in Thailand in 2004. While no acts of international terrorism were committed in China in 2004, there were several reports of bombings and bomb threats in various parts of China. It is unclear whether these were acts of terrorism or criminal attacks. Chinese authorities assert that ethnic Uighur terrorists, primarily based in Xinjiang Uighur Autonomous Region, continue to operate on Chinese territory.

Indonesia

In 2004, Indonesia continued building on its successes combating terrorism, but the bombing of the Australian Embassy in Jakarta in September that killed 10 demonstrates the continued threat posed by terrorists operating in Indonesia. The Indonesian National Police continued to take effective steps to counter the threat posed by the regional terrorist network Jemaah Islamiya (JI). Indonesian police arrested approximately two dozen terrorist suspects in 2004. Those arrested or convicted in 2004 include suspected senior JI leaders, former instructors at JI training camps, financiers of attacks, and members of splinter networks who joined with JI to carry out attacks. Since the October 2002 Bali bombings, Indonesian prosecutors and courts have convicted more than 100 members of JI or affiliated groups on terrorism charges.

Indonesian prosecutors and courts became a focal point of counterterrorism efforts in 2004, as more than 45 JI members stood trial on terrorism charges in Jakarta, Central Sulawesi, and Sumatra. As in previous years, the Government continued to mount effective prosecutions and the courts continued to convict those arrested in cases such as the Marriott bombing, although prosecution cases could have been strengthened in many instances. Additionally, prosecutors have begun levying terrorism charges against suspects involved in sectarian violence in Maluku and Central Sulawesi.

In September 2003, the Indonesian Supreme Court found suspected JI Emir Abu Bakar Ba'asyir guilty of document fraud and immigration violations, but exonerated him on charges of leading and participating in treasonous acts, accepting defense arguments that prosecutors had shown no connection between Ba'asyir and JI. A Supreme Court decision in January 2004 reduced his sentence from three years to 18 months. As Ba'asyir completed that sentence in April 2004, Indonesian police rearrested him and charged him with conspiracy to commit terrorist acts, linking him to the Bali and Marriott bombings as well as to a cache of arms and explosives found in central Java. His trial began in October 2004 and was ongoing at year's end.

In July, the Constitutional Court struck down the retroactive application of the 2003 Anti-Terror Law, passed after the Bali attack. In a divided decision, the Court ruled that the Bali bombings did not constitute an extraordinary crime. Both the Constitutional Court and Supreme Court officials said publicly the ruling would not affect Bali bombing cases already adjudicated. At the time of writing, no sentences of those convicted of Bali-related charges have been appealed based on the Constitutional Court ruling.

In October, an Indonesian court convicted and sentenced Rusman "Gun Gun" Gunawan, an Indonesian connected to the bombing of the J.W. Marriott hotel in Jakarta, to four years in prison for his role in helping facilitate the transfer of funds for that attack.

The South Jakarta District Court handed down an important verdict in November when it found JI member Mohammad Qital guilty under corporate criminal liability provisions of the Anti-Terror Law. In its decision, the court officially recognized the existence of JI and acknowledged that it engaged in terrorist actions. The court then found Qital guilty of terrorist activities through his duties as a JI member. However, at year's end, JI was not a banned organization in Indonesia. The Government has also established and is implementing an interagency process for responding to UN 1267 Sanctions Committee designations. The Government of Indonesia notified the UN Resolution 1373 Committee that it has frozen 18 accounts, but the details of those freeze orders are unclear.

By year's end, newly-elected President Yudhoyono had identified the capture of fugitive JI bomb-makers Noordin Mohammad Top and Azahari Hussein as a top priority. The Indonesian Government demonstrated commitment to regional leadership in counterterrorism efforts by working with the Australians to establish the Jakarta Center for Law Enforcement Cooperation (JCLEC), which will develop into a regional counterterrorism training institute.

Japan

Japan continued its strong counterterrorism stance, both domestically and abroad, in 2004. In May, the Diet ratified a mutual legal assistance treaty with the United States. The treaty will make cooperation in investigations and prosecution of terrorists easier.

Japan is active regionally in building counterterrorism cooperation and capacity among Asian countries. In June, Japan announced its APEC Counterterrorism Capacity Building Initiative and its plans to provide assistance to address aviation, port, and maritime security, as well as terrorism financing shortfalls in the region. The Japanese Coast Guard invited students from Southeast Asian countries to study at its academy, provided training for maritime law enforcement activities, and conducted a human resource development project to modernize and further professionalize the Philippine Coast Guard. Japanese officials have led regional seminars on terrorist finance, customs cooperation, law enforcement, immigration control, and export control. To help stem the flow of terrorist financing to al-Qaida and the Taliban, Japan designated under its asset-freezing program all entities and individuals included on the UN 1267 Sanctions Committee's consolidated list and sponsored an experts seminar on establishing financial intelligence units for Southeast Asian countries in December 2004.

There were no serious incidents of international or domestic terrorism in Japan during 2004. The leader of Aum Shinrikyo, a US-designated foreign terrorist organization accused of perpetrating the sarin gas attack on the Tokyo subway system in 1995, was sentenced to death in February. Appeals are pending. The Public Security Intelligence Agency is continuing its surveillance of the group through 2005, as authorized by the Public Security Commission in December 2002.

Laos

Laos has continued to support the global war on terrorism, but lacks specific counterterrorism laws. The Office of the Prosecutor General is drafting amendments to existing criminal law, under which acts of terrorism fall, to make more explicit the descriptions of and punishments for terrorism-related crimes. Efforts to implement the counterterrorism provisions of multilateral agreements are hampered by weak enforcement procedures and inefficiency of security organizations. The Government cooperated bilaterally on counterterrorism issues with the United States and other nations, and multilaterally with the United Nations and the Association of Southeast Asian Nations (ASEAN).

Laos suffered a handful of incidents of domestic terrorism in 2004, carried out by groups opposed to the Lao Government. A group calling itself the Free Democratic People's Government of Laos claimed credit for several small bombings, which resulted in one death and a number of injuries. This group also claimed responsibility for several explosions in Vientiane designed to disrupt the ASEAN Summit in late November 2004.

Malaysia

The Malaysian Government continues to be a strong partner in the war on terrorism, taking on a leading role to facilitate regional cooperation, most notably through its Southeast Asia Regional Center for Counter Terrorism (SEARCCT). Malaysia has detained more than 100 suspected terrorists under the Internal Security Act (ISA) since May 2001. According to the Internal Security Ministry, 87 such suspects remained in custody. Malaysia issued eight and renewed 32 two-year detention orders for terrorist suspects in 2004. Five detained terrorist suspects were granted conditional release in 2004.

The SEARCCT, established in 2003, focused primarily on training for regional authorities in law enforcement, banking, and other sectors. US trainers conducted courses for officials throughout the region at SEARCCT, and Malaysian, Japanese, Australian, South Korean, British, Croatian, and Canadian trainers also participated in regional counterterrorism courses, seminars, lectures, and workshops.

The Malaysian Government has worked to ensure that separatist violence in southern Thailand, which has wounded Malaysian tourists, does not spill over into Malaysia. Malaysia has strengthened border controls along the frontier between the two countries.

New Zealand

New Zealand has a strong capacity to develop and implement counterterrorism policies, and further strengthened its role in the global war on terror in 2004 through domestic legislation and regional involvement. In May, New Zealand hosted a counterterrorism meeting for Pacific Island Forum members. The meeting, which was funded through the Government's Pacific Island Security Fund, discussed the region's counterterrorism obligations and the range of international assistance available to help Pacific Island nations meet these requirements. In December, the Government introduced a bill into Parliament to extend until 2007 New Zealand's UN Security Council-related designations of terrorist organizations. By year's end, New Zealand had designated 420 terrorist organizations and was considering adding more to the list. In its 2004 budget, New Zealand allocated funds for the creation of specially-dedicated National Security Teams to combat terrorism.

Philippines

The Philippines continues to cooperate on a range of bilateral and multilateral counterterrorism efforts. Indigenous terrorist groups, as well as operatives of Jemaah Islamiya, continue to threaten the security of the country. The Philippines suffered the worst terrorist attack in its history when a bomb planted by Abu Sayyaf Group (ASG) terrorists sunk SuperFerry 14 in Manila Bay, killing approximately 130 passengers. In December, a bomb exploded in a crowded market in General Santos City, Mindanao, killing a reported 17 people. No group claimed responsibility for the attack.

Philippine authorities had a number of successes against terrorists in 2004. In March, they arrested seven ASG members responsible for the SuperFerry bombing and uncovered their plans to bomb the US Embassy, shopping malls, and other targets in Metro Manila. In April, a Philippine military unit killed six ASG members on Basilan Island, including Hamsiraji Sali, a senior ASG leader wanted by the United States for his role in the kidnappings of Americans Guillermo Sobero and Gracia and Martin Burnham and Sobero's and Martin Burnham's subsequent deaths. One of the three US-trained Light Reaction Companies bloodlessly apprehended two New People's Army (NPA) commanders in June, and an August air strike against the Pentagon Gang destroyed its leadership and virtually eliminated it as an organization. A court in August sentenced 17 ASG members to death, although four were convicted in absentia after having escaped from jail. In October, authorities arrested two men and one woman for their roles in bomb attacks at the Davao airport and ferry port.

President Gloria Macapagal-Arroyo announced the creation of a multi-agency Anti-Terrorism Task Force (ATTF) in March. During the first five months of its existence, ATTF operatives, backed up by law enforcement, captured over 60 suspected terrorists, seven of them foreigners believed to be elements of al-Qaida and JI.

The Philippines has made progress in tracking, blocking, and seizing terrorist assets. The main body tasked with investigating terrorist finance cases—the Anti-Money Laundering Council (AMLC)—completed the first phase of its information technology upgrades in 2004. The arrests in May and September, respectively, of ASG suspects Khair Mundus and

Satrap Tilao on the first-ever money laundering charges against terrorists grew out of an investigation initiated by the US Department of Homeland Security (DHS) in coordination with Philippine officials. On December 17, the Philippines agreed to co-sponsor, with the United States, the submission of ASG leader Khadaffy Janjalani for inclusion on the United Nations 1267 Sanctions Committee list.

Major evidentiary and procedural obstacles in the Philippines, such as the absence of a law defining and codifying terrorist acts and restrictions on gathering of evidence, hinder the building of effective terrorism cases. Although several new counterterrorism bills were introduced in the new session of Congress in July, the Philippines failed to enact new antiterrorism legislation in 2004. Generic problems in the law enforcement and criminal justice systems also hamper bringing terrorists to justice. Among them are corruption, low morale, inadequate salaries, recruitment and retention difficulties, and lack of effective cooperation between police and prosecutors.

US and Philippine authorities worked closely during 2004 to energize rewards programs targeting terrorist groups. Using its Rewards Program, the US Department of Defense made two payments of $15,000 and $9,800 to Filipino informants for their roles in the capture of ASG cell leaders Galib Andang (aka "Commander Robot") and Alhamzer Limbong (aka "Kumander Kosovo"). The US Department of State, through its Rewards for Justice program, made a payment of $1 million to the three Philippine informants who played a crucial role in the attempted capture of Hamsiraji Sali, during which Sali was killed.

Singapore

Singapore continued its strong opposition to terrorism and worked vigorously to advance the counterterrorism agenda in bilateral and multilateral contexts. While there were no acts of international or domestic terrorism in Singapore in 2004, Singaporean authorities pressed their investigation of the regional terrorist group Jemaah Islamiya (JI), and continued to detain JI members who plotted to carry out attacks in Singapore in the past.

Over the course of the year, the number of terrorism-related detainees held under the Internal Security Act decreased from 37 to 35. Detainees include members of JI and two members of the Moro Islamic Liberation Front (MILF). The "Restriction Orders" authorizing detention require these persons to undergo a program of religious counseling with a group of volunteer religious counselors.

During 2004, Singapore continued its intelligence and law enforcement cooperation with a variety of governments, including the United States, to investigate terrorist groups, especially JI. Singapore provided information to Indonesia to assist in the second trial of Abu Bakar Ba'asyir. It has requested that Indonesia extradite to Singapore several JI members to face trial for engaging in a conspiracy to commit terrorist acts.

In 2004, authorities updated the Monetary Authority of Singapore Act (Anti-Terrorism Measures) and the United Nations Act (Anti-Terrorism Measures). These regulations prohibit the provision of any funds or other assistance to terrorists, and provide the authority for the seizure of financial or other assets.

Singaporean officials have taken strong measures to enhance maritime security in nearby waters, especially the Strait of Malacca. These measures are focused on addressing terrorist threats as well as piracy and other criminal attacks. The Maritime and Port Authority (MPA) of Singapore issued new security control measures on ships calling at the Port of Singapore, including pre-arrival notification requirements. In July, the navies of Singapore, Indonesia, and Malaysia initiated coordinated patrols in the Strait of Malacca. The Government of Singapore has scheduled a Proliferation Security Initiative maritime interdiction exercise in August 2005. Based on an initiative by Japan, 16 countries, including Singapore, agreed to the regional Cooperation Agreement on Combating Piracy and Armed Robbery against Ships in Asia. The countries agreed to establish a center, based in Singapore, to coordinate information exchange on maritime piracy. Singapore and the other members of the Five Power Defense Arrangement (Malaysia, Australia, United Kingdom, and New Zealand) announced that their agreement would be expanded to deal with terrorism and other unconventional threats, including maritime security.

Singapore actively participated in counterterrorism efforts through various international fora, including the ASEAN Regional Forum, and has worked to enhance regional counterterrorism capabilities. Singaporean police conducted a regional workshop on "Explosives and Suicide Bomber Counter-Measures" to enhance the capabilities of police units in other ASEAN member countries. Singapore hosted an APEC Counterterrorism Task Force meeting to further develop proposals to enhance the counterterrorism capabilities of APEC members, as committed by leaders in November 2003.

Taiwan

Taiwan remains a responsive partner in the global war on terrorism, although it is frequently prevented from participating in international and regional fora on counterterrorism issues.

In November 2004, Taiwan authorities announced the creation of a counterterrorism policy committee chaired by the Premier of the Executive Yuan and composed of seven multi-agency task forces. Each task force is required to collect information and develop operational plans to deal with such contingencies as terrorist attacks on public infrastructure and telecommunication networks. The National Police Administration (NPA) also established a special SWAT team to respond to terrorist incidents and continues to send law enforcement personnel abroad for counterterrorism training.

Cooperation on maritime security issues advanced in 2004, as Taiwan and the United States agreed on a framework to implement the US Department of Homeland Security's Container Security Initiative (CSI) in the southern port city of Kaohsiung. Kaohsiung is one of the busiest container ports in the world and will be the eleventh port in the East Asia Pacific region to implement CSI standards designed to protect shipping containers against exploitation by terrorists and criminal elements. US customs and border protection officers are tentatively scheduled to begin operations with their Taiwanese counterparts in 2005.

Although not a member of the United Nations and therefore unable to become a party to international treaties, Taiwan has nonetheless committed to implement the 12 UN conventions and protocols related to international terrorism, and has taken some unilateral measures to combat illicit money flows. In 2004, Taiwan's legislative Yuan amended the Money Laundering Control Act, strengthening provisions to identify and seize terrorist assets and property. Taiwanese authorities also continue to maintain a centralized database to verify and track remittances.

Thailand

There were no significant acts of international terrorism in Thailand during 2004. However, there was a significant increase in acts of domestic violence fueled by a renewed separatist insurgency based in the far southern provinces of Thailand. The violence has been primarily concentrated in the Muslim majority provinces of Pattani, Yala, and Narathiwat, which are located along the Thai-Malaysian border. Most estimates put the number of deaths this year directly related to the violence at over 500. The victims include government officials and civilians, both Buddhist and Muslim. The Thai Government has expressed concern that Thai militants may be seeking refuge across the border; Malaysia has denied these allegations.

There is no evidence of a direct connection between militants in southern Thailand and international terrorist organizations such as Jemaah Islamiya and al-Qaida. However, there is concern that transnational groups may attempt to capitalize on the increasingly violent situation for their own purposes. Long-standing Muslim separatist organizations in southern Thailand continue to be active to some degree, but there is little direct evidence that these groups are actively organizing the violence. Thai separatist groups by all indications remained focused on seeking autonomy or independence for the far southern provinces. Violence in the south remains focused on government officials and other symbols of Thai authority, as well as civilians.

Thailand has commitments to work with neighboring countries on counterterrorism issues and is a participant in the Southeast Asia Regional Center for Counterterrorism (SEARCCT) in Malaysia.

Thailand is also enhancing the security of its borders by implementing more effective controls. In cooperation with the G8 Counterterrorism Action Group (CTAG) member governments, Thailand has increased efforts to combat document fraud. During 2004, Thailand enhanced its ability to internally coordinate its response to terrorist financing activities. Thailand has embarked on an aggressive program to equip its air, land, and sea ports of entry with a computerized terrorist watch listing system. The system will be operational at a limited number of locations in 2005, with completion forecast for 2006.

Europe and Eurasia Overview

Major terrorist events occurred in Europe in 2004, with hundreds dying in horrific attacks in Spain, Russia, and Uzbekistan, accompanied by major successes, including broad-based international cooperation to secure the Olympics in Greece, and deepened multilateral efforts to improve capabilities to combat the threat of terrorism. European nations continued to work in close partnership with the United States in the global counterterrorism campaign and, galvanized by the Madrid bombings and growing awareness of their own vulnerabilities, took significant steps to enhance their capability to combat terrorists and their supporters. The contributions of European countries in sharing intelligence, arresting members of terrorist cells, and interdicting terrorist financing and logistics continued to be vital elements in the war on terrorism.

The European Union (EU) remained a key partner in the war on terrorism and has moved to strengthen Community legal and administrative capacity, and that of EU member states, to combat terrorism. The EU created the position of Coordinator for Counterterrorism following the Madrid attacks in March. International judicial cooperation advanced as EU members brought into effect the European Arrest Warrant and enacted implementing legislation for US-EU Extradition and Mutual Legal Assistance Treaties. The June US-EU Summit Declaration on Combating Terrorism reaffirmed a wide range of transatlantic commitments to cooperate closely and continue to work together to develop measures to maximize capacities to detect, investigate and prosecute terrorists and prevent terrorist attacks, prevent access by terrorists to financial and other economic resources, enhance information sharing and cooperation among law enforcement agencies, and improve the effectiveness of border information systems. The United States and EU initiated a dialogue on terrorism finance issues in September.

European nations are active participants in a variety of multilateral organizations that have made contributions in counterterrorist efforts, including the G8, NATO, the Financial Action Task Force (FATF), the Organization for Security and Cooperation in Europe (OSCE), the International Maritime Organization (IMO), and the International Civil Aviation Organization (ICAO). They worked actively with the United States and other partners through these organizations to establish and implement best practices, build the counterterrorism capabilities of "weak but willing" states, and institutionalize the war against terrorism globally. OSCE members have committed themselves to becoming parties to the 12 UN terrorism conventions and protocols, to work together to modernize travel documents and shipping container security, and to prevent and suppress the financing of terrorist organizations.

Terrorist activity and the presence of terrorist support

networks in Europe remain a source of concern. Efforts to combat the threat in Europe are sometimes hampered by legal protections that make it difficult to take firm judicial action against suspected terrorists, asylum laws that afford loopholes, inadequate legislation, or standards of evidence that limit use of classified information in holding terrorist suspects. Ease of travel within Schengen visa countries also makes Western Europe attractive to terrorists. Some European states have at times not been able to prosecute successfully or hold some of the suspected terrorists brought before their courts. The Clearinghouse mechanism for authorizing EU-wide terrorist designations was unable to generate consensus on action to block the assets of charities associated with HAMAS and Hizballah.

In March, Islamic extremists linked to the Moroccan Islamic Combatant Group (GICM) detonated 10 bombs on commuter trains during the Madrid rush hour, killing 191 persons and wounding hundreds more; several suspects later blew themselves up in order to avoid arrest.

Russia endured a series of deadly terrorist attacks in February, August and September 2004, including explosions on the Moscow subway, suicide bomb attacks that brought down two Russian airliners simultaneously, a suicide bomber attack outside a Moscow metro station, and the seizure of approximately 1,200 hostages, most of whom were school children, at a school in Beslan, North Ossetia, that left at least 331 people dead, more than half of them children, and hundreds of others injured.

In Uzbekistan in March and April 2004, suicide bombers attacked a popular bazaar and other locations resulting in the death of more than a dozen police officers and innocent bystanders. A further round of bombings in July outside the US and Israeli Embassies and the Uzbekistani General Prosecutor's Office resulted in the death of four Uzbekistani security officers.

Deploying thousands of security personnel and working closely with partners from across the globe, Greece staged successful and secure summer Olympic Games.

The Netherlands was rocked by the brutal assassination of a prominent film director by a Dutch-born Moroccan dual national. The killing and its aftershocks, like the Madrid bombings, focused attention throughout Europe on the potential threat from extremist groups recruited from within Europe.

Cooperation among European law enforcement authorities continued to be key to counterterrorism successes. Intra-European information exchanges shed light on the continent-wide linkages of the Madrid bombers and facilitated the April arrests across Europe of suspects connected to the Turkish Revolutionary People's Liberation Party/Front (DHKP/C).

Enhancing regional counterterrorism cooperation has been a priority for the United States. Toward that end, the US Department of State co-hosted with the Swiss Government the sixth Counterterrorism Conference for Eurasian states in Zurich, Switzerland, in December 2004. Participants included most of the Eurasian states, Turkey, and representatives from the World Health Organization, the EU, Interpol, OSCE, NATO, and Poland's recently developed Foundation for the Prevention of Terrorism and Biological Threats. The conference provided participants an opportunity to describe and identify components of their national programs to respond to a bioterrorism attack, and to see how their various governments would respond together to a transnational bio-emergency. The Dutch EU Presidency hosted an EU-wide conference on terrorism finance in Brussels in September, which included participation by the United States as well as other third countries and international organizations, including the United Nations.

The North Atlantic Treaty Organization (NATO) also played a key role in combating terrorism at the regional level in Europe. First and foremost, NATO continues Operation Active Endeavor (OAE), a naval operation aimed at combating terrorism by monitoring maritime traffic in the Mediterranean. Thus far, Alliance warships have hailed over 57,000 vessels and have boarded nearly 100 vessels. Currently, NATO is discussing expanding OAE into the Black Sea and strengthening the mandate's directives for searching for WMD materials. Additionally, during the Olympics, NATO provided critical chemical, biological, radiological, nuclear (CBRN), and air patrol capabilities to the Government of Greece.

Despite limited resources, the countries of southeast Europe have actively supported the international coalition against terrorism. Through the Southeast European Cooperation Initiative (SECI) Regional Center to Combat Transborder Crime, based in Romania, the twelve states of Albania, Bosnia and Herzegovina, Bulgaria, Croatia, Greece, Hungary, Macedonia, Moldova, Romania, Serbia and Montenegro, Slovenia, and Turkey cooperated to combat organized crime and various forms of trafficking, enhance border security, and improve training for border security personnel.

In October Belarus, China, Kazakhstan, Kyrgyzstan, Tajikistan, and Russia created the Eurasia Group, a regional anti-money laundering organization or Financial Action Task Force-style regional body (FSRB).

Albania

Despite limited resources, Albania continued to support the global war on terrorism and made progress in implementing its national action plan against terrorism, originally approved in 2002. Albania has steadfastly supported US actions against terrorism, sharing information and investigating terrorist-related groups and activities. In 2004, the Government froze the assets of terrorist financiers, curtailed the activities of suspect Islamic NGOs, and detained or expelled individuals suspected of having links to terrorism or attempting to foment religious intolerance. In July, Parliament passed legislation to implement asset freezes against persons designated as terrorists or terrorist financiers by the United Nations. Albania has begun cracking down on ethnic Albanian extremists, including leaders of the ultranationalist Albanian

National Army. In December, police apprehended four arms traffickers dealing in surface to air missiles likely intended for regional extremists.

Armenia

In 2004, Armenia continued to be a full and active participant in the global war against terrorism. A new Armenian criminal law more clearly defining terrorist acts replaced Soviet-era legislation in 2003. The National Assembly passed legislation outlawing money laundering and financing of terrorism in December 2004, bringing Armenian legislation in line with its international obligations to combat terrorist finance, and strengthening the ability of the Government to prosecute terrorist-related offenses. Border Guards seized 42 grams of non-weapons-grade radioactive material in 2004. While none of the material was likely destined for terrorist organizations, the Border Guards have shown that they are capable of detecting and interdicting nuclear material. The Armenian Central Bank fully cooperated with efforts to freeze terrorist assets but reported finding none in 2004.

Austria

Austria continued its participation in multilateral missions, its cooperation with US law enforcement agencies, and its leadership in regional anti-terrorism initiatives. In 2004, the Government made efforts to tighten financial oversight of suspected terrorism financing.

In 2004, the Interior Ministry's intelligence arm, the Federal Office for the Protection of the Constitution and for Terrorism (BVT), stepped up surveillance of suspected Islamic extremists; it also increased monitoring of suspected extremist prayer houses in Vienna and surveillance of the Egyptian al-Jama'ah al-Islamiyah movement and of suspected Afghan extremists entering Austria as asylum seekers. Austria passed legislation to allow police video surveillance of public spaces. Austria's legal and institutional framework to combat terrorism was strengthened. Its money laundering and terrorist financing legislation is now in compliance with FATF 40+9 Recommendations, and the EU-wide arrest warrant became effective in 2004.

Azerbaijan

Azerbaijan and the United States have a very good record of cooperation on counterterrorism issues that predates the September 11, 2001, attacks. With the 2004 ratification of the Convention on Offenses and Certain Other Acts Committed on Board Aircraft and the Convention on the Physical Protection of Nuclear Material, Azerbaijan has acceded to all 12 international conventions and protocols relating to terrorism. While Azerbaijan has served as a route for international mujahedin with ties to terrorist organizations seeking to move men, money, and materiel throughout the Caucasus, the Azeri Government has stepped up its efforts and succeeded in reducing their presence and hampering their activities. Azerbaijan has taken steps to combat terrorist financing and identify possible terrorist-related funding by distributing lists of suspected terrorist groups and individuals to local banks. An experts group, led by the National Bank of Azerbaijan, has prepared draft anti-money laundering legislation that would establish a financial intelligence unit (FIU) and expand the predicate crimes for money laundering beyond narcotics trafficking.

In 2004, the Government continued to make significant arrests of individuals associated with terrorist groups. Members of Jayshullah, an indigenous terrorist group, who were arrested in 2000 and tried in 2001 for plotting to attack the US Embassy in Baku, remain in prison.

Belgium

In 2004, the Belgian Government continued anti-terrorist cooperation with European neighbors and the US Government on multiple levels. Belgium remained active in sharing information with the United States regarding terrorist threats to US interests or persons. In 2004, Belgium and the United States broadened cooperation under the Container Security Initiative—in place for the Port of Antwerp since 2003—to include a second Belgian port, Zeebrugge. The two governments also agreed to place radiation detection equipment in the Port of Antwerp under the Department of Energy's Megaports program.

The Belgian judicial system applied the rule of law to terrorist conspirators in 2004, when it charged 10 suspects with criminal conspiracy related to possible terrorist activities. Eight of the defendants were found guilty, receiving sentences ranging from 11 months to five years. One of those convicted, Tarek Maaroufi, had been found guilty in the 2003 terrorist trial in Belgium and will serve a total of seven years in prison based on that previous conviction. A Belgian appellate court rejected appeals filed by nine of the 18 convicted in Belgium's 2003 terrorist trial, including Maaroufi and Nizar Trabelsi, a Tunisian national and al-Qaida associate. The court actually increased Maaroufi's sentence from six to seven years, while maintaining the ten-year sentence of Trabelsi and the shorter sentences of three other defendants. Another of the appellants, Mouloud Haiter, had his sentence increased from three to four years, while Abelhouaid Aberkan's sentence was reduced from three to two years. A final appellant, who cooperated with authorities in the initial trial, had his sentence suspended.

The Belgian authorities, in cooperation with Spanish, Italian, and Dutch investigators, continued criminal investigations of over 20 other suspects in Belgium for possible terrorism activities, including possible links to the March Madrid bombing and the November murder of Dutch filmmaker Theo van Gogh. Belgian legislation adopted in 2003 to implement the EU's Framework Decision of June 2002 on combating terrorism and the European Arrest Warrant came into effect in December 2003 and January 2004, respectively.

Bosnia and Herzegovina

The Government of Bosnia and Herzegovina (BiH) remained a strong and active partner in the global war on terrorism. The country's ethnic divisions, its complex and multi-level government structure, and its still weak central institutions complicate its efforts against terrorism, but Bosnia made great strides in institutionalizing its counterterrorism capabilities. State-level Ministries of Defense and Security were established in 2004, and the two entity-level (Federation and Republika Srpska) intelligence services were merged into a single state-level service. US Government assistance helped establish the State Investigative and Protection Agency (SIPA), an FBI-like agency responsible for investigating complex crimes including terrorism, illegal trafficking, organized crime, and smuggling of weapons of mass destruction. SIPA will have a financial intelligence unit (FIU), and a sub-unit of its Criminal Investigation Department will be dedicated to counterterrorism and WMD. However, these units of SIPA are not yet fully staffed or fully operational, and state institutions in general are largely under-funded, under-resourced, and lack sufficiently trained personnel.

In June, Bosnia adopted a package of laws that, when fully implemented, will dramatically strengthen state-level law enforcement capabilities. The set of laws includes legislation giving SIPA law enforcement and investigative authority for state-level crimes, including terrorism, and a law on prevention of money laundering. The law, which came into force on December 28, determines the measures and responsibilities for detecting, preventing, and investigating money laundering and terrorist financing, and prescribes measures and responsibilities for international cooperation. Bosnia lacks established procedures for dealing with such issues as denaturalization, extradition, and preventive detention.

The BiH Government took decisive action in apprehending suspects and shutting down NGOs and bank accounts tied to terrorist-linked organizations. In the past year and a half, Bosnian Federation authorities shut down NGOs with terrorist links and froze accounts of terrorist supporters. In 2004, the Government disrupted the operations of al-Furqan (a.k.a. Sirat Istikamet), al-Haramain and al-Masjed al-Aqsa Charity Foundation, and Taibah International, organizations listed by the UN 1267 Committee as having direct links with al-Qaida. Of continuing concern are the foreign Islamic extremists who remain in Bosnia as a legacy of the 1992–95 war.

Bulgaria

Bulgaria is a staunch ally of the United States in the global war against terror. During 2004, the Bulgarian Government continued its high level of cooperation with the United States in preventing acts of terrorism in Bulgaria and elsewhere. This included information sharing on potential terrorist threats. Bulgarian officials have aggressively pursued and developed leads and provided extensive cooperation to US officials. Cooperation with US and regional officials on export and border controls continued to be outstanding.

Czech Republic

Czech authorities have cooperated closely with the US Government and other European governments to prevent terrorist activity. In 2004, the Czechs blocked several exports of weapons and explosives that were linked to possible terrorist activity. Czech authorities responded effectively to requests for increased protection of US facilities, including at the Prague headquarters of Radio Free Europe/Radio Liberty.

Finland

Finland enhanced its ability to combat terrorism in 2004, implementing legislation that allowed it to freeze assets without prior action by the EU or UN. Finland amended its criminal code to make it possible to sentence leaders of terrorist groups to 15 years in jail, although the group has to have actually committed acts of terrorism in Finland before investigation and prosecution can begin. In January, the Finnish Security Police created a special unit concentrating solely on fighting terrorism, the first of its kind in Finland.

France

Throughout 2004, France continued to pursue one of Europe's most effective and aggressive counterterrorism policies and made significant terrorism-related arrests. In April, French authorities shut down a cell of the Moroccan Islamic Combatant Group (GICM) that was considered to be extremely dangerous. In July, the Government took custody of four former detainees at Guantanamo Bay and charged them with terrorist conspiracy; all four remain in pretrial detention with trials expected to begin in 2005. In October, French and Spanish authorities struck a significant blow to ETA terrorism through the arrest in France of two top ETA leaders and the seizure of significant arms and materials caches. Judicial and police investigations following the high-profile arrests in 2003 of German national Christian Ganczarski and Moroccan national Karim Mehdi continued in 2004. Ganczarski and Mehdi, who are suspected of ties to al-Qaida, remain in pretrial detention in France. The investigation into the activities of suspected terrorist Djamel Beghal concluded in late 2004. His trial, as well as the trials of seven associates, will begin in January 2005. The Beghal network is suspected of planning a number of terrorist acts, including an attack on the US Embassy in Paris.

The Ministry of Finance's terrorism financing coordination cell TRACFIN maintained direct coordination with the US Treasury Department. At the level of the European Union, France played an active role in the Clearinghouse, the Union's terrorism financing coordination body. France has not designated HAMAS-affiliated charities, arguing that they have no links to terrorism, and continues to oppose designating Lebanese Hizballah as a terrorist organization. France took rapid action in support of US requests to freeze Taliban, al-Qaida, and other terrorist financial assets.

In 2004, France expanded its international judicial cooperation. In addition to bringing into force the European Arrest Warrant, France signed with the United States two new agreements in September that updated a bilateral extradition treaty and improved overall counterterrorism cooperation.

Georgia

The Georgian Government remained deeply committed to combating international and domestic terrorism in 2004 and has consistently and publicly condemned acts of terror. Georgia is still used to a limited degree as a terrorist transit state, although much less so since the government crackdown on the Pankisi Gorge in late 2002. Stepped-up Georgian law enforcement counterterrorism operations in late 2004 in Pankisi, in the wake of the Beslan terrorist attack in September 2004 in Russia, have further eroded the ability of transnational terrorist groups to use the Pankisi Gorge as a transit area.

Georgian law enforcement capabilities are limited, although improving through internal reform and US Government and Western donor technical and financial assistance. In particular, the United States is providing counterterrorism training via the State Department's Antiterrorism Assistance Program. The Procuracy has a special unit of six prosecutors and investigators solely dedicated to terrorism financing and money laundering cases. Efforts to reform the Ministry of Internal Affairs and Ministry of State Security and enhance their counterterrorism capabilities are constrained by lack of adequate resources, equipment, and, mostly, training. These reform efforts, coupled with frequent personnel turnover, have created confusion and prevented development of an overall counterterrorism policy. Border guard and customs reform is continuing, and over the past few years, maritime, air, and communications capabilities have improved considerably.

Germany

Germany continued to be a dedicated and important participant in the global coalition against terrorism; cooperation with the United States remained solid. Throughout 2004 German law enforcement authorities conducted numerous actions against individuals, organizations, and mosques suspected of involvement in terrorism. In some cases, hundreds of individuals and vehicles were searched, which resulted in arrests for document fraud, illegal residency, and weapons violations.

To improve coordination of state and federal law enforcement and intelligence agencies, in December 2004 Interior Minister Schily announced establishment of a Berlin-based "Information and Analysis Center" that will bring together all agencies involved in the German fight against terrorism. In 2004, the German Federal Criminal Office also established an Office for International Coordination to improve counterterrorism collaboration with foreign law enforcement authorities. In July, Germany adopted a new immigration law containing provisions to strengthen Germany's fight against terrorism. The new law took effect in January 2005.

Germany is currently investigating almost 200 cases of terrorism nationwide, but has at times had difficulties in convicting terrorist suspects. The 2003 conviction of Moroccan citizen Mounir el Motassadeq for accessory to murder and membership in the "Hamburg cell" that had formed around 9/11 suicide pilot Mohammed Atta was overturned and Motassadeq was released in April pending a retrial, despite what the court called "strong evidence" of his membership in a terrorist organization. His retrial began in August. A trial on similar charges against another "Hamburg cell" suspect, Moroccan citizen Abdelghani Mzoudi, ended with his acquittal in February. Prosecutors filed an appeal. German authorities have initiated deportation proceedings against both Motassadeq and Mzoudi.

Other notable 2004 arrests and indictments include the cases of several alleged members of the Iraq-based terrorist group Ansar al-Islam. Three Iraqi alleged members of Ansar al-Islam were arrested in December on charges of plotting an attack on Iraqi Prime Minister Ayad Allawi during his visit to Berlin. Tunisian national Ishan Garnoui was indicted by the Federal Prosecutor in January 2004 for attempted formation of a terrorist organization with the intention to unleash explosive attacks on US and Jewish targets in Germany. He was convicted in April 2005 on charges of tax evasion, illegal possession of weapons, and violation of the immigration law, but was acquitted on terrorism charges.

German authorities deported Turkish extremist Metin Kaplan to Turkey, where authorities detained him to face numerous charges, including treason. German authorities made several indictments and arrests related to the Turkish terrorist group PKK/KADEK/Kongra-Gel, although one prominent PKK suspect was later released.

German prosecutors were unsuccessful in bringing indictments against several prominent al-Qaida suspects, including German national Christian Ganczarski, a suspect in the April 2002 bombing of a Tunisian synagogue in which several German citizens were killed. Similarly, authorities were unable to indict Syrian-German dual national Mamoun Darkazanli, but he is in custody and authorities are seeking to extradite him to Spain, where a 2003 arrest warrant accuses him of membership in and providing logistical and financial support to al-Qaida. In November, the Federal Constitutional Court blocked his extradition pending its review of the constitutionality of the new European Arrest Warrant.

In 2002 the German Interior Ministry banned the al-Aqsa Foundation on the grounds of providing financial support to HAMAS. In July 2003, a German court temporarily lifted the ban pending a final court ruling, although it also imposed financial reporting requirements on al-Aqsa. In December 2004, following a court ruling upholding the 2002 ban on the al-Aqsa Foundation, German law enforcement officials searched more than 30 al-Aqsa offices nationwide. The Interior Ministry has banned the extremist Islamic association Hizb ut-Tahrir—based outside Germany—from any activity within the country and has seized the association's assets in Germany. The US Government has no evidence that Hizb ut-Tahrir has committed any terrorist acts, but the group's radical anti-US and anti-Semitic ideology is sympathetic to acts of violence against the United States and its allies, and it has publicly called on Muslims to travel to Iraq and Afghanistan to fight Coalition forces.

Greece

Greece continued to strengthen its ability to fight terrorism and held the 2004 Olympic and Paralympic Games in Athens without incident. In June, the Greek Parliament passed new counterterrorism legislation that brought Greece into compliance with the EU Framework Decision on Combating Terrorism, including approval of the EU Arrest Warrant. This legislation made specific reference to terrorist crimes and groups for the first time. Among its provisions, the legislation extends the statute of limitations on terrorist-related killings from 20 to 30 years, established a framework for EU-wide probes and rapid extradition of terrorist suspects within the EU bloc, and provided for harsher treatment of terrorist leaders and those who provide money and logistics to terrorists.

In October, after an eight month process, a Greek court sentenced four of five accused members of the domestic terrorist group Peoples' Revolutionary Struggle (ELA) to what amounts to 25 years imprisonment, the maximum allowed under Greek law, for bombings/attempted murders, possession of firearms/explosives, and involvement in the 1994 assassination of a police officer. The ELA defense immediately appealed these sentences; by year's end there was no decision on the timing of the appeals. In July the Athens Court of Appeals indicted longtime suspected ELA leader Yannis Serifis for his role in the 1994 assassination; the trial is set to begin in February 2005.

A Greek court announced in October that the appeals process for members of the 17 November (17N) terrorist group, convicted in December 2003 of hundreds of crimes over the years, including the murder of five US Government employees, would begin in December 2005. Top Greek law enforcement officials have stated that further investigation of 17N suspects/evidence will continue and that the case is not considered closed.

Anarchists and domestic terrorists continued to conduct numerous small-scale arson attacks, most involving gas canister or other crude improvised explosive devices (IEDs), against an array of perceived establishment and so-called "imperialist targets," such as banks, US fast food restaurants, courts, and personal vehicles. In May, exactly 100 days before the start of the Olympic Games in Athens, a group calling itself "Revolutionary Struggle" took responsibility for three IEDs which detonated near a police station in the Athens suburb of Kallithea, causing significant property damage but no injuries. The reported number of IED attacks dropped dramatically during the Olympic and Paralympic Games (August-September), but increased soon after.

In October, in a departure from crude IED attacks against property that usually occur in the dead of night, a remotely-controlled device detonated during the morning rush hour near two police buses that were carrying officers to the Korydallos prison (where 17N members are imprisoned). The explosion caused no injuries and only minor damage. No group has thus far claimed responsibility for this attack and Greek authorities have continued their investigation. In December, unknown assailants shot and killed a Greek Special Guard at his post outside the residence of the British Defense Attaché. While the case has not yet been solved, police are treating the case as a domestic terrorist incident.

Hungary

In early 2004, the Hungarian Parliament passed far-reaching legislation on reporting requirements for financial transactions. This follows Hungarian initiatives on money laundering and terrorist financing that brought it into full compliance with EU and Financial Action Task Force norms. Hungary has been fully supportive of the war against terrorism and US initiatives against al-Qaida and other terrorist organizations both within its borders and abroad.

Cooperation with US and regional officials on export and border controls is outstanding. In several cases in 2004, Hungarian officials aggressively pursued and developed leads and provided extensive cooperation to US officers that have stopped the transshipment of hazardous goods. Hungary is actively improving its technical ability to track and control dangerous materials, and its accession into the EU is accelerating this process.

Italy

Italy has been a staunch ally in the war against terror. The commitment of the Government of Italy to the global war on terrorism remained steadfast, despite two separate hostage-takings in Iraq, the brutal murders of an Italian journalist and another Italian hostage, and terrorist threats throughout the year against Italy for its participation in the OEF coalition and in the reconstruction of Iraq, and for its active efforts against terrorism.

Italy's law enforcement authorities maintained the initiative against Italy-based terrorist suspects through investigations, detentions, prosecutions, and expulsions. According to Ministry of Interior data and the media, Italian authorities in 2004 arrested more than 60 individuals suspected of planning or providing support to terrorist activity, both international and internal. Many of those arrested were suspected al-Qaida sympathizers and recruiters supporting anti-coalition activities in Iraq. Many were also suspected of having ties to Ansar al-Islam and other al-Qaida-linked extremist organizations. Included among those arrested was Rabei Osman Sayed Ahmed, who was suspected of involvement in the March Madrid bombings. In April, Italy coordinated with four of its European neighbors the arrests of multiple suspects believed to have ties to the Turkish DHKP/C and in September, Italian intelligence and law enforcement agencies joined with Lebanese authorities to thwart a plot to attack the

Italian Embassy in Beirut. Italy's Minister of Interior continued to expel terrorist suspects he believed posed a serious terrorist threat.

The domestic leftwing terrorist group, the new Red Brigades-Communist Combatant Party (BR-CCP), presents a diminished threat due to Italian authorities' continued efforts to dismantle the organization. In June, the BR-CCP's presumed leader, Desdemona Lioce, was given a life sentence for killing one police officer and wounding a second during a train shootout in 2003.

Kazakhstan

After the July 30 suicide bombings in Tashkent, Uzbekistan, the Government of Kazakhstan aggressively sought leads and prosecuted individuals involved with extremist groups targeting Western interests in the region. The Government's cooperation and timeliness in sharing information with the United States has greatly improved since 2003. The Government is pursuing legislation to make banking laws more transparent to facilitate terrorist finance investigations. In October, Kazakhstan, along with Belarus, China, Kyrgyzstan, Tajikistan, and Russia joined the Eurasia Group, a regional anti-money laundering organization or Financial Action Task Force-style regional body. Kazakhstan, along with China, Kyrgyzstan, Russia, Tajikistan, and Uzbekistan, is a member of the Shanghai Cooperation Organization, which established a Regional Antiterrorism Center in Tashkent in June.

In October, the Supreme Court recognized al-Qaida, the East Turkistan Islamic Party, the Kurdish People's Congress, and the Islamic Movement of Uzbekistan (IMU) as terrorist groups, a decision that prohibits them from any activity in the country. Lacking legislative means for prosecuting suspected terrorists, the Government must use other provisions of its criminal code. In 2004, Kazakhstan arrested and tried more than 60 individuals suspected of participation in Hizb ut-Tahrir activities. They were prosecuted under the criminal code for "participating in activities of illegal organizations" (although Hizb ut-Tahrir has not been banned by name in Kazakhstan) and "inciting social, national, tribal, racial, or religious hatred." Several thousand members of Hizb ut-Tahrir, an extremist political movement advocating the establishment of a borderless, theocratic Islamic state throughout the entire Muslim world, are present in Kazakhstan, Kyrgyzstan, Tajikistan, and Uzbekistan as well as in countries outside the Central Asian region. The US Government has no evidence that Hizb ut-Tahrir has committed any terrorist acts, but the group's radical anti-US and anti-Semitic ideology is sympathetic to acts of violence against the United States and its allies, and it has publicly called on Muslims to travel to Iraq and Afghanistan to fight Coalition forces.

In November, the Government announced that Kazakhstani security agencies had detained leaders and accomplices of the Central Asia Mujahedeen Jamaat (more frequently referred to in English as the Islamic Jihad Group). More than a dozen suspects were detained, including four women who were allegedly preparing to be suicide bombers. This group was alleged to have links to the July 30 bombings in Tashkent.

Kosovo (Serbia and Montenegro)

Kosovo, currently under the administration of the United Nations Interim Administration Mission in Kosovo (UNMIK) pursuant to UN Security Council Resolution 1244, successfully prosecuted individuals for terrorism and developed new tools to combat terrorist financing. Radical Islamic organizations, some with links to terrorism, have attempted to recruit followers among Kosovo Albanian Muslims but these attempts have largely failed. In June 2004, authorities in Albania arrested and extradited Florim Ejupi to Kosovo, a suspect in a deadly 2001 terrorist attack against a bus carrying Kosovo Serbs; Ejupi was later indicted by a local Kosovo District Court for terrorism and murder. In February, UNMIK passed a regulation and later established a Financial Information Center to monitor suspicious financial transactions and deter money laundering and identify sources of terrorist financing. UNMIK, as well as Kosovo's local Provisional Institutions of Self-Government (PISG), continue to cooperate closely with the United States and other governments in sharing information and investigating terrorist-related groups and activities.

Kyrgyzstan

Kyrgyzstan in 2004 remained a dependable and outspoken ally in the global war on terrorism, taking political, legislative, and law enforcement initiatives to disrupt and deter terrorism.

Kyrgyzstan suffered a deadly act of terrorism in 2004. An explosion in the southern city of Osh in November killed one police officer and one suspected terrorist. The Ministry of Interior announced in December that it would open a temporary antiterrorism center in Osh. In December the Kyrgyz Parliament began consideration of a law on terrorism financing that, if passed, will considerably strengthen Kyrgyzstani efforts in this area. In April, Kyrgyzstan added Hizb ut-Tahrir to the list of banned religious extremist groups, though members are typically only arrested for distributing literature that "incites religious, ethnic or racial hatred." Several thousand members of Hizb ut-Tahrir, an extremist political movement advocating establishment of a borderless, theocratic caliphate throughout the entire Muslim world, are present in Kazakhstan, Kyrgyzstan, Tajikistan, and Uzbekistan as well as in countries outside the Central Asian region. Hizb ut-Tahrir pamphlets, filled with anti-US propaganda, have been distributed throughout the southern region of the country and even appeared in Bishkek and other parts of the north. The US Government has no evidence that Hizb ut-Tahrir has committed any terrorist acts, but the group's radical, anti-US and anti-Semitic ideology is sympathetic to acts of violence against the United States and its allies, and it has publicly called on Muslims to travel to Iraq and Afghanistan to fight Coalition forces.

Kyrgyzstan's military and internal forces worked to improve their counterterrorism capabilities and to expand their cooperation with regional partners in 2004. The Kyrgyz, Tajik, and Kazakh Border Services held joint exercises along their common borders in June to improve regional cooperation against terrorists. In July, Russia, Armenia, Belarus, Tajikistan, Kazakhstan, and Kyrgyzstan held joint military counterterrorism exercises in Kyrgyzstan. In April, the National Border Service opened an Interagency Training Center, which will focus on training to fight illegal migration and terrorism. Kyrgyzstan and China signed a bilateral agreement in September on cooperation against terrorism, separatism, and extremism.

Kyrgyzstan hosts a Commonwealth of Independent States (CIS) counterterrorism center in its capital, Bishkek. Kyrgyzstan, along with China, Kazakhstan, Russia, Tajikistan, and Uzbekistan, is a member of the Shanghai Cooperation Organization, which established a Regional Antiterrorism Center in Tashkent in June. In October, Kyrgyzstan, along with Belarus, China, Kazakhstan, Tajikistan, and Russia, formed the Eurasia Group, a regional anti-money laundering organization or Financial Action Task Force-style regional body.

The Netherlands

In November 2004, the Netherlands was rocked by the murder of prominent Dutch film director Theo van Gogh by a Dutch Moroccan acting out of radical Islamic convictions, prompting a national debate on the need to toughen immigration and counterterrorism legislation.

In June, the Dutch for the first time successfully convicted two individuals of terrorist activity; two men suspected of plotting to bomb the US Embassy in Paris were sentenced to six and four-year jail terms, respectively. The appeals court ruled information by the General Intelligence and Security Service (AIVD) served as a legitimate base for starting criminal investigations, thereby allowing use of AIVD intelligence as evidence. Justice Minister Donner submitted legislation codifying the court's ruling to allow the use of intelligence information in criminal proceedings. The bill is still awaiting parliamentary action.

The Act on Terrorist Crimes, implementing the 2002 EU framework decision on combating terrorism, became effective in August. The Government also reorganized its counterterrorism efforts to centralize and coordinate information sharing, currently shared by multiple ministries and agencies. As part of this effort, the Justice and Interior Ministries have proposed additional legislation to enhance the ability of law enforcement to detect and prevent terrorist activity and to hold and prosecute terrorists.

The six-month Dutch EU Presidency placed a priority on counterterrorism issues. The US and the EU initiated a dialogue on terrorism finance issues in September. The Netherlands finance ministry and Europol hosted a joint US-EU workshop for prosecutors and investigators of terrorism finance cases in November. EU leaders approved updated Presidency action plans on counterterrorism and terrorist financing in December.

Using national sanctions authority, the Dutch blocked the accounts and financial transactions of a HAMAS fundraiser, the al-Aqsa Foundation, and al-Qaida-affiliated Benevolence International Nederland. In July, the Netherlands froze all financial assets of the Dutch branch of al-Haramain. The Dutch have also been active in seeking support for an EU designation of Hizballah as a terrorist group.

The Netherlands continued its cooperation with the United States on shipping and port security. Under the Department of Energy's (DOE) Megaport/Second Line of Defense Initiative, four radiological monitors (provided by DOE) became operational in the port of Rotterdam in February. An estimated 31 additional monitors (funded by the Dutch) will be installed by the end of 2006. Improved security targeting at the port resulted from bilateral discussions. In July, the Government approved an experiment with air marshals on certain transatlantic flights, and the Dutch also permitted US immigration officials to return to Schiphol Airport to assist with US-bound passenger screening (now part of the Immigration Assistance Program).

Norway

Norway remained a stalwart ally in the war against terror. Due to lack of evidence admissible in Norwegian courts, authorities dropped their criminal case against suspected Ansar al-Islam leader (and Norway resident) Mullah Krekar but ordered his expulsion from Norway on national security grounds. The administrative and legal processes related to the expulsion order have extended into 2005.

Poland

Poland continued to play an active role in the war on terrorism as a leader in Central and Eastern Europe. In 2004, Poland's active Financial Intelligence Unit—the General Inspectorate for Financial Information (GIIF)—amended legislation to include non-profit organizations and legal practitioners as institutions obligated to file reports. The GIIF suspended five transactions worth 650,000 Euros, and blocked 12 accounts worth 2.1 million Euros in cases involving money laundering.

Portugal

In response to the March 11 train bombings in Spain, Portuguese security forces reassessed the security situation for the June-July EURO 2004 soccer tournament, increasing security at all levels within the country, enhancing cooperation with neighboring countries, and soliciting NATO air support during the games. While the games went forward without incident, the Portuguese addressed certain vulnerabilities, most notably the use of false documentation, and the relative ease with which terrorists could enter the country. In November, the media revealed that Portugal had apprehended ten suspected terrorists, predominantly Moroccan nationals, on the eve of the EURO 2004 opening ceremony in Porto. The suspected terrorists were deported both to Morocco and the Netherlands. One was later linked to the terror cell that carried out the murder of Dutch filmmaker Theo van Gogh. In addition, accused Indian terrorist Abu Salem remained in Portuguese custody pending extradition to India.

Romania

Romania is a staunch ally of the United States in the global war against terrorism, providing full public and diplomatic support for US goals to counter terrorism. The Romanian Government has established internal mechanisms to combat terrorism, including adoption of a national antiterrorism strategy and guidelines to prevent the use of the Romanian financial and banking system for the purpose of financing terrorist acts. As part of its national strategy, Romania adopted legislation in 2004 that delineates the responsibilities of Romanian Government institutions in battling terrorism, providing a clearer framework for interagency coordination and cooperation. Bucharest hosts the headquarters of the Southeast European Cooperation Initiative's regional center that provides law enforcement training and intelligence sharing on transborder criminal activities, including terrorism, for 12 member countries in Southeastern and Central Europe.

Russia

Russia pursued several major domestic and global counterterrorism initiatives in 2004, expanding its role in the global war on terrorism. Russia's leadership and public assigned increasing importance to counterterrorism following a series of deadly terrorist attacks in 2004. Separatist terrorists based in the North Caucasus were responsible for the murder of hundreds of Russian citizens. There is evidence of a foreign terrorist presence in Chechnya and of international financial ties with Chechen groups, although much of the actual terrorist activity in the region and elsewhere in Russia is homegrown and linked to the Chechen separatist movement.

Throughout the year, Russia continued revamping its domestic counterterror legislation and restructuring its law enforcement and security services in response to the terrorist threat. It facilitated effective interdiction of terrorist finance flows as a full member of the Financial Action Task Force (FATF). In October, Russia fulfilled its pledge to create a Central Asian FATF-style regional body (FSRB)—the Eurasia Group—whose members include Belarus, China, Kazakhstan, Kyrgyzstan, Tajikistan, and Russia. As chair of that new group, Russia declared its intention to create a training center in Moscow to bolster regional cooperation.

On September 13, immediately following the Beslan tragedy, President Putin announced political reforms (including the presidential nomination of governors) that the Government said would result in greater domestic security. Some Russians view those reforms as anti-democratic, and the United States expressed concerns about the nature of some of the proposals and the degree to which they would address Russia's counterterrorism efforts.

Examples of noteworthy law enforcement and judicial actions undertaken by Russia in 2004 include: Zarema Muzhikhoyeva, a failed Chechen suicide bomber, was convicted of terrorism by a Moscow court in April and sentenced to 20 years in prison. In November, Russian law enforcement officials arrested Alisher Usmanov, whom the Russian authorities allege was the leader of a terrorist cell. Usmanov was reportedly carrying explosives and al-Qaida training manuals at the time of his arrest. Abdulla Aliyev, an aide to Chechen terrorist Shamil Basayev, was convicted of involvement in Basayev's 1999 incursion into Dagestan after returning to Dagestan from self-imposed exile in Turkey and confessing to prosecutors. He was given an eight-year suspended sentence.

Russia increasingly oriented its foreign policy to strengthening efforts to fight terrorism and engaged in bilateral counterterrorism cooperation with numerous countries, including the United Kingdom, India, France, Pakistan, Japan, and Germany. President Putin created the post of Special Envoy for International Counterterrorism Cooperation and appointed former Deputy Foreign Minister Anatoliy Safonov to fill that role. Safonov co-chaired many of the bilateral meetings.

The US-Russia Counterterrorism Group met in March and October, fostering cooperative operational links between numerous US agencies and their counterparts in Russia. The Russian Federal Security Service (FSB) and the US Federal Bureau of Investigation (FBI) regularly exchanged operational counterterrorism information, and several joint investigations were underway in 2004. The FSB and Russia's Foreign Intelligence Service (SVR) have provided information to US agencies that has helped identify potential terrorism financing flows and suspect bank accounts and transactions. During FBI Director Mueller's December 2004 visit to Moscow, he and FSB Chief Patrushev signed a comprehensive memorandum of cooperation between the two agencies on counterterrorism, specifically committing them to the timely sharing of terrorist threat information. The FSB and FBI agreed to expand their cooperative exchange program to include information on weapons of mass destruction. Russia also cooperated extensively with the DHS Transportation Security Agency to increase airport security following terrorists' downing of two Russian airliners in August. The US Department of Treasury and Russia's Federal Service for Financial Monitoring (FSFM) submitted a joint report to Presidents Bush and Putin in July 2004 on Cooperative Strategies for Countering Terrorist Finance.

Russia was the chief sponsor of UN Security Council Resolution 1566, passed October 8, which created a working group to explore ways to sanction terrorist groups not covered by the al-Qaida/Taliban Sanctions Committee and strengthened the UN's Counter-Terrorism Committee (CTC). Russia chaired the CTC in the latter half of 2004 and was active in numerous other international fora in building cooperative mechanisms and programs to counter terror. For example, Russia led efforts in the Asia-Pacific Economic Cooperation (APEC) and the Shanghai Cooperation Organization (SCO) to focus those organizations on counterterrorism cooperation. Russia signed a joint declaration on international counterterrorism cooperation with the Association of Southeast Asian Nations (ASEAN) in Jakarta in July, and has pushed that organization's members to create a Russia-ASEAN counterterrorism task force. Russia has urged the OSCE and other organizations to orient their missions and goals to the global counterterrorist fight. The NATO-Russia Council adopted a joint counterterrorism plan at its December meeting in Brussels. Russia signed an agreement at the same meeting to begin permanent participation in 2005 in NATO's Operation Active Endeavor by providing naval assets to the ongoing sea interdiction operation in the Mediterranean.

Major terrorist acts perpetrated against Russia during 2004 included, in chronological order:

On February 6, suicide bombers blew up a Moscow subway train, killing at least 41 and wounding more than 100.

On April 6, a suicide bomber tried to assassinate Ingush President Murat Zyazikov by ramming an explosive-laden vehicle into Zyazikov's motorcade. The blast wounded four of Zyazikov's bodyguards and two civilians. Zyazikov was lightly wounded.

On May 9, Chechen President Akhmed Kadyrov was assassinated during Victory Day celebrations in a Grozny stadium.

On June 22, armed militants seized a Ministry of Interior building in Ingushetia, killing at least 92 people.

On August 24, suicide bombers simultaneously brought down two Russian airliners, killing 88 passengers and crew.

On August 31, a female suicide bomber killed at least eight persons and wounded more than 50 others when she detonated explosives outside a Moscow subway station.

September 1–3, terrorists seized approximately 1,200 hostages, more than half children, at a school in Beslan, North Ossetia. Two days later, an explosion inside the gymnasium where hostages were held sparked a fierce gun battle between terrorists and security forces. According to official figures, 331 people were killed, 172 of them children, though many believe the actual number of deaths was higher. Hundreds of others were injured.

Slovenia

Slovenia hosted a regional anti-money laundering conference for eight of its Balkan neighbors in October 2004. In 2004, Slovenia changed its penal code, increasing the prison term for money laundering from three to five years. Slovenia is actively involved in regional efforts to combat money laundering and terrorism financing, working throughout the Balkans and Eastern Europe, especially with Serbia and Montenegro, Ukraine, Macedonia, and Russia, through its Office for Money Laundering Prevention (OMLP). In 2004, Slovenia provided police trainers in Amman, Jordan, to train Iraqi policemen. Slovenia provides training to its non-EU member neighbors on border security and enforcement against financial crimes.

Spain

Spain remained a strong ally in the global war against terrorism and suffered a massive terrorist attack in March, when Islamic extremists attacked commuter trains in Madrid, killing 191 and wounding hundreds of others.

On the morning of March 11, 2004, terrorists detonated bombs on commuter trains, including five near Atocha, the city's biggest train station. Police discovered that extremists associated with the Moroccan Islamic Combatant Group (GICM), most of them North African residents of Spain, had carried out the attacks. On April 2, authorities located an explosive device under the high-speed railway connecting Madrid and Seville that failed to detonate. On April 3, seven suspects sought by police in connection with the March 11 bombings detonated explosives in an apartment in a Madrid suburb in order to avoid arrest. All seven suspects and one police officer were killed in the explosion. Authorities are holding approximately two dozen individuals in connection with the March 11 bombings. Those charged in the case are pending trial on charges of murder and belonging to a terrorist organization.

Spain has arrested and indicted scores of individuals with possible links to al-Qaida since September 11. In November, Spanish police arrested more than 30 suspected members of a radical Islamic organization, disrupting apparent plans to bomb Spain's High Court, Madrid's largest soccer stadium, the headquarters of the opposition Popular Party, an office building, and other public landmarks. Spain requested the extradition from Switzerland of Mohamed Achraf, the alleged leader of this terrorist conspiracy, also known as "Mikael Etienne Christian Lefevre." Extradition was authorized in January 2005 by the Swiss Federal Office of Justice, and in April 2005, Achraf's appeal against extradition was denied. In May, a Spanish judge ordered the detention of three Algerian nationals and one Spanish national for their ties to an al-Qaida cell in Hamburg, Germany. Police in Barcelona arrested ten Pakistani nationals suspected of providing logistical and financial support to Islamic extremist groups outside of Spain. At the time of their arrest, Spanish officials explicitly said these individuals were not known to be linked to al-Qaida. On December 17, Spanish police arrested Moroccan national Hassan El Haski and three other members of the Moroccan Islamic Combatant Group in the Canary Islands on charges of participating in the March 11 train bombings.

Spain has had some success in prosecuting terrorism cases. In November, a Spanish judge issued the first sentence connected to the March 11 train bombings, sentencing a 16-year-old male to six years in a juvenile prison facility and five years probation for helping the conspirators obtain the explosives used in the blasts. In November, a judge ordered the detention of an al-Jazeera television network journalist with alleged ties to the Spain-based al-Qaida network of Imad Eddin Barakat Yarkas. The journalist had been released on bail in 2003 for health reasons. The trial of 24 suspects charged in the Barakat Yarkas case is scheduled to begin in April 2005. The prosecutor is requesting 25-year prison terms for each victim of the 9/11 attacks for several members of the Barakat Yarkas cell.

Spain scored significant successes in its decades-old campaign to eliminate domestic terrorist groups, including the Basque Fatherland and Liberty (ETA) organization, a radical terrorist group. Spanish police arrested more than 70 individuals in 2004 for association with or membership in ETA and dismantled several ETA operational terrorist cells, dealing a blow to ETA's logistic, recruitment, and operational capabilities. In October, a joint French-Spanish investigation led to the arrest in France of high-ranking ETA terrorists Mikel Antza and Soledad Iparragirre. Antza was the leader of ETA at the time of his arrest and Iparragirre was sought in connection with 14 murders. ETA carried out a series of bombings of tourist areas during the summer and detonated 12 bombs on December 3 and 6 in Madrid and eight other cities, resulting in minor injuries to approximately a dozen people. Spanish and French authorities also made joint advances against the domestic terrorist group First of October Antifascist Resistance Group, all but eliminating the group.

US Attorney General John Ashcroft visited Spain on December 17 to sign the bilateral protocols to the US-EU Mutual Legal Assistance Treaty and Extradition Agreement, deepening bilateral judicial cooperation. In December, Spain signed a Memorandum of Understanding with the US Department of Energy for the installation of nuclear material detectors at the port of Algeciras. Spain is also cooperating with the Department of Homeland Security on the Container Security Initiative to scan containers bound from Algeciras to the United States for hazardous materials. Spain led the effort in the EU to approve the EU-wide common arrest and detention order, which the EU approved in late 2001. Spain co-chairs with the United States the Financial Action Task Force (FATF) Terrorism Finance Working Group and is pressing to become a standing member of the G8's Counterterrorism Action Group on the basis of its high level of technical counterterrorism assistance to third countries.

Tajikistan

The Government of Tajikistan continues to be a staunch supporter of the United States in the global war on terrorism. The Tajik Government directs intelligence and law enforcement resources against terrorist groups operating within its borders such as the Islamic Movement of Uzbekistan. In addition, Tajikistan combats terrorist financing by distributing lists of designated terrorist groups and individuals to local banks and other financial institutions. On the international level, Tajikistan participates in antiterrorist initiatives advanced by the Shanghai Cooperation Organization (SCO) and the Community of Independent States Antiterrorist Center. The SCO established a Regional Antiterrorism Center in Tashkent in June. In 2004, Tajikistan, with Russia, Kazakhstan, Kyrgyzstan, China, and Belarus, co-founded the Eurasia Group, a regional anti-money laundering organization or Financial Action Task Force-style regional body. The United States currently provides technical aid to the antiterrorist units of the Tajik Government. With the assistance of the United States and other foreign countries, Tajikistan's law enforcement personnel receive training in such areas as crisis management, bomb detection, and post-blast investigation. In 2004, Tajikistan worked with Russia to extradite a Tajik citizen to Russia to stand trial for accusations of terrorist acts in 2000.

Turkey

Turkish authorities, long staunch counterterrorism allies, continued to provide strong support in the global war on terrorism. Domestic and transnational terrorist groups have targeted Turks and foreigners, occasionally including US Government personnel, for over 40 years. International and domestic terrorist groups operating in Turkey include Marxist-Leninist, radical Islamist, separatist, and pro-Chechen-separatist groups. In response to these threats the Government has developed strong determination and the capability to fight most domestically-based terrorism. The Marxist-Leninist Revolutionary People's Liberation Party-Front (DHKP/C) continued to be active, and allegedly was responsible for a blast on an Istanbul bus in June that killed four and injured more than a dozen, as well as a number of smaller "sound" bombs. Turkish law enforcement authorities pursued several successful operations against DHKP/C cells.

In the summer of 2004, PKK/KADEK/Kongra-Gel renounced its self-proclaimed cease-fire and threatened to renew its separatist struggle in both the Southeast and Turkey's western cities. The Turkish press subsequently reported multiple incidents in the Southeast of PKK/KADEK/Kongra-Gel terrorist actions or clashes between Turkish security forces and PKK/KADEK/Kongra-Gel militants. PKK/KADEK/Kongra-Gel maintains approximately 500 armed militants in Turkey and an estimated 3,000 to 3,500 armed militants in northern Iraq, according to Turkish government sources and NGOs.

A new group calling itself the Kurdistan Liberation Hawks (TAK) used pro-PKK/KADEK/Kongra-Gel media sources in Germany to claim responsibility for several attacks on civilian targets this year, including two Istanbul hotels, the governor of Van province, and a music festival in Mersin. Several civilians, including international tourists, were killed and dozens were wounded in these attacks.

A criminal trial is underway for dozens of defendants charged with involvement in the November 2003 bombings of banks and synagogues in Istanbul. The lead defendants have admitted to contacts with al-Qaida and warned of further attacks if Turkey continues to cooperate with the United States and Israel. However, most of the other defendants denied any responsibility for or knowledge of the bombings. Verdicts are not expected until sometime in 2005.

On March 9, a suicide attack against an Istanbul Masonic lodge killed one attacker and one other person and wounded several others. Statements made by the surviving attacker suggest the attack was conducted by Islamic extremists against what they believed was a "Zionist" or Jewish target. Thirteen suspects have been charged in this attack, including one who is also a defendant in the trial related to the November 2003 bombings.

In May, Turkish authorities announced that they had foiled a plot to attack the NATO Summit in Istanbul. Turkey charged nine alleged members of the Ansar al-Islam terrorist group—which has ties to al-Qaida—with planning the bombing.

Turkmenistan

The Government of Turkmenistan has been a cautious member of the international coalition against terrorism, taking limited action to secure its border with Afghanistan, demonstrating greater willingness to accept some border security expertise and equipment from the international community, and instituting new airport security measures.

There was a significant change in the Government's attitude toward terrorism, specifically "domestic terrorism," following the November 25, 2002, attack on President Niyazov's motorcade. The intent of the new antiterrorism laws and strictures, however, has been to strengthen internal security controls to ensure the survival of the Niyazov government. The effect of these new laws has been a serious infringement on civil liberties and violations of human rights.

To build on its Law on Fighting Terrorism, adopted in August 2003, the President issued a decree in September 2004 approving the creation of the State Commission on Fighting Terrorism. The Department for Organized Crime at the Ministry of Internal Affairs also took on the responsibility for counterterrorism activities in 2004, becoming the Department for Counterterrorism and Organized Crime.

Ukraine

The fight against terrorism is a top foreign policy priority for the Government of Ukraine. Ukraine does not suffer from a domestic terrorism problem. In 2004, Ukrainian courts carried out no prosecutions on charges of international terrorism, although in May Ukrainian authorities arrested an Iraqi, two Greeks, and a Pakistani in a sting operation to foil an attempt to buy weapons for use in Iraq by the Iraqi insurgency; the four were convicted in late December, given suspended sentences, and deported.

United Kingdom

The United Kingdom has been and remains one of the United States' strongest partners in the global fight against terrorism. In what was reportedly the largest counterterrorism operation in the UK since 9/11, police in March arrested eight men, all British citizens of Pakistani descent, and seized a half-ton of ammonium nitrate. The men were charged under the Terrorism Act for involvement in a plot to manufacture and deploy an improvised explosive device. The UK has not commented publicly on the eight plotters' likely target. Their trials are expected to begin in 2005. In an unrelated case, police arrested eight men in August for planning a terrorist attack in the UK. All eight were charged with terrorism-related offenses, and at the time of their arrests, it was widely reported that police suspected them of having links with al-Qaida. Their trials are expected to begin in late 2005. The first trials for individuals arrested in connections with the 2003 "ricin plot" began in September. A second group of trials related to the ricin plot are likely to begin after the first group concludes.

UK law enforcement authorities may detain without charge individuals suspected of having committed a terrorism-related offense for up to 48 hours. Until January 2004, this period could be extended by court order to seven days. In January, a new law came into force allowing court ordered detention without charge for up to 14 days. In December, the UK's highest court ruled that special immigration powers that allowed the Home Secretary to detain indefinitely certain foreign nationals were incompatible with the European Convention on Human Rights (ECHR). In response to the ruling, the detention powers were allowed to lapse and Parliament adopted the Prevention of Terrorism Act. The Act gives the Home Secretary powers to make control orders that impose a range of conditions, including a ban on Internet or mobile phone use, restrictions on movement and travel, restrictions on association with named individuals, curfews, and tagging. These may be applied to both UK citizens and foreign nationals suspected of involvement in international terrorism.

The UK continued to assist with the US request for the extradition of Khaled al-Fawwaz, Adel Abdel Bary, and Ibrahim Eidarous for their involvement in the 1998 bombings of two US embassies in East Africa. However, all three have exercised their legal right to make representations to the Home Secretary against their surrender to the United States. The United States has also requested the extradition of Abu Doha in connection with the December 1999 plot by Ahmed Ressam and others to attack Los Angeles International Airport. As in the case of the Embassy bombers, his case is before the Home Secretary. In May, British officials arrested the radical cleric, Abu Hamza, on a US extradition warrant. The UK Government subsequently arrested Hamza on separate terrorism-related charges and in October the Crown Prosecution Service charged him with 16 criminal offenses, including soliciting murder, inciting racial hatred, and possessing a document that contained information "of a kind likely to be useful to a person committing or preparing an act of terrorism." The British case against Hamza takes legal precedence over the US extradition request, which has been suspended until the British case is settled. In August, the United States requested the extradition of Babar Ahmed, an alleged terrorist recruiter.

UK law enforcement and intelligence authorities work closely with their US counterparts. The regular exchange of law enforcement reporting and intelligence has resulted in the successful disruption of several significant plots to commit terrorist attacks against unspecified targets in the UK and the United States. The Metropolitan Police have also assisted other international partners with terrorism-related investigations, including Turkey, Saudi Arabia, Indonesia, and Iraq.

The United States and the United Kingdom are also strong allies in combating terrorism finance. Both work closely together and with other partners within the United Nations and the Financial Action Task Force (FATF) and the G8 Counterterrorism Action Group to promote initiatives to deny terrorists and their supporters access to the international financial system. The UK has strong legal provisions for freezing assets related to terrorist financing.

In 2004, the United States and the UK co-sponsored a proposal to the UN 1267 Sanctions Committee to include on its consolidated list the Jama'at al-Tawhid wa'al-Jihad (subsequently renamed al-Qaida of the Jihad Organization in the Land of the Two Rivers), the organization which was responsible for the bombing of UN headquarters in Baghdad and the brutal abduction and execution of seven civilians in Iraq.

In Northern Ireland, Republican and Loyalist paramilitary organizations have increasingly shifted their activity from political actions to criminal racketeering. This shift began with the 1994 ceasefires of the Provisional Irish Republican Army (PIRA), the Ulster Defense Association (UDA), and the Ulster Volunteer Force (UVF), and has accelerated since the signing of the Good Friday Agreement in 1998. Two relatively small "dissident" Republican paramilitaries—Continuity Irish Republican Army (CIRA) and Real Irish Republican Army (RIRA)—are not observing a ceasefire, and continue to advocate the use of armed violence to support their goal of uniting the northern and southern parts of Ireland. The activities of Loyalist paramilitaries take place almost exclusively within Northern Ireland, while Republican paramilitaries also have a presence in the Republic of Ireland.

In December, unknown persons suspected of being linked to PIRA robbed a Belfast bank of some $50 million dollars.

Uzbekistan

Uzbekistan has played an active role in multilateral regional efforts to address terrorism. In June, the Shanghai Cooperation Organization (SCO) Regional Antiterrorism Center was established in Tashkent and is in the early stages of development. The SCO membership includes China, Kazakhstan, Kyrgyzstan, Russia, Tajikistan, and Uzbekistan. After an explosion at a safe house in Bukhara, suicide bombers attacked a popular bazaar and other locations in Tashkent in March and April, resulting in the deaths of more than a dozen police officers and innocent bystanders and dozens of injuries. These were the first suicide bombings to occur in Central Asia. A further round of bombings took place in July outside the US and Israeli Embassies and the Uzbek General Prosecutor's Office, resulting in several injuries and the death of two Uzbekistani police officers at the US Embassy, one Uzbekistani National Security Service Officer, and an Uzbekistani guard at the Israeli Embassy. The Government of Kazakhstan has recently detained individuals suspected of organizing these latest attacks.

Uzbekistan continues to make countering terrorism and anti-government threats a high priority. In August and September, Uzbek courts convicted more than 80 individuals of terrorist activities for their involvement in the March and April attacks.

Middle East and North Africa Overview

The Middle East and North Africa region continues to be the region of greatest concern in the global war on terrorism. Iraq witnessed extensive terrorism and violence by foreign jihadists, former regime elements, and Islamic extremists. Numerous attacks in Iraq targeted foreign aid workers, contractors, and other non-combatants. Major terrorist attacks also occurred in Egypt, Saudi Arabia, and Israel. Active groups in the Middle East included al-Qaida, the Islamic Resistance Movement (HAMAS), Hizballah, Palestinian Islamic Jihad (PIJ), the al-Aqsa Martyrs Brigade (Fatah's militant wing), the Popular Front for the Liberation of Palestine (PFLP), Ansar al-Islam and its offshoot Ansar al-Sunna, and Abu Mus'ab al-Zarqawi's organization Tanzim Qaidat al-Jihad fi Bilad al-Rafidayn, or the al-Qaida Jihad Organization in the Land of the Two Rivers (formerly Jama'at al-Tawhid wa'al-Jihad). There was an increase in terrorist groups affiliating themselves with al-Qaida or expressing support for al-Qaida's ideology. In December, the United States amended the Foreign Terrorist Organization (FTO) designation of Zarqawi's group to include its new name and aliases and designated the Libyan Islamic Fighting Group (LIFG) as an FTO. Lebanese Hizballah's television network, al-Manar, was also added to the Terrorist Exclusion List (TEL).

Almost all countries in the region continued significant international counterterrorism cooperation and undertook efforts to strengthen their counterterrorism capabilities and effectiveness. Many countries continued to provide support to Coalition efforts to bring peace and stability to Iraq and Afghanistan. The United States continued to provide training throughout the region to assist US allies to enhance their counterterrorism capacity. In November, Bahrain hosted the first meeting of the newly-established FATF-style regional body, the Middle East and North Africa Financial Action Task Force (MENA FATF), the creation of which should strengthen members' efforts to combat money laundering and terrorist financing in countries in the region.

Iraq's designation as a state sponsor of terrorism was officially rescinded on October 20, and the United States continued to work closely with the Iraqi Interim Government (IIG) and Iraqi Security Forces to combat terrorism in Iraq. Nevertheless, terrorists and insurgents endeavored to prevent the establishment of a free, sovereign, and democratic Iraq through numerous attacks, including bombings, assassinations, kidnappings, and beheadings.

Saudi Arabia, Jordan, and Kuwait undertook aggressive actions to prevent terrorists and insurgents from crossing their borders into Iraq. Syria also took some measures to intercept Iraq-bound foreign jihadists, but those efforts were only partly successful.

Terrorist attacks in Israel in 2004 killed almost 100 people, a significant decrease from the year before. HAMAS claimed responsibility for the deadliest attack of the year, the August 31 double suicide bombing of two buses in Beersheva that killed 16 people and wounded 100.

In Egypt on October 7, terrorists attacked three tourist targets in Taba and Nuweiba on the Sinai peninsula, killing 34 people, including Egyptians, Israelis, Italians, a Russian, and an American-Israeli dual national, and injuring over 140. By the end of the year, the Egyptian Government assessed that of the nine individuals responsible for the attacks, two had been killed in the attacks, five were in custody, and two were still at large.

In Saudi Arabia, terrorists killed dozens of foreigners and Saudi citizens in 2004, including six Americans. Saudi authorities aggressively pursued terrorists and succeeded in capturing or killing many on their most-wanted list. On December 6, an attack on the US Consulate in Jeddah killed four Consulate locally engaged staff and one contract guard, and significantly injured ten employees. Three of the attackers were killed at the site, and one died later of his injuries. The fifth is in Saudi custody. Two groups associated with al-Qaida claimed responsibility for the attack.

Jordan's State Security Court sentenced eight men to death, including Abu Mus'ab al-Zarqawi, for the 2002 murder of USAID official Laurence Foley. In Yemen, the Sana'a Primary Court, in separate trials, convicted the defendants in the USS Cole and French M/V Limburg attacks. Both cases were under appeal at the end of 2004.

Algeria killed or apprehended key leaders of the Salafist Group for Call and Combat (GSPC) and the Armed Islamic Group (GIA), and arrested more than 400 other GSPC and GIA terrorists during 2004. On October 12, Algerian President Abdelaziz Bouteflika opened the African Union's Center for Study and Research on Terrorism in Algiers.

Morocco continued its aggressive action against suspects in the May 2003 Casablanca bombing.

Algeria

Algeria continued strong support for US counterterrorism efforts and demonstrated its overall support of the global war on terror. Algeria made impressive gains against both the Salafist Group for Call and Combat (GSPC—also known as the Salafist Group for Preaching and Combat) and the Armed Islamic Group (GIA). In June, GSPC "Emir" Nabil Sahraoui (aka Abu Ibrahim Mustapha) was killed by security forces during an armed clash. In October, Amari Saifi, a.k.a. Abderazak al-Para, the GSPC leader responsible for the 2003 kidnapping of 32 European hostages in Algeria, was apprehended through cooperation with the Chadian and Libyan authorities, and returned to Algeria after being held by a Chadian rebel group, the Movement for Democracy and Justice, for several months. In early November, Algerian security forces captured GIA leader Nouredine Boudiaf and three of his associates along with a large cache of weapons near the Algiers airport. Algerian authorities arrested more than 400 other GSPC and GIA terrorists during 2004.

According to Algerian authorities, fewer than 800 terrorists remain active in Algeria, down from a possible high of 28,000 terrorists in the mid-1990s. The Government's success in capturing or killing a number of GSPC and GIA leaders has further weakened the effectiveness of these two groups. The GSPC, however, carried out several operations in Algeria in 2004, including the August ambush of a military convoy in which 40 members of the security forces were killed. On June 21, GSPC terrorists exploded a vehicle-borne explosive device outside the El-Hamma electric power generating facility in central Algiers, causing no casualties but knocking out 210 MW of generating capacity for several months. Members of the cell responsible for the El-Hamma bombing were reportedly killed by security forces in October. Numerous smaller incidents occurred in 2004, mainly in the Boumerdes area and in parts of Kabylie.

Algeria's neighbors, including Mali, Niger, Chad, and Mauritania, continue to be affected by the GSPC's activities. The GSPC conducts smuggling activities between Algeria and neighboring countries. There are also financial links between GSPC cells in Europe and Algeria. The GSPC issued several communiqués on its website threatening foreigners in Algeria and pledged renewed allegiance to al-Qaida and global jihad. Algeria cooperates closely with its neighbors in the Sahel. This cooperation led to the apprehension of Abderrazak al-Para.

On October 12, President Abdelaziz Bouteflika hosted a high-level African Union (AU) conference on counterterrorism in Algiers and opened the new AU Center for Study and Research on Terrorism. This center is intended to facilitate information exchange and training for AU member states in the fight against terrorism. In the financial arena, Algeria drafted legislation to criminalize money laundering activities. A financial intelligence unit (FIU), which turns over actionable information to the courts, became operational.

Bahrain

Bahrain provides important support to US counterterrorism efforts, particularly efforts to block the financing of terror groups. Bahrain has continued to respond positively to requests for assistance to combat terror financing and has frozen about $18 million in terrorist-linked funds. In November, Bahrain hosted the inaugural meeting of the Middle East and North Africa Financial Action Task Force (MENA FATF). Bahrain worked closely with FATF for several years to establish this regional body. Located in Bahrain, the new MENA FATF secretariat will promote FATF recommendations to combat money laundering and terrorist financing.

Bahrain is an active participant in the US Government's Antiterrorism Assistance Program. Bahrain continued to cooperate with the US on intelligence and law enforcement matters.

The Government actively monitored terrorist suspects, but domestic legal constraints, including the absence of comprehensive conspiracy legislation, have at times hamstrung the Government's ability to detain and prosecute suspects. In June, the Government arrested six Bahrainis and placed one Bahraini under house arrest on suspicion of plotting terrorist attacks. All seven were released within two days. The Government re-arrested the six individuals in mid-July. The court ordered the release of two of the individuals in mid-September and ordered the release of the remaining four in early November pending trial. Preliminary hearings for the case began in early December. The court referred to the Constitutional Court a motion contesting the constitutionality of the charges against the suspects. One of the four escaped the courtroom during a hearing in mid-September and was recaptured the same day. He was convicted in mid-November for the escape attempt and began serving a six-month sentence.

Egypt

The Egyptian and US Governments maintained close cooperation on a broad range of counterterrorism and law enforcement issues in 2004. A high-level Egyptian judicial delegation visited the United States in June and met with representatives of the US Departments of Justice, State, and the FBI to discuss cooperation in the areas of counterterrorism, law enforcement, and the mutual legal assistance treaty. In September, 20 generals from Egyptian security services attended a crisis management seminar in Washington funded by the Department of State's Antiterrorism Assistance Program.

The Egyptian and US Governments also exchanged information on a variety of terrorism, security, and law enforcement matters during the course of the year. In the past two years, Egypt has tightened its assets-freezing regime in keeping with relevant UN Security Council Resolutions. Egypt passed strong anti-money laundering legislation in 2002 and established a financial intelligence unit in 2003. Egypt maintained its strengthened airport security measures and security for the Suez Canal, and continued to institute more stringent port security measures.

Egypt was a victim of terrorism in 2004. On October 7, terrorists attacked tourist targets in Taba and Nuweiba on the Sinai peninsula in three separate but coordinated actions. Thirty-four people were killed, including Egyptians, Israelis, Italians, a Russian, and an American-Israeli dual national, and over 140 were injured. On October 25, the Minister of Interior announced that the Government had identified nine individuals responsible for the attack. According to the Egyptian Government, a Palestinian resident in North Sinai was the group's ringleader. The Government reported that the Palestinian and an accomplice were killed in the course of the attack in Taba, and that five others had been taken into custody. At year's end, two of the nine named by the Government remained at large. The Government asserted that the nine perpetrators were not part of a wider conspiracy and did not receive assistance from international terrorist organizations.

The Egyptian judicial system does not allow plea bargaining in most cases, and terrorists have historically been prosecuted to the full extent of the law. Defendants are tried in military tribunals or emergency courts. In March, an emergency court pronounced its verdict in the trial of 26 persons accused of attempting to reconstitute the Islamic Liberation Party (Hizb al-Tahrir al-Islami), which was banned in Egypt in 1974 for its efforts to overthrow the Egyptian Government. The court sentenced 12 of the defendants (including three UK citizens) to prison. In April, Ahmad Hussein Agiza, an Islamist militant returned to Egypt by Sweden in 2001, was sentenced by a military court to 25 years in prison for membership in a banned organization, although his sentence was subsequently commuted to 15 years.

Egypt continued to release from prison members of the terrorist Islamic Group (IG) who recanted their past actions and renounced the use of violence. Approximately 700 people were released over the course of the year, of which the majority were reportedly IG members. The Government characterized the releases as the result of a transformation in the ideological and theological positions of the imprisoned IG leadership, reflected in a number of books, pamphlets, and interviews in which they espoused a new non-violent philosophy. Some IG members in Egypt and abroad rejected the leadership's move to adopt nonviolence.

Egypt continued to work with Israel to crack down on long-established smuggling tunnels through the Sinai to Gaza. Egypt has destroyed more than 40 tunnel openings since 2003 and long ago cleared sensitive portions of the border area spanning the tunneling area. Egypt has actively engaged Palestinian leaders on the question of reorganizing the Palestinian Authority's security services to better police the border area.

Iraq

Iraq remains the central battleground in the global war on terrorism. Former regime elements as well as foreign fighters and Islamic extremists continued to conduct terrorist attacks against civilians and non-combatants. These elements also conducted numerous insurgent attacks against Coalition and Iraqi Security Forces, which often had devastating effects on Iraqi civilians and significantly damaged the country's economic infrastructure. Following the return of sovereignty to the Iraqi Interim Government (IIG) on June 28, 2004, Iraqi authorities began to implement a new legal regime and to undertake needed law enforcement action to counter terrorist activity. Iraqi Security Forces (including the Police, Border Enforcement, National Guard, and Iraqi Armed Forces) worked closely with the Multi-National Forces-Iraq (MNF-I) to combat terrorism in Iraq. On October 20, 2004, Iraq's designation as a state sponsor of terrorism was rescinded by the United States.

Prior to the IIG, the governing Coalition Provisional

Authority (CPA) implemented several orders (binding instructions or directives that have the force of law) governing the creation of a revised penal code, new policies on border security, management of the court system, and new security forces. IIG cooperation with MNF-I forces was enshrined in Article 59 of the Transitional Administrative Law (TAL), which established the framework for Iraq's transition from the CPA through the sovereign IIG and eventually to a permanent sovereign Iraqi Government. The TAL names the Iraqi Armed Forces as the MNF-I's "principal partner... pursuant to the provisions of United Nations Security Council Resolution 1511 (2003)... until the ratification of a permanent constitution."

At the United Nations, the IIG consistently responded positively to US requests to co-sponsor the listing of al-Qaida-related entities and individuals pursuant to UN Security Council Resolution 1267 and related resolutions that provide for the imposition of sanctions against entities associated with Usama bin Ladin, al-Qaida and the Taliban.

Terrorist attacks against a variety of targets increased in late 2004 in the run-up to the January 30, 2005, elections for the Transitional National Assembly and regional parliamentary bodies.

Jordanian-born Abu Mus'ab al-Zarqawi and his organization emerged in 2004 to play a leading role in terrorist activities in Iraq. In October, the US Government designated Zarqawi's group, Jama'at al Tawhid wa'al-Jihad, as a Foreign Terrorist Organization (FTO). In December, the designation was amended to include the group's new name Tanzim Qaidat al-Jihad fi Bilad al-Rafidayn (or "The al-Qaida Jihad Organization in the Land of the Two Rivers") and other aliases following the "merger" between Zarqawi and Usama bin Ladin's al-Qaida organization. Zarqawi announced the merger in October, and in December, bin Ladin endorsed Zarqawi as his official emissary in Iraq.

Zarqawi's group claimed credit for a number of attacks targeting Coalition and Iraqi forces, as well as civilians, including the October massacre of 49 unarmed, out-of-uniform Iraqi National Guard recruits. Attacks that killed civilians include the March 2004 bombing of the Mount Lebanon Hotel, killing seven and injuring over 30, and a December 24 suicide bombing using a fuel tanker that killed nine and wounded 19 in the al-Mansur district of Baghdad.

In February, Zarqawi called for a "sectarian war" in Iraq. He and his organization sought to create a rift between Shi'a and Sunnis through several large terror attacks against Iraqi Shi'a. In March 2004, Zarqawi claimed credit for simultaneous bomb attacks in Baghdad and Karbala that killed over 180 pilgrims as they celebrated the Shi'a festival of Ashura. In December, Zarqawi also claimed credit for a suicide attack at the offices of Abdel Aziz al-Hakim, leader of the Supreme Council for the Islamic Revolution in Iraq (SCIRI), one of Iraq's largest Shi'a parties, which killed 15 and wounded over 50. Zarqawi has denied responsibility for another significant attack that same month in Karbala and Najaf, two of Shi'a Islam's most holy cities, which killed 62 Iraqi civilians and wounded more than 120.

Terrorists operating in Iraq used kidnapping and targeted assassinations to intimidate Iraqis and third-country nationals working in Iraq as civilian contractors. Nearly 60 noncombatant Americans died in terrorist incidents in Iraq in 2004. Other American noncombatants were killed in attacks on coalition military facilities or convoys. In June, Zarqawi claimed credit for the car bomb that killed the chairman of the Coalition-appointed Iraqi Governing Council. In April, an American civilian was kidnapped and later beheaded. One month later, a video of his beheading was posted on an al-Qaida-associated website. Analysts believe that Zarqawi himself killed the American as well as a Korean hostage, kidnapped in June. Zarqawi took direct credit for the September kidnapping and murder of two American civilians and later their British engineer co-worker, and the October murder of a Japanese citizen.

In August, the Kurdish terrorist group Ansar al-Sunna claimed responsibility for the kidnapping and killing of 12 Nepalese construction workers, followed by the murder of two Turkish citizens in September. Many other foreign civilians have been kidnapped. Some have been killed, others released, some remain in their kidnappers' hands, and the fate of others, such as the director of CARE, is unknown.

Other terrorist groups were active in Iraq. Ansar al-Sunna, believed to be an offshoot of the Ansar al-Islam group founded in Iraq in September 2001, first came to be known in April 2003 after issuing a statement on the Internet. In February 2004, Ansar al-Sunna claimed responsibility for bomb attacks on the offices of two Kurdish political parties in Irbil, which killed 109 Iraqi civilians. The Islamic Army in Iraq has also claimed responsibility for terrorist actions.

Approximately 3,800 disarmed persons remained resident at the former Mujahedin-e Khalq (MeK) military base at Camp Ashraf; the MeK is a designated US Foreign Terrorist Organization (FTO). More than 400 members renounced membership in the organization in 2004. Forty-one additional defectors elected to return to Iran, and another two hundred were awaiting ICRC assistance for voluntary repatriation to Iran at the end of the year. PKK/ KADEK/Kongra Gel, a designated foreign terrorist group, maintains an estimated 3,000 to 3,500 armed militants in northern Iraq, according to Turkish Government sources and NGOs. In the summer of 2004, PKK/KADEK/Kongra Gel renounced its self-proclaimed cease-fire and threatened to renew its separatist struggle in both Turkey's Southeast and urban centers. Turkish press subsequently reported multiple incidents in the Southeast of PKK/KADEK/ Kongra Gel terrorist actions or clashes between Turkish security forces and PKK/KADEK/ Kongra Gel militants.

Israel, the West Bank, and Gaza

Israel maintained staunch support for US-led counterterrorism efforts in 2004. Palestinian terrorist groups conducted a large number of attacks in Israel, the West Bank, and Gaza Strip in 2004. HAMAS, Palestinian Islamic Jihad (PIJ), the al-Aqsa Martyrs Brigade, and the Popular Front for the Liberation of Palestine (PFLP)—all US-designated Foreign Terrorist Organizations—were responsible for most of the attacks, which included suicide bombings, shootings, and mortar and rocket firings against civilian and military targets. Terrorist attacks in 2004 killed almost 100 people (mostly Israelis, as well as a number of foreigners, including one US citizen), a decrease from the almost 200 people killed in 2003.

The October 15, 2003, attack on a US diplomatic convoy in Gaza that killed three Americans is the most lethal attack ever directly targeting US interests in Israel, the West Bank, or Gaza. The Popular Resistance Committees (PRC), a loose association of Palestinians with ties to various Palestinian militant organizations such as HAMAS, PIJ, and Fatah, claimed responsibility, although that claim was later rescinded. Official investigations continued and resulted in the arrests of four suspects. A Palestinian civil court ordered the four suspects freed on March 14, citing a lack of evidence. Palestinian Authority (PA) Chairman Arafat rescinded the order and kept the suspects in custody until Palestinian gunmen attacked the Gaza prison and released the four suspects on April 24. Since the April 24 incident, the PA has failed to re-arrest the four suspects or to identify and bring to justice the perpetrators of the October 2003 attack.

Palestinian terrorist groups in Israel, the West Bank, and Gaza continue to focus their attention on the Palestinians' historical conflict with Israel, attacking Israel and Israeli interests within Israel and the Palestinian territories, rather than engaging in operations worldwide.

Israel employed a variety of military operations in its counterterrorism efforts. Israeli forces launched frequent raids throughout the West Bank and Gaza, conducted targeted killings of suspected Palestinian terrorists, destroyed homes —including those of families of suicide bombers—imposed strict and widespread closures and curfews in Palestinian areas, and continued construction of an extensive security barrier in the West Bank. Israeli counterterrorism measures appear to have reduced the lethality of attacks; continuing attacks and credible threats of attacks, however, show that the terrorist groups remained potent.

Israel also took action in February to block what it labeled terrorist funding in two Palestinian banks. The Israeli Defense Forces (IDF) and Shin Bet raided the West Bank offices of the Arab Bank and the Cairo-Amman Bank, seizing almost $9 million in cash from 310 accounts. Israeli law does not allow seizure of funds via correspondent accounts in Israel, and the Israeli Government claimed that the PA had failed to act on earlier intelligence. PA officials asserted that the funds belonged to reputable clients, with no connection to terrorism. The funds remain seized by order of an Israeli court.

HAMAS was particularly active in 2004, carrying out attacks that included shootings, suicide bombings, and stand-off mortar and rocket attacks against civilian and military targets, many of them joint operations with other militant organizations. HAMAS was responsible for the deadliest attack of the year in Israel—the August 31 double suicide bombing of two buses in Beersheva that killed 16 people and wounded 100. HAMAS was also responsible for an increase in Qassam rocket attacks. A rocket attack on Sderot on June 28 was the first fatal attack against Israelis using Qassam rockets. Two Israelis died in the attack. In September, two Israeli children were killed in Sderot from another Qassam rocket attack. In response to the continued Qassam rocket fire, the IDF launched a three-week operation on September 28, in which 130 Palestinians (among them 68 HAMAS and Palestine Islamic Jihad militants) and five Israelis died, according to press reports.

The Popular Front for the Liberation of Palestine (PFLP) was active in 2004. The group was responsible for the November 1 suicide bombing at the Carmel Market in Tel Aviv, which killed three people and wounded 30. Palestinian Islamic Jihad conducted numerous attacks on Israeli settlements and checkpoints, including the April 3 attacks on the Avnei Hafetz and Enav settlements in the West Bank which killed one Israeli and seriously wounded a child.

Fatah's militant wing, the al-Aqsa Martyrs Brigade, conducted numerous shooting attacks and suicide bombings in 2004. It was responsible for two suicide bus bombings in Jerusalem during January and February. The attacks killed 21 people and wounded over 110. Al-Aqsa also claimed responsibility along with HAMAS for the March 14 suicide attack in the port of Ashdod. The double suicide attack killed ten people and wounded at least 15. The group also claimed responsibility for a suicide bomber attack which killed two people and wounded 17 at a checkpoint near Jerusalem on August 11. On May 2, Palestinian gunmen belonging to the al-Aqsa Martyrs Brigade and PIJ shot and killed an Israeli settler and her four daughters in the Gaza Strip. The group also claimed responsibility for a suicide bomber attack which killed two people and wounded 17 at a checkpoint near Jerusalem on August 11.

Lebanese Hizballah remained a serious threat to the security of the region, continuing its call for the destruction of Israel and using Lebanese territory as a staging ground for terrorist operations. Lebanese Hizballah was also involved in providing material support to Palestinian terrorist groups to augment their capacity and lethality in conducting attacks against Israel.

In December, Israel convicted and sentenced an Israeli man for membership in the "New Jewish Underground," a terrorist organization that aimed to carry out attacks on Arab civilians. On September 29, a group of five Israeli settlers attacked and seriously wounded two US citizens, members of an NGO, who were escorting Palestinian children to school near Hebron. As of the end of 2004, the Israeli police had not arrested those responsible.

The Palestinian Authority's efforts to thwart terrorist operations were minimal in 2004. The PA security services remained fragmented and ineffective, hobbled by corruption, infighting, and poor leadership. Following the November 11 death of PA Chairman Arafat, Prime Minister Ahmed Qurei and then PLO Chairman Mahmoud Abbas engaged in an effort to convince militant Palestinian groups to agree to a cease-fire. Cease-fire talks were inconclusive by the end of 2004. Palestinian officials, including Mahmoud Abbas, and some Palestinian intellectuals have called for an end to armed attacks against Israelis.

Jordan

Jordan continued its strong support for the global war on terrorism in 2004. Jordanian security services disrupted numerous terrorist plots during the year, including several that targeted US interests in Jordan. It has aggressively pursued the network of fugitive Jordanian terrorist Abu Mus'ab al-Zarqawi, deemed responsible for numerous plots and attacks in Jordan and Iraq. In the most serious plot disrupted to date in Jordan, security services in April arrested Zarqawi affiliates in the advanced stages of a plan to launch truck bombs against Jordanian Government targets and the US Embassy in Amman. In an unprecedented move, the Jordanian Government aired the plotters' confessions on state-run television, emphasizing their plans to kill thousands, including Jordanian citizens. In late April, Government officials, including Queen Rania, joined thousands of Jordanians in a street march against terrorism. The Government publicly condemned terrorist acts throughout the world. King Abdullah was an outspoken critic of terrorism and Islamic extremism, and in September directed religious authorities to deliver the "Amman Message," a declaration that rejects religious extremism and terrorism, and seeks to promote moderate Islam and dialogue.

Jordan's State Security court, which has purview over terrorism-related cases, maintained a heavy caseload over the year, most of which involved Zarqawi-affiliated suspects. The Court in April sentenced eight men to death, including Zarqawi and five others in absentia, for the murder of USAID official Laurence Foley in front of his Amman home on October 28, 2002. The Government announced in July that Muammar al-Jaghbir, sentenced to death in absentia for his role in the Foley murder, was in Jordanian custody and would be re-tried according to Jordanian law. In May, the Court found guilty three Jordanians—including one of Zarqawi's nephews—for plotting attacks against US and Israeli tourists in the country. In June, the Court sentenced Ahmad al-Riyati and eight men being tried in absentia (including Zarqawi and reputed Ansar al-Islam leader Mullah Krekar) to prison for plotting against US interests. In October, the Court sentenced Bilal al-Hiyari, a Zarqawi fundraiser, to six months in jail for his activities. It also indicted suspected Zarqawi affiliate Miqdad al-Dabbas for planning attacks against Jordanian interests in Iraq. In November, the Court began the trial of the 13 suspects accused in the April plot, including Zarqawi in absentia.

In one of the few non-Zarqawi related terrorism cases, the State Security Court in September indicted two Jordanians for plotting to attack foreign diplomats in Amman. Separately, the Court in November acquitted four men of charges they plotted attacks against US and Israeli targets in Jordan, although they were sentenced to one year in jail for possession of an automatic weapon. In late December, the court convicted 11 men on weapons charges in a plot against the US Embassy and US military forces in Jordan.

The State Security Court also moved forward on other long-standing terrorism cases. In June, the Court affirmed its guilty verdict (first handed down in September 2000) against ten men accused of plotting attacks during Jordan's millennial celebrations, sentencing two to death. In October, Jordan's Court of Cassation, which hears appeals from the State Security Court, upheld the lower court's guilty verdict of US-Jordanian citizen Ra'ed Hijazi, one of those sentenced to death for his role in the plot, but commuted the death sentence, sentencing him to 20 years in jail with labor. The decision is final, and no more appeals will be heard.

Border security remained a top concern of Jordanian officials in 2004, as the Jordanian Government continued to interdict weapons and potential infiltrators at its borders. In July, Jordanian border officials intercepted and killed armed individuals attempting to infiltrate northern Israel from Jordan. Jordanian border officials allegedly intercepted suspects involved in the April Zarqawi plot as they tried to enter Jordan from Syria. In November, a terrorist driving a vehicle loaded with explosives tried to cross the Iraqi-Jordanian border, but was stopped before the explosives detonated.

Kuwait

Kuwait continued to engage with the US Government and its neighbors to thwart domestic threats to Kuwaiti and foreign interests. It also continued to provide significant support to US efforts to stem terror financing. Following the four terror attacks carried out against Operation Iraqi Freedom and Coalition forces in Kuwait between October 2002 and December 2003 that resulted in the death of one US Marine and a US defense contractor, the Government of Kuwait sought to strengthen domestic counterterrorism efforts, but the potential for further attacks remains a serious concern.

The Kuwaiti Government has taken significant measures to bolster security and enhance protection for Coalition forces transiting Kuwait. Kuwait responded quickly to US concerns about a possible terror attack in December 2004. Kuwaiti officials have heightened security along their border with Iraq to prevent terrorist infiltration and have also worked with Syria and Iran to develop procedures to increase intelligence sharing and enhance customs and border-monitoring cooperation. In July, Syria repatriated to Kuwait seven people recruited to carry out suicide bomb attacks in Iraq. Kuwait subsequently arrested a dozen Kuwaitis reportedly being trained to attack US and Coalition forces in Iraq. By the end of 2004, all but two of them had been released on bail.

The Kuwaiti Government was able to identify and arrest terror suspects in some cases, but was on occasion unable to secure convictions, citing a lack of evidence for use in court. Those actually sentenced to jail on terrorism charges often had their sentences reduced.

As part of its campaign against terror, the Government formed in October a ministerial committee chaired by the Minister of Islamic Endowments and Islamic Affairs to develop strategies to combat terror and extremists. In November, the Government forbade Kuwaiti ministries and religious institutions from extending official invitations to 26 Saudi clerics who reportedly signed a statement in support of jihad in Iraq. No entry ban was imposed, however, and at least one cleric visited the homes of some Members of Parliament and other private gatherings, sparking widespread public criticism of the cleric's presence. The Islamic political bloc in the Kuwaiti Parliament has been critical of the Government's methods in confronting and dealing with Islamic extremists.

Lebanon

Lebanon remains host to numerous US-designated terrorist groups. Beirut continued to demonstrate an unwillingness to take steps against Lebanese Hizballah, Palestinian Islamic Jihad (PIJ), the Popular Front for the Liberation of Palestine-General Command (PFLP-GC), the Abu Nidal organization (ANO), and HAMAS. In contrast, the Lebanese Government moved vigorously through legal and operational initiatives against Sunni extremist groups, including those similar in ideology to al-Qaida.

The Lebanese Government recognized as legitimate resistance groups organizations that target Israel and permitted them to maintain offices in Beirut. Lebanon also exempts what it terms "legal resistance" groups, including Lebanese Hizballah, from money laundering and terrorism financing laws. Lebanese leaders, including President Emile Lahud, reject assessments of Lebanese Hizballah's global terror activities, though the group's leadership has openly admitted to providing material support for terror attacks inside Israel, the West Bank, and Gaza. Hizballah, which holds 12 seats in the Lebanese parliament, is generally seen as a part of Lebanese society and politics.

The Lebanese Government has failed to comply with numerous UN resolutions to extend sole and effective authority over all Lebanese territory. The Lebanese security forces remain unable or unwilling to enter Palestinian refugee camps, the operational nodes of terrorist groups such as Asbat al-Ansar and other Palestinian terror groups, and to deploy forces into areas dominated by Lebanese Hizballah, including the Beka'a Valley, southern Beirut, and the south of the country up to the UN-demarcated Blue Line.

Syria's predominant role in Lebanon facilitates the Lebanese Hizballah and Palestinian terrorist presence in portions of Lebanon. In addition, Syrian and Iranian support for Lebanese Hizballah activities in southern Lebanon, and for Palestinian terrorist groups throughout the country, help promote an environment where terrorist elements flourish.

The Lebanese and Syrian Governments have not fully complied with UN Security Council Resolution 1559, which calls for, among other things, respect for the sovereignty and political independence of Lebanon, and the disarming and disbandment of all Lebanese and non-Lebanese militias. Lebanese Hizballah militiamen operate freely in southern Lebanon without interference from Lebanese security forces. Lebanese Government officials have openly and publicly condoned Lebanese Hizballah operations against Israel.

Lebanese authorities further maintain that the Government's provision of amnesty to Lebanese individuals involved in acts of violence during the civil war prevents Beirut from prosecuting many cases of concern to the United States, including the hijacking in 1985 of TWA 847 and the murder of a US Navy diver on the flight, and the abduction, torture, and murder of US hostages from 1984 to 1991. US courts have brought indictments against Lebanese Hizballah operatives responsible for a number of those crimes, and some of these defendants remain prominent terrorist figures. Despite evidence to the contrary, the Lebanese Government has insisted that Imad Mugniyah, wanted in connection with the TWA hijacking and other terrorist acts, who was placed on the FBI's list of most-wanted terrorists in 2001, is no longer in Lebanon. The Government's legal system also has failed to hold a hearing on the prosecutor's appeal in the case of Tawfic Muhammad Farroukh, who—despite the evidence against him—was found not guilty of murder for his role in the killings of US Ambassador Francis Meloy and two others in 1976.

Lebanon's Special Investigation Commission (SIC), and independent legal entity with judicial status empowered to investigate suspicious transactions, investigated over 176 cases involving allegations of money laundering and terrorist financing activities in 2004.

Lebanon has taken other counterterrorism measures in 2004, primarily directed against Sunni extremists. In March, a Lebanese military tribunal sentenced eight alleged Sunni extremists, for periods varying from five to 20 years imprisonment with hard labor, who were accused of carrying out terrorist attacks against foreign interests in Lebanon (including bombings of McDonalds and Pizza Hut restaurants) and plotting to assassinate the US Ambassador. Lebanese security services, in concert with Italian and Syrian authorities, rounded up members of a Sunni extremist cell in September that was allegedly planning to bomb the Italian and Ukrainian Embassies, and assassinate Western diplomats. The alleged cell leader later died in Lebanese custody. In October, a Lebanese military tribunal found guilty and sentenced two people to imprisonment with hard labor on charges of bringing an explosives device to US Embassy premises. One was sentenced for seven years and the other for three years.

Morocco

The Government of Morocco continues to be a staunch ally in the war on terror. King Mohammed VI has been a steadfast supporter of efforts to confront terrorism, in particular by promoting internal reforms designed to combat sources of terrorism over the long-term. Towards this end, during 2004 Morocco implemented reforms to the Ministry of Islamic Affairs to promote religious moderation and tolerance. Domestically, Morocco's historical record of strong vigilance against terrorist activity remained unwavering.

Following the May 16, 2003, Casablanca attacks in which suicide bombers from the "Salafiya Jihadiya" group killed 42 and wounded approximately 100 others, the Government arrested several thousand people, prosecuted 1,200 and sentenced about 900 for various terrorism-related crimes. The Minister of Justice announced that these arrests represented approximately 90 percent of those sought by the Government. The remaining ten percent were subjects of international arrest warrants. A spate of May 16-related terrorist arrests since June 2004, however, in Agadir, Beni Mellal, Fes, Khourigba, and Meknes suggests that the number of at-large suspects has likely decreased further. The Government also aggressively pursued Salafiya Jihadiya terrorist cells in several Moroccan cities.

The al-Qaida-affiliated Moroccan Islamic Combatant Group (GICM) continues to pose a threat in Morocco as well as in Europe. Moroccan extremists, associated with the GICM, were among those implicated in the March 11 terrorist attacks in Madrid.

Oman

Oman continued to provide support for the global war on terrorism, and has been responsive to requests for Coalition military and civilian support, making arrests as well as working with its neighbors to improve cross-border security. During the last three years, the Government of Oman has implemented a tight anti-money laundering regime, including surveillance systems designed to identify unusual transactions, with plans to require financial institutions to verify customer identities using sophisticated biometric technology. Omani financial authorities have also demonstrated their commitment to freeze the assets of any UN-listed individual found in Oman.

Qatar

The Government of Qatar provided the United States with significant counterterrorism support during 2004, building on the bilateral cooperation it has maintained since September 11, 2001.

No terrorist attacks occurred in Qatar in 2004, and the Qatari security services had some successes against terrorist targets. In March, Qatar passed the Combating Terrorism Law. The law defines terrorism and terrorist acts, lists specific punishments for terrorist crimes to include the death penalty, provides measures against terrorist financing or fundraising activities, and gives the Government sweeping authority to take action against terrorist crimes and activities. The law incorporates existing laws such as Qatar's penal code, criminal procedures code, judicial law, law on weapons, ammunitions and explosives, and the anti-money laundering law.

In March, the Government passed a new law to establish the Qatar Authority for Charitable Works, which monitors all domestic and international charitable activities. The Secretary General of the Authority approves international fund transfers by the charities. The Authority has primary responsibility for monitoring overseas charitable, developmental, and humanitarian projects, and is to report annually to concerned Government ministries on the status of all projects. The Authority was still in the process of developing concrete measures to exert more control over domestic charity collection.

In October, the Government appointed a member of the ruling al-Thani family as director of its financial intelligence unit (FIU). The FIU is responsible for reviewing all financial transaction reports, identifying suspicious transactions and financial activities of concern, and ensuring that all Government ministries and agencies have procedures and standards to ensure proper oversight of financial transactions.

Saudi Arabia

In 2004, the Kingdom of Saudi Arabia continued to support the global war on terror. Terrorists killed dozens of foreigners and citizens, including six Americans, in attacks throughout the country. The attacks consisted of kidnappings, armed assaults, targeted shootings, bombings, and beheadings. In the first half of 2004, the al-Qaida presence in Saudi Arabia kept up a steady tempo of attacks, surpassing the number and lethality of attacks conducted in the previous year. In the second half of the year, facing concerted pressure from Saudi authorities, the network appeared to be largely on the defensive, and did not mount a major operation until the December 6 attack on the US Consulate General in Jeddah. Five foreign nationals—four locally engaged staff and one local guard—working at the Consulate were killed. This attack was later claimed by "al-Qaida in the Arabian Peninsula," which also claimed credit for other deadly attacks against American citizens in 2004. Two car bombs, one aimed at the Ministry of Interior, exploded December 29, killing one passer-by and injuring several others.

In response to the wave of terrorist violence in the Kingdom, the Saudi Government aggressively pursued terrorists and achieved successes, including the capture or killing of all but seven of the Kingdom's 26 most-wanted terrorists and most of the known terrorist leadership in Saudi Arabia. Saudi forces launched dozens of security sweeps throughout the country, dismantling several al-Qaida cells, some of which were directly involved in attacks against US citizens and interests. More than thirty members of the Saudi security forces lost their lives in this campaign.

Saudi Arabia continued a public outreach campaign in the war against terror. As custodian of the two holy mosques in Mecca and Medina, the Saudi Government worked to delegitimize the inappropriate use of Islam to justify terrorist attacks. During the year, Saudi authorities aired confessions of militants and interviews with fathers of wanted men as part of a campaign to rally the public against radicals who carried out attacks in the Kingdom. In June, the Grand Mufti Shaykh Abd al-Aziz Al al-Shaykh issued a fatwa condemning terrorist acts and calling on citizens to report "saboteurs and anyone planning or preparing to carry out terrorist acts to the concerned authorities." Also in June, six senior religious leaders issued a statement denouncing terrorist attacks as "heinous crimes." A November "fatwa" issued by 26 radical Saudi clerics, who called on Iraqis to resist Coalition forces in Iraq by force, was rebutted by senior members of the Saudi official religious establishment, including the Grand Mufti. The Government also focused on internal social, political, and economic reforms as a method to reduce the appeal of radical ideologies. The media reported widely on each of the attacks conducted by terrorists in the Kingdom and the subsequent Government crackdown, leading to widespread public recognition that terrorism is a serious threat in the Kingdom, not only to foreigners, but to Saudis as well.

During the year, the Government launched intensive searches and counterterrorism sweeps in the country, often involving thousands of Saudi security personnel. On June 23, Crown Prince Abdullah issued an ultimatum to terrorists: surrender in 30 days or suffer the full force of the state. The ultimatum prompted several notable extremists to turn themselves in, including one terrorist suspect on Saudi Arabia's 26 most-wanted list. On June 29, the Prince Nayif Security Academy began training employees of the national oil company (Saudi ARAMCO) on counterterrorism measures. On the same day, the Ministry of Interior announced a 60-day pardon for persons to surrender unlicensed weapons.

In July, reporting on the results of a mutual evaluation conducted in 2003, the Financial Action Task Force (FATF) concluded that Saudi Arabia's financial regime met the general obligations of the organization's recommendations for combating money laundering and financing of terrorism. The Government continued to take steps to make operational a financial intelligence unit (FIU) established in 2003 under anti-money laundering and antiterrorist financing law. Concerned about the possible misuse of charitable organizations for terrorist purposes, the Government issued a set of bylaws for the Commission for Relief and Charitable Work Abroad, designed to oversee all Saudi charities. In this regard, the Government ordered the closure of the al-Haramain Foundation, a Saudi charity with a number of overseas offices that had been designated by the UN Sanctions Committee for providing support for terrorist activities. The Government also maintained its prohibition, imposed in 2003, on the collection of cash donations at mosques or commercial establishments and its restrictions on the bank accounts of charities, including prohibiting fund transfers out of the country. The media reported during the year that Saudi banks froze more than 250,000 accounts for noncompliance with anti-money laundering and terrorist finance laws. During the year, the Saudi Government requested that the UN 1267 Sanctions Committee add entities and individuals suspected of terrorist activities or of supporting terrorists to its consolidated list.

Tunisia

The Government of Tunisia publicly supported the international coalition against terrorism and responded positively to US requests for information and assistance in blocking financial assets. Tunisia's active stance against terrorism has been reinforced by its own experience with international terrorism. In April 2002, a suicide truck bomb detonated outside the el-Ghriba synagogue on the island of Djerba, killing at least twenty.

The Government of Tunisia has taken steps to strengthen counterterrorism laws. The Tunisian legislature in December 2003 passed a comprehensive law to "support the international effort to combat terrorism and money laundering." The first prosecution of suspected terrorists under the law's provisions commenced in February 2004. Tunisia has consistently emphasized the threat that terrorism poses to security and stability in the region. Further, it has encouraged Libya to abandon terrorism. Domestically, the Tunisian Government has prohibited the formation of religious-based political parties and groups, which it believes pose a terrorist threat.

United Arab Emirates

In 2004, the United Arab Emirates continued to provide staunch assistance and cooperation to the global war against terrorism. In July, late President Sheikh Zayed issued an antiterrorism law defining terrorist crimes and punishment, and specifically criminalizing the funding of terrorist organizations. In December, the United States and the Emirate of Dubai signed a Container Security Initiative Statement of Principles aimed at screening US-bound containerized cargo transiting Dubai's ports. The UAE also undertook several security measures along its land border and at sea to deter terrorists from reaching UAE soil.

In October, the UAE hosted an international conference on Islam intended to encourage moderation and condemn terrorism and extremism. The conference included sessions by prominent international and Emirate Muslim religious figures, and called for moderate Islamic preaching, increased training of imams, and reforms of the Islamic studies education curriculum.

In suppressing terrorist financing, the UAE Central Bank continued to enforce anti-money laundering regulations aggressively. Tightened oversight and reporting requirements for domestic financial markets resulted in a stronger legal and regulatory framework to deter abuse of the UAE financial system. The Central Bank has provided training programs to financial institutions on money laundering and terrorist financing. In April, the Central Bank hosted the Second International Hawala Conference, which was attended by 375 participants from around the world to discuss how to better monitor money flows occurring outside the formal banking structure. (Hawalas are informal money remittance and exchange businesses common in the Middle East and South Asia.) The conference included interactive panels, overviews of anti-money laundering systems in various other countries, and presentations from multilateral organizations such as the International Monetary Fund, World Bank, FATF, and the United Nations Office on Drugs and Crime. The Central Bank has also investigated financial transactions and frozen accounts in response to UN resolutions and internal investigations, and continued the process of registering hawala dealers.

Yemen

In 2004, the Republic of Yemen continued to provide support for the global war on terrorism and took action against al-Qaida and local extremists, arresting several individuals suspected of having al-Qaida ties and prosecuting the perpetrators of several terrorist acts.

On August 28, the Sana'a Primary Court convicted 14 al-Qaida members for the October 2002 attack on the French tanker M/V Limburg, the murder of a Ministry of Interior officer during the November 2002 attack on an oil company helicopter, a plot to attack the Civil Aviation and Meteorology Authority, a plot to attack four foreign embassies in Sana'a and to kill the US Ambassador, and for forging documents for the purpose of carrying out terrorism. Two defendants received death sentences, one in absentia. The other defendants were sentenced to prison terms ranging from three to ten years. Under Yemeni law, both defendants and the prosecution have the right to appeal rulings. All defendants have appealed their sentences, as has the prosecution, the latter arguing that some of the sentences were too light. The appeals process is expected to conclude in early 2005.

On September 10, the Sana'a Primary Court concluded the trial of five defendants for the October 12, 2000, attack on the USS Cole in Aden that killed 17 US sailors and injured 35. This included suspects Jamal al-Badawi and Fahad al-Quso, who were re-apprehended on March 10 by Yemeni authorities following their escape from an Aden prison in April 2003. On September 29, the court issued two death sentences for the ringleaders of the bombing (al-Badawi and Abd al-Rahim al-Nashiri in absentia). Three others were convicted and sentenced to prison terms ranging from five to ten years for their roles in the attack. These cases were under appeal by both the Government and the defense at the end of 2004.

The Yemeni Supreme Court heard appeals on the death sentences of Abed Abdulrazak al-Kamel and Ali Ahmed Mohamed Jarallah for the December 30, 2002, shootings of three American citizens in Jibla. No final decision has been issued in these cases.

Yemen has expressed a willingness to fight international terrorists by denying them the use of its territorial seas and ports. Over the past year, Yemen has increased its maritime security capabilities. The US Government provided extensive training and eight boats to the Yemeni Coast Guard, which is now a visible patrolling force along the coastline. Coast Guard operations are expanding to stem the use of Yemen as a way station for smuggling of persons, drugs, weapons, and explosives.

Land border security along Yemen's extensive frontier with Saudi Arabia remains a major concern. In February, Yemen and Saudi Arabia agreed to bolster cooperation in order to combat the cross-border smuggling of arms and people. The two countries also agreed to establish joint patrols and increase monitoring.

The Government's capacity for stemming terrorism financing remains limited. In February, the UN 1267 Sanctions Committee designated prominent Yemeni sheikh and opposition Islah party leader Abd al-Majid al-Zindani for his association with al-Qaida. The Yemeni Government has taken no action to bar his travel or to freeze his assets in compliance with its UN obligations, and Zindani continues to appear prominently at public events.

Yemen utilized its Islamic Dialogue Committee, headed by a leading judge, to continue its dialogue with detainees arrested for connections to terrorist groups and extremist elements. In a 2004 Ramadan amnesty the Government released over 100 security detainees, claiming that they had been rehabilitated and had made commitments to uphold the Yemeni constitution and laws, the rights of non-Muslims, and the inviolability of foreign interests.

Several terrorist organizations continued to maintain a presence in Yemen throughout 2004. HAMAS and Palestinian Islamic Jihad (PIJ) are recognized as legal organizations, and HAMAS maintains offices in Yemen. Neither organization has engaged in any known terrorist activities in Yemen, and PIJ does not have any known operational presence. HAMAS conducts extensive fundraising through mosques and other charitable organizations throughout the country. While al-Qaida's operational structure in Yemen has been weakened and dispersed, concerns remain about the organization's attempts to reconstitute operational cells in Yemen.

South Asia Overview

South Asia continued in 2004 to be a major theater of the global war on terrorism, and partner countries achieved several notable successes in countering terrorist groups. Afghanistan ratified a new constitution in January, and Hamid Karzai became the country's first popularly elected leader in October's presidential election. The Afghan National Army (ANA), while still limited in its capabilities, has lent support to US-led Coalition forces against antigovernment elements in the country's southern and eastern regions. The number of trained Afghan National Police (ANP) also continued to grow, playing an increasingly important role in deterring terrorist and extremist activity.

Security remained a key concern in the region. Insurgent and terrorist elements in Afghanistan continued to target international military forces, international and nongovernmental organizations (IOs and NGOs), the Afghan Government, and Afghan civilians. The Coalition sought to address security concerns by extending its activities into the Afghan provinces, aided by a growing network of provincial reconstruction teams (PRTs). For its part, the NATO-led International Security Assistance Force (ISAF) expanded into northern Afghanistan and worked on plans to extend its reach into the country's western regions.

Pakistan also achieved notable gains in the war on terrorism. Assassination attempts against key Government officials and numerous terrorist attacks were thwarted, as Pakistan continued its close cooperation with the United States. Counterterrorist activities and military operations in the Federally Administered Tribal Areas, where elements of al-Qaida and other groups continue to hide, disrupted terrorist command and control capabilities and killed or captured hundreds of militants. Authorities continued to arrest members of al-Qaida and other terrorist groups throughout the country while providing many new leads for future investigations and arrests.

India joined the United States in a renewed commitment to cooperate in a broadening range of counterterrorism measures. India suffered hundreds of attacks from both foreign and domestic terrorists this year, but security forces were increasingly effective, particularly in Kashmir, where the level of terrorist violence declined. The Indian Government cooperated with both Nepal and Bhutan in these countries' counterterrorist efforts. The Indian legislature modified its counterterrorism law regime in December, removing controversial elements while maintaining or strengthening provisions essential to fighting the war on terror.

Sri Lanka, Nepal and Bangladesh experienced mixed results in 2004. Violence in Sri Lanka increased as fighting broke out between differing factions of the Liberation Tigers of Tamil Eelam (LTTE). While the ceasefire between the Government and the LTTE was generally observed, the LTTE repeatedly struck at dissident members of the Tamil community. Both sides failed to resume the negotiations broken off by the LTTE in 2003, but the December 26 tsunami may have an impact on reconciliation in 2005. In Nepal, the Maoist insurgency continued, accompanied by increased anti-US and anti-Indian rhetoric. The Maoists threatened numerous companies, shut down business operations, and called for several general strikes throughout the country. They continued to extort money from Nepalis and foreign tourists. In September, suspected Maoists bombed the American Center in Kathmandu. Political violence increased in Bangladesh, where political rallies suffered from attacks with explosives. The United States concentrated its assistance on strengthening Bangladesh's weak institutions and laws to combat terror.

Afghanistan

Afghanistan made great strides towards building democracy and rebuilding the country in 2004. In January, Afghan delegates ratified a new national constitution that embraced democracy and pluralism in the context of Afghan and Islamic traditions. On October 9, over eight million citizens defied terrorist and extremist threats and small-scale attacks by voting in Afghanistan's first democratic presidential election. Hamid Karzai became the country's first popularly elected leader and was inaugurated as Afghanistan's president on December 7. Both the election and inauguration occurred without any major security incidents, despite Taliban threats to disrupt the democratic process. Other achievements included: the growing effectiveness of the Afghan National Army (ANA), with over 18,000 personnel in its ranks; a build-up to 33,000 personnel in the Afghan National Police (ANP); major gains in the Disarmament, Demobilization, and Reintegration (DDR) process; arrests of suspects in the August and October Kabul street bombings; and the expansion of reconstruction efforts. In the coming year, Afghans will face the challenge of building upon these gains, especially through holding parliamentary, provincial, and district elections.

President Karzai and his Government remained strongly committed to the war on terrorism. The ANA stepped up its role alongside the US-led Coalition in fighting insurgents and terrorists in Afghanistan's south and east. The ANA and ANP, along with the Coalition and the International Security Assistance Force (ISAF), played a key role in thwarting extremist attempts to disrupt the October presidential election. The Afghan people were also instrumental in thwarting terrorist threats against the election, providing information that in some cases resulted in the discovery of improvised explosive devices (IEDs).

Terrorist and insurgent elements targeted Afghan Government, US, Coalition, and ISAF assets in Kabul, as well as in southern and eastern provinces. Four American noncombatants are known to have died in international terrorist incidents in Afghanistan in 2004. Terrorists and other extremists hampered reconstruction efforts with attacks on NGOs and UN facilities and personnel in an unsuccessful attempt to drive the international community out of Afghanistan. These elements also targeted Afghan citizens who were trying to participate in their country's political process, in some cases reportedly killing people for possessing voter registration cards. Despite these concerted efforts, they failed to disrupt the October 9 presidential election.

Afghan troops continued to carry out joint operations with Coalition forces against the Taliban, al-Qaida, and other anti-government elements. The Tripartite Commission, formed in 2003 by the United States, Afghanistan, and Pakistan, continued to improve the sharing of information and coordination of border security efforts and to discuss other political issues between Afghanistan and Pakistan.

Bangladesh

Bangladesh supports the global war on terror but its ability to combat terrorism is undermined by weak institutions, porous borders, limited law enforcement capabilities, and debilitating in-fighting between the two major political parties.

Bangladesh's long tradition of inclusive, moderate Islam is increasingly under threat from extremist alternatives, already offering an attractive breeding ground for political and sectarian violence. Endemic corruption, poverty, and a stalemated political process could further contribute to the type of instability and widespread frustration that has elsewhere provided recruits, support, and safe haven to international terrorist groups.

There was an increase in political violence using explosives in 2004. In May, the British High Commissioner and more than 70 others were injured in a grenade attack in Sylhet. In August, approximately 20 Awami League supporters were killed, and 200 injured during an attack on the party's opposition rally in Dhaka.

Bangladesh, with US technical assistance, is strengthening police institutions with a professionalization program, enhancing police and banking capabilities to combat terrorist financing, and strengthening border control systems to detect suspicious travel and improve the integrity of Bangladeshi travel documents. The United States is assisting Bangladesh in developing new, stronger laws to enhance banking oversight and enforcement and in creating a financial intelligence unit (FIU). The Government is committed to enforcing UN Security Council resolutions and actions related to terrorism, including the identification and freezing of assets of individuals and organizations designated as terrorists or terrorist supporters, such as the Saudi-based charity al-Haramain Foundation. It also ordered the closure of the local Rabita Trust office and the departure from Bangladesh of its expatriate staff.

The Bangladesh military maintains a large presence in the Chittagong Hill Tracts, and has been successful in locating hidden weapons. In April it seized a large cache of weapons in Chittagong harbor. Bangladesh is taking steps to improve its effectiveness in preventing maritime smuggling and its capabilities in terrorist interdiction operations.

India

India remains an important ally in the global war on terror. Cooperative counterterrorism training expanded during the year, with hundreds of Indian military and law enforcement officers trained under State Department and Department of Defense programs. In 2004, both the US-India Counterterrorism Joint Working Group (CTJWG) and the Indo-US Cyber Security Forum, which includes counterterrorism prevention and detection discussions, met in New Delhi and Washington, respectively. These consultations improved information exchanges and underlined political commitment in both countries to counterterrorism cooperation as a strong pillar of the bilateral relationship. In November, the Indian Cabinet ratified the US-India Mutual Legal Assistance Treaty, which will come into force once the instruments of ratification are exchanged.

Separatist terrorists and insurgents staged hundreds of attacks on people and property in 2004, especially in Jammu and Kashmir, in the northeastern states, and the "Naxalite (Maoist) belt" in eastern India. The Government noted a significant decline in infiltration from Pakistani Kashmir during 2004, attributing the drop in large part to the fence it constructed during the year-long cease-fire with Pakistan and more effective counter-insurgency methods. Nevertheless, in Jammu and Kashmir insurgent and terrorist groups made numerous attempts to kill Indian and Kashmiri politicians, targeted public areas frequented by tourists, and attacked security forces. More than 500 civilians were killed in these attacks. Foreign Terrorist Organizations Lashkar e-Tayyiba (LT) and Jaish-e-Mohammad (JEM), operating through front groups in India under a number of new names, claimed responsibility for attacks on prominent Indian politicians and for killing the uncle of a prominent Kashmiri religious and political leader. In eastern India, the primary Naxalite groups took steps towards consolidation by combining to form the Communist Party of India (Maoist). Naxalite violence dropped significantly in 2004, but the future of peace talks was uncertain at year's end.

The Government further engaged other neighbors in the region, supporting Bhutanese and Nepalese counterterrorism efforts, and continues to pursue counterterrorism diplomacy at international and multilateral fora.

In December, India modified its counterterrorism legislation, repealing the Prevention of Terrorism Act (POTA) and simultaneously amending the Unlawful Activities Prevention Act (ULPA). The new legislation retained POTA's salient aspects and maintained India's compliance with UNSCR 1373, expanded the legal definition of terrorism to include extraterritorial acts, and strengthened Government wire-tapping authority in terrorism cases. In November, the Government also announced a review of its policy on the resolution of hostage crises.

Indian authorities began issuing machine-readable passports in New Delhi and Mumbai, and plan to expand this program to other major cities. The Cabinet approved the establishment of a financial intelligence unit (FIU) in November, although by year's end had yet to issue the regulations needed to make this unit fully effective. The Government was also unable to complete the requirements to accept the Financial Action Task Force's long-standing invitation to join.

Nepal

In April 2003, Nepal signed an agreement with the US Government establishing an antiterrorism assistance program. The Government continued its strong support of the global coalition against terrorism in 2004, and was responsive to both US and multilateral efforts to police international terrorism. Nepal's primary focus, however, remained the Maoist insurgency, active in Nepal since February 1996.

After unilaterally withdrawing from a seven-month cease-fire in August 2003, the Maoists resumed full-scale hostilities. In 2004 alone, Maoists were responsible for the deaths of at least 383 civilians and 214 Government security forces, with some estimates running as high as 831 victims. The Government has stated that Nepalese security forces have arrested thousands of suspected Maoists and killed more than 1,555 during the year.

Repeated anti-US rhetoric suggests the Maoists view US support for Kathmandu as a key obstacle to their goal of establishing a communist dictatorship in Nepal. Maoist supreme commander Prachanda issued a press statement in July 2004 threatening to use "more violent means" if peace talks with the Government of Nepal were not forthcoming or were unsuccessful. In August and September, Maoists threatened almost 50 companies and forced them to shut down operations. In August, a Maoist-affiliated group stated that it had decided to close down all multinational corporations in Nepal with US investment permanently. All companies reopened in mid-September after an agreement was reached between the Maoist-affiliated group and the Government of Nepal.

In addition to the threats against American-affiliated business enterprises, Maoists have threatened attacks against US and international NGOs, including those associated with Peace Corps programs. In September, Maoists attacked an American NGO worker in midwestern Nepal. They sought to extort money from Nepalis and foreigners to raise funds for their insurgency. The Maoists' public statements have criticized the United States, the United Kingdom, and India for providing security assistance to Nepal. On September 10, Maoists bombed the American Center in Kathmandu. The attack occurred during non-duty hours and there were no injuries, but the blast damaged the facility.

Security remains weak at many public facilities, including Tribhuvan International Airport in Kathmandu. The United States and other donor countries are actively working to improve this situation, but limited Government finances, weak border controls, and poor security infrastructure could make Nepal a convenient logistic and transit point for outside militants and international terrorists.

Pakistan

Pakistan continues to be one of the United States' most important partners in the war on terrorism. Few countries suffered as much from terrorism in 2004 as Pakistan, and few did as much to combat it. After the two near-miss assassination attempts against President Musharraf in December 2003, groups linked to al-Qaida tried to assassinate a corps commander in Karachi in June, and the Finance Minister (now Prime Minister) in July. Nearly 200 people were killed in major Sunni-Shia sectarian attacks. Al-Qaida declared the Government of Pakistan to be one of its main enemies, and called for its overthrow.

The Government of Pakistan continues to pursue al-Qaida and its allies aggressively through counterterrorist police measures throughout the country and large-scale military operations in the Federally Administered Tribal Areas (FATA) along the rugged Afghanistan-Pakistan border. Pakistani Army and Frontier Corps units destroyed key al-Qaida safe havens in South Waziristan Agency (part of the FATA), killing over 100 foreign terrorists and dispersing several hundred more. These operations significantly degraded al-Qaida's command and control capabilities in the region, but at a cost of approximately 200 Pakistani servicemen killed in action. Parallel to this military effort, the Government pursued a strategy to win the support of the tribes in the FATA with a combination of negotiations and economic development investments.

In addition to counterterrorism operations in the tribal areas, Pakistani security services are cooperating closely with the United States and other nations in a successful campaign to eliminate terrorism both within Pakistan and abroad. Over 600 suspected operatives of al-Qaida and other groups have been killed or captured by Pakistani authorities since September 2001. Individuals detained in 2004 have provided leads that aided investigations by security agencies around the world. Particularly notable in 2004 were the capture of al-Qaida communications expert and Heathrow bomb plot suspect Naeem Noor Khan in July, the arrest of 1998 US Embassy bombing suspect Ahmed Khalfan Ghailani the same month, and the killing of Daniel Pearl murder-suspect Amjad Farooqi in September. The Government also cracked down on several groups that had been active in the Kashmir insurgency, detaining the head of Harakat ul-Mujahidin (HUM) for several months and arranging the extradition of the head of Harakat ul-Jihad-I-Islami (HUJI).

Pursuant to its obligations under UN Security Council Resolution 1267 and subsequent resolutions, Pakistan continues to work with the UN 1267 Sanctions Committee to freeze the assets of individuals and groups identified as terrorist entities linked to al-Qaida and the Taliban. Pakistan's Parliament passed an amendment to the 1997 Antiterrorism Act that increased penalties and prohibited bail for those who finance terrorism. Pakistan also drafted and won agreement for a regional convention against terrorist financing. However, the Government's failure to pass an anti-money laundering or counterterrorist financing law that meets international standards has inhibited Pakistan's ability to cooperate internationally on counterterrorism finance issues.

Pakistan's Antiterrorism Courts continue to prosecute terrorism cases. In 2004, the courts convicted a suspect in the 2003 bombing of the US Consulate in Karachi, several suspects in the assassination attempts against President Musharraf, seven suspects in the 2002 attack on a Christian school, and nine suspects in the bombing of the Macedonian Consulate in Karachi.

US-Pakistan joint counterterrorism efforts have been extensive. They include cooperative efforts in border security and criminal investigations, as well as several long-term training projects. A Joint Working Group on Counterterrorism and Law Enforcement, established in 2002, met in September to assess joint efforts and discuss enhanced cooperation.

Sri Lanka

Sri Lanka supports the global war on terror and continues to demonstrate a strong commitment to combating terrorism. The Sri Lankan Government has cooperated with US efforts to track terrorist financing, although no assets have been identified in Sri Lanka to date. The United States has worked with the Government of Sri Lanka to develop anti-money laundering legislation, develop a Sri Lankan financial intelligence unit, and provide training for relevant Government agencies and the banking sector. Sri Lankan police provided investigative assistance in response to US requests.

The 2002 ceasefire between the Sri Lankan Government and the Liberation Tigers of Tamil Eelam (LTTE), a designated Foreign Terrorist Organization, continued to hold despite lack of progress in resuming the negotiations broken off by the LTTE in April 2003. The Sri Lankan Army remains deployed across the country for counter-insurgency purposes. The paramilitary Special Task Force police (STF) is deployed in the east.

Numerous violations of the ceasefire agreement were reportedly committed, primarily by the LTTE, during the year. Fighting broke out between a dissident LTTE faction, led by eastern military commander Karuna, and the mainstream LTTE in March, leading initially to the deaths of at least 120 LTTE cadres and civilians in the east. Following the split, the LTTE began a campaign of targeted assassinations against political opponents, members of the Karuna faction, and suspected Sri Lankan Army informants, killing at least another 80 individuals during the year. In addition, at least 26 members of the mainstream LTTE were killed by suspected Karuna sympathizers, while six members of the Sri Lankan security forces were killed in isolated incidents by suspected LTTE terrorists. On July 7, a suspected LTTE suicide bomber detonated herself while being questioned inside a Colombo police station, killing herself and four policemen. Her intended target was believed to be the Minister of Hindu Affairs, a Tamil politician opposed to the LTTE.

The renewed violence in Sri Lanka has done much to dissipate the cautious optimism that surrounded the process last year. In September, State Department Coordinator for Counterterrorism Cofer Black affirmed that the United States would maintain the designation of the LTTE as a Foreign Terrorist Organization until it unequivocally renounces terrorism in both word and deed.

Western Hemisphere Overview

Terrorism in the Western Hemisphere historically has been perpetrated by groups advocating internal political change and by criminal organizations seeking to intimidate society and governments to allow them to exist and operate unfettered. The focus of terrorist groups has been primarily domestic. In the last year alone, Colombia's three US-designated Foreign Terrorist Organizations (FTOs)—the Revolutionary Armed Forces of Colombia (FARC), the National Liberation Army (ELN), and the United Self-Defense Forces of Colombia (AUC)—were responsible for murdering approximately 3,000 people, mostly Colombians. Shining Path's bloody 30-year campaign in the 1980s and early 1990s left over 35,000 Peruvians dead.

Terrorists in the region are becoming increasingly active in illicit transnational activities, including the drug trade, arms trafficking, money laundering, contraband smuggling, and document and currency fraud. The Western Hemisphere's lightly-defended "soft" targets—its tourism industry, large American expatriate communities, thriving aviation sector, and busy ports—as well as systemic disparities between countries in border security, legal and financial regulatory regimes, and the difficulty of maintaining an effective government presence in remote areas—represent targets and opportunities for domestic and foreign terrorists to exploit.

Although the threat of international terrorism in the Western Hemisphere remained relatively low during 2004 compared to other world regions, terrorists may seek safehaven, financing, recruiting, illegal travel documentation, or access to the United States from the area and pose serious threats. International terrorists have not hesitated to make the Western Hemisphere a battleground to advance their causes. The attacks of September 11, 2001, in the United States and the bombings of the Israeli Embassy in Buenos Aires in 1992 and the Argentine-Jewish Cultural Center in 1994 are stark reminders of this. Americans have fallen victim to terrorists elsewhere in the region; since 1992, the FARC has murdered at least 10 US citizens and currently holds three US Government civilian contractors hostage.

Various countries participated in joint counterterrorism training and simulations during 2004, including "Panama 2004" in August and "Fuerzas Comando 2004" (El Salvador) in July. Many countries in the Western Hemisphere are also active participants in the Counterterrorism Action Group (CTAG) meetings hosted by local US embassies. An initiative coming out of the US Government's chairmanship of CTAG in 2004, these meetings bring together local representatives of the G8, host government, and other regional governments to discuss counterterrorism capacity-building assistance. The countries of the hemisphere are also active in the OAS Inter-American Committee Against Terrorism (Spanish acronym, CICTE).

Significant developments in specific countries and subregions:

Colombia suffered continued terrorist violence as the Revolutionary Armed Forces of Colombia (FARC) and other narcoterrorist groups conducted car bombings, kidnappings, and political murders, as well as targeted critical infrastructure (water, oil, gas, electricity) and transportation systems. Three Americans, whose plane made an emergency crash landing in southern Colombia on February 13, 2003, continue to be held hostage by the FARC.

At the time of the crash, the FARC murdered a fourth American and a Colombian soldier. Under President Uribe, the Colombian military, police, and intelligence forces continued successfully to disrupt the activities of Colombian terrorist groups. Acts of terrorism, homicides, massacres, and kidnappings dropped significantly in 2004, while the Colombian Government captured FARC leaders, including Nayibe Rojas Cabrera (aka "Sonia") and Juvenal Ovidio Ricardo Palmera (aka "Simon Trinidad") who were extradited to the United States. Colombia demobilized thousands of AUC members, and continued aggressive coca and poppy eradication.

The United States continued strong cooperative relationships with Canada and Mexico on a range of counterterrorism issues, including border, aviation, maritime, and transportation security. In September 2004, Canada hosted a border symposium for the 34 OAS member states in Vancouver to demonstrate US-Canada cooperation on border security and encourage more active border security measures by CICTE members.

The primary focus in 2004 for many of the countries in the region was to strengthen capabilities to prevent or disrupt possible terrorist fundraising activity in their territories, and to bolster their ability to combat transnational crime, including activities that terrorists could undertake to support terrorism.

In Central America, governments concentrated on strengthening intelligence collection and sharing capabilities, and on their ability to respond to terrorist threats and incidents. Efforts were made more difficult by widespread, unfounded media reports alleging formal links between transnational criminal gangs and Islamic extremists in the region.

The United States strengthened its cooperative dialogue with the "Three Plus One" partners Argentina, Brazil, and Paraguay, and provided advice and training support to El Salvador after Islamic terrorists threatened attacks to punish El Salvador's participation in the Coalition fighting to liberate Iraq. In the Caribbean, the US Government began a series of assessments requested by countries to determine ways to improve their counterterrorism regimes, and assisted countries to comply with new international norms for port security. Governments stepped up efforts to tighten border security and in general, vigilance against the development of Islamic extremism or other potential misuse of their territories, whether from within or from abroad.

Bolivia

Despite considerable political and economic instability in 2004, Bolivia continued to work closely with the US Government to combat terrorism both domestic and foreign. In late 2004, Bolivia's Financial Investigation Unit collaborated with the US Government to share information about possible terrorist-linked financial transactions and enhance the monitoring and enforcement of financial networks. The Bolivian Government established in 2004 a counterterrorism coordination unit in the Ministry of the Presidency, including elements of the Bolivian National Police and military, to develop national counterterrorism policy, manage terrorism-related information, and coordinate Bolivian Government agencies (military, police, diplomatic, intelligence) to address terrorist threats and activities. The Bolivian Government is an active participant in Counterterrorism Action Group (CTAG) meetings.

Although no significant acts of international terrorism occurred in Bolivia in 2004, domestic terrorism related mainly to the drug trade continued to be a threat, though relatively less than in 2003. Bolivia remains vulnerable to terrorists seeking to exploit its porous borders, resource constraints, corruption, and lack of investigative expertise to disrupt recruiting and fundraising. Members of the Revolutionary Armed Forces of Colombia (FARC), Peru's Shining Path (SL, in Spanish) and Tupac Amaru Revolutionary Movement (MRTA) have at times been identified in Bolivia; FARC and SL are US Government-designated Foreign Terrorist Organizations (FTOs). More than 300 members of Shining Path and MRTA have been resettled in El Alto under United Nations auspices. Many maintain contacts in Peru and may have contributed to politically motivated violence in Bolivia. The widespread availability of explosives and miners skilled in detonation techniques has complicated Bolivia's counterterrorism efforts. On at least two occasions, domestic groups planned to attack the Congress with dynamite and small arms. Police acted quickly to quell the threats, although one distraught miner in March 2004 detonated charges inside the parliament, killing two policemen and himself, while injuring bystanders.

Colombian National Liberation Army (ELN) member Francisco "Pacho" Cortes—arrested in 2003 on espionage and terrorism charges while attempting to create an ELN-Bolivia branch—remains in custody, but the presiding judge in the case has ruled Cortes eligible for bail. NGOs and Cortes' supporters are attempting to raise funds for his release. The Bolivian Government continues to hunt for organized crime head Marco Marino Diodato, who escaped from prison in early 2004. Diodato is suspected of orchestrating the fatal car bombing of Bolivian prosecutor Monica von Borries in mid-2004, and has reportedly made threats against members of the US Embassy and other Americans in Bolivia. Little progress was made in the investigation of the 2000 torture and murder of police officer David Andrade and his wife, and the suspects remain at large.

Bolivia maintained its policy of forced coca eradication in the Chapare growing region, despite continued threats of violence against Government eradicators there. Violence in the Chapare dropped off, however, after the Government and coca grower syndicates signed an accord in October 2004 allowing for a limited exception of 3,200 hectares to remain untouched for one year. At the same time, there were incidents of violence in the Yungas growing region, a lawless area of both legal and illegal coca cultivation. Coca growers dynamited USAID alternative development projects, threatened police and other government officials, and delayed construction of a police checkpoint.

Bolivia has signed the Inter-American Convention Against Terrorism and the August 2003 Asuncion Declaration, in which several South American nations committed themselves to support the Colombian Government in its ongoing struggle against terrorism and drug trafficking.

Canada

The Canadian Government continued in 2004 to be a strong ally of the United States in the fight against international terrorism. Counterterrorism cooperation with Canada remains excellent. The Canadian Government has responded quickly to requests from the United States for assistance in areas ranging from information-sharing to disrupting terrorism activities.

Day-to-day cooperation between US and Canadian law enforcement agencies is close and continuous. Canada's 2001 Antiterrorism Act strengthened its ability to identify, deter, disable, prosecute, convict, and punish terrorist groups. It also provides investigative tools for Canadian law enforcement agencies, while providing substantial safeguards to privacy and due process. In December 2003, the Canadian Government established Public Safety and Emergency Preparedness Canada (PSEPC), a counterpart of the US Department of Homeland Security, and gave it the mandate of protecting Canadians from criminals and terrorists.

Canada cooperates closely with the United States on investigations. There is a heavy volume of extradition requests between the two countries. Canadian privacy laws, limited resources, and criminal procedures limit a fuller and more timely exchange of information with the United States.

The diplomatic engagement between the United States and Canada on counterterrorism issues remains strong, maintained in long-standing bilateral fora. For over 15 years, the US-Canada Bilateral Consultative Group (BCG) has brought together government officials to develop ways to enhance cooperation on a broad range of counterterrorism issues, including technical research and development, terrorist designations, threat alerts, and cross-border crime. Canada plans to host the next round of the BCG in 2005.

On December 12, 2001, the United States and Canada signed the Smart Border Declaration, which sets forth a 30-point (later expanded to 32-point) action plan based on four pillars: the secure flow of people, the secure flow of goods, secure infrastructure, and coordination and information-sharing in the enforcement of these objectives. Under the Smart Border Declaration, 15 Integrated Border Enforcement Teams (IBETS) are coordinating US and Canadian efforts to disrupt cross-border criminal and potential terrorist activity. Canada and the United States cooperate on shared immigration issues through the Border Vision process, which began in 1997 and seeks to develop a joint regional approach to migration through information and intelligence sharing, policy coordination, joint overseas operations, and border cooperation.

Canada and the United States coordinate judicial efforts at the US-Canadian Cross-Border Crime Forum, which last met in Ottawa in October 2004 and has a sub-group on counterterrorism. Through the 1995 Shared Border Accord, Canada and the United States continue to streamline processes for legitimate travelers and commercial goods, provide enhanced protection against drug smuggling and the illegal entrance of people, and promote international trade. Canada was the first country to join the United States in developing the Container Security Initiative (CSI) to screen incoming container shipments, and Canada has been an active participant in the Proliferation Security Initiative.

Canada and the United States also work multilaterally, in fora such as in the G8's Counterterrorism Action Group (CTAG) and the OAS Inter-American Committee Against Terrorism (CICTE), to build legal and financial counterterrorism capacity globally and to strengthen security at ports, airports, and land borders around the world. In September 2004, Canada hosted a border symposium, which brought representatives from the 34 OAS member states to Vancouver to view US-Canada cooperation on border security (land, air, and sea). Participants are expected to report on their border security programs to CICTE.

Canada implements terrorist finance listings in compliance with UN requirements and coordinates closely with the United States on plans to freeze assets. Efforts to counter terrorist financing include implementing the provisions of UN Security Council Resolution 1373, promoting the Special Recommendations on Terrorist Financing of the Financial Action Task Force (FATF), and actively participating in the G7, G8, and G20. Under Canadian law, all terrorist entities listed by the United Nations are automatically designated on a domestic basis within Canada as well. Although they are subject to prosecution under the Criminal Code of Canada, the law remains untested and no prosecutions have yet taken place.

Chile

Chile is a steadfast ally in the global war on terrorism. In 2004 Chile served as chair of the UN's al-Qaida and Taliban sanctions committee, and moved to address the potential threat from Islamic extremist fundraising in its free trade zone of Iquique. As host of the 2004 Asia-Pacific Economic Cooperation (APEC) Summit, Chile emphasized security and counterterrorism issues on the agenda.

There were no significant incidents of international terrorism in Chile in 2004, although various domestic groups firebombed a McDonald's restaurant and planted or detonated low-powered bombs outside banks, ATM machines, a subway, and in a restroom in the Brazilian consulate in Santiago. There were no injuries or deaths.

Chilean law enforcement agencies were consistently cooperative in investigating links to international terrorism, but, hampered by a restrictive law, the Investigative Police were unable to bring any investigation to prosecution. Chile has a 200-person designated counterterrorist force in the national uniformed police. In October 2004, a new National Intelligence Agency became fully operational as the coordinator of intelligence gathering for Chile. A number of Chilean Government entities and officials benefited from US-sponsored training during 2004, including the Chilean Air Force and law enforcement personnel at various levels.

Chile's money laundering statute covers terrorist financing and expands the Government's ability to freeze and seize assets, although the Government has yet to charge anyone under that law or to apply it against terrorist assets identified by other governments or international institutions. Chile launched in June 2004 its financial analysis unit (UAF) charged with investigating suspicious transactions. However, the Constitutional Tribunal ruled some of the UAF provisions to be unconstitutional. Efforts are underway to amend the laws to provide the UAF with greater investigative authority.

Colombia

Colombia remained a steadfast ally of the United States in the fight against narcoterrorism in 2004. The Colombian Government, through bilateral, multilateral, military, and economic activities, continued to assist US Government counterterrorism efforts and to disrupt terrorist acts, block terrorist finances, and extradite terrorists to face justice in the United States.

The US Government has designated three Colombian armed groups as Foreign Terrorist Organizations (FTOs): the Revolutionary Armed Forces of Colombia (FARC), the National Liberation Army (ELN), and the United Self-Defense Forces of Colombia (AUC). In February 2004, the US Government also designated the FARC and the AUC as significant foreign narcotics traffickers under the Kingpin Act. All three Colombian FTOs are primarily focused on domestic change in Colombia and on maintaining their own influence and viability but recently have been suspected of assisting violent groups in other countries such as Paraguay. In 2004, the three FTOs conducted car bombings, kidnappings, political murders, and the indiscriminate use of landmines. They also targeted critical infrastructure (water, oil, gas, electricity), public recreational areas, and modes of transportation.

Some examples in 2004 included the FARC's Christmas Eve kidnapping of seven people in Antioquia Department (Province) and New Year's Eve massacre of at least 17 people for suspected affiliation with the AUC; the FARC's bombing in May of a popular nightclub in Apartado, Antioquia, which killed five and injured almost 100; the suspected FARC bombing in August of Medellin's annual flower festival that injured approximately 38; the FARC's attempted mass kidnapping in February in a condominium complex in Neiva, Huila Department (one hostage was released two months later and three hostages remain in captivity); and the ELN's July kidnapping of the Bishop of Yopal, Casanare Department. Paramilitaries continued to displace forcibly civilians who resided along drug and weapons transit corridors or who were suspected of being guerrilla sympathizers. In late June, the AUC kidnapped former Senator Jose Eduardo Gnecco and his family. Both FARC and the ELN continued attacks against the country's infrastructure and oil pipelines, albeit at reduced levels. Many more attacks were thwarted nationwide by the Colombian Government's excellent intelligence and security work.

All three FTOs carried out attacks in and around major urban areas in Colombia, including at supermarkets, places of entertainment, and other areas frequented by US citizens and expatriates. Colombia's FTOs continued to threaten and target US citizens in 2004. Historically, American victims of kidnappings and murders have included journalists, missionaries, scientists, human rights workers, US Government employees, and business people, as well as tourists and family visitors, and even small children. On February 13, 2003, a plane carrying five crew members (four US citizens who were US Government defense contractors and one Colombian citizen) crashed in a remote section of Colombia. Two crew members (the Colombian and one of the Americans) were killed by the FARC and the remaining crew members were taken hostage. The FARC continues to hold captive the three US citizens. In the past four years, 30 American citizens have been reported kidnapped in Colombia.

President Uribe's Government has made significant progress in achieving the goals of his national security strategy: to regain control of national territory from Colombia's FTOs, promote desertion and reintegration of former illegal armed militants, and demobilize AUC blocs. Colombian statistics for 2004 indicate that acts of terrorism fell by 42 percent, homicides by 13.2 percent, massacres by 43.5 percent, and kidnappings by 42.4 percent. At least 20 mid-level FARC leaders and financiers and at least 11 paramilitary field commanders have been killed or captured. Nayibe Rojas Cabrera (aka "Sonia"), who managed the finances and drug trafficking of the FARC's Southern Bloc, was captured in February 2004 and later extradited to the United States. In November, the Colombian Army killed FARC's Teofilo Forero Mobile Column Deputy and Operations Chief Humberto Valbuena (aka "Yerbas"), who had replaced Victor Hugo Navarro (aka "El Mocho") after he was killed by the Colombian Army in October 2003. On December 13, the Colombian Government arrested Rodrigo Granda Escobar, a reported FARC General Staff member, considered the FARC's "foreign minister." Nearly 7,000 insurgents and paramilitaries have been captured and more than 4,000 terrorists have deserted their FTOs. Approximately 1,100 extortionists and 400 kidnappers have been captured and 120 civilian hostages have been rescued. Government presence has been restored in all municipalities and internal displacement is down 50 percent.

The US-Colombian extradition relationship continues to be one of the most successful in the world; President Uribe's administration has extradited more than 180 individuals to the United States through the end of 2004. On December 31, the Colombian Government extradited senior FARC commander Juvenal Ovidio Ricardo Palmera (aka "Simon Trinidad") to the United States on charges of kidnapping, providing material support to terrorists, and narcotics trafficking. The threat of extradition has been cited as a significant concern of the FARC, ELN, and AUC leaders.

The Colombian Government's peace process with the AUC, involving AUC demobilization, made substantial progress in 2004 with the removal of nearly 3,000 AUC paramilitaries from combat in November and December 2004. This effort should further reduce overall violence and atrocities, disrupt drug trafficking, and serve as a model for future peace processes with the FARC and ELN.

Although kidnappings have declined, Colombia still suffers from the world's highest kidnapping rate (over 1,500 in 2004). The US Government has provided $25 million to support the Colombian Government's Anti-Kidnapping Initiative, which trains and equips Colombian Army and Colombian National Police anti-kidnapping units (GAULAs); is developing an anti-kidnapping database to collect, analyze, and disseminate information on kidnappings; and has established a training facility near Bogota. US-trained GAULA units have rescued over 48 hostages, arrested over 200 hostage takers, and seized over $7 million paid as ransom money.

In September, Colombia's Constitutional Court struck down the 2003 Antiterrorism Bill (proposed by President Uribe) that would have allowed the Colombian Government to conduct wiretaps, search residences, and detain suspects more easily.

Colombia continued to cooperate internationally in the war against terror. On December 16, 2004, the Bogota Appeals Court reversed an earlier decision to acquit three IRA members of providing support to the FARC, sentenced them to 17 years in prison, levied heavy fines, and ordered their recapture. It is unclear, however, whether they are still in Colombia, having been released under conditional parole based on earlier acquittal. This case reportedly came from an exchange of information by Interpol in 2000 about a possible three-way link among the FARC, the IRA, and ETA. Less than a year later, Colombian authorities arrested the IRA members, who had been preparing to leave the country; one of the three was the official Sinn Fein representative to Havana. Even though the IRA-ETA link is well established, there is little indication that ETA has ever actively engaged with the FARC.

Counterterrorism cooperation has paid dividends for Colombia, as illustrated by Ecuador's capture and deportation to Colombia in January 2004 of "Simon Trinidad." Canada and the European Union have added the FARC, ELN, and AUC to their terrorist lists. Mexico closed the official FARC office there in April 2002. Colombia continued to take an active role in the OAS Inter-American Committee Against Terrorism (CICTE) to enhance hemispheric counterterrorism cooperation, information-sharing, and capacity-building. In August 2003, the Chiefs of State of Argentina, Bolivia, Brazil, Chile, Paraguay, Peru, and Uruguay signed the Asuncion Declaration supporting Colombia's struggle against terrorism and condemning terrorism and narcotic trafficking.

The use of areas along Colombia's porous border by the FARC, ELN, and AUC to find logistical support and rest, as well as to transship arms and drugs, poses a serious challenge to Colombia. Colombia seeks to cooperate with its neighbors to enhance border security. The situation on the Venezuelan side of the Colombian border, which all three Colombian FTO's exploit, is especially disconcerting. Even though the Colombian Government repeatedly made offers to Venezuela to enhance counterterrorism cooperation, the level and quality of cooperation from Venezuela has been very limited. This is despite the issuance by the Colombian Government of a strong statement condemning an alleged paramilitary plot against Venezuelan President Hugo Chavez in May 2004, and the release of prison records and criminal information on all individuals arrested.

Colombia continued to cooperate fully with the United States in blocking terrorist assets. The Colombian Financial Information and Analysis Unit collaborated with the US Government to close suspicious bank accounts. In August, the Colombian military, police, and investigative units produced an estimate of FARC finances. The Government plans to continue this research and expand it to include other terrorist groups in Colombia, which will assist in further developing strategies to cut off the FARC's financial resources. In September, US Secret Service and Colombian National Police seized $3.6 million counterfeit dollars from the FARC, which had planned to use them to purchase weapons and explosives. The Government also took steps to reorganize and streamline its Inter-Institutional Committee Against Subversive Finances.

Colombia made significant strides in combating narcotrafficking, the primary source of revenue for Colombia's terrorist organizations. Eradication programs targeting coca and opium poppies continued throughout the year with record results for the third straight year. Interdiction operations also resulted in record seizures this year.

Ecuador

The Ecuadorian Government continued in 2004 to support US efforts to combat terrorism. Ecuadorian security forces were receptive to US requests to investigate domestic terrorist incidents and assist with international terrorism investigations. Ecuador shared terrorism-related information with US counterparts. Ecuador's Banking Superintendency cooperated in requesting that Ecuadorian financial institutions report transactions involving known terrorists, as designated by the US Government or by the UN 1267 Sanctions Committee.

In 2004, the Ecuadorian Armed Forces (FFAA) and National Police (ENP) sustained an aggressive campaign to prevent Colombia's narcoterrorism from spreading to Ecuador, and in doing so, disrupted several Colombian narcoterrorist encampments in Ecuador. The FFAA in January and November conducted large-scale operations in Sucumbios province near the Colombian border, capturing several FARC members. FFAA has reportedly tripled its force posture to approximately 8,000 soldiers along its northern border with Colombia. Since 2003, Ecuadorian armed forces have interdicted thousands of gallons of smuggled petroleum ether, a precursor used in Colombian cocaine laboratories. The US Government provides assistance to Ecuadorian security forces to enhance border security along its northern border with Colombia.

Although no significant international acts of terrorism occurred in Ecuador in 2004, Ecuadorian police suspect several groups of domestic subversion and probable involvement in a dozen pamphlet and incendiary bombs. Prime among the suspected groups is the "Popular Combatants Group" (GCP, in Spanish), which reportedly numbers roughly 200 and is an armed faction of the Marxist-Leninist Communist Party of Ecuador.

Ecuador's porous borders, endemic corruption, and well-established illegal migrant networks may serve as attractive gateways for terrorists to exploit. The Revolutionary Armed Forces of Colombia (FARC), a US-designated Foreign Terrorist Organization, continues to utilize Ecuador for resupply, rest, and recuperation. However, the FARC realizes that Ecuador is less hospitable than before. Limited law enforcement (especially prosecutorial capacity) and military resources limit Ecuador's counterterrorism capabilities.

High rates of migrant smuggling from Ecuador to the United States remain a concern. In response, the Ecuadorian Government operates a US Government-supported antismuggling police unit (COAC, in Spanish), which supplied information that led to the 2004 conviction in the United States of an Iranian smuggler, Mehrzade Arbade, whom the COAC had arrested in Ecuador in 2003. In December 2004, the

Ecuadorian Government sought US Government assistance and technology to establish a comprehensive entry/exit control system. Ecuador's four international ports met International Ship and Port Facility Security Code (ISPS) technical requirements in 2004.

Cooperation between Colombian and Ecuadorian police forces improved in 2004. On January 3, Juvenal Ovidio Ricardo Palmera (aka "Simon Trinidad"), the most senior FARC official to be captured in decades, was detained by the ENP in Quito and deported to Colombia. Cooperation between the two countries continued to grow through the year, leading to a meeting of Colombian and Ecuadorian law enforcement in Pasto, Colombia, in December 2004.

The Ecuadorian Government has signed and submitted for ratification to its Congress the Inter-American Convention Against Terrorism. In 2004, the Ecuadorian Government also submitted comprehensive anti-money laundering legislation that is moving through its legislature.

Mexico

Mexico is a key ally of the United States in combating terrorism. The Mexican Government works closely with the US Government to enhance aviation, border, maritime, and transportation security; protect US citizens, businesses, and Government facilities and personnel in Mexico; secure critical infrastructure; and combat terrorism financing.

The Mexican and US Governments have participated in a range of bilateral fora that sought to address shared counterterrorism-related concerns, including the US-Mexico Border Partnership Action Plan, Senior Law Enforcement Plenary, the Bi-National Commission, and the Mexico-US Committee on Transborder Critical Infrastructure Protection. On the multilateral front, Mexico hosted the Special Summit of the Americas in Monterrey on January 12–13, 2004, during which issues of regional counterterrorism cooperation were advanced.

In 2004, Mexico continued to offer outstanding cooperation in improving border security. The United States and Mexico continued to follow through on implementation of the US-Mexico Border Partnership Action Plan, signed in March 2002 in Monterrey, to improve infrastructure at ports of entry, expedite legitimate travel, and increase security related to the movement of goods. The US Government has provided $25 million in support. Law enforcement officials on both sides of the border participated in a workshop on emergency responses to chemical incidents and terrorist attacks. Mexico's Plan Centinela, initiated in 2003, continued to integrate security efforts to manage issues along the northern and southern Mexican border, to protect infrastructure, and to enhance airport security.

The Mexican military continued to take steps to improve the capabilities of their counterterrorism forces with additional training and equipment. The Secretariat of the Navy increased security operations for passenger cruise ships and military vessels calling on Mexican ports. The Mexican Navy also established an offshore rapid response base for the protection of oil production infrastructure. Mexico has effectively undertaken implementation of International Ship and Port Facility Security Code (ISPS) and related port security efforts.

A continuing issue of strategic concern in 2004 to US-Mexico counterterrorism efforts remained the existence and continued exploitation of smuggling channels traversing the US-Mexico border. Despite active and prolonged cooperation by the Mexican Government to address these smuggling routes, many smugglers have avoided prosecution. The Mexican Government continued in 2004 to step up efforts to address the flow of illegal migrants into Mexico, many of whom sought eventually to reach the United States. In October and November, a comprehensive operation targeting gangs and migrant smugglers began along Mexico's southern border that resulted in hundreds of arrests.

Panama

Panama is a stalwart supporter of the United States in the war on terror. As the custodian of key infrastructure astride a strategic location, Panama takes the threat of terror seriously, and is taking appropriate measures.

There were no significant incidents of international terrorism in Panama in 2004.

Panama's immediate terrorism concern is incursions by Colombian narcoterrorists into Panama's remote Darien region. Following the murder of four Panamanians by narcoterrorists in 2003, Panama entered into a border security cooperation agreement with Colombia and strengthened police presence in Darien, and along the frontier. To confront challenges in the medium and longer term, Panama is taking other steps.

Panama's new antiterrorism legislation mandates severe penalties for a variety of activities in support of terrorists. Heavy caseloads, lack of expertise for complex international investigations, and extra-legal influence hinder the police and judicial system, however. Panama's security and anti-money laundering authorities have taken good advantage of US-provided training opportunities and equipment. The Government could bolster its already strong political will to combat terrorism by devoting more of its own resources to counterterrorism efforts.

Panama has increased the security of its key infrastructure and of the Panama Canal significantly. The Government has installed surveillance technology at critical points, such as the Bridge of the Americas and container ports. The Panama Canal Authority has improved its collection of information on ships that use the Canal and has modernized its incident management center. Panama has also strengthened the capabilities of its national security authorities to collect, analyze, and disseminate intelligence. Anti-money laundering authorities are extremely cooperative in preventing terror financing through Panamanian institutions.

In 2004, Panama signed an agreement with the United States under the Proliferation Security Initiative (PSI) that facilitates boarding procedures to search vessels suspected of carrying cargoes of proliferation concern. Panama also provided enhanced force protection for US warships transiting the Canal.

Shortly before leaving office in September 2004, President Moscoso pardoned four foreigners arrested in 2000 and jailed for illegal possession of explosives. The Government of Cuba alleged that the suspects were plotting to kill Fidel Castro, who was attending the Ibero-American summit in Panama, and sought their extradition. Panama refused, on grounds that they would not be accorded a fair trial in Cuba. Upon their release, the Cuban Government suspended diplomatic relations with Panama. Relations were later restored.

Panama has a significant Muslim population, augmented recently by an influx of South Asian immigrants, that has traditionally remained apolitical and focused on business interests centered around the Colon Free Trade Zone and provincial towns. While rumors persist of ties between Panama's Muslim community and terrorist groups in the Middle East, there has been no credible evidence to support such speculation. The Panamanian Government remains cognizant of the potential threat posed by immigrants from countries associated with Islamic extremism.

Peru

Peru remained a supporter of US counterterrorism efforts in 2004. Even though the Shining Path (Sendero Luminoso, or SL), a US Government-designated Foreign Terrorist Organization (FTO), remains small and isolated, SL continues to pose a threat to US and Peruvian interests. SL conducted several deadly attacks in remote Peruvian areas in 2004. SL has a few hundred armed members concentrated in the coca-growing valleys where they reportedly are increasing their involvement in the drug trade, gaining more resources for terrorist activities. Lack of an effective Government presence in these areas has complicated efforts to disrupt SL activity. A purported SL leader threatened attacks against US and Peruvian coca eradication efforts in Huanaco Department (Province). Armed terrorist incidents fell to 40 in 2004 from 100 in 2003. Reports suggest that SL is trying to rebuild support in the universities where they exercised considerable influence in the 1980s. The Peruvian Government arrested 161 suspected SL members, including alleged key leader Gavino Mendoza. Peru successfully extradited from Spain suspected SL leader Adolfo Olaechea in 2003; his case will be tried in 2005.

The Tupac Amaru Revolutionary Movement (MRTA) was significantly reduced in numbers in recent years, but it appears to be quietly trying to rebuild its membership. The MRTA has not conducted a significant terrorist attack since the December 1996 hostage siege at the Japanese Ambassador's residence in Lima, and posed a very limited threat in 2004. The Peruvian Communist Party (Patria Roja) has not engaged in terrorist acts but has been suspected of advocating violent confrontation with Peruvian security forces.

There is only limited evidence of the Revolutionary Armed Forces of Colombia (FARC) or Colombia's National Liberation Army (ELN) operating inside Peru or working with SL. In January 2004, a FARC member and several Peruvians were arrested for arms trafficking in northern Peru. In 2004, Peru, Colombia, and Brazil signed a border security agreement to enhance cooperation to combat terrorism and arms trafficking.

President Toledo has pledged increased funding for security forces and social development projects in areas where SL and other terrorist groups operate. The Peruvian Congress approved the President's request to create a National Defense and Security Fund, totaling $40 million for 2005. The Peruvian Congress created a national security system designed to improve inter-governmental cooperation and strengthen prosecutors. The National Police (PNP) Directorate of Counterterrorism (DIRCOTE) is the primary Peruvian agency coordinating counterterrorism efforts, along with the Peruvian Army, which operates approximately 75 bases.

President Toledo has repeatedly extended a state of emergency, which suspends some civil liberties and gives the Armed Forces authority to maintain order, for successive periods of up to 60 days in parts of Peru's five departments where SL is believed still to have armed members. The Peruvian Government and civil society are working to implement the 2002 recommendations of the Truth and Reconciliation Commission to heal wounds from the terrorist conflict of the 1990s. President Toledo's Peace and Development Commissions, formed in 2002, continued to promote cooperation between police, military, and residents in the areas where SL and MRTA conflicts had been the greatest.

The Government continued to prosecute terrorist suspects aggressively. Peru's special antiterrorism court is retrying around 750 of the 1,900 overturned convictions, in conformance with the findings of the Inter-American Court of Human Rights (IACHR), of SL and MRTA defendants who had been tried on Fujimori-era decree laws on terrorism. All the cases must be re-tried by January 2006 or the defendants will be released in accordance with Peruvian law. A retrial ("megatrial") of SL founder Abimael Guzman and 15 co-defendants began in November 2004. The retrial of 13 MRTA leaders, including its founder Victor Polay, together in another "megatrial" began in December 2004. Six SL members remain in various stages of trials and appeals for complicity in the March 2002 bombing near the US Embassy that killed ten people; two defendants were released for lack of evidence. A principal SL leader, Osman Morote, was acquitted of charges relating to a 1992 television station bombing, although three other SL members were convicted and sentenced. Morote continues to serve an 18-year sentence on a previous terrorism conviction and is one of the "megatrial" defendants.

In May 2004, the IACHR issued its decision in the case brought by Lori Berenson, a US citizen and convicted MRTA member, who claimed that the terrorism law enacted to deal with the overturned terrorist convictions still violated international due process of law. While the Court found against Peru on some claims, the Court did not invalidate Berenson's conviction or 20-year sentence.

Peru passed legislation in July 2004 to strengthen and expand the authorities of its financial intelligence unit (FIU). The new legislation included counterterrorist finance activities among the FIU's functions; greatly expanded the FIU's capacity to engage in joint investigations and information-sharing with foreign FIU's; enhanced the FIU's capacity to exchange information and pursue joint cases with other agencies of the Peruvian Government; and required that individuals and entities transporting more than $10,000 in currency or monetary instruments into or out of Peru file reports with Peruvian Customs. The US Government continued to provide assistance, including a technical advisor and funding for hardware and software, to help Peru fight money laundering and other financial crimes.

All of Peru's major seaports achieved UN and private sector security certifications. The US Government supports a port security program in Peru that focuses on narcotrafficking but also counters terrorist threats and arms smuggling. Airport security in Peru has been enhanced with US assistance.

Peru has ratified the Inter-American Convention Against Terrorism and signed the August 2003 Asuncion Declaration, by which several South American nations committed themselves to support the Colombian Government in its ongoing struggle against terrorism and drug trafficking. Peru has been an active participant in the United Nations and OAS Inter-American Committee Against Terrorism (CICTE).

Triborder Area (Argentina, Brazil, and Paraguay)

The countries of the Triborder Area (TBA)—Argentina, Brazil, and Paraguay—have long been concerned about the pervasiveness of transnational crime in the region where the three nations converge. In the early 1990s, the countries established a mechanism for addressing jointly arms and drug trafficking, contraband smuggling, document and currency fraud, money laundering, and the manufacture and movement of pirated goods. In 2002, at their invitation, the United States joined them in a consultative mechanism—the "Three Plus One" Group on Triborder Area Security—to strengthen the capabilities to fight cross-border crime and thwart money laundering and terrorist fundraising activities. The United States remains concerned that Hizballah and HAMAS raise funds among the sizable Muslim communities in the region, and that the high incidence of illicit activity could tempt terrorist groups to seek to establish safehavens in this largely uncontrolled area. Persons suspected of ties to terrorist groups have been spotted in the TBA, but no operational activities of terrorism have been detected.

In December 2004, the United States hosted the fourth high-level meeting of the "Three Plus One," at which the partners exchanged views on measures taken and progress confronting the region's security challenges. Argentina, Brazil, and Paraguay agreed to develop guidelines for detecting and monitoring potentially illegal flights in the TBA, to exchange information on cargo flights, and to explore the feasibility of conducting joint patrols on Iguacu waterways. They also agreed to meet in 2005 to strengthen institutional ties among prosecutors, to consider integrated border and customs controls, to enhance cooperation among their financial analysis units, and to begin looking at charities to prevent their abuse of fundraising. Brazil announced the creation of a Regional Intelligence Center in Foz do Iguacu, and Argentina and Paraguay committed to designate liaisons to it. The parties agreed to continue to work among themselves and with the United States to confront transnational crime and continue to deny the TBA to terrorists.

Individually, the TBA countries maintained strong stances against international terrorism.

Argentina continued to cooperate with the United Nations, the OAS, its neighbors, and the United States on a number of counterterrorism initiatives. Argentine security forces have been especially vigilant in monitoring illicit activity and its potential links to Islamic radical groups in the TBA. There is no credible evidence that operational Islamic terrorist cells exist in Argentina. Argentina maintains a leading role in the OAS Inter-American Committee Against Terrorism (CICTE), established on Argentina's initiative in the 1990s.

There were no significant acts of international terrorism in Argentina in 2004. In November, small explosive devices set to detonate after hours at three foreign bank branches (one US) killed a security guard and injured a policeman. No group has claimed responsibility. In September, a three-judge panel acquitted all 22 Argentine defendants charged in connection with the 1994 terrorist bombing of the Buenos Aires Jewish Community Center, in which at least 85 persons were killed. The panel faulted the investigation of the original judge and prosecutors and called for an investigation of their handling of the case and trial. An Argentine criminal court judge reconfirmed the validity of international arrest warrants against 12 Iranian nationals, including diplomats stationed in Buenos Aires in 1994, and one Lebanese official believed to head Hizballah's terrorist wing. There were no new developments in the investigation of the 1992 bombing of the Israeli Embassy, in which at least 29 persons were killed.

Draft legislation to criminalize terrorist financing introduced in the Argentine Chamber of Deputies in 2003 remained stalled through 2004. The draft provides penalties for violations of international conventions, including the UN's Convention for the Suppression of the Financing of Terrorism. Argentina's lower legislative chamber will consider the new legislation once it ratifies the UN pact, as well as the Inter-American Convention Against Terrorism.

Argentine executive branch officials and the Central Bank continued to be extremely cooperative in 2004, responding quickly and effectively to ensure that the assets of terrorist groups identified by the United States or the UN would be frozen if detected in Argentine financial institutions. New regulations require travelers to report the cross-border transport of currency in excess of $10,000, whether inbound or outbound and the country is establishing an automated entry/exit system at ports of entry.

Brazil continues to extend practical and effective support for US counterterrorism efforts on all fronts, including intelligence, law enforcement, and finance. There were no international terrorism incidents of significance in Brazil in 2004, and no credible evidence of the existence of operational terrorist cells. The United States remained concerned about the possible use of Brazilian territory for transit by terrorists using established illegal migrant smuggling groups or for fundraising for terrorist groups.

In May 2004, the Government of Brazil created a technical team from five key ministries and the Armed Forces to formulate a national policy to combat terrorism. The group's recommendations are intended as the basis of a bill to establish a national authority for combating terrorism. By the end of 2004, however, the administration of President Lula da Silva had yet to submit a bill to the legislature. Also awaiting legislative action were a bill introduced in 2003 aimed at preventing terrorist attacks on Brazil's cyber infrastructure and measures to update Brazil's money laundering law that dates back to 1978. There are no significant impediments to the prosecution or extradition of suspected terrorists by Brazil, although Brazil's legal procedures can be protracted.

Brazil is increasingly capable of monitoring domestic financial operations and effectively utilizes its Financial Activities Oversight Council (COAF, in Portuguese) to identify possible funding sources for terrorist groups. The United States recently provided assistance and training to COAF to upgrade its database and data collection mechanism. In January 2005, the Brazilian Federal Police will inaugurate a regional field office in Foz do Iguacu to coordinate its law enforcement efforts in the TBA.

Paraguay has cooperated in the global war against terrorism by actively supporting counterterrorism initiatives at the UN and the OAS. In December 2004, at the fourth meeting of the "Three Plus One", Paraguay offered to host a conference of TBA financial intelligence units in the first half of 2005.

In September 2004, Cecilia Cubas, the daughter of a former president of Paraguay, was abducted and subsequently murdered. The Paraguayan Government charged, credibly, that what appeared as a kidnap for profit gone awry was really the work of a radical leftist group with possible ties to the Revolutionary Armed Forces of Colombia (FARC).

Paraguay remained vigilant throughout 2004 against extremists seeking to raise funds among Paraguay's Muslim community for terrorist activities outside Paraguay. There was no credible evidence of operational Islamic terrorist cells in Paraguay.

The executive branch's strong political will to combat terrorism notwithstanding, the Government remained hampered by weak or non-existent legislation and by limited law enforcement and intelligence capabilities. In particular, Paraguay lacks an antiterrorism law that would afford authorities the special powers needed to investigate and prosecute terrorism-related crimes. Lacking such a law, and adequate money laundering legislation, the Government is only able to prosecute suspected terrorist financiers for tax evasion or other crimes. To address these deficiencies, the Government in 2004 prepared for consideration by the legislature draft legislation to strengthen Paraguay's anti-money laundering regime and an antiterrorism bill that would outlaw support for terrorists. Both need to be adopted by the legislature. These initiatives are key to Paraguay meeting its international counterterrorism obligations as set forth in UN Security Council Resolutions.

Despite the lack of specific antiterrorist statutes, Paraguay has actively prosecuted suspected terrorist fundraisers under other statutes. Hizballah fundraisers Sobhi Fayad and Ali Nizar Dahroug were sentenced to lengthy prison terms in November 2002 and August 2003, respectively, for tax evasion. A major accomplishment in 2004 was the successful prosecution and conviction in May of Hizballah fundraiser Assad Ahmad Barakat on charges of tax evasion, following his extradition from Brazil. He was sentenced to six and one-half years. The Government is considering additional charges of bank fraud, pending concurrence by Brazil. (The terms of the Paraguay-Brazil extradition treaty prohibit prosecution of extradited suspects on charges other than those that were the basis for extradition.) Separately, in March Paraguay opened a case of tax evasion against a money exchange house and 46 individuals suspected of involvement in money laundering. In August, Paraguay brought charges of document fraud against Barakat's brother Hatem Barakat, also a suspected terrorist financier. Paraguay's antiterrorist police Secretariat for the Prevention of International Terrorism (SEPRINTE) continued to provide excellent support in these and other investigations.

Uruguay

The Government of Uruguay cooperates fully with the United States and international institutions in the war on terrorism, but has not devoted great resources to the effort. There were no significant incidents of international terrorism in Uruguay in 2004.

Uruguayan banking and law enforcement agencies profess to search for financial assets, individuals, and groups with links to terrorism, but they have not discovered any terrorist assets in Uruguayan financial institutions, nor any terrorist operatives in Uruguay. The Government has occasionally assisted in monitoring the possibility of extremists raising funds for terrorist groups from Muslim communities in the Triborder area and along Uruguay's northern frontier with Brazil.

In September 2004, Uruguay approved legislation that significantly strengthened its anti-money laundering regime. It also signed the Asuncion Declaration in support of Colombia's efforts against terrorism and drug trafficking. Uruguay seconded personnel to the Executive Secretariat of the Organization of American States' Committee to Combat Terrorism (CICTE) and, as CICTE Chair, hosted the annual meeting in Montevideo in January 2004.

Venezuela

In 2004, Venezuelan-US counterterrorism cooperation continued to be inconsistent at best. Public recriminations against US counterterrorism policies by President Chavez and his close supporters overshadowed and detracted from the limited cooperation that exists among specialists and technicians of the two nations.

Venezuela continued in 2004 to be unwilling or unable to assert control over its 1,400-mile border with Colombia. Consequently, Colombia's three US-designated Foreign Terrorist Organizations (FTOs)—the Revolutionary Armed Forces of Colombia (FARC), the National Liberation Army (ELN), and the United Self-Defense Forces of Colombia (AUC)—continued to regard Venezuelan territory near the border as a safe area to conduct cross-border incursions, transship arms and drugs, rest, and secure logistical supplies, as well as to commit kidnappings and extortion for profit. Weapons and ammunition—some from official Venezuelan stocks and facilities—continued flowing from Venezuelan suppliers and intermediaries into the hands of Colombia's FTOs. It is unclear to what extent and at what level the Venezuelan Government approves of or condones material support to Colombian terrorists. President Chavez's close ties to Cuba, a US-designated state sponsor of terrorism, continue to concern the US Government.

Current Venezuelan law does not specifically mention crimes of terrorism, although the UN Convention on Terrorist Bombings of 1997 and the UN Convention on Terrorism Financing of 1999 became law in Venezuela in July 2003. Venezuela neither maintains a foreign terrorist list nor designates groups as such. Venezuela signed the OAS Inter-American Convention Against Terrorism in June 2002 and ratified it in January 2004. Legislation considered throughout 2004—including the organized crime bill, anti-terrorism bill, and proposed changes to the penal code—defined terrorist activities, established punishments, facilitated investigation and prosecution, and froze the assets of terrorism financiers. However, other proposed changes to the penal code would undercut political freedoms. The law modifying the penal code passed in the Assembly on January 6, 2005, and is awaiting Chavez's signature.

President Chavez's stated ideological affinity with FARC and ELN—both US-designated Foreign Terrorist Organizations (FTOs)—further limited Venezuelan counterterrorism cooperation with Colombia, which in 2004 continued to receive less cooperation from Venezuela than from its other neighbors. Venezuelan and Colombian military and police cooperated on some terrorism and drug-related cases. Moreover, the September 17 murder of at least six Venezuelan National Guard members and a civilian engineer near the border with Colombia, reportedly by FARC forces, publicly upset Chavez and raised expectations that border policing would be stepped up with additional resources and political will.

However, President Chavez's and the Venezuelan Government's acerbic reaction to the December 13 detention of Rodrigo Granda Escobar, a reported FARC General Staff member who is considered the FARC's "foreign minister," complicated efforts to enhance Venezuelan-Colombian counterterrorism cooperation. Granda had reportedly been captured in Venezuela by bounty hunters, and then brought to Cucuta, Colombia (near the Venezuelan border), where he was detained by Colombian officials. President Chavez and the Venezuelan Government publicly accused the Colombian Government of infringing on Venezuela's sovereignty, suspended trade and business accords with Colombia, and recalled Venezuela's Ambassador to Colombia. President Chavez rejected Colombian President Uribe's offer to meet face-to-face to resolve the impasse and conditioned any meeting with Uribe—as well as the resumption of trade relations and return of Venezuela's Ambassador to Colombia—on Uribe's apologizing to Chavez and accepting responsibility for violating Venezuela's sovereignty. In early 2005, Chavez and Uribe resolved to move past this incident. However, future counterterrorism cooperation between Venezuela and Colombia remains uncertain.

Following the killing of prosecutor Danilo Anderson on November 18, 2004, President Chavez ordered Venezuela's National Defense Council to define an antiterrorism strategy to include tighter border and communications security. At President Chavez's instruction, the National Assembly formed a committee to develop an antiterrorism law, and the Supreme Court designated a group of judges to handle terrorism cases. Nevertheless, there are concerns within Venezuela, based on preliminary details of the antiterrorism law, that Chavez's recent attention to "terrorism" may be intended to target domestic opponents of his Government. An increasingly politicized judiciary and the recent appointment of Venezuelan Government supporters to fill the 12 new seats added to the Supreme Court (plus five vacancies) cast serious doubts on the judges' independence and impartiality.

Terrorist tactics were employed throughout 2004 by unidentified domestic groups attempting to influence the tenuous political situation, particularly in Caracas. A series of small bombs and threats throughout the year were in some cases blamed on supporters of President Chavez or on the Government's political opponents. The Venezuelan Government alleged in 2004 that exile groups and the US Government sought to overthrow or assassinate President Chavez, but offered no proof to support its claims. The Government claimed on May 8 that some 100 Colombian paramilitaries were training secretly near Caracas; those detained turned out to be unarmed Colombian agricultural workers.

Venezuela's limited document security, especially for citizenship, identity, and travel documents, makes it an attractive venue for persons involved in criminal activities, including terrorism. Venezuela could serve as a transit point for those seeking illegal entry into the United States, Europe, or other destinations.

Most examples of positive counterterrorism cooperation with the United States pre-date 2004. In the wake of 9/11, Venezuela supported the invocation of the Inter-American Treaty of Reciprocal Assistance ("The Rio Treaty"), which calls for the collective self-defense of OAS member states in response to an attack on any member. Venezuela had provided limited cooperation to the US Government on counterterrorism and counterterrorist finance efforts, as well as US Government counternarcotics initiatives. In November 2002, a US Financial Systems Assessment Team (FSAT) visited Venezuela and met with Venezuelan Government officials to assess Venezuela's counterterrorism finance regime. Venezuelan officials have participated in various US Government counterterrorism finance courses, identified by the FSAT. The Venezuelan military has received anti-kidnapping training from the US military. Venezuela helped provide evidence that led to the indictment of FARC members for the 1999 murder of three American indigenous activists. Future counterterrorism cooperation with the United States remains uncertain, especially given President Chavez's and the Venezuelan Government's actions in 2004.

Global Jihad: Evolving and Adapting

The 2004 Country Reports on Terrorism *included the following description of "Global Jihad: Evolving and Adapting."*

The global jihadist movement—including its most prominent component, al-Qaida—remains the preeminent terrorist threat to the United States, US interests and US allies. While the core of al-Qaida has suffered severe damage to its leadership, organization, and capabilities, the group remains intent on striking US interests in the homeland and overseas. During the past year, concerted antiterrorist coalition measures have degraded al-Qaida's central command infrastructure, sharply decreasing its ability to conduct massive attacks. At the same time, however, al-Qaida has spread its anti-US, anti-Western ideology to other groups and geographical areas. It is therefore no longer al-Qaida itself but groups affiliated with al-Qaida, or independent ones adhering to al-Qaida's ideology that present the greatest threat of terrorist attacks against US and allied interests globally.

US and coalition successes against al-Qaida have forced these jihadist groups to compensate by showing a greater willingness to act on their own and exercising greater local control over their strategic and tactical decisions. As a result of this growing dispersion and local decision-making, there is an increasing commingling of groups, personnel, resources, and ad hoc operational and logistical coordination. These groups affiliated with al-Qaida or indoctrinated with al-Qaida's ideology are now carrying out most of the terrorist attacks against US and allied interests. Their decreased power projection and limited resources mean that an increasing percentage of jihadist attacks are more local, less sophisticated, but still lethal. Some groups, however, are seeking to replicate al-Qaida's global reach and expertise for mass casualty attacks. This trend underscores that America's partners in the global war on terror require the capabilities to identify and eliminate terrorist threats in their countries for their own security and ultimately to stop terrorists abroad before they can gain the ability to attack the US homeland.

Al-Qaida

Despite intensive US and partner operations that have led to the killing or capture of much of al-Qaida's senior leadership, Usama bin Ladin and his deputy, Ayman al-Zawahiri, remain at large. In late 2004, they made videotaped statements addressed directly to the US public that warned of more attacks. The two have also publicly threatened at least three dozen countries in Europe, Africa, the Middle East, and South Asia.

The apparent mergers or declarations of allegiance of groups such as Abu Mus'ab al-Zarqawi's organization with al-Qaida suggest that al-Qaida is looking to leverage the capabilities and resources of key regional networks and affiliates —a trend that al-Qaida could also use to try to support new attacks in the United States and abroad.

The Global Jihadist Movement

The global jihadist movement predates al-Qaida's founding and was reinforced and developed by successive conflicts in Afghanistan, Bosnia, Chechnya, and elsewhere during 1990s. As a result, it spawned several groups and operating nodes and developed a resiliency that ensured that destruction of any one group or node did not destroy the larger movement. Since 2001, extremists, including members of al-Qaida and affiliated groups, have sought to exploit perceptions of the US-led global war on terrorism and, in particular, the war in Iraq to attract converts to their movement. Many of these recruits come from a large and growing pool of disaffected youth who are sympathetic to radical, anti-Western militant ideology. At the same time, these extremists have branched out to establish jihadist cells in other parts of the Middle East, South Asia, and Europe, from which they seek to prepare operations and facilitate funding and communications.

Foreign fighters appear to be working to make the insurgency in Iraq what the resistance movement to the Soviet occupation of Afghanistan was to the earlier generation of jihadists—a melting pot for jihadists from around the world, a training ground, and an indoctrination center. In the months and years ahead, a significant number of fighters who have traveled to Iraq could return to their home countries, exacerbating domestic conflicts or augmenting with new skills and experience existing extremist networks in the communities to which they return.

The Spread of Al-Qaida's Ideology

Al-Qaida's ideology resonates with other Sunni extremist circles. Some affiliated groups—including Jemaah Islamiyah in Southeast Asia—look to their own spiritual leaders, yet historically have shared close ideological and operational ties to al-Qaida. In recent years, however, the resonance of al-Qaida's message has contributed to the formation of an assortment of grassroots networks and cells among persons that previously have had no observable links to bin Ladin or al-Qaida aside from general ideological and religious affinity.

Examples of this trend include Salafiya Jihadia, a loosely-organized Moroccan movement involved in carrying out the bombings in May 2003 in Casablanca, and the terrorists who executed the March 2004 attack in Madrid. Although these cells do not appear to have been acting directly on al-Qaida orders, their attacks supported al-Qaida's ideology and reflected al-Qaida's targeting strategy.

Terrorist capabilities for attacks will remain uneven, given the varying degrees of expertise and increasing decentralization within the movement. Most groups will be capable only of relatively unsophisticated, but still deadly small-scale attacks. Others, however, may seek to acquire or replicate al-Qaida's expertise and material support for mass-casualty attacks. The explosive growth of media and the Internet, as well as the ease of travel and communication around the world have made possible the rapid movement of operatives, expertise, money, and explosives. Terrorists increasingly will use media and the Internet to advance key messages or rally support, share jihadist experiences and expertise, and spread fear.

Although the jihadist movement remains dangerous, it is not monolithic. Some groups are focused on attacking the United States or its allies, while others view governments and leaders in the Muslim world as their primary targets. The United States and its partners in the global war on terrorism will continue to use all the means available to identify, target, and prevent the spread of these jihadist groups and ideology.

April 27, 2005

Release of Country Reports on Terrorism for 2004

U.S. Department of State

In the transcript below, Philip Zelikow, counselor of the Department of State, and John Brennan, interim director of the National Counterterrorism Center, offer remarks related to the release of the Country Reports on Terrorism *on 27 April 2005.*

Mr. Ereli: Greetings, everyone. Thank you for coming on short notice. We're very pleased today to have two distinguished Administration officials to brief on the State Department Country Reports on Terrorism, and the statistical reports are prepared by the National Counterterrorism Center.

We will begin with an overview by Philip Zelikow, the Counselor of the State Department, and then hear from Interim Director of the National Counterterrorism Center, Mr. John Brennan, on the statistical side of things. And then they'll be available to answer your questions.

So let's start with Dr. Zelikow.

Mr. Zelikow: Thanks, Adam. What I'd like to do is to start with the substance and then go to the process.

So first, on substance. Terrorism remains a global threat from which no nation is immune. Despite ongoing improvements in U.S. homeland security, our campaigns against insurgents and terrorists, and the deepening counterterrorism cooperation among the nations of the world, international terrorism continued to pose a significant threat to the United States and its partners in 2004.

The slaughter of hundreds of innocents in the Beslan school, in the commuter trains of Madrid, on a Philippines ferry and in a Sinai resort proved again that the struggle against terrorism is far from over.

In 2004, the United States broadened and deepened its international cooperation on counterterrorism issues. Increased diplomatic, intelligence, law enforcement, military and financial cooperation contributed directly to homeland security and the interdiction or disruption of terrorists around the globe.

We'll offer a number of examples in the Country Report that we are releasing today. A few of them, for example, are as follows: Close cooperation with British, French and other authorities, coordinated through the State Department and U.S. Embassies in London, Paris and elsewhere, was pivotal to managing threats to airline security during the '03–'04 new year period. Information sharing with the United Kingdom and Pakistan led to the disclosure and disruption of al-Qaida attack planning against U.S. financial institutions.

U.S. diplomatic and military assistance facilitated cooperation among Algeria, Mali, Mauritania, Niger, Libya and Chad that led to the capture and return of wanted GSPC faction leader El Para to Algeria to stand trial.

Law enforcement officers in Iraq, Colombia, Indonesia, the Philippines, Saudi Arabia and Pakistan, among others, applied U.S. specialized counterterrorism training to bring terrorists to justice. And there are a number of examples of that that we'd be glad to elaborate—some remarkable stories, really.

Working with a broad spectrum of domestic and international partners, the United States has identified and disrupted many sources of terrorist finance. And the United States used its G-8 Presidency in 2004 to advance new international transportation security measures and to coordinate international counterterrorism assistance among the G-8 and other donors.

Notably, 2004 was also marked by progress in decreasing the threat from states that sponsor terrorism—state-sponsored terrorism. Iraq's designation as a state sponsor of terrorism was formally rescinded in October 2004. Though they are still on the list, Libya and Sudan took significant steps to cooperate in the global war on terrorism. Unfortunately, Cuba, North Korea, Syria, and in particular, Iran continued to embrace terrorism as an instrument of national policy. Most worrisome is that these countries also have the capabilities to manufacture weapons of mass destruction and other destabilizing technologies that could fall into the hands of terrorists.

Iran and Syria are of special concern for their direct, open, and prominent role in supporting Hezbollah and Palestinian terrorist groups, for their unhelpful actions in Iraq and in Iran's case, the unwillingness to bring to justice senior al-Qaida members detained in 2003, including—I will add personally—senior al-Qaida members who were involved in the planning of the 9/11 attacks.

The United States will continue to broaden and deepen international cooperation to protect U.S. citizens. The trend away from centralized planning of terrorist activities and towards inspiration of local groups to commit acts of terror make it even more crucial to have deeper international cooperation to defeat the emerging violent extremist groups. The United States and its partners must intensify their efforts to bolster the political will and the intelligence, law enforcement, financial, and military capabilities of partner nations to combat terrorism, on their own or with us.

The United States will step up cooperation with its partners to prevent the spread of al-Qaida's ideology and the growth of jihadist terror. The United States will continue its efforts to defeat non-al-Qaida terrorist groups, discourage state sponsorship of terrorism, and mobilize international will and build capacity to prevent terrorist access to weapons of mass destruction.

Now let me turn to the process issues. For years, as many of you know, statistical data on global terrorism has been published as part of an annual State Department report called Patterns of Global Terrorism, that was last provided to Congress in April 2004.

The law itself requires basically two things: It requires detailed assessments of specified countries, and information about specified terrorist groups.

The compilation of data about terrorist attacks is not a required part of the report, but traditionally had been provided by the State Department, going back to the years in which the State Department was basically the public voice of the U.S. Government on international terrorism, generally.

Of course, that situation has been changing in recent years. In July 2004, the 9/11 Commission recommended creation of a National Counterterrorism Center to provide an authoritative agency for all-source analysis of global terrorism. I would be glad to answer any questions how the 9/11 Commission reached that conclusion.

The President implemented the recommendation by Executive Order in August. And the agency was created by statute in December 2004, in the Intelligence Reform and Terrorism Prevention Act, which is Public Law 108-458, for those of you who wish to look it up right away.

But what's important for our purposes is what the law said the NCTC should do. It said the NCTC was the primary organization for analysis and integration of—and I'm quoting from the law now—"All intelligence possessed or acquired by the United States Government pertaining to terrorism or counterterrorism." The law further stated that the NCTC would be the United States Government's "shared knowledge bank on known and suspected terrorists and international terror groups, as well as their goals, strategies, capabilities, and networks of contact and support."

Therefore, given that statutory mandate, the State Department has focused its own report to Congress on the issues in its mandate, renamed Country Reports on Terrorism: Assessing Countries and Providing Information on Terrorist Groups, which we are still statutorily required to do. And it is deferred to the National Counterterrorism Center to assume its prescribed role as the "shared knowledge bank" for data on global terrorism.

We are publicly presenting our required report to Congress and the public today. In conjunction with that presentation, the NCTC will present current 2004 terrorist incident data that is compiled using the old statutory criteria, the old counting rules and past practices. We're presenting this data today in a period of transition to what should ideally be the proper way to present this data in the future, which NCTC is developing. NCTC will present its own approach to compiling statistics that need to be and will be significantly revised and improved, including its plans for providing a more comprehensive accounting of global terrorism incidents by June of this year. And to describe that effort further, I turn the floor over to Mr. Brennan, the Acting Director of the National Counterterrorism Center.

Mr. Brennan: Thank you, Philip. Good afternoon. My name is John Brennan. I am the interim Director of the National Counterterrorism Center. I am also formerly the Director of the Terrorist Threat Integration Center, the functions and responsibilities of which transferred to the NCTC as of 6 December last year.

Now, before I discuss specific numbers that are being released today, I would like to address two key issues. First, after the problems associated with last year's Patterns publication, the NCTC, along with the Department of State, engaged in a rigorous internal review of processes and procedures used to support the publications of Patterns. We also worked very closely with the Department's Inspector General, and we took the Inspector General's recommendations fully into account in the reengineering of that process.

To ensure a more comprehensive accounting of terrorist incidents, we in the NCTC significantly increased the level of effort from three part-time individuals to 10 full-time analysts, and we took a number of other steps to improve quality control and database management. This increased level of effort allowed a much deeper review of far more information and, along with Iraq, are the primary reasons for the significant growth in a number of terrorist incidents being reported.

Now, this increase in the number of incidents being reported today does not necessarily mean that there has been a growth in actual terrorist incidents. In other words, the data you will see today represent a break from previous years, and the numbers can't be compared to previous years in any meaningful way. This point was made to congressional staffers earlier this week, but has not been accurately captured in the various press articles over the past couple of days.

Now, second. In our scrub of last year's data, it became increasingly clear that there were methodological problems associated with statutory language and counting rules. These criteria dated to a period of focus on state-sponsored terrorism in the early 1980s and not the transnational phenomena we confront now. I will discuss some of these methodological problems and what we're doing to improve the process of accounting for global terrorist incidents. I would like to first turn to our charts. Using the statutory criteria found in Title 22, Section 2656-F of the U.S. Code, along with counting rules that were provided to the National Counterterrorism Center, we compiled data on 651 attacks that met the criteria for significant international terrorist incidents. Now, there are several points of note. As you can see on the left-hand side, there were over 9,000 victims of significant international terrorism last year, of which 1,907 were killed. On the right-hand side, you can see the regional breakdown of total attacks and the relative share of the 1,907 individuals killed.

Now, a couple of points of note. Much has been made in the press about Kashmir and clearly there was, on average, an attack nearly every day in Kashmir. In fact, there were a total of 284 attacks in Kashmir that met the statutory criteria for significant terrorist incidents. Now, the total number of people killed in South Asia was about 500. In other words, the attacks were often conducted against one or two people. By contrast, there were very few attacks in Europe—it's represented here on the blue bar, in Europe—but there was a very high death toll. This reflects the very deadly attacks in places like Madrid and Beslan, Russia, where many hundreds of people were killed in single incidents.

As you can see in the lower left-hand corner, the methodology, chronology, and selected statistical charts are being posted and are already posted on www.tkb.org. This is the website for the Memorial Institute for the Prevention of Terrorism in Oklahoma City, and we are most appreciative of the institute for partnering with us to make the data available to the American public.

Now, the next chart. This second chart reflects the subset of significant international attacks conducted against U.S. interests. As you can see on the left, 64 attacks, approximately 10 percent of the total number of attacks worldwide, were conducted against U.S. interests. The vast majority of these anti-U.S. attacks took place in the Middle East, where 83 percent of those attacks occurred. As you can see on the pie charts on the right-hand side of the briefing board, a far lower percentage of U.S. citizens were actually wounded or killed. Of the roughly 9,300 individuals wounded in significant international terrorist incidents, 103 were Americans. Total U.S. victims: 103. And of the more than 1,800 people killed last year in significant international terrorist incidents, 68 were Americans.

Now, as I said at the outset, the process of compiling this data highlighted some significant methodological shortcomings that are based on statutory criteria. I'd like to spend a few moments discussing these shortcomings, provide some examples of the misleading results, and then discuss what we're doing to provide what we believe will be a more accurate accounting of terrorist incidents.

To constitute a significant international terrorist incident, the statutory criteria and counting rules provided to NCTC were applied. Terrorism is defined in the statute, as noted in the left-hand column. It is a violent act. It involves non-combatants. It is premeditated, perpetrated by a sub-national or clandestine agent, and politically motivated. And for non-combatants in non-warlike areas, combatants who are in a non-combatant status are also included.

"International" is also defined in the statute as "involving the citizens or territory of more than one country." And as I'll show you on the next chart, this definition, while appropriate for state-sponsored terrorism, is simply not as useful for the current trans-national threat we now face. And thirdly, "significant" has been traditionally defined as not only killings or severe woundings, but also property damage of over $10,000. So, to be significant, deaths, more than superficial woundings, kidnappings, or property damage over $10,000.

As I mentioned at the outset, there is simply no question that these statutorily based criteria, coupled with counting rules provided to the National Counterterrorism Center, resulted in a series of anomalies and misleading results. Here are a few examples of what was and wasn't counted.

Many incidents were not viewed as terrorism and are not reflected in our numbers. For instance, other types of political violence, such as hate crimes, were not counted. In one instance, 19 immigrants were wounded in a bomb blast against a Vietnamese dormitory in Moscow. That is not included in the tally because it does not meet the definition for international terrorism.

Far more problematic from our perspective was the statutory definition of international terrorism, which requires the involvement of citizens or territory of more than one country. On 27 February of last year, a member of the Abu Sayyaf Group in the Philippines—a terrorist organization—sank Superferry 14, killing over 100 people. Now, obviously, this was an act of terrorism directed against innocent civilians. But because the perpetrator and the victims were all Filipino, this incident didn't meet the statutory definition and is not reflected in the chronology.

Iraq is a particularly difficult case. In the case of Iraqis attacking Iraqi election officials, this clearly did not meet the statutory definition. It was an attack in Iraq against Iraqis by Iraqis, and we generally found it virtually impossible to distinguish between insurgency and terrorism. Iraqis, for instance, fight for the terrorist, Abu Musab al-Zarqawi, as well as for insurgent forces; but there is no defensible way to distinguish between the two: insurgents and terrorists. As such, our chronology focuses on attacks that killed or wounded non-Iraqi civilians in Iraq, and they are included in the chronology.

In the case of Uzbekistan, this instance on the board was undoubtedly Sunni extremism as three attacks took place on the same day, 30 July of last year: one attack against the U.S. Embassy, one attack against the Israeli Embassy, and one attack against an Uzbek Government building. Under the statutory definition, the latter, the attack against the Uzbek building, is considered indigenous because the perpetrator and victims were Uzbek.

And finally, on 24 August of last year, two Chechen suicide bombers blew up two Aeroflot flights. One flight contained all Russian citizens and under the statutory definition, does not constitute international terrorism. That flight isn't in the chronology. The other flight on that day had one individual with Israeli citizenship and therefore, under the statutory definition, constitutes international terrorism and is reflected in the chronology. The attack against the school in Beslan is considered to be international terrorism because one perpetrator was Uzbek and one perpetrator was Kazakh. If they were not, that would not have been included in the tally.

As far as the air flights are concerned, this is perhaps the poster child for what is wrong with the methodology. Two attacks against two airliners. One airliner had an Israeli citizen, the other did not. One counts, one doesn't. Now more generally, in our view, it simply makes no sense that a determination whether to count an incident as international terrorism would hinge on reviewing a manifest or determining citizenship of everyone involved.

And lastly, we had anomalies based on counting rules and the definition of "significant." On two separate occasions, bombs went off outside four HSBC banks in Turkey on the same day last year. While this would constitute international terrorism, no single bomb caused $10,000 worth of damage and, therefore, did not meet the threshold. Now, as I believe should be readily apparent, the statutory criteria and legacy counting rules used to support Patterns simply do not reflect the nature of the global terrorism problem we now confront. Accordingly, the National Counterterrorism Center is in the midst of compiling 2004 data in a more comprehensive manner that will not only address the many anomalies I've already highlighted, but will also address the kinds of indigenous terrorism conducted by such groups as the ETA and FARC against their own citizens. These, of course, also are not reflected in the data provided today because it's indigenous terrorism. In other words, our intent is to capture any incident where a non-combatant is targeted or indiscriminately attacked and the attack is politically motivated.

Now, we recognize that users of this information will want to query the data in various fashions, so we will be rolling out in June not only a more comprehensive data set, but also a database that will empower the user and support interactive queries.

What we'll be rolling out in June is a comprehensive chronology of all attacks where non-combatants are targeted or indiscriminately attacked and where the attack is politically motivated, which is not a crime or genocide. It will be (inaudible) terrorism and it will be available on www.tkb.org. It will have more data, will be accessible and searchable, it will be used for empowering, it will be open and transparent, and it will be regularly updated.

And finally, we look forward to interacting with both private and public experts to further refine our methodology and continually improve the approach for counting terrorist incidents.

Voice: Thank you, John. Have a seat—you don't need to go. Arshad?

(Laughter.)

Question: Three questions if I may, very simple ones. In your last statement, is NCTC therefore committing to, on a regular basis, going forward, providing this more comprehensive data set on acts of terrorism? Second, you said that one reason for the increase this year, aside from the greater resources devoted to monitoring, was Iraq. What were the figures for Iraq in '04 and '03? Thirdly, why didn't you go back and redo the 2003 data in a more comprehensive manner so that there would be comparable data for at least '03 and '04? Those are addressed all to Mr. Brennan, of course.

Mr. Brennan: First of all, yes, we are committing to make available on a regular basis the incidents that meet what we believe is a more comprehensive definition of international terrorism, so we are going forward. We are releasing this. We have released it today. We'll continue to do so.

Secondly, as far as the number in Iraq, in 2003 the number of incidents were 22. In 2004, the incidents were 201. I might add, that reflects the increasing number of civilians and contractors and others who were in Iraq who are participating in the rebuilding of the Iraqi economy and nation. And then the final question?

Question: The final question was, why didn't you go back and redo the '03 data so that—

Mr. Brennan: I think, as we tried to make clear, there are some serious shortcomings in the methodology used to date. What we wanted to do this year was to put out the information based on that methodology, based on a very rigorous application of that methodology with a very exhaustive data search. And I think what we demonstrated here today is that there are serious shortcomings. To apply very precious resources to go back and do 2003 or 2002 with a deficient methodology, I think, would not be in the best interests of the U.S. Government or the American people. What we're trying to do is to look forward. We want to, in fact, apply these resources, our new understanding, and the lessons that we've learned to the data compilation in the future.

Question: Do you regard the Iraq numbers that you just gave us—for which, thank you—as comparable? And the reason I ask is that I've got to figure that if there's one piece of real estate that the U.S. intelligence community has devoted enormous resources to in the last two years, it's got to be—two-and-a-half years—it's Iraq. Therefore, do you think those figures are comparable, '03 to '02?

Mr. Brennan: In terms of what the term you're using—"comparable"—to sort of denote here, I'm not certain. The rigor that we applied worldwide for the 2004 data also applied to Iraq. So it was Iraq, Kashmir, and others. So that number, I think, is the result of exhaustive search and research on that. Also, as I pointed out, the number of civilians that have come not just from the United States, but also from other countries—the number of individuals who, in fact, are in different places in Iraq that have been involved in some of the attacks that have taken place there, I think that is the reason why, in fact, we're seeing an increase in that number.

Question: The reason I ask the question, and I'm using the term "comparable" not in any complex sense, but in the same way that you used in saying that the overall '04 numbers are not comparable to the overall '03 numbers, because the greater rigor and—

Mr. Brennan: Right.

Question: —and so on, the monitoring. My question on Iraq, I think, is germane because there has been enormously rigorous study by the U.S. Government on what has been happening in Iraq in '03 and '04. So if we were to say, "Look, 201 versus 22," that jump isn't the result of just more rigorous monitoring in '04 but in fact reflects the underlying reality.

Mr. Brennan: Don't know the answer to that question because as you say, you know, we are not applying then this methodology, as the rigorous research to the 2003 data. We have not gone back and looked at it, at this point, in terms of Iraq. So all I can do is stand behind, very strongly, the figures for Iraq for 2004.

Question: And henceforth, I presume, you're never going to —are you ever going to go back and redo data in future, based in these methodologies that you feel are so inadequate that had been the case?

Mr. Brennan: As I said, we are trying to look to the future in applying methodology to the future.

Mr. Ereli: Elise.

Question: A couple of questions. For Mr. Brennan, just a follow up on what Arshad was saying.

Basically, what you said is that, you know, you proved today that there are serious shortcomings in the methodology that was currently used. So did you do all that exhaustive effort—don't you think that the efforts would have been served, kind of, moving forward than just to do this to make a point that there are such serious shortcomings?

I mean, you already kind of handicapped your own numbers, don't you think, in a way that will, you know, kind of makes us question why you put them out. Why don't you just wait to, kind of, June and say, you know, this is the new methodology—

Mr. Brennan: Yeah. Well, first of all, we wanted—we made a commitment to the State Department that we were going to revamp this process and provide the State Department everything they needed in support of their annual requirement as far as reporting to the Congress.

We learned a lot of things over the past nine months as we looked back at this information. And the lessons learned, the anomalies and other things, really became quite stark. We grappled with that last year when, in fact, we had to do a revised version of Patterns as a result of some flaws in terms of the publication process and how the information came out.

But we wanted to do is to make sure we really understood the totality of the issue. And so what we wanted to do, as a result of this thorough research, is to look at the shortcomings in the individual criteria and in the methodology. And we found out what the problems were. So what we did, as a result of this, we made the State Department aware of these anomalies and we worked very closely with them. And I think that's why, right now today, we have, in fact, NCTC and the Department of State issuing concurrent reports. What we want to do—and I think this has been in the press recently —in terms of full transparency to the American public, there was never any effort—and I want to make that very clear—never any effort that was applied to the NCTC to either suppress these numbers or not to release them.

We had moved forward on this, hand in hand with the State Department. We were committed to doing it. But once we realized that there were going to be shortcomings here, we wanted to make sure that it was understood when it was going to be presented, what those problems were.

But not just put them out and say, "There are shortcomings here, that's it." We wanted to say, "Okay, what are we going to do about it." And that's what we said today. We have something now in process, and by June there's going to be this comprehensive data set that's going to be made available, regularly updated, that is going to be much more user friendly, that can be a tool for individuals to research and to really look at the phenomena in international terrorism.

Mr. Zelikow: Now, let me just add on that question. I mean, the reason—I think it's a good question as to why we put out these numbers today. I asked that question myself some time back. And the reason we did it is because you wanted us to. And the Hill wanted us to. Because if we didn't put out these numbers, you'd say we were withholding data. That's why we're putting them out.

So we had this dilemma. We could either not put out the numbers and wait until we felt like we had good numbers and then put those out. And then you write stories saying we're withholding data. Or we put out numbers that are basically in transition, you know, like: okay, come visit us in the middle of this transitional process and we'll show you the numbers as they exist right now, and just tell you, as openly as we can, these aren't very good. That's why we're making them better and we'll have the good numbers ready for you in a couple of months. But just so you're not suspicious about what we're doing, let's be totally transparent and show you where we are right now.

And so we just chose the path of transparency.

Question: Just one more for you, Mr. Zelikow. What do you say about the issue that this is no longer—the State Department, yes, is putting out these Country Reports, but it's no longer what it used to be, which is Patterns of Global Terrorism. Is that what the NT—Counterterrorism Center is going to do? If you could talk a little bit about your decision to—and the State Department's decision to shift over to NCTC, and a little bit more in the—there's a little bit in the report about global jihad phenomenon and how that, kind of, came as an off-shoot of al-Qaida. I know that's a bit but—thank you.

Mr. Zelikow: Sure. I came into the State Department earlier this year, as you know, and so I had not been a part of these issues in the past. I also came into the Department believing rather strongly in the importance of the NCTC. I'd been the director of the 9/11 Commission last year. I'd played a part in recommending the creation of that Center. I testified publicly to Congress in support of its creation and participated in the drafting of the statutory language that I quoted to you.

So when I come into the State Department and I kind of find out—my instinctive reaction is, why isn't NCTC doing this? Congress mandated that they should do this, as I know well. And so my instinct was, we need to focus the State Department on country policies, which is what the State Department does. And since the statute requires us to describe international terrorist groups, we have to do that. Although I think NCTC is the more proper center to provide authoritative descriptions of those groups, but we're required to do that so we have to do that. So that's in the report, along with the discussion of global jihadism, because of the language in the statute that refers to umbrella groups, the umbrella conception being the notion of Islamism and violent global Jihad and so that's described in the report as well, in order to comply with the mandate.

But very early on, I actually spoke to John and said, "John, you should do this." And in principle John agreed. And so there—

Question: But what about the idea—

Mr. Zelikow:—we went forward from there.

Question:—what about the idea that you're not really putting forward? You're kind of putting out a lot of statistics and a lot of information about a lot of different stuff. But it's not being kind of put together in terms of what are the patterns of global terrorists.

Mr. Zelikow: Well, in part, because the overall depiction of the trend lines and analysis of global terrorism as a phenomenon really is anointed as the business of the NCTC explicitly in the statute. And to the extent we can, we plan to defer to that. You could make the counter argument. The counter argument would be: Well, why don't you guys do it, too, and set yourselves up as a rival voice on this issue with NCTC? And that would, of course, replicate the precise phenomena we decried last year.

Question: (Inaudible) basically, everybody agrees there's a significant increase in the number of terrorist attacks last year, right?

Mr. Zelikow: No. We don't. We agree that we made a more aggressive effort to compile the data and therefore have a much larger dataset.

Question: I remember somebody said that—

Mr. Zelikow: I mean, we have really no way of knowing whether the actual number of attacks, had we equally aggressively compiled the data in previous years, whether the numbers would have gone up or down, if you had held the data compilation efforts constant. We have actually no way of knowing whether the attack numbers would have gone up or down.

Question: Without numbers, how would you say that terrorism is a significant threat?

Mr. Zelikow: Well, here's what we can—you'll notice from —John, I'm going to ask you to comment on this, too. You notice on the charts that there are thousands of people being killed and the implications of the counting rule problems are mostly about things that are excluded. So there are at least thousands of people killed. And if you had adopted different kinds of counting rules, the numbers both in '04 and '03 and '02 probably would be significantly enlarged. But at a point where you have groups killing thousands of people, even under these relatively straightened and odd counting rules, and plus trans—once you redefine from international to transnational, killing hundreds, possibly thousands more, that's a very significant problem.

Mr. Brennan: Just might add, the top five incidents of last year in terms of casualties resulted in over 4,000 deaths. That's five attacks. The attack in Spain—4,000 casualties, not deaths; 4,000 casualties. It's the attack in Spain against the railway, the attack in Russia against the school, and three attacks in Iraq—two attacks on the second of March of last year in Karbala where there were suicide bombers that set off bombs against the Shia Muslim community there and another attack in Iraq on 1 February of last year in Irbil. So between those five attacks, over 4,000 casualties, it shows that, in fact, if you count those as five and then you take five attacks somewhere maybe in Kashmir, you really cannot compare the two because those five resulted in over 4,000 casualties, where maybe five attacks in Kashmir, you know, resulted in just a couple.

Let's go to Tammy.

Question: I was wondering if I could ask Mr. Brennan about the Iraq figures. The 2,000—or I'm sorry—the 201 number that you have according to the current counting rules, was culled from a larger universe. Do you have a figure that you can provide today of the numbers of attacks you believe took place—terrorist attacks—not according to the counting rules?

Mr. Brennan: No, not today because, in fact, we're still in the process of compiling that information. As I said, it'll be made available in June on this website. That's what we want to do, is to make sure that people are able to see things. Now, Iraq and Afghanistan and other war-like conditions are, in fact, a little bit sort of unique. What we'll want to do is to, as we put this out in June, is to make as much data available. You know, we're talking about thousands of entries, you know, based on the totality then of incidents that constitute some form of terrorism, whether it be indigenous or transnational, whatever. So I think you're going to have to wait until June. We want to make sure that's right. We don't want to put out any numbers or anything else here that we really haven't scrubbed carefully.

Question: Mr. Brennan, I just wanted to follow up what Mr. Zelikow was just saying. If you used the criteria that you all would prefer to use the numbers for 2004 would likely go up, correct?

Mr. Brennan: I think what you'll see in June when we put out, in fact, this database, that the total number of incidents is going to increase, and it's going to increase probably significantly because it's going to take into account a lot of indigenous attacks. You know, within Colombia, a number of those incidents that I pointed out that are not included because of the limitations as far as the statutory criteria. So what we're trying to do is to have a much more comprehensive data set of all incidents that appear to be terrorism in nature, as far as being directed against noncombatants and are politically motivated. And so this will give people an opportunity to really sort of slice and dice these numbers according to a number of different criteria that—we shouldn't be, you know, having a rigid one that will exclude some and not include the others because then we're never going to be able to sort of service the people who are looking really comprehensively around the world to get a better understanding of politically motivated terrorism violence.

Mr. Zelikow: Let me add, I know this may be counterintuitive because the whole direction of the press commentary on this was like we're trying to hold the numbers down. In fact, we're revising the accounting rules that are going to raise the numbers up to show that transnational terrorism is at least as great a threat and, in fact, worse. But then you get into the phenomena of, well, is there a significant—a statistical change then over the last few years, which is the question you asked. And again, this is just an elementary statistics point. I mean, you have to hold some of these variables constant. So if you held constant accounting rules and the compilation efforts, then we have no idea of whether, in fact—what the graph would show. It's not at all obvious that the numbers in past years wouldn't have been hugely larger if we had compiled equally thoroughly and counted on transnational counting rules. We just don't know.

And in fact, just to tell you in a very straightforward way, what I think the global assessment would show is, you'd find it varied significantly by region and by country, that in some countries things have gone down and in other countries things have gone up, and that some of this is due to the success or failure of indigenous law enforcement efforts; and you'd have a fairly complex mosaic to examine.

Question: Um, 651 attacks in 2004, compared to 175 attacks in your report in 2003. That's a sharp increase in terrorist attacks. What does that tell us about the war on terrorism—the global war on terrorism and the cooperation?

Mr. Brennan: I will tell you, but I just want to make sure it's clear: It does not necessarily represent a sharp increase in the number of terrorist attacks. What a sharp increase is in the number of incidents being reported now annually, again as a result of much more rigorous research and identification of all these incidents. So I want to make sure it's understood that the numbers cannot be compared in a meaningful way because the number now is what is being reported as far as terrorist incidents. If we were to go back and apply that much more extensive research with a (inaudible) against that against that dataset in 2003, I bet you that we're probably going to see more. But again, what we want to do is to use those resources to continue to engage in counterterrorism activities looking in the future.

Mr. Zelikow: I mean, the short answer is it doesn't tell us anything about the war on terror. The statistics are simply not valid for any inference about the progress, either good or bad, of American policy. I think that's the honest answer. If you just look at what the statistics are and what kind of inferences can legitimately be drawn from them, I can't come up with a defensible inference.

Question: But, why do you issue a report like this? I mean, if it does not tell us anything about where the war on terror is heading, how can we evaluate this war and where it is right now?

Mr. Zelikow: What we think would be fair is, we can compile the data we can compile. For example, when you look at the NCTC dataset, there is a chronology and of many terrorist incidents. It's a subset of the transnational terrorist total, but that's interesting. It's just hard to—it's not a homogenous set for comparison with past years. There is interesting data there about—let's say you wanted to find out some of the terrorist incidents that occurred in the Philippines. It would be a reference for some of those incidents, for example. Or there may be other uses to which people can put it. But fundamentally, the reason we're putting out these numbers now when they're still in a transitional condition are the reasons I gave in answer to a question earlier.

Question: (Inaudible) about the states that sponsor terrorism. In the report you say that Cuba, North Korea, and Syria have the capacity to manufacture weapons of mass destruction. And I wonder if you could elaborate on Cuba. How can Cuba—I mean, in what way or—?

Mr. Zelikow: If you expect me to walk into the minefield of discussing the Cuban biological weapons program, I'm going to disappoint you. (Laughter.) However—

Question: (Inaudible.)

Mr. Zelikow: No. The Cuban Government has the capability to manufacture some weapons of mass destruction. The U.S. Government has discussed what those capabilities are in other settings and I don't want to get into that here. The same is true for Syria and the other countries we named. What we're focusing on here principally is less what is the WMD capability of the states, is simply what is the role of those states in state sponsorship of terrorism. And then please look at that against the background of what we have already said publicly about the capabilities of those states in the WMD world. And then you can draw some inferences about whether that's disturbing or not.

Question: (Inaudible) the report about terrorism and weapons of mass destruction, so then you explain a little bit in what way—

Mr. Zelikow: It is—

Question:—(inaudible) do it because I look in the country description and there is no information on that.

Mr. Zelikow: No information on?

Question: On weapons of mass destruction.

Mr. Zelikow: No, because the report is not on—this is not a weapons of mass destruction report. It's a report about sponsorship of terrorism and relationship to terrorism. We simply point out that if you look at the state—at some of these state sponsors of terrorism and you note that they also have been described in other U.S. Government statements of being involved in WMD production, some might consider that a disturbing combination.

Question: Hi. I'm Janine (inaudible), Bloomberg News. Two questions. Were NCTC figures released in response to Hill pressure because it was not included in the State Department version? And secondly, I was a little confused about the new numbers that are going to come out, Mr. Brennan. Are you not mandated under the same statutes to define terrorist acts—international terrorist acts, the way the Congress says because it's coming out of your group instead of the State Department?

Mr. Zelikow: Let me start on that. The decision to release these numbers today for '04 was not made this week. So it is not a response to articles in the press this week or to pressure from Hill staffers this week. That decision had already been made. The statement that I read you on process today was given practically word-for-word identically in a briefing of Hill staffers on Monday.

So it's been our view all along that we needed to go ahead and give you the data in this transitional form because we already anticipated that if we did not do so, there would be accusations that we were hiding something. So we thought transparency was the better route.

Mr. Brennan: And we did not release any numbers as a result of any pressure from the Hill or elsewhere.

Question: And the question about how—we understand what you said is that Congress says you have to define international terrorism in a certain way. You are now going to define it in a new way, including a Russian attack—an attack on a plane with only Russians are killed. Are you allowed to do that because you are releasing it and not State?

Mr. Brennan: In the statute that requires State to issue this annual report, it defines international terrorism, it sets a definition there in terms of citizens or territory of more than one country. So therefore, in the report that the State Department puts out, it is bound by that statutorily defined criteria.

As we, now, in the NCTC are looking at the phenomenon of worldwide terrorism, we want to make sure that we are looking at it as openly and as exhaustively as possible. And therefore, in this effort—and since we are compiling this data—we are going to be making that data available to other U.S. Government departments and agencies, and as a result of the effort while we're working with the State Department now, making that available also to the U.S. public because it is based on information that is available in the press. So if we're doing that, it's a service that is going to be provided then and made available to the public.

Mr. Zelikow: Now let me just clarify. Now do you see the source of the statistical anomaly, in part, and why these counting rules are so peculiar is because the definitions were not definitions for the construction of a database. The definitions were created for the specification of countries on which you must report and groups that you must describe.

But since those were the only definitions in the statute and since we were compiling a database, we therefore fell into the habit of applying those definitions to the construction of a database, which turns out, on reflection, to be unsuitable.

Therefore, you have transnational terrorism. There is no statutory guidance on how to define it, so in a way the NCTC is free to simply try to do this right and come up with an—which and they would then publicize it and then they will have to defend that and people can argue whether or not it's defined correctly or not.

Question: Just to clarify—

Mr. Zelikow: Go ahead.

Question: Just to clarify, are you now saying you're—I'm interested in both Mr. Zelikow and Mr. Brennan's opinion on this—are we now saying that all previous reports should be considered suspect because of the issues that the NCTC managed to identify in its review of the report for this year's report? In other words, should we consider that there is not a useful evaluation of terrorist activity in all previous reports, first of all.

And second of all, you've talked about the changes in your methodology and your information collection, that you've had ten people working full time to gather incidents, for example—but I'm less clear on what changes in methodology you're saying. In other words, aside from potentially gleaning more terrorist incidents that were out there that you might not have in previous years, have you made other substantial changes in your methodology from previous years?

Mr. Zelikow: Let me do the first one and if you understood the second question, John, I'll let you try to answer; it was hard for me.

On the first question, what does this say about the quality of the data compilations in previous years, I think it speaks for itself. I think now you have to—people should examine those compilations in previous years with their eyes wide open as to the level of effort involved in compiling the data and the counting rules they labored under. Rules, which as John described earlier, seemed to make good sense in the 1980s when they began regularly doing this. And then you can judge the quality of how that worked over the years.

This is, by the way, not an unusual problem in the social sciences, where there are lots of phenomenon that we try to measure—poverty, unemployment and so forth—and advancing methodology and questions then as how you regard previous statistics calculated by different methods. And this is, yet, another one of those stories.

Mr. Brennan: I think looking back at previous years' data, there is, I think, a degree of confidence that the methodology and criteria, as defined by the statute, were applied as the counts were done on an annual basis. Might there have been some underreporting? Yeah, I think so. But it was partly a result of that limitation that was imposed by the statutory definition, as well as the practices that were used as far as trying to define some of these other aspects of terrorism.

Now, as far as the changes for the future, we are in fact now stripping away some of those limitations that I tried to explain, as far as why the one Aeroflot flight was not counted. We are not going to limit this database to only those instances that involved citizens and territory of more than one country. I think we have ample evidence of terrorism conducted by groups that are designated by the U.S. Government, as well as other governments, as being foreign terrorist organizations perpetrating attacks. And we want to make sure that that information is included.

So again, it's going to result in an increase in the number of incidents that are included in the database. But as Phil pointed out, the NCTC does not have to adhere to that statutory definition because that statutory definition only applies to the annual State Department obligation.

What we're trying to do, and be based on the legislative language that created the NCTC that we have primary responsibility in U.S. Government for analysis and integration of all information dealing with terrorism and counterterrorism. And so that's why it's going to be a much more comprehensive data set.

Mr. Zelikow: Does that answer the question?

Question: Well, I'm just trying to figure out just one more time, maybe I wasn't clear. Did you make any other significant changes in what you were allowing or not allowing? I thought that you said that the numbers that you are releasing today, in this transition period, were based on the statutory criteria. And that the main difference that—I've heard you say today, the main difference is simply that you had more manpower devoted to making sure that you got all the terrorist incidents.

Question: (Inaudible).

Mr. Brennan: Right, I mean, there are several different issues here that are at play. One is that, you're absolutely right, we applied much more rigor, more manpower, better quality control to the effort over the past year than in previous years, which has resulted in a much more comprehensive data set that we looked at. By multiple measures, we looked at much more information.

As a result of that more comprehensive research then, we identified more incidents that met that definition and the criteria. And so that is one of the reasons, I think, one overwhelming reason for this increase in the number that are being reported, as far as terrorist incidents.

Are there other factors that come into play also? I think that there are. There are some things that we're looking at now in terms of individual countries. What's the reason for, or in fact, the number of incidents that took place there?

Again, trying to compare it with past practices that were less than one-third or one-fourth of the effort that was expended, I don't think it would be a fair comparison to take a look at the numbers that we're issuing today and the numbers in previous reports. And so, we've learned from that and we're making adjustments accordingly.

Mr. Zelikow: Especially since the effects of the more aggressive data is just, "Well, okay, so we've discovered, you know, hundreds of additional incidents in Kashmir," because we actually—people went out and looked at local newspapers from Kashmir and so on and said, "Okay, now what larger inference should I then draw from that for the conduct of the global war on terror," (inaudible). Hard argument.

Question: Can we move back to the Country Report for a minute, Mr. Zelikow, and just—you've—

Mr. Zelikow: I don't care.

Question:—gone—you know, pretty tough against al-Qaida and have said that you've eliminated—you know, a lot of the leadership of al-Qaida but that there's this new phenomenon of global—you know, kind of jihadist sympathizing with that. Is that the new face of terrorism as you see it? And if you could flesh that out a little bit more.

Mr. Zelikow: Yes, that's—I think that's a fair summary. A declining role for a significantly degraded, highly organized al-Qaida network of the kind that had built up before 9/11;

rising emergence of decentralized, more local groups that are loosely affiliated or inspired by the Islamist ideology espoused by al-Qaida, creating a different kind of transnational terrorist phenomenon for us to tackle.

Question: Do you believe that the United States and its allies are winning the war on terrorism?

Mr. Zelikow: I do think we are winning the war on terrorism, but I think it's a very long struggle. Just looking back on this from a historical perspective and a little bit having looked at the pre-9/11 period before, obviously a period in which the terrorists essentially owned a state and could more or less unhindered organize and mount transnational catastrophic terrorist attacks from within that kind of shelter, building up a very large, complex global organization can, I think, be favorably contrasted with their ability to mount catastrophic, long-range attacks today. And I think one indicator of that is the absence of attacks on the homeland of the United States in a situation where, obviously, they would have wanted by now to carry out such attacks. So there is some issue of capacity.

But I want to underscore—let me triple-underscore: no complacency, no reason to think that the danger has now passed. The language of the 9/11 Commission report last July said, "We are safer, but we are not safe", and I think that the administration today would continue to echo those words.

Question: Could I follow up on one aspect of that? Well, actually, if I may just do—on the Country Reports. On Libya, you said that you've expressed your concerns about the alleged plot to kill Saudi Crown Prince Abdallah. Have the Libyans yet allayed those concerns, or are those concerns still there?

And secondly, you say that Sudan took significant steps to improve its counterterrorism cooperation but concerns remain. Reading the quick summary, I didn't perceive what those concerns were. Could you outline the concerns about Sudanese support for—state support for terrorism?

Mr. Zelikow: First on the Saudi issue and Libya, we continue to address those concerns with the Libyan Government. On the second question having to do with Sudan, both the reasons why we think they've cooperated more cannot be elaborated fully in public, and the full nature of our continuing concerns, I'm afraid, also cannot be fully elaborated in public.

The point is we want to acknowledge an improvement in their counterterrorist cooperation, while we have not removed them yet from the designation list because we still feel there's—a further along that road they still have to travel.

Question: Briefly, I remembered the thing I wanted to ask you. On the question of when the decision was actually taken to release this? It was explained to me, and perhaps I misunderstood, that technically, no decision was taken for NCTC to release the numbers because NCTC falls under the DNI. The DNI didn't actually get confirmed, I think, until Friday. So when—I just want to understand to make sure that you're statement is accurate. When did DNI Negroponte actually decide to release this, or was the decision taken by the President or somebody else, you know, a couple of weeks ago or months ago?

Mr. Zelikow: All right, let me clarify what the State—the timing of the State Department. There are two separate decisions. There's a decision by the State Department and a decision by the NCTC. And I can only speak to the former.

On the decision by the State Department, the Secretary took the decision as to how to restructure the report some weeks ago, and with the knowledge and expectation that NCTC would pick up the statistical compilation in a fashion that they needed to determine and they needed to decide how and when they wished to make that public and in what form because it would be [their] responsibility.

That then led to a decision-making process within NCTC involving both the CIA, it's current owner, and its future owner; and John should comment on that.

Mr. Brennan: Ambassador Negroponte was confirmed by the Senate and sworn in by the President last Thursday afternoon. Before then, the NCTC reported to the Director of Central Intelligence. Once the Director of National Intelligence, Ambassador Negroponte, he was sworn into office, we then fell under the Director of National Intelligence.

We had engaged with the Office of the Director of National Intelligence and with Ambassador Negroponte on the plans to support what we were going to be doing this week, as far as the rollout on the 29th. And so we wanted to make sure that he was aware, first of all, and had seen the information report. Since we fall under him, I wanted to respect that chain of command; but we had every intention to move forward on it.

And so there were, I think, a lot of misunderstandings that were out there as far as that were—we're not going to commit to it or it was not going to happen. No; the plan was, we were going to move forward. But in the first few days in office, you can imagine Ambassador Negroponte had a number of things. And so what we wanted to do was to do it in the right order and to respect the DNI's—

Question: When did he actually sign off on it then, because obviously he couldn't sign off on it prior to his having been confirmed and sworn in, so when did he actually say "go"?

Mr. Brennan: Well, I was engaged with Ambassador Negroponte's office extensively this morning since we moved this up so we'd (inaudible) today. So, as of this morning.

Question: So he signed off this morning?

Mr. Brennan: It was acknowledged that we were going to hold this press conference and the release had to be done today, so you can imagine we had to do a number of last minute, you know, a sort of a hurry up as far as making sure that we could push it out. It was done this afternoon, so he had no problem or his office, and I was engaged with them extensively.

Mr. Ereli: Just a few more questions.

Question: Based on the new methodology that's used to capture the statistics on terrorism. Will this be used as a basis for also determining foreign terrorist organizations?

Mr. Brennan: No. There is—foreign terrorist organizations and their designation is the creature of still more law and regulation governed by its own set of definitions and procedures, which we patiently study and attempt to apply.

Question: Because there's a clear division here between indigenous attacks and attacks involving foreigners.

Mr. Brennan: Correct.

Question: So would you use the same—

Mr. Brennan: Yet one more area of legacy law, which we continue to apply. Though we have found that the designation of foreign terrorist organization is still pretty meaningful, and works for a lot of the different organizations that we have to cover so it doesn't present some of the same kinds of problems that we're trying to address in the statistical compilation, but it's a whole separate story all its own.

Mr. Ereli: One last question. Arshad.

Question: Can you give us, Mr. Brennan, can you give us the 2003 figure for Kashmir related violence? And just to be precise about it, should one refer to this as violence that is related to Kashmir but took place in India and Pakistan? Or did you mean to, quite precisely, say that it took place in Kashmir and therefore, how do you define Kashmir?

Mr. Zelikow: I'll take that latter one for you.

Mr. Brennan: Okay. The numbers for 2003 in Kashmir: there were 52 incidents in Kashmir that were included in the chronology that was issued last year; 284 in 2004. The number of victims in Kashmir in 2003 was 776; in 2004, it was 1,872. The number of killed in Kashmir in 2003 was 111; and in 2004, it was 434. And in the chronology that we are issuing, you will see that is listed under—for each of the individual incidents, listed under India, but it identifies Kashmir as the location for the attack.

Question: Can you give us the killed and wounded also for Iraq, since that was the other one you broke up for us in terms of attacks?

Mr. Brennan: Incidents: 22 in 2003, 201 in 2004. Number of victims in 2003, 501. Number of victims in 2004, 1,709. Number of killed in 2003, 117; in 2004, 554.

Now again, this is what we had pulled out from it this morning, but it's out on the database there right now, so I just wanted to make sure that was—are consistent with what's out.

Mr. Zelikow: And just to clarify, of course, all attacks in Kashmir occurred in either India or Pakistan. (Laughter.) But—

Question: (Inaudible) We can consider the UN line—

Mr. Zelikow: You certainly can.

Question: Yes, well, did they happen in India but—

Mr. Zelikow: We're not trying to make any new policy on defining the international status of Kashmir.

Mr. Ereli: Thank you, everyone. Thank you to our guests.

Reviewing the State Department's Annual Report on Terrorism

U.S. House of Representatives, Committee on International Relations, Subcommittee on International Terrorism and Nonproliferation

Below is the transcript of a hearing held on 12 May 2005, concerning the U.S. Department of State's Annual Report on Terrorism. *Witnesses at the hearing included: Philip Zelikow, counselor of the Department of State; John Brennan, interim director of the National Counterterrorism Center; Raphael F. Perl, specialist in international terrorism policy, Congressional Research Service; Larry C. Johnson, managing director, BERG Associates.*

Royce Statement on Annual Terrorism Report

Hearing Examines the State Department's 2004 Report on Terrorism

WASHINGTON, D.C.—Today, the House Subcommittee on International Terrorism and Nonproliferation (ITNP) held a hearing to review the State Department's annual report on terrorism. ITNP Chairman U.S. Rep. Ed Royce (R-CA-40) issued the following opening statement:

"The State Department's last two editions of its yearly report on international terrorism have been mired in controversy. The 2003 edition had to be reissued after significant errors were detected—errors that underreported the number of terrorist attacks for 2003. This year, the State Department issued its 2004 report minus its traditional annex statistically reporting on the number of terrorist attacks worldwide.

"This change leaves us with two documents: a *Country Reports on Terrorism,* produced by the State Department, and *A Chronology of Significant International Terrorism,* produced by the National Counterterrorism Center (NCTC). We used to have one report: *Patterns of Global Terrorism.*

"*Patterns* had been around since 1983. It was widely used throughout the world, because it was authoritative and comprehensive. In truncating this document, a good brand name was jettisoned. Post-9/11, when we are finding that much of what we have been doing for years in the terrorism field has been ineffective, it is an odd time to play with success.

"The new *Country Reports on Terrorism* is a bit like a one-sided baseball card. We have the terrorist's picture on the front. We see what team he is on. What is missing are the statistics on the back. In this case, it is the grisly statistics of attacks committed and deaths, injuries, and damage inflicted. Looking to next year, I would ask the Administration to revisit its decision to split this report in two. One report makes sense.

"I am not concerned, as are some, about the change in methodology that the NCTC is undertaking. There is room for improvement in classifying terrorist attacks, which is not an easy task. If the Administration needs a legislative fix to allow NCTC to input new statistics into a revived *Patterns* report, many of us would want to help. But, I should comment that after the problems with the 2003 report, in which Members of this Committee were very interested, I do not understand why the Committee was not consulted as the decision to alter *Patterns* was made. To some this may be just a report, but it is a congressionally mandated report dealing with the central security challenge facing our nation.

"Regarding some of the rhetoric surrounding this debate, the spike in terrorist attacks from 2003 to 2004 is not proof that we are losing the battle against terrorism. The Administration invited this charge though when it trumpeted its initial set of 2003 *Patterns'* numbers to claim that we were winning the battle. Let's get some perspective.

"The struggle against terrorism goes beyond the statistics of *Patterns*. Terrorism is a complex phenomenon. Key to fighting it is countering anti-Americanism, militant Islam, and various creeds that inspire terrorism and create a climate conducive to terrorist operations. *Patterns'* statistics said nothing about this crucial effort. This is not to disparage *Patterns*, as some have who call its statistics bad or worthless. This report is, or at least was, a useful tool. But again, it is not the ultimate scorecard in the battle against terrorism. It is not that simple. My hope for this hearing is that we examine the issues and look ahead. A commitment from the Administration to work with Congress on producing the best possible report on international terrorism would be a good start."

Testimony by Dr. Philip D. Zelikow

The Department of State has the lead responsibility for advancing our counterterrorism goals with other countries and welcomes the opportunity to submit a report to the Congress on those issues. After I say a few words on that subject, I will address the composition of the report and why we made the decision to revamp the Department's report to reflect the creation of the National Counterterrorism Center (NCTC), allowing each agency to concentrate in the area of its expertise.

International terrorism continued to pose a significant threat to the United States and its partners in 2004. Despite ongoing improvements in U.S. homeland security, our campaigns against insurgents and terrorists, and the deepening counterterrorism cooperation among the nations of the world, the slaughter of hundreds of innocents at Beslan school and major attacks in Madrid, on a Philippines ferry, and in Sinai, demonstrated the danger that international terrorism poses to friendly countries. Although fortunately there were no attacks on the homeland during 2004, the loss of American citizens in Iraq, Afghanistan, Saudi Arabia, Egypt, and Gaza this year reminds us that the U.S. homeland, U.S. citizens and interests, and U.S. friends and allies remain at risk.

In 2004, the United States broadened and deepened its international cooperation on counterterrorism issues. Increased diplomatic, intelligence, law enforcement, military and financial cooperation contributed directly to homeland security and the interdiction or disruption of terrorists around the globe. We have discussed these efforts extensively in *Country Reports on Terrorism 2004* our annual report to Congress transmitted to you on April 27.

In that report, we offered a number of examples of this cooperation. For example:

- Close cooperation with British, French and other authorities, coordinated through the State Department and U.S. Embassies in London, Paris and elsewhere, was pivotal to managing threats to airline security during the '03-'04 new year period.
- Information sharing with the United Kingdom and Pakistan led to the disclosure and disruption of al-Qaida attack planning against U.S. financial institutions.
- U.S. diplomatic and military assistance in Africa facilitated cooperation among Algeria, Mali, Mauritania, Niger, Libya and Chad that led to the capture and return of wanted GSPC faction leader El Para to Algeria to stand trial.
- Law enforcement officers in Iraq, Colombia, Indonesia, the Philippines, Saudi Arabia and Pakistan, among others, applied U.S. specialized counterterrorism training to bring terrorists to justice.

Notably, 2004 was also marked by progress in decreasing the threat from state-sponsored terrorism. Iraq's designation as a state sponsor of terrorism was rescinded in October 2004. Although still designated as state sponsors of terrorism, Libya and Sudan took significant steps to cooperate in the global war on terrorism. Unfortunately, Cuba, North Korea, Syria, and in particular, Iran continued to embrace terrorism as an instrument of national policy. And, as we have noted before, we find it most worrisome that these countries all have the capabilities to manufacture weapons of mass destruction and other destabilizing technologies that could fall into the hands of terrorists.

Iran and Syria are of special concern to us for their direct, open, and prominent role in supporting Hezbollah and Palestinian terrorist groups, for their unhelpful actions in Iraq and in Iran's case, the unwillingness to bring to justice senior al-Qaida members detained in 2003, including senior al-Qaida members who were involved in the planning of the 9/11 attacks.

Now let me turn to the process issues. For years, as many

of you know, statistical data on global terrorism has been published as part of an annual State Department report called *Patterns of Global Terrorism,* that was last provided to Congress in April 2004.

The law itself requires basically two things. It requires detailed assessments of specified countries, and information about specified terrorist groups.

The compilation of data about terrorist attacks is not a required part of the report. And, in fact, the Department of State itself has never compiled statistical data on international terrorist incidents. This function has always been performed by the intelligence community, although the State Department has traditionally released this data, going back to the years in which the State Department was the public voice of the U.S. Government on international terrorism generally.

Of course, that situation has been changing in recent years. In July 2004, the 9/11 Commission recommended creation of a National Counterterrorism Center to conduct all-source analysis of global terrorism.

The President implemented this recommendation by Executive Order in August and the center was created by statute in December 2004, in the Intelligence Reform and Terrorism Prevention Act.

But what's important for our purposes here is what the law that Congress adopted said the NCTC should do. The law states that the NCTC is the primary organization for analysis and integration of "all intelligence possessed or acquired by the United States Government pertaining to terrorism or counterterrorism." The law further states that the NCTC will be the United States Government's "shared knowledge bank on known and suspected terrorists and international terror groups, as well as their goals, strategies, capabilities, and networks of contact and support."

Given that statutory mandate, the State Department has focused its own report to Congress on the issues in its mandate, renamed *Country Reports on Terrorism 2004,* assessing countries and providing information on terrorist groups, which we are still statutorily required to do. And we respect and defer to the National Counterterrorism Center to assume its new mandate as the "shared knowledge bank" for data on global terrorism.

We are gratified by the way some serious experts on terrorism analysis have responded to these innovations. Former terrorism prosecutor Andrew C. McCarthy in "The National Review Online" noted that under our new approach, State and NCTC "have labored to make terrorism information more reliable, more accessible, and more reflective of common sense." Oxford Analytica noted that despite a new title and format "Country Reports on Terrorism 2004 continues to provide a detailed account of global antiterror cooperation." Noted national security commentator Tony Cordesman at the Center for Strategic and International Studies wrote in a report called "Good Riddance to Meaningless Rubbish," "The news that the State Department has dropped the statistical appendices from its annual report (on terrorism) should not come as a shock to anyone. The State Department report has been (and is) extremely useful for its characterization of terrorist groups. It never, however, produced useful numbers on the patterns of terrorism." An analysis of the report by the Washington Institute for Near East Policy noted that the controversy over numbers "diverted attention from other, more significant aspects of the report. Country Reports 2004 provides a fairly balanced assessment of the evolving global jihadist threat, illustrating why and how jihadist groups pose a serious danger not only to the United States, but also to many other countries."

On April 27, NCTC committed to developing a new approach to compiling statistics that needs to be and will be significantly revised and improved, including NCTC's plans for providing a more comprehensive accounting of global terrorist incidents by June of this year. My colleague, John Brennan, is here with me today to discuss this with you.

The Department of State would support legislative changes that specifically task NCTC with the annual responsibility for statistical analysis of terrorism consistent with its basic mandate. The State Department would continue to prepare an annual report addressing state sponsors of terrorism, multilateral and bilateral cooperation on terrorism, terrorist groups and terrorist sanctuaries, as well as the new Section 7120 reporting requirements that lie within State's area of expertise. The Department has begun consultations on this topic. We will be working with DNI and NCTC to shape a joint understanding on this topic. We will be back in touch with the Committee at a later date with a formal proposal.

Thank you, Mr. Chairman, for this opportunity to testify before the Committee.

Statement for the Record of John O. Brennan

Good morning Mr. Chairman. I am pleased to be here to address the role that the Terrorist Threat Integration Center (TTIC) and the National Counterterrorism Center (NCTC) have played over the past year in compiling a chronology of international terrorism incidents.

By way of background, the Intelligence Community (IC) has traditionally provided input to the State Department publication of Patterns of Global Terrorism. This has included, among other things, Appendix A, that laid out in some detail those incidents of "international terrorism" that were considered "significant." Because Patterns was produced in response to statutory directive, Intelligence Community input was consistent with the statutory criteria that, for instance, defined "international terrorism" as "terrorism involving citizens or the territory of more than one country." In many cases, the key statutory criteria, such as the definition of "noncombatant," whether an attack in a specific region should be considered "international" and what constituted "significant" were open to interpretation. In such cases the IC looked to the State Department to provide counting rules; these counting rules, coupled with past practices and our own judgment were then used to evaluate specific incidents.

With the standup of the Terrorist Threat Integration

Center in May 2003, responsibility to support Patterns shifted from the CIA to TTIC. However, during the hectic early days of TTIC, the database to support Patterns received insufficient attention and resources. Adequate quality control was lacking, incidents were missed, and the document was published with numerous errors. As you are aware, these shortcomings were noted by academics and the press, and Appendix A was ultimately reissued. To avoid a repeat of such problems TTIC/NCTC took a number of actions last year:

- Increased personnel assigned to the database from three part-time to ten full-time individuals;
- Reengineered the database itself to improve data integrity;
- Established an Incident Adjudication Board, drawn from Intelligence Community officers assigned to the TTIC/NCTC to ensure quality control;
- And took on board, as appropriate, recommendations of the Department of State Inspector General's Report which had reviewed the 2003 production process.

In the process of compiling the statistics for 2004, a number of issues became apparent. Because of the significant increase in the resources devoted to maintaining the database, far more source material was reviewed and a substantially higher number of incidents meeting the statutory criteria were compiled; significant international incidents rose from under 200 in 2003 to approximately 650 last year—a copy of the entire chronology of significant international attacks is provided for the written record. While some of the global increase was attributable to incidents in Iraq, the overall growth in total incidents represented a statistical discontinuity—a function of increased resources dedicated to research and not necessarily any change in the nature of global terrorism. The impact of such additional research is seen most clearly in Kashmir, where a dramatic growth is noted over previous years' data; there is little doubt that a more accurate accounting of the incidents in Kashmir would have reflected far higher totals than was the case in 2003 Patterns. In other words: the numbers compiled for 2004 cannot be compared to those of previous years in any meaningful way.

A rigorous application of the statutory criteria and counting rules clearly gave rise to a significant increase in the number of international terrorist incidents. However, in compiling the results, TTIC/NCTC became increasingly concerned with both the statutory criteria themselves as well as the definitions that we were being asked to use: Of primary concern was the statutory definition of "international terrorism." This definitional approach may be valid for a state sponsored threat, but is far less useful with the kind of transnational threat that we confront now. For instance, the requirement that international terrorism involve the citizens or territory of more than one country necessarily implied that if a suicide bomber from Country A blows up a café in Country A and kills only citizens of Country A, it doesn't count. But... if a suicide bomber from Country A blows up a café in Country A and there happens to be a tourist from Country B in the café who is killed or seriously wounded, it counts. In other words, the end results were arbitrary and often a function of serendipity; analysts were left trying to determine citizenship of those people present at an attack or the makeup of an aircraft manifest. Representative problems from 2004 included:

- On 2 November the Dutch filmmaker, Theo Van Gogh, was killed by Mohammed Bouyari, a Dutch Moroccan and Islamic extremist. The murder was clearly a terrorist attack, but because they were both Dutch citizens this attack did not meet the statutory definition of "international terrorism."
- On 24 August two Russian airliners were destroyed in mid air by Chechen female suicide bombers. One aircraft apparently had all Russian passengers and crew and therefore, did not meet the criteria for international terrorism. The other aircraft had a single dual Israeli citizen onboard and therefore, is reflected in the international terrorism statistics.
- On 26 February a member of the Abu Sayyaf Group sank a Superferry, killing 118 people and leaving many more missing. Because the reported victims and perpetrator were all from the Philippines, the attack did not constitute international terrorism.

These are not unique instances. We have also identified over 100 other attacks conducted by Foreign Terrorist Organizations that do not meet the criteria for international terrorism.

In our compilation of 2004 data, we found problems not only with the statutory definition of "international terrorism," but also with incidents occurring in Iraq and Afghanistan. Determining "noncombatant" status in such an environment is hard enough. But in such "war-like" circumstances, it was often impossible to distinguish between terrorism and insurgency; for instance, in some cases Iraqis were part of the Zarqawi network (a terrorist network) and in other cases they were Former Regime Elements (insurgency). Under the statutory definition, as noted above, attacks by Iraqis on Iraqis wouldn't meet the definition of international terrorism. But in the context of attacks against the U.S. military, we had little practical or intellectually defendable way of distinguishing between terrorism and insurgency; as such, with State's concurrence, we focused on attacks against international civilians.

Finally, we were advised by Department of State to continue to use the Community definition of "significant" as attacks that involve death, serious injury, or property damage over $10,000; that amount presents a very low bar, but it is the standard that has been used for many years.

These are just a few of the difficulties associated with counting international terrorist incidents. The Department of State and many others shared our concerns regarding the often arbitrary nature of the designations, and a consensus began to emerge on the need for a methodological change that more accurately captured the nature of the terrorist threat. I must emphasize that at no point did the Department of State attempt to pressure NCTC to lower its numbers, or indicate to us that the numbers would not be included in Patterns because they were "too high."

Looking Ahead

Under the Intelligence Reform and Terrorism Prevention Act of 2004, NCTC has been given unique responsibilities to "serve as the central and shared knowledge bank on known and suspected terrorists and international terror groups, as well as their goals, strategies, capabilities, and networks of contacts and support." As such, I believe that this is an opportune time to reexamine how terrorist incidents are reported; we do not pretend to have all the answers and, thus, will be reaching out to subject matter experts both inside and outside the government.

Given the concerns highlighted above, we have serious misgivings about the utility of the data that was released on the 27th of April. As such, we will make available, by the end of June of this year, a more comprehensive accounting of worldwide terrorism incidents. The precise nature of this accounting is still being worked, but we will undoubtedly extend reporting beyond those incidents that only involve citizens or territory of two or more countries. Depending on what precisely is counted, this could raise the global totals to several thousand incidents. Several points are worthy of note:

- First, as is hopefully self evident, this will totally invalidate any comparisons with past Patterns reports. Beyond the differing levels of effort used this past years in comparison to previous years, methodologically, we will be counting very different things.
- Second, this must be seen as a work in progress. The definition of terrorism, relative to all other forms of political violence, has never been clear-cut. We envision reaching out to experts across the Government and academia to further develop and refine a more meaningful approach.
- Third, as we have done with the data released on 27 April, we will make both the methodology and the results as transparent as possible, ideally providing an interactive search capability on the INTERNET; we are currently reviewing precisely what can be accomplished by June. And in this vein, I also want to express my deep appreciation for the efforts of the Memorial Institute for the Prevention of Terrorism in Oklahoma City (MIPT). MIPT is partnering with us to make the data as accessible as possible to the American public. The data to be released in June, like that released the end of last month, will be available at www.tkb.org.
- Finally, I would caution against the natural inclination to want to use terrorist incidents as a simple metric to judge progress in the Global War on Terrorism. While we anticipate this new approach will provide data that can be used to more accurately depict the nature of terrorism around the world, it won't necessarily translate into a simple basis for judging whether we are prevailing in the struggle against terrorism.

Mr. Chairman, I appreciate the opportunity to discuss NCTC's role in this important issue and look forward to taking your questions.

The Department of State's Annual Report on Terrorism: Testimony of Raphael F. Perl

Mr. Chairman, distinguished Members of the Subcommittee, my name is Raphael Perl. I am a senior foreign policy specialist with the Congressional Research Service of the Library of Congress. I thank you for the opportunity to be here today and to address issues relating to the Department of State's annual report to Congress on global terrorism, which is entitled this year, *Country Reports on Terrorism 2004*. In previous years this report was entitled *Patterns of Global Terrorism*, and prior to that, *Patterns of International Terrorism*. In my testimony I refer to this new report version as "*Country Reports*."

Focus of Testimony

My testimony will focus on two areas of potential concern to Congress:

1. The importance of numbers and data to sustain credibility of the report; and,
2. Options for consideration by Congress to strengthen the Department of State's reporting role in this area so vital to the security of our nation.

In discussing options, I remind the Committee that the Congressional Research Service (CRS) does not recommend any particular policy option or approach. Although I confine my discussion to selected options, CRS is prepared to address the merits and downsides of a full range of additional issues and options at the Subcommittee's behest.

This year's annual report to Congress has both a new title and a modified format. Country Reports continues to provide information on anti-terror cooperation by nations worldwide. It continues to list state sponsors of terrorism, which are subject to sanctions. However, this year statistical data on terrorist incidents are not included as an integral part of the report. They are provided and released concomitantly with the publication of Country Reports by the newly created National Counter Terrorism Center (NCTC). The NCTC will likely release more detailed statistical data later this year—perhaps as early as June 17th, the date that a new, congressionally-mandated report on terrorist sanctuaries is due.

It should be noted that this separation of the NCTC data from the Country Reports may not be very user-friendly for readers of the reports. One option would be to include the NCTC data as an appendix.

The Importance of Data

As a researcher who has served both at the Congressional Research Service and at the National Academy of Engineering, I must stress the core importance of data. Data provide the context of, and basis for, subsequent analysis. Analysis without underlying data often lacks credibility. In the academic and scientific community, analysis without reference to data —even if logical and persuasive—is viewed with skepticism.

For the purpose of maintaining credibility, an annual report to Congress on global terrorism would benefit from the availability of a significant compilation of relevant data. Although in most cases data are integrated either in the text or in an appendix of a report, at the very least data should be in some manner readily available elsewhere, in print or on the Internet, as appropriate.

Strengthening the Report

Overview

Looking at things afresh, what areas might an annual global report on terrorism address? What trends might it home in on? How might it be structured? How rigid or how loose might congressional reporting requirements be?

It has been some fifteen years since Congress mandated the first annual report on global terrorism. When the report was originally conceived as a reference document, the primary threat from terrorism was state-sponsored. But, since then, the threat has evolved, with Al Qaeda-affiliated groups and non-state sponsors of terrorism increasingly posing a major and more decentralized threat.

The terrorist threat we face today has greatly increased in complexity and danger. It has evolved to have a major economic aspect. Technology and the Internet are both major facilitators and mitigators of this threat, aiding both terrorists and those who seek to interdict them. It appears that, in today's globally interconnected world, the distinction between domestic and international is becoming increasingly blurred. And it appears that some terrorist groups may look to an expanding range of criminal activity to provide financial and logistical support for their causes.

Clearly the threat is becoming ever more global. The terrorist of the past wanted to change his country. The terrorist of today often wants to change the world. And as the gap between the haves and the have nots widens globally, increasingly the use of terror may become the "ballot box" for the dispossessed.

Many analysts suggest that terrorism today is rapidly assuming the characteristics of a global insurgency, with strong ideological and often religious motivations. More and more, the conflict is seen as a struggle for hearts and minds of the vulnerable, with the media at the center of the battlefield.

Given these important changes since the report was originally conceived, how might they best be reflected in future reports?

Structural Issues and Options

The current report begins with several short chapters: legislative requirements, an overview, a brief analysis of global jihad and a description of international antiterrorism efforts. This is followed by country reports broken down by region, and finally, by a chapter on terrorist groups.

Much of the current report corresponds to the Department of State's structure of regional bureaus, which include Africa, Europe, East Asia and Pacific, Europe and Eurasia, the Near East and North Africa, South Asia and the Western Hemisphere. However, as international terrorism and, more particularly, Islamist militancy become more decentralized, regional or country-specific presentations alone may not reflect the wider picture, and an expanded transregional focus may add value.

A report which also includes a number of supplemental categories of information about terrorism could prove useful for congressional purposes, especially if it presents facts and data, along with understandable tables and graphics.

An integral question is who should prepare and publish such data and what should they measure? The NCTC might well be tasked by Congress or its own administrators to develop meaningful data compilations on terrorism, including and going beyond those eliminated from the State Department report this year. Ideally, some flexibility should be granted in the development and publication of this data. A series of seminars and workshops to explore these possibilities, with congressional participation, might prove useful in this regard.

Analysis, including impacts—not merely reformulating the numbers—is another important element; Congress could specify subject areas of particular interest, such as terrorist involvement with weapons of mass destruction or narcotics trafficking.

Also useful would be a set of meaningful predictions, where possible based on trends, projections, survey data and intelligence inputs where available. Finally, clearly enunciated policy statements might be set forth, including goals and objectives, as well as criteria to measure progress.

The Government Accountability Office uses goals, objectives and measurement criteria in order to report on operational efficiency. These are also needed to facilitate decisions on funding and resource allocation. The Government Performance and Results Act (GPRA) has similar requirements. And the Department of State already includes such criteria in its Mission and Bureau performance plans, and might be able to develop some variation appropriate to its report.

The more specific Congress can be about requirements and structure of the report, the more pertinent and responsive the product is likely to become. To the degree that many perceive the presentation by region and country as providing a useful and informative guide to international cooperation, this format could be retained. State might then also present analysis and predictions in a manner tailored to its own functional organization, which includes Political, Economic, Consular, Administrative, Public Diplomacy and Commercial components, plus Diplomatic Security and other lateral offices, with each component providing relevant but different outlooks on the challenges and impacts of terrorism.

In addition to required information and structure, the Department of State might be encouraged to provide supplementary facts, analysis, predictions, and other relevant information in separate chapters or annexes without prejudice for future years. This flexibility could maximize the use of the Department's expertise by including such topics as the linkage of terrorism to weapons of mass destruction, terrorist narcotics activities, and other areas of interest without the possibility of creating requirements that may outlive their usefulness. Some of this has already been legislated by Congress in Public Laws 108-458 and 108-487.

The public diplomacy elements of the report are of great relevance to terrorism policies, given the amalgamation several years ago of the Department of State and the U.S. Information Agency. Since the decommissioning of the Strategic Information Initiative, State appears to have the sole departmental charter for winning hearts and minds abroad, a critical strategic component of any long-term, reality-based, and forward-looking antiterrorism strategy.

Arguably, the report is an appropriate vehicle for describing, among other results, the trends in public opinion polls abroad concerning aspects of terrorism or Islamist militancy, when available or significant. The report might discuss current public diplomacy initiatives which attempt to mitigate support for terrorism and how successful they have been.

The report's usefulness to Congress would likely be enhanced by inclusion of classified appendices to inform Congress about sensitive issues and analysis. Often countries do not want it made public that they go out of their way to assist the United States in certain sensitive anti-terrorist operations. And often it may not be productive to strongly criticize countries in a public document if the feeling is that they can be won over. Yet, clearly this is information of interest and importance to Congress.

After the structure of the report is generally determined, the baseline content could also be defined. Further options concerning content and subject matter are discussed below.

Report Content

Regardless of whether information is presented in country reports or in separate chapters (or both), the report might include, at a minimum, information of potential interest to Congress such as the following, some of which is already present:

- *Levels of state cooperation* (or lack thereof) in antiterrorism efforts. Which states support or incite terror? Which states countenance or allow terror? Which states stand firmly opposed to it? Which countries are cooperative, but vulnerable? Which are exemplary?
- *Responsiveness of international organizations* to antiterrorism programs, going beyond the United Nations to encompass regional organizations and others, such as Interpol and the Financial Action Task Force (FATF).
- *Profiles and data on major terrorist groups,* as well as on emerging groups, including activities, capabilities and attributed significant incidents.
- *Trends,* including all reported incidents of major significance, categorized by location, target and method of attack, with emphasis on incidents affecting U.S. interests. Data on fund-raising and recruiting trends would likely be of interest to Congress as well.
- *Attitudes/factors contributing to terrorism* and its support.

- *Economic consequences of terrorism.*
- *Special Topics*: some options might include:
    —Terrorism and weapons of mass destruction.
    —Links to narcotics and organized crime.
    —Fund-raising and money laundering.
    —Economic impact of specific major attacks.
    —Impact of technology, including the internet, on terror and counter-terror.
- *Proposed action agenda*; goals and objectives for the year ahead.

Conclusion

In combating terrorism, we are engaged in an ongoing campaign, not a war in the traditional sense. Both Congress and the Administration are heavily committed to this open-ended effort. Communicating the best information available as clearly as possible to the Congress will benefit the United States in this campaign.

As in the past, a major component of any meaningful annual report to Congress on international terrorism will likely focus on the successes and failures of diplomacy and the levels of cooperation provided by states in the global campaign against terror. A well-structured, comprehensive report could include supporting information, profiles on major and emerging terrorist groups, discussion of major developments or trends in terrorist activity—especially those directed against U.S. personnel or interests—and evaluation of the impact of terrorism on individual nations and the global economy.

The report would likely continue to include a potentially changing array of special topics, supplemented by presentation of a policy-driven action agenda with both short-term and long-term goals and objectives, in which the "war of ideas" plays a significant role. Such a report could serve congressional needs by providing an important reference tool and policy instrument in support of the nation's global campaign against terror. Providing the Department of State with flexibility while mandating a periodic review of both structure and content could help ensure its ongoing effectiveness.

Mr. Chairman, this concludes my formal testimony. I would be honored to answer any questions the Subcommittee might have.

Thank you.

Terrorism: Why the Numbers Matter—Testimony of Larry C. Johnson

In the wake of the attacks on September 11, 2001, fighting terrorism has become a growth business in the United States. We are spending money like wild fire to harden airports, equip first responders, deploy explosive detection equipment, and beef up border patrols. I understand how in the immediate aftermath of the September 11th attacks there was enormous political pressure to do something. As a result Federal and State governments are spending a lot of money to deter and prevent this threat.

While we assume that the threat of terrorism is very grave, little attention has been paid to trying to assess the actual threat. If we are going to spend a lot of money to detect and deter a particular threat it stands to reason we should have some method of identifying and monitoring the persons and groups who threaten us. I believe we have an obligation to the taxpayers to somehow measure the effectiveness of our nation's efforts to combat the threat of terrorism. Yet some have argued that we cannot use statistics to help gauge the actual threat. If we accept that argument then what standards or methods should we use to determine if a threat exists? Feelings? Mind reading? I am not trying to be flippant. But surely we should be able to have an objective, empirical discussion about terrorism because ultimately it is an activity carried out by flesh and blood human beings.

Although a terrorist act can have a psychological effect on a population, it is more than a state of mind—it is a tangible, organized physical activity. It is a pre-meditated act. And when I say "pre-meditated" I am referring to a host of activities ranging from the recruitment of personnel, training, intelligence collection, acquisition of explosives, and the provision of such mundane things as food and a place to sleep. People who want to engage in terrorist operations need a place to train. It does not require a large base with elaborate barracks and shooting houses. It can be done on the cheap. But it does require one or more physical locations where prospective murderers can plan and prepare.

I take the threat of terrorism seriously. I believe that Americans, regardless of political affiliation, take the threat seriously. We recognize that there are people in the world who, if given the opportunity, would like to kill large number of Americans. Fortunately for us, desire does not equal capability.

If we are going to confront this threat intelligently we must be serious about measuring and monitoring the activity. We must also be willing to take an honest, objective look at the facts and put terrorism in its proper perspective. We ought to acknowledge that terrorism, thankfully, is a relatively infrequent activity and that the number of lives lost at the hands of terrorists over the past 30 years are relatively few compared to the thousands who die from drug abuse, or cancer or automobile accidents in any given year. Nonetheless, terrorism has the potential to cause great harm and should not be ignored or trivialized.

We are here today in part because the State Department, in a break with previous policy, has claimed that the numbers on terrorism do not matter. When I learned in mid-April that the Department was planning to quietly submit the legally required report to Congress without including the 2004 terrorism statistics I was shocked. (I decided to publish this development on the Counter Terrorism Blog—counterterror.typepad.com.) I was told by friends in the intelligence community that the Seventh Floor at State (this is a State Department euphemism for the Secretary of State and her staff) was alarmed by the data, which showed a dramatic increase in significant terrorist attacks and fatalities. Rather than explain the meaning of these numbers to the Congress and the American people, the Seventh Floor wanted to shift the burden of explanation to the National Counter Terrorism Center. It was only after a minor media and Congressional firestorm that the State Department decided to release the report in tandem with the statistical data from the National Counter Terrorism Center.

I was amazed by the audacity of Phil Zelikow and John Brennan at the State Department press conference on April 28th, who insisted that the numbers did not matter and could tell us little about the progress of our national policy in dealing with terrorism. At a minimum this is intellectually dishonest. If we are to be successful in finding and defeating those groups and individuals who want to employ terrorism against us we must have the courage to call a spade a spade. I hope we have not entered a world created by Lewis Carroll, where up is down and bigger is smaller. If we refuse to accept objective facts about terrorist activity then I do not know how we can keep track of what is happening around the world.

Last year's facts on terrorism are disturbing because they point to a trend of increased lethality by Islamic extremist groups. The 651 attacks marks the highest number of significant incidents of terrorism the intelligence community has recorded since 1968. (An incident is counted as significant if an attack results in death, injury or kidnapping of one or more persons, or property damage is in excess of $10,000). This surpasses the previous high of 273 significant attacks in 1985. It also was the second highest death toll from terrorist attacks. The 1,907 people who died in international terrorist attacks last year marks the second highest death toll in 36 years, with 2001 still holding that horrific record.

Why are the numbers important? For starters the raw data on terrorist incidents tells us who is getting killed, where they are being killed, and who are the likely culprits. That information should help our policymakers set priorities for employing our diplomatic, intelligence, law enforcement, and military resources in going after groups who have killed or are planning to kill Americans.

Beyond helping establishing priorities, the numbers also flag trouble spots that require intense focus. Take last year, for example. The numbers show that most of the attacks and fatalities occurred in Iraq, India, and Russia. If we are going to confront the threat of terrorism effectively our efforts ought to concentrate on these areas. The terrorist attacks in these three countries share a common tie—the attacks were carried out by groups with links to international Islamic jihadists.

Let us take a closer look at the threat in India's Kashmir region. Some of the groups carrying out those terrorist attacks —the Lashkar Tayiba and Harakat ul-Ansar—have received direct support, including financing and training, from senior Pakistani intelligence officers. It is worth recalling that the cruise missiles fired by President Clinton in August of 1998 in retaliation for the Al Qaeda bombing of the US Embassies in Kenya and Tanzania struck a camp in Afghanistan and killed members of Harakat as well as two Pakistani intelligence officers. In the war against Islamic extremists Kashmir matters.

Pakistan poses a delicate policy dilemma. On the one hand it has been an important ally in the war against Al Qaeda. Pakistan has helped apprehend and turn over to US authorities terrorists such as Khalid Sheik Mohammed, Ramsi Yousef, and Mir Aimal Kansi. On the other hand there are Pakistani officials who are financing and training groups responsible for international terrorist attacks. The statistics on terrorist activity in Kashmir tell us a very uncomfortable story—our ally in the war on terrorism is also a sponsor of terrorism.

The terrorism statistics can create some uncomfortable policy dilemmas. I am not suggesting that they should take precedence over all other considerations. During my time at State Department, for example, there was a behind the scenes debate about whether or not to put Greece as well as Pakistan on the list of State Sponsors of Terrorism. If we had relied solely on the terrorism data then both countries should have been put on the list. But State Department also looked at other issues. This is the grey area where intelligence data and policy considerations collide. In retrospect I do not think previous versions of Patterns of Global Terrorism went far enough in putting both Greece and Pakistan on notice that their support for terrorism was unacceptable behavior. Frankly if the data concerning their role in supporting groups responsible for terrorist attacks had been more fully disclosed it might have generated enough pressure to persuade them to back off of that support.

What Should We Do about the Numbers?

I have no beef with NCTC taking over the job from CTC of compiling the statistics on terrorism. I also welcome the news that 10 analysts are now focused on this task. If that leads to better, more comprehensive data on terrorist activities it will provide an important resource to finding and rooting out those groups who threaten us. However, we still do not have a good explanation of why the CIA's CTC was able to do a credible job of tracking terrorist activity but TTIC could not. Why did TTIC only assign three part time workers to the task of monitoring and counting terrorist incidents? What is NCTC, the TTIC successor, doing differently?

I think it is a big mistake to separate the statistics from the policy analysis in the Annual Report. I believe that State Department should continue to be responsible for issuing an annual report on terrorism that includes the statistical data. This is not a fight over turf, nor am I trying to protect a status quo. The State Department role in producing the Patterns of Global Terrorism, at least until this year, was pretty straightforward. S/CT was never in charge of collecting or compiling the statistics. That task was carried out by CTC (and later TTIC) with the help of INR. In the future I would hope that NCTC and INR analysts would again meet on a regular basis to make the decision about what should be classified as an incident of international terrorism. The analysts in NCTC and INR should continue to draft the narrative of the report. For its part S/CT should continue to do the policy overview and the policy summaries at the start of each regional section. The Office of the Coordinator for Counter Terrorism should retain the job of editing and producing the final report. The key to this process is a joint, closely coordinated effort with the NCTC and INR.

There is a need for better information in the report. Summary statistics, such as total attacks or total fatalities, are of little use in helping further our understanding of what is going on in the world of international terrorism. NCTC needs to provide more "micro" data. By "micro" I mean specifically identifying which groups are responsible (or believed to be responsible) for terrorist attacks that produce fatalities. If you consult the previous editions of Patterns of Global Terrorism, for example, you would be hard pressed to answer the question: How many attacks has Hezbollah carried out? How many fatalities did Hezbollah attacks cause?

One piece of analysis sorely lacking in previous editions of Patterns concerns identifying emerging trends in terrorist attacks. Last year, for example, I created charts using the data I summarized from incidents listed in Appendix A of previous editions of Patterns of Global Terrorism that showed a dramatic, steady rise in the number of significant attacks, even though the total number of attacks was declining. When I looked more closely at the data I realized that in 2003, for example, over 95% of the casualties were caused by attacks by Islamic extremists in just 10 countries. The annual report to Congress needs more precise data and more thoughtful analysis.

The definition of "international terrorism" needs to be reconsidered. From an analytical standpoint I think it would be useful for NCTC to keep track of all violence, not just terrorism, as a means of establishing a benchmark. I do not think we have sufficient data today to indicate whether or not there is a direct correlation between violence and terrorism. From an analytical standpoint it is important to differentiate between groups like Colombia's FARC, who rarely targets US and European citizens, from a group like Islamic Jihad that takes pride in encouraging such attacks.

NCTC's methodology should been expanded to include under the umbrella of international terrorism those groups that receive assistance of any kind from outside their national territory. This would allow us to capture the terrorist attacks carried out over the last several years by the Chechens. While it is true that most Chechen attacks have killed Russians in Russia there is overwhelming evidence that they are closely aligned with Al Qaeda. In March 2002, for instance, Chechen fighters killed US soldiers in the mountains of Afghanistan.

The State Department and NCTC should also follow up on the recommendation by the State Department's Inspector General that some statistics be made available on a quarterly basis. I fail to see how having more information about terrorist events is harmful or counterproductive.

I believe that part of the reason the statistics became an issue again this year is because of the failure to keep the position of the Coordinator for Counter Terrorism filled with a competent Presidential appointee. That slot has been vacant now for almost six months. While the conventional wisdom is that State Department's role in combating terrorism consists of sending stern diplomatic notes to terrorists, it is an unfair and inaccurate perception. State Department's role as the lead for coordinating international terrorism emerged in the mid-1980s in the wake of devastating attacks in Lebanon. A National Security Decision Directive signed by President Reagan in early 1986 gave State the responsibility of coordinating international terrorism policy. This was in response to an interagency fight that broke out during an effort to apprehend the terrorists responsible for the hijacking of the Achille Lauro cruise ship. While flying over Italy in late 1985 in pursuit of Abu Abbas, a State Department official and a CIA officer argued heatedly over who was in charge of the mission. Recognizing the need for a clear chain of command the Department of State was put in charge of coordinating the efforts of CIA, DOD, and FBI efforts to track and deal with terrorism. The first man put in charge of this effort was L. Paul (Jerry) Bremer.

The Coordinator for Counter Terrorism at State Department (S/CT) plays a variety of roles, including facilitating the travel of military special operations personnel into countries where terrorists are operating or are receiving safehaven. S/CT also has played a direct role in helping FBI and other law enforcement personnel move into countries to apprehend terrorists or provide assistance to local forces, who in turn root out and capture terrorist suspects. And, within Foggy Bottom, S/CT pokes a finger in the eye of the regional bureaus. While the incentive of the desk officer for a country like Pakistan, for example, is to be accommodating of Pakistani concerns, a bureau like S/CT is there to bring up the uncomfortable facts about Pakistan's support for terrorist activities. Not having a Coordinator for Counter Terrorism is inexcusable and unfortunately says a lot about the true importance assigned to that function.

At the end of the day we need more and better coordination between the intel community and the policy community not less. While there have been problems with Patterns of Global Terrorism in the past, the basic process of the coordination of the two elements was sound. I am struck by the irony that the staff director of the 9-11 Commission that correctly criticized the stove piping of information and the lack of coordination, was a key decision maker in taking collaborative process and splitting it into separate components that will make cooperation and coordination more difficult. I encourage this Committee to take the appropriate steps to require these two important agencies—State and NCTC—to work closely together on one report on terrorism.

CRS Report for Congress

The National Counterterrorism Center: Implementation Challenges and Issues for Congress

Todd M. Masse
Specialist in Domestic Intelligence and
Counterterrorism Domestic Social Policy Division

Summary

In July 2004, the National Commission On Terrorist Attacks Upon the United States recommended the establishment of a National Counterterrorism Center (NCTC) to serve as a center for "... joint operational planning *and* joint intelligence, staffed by personnel from the various agencies. . . ." On August 27, 2004, President George W. Bush signed Executive Order (EO) 13354, *National Counterterrorism Center,* which established the National Counterterrorism Center and stipulated roles for the NCTC and its leadership and reporting relationships between NCTC leadership and NCTC member agencies, as well as with the White House. In December 2004, Congress passed the Intelligence Reform and Terrorism Prevention Act of 2004, P.L. 108-458. Like the preceding executive order, among many other reform initiatives, the act prescribes roles and responsibilities for the NCTC and its leadership.

The purpose of this report is to outline the commonalities and potential differences between EO 13354 and P.L. 108-458, as these conceptual differences could be meaningful in the implementation process of P.L. 108-458 and/or should the issue of intelligence reform be re-visited by the 109th Congress. The report examines some aspects of the law related to the NCTC, including the relationship between the NCTC's Director and the Director of National Intelligence (DNI), which may have implications related to policy and implementation of an effective and efficient nationally coordinated counterterrorism function. Moreover, the report examines several issues that may be of interest to Congress as the NCTC matures and evolves, including potential civil liberties implications of collocating operational elements of the traditional foreign intelligence and domestic intelligence entities of the U.S. Intelligence Community. While the appointment and confirmation of a DNI may resolve some of the uncertainty regarding the NCTC, the NCTC is only one of a myriad of complex issues that will be competing for the time and attention of the recently nominated DNI.

An issue for Congress is whether to let the existing intelligence reform law speak for itself (and let certain ambiguities be resolved during implementation), or to intervene to address apparent ambiguities through amendments to the law now. Alternatively, the executive branch may choose to intervene to clarify apparent ambiguities within P.L. 108-458, or between EO 13354 and P.L. 108-458. In any event, congressional oversight of the status quo and implementation of the present law could prove useful.

This product will be updated as necessary.

Introduction

Currently there are two legal mechanisms governing the establishment of the National Counterterrorism Center (NCTC).[1] The NCTC was initially established by Executive Order 13354, signed by President George W. Bush on August 27, 2004. Section 3 of EO 13354 outlined the functions of the NCTC which included, among others, (1) serving as the primary organization within the U.S. government for analyzing and integrating all intelligence possessed by the U.S. government pertaining to terrorism and counterterrorism, (2) conducting strategic operational planning for counterterrorism activities, (3) assigning operational responsibilities to lead agencies for counterterrorism activities, and (4) serving as a shared knowledge bank on known and suspected terrorists and international terror groups. Less than two months later, the Intelligence Reform and Terrorism Prevention Act of 2004 (hereinafter the act) became P.L. 108-458. Section 1021 of the act amends the National Security Act of 1947, as amended (50 U.S.C. 402 et. seq.) to establish within the Office of the Director of National Intelligence, a National Counterterrorism Center. The primary NCTC missions outlined in the act are largely consistent with those stipulated in EO 13354. However, there are some differences between these two legal mechanisms that may be worthy of congressional consideration. Moreover, within Section 1021 of the act itself there are some provisions that may prove problematic if efficient and effective implementation of a nationally coordinated counterterrorism function is to take place in a timely manner.

---

1 For an analysis of the debate and rationale for the establishment of the NCTC, see CRS Report RL32558, *The 9/11 Commission and a National Counterterrorism Center: Issues and Options for Congress.*

Executive Orders and Statutes[2]

The President's constitutional authority to issue executive orders (EO) related to national security is derived from Article II, Section 2, Clause 1 of the U.S. Constitution, which identifies, among other powers, that the President serves as the "... Commander in Chief of the Army and Navy of the United States...."[3] In general, the President can also issue executive orders based on congressionally delegated statutory authority. The preamble to EO 13354 titled, *National Counterterrorism Center,* states that the President's authority to issue the executive order flows from the "... authority invested in (the) President as by the Constitution and laws on the United States of America, including section 103(c)(8) of the National Security Act of 1947 (as amended)...."[4] At the time the executive order was issued this section of the National Security Act stipulated that the Director of Central Intelligence (DCI), acting as head of the IC shall "... perform such other functions as the President or the National Security Council may direct."[5]

One of the issues for the 109th Congress with respect to the implementation of the functions outlined for the NCTC, or the role and responsibilities of its Director, is the extent to which the executive order and Intelligence Reform and Terrorism Prevention Act of 2004 (hereinafter Act) are consistent, or at least not contradictory. In general, executive orders are interpreted as having the force of law, unless they contravene existing law.[6] Given that the NCTC, its roles and responsibilities, and those of its Director, have been established in both an executive order and in statute, it is reasonable for one to conclude that any differences or inconsistencies would be resolved in favor of the statutory language. While this is true generally, given that the intelligence reform legislation passed in the 108th Congress is open to interpretation in some areas,[7] the basis for this interpretation could be either the legislative history of P.L. 108-458 or EO 13354. As a result, legislative oversight and potential amendments to the act in the 109th Congress are possible. As a means of understanding the varying conceptual underpinnings for the NCTC, its Director, and how its Director relates to the established Director of National Intelligence, it may be useful to outline the areas of commonality and difference between these two legal authorities.

Genesis of the NCTC

In the aftermath of the terrorist attacks of September 11, 2001, two authoritative reports concluded that the lack of adequate and timely coordination and communication within the Intelligence Community (IC) was one factor contributing to the inability of the IC to detect and prevent the terrorist attacks. The *Joint Inquiry Into Intelligence Community Activities Before and After the Terrorist Attacks of September 11, 2001* (hereinafter Joint Inquiry) concluded, in part, that

> Within the Intelligence Community, agencies did not adequately share relevant counterterrorism information, prior to September 11. This breakdown in communications was the result of a number of factors, including differences in agencies' missions, legal authorities and cultures. Information was not sufficiently shared, not

---

2 This report is not intended to provide an authoritative legal interpretation of the relationship between executive orders and statutes. Others have done that elsewhere. See CRS Report RS20846, *Executive Orders: Issuance and Revocations,* by T.J. Halstead. See also Phillip J. Cooper, *By Order of the President: The Use and Abuse of Executive Direct Action,* Lawrence, Kansas: University Press of Kansas, 2002. The case of *Youngstown Sheet and Tube* v. *Sawyer,* is often cited as offering an appropriate framework for determining the constitutionality of an executive order. In this case, the Supreme Court ruled that an executive order issued by President Truman in 1952, directing the Secretary of Commerce to seize U.S. steel mills and continue their operation in order to avert a strike, was unconstitutional. As one of five concurring opinions, Justice Black developed a three-pronged test against which to weigh the presidential power to issue executive orders. The first leg of the triad concludes that the presidential power to issue an authoritative executive order was at its maximum when "... the president acts pursuant to an express or implied authorization of Congress." The second leg of the triad stipulates that presidential authority to issue authoritative executive orders is in "... a zone of twilight in which he and Congress may have concurrent authority, or in which its distribution is uncertain...." In this area, presidential power is "... likely to depend on the imperatives of events and contemporary imponderables rather than on abstract theories of law...." The third leg of the triad concludes that the president's power is at its "lowest ebb" when the president "... takes measures incompatible with the expressed implied will of Congress... for then he can rely only upon his own constitutional powers minus any constitutional powers of the Congress over the matter...." Arguably, the President's decision to issue EO 13354 lies somewhere between the first and second leg of Justice Black's test. The majority and minority opinions may be found at *Youngstown Sheet and Tube v. Sawyer* 343 U.S. 579, 72 S. Ct. 863, 96 L. Ed. 1152 (1952).

3 Presidential authority to issue executive orders can also be derived from the vesting of executive power of the U.S. government in the President in Article II, Section 1, clause 1, and from Article II, Section 3 which states that the President shall take care that the laws "... be faithfully executed...."

4 Executive Order 13354, "National Counterterrorism Center," 69 *Federal Register* 53589, Sept. 1, 2004.

5 As amended by the Intelligence Reform and Terrorism Prevention Act of 2004, Section 1011(a), the prior Sections 102 through 104 of the National Security Act were replaced with (new) Sections 102 through 104. Under new Section 102A(f)(7) of the National Security Act, the newly created Director of National Intelligence is directed, in part, to "perform such other functions as the President may direct." Section 1012 of P.L. 108-458 established the NCTC in the Office of the Director of National Intelligence and sets out its duties and responsibilities.

6 See Bradley H. Patterson, Jr., *The White House Staff: Inside the West Wing and Beyond* (Washington, DC: Brookings Institution Press, 2000).

7 See Walter Pincus, "National Intelligence Director Proves to be Difficult to Post to Fill," Washington Post, Jan. 31, 2005, p. A4.

only between Intelligence Community agencies, but also within agencies, and between the intelligence and law enforcement agencies.[8]

While the Joint Inquiry did not recommend the creation of a National Counterterrorism Center *per se,* it did recommend the following measures, which are largely consistent, in a conceptual sense, with the creation of the NCTC: (1) the development, within the Department of Homeland Security (DHS), of an "all-source terrorism information fusion center," and (2) congressional consideration of legislation, modeled on the Goldwater-Nichols Act of 1986 (P.L. 99-433), to "... instill the concept of "jointness" throughout the intelligence community." With respect to the all-source terrorism information fusion center, the Homeland Security Act of 2002 (P.L.107-296) created within DHS an Information Analysis and Infrastructure Protection (IAIP) Directorate which has, among other functions, legal responsibility for the fusion of federal, state and local intelligence information to "identify and assess the nature and scope of terrorist threats to the homeland."[9] Subsequently, in his State of the Union Address on January 28, 2003, President George W. Bush announced the creation of a new organization, the Terrorist Threat Integration Center (TTIC) designed to "... merge and analyze all threat information in a single location." While the IAIP continues to exist within DHS, TTIC and its fusion functions have been absorbed into the newly-created NCTC Directorate of Intelligence.[10]

Like the Joint Inquiry, the National Commission on Terrorist Attacks Upon the United States (hereinafter The Commission) also found, among other factors,[11] that the lack of information sharing and coordination within the IC led to numerous missed operational opportunities[12] to detect and prevent the attacks. However, it also expounded on the virtues of "jointness" with respect to operational planning, unification of effort, and analysis. Seeking "unity of effort across the foreign domestic divide" and deliberate avoidance of the proliferation of intelligence "fusion" centers, one of the Commission's central recommendations was the creation of an NCTC which would have responsibilities for both joint counterterrorism operational planning, and joint intelligence analysis.[13] The central tenets of this recommendation were incorporated into both EO 13354 and P.L. 108-458, albeit in somewhat different forms.

Commonalities Between EO 13354 Approach and P.L. 108-458[14]

There is a high degree of consistency between section three of EO 13354 "Functions of the Center," and the "Primary Missions" provisions of P.L. 108-458.[15] Under each of these legal mechanisms, the NCTC is to (1) be the primary organization for analysis and integration for "... all intelligence possessed or acquired by the United States Government pertaining to terrorism and counterterrorism..."[16] (2) conduct strategic operational planning for counterterrorism activities, "integrating all instruments of national power, including diplomatic, financial, military, intelligence, homeland security, and law enforcement activities..." within and among agencies; (3) assign operational responsibilities to lead departments or agencies, as appropriate, with the limitation that the Center "... shall not direct the execution" of operations; (4) serve as a "shared knowledge bank on known and suspected terrorists and international terror groups, as well as their goals, strategies, capabilities, and networks of contact and support;" and

---

8 See U.S. Congress, Senate Select Committee on Intelligence, and the U.S. House Permanent Select Committee on Intelligence, *Joint Inquiry Into Intelligence Community Activities Before and After the Terrorist Attacks of September 11, 2001,* 107th Cong., 2nd sess., S.Rept. 107-351, H.Rept. 107-792, p. xvii, Dec. 2002.

9 See Title 6 U.S.C. §121.

10 See Section 119 (I) of the National Security Act of 1947, 50 U.S.C. §402 (I), as amended by P.L. 108-458 §1021.

11 The Commission outlined what it considered four broad areas of failure—including (1) imagination, (2) policy, (3) capabilities, and (4) management. See *The Final Report of the National Commission on Terrorist Attacks Upon the United States,* chapter 11, pp. 339–360.

12 See *The Final Report of the National Commission on Terrorist Attacks Upon the United States,* July 22, 2004, pp. 355–356.

13 As recommended by the Commission, the joint intelligence element of the NCTC would be "built on the foundation of the existing Terrorist Threat Integration Center...." This has occurred, as the TTIC has been incorporated into the NCTC's Directorate of Intelligence. The NCTC currently has over 300 personnel on board—either as employees or assignees from over ten different federal agencies, and continues to hire additional staff. See Faye Bowers, "U.S. Intelligent Agencies Make Headway on Reform," *Christian Science Monitor,* May 14, 2005, p. 2.

14 Quotes in this section of the report illustrate identical language in the executive order and the act. The NCTC continues to function under EO 13354 until the DNI is confirmed.

15 See new section 119(d) of the National Security Act of 1947, as amended by P.L. 108-458, Section 1021.

16 Both EO 13354 and PL 108-458 exclude intelligence pertaining exclusively or purely to domestic terrorists and domestic counterterrorism from the NCTC's analytical responsibility. See EO 13354 Section 3(a) and new Section 119(d)(1) of the National Security Act of 1947, as amended by Section 1021 of P.L. 108-458. However, the act allows the NCTC to receive, retain, and disseminate domestic counterterrorism intelligence to fulfill its responsibilities. See Section 119A(e) of the National Security Act of 1947, as amended by Section 1021 of P.L. 108-458. This exclusion is generally interpreted to mean that the NCTC will not be responsible for comprehensive threat analysis concerning terrorist groups based largely in the United States and engaging in politically motivated violence within the United States. For example, domestic terrorist groups, such as the Earth Liberation Front or the Animal Liberation Front, do not generally take direction from any foreign group. See "The Threat of Eco-Terrorism," testimony of James F. Jarboe, Domestic Terrorism Section, Counterterrorism Division, FBI, Before the House Resources Committee, Subcommittee on Forests, and Forest Health, Feb. 12, 2002.

(5) ensure that agencies "... have access to and receive" all-source intelligence "needed to execute their counterterrorism plans, or perform independent, alternative analysis."

Potential Inconsistencies Between EO 13354 Approach and P.L. 108-458

It is clear that at least with respect to the baseline functions of the NCTC, there is general agreement between the executive and legislative branches of government. However, as it pertains to the roles and responsibilities of the Director of the NCTC, who has yet to be named, and reporting relationships for the Director of the NCTC to the DNI and to the President, there is less agreement between these two legal mechanisms. The executive order specifies how the President prefers to implement the functions of the NCTC. However, the act altered some of the processes and structures underlying the executive order. While the explicit Act will take precedence legally, ambiguities in implementation may cause confusion, which could undermine the intent of integrating the counterterrorism function nationally.

There are at least two areas in which there are inconsistencies between the executive order and the act: (1) the appointment of the Director of the NCTC, and (2) the roles and responsibilities of the Director of the NCTC, including the reporting relationships associated with this position. **Appendix 1** outlines some of the potential inconsistencies or factors which may complicate effective implementation of the NCTC's mission between the executive order and the act, and within the act itself, which may be of congressional interest. To the extent that there are inconsistencies or contradictions between these two legal mechanisms specific provisions of the act would take precedence over the executive order.

NCTC Director Appointment.

First, with respect to the appointment of the Director of the NCTC, the executive order stipulates that this individual will be appointed by the DCI with the approval of the President. As a result of P.L. 108-458, however, the position of DCI, as envisioned in the National Security Act of 1947, as amended, no longer exists.[17] Under the act, the Director of the NCTC is appointed by the President with the advice and consent of the Senate. Although the NCTC now has an acting director, former head of the TTIC, John O. Brennan, it is not known at this time whether he will be asked by the President to assume the statutorily defined role of Director of the NCTC. It is possible that the nomination of the Director of the NCTC may not occur unless and until the U.S. Senate confirms Ambassador John Negroponte, the President's nominee for DNI.

NCTC Director Reporting Relationships

Second, a possibly more stark contradiction exists between the executive order and the act with respect to the reporting relationships for the Director of the NCTC. Under the executive order, the reporting chain of command for the Director of the NCTC would have the individual reporting directly to the DCI who, in turn, would report to the President. Even if one changed the language in the executive order—replacing DCI with DNI—a substantial difference between the executive order and the act in the reporting relationships of the Director of the NCTC would remain. Under the executive order, the DCI would have "... authority, direction, and control over the Center and the Director of the Center." In contrast, the act has the Director of the NCTC's reporting responsibilities bifurcated. According to P.L. 108-458, the Director of the NCTC reports to the DNI with respect to (1) budget and programs of the NCTC, (2) activities of the NCTC's Directorate of Intelligence, and (3) the conduct of intelligence operations implemented by other elements of the IC. However, according to the act, the Director of the NCTC also reports directly to the President with respect to the "... (other than intelligence operations)."

Issues for Congress

The differences between the executive order and Act are summarized here only to highlight alternative perspectives with regard to the NCTC. Should Congress consider amending P.L. 108-458, it may want to examine elements within the act that may contribute to a lack of clarity within the NCTC and the broader IC. While clarity can be a byproduct of experience, specific guidance may prove useful in facilitating the more rapid development of effective and efficient operations.

There are at least two areas within Section 1021 of P.L. 108-458 that may be worthy of additional congressional scrutiny. The first concerns the bifurcated reporting relationships the act outlines for the Director of the NCTC. Through this mechanism the Director of the NCTC reports directly to President with regard to "the planning and progress of joint counterterrorism operations (other than intelligence operations)." This language could be construed to mean that under the act the Director of the NCTC will be reporting to the President on the planning and progress of joint military counterterrorism operations, a role traditionally reserved to components of the Department of Defense (DOD). As noted earlier, the Director of the NCTC also reports to the DNI with respect to (1) the budget and programs of the NCTC; (2) the activities of the NCTC's Directorate of Intelligence; and (3) the conduct of intelligence operations implemented by other elements of the IC. The act, then, differentiates

---

17 Sections 102–104 of the National Security Act of 1947 were deleted and replaced with new language regarding the new position of DNI. Unlike the former DCI who held simultaneously the positions of DCI and the Director of the Central Intelligence Agency, the DNI is prohibited from concurrently serving as the Director of the CIA, or any other element of the IC. (See P.L. 108-458, Title I, §102).

Appendix 1 Functional Comparison EO 13354 and P.L. 108-458

Issue	Executive Order 13354	P.L. 108-458	Consistency	Implications
NCTC Functions	(1) Analysis and integration of intelligence; (2) coordination of strategic operational planning; (3) assigning operational responsibilities to agencies; (4) serving as a shared knowledge bank; and (5) ensuring agencies have appropriate access to intelligence.	Identical language	Consistent	Experience in implementation of this core mission may have important policy implications. For example, as the NCTC is an Intelligence Community entity staffed largely with detailees, it has the burden of proving that it will put the Community's interests above those arguably more parochial interests of its constituent member agencies. The burden of this responsibility may lie mostly with NCTC leadership, as well as with the Director of National Intelligence. In short, the NCTC may need to protect its "jointness."
Limitations	Does not execute operations	Identical language	Consistent	N/A
Appointment of Director, NCTC	DCI appoints with approval of President	Appointed by President with advice and consent of Senate	Inconsistent	P.L. 108-458 supercedes. Within the act, does the fact that the Director, NCTC is a Senate approved presidential nominee make the Director, NCTC more of a principal policy aide than expert staff?
Duties and Responsibilities Director, NCTC	(1) Access information necessary for NCTC function; (2) correlate, analyze, evaluate, integrate and produce reports on terrorism information; (3) disseminate terrorist information to the President, Vice President in the performance of executive functions; (4) support DoJ and DHS in dissemination mission; (5) establish information systems and architecture; (6) assist DCI in establishing and prioritizing intelligence collection requirements relating to CT; and (7) identify specific CT planning efforts.	Identical with the exception of establishing information systems. In addition to the duties outlined in the EO, the act also includes the following provisions: (1) Serve as principal intelligence adviser to the DNI on intelligence operations relating to CT; (2) provide strategic operational plans for civilian and military CT efforts; (3) advise DNI on extent to which NCTC budget meets presidential [sic]	Some inconsistencies	Does the direct reporting role of the NCTC Director to the President for intelligence operations relating to counterterrorism matters potentially undermine the authority of the DNI?
Operations and Legal Authorities	Specifies that "…each agency representative to the Center…shall operate under the authorities of the representative's agency."	None	Possibly inconsistent	Collocation is not necessarily integration. However, could potential and unintentional mission creep and operational zeal lead to situations in which rules designed to guide traditional foreign intelligence collection may be applied to U.S. persons?
Reporting Relationships Director, NCTC	Director, NCTC reports to DCI.	Director, NCTC reports directly to President for "planning and progress of joint CT operations (other than intelligence operations)." Reports to DNI on all other matters.	Inconsistent	Does the direct report role of the Director, NCTC undermine the authority of the DNI?

between joint counterterrorism "intelligence operations" and other (presumably military) counterterrorism operations. This bifurcated structure was intentionally designed to reflect what the Commission and the Congress believed should be the dual missions of the NCTC. Its first mission is to integrate and analyze all counterterrorism intelligence available to U.S. government departments and agencies and to serve as a knowledge bank on known and suspected terrorist and international terrorist groups. Given that this function is directly germane and limited to intelligence-related activities, the act stipulates that the Directorate of Intelligence report to the DNI. It is the second function—strategic counterterrorism operational planning—that gave rise to the unique reporting structure that has the Director of the NCTC reporting directly to the President for planning and progress of joint counterterrorism operations. According to Senator Joseph I. Lieberman, a cosponsor of the act and the ranking member of the then named Senate Governmental Affairs Committee, the strategic operational planning function is an "... an Executive branch wide planning—which is beyond the DNI's jurisdiction."[18]

While such reporting mechanisms and processes may be necessary to achieve "jointness," it is not implausible to foresee potential conflicts between the DNI and the Director of the NCTC concerning who is the President's primary advisor with respect to joint counterterrorism operational initiatives. Is the role of the DNI as "... principal adviser to the President, to the National Security Council, and the Homeland Security Council for intelligence matters relating to national security ..."[19] undermined by establishing a separate reporting channel to the President for certain counterterrorism operations? Moreover, given that the Director of the NCTC is a confirmed Presidential appointee, a question could be raised as to whether the individual will serve more of a policy advisory role to implement the Administration's agenda, or will serve as an unbiased professional civil servant.[20] Some believe, however, that the NCTC Director will have greater analytical independence and objectivity because the incumbent will be confirmed by the Senate.[21]

A second issue which may be of interest to appropriate congressional oversight committees is the collocation of what has traditionally been foreign and domestic intelligence operators. In general, national security professionals look favorably upon the concept of "jointness,"[22] at least in part as a result of the positive results yielded from the Goldwater-Nichols Department of Defense Reorganization Act of 1986. This favorable predisposition generally extends to the intelligence arena, especially with respect to joint intelligence analysis projects. Alternative analysis, "red teaming," and competing analysis conducted creatively and without undue duplication, are all generally thought to result in better analysis. However, with respect to joint intelligence *operations* and the integration of traditionally foreign and domestic intelligence operations, there seems to be less of a consensus. At a macro level, it is clear that coordination[23] in intelligence operations is a common good. Yet, the legal mechanisms and regulations that underlie and guide foreign intelligence collection and domestic intelligence collection, particularly as it relates to U.S. persons,[24] are substantially different.[25]

---

18 See *Congressional Record*, December 8, 2004, Senate consideration of the conference report to accompany S.2845. Senator Lieberman continued that the then-proposed NCTC Directorate of Strategic Operational Planning would conduct planning for "... the entire Executive branch—ranging from the combatant commands, to the State Department, to the FBI's Counterterrorism Division to the Department of Health and Human Services to the CIA."

19 See P.L. 108-458, Title I, Subtitle A, Establishment of a Director of National Intelligence.

20 See Walter Pincus, "The Hill, Bush, Differ on Counterterror Center," in *Washington Post*, Nov. 28, 2004, p. A6.

21 See remarks of Senator Carl Levin in Congressional Record, p.S9882, Sept. 29, 2004.

22 While collocation may facilitate "jointness," without harmonization of business practices, training, and perhaps even doctrine, it will not, in and of itself, yield jointness.

23 Jurisdictions defining which IC agency may have the lead in certain intelligence operations can be nebulous. For example, both the FBI and the Central Intelligence Agency's domestically-oriented division have jurisdiction to collect foreign intelligence within the United States. See EO 12333, Section 1.8 for Central Intelligence Agency responsibilities, and Section 1.14 for FBI responsibilities. Depending on circumstances and location of an operation, one agency or the other may be in the lead, with the support of the other. However, transcending questions about which agency is lead and which is support is the national imperative for timely coordination and sharing of the information between IC agencies involved in CT operations. See "Spies Clash as FBI Joins CIA Overseas: Sources Talk of Communication Problem in Terrorism Role," the Associated Press, Feb. 15, 2005. See also Richard B. Schmitt and Greg Miller. "FBI In Talks to Extend Reach," *Los Angeles Times*, Jan. 28, 2005.

24 The Foreign Intelligence Surveillance Act of 1978 (50 U.S.C. §1801 *et seq.*), as amended defines U.S. persons as "... a citizen of the United States, an alien lawfully admitted for permanent residence (as defined in section 101(a)(20) of the Immigration and Nationality Act), an unincorporated association a substantial number of members of which are citizens of the United States or aliens lawfully admitted for permanent residence, or a corporation which is incorporated in the United States, but does not include a corporation or an association which is a foreign power, as defined in subsection (a) (1), (2), or (3).

25 The roles and responsibilities of the IC are set forth in numerous legal mechanisms including, but not limited to, The National Security Act of 1947, as amended; certain sections of Titles 10 and 50 of the U.S. Code; numerous classified and unclassified executive orders, such as 12333, titled *United States Intelligence Activities*; and a series of classified and unclassified regulations and guidelines known as DCI Directives. In addition to some of the aforementioned IC guidelines, the FBI is also required to execute its intelligence activities in a manner that is consistent with, among other regulations, the (1) Attorney General Guidelines for FBI National Security Investigations and Foreign Intelligence Collection (U), and (2) Attorney General Guidelines on General Crimes, Racketeering Enterprises, and Terrorism Enterprise Investigations. For an assessment of the potential tradeoffs between civil liberties and domestic intelligence collection,

The act defines strategic operational planning as "... the mission, objectives to be achieved, tasks to be performed, interagency coordination of activities, and the assignment of roles and responsibilities."[26] The executive order does not directly define strategic operational planning, other than to state generally that it involves the integration of all instruments of national power. As stated above, under both the executive order and the act, the NCTC itself is expressly prohibited from executing operations; it assigns roles and monitors overall counterterrorism operational progress. It is explicitly stated in the executive order that "... each agency representative to the Center, unless otherwise specified by the DCI, shall operate under the authorities of the representative's agency." That is, while strategic planning may be joint, if the NCTC Director assigns the FBI, CIA, and Department of Defense certain counterterrorism operational responsibilities, each agency operates under its own legal authorities. While it may be implicit, no such similar and explicit legal authority guidance was provided in P.L. 108-458.

The FBI has physically moved a substantial portion of its operational and analytical counterterrorism personnel from FBI Headquarters to offsite locations in the interest of closer coordination with the rest of the IC's counterterrorism entities.[27] While not necessarily "integrated" into the NCTC, these individuals are now "collocated" with elements of the NCTC. As envisioned by the Commission and P.L. 108-458, this collocation could yield substantial analytical dividends, particularly when information systems are integrated in a manner that allows for closer analytical collaboration across the IC. The collocation of IC personnel engaged in counterterrorism operations may also lead to substantially improved and informed counterterrorism operations. Human assets recruited by the IC can be highly mobile. As these individuals move between the United States and overseas locations, coordination amongst and between IC agencies having sole or shared jurisdiction can add substantial value to an operation, and avoid inefficient as well as potentially embarrassing operational overlaps. Recent media coverage suggests tension between the FBI and the domestic intelligence arm of the CIA on domestic intelligence activities.[28] While a distinction must be made between *collocation*, which implies reliance on existing legal authorities, and *integration*, which implies the creation of a new body of law and regulations, the possibility exists that unintentional mission creep and operational zeal could lead to situations in which rules designed to guide traditional foreign intelligence collection may be applied to U.S. persons. That is, the civil liberties of U.S. persons could be at risk if domestic intelligence collection is directed against them in a manner that may not be consistent with or constrained by appropriate Attorney General Guidelines.[29]

Finally, with respect to the resolution of disputes between the NCTC and its constituent agencies, the act stipulates that the DNI shall resolve conflicts. In the event that the heads of constituent agencies disagree with the DNI's resolution, they may appeal the resolution to the President. Given the NCTC's role to "... monitor the implementation of strategic operational plans," it is possible to envision conflicts between the NCTC and an agency with respect to what exactly constitutes "implementation" and how, specifically, operational success is defined. This may be exacerbated by the act's distinction between joint *intelligence* counterterrorism operations, and joint counterterrorism operations *other than intelligence*. Regardless, resolution of potential disputes within the NCTC is one area that may be worthy of congressional oversight.

Options for Congressional Consideration

An issue for Congress is whether to let the existing intelligence reform act speak for itself (and let certain ambiguities be resolved during implementation), or to intervene to address apparent ambiguities through amendments to the act now. Alternatively, the Executive Branch may choose to intervene to clarify apparent ambiguities within P.L. 108-458 or between EO 13354 and P.L. 108-458.[30] In any event, congressional oversight of the status quo and implementation of the present act could prove useful.

Should Congress amend intelligence reform legislation in the 109th Congress, or introduce new legislation (possibly through the annual intelligence authorization process) related to the NCTC, there are at least two areas in which it might consider action. The first concerns the reporting relationships of the Director of the NCTC to the DNI and to the President. While the coordination of planning for counterterrorism operations is necessarily an executive branch wide endeavor, the daily implementation of such practice remains a relatively nebulous function and may, therefore, be a topic for close congressional oversight. Some might argue that if a close professional and personal bond develops between the President and

---

see Kate Martin, "Domestic Intelligence and Civil Liberties," *SAIS Review*, vol., XXIV, no. 1 (Winter-Spring 2004). For an assessment of the differences between law enforcement and intelligence, see Stuart A. Baker, "Should Spies Be Cops?" in Foreign Policy, Winter 1994/95.

26 See Section 119(j)(2) of the National Security Act of 1947, as amended by P.L. 108-458, Section 1021, 50 U.S.C. §402 (j)(2).

27 Approximately $35.5 million was appropriated for the "... relocation of portions of the Counterterrorism Division...," in the FY2005 Consolidated Appropriations Act, P.L. 108–447.

28 See "Spies Clash as FBI Joins CIA Overseas: Sources Talk of Communication Problem in Terrorism Role," the *Associated Press*, Feb. 15, 2005. See also Richard B. Schmitt and Greg Miller, "FBI In Talks to Extend Reach," *Los Angeles Times*, Jan. 28, 2005.

29 The Foreign Intelligence Surveillance Act of 1978, as amended (50 U.S.C §1801 *et seq.*) authorizes, under certain circumstances and subject to a court order, electronic surveillance directed against U.S. persons.

30 See comments of Rand Beers, former National Security Council official, in Walter Pincus, "Negroponte's First Job Is Showing Who's Boss: Intelligence Director Must Assert Authority, Experts Say," in *Washington Post*, Mar. 1, 2005, p. A13.

the DNI,[31] then a direct reporting chain for the Director of the NCTC to the President for certain joint operations relating to counterterrorism is unlikely to undermine the DNI's new authority. The frequency, substance, and duration of the direct meetings between the President and the Director of the NCTC may pale in comparison to those between the President and the DNI. However, it is possible that confusion could develop because the act differentiates between *intelligence* joint counterterrorism operations and joint counterterrorism operations *(other than intelligence operations)*—presumably military operations. This distinction may prove difficult to make in practice because, generally, even joint military counterterrorism operations require sound tactical intelligence to achieve their objectives.

Second, Congress may wish to consider adding to its expressed prohibition for the NCTC to execute operations, language which would explicitly clarify the legal authorities of constituent NCTC members with respect to counterterrorism operations. Alternatively, Congress could consider specifically stating in law that the Privacy and Civil Liberties Oversight Board established in P.L. 108-458,[32] has explicit responsibility for oversight of the joint counterterrorism operations of the NCTC, particularly when these operations involve U.S. persons.

Finally, another potential area for congressional scrutiny may be the appropriate arrangements and congressional committees that have jurisdiction over the activities of the NCTC. While the Directorate of Intelligence's activities are largely bounded by traditional intelligence functions, such as the setting of collections requirements, collection of raw intelligence, and the conduct of intelligence analysis, the Directorate of Strategic Operational Planning's activities go beyond intelligence. As such, the universe of committees having oversight over the executive branch wide functions associated with strategic operational planning may exceed those that will conduct oversight over the NCTC's Directorate of Intelligence. One could envision a situation in which, not unlike the activities of the Department of Homeland Security, the number of committees claiming jurisdiction over the NCTC's Director of Strategic Operational Planning could be substantial. The challenge would then be to coordinate congressional oversight in a manner that is rigorous and meaningful without unduly burdening NCTC leadership.

Conclusion

The ostensible purpose for the creation of intelligence "centers," including the NCTC, is to bring together the disparate elements of the IC having different intelligence foci and missions in order to achieve common intelligence and national security objectives. Given the positive results of "jointness" achieved in the armed forces context as a result of the Goldwater-Nichols Defense Reorganization Act of 1986, there is an inherent attraction to apply such "best practices" to the IC. Yet the cohesive integration of functions across the IC requires relatively clear guidance, or at least the absence of contradictory or confusing authorities. With respect to the NCTC, the act outlines some authorities which may cause a lack of clarity, which may, in turn, undermine the effective and efficient implementation of a truly national approach to counterterrorism. The bifurcated reporting relationships the act outlines for the Director of the NCTC, ill-defined distinctions between joint counterterrorism intelligence operations and joint counterterrorism operations (*other than intelligence*), as well as the authority of the NCTC to define operational success and have the tools necessary to ensure compliance with its joint plans, are all areas in which unclear authority could lead to inefficient business practices. Professionalism, and a high degree of commitment among the counterterrorism cadre assigned to the NCTC, may go a long way toward ameliorating these ambiguities and thus negate the need for legislative action. It is also possible, however, that the ambiguities outlined in the act may only complicate the inevitable growing pains associated with establishing an effective, nationally coordinated counterterrorism intelligence effort.

As such, narrowly targeted and clarifying oversight guidance or legislative remedies may assist the NCTC in reaching optimal effectiveness in the least amount of time.

Order Code RL32816, Updated March 24, 2005

---

31 President Bush stated in his press briefing announcing the nomination of the current U.S. Ambassador to Iraq John Negroponte as DNI that his nominee: "... will have access on a daily basis in that he'll be my primary briefer...." See White House Press Conference, Feb. 17, 2005, at [www.whitehouse.gov/news/releases/2005/02/print/20050217-2.html].

32 See Title I, Subtitle F—Privacy and Civil Liberties, in P.L. 108-458. As currently drafted, the act would likely allow such oversight, as it is stated that the Board "... shall continually review, regulations, executive branch policies, and procedures (including implementation of such regulations, policies, and procedures) ... to ensure that privacy and civil liberties are protected."

PART 4

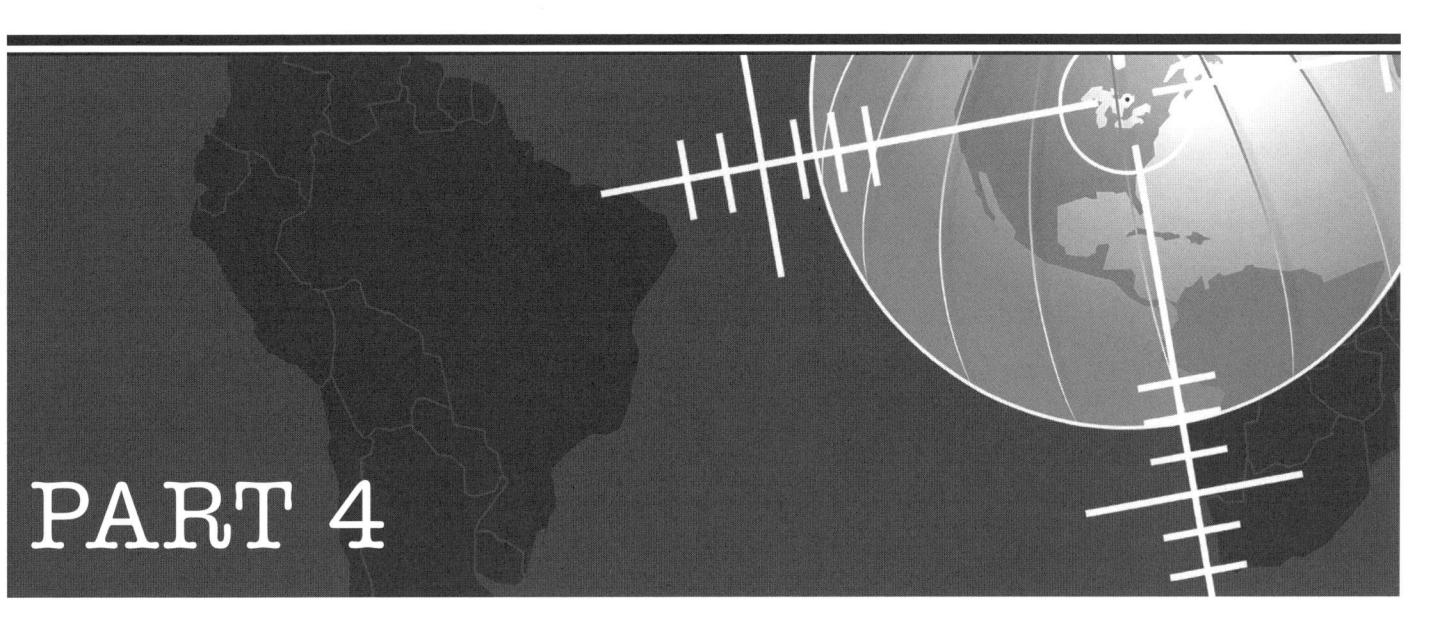

CHRONOLOGY OF SIGNIFICANT TERRORIST INCIDENTS 1961–2005

Chronology of Significant Terrorist Incidents 1961–2005

Overview of the Chronology of Significant Terrorist Incidents 1961–2005

Anna Sabasteanski

Various U.S. government departments have monitored terrorist activities for many years, but the practice of reporting significant attacks began as a research project at the Central Intelligence Agency (CIA) in the 1970s and gradually shifted to the Department of State in the 1980s. Although the State Department is the governmental department responsible for preparing the yearly report on terrorism, it gets information from other departments, including overseas posts and bureaus that provide country-specific data. Formerly the CIA's Counterterrorist Center (CTC) was responsible for maintaining the database of international terrorist-related information; that task was later given to the Terrorist Threat Integration Center (TTIC), which in December 2004 was superseded by the National Counterterrorism Center (NCTC). NCTC uses the information in the database for analysis, and the database provides the material that is evaluated for inclusion in the Department of State reports.

Title 22 of the United States Code, Section 2656f(d), the law that established the requirement for an annual report on terrorism, defines terrorism as "premeditated, politically motivated violence perpetrated against noncombatant targets by subnational groups or clandestine agents, usually intended to influence an audience" but does not define what makes a terrorist attack significant.

The secretary of state makes this determination. As the process has evolved, criteria have been developed based on casualties and financial impact. Today, an incident is included if it involves significant loss of life; abduction, kidnapping, or serious injury to people; and major property damage in excess of $10,000. A failed attack may also be considered significant if it is deemed likely that it could have led to similar casualties, incidents, or damage. That definition still leaves room for interpretation, and a committee of experts is involved in conducting the annual evaluation. A detailed description of this process can be found in the Department of State inspector general's *Review of the Department's Patterns of Global Terrorism—2003 Report*.

The National Counterterrorism Center was established by executive order to take the place of the TTIC following recommendations of the 9/11 Commission. According to the executive order issued on 27 August 2004 (http://www.whitehouse.gov/news/releases/2004/08/20040827-5.html), The NCTC has the following responsibilities:

(a) serve as the primary organization in the United States Government for analyzing and integrating all intelligence possessed or acquired by the United States Government pertaining to terrorism and counterterrorism, excepting purely domestic counterterrorism information. The Center may, consistent with applicable law, receive, retain, and disseminate information from any Federal, State, or local government, or other source necessary to fulfill its responsibilities concerning the policy set forth in section 1 of this order; and agencies authorized to conduct counterterrorism activities may query Center data for any information to assist in their respective responsibilities;

(b) conduct strategic operational planning for counterterrorism activities, integrating all instruments of national power, including diplomatic, financial, military, intelligence, homeland security, and law enforcement activities within and among agencies;

(c) assign operational responsibilities to lead agencies for counterterrorism activities that are consistent with applicable law and that support strategic plans to counter terrorism. The Center shall ensure that agencies have access to and receive intelligence needed to accomplish their assigned activities. The Center shall not direct the execution of operations. Agencies shall inform the National Security Council and the Homeland Security Council of any objections to designations and assignments made by the Center in the planning and coordination of counterterrorism activities;

(d) serve as the central and shared knowledge bank on known and suspected terrorists and international terror groups, as well as their goals, strategies, capabilities, and networks of contacts and support; and

(e) ensure that agencies, as appropriate, have access to and receive all-source intelligence support needed to execute their counterterrorism plans or perform independent, alternative analysis.

In 2005, the NCTC took over responsibility for producing the annual reports that used to be included in *Patterns of Global Terrorism,* which was replaced with *Country Reports on Terrorism.* This change is covered in depth in the section of this collection that covers terrorism in the new millennium.

An NCTC database is available to the public through the National Memorial Institute for the Prevention of Terrorism's "Terrorism Knowledge Base," which includes data from the RAND Terrorism Chronology, 1968–1997, from the RAND-MIPT terrorism incident database (1998–present); from the terrorism indictment database of the University of Arkansas, and from DFI International's research on terrorist organizations. The NCTC's Worldwide Incidents Tracking System (WITS) is a searchable database that can be accessed at http://www.tkb.org/.

This section includes significant incidents listed in the Department of State's summary for the years prior to 1985, the complete chronologies included in *Patterns of Global Terrorism* from 1985 to 2003, and the NCTC's *A Chronology of Significant International Terrorism for 2004.* Additional incidents that occurred in the first half of 2005 have been collated from the TerrorismCentral Newsletter.

Chronology of Significant Terrorist Events 1961–2005

1961

1 May   **United States**
The first US aircraft was hijacked by Puerto Rican born Antuilo Ramierez Ortiz, who forced at gunpoint a National Airlines plane to fly to Havana, Cuba, where he was given asylum.

1968

28 August   **Guatemala**
US Ambassador to Guatemala John Gordon Mein was murdered by a rebel faction when gunmen forced his official car off the road in Guatemala City and raked the vehicle with gunfire.

1969

30 July   **Japan**
US Ambassador to Japan A.H. Meyer was attacked by a knife-wielding Japanese citizen.

3 September   **Brazil**
US Ambassador to Brazil Charles Burke Elbrick was kidnapped by the Marxist revolutionary group MR-8.

1970

10 February   **West Germany**
Three terrorists attacked El Al passengers in a bus at the Munich Airport with guns and grenades. One passenger was killed and 11 were injured. All three terrorists were captured by airport police. The Action Organization for the Liberation of Palestine and the Popular Democratic Front for the Liberation of Palestine claimed responsibility for the attack.

31 July   **Uruguay**
In Montevideo, Uruguay, the Tupamaros terrorist group kidnapped US Agency for International Development adviser Dan Mitrione; his body was found on August 10.

1972

21 July   **Northern Ireland**
An Irish Republican Army (IRA) bomb attack killed eleven people and injure 130 in Belfast, Northern Ireland. Ten days later, three IRA car bomb attacks in the village of Claudy left six dead.

5 September   **West Germany**
Eight Palestinian "Black September" terrorists seized 11 Israeli athletes in the Olympic Village in Munich, West Germany. In a bungled rescue attempt by West German authorities, nine of the hostages and five terrorists were killed.

1973

2 March   **Sudan**
US Ambassador to Sudan Cleo A. Noel and other diplomats were assassinated at the Saudi Arabian Embassy in Khartoum by members of the Black September organization.

4 May   **Mexico**
US Consul General in Guadalajara Terrence Leonhardy was kidnapped by members of the People's Revolutionary Armed Forces.

17 December   **Rome**
Five terrorists pulled weapons from their luggage in the terminal lounge at the Rome airport, killing two persons. They then attacked a Pan American 707 bound for Beirut and Tehran, destroying it with incendiary grenades and killing 29 persons, including 4 senior Moroccan officials and 14 American employees of ARAMCO. They then herded 5 Italian hostages into a Lufthansa airliner and killed an Italian customs agent as he tried to escape, after which they forced the pilot to fly to Beirut. After Lebanese authorities refused to let the plane land, it landed in Athens, where the terrorists demanded the release of 2 Arab terrorists. In order to make Greek authorities comply with their demands, the terrorists killed a hostage and threw his body onto the tarmac. The plane then flew to Damascus, where it stopped for two hours to obtain fuel and food. It then flew to Kuwait, where the terrorists released their hostages in return for passage to

an unknown destination. The Palestine Liberation Organization disavowed the attack, and no group claimed responsibility for it.

1974

19 August — **Cyprus**
US Ambassador to Cyprus Rodger P. Davies and his Greek Cypriot secretary were shot and killed by snipers during a demonstration outside the US Embassy in Nicosia.

1975

27–29 January — **United States**
Puerto Rican nationalists bombed a Wall Street bar, killing four and injuring 60; two days later, the Weather Underground claims responsibility for an explosion in a bathroom at the US Department of State in Washington.

1976

27 June — **Uganda**
Members of the Baader-Meinhof Group and the Popular Front for the Liberation of Palestine (PFLP) seized an Air France airliner and its 258 passengers. They forced the plane to land in Uganda. On July 3 Israeli commandos successfully rescued the passengers.

21 September — **United States**
Exiled Chilean Foreign Minister Orlando Letelier was killed by a car-bomb in Washington.

1978

16 March — **Italy**
Premier Aldo Moro was seized by the Red Brigade and assassinated 55 days later.

1979

14 February — **Afghanistan**
Four Afghans kidnapped US Ambassador Adolph Dubs in Kabul and demanded the release of various "religious figures." Dubs was killed, along with four alleged terrorists, when Afghan police stormed the hotel room where he was being held.

4 November — **Iran**
After President Carter agreed to admit the Shah of Iran into the United States, Iranian radicals seized the US Embassy in Tehran and took 66 American diplomats hostage. Thirteen hostages were soon released, but the remaining 53 were held until their release on 20 January 1981.

20 November — **Saudi Arabia**
Two hundred Islamic terrorists seized the Grand Mosque in Mecca, Saudi Arabia, taking hundreds of pilgrims hostage. Saudi and French security forces retook the shrine after an intense battle in which some 250 people were killed and 600 wounded.

1981

31 August — **West Germany**
The Red Army Faction [an offshoot of the Baader-Meinhof Group] exploded a bomb at the US Air Force Base at Ramstein, West Germany.

6 October — **Egypt**
Soldiers who were secretly members of the Takfir Wal-Hajira sect attacked and killed Egyptian President Anwar Sadat during a troop review.

4 December — **El Salvador**
Three American nuns and one lay missionary were found murdered outside San Salvador, El Salvador. They were killed by members of the National Guard, and the killers are currently in prison.

1982

14 September — **Lebanon**
President Bashir Gemayel was assassinated by a car bomb parked outside his party's Beirut headquarters.

1983

8 April — **Colombia**
A US citizen was seized by the Revolutionary Armed Forces of Colombia (FARC) and held for ransom.

18 April — **Lebanon**
Sixty-three people, including the CIA's Middle East director, were killed and 120 were injured in a 400-pound suicide truck-bomb attack on the US Embassy in Beirut, Lebanon. The Islamic Jihad claimed responsibility.

25 May — **El Salvador**
A US Navy officer was assassinated by the Farabundo Marti National Liberation Front.

9 October — **Burma**
North Korean agents blew up a delegation from South Korea in Rangoon, Burma, killing 21 persons and injuring 48.

23 October — **Lebanon**
Simultaneous suicide truck-bomb attacks were made on American and French compounds in Beirut, Lebanon. A 12,000-pound bomb destroyed the US compound, killing 242 Americans, while 58 French troops were killed when a 400-pound device destroyed a French base. Islamic Jihad claimed responsibility.

15 November   Greece
A US Navy officer was shot by the 17 November terrorist group in Athens, Greece, while his car was stopped at a traffic light.

1984

16 March   Lebanon
The Islamic Jihad kidnapped and later murdered US Embassy Political Officer William Buckley in Beirut, Lebanon. Other US citizens not connected to the US government were seized over a succeeding two-year period.

12 April   Spain
Eighteen US servicemen were killed and 83 people were injured in a bomb attack on a restaurant near a US Air Force Base in Torrejon, Spain.

5 June   India
Sikh terrorists seized the Golden Temple in Amritsar, India. One hundred people died when Indian security forces retook the Sikh holy shrine.

31 October   India
Premier Indira Gandhi was shot to death by members of her security force.

1985

1 January   Japan
Three homemade rockets were launched by a time-delay mechanism at the US Consulate General in Kobe. The rockets caused neither damage nor casualties. The radical leftist group Chukaku-ha (Nucleus Faction) claimed credit.

8 January   Lebanon
In West Beirut, Reverend Lawrence Jenco, US director of Catholic Relief Services in Beirut, was kidnapped as he was being driven to work from his residence. Islamic Jihad claimed responsibility. Reverend Jenco was released in July 1986.

15 January   Belgium
The Communist Combatant Cells set off a car bomb in front of the US NATO Support Activity building outside Brussels. The bomb heavily damaged the building and blew out windows as far away as 100 meters. One US military policeman was injured.

25 January   France
Gen. Rene Audran, the French Defense Ministry official in charge of international arms sales, was assassinated by an unknown assailant outside his home in Paris. An anonymous telephone caller claimed credit for the attack in the name of "Commando Elizabeth Van Dyck of Action Directe."

28 January   Portugal
Popular Forces of 25 April launched a mortar attack at NATO warships anchored in Lisbon harbor. None of the vessels was struck.

1 February   West Germany
In Munich two terrorists forced their way into the home of West German industrialist Ernst Zimmermann, tied him to a chair, and shot him in the head. He died 12 hours later. The Red Army Faction claimed responsibility for the attack in the name of Commando Patrick O'Hara, a member of the Irish National Liberation Army who died in a hunger strike in 1981.

2 February   Greece
A popular bar in the Athens suburb of Glyfada was bombed by unknown terrorists, injuring 78 persons, included 57 US servicemen and their dependents. The Cypriot group National Front claimed responsibility, but Middle Eastern terrorists are considered possible suspects.

21 February   Greece
The leftist terrorist organization 17 November gunned down a conservative Greek publisher on a busy Athens street and critically wounded his driver. Leaflets found at the scene strongly denounced Greece's socialist government.

22 February   France
In Paris terrorists exploded a bomb near the rear entrance of the Marks and Spencer department store shortly after the store opened, killing one person and injuring 15 others. In May 1986 French police arrested a Tunisian suspect linked to Middle Eastern terrorists in connection with this and other bombings.

28 February   Kuwait
Four gunmen shot the assistant cultural attaché of the Iraqi Embassy and his son in their Kuwaiti home. No group claimed responsibility.

Austria
The former Libyan Ambassador to Austria was severely wounded by two shots fired from a car outside his home in Vienna. The victim had supported Qadhafi's seizure of power in 1969 but resigned his position in disgust at the regime in 1980.

1 March   Northern Ireland
The Provisional Irish Republican Army launched nine mortar rounds at a Royal Ulster Constabulary compound in Newry. Several rounds made direct hits on a trailer serving as a temporary canteen for the police station. Nine officers were killed and 37 other persons, including 25 civilians, were wounded.

8 March   Lebanon
In south Beirut an estimated 250 kilograms of explosives concealed in a car detonated near the home of Hizballah spiritual leader Muhammad Husayn Fadlallah, killing 80 persons

and wounding more than 250 others. No group claimed responsibility.

12 March   Canada
In Ottawa three members of the Armenian Revolutionary Army seized the Turkish Embassy, killing a guard. Turkish Ambassador Coskum Kirca escaped by jumping out of an upper story window but was injured by the fall. After four hours, the terrorists surrendered.

14 March   Guadeloupe
In Point-a-Pitre, a bomb exploded at lunchtime in a crowded restaurant, killing one person and injuring 11 others. Four Americans were slightly injured. No group claimed responsibility for the incident, but the separatist Caribbean Revolutionary Alliance is suspected.

16 March   Lebanon
In West Beirut gunmen abducted Terry Anderson, the chief Middle East correspondent for Associated Press. An anonymous caller claimed that Islamic Jihad was responsible.

21 March   Greece, Italy, Cyprus
In Athens, Rome, and Nicosia, Jordanian airline offices were the targets of grenade attacks that injured five persons. In telephone calls to press agencies, claims of responsibility were made in the name of Black September, a cover name used by the Abu Nidal Group.

27 March   Italy
In Rome the Red Brigades assassinated Rome University professor Enzo Tarantelli, an eminent labor economist involved with the Christian Democratic-oriented Confederation of Italian Labor.

Iraq
In Tikrit, President Saddam Hussein's hometown, two car bombs exploded, killing 36 persons and injuring many more. One vehicle bomb reportedly exploded outside a Women's Federation office and the other near the town's Labor Federation office. No one claimed credit for the attacks.

6 April   West Germany
In Bonn, an anti-Qadhafi Libyan student was killed by a Libyan gunman. The assassin also wounded two German passers-by, one seriously. The Libyan victim had been a target of the Qadhafi regime for at least two years.

12 April   Spain
The El Descanso restaurant outside Madrid was bombed, killing 18 Spaniards and wounding another 82 persons, including 15 Americans. Individuals claiming to represent several terrorist groups—including the First of October Antifascist Resistance and Islamic Jihad—claimed responsibility. Middle Eastern terrorists are among the prime suspects.

10–12 May   India
A coordinated bombing campaign by Sikh extremists left 85 persons dead and more than 150 wounded in New Delhi and other cities. More than a dozen bombs exploded in buses, bus stations, and other public places.

11, 15 May   France
In Corsica the National Front for the Liberation of Corsica is suspected of setting off 15 bombs on 11 May and 17 more on 15 May. The blasts damaged cars, banks, and shops of mainland Frenchmen but caused no casualties.

14 May   Sri Lanka
Tamil separatist guerrillas killed some 150 men, women, children, and Buddhist monks and nuns in a machinegun attack on the Buddhist shrine of Anuradhapura. The perpetrators escaped into a wildlife refuge and were never apprehended.

25 May   Kuwait
In Kuwait members of the Iranian-backed Dawa party carried out a car bombing on the motorcade of the Amir of Kuwait. Six people died in the explosion and ensuing melee, and 12 were injured. The Amir suffered minor injuries. Islamic Jihad claimed responsibility.

28 May   Lebanon
In West Beirut six gunmen kidnapped David Jacobsen, the US administrator of the American University Hospital, as he was walking from the campus to the adjacent hospital compound. Islamic Jihad claimed responsibility.

10 June   Lebanon
Gunmen kidnapped Thomas Sutherland, US dean of agriculture at the American University of Beirut, as he was leaving Beirut International Airport. Islamic Jihad claimed responsibility.

14 June   Lebanon
Lebanese Shi'a gunmen hijacked TWA flight 847 en route from Athens to Rome and forced it to land in Beirut after two round trips from Beirut to Algiers. The hijackers released the hostages 17 days later, but, before they did, they killed US Navy diver Robert Stethem.

19 June   West Germany
A bombing of the international terminal at Frankfurt's Rhein-Main Airport left four persons dead and 60 injured. Among the groups that claimed responsibility were the Arab Revolutionary Organization, the Red Army Faction, and the so-called Peace Conquerors.

El Salvador
An armed attack on a café in San Salvador's Zona Rosa district killed 13 persons, including six Americans. The Mardoqueo Cruz Urban Commandos of the Central American Revolutionary Worker's Party took credit for the attack.

20–21 June   Nepal
Five bombs exploded in the capital of Katmandu and the western city of Pokhara on 20 June, leaving seven dead and at least 19 others injured. On 21 June three more bombs went off in the southern border town of Birgunj, killing one

other person. These were the first terrorist bombings ever recorded in Nepal. Two previously unknown groups claimed credit.

23 June   **North Atlantic**
A Shannon-bound Air India flight from Toronto was bombed over the North Atlantic, killing 329 passengers and crewmembers. Two Sikh organizations and a Kashmir separatist group claimed responsibility, but Sikh extremists probably carried out the attack.

Japan
A few hours after the explosion aboard the Air India flight, a bomb exploded in the baggage handling area of Tokyo's Narita Airport, killing two Japanese workers. The suitcase containing the explosive device had arrived from Canada and was being transferred to another Air India jet bound for India. Although no group claimed credit for this incident, Sikh extremists are believed responsible.

1 July   **Spain**
In Madrid a bomb exploded at the British Airways ticket office, killing one person and injuring 27 others. The blast gutted the premises and also wrecked a TWA office located directly above. Minutes later, a grenade was lobbed in to nearby offices of Royal Jordanian Airlines, and the front of the building was raked with small-arms fire. The Organization of the Oppressed, Revolutionary Organization of Socialist Muslims, and Black September claimed responsibility.

11 July   **Kuwait**
In Kuwait two powerful bombs exploded within minutes of each other in two crowded outdoor cafes, killing eight people and injuring 89 others. The Arab Revolutionary Brigades, a cover name used by the Abu Nidal Group, claimed responsibility.

22 July   **Denmark**
In Copenhagen simultaneous bombings damaged the Northwest Orient Airlines office and a synagogue, injuring 32 persons. A caller claiming to represent Islamic Jihad took responsibility.

29 July   **Spain**
The Basque Fatherland and Liberty-Military Wing claimed credit for the machinegun attack that killed Vice Adm. Fausto Escrigas Estrada, the Director General of Defense Policy, as he drove to work in Madrid.

6 August   **Mozambique**
The Mozambique National Resistance killed 33 persons in an attack on a funeral cortege in Tete Province near the Malawi border.

8 August   **West Germany**
A car bombing at Rhein-Main airbase near Frankfurt killed two Americans and wounded 17 other persons. The West German Red Army Faction and the French Action Directe both claimed responsibility.

16 August   **Columbia**
The 19th of April Movement claimed responsibility for the kidnapping in Bogota of an American oil company executive, Michael Stewart. Stewart, an employee of a Tenneco subsidiary, was released on 23 December.

20 August   **Egypt**
In Cairo the Israeli administrative attaché was assassinated by gunmen in a passing car. His wife and secretary were wounded. The previously unknown group Egyptian Revolution claimed credit.

3 September   **Greece**
Two grenades were thrown into the lobby of a Greek hotel in Glyfada, wounding 19 Britons. A caller to an Athens newspaper stated that Black September would conduct numerous attacks in Athens if Greek authorities did not release one of its members.

9 September   **Spain**
In Madrid the Basque Fatherland and Liberty-Military Wing claimed responsibility for a remote-controlled car-bomb attack that injured 18 Spanish Civil Guardsmen and an American passer-by; the American later died of his injuries.

10 September   **El Salvador**
President Duarte's daughter Inez and a companion were kidnapped on a San Salvador university campus during a scuffle that left one security guard dead and another mortally wounded. Inez Duarte was held for nearly two months before being released in a prisoner swap involving approximately two dozen captured guerrillas. The Pedro Pablo Castillo Front claimed responsibility.

16 September   **Italy**
Terrorists lobbed grenades into the Café de Paris restaurant in Rome, wounding 38 tourists, including nine Americans. The Revolutionary Organization of Socialist Muslims, a cover name used by the Abu Nidal Group, claimed responsibility.

25 September   **Italy**
In Rome a bomb exploded in the British Airways office, injuring 15 persons. An Arab arrested while fleeing the scene claimed to be a member of the Revolutionary Organization of Socialist Muslims, a cover name used by the Abu Nidal Group.

30 September   **Lebanon**
In Beirut three Soviet diplomats and a Soviet Embassy doctor were kidnapped. The body of one of the captives was found in a West Beirut suburb on 2 October; the remaining hostages were released on 30 October. A Sunni Muslim group, Islamic Liberation Organization, claimed responsibility.

7 October   **Mediterranean Sea**
The Italian cruise ship *Achille Lauro* was seized as it departed Alexandria, Egypt, for Port Said. Before surrendering to Egyptian authorities on 9 October, the terrorists killed US

tourist Leon Klinghoffer. Abu Abbas' Palestine Liberation Front was responsible.

6   November   Colombia
Guerrillas belonging to the 19th of April Movement seized the Palace of Justice and held it for more than 27 hours. By the time the incident came to an end—after government troops stormed the building—some 90 people were dead, including 12 Supreme Court judges and more than 50 guerrillas.

23   November   Malta
An Egyptian jetliner was hijacked from Athens to Malta. Before Egyptian commandos stormed the plane—killing some 60 persons who remained aboard—the terrorists murdered several persons, including an American woman, and wounded the other Americans on board. The Arab Revolutionary Brigades—a cover name used by the Abu Nidal Group—claimed responsibility for the hijacking jointly with the Egyptian Revolution.

24   November   West Germany
A car bomb exploded in a parking lot adjacent to a US military shopping center in Frankfurt, wounding 32, mostly US military personnel and dependents. No group claimed responsibility, but Middle Eastern terrorists are suspected.

29   November   Japan
Chukaku-ha cut National Railway communications cables in at least 16 places, firebombed a railway station, and burned a transformer facility in a well-executed assault that ultimately stranded 11 million commuters.

7   December   France
The bombing of two department stores in Paris left about 35 holiday shoppers wounded. The Palestine Liberation Front, the Armenian Secret Army for the Liberation of Armenia, and Islamic Jihad all claimed responsibility.

10   December   Columbia
Approximately 60 armed guerrillas of the People's Liberation Army attacked a Bechtel Corporation construction site in northern Colombia and kidnapped two US engineers, demanding $6 million for their release. One of the Americans died in captivity in early 1986; the other was released shortly thereafter.

27   December   Italy and Austria
Near-simultaneous machinegun and grenade attacks at the Rome and Vienna airports left more than 20 persons dead, including five Americans, and some 120 wounded, including 20 Americans. Both incidents were carried out by the Abu Nidal Group.

1986

17   January   Lebanon
A Spanish security official and two Lebanese employees of the Spanish Embassy were kidnapped at gunpoint in West Beirut on the same day Spain normalized relations with Israel. All three were released in February.

31   January   Lebanon
Chae Do-sung, a South Korean diplomat, was kidnapped in Beirut. His abduction was later claimed by the "Fighting Revolutionary Cells"; his fate is unknown.

18   February   Portugal
A bomb exploded in a car being inspected at the gate of the US Embassy in Lisbon. There were no casualties. The Portuguese terrorist group Popular Forces of 25 April claimed responsibility.

28   February   Sweden
A lone gunman assassinated Prime Minister Olaf Palme on a Stockholm street. Although suspicion has centered on Kurdish groups, there have been no arrests and the murder remains unsolved.

8   March   Lebanon
A four-man French TV crew was abducted in Beirut, probably by elements of Hizballah. Three of the captives were subsequently released.

13   March   Syria
A powerful bomb exploded in a refrigerator truck under a bridge in a suburb of Damascus, killing perhaps 60 persons and wounding more than 100 others. The attack was probably related to Syria's military role in Lebanon.

19   March   Egypt
The wife of an Israeli Embassy employee was killed and three other Israelis were wounded when their care was fired on as they left the Cairo Trade Fair. Egypt's Revolution, a Nasserite group, took credit.

29   March   Lebanon
British citizens Leigh Douglas and Philip Padfield were kidnapped as they dined in West Beirut. They were found murdered three weeks later. Libya is believed responsible.

30   March   West Berlin
A bomb destroyed the German-Arab Friendship Association, injuring seven persons. A Jordanian later convicted in the case admitted receiving the bomb from the Syrian Embassy in East Berlin. West Germany temporarily recalled its Ambassador to Damascus over the incident.

2   April   Greece
A bomb exploded aboard TWA Flight 840 as it approached Athens airport, killing four American citizens. The device was similar to bombs used earlier in the decade by the Palestinian 15 May Organization, and a Lebanese woman who left the plane at an earlier stop is the leading suspect.

5   April   West Berlin
A bomb exploded in a crowded discotheque, killing two American soldiers and a Turkish woman and wounding more

than 200 others, including more than 70 Americans. Evidence of Libyan complicity led to the US bombing raids on Tripoli and Benghazi on 15 April.

11 April — Lebanon
Unidentified gunmen abducted Brian Keenan, an Irish lecturer at the American University of Beirut. No group claimed responsibility, and his fate is unknown.

17 April — United Kingdom
An Irish woman boarding an El Al jet in London was found to have a bomb in her carry-on luggage. Her Jordanian boyfriend was convicted in the attempt and implicated the Syrian Ambassador and his staff, who provided the bomb. Britain broke diplomatic relations with Syria over the incident.

Sudan
A communications officer of the American Embassy was shot and severely wounded in Khartoum. Libya is believed to have sponsored the attack in retaliation for the 15 April raids.

Lebanon
The bodies of American hostage Peter Kilburn (kidnapped in 1984) and British hostages Douglas and Padfield were discovered in Beirut. A group calling itself the Arab Revolutionary Cells claimed responsibility for the murders in retaliation for the US raid and British assistance to it.

Lebanon
The Revolutionary Organization of Socialist Muslims—a cover name used by the Abu Nidal organization—claimed to have "executed" British hostage Alec Collett (kidnapped in 1985) in retaliation for UK support of the US raids on Libya. No body was found, however, and his death cannot be confirmed.

Lebanon
British TV journalist, John McCarthy, was kidnapped by unknown assailants while en route to Beirut airport. His fate is unknown.

18 April — Turkey
Authorities arrested two Libyan men as they approached a US officers' club in Ankara with hand grenades. At their trial, they admitted receiving the grenades from the Libyan People's Bureau, which had ordered the attack.

25 April — North Yemen
A US Embassy communications officer was shot and severely wounded as he was driving his car in Sanaa. Libya is thought to have sponsored or inspired this attack as it did the one on 17 April in Khartoum.

3 May — Sri Lanka
An explosion blew the tail off an Air Lanka jet preparing to leave Colombo airport for the Maldives. The dead included three Britons, three Frenchmen, three Sri Lankans, two Japanese, two Maldivians, two West Germans, and the wife of a PLO official. Tamil separatist guerrillas were responsible.

4 May — Japan
The leftist radical group Chukaku-ha (Nucleus Faction) fired five homemade mortar shells as the heads of state were arriving for the opening session of the Western Economic Summit in Tokyo. The shells all missed their targets and caused no casualties.

7 May — Lebanon
French businessman Camille Sontag was abducted in West Beirut, probably by Hizballah elements. He was released in November.

14 May — Indonesia
Homemade mortar shells were fired at the US and Japanese Embassies in Jakarta and a car bomb exploded in the parking lot of the Canadian Embassy; there were no injuries and damage was limited to six parked cars. A previously unknown group calling itself the Anti-Imperialist International Brigade took credit. A member of the Japanese Red Army had rented the hotel room from which some of the projectiles were fired.

25 June — Peru
Sendero Luminoso planted a bomb aboard a tourist train bound for the Inca ruins of Machu Picchu. When the bomb detonated, seven persons were killed and scores were wounded. Among the dead were two US citizens, one of them a little girl.

26 June — Spain
A bomb placed in a suitcase partially detonated at Madrid's Barajas Airport, wounding 11 persons. The device was meant to explode aboard an El Al flight to Tel Aviv. Police arrested a man claiming to belong to the Palestinian Abu Musa Fatah rebels.

9 July — West Germany
The Red Army Faction murdered Seimens executive Dr. Karl-Heinz Beckurts with a remotely controlled bomb. The group singled out his role in the nuclear industry and research into the Strategic Defense Initiative in its claim letter.

12 July — Philippines
American missionary, Brian Lawrence, was kidnapped from his home in Mindanao by a political faction opposed to the government of President Corazon Aquino. He was released the following month.

14 July — Colombia
Guerrillas of the National Liberation Army (ELN) attacked two sections of the Occidental-Shell-Ecopetrol pipeline near the Venezuelan border. This was the first of dozens of similar attacks on the pipeline during 1986.

26 July — Lebanon
American hostage Father Lawrence Jenco was set free in Beirut. He had been kidnapped in January 1985.

3 August   **Cyprus**
At least three teams of gunmen attacked the British base area at Akrotiri with automatic weapons and mortars, slightly wounding two women. The attackers, probably sponsored by Libya and seeking revenge for Britain's role in the 14 April US raids on Libya, withdrew without penetrating the base's perimeter.

11 August   **Colombia**
The body of American Edward Sohl was discovered. He had been abducted by the People's Liberation Army in northern Colombia in December 1985. Sohl may have died in May; another engineer taken captive with him was released unharmed.

5 September   **Pakistan**
Four Palestinian gunmen stormed aboard a Pan Am 747 in Karachi in an abortive hijacking attempt. By the time security personnel boarded the plane the next day, 21 persons, two of them Americans, had been killed. The four terrorists and an accomplice, members of the Abu Nidal organization, probably will be brought to trial in 1987.

6 September   **Turkey**
Two Palestinian gunmen, members of the Abu Nidal organization, attacked a synagogue in Istanbul with grenades and automatic weapons, killing 22 persons and wounding seven others before blowing themselves up.

7 September   **Chile**
Approximately 30 members of the Manuel Rodriguez Patriotic Front ambushed the motorcade of President Augusto Pinochet in Santiago, killing at least five security guards and wounding others. Pinochet himself was unharmed in the rocket and machinegun attack.

9 September   **Lebanon**
Unidentified gunmen kidnapped Frank Reed, an adviser to the Lebanese International School, in Beirut. A caller took credit in the name of Islamic Jihad, but the group later denied responsibility. The "Revolutionary Justice Organization" also claimed credit.

12 September   **Lebanon**
The Revolutionary Justice Organization took responsibility for abducting Joseph Cicippio in Beirut. Cicippio was the deputy comptroller of the American University.

14 September   **South Korea**
A bomb exploded in a trash can at Seoul's Kimpo Airport on the eve of the Asian Games. Five persons were killed and 29 others were wounded; all the casualties were South Koreans. The government blamed North Korean agents for the incident.

17 September   **France**
Seven persons were killed and more than 60 others injured in Paris when a device went off in front of the crowded Tati clothing store. This was the 13th bombing in Paris conducted in two waves—February–March and September. Middle Eastern radicals seeking the release of three jailed terrorists claimed responsibility for both series of attacks.

15 October   **West Bank**
Two attackers hurled hand grenades into a crowd of civilians and soldiers in a bus parking lot at East Jerusalem's Western Wall. One person was killed and nearly 70 others wounded. Several Palestinian groups claimed responsibility for the incident.

21 October   **Lebanon**
Freelance writer Edward Tracy was kidnapped in Beirut. The Revolutionary Justice Organization took responsibility. As of the end of the year, Reed, Cicippio, and Tracy—all of whose kidnappings were claimed by that group in 1986—were still being held.

3 November   **Lebanon**
American hostage, David Jacobsen, was freed by his captors in Beirut. He had been held since May 1985 by elements of Hizballah.

5–29 November   **Colombia**
Guerrillas of the ELN intensified their attacks, begun in July, on a partially American-owned oil pipeline near the Venezuelan border. They conducted 11 attacks in November alone and, on at least one occasion, staged two attacks on different sections on the same day.

17 November   **France**
Members of the leftist terrorist group Action Directe murdered Georges Besse, president of Renault, near his Paris home. Besse may have been targeted because of an earlier role he played in developing the French nuclear industry.

25 December   **Saudi Arabia**
An Iraqi airliner crashed in Saudi Arabia following a hijacking attempt; at least 62 of the 107 persons on board were killed, including two of the four hijackers. Several groups claimed credit, but Iranian-backed terrorists probably were responsible.

1987

21 February   **France**
French police arrested the four top leaders of the terrorist group Action Directe (AD) in a farmhouse near Orleans. The arrests dismantled the leadership of AD's international wing, leaving it with little, if any, operational capability. The group had conducted several attacks in 1986, including the assassination of Renault president Georges Besse.

18 March   **Djibouti**
A bomb exploded at the "Café Historil," known to be frequented by Europeans, killing five French citizens (four of whom were military), three West Germans, and three Djiboutians. Fifty persons were wounded, including 25 French

nationals. The bomb was a delayed action device and was timed to go off when the café was crowded. The bomber was arrested a short time later: he was a Palestinian believed to have been working for Libya. His motive may have been to avenge recent Libyan defeats in Chad, attributed to French intervention.

20 March   Italy
Italian Air Force Gen. Licio Giorgieri was shot and killed by two terrorists on a motorcycle while he was being driven home. Giorgieri was director general of armaments in the aerospace sector of the Italian defense ministry. The Red Brigades—Union of Combatant Communists (BR-UCC)—claimed responsibility for the attack. The murder spurred a major counter-terrorist effort by Italian authorities, and by the end of June more than 60 members of the group had been arrested in Italy, France, and Spain.

23 March   West Germany
A large car bomb exploded outside an officers' club at the British Army base at Rheindahlen, injuring over 30 persons, most of whom were West German military officers and their spouses, although they were not the intended targets. The Provisional Irish Republican Army PIRA) claimed responsibility.

24 April   Greece
Sixteen American service men were injured when a bomb exploded alongside a Greek Air Force bus in which they were riding. The bomb had been placed in a metal container on a road near Piraeus and then detonated by remote control. Revolutionary Organization 17 November claimed responsibility for the attack. Although responsible for several previous assassinations of US citizens, this attack was the first time the group had used a bomb in an attempt to cause large numbers of casualties.

9 June   Italy
In a series of incidents in Rome, a car bomb exploded outside the US Embassy, two crude rocket devices were launched into the US Embassy compound, and a bomb of similar construction was launched into the British Embassy compound. Some of the devices failed to explode. In all instances, damage was minor. The Anti-Imperialist International Brigade (AIIB)—believed to be a group associated with, if not part of, the Japanese Red Army—claimed responsibility for the attacks, which appear to have been timed to coincide with the Summit Seven economic conference in Venice.

17 June   Lebanon
US journalist Charles Glass was kidnapped in Beirut along with the son of the Lebanese Defense Minister and their Lebanese driver. After intense Syrian pressure, the two Lebanese were released on 24 June and Glass claimed to have escaped on the night of 17–18 August. The Organization for the Defense of Free People—probably a cover name for Hizballah—claimed responsibility for the kidnapping.

14 July   Pakistan
Two car bombs exploded in a busy shopping center in Karachi within minutes of each other, killing at least 70 and wounding more than 200 persons. The explosions occurred at peak hours in a crowded urban area. No group claimed responsibility, but we believe that the bombings were perpetrated by agents of the Afghanistan Ministry of State Security (WAD) as part of a ruthless campaign to deter the Pakistan Government from supporting anti-Communist guerrillas fighting in Afghanistan.

**24 July   Central African Republic/
                                                 Italy/Switzerland**
A lone gunman who boarded an Air Afrique flight in Bangui, Central African Republic, hijacked the plane as it left Rome. After landing in Geneva, the hijacker killed a French passenger and demanded the release from prison of the Hammadi brothers in West Germany, the Hizballah-backed terrorists in France, and Shia detainees in Israel. The incident ended the same day, after passengers aboard the airliner overpowered the hijacker.

8 August   Honduras
A pipe bomb exploded outside a Chinese restaurant in Comayuga frequented by US servicemen stationed at the nearby Palmerola Airbase. Five US servicemen, one US contractor, and six Hondurans were injured. No group claimed responsibility for the attack; we believe it was carried out by Honduran leftists.

10 August   Greece
A remotely controlled but apparently prematurely detonated bomb secreted in a parked car injured 10 members of a US Air Force flight crew as they traveled past in a bus. The bus, which was unmarked, was used exclusively to transport US Strategic Air command crewmembers to and from Hellenikon Airbase and their hotel. The Revolutionary Organization 17 November claimed responsibility for the attack.

26 October   Philippines
Assassination units, known as sparrow squads, from the Communist New People's Army murdered two US servicemen, a former US serviceman, and a Filipino businessman in four separate incidents near Clark Airbase. After a wait of several weeks, the Central Committee of the Communist Party of the Philippines claimed responsibility for the incidents.

30 October   France
French authorities seized the vessel *Eksund II* off the coast of Brittany with over 150 tons of Libyan-supplied arms destined for the Provisional Irish Republican Army (PIRA) on board. The weapons included surface-to-air missiles. Five crewmen with PIRA ties were arrested.

8 November   Northern Ireland
The PIRA took responsibility for detonating a large bomb at Enniskillen 65 miles southwest of Belfast, which killed 11

civilians and injured more than 60 who were attending a memorial ceremony for Britain's war dead.

25 November   **Zimbabwe**
Zimbabwean dissidents attacked a farm operated by missionaries near Bulwayo and murdered 16 persons, including two US citizens. The victims were tied with barbed wire and then hacked to death with machetes, after which their bodies were burned.

29 November   **Burma/Andaman Sea**
Korean Air Lines Flight 858 disappeared over the Andaman Sea off Burma, killing all 115 persons on board. Two North Korean intelligence agents—an elderly man and a young woman—were arrested in Bahrain on 4 December: the man committed suicide by taking a cyanide pill, the woman tried but failed. The survivor was expelled to South Korea where she subsequently confessed on television that she and her companion had planted a bomb on board the airliner when they boarded it in Baghdad. The two later disembarked in Abu Dhabi. The woman also stated that the operation had been planned by North Korean intelligence officials as part of a plan to destabilize the South Korean Government and disrupt the 1988 Olympic Games to be held in Seoul in September and October.

26 December   **Spain**
Two grenades were thrown into a bar in Barcelona operated by the US United Services Organization (USO). One US sailor was killed and nine others wounded. Two Catalan separatist terrorist groups, the pro-Communist Terra Lliure and the Catalan Red Liberation Army, claimed responsibility for the attack.

1988

18 January   **Japan**
Unknown assailants launched five homemade rockets in the vicinity of Narita Airport. The airport tower, located near the passenger terminal, was the intended target. Authorities suspect Chukaku-ha (the Middle Core Faction), known for its opposition to the second-phase construction of the airport, was responsible for the attack.

21 January   **Greece**
17 November failed in an attempt with a bomb to kill a Drug Enforcement Administration official outside his home in Athens.

17 February   **Lebanon**
Pro-Iranian Hizballah terrorists kidnapped Lt. Col. William Higgins, USMC, Commander of the United Nations Truce Supervisory Organization's Observer Group in Lebanon. The Organization of the Oppressed on Earth claimed responsibility.

20 February   **Senegal**
Two Libyan terrorist operatives and one Senegalese were arrested at Dakar Airport for possession of arms and explosives.

23 March   **Colombia**
An M-19 terrorist fired a light antitank rocket at the US Embassy, causing minor damage but no injuries.

25 March   **India**
A lone gunman attacked a bus occupied by an Alitalia flight crew at the airport in Bombay and injured the aircrew's captain. Indian authorities suspected the ANO, using a cover name, was responsible. The real target may have been an American crew.

5 April   **Middle East**
Hizballah terrorists hijacked Kuwait Airways Flight 422 en route from Bangkok, Thailand, to Kuwait. Before the hijacking ended in Algeria on 20 April, the aircraft landed in Iran and Cyprus. The hijackers' demand for the release of 17 Shia terrorists jailed in Kuwait was rejected, but they killed two Kuwaiti passengers in order to dramatize their demands.

14 April   **Italy**
A car bomb exploded outside the USO club in Naples, killing five persons, including a US Navy enlisted woman. The Organization of Jihad Brigades (a JRA-associated group) claimed responsibility for the attack on the anniversary of the US bombing of Libya on 15 April 1986.

Colombia
Gunmen set off explosives in the USIS bi-national center in Medellin. This attack was claimed by M-19, which has received training and money from Libya.

15 April   **Spain**
A bomb exploded outside a US Air Force communications facility near Humosa. The bomb substantially damaged the facility but caused no casualties. The timing of the attack suggested it was a protest against the 1986 bombing of Libya.

16 April   **Italy**
The BR killed Italian Senator Roberto Ruffilli in his home.

Tunisia
Fatah Deputy Commander (Khalil al-Wazir Abu Jihad) was assassinated in Tunis. No group has claimed responsibility, but Palestinians publicly blamed Israel.

Peru
MRTA, which has Libyan links, claimed responsibility for two attacks against USIS bi-national centers in Lima, Peru.

19 April   **Costa Rica**
A bomb exploded near the USIS bi-national cultural center in San Jose in which several persons were injured. A group with ties to Libya is the prime suspect.

28 April   **Greece**
Hagop Hagopian, the Leader of ASALA, was shot and killed outside his home in Athens. Disgruntled members of the group may have been responsible.

1 May   **Netherlands**
PIRA carried out two attacks on British soldiers as they left two nightclubs. The car bombing and shooting killed three and wounded another three servicemen.

10 May   **India**
A powerful bomb exploded at the Citibank branch in New Delhi, killing one person and wounding at least 13 others. No group claimed responsibility, but Indian authorities believe a non-Indian group, possibly the JRA, rather than Sikh extremists, conducted the attack.

11 May   **Cyprus**
A car bomb detonated near the Israeli Embassy, killing the driver and two others. The ANO claimed responsibility.

15 May   **Sudan**
ANO terrorists, in nearly simultaneous attacks, fired machine guns and threw grenades in the British Sudan Club and the Acropole Hotel in Khartoum. Eight persons, including five UK citizens, were killed.

9 June   **Peru**
Members of the MRTA fired three mortar rounds at the US Ambassador's residence.

13 June   **Peru**
SL terrorists killed a US citizen and Peruvian coworker in an ambush near Quicha Baja.

28 June   **Greece**
17 November, with a car bomb, killed the US defense attaché near his home in Athens.

11 July   **Greece**
The ANO is suspected in the attack aboard The City of Poros day-excursion ship that killed nine persons and wounded approximately 100. A bomb explosion in a car at the ship's pier killed two suspected terrorist occupants. They may have been planning to carry out additional attacks on the ship when it arrived.

13 July   **West Germany**
PIRA detonated a bomb at the British military barracks near Duisburg, injuring nine soldiers.

17 July   **Honduras**
Cinchonero terrorists claimed credit for an attack on nine US servicemen in San Pedro Sula, wounding several.

8 August   **Bolivia**
The Simon Bolivar Guerrilla Commando probably was responsible for detonating a bomb alongside the highway as US Secretary of State Shultz's motorcade drove by on its way to La Paz.

11 September   **Japan**
Police seized mortar launchers and a large amount of explosives in a raid on a warehouse on the outskirts of Niigata City. The warehouse was rented by Chukaku-ha (the Middle Core Faction) in the name of a construction company.

20 September   **West Germany**
The RAF failed in an attempt to murder a West German Finance Ministry official involved in organizing the IMF/World Bank Conference in West Berlin.

26 October   **West Germany**
West German authorities arrested 14 members of the PFLP-GC led by central committee member Dalkamoni and seized weapons, ammunition, and Semtex explosives in a Frankfurt safe house.

5 November   **El Salvador**
Suspected members of the FMLN fired a rocket at the Sheraton Hotel in San Salvador, causing minor damage but no injuries.

5 December   **Peru**
SL terrorists brutally murdered two French development workers along with two Peruvian technicians in the south central department of Apurimac.

21 December   **Scotland**
A Pan American 747 aircraft was destroyed in flight over Scotland by a bomb, most likely planted by terrorists although the investigation is not complete, killing 259 persons on board, including 189 Americans, and 11 others on the ground.

1989

10 January   **Greece**
17 November fatally wounded Greek Public Prosecutor Kostas Androulidakis in Athens.

11 January   **France**
Police arrested one of the top three leaders of the Spanish terrorist group Basque Fatherland and Liberty (ETA).

18 January   **Greece**
17 November wounded Greek Supreme Court Deputy Public Prosecutor Panaylotis Tarasouleas in Athens.

23 January   **Greece**
1 May assassinated Greek Supreme Court Deputy Public Prosecutor Anastasios Vernardos in Athens.

19 February   **Honduras**
A bus carrying US military personnel near Comayagua was hit by a bomb blast, injuring three US military and two Hon-

duran civilians. The Morazanist Patriotic Front (FPM) claimed responsibility.

27 February — Peru
A bomb was thrown at the US Chancery in Lima, causing minor damage. Police arrested a member of Sendero Luminoso (SL) suspected of having thrown the bomb.

29 March — Belgium
An unknown gunman shot and killed the Saudi Arabian Sunni Imam of Brussels' largest mosque and his Tunisian librarian. The murder was probably a reaction to the Imam's public opposition to Ayatollah Khomeini's demand for the execution of author Salman Rushdie.

21 April — The Philippines
"Sparrow units" of the New People's Army assassinated US Army Col. James Rowe while en route to his office in Manila.

27 April — Dominican Republic
Three bombs exploded in Santo Domingo: one at the USIS Binational Center, killing a child and injuring the mother; one at a restaurant, and another on a street in the capital's business section. No group claimed responsibility.

4 May — Greece
17 November wounded former Greek Minister of Public Order George Petsos with a car bomb as he was driving to work in Athens.

16 May — Lebanon
Suspected radical Palestinian terrorists kidnapped two German relief workers, possibly in an attempt to influence the pending verdict on the accused Lebanese hijacker, Muhammad Ali Hammadi, which was before a West German court.

17 May — West Germany
The Hesse State Supreme Court convicted and sentenced Hammadi to life imprisonment for his role in the June 1985 hijacking of TWA Flight 847 to Beirut, the murder of US Navy diver Robert Stethem, and the possession of explosives.

24 May — Bolivia
Two Mormon missionaries were assassinated in La Paz by the Zarate Willka Forces of Liberation (FAL). The killings were probably meant to protest US counter narcotics efforts in Bolivia.

4 June — United Arab Emirates
An Iranian dissident was assassinated, probably by Iranian intelligence officers.

5 July — Peru
Thirty-three Soviet tourists were injured when a bus was bombed in Lima by the Sendero Luminoso.

13 July — Austria
Three Iranian dissidents were assassinated in Vienna by Iranian agents. The victims were Kurdish activists, and one was the leader of the Iranian Kurdish Democratic Party. Later in the year, a Vienna court issued arrest warrants for three Iranians suspected of the murder.

— Honduras
A bomb thrown from a car wounded seven US soldiers outside a discotheque in La Ceiba. The FPM carried out the attack to protest the presence of US troops in Honduras.

14 July — France
Police arrested three important members of the Provisional Irish Republican Army (PIRA). The three were allegedly preparing for a terrorist attack against British military targets in West Germany.

26 July — Saudi Arabia
Two bombs exploded during the hajj ceremonies, killing one and injuring over twenty others.

3 August — United Kingdom
A Shia terrorist was killed assembling a bomb in a London hotel room. The terrorist was reportedly planning an attack to protest Salman Rushdie's book, *The Satanic Verses*.

28 August — Cyprus
One Iranian dissident was assassinated, another injured in an attack by armed gunmen. Iranian intelligence officers probably were responsible for carrying out the assassination.

2 September — France
Police arrested five members of a Parisian cell of the Italian Red Brigades-Fighting Communist Party faction.

5–6 September — Italy
Police arrested four members of the Red Brigades who were linked to a cell arrested in France days before.

7 September — West Germany
PIRA killed the West German wife of a British soldier in a Dortmund military housing area.

12 September — Spain
ETA gunmen assassinated Carmen Tagle, a public prosecutor in Madrid, in the first successful attack by ETA against a member of the Spanish judicial system.

19 September — Niger
A bomb exploded aboard UTA Flight 772 over Niger, killing 171 persons, including seven US citizens. Individuals alleging affiliation with either Hizballah or Chadian separatists claimed responsibility for the attack.

22 September — United Kingdom
PIRA killed 10 British servicemen in a bombing at the Royal Marine School of Music in Kent.

26 September — Chile
The Arnoldo Camu Command (ACC) detonated a bomb across the street from the US Embassy in Santiago, slightly injuring a contract guard.

The Philippines

The New People's Army killed two US civilian Department of Defense contractors in their vehicle north of Clark Airbase, apparently timed to coincide with the arrival of the US Vice President in Manila.

Greece

17 November assassinated Pavlos Bakoyannis, a member of the Greek Parliament and son-in-law of the leader of the New Democracy Party.

3 October — Belgium

A prominent Jewish leader in Brussels was assassinated. The "Soldiers of the Right" claimed responsibility.

6 October — Lebanon

Radical Palestinians were probably responsible for the kidnapping of two Swiss International Red Cross workers outside Sidon, possibly to embarrass PLO Chairman Arafat or to obtain ransom for the hostages.

16 October — Turkey

A Saudi diplomat was seriously injured when a bomb exploded in his car. Islamic Jihad claimed responsibility for the attack.

22 October — Greece

Revolutionary Popular Struggle firebombed three cars belonging to US Air Force personnel in Athens. The next day, an incendiary device was found under another airman's car.

24 October — The Netherlands

A bomb destroyed the Spanish Consulate General's private vehicle parked near his residence in The Hague. The Spanish terrorist group ETA claimed responsibility.

25 October — Peru

SL probably was responsible for detonating a car bomb in front of the US Marine House in Lima; two other bombs exploded outside the Soviet and Chinese Embassies within 20 minutes of each other.

26 October — West Germany

PIRA murdered a British soldier and his six-month-old daughter in a shooting in Wildenrath.

27 October — The Netherlands

Bombs exploded at two separate offices of the Spanish Embassy in The Hague. ETA claimed responsibility.

1 November — Lebanon

A Saudi official was assassinated by three gunmen in West Beirut. Islamic Jihad claimed responsibility for the attack.

30 November — West Germany

The Red Army Faction (RAF) claimed responsibility for the bombing that killed Deutsche Bank Chairman Alfred Herrhausen and injured the driver of his armored car. The bomb was concealed in the saddlebags of a bicycle propped against a road marker near Herrhausen's residence outside Frankfurt. The bomb was wired to an electrical device hidden in nearby bushes and triggered by a light beam that spanned the road.

6 December — The Netherlands

Rockets were launched at the Spanish Ambassador's residence, which is co-located with the Spanish Embassy in The Hague. Damage was minimal and no injuries resulted. ETA claimed responsibility.

16 December — Belgium

A Syrian diplomat escaped an attempted assassination when two grenades were discovered attached to the undercarriage of his car in Brussels.

20 December — Bolivia

The FAL claimed responsibility for detonating a bomb outside the US Embassy in La Paz to protest US military action in Panama.

21 December — Sweden

A Swedish Court convicted four Palestinians of complicity in a series of bombings in Stockholm, Copenhagen, and Amsterdam in 1985–86.

1990

13 January — Peru

Sendero Luminoso (SL) terrorists singled out and shot two French tourists aboard a bus traveling in the Apurimac department. Peruvian passengers were forced to pay the terrorists money but were unharmed.

15 January — Peru

Tupac Amanu Revolutionary Movement (MRTA) terrorists bombed the US Embassy in Lima, injuring three guards.

19 January — The Philippines

Members of the Moro National Liberation Front killed two Swiss Red Cross workers and wounded a third during an ambush on Mindanao.

1 February — Thailand

Three officials of the Saudi Arabian Embassy in Bangkok were assassinated in two separate attacks. One official was gunned down at his home, and the other two were shot in a car outside their residences. Iranian surrogates are believed to have been responsible.

4 February — Egypt

Palestinian Islamic Jihad (PIJ) terrorists attacked an Israeli tour bus en route from Rafah to Cairo, killing 11 persons—including nine Israeli citizens—and wounding 17 others.

8 February — Peru

An American tourist was shot and killed at an Inca fortress near Cuzco. Sendero Luminoso may have been responsible, although a criminal motive has not been ruled out.

19 February — Greece
The Revolutionary Solidarity terrorist group shot and killed a Greek psychiatrist in Athens as he was walking to his car. In a letter, the group stated he was killed because of his work at the Korydallos prison.

2 March — Panama
An unidentified assailant tossed a grenade inside a bar frequented by Americans, killing one US serviceman and injuring 15 others. Fourteen Panamanians were also injured in the attack.

6 March — The Philippines
An American citizen was assassinated by members of the New People's Army (NPA) for refusing to pay "revolutionary taxes" levied against his ranch.

30 March — Lebanon
The Polish Ambassador and his Lebanese wife were shot and wounded in Beirut. A previously unknown Arab group claimed responsibility for the attack, threatening to strike again if Poland continued to assist the emigration of Soviet Jews to Israel.

31 March — Honduras
Four terrorists attacked a US Air Force bus near Tegucigalpa, injuring eight persons. The Morazanist Patriotic Front claimed responsibility.

3 April — Pakistan
A bomb concealed in a box of apples exploded in a crowded bazaar in Lahore, killing five persons and wounding 50. The Afghan secret police is believed responsible.

14 April — Chile
Suspected members of the Manuel Rodriguez Patriotic Front (FPMR) hurled explosive devices into the US Consular annex compound in Santiago, injuring one contract guard and damaging two vehicles.

24 April — Switzerland
An exiled Iranian political leader was shot and killed near Geneva while driving home. Agents of the Iranian Government are believed responsible.

13 May — The Philippines
NPA assassins shot and killed two US Air Force airmen near Clark Airbase. The killings came on the eve of the Philippines-US exploratory talks on the future of the US military bases in the Philippines.

27 May — The Netherlands
Two Australian tourists where shot and killed in Roermond by members of the Provisional Irish Republican Army (PIRA). The claim letter acknowledged the group had killed the Australians by mistake, believing them to be British soldiers.

28 May — Israel
One person was killed and nine wounded in a pipe-bomb explosion at a market in Jerusalem. Several Palestinian groups claimed responsibility.

30 May — Israel
Israeli forces aborted a sea borne attack on the beaches at Tel Aviv mounted by the Palestine Liberation Front (PLF). Four PLF members were killed and 12 arrested.

2 June — Germany
A British Army artillery officer was shot and killed by three attackers in Dortmund while returning home from a social event with his wife. PIRA issued a statement in Dublin claiming responsibility.

6 June — Lebanon
A rocket was fired at the Romanian Embassy in Beirut, injuring one person. The "Revolutionary Action Organization" claimed the attack was to protest Romania's role in facilitating Jewish immigration to Israel.

10 June — Bolivia
A prominent Bolivian businessman was kidnapped in La Paz by the Nestor Paz Zamora Commission (CNPZ), which demanded payment of a ransom. In December he was shot and killed moments before local police stormed the building in which he was held.

Greece
A rocket fired from a bazooka was launched at the offices of Proctor and Gamble in Athens, causing extensive property damage but no injuries. Revolutionary Organization 17 November claimed responsibility for the attack.

13 June — The Philippines
An American Peace Corps worker was abducted from his home by NPA terrorists. No ransom was paid, and he was released unharmed on 2 August.

23 June — Israel
A pipe bomb exploded on a crowded beach at Ein Gedi, wounding two Israelis and two West Germans.

18 July — Peru
MRTA exploded a dynamite bomb at the US Bi-national Center in Cuzco, injuring four students.

27 July — Germany
The Red Army Faction attempted to kill interior Ministry State Secretary Hans Neusel with a bomb attached to a guardrail on a highway exit ramp near the Interior Ministry.

28 July — Israel
A pipe bomb exploded on a beach in Tel Aviv, killing a Canadian tourist and wounding 20 others.

30 July — United Kingdom
Member of Parliament Ian Gow was killed in front of his home by a bomb planted by the Provisional Irish Republican Army.

26 September — Turkey
Gunmen assassinated the former Deputy Director of the Turkish National Intelligence Agency in Istanbul. The Dev Sol group claimed responsibility.

27 September — Djibouti
Grenades thrown from a passing car exploded in the Café de Paris, killing a French boy and injuring 15 other French citizens. At approximately the same time, grenades were also thrown at the Café L'Historil but did not explode. A previously unknown group, the Djibouti Youth Movement, claimed responsibility.

10 October — Bolivia
Members of the Nestor Paz Zamora Commission exploded a bomb and fired automatic weapons at the US Embassy Marine Guard residence in La Paz, killing one Bolivian guard and wounding another. The explosion caused major structural damage to the building.

12 October — Egypt
Local Islamic extremists killed Egypt's Assembly speaker during an assault on his motorcade in Cairo.

23 October — France
An Iranian dissident leader of the Flag of Freedom Organization was assassinated in his Paris apartment. Agents of the Iranian Government were probably responsible.

24 October — Northern Ireland
A PIRA car bomb, driven by a civilian whose family was being held hostage, killed five soldiers and the civilian driver at a Londonderry checkpoint.

3 November — Chile
A bomb exploded in front of a restaurant in Vina del Mar, injuring eight persons, including three US sailors. The Manuel Rodriguez Patriotic Front-Dissident Faction (FPMR/D) was probably responsible.

8 November — Peru
MRTA exploded a bomb in the park adjacent to the US Ambassador's residence and attacked his home with automatic weapons. No injuries resulted.

17 November — Chile
A bomb concealed in a softball bat exploded at the national stadium in Santiago during a softball game between the University of Chile and the American Chamber of Commerce. One Canadian was killed, and a US Embassy officer was wounded. The FPMR/D was probably responsible.

20 November — Greece
The car in which a Greek industrialist was riding narrowly missed being struck by three rockets fired at close range by the Revolutionary Organization 17 November.

10 December — Peru
Sendero Luminoso terrorists exploded a car bomb near the US Embassy in Lima. No injuries or damage resulted.

Peru
Terrorists armed with dynamite destroyed a Mobil Oil Company exploration camp in the Upper Huallaga Valley. They also used the camp's helicopters to dynamite other nearby Mobil installations. Sendero Luminoso was probably responsible.

16 December — Chile
The Lautaro Youth Movement fired automatic weapons and threw incendiary bombs at a Mormon church in Santiago. The church was destroyed, but no injuries resulted.

1991

2 January — El Salvador
Two US crewmen, Lt. Col. David Pickett and crew chief PFC Earnest Dawson, were executed after their helicopter was downed by Farabundo Marti National Liberation Front (FMLN) militants in San Miguel department. A third American, Chief Warrant Officer Daniel Scott, died of injuries he received when the helicopter was shot down.

12 January — Afghanistan
Hezb-I-Islami (Hekmatyar) kidnapped four Swiss Red Cross workers outside Qandahar.

18 January — Indonesia
A bomb was discovered outside the US Ambassador's residence in Jakarta. The device was probably place by Iraqi agents.

19 January — Philippines
A bomb carried by two Iraqi agents detonated prematurely near the USIS library in Manila. One was killed; the second was seriously injured.

31 January — Yemen
Gunmen threw dynamite at the residences of the Turkish and Japanese Ambassadors and attacked the US Embassy.

Peru
MRTA terrorists fired shots and an antitank weapon at the US Embassy.

3 February — Saudi Arabia
Unknown assailants fired upon a bus transporting US Air Force personnel, wounding two US airmen and a Saudi guard.

Chronology of Significant Terrorist Incidents 1961–2005

7 February — United Kingdom
Provisional Irish Republican Army (PIRA) conducted an improved mortar attack against the residence of Prime Minister John Major in London. Three mortar rounds were fired from a parked van nearby. There were no deaths or serious injuries.

Turkey
Dev Sol shot and killed a US citizen contractor as he was getting into his car to travel to work at Incirlik Air Base in Adana.

13 February — Germany
The Red Army Faction (RAF) claimed responsibility for firing approximately 250 rounds of small-arms fire at the US Embassy in Bonn. This was the first RAF attack against a US target since 1985.

16 February — Chile
Manual Rodriguez Patriotic Front dissidents (FPMR/D) claimed responsibility for an antitank rocket attack on a US Marine security guard van in Santiago, injuring one marine.

20 February — Iran
Concussion grenades were thrown at the British, Italian, and Turkish Embassies in Tehran. A claim of responsibility was issued by Islamic Jihad.

23 February — Japan
Chukaku-ha attacked a US Navy housing compound in Yokohama with projectiles, causing minor damage.

28 February — Turkey
Two Dev Sol gunmen shot and wounded a US Air Force officer as he entered his residence in Izmir.

2 March — Sri Lanka
State Minister for Defense Wijerate was killed in a car bombing in Colombo along with 50 other victims. Liberation Tigers of Tamil Eelam (LTTE) probably was responsible.

12 March — Greece
US Air Force Sergeant Ronald Odell Stewart was killed by a remote control bomb detonated at the entrance of his apartment building in Athens. The Revolutionary Organization 17 November claimed the attack was in response to "the genocide of 13,000 Iraqis."

22 March — Turkey
Three members of Dev Sol assassinated John Gandy, a US civilian contractor, in his Istanbul office.

26 March — Singapore
Four Pakistanis claiming to be members of the Pakistani People's party hijacked a Singapore Airlines flight en route from Kuala Lumpur to Singapore and demanded the release of several people reportedly imprisoned in Pakistan. Singapore counter terrorism units stormed the plane and killed the hijackers.

28 March — Saudi Arabia
Three US marines were shot at and injured by an Arab while driving near Camp Three, Jubial.

31 March — India
A Kashmiri separatist group, the Muslim Janbaz Force (MJF), kidnapped two Swedish engineers. They escaped on 5 July.

1 April — Germany
RAF killed Detlev Rohwedder, a leading German businessman, in a sniper attack on his Duesseldorf home.

19 April — Greece
Seven people, including six Greeks, were killed in Patras when explosives carried by a Palestinian student detonated prematurely.

France
An Iranian dissident leader was stabbed and killed in the lobby of his apartment building in Paris.

17 May — Peru
Sendero Luminoso (SL) killed the Canadian director of the humanitarian organization World Mission and seriously injured his Colombian assistant in a Lima suburb.

21 May — India
Former Prime Minister Rajiv Gandhi was assassinated by a suspected LTTE suicide bomber while campaigning in southern India. Seventeen others also died in the bombing.

22 May — Peru
An Australian nun and four Peruvian officials were executed by SL after a "people's trial" in a rural village.

29 May — Spain
Basque Fatherland and Liberty (ETA) claimed responsibility for a car bombing that destroyed a Civil Guard barracks near Barcelona, killing nine and injuring over 50.

5 June — Peru
A Soviet textile technician was ambushed and killed by four SL members in Lima.

23 June — Honduras
The Morazanist Patriotic Front (FPM) launched an RPG-7 rocket at the UN Observer Group headquarters in Tegucigalpa, causing some damage.

26 June — India
A Kashmiri separatist group kidnapped one Dutch and seven Israeli tourists in Srinagar. One Israeli was killed in an escape attempt.

1 July — India
A Soviet engineer was killed trying to escape after being kidnapped (along with 14 Indians) by United Liberation Front of Assam (ULFA) militants in Assam.

3, 12 July   Italy, Japan

The Italian translator of Salman Rushdie's book *The Satanic Verses* was stabbed and beaten by a man believed to be Iranian on 3 July in Milan. The Japanese translator of the book was stabbed to death in Tokyo on 12 July.

7 July   Afghanistan

Two private American agricultural consultants were kidnapped by Afghan militants in Joghere. One man was released in mid-October, the other in December.

11 July   France

A founder and former director of Dev Sol was assassinated in Paris by probable Dev Sol members.

12 July   Peru

Three Japanese agronomists were assassinated by 10 SL members at a Japanese-funded rural research center.

16 July   Greece

A remote control car bomb injured the Turkish Charge D'Affaires and two other members of the Turkish Embassy in Athens. 17 November claimed responsibility for the attack.

2 August   Turkey

The Kurdish Worker's Party (PKK) kidnapped 10 German tourists near Lake Van. The tourists were released on 9 August.

6 August   France

Former Iranian Prime Minister Shapur Bakhtiar and his aide were assassinated in Paris.

8 August   Lebanon

British hostage John McCarthy was released from captivity. A French aid worker was kidnapped in Beirut by probably Hizballah elements in protests of the McCarthy release. The Frenchman was freed by his captors 11 August.

9 August   Peru

Two Polish priests were shot and killed by SL members in a remote rural area; a local mayor was also murdered, and an Italian nun was held for several hours.

10 August   Philippines

A grenade attack on a cultural show killed two youth missionaries—a Swede and a New Zealander. Muslim separatists are suspected in the attack.

11 August   Lebanon

American hostage Edward Tracy was released from captivity.

19 August   Turkey

Dev Sol claimed responsibility for the fatal shooting of a British businessman in his Istanbul office.

20 August   Romania

The Indian Ambassador to Romania was wounded in a drive-by assassination attempt in Bucharest. The Khalistan Liberation Front (KLF), a Sikh terrorist group, claimed credit.

25 August   Peru

An Italian priest was killed in an ambush on his car by SL members.

30 August   Turkey

Suspected PKK terrorists kidnapped three Americans, a Briton, and an Australian near Bingol. The hostages were released unharmed on 21 September.

6 September   Former USSR

An unsuccessful assassination attempt was made against the Azerbaijani President. The opposition Azeri Popular Front (APF) is suspected.

13 September   Lebanon

Palestinian guerrillas seized a group of UN peacekeeping soldiers in south Lebanon after the guerrillas failed to reach Israel by sea. They had apparently intended to carry out a terrorist attack in Israel. One Swedish officer was killed and five other officers were wounded in an ensuing gun battle between the guerrillas and a force of Israeli troops and Lebanese militiamen.

24 September   Lebanon

British hostage Jack Mann was released from captivity.

7 October   Greece

A Turkish Embassy press attaché was shot and killed near his home in Athens by two 17 November assassins. The group denounced the Turkish presence in Cyprus.

9 October   India

The Khalistan Liberation Front kidnapped the Romanian Charge D'Affaires in New Delhi in an unsuccessful effort to force the release of other terrorists jailed in India. He was released 26 November.

14 October   India

A French engineer was kidnapped by the Muslim militant group, Al Fatah, in Kashmir. The group demanded the release of 11 jailed members.

22 October   Lebanon

American hostage Jesse Turner was released from captivity.

28 October   Turkey

Two car bombings killed a US Air Force sergeant and severely wounded an Egyptian diplomat. Turkish Islamic Jihad claimed responsibility.

  West Bank

Gunmen fired on a bus carrying Israeli settlers, killing two Israelis and wounding several others. The PIJ and The PFLP claimed responsibility.

29 October   Lebanon

A rocket struck the edge of the US Embassy in Beirut. There were no casualties.

30 October   Pakistan
The Afghan director of the Austrian Relief Committee was wounded when unidentified gunmen fired upon his vehicle near Peshawar.

3 November   Lebanon
A 100-kg car bomb destroyed the Administration Building of the American University in Beirut, killing one person and wounding at least a dozen.

18 November   Lebanon
American hostage Thomas Sutherland and British hostage Terry Waite were released from captivity.

25 November   Pakistan
The Afghan director of an English language program run by the International Rescue Committee was assassinated by unidentified gunmen in Peshawar.

2 December   Lebanon
American hostage Joseph Cicippio was released from captivity.

3 December   Lebanon
American hostage Alann Steen was released from captivity.

4 December   Lebanon
American hostage Terry Anderson was released from captivity.

19 December   Hungary
ASALA claimed responsibility for a failed attempt on the life of the Turkish Ambassador in Budapest.

22 December   Lebanon
The remains of American hostage Col. William R. Higgins were recovered and flown back to the United States for burial at Quantico National Cemetery.

27 December   Lebanon
The remains of American hostage William Buckley were recovered and flown back to the United States for burial at Arlington National Cemetery.

28 December   Hungary
A car bomb exploded near a bus transporting Soviet Jewish immigrants to Israel, injuring two policemen who were guarding the bus.

1992

9 January   Pakistan
An Afghan working for the UN Operation Salam mine awareness program was shot and killed outside his home Peshawar.

17 January   Philippines
Michael Barnes, Vice President and General Manager of Philippine Geothermal, Incorporated, and Vice President of the American Chambers of Commerce, was kidnapped in Manila by members of the Red Scorpion Group, a gang comprised of some former New People's Army members and criminal elements. On 18 March he was rescued by elements of the Philippine National Police and other government forces during a coordinated raid.

21 January   Colombia
US citizen Edward Faught was kidnapped in Bagre, Antioquia Department, by suspected National Liberation Army terrorists. He was released from captivity on 30 November 1992 in El Bagre, Colombia.

**   Colombia**
Suspected Revolutionary Armed Forces of Colombia (FARC) guerrillas kidnapped US citizen Michael James, a geologist, in Mutata, Antioquia Department. James was released on 3 March near the place from which he had been taken.

11 February   Peru
Probable Sendero Luminoso terrorists car-bombed the US Ambassador's residence in Lima. The blast killed three policemen and wounded a fourth and several passers-by.

7 March   Turkey
A bomb place under a car exploded in the Cankaya District of Ankara, killing the Israeli Embassy's security attaché and seriously injuring two Turkish boys.

17 March   Argentina
Hizballah terrorists truck-bombed the Israeli Embassy in Buenos Aires. Islamic Jihad—a cover name for Hizballah—publicly claimed responsibility for the attack and provided a videotape of the Embassy taken before the bombing to authenticate the claim. The three-story Embassy was leveled, and a nearby church, school, retirement home, and private residences were seriously damaged. Casualties totaled 29 dead and 242 wounded.

20 March   Iraq
Assailants in Baghdad attacked a car belonging to the Embassy of the Islamic Republic of Iran. Two Iranian diplomats were beaten during the attack.

27 March   Colombia
A bomb destroyed the façade of the US-owned Diners Club in Bogota and killed one employee. Five passersby were injured. FARC claimed responsibility for the attack.

22 April   Afghanistan
An Icelandic employee of the International Committee of the Red Cross (ICRC) was murdered by an unidentified mujahid in the town of Kowt-e Ashrow (Maidanshar) outside Kabul.

23 April   India
A bomb exploded in New Delhi at the Loomis Restaurant in the Vivek Hotel. Thirteen foreign tourists and two Indian waiters were injured.

20 May — Kuwait
Two Romanian circus performers were wounded when four assailants attacked their bus with machine guns. No one claimed responsibility.

10 June — Panama
A US Army vehicle was raked with gunfire between Panama City and Colon, killing the driver and wounding the passenger and a civilian bystander.

14 June — Pakistan
Unidentified assailants killed a Japanese engineer working in Peshawar for the United Nations.

3 July — Spain
Two bombs exploded in an underground parking lot on the main street of San Sebastian, where the first Tour de France bicyclists were expected to arrive on 4 July. The explosion caused one injury and two cars were damaged.

6 July — Iraq
The wife of French President Francois Mitterrand escaped injury in a car-bomb attack near the town of Hawana, Iraq. Four people were killed, and at least 19 others were injured.

8 July — Iraq
Two UN soldiers were wounded in a grenade attack in Irbil.

15 July — Egypt
Three armed assailants attacked a tour bus near Luxor, slightly injuring four tourists.

17 July — Iraq
A UN guard was assassinated in Dahuk.

20 July — Iraq
A bomb explosion destroyed a UN vehicle near Sulaymaniyah. Two UN soldiers were injured.

21 July — Peru
Suspected Sendero Luminoso terrorists detonated a car bomb near the front entrance of the Bolivian Embassy in Lima. The bomb injured 15 people and caused severe structural damage.

24 July — Peru
Five American Airlines workers in charge of cleaning and loading tasks were wounded by a bomb that exploded at Lima's Jorge Chavez Airport.

4 August — Germany
A dissident Iranian poet was stabbed and killed in Bonn.

25 August — Algeria
A bomb exploded in Algiers at the Houari Boumedienne International Airport, near the Air France ticket counter, killing 12 people and inuring at least 128.

5 September — Colombia
The Simon Bolivar National Guerrilla Coordinating Board detonated an explosive device on a pipeline, spilling an estimated 10,000 barrels of oil. Three children died and five persons were injured.

9 September — Turkey
Probably Kurdistan Workers Party terrorists attacked the Mobil exploration site neat the city of Batman. Several non American workers were wounded.

17 September — Germany
Four Kurdish separatists from Iran were assassinated at a Greek restaurant in Berlin. One of the three was the leader of the Kurdish Democratic Party of Iran whose predecessor was assassinated by Iranian agents in Austria in 1989.

2 October — Peru
Five Sendero Luminoso terrorists assassinated an Italian lay missionary Jangas.

12 October — Iraq
A US soldier serving with the United Nations was stabbed and wounded near the port of Umm Qasr.

21 October — Egypt
A bus carrying foreign tourists was attacked by two unidentified gunmen in Dayrut, southern Egypt. One British tourist was killed, and two others were wounded.

23 October — Colombia
British businessman Arthur Kessler was kidnapped in Magdalena by the FARC guerrilla movement. He was killed by the FARC the next day during a Colombian military rescue attempt.

2 November — Iraq
A bomb exploded in a market near the headquarters of the UN guard contingent in Irbil. One person was killed, and 16 were injured.

7 December — Jordan
Two assailants shot and killed an Iraqi nuclear scientist near his residence in Amman.

25 December — Rwanda
Twenty people, including four French soldiers, were injured when a bomb exploded in a Kigali nightclub.

28 December — Peru
Sendero Luminoso guerrillas detonated car bombs at the Japanese and Chinese Embassies in Lima, causing injuries and damaging more than 60 homes and buildings. At least 12 people were injured by the car bomb at the Japanese Embassy; all were bystanders, neighbors, or in passing vehicles.

29 December — Yemen
An explosion at the Gold Mihor Hotel in Aden killed an Austrian national and seriously injured his wife. About 100 US soldiers, part of Operation Restore Hope in Somalia, had been staying in Aden since mid-December.

1993

22 January — Peru
Terrorists detonated a van bomb at a Coca-Cola plant in central Lima, causing serious damage to the plant. At least two persons were killed, and two others were injured. Later that day, a car bomb detonated at another Coca-Cola plant in Lima, causing only slight material damage.

26 January — Turkey
Well-known Turkish journalist Ugur Mumcu, noted for his criticism of Islamic extremism and separatism, was killed when a bomb exploded under his car outside his apartment in Ankara.

28 January — Turkey
Police bodyguards foiled an attempt to ambush the motorcade of a prominent Jewish businessman and community leader in Istanbul. Police recovered an RPG-18 rocket at the scene and, on 30 January, arrested two of the terrorists as they fled toward the Iranian border.

Peru
Terrorists exploded a car bomb in front of the IBM headquarters building in Lima. Major damage was caused, and 11 passers-by and employees were injured.

31 January — Panama
A large group of FARC terrorists from Colombia kidnapped three US missionaries—Mark Rich, David Mankins, and Rick Tenenoff—from the New Tribes Mission at a location near the Colombian border. A $5 million ransom has been demanded. FARC produced proof that the three missionaries were still alive in December through taped messages from the hostages to their wives. FARC is still holding the hostages.

4 February — Egypt
A molotov cocktail bomb was lobbed at a tour bus as South Korean passengers waited to embark at a hotel outside Cairo. The Islamic extremist terrorist group al-Gama'a al-Islamiyya claimed responsibility for the attack.

23 February — Colombia
Eight ELN terrorists kidnapped US citizen Lewis Manning, an employee of the Colombian gold-mining company Oresom, in the Choco area. In December, the International Committee of the Red Cross received a photograph of the hostage as proof that he was still alive.

26 February — Egypt
A Swedish, Turkish, and an Egyptian citizen were killed when a bomb exploded inside a cafe in downtown Cairo. US citizens Jill Papineau and Raymond Chico, a Canadian, and a Frenchman, and 14 others were wounded.

United States
Terrorists exploded a massive van bomb in an underground parking garage below the World Trade Center in New York City. Six people were killed, and some 1,000 others were injured. A group of Islamic extremists was later arrested.

3 March — Former Yugoslavia
Terrorists exploded a small bomb, probably a handgrenade, in front of the US Embassy in Belgrade, causing minor damage.

7 March — Germany
Terrorists firebombed the Turkish Consulate in Hamburg, causing little damage. Police arrested four people.

8 March — Costa Rica
Four terrorists took 25 persons hostage in the Nicaraguan Embassy in San Jose, including the Nicaraguan Ambassador. The hostages were held for several days while negotiations were conducted. On 21 March, the occupation of the Embassy concluded peacefully, and, after the hostages were released, the terrorists were permitted to leave the country.

16 March — Italy
Two terrorists on a motorscooter shot and killed a leading Iranian dissident while he was traveling in his car in Rome.

22 March — Iraq
A Belgian official from a nongovernment organization involved in relief efforts in northern Iraq was shot and killed while traveling on the road between Irbil and Sulaimaniyah.

15 April — Kuwait
Kuwaiti authorities arrested 17 people as they attempted to infiltrate Kuwait from Iraq. Another person was arrested later, and a large car bomb and weapons were recovered. Fourteen are charged with being part of an Iraqi Government plot to assassinate former President Bush while he was visiting Kuwait.

20 April — Egypt
Terrorists attempted to assassinate Egyptian Information Minister Safwat Sharif in Cairo by firing shots at his motorcade. The Minister was slightly injured, and his bodyguard was seriously wounded. Al-Gama'a al-Islamiyya claimed responsibility for the attack.

13 May — Chile
Three terrorists entered a Mormon church in Santiago, overpowered the Bishop, sprayed the church with fuel, and set it afire. The church was completely destroyed. The terrorists left pamphlets at the scene in which the Mapu Lautaro group—United Popular Action Movement—claimed responsibility.

19 May — Peru
Terrorists detonated a car bomb in front of the Chilean Embassy in Lima at the end of a strike called by the Sendero Luminoso terrorist group. The explosion damaged the Embassy and nearby houses.

8 June — Egypt
Terrorists exploded a bomb underneath an overpass as a tour bus traveled to the Giza pyramids. Two Egyptians were killed,

and six British tourists, nine Egyptians, three Syrians, and at least three others were injured.

22 June   **Lebanon**

Two terrorists were killed and another was injured while attempting to plant a bomb on a bridge near the Al-Balamand Monastery. The target of the failed bomb attempt may have been a bus carrying 22 church members from around the world who were attending a meeting of the Commission for Dialogue Between the Catholic and Orthodox Churches.

24 June   **Western Europe**

Terrorists from the Kurdistan Workers Party (PKK) staged a wave of coordinated attacks in more than 30 cities of six West European countries. The attacks consisted primarily of vandalism against Turkish diplomatic and commercial targets, and included the takeover of a Turkish Consulate.

27 June   **Turkey**

Terrorists threw handgrenades at several hotels and restaurants frequented by tourists in the Mediterranean resort area of Antalya. Among the 28 people injured, 12 were foreigners. Earlier, on 9 June, PKK leader Abdulla Ocalan threatened violence by the PKK against tourist facilities in western Turkey.

1 July   **Japan**

A few days before President Clinton's arrival at the US Air Force base in Yokota before the Group of Seven summit in Tokyo, terrorists fired two homemade rockets, causing minimal damage.

7 July   **Japan**

Terrorists exploded a homemade bomb at the UN Technology Center in Osaka, causing minor damage. On 9 July, the Chukaku-Ha terrorist group claimed responsibility. Terrorists fired four homemade projectiles at the headquarters of the US Air Force at Camp Zama. None of the projectiles exploded and little damage was caused.

                                                                                    Peru

Police discovered the bodies of two European tourists in a remote area of Ayacucho. The two had been traveling together in a region contested by Sendero Luminoso terrorists.

5 July–14 October   **Turkey**

In eight separate incidents, the PKK kidnapped 19 Western tourists traveling in southeastern Turkey. The hostages, including US citizen Colin Patrick Starger, were released unharmed after being held for several weeks.

25 July   **Turkey**

A terrorist bomb planted in a trash can next to an automatic teller machine in the Hagia Sophia District of Istanbul exploded and wounded two Italian tourists.

27 July   **Peru**

After first spraying the building with automatic weapons, terrorists exploded a van bomb outside the US Embassy in Lima, injuring an Embassy guard. The explosion caused extensive damage to the Embassy's facade and perimeter fence. Subsequent small fires caused only minor damage. The nearby Spanish Embassy, as well as stores and a US-owned hotel, were also damaged. Two hotel employees and a hotel guest were injured. The explosion coincided with an "armed strike" called by Sendero Luminoso.

18 August   **Turkey**

Terrorists threw a handgrenade underneath a Hungarian tourist bus in front of a hotel. Three foreign tourists and five Turkish bystanders were injured.

                                                                                    Egypt

A motorcycle bomb killed five persons and wounded 15 others on a road in Cairo. The bomb was directed at Egyptian Interior Minister Alfi, who was slightly injured. The Islamic extremist group New Jihad claimed responsibility.

25 August   **Turkey**

Four terrorists, masquerading as Turkish security officials, kidnapped Iranian dissident Mohammad Khaderi from his residence. On 4 September, his body was discovered by the side of the Kiursehir-Boztepe Highway.

28 August   **Turkey**

Iranian dissident Behram Azadfer was assassinated by terrorists in Ankara.

2 September   **Italy**

Three terrorists threw a handgrenade over the fence and fired shots at the US Air Force base in Aviano. The Red Brigades terrorist group later claimed responsibility.

9 September   **Chile**

Terrorists placed small bombs at two McDonald's restaurants and a Kentucky Fried Chicken restaurant in the Santiago area. The two bombs in the McDonald's restaurants exploded, causing some damage but no casualties. The bomb in the Kentucky Fried Chicken restaurant was found and deactivated. In all three instances, a man claiming to be a member of the Movement of the Revolutionary Left (MIR) telephoned to claim responsibility.

20 September   **Algeria**

One Moroccan and two French surveyors were kidnapped by terrorists as they drove between Oran and Sidi Bel Abbes. The Morrocan citizen was released unharmed, but the two Frenchmen were later found murdered.

26 September   **Iraq**

A UN truck carrying 12 tons of medical supplies was destroyed by a bomb while traveling near Irbil. The bomb had been attached to the truck's fuel tank. The driver and 12 civilians were injured.

11 October   **Norway**

The Norwegian publisher of Salman Rushdie's book *The Satanic Verses* was shot and seriously wounded at his home near Oslo.

16 October   **Algeria**

Terrorists shot and killed two Russian military officers and wounded a third outside an apartment building near the Algerian military academy. The Russians were instructors at the academy.

19 October   **Algeria**

Terrorists kidnapped a Peruvian, a Filipino, and a Colombian, technicians employed by the firm, from the cafeteria of an Italian construction firm in Tiaret. On 21 October, the three were found dead with their throats cut 50 km from the abduction site. On 26 October, the extremist Armed Islamic Group claimed responsibility for this and other attacks against foreigners.

24 October   **Algeria**

Three French diplomats were kidnapped as they left their apartment in Algiers. A police officer who attempted to prevent the kidnapping was shot and killed. On 26 October the Armed Islamic Group claimed responsibility for the incident. The three diplomats were released unharmed on the night of 31 October.

                                                                                    Israel

Two small explosive charges were detonated near the French Embassy in Tel Aviv. There was no damage or casualties. A member of the Jewish extremist Kahane Chai movement claimed responsibility for the explosions, saying the attack was carried out to protest PLO leader Yasir Arafat's visit to France and agreements he signed there.

25 October   **Nigeria**

Four members of a Nigerian dissident group hijacked a Nigerian Airways Airbus-310 airliner with 150 passengers and crew on board shortly after it took off from Lagos. After trying unsuccessfully to land the aircraft at N'Djamena, Chad, the terrorists ordered the plane to land at Niamey, Niger. The hijackers then released two groups of passengers. After lengthy but fruitless negotiations, Nigerian police stormed the aircraft on 28 October. All four of the hijackers surrendered, but one of the crew and one of the hijackers were killed during the rescue operation.

                                                                                    Peru

Terrorists exploded a large bomb under a minibus in the parking lot near the departure terminal at Lima's international airport. The driver of a hotel shuttle bus was killed and about 20 others were injured. The American Airlines cargo office, which was located nearby, sustained some damage.

29 October   **France**

Three terrorists threw a firebomb into the Turkish-owned Bosporus Bank in central Paris. No serious damage was caused, but four people were injured, one seriously.

4 November   **Western Europe**

The PKK staged a second round of coordinated attacks against Turkish diplomatic and commercial facilities in six West European countries. The assaults consisted mainly of firebombings and vandalism, but one person was killed and about 20 others were injured.

8 November   **Iran**

Two handgrenades were thrown into the courtyard of the French Embassy in Tehran, causing little damage. On the same day, a French citizen was injured when a hand grenade was thrown into the Tehran offices of Air France. A group called the Hizballah Committee claimed responsibility for both attacks, saying they were carried out to protest the French Government's support for the Mujahedin-e-Khalq.

14 November   **Philippines**

Terrorists from the Islamic extremist group Abu Sayyaf kidnapped a US missionary, Charles M. Watson, in Pangutaran Island, Sulu Batu. The missionary worked for the Summer Institute of Linguistics. He was released unharmed in Manila on 7 December.

20 November   **Peru**

Terrorists exploded a satchel bomb outside the offices of the US-Peruvian Binational Center in Lima. The bomb caused minor damage.

25 November   **Egypt**

A car bomb exploded near the motorcade of Prime Minister Atef Sedky; the Prime Minister was unhurt, but one bystander, a teenaged girl, was killed and at least 18 people were wounded. The "Jihad Group" later claimed responsibility.

29 November   **Iraq**

Terrorists shot and seriously wounded the senior fuel coordinator for the Australian CARE organization in Atrush.

2 December   **Algeria**

A Spanish businessman was shot and killed at an illegal roadblock manned by terrorists while driving between Oran and Annaba.

4 December   **Algeria**

An Italian businessman was shot and wounded by a terrorist as he left his residence in a suburb of Algiers.

5 December   **Algeria**

Terrorists shot and killed a Russian woman as she was shopping in a market in Algiers.

7 December   **Algeria**

Terrorists shot and killed a British subject at a gas station in Arzew.

Terrorists shot and killed a retired French citizen in Larba. At the time, the Frenchman was in his hut on the grounds of a company for which he had once worked.

9 December   **Egypt**

A police officer was killed and six others were injured when a group of terrorists opened fire on two movie houses that were showing foreign films. On 12 December, al-Gama'at al-Islamiyya claimed responsibility, stating that the attack retaliated for the screening of "immoral" films.

11   December   Egypt
Libyan dissident, human rights activist, and former Foreign Minister Mansour Kikhia was kidnapped from his hotel in Cairo. Ambassador Kikhia was visiting Cairo to attend a human rights conference. He has not been heard from since.

13   December   Iraq
One person was killed and six others were injured in Sulaimaniyah when a terrorist bomb destroyed a relief center operated by the Belgian humanitarian group Handicap International.

14   December   Algeria
A large group of armed terrorists attacked a work camp of a hydroelectric project in Tamezquida and abducted 14 Croatian citizens. Twelve were murdered by having their throats slit, but two others escaped with injuries. On 16 December, the Armed Islamic group claimed responsibility, stating that the attack was part of an ongoing campaign to rid Algeria of all foreigners and to avenge Muslims killed in Bosnia.

27   December   Egypt
Eight Austrian tourists and eight Egyptians were wounded when terrorists fired on a tour bus traveling in the old district of Cairo. A small bomb that was thrown at the bus rolled near a cafe and exploded.

29   December   Algeria
Terrorists murdered a Belgian couple as they slept in their home in Bouira. The man's throat was cut, and his wife was shot.

1994

4   January   Ireland
The Ulster Volunteer Force (UVF) claimed responsibility for two mail bombs sent to Sinn Fein's Dublin offices.

Turkey
Iranian state agents are believed responsible for the assassination of a member of the Iranian KDP Central Committee in Corum.

9   January   Iran
An armed attack was carried out against the British Embassy in Tehran. No one was injured, and no one has claimed responsibility for the attack.

10   January   Italy
A bomb detonated in front of the NATO Defense College building in Rome. That evening, copies of an eight-page Red Brigades bulletin, claiming responsibility on behalf of the "Combatant Communist Nuclei" (NCC), were found in several provinces.

11   January   Peru
A suspected Sendero Luminoso (SL) satchel bomb exploded in front of the Peruvian-Japanese cultural center in Lima, causing minimal damage to the structure.

14   January   Colombia
Suspected members of the National Liberation Army (ELN) kidnapped US citizen Russell Vacek, his wife, Elizabeth, and other family members as they were traveling in El Playon.

29   January   Lebanon
A Jordanian diplomat was shot and killed outside his home in Beirut. The Government of Lebanon arrested and prosecuted ANO terrorists for the attack.

2   February   Azerbaijan
Several bombs exploded inside railcars, killing five persons and injuring several others at the Baku train station.

3   February   Greece
A bomb detonated at the German Goethe (culture) Institute in Athens. A local newspaper received a warning a half hour before the detonation from the Revolutionary People's Struggle (ELA) terrorist group.

Italy
A bomb was placed underneath the car of a Spanish Military Attache, Lt. Col. Fernando Sagristano, in Rome. The device severely injured an embassy driver.

19   February   Egypt
Unknown assailants fired upon a passenger train and wounded a Polish woman, a Thai woman, and two Egyptian citizens in Asyut. The al-Gama'at al-Islamiyya (Islamic Group) claimed responsibility for the attack.

23   February   Egypt
A bomb explosion aboard a passenger train in Asyut injured six foreign tourists—two New Zealanders, two Germans, and two Australians—and five Egyptian citizens. The Islamic Group (IG) claimed responsibility for the incident.

4   March   Egypt
Unknown gunmen opened fire at a Nile cruise ship and wounded a German tourist near the Sohag Governorate. The Islamic Group (IG) claimed responsibility for the incident.

Iraq
Unidentified gunmen fired on a European Relief Organization vehicle and wounded two local guards near Irbil.

9–13   March   United Kingdom
The Provisional Irish Republican Army (PIRA) fired mortars at London's Heathrow International Airport in three separate attacks. There were no injuries because the fully primed mortars failed to detonate.

13 March — Lebanon
A grenade detonated on the British Embassy compound, causing minor damage and no injuries. No arrests or claims of responsibility were reported.

24 March — Turkey
The Kurdistan Workers' Party (PKK) is believed responsible for bombing the Central Bazaar in Istanbul's historic tourist district. Four tourists, including two Romanian women, were injured by the blast.

27 March — Turkey
A bomb detonated in the gardens of the Saint Sophia Mosque and Museum in Istanbul, injuring three tourists: one German, one Spanish, and one Dutch. The Metropole Revenge Team of the political wing of the PKK claimed responsibility.

29 March — Iraq
Six assailants fired on a United Nations guard contingency bus traveling from Irbil to Mosul and seriously wounded two Austrian guards.

1 April — Colombia
Six members of the Revolutionary Armed Forces of Colombia (FARC) kidnapped US citizen Raymond Rising, Security Chief of the Summer Linguistic Institution, as he rode his motorcycle from the Municipal Capital of Puerto Lleras.

2 April — Turkey
The Kurdistan Workers' Party (PKK) claimed responsibility for bombing the IC Bedesten, the old bazaar at the center of the bazaar complex, in Istanbul. Two foreign tourists, one Spanish and one Belgian, were killed, and 17 others were injured.

3 April — Iraq
Assailants fired on a German journalist and her bodyguard while they were traveling in their car near Suleymaniyah. Both occupants of the vehicle were killed instantly.

8 April — Sri Lanka
A small bomb exploded inside a bathroom at the Marriott Hotel in Colombo, causing minor damages and no casualties.

11 April — Greece
The 17 November terrorist group claimed responsibility for planting rockets aimed at a British aircraft carrier, the Arc Royal. The rockets were defused by explosives experts.

13 April — Lebanon
Five individuals, including two Iraqi diplomats, were arrested for assassinating Iraqi opposition figure Shaykh Talib Ali al-Suhayl in his house near West Beirut.

27 April — South Africa
A car bomb exploded at Jan Smuts Airport in Johannesburg, injuring 16 persons, including two Russian diplomats and a Swiss Air pilot. Although no group has claimed responsibility, white separatists opposed to South Africa's first multiracial election are believed responsible.

8 May — Algeria
Two French priests were shot and killed by two male assailants in the lower Casbah district of Algiers. In its weekly publication, the Armed Islamic Group (GIA) claimed responsibility.

17 May — Greece
A timedetonated rocket was fired at an IBM office in downtown Athens. The 17 November terrorist group claimed responsibility in a warning call to a radio station.

29 May — Iraq
At least two unknown assailants shot and killed an Iranian dissident, Seyeed Ahmad Sadr Lahijani, as he drove his car through Ghalebieh.

17 June — Uganda
A driver for the Catholic Relief Services was badly beaten by Lord's Resistance Army (LRA) rebels who ambushed the truck he was driving.

21–22 June — Turkey
In the coastal towns of Fethiye and Marmaris, bombs killed one foreign national and injured 10 others at tourist sites. The PKK claimed responsibility for the attacks on German television.

22 June — Turkey
Two bombs detonated within minutes of each other at a beach and park in the resort town of Marmaris, wounding 12 persons, including four British nationals, one of whom died five days later.

24 June — Greece
The Revolutionary People's Struggle (ELA/1 May) claimed responsibility for a bombing outside the offices of the European Community in downtown Athens. There were no injuries reported.

4 July — Greece
A senior Turkish diplomat in Athens, Omer Sipahioglu, was killed by three gunmen as he sat in his car. "November 17–Theofilos Georgiadis Commandos" claimed responsibility for the attack.

11 July — Greece
A bomb detonated in a Lindos restaurant on the Island of Rhodes, seriously injuring an Italian tourist and a Greek citizen.

18 July — Argentina
A car bomb exploded at the Israeli-Argentine Mutual Association (AMIA), killing nearly 100 persons and wounding more than 200 others. The explosion caused the seven-story building to collapse and damaged adjacent buildings.

19 July — Panama
A commuter plane exploded in flight over the Santa Rita mountains. Among the 21 victims were Israeli nationals, dual Israeli-Panamanian citizens, three US citizens, and 12 Jewish persons.

23 July — West Bank
Two unknown Palestinians stabbed and seriously injured a US woman in the Arab quarter of the Old City of Jerusalem. The assailants escaped unharmed.

26 July — Cambodia
The Khmer Rouge attacked a train traveling in Kompong Trach and kidnapped a number of passengers, among them an Australian, a Briton, and a Frenchman.

United Kingdom
A car bomb exploded at the Israeli Embassy in London, injuring 14 persons. Police said the bomb was planted by a woman who was driving an Audi.

27 July — United Kingdom
A car bomb detonated outside a building that houses Jewish organizations in London. Five persons were injured in the attack.

3 August — Algeria
Five French Embassy employees were killed and one injured when guerrillas from the Armed Islamic Group (AIG) attacked a French residential compound in Algiers.

8 August — Turkey
The PKK kidnapped two Finnish nationals, stating that they did not have "entry visas for Kurdistan." The Finns were held for 22 days before being released unharmed.

12 August — Turkey
A bomb detonated in the Topkapi Bus Terminal, killing one Romanian consular official and wounding seven other people. The PKK is suspected.

18 August — Chile
A bomb exploded at a Santiago office building that houses the American company Fluor Daniel. The Manuel Rodriguez Patriotic Front (FPMR) claimed responsibility and stated that the incident was carried out in solidarity with Cuba and against the US economic blockade of the island.

26 August — Angola
A Portuguese priest and four nuns were kidnapped by suspected National Union for the Total Independence of Angola (UNITA) rebels near Choba.

27 August — Philippines
Seven South Korean engineers and 30 Filipino workers were taken captive by the Moro Islamic Liberation Front (MILF).

23 September — Colombia
Twelve terrorists from the Revolutionary Armed Forces of Colombia (FARC) kidnapped US citizen Thomas Hargrove when he stopped at a guerrilla roadblock.

27 September — Egypt
Three persons were killed and two were wounded when an assailant fired on a downtown tourist area in Hurghada. Two Egyptians and one German were killed in the attack. The Islamic Group claimed responsibility for the attack.

9 October — Israel
Two Arabs armed with assault rifles and grenades attacked pedestrians in Jerusalem. The gunmen killed two persons and injured 14 others. Two US citizens were among the injured. HAMAS has claimed responsibility for the incident.

18 October — Algeria
Approximately 30 members of the Armed Islamic Group (AIG) attacked an oil base, killing a French and an Italian worker.

23 October — Egypt
Assailants shot and killed a British tourist and wounded three others in an attack on a bus near Luxor. The Islamic Group is believed responsible for the attack.

11 December — Philippines
The Abu Sayyaf Group (ASG) claimed responsibility for an explosion aboard a Philippine airliner. One Japanese citizen was killed, and at least 10 others were injured.

12 December — Turkey
The Kurdistan Workers' Party (PKK) is believed responsible for a bomb blast outside a store in Istanbul, which injured eight persons, including four Romanian tourists.

24 December — Algeria
Members of the Armed Islamic Group (AIG) hijacked an Air France flight in Algeria. The plane arrived in Marseille, France, on 26 December. A French antiterrorist unit stormed the plane, ending the 54-hour siege in which three hostages were killed by the terrorists. All four terrorists were killed during the rescue.

25 December — Israel
An American was among 12 persons injured when a HAMAS supporter carrying a bag of explosives blew himself up at a West Jerusalem bus stop.

27 December — Algeria
The Armed Islamic Group (AIG) claimed responsibility for the murders of four Catholic priests. The murders were apparently in retaliation for the deaths of four GIA hijackers the previous day in Marseille.

1995

8　January　　　　　　　　　　　Algeria
Armed assailants attempted to kill two priests, one French and one Swiss, belonging to the order of the White Fathers. The priests escaped unharmed. The Armed Islamic Group (GIA) is suspected in the attack.

12　January　　　　　　　　　　　Egypt
Suspected members of al-Gama'at al-Islamiyya (Islamic Group or IG) opened fire on a passenger train. Six passengers, including two Argentine tourists, were injured.

15　January　　　　　　　　　　Cambodia
A US tourist was killed and her husband was seriously wounded when Khmer Rouge rebels attacked their sightseeing convoy. A tour guide also was killed when the assailants fired a rocket at the van.

18　January　　　　　　　　　　Colombia
Members of the People's Liberation Army kidnapped a US citizen, working as an administrative support officer for Cerrejon Coal Mine of Riohacha, in La Guajira.

Sierra Leone
Five Europeans and at least three Sierra Leoneans were kidnapped by Revolutionary United Front (RUF) rebels. All of the victims were employed by the Swiss-owned Sierra Leone Ore and Metal Company (Sieromco).

22　January　　　　　　　　　　　Algeria
Gunmen shot and killed a Frenchman as he drove through a park. A woman also was injured in the attack. The GIA is suspected.

24　January　　　　　　　　　United Kingdom
An unidentified assailant shot and killed a Sikh newspaper editor, a known advocate for an independent Sikh state. No one claimed responsibility for the attack.

25　January　　　　　　　　　　Sierra Leone
The Revolutionary United Front (RUF) raided a mission near the Guinea border, taking 100 hostages. Seven nuns—six Italians and one Brazilian—were among the captives.

26　January　　　　　　　　　　Colombia
Seven guerrillas of the National Liberation Army (ELN) kidnapped three Venezuelan Corpoven engineers and killed a fourth near La Victoria.

31　January　　　　　　　　　　Colombia
Suspected guerrillas kidnapped two Brazilian engineers at an abandoned hydroelectric dam. The engineers are employed by the Swiss Company, ASEA.

14　February　　　　　　　　　　Pakistan
Three gunmen shot and killed a former Afghan Brigadier at his residence. The victim was affiliated with the moderate, pro-Afghanistan Council for Understanding and National Unity (CUNA). No group claimed responsibility, but Gulbuddin Hikmatyar's Hizb-I-Islami organization is suspected.

24　February　　　　　　　　　　Jordan
A French diplomat posted to the French Embassy was shot and wounded by two assailants while he was sightseeing with his wife. No group claimed responsibility for the attack.

27　February　　　　　　　　　　Greece
Khidir Abd al-Abbas Hamza, a defecting Iraqi former nuclear scientist, was abducted in Athens while he was attempting to call a newspaper office from a phone booth. The Iraqi Ambassador in Athens has denied any Iraqi involvement, but the incident is similar to other Iraqi Government sponsored abductions.

28　February　　　　　　　　　　Peru
An explosive device containing about 500 grams (one pound) of dynamite detonated on the sidewalk across the street from the US Embassy in Lima.

3　March　　　　　　　　　　Algeria
A Palestinian student attending the Algerian Arab College was murdered by an armed group who stormed the area where he and his family lived. The Armed Islamic Group (GIA) is suspected.

8　March　　　　　　　　　　Pakistan
Two unidentified gunmen armed with AK-47 assault rifles opened fire on a US Consulate van in Karachi, killing two US diplomats and wounding a third. The Pakistani driver was not hurt.

27　March　　　　　　　　　　Bahrain
A Pakistani man burned to death when a video store was set on fire. No group claimed responsibility for the attack.

31　March　　　　　　　　　　Israel
One Israeli civilian was killed and 20 others were wounded when suspected Hizballah members fired Katyusha rockets into western Galilee.

5　April　　　　　　　　　　Honduras
Morazanist Patriotic Front (FPM) guerrillas claimed responsibility for a leaflet propaganda bomb that exploded in front of a Tegucigalpa building that houses US, German, and Spanish press agencies. The attack caused minor damage to nearby buildings.

9　April　　　　　　　　　　Gaza Strip
A suicide bomber crashed an explosive-rigged van into an Israeli bus, killing a US citizen and seven Israelis. Over 50 other persons, including two US citizens, were injured. The Palestine Islamic Jihad (PIJ)-Shaqaqi Faction claimed responsibility for the attack.

Georgia
Assailants attacked the T'bilisi residence of the Russian special envoy and the headquarters of Russian troops in the

Transcaucasus. There were no injuries. A group calling itself the Algeti Wolves claimed responsibility for the attack in revenge for events in Chechnya and for the signing of the treaty on Russian military bases in Georgia.

19   April   Colombia
Members of the National Liberation Army (ELN) kidnapped two Italian oil workers from their car and killed their Colombian driver near Barrancabermeja.

21   April   Turkey
An attempted car bombing in front of the Iranian Consulate General in Istanbul killed a tow truck driver. The illegally parked vehicle was towed to an open parking lot where it detonated, killing the driver and damaging 18 other vehicles. No group has claimed responsibility.

22   April   Netherlands
Two Turkish citizens were shot by Kurdish extremists at a coffeehouse in The Hague. Four men were arrested in connection with the attack.

29   April   Somalia
A foreign businessman was killed near Chisimayu by Islamic fundamentalists.

5   May   Algeria
Suspected members of the Armed Islamic Group (GIA) attacked employees of a pipeline company, killing four foreigners. An Algerian security guard was also killed and at least six other guards were injured.

**   Israel**
Hizballah launched at least eight Katyusha rockets that struck near Qiryat Shemona. Four Israeli civilians were wounded in the attack.

7   May   Algeria
Armed assailants ambushed a two-vehicle advance for a convoy of foreigners, including Britons and Canadians, being escorted from a worksite to their accommodation camp. Several security forces were killed or wounded, but there were no foreign casualties.

15   May   Peru
Five alleged Sendero Luminoso (SL) members held up a bus near Chimbote and robbed some 50 passengers. The assailants, wearing masks painted with a red hammer and sickle, threatened passengers with machine guns and grenades.

22   May   Colombia
Approximately one kilo of dynamite detonated under a metal security door of a Dunkin Donuts restaurant in Bogota. The damage was estimated at $18,000. No injuries were reported and no group has claimed responsibility for the attack.

23   May   Sierra Leone
Revolutionary United Front (RUF) rebels abducted three Lebanese businessmen during attacks on towns in the Lebanese community of the diamond district of Kono.

24   May   Peru
Presumed members of Sendero Luminoso (SL) detonated a 50-kg car bomb in front of the Maria Angola Hotel in a suburb of Lima, killing three hotel employees and a passerby. About 30 others were injured.

31   May   Colombia
Seven National Liberation Army (ELN) guerrillas kidnapped a US citizen and three Colombians at the Verde Limon Gold Mine in Zaragoza. Shortly afterward, the Colombian Army freed the captives in a confrontation that left one Colombian hostage and two guerrillas dead.

5   June   Nicaragua
Three members of the Recontra 380 occupied the Chilean Embassy in Managua and took hostage the husband of Ambassador Laura Sota. The abductors left a package they claimed was a bomb and fled without making any reported statements or demands. The kidnap victim was released unharmed a few hours later.

7   June   Algeria
Suspected members of the Armed Islamic Group (GIA) shot and killed a French couple in Algiers. No one claimed responsibility for the attack.

24   June   Colombia
Unknown guerrillas abducted the son of a British Exxon employee in Formeque and demanded a ransom of $500,000. On 12 August, during the course of negotiations, the victim's body was found.

25   June   Pakistan
Five gunmen kidnapped three German engineers and a Pakistani driver in the North-West Frontier Province. The kidnappers demanded a ransom of ten million rupees. One of the Germans and the Pakistani were released on 3 July, at which time the kidnappers added the release of four prisoners in Peshawar to their demands. The other two hostages were freed unharmed on 13 July. It does not appear that the demands were met.

26   June   Ethiopia
Al-Gama'at al-Islamiyya claimed responsibility for a failed assassination attempt against Egyptian President Hosni Mubarak in Addis Ababa. As his motorcade headed from the airport to a meeting of the Organization of African Unity, two vehicles tried to block the road, and several gunmen fired at his armored limousine. President Mubarak was not injured. Two Ethiopian military guards died and one was wounded in the exchange of gunfire; two gunmen were killed and two others captured. The Palestinian Ambassador to Ethiopia also was injured.

3 July — Germany
Attackers smashed the windows of three vehicles at a Chrysler car dealership in Kassel. They also broke the salesroom window and scrawled graffiti protesting the scheduled execution of Mumia Abu Jamal, a convicted murderer, in Pennsylvania.

4–8 July — India
Six tourists—two US citizens, two Britons, a Norwegian, and a German—were taken hostage in Kashmir by the previously unknown militant group Al-Faran, which demanded the release of Muslim militants held in Indian prisons. Al-Faran may be part of the Kashmiri separatist group Harakat ul-Ansar based in Pakistan. One of the US citizens escaped on 8 July. On 13 August, Al-Faran murdered the Norwegian; his decapitated body was found with the name Al-Faran carved on his stomach and a note stating that the other hostages also would be killed if the group's demands were not met. The Indian Government has refused to comply with their demands.

11 July — France
Two assailants assassinated a cofounder of the Algerian Islamic Salvation Front and his bodyguard in a Paris mosque. No one claimed responsibility for the murders. Earlier this year Algerian publications reportedly received a communique from the Armed Islamic Group (GIA) listing their priority targets, including the victim.

13 July — Turkey
Kurdish separatists abducted a Japanese tourist at a rebel checkpoint near Siirt. No demands were made, and the kidnappers released the hostage unharmed on 17 July. The Kurdistan Workers' Party (PKK) is suspected.

25 July — France
A bomb detonated aboard a Paris subway train as it arrived at St. Michel station, killing seven commuters and wounding 86.

5 August — Greece
A small improvised bomb detonated at a Citibank branch in Athens, causing minor damage. The Anti-Regime Nuclei (ARN) later claimed responsibility.

10 August — Germany
Assailants firebombed a vehicle parked at a Usawned Chrysler dealership in a small German city. No one was injured. A letter left at the scene identified the perpetrators as members of the Anti-Imperialistic Group Liberty for Mumia Aba Jamal.

12 August — Colombia
Members of the Jaime Bateman Cayon Front, a remnant of the 19 April Movement, kidnapped a British diplomat and a Colombian colleague along a highway near Tolima Department. On learning of the British official's diplomatic status, the terrorists demanded an unspecified ransom to free him. They released the Colombian national.

17 August — France
A nail-filled bomb detonated in a trash bin near a subway entrance in Paris injuring 17 people. Among those injured were four Hungarians, four Italians, three Portuguese, one German, and one Briton. Authorities determined a similar explosive device was used in the Paris subway bombing on 25 July.

20 August — France
Assailants threw a molotov cocktail at a building in Paris that houses a Turkish sporting and cultural association, injuring six persons and causing minor damage. Witnesses reported seeing three people flee the scene. The Kurdistan Workers' Party (PKK) may be responsible for the attack.

21 August — Israel
A bomb exploded on a bus in Jerusalem, killing six persons, including one US citizen, and wounding two other US citizens and over 100 others. The Izz al-Din al-Qassem Brigades, the military wing of the Islamic Resistance Movement (HAMAS), claimed responsibility.

24 August — Pakistan
Sixteen men armed with steel pipes and at least one gun vandalized the BBC office in Islamabad. The attackers destroyed equipment and files, bombed the entry hall, and destroyed two cars. The BBC chief correspondent, a Canadian, and a Pakistani BBC staff member escaped with minor injuries. The radical Sunni organization Sipah-l-Sahaba Pakistan (SSP) claimed responsibility, although the group's leader stated that he had ordered only a peaceful demonstration to protest the BBC airing of a documentary about the group.

27 August — Spain
Arsonists in San Sebastian doused a car bearing French license plates with gasoline and ignited it. There were no injuries. Authorities believe a support group of the Basque Fatherland and Liberty (ETA) is responsible.

1 September — Colombia
Guerrillas intercepted and kidnapped a US businessman and his Colombian partner in Cali. The captors, five armed masked men, took the two men to a jungle camp. The Colombian negotiated a $30,000 ransom for his US partner, who was released on 22 September. No group has claimed responsibility.

Colombia
In Santa Marta, Revolutionary Armed Forces of Colombia (FARC) guerrillas destroyed containers of bananas belonging to the US company Dole.

2 September — Algeria
Suspected Armed Islamic Group (GIA) militants shot and killed an Italian national in Oran.

3 September — Algeria
Unidentified assailants shot and killed two nuns in the Belcourt district of Algiers. One of the victims was French and

the other Maltese. Authorities suspect the Armed Islamic Group (GIA).

5　September　　　　　　　　　　West Bank
Unknown assailants stabbed to death an Israeli settler of British origin and wounded his US-born wife in the settlement of Ma'ale Mikmas, near Ram Allah. An anonymous caller claimed responsibility in the name of the Popular Front for the Liberation of Palestine (PFLP). The caller stated the attack was in retaliation for the arrest of three PFLP activists and the continued detention of a PFLP politburo member, imprisoned for three years.

Germany
Arsonists attacked two Turkish-owned facilities. In Luebeck, arsonists set fire to a bistro. Two persons died and 20 were injured. Arsonists also firebombed a nightclub in Freital. There were no injuries. Authorities suspect the Kurdistan Workers' Party (PKK).

7　September　　　　　　　　　　　India
A woman claiming to be from the militant group Dukhtaran-e-Millat delivered a parcel bomb to the office of the BBC in Srinagar, Kashmir. The bomb exploded later in the hands of a freelance photographer for Agence France-Press, who died on 10 September from his injuries. The blast wounded two others and caused major damage. Dukhtaran-e-Milat denied responsibility for the bombing.

13　September　　　　　　　　　　Russia
Unidentified assailants fired a rocket-propelled grenade at the US Embassy in Moscow, causing minor damage to a sixth-floor office. No injuries were reported. Authorities suspect the attack was in retaliation for US participation in NATO airstrikes against Bosnian Serb targets.

20　September　　　　　　　　　　Austria
In Vienna, assailants attempted to firebomb a German pharmaceutical firm, but the molotov cocktails failed to ignite. The German firm was hosting a US delegation and had raised the US flag outside the building.

21　September　　　　　　　　　　Austria
Assailants threw lit bottles containing heating oil and paint thinner into two rooms of the American International School in Vienna. There were no injuries. The Austrian press later received a letter in which the Cell for Internationalism claimed responsibility. Authorities believe there may be a connection with the previous day's bombing.

13　October　　　　　　　　　　Colombia
A letter bomb sent to the Italian Embassy in Bogota exploded when opened by a staff member, who was wounded. The injured employee is responsible for Italian cooperation with Colombia under their countries' economic drug-fighting agreements. No group has claimed responsibility for the bombing.

20　October　　　　　　　　　　Croatia
A car bomb detonated outside the local police headquarters building in Rijeka, killing the driver and injuring 29 bystanders. The Egyptian al-Gama'at al-Islamiyva claimed responsibility, warning that further attacks would continue unless authorities released an imprisoned Gama'at militant, Tala'at Fuad Kassem, who had been arrested in September 1995.

20　October　　　　　　　　　　　Turkey
A pipe bomb exploded outside a Coca-Cola Company warehouse in Istanbul, causing minor damage to the building and to a vehicle. No one has claimed responsibility for the attack.

27　October　　　　　　　　　　　Angola
National Union for the Total Independence of Angola (UNITA) soldiers killed two persons and kidnapped 32 others in Lunda Norte. Four of the hostages are South African citizens employed by the SA Export Company, Ltd.

8　November　　　　　　　　　　　Egypt
Islamic extremists opened fire on a train enroute to Cairo from Aswan, injuring a Dutchman, a French woman, and an Egyptian. Al-Gama'at al-Islamiyya (Islamic Group or IG) claimed responsibility for the attack.

9　November　　　　　　　　　　　Algeria
Unidentified assailants set fire to the off-compound US Embassy warehouse in Algiers, destroying the facility and its contents. The Armed Islamic Group (GIA) may be responsible for the attack.

10　November　　　　　　　　　Switzerland
Unknown assailants firebombed a Turkish-owned shop in Basel, injuring three persons and causing major damage. No one has claimed responsibility for the attack.

13　November　　　　　　　　　Saudi Arabia
A car bomb explosion in the parking lot of the Office of the Program Manager/Saudi Arabian National Guard (OPM/SANG) in Riyadh, killed seven persons and wounded 42 others. The deceased include four US federal civilian employees, one US military person, and two Indian Government employees. The blast severely damaged the three-story building, which houses a US military advisory group, and several neighboring office buildings. Three groups, including the Islamic Movement for Change, claimed responsibility for the attack.

Switzerland
An Egyptian diplomat was shot and killed in the parking garage of his apartment building in Geneva. On 15 November the International Justice Group claimed responsibility for the attack.

15　November　　　　　　　　　　Japan
An electric company employee discovered an explosive device burning on a powerline to a US military housing complex in Sagamihara, Kanagawa Prefecture. The explosion caused

minor damage. No group has claimed responsibility, but both the Chukaku-Ha and the Kakuro-kyo-Ha had announced plans to disrupt the Asia Pacific Economic Council (APEC) summit in Osaka, held during 13 to 19 November.

19   November   Pakistan
A suicide bomber drove a vehicle into the Egyptian Embassy compound in Islamabad, killing at least 16 persons and injuring some 60 others. The bomb destroyed the entire compound and caused damage and injuries within a half-mile radius. The Japanese and Indonesian Embassies, the Canadian High Commission, the UK housing compound, and Grindlays Bank were among the damaged buildings. Al-Gama'at al-lslamiyya (Islamic Group or IG), Jihad Group, and the International Justice Group all claimed responsibility for the bombing.

21   November   India
A powerful bomb exploded outside a restaurant in the Connaught Place shopping area in New Delhi. The blast injured 22 persons, including two Dutch citizens, one South African and one Norwegian, and caused major damage to shops and parked cars. Both the Jammu and Kashmir Islamic Front, a Kashmiri Muslim separatist group, and the Khalistan Liberation Tger Force, a Sikh separatist group, claimed responsibility for the bombing.

30   November   Algeria
Four suspected Islamic extremists shot and killed two Latvian seamen and wounded a third. No one has claimed responsibility, but the Armed Islamic Group (GIA) is suspected.

9   December   France
Assailants in Bayonne set fire to a stolen vehicle and firebombed a bank after the French Government expelled a member of the Basque Fatherland and Liberty (ETA).

10   December   Ecuador
Three FARC militants kidnapped the treasurer for the Nazarine missions, who is a US citizen. A captured member of FARC led a rescue team to a mountainous area near Quito, where they rescued the victim. Three kidnappers were killed and two others escaped.

11   December   Austria
Two letter bombs detonated inside a mailbox located outside a local post office in Graz, wounding a passer-by. One was addressed to the UN High Commissioner for Refugees' office. Remnants of a claimant letter were discovered at the scene. Two other letter bombs were discovered intact. Authorities suspect the Bavarian Liberation Army may be responsible.

16   December   Spain
Several bombs detonated in different areas of a department store in Valencia, killing one person and wounding eight others, including a US citizen. Basque Fatherland and Liberty (ETA) claimed responsibility for the attack.

23   December   Germany
A bomb detonated outside an office building in Duesseldorf that housed the Peruvian Honorary Consulate, causing major damage. On 27 December the Anti-Imperialist Cell (AIZ) claimed responsibility for the attack in a letter stating that the Peruvian Government's domestic policies are "unbearable for the majority of Peruvians."

27   December   Philippines
Twenty Abu Sayyaf militants kidnapped at least 16 vacationers, including six US citizens, at Lake Sebu, Mindanao. Two of the hostages escaped and four were released, carrying a ransom demand of $57,700. On 31 December the kidnappers released the remaining hostages in exchange for government promises of improvements in the south.

30   December   France
A bomb detonated outside a Paris branch of Citibank, causing major damage. Suspicion centered on sympathizers of the Armed Islamic Group (GIA) who may be responsible.

1996

1   January   Iraq
Three individuals attempted to leave a vehicle containing explosives near UN offices in Irbil. The driver abandoned the vehicle after a security guard ordered him to move it.

8   January   Indonesia
Two hundred Free Papua Movement (OPM) guerrillas abducted 26 individuals in the Lorenta nature preserve, Irian Jaya Province. The hostages were on a research expedition for the Worldwide Fund for Nature. Among the hostages were seven persons from the United Kingdom, the Netherlands, and Germany. The OPM demanded the withdrawal of Indonesian troops from Irian Jaya, compensation for environmental damage and for the death of civilians at the hands of the military, and a halt to Freeport Indonesia mining operations. On 15 May Indonesian Special Forces members rescued the last nine hostages after locating them with a pilotless drone.

16   January   Turkey
Seven Turkish nationals of Chechen origin hijacked a Russia-bound Panamanian ferry in Trabzon. The hijackers initially threatened to kill all Russians on board unless Chechen separatists being held in Dagestan, Russia, were released. On 19 January the hijackers surrendered to Turkish authorities outside the entrance to the Bosporus. The passengers were unharmed.

18   January   Ethiopia
A bomb exploded at the Ghion Hotel in Addis Ababa, killing at least four persons and injuring 20 others. The injured included citizens from the United Kingdom, Mali, India, and France. In March, al-Ittihaad al-Islami (The Islamic Union), an ethnic Somali group, claimed responsibility for the bombing.

19 January — Colombia
Six suspected Revolutionary Armed Forces of Colombia (FARC) guerrillas kidnapped a US citizen and demanded a $1 million ransom. The hostage was released on 22 May.

26 January — Yemen
Al-Aslam tribesmen kidnapped 17 elderly French tourists in the Ma'rib Governate to pressure authorities into releasing one of their tribesmen. The kidnappers released the hostages unharmed on 29 January.

31 January — Sri Lanka
Suspected members of the Liberation Tigers of Tamil Eelam (LTTE) rammed an explosives-laden truck into the Central Bank in the heart of downtown Colombo, killing 90 civilians and injuring more than 1,400 others. Among the wounded were two US citizens, six Japanese, and one Dutch national. The explosion caused major damage to the Central Bank building, an American Express office, the Intercontinental Hotel, and several other buildings.

6 February — Colombia
National Liberation Army (ELN) rebels kidnapped three cement industry engineers including a Briton, a Dane, a German, and their Colombian companion in San Luis; they were abducted from their vehicle at a makeshift roadblock. The hostages were freed later.

9 February — United Kingdom
A bomb detonated in a parking garage in the Docklands area of London, killing two persons and wounding more than 100 others, including two US citizens. The Irish Republican Army (IRA) claimed responsibility.

11 February — Bahrain
A bomb exploded at the Diplomat Hotel in Manama, injuring a British guest and two employees and causing significant damage to the hotel. The London-based Islamic Front for the Liberation of Bahrain claimed the bombing, but later denied responsibility.

15 February — Greece
Unidentified assailants fired a rocket at the US Embassy compound in Athens, causing minor damage to three diplomatic vehicles and some surrounding buildings. Circumstances of the attack suggest it was a 17 November operation.

16 February — Colombia
Six alleged National Liberation Army (ELN) guerrillas kidnapped a US citizen in La Guajira Department. No ransom demand was made. The hostage was released on 15 November.

17 February — Venezuela
Two alleged National Liberation Army (ELN) guerrillas killed two Venezuelan guards at a gasoline station near the Colombian-Venezuelan border in La Victoria. The two men took the guards' rifles and fled in a small boat down the international waters of the Arauca River.

20 February — Turkey
Two members of Mujahedin-e Khalq (MEK), an Iranian dissident group, were found dead in their Istanbul apartment. In April 1996 authorities apprehended three Islamic militants and several Iranian and Turkish nationals in connection with the killing. The militants later claimed they had received their orders from Iranian diplomats stationed in Turkey.

25 February — Jerusalem
A suicide bomber blew up a bus, killing 26 persons, including three US citizens, and injuring some 80 persons, including three other US citizens. HAMAS's Izz al-Din al-Qassem Battalion claimed responsibility for the bombing in retaliation for the Hebron massacre two years before, but later denied involvement. HAMAS also issued a leaflet assuming responsibility for the bombing signed by the Squads of the New Disciples of Martyr Yahya Ayyash, the Engineer, claiming the bombing was in retaliation for Ayyash's death on 5 January 1996.

3 March — Jerusalem
Another suicide bomber detonated an explosive device on a bus, killing 19 persons, including six Romanians, and injuring six others. The Students of Yahya Ayyash, a splinter group of HAMAS, claimed responsibility for the attack.

4 March — Israel
A suicide bomber detonated an explosive device outside the Dizengoff Center, Tel Aviv's largest shopping mall, killing 20 persons and injuring 75 others, including two US citizens. HAMAS and the Palestine Islamic Jihad (PIJ) both claimed responsibility for the bombing.

14 March — Bahrain
Assailants poured gasoline at the entrance to a restaurant in Sitrah and threw Molotov cocktails inside, killing seven Bangladeshi employees and destroying the restaurant.

23 March — Venezuela
Suspected National Liberation Army (ELN) guerrillas killed one policeman and injured another policeman and a civilian in La Victoria.

26 March — Cambodia
Suspected Khmer Rouge guerrillas abducted 26 Cambodian mine disposal experts, their British supervisor, and his translator near the Angkor Wat temple complex. Six of the hostages escaped, leaving the British national and his interpreter captive. At least five police officers and soldiers were killed by landmines while searching for the hostages.

27 March — Algeria
Armed Islamic Group (GIA) extremists kidnapped seven French monks from their monastery in the Medea region. On 26 April the GIA offered to free the monks in exchange for the release of GIA members held in France. On 21 May the group stated that they killed the monks in response to the French Government's refusal to negotiate with them.

31 March   Venezuela
Four guerrillas from the Colombian People's Liberation Army (EPL) kidnapped a rancher from a store in La Gabarra. The rancher had been warned he would be kidnapped if he didn't pay $50,000 in protection money. The four abductors, who opened fire on security forces as they fled, were killed and the hostage escaped.

18 April   Egypt
Four al-Gama'at al-Islamiyya (IG) militants opened fire on a group of Greek tourists in front of the Europa Hotel in Cairo, killing 18 Greeks and injuring 12 Greeks and two Egyptians. The IG claimed they intended to attack a group of Israeli tourists they believed were staying at the hotel, as revenge for Israeli actions in Lebanon.

24 April   Poland
A bomb placed at a Shell gas station in Warsaw detonated, killing one policeman who was preparing to defuse the device. A group calling itself GN 95 later claimed responsibility and demanded $2 million from the Royal Dutch Shell Group. The group justified the attack by stating its opposition to expansion of foreign investment in Poland.

5 May   India
Islamic separatists killed eight Hindu Nepalese migrant workers near Srinagar. No group claimed responsibility.

8 May   Cambodia
Forty Khmer Rouge militants kidnapped seven Thai quarry workers in the Kampong Spoe Province and demanded $350,000 in ransom. The quarry is owned by three Thai companies: ASCO, Seaboard, and the Italian-Thai Construction Co., a subcontractor for the US Fischbach International Company. On 9 May the militants released the hostages after the companies each paid a $100,000 ransom.

13 May   West Bank
Arab gunmen opened fire on a bus and a group of Yeshiva students near the Bet El settlement, killing a dual US/Israeli citizen and wounding three Israelis. No one claimed responsibility for the attack, but HAMAS is suspected.

16 May   Peru
Sendero Luminoso (SL) terrorists detonated a car bomb, injuring at least four persons and destroying a portion of the joint Shell-Mobil offices and warehouse in Lima. The explosion at a Shell gas station also destroyed five automobiles and damaged six Shell tankers. Three days earlier, the Peruvian Government had announced an agreement with a consortium led by the US Mobil Corporation and Royal Dutch Shell to develop the expansive Camisea gas reserves. SL terrorists left leaflets at the scene lauding the group and the armed struggle and proclaiming "No to the sale of the country."

28 May   France
Unidentified gunmen shot and killed a former Iranian deputy education minister under the Shah at his home in Paris. No one claimed responsibility for the killing.

Greece
A bomb exploded at a building housing the main offices of IBM in Athens, causing extensive structural damage but no injuries. The group Fraxia Midheniston (Nihilist Faction) claimed responsibility in a call to a local television station.

31 May   Nicaragua
A gang of former Contra guerrillas kidnapped a US employee of USAID who was assisting with election preparations in rural northern Nicaragua. She was released unharmed the next day after members of the international commission overseeing the preparations intervened.

4 June   Tajikistan
Gunmen shot and killed two Russian servicemen's wives while the victims were visiting a cemetery in Dushanbe. No one claimed responsibility. The Tajikistan Internal Affairs Ministry believes the gunmen were members of "Muzlokandov's Gang," an Islamic extremist group.

8 June   Venezuela
In Apure State, just over the Colombian border, 10 Colombian National Liberation Army (ELN) gunmen killed a Venezuelan man whom they believed was an informant for Venezuela's national guard.

9 June   Israel
Unidentified gunmen opened fire on a car near Zekharya, killing a dual US/Israeli citizen and an Israeli. The Popular Front for the Liberation of Palestine (PFLP) is suspected.

15 June   United Kingdom
A truck bomb detonated at a Manchester shopping center, wounding 206 persons, including two German tourists, and causing extensive property damage. The Irish Republican Army (IRA) claimed responsibility.

25 June   Saudi Arabia
A fuel truck carrying a bomb exploded outside the US military's Khubar Towers housing facility in Dhahran, killing 19 US military personnel and wounding 515 persons, including 240 US personnel. Several groups claimed responsibility for the attack, which remains under investigation.

27 June   Bosnia and Herzegovina
Assailants detonated a bomb at a building in Zvornik that houses the Socialist Party of the Serb Republic, the International Police Task Force, the Organization for Security and Cooperation in Europe, and the European Community Monitoring Mission. The explosion caused major damage but no injuries.

8 July — Ethiopia
Two Somali gunmen opened fire on the Minister of Transport and Communications as he arrived at his office in Addis Ababa, wounding him and killing two guards and two passersby. Al-Ittihaad al-Islami claimed responsibility for the attack.

12 July — Austria
Four Kurdish militants occupied a Reuter news agency office in Vienna and held two employees hostage for several hours before surrendering. The attackers are suspected Kurdistan Workers' Party (PKK) sympathizers.

14 July — Colombia
Armed men forced an Italian engineer out of his vehicle and took him hostage in Antioquia Province. No ransom demand was made. Authorities suspect the National Liberation Army (ELN) or the Revolutionary Armed Forces of Colombia (FARC).

20 July — Spain
A bomb exploded at Tarragona International Airport in Reus, wounding 35 persons, including British and Irish tourists. Basque Fatherland and Liberty (ETA) is suspected.

24 July — Germany
Turkish leftist militants seized a German Social Democratic Party (SPD) office in Frankfurt for several hours, taking four party officials hostage. The activists demanded improved conditions for political prisoners in Turkey and SPD support for their plight. Police forces stormed the office and arrested them.

26 July — Germany
Armed assailants briefly occupied a Turkish consulate office in Berlin. The attackers tied up four staffers and painted leftist slogans on the walls. The Turkish Communist Party Marxist/Leninist (TKP-ML) is suspected.

Tajikistan
Two gunmen arrived at a Dushanbe airport in a taxi, shot the driver, and went to the airport's military section where they shot two Russian soldiers. Several others were wounded in the attack. Russian military personnel immediately arrested the gunmen.

1 August — Algeria
A bomb exploded at the home of the French Archbishop of Oran, killing him and his chauffeur. The attack occurred after the Archbishop's meeting with the French Foreign Minister. The Armed Islamic Group (GIA) is suspected.

5 August — Bosnia and Herzegovina
After receiving a telephoned bomb threat, security officers evacuated two buildings in Sarajevo that house the offices of the Organization for Security and Cooperation in Europe (OSCE). Authorities located and defused the bomb. No one claimed responsibility.

Ethiopia
A bomb exploded in the lobby of the Wabbe Shebelle Hotel in Addis Ababa, killing two persons and injuring 17 others, including a Belgian citizen. No one claimed responsibility for the attack.

France
Unidentified assailants killed the local chief representative of the Kurdistan Democratic Party at his Paris residence. No one claimed responsibility for the killing.

9 August — Colombia
Suspected leftist guerrillas kidnapped an Italian restaurateur and longtime Colombian resident.

10 August — Panama
Some 50 suspected Colombian guerrillas kidnapped the former representative for the Democratic Revolutionary Party in Boca de Cupe, Darien. Revolutionary Armed Forces of Colombia (FARC) or National Liberation Army (ELN) guerrillas are suspected.

11 August — Somalia
Suspected Al-Ittihaad al-Islami gunmen killed two Ethiopian businessmen in Beledweyne to avenge Ethiopia's two-day military incursion into Somalia earlier that month.

14 August — Colombia
Suspected National Liberation Army (ELN) rebels kidnapped two Brazilian engineers working on a highway in Meta Department.

Sri Lanka
Liberation Tigers of Tamil Eelam (LTTE) rebels bombed the offices and residences belonging to two South Korean companies, Korea Telecom International and Samsung Electronics, causing serious damage but no injuries. This was the first LTTE attack against foreign investors in Sri Lanka.

15 August — Tajikistan
A remote-controlled explosive device—placed in a drainage culvert under a road in Dushanbe—detonated as a Russian troop transport vehicle passed over it, killing the driver and wounding a passenger. No one claimed responsibility.

17 August — France
A bomb exploded at the construction site for a McDonald's restaurant in Saint-Jean-de-Luz, causing extensive structural damage. Basque separatist groups are suspected.

Sudan
Sudan People's Liberation Army (SPLA) rebels kidnapped six missionaries in Mapourdit, including a US citizen, an Italian, three Australians, and a Sudanese. The SPLA released the hostages on 28 August.

21 August — Colombia
Gunmen kidnapped an Italian engineer working on an oil pipeline in northern Colombia.

25 August — **Bahrain**
Three Bahrainis shot and wounded a Pakistani policeman guarding the Russian Consulate. No one claimed responsibility for the attack.

27 August — **Germany**
Turkish leftist militants shot at a vehicle carrying two members of a rival exiled-leftist organization, killing one of the occupants and injuring the other.

11 September — **Iraq**
Kurdish refugees seized nine UN employees near Sairanbar. A World Food Program official, a UNICEF official, and a UNHCR employee were among those taken. A crowd of refugees demonstrating near the UN offices seized the workers as thousands chanted anti-US slogans and threw rocks at UN employees. The refugees later released all the hostages.

13 September — **Iraq**
Patriotic Union of Kurdistan (PUK) militants kidnapped four French workers for Pharmaciens Sans Frontieres (Pharmacists Without Borders), a Canadian UNHCR official, and two Iraqis.

14 September — **Bahrain**
Three assailants threw a flammable liquid into a parts shop in An Nuwaydirat and set it on fire. The attackers then pulled the rolling metal door down, preventing an Indian employee from escaping. The employee died from his burns the next day.

Venezuela
National Liberation Army (ELN) guerrillas opened fire on a military post in Los Bancos, killing one soldier and wounding two civilians.

1 October — **Russia**
In Vladivostok, two or three assailants attacked and killed a South Korean consul near the victim's apartment. He reportedly died of a head wound. No one claimed responsibility. South Korean authorities believe that the attack was carried out by professionals and that the assailants were North Koreans. North Korean officials denied the country's involvement in the attack.

5 October — **Ethiopia**
Unidentified assailants shot and killed a German botanist near a shopping area called the Taiwan Market in Dire Dawa. No one claimed responsibility for the attack.

10 October — **Venezuela**
Suspected National Liberation Army (ELN) guerrillas kidnapped a Venezuelan cattleman at the border with Colombia. A few hours later the victim was found dead in Libertador.

16 October — **Ethiopia**
In two separate incidents, unknown assailants shot and killed a French national and a Yemeni national near the Taiwan Market in Dire Dawa.

20 October — **Cambodia**
Approximately 40 suspected Khmer Rouge militants abducted three Frenchmen and five Cambodians who were traveling by motorcycle in Kampong Chhnang Province. The kidnappers released the hostages unharmed about 24 hours later.

Yemen
Assailants abducted a French diplomat while he was driving in Sanaa. On 26 October the diplomat was turned over to local tribe members who then detained him until 1 November, when the government agreed to their conditions for his release.

24 October — **Uganda**
Several gunmen attacked a Sudanese refugee camp in Palorinya, western Moyo, killing 16 Sudanese refugees and wounding five others. No one claimed responsibility for the attack.

26 October — **Colombia**
Leftist rebels abducted a French geologist and a Colombian engineer in Meta Department after attacking the convoy in which the pair was traveling. No one claimed responsibility, but authorities suspect the National Liberation Army (ELN) or the Revolutionary Armed Forces of Colombia (FARC).

France
Gunmen assassinated the international treasurer of the Liberation Tigers of Tamil Eelam (LTTE) and a companion in Paris. Authorities believe the LTTE killed the official for misappropriating funds for personal use.

1 November — **Sudan**
A breakaway group from the Sudanese People's Liberation Army (SPLA) kidnapped three International Committee of the Red Cross (ICRC) workers, including a US citizen, an Australian, and a Kenyan. On 9 December the rebels released the hostages in exchange for ICRC supplies and a health survey for their camp.

12 November — **Bahrain**
Two propane gas cylinders exploded behind a strip mall near the Shia village of Wattyan, damaging the Gulf Motors Agency Hyundai dealership and injuring a security guard.

15 November — **Algeria**
Unidentified assailants beheaded a Bulgarian businessman who was the former Bulgarian defense attache to Algeria. The victim was found at the entrance to Bainem Forest, west of Algiers. No one claimed responsibility for the attack.

17 November — **Turkey**
A fire broke out at the Tozbey Hotel in Istanbul, killing 17 Ukrainians and injuring more than 40 persons. On 22 November the group Turkish Islamic Jihad (TIJ) claimed responsibility for starting the fire, although authorities believed it may have been caused by faulty wiring and negligence by the hotel's guests.

3 December — France

A bomb exploded aboard a Paris subway train as it arrived at the Port Royal station, killing two French nationals, a Moroccan, and a Canadian, and injuring 86 persons. Among those injured were one US citizen and a Canadian. No one claimed responsibility for the attack, but Algerian extremists are suspected.

8 December — Tajikistan

Guerrillas attacked a jointly owned Tajik-British gold mine in Darvaz, abducting four employees, including a Briton and a South African. The assailants occupied the mine for five days. After negotiations with representatives from the UN, the Red Cross, British diplomats, and an inter-Tajik joint commission monitoring the current peace accord, the hostages were released on 28 December in Childara village.

11 December — Colombia

Five armed men claiming to be members of the Revolutionary Armed Forces of Colombia (FARC) kidnapped a US geologist at a methane gas exploration site in La Guajira Department. (The geologist was killed, and his body was retrieved by Colombian authorities in February 1997.)

17 December — Peru

Twenty-three members of the Tupac Amaru Revolutionary Movement (MRTA) took several hundred people hostage at a party given at the Japanese Ambassador's residence in Lima. Among the hostages were several US officials, foreign ambassadors and other diplomats, Peruvian Government officials, and Japanese businessmen. The group demanded the release of all MRTA members in prison and safe passage for them and the hostage takers. The terrorists released most of the hostages in December but still held 81 Peruvians and Japanese citizens at the end of the year.

Russia

Gunmen broke into a residential area for the International Committee of the Red Cross (ICRC) in Novyy Atagi, Chechnya, fatally shooting six staff employees and wounding a seventh. The victims included two Norwegians, a Dutch national, a Canadian, a New Zealander, a Spaniard, and a Swiss national. No group claimed responsibility.

20 December — Tajikistan

An armed group stopped a convoy between Fayzabad and Gharm and seized 23 hostages, including seven foreign national UN military observers and Tajik Government officials. The group claimed it was loyal to Rezvon Sodirov, the leader of an armed gang, and demanded that several of their supporters be returned to them. The hostages were subsequently released.

27 December — Eritrea

Unknown assailants ambushed and killed five Belgian tourists and their Eritrean driver as they returned to Asmara from a field trip. No one claimed responsibility for the attack.

31 December — Bahrain

Eight assailants surrounded a building in a Shia village, set several tires on fire, and threw Molotov cocktails inside, killing an Asian man and injuring two others.

1997

2 January — Tajikistan

Unidentified gunmen shot and killed a Russian medical service major and an ethnic Tajik senior medical nurse in an apartment in Dushanbe. There is speculation the killings were domestically motivated or carried out by Islamist opposition fighters.

2–13 January — United States

A series of letter bombs with Alexandria, Egypt, postmarks were discovered at Al-Hayat newspaper bureaus in Washington, DC; New York City; London, United Kingdom; and Riyadh, Saudi Arabia. Three similar devices, also postmarked in Egypt, were found at a prison facility in Leavenworth, Kansas. Bomb disposal experts defused all the devices, but one detonated at the Al-Hayat office in London, injuring two security guards and causing minor damage.

4 January — Tajikistan

A car bomb exploded near a major marketplace in Dushanbe, killing one Russian soldier and wounding three others, and wounding a Tajik driver employed by the Commonwealth of Independent States (CIS) joint peacekeeping forces. CIS officials believe professionals may have carried out the bombing. Islamist opposition fighters are suspected.

5 January — South Africa

The Boere Aanvals Troepe claimed responsibility for exploding a bomb at a mosque in Rustenburg, injuring a Sudanese citizen and a South African.

18 January — Rwanda

Hutu militants shot and killed three Spanish aid workers from Doctors of the World and wounded one US citizen, who had to have his leg amputated.

19 January — Russia

Near Samashki village in Chechnya, assailants kidnapped two Russian journalists who were traveling to the Ingush region's capital, Nazran. The kidnappers demanded a ransom of $500,000. The hostages were released on 18 February. There is reporting that no ransom was paid. A Jordanian militant is suspected of leading the kidnappers.

20 January — Bosnia and Herzegovina

A Bosnian-Croatian businessman died after he tripped a boobytrap explosive attached to the front door of his apartment.

21 January — Iraq

At the Atrush refugee camp approximately 400 militants took 1,500 Turkish male refugees hostage and fled to nearby

Garo mountain after the United Nations High Commission for Refugees (UNHCR) closed the camp. There are approximately 5,000 to 8,000 persons remaining at the camp. UNHCR and Turkish Government officials believe the Kurdistan Workers' Party (PKK) is responsible.

23 January   Tajikistan
In Dushanbe, gunmen shot and killed a retired Cossack military commander, his mother, and his fiancee.

2 February   Rwanda
An unidentified gunman entered a church in Ruhengeri and shot and killed a priest as he served communion.

4 February   Rwanda
Suspected Hutu militants killed five team members of the Human Rights Field Operation in Rwanda (HRFOR) in Cyangugu Prefecture, using firearms, grenades, and machetes. The victims include a Briton, a Cambodian, and three Rwandans.

                                                        Tajikistan
Near Komsomolabad, a paramilitary group led by Bakhrom Sodirov abducted four UN military observers. The victims included two Swiss, one Austrian, one Ukrainian, and their Tajik interpreter. The kidnappers demanded safe passage for their supporters from Afghanistan to Tajikistan. On 11 February the group released the Austrian hostage who was ill. By 17 February all the hostages were released after the group's demand was met.

5–17 February   Tajikistan
In four separate incidents occurring between Dushanbe and Garm, Bakhrom Sodirov and his group kidnapped two International Committee for the Red Cross members, four Russian journalists and their Tajik driver, four UNHCR members, and the Tajik Security Minister, Saidamir Zukhurov. Sodirov demanded safe passage for his brother, Rezvon Sodirov, and his followers from Afghanistan to Tajikistan. The group released the hostages when the Tajikistan and Russian Governments complied with their demand.

7 February   Colombia
Several Revolutionary Armed Forces of Colombia (FARC) guerrillas kidnapped two German and two Austrian tourists in Los Katios National Park, demanding a $15 million ransom. On 4 March Colombia soldiers patrolling an area in Choco Department spotted them along with their captors. The rebels killed two of the hostages when the troops discovered their hideout. The military forces engaged in a gun battle with the captors, killing four guerrillas. The military rescued the two remaining hostages.

8 February   Angola
Separatists from the Cabinda Liberation Front-Cabindan Armed Forces (FLEC-FAC) kidnapped one Malaysian and one Filipino forest engineer. A FLEC-FAC official charged the two with spying for the Angolan Government and said they would be punished by expulsion or death. FLEC-FAC issued an ultimatum to Western companies to leave the enclave of Cabinda or become targets in the guerrilla struggle for independence.

11 February   Ethiopia
Two unidentified Ethiopian gunmen tried to bypass security guards at the Belaneh Hotel in Harer, killing one security officer and wounding one other person. The gunmen then threw grenades into the hotel lounge, wounding three Britons, one German, one Dutch and one French citizen.

12 February   Venezuela
Two oil engineers were kidnapped from oilfields by presumed Colombian guerrillas in Apure.

14 February   Venezuela
Six armed Colombian guerrillas kidnapped a US oil engineer and his Venezuelan pilot in Apure. The kidnappers released the Venezuelan pilot on 22 February. According to authorities, the FARC is responsible for the kidnapping.

15 February   Ecuador
Achuar Indians kidnapped a US geologist, a British technical assistant, and two Ecuadorian scientists in Shimi. The hostages work for an Argentine company, conducting environmental research in an area being explored for oil. The kidnappers released the two Ecuadorians the next day and released the two others on 22 February.

20 February   Colombia
Suspected National Liberation Army guerrillas kidnapped a Norwegian employee of a Swedish-owned construction company in Urra.

                                                          Pakistan
Unidentified gunmen shot and killed the Chief of the Iranian Cultural Center and six others.

21 February   Azerbaijan
Unidentified assailants killed a prominent member of parliament in the lobby of his Baku apartment building.

22 February   Georgia
In Gali, Abkhazia, a landmine exploded when a Russian armored personnel carrier passed by, killing three Russian peacekeeping soldiers and wounding another. An ambulance responding to the first blast ran over a second landmine, killing three Russian medics. Both blasts caused major damage. A group calling itself the White Legion and other Georgian partisans are suspected. The White Legion denied responsibility.

23 February–12 April   Russia
Four gunmen kidnapped an Italian photojournalist traveling between Chernorechye village and Grozny. In late March the kidnappers demanded a ransom of $1 million. Russian and Chechen authorities and the humanitarian agency Intersos helped bring about the hostage's release. Chechen militants

are suspected of carrying out the abduction in an attempt to undermine ongoing talks between Moscow officials and the recently elected Chechen government.

23 February — United States
A Palestinian gunman opened fire on tourists at an observation deck atop the Empire State building in New York City, killing a Danish national and wounding visitors from the United States, Argentina, Switzerland, and France before turning the gun on himself. A handwritten note carried by the gunman claimed this was a punishment attack against the "enemies of Palestine."

24 February — Colombia
ELN guerrillas kidnapped a US citizen employed by a Las Vegas gold corporation who was scouting a gold mining operation in Colombia. The ELN demanded a ransom of $2.5 million.

4 March — Yemen
Fifty Yemeni tribesmen kidnapped six German tourists and their German tour guide in Wadi al-Dabaat, demanding $12 million from the Yemen Government. On 12 March the tribesmen released the seven hostages.

7 March — Colombia
FARC guerrillas kidnapped a US mining employee and his Colombian colleague who were searching for gold in Colombia. On 16 November the rebels released the two hostages after receiving a $50,000 ransom.

21 March — Germany
Suspected members of the Kurdistan Workers' Party (PKK) detonated an improvised explosive device next to propane/butane gas tanks outside a Turkish-owned fast-food restaurant in Bad Vilbel, injuring one person and causing extensive damage.

22 March — Nigeria
Armed members of the Ijaw community, protesting the redrawing of regional boundaries, occupied Shell buildings, holding 127 Nigerian employees of the Anglo-Dutch-owned Shell Oil Company. The protesters released 18 hostages on 25 March and the remaining 109 on 27 March. Three of the hostages had been injured.

25 March — Netherlands
Suspected members or sympathizers of the Turkish Grey Wolves organization or the PKK set a fire at a home in a predominantly Turkish neighborhood in The Hague, killing a mother and her five children, and causing extensive damage.

27 March — Yemen
Yemeni tribesmen kidnapped four German tourists who were returning to Sanaa from Marib. A letter was sent to the German Embassy threatening to kill the hostages if the Yemeni Government did not pay a ransom of roughly $3 million. On 6 April 1997 the tribesmen released the hostages. No ransom was paid.

29 March — Colombia
Five uniformed, heavily armed Colombian Simon Bolivar Guerrilla Coordinating Board members kidnapped a Venezuelan cattle rancher who is the godparent of Venezuela's president in Zulia municipality.

30 March — Cambodia
Unknown assailants threw four grenades into a political demonstration in Phnom Penh, killing up to 16 persons and wounding more than 100 others. Among the injured were a US citizen from the International Republican Institute, a Chinese journalist from the Xinhua News Agency, and opposition leader Sam Rainsy, who led some 200 supporters of his Khmer National Party in the demonstration against the governing Cambodian People's Party.

1 April — Venezuela
Thirty suspected Colombian ELN guerrillas killed two Venezuelan naval officers in El Ripial, Apure state. The officers were part of a patrol group sailing on a river located along the Venezuelan shore when the guerrillas opened fire on them.

3 April — Ethiopia
A Danish nurse who had worked in Ethiopia for the Danish Ethiopian Mission since 1993 was found murdered in the southern region of Bale. She had been missing since her car was stopped by armed men in late March.

8 April — Colombia
FARC guerrillas bombed a rail line at a mining complex in El Cerrejon, derailing 27 railcars, spilling 2,700 tons of coal and 3,700 gallons of diesel fuel, and damaging 550 yards of rail line. The mine is operated under concession by Intercor, a subsidiary of Exxon Corp.

11–12 April — Bosnia and Herzegovina
Police discovered and defused 23 landmines under a bridge that was part of Pope John Paul II's motorcade route in Sarajevo, several hours before the Pope's arrival.

22 April — Cambodia
Khmer Rouge guerrillas attacked two trucks in the Barkeo district of Ratanakkiri Province, killing three Vietnamese citizens, wounding six others, and destroying the trucks.

27 April — Cambodia
Khmer Rouge guerrillas attacked Vietnamese fishermen and wood cutters in Barkeo district of Ratanakkiri, killing nine persons and wounding 10 others.

28 April — Russia
In Grozny, Chechnya, assailants kidnapped the son of the late Georgian President Zviad Gamsakhurdia. The kidnappers threw the hostage out of their vehicle when police pursued them.

5   May   **Colombia**
ELN rebels kidnapped a Brazilian construction worker. The ELN released the hostage on 15 October in Santa Marta. The Red Cross helped the construction company negotiate with the kidnappers. Claiming security reasons, the construction company did not report whether it paid any ransom.

16   May   **Venezuela**
In Urena municipality four armed men kidnapped a Venezuelan politician. The victim was forced into a vehicle and taken to Colombia where he attempted to escape and was shot and killed by his captors. ELN and FARC both operate in the area where the politician was abducted.

13   June   **Bahrain**
Arsonists set fire to an upholstery shop in Manama, killing four Indian expatriates who were trapped in their home above the shop. Shia extremists are suspected.

17   June   **Tajikistan**
A gunman opened fire on two Russian CIS Collective Peacekeeping Force officers in Dushanbe, killing one and wounding the other.

22   June   **Algeria**
Unknown assailants killed a French woman in Bouzeguene and dumped her body in a well. The Armed Islamic Group is suspected.

27   June   **Colombia**
In San Pablo, 60 ELN guerrillas kidnapped three employees of a Brazilian company contracted to repair railroad track in Cesar and Magdalena departments. Two workers were released on 1 July unharmed. The rebels still hold a Spanish engineer and are asking a ransom of $9,000 worth of food "for the people" to release the hostage.

1   July   **Sri Lanka**
Guerrillas from the Liberation Tigers of Tamil Eelam (LTTE) captured an Indonesian flag passenger ferry, taking two Indonesian and seven Sri Lankan crewmembers hostage and then torching the ship. The terrorists released the Indonesians, but the fate of the Sri Lankan hostages is unknown.

6   July   **Bahrain**
Arsonists set fire to a store in Sitra, killing a Bangladeshi and injuring another. Shia extremists are suspected.

7   July   **Sri Lanka**
LTTE guerrillas hijacked a North Korean food ship, killing one North Korean crewmember and holding 37 others hostage. On 12 July the LTTE released the hostages to the International Committee of the Red Cross.

12   July   **Cuba**
A bomb exploded at the Hotel Nacional in Havana, injuring three persons and causing minor damage. Among the injured were one Jamaican man and one Cuban woman. The Hotel Nacional is a five-star hotel located 200 meters from a hotel that was bombed 10 minutes earlier. The Cuban Government stated that "the people responsible for the bombings and also the material used in them came from the United States." In a series of telephone calls to news organizations in Madrid and other foreign capitals, a previously unknown group calling itself the Military Liberation Union claimed responsibility for the recent bombings in Havana. The group claims to be made up of disenchanted Cuban soldiers who intend to spark revolt against Fidel Castro. Their claims are supported by an ex-Cuban air force colonel, who says dissident soldiers are stealing explosives from military arsenals. On 10 September the Ministry of Interior announced the arrest of a Salvadoran citizen who confessed responsibility for the bombing.

19   July   **Colombia**
ELN guerrillas kidnapped a dual Canadian-Colombian citizen and a Colombian citizen in El Bagre. The dual citizen may have been hired by a US mining company to negotiate the release of its US employee who is being held captive by the FARC.

22   July   **Colombia**
Rebels kidnapped six persons who were flying to a remote area in Antioquia to work on electrical lines and seized their helicopter. A group calling itself the Guevarista Revolutionary Army claimed responsibility, demanding a $500,000 ransom and stating that they mined the jungle site where the six were taken and have loaded the helicopter with explosives. The helicopter engineer is a Nicaraguan citizen. On 30 July, Colombian troops found three of the hostages, unharmed, and recovered the helicopter.

26   July   **Yemen**
Unknown assailants kidnapped two Italian tourists and their Yemeni driver near Kohlan. Security forces freed the hostages the next day.

30   July   **Colombia**
ELN guerrillas bombed the Cano Limon-Covenas oil pipeline in Norte de Santander. The rebels wrapped sticks of dynamite around the pipes of the pump, causing a major oil spill and suspending pumping operations for more than a week, which resulted in several million dollars in lost revenue.

                                                 Israel
Two bombs detonated in the Mahane Yehuda market in Jerusalem, killing 15 persons, including two suspected suicide bombers, and wounding 168 others. A dual US-Israeli citizen was among the dead, and two US citizens were among the wounded. The Izz-el-Din al-Qassam Brigades, the military wing of the Islamic Resistance Movement (HAMAS), claimed responsibility for the attack.

6   August   **Yemen**
Yemeni tribesmen kidnapped an Italian tourist they randomly picked out among six others traveling between Rada and Aman. The tribesmen released the tourist on 10 August.

They reportedly kidnapped him to pressure the government to recover a car confiscated in 1994.

7 August — Colombia
In Yopal municipality, unidentified guerrillas attacked the installations of a Colombian firm that works for British Petroleum, harassing workers and setting machinery on fire. Damage is estimated at $2 million.

13 August — Yemen
Tribesmen kidnapped six Italian tourists traveling to Aden from Mukallah. They released the hostages on 15 August.

14 August — Yemen
Tribesmen kidnapped four Italian tourists in Khami. They released the hostages the next day.

15 August — Peru
Sixty Sendero Luminoso (SL) guerrillas kidnapped 30 oil workers in Junin Department. The workers are employed by a firm that is contracted by a French transnational oil company. On 17 August the SL rebels released the oil workers unharmed in exchange for a ransom of food, medicines, clothing, and batteries.

Venezuela
Fifteen Colombian guerrillas kidnapped a Venezuelan army lieutenant and an unidentified resident in Chorrosquero. Three other army officers escaped capture by jumping into a nearby river. Authorities believe the two victims were immediately taken to Colombian territory. Both the ELN and FARC operate near the area.

4 September — Cuba
A bomb exploded at the Copacabana hotel, killing an Italian tourist and causing minor damage. The tourist was killed by flying shards of glass from the explosion. Minutes earlier two other hotels frequented by foreign tourists were also bombed. On 10 September the Interior Ministry announced the arrest of a Salvadoran citizen, who confessed to these three bombings and two others on 12 July.

Israel
Three suicide bombers detonated bombs in the Ben Yehuda shopping mall in Jerusalem, killing eight persons, including the bombers, and wounding nearly 200 others. A dual US-Israeli citizen was among the dead, and seven US citizens were wounded. The Izz-el-Din al-Qassam Brigades, the military wing of the Islamic Resistance Movement (HAMAS), claimed responsibility for the attack.

9 September — Philippines
Suspected members of the Abu Sayyaf Group (ASG) kidnapped a German business executive in Zamboanga City. The ASG released the hostage on 26 December.

Sri Lanka
Guerrillas from the Liberation Tigers of Tamil Eelam (LTTE) attacked a merchant ship with rocket-propelled grenades, causing major damage to the ship. Up to 20 persons were reported killed, wounded, or missing, including five Chinese crewmen. The ship was owned by the China Ocean Shipping Company, registered in Panama, and chartered by the US company ACI Chemicals. The LTTE claimed responsibility.

16 September — Georgia
Three men carrying AK-47s kidnapped one Egyptian and one Jordanian UNOMIG military observer and their local interpreter near the Georgian side of the Injuri River. The kidnappers released the Egyptian, demanding $50,000 for the release of the Jordanian. The kidnappers released the second observer after the United Nations paid them $7,000.

18 September — Egypt
Gunmen attacked a tourist bus in front of the Egyptian National Antiquities Museum in Tahrir Square, Cairo, killing nine German tourists and their Egyptian busdriver, and wounding eight others.

22 September — Jordan
Unknown assailants shot and wounded two Israeli security personnel as they sat in a parked vehicle outside an apartment building housing an Israeli Embassy family in Amman. The Jordanian Islamic Resistance claimed responsibility for the attack. The group demanded the release of a Jordanian soldier serving a life sentence for killing seven Israeli schoolchildren and threatened further attacks if Israeli diplomatic personnel did not leave within a month.

1 October — India
Three bombs exploded on a passenger train as it approached Ghaziabad, in Uttar Pradesh, killing two persons and injuring 38 others, including one Japanese and four Australian passengers.

13 October — Turkey
Nine PKK terrorists kidnapped two Bulgarian and one Turkish engineer from a coal mine. The Turkish engineer was found dead, but the Bulgarians were released unharmed on 16 October.

15 October — Sri Lanka
LTTE guerrillas detonated a massive truck bomb in the parking lot of a major hotel next to the new World Trade Center in Colombo, killing 18 persons and injuring at least 110 others. Among the injured were seven US citizens and 33 other foreign nationals. The explosion caused extensive damage to several international hotels and the World Trade Center.

Yemen
Bani Dabian tribesmen kidnapped a British businessman and two Yemenis near Sumayr. The tribesmen demanded financial aid for their tribe and completion of electricity and water projects in the region. They released the hostages on 30 October.

Yemen

Yemeni tribesmen kidnapped four French tourists in Saada. The tribesmen demanded the return of a car they claimed the government confiscated because of lack of proper documentation. Authorities freed the hostages the next day.

22 October   **Yemen**

Al-Hadda tribesmen kidnapped two Russian doctors and their wives in the Zamar region to pressure the government into handing down death sentences to four residents who raped a boy from their tribe. The tribesmen released the four hostages on 10 November.

23 October   **Colombia**

ELN rebels kidnapped two foreign members of the Organization of American States (OAS) and a Colombian human rights official at a roadblock. One observer is Chilean, and the other is Guatemalan. The ELN claimed that the kidnapping was intended "to show the international community that the elections in Colombia are a farce." In a letter to the Antioquia governor, the ELN stated that it would release the hostages after the elections, but that a nationwide "armed strike" would aim to prevent the elections from being held. On 28 October the ELN rebels issued the following conditions for the hostages' release: lift the army checkpoints on the highway between Bogota and Medellin, clear La Pinuela base, clear Granada municipality, and halt army operations for eight consecutive days from the time of the release. On 1 November masked ELN guerrillas dressed in Colombian national police uniforms turned the hostages over to representatives of the Red Cross, Catholic Church, national and local peace commission members, and other witnesses in front of a parish church in Santa Ana. The men had been held elsewhere and were transferred by helicopter to the village.

27 October   **Philippines**

Suspected Moro Islamic Front (MILF) guerrillas kidnapped an Irish Roman Catholic priest in Marawi, demanding $192,000 in ransom and the release of livelihood funds promised under the amnesty program. On 4 November the captors freed the priest.

29 October   **Yemen**

Gunmen opened fire on the Qatari Ambassador to Yemen's car in Sanaa. The ambassador escaped the attack. Militants opposed to the mid-November Middle East and North Africa economic conference in Qatar may be responsible.

30 October   **Yemen**

Al-Sha'if tribesmen kidnapped a US businessman near Sanaa. The tribesmen sought the release of two fellow tribesmen who were arrested on smuggling charges and several public works projects they claim the government promised them. They released the hostage on 27 November.

31 October   **Uganda**

Unknown assailants hurled two handgrenades into a backpackers' hostel in Kampala, Uganda, injuring one South African, one Briton, and one unidentified foreign tourist.

11 November   **Colombia**

Unknown assailants kidnapped a German industrialist in Cundinamarca, Colombia. No group claimed responsibility.

12 November   **Colombia**

FARC rebels kidnapped one Mexican and one Colombian engineer from a hydroelectric plant. The rebels also stole dynamite and two vehicles they used to flee the scene.

Pakistan

One day, after the conviction of Mir Aimal Kansi, two unidentified gunmen shot to death four US auditors from Union Texas Petroleum and their Pakistani driver after they drove away from the Sheraton Hotel in Karachi. The Islami Inqilabi Council, or Islamic Revolutionary Council, claimed responsibility in a call to the US Consulate in Karachi. The Aimal Secret Committee, or Aimal Khufia Action Committee, also claimed responsibility in a letter to Pakistani newspapers.

17 November   **Egypt**

Al-Gama'at al-Islamiyya (IG) gunmen shot and killed 58 tourists and four Egyptians and wounded 26 others at the Hatshepsut Temple in the Valley of the Kings near Luxor. Thirty-four Swiss, eight Japanese, five Germans, four Britons, one French, one Colombian, a dual-national Bulgarian/Briton, and four unidentified persons were among the dead. Twelve Swiss, two Japanese, two Germans, one French, and nine Egyptians were among the wounded. The IG militants left a leaflet at the scene calling for the release of Umar Abd al-Rahman, the IG spiritual leader imprisoned in the United States.

18 November   **Philippines**

Two suspected former members of the Moro National Liberation Front (MNLF) kidnapped a Belgian Roman Catholic priest in Ozamis as he returned home from a farewell party for the Irish priest who had been kidnapped 10 days earlier. The kidnappers released the Belgian priest on 19 November.

Tajikistan

A French couple was kidnapped by the brother and friends of jailed militant Bahrom Sodirov in hopes of gaining his release. On 29 November the kidnappers released the male hostage, but the woman was shot and later died when Tajik authorities stormed the building. Five terrorists died in the battle.

20 November   **Israel**

Unknown gunmen shot and killed a Hungarian Yeshiva student and wounded an Israeli student in the Old City of Jerusalem.

21 November   **Somalia**

In Elayo Village in the self-proclaimed republic of Somaliland, approximately 20 unidentified gunmen kidnapped five United Nations and European aid workers. The hostages included one Briton, one Canadian, two Kenyans, and one Indian and were released on 24 November.

22 November   **Algeria**

Unidentified hooded attackers killed a German-born man in his home in Ain el Hajar, Saida Province. The victim had lived in Algeria since 1952, had converted to Islam, and was married to an Algerian woman.

25–26 November   **Yemen**

Yemeni tribesmen kidnapped a US citizen, two Italians, and two unspecified Westerners near Aden to protest the eviction of a tribe member from his home. The kidnappers released the five hostages on 27 November without incident.

10 December   **Turkey**

Authorities defused a powerful time bomb found inside a gas cylinder at a Turkish facility adjoining the international ATAS oil refinery in Mersin. The ATAS refinery is a joint venture of Royal Dutch/Shell group, Mobil Oil, British Petroleum (BP), and Turkey's Marmara Petrol.

13 December   **Nigeria**

Employees and villagers kidnapped one US citizen, one Australian, and two British oil workers, and at least nine Nigerian staff members of Western Geophysical, a US-owned oil exploration company off the coast of Nigeria. The victims were released in stages on 17 and 18 December.

17 December   **Chechnya**

Fifteen armed men kidnapped five Polish nationals working for the Catholic charity Caritas, Poland.

18 December   **Colombia**

ELN rebels kidnapped four Colombian Coca-Cola employees at a roadblock in Norte de Santander. The rebels seek individual ransoms and a payoff from Coca-Cola to prevent further kidnappings and have approached other Coca-Cola officials demanding a protection payoff.

23 December   **Pakistan**

Unidentified assailants fired shots at the teachers' residential compound of the Karachi American School, wounding one Frontier Constabulary guard. The compound is home to nine US citizens and six Canadian teachers and is one block from the school compound in a neighborhood with seven other consulate residences. The guard post has been in place since the 12 November murders of four Union Texas Petroleum employees.

1998

5 January   **Yemen**

Two Yemeni tribesmen kidnapped three South Korean citizens, including the wife and daughter of the First Secretary of the Korean Embassy, in Sanaa. The hostages were released on 9 January.

8 January   **Russia**

Two Swedish missionaries were kidnapped in Makhackala. An anonymous telephone caller claiming to represent the Dagestani kidnappers stated the hostages had been moved to Chechnya. The hostages were released on 24 June 1998.

14 January   **Israel**

A boobytrapped videocassette exploded at the Israel-Lebanon border crossing near Metulla, injuring three Israelis and three Lebanese, including the man who carried it. The Amal claimed responsibility, stating that the intended target was a senior Israeli intelligence officer.

21 January   **Yemen**

Armed tribesmen abducted two engineers in two separate incidents. The tribesmen released the hostages, one German and one Chinese, the next day.

25 January   **India**

Heavily armed masked militants attacked four Hindu families in Wandhama, on the Pakistani side of the Kashmir Line of Control, killing at least 23 men, women, and children. A lone survivor described the militants as Urdu-speaking foreigners, who first took tea with the Hindu families before opening fire. The militants also set fire to a Hindu temple and some homes.

3 February   **Chad**

Five armed members of a Chadian opposition group kidnapped four French nationals in Manda National Park in Moyen-Chari Prefecture, releasing them unharmed on 8 February. The Union of Democratic Forces (UFD) claimed responsibility.

    Greece

Bombs detonated at two McDonald's restaurants in the Halandri and Vrilissia suburbs of Athens, causing extensive damage. Authorities suspect anarchists carried out the attacks in retaliation for the arrest of the alleged leader of the Fighting Guerrilla Formation (MAS).

9 February   **Yemen**

Yemeni tribesmen kidnapped a Dutch tourist in Sanaa. The kidnappers demanded the release of three members of their clan who had been arrested for stealing a United Nations vehicle. The hostage was released on 25 February.

19 February   **Georgia**

Armed supporters of late Georgian president Zviad Gamsakhurdia abducted four United Nations military observers from Sweden, Uruguay, and the Czech Republic. On 22 February one Uruguayan military observer was released. The remaining hostages were released after President Shevardnadze met with the Gamsakhurdia opposition on 25 February. Eight of the kidnappers were captured. (The leader, a key figure in the assault on 9 February on President Shevardnaze's motorcade, remained at large until Georgian authorities tracked him to western Georgia and killed him in a shootout on 31 March.)

19 February   Yemen
Yemeni al-Hadda tribesmen kidnapped a Dutch agricultural expert in Dhamar. The kidnappers demanded development projects in their area and released the hostage the next day.

21 February   Pakistan
Unidentified gunmen killed two Iranian engineers near the Iranian Cultural Center in Karachi. The shooting may have been conducted to mark the anniversary of the attack on 20 February 1997 on the Iranian Cultural Center in Multan.

25 February   Ethiopia
An armed group kidnapped an Austrian national as she traveled from Gode to Denan, according to press reports. The Ogaden National Liberation Front (ONLF) claimed responsibility. The ONLF released the hostage 23 March after announcing on a radio broadcast its intent to release her.

14 March   Colombia
Revolutionary Armed Forces of Colombia (FARC) guerrillas kidnapped two French businessmen in Meta Department, according to press accounts. The hostages are brothers who run a hotel in the department. One hostage was released shortly after the abduction with a huge ransom demand by the rebels for his brother's release.

21 March   Colombia
FARC rebels kidnapped a US citizen in Sabaneta. According to multiple media sources, the hostage was released to the International Red Cross on 6 September 1998.

22 March   Chad
Gunmen kidnapped six French and two Italian nationals in the Tibesti region. Chadian forces freed all but one hostage within hours. A group called the National Front for the Renewal of Chad (FNTR) claimed responsibility in a statement to the press, saying it would release the remaining hostage on the condition that French troops withdraw from Chad and that Western oil companies halt exploration and exploitation of all resources in Chad. On 27 March, Chadian security forces freed the last hostage.

23 March   Angola
Rebels from the Front for the Liberation of the Cabinda Enclave-Cabinda Armed Forces (FLEC-FAC) abducted two Portuguese citizens in Cabinda. The victims are employed by Mota & Company, a Portuguese construction company. The FLEC-FAC demanded $500,000 in ransom, the intervention of Portuguese authorities, and negotiations for the withdrawal of Portugal from Angola. On 24 June the FLEC-FAC released the hostages. It is not known if a ransom was paid.

         Colombia
FARC rebels killed three persons, wounded 14, and kidnapped at least 27 others at a roadblock near Bogota. Four US citizens and one Italian were among those kidnapped, as well as the acting president of the National Electoral Council (CNE) and his wife. On 25 March the rebels released the CNE president and his wife. The rebels released nine of the Colombian hostages two days later. On 2 April one of the US hostages escaped his captors. On 25 April the last two hostages were released.

25 March   Colombia
At the British Petroleum oil field in Cupiagua, a bomb blast injured one US citizen and two British workers. At least one bomb was placed near the oil workers' sleeping trailers and detonated around midnight. Police blame the attack on the National Liberation Army.

Early April   Morocco
An armed Islamic group killed 10 Moroccans near the border town of Oujda in early April, according to news reports.

4 April   Uganda
The US Embassy reported that bombs exploded at two restaurants in Kampala, killing five persons—including one Swedish and one Rwandan national—and wounding at least six others. The restaurants, the Nile Grill and the cafe at the Speke Hotel, are within walking distance of the US Embassy and the Sheraton Hotel. A Ugandan Government official reported to local press that the Allied Democratic Forces may be responsible.

10 April   Turkey
Two Kurdistan Workers' Party (PKK) members on a motorcycle threw a bomb into a park near the Blue Mosque in Istanbul, according to press reports. The explosion injured two Indian tourists, one New Zealander, four Turkish civilians, and two Turkish soldiers. On 12 April authorities arrested the two PKK members involved in the attack.

15 April   Somalia
Multiple media sources reported that militiamen abducted nine Red Cross and Red Crescent workers at an airstrip north of Mogadishu. The hostages included a US citizen, a German, a Belgian, a French, a Norwegian, two Swiss, and one Somali. The gunmen are members of a subclan loyal to Ali Mahdi Mohammed, who controls the northern section of the capital. On 24 April the hostages were released unharmed, and no ransom was paid.

17 April   **Cambodia**

Approximately 60 armed suspected Khmer Rouge militants attacked two fishing villages on the Tonle Sap lake in Kampong Chhnang Province, killing 21 persons and wounding at least nine others, according to press accounts. Twelve of the victims were Vietnamese nationals. The attack occurred in the early morning when the victims were asleep.

Yemen

Press reported that tribesmen kidnapped a British Council official, along with his wife and son, as they traveled from Aden to Sanaa. The kidnappers released the hostages on 3 May.

18 April   **India**

Muslim militants attacked Barankot village in Udhampur district, Kashmir, killing 29 persons, according to press reports. Lashkar-i-Taiba claimed responsibility for the massacre.

19 April   **Venezuela**

Unidentified Colombian guerrillas kidnapped a Venezuelan cattleman in Los Flores hacienda. On 23 April the Venezuelan Directorate of Intelligence and Prevention Services rescued the hostage.

22 April   **Angola**

Suspected secessionists from the Front for the Liberation of the Cabinda Enclave abducted a Portuguese citizen and nine Angolans in Cabinda, according to press reports. The victims are employed by Mota & Company, a Portuguese construction company. The Portuguese hostage was released unharmed on 24 June.

Iraq

A gunman shot and killed an Iranian clergyman and injured his two companions in An Najaf, according to press reports. No one claimed responsibility for the attack.

23 April   **Yemen**

A police officer from the Al-Marakesha tribe kidnapped a Ukrainian citizen on his way to Sanaa and handed him over to the tribe, according to press reports. Tribesmen released the hostage the next day.

24 April   **Yemen**

A bomb exploded in the courtyard of the Al-Kheir mosque after midday prayers in Sanaa, according to US Embassy reporting. The explosion killed two persons and wounded 26 others, including two United States citizens, one Canadian, one Libyan, and several Somalis.

25 April   **Colombia**

FARC guerrillas kidnapped a Palestinian connected to the Palestine Liberation Organization in Bogota. The victim is a Colombian citizen who has resided in Colombia for the past 20 years. On 17 July the FARC rebels released the hostage, reportedly at the request of the International Red Cross and of a special envoy of the Palestinian Authority.

Late April   **Angola**

Militants thought to be from the National Union for the Total Independence of Angola (UNITA) abducted a Portuguese couple involved in trading, according to the press. An administrative source told the Angolan Press Agency that the abduction occurred after 150 armed men occupied the commune of Ebanga. UNITA does not have a history of kidnapping foreigners, and the motive is unclear.

1 May   **India**

A bomb exploded under a crowded bus in Shupiyan, injuring six persons, according to press reports. Muslim militants are suspected.

4 May   **India**

Near Manchar, east of Jammu, Kashmir, police reported that suspected Muslim militants killed four members of a village defense committee, four other villagers and one police officer.

5 May   **India**

Armed Islamic militants reportedly entered a home in Surankote, north of Jammu and killed four persons.

6 May   **India**

Suspected Muslim militants killed five Hindu family members during a funeral procession outside the town of Punch, Kashmir, according to US Embassy reports.

16 May   **Colombia**

Six unidentified heavily armed men kidnapped an Italian engineer near Medellin. The engineer, who was overseeing the construction of a tunnel, was taken from his car and forced to enter a taxi with the gunmen, according to police reports. Police said it was unclear whether the kidnappers were leftist guerrillas.

India

In Binola Chuora village, Kashmir, militants killed at least seven persons. According to press accounts, the victims were former militants who had become police informants or members of village defense groups opposed to the militants.

19 May   **Angola**

Armed assailants attacked a marked United Nations vehicle at Calandula, killing one Angolan interpreter working for the UN and wounding two other UN employees and one Angolan police officer. A UN spokesperson blamed UNITA.

22 May   **Sudan**

Guerrillas from the Sudan People's Liberation Army (SPLA) abducted a British contractor for the World Food Program (WFP) and held him for ransom in an SPLA-controlled area of southern Sudan, according to official sources. The victim is employed by Terra Firma and was on a survey mission for WFP when he was abducted. SPLA demanded $58,000 and 125 drums of diesel fuel. The contractor was released on 19 June.

23 May   India
A provincial legislator, his driver, a bodyguard, and three others were injured seriously when a bomb detonated on the outskirts of Srinagar, according to police reports. Their armored car was totally destroyed. Pakistani-supported Muslim militants are suspected.

26 May   Venezuela
Three armed FARC guerrillas kidnapped a Venezuelan engineer in La Victoria. On 18 June the rebels released the engineer and gave him money to travel home. The hostage told authorities that the FARC stated they intended to kidnap a businessman from that area but took him by mistake.

27 May   Colombia
In Santa Marta, 20 National Liberation Army (ELN) rebels bombed the offices of a subsidiary of the US-owned Dole company. The guerrillas overpowered the guards, gagged the employees, and destroyed files before detonating four bombs, partially destroying the headquarters. The rebels painted graffiti accusing the company owners of assisting paramilitary groups in the region. The rebels opened fire on the police as they escaped.

1 June   India
Local press reported that a bomb exploded at a busy market in the heart of Jammu, Kashmir, killing one child and injuring 19 other persons. At least 10 shops were damaged. Indian officials suspect that Muslim militants are responsible.

India
A bomb exploded at an Army base in Jammu, Kashmir, killing two civilians and damaging the Army's intelligence wing. Indian officials suspect that Muslim militants are responsible.

3 June   Turkey
Armed PKK militants kidnapped a German tourist and a Turkish truck driver at a roadblock in Agri, according to press reports. The German tourist was found unharmed the next morning near the kidnapping site, but the truck driver still is missing.

7 June   Pakistan
Police reported that a bomb ripped through an 18-car passenger train en route from Karachi to Peshawar, killing 23 persons and wounding at least 32 others, and destroying one railcar. Pakistan blames India's Research and Analysis Wing for the bombing. Indian officials deny the accusation.

18 June   Iraq
Unidentified assailants shot and killed an Iranian Shiite cleric, two of his relatives, and his driver. The victims were driving back to An Najaf after a pilgrimage to a shrine in Karbala'.

Yemen
Tribesmen kidnapped nine Italian tourists and their Yemeni driver in Husn al-Ghurab in the Bir Ali area of Mayfaah District. The tribesmen demanded the government pay them 800,000 riyals that were pledged to them in a previous agreement, compensation for a car lost in the civil war in 1994, and construction of a school and health facility in their region. The kidnappers released two elderly women and the driver on 19 June and the remaining seven hostages on 21 June.

19 June   India
Five armed militants attacked Hindu villagers in Champnari village in Jammu's Doda District, killing at least 25 persons and injuring seven others, according to police reports. The victims were members of two wedding parties. Indian officials blame Pakistani-backed Muslim militants.

21 June   Lebanon
Unknown assailants fired four rocket-propelled grenades in the direction of the US Embassy in Beirut. The rockets exploded immediately after being launched, missing the Embassy.

23 June   India
A remote-controlled bomb exploded under the Delhi-bound Shalimar Express in Kashmir, injuring at least 35 of the 2,000 passengers and derailing seven cars, according to press reports. A police spokesperson stated that Muslim militants are suspected.

25 June   Ethiopia
Six staff members of the International Committee of the Red Cross were abducted when they were traveling from Gode to Degeh Bur in three marked vehicles. The ICRC members include one Swiss national and five ethnic Somalis. On 3 July the Islamic group al-Ittihad al-Islami claimed responsibility, stating that the hostages were under investigation for spying. On 10 July the hostages were released.

Colombia
FARC rebels kidnapped a Canadian, a Bolivian, and a Colombian citizen in Santander Department. The Bolivian citizen works for a Colombian-German firm, while both the Canadian and Colombian work for a Canadian mining company. The three men were kidnapped while driving on a rural road.

28 June   India
According to press reports, a bomb hidden in a lunchbox detonated in Achaval Gardens, a popular picnic site in Anantnag, Kashmir. Two persons were killed and at least fifteen persons were injured in the blast.

8 July   Uganda
A United Nations World Food Program (WFP) worker was killed instantly when guerrillas from the Uganda National Rescue Front II fired a rocket-propelled grenade at his WFP truck.

14 July   Colombia
FARC rebels kidnapped an Ecuadorian citizen near Medellin. The victim, a US resident, was enroute to visit his family in Ecuador when he was abducted. The FARC demanded $1 million for his release.

1 July   India
An unidentified militant threw a grenade in the Jehangir Chowk area in Srinagar, Kashmir, injuring 13 persons, according to press accounts. A police official stated that the grenade was thrown at a Border Security Force post but exploded in the road instead. No one claimed responsibility, but police believe that Muslim militants are behind the attack.

18 July   Ecuador
The Indigenous Defense Front for Pastaza Province (FDIP) kidnapped three employees of an Ecuadorian pipeline maker subcontracted by a US oil company in Pastaza Province. The group accuses the company of causing environmental damage in its oilfield developments. On 28 July the FDIP released one hostage, and it released the remaining two hostages the next day.

20 July   Tajikistan
Unidentified assailants ambushed and killed four members of the United Nations Mission of Observers in the Tavildara area. The victims included military observers from Poland and Uruguay, a Japanese Civil Affairs officer, and a Tajikistani interpreter.

22 July   Yemen
An assailant possibly associated with the Abu Nidal organization murdered an Egyptian citizen in Sanaa. The victim, Muhammad Salah Sha'ban, was the Imam of al-Husayni Mosque in Sanaa. The motive for the murder of Sha'ban— reportedly a member of the Egyptian al-Gama'at-al-Islamiyya —is unclear.

24 July   India
A bomb exploded near the railroad tracks moments after the Shalimar Express passed by in Jammu and Kashmir, killing one soldier and injuring two civilians. Indian officials believe that Muslim militants are responsible.

25 July   Yemen
A Yemeni shot and killed three Catholic nuns, one Filipino, and two Indians in the Red Sea port city of Al Hudaydah. Press reports stated that the assailant considers himself a Muslim fundamentalist and that he trained in Bosnia as a fighter, but Yemeni officials described him as "deranged."

26 July   India
A bomb exploded on an empty bus parked at the interstate bus terminal in New Delhi, killing two persons and injuring at least eight others, according to police reports. The bomb destroyed the bus and caused major damage to six others.

28 July   India
According to police reports, suspected Muslim militants killed ten villagers in a predawn attack northwest of Doda, Kashmir. Five persons are reported missing.

India
In Doda, Kashmir, suspected Muslim militants killed at least eight members of two Hindu families and wounded three others. Eyewitnesses reported that the gunmen lined up the victims and shot them at point blank range.

1 August   Northern Ireland
A 500-pound car bomb exploded outside a shoe store in Banbridge, injuring 35 persons and damaging at least 200 homes. Authorities had received a warning telephone call and were evacuating the area when the bomb went off. The Real IRA, the Republic of Ireland-based military wing of the 32 County Sovereignty Council, claimed responsibility.

4 August   India
Suspected militants from the Harakat ul-Mujahidin (HUM) gunned down 19 persons near Surankot, Kashmir, according to the Indian Border Security Force and press reports. Two survivors traveled six hours on foot to report the attack to authorities. The victims were family members of a rival group that reportedly had been collaborating with Indian security forces.

India
Unidentified assailants with automatic rifles opened fire on a group of sleeping laborers at a remote construction site in Himachal Pradesh, killing 26 persons and wounding eight others. As the militants headed back to Kashmir they attacked a second group of workers, killing eight persons and wounding three others. Authorities suspect Pakistani-backed militants.

India
According to eyewitness reports, militants detonated a grenade in a crowded marketplace in Lal Chowk, Srinagar, Kashmir, injuring seven persons.

7 August   Kenya
A bomb exploded at the rear entrance of the US Embassy in Nairobi, killing 12 US citizens, 32 Foreign Service Nationals (FSNs), and 247 Kenyan citizens. Approximately 5,000 Kenyans, six US citizens, and 13 FSNs were injured. The US Embassy building sustained extensive structural damage. The US Government is holding terrorist financier Usama Bin Ladin responsible.

Tanzania
Almost simultaneously, a bomb detonated outside the US Embassy in Dar es Salaam, killing seven FSNs and three Tanzanian citizens, and injuring one US citizen and 76 Tanzanians. The explosion caused major structural damage to the US Embassy facility. The US Government holds Usama Bin Ladin responsible.

10 August — India
Unidentified assailants threw a grenade and fired automatic weapons into a crowded bus in Anantnag, Kashmir, killing four persons and injuring seven others, according to police reports. Authorities suspect Pakistani-backed separatists.

12 August — Democratic Republic of the Congo
Suspected former Rwandan soldiers abducted six tourists—one Canadian, two Swedes, and three New Zealanders—after the tourists crossed into the Congo from Uganda. Two of the New Zealanders escaped one week later, and the Canadian was released on 19 August with a statement from a previously unknown group called People in Action for the Liberation of Rwanda. The group claimed responsibility and stated that the remaining captives would be freed if a message from the group was read over BBC broadcasts in Africa. The remaining hostages reportedly were sighted in the forests in eastern Congo.

14 August — Sri Lanka
The Liberation Tigers of Tamil Eelam (LTTE) seized a Dubai-owned cargo ship and abducted 21 crew-members, including 17 Indian nationals. The LTTE evacuated the crew before the Sri Lankan Air Force bombed and destroyed the ship, on the suspicion that the vessel was transporting supplies to the LTTE. The 17 Indian hostages were released to the International Committee of the Red Cross on 19 August. The LTTE continues to hold four Sri Lankans hostage.

15 August — Northern Ireland
A 500-pound car bomb exploded outside a local courthouse in Omag's central shopping district, killing 29 persons and injuring more than 330. Authorities were in the process of clearing the shopping area around the courthouse when the bomb exploded. On 17 August authorities arrested five local men suspected of involvement in the bombing. The Real IRA claimed responsibility.

25 August — India
Separatist guerrillas threw a grenade at a vehicle carrying security personnel in Srinagar. According to police, the grenade missed its target and exploded in the crowded street, injuring 12 persons.

India
Police reported that unidentified militants threw a grenade in downtown Srinagar, killing one civilian and injuring 11 others.

South Africa
A bomb exploded in the Planet Hollywood restaurant in Capetown, killing one person and injuring at least 24 others—including nine British citizens—and causing major damage. The Muslims Against Global Oppression (MAGO) claimed responsibility in a phone call to a local radio station, stating that the bomb was in retaliation for the US missile attacks on terrorist facilities in Sudan and Afghanistan. Police believe that People Against Gangsterism and Drugs (PAGAD) are responsible.

29 August — Belgium
Arsonists firebombed a McDonald's restaurant in Puurs, destroying the restaurant and causing up to $1.4 million in damage. The Animal Liberation Front (ALF) claimed responsibility for the attack.

2 September — India
Police reported that Muslim militants detonated a landmine under a bus carrying troops from Jammu to Punch, killing the civilian driver and seriously injuring 15 soldiers.

8 September — Philippines
Approximately 30 suspected Muslim militants armed with rifles and grenade launchers abducted an Italian priest and 12 Filipinos from a cooperative store in the parish church. The Filipino hostages were released the next day, but the priest still is being held. No ransom has been demanded. Police suspect either the Abu Sayyaf Group (ASG) or the Moro Islamic Liberation Front (MILF).

9 September — Philippines
Suspected ASG members kidnapped three Hong Kong businessmen in Mindanao. The victims are employed by the Jackaphil Company. No ransom demand has been made. On 23 December the three kidnapped victims were released unharmed.

21 September — Georgia
Unidentified assailants opened fire on a bus in Sukhumi, wounding three UN military observers and one other UN mission employee, according to UN officials. The injured include two Bangladeshis and one Nigerian.

22 September — Colombia
Suspected FARC members kidnapped a Japanese businessman from his farm in Bogota.

India
Police and doctors reported that unidentified gunmen shot and wounded a French tourist near the Jama Masjid mosque in Srinagar. Witnesses said that two assailants fired at the victim. Muslim guerrillas are suspected.

29 September — Ecuador
A bomb exploded at the Ecuadorian Bishops' Conference, injuring one Spanish missionary and causing major damage. The explosion released leaflets calling for improved cost of living and utility services. Police believe the bombing is linked to a national strike protesting the economic package implemented by the Ecuadorian President.

3 October — Russia
On 3 October 1998 in Groznyy, Chechnya, 20 unidentified armed assailants kidnapped three Britons and one New Zealander. On 8 December partial remains of the hostages were discovered on a roadside.

5 October — Ecuador
Three employees of the Santa Fe Oil Company, two US citizens and one Ecuadorian, were kidnapped, according to local press accounts. One US citizen escaped the next day.

6 October — India
According to police reports, suspected Muslim militants threw a bomb at a vehicle carrying a prominent former militant in Tral, Kashmir, killing him and 10 others.

8 October — India
According to police officials, Muslim militants threw a grenade at a police post in Srinagar, Kashmir, injuring five civilians, four police officers and four soldiers.

India
Police reported that Muslim militants detonated a bomb near the state secretariat building in Srinagar, Kashmir, injuring 13 persons and causing minor damage.

9 October — Pakistan
Police reported that unidentified assailants opened fire on the Iranian Cultural Center in Multan, killing one Pakistani security guard and wounding another.

12 October — Colombia
People's Liberation Army (EPL) rebels kidnapped 20 persons, including four foreigners at a road block on the Northeastern Highway. The rebels burned three cars and released two hostages to report the situation to the media.

18 October — Colombia
A bomb exploded on the Ocensa pipeline in Antioquia Department, killing approximately 71 persons and injuring at least 100 others. The explosion caused major damage when the spilled oil caught fire and burned nearby houses in the town of Machuca. The pipeline is jointly owned by the Colombia State Oil Company Ecopetrol and a consortium including US, French, British, and Canadian companies. On 19 October the ELN claimed responsibility.

26 October — Colombia
Guerrillas abducted a Danish engineer and two Colombians at a roadblock in San Juan. Local authorities suspect the FARC or ELN is responsible. (On 21 January 1999 in Carmen de Bolivar EPL rebels freed the Danish hostage. There have been no reports on the two Colombians.)

28 October — Yemen
Armed tribesmen in the Mahfad region kidnapped two Belgian citizens, demanding the release of a tribesman sentenced to death by a Yemeni court. On 29 October tribesmen released the hostages.

8 November — Angola
In Lunde Norte Province at least 50 armed assailants attacked a Canadian-owned diamond mine, killing one Portuguese national, two Britons, three Angolans, and wounding 18 others. The assailants also took four workers hostage, including one South African, one Briton, and two Filipinos. Angolan officials blame the attack on UNITA. The secretary general of UNITA claimed responsibility for the attack but denied taking hostages.

14 November — India
In Budgam, near Srinagar, Kashmir, a police spokesman reported that militants threw a grenade near a telephone booth, seriously injuring one person.

India
Police reported an explosion at a taxi stand near Srinagar that injured four persons and damaged four vehicles.

15 November — Colombia
Armed assailants followed a US businessman and his family home in Cundinamarca Department and kidnapped his 11-year-old son after stealing money, jewelry, one automobile, and two cell phones. The kidnappers demanded $1 million in ransom. On 21 January 1999 the US Embassy reported that the kidnappers released the boy to his mother and uncle in Tolima Department. It is not known if any ransom was paid. The kidnappers claim to be members of the Leftist Revolutionary Armed Commandos for Peace in Colombia.

Sierra Leone
Sierra Leone authorities report that rebels led by Sierra Leone's ousted junta leader, Solomon Musa, kidnapped an Italian Catholic missionary from his residence. Musa leads a faction of the Armed Forces Revolutionary Council. Musa demanded a satellite telephone, medical supplies, and radio contact with his wife for release of the priest. His wife, Tina Musa, was arrested in September and is being detained in Freetown.

17 November — Greece
According to press reports, a bomb exploded outside a Citibank branch in Athens, causing major damage. An unidentified telephone caller to a local newspaper claimed the attack was to protest against arrests made during a student march.

India
A bomb exploded near the Madana bridge in Surankot, Kashmir, killing four persons and injuring several others, according to press reporting. Muslim militants are suspected.

India
Press reported a bomb detonated near a crowded bus stand in Anantnag, killing three persons and wounding 38 others.

India
Police reported Muslim militants detonated a grenade in Anantnag, killing three persons and injuring 35 others.

24 November — Yemen
A car bomb exploded near the German Embassy in Sanaa, killing two persons and injuring several others, according to

reports from German and Yemeni officials. The German Embassy confirmed that no Germans were killed or injured.

25 November — India
In Handwara, Kashmir, police reported that Muslim militants threw a grenade at a wedding party, injuring 11 persons.

27 November — Uganda
Ugandan officials state that 30 Lord's Resistance Army rebels attacked a World Food Program (WFP) convoy, killing seven persons and wounding 28 others. An eyewitness reported the rebels also abducted five persons believed to be WFP officials, and one other person.

3 December — Colombia
Guerrillas kidnapped one German citizen and two Colombians from a bus at a false roadblock in Cauca Department. The guerrillas set the bus on fire and dynamited a tollbooth after stealing the money. Authorities suspect the FARC or ELN is responsible. On 8 January the ELN released the German citizen unharmed.

6 December — Yemen
Local press reported that armed tribals kidnapped four German tourists in Sanaa, demanding $500,000 ransom and improvements to local health and educational facilities. On 30 December the guerrillas released the hostages.

7 December — Italy
During the week of 7 December the ALF sent panettone cakes laced with rat poison to two branches of the Italian news agency ANSA. Two Italian subsidiaries of Swiss Nestle were forced to halt production, costing the company $30 million. According to Italy's ALF founder, the poisoned cakes were sent to protest Nestle's genetic manipulation of food.

8 December — Colombia
A Spanish newspaper reported that FARC guerrillas kidnapped one Spanish citizen and three Colombians. No ransom demands have been made.

9 December — India
A bomb exploded in a shop in the Punch District of Kashmir, wounding the shopkeeper. Police suspect Muslim militants are responsible.

India
In Bandipura, Kashmir, local press reported that Muslim militants threw a grenade at a group near a bus station, killing three persons and injuring 20 others.

Yemen
In Sanaa, Yemeni passengers on a chartered Egyptian airliner demanded to be flown to Libya. The Egyptian pilot landed the plane in Tunisia and told the 150 passengers he could not fly the plane to Libya due to the UN sanctions. The plane and passengers remained on the ground for 15 hours before returning to Yemen.

23 December — India
Muslim militants forced their way into three homes in three separate villages in Kulham District, Kashmir, killing nine persons, according to police reports. The victims were all close relatives of former militants who now support the pro-Indian government militia. Kashmir authorities blame the attacks on the Hizbul Mujahidin.

26 December — Angola
United Nations officials report that a transport plane carrying 10 UN officials and four crew members was shot down over an area of intense fighting between UNITA rebels and government troops. National Radio Services state that UNITA shot down the plane. A UN rescue team arrived at the crash site on 8 January 1999, reporting that no one survived the crash and that the bodies of all 14 persons aboard the plane were accounted for.

28 December — Yemen
Armed militants kidnapped a group of tourists traveling on the main road from Habban to Aden. The victims included two US citizens, twelve Britons, and two Australians. On 29 December Yemeni security forces undertook a rescue attempt, during which three Britons and one Australian were killed, and one US citizen was injured seriously. Yemeni officials reported that the kidnappers belong to the Islamic Jihad, but the investigation is ongoing.

1999

2 January — Angola
A United Nations (UN) plane carrying one US citizen, four Angolans, two Philippine nationals and one Namibian was shot down, according to a UN official. No deaths or injuries were reported. Angolan authorities blamed the attack on National Union for the Total Independence of Angola (UNITA) rebels. UNITA officials deny shooting down the plane.

4 January — India
Unidentified Muslim militants fired four rockets at a police complex in Pattan, Kashmir, killing one officer and his wife and seriously injuring their five-year-old child, according to police reports.

6 January — Angola
Thirty armed UNITA rebels ambushed a vehicle, killing one Briton, one Brazilian, and two Angolan security guards, according to reports from the Australian-owned Cuango mine.

Sierra Leone
The Italian Embassy reported Armed Forces Revolutionary Council rebels kidnapped two Italian missionaries. The missionaries were rescued on 13 January by government-sponsored forces.

8 January — South Africa
Five unidentified youths firebombed a Kentucky Fried Chicken (KFC) restaurant in Cape Town, causing major damage but no

injuries, according to a KFC representative. No one claimed responsibility.

9 January — Yemen
Unidentified assailants abducted a British oil worker from an oilfield operated by a US company, according to press reports. On 13 January the kidnappers released the hostage unharmed.

11 January — Colombia
In Chinacota two vacationing Italian citizens and one Colombian were kidnapped at a false roadblock, according to local media reports. On 9 March in Norte de Santander, the National Liberation Army (ELN) released one of the Italian hostages.

12 January — Pakistan
Unidentified assailants entered the Peshawar home of Abdul Haq, a well-known Afghan moderate, and murdered his wife, 11-year-old son, and a guard. Police reported that Haq was not at home and the victims were sleeping when the attack occurred. No one claimed responsibility.

Sierra Leone
Revolutionary United Front (RUF) rebels kidnapped a Spanish missionary, according to reports from the Xaverian Monastic Order. On 22 January church officials reported soldiers from the Economic Community of West African States Cease-Fire Monitoring Group (ECOMOG) rescued the missionary.

17 January — Yemen
Armed tribesmen kidnapped two Dutch aid workers, their two sons, and two British aid workers. The kidnappers demanded the release of an imprisoned tribesman, according to news reports. On 2 February the six hostages were released unharmed.

Yemen
Armed tribesmen attempted to kidnap two US Embassy employees as they drove to work. The victims drove around their attackers and escaped, according to the Embassy.

18 January — Bangladesh
Two assailants attempted to assassinate celebrated Bangladeshi poet Samsur Rahman, according to local police. Rahman, who has been outspoken against Islamic extremism, escaped unharmed, but his wife suffered knife wounds. Police arrested one Pakistani and one South African, who told investigators that they received financial support from Usama Bin Ladin for training and recruiting mujahidin in Bangladesh. Police suspect the Harakat ul-Jihad Islami (HUJI) is responsible and arrested at least 47 members of the HUJI and Harakat ul-Mujahidin (HUM).

25 January — Sierra Leone
Military sources reported RUF rebels robbed and kidnapped a Japanese businessman. On 29 January the RUF released the hostage.

26 January — Venezuela
In the Alto Apure region, the ELN kidnapped five Venezuelan engineers working for the Venezuelan Petroleum Company. The ELN released one hostage on 15 February and the four others two days later.

27 January — Yemen
Tribesmen kidnapped three German nationals and five Yemenis, according to press reports. Kidnapped were a German midwife, her Yemeni husband and three children, her visiting mother and brother, and their driver. On 28 January the kidnappers released the five Yemeni citizens. No demands were made for the release of the German hostages. The German foreign minister urged Yemeni officials to avoid any rescue attempts that would endanger the hostages.

31 January — Yemen
Tribesmen abducted a British oil worker employed by the US-owned Hunt Oil, releasing him six hours later, according to news reports.

8 February — Greece
A bomb exploded near the Turkish Consulate in Komotini, wounding a member of the bomb squad and causing minor damage. The US Embassy reported that a telephone caller to local authorities warned of and later claimed responsibility for the bomb on behalf of a group called the Support to Ocalan—The Hawks of Thrace.

9 February — India
Police reported that suspected Muslim militants threw a grenade at a security patrol in Pulwama Chowk, injuring 12 civilians and two security personnel.

Nigeria
Officials for an unidentified oil company reported that unknown assailants kidnapped two employees, one British and one Italian. The Italian citizen was released shortly after being abducted. No demands were made, and no group claimed responsibility.

10 February — Angola
Church officials reported UNITA rebels kidnapped two Portuguese nationals and two Spaniards who work for Navacong, a company tasked with renovating M'Banza Congo's public infrastructure. The rebels kidnapped the victims from a church where they had sought shelter.

11 February — Angola
A representative of SDM/Ashton mining company reported UNITA rebels attacked the scout vehicle for a convoy of diamond mine vehicles, killing three Angolan security guards and wounding five others. Angolan and Australian mining companies jointly own SDM/Aston mining.

12 February — Sierra Leone
The Rome-based news agency, MISNA, reported the RUF kidnapped an Italian missionary from a church. No demands

were made. The rebels released the hostage unharmed on 8 April.

13 February — **India**
According to authorities, suspected Lashkar-I-Tayyiba militants attacked a village, killing a family of four and injuring one other person. The victims were relatives of a member of the local village defense committee.

14 February — **Nigeria**
Officials for Shell oil company reported three armed youths kidnapped one British employee and his young son. The captors released their victims unharmed on 15 February. No ransom was paid, and no one claimed responsibility.

Uganda
Police reported a pipe bomb exploded inside a bar, killing five persons and injuring 35 others. One Ethiopian and four Ugandan nationals died in the blast, and one US citizen working for USAID, two Swiss nationals, one Pakistani, one Ethiopian, and 27 Ugandans were injured. Eyewitnesses stated two unidentified Asians and one Ugandan police officer also were wounded. The explosion caused extensive damage to the bar. Ugandan authorities blamed the attack on the Allied Democratic Forces (ADF).

15 February — **India**
Police reported that Muslim militants shot and critically injured the owner of a video shop in Srinagar, Kashmir.

India
In an attempt to ban Western broadcasts, Muslim militants shot and wounded three cable television operators in Srinagar, Kashmir, according to police. The operators were shot in the legs and ordered to broadcast only news and current affairs.

India
A bomb exploded in a crowded marketplace in Srinagar, Kashmir, injuring six persons. Police suspect Muslim militants were responsible.

16 February — **Austria**
Kurdish protesters stormed and occupied the Greek Embassy in Vienna, taking the Greek Ambassador and six other persons hostage. Several hours later the protesters released the hostages and left the Embassy. The attack followed the Turkish Government's announcement of the successful capture of the Kurdistan Workers' Party (PKK) leader Abdullah Ocalan.

France
Sixteen Kurdish protesters occupied the Kenyan Embassy in Paris and took seven Kenyan officials hostage. According to press reports, local police were able to end the occupation and gain the hostages' release without injuries.

Germany
Kurdish protesters occupied the Kenyan Embassy in Bonn and held one person hostage for 12 hours before surrendering to police, according to press reports.

Germany
Approximately 40 Kurdish protesters stormed the Kenyan National Tourist office in Frankfurt and took four employees hostage. The protesters released the hostages several hours after being assured no arrests would be made.

Germany
Approximately 75 Kurdish protesters occupied a travel agency located in a building housing the Greek Consulate in Leipzig. Three travel agents were held hostage until authorities stormed the premises and freed them, according to press reports.

Germany
According to press reports, Kurdish protesters occupied the Greek Embassy in Bonn and held one person hostage for 12 hours before surrendering to police.

Italy
Approximately 30 Kurdish protesters occupied the Greek Consulate in Milan and held six persons hostage for four hours before surrendering, according to press reports.

Netherlands
Approximately 150 Kurdish protesters stormed the Greek Ambassador's residence in The Hague, taking the Ambassador's wife, their eight-year-old son, and a Filipino servant hostage. The protesters released the hostages early the next day and were arrested.

Switzerland
According to media reports, Kurdish protesters stormed the Greek Consulate in Zurich, taking the building's owner and a Swiss police officer hostage. On 17 February, US Embassy officials reported the release of both hostages unharmed.

United Kingdom
Approximately 100 Kurdish protesters stormed and occupied the Greek Embassy in London, taking one night watchman hostage. On 18 February the protesters left the Greek Embassy and surrendered to British authorities.

17 February — **Germany**
Approximately 200 Kurdish protesters armed with clubs broke into the Israeli Consulate in Berlin and briefly took one Consulate worker hostage. Israeli guards shot and killed three protesters and wounded 15 others during the attack.

18 February — **Colombia**
Local press reported the Revolutionary Armed Forces of Colombia (FARC) kidnapped two Spaniards, one Algerian, and two Colombians. On 2 November, FARC rebels released the Spaniards and the Algerian unharmed.

Sudan

Sudanese officials reported the Sudan People's Liberation Front (SPLA) kidnapped seven International Committee of the Red Cross (ICRC) workers. Two hostages were Swiss citizens and five were Sudanese nationals. On 12 March the rebels released the two Swiss nationals. The SPLA executed the five Sudanese hostages on 1 April.

20 February — India

Indian press reported that Muslim militants massacred 20 persons in two districts in Jammu. A military spokesman said the Lashkar-I-Tayyiba is suspected.

21 February — Colombia

The FARC kidnapped two Spanish citizens and seven Colombians, according to a Colombian antikidnapping unit. The rebels released one Spanish hostage and two Colombians and demanded 300 million pesetas for the release of the second Spanish hostage. The rebels released the Spanish hostage on 28 February. No ransom was paid.

22 February — India

Police reported that suspected Muslim militants shot and killed a politician from the National Conference party in Kashmir.

India

Suspected Muslim militants killed two persons and wounded two others in Jigrayi, Kashmir, according to police reports.

India

In Udhampur District, Kashmir, police reported that suspected Lashkar-I-Tayyiba militants killed three persons and shot one other.

24 February — Nigeria

The US Embassy reported armed youths kidnapped a US citizen, holding him for ransom. A local militant group rescued the hostage but then demanded ransom for his release. Bristow Helicopters, the victim's employer, paid the demanded $53,000. The group released the hostage unharmed on 4 March.

25 February — Colombia

The FARC kidnapped three US citizens, according to media reports. The victims worked for the Hawaii-based Pacific Cultural Conservancy International. On 4 March the bodies of the three victims were found in Venezuela. FARC leaders claimed rogue elements within the organization were responsible.

26 February — Colombia

Police reported an unidentified assailant detonated a powerful explosive device at the headquarters of the Colombian Daily Company, a subsidiary of Swiss-owned Nestle Multinational. The explosion caused major damage but no injuries.

India

Official sources reported that unidentified militants abducted and killed five police officers near Hindwara, Kashmir.

28 February — Zambia

The US Embassy reported 16 bombs exploded in and around Lusaka. An explosion inside the Angolan Embassy killed one person and caused major damage. Other bombs detonated near major water pipes and powerlines and in parks and residential districts, injuring two persons and causing major damage. Bomb experts detonated five more bombs and defused two others. No one claimed responsibility. Zambian officials blame agents of neighboring Angola.

March — Zambia

The ICRC reported a French citizen died of natural causes while a captive of the ELN. The ELN had kidnapped the French national on 23 November 1998.

1 March — Uganda

According to French diplomatic reports, 150 armed Hutu rebels attacked three tourist camps, killed four Ugandans, and abducted three US citizens, six Britons, three New Zealanders, two Danish citizens, one Australian, and one Canadian national. On 2 March, US Embassy officials reported the Hutu rebels killed two US citizens, four Britons, and two New Zealanders. The rebels released the remaining hostages.

2 March — Nigeria

The US Embassy reported at least 20 armed assailants attacked a compound housing a large Italian construction company and its workers, injuring six persons. No group claimed responsibility.

7 March — Colombia

Local press reported suspected guerrillas from the ELN or the FARC kidnapped an Argentine citizen from a false checkpoint. No demands were made.

Colombia

Local press reported the ELN or the FARC kidnapped one Swiss citizen and seven Colombians from a false checkpoint. No one claimed responsibility.

9 March — Nigeria

The US Embassy reported unidentified assailants kidnapped a US citizen from his office. No demands were made, and no one claimed responsibility.

Venezuela

Local press reported suspected ELN or FARC guerrillas attacked a Venezuelan patrol unit, injuring one civilian and kidnapping three others.

10 March — Angola

Government officials reported an unidentified group kidnapped five oil workers—two French citizens, two Portuguese nationals, and one Angolan. According to local press, all hostages were released unharmed on 7 July. Members of he Front for the Liberation of Cabinda (FLEC) may be responsible.

1 March   India
Unidentified militants shot and killed a man and his two daughters and wounded his wife and three other relatives in Srinagar, Kashmir, according to Indian officials.

23 March   Colombia
The US Embassy reported armed guerrillas kidnapped a US citizen in Boyaca. The ELN claimed responsibility and demanded $400,000 ransom. On 20 July, ELN rebels released the hostage unharmed following a ransom payment of $48,000.

Colombia
Government officials in Antioquia reported the FARC kidnapped two engineers—one German and one Swiss—from the El Cairo Cement Works. No demands were made.

25 March   Macedonia
In Skopje approximately 200 protesters occupied the US Embassy compound, according to military reporting. The protesters, armed with rocks and Molotov cocktails, set fire to several diplomatic vehicles, causing major damage to the exterior of the Embassy. The protesters did not gain entry into the Embassy, and police eventually dispersed them.

26 March   Greece
The US Embassy reported approximately 500 Greek and Serbian protesters broke down the gate at the British Embassy in Athens and entered the British Ambassador's residence, injuring three local guards and causing major damage.

Serbia
Serbian demonstrators burned down the United States Information Service (USIS) American center.

27 March   Pakistan
In Peshawar the US Embassy reported unidentified assailants assassinated Mohammed Jehanzeb, an Afghan national and secretary to Taliban opponent Haji Qadir. Qadir was the brother of Afghan moderate Abdul Haq, whose wife and son were murdered in Peshawar on 12 January.

Uganda
In Kisoro suspected Rwandan rebels armed with machetes attacked a village, killing three persons. According to military reporting, the attackers crossed into Uganda from the Democratic Republic of the Congo.

28 March   India
Police reported suspected Muslim militants threw a grenade into a crowd in Anantnag, injuring at least 28 people

1 April   India
Suspected Muslim militants shot and killed three family members in their home in Kashmir, according to police reports.

2 April   India
In Poonch District, Kashmir, police reported suspected Muslim militants shot and killed five family members.

3 April   Bosnia-Herzegovina
According to press accounts, unidentified assailants opened fire on a Stabilization Force (SFOR) vehicle carrying two Bosnian employees, injuring one. No one claimed responsibility, but authorities believe SFOR was the target.

Ethiopia
Government officials in Addis Ababa reported an unidentified armed group kidnapped a French aid worker, two Ethiopian staff workers, and four Somalis. On 4 May the Ogaden National Liberation Front released the French diplomat.

9 April   Colombia
The ELN abducted two Swiss nationals, one Israeli, and one Briton in Cauca Department,

12 April   Colombia
Police in Bucaramanga reported the ELN hijacked Avianca Airlines flight 9463 carrying one US citizen, one Italian, one Ecuadorian, and several Colombians. On 13 April six hostages were released, three more on 16 April, and seven more on 7 May. The ELN released eight additional hostages on 18 June, seven on 5 September, and the US citizen on 2 October.

Venezuela
The FARC kidnapped a rancher in Cunaviche, Apue State, according to press accounts. The victim reported that the FARC released him in Caracolito, Norte De Santander Department, on 18 April.

14 April   Angola
Unidentified assailants attacked a Save the Children vehicle in Salina, killing six Angolans, according to US Embassy reporting. UNITA is suspected.

15 April   Greece
Two explosive devices detonated at the Detroit Motors car dealership in Athens, causing no injuries but extensive damage. A group calling itself the Enraged Anarchists claimed responsibility.

20 April   Colombia
On the Pamplona-Bucaramanga road, FARC guerrillas stopped four vehicles at a fake roadblock, kidnapping four prison guards and two truck drivers. The FARC guerrillas also stole three tractor-trailers transporting 27 vehicles from Venezuela and a cargo truck. The rebels later released the two drivers.

India
In Rajauri, Kashmir, a bomb exploded in a goldsmith shop, killing five persons, injuring 47 others, and causing major damage, according to press reports. No one claimed responsibility, but police suspect Muslim militants.

21 April   Liberia

Government officials reported unidentified assailants from Guinea crossed the border and attacked the town of Voinjama, kidnapping the visiting Dutch Ambassador, the First Secretary of Norway, a European Union representative, and 17 aid workers. The hostages were released later that day. Eyewitnesses stated the assailants were members of the militia groups ULIMO-K and ULIMO-J.

27 April   Greece

A bomb exploded at the Intercontinental Hotel, killing one person and injuring one other, according to press reports.

30 April   India

In Kupwara District in Kashmir, Muslim militants stormed the home of a police informant, killing him and eight other persons and wounding three others, according to press accounts.

11 May   India

Suspected Muslim militants killed four members of one family in Kupwara District, Kashmir, according to police reports.

13 May   Angola

UNITA fired surface-to-air missiles to bring down a privately owned plane, abducting the three Russian crewmembers and three Angolan passengers, according to the US Embassy.

Colombia

Four unidentified assailants kidnapped a US helicopter technician in Yopal, according to press accounts. Police suspect the FARC or ELN.

15 May   Russia

The ICRC reported unidentified gunmen abducted two employees—one New Zealander and one Russian. The Russian was released the same day. No one claimed responsibility, and no demands were made. The New Zealander was released on 19 July.

19 May   India

The press reported an explosion on a bus in Jammu killed one person, injured eight others, and destroyed six buses, two tankers, and a gas pump. Kashmiri militants are suspected.

30 May   Colombia

In Cali local press reported heavily armed ELN militants attacked a church in the neighborhood of Ciudad Jardin, kidnapping 160 persons, including six US citizens and one French national. The rebels released approximately 80 persons, including three US citizens, later that day. On 3 June the ELN released an additional five hostages. On 15 June the rebels released 33 hostages including two US citizens, according to US Embassy reporting. On 10 December local press reported the rebels released the remaining hostages unharmed.

6 June   Colombia

The US Embassy reported ELN militants kidnapped nine persons, including one US citizen, near Barranquilla. On 24 September, ELN militants released the US citizen.

7 June   Spain

Authorities safely defused a letter bomb sent to an Italian diplomat in Burgos. The Italian Red Brigades were suspected.

Spain

Authorities safely defused a letter bomb sent to the Italian Consulate in Barcelona. Authorities suspect the Italian Red Brigades.

8 June   Spain

Authorities safely defused a letter bomb sent to the Italian Consulate in Zaragoza. Authorities suspect the Italian Red Brigades.

9 June   Iraq

In Baghdad, according to press reports, a car bomb exploded next to a bus carrying members of the Iranian opposition movement Mujahedin-e-Khalq Organization (MEK), killing seven members and injuring 23 others, including 15 Iraqi civilians. MEK officials suspect the Iranian Government is responsible.

12 June   Philippines

According to press reports, in Zamboanga armed militants kidnapped two Belgium nationals. The Abu Sayyaf Group and the separatist Moro Islamic Liberation Front (MILF) were suspected. One Belgian was released on 18 June and the other on 23 June.

13 June   Serbia

Suspected Serbian gunmen shot and killed two German journalists, according to military reporting. No one claimed responsibility.

15 June   Iran

According to Iranian Government authorities, three armed assailants kidnapped three Italian steel experts in Bam. On 20 June the hostages were released unharmed.

16 June   United Kingdom

In Whitely Bay, Tyneside, an unidentified assailant shot and wounded a former Special Branch Agent. Authorities suspect the Irish Republican Army's Belfast Brigade was responsible.

22 June   India

The United Liberation Front of Assam, with the backing of Pakistan's Inter-Service Intelligence, claimed responsibility for the bombing at the Julpaiguri railroad station that killed 10 persons and injured 80 others, according to senior government officials.

27 June   Nigeria

In Port Harcourt, a Royal Dutch Shell official reported five heavily armed youths stormed a Shell oil platform, kidnapping one US citizen, one Nigerian national, and one Australian citizen, and causing undetermined damage. The assailants hijacked a helicopter and forced the hostages to fly them to a village near Warri. On 16 July an Australian Government official reported the youths released the hostages unharmed for an undisclosed ransom. A group calling itself "Enough is Enough in the Niger River" claimed responsibility.

29 June   Indonesia
Armed militants attacked a United Nations Mission in an East Timor outpost, injuring 12 persons, according to press reports.

Nigeria
According to US Embassy officials, armed militants kidnapped two Indian nationals as they drove through the city of Lagos. On 14 July the militants released the hostages unharmed.

Colombia
Near Medellin, US Embassy officials reported six armed FARC rebels kidnapped a US citizen from his home in Antioquia Department. The rebels demanded $60,000. On 26 July, FARC rebels released the hostage unharmed, but no ransom was paid.

30 June   Angola
Local press reported UNITA rebels shot down an Angolan-owned plane with five Russian crewmen aboard near Capenda-Camulemba. One crewmember died when the plane crashed in UNITA-held territory. A UNITA official confirmed they captured the four crewmen. No demands were made for the hostages' release.

Burundi
World Food Program (WFP) officials reported suspected Hutu rebels fired on a WFP vehicle near Bujumbura, injuring one person.

1 July   Nigeria
Near Aleibiri, US Embassy officials reported armed Oboro youths kidnapped one US citizen, one British national, and one Nigerian citizen. The assailants demanded a ransom of $80,000 for the release of the hostages. On 12 July the youths released the hostages unharmed. No ransom was paid.

4 July   Indonesia
Armed militants ambushed a United Nations convoy kidnapping an Australian and 15 others. A driver and two other persons were wounded. The militants are believed to be members of the Besi Merah Putih Militia group.

6 July   Angola
Local press reported UNITA rebels ambushed a German humanitarian convoy, killing 15 persons, injuring 25 others, and causing major damage. The convoy was transporting goods for Catholic Relief Service.

9 July   Georgia
A bomb exploded outside the United Nations Observer Mission in Georgia in Sukhumi, causing minor damage. According to military reporting, authorities discovered and safely defused a second bomb near the blast site. No one claimed responsibility.

16 July   Yemen
Tribesmen in Omran kidnapped four Belgian tourists, according to local officials. On 18 July the four hostages were released unharmed. No one claimed responsibility.

20 July   Nigeria
A Royal Dutch Shell representative reported armed youths stormed an oil rig in Osoko, detaining seven British nationals and 57 Nigerian citizens. No one was injured. On 22 July the youths released the hostages unharmed.

21 July   Angola
According to Angolan military sources, UNITA militants fired mortars and long-range artillery at World Food Program and International Committee for the Red Cross aircraft parked at the Huambo airport. No one was injured, and no damage occurred.

23 July   Germany
According to police officials, an unidentified assailant threw a bomb into a Turkish travel agency in Munich, injuring two persons and causing minor damage. Authorities suspect the attack was connected to the conviction of PKK leader Abdullah Ocalan.

27 July   Pakistan
According to police reports, a bomb exploded on a passenger bus, killing eight persons and wounding 40 others. No one claimed responsibility.

28 July   Yemen
In Shabwa Province, armed tribesmen kidnapped a Canadian citizen working on the US-owned Hunt Oil pipeline, according to authorities. Tribesmen released the hostage unharmed the following day.

30 July   Venezuela
US Embassy officials reported suspected FARC rebels hijacked a domestic Avior Express flight out of Barinas. No one was injured in the attack. On 10 August local press reported FARC rebels released the hostages unharmed near the Colombian-Venezuelan border. No ransom was paid. FARC officials denied hijacking the plane.

4 August   Sierra Leone
UN officials reported an Armed Forces Revolutionary Council (AFRC) faction kidnapped 33 UN representatives near Occra Hills. The hostages included one US citizen, five British soldiers, one Canadian citizen, one representative from Ghana, one military officer from Russia, one officer from Kyrgystan, one officer from Zambia, one officer from Malaysia, a local bishop, two UNICEF officials, two local

journalists, and 16 Sierra Leonean nationals. No one was injured in the attack. The rebels demanded the release of imprisoned leader John Paul Karoma. On 5 August the rebels released one US citizen and one local journalist. On 10 August the rebels released all remaining hostages.

6 August   Kyrgyzstan
In the Batken district, according to local press, unidentified Tajikistani rebels kidnapped four Kyrgyzstani Government officials. On 13 August the rebels released the hostages unharmed for an unspecified amount of ransom.

10 August   Nigeria
In the Niger-Delta Region, local press reported armed youths kidnapped three British nationals from a US-operated oil platform. No one was injured, and no one claimed responsibility. On 11 August the youths released the hostages unharmed. No ransom was paid.

In a different incident, a spokesperson for the British-owned Niger-Benue Transport Company reported unidentified youths kidnapped two British citizens in the Niger-Delta Region. No one claimed responsibility, and no demands were made. The hostages were released on 11 August.

11 August   Liberia
In Kolahun the British Foreign Office reported an armed gang kidnapped four British nationals, one Norwegian citizen, and one Italian national. The victims worked for an unidentified humanitarian aid service. On 13 August a British official reported the rebels released all the hostages unharmed. No one claimed responsibility.

14 August   Pakistan
According to police reports, a bomb exploded in a van in Dina, killing six persons and injuring 14 others.

15 August   Iran
In Kerman, according to press reports, armed militants kidnapped four tourists, three Spanish and one Italian. On 31 August the militants released the hostages unharmed. No one claimed responsibility.

16 August   Russia
In Dagestan local police reported unidentified assailants kidnapped two Polish citizens and two Russian nationals. The kidnappers demanded $50,000 ransom. On 7 January 2000 the Chechen Parliament reported the hostages were released unharmed in December.

21 August   Ethiopia
Near Dire Dawa, US Embassy officials reported suspected al-Ittihad al-Islami operatives detonated a mine beneath a train carrying 400 Djiboutian nationals. The explosion severely wounded two Ethiopian conductors, destroyed one locomotive, and caused extensive damage to the railway line, shutting it down for four days. No one claimed responsibility.

22 August   Kyrgyzstan
In Bishkek, government officials reported unidentified Uzbekistani gunmen kidnapped four Japanese geologists, their interpreter, and eight Kyrgyzstani soldiers. On 13 October four Kyrgyzstani soldiers were released unharmed. On 18 October another two Kyrgyzstani hostages were freed. On 25 October the remaining hostages were released unharmed. No ransom was paid.

Yemen
In Marib Governorate, according to police reports, armed tribesmen kidnapped a French diplomat and his wife when the driver of their vehicle stopped for late afternoon prayers. On 2 September the hostages were released unharmed. No one claimed responsibility.

23 August   Venezuela
Colombian Embassy officials reported a small bomb exploded outside the Colombian Consulate in Caracas, causing minor damage but no injuries. Security officials defused a second explosive device at the Consulate. Venezuelan police located and safely defused a bomb found on the first floor of Credival Tower, the building housing the Colombian Embassy. The Tupamaro Revolutionary Movement claimed responsibility.

27 August   Russia
In Volograd unidentified assailants kidnapped the General Director of the Coca-Cola Volograd Company and demanded a $50,000 ransom, according to police officials. The hostage, a Filipino citizen, escaped later the same day. No one claimed responsibility.

28 August   Columbia
According to police officials, near Yopal City, police suspected FARC or ELN militants abducted a Scottish oil engineer working for the US-UK owned British Petroleum-Amoco Corporation. No one claimed responsibility, and no demands were made.

30 August   India
Muslim separatists opened fire on a taxi, killing four police officers and their driver in Hanjiweera, according to police authorities.

31 August   Colombia
Local press reported armed FARC militants stormed the Anchicaya hydroelectric plant near Buenaventura, detaining 168 persons. No one was injured. The rebels released several hostages unharmed later that day. The FARC released 58 hostages on 4 September and all remaining hostages unharmed on 5 September. The Pacific Energy Enterprise power plant is operated jointly by US, Colombian, and Venezuelan companies.

Chronology of Significant Terrorist Incidents 1961–2005

6 September — Yemen
Armed tribesmen kidnapped three Sudanese teachers in the Marib region, according to press reports. On 17 September the tribesmen released the teachers unharmed.

8 September — India
On the Surankote-Poonch Road a bomb exploded in front of a motorcade carrying the Chief Minister of Jammu and Kashmir, causing no injuries or damage. According to military reporting Muslim militants were suspected.

India
A bomb exploded at a polling booth in Thanamandi, Kashmir, causing major damage but no injuries. Military officials suspect Muslim separatists.

Nigeria
In Bayelsa State, according to local press, gunmen kidnapped an Indian citizen. On 15 September the gunmen released the hostage unharmed. No one claimed responsibility, no demands were made, and no ransom was paid. Ijaw youths were suspected.

9 September — India
A Kashmiri militant threw a handgrenade into a jeep, injuring two police officers and eight other individuals in Doda, according to military reporting.

11 September — Ecuador
Police officials reported 25 to 30 FARC rebels kidnapped 12 Westerners. Eight hostages, one US citizen and seven Canadian nationals, worked for a US-based oil pipeline company. The other hostages, three Spanish nationals and one Belgian citizen, were tourists. Ecuadorian police rescued one Canadian hostage later that day. No demands were made. FARC officials denied participating in the kidnapping.

13 September — India
Near Tangmarg, Muslim insurgents ambushed a convoy carrying a government minister, injuring a bodyguard and three civilians, according to military reporting. The Hizbul Mujahedin group claimed responsibility.

17 September — India
According to press reports, an unidentified militant threw a handgrenade at an army patrol near a bus station in Shopian, injuring two soldiers and 24 other persons. Muslim militants were suspected.

India
Local authorities reported that Muslim militants shot and killed a politician in Baramulla.

20 September — India
Unidentified militants shot and killed a National Conference party member in his home, according to press reports. Muslim militants were suspected.

29 September — India
According to press reports, unidentified militants threw grenades at a government building in Srinagar, killing one police officer and causing undetermined damage. The Harakat ul-Mujahidin (HUM) claimed responsibility.

Nicaragua
US Embassy officials reported rebels belonging to the Andres Castro United Front (FUAC) kidnapped one Canadian citizen and one Nicaraguan military officer in Bonanza Municipality. The rebels demanded $1 million and a renegotiation of agreements made between the FUAC and the Nicaraguan Government in 1997.

1 October — India
Suspected Muslim militants shot and killed a local politician at his residence, according to press sources.

Thailand
Five armed Burmese dissidents stormed the Burmese Embassy in Bangkok, taking 89 persons hostage. The hostages included three French nationals, three Canadians, one German, one US citizen, and several citizens from Malaysia, Singapore, and Thailand. The group, calling itself the Vigorous Burmese Student Warriors, demanded the release of all political prisoners held in Burma. On 2 October the hostages were released unharmed, and the militants were flown to the Burmese border.

4 October — India
Local police reported a landmine exploded near a polling station in Pampore, killing one election officer, wounding one other, and injuring three police officers. Authorities suspect Muslim militants.

8 October — Nigeria
The US Embassy reported armed youths attacked a US oil-company compound housing employees from the United States, United Kingdom, and Nigeria. The attackers injured four US citizens and four Nigerian nationals and caused massive damage to the compound. The youths demanded the oil facility replace its existing Nigerian staff with local workers. On 11 October government officials reported the attackers left the compound without further incident.

12 October — Burundi
US Embassy officials reported suspected Rwandan Hutu rebels attacked humanitarian aid workers in Rutana. One Chilean UNICEF official, one Dutch World Food Program employee, four local military officers, and six Burundi nationals died in the attack. One Belgian and one Burundi national working for the UN and four Burundi citizens were wounded. No one claimed responsibility.

13 October — Georgia
In Sukhumi unidentified masked gunmen kidnapped six UN military observers—from Germany, the Czech Republic, Greece, Switzerland, Sweden, and Uruguay. A Georgian

interpreter also was kidnapped. The abductors demanded a $250,000 ransom. Four hostages were released unharmed on 14 October, and the remaining three hostages were freed the next day.

15 October — Sierra Leone
In Masombo the Missionary News Agency reported unidentified persons kidnapped three clergymen—two Italian and one Sierra Leonian. No one claimed responsibility, and no demands were made. AFRC rebels are suspected.

21 October — India
Kashmiri militants kidnapped and beheaded a father and daughter suspected of spying for the Indian Army in Kupwara, according to government officials.

26 October — Yemen
Unidentified armed tribesmen kidnapped three US citizens. The tribesmen demanded the government release five fellow tribesmen, according to press reports. The hostages were released unharmed on 28 October.

28 October — India
Local police reported Muslim militants fired six grenades at the secretariat building, killing one person and injuring 11 others.

30 October — Nigeria
Local press reported armed youths seized a helicopter near Warri, kidnapping three British citizens. The kidnappers forced the hostages, pilots for the petroleum company Royal Dutch Shell, to fly to an undisclosed location. No demands were made, but negotiations for release of the hostages were initiated.

1 November — Nigeria
US Embassy officials reported armed youths seized a US vessel near Bonny Island, kidnapping one US citizen, one Polish national, and 12 Nigerian locals. No one was injured in the attack, and the ship sustained minimal damage. The attackers released all the hostages unharmed on 3 November. No one claimed responsibility.

3 November — Panama
Police officials reported suspected FARC rebels hijacked two Panamanian helicopters carrying four Colombian nationals, two Ecuadorian citizens, and two Panamanian pilots near Colon. No one was injured in the attack. The guerrillas released all the hostages unharmed later that day but retained the helicopters.

8 November — Nigeria
The US Embassy reported that 14 youths armed with machetes boarded a Belize-owned vessel near Escravos, in Delta State, and kidnapped one US citizen and one Nigerian national. The youths released the hostages unharmed on 12 November. No ransom was paid.

10 November — Colombia
A representative for the International Committee for the Red Cross (ICRC) reported FARC militants kidnapped a British national working for the ICRC. On 14 November the rebels released the hostage unharmed following a meeting between FARC and ICRC officials. No ransom was paid.

12 November — India
A bomb exploded on the Punjab Express bound for New Delhi, killing 13 persons and injuring some 50 others. No one claimed responsibility, but authorities suspect Muslim separatists were responsible.

— Pakistan
According to local press accounts, unidentified assailants fired seven rockets from three vehicles parked at various locations, injuring six persons and causing minor damage. One vehicle was parked in a lot at the US Cultural center, another near the building housing UN offices, and the third near the US Embassy.

23 November — India
Local police reported a bomb exploded outside a political party headquarters in Srinagar, injuring five persons and causing major damage. Tehrik-i-Jihad claimed responsibility.

7 December — Sierra Leone
Near Buedu, Revolutionary United Front militants kidnapped one German national and one Belgian citizen, both of whom work for the humanitarian group Doctors Without Borders (Medicins Sans Frontieres). No one was injured in the attack. The rebels released both hostages unharmed on 16 December. No ransom was paid.

18 December — Pakistan
A bomb exploded in a marketplace, killing 10 persons, injuring 17 others, and causing major damage, according to press reports.

22 December — India
An unidentified militant lobbed a grenade into a crowd in Anatnag, injuring 12 people, according to press reports. Authorities suspect Muslim Separatists were responsible.

23 December — Colombia
In the Santander Mountain region, local press reported Popular Liberation Army militants kidnapped a US citizen. After deciding that their captive had no ties to the US Government, the rebels released the hostage unharmed on 13 January 2000. No ransom was paid.

24 December — Colombia
US Embassy officials reported a bomb exploded outside the Colombo-American Bi-National Center in Cali, causing an unreported number of minor injuries and major damage to the building. A group calling itself the Colombian Patriotic Resistance claimed responsibility, but police suspect ELN members carried out the attack.

Nepal

Five heavily armed militants hijacked an Indian Airlines Airbus carrying 189 passengers and 11 crewmembers en route from Katmandu to New Delhi. After refueling in Pakistan, the plane was diverted to Dubai, United Arab Emirates, where the hijackers released 27 hostages along with the body of a hostage they had murdered. The hijackers then flew to Qandahar, Afghanistan, and demanded the release of 36 militants imprisoned in India. On 31 December the Indian Government agreed to release three imprisoned militants in exchange for the hostages' safe return. The plane and remaining hostages were released unharmed later that day.

31 December   **Colombia**

Police officials reported three unidentified persons kidnapped a Spanish citizen from his residence in the Santa Ana neighborhood of Barrancabermeja. The hostage, an engineer, was employed by a Venezuelan firm. No one claimed responsibility. The attack bore the hallmark of the ELN.

2000

3 January   **Namibia**

Unidentified assailants attacked four vehicles in Rundu, killing three French children and wounding their parents. The gunmen also injured two humanitarian aid workers—one Scottish citizen and one Namibian national. National Union for the Total Independence of Angola (UNITA) guerrillas are suspected, but UNITA leaders denied the group's involvement in the attack.

8 January   **Sudan**

Humanitarian Aid Commission officials reported Sudanese People's Liberation Army (SPLA) rebels attacked a CARE vehicle in Al Wahdah State, killing the CARE office director and his driver, and abducting two others. An SPLA spokesperson denied the group's involvement.

9 January   **Namibia**

Five suspected UNITA rebels entered a private residence in western Kavango and attacked the occupants, killing two Namibian nationals and injuring one other, according to police officials. No one claimed responsibility.

14 January   **Namibia**

Military officials reported UNITA gunmen attacked a privately owned vehicle near Divundu, killing four persons and injuring five others.

18 January   **Yemen**

Armed tribesmen kidnapped two French nationals and their two Yemeni guides, according to press reports. The Al-Shamian tribe claimed responsibility. The tribesmen released the hostages on 18 January but recaptured them the same day after authorities attempted to arrest the kidnappers. The hostages were released again unharmed on 19 January.

21 January   **Namibia**

UNITA gunmen entered a private residence near Mayara and opened fire, killing three persons and injuring six others, according to local press accounts.

25 January   **Angola**

Local press reported UNITA militants ambushed a vehicle near Soyo, killing one Portuguese national. No one claimed responsibility.

26 January   **Yemen**

Armed tribesmen in Ma'rib kidnapped a US citizen working for the Halliburton Company, according to press reports. On 10 February, the kidnappers released the hostage unharmed.

27 January   **Spain**

Police officials reported unidentified individuals set fire to a Citroen car dealership in Iturreta, causing extensive damage to the building and destroying 12 vehicles. The attack bore the hallmark of the Basque Fatherland and Liberty (ETA).

29 January   **Colombia**

According to press reporting, suspected Revolutionary Armed Forces of Colombia (FARC) or National Liberation Army (ELN) rebels bombed a section of the Cano-Limon pipeline in Arauquita, causing major damage and suspending oil production for three days.

2 February   **Yugoslavia**

Government officials reported unidentified individuals fired an antitank missile at a refugee convoy escorted by KFOR soldiers in Mitrovica, killing two Serbians and injuring five others. No one claimed responsibility.

3 February   **Colombia**

In Putumayo, according to press reporting, suspected FARC or ELN rebels bombed a section of the Cano-Limon pipeline, causing major damage, including an oil spill, and halting production for three days.

8 February   **Colombia**

Government officials reported suspected ELN guerrillas bombed the ONCESA (Canadian-British-Colombian consortium) oil pipeline near Campo Hermoso, causing extensive damage to the pipeline, an oil spill, and a forest fire.

11 February   **Spain**

Four individuals set fire to and destroyed a Citroen car dealership in Amorebieta, according to press reports. The attack bore the hallmark of the ETA.

13 February   **Yugoslavia**

According to press accounts, unidentified individuals shot and wounded two French KFOR soldiers in Mitrovica. No one claimed responsibility.

27 February   **India**

A bomb exploded at a railroad station in New Delhi, injuring eight persons and causing major damage, according to military reporting. Indian authorities suspect Kashmiri militants or Sikhs were responsible.

29 February — Yugoslavia

According to press accounts, an unidentified assailant shot and killed a Russian KFOR soldier while he was on patrol in Srbica. An ethnic Albanian youth was arrested.

Near Pristina, an unidentified gunman shot a UN official, according to press reports. No one claimed responsibility.

2 March — Yemen

Armed tribesmen kidnapped the Polish Ambassador in Sanaa, according to press reports. The Khawlan tribe claimed responsibility. On 4 March, the Ambassador was released unharmed.

3 March — India

A bomb exploded on a bus in Sirhand, Punjab, killing eight persons and injuring seven others. The Indian Government suspects either Kashmiri militants or Sikhs were responsible.

4 March — Uganda

Armed militants kidnapped two Italian missionaries in Kampala, according to press reports. The hostages were released unharmed several hours later. The Lord's Resistance Army (LRA) probably was responsible.

10 March — El Salvador

US Embassy officials reported unidentified gunmen kidnapped a US citizen and his El Salvadoran nephew from their vehicle near San Antonio Pajonal. On 21 March, the hostages were released unharmed following a ransom payment of $34,000.

14 March — Nigeria

Press reported armed youths occupied Shell Oil Company buildings in Lagos and held hostage 30 Nigerian employees and four guards of the Anglo-Dutch-owned company. No group claimed responsibility. On 15 March the Nigerian army rescued the 34 hostages unharmed.

21 March — India

Armed militants killed 35 Sikhs in Chadisinghpoora Village, according to press reports. Police officers arrested Muslim militants, who confessed to helping two groups suspected in the massacre—the Lashkar-e-Tayyiba and the Hizb ul-Mujahedin—two of the principal Muslim groups in Kashmir.

27 March — India

Armed militants threw a grenade at a group of police officers, missing their target but killing three civilians and injuring 11 others in Srinagar, according to press reports. The Hizb ul-Mujahedin may be responsible.

4 April — Pakistan

Armed militants fired on an Afghan vehicle, killing the Governor of the Taliban-held northern Afghan province of Kondoz and his militia commander, and wounding his driver and another passenger, according to press reports. No one claimed responsibility.

7 April — Nigeria

Armed militants kidnapped 40 persons—15 British, 15 French, and 10 Korean citizens—from residences belonging to the Elf Aquitaine Oil Company in Port Harcourt, according to press reports. The 40 hostages were released unharmed several hours later. Disgruntled landowners were suspected.

12 April — Colombia

Police officials reported ELN rebels kidnapped a Mexican citizen in Cali and demanded $5 million ransom. On 16 April, police arrested three of the kidnappers and freed the hostage unharmed.

India

Militants using a remote-controlled device detonated a car bomb near an army convoy in Srinagar, killing one bystander, according to press reports. No one claimed responsibility.

13 April — Colombia

Press reported a bomb exploded on the Cano-Limon oil pipeline near La Cadena, causing major damage and suspending oil production for several days. Police suspect either FARC or ELN rebels were responsible.

14 April — Nigeria

In Warri, armed militants kidnapped 19 employees of the Noble Drilling Oil Company, a firm contracted by the Anglo-Dutch-owned Shell Oil Company, according to press reports. Ijaw youths probably were responsible.

15 April — India

Armed militants killed 12 persons, wounded seven others, and torched several huts in Tripura, according to press reports. No one claimed responsibility.

19 April — France

Press reported a bomb exploded at a McDonald's restaurant in Quevert, killing one person and causing major damage. Although no group claimed responsibility, authorities suspect the Breton Liberation Army (ARB). Nine persons associated with ARB were arrested.

20 April — Pakistan

A bomb exploded near the Jamaat-E-Islami headquarters in Mansuren, injuring two persons in a nearby residence, according to press reports. No one claimed responsibility.

24 April — Malaysia

In Kampong Pulau Tiga, Abu Sayyaf Group (ASG) militants kidnapped 21 persons—two French, three Germans, two South Africans, two Finns, two Filipinos, one Lebanese, and nine Malaysians—according to press reports.

Tajikistan

According to government officials, a group of armed Afghans broke into a residence in Khatlon Oblast and opened fire, killing one person, injuring another, and kidnapping one other. No one claimed responsibility.

28 April   **India**

A bomb exploded at a police checkpoint in Srinagar, killing one civilian and wounding four police officers and one civilian, according to press reports. No one claimed responsibility. In Srinagar, militants threw a grenade at a security patrol but hit a bus stop instead, injuring two civilians, according to press accounts. No one claimed responsibility.

1 May   **Sierra Leone**

On 1 May in Makeni, Revolutionary United Front (RUF) militants kidnapped at least 20 members of the United Nations Assistance Mission in Sierra Leone (UNAMSIL) and surrounded and opened fire on a UNAMSIL facility, according to press reports. The militants killed five UN soldiers in the attack.

In Kailahun, RUF militants kidnapped 27 members of the UNAMSIL. The hostages were released unharmed on 28 May.

2 May   **Sierra Leone**

Unidentified militants kidnapped five Kenyan soldiers from the UNAMSIL peacekeeping force in Magburaka, according to press reports. RUF militants were probably responsible. On 10 May, the hostages escaped.

3 May   **Angola**

Armed militants attacked a World Food Program humanitarian convoy in Luanda, killing one person, wounding one other, and setting the trucks on fire. The UNITA was probably responsible.

5 May   **Sierra Leone**

RUF militants kidnapped 300 UNAMSIL peacekeepers throughout the country, according to press reports. On 15 May in Foya, Liberia, the kidnappers released 139 hostages. On 28 May, on the Liberia and Sierra Leone border, armed militants released unharmed the last of the UN peacekeepers.

8 May   **Sierra Leone**

In Freetown, armed militants shot down a United Nations helicopter, causing major damage to the helicopter but no injuries, according to press reports. The RUF was probably responsible.

9 May   **Sierra Leone**

In Freetown, armed militants kidnapped two British citizens working for a humanitarian organization, according to press reports. The RUF was probably responsible. On 19 June one of the hostages was released unharmed.

10 May   **India**

In Kupwara, armed militants kidnapped a civilian from his residence and then killed him, according to press reports. No one claimed responsibility.

11 May   **India**

In Bihar, according to press reports, armed militants killed 11 persons and injured four others. No one claimed responsibility.

14 May   **Colombia**

Press reported unidentified individuals kidnapped an Australian missionary and three Colombians in Canito. Several hours later, the Colombian hostages were released unharmed. No group claimed responsibility.

Iran

A bomb exploded in the cultural/sports center in Kermanshah, injuring two civilians, according to press reports. The Mujahedin-e Khalq claimed responsibility.

15 May   **India**

A landmine exploded in Chabran, killing Kashmir's power minister and four other government employees and destroying their vehicle, according to press reports. No one claimed responsibility.

19 May   **India**

In Amludesa, armed militants killed six persons—one magistrate, four police officers, and one civilian—according to press reports. No one claimed responsibility.

A rocket hit a private residence in Srinagar, injuring six persons, according to press reports. No one claimed responsibility.

20 May   **India**

Armed militants threw several bombs at a government vehicle near a bus stop in Srinagar, injuring four police officers and three civilians, according to press reports. No one claimed responsibility.

23 May   **India**

Militants fired six grenades at the Civil Secretariat building in Kashmir, killing one civilian and injuring three others, according to press reports. No one claimed responsibility.

24 May   **Angola**

Press reported suspected Front for the Liberation of the Cabinda Enclave rebels kidnapped three Portuguese construction company workers in Cabinda. No one claimed responsibility.

25 May   **Sierra Leone**

In Freetown, according to press reports, armed militants ambushed two military vehicles carrying four journalists. A Spaniard and one US citizen were killed, and one Greek and one South African were injured in the attack. The RUF was probably responsible.

27 May   **Indonesia**

According to press reporting, armed militants, who claimed to be members of the Free Aceh Movement, occupied a Mobil Oil production plant. The rebels ordered the workers and all Indonesian nationals to shut down production and held six hostages for several hours before releasing them unharmed and allowing production to resume. The militants demanded $500,000 ransom to restore operations.

1 June   **Georgia**

In Kodori Gorge, police officials reported unidentified gunmen kidnapped two Danish UN military observers, a British Government employee, and two Abkhaz citizens, demanding a $500,000 ransom. On 3 June, one Abkhaz hostage was released. On 5 June, the remaining hostages were released unharmed.

2 June   **Namibia**

In Mut'jiku, press reported suspected UNITA militants kidnapped a woman from her residence. No one claimed responsibility.

In Rundu, according to press accounts, suspected UNITA militants kidnapped a man.

India

Police officials reported a bomb exploded at a religious meeting in Srinagar, killing 12 persons and injuring seven others, including a senior legislator. The Hizbul-Mujahedin claimed responsibility.

6 June   **Sierra Leone**

Suspected RUF rebels kidnapped 21 Indian UN peacekeepers in Freetown, according to press accounts. No one claimed responsibility.

8 June   **Greece**

In Athens, press reported two unidentified gunmen killed British Defense Attache Stephen Saunders in an ambush. The Revolutionary Organization 17 November claimed responsibility.

India

Press reported unidentified individuals threw a handgrenade into a crowded marketplace in Sopur, injuring 30 civilians and causing major damage. No one claimed responsibility.

11 June   **Yemen**

Four unidentified gunmen kidnapped a Norwegian diplomat and his son, according to press reports. Later the same day, Yemeni police opened fire on the kidnappers, killing the diplomat and one gunman. The son escaped unharmed. The three remaining assailants escaped. No one claimed responsibility.

16 June   **Yemen**

In the Ma'rib region, according to press reports, armed tribesmen kidnapped an Italian archaeologist. On 20 July, the kidnappers released the hostage unharmed. Yemeni tribesmen claimed responsibility.

17 June   **India**

Armed militants shot and injured four civilians in Jammu and Kashmir, according to press reports.

18 June   **Nigeria**

In the Niger Delta region, press reported armed militants kidnapped 22 Nigerian citizens and two unidentified foreign nationals working for Chevron, a US-owned oil company. The militants later released the two foreign nationals and four Nigerians. No one claimed responsibility.

26 June   **Yugoslavia**

In Prizren, press reported a bomb exploded outside a shop located below a UN police officer's residence, slightly injuring the officer and destroying the shop. No one claimed responsibility.

27 June   **Colombia**

In Bogota, according to press reporting, ELN militants kidnapped a five-year-old US citizen and his Colombian mother, demanding an undisclosed ransom.

30 June   **India**

A landmine exploded in Srinagar, killing one person, injuring three military personnel and five civilians, damaging several vehicles, and shattering the windows in several nearby hotels, according to press reports. No one claimed responsibility.

2 July   **Philippines**

Unidentified militants kidnapped a German journalist working for *Der Spiegel* magazine, according to police authorities. The Abu Sayyaf Group (ASG) claimed responsibility. On 27 July, the journalist was released unharmed.

4 July   **India**

In Jammu and Kashmir, armed militants killed one person and injured one other, according to press reports. No one claimed responsibility.

9 July   **Democratic Republic of the Congo**

Near the Rwandan border, Rwandan Interahamwe militiamen attacked a refugee camp, killing 30 persons and kidnapping four others, according to press accounts.

10 July   **Afghanistan**

Press reported a bomb exploded at the Pakistani Embassy, causing major damage but no injuries. No one claimed responsibility.

13 July   **India**

In Leh, Kashmir, armed militants killed three Buddhist monks, according to press reports. No one claimed responsibility.

14 July   **India**

In the Himalaya Mountains, press reported armed militants attacked two German hikers, killing one and injuring the other. No one claimed responsibility.

Chronology of Significant Terrorist Incidents 1961–2005

15 July   **India**
In Doda, Kashmir, armed militants killed the Doda National Conference district president and his bodyguard, according to press reports. No one claimed responsibility.

Sierra Leone
Press reported suspected RUF militants attacked UNAMSIL troops, near Kailahun, killing one Indian soldier and wounding one other Indian soldier. No one claimed responsibility.

India
In Srinagar, Kashmir, militants fired nine rifle grenades toward the Civil Secretariat building, according to press reports. The Chief Minister was in his office at the time but was unharmed in the attack, which injured four civilians and damaged two vehicles nearby. The Jaish-e-Mohammed claimed responsibility.

India
In Tangmarg, Kashmir, armed militants killed one Indian soldier and one civilian, according to press reports. No one claimed responsibility.

16 July   **Sierra Leone**
Unidentified militants killed a Nigerian UNAMSIL soldier in Rogberi, press reported. No one claimed responsibility.

Germany
In Ludwigshafen, the US Consulate reported unidentified individuals firebombed a refugee shelter housing Albanian Kosovars, injuring three children and causing minor damage. No one claimed responsibility.

18 July   **Angola**
Press reported UNITA troops kidnapped 14 clergy members from the Dunge Catholic Mission in Benguela. According to press accounts, two persons were killed and several escaped during the kidnapping. On 26 July all remaining hostages were released unharmed.

20 July   **Angola**
Unidentified militants kidnapped four Namibian citizens from their residence in Kavango, according to press accounts. The militants shot and killed two of the hostages. A third hostage was injured but escaped with a child. UNITA is suspected.

24 July   **India**
A bomb exploded on a private bus in Ballen, killing six persons and injuring 10 others, according to press reports. Kashmiri militants or Sikhs may have been responsible.

27 July   **Colombia**
In Bogota, suspected Guevarist Revolutionary Army (ARG) militants kidnapped a French aid worker affiliated with Doctors Without Borders, according to press reports. The ARG is a suspected faction of the ELN.

29 July   **Namibia**
In Nginga, suspected UNITA rebels crossed into Namibia and kidnapped five Namibian men, according to press reports. No one claimed responsibility.

30 July   **India**
Militants threw a grenade into a crowded marketplace in Gulmarg, killing one person and injuring five others, according to press reports. No one claimed responsibility.

Sierra Leone
In Masiaka, suspected RUF militants fired on Jordanian UNAMSIL troops, killing one soldier and wounding three others, according to press accounts. No one claimed responsibility.

31 July   **India**
A remote-controlled landmine exploded in Gulmarg, killing one person, injuring five others, and destroying their vehicle, according to press reports. No one claimed responsibility.

Nigeria
Press reported armed youth stormed two oil drilling rigs, taking 165 persons hostage. The hostages included 145 Nigerians, seven US citizens, five Britons, and eight Australian and Lebanese nationals. All were employed by service contractors of Shell Oil Company. No one claimed responsibility, but the gunmen were believed to be ethnic Ijaw. On 4 August all hostages were released unharmed.

Sierra Leone
Press reported RUF militants ambushed a UNAMSIL patrol in Freetown, killing one Nigerian soldier. No one else was injured.

2 August   **India**
In Rajwas, armed militants killed 30 persons and injured 47 others when they threw a grenade and then opened fire on a community kitchen, according to press reports. The Lashkar-e-Tayyiba claimed responsibility.

4 August   **Georgia**
Ethnic Kists kidnapped two Red Cross workers and their driver in Pankisi. No injuries were reported, and all hostages were released on 13 August.

Namibia
Press reported suspected UNITA rebels shot and killed one Namibian rebel inside her residence in Mwitjiku. No one claimed responsibility.

8 August   **Angola**
Suspected UNITA rebels attacked a diamond mine in Lunda Norte Province, killing eight South African security personnel, according to press accounts. No one claimed responsibility.

9 August   **Angola**
Press reported suspected UNITA rebels shot and killed one South African national and abducted seven Angolan workers

during a raid on a diamond mine in northeast Angola. No one claimed responsibility.

10 August   **India**
A remote-controlled car bomb exploded in Srinagar, killing nine persons, injuring 25 others, and damaging four cars, according to press reports. Eight police officers were among those killed, and five journalists were among the wounded. No one claimed responsibility.

11 August   **Colombia**
Police authorities reported suspected ELN militants kidnapped a group of 27 tourists in Antioquia. A US professor and a German student were among the hostages. On 12 August the rebels released all hostages unharmed.

In Tolima, according to press reports, the FARC kidnapped then killed two persons—one Colombian and one Irish citizen.

12 August   **India**
A grenade exploded near a historic mosque in Srinagar, injuring four persons—two Hungarians and two Indians—according to press accounts. No one claimed responsibility.

Kyrgyzstan
In the Kara-Su Valley, according to press accounts, Islamic Movement of Uzbekistan rebels took four US citizens and one Kyrgyzstani soldier hostage. The rebels killed the soldier, but the four US citizens escaped on 18 August.

14 August   **India**
Armed militants kidnapped three persons from their residences in Kot Dhara and later killed them, according to press reports. No one claimed responsibility.

India
Militants threw a grenade at a bus in Pulwama, injuring 14 passengers. No one claimed responsibility.

16 August   **Greece**
Militants in Athens set fire to a car belonging to an Italian Embassy official, according to press accounts. No one was injured. The Mavro Asteri (Black Star) called a local newspaper and claimed responsibility.

6 September   **Indonesia**
A militia-led mob attacked a UNHCR aid office in Atambua, West Timor, killing three aid workers—one US citizen, one Ethiopian, and a Croatian—and destroying the compound.

7 September   **Guinea**
Suspected RUF rebels kidnapped three Catholic missionaries—one US citizen and two Italian priests—in Pamlap, according to press accounts. In early December, the two Italian priests escaped.

13 September   **Colombia**
According to press reports, ELN militants set up a fake roadblock in Antioquia and kidnapped two Russian civil engineers. On 21 September the hostages were freed.

15 September   **Colombia**
According to police officials, a group of armed militants kidnapped three Italians in Medellin. No one claimed responsibility.

17 September   **Guinea**
Unidentified rebels attacked and killed a Togolese United Nations refugee agency employee in Macenta, according to press accounts. The rebels also kidnapped an Ivorian secretary. No one claimed responsibility.

30 September   **India**
Armed militants killed five persons in their private residence in Jammu, according to press reports. No one claimed responsibility.

1 October   **Tajikistan**
Unidentified militants detonated two bombs in a Christian church in Dushanbe, killing seven persons and injuring 70 others, according to press reports. The church was founded by a Korean-born US citizen, and most of those killed and wounded were Korean. No one claimed responsibility.

2 October   **Uganda**
Press reported LRA rebels shot and killed an Italian priest as he drove to church in Kitgum. No one else was injured.

12 October   **Ecuador**
In Napo, according to press reports, possible FARC members hijacked an Ecuadorian-owned helicopter and took hostage 10 aviation company employees and oilworkers—five US citizens, two French nationals, one Argentine, one Chilean, and one Ecuadorian. On 16 October the two French citizens escaped. (On 31 January, the US Embassy in Quito confirmed the death of one US hostage.)

Yemen
In Aden, a small dinghy carrying explosives rammed the US destroyer, *USS Cole,* killing 17 sailors and injuring 39 others. Supporters of Usama Bin Ladin are suspected.

13 October   **Bosnia**
In Sarajevo, four German NATO-led Stabilization Force (SFOR) soldiers were injured when they attempted to arrest a Bosnian, according to press accounts. The suspect detonated a handgrenade, killing himself and wounding the soldiers and one civilian.

Indonesia
A powerful bomb exploded in Lombok, damaging the offices of the PT Newmont Nusa Tenggara Mining Company, which is jointly owned by the United States, Japan, and Indonesia, according to press reports. No one claimed responsibility.

Yemen

A small bomb detonated on the compound of the British Embassy in Sanaa, but there were no injuries.

14 October — South Africa

Demonstrators, possibly supported by PAGAD members, vandalized and threw rocks at a McDonald's restaurant in Cape Town, according to press reports. No one was injured, but significant damage was done to the restaurant and customers' vehicles.

19 October — Sri Lanka

In Colombo, a suicide bomber detonated the explosives he was wearing near the town hall, killing four persons and wounding 23 others, including two US citizens, according to press reports. The Liberation Tigers of Tamil Eelam (LTTE) were probably responsible.

14 November — Yemen

In Sanaa, an armed group from the Gahm Tribe kidnapped a Swedish employee of a local power station. On 30 November the hostage was released.

19 November — Namibia

Armed militants in Mahane Village kidnapped seven men and their cattle and moved them to Angola. Three men escaped. UNITA rebels were probably responsible.

Jordan

In Amman, armed militants attempted to assassinate the Israeli Vice Consul, according to press reports. The Movement for the Struggle of the Jordanian Islamic Resistance Movement and Ahmad al-Daqamisah Group both claimed responsibility.

24 November — India

In Akhala, armed militants kidnapped six persons from a bus stop and killed five of them, according to press reports. The fate of the sixth individual was unknown. The Lashkar-e-Tayyiba was probably responsible.

27 November — Chile

In Santiago, a bomb planted in front of the Colombian Embassy exploded, causing some property damage. No one was injured. No one claimed responsibility.

1 December — India

A grenade thrown at a passing security vehicle missed its target and exploded in a crowded street in Pattan, injuring 12 persons, according to press reports. No one claimed responsibility.

India

Press reported armed militants barged into the private residence of a village defense committee member in Udhampur, killing four children and injuring two others. No one claimed responsibility.

India

Militants threw a grenade at a military vehicle in Srinagar, missing their target but injuring three civilians. No one claimed responsibility.

5 December — Burundi

Small-arms fire struck a Sabena airliner as it was landing in Bujumbura, injuring two persons, a Belgian stewardess, and a Tunisian passenger, according to press reports. The airliner was on a routine flight from Brussels. No one claimed responsibility.

Jordan

In Amman, an unidentified assailant shot and wounded an Israeli diplomat as he, his wife, and his bodyguard were leaving a grocery store. The Movement for the Struggle of the Jordanian Islamic Resistance claimed responsibility.

6 December — India

A bomb destroyed a vendor's cart, injuring four persons and damaging roadside shops in Muzaffarabad, according to press reporting. No one claimed responsibility.

7 December — India

Armed militants threw a grenade at a bus stop in Kupwara, injuring 24 persons, including one special police officer, according to press reports. No one claimed responsibility.

India

A bomb exploded near a mosque in Shopian, injuring 31 persons, including three police officers, according to press reports. No one claimed responsibility.

India

A bomb exploded in Gohlan, killing a father and injuring his son, according to press reports. No one claimed responsibility.

9 December — India

A bomb exploded in Neelum Valley, killing three persons, including a young boy, according to press accounts. No one claimed responsibility.

12 December — India

A grenade thrown at an outdoor marketplace in Chadoura injured 12 civilians and four police officers, according to press reports. The Jaish-e-Mohammed was probably responsible.

India

In Qamarwari, a police vehicle activated a remote-controlled bomb, killing five police officers and injuring five civilians. The Jaish-e-Mohammed claimed responsibility.

13 December — Nambia

A landmine placed near a private residence in Shighuru exploded, injuring the owner, according to press reports. UNITA was probably responsible.

25   December   India
A car bomb exploded at the main gate of a military base in Srinagar, killing nine persons—six military personnel and three civilians—and injuring 23 civilians, according to press reports. The Jaish-e-Mohammed and Jamiat-ul-Mujahedin claimed responsibility.

Greece
A bomb placed at a Citibank ATM in Athens exploded, causing major damage to the exterior ATM and to the bank interior, according to press reports. The Anarchists Attack Team claimed responsibility for the attack to show support for the dead prisoners in Turkey.

30   December   Philippines
A bomb exploded in a plaza across the street from the US Embassy in Manila, injuring nine persons, according to press reports. The Moro Islamic Liberation Front was possibly responsible.

31   December   Thailand
Armed militants attacked a grocery store in Suan Phung during New Year celebrations, killing six persons, according to press reports. The Burmese group, God's Army, was probably responsible.

Spain
A vehicle carrying explosives exploded in Seville, but no injuries resulted. The vehicle had been stolen from Toulouse, France. No one claimed responsibility.

2001

3   January   Switzerland
In Zurich, a bomb exploded outside the glass entrance doors to the office of El Al Airlines, causing damage to the doors, according to press reports. The Revolutionary Perspective claimed responsibility in a message faxed to the Associated Press.

Yemen
In Sanaa, the US Ambassador to Yemen and the Yemeni Ambassador to Washington were aboard a Yemeni airliner that was hijacked by a Yemeni national during an internal flight according to press reports. The plane, which had 91 passengers on board, landed safely at Djibouti Airport. No passengers or crew were injured.

5   January   India
In Srinagar, a grenade exploded in the downtown area injuring 27 persons, including four police officers, according to press reports. The grenade was thrown at a police picket but fell short of its target. No one claimed responsibility.

6   January   Greece
In Athens, press reported an incendiary bomb placed under the vehicle of a Turkish commercial attache exploded, resulting in no injuries but causing major damage to the car. A group calling themselves the "Crazy Gas Cannisters" claimed responsibility.

8   January   Algeria
In Annaba, according to press reports, armed militants killed six Russian citizens. The Armed Islamic Group is probably responsible.

9   January   Russia
In Chechnya, according to press accounts, a US citizen working for Medecins Sans Frontieres, was kidnapped. On 4 February the hostage was released unharmed.

17   January   Yemen
In Sanaa, according to press reports, armed militants abducted a German citizen working for the German Company, Preussag Energy. The hostage was released unharmed the next day. No one claimed responsibility.

21   January   India
In Rajpura, Kashmir a grenade thrown at a security patrol missed its target, killing two civilians and a policeman and injuring 20 others, according to press reports. No one claimed responsibility.

India
In Jammu, a bomb exploded near the headquarters of the National Conference Party, injuring six persons in three passenger buses parked nearby and damaging several private vehicles, according to press reports. No one claimed responsibility.

22   January   India
In Kareri, a public bus hit a landmine, killing four civilians and two soldiers and injuring 16 civilians and eight soldiers, according to press reports. No one claimed responsibility.

Indonesia
According to press reports, in Merauke, armed militants kidnapped 17 persons—four Koreans and 13 Indonesians—working on a forest logging project. The kidnappers demanded $1 million dollars in compensation for "environmental damage," a halt to all future logging, and withdrawal of police mobile brigade forces from the district. They also demanded that the Indonesian Government open a dialog with the Free Papua Movement (OPM) regarding the status of Irian Jaya. The Willem Onde Group, a splinter group of the OPM, is probably responsible. On 7 February, the last three hostages were released unharmed. No ransom was paid.

27   January   India
According to press reports, armed militants kidnapped a district president of Shah's Awami National Conference when he was moving out of his private residence without his security forces. No one claimed responsibility.

28 January — **India**
In Srinagar, militants threw a grenade at a police post, missing their target but injuring two civilian passers-by, according to press reports. No one claimed responsibility.

29 January — **Indonesia**
In Lombok, a bomb exploded causing no injuries but damaging the subsidiary office of the US firm Newmont Mining Corporation, according to press reports. No one claimed responsibility.

Nigeria
In southern Nigeria, armed militants stormed oil flow stations causing the loss of 40,000 barrels per day, according to press reports. The Ijaw Youths are probably responsible.

2 February — **Colombia**
In Cesar, according to press reports, an explosion caused major damage to the railroad tracks used to transport coal by the US multinational firm Drummond. According to Drummond officials, the company was being extorted and blackmailed by the Revolutionary Armed Forces of Colombia (FARC) rebels.

Colombia
In Arauca, according to press reports, six bombs exploded along the Cano Limon–Covenas pipeline, derailing a nine-car train and forcing the suspension in the pumping of crude oil. FARC rebels are suspected.

4 February — **India**
Armed militants killed four Sikhs and injured four other persons in Srinagar, according to press reports. No one claimed responsibility.

9 February — **India**
In Rajaori, armed militants set fire to several private residences, killing 15 persons, according to press reports. No one claimed responsibility.

Tanzania
In Kasulu, rebels raided a refugee camp, kidnapping 13 persons and killing one other, according to press reports. The Forces for the Defense of Democracy are probably responsible.

16 February — **Bangladesh**
In Rangamati, armed tribesmen at a roadblock, kidnapped two British citizens and two Danes working for a Danish consulting firm engaged in road work, according to press reports. The driver of the vehicle and one British citizen were later released to deliver a ransom note to the authorities.

17 February — **Turkey**
In Istanbul, press reported a bomb was found at a McDonald's restaurant and safely defused by police. No one claimed responsibility.

18 February — **Angola**
In Cassanguidi, rebels ambushed and burned a vehicle, killing two persons and wounding two others. The National Union for the Total Independence of Angola (UNITA) claimed responsibility.

22 February — **Colombia**
In Bogota, armed rebels abducted a Japanese businessman and his driver. The rebels demanded $8 million ransom for the release of the Japanese businessman but released the driver, according to press reports. The FARC are probably responsible.

5 March — **Algeria**
In Kolea, armed rebels attacked a home, killing two persons. The GIA is probably responsible.

7 March — **India**
In Srinagar, a bomb exploded near a Border Security Force, injuring two police officers and six civilians, and setting on fire several private residences, according to press reports. No one claimed responsibility.

8 March — **Sudan**
In Kiech Kuon, armed rebels attacked a village, abducting four NGO relief workers—two Kenyan and two Sudanese—and killing two persons, according to US Embassy and press reports. The Sudanese Government obtained their release after initiating negotiations. The Sudan Peoples Liberation Army (SPLA) is probably responsible.

9 March — **Angola**
In the enclave province of Cabinda, armed rebels abducted six persons five Portuguese and one Angolan according to press reports. On 23 May, the hostages were released unharmed. The Front for the Liberation of Cabinda Enclave-Renewed (FLEC-Renewed) claimed responsibility.

15 March — **Turkey**
In Istanbul, according to press reports, a plane carrying 162 passengers was hijacked to Saudi Arabia where authorities stormed the plane, killing three Russian passengers and injuring one Turkish passenger. No one claimed responsibility.

18 March — **Burundi**
In Ruyigi, according to press reports, armed rebels attacked a village, burning 20 houses, looting shops, and stealing cows. The Force for the Defense of Democracy is probably responsible.

19 March — **Colombia**
In Prado, according to press reports, armed rebels abducted a German hotel businessman. No one claimed responsibility.

20 March — **Namibia**
In Mayenzere, according to press reports, armed rebels attacked a home, abducting two young persons and looting property. On 20 March, the hostages escaped their captors, according to press reports. UNITA is probably responsible.

26 March   Turkey
In Ankara, according to press reports, an Iranian national poured oil on the main gate to the Iranian Embassy, then set it on fire, causing an undetermined amount of damage. No one claimed responsibility.

27 March   Somalia
In Mogadishu, militiamen attacked and overran the Medecins Sans Frontieres facility, killing 11 persons, wounding 40 others, and kidnapping nine international aid workers and two UNICEF officials. By 4 April, the foreign national aid workers—including the UNICEF officials—had been released, according to US Embassy and press reports. Militiamen loyal to warlord, Musa Sude Yalahow are responsible.

28 March   Israel
In Kefar Sava, at a bus stop, a suicide bomber detonated explosives he was wearing, killing two persons and injuring four others, according to press reports. A US citizen was one of the four injured. The Izz-al-Din-al-Qassam Battalions, the military wing of HAMAS, claimed responsibility.

29 March   Philippines
According to press reporting, armed militants kidnapped a Chinese-Philippine attorney and her daughter. On 20 June, in Tungawan, Philippines, after a small payment for room and board, the hostages were released unharmed. The Moro Islamic Liberation Front claimed responsibility.

3 April   Burundi
In Ruyigi, rebels ambushed a United Nations (UN) convoy, wounding four persons. The convoy consisted of two World Food Program (WFO) vehicles, according to radio reports. The Force for the Defense of Democracy is probably responsible.

6 April   Greece
In Kholargos, according to press reports, armed militants set two foreign bank branches on fire. The Anarchic Attack Groups claimed responsibility.

13 April   India
In Baramula, according to press reports, armed militants threw a grenade towards a moving security vehicle. The grenade missed its target and exploded in a crowded bazaar, injuring 16 persons. No one claimed responsibility.

India
In Kashmir, armed militants killed a National Conference block president as he was returning home from morning prayers, according to press reporting. No one claimed responsibility.

15 April   Burundi
In Gitega, armed rebels launched an attack, killing 10 persons. The rebels retreated into Tanzania, according to press reports. No one claimed responsibility.

16 April   Burundi
In Butaganzwa, armed gangs attacked the community, setting fire to the health center and the primary school headmaster. The armed gangs returned to Tanzania, according to press reports. No one claimed responsibility.

17 April   Greece
In Athens, according to press reports, two diplomatic vehicles were set on fire—one belonging to the Israeli Embassy and the other to the Thai Embassy. No one claimed responsibility.

19 April   Burundi
In Ruyigi, according to press reports, rebels ambushed a college vehicle, killing 18 persons. The Force for the Defense of Democracy is probably responsible.

22 April   Democratic Republic of the Congo
In Nord-Kivu Province, an armed group abducted a priest of the Italian-based Missionary Service, according to press reports. No one claimed responsibility.

India
In Sopur, a bomb placed in a vegetable cart parked in a crowded marketplace exploded, killing one policeman, injuring nine civilians, and damaging a police station, and nearby houses, according to press reports. No one claimed responsibility.

Turkey
In Istanbul, armed Chechen gunmen held 120 persons hostage, including four Russians, 16 Swiss, and several other nationals. On 23 April, after negotiating with officials, the gunmen released all hostages unharmed, according to press reports.

23 April   Colombia
In Bogota, the Colombian National Liberation Army (ELN) released a Danish citizen from captivity whom the militants had held since 17 March. A friend of the Danish citizen who was captured at the same time also was released recently, according to press reports.

India
In Kishtwar, a bomb exploded at a bus stop, injuring five persons, according to press reports. No one claimed responsibility.

India
In Srinagar, a grenade was thrown at the Hurriyat Conference center, injuring five persons, according to press reports. Kashmiri separatist members were meeting to discuss holding peace talks with India. No one claimed responsibility.

Namibia
In the village of Karangana, armed rebels abducted eight persons and took them to Angola, according to press reports. UNITA is probably responsible.

24 April   **Burundi**
In Gisagara, armed groups killed six persons, kidnapped two others, and stole 100 cows, according to press reports. No one claimed responsibility.

26 April   **Ethiopia**
In Debre Zeyit, a group of five Ethiopian Air Academy students hijacked a military aircraft carrying 50 passengers, according to press reports.

Democratic Republic of the Congo
In the Province of Ituri, tribesmen abducted International Committee of the Red Cross (ICRC) workers, killing six persons—one Columbian, one Swiss, and four Congolese, according to press reports. No one claimed responsibility.

27 April   **India**
In Srinagar, a grenade thrown at the main telegraph office injured five police officers, according to press reports. No one claimed responsibility.

India
In Chadoora, a grenade exploded at a crowded bus terminal, killing two persons and injuring 29 others, according to press reports. No one claimed responsibility.

30 April   **India**
In Tuibana, armed militants killed two persons in their residence, according to press reports. No one claimed responsibility.

India
In Gundpora, armed militants killed one person in his residence, according to press reports. No one claimed responsibility.

India
In Lobal, two persons abducted from their homes were found decapitated, according to press reports. No one claimed responsibility.

India
In Lalpor, a grenade thrown at a police installation missed its mark and exploded, killing one person, according to press reports. No one claimed responsibility.

2 May   **Saudi Arabia**
In Dhahran, a letter bomb that was delivered to a US physician at the Saad Medical Center exploded, severely injuring the doctor, according to US Embassy reports. No one claimed responsibility.

5 May   **Afghanistan**
In Herat, a bomb placed near a mosque exploded, killing 12 persons—one Iranian cleric and 11 civilians—injuring 28 others, and damaging the Iranian Consulate and 12 cars parked nearby, according to press reports. No one claimed responsibility.

6 May   **Angola**
In Caxito, armed rebels attacked the town, killing 100 persons and kidnapping 120 others, according to press and media reports. UNITA is responsible.

7 May   **Pakistan**
In Sanni, armed militants attacked a vehicle convoy on an oil exploration mission, killing one person and injuring three others, including a Chinese engineer working for the Chinese oil and gas exploration company, BGP. No one claimed responsibility.

9 May   **India**
In Kashmir, a bomb exploded, killing six persons. In an exchange of gunfire between the militants and the police following the explosion, four more persons were killed, according to press reports. No one claimed responsibility.

West Bank
In the Israeli settlement of Teqoa, two teens who were out hiking, US citizen Yaakov Nathan Mandell and an Israeli, were stoned to death. Their bodies were found in a nearby cave, according to media reports. A group calling itself "Palestinian Hizballah" claimed responsibility.

10 May   **Gaza Strip**
In Kissufim Crossing, a bomb exploded next to a border fence being repaired by three workmen, killing two Romanian workers hired by the Israeli Defense Force (IDF) and wounding an Israeli citizen, according to US Embassy and media reports. No one claimed responsibility.

11 May   **Burundi**
In Kibago, rebels stopped a Dutch NGO's mobile-clinic vehicle, kidnapping six persons, according to press reports. The Force for the Defense of Democracy is probably responsible.

15 May   **Democratic Republic of the Congo**
In eastern Democratic Republic of the Congo, tribal warriors kidnapped 20 Thailand Timber Company employees—including 12 Thai, one Kenyan, and one Swedish national, according to media reports. Mai Mai tribal warriors claimed responsibility.

16 May   **India**
In Kashmir, a grenade thrown at the private residence of the Forest Minister fell short of its target, landing outside the main gate, resulting in no injuries or damage, according to press reports. No one claimed responsibility.

21 May   **Namibia**
In the village of Mwitjiku, armed militants attacked the community, killing one person and wounding one other, according to press reports. UNITA is probably responsible.

26 May   **Philippines**
In Palawan, the Abu Sayaaf Group (ASG) kidnapped 20 persons including three US citizens and 17 Filipinos from a beach resort and took them to Basilan Island in Sulu

Archipelago, according to press reports. On 31 May, three captives were released unharmed. On 2 June, the kidnappers, with their hostages in tow, raided a hospital and church in Lamitan, Basilan, temporarily taking 200 persons hostage. They managed to escape from an ensuing gun battle with Philippine military forces and added five hospital employees to their group of hostages. On 4 June, the ASG released two female hostages after ransom was paid, according to press reports. Three more Philippine hostages were released on 16 June. On 26 June, two more Philippine civilians were taken hostage. In June, the ASG beheaded one of the US hostages. At year's end, two of the 20 original hostages (both US citizens) and one Filipino from the Lamitan hospital remained captive.

Yemen

In Sanaa, armed tribesmen kidnapped a German teacher and demanded the release of six members of their tribe serving prison sentences. On 13 June, the teacher was released unharmed, according to press reports. The Al Ali bin Falah tribe is responsible.

29 May   West Bank
In the Israeli settlement of Newe Daniyyel, assailants fired on a passing vehicle, killing two persons US citizen Sara Blaustein and one Israeli and wounding four others including two US citizens, according to press reports. The al-Aqsa Martyrs Brigade claimed responsibility.

1 June   Israel
In Tel Aviv, a suicide bomber detonated a bomb he was wearing in front of a busy club, killing 18 persons including a Ukrainian national and wounding 119 others, according to press reports. HAMAS was the likely perpetrator.

2 June   Angola
In Talamanjaba, rebels ambushed a truck and car, killing seven persons including a Portuguese citizen, and wounding three others, according to press reports. UNITA is probably responsible.

India

In Kupwara, a bomb exploded at a crowded bus stop, killing two persons and injuring 32 others, according to press reports. No one claimed responsibility.

8 June   Angola
In Luena, armed militants launched a surface-to-air missile at a UN World Food Program chartered Boeing 727, severely damaging one engine causing the pilot to make a forced landing at the airport, according to press reports. UNITA claimed responsibility.

India

In Tsrar Sharif, a bomb placed near a mosque exploded, killing four persons and injuring 54 others, according to media reports. No one claimed responsibility.

Colombia

In Florida, a Spaniard was kidnapped after leaving the hospital where she worked, according to press reports. On 7 July, the Spaniard was released and left on the mountains in southwestern Colombia. Motives for the kidnapping were unclear, no ransom was collected, and no one claimed responsibility. Authorities found that her captives, a group of guerrillas from the 19 April Movement (M-19), also referred to as the Jaime Bateman Canyon Movement, were responsible.

12 June   West Bank
In the Israeli settlement of Ma'ale Adummim (east of Jerusalem), militants fired upon a passing car, killing the driver, a Greek monk, according to press reports. No one claimed responsibility.

14 June   Nigeria
In Abereke, militant youths kidnapped two Nigerian oil employees working for the US Oil Group Chevron who were inspecting an oil spillage, according to press reports. No one claimed responsibility.

16 June   Tajikistan
In Tovildara region, assailants kidnapped 15 employees of a German humanitarian group—four Germans, nine Tajikistanis, a Russian, and a US citizen. The kidnappers immediately released four hostages—two Germans, the Russian, and a Tajikistani—and demanded the release of four members of their group who were arrested and charged with the murder of the Deputy Interior Minister in April. On the same day in Tolvildara region, four officers from the Tajik Security Ministry who came to talk to the kidnappers also were taken hostage. On 17 June all remaining hostages were released unharmed. No one claimed responsibility, but Tajikistani authorities found that a former United Tajik Opposition fighter was responsible for the kidnapping, according to press reporting.

19 June   Indonesia
In Nabire, two Belgian filmmakers were kidnapped, according to press and US Embassy reporting. On 22 August, the two filmmakers were released unharmed. Dani tribesmen claimed responsibility.

20 June   Philippines
In North Cotabato, the "Pentagon Gang" abducted a Chinese engineer working for a Japanese-funded irrigation project, according to press reports. On 12 August, three Chinese nationals and a local Philippine businessman were kidnapped when they tried to deliver the ransom payment for the engineer. On 19 August, the Philippine military attempted a rescue, which left two Chinese dead, one injured but rescued. On 19 October, the one remaining Chinese hostage was released, reportedly after a ransom was paid.

22 June   Burundi
In Ruvumu, rebels ambushed a van, killing one person and kidnapping three others. The vehicle is owned by the British NGO Children Aid Direct. In a search effort later, authorities

found the three persons who were kidnapped, according to press reports. No one claimed responsibility.

15   July   Somalia
In Mogadishu, militiamen attacked a WFP convoy, killing six persons and wounding several others, according to press reports. Militiamen loyal to Usman (Hasan Ali) Ato are probably responsible.

18   July   Colombia
In Silvia, FARC guerrillas claimed responsibility for kidnapping three German experts who were assisting rural peasant communities with several agricultural projects, according to press reports.

21   July   India
In Sheshang, a bomb exploded, killing six persons and two policemen and wounding 15 civilians, according to press reports. No one claimed responsibility.

22   July   India
In Chirji, armed militants killed 15 persons, according to press reports. No one claimed responsibility.

India
In Chatroo, armed militants kidnapped five persons, according to press reports. No one claimed responsibility.

24   July   Sri Lanka
In Colombo, armed militants attacked the international and military airports, killing six persons—four military and two civilians—and injuring nine others. Also destroyed were five commercial and eight military aircraft, several ammunition dumps, and oil storage depots, according to press reports. The Liberation Tigers of Tamil Eelam claimed responsibility.

27   July   Yemen
In Sanaa, armed men stopped a German diplomat's car, kidnapping and taking the Embassy employee to the provincial capital of Dhamar, according to US Embassy reports. Tribal militants in the Seruwa region are probably responsible.

4   August   India
In Atholi, armed militants killed 17 persons at a trading post, according to press reports. No one claimed responsibility.

9   August   Israel
In Jerusalem, a suicide bomber walked into a busy downtown restaurant and detonated a 10-pound bomb he was wearing, killing 15 persons including US citizens Judith Greenbaum and Malka Roth and five Dutch and wounding 130 others including four US citizens, according to press reports. HAMAS claimed responsibility.

10   August   India
In Narbal, a bomb exploded, killing one person and injuring five others, according to press reports. No one claimed responsibility.

India
In Kashmir, a bomb exploded at a Muslim shrine, killing six persons and injuring 24 others, according to press reports. No one claimed responsibility.

India
In Srinagar, a bomb exploded, killing one person and injuring five others, according to press reports. No one claimed responsibility.

13   August   India
In Damhalhanjipora, armed militants using firearms and rifle grenades fired on the Kashmir Tourist Minister's residence, killing a policeman and three mercenaries, according to press reports. No one claimed responsibility.

14   August   India
In Riasi, armed militants killed three persons, then placed grenades under the bodies that exploded when they were examined, killing two more persons, according to press reports. No one claimed responsibility.

18   August   Spain
In Salou, a car bomb exploded at a hotel, injuring 13 persons five Spanish, two Russian, two Irish, two French, one Portuguese, and one Briton—according to press reports. No one claimed responsibility, but authorities suspect the Basque Fatherland and Liberty.

21   August   Philippines
In Cotabato, armed militants killed an Irish parish priest in a botched kidnapping attempt, according to press reports. No one claimed responsibility, but police named the son of a former Moro National Liberation Front commander as a suspect.

23   August   Nigeria
In Lagos, militant youths overran an oilrig operated by Trans-Ocean SEDCO/Trident, a subcontractor to Shell, kidnapping 19 foreign nationals and 80 nationals, according to press reports. Five days later the hostages were released unharmed. No one claimed responsibility.

1   September   Uganda
In Nimule, armed militants ambushed a vehicle belonging to the Catholic Relief Services, killing five persons and wounding two others, according to press reports. The Lord's Resistance Army is probably responsible.

4   September   India
In Jamiapura, a bomb exploded near a school, killing three persons and injuring three others, according to press reports. No one claimed responsibility.

8   September   India
In Pahalgam, a schoolbus hit a landmine that exploded, killing one person and injuring 20 others, according to press reports. No one claimed responsibility.

11 September   United States—New York
Five terrorists hijacked American Airlines Flight 11, which departed Boston for Los Angeles at 7:45 a.m. An hour later it was deliberately piloted into the North Tower of the World Trade Center in New York City.

Five terrorists hijacked United Airlines Flight 175, which departed Boston for Los Angeles at 7:58 a.m. At 9:05 the plane crashed into the South Tower of the World Trade Center. Both towers collapsed shortly thereafter, killing approximately 3000 persons, including hundreds of firefighters and rescue personnel who were helping to evacuate the buildings. Usama Bin Ladin and his organization al-Qaida are responsible.

United States—Pennsylvania
Near Shanksville, terrorists using knives and boxcutters hijacked a United Airlines plane Flight 93, a Boeing-757 commercial airliner carrying 44 passengers and crew en route from Newark International Airport to San Francisco International Airport. The hijackers took over the plane's controls and were heading the aircraft in the direction of Washington, D.C. In attempting to retake control of the airplane, the passengers crashed it into the Pennsylvania countryside, according to press reports. Usama Bin Ladin and his organization al-Qaida are responsible.

United States—Virginia
Near Washington D.C., terrorists using knives and box cutters hijacked an American Airlines Flight 77, a Boeing 757 commercial airliner carrying 64 persons on board en route from Dulles International Airport to Los Angeles International Airport. The terrorists took over the controls and flew the plane into the west side of the Pentagon, destroying the left side of the building. Casualties included 64 passengers and crew and 125 military and civilian personnel killed with 80 injured in the partially collapsed side of the Pentagon, according to press reports. Usama Bin Ladin and his organization al-Qaida are responsible.

16 September   Philippines
In Tawitawi, armed militants kidnapped from his residence a Sierra Leonean professor who later escaped his captors, according to press reports. No one claimed responsibility.

24 September   Colombia
In Bogota, leftist rebels kidnapped a Slovak missionary, a Czech priest, and another seven persons from a bus heading to the capital, according to press reports. The Slovak missionary was released three days later. No one claimed responsibility, but authorities suspect the ELN.

27 September   Chile
In Santiago, bomb-squad experts, safely detonated a letter bomb delivered to the US Embassy, according to US Department of State reporting. No one claimed responsibility.

28 September   India
In Doda, a bomb exploded at a bus stop, injuring five persons, according to press reports. No one claimed responsibility.

Turkey
In Istanbul, a bomb exploded at a McDonald's restaurant, injuring three persons and causing property damage, according to press reports. No one claimed responsibility.

1 October   India
In Kashmir, a car bomb exploded at the State Legislative Assembly Building, killing 15 persons and injuring 40 others, according to press reports. The Jaish-e-Mohammad may be responsible.

6 October   Saudi Arabia
In Al Khubar, a suicide bomber exploded a device in a busy shopping area, killing one person—US citizen Michael Jerrald Martin, Jr.—and injuring five others—two US citizens, one Briton and two Filipinos—according to press reports. No one claimed responsibility.

11 October   Saudi Arabia
In Riyadh, unidentified assailants threw a Molotov cocktail at a car carrying two Germans, but no injuries resulted, according to press reports. No one claimed responsibility.

16 October   Spain
In Catalan, a letter bomb sent to the Catalan Prison Employees' Union Chatac failed to explode, according to press reports. The Italian Anarchist Black Cross claimed responsibility.

4 November   Israel
In east Jerusalem near French Hill, US citizen Shoshana Ben Yashai was killed in a shooting attack on a bus, and 35 others were injured, according to press reports. The assailant was also killed in the attack, which was claimed by the Palestine Islamic Jihad.

11 November   Colombia
In Antioquia, a technician for the Italian engineering company Ansaldo was kidnapped by guerrillas just hours before they released another Italian technician who had been held captive since 15 September, according to press reports. No one claimed responsibility, but authorities suspect the ELN.

1 December   Israel
On 1 December, two suicide bombers detonated explosives on a busy downtown pedestrian mall, killing at least 10 persons and wounding 120 others. A simultaneous car bomb may have targeted first responders. HAMAS claimed responsibility.

13 December   India
In New Delhi, an armed group attacked India's Parliament while it was in full session, killing 13 terrorists and security

personnel. India has blamed Lash-kar-e-Tayyiba and Jaish-e-Mohammed for the attack.

21 December   **Philippines**
In Manila, according to press reports, authorities safely defused a bomb placed outside the Allied Bank building housing the Canadian Embassy and next door to the British Embassy. The bomb weighed between 50–60 pounds, was composed of ammonium nitrate soaked in gasoline, and contained two electric blasting caps. No one claimed responsibility.

2002

12 January   **Venezuela**
In El Amparo, armed militants kidnapped two persons, an Italian and Venezuelan citizen. On 17 May, a rebel defecting from the Revolutionary Armed Forces of Colombia (FARC) released the two hostages.

15 January   **West Bank**
In Bayt Sahur, militants attacked a vehicle carrying two passengers, killing one person, who was a US-Israeli citizen, and wounding the other. The Al-Aqsa Martyrs Battalion claimed responsibility.

22 January   **India**
In Kolkata (Calcutta), armed militants attacked the US Consulate, killing five Indian security forces and injuring 13 others. The Harakat ul-Jihad-I-Islami and the Asif Raza Commandoes claimed responsibility.

India
In Jammu, Kashmir, a bomb exploded in a crowded retail district, killing one person and injuring nine others. No one claimed responsibility.

23 January   **Pakistan**
In Karachi, armed militants kidnapped and killed a US journalist working for the *Wall Street Journal* newspaper. No one claimed responsibility.

24 January   **Algeria**
In Larbaa-Tablat Road, militants set up an illegal roadblock, killing three persons, including one Syrian. No one claimed responsibility.

31 January   **Philippines**
Two hikers on the slopes of the Pinatubo volcano were attacked by militants. One of the hikers, a US citizen, was killed.

9 February   **France**
In Saint-Jean-De-Luz, unidentified persons threw gasoline bombs at a police headquarters, causing material damage to police barracks and three parked vehicles but resulting in no injuries. No one claimed responsibility, but authorities suspect radical groups associated with the Basque Fatherland and Liberty.

16 February   **West Bank**
In Karnei Shomron, a suicide bomber attacked a pizzeria in an outdoor food court, killing four persons, two of whom were US citizens and wounding 27 others including two US citizens. The Popular Front for the Liberation of Palestine (PFLP) claimed responsibility.

28 February   **Colombia**
In Antioquia, an Italian tourist was kidnapped at a checkpoint armed rebels had illegally set up. On 17 March in San Francisco, the rebels released the Italian tourist.

Jordan
In Amman, a bomb placed in a car was detonated by a timing device, killing an Egyptian and an Iraqi laborer who worked in a nearby food shop. The car belonged to the wife of the head of the Jordanian Anti-Terrorism Unit and was parked near their home. No one claimed responsibility.

7 March   **West Bank**
In Ariel, a suicide bomber entered a large supermarket collocated with a hotel and detonated the explosive device he was wearing, wounding 10 persons including a US citizen, according to media and US Embassy reporting. The PFLP claimed responsibility.

9 March   **Israel**
In Jerusalem, a suicide bomber entered a restaurant/cafe detonating the explosive device he was wearing, killing 11 persons and wounding 52 others including a US citizen, according to media and US Embassy reporting. The Al-Aqsa Martyrs Brigade claimed responsibility.

14 March   **Colombia**
In Cali, two US citizens were shot and killed by motorcycle-riding gunmen. The two US citizens were brothers who arrived in town the day before to negotiate the release of their father who had been taken captive by the FARC. No one claimed responsibility.

17 March   **Pakistan**
In Islamabad, during a Protestant service, several grenades were thrown inside a church used by diplomatic and local personnel, killing five persons—including two US citizens and 46 others, according to press reports. The Lashkar-e-Tayyiba probably is responsible.

18 March   **Georgia**
In Abkhazia, Georgian guerrillas kidnapped four Russian peacekeepers to negotiate an exchange for two Georgian gunmen who were being held by Russian authorities. On 21 March, the four Russian peacekeepers and their weapons were released in exchange for the two Georgian gunmen. Georgian guerrillas claimed responsibility.

20 March   **Peru**
In Lima, a vehicle bomb exploded at a shopping center some 50 meters from the US Embassy, killing nine persons, injuring 32 others, and causing major damage. Authorities suspect

the Maoist Shining Path rebels and/or the Tupac Amaru Revolutionary Movement. The dead included two police officers and a teenager but no US citizens. The attack occurred three days before the US President's planned visit to Peru.

21   March   Israel
In Jerusalem, a suicide bomber detonated the explosive device he was wearing, killing three persons and wounding 86 others, including two US citizens, according to US Consulate and media reporting. The Palestinian Islamic Jihad claimed responsibility.

22   March   India
In Shopiyan, Kashmir, militants threw several grenades into a busy market at midmorning, injuring 35 persons. No one claimed responsibility.

India
In Anantnag, Kashmir, militants tossed several grenades at a busy bus stand, injuring 17 persons. No one claimed responsibility.

India
In Rajouri, Kashmir, a bomb exploded in a sweet shop, injuring five persons. No one claimed responsibility.

Uganda
In Kalosaric, gunmen stopped a vehicle traveling on the Moroto-Kotido Road, killing three persons—an Irish Catholic priest, his driver, and his cook. Karamojong gunmen are probably responsible.

23   March   India
In Kadal, Kashmir, a grenade hurled at a police installation missed its target and landed in a group of civilians, killing two persons and injuring 20 others, including nine policemen. No one claimed responsibility.

26   March   Senegal
In Kafountine, Casamance Province, rebels attacked the coastal resort, killing five persons and wounding four others including a French citizen. The Casamance Movement of Democratic Forces is probably responsible.

West Bank
In Hebron, gunmen stopped and fired on a vehicle owned and operated by the Temporary Presence in Hebron (TIPH), killing two persons—a Turkish Army officer and a Swiss office worker—and wounding a Turkish Army officer, according to media and government reports. No one claimed responsibility. The Palestinian Authorities and the Israeli Army accuse each other of the incident.

27   March   Israel
In Netanya, a suicide bomber entered the crowded restaurant of a hotel and detonated the explosive device he was wearing, killing 22 persons including one US citizen and wounding 140 others. The Islamic Resistance Movement (HAMAS) claimed responsibility.

30   March   India
In Jammu, Kashmir, a bomb exploded at a Hindu temple, killing 10 persons, according to press reports. The Islamic Front has claimed responsibility.

31   March   West Bank
In Efrat, a suicide bomber standing next to an ambulance station detonated the explosive device he was wearing, injuring four persons including one US citizen, according to press and US Consulate reporting. The Al-Aqsa Martyrs Brigades claimed responsibility.

1   April   Nigeria
In Niger Delta, 10 oil workers contracted to the Royal Shell Oil Group were kidnapped by militant youths, according to press reports. Six of the hostages were foreign nationals, including one US citizen, one Filipino, and four Ghanaians.

10   April   India
In Gando, Kashmir, armed militants killed five persons and injured four others in their residence. No one claimed responsibility.

11   April   Tunisia
In Djerba, a suicide bomber crashed and detonated a propane gas truck into the fence of a historic synagogue, killing 16 persons including 11 German citizens, one French citizen, and three Tunisians and injuring 26 German citizens. The Islamic Army for the Liberation of the Holy Sites claimed responsibility.

12   April   Israel
In Jerusalem, a suicide bomber detonated the explosive vest she was wearing, killing six persons, including two Chinese citizens, and wounding 90 others. The Al-Aqsa Martyrs Brigade claimed responsibility.

14   April   India
In Pulwama, Kashmir, a grenade fired at a police vehicle missed its target, landing in a crowded bus stop, killing one person and injuring 13 others. No one claimed responsibility.

16   April   India
In Balhama-Rafiabad, armed militants killed five persons and injured two others. The Ikhwan are probably responsible.

26   April   India
In Gharat, Kashmir, a bomb planted under a bus was detonated by remote control, killing one person and injuring 21 others—nine security personnel and 12 civilians. No one claimed responsibility.

28   April   Colombia
In Bogota, according to US Embassy reporting, a car packed with 88 pounds of explosives was discovered adjacent to the World Business Port commercial building that houses the US Agency for International Development (USAID) and other international organizations. A policeman identified the vehicle

as suspicious and called the bomb squad who disarmed the device. No one claimed responsibility.

4 May   Istanbul

In Istanbul, an armed gunman entered a large tourist hotel and took several Turkish nationals and one Bulgarian hostage, according to press and US Embassy reporting. About an hour later, all the hostages were released unharmed, and the gunman surrendered. No group claimed responsibility.

7 May   Colombia

In Quebradas, a section of the Cano Limon-Covenas pipeline was bombed, killing two persons, wounding four others, and causing millions of dollars in property damage. The FARC or National Liberation Army (ELN) is probably responsible.

8 May   Pakistan

In Karachi, a vehicle parked next to a Navy shuttle bus exploded, killing 10 French nationals and two Pakistanis and wounding 19 others—11 French nationals and eight Pakistanis—shattering windows in nearby buildings and leaving a large crater in the road, according to press reports. Al-Qaida is probably responsible.

9 May   Lebanon

In Tripoli, a bomb placed beside a US fast food restaurant—Kentucky Fried Chicken (KFC)—detonated, wounding an employee, according to press reports. No one claimed responsibility.

Russia

In Kapiisk, Dagestan, militants detonated a remote-controlled bomb in the bushes as the May Day Parade was passing by on Main Street, killing 42 persons, including 14 soldiers, and wounding 150 others, including 50 soldiers, according to press reports. Islamist militants linked to al-Qaida are probably responsible.

Thailand

In Tachilek, a bomb exploded at a hotel, killing one Burmese national and injuring three others. No one claimed responsibility.

10 May   United Kingdom

In London, a timer-detonated bomb exploded at the Armenian Embassy. No casualties were reported, and no one claimed responsibility.

14 May   India

In Kaluchak, Jammu, militants fired on a passenger bus, killing seven persons, then entered a military housing complex killing three soldiers, four soldiers' wives, and three children. The Al-Mansooran and Jamiat ul-Mujahedin claimed responsibility.

17 May   India

In Srinagar, Kashmir, a bomb exploded outside the high-security civil secretariat area, injuring six persons. No one claimed responsibility.

In Jammu, Kashmir, a bomb exploded at a fire services headquarters, killing two persons and injuring 16 others. No one claimed responsibility.

21 May   Colombia

In Srinagar, armed gunmen killed a senior Hurriyat conference leader, according to press reports. No one claimed responsibility.

30 May   India

In Kashmir, armed militants shot and injured a subeditor of a local English language newspaper, *Kashmir Images*. No one claimed responsibility.

1 June   India

In Kulgam, Kashmir, a grenade thrown into a crowd killed one person and injured seven others. No one claimed responsibility.

India

In Srinagar, armed militants threw a grenade into a paramilitary foot patrol, killing one person and injuring 13 others. No one claimed responsibility.

India

In Anantnag, armed militants threw a grenade into a police station, injuring 18 persons. No one claimed responsibility.

7 June   India

In Pindi, armed militants killed one person, injured three others, and damaged several houses. No one claimed responsibility.

India

Philippine military units on a rescue mission engaged terrorists from the ASG in a firefight that took the life of US citizen Martin Burnham, who had been held hostage along with his wife, for more than a year. She was wounded and freed.

9 June   India

In Rajouri, Kashmir, armed militants wounded six persons including three security personnel and damaged a television tower building. No one claimed responsibility.

14 June   Pakistan

In Karachi, a vehicle bomb exploded on the main road near the US Consulate and Marriott Hotel, killing 11 persons, injuring 51 others, including a US and a Japanese citizen, and damaging nearby buildings. Al Qaida or Al-Qa'nun is possibly responsible.

19 June   Israel

In Jerusalem, a suicide bomber jumped out of a car, ran into the concrete shelter at a bus stop, and detonated the explosive device he was wearing, killing six persons and wounding

43 others, including two US citizens. The Al-Aqsa Martyrs Brigades claimed responsibility.

20 June   Pakistan
In Neelum Valley, armed militants fired on a passenger bus sending it over a cliff, killing the driver and nine passengers and injuring 12 others. No one claimed responsibility.

21 June   Spain
In Fuengirola, a vehicle bomb exploded in a parking lot adjacent to a beach hotel/apartment building injuring six persons, including four Britons, one Moroccan, and one Spaniard. The Basque Fatherland and Liberty is probably responsible.

24 June   India
In Kupwara, Kashmir, a bomb exploded at the State Law and Parliamentary Minister's residence, injuring five police officers guarding the home. No one claimed responsibility.

30 June   India
In Nishat, Kashmir, armed militants killed a National Conference leader. No one claimed responsibility.

5 July   Algeria
In Larbaa, rebels detonated a homemade bomb in the downtown area, killing 35 persons, including two Nigerian citizens, and wounding 80 others. The Armed Islamic Group is possibly responsible.

8 July   India
In Indh, Kashmir, a bomb exploded near a water tank, killing three persons. No one claimed responsibility.

13 July   India
In Jammu, armed militants attacked a village, killing 27 persons. The Lashkar-e-Tayyiba is probably responsible.

Pakistan
In Mansehra, a grenade thrown into a group of European tourists visiting at an archeological site exploded, injuring 12 persons—seven Germans, one Austrian, one Slovak, and three Pakistanis. No one claimed responsibility.

17 July   India
In Anantnag, Kashmir, a bomb exploded in a government building, killing three persons and injuring nine others. No one claimed responsibility.

Israel
In Tel Aviv, two suicide bombers carried out an attack simultaneously near the old bus station, killing five persons, including one Romanian and two Chinese, and wounding 38 others, including one Romanian. The Islamic Jihad claimed responsibility.

22 July   India
In Sumber, Kashmir, armed militants killed three persons, all members of the Village Defense Committee. No one claimed responsibility.

24 July   India
In Rajouri, Kashmir, a grenade exploded in a crowded marketplace, killing one person and injuring 27 others. No one claimed responsibility.

25 July   India
In Batmaloo, Kashmir, militants threw a grenade into a crowded marketplace, injuring 15 persons. No one claimed responsibility.

31 July   West Bank
In Jerusalem, a bomb hidden in a bag that was placed on a table in the Frank Sinatra International Student Center, Hebrew University, detonated, killing nine persons including five US citizens and four Israeli citizens and wounding approximately 87 others including four US citizens, two Japanese citizens, and three South Korean citizens, according to media reports. The Islamic Resistance Movement (HAMAS) claimed responsibility.

4 August   Israel
In Safed, a suicide bomber boarded a bus and detonated the explosive device he was wearing, killing nine persons, including two Philippine citizens, and injuring 50 others, including an unspecified number of military personnel returning from leave. HAMAS claimed responsibility.

5 August   India
In Malik, Kashmir, a grenade was thrown into a crowded marketplace injuring 10 persons. No one claimed responsibility.

Pakistan
In Murree, gunmen attacked a Christian School attended by 146 children of missionaries from around the world, killing six persons—two security guards, a cook, a carpenter, a receptionist, and a private citizen—and injuring a Filipino citizen visiting her son. A group called al-Intigami al-Pakistani claimed responsibility.

6 August   Colombia
In Cuanata, a bomb exploded on a segment of the Canadian-owned Ocensa oil pipeline, causing oil spillage and environmental damage. The explosion forced the suspension of crude oil transport to the Port of Covenas. The FARC is responsible.

India
In Pahalgam, Kashmir, armed militants threw several grenades and then fired into a group of Hindu pilgrims, killing nine persons and injuring 32 others. The Lashkar-e-Tayyiba claimed responsibility.

13 August   **India**
In Anantnag, Kashmir, a bomb exploded at a bus stop, killing one person and injuring 21 others. No one claimed responsibility.

20 August   **Germany**
In Berlin, militants occupied the Iraqi Embassy, taking hostage six Iraqi nationals and injuring two persons. German police ended the five-hour siege and arrested the five militants. The Democratic Iraqi Opposition is responsible.

25 August   **Afghanistan**
In Kabul, a bomb exploded outside the United Nations main guesthouse, injuring two persons. There were 50 persons living at the guesthouse. No one claimed responsibility.

28 August   **Ecuador**
In Guayaquil, a pamphlet bomb exploded at a McDonald's restaurant, injuring three persons and causing major property damage. The Revolutionary Armed Forces of Ecuador is responsible.

31 August   **India**
In Mahore, armed militants entered the private residence of a Revenue Department official who had been deployed on election duty, killing three persons. No one claimed responsibility.

3 September   **India**
In Langet, Kashmir, armed militants attacked a political rally, killing three persons and injuring four others. No one claimed responsibility.

In Kishtwar, Kashmir, a bomb exploded near the downtown area, injuring 19 persons. The Hizb ul-Mujahedin is possibly responsible.

6 September   **Macedonia**
In Skopje, a bomb exploded in a restaurant, injuring two persons including one Turkish citizen. No one claimed responsibility.

8 September   **India**
In Dodasanpal, Kashmir, armed militants killed five persons and injured one other. No one claimed responsibility.

11 September   **India**
In Dhamhal Hanjipora, Kashmir, militants hurled a grenade at the private residence of the Minister of Tourism, injuring four persons inside. No one claimed responsibility.

In Tikipora, Kashmir, armed militants killed the Law Minister and six security guards escorting him while he was out campaigning. Three different groups claimed responsibility: Lashkar-e-Tayyiba, Jamiat ul-Mujahedin, and Hizb ul-Mujahedin.

15 September   **India**
In Dhamhal Hanjipora, Kashmir, armed militants fired on then threw an improvised explosive device at the motorcade carrying the Minister of Tourism, killing a police officer and injuring two others. The Minister of Tourism escaped unharmed. No one claimed responsibility.

17 September   **India**
In Srinagar, Kashmir, armed militants shot and injured the leading editor of the *Urdu Daily Srinagar Times* at his private residence. No one claimed responsibility.

In Srinagar, militants lobbed a grenade at the office of a local political party, injuring a security guard. No one claimed responsibility.

18 September   **West Bank**
In Yahad, gunmen ambushed and overturned a vehicle on the Mevo Dotan-Hermesh Road, killing one person, an Israeli, and wounding a Romanian worker. The Al-Aqsa Martyrs Brigades claimed responsibility.

19 September   **Israel**
In Tel Aviv, a suicide bomber boarded a bus and detonated the explosive device concealed in his backpack, killing five Israelis and one UK citizen and wounding 52 others, according to media and US Embassy reporting. HAMAS claimed responsibility.

20 September   **India**
In Jammu, Kashmir, armed militants killed a senior National Conference Party worker in his home. No one claimed responsibility.

In Srinagar, Kashmir, armed militants opposed to Indian held elections, killed a political activist of the ruling National Conference Party. A National Conference leader stated that the Hizb ul-Mujahedin may be responsible.

22 September   **India**
In Shopian, Kashmir, armed militants threw grenades and then fired at the residence of the ruling National Conference legislator who was in residence at the time but was unharmed in the attack. No one claimed responsibility.

In Bandgam, Kashmir, armed militants shot and killed the Ruling Block president. No one claimed responsibility.

23 September   **India**
In Bijbiara, Kashmir, militants hurled a grenade at a vehicle belonging to the Jammu and Kashmir's Peoples Democratic Party. The grenade missed its target and exploded on the roadside, injuring eight persons. No one claimed responsibility.

                                                                       India
In Sangam, Kashmir, armed militants attempted to hurl a grenade at a political rally, but it missed the intended victims, exploded near a group of private citizens and injured eight persons. No one claimed responsibility.

                                                                       India
In Srinagar, Kashmir, militants hurled a grenade at an army vehicle but missed its target and exploded in a crowded marketplace, injuring 12 persons and two police officers. No one claimed responsibility.

27 September — India
In Pulwama, Kashmir, a grenade exploded on the road, injuring 17 persons and five soldiers. The attack came right before India's scheduled elections.

28 September — India
In Devsar, Kashmir, a landmine exploded under a vehicle carrying a National Congress Party member and three other persons. The explosion killed the three passengers and injured the National Congress Party member. No one claimed responsibility.

29 September — India
In Tral, Kashmir, militants threw a grenade at a bus station, killing one person and injuring 12 others, according to press reports. No one claimed responsibility.

India
In Ganderbal, Kashmir, armed militants killed a political activist belonging to the ruling National Conference Party. No one claimed responsibility.

30 September — India
In Manda Chowk, Kashmir, a timed device exploded on a bus carrying Hindu pilgrims, killing one person and injuring 18 others. No one claimed responsibility.

1 October — India
In Kathu, Kashmir, militants hijacked a minivan, driving it into a utility pole near an open-air vegetable market. The gunmen fired grenades at the minivan, killing all nine passengers. The Al-Arifeen, an offshoot group of the Lashkar-e-Tayyiba, claimed responsibility.

2 October — India
In Haihama, Kashmir, armed militants killed three political activists working with India's ruling National Conference Party. The Al-Arifeen, an offshoot group of the Lashkar-e-Tayyaiba, claimed responsibility.

6 October — Yemen
In al-Dhabbah, a small boat carrying a large amount of explosives rammed the hull of the French oil tanker Limburg as it was anchored approximately 5 miles from port. The attack killed one person and wounded four others. Al-Qaida is probably responsible.

8 October — India
In Doda, Kashmir, armed militants hurled grenades and then fired into a polling station, causing no injuries. No one claimed responsibility.

India
In Kashmir, militants attempted to throw a grenade at a security patrol, but the grenade missed the target and exploded in a crowded marketplace, injuring 14 persons. No one claimed responsibility.

Kuwait
On Failaka Island, gunmen attacked US soldiers while they were conducting a non-live-fire exercise, killing one US Marine and wounding one other. Al-Qaida claimed responsibility.

12 October — Indonesia
In Manado, a bomb exploded near the Philippine Consulate, damaging the front gate and breaking several windows. No one claimed responsibility.

Indonesia
In Bali, a car bomb exploded outside the Sari Club Discotheque on Legian Street, a busy tourist area filled with nightclubs, cafes, and bars, killing at least 187 international tourists and injuring about 300 others. The resulting fire also destroyed the nearby Padi Club and Panin Bank and other buildings and cars. Al-Qaida claimed responsibility for this attack.

20 October — India
In Onagam, armed militants killed three persons and injured two others near a mosque. No one claimed responsibility.

23 October — Russia
In Moscow, 50 armed Chechen rebels took control of the Palace of Culture Theater to demand an end to the war in Chechnya. The theater was rigged with landmines and explosive devices to control hostages and promote leverage with Russian authorities. The rebels held more than 800 hostages including foreign nationals from the United Kingdom, France, Belarus, Germany, Azerbaijan, Georgia, Bulgaria, Netherlands, Ukraine, Israel, Austria, United States, and two permanent residents of the United States. During the three-day siege, rebels killed one Russian police officer and five Russian hostages.

On 26 October, the third day of the siege, Russian Special Forces administered the anesthetic gas fentanyl through the ventilation system. Commandos stormed the theater and killed all of the Chechen rebels after a brief gun battle. In the rescue attempt, 124 hostages died including citizens from Russia (115), United States (1), Azerbaijan (1), Netherlands (1), Ukraine (2), Armenia (1), Austria (1), Kazakhstan (1), and Belarus (1). Chechen rebels led by Movsar Barayev claimed responsibility.

25 October — Russia
In Moscow, an explosive device described as a shrapnel-filled artillery shell equivalent to five kilograms of TNT exploded in an automobile parked in a McDonald's parking lot, killing one person and injuring eight others. The explosion caused major damage to the restaurant. The explosive device was similar to the type commonly used in Chechnya. Russian authorities arrested a Chechen male in connection with the explosion. No one claimed responsibility.

28 October — Jordan

In Amman, press reports stated that gunmen shot and killed a US diplomat, the senior administrator at the US Agency for International Development (USAID). The Honest People of Jordan claimed responsibility.

18 November — Turkey

In Istanbul, an Israeli Arab attempted to hijack El Al Flight 581, 15 minutes before landing. The passenger ran toward the cockpit, attacked the stewardess with a penknife, and demanded that she open the cockpit door. Security guards simultaneously overpowered the man and took him into custody. Shin Bet stated that his actions were nationalistically motivated. No one claimed responsibility.

21 November — Israel

In Jerusalem, a suicide bomber entered a bus on Mexico Street near Kiryat Menachem and detonated the explosive device he was wearing, killing 11 persons including a Romanian citizen and wounding 50 others, according to media and US Consulate reports. HAMAS claimed responsibility.

Kuwait

In Kuwait City, a Kuwaiti police officer stopped and shot two US soldiers driving a rental car, wounding both, according to media and US Embassy reports. The military personnel were both in uniform and armed but did not return fire. No group claimed responsibility.

Lebanon

In Sidon, a gunman shot and killed a US citizen who was an office manager/nurse for a church-run health facility, according to media and US Embassy reports. The female victim, married to a citizen of the United Kingdom, was shot as she entered the facility. An Asbat al-Ansar–linked extremist is probably responsible.

24 November — India

In Jammu, Kashmir, armed militants attacked the Reghunath and Shiv temples, killing 13 persons and wounding 50 others. The Lashkar-e-Tayyiba claimed responsibility for this attack.

28 November — Kenya

In Mombasa, a vehicle containing three suicide bombers drove into the front of the Paradise Hotel and exploded, killing 15 persons including three Israelis and 12 Kenyans and wounding 40 others including 18 Israelis and 22 Kenyans. Al-Qaida, the Government of Universal Palestine in Exile, and the Army of Palestine claimed responsibility. Al-Ittihad al-Islami (AIAI) is probably linked to the attack.

Kenya

In Mombasa, two SA-7 Strela antiaircraft missiles were launched but missed downing a Arkia Boeing 757 taking off from Mombasa enroute to Israel. The aircraft carried 261 passengers and continued its flight. Al-Qaida, the Government of Universal Palestine in Exile, and the Army of Palestine claimed responsibility. AIAI is probably linked to the attack according to reports.

30 November — India

In Awantipora, Kashmir, a grenade exploded, injuring four persons. No one claimed responsibility.

In Srinagar, Kashmir, a bomb exploded near a police vehicle, injuring seven persons. No one claimed responsibility.

4 December — India

In Srinagar, Kashmir, authorities safely defused a bomb found at a bus station. No one claimed responsibility.

5 December — Pakistan

In Karachi, a bomb exploded at the Macedonia Consulate destroying the consulate building. When the authorities searched through the debris, they found three local workers with their throats slit. No one claimed responsibility.

6 December — India

In Rajpora Chowk, Kashmir, militants threw a grenade toward a vehicle carrying several military officers, but it missed its mark and landed near a group of private citizens, injuring eight persons. No one claimed responsibility.

India

In Damhal Hanjipora, Kashmir, militants threw a grenade and fired shots at the private residence of a former minister. The Lashkar-e-Tayyiba probably is responsible. In Pulwama, Kashmir, armed militants killed the brother of the recently slain Law Minister outside his private residence. The militants threw a grenade then fired shots at him. The Lashkar-e-Tayyiba claimed responsibility in a communique to a local television station.

India

In Bombay, a bomb exploded at a local McDonald's restaurant located in a busy rail station mall, injuring 23 persons. The bomb consisted of gunpowder, nails, and iron balls and followed a bomb attack on 6 December at a McDonald's outlet in the Indonesian city of Makassar. No one claimed responsibility.

Indonesia

In Makassar, a bomb exploded in a McDonald's restaurant, killing three persons, injuring 11 others, and causing major damage to the restaurant. No one claimed responsibility though police are focusing on a hardline Islamic group, Laskar Jundullah.

18 December — India

In Yaripora, Kashmir, militants lobbed a handgrenade at a parked military vehicle, but it missed its target and landed near a group of private citizens, injuring 15 persons, three military personnel, and causing major damage to the military vehicle. No one claimed responsibility.

20   December   India
In Kashmir, armed militants killed a newly elected state legislator. No one claimed responsibility.

24   December   Pakistan
In Islamabad, authorities safely dismantled several grenades and about 30 rounds of ammunition, which had been placed in a bag near a church where local and Western worshippers were to gather for Christmas services. An anonymous phone call to the local authorities had warned that a bomb had been placed near the church. No one claimed responsibility.

26   December   Philippines
In Zamboanga del Norte, armed militants ambushed a bus carrying Filipino workers employed by a local Canadian mining company, killing 13 persons and injuring 10 others. Police said that the Moro Islamic Liberation Front (MILF) had been extorting money from the workers' employer, the Calgary-based mining firm Toronto Ventures Inc. Pacific. The Catholic charity Caritas-Philippines said that the Canadian mining company has been harassing tribesmen opposed to mining operations on their ancestral lands. Authorities have accused the MILF of carrying out the attack.

27   December   Chechnya
In Grozny, suicide bombers drove two trucks packed with explosives to the headquarters of Chechnya's pro-Moscow government building and detonated them, killing 72 persons and wounding 210 others. Chechen officials believe the explosives had the force of one ton of TNT and left a 20-foot-wide crater. The explosions destroyed the government building and caused extensive damage to surrounding government facilities. The Kavkaz Center, which operates a Chechen Web site, reported that Chechen shaheeds (martyrs) were responsible.

30   December   Yemen
In Jibla, a gunman entered a Baptist missionary hospital, killing three persons and wounding one other, all US citizens. The gunman is believed to have acted alone. He admitted, however, to being affiliated with the Islah party.

2003

5   January   India
In Kulgam, Kashmir, a hand grenade exploded at a bus station injuring 40 persons: 36 private citizens and four security personnel, according to press reports. No one claimed responsibility.

**   Pakistan**
In Peshawar, armed terrorists fired on the residence of an Afghan diplomat, injuring a guard, according to press reports. The diplomat was not in his residence at the time of the incident. No one claimed responsibility.

**   Israel**
In Tel Aviv, two suicide bombers attacked simultaneously, killing 23 persons including: 15 Israelis, two Romanians, one Ghanaian, one Bulgarian, three Chinese, and one Ukrainian and wounding 107 others—nationalities not specified—according to press reports. The attack took place in the vicinity of the old central bus station where foreign national workers live. The detonations took place within seconds of each other and were approximately 600 feet apart, in a pedestrian mall and in front of a bus stop. The al-Aqsa Martyrs Brigade was responsible.

12   January   Pakistan
In Hyderabad, authorities safely defused a bomb placed in a toilet of a Kentucky Fried Chicken restaurant, according to press reports. Two bomb explosions in Hyderabad in recent months have killed a total of four persons and injured 33 others, all Pakistanis. No one has claimed responsibility.

21   January   Kuwait
In Kuwait City, a gunman ambushed a vehicle at the intersection of al-Judayliyat and Adu Dhabi, killing one US citizen and wounding another US citizen. The victims were civilian contractors working for the US military. The incident took place close to Camp Doha, an installation housing approximately 17,000 US troops. On 23–24 January, a 20-year-old Kuwaiti civil servant, Sami al-Mutayri, was apprehended attempting to cross the border from Kuwait to Saudi Arabia. Al-Mutayri confessed to the attack and stated that he embraces al-Qaida ideology and implements Usama Bin Ladin's instructions although there is no evidence of an organizational link. The assailant acted alone but had assistance in planning the ambush. No group has claimed responsibility.

22   January   Colombia
In Arauquita, military officials reported either the National Liberation Army (ELN) or the Revolutionary Armed Forces of Colombia (FARC) terrorists bombed a section of the Cano Limon-Covenas oil pipeline, causing an unknown amount of damage. The pipeline is owned by US and Colombian oil companies.

24   January   Colombia
In Tame, rebels kidnapped two journalists working for the *Los Angeles Times*, one was a British reporter and the other a US photographer. The ELN is responsible. The two journalists were released unharmed on 1 February 2003.

27   January   Afghanistan
In Nangarhar, two security officers escorting several United Nations vehicles were killed when armed terrorists attacked their convoy, according to press reports. No one claimed responsibility.

31   January   India
In Srinagar, Kashmir, armed terrorists killed a local journalist when they entered his office, according to press reports. No one claimed responsibility.

1 February — Turkey
In Istanbul, press reports stated that a time bomb had been discovered in a McDonald's restaurant. The cleaning man spotted the explosive device by identifying the timer and cables attached to the box located under a table. The authorities were notified immediately, and police experts defused it. No casualties were reported, and no one claimed responsibility.

5 February — Saudi Arabia
In Riyadh, television reports stated that three gunmen fired on a UK citizen as he was traveling from work to home. Five bullets were fired at the vehicle, but the employee of British Airways was not injured except for possible superficial wounds from broken glass. No one claimed responsibility.

6 February — Colombia
In Arauquita, military officials reported either ELN or FARC terrorists bombed a section of the Cano Limon-Covenas oil pipeline, causing an unknown amount of oil to spill. The pipeline is owned by US and Colombian oil companies.

13 February — Colombia
In Bogota, a Southern Command–owned airplane carrying five crew and five passengers—four US citizens and one Colombian—crashed in the jungle. All five passengers survived the crash—two of the crewmembers were injured. Terrorists later killed a Colombian army officer and a US citizen, while three other US citizens are missing, according to press reports. FARC claims they are holding the three missing persons. On 31 March, press reports stated that the three missing US citizens were still captives of FARC. There are upward of 4,500 individuals involved in nonstop, US-financed search efforts. On 22 April, press reports identified the three missing US citizens: Keith Stansell, Marc D. Gonsalves, and Thomas R. Howes—civilians doing drug surveillance for the Department of Defense.

United Kingdom
In London, press reports stated that a person arriving on a British Airways flight was arrested for concealing a live hand hand grenade in his luggage. The man, a Venezuelan of Bangladeshi origin, was arrested under the Terrorism Act by officers from Sussex Police and later charged by authorities. The flight BA 2048 from Bogota, Colombia, with a stop in Caracas, Venezuela, landed at Gatwick Airport. The discovery caused the closure of the North Terminal for approximately two hours. No one claimed responsibility.

15 February — Colombia
In Saravena, military officials reported either ELN or FARC terrorists bombed a section of the Cano Limon-Covenas oil pipeline, causing an unknown amount of damage. The pipeline is owned by US and Colombian oil companies.

20 February — India
In Varmul, Kashmir, a landmine planted near a busy marketplace exploded, killing six persons and injuring three others, according to press reports. No one claimed responsibility.

20 February — Algeria
In the Sahara Desert, four Swiss citizens went missing while touring in a small group without a guide, according to Swiss Embassy and press reports. The tourists were later confirmed kidnapped by terrorist members of the Salafist Group for Preaching and Combat (GSPC). From mid-February to mid-May, the GSPC kidnapped a total of 32 European tourists—17 of whom were freed by Algerian forces in a rescue operation on 13 May. The Swiss tourists are still being held hostage.

Saudi Arabia
In Riyadh, a gunman ambushed a car at a stoplight, killing one person—a UK citizen employed by British Aerospace Engineering, according to press reports. The gunman—a Yemen-born naturalized Saudi who had recently traveled to Pakistan and named his youngest son Osama—was arrested by Saudi police. No group claimed responsibility.

22 February — Algeria
In the Sahara Desert, four German citizens went missing while touring in a small group without a guide, according to German Embassy and press reporting. The tourists were later confirmed kidnapped by the GSPC. On 18 August in Gao, Mali, the last of the 14 hostages were released unharmed after German authorities paid $5 million ransom for their release to the GSPC leader.

Turkey
In Istanbul, press reports stated that two unidentified persons threw a bomb into a British Airways office shattering windows. No casualties were reported, and no one claimed responsibility.

25 February — Saudi Arabia
In al-Dammam, an incendiary bomb was thrown at a McDonald's restaurant, according to press reports. Two persons in a car approached the business; the passenger got out and hurled the bomb, which failed to explode. The passenger attempted—without success—to re-ignite the canister before he fled. The police arrested a person whose clothes contained the same substance as in the bomb and who was later identified by witnesses. No group claimed responsibility.

Venezuela
In Caracas, two bombs exploded within minutes of each other, injuring four persons—one Colombian and three Venezuelans—and damaging the Spanish and Colombian Embassies and other buildings nearby. No one claimed responsibility.

2 March — Venezuela
In Maracaibo, a car bomb exploded damaging surrounding buildings, including a local office of the US oil company Chevron Texaco, according to press reports. The car bomb was composed of C-4 semtex, similar to that used in the detonations at the Spanish and Colombian Embassies the previous week. The explosion occurred outside the home of controversial cattle livestock producer, Antonio Melian.

Mr. Melian is a leading activist in Zulia State, and he has been the center of opposition-government debate in the wake of the two-month nationwide labor-management stoppage that failed to bring down the Chavez Frias government. No one claimed responsibility.

4   March   Philippines
In Davao, a bomb hidden in a backpack exploded in a crowded airline terminal killing 21 persons—including one US citizen—and injuring 146 others (including three US citizens), according to press reports. The Moro Islamic Liberation Front (MILF) claimed responsibility.

5   March   Israel
In Haifa, a suicide bomber boarded a bus on Moriya Boulevard in the Karmel neighborhood and detonated an explosive device, killing 15 persons—including one US citizen—and wounding 40 others, according to press and US Embassy reports. The Islamic Resistance Movement (HAMAS) claimed responsibility.

7   March   Israel
Two US citizens were killed when a Palestinian gunman opened fire on them as they were eating dinner in the settlement of Kiryat Arba.

9   March   India
In Doda District, Kashmir, armed terrorists kidnapped and killed a private citizen, according to press reports. No one claimed responsibility.

India
In Sogam, Kashmir, a bomb injured a student, according to press reports. No one claimed responsibility.

11   March   India
In Rajouri, Kashmir, a bomb exploded in a candy store, killing two persons and injuring four others, according to press reports. No group has claimed responsibility.

13   March   India
In Rajouri, Kashmir, a bomb exploded on a bus parked at a terminal, killing four persons, according to press reports. No one claimed responsibility.

16   March   India
In Indh, Kashmir, armed terrorists attacked a police installation, killing nine police officers and two civilians and wounding eight police officers and one civilian, according to press reports. No one claimed responsibility.

20   March   Greece
In Kholargos, terrorists placed four gas canisters at the entrance to the Citibank and then set them on fire, causing minor damage. No one claimed responsibility.

21   March   Norway
In Oslo, antiwar protesters threw a Molotov cocktail into a McDonald's restaurant before opening time, causing limited damage. No one was hurt in the attack.

22   March   Greece
In Koropi, a makeshift incendiary device exploded in an ATM outside a Citibank branch. The explosion and subsequent fire caused severe damage to the ATM. No one claimed responsibility.

Iraq
In Sayed Sadiq, an Australian journalist/cameraman died instantly when a taxi raced up beside him and exploded. The journalist's colleague, also an Australian on assignment for the Australian Broadcasting Corporation, suffered shrapnel wounds. At least eight other persons were injured in the bombing. Ansar al-Islam is believed to be responsible.

23   March   Ecuador
In Guayaquil, a bomb exploded at the British Consulate. Although it did not cause serious damage or personal injury, the explosion left a hole in the ground, destroyed two windows and a bathroom, and damaged the building's electrical control board. The People's Revolutionary Militias group (MRP) sent an e-mail claiming responsibility for the attack.

24   March   India
In Nadi Marg, Kashmir, armed terrorists dressed in military uniforms entered a village and killed 24 persons, according to press reports. No group claimed responsibility.

25   March   Italy
During 25–26 March in Vicenza, terrorists firebombed three cars belonging to US service members. The Anti-Imperialist Territorial Nuclei (NTA), an extremist group believed to be close to the new Red Brigades, claimed responsibility for the attacks.

Lebanon
In Beirut, an explosive device weighing approximately 400 grams exploded on the US Embassy wall. No casualties were reported, but the building sustained light damage. No one claimed responsibility.

26   March   India
In Narwal, Kashmir, a bomb placed inside the engine of an empty oil tanker parked outside a fuel storage area exploded and caught fire, killing one person and injuring six others, according to press reports. No one claimed responsibility.

27   March   Chile
In Santiago, antiwar protesters exploded a small bomb at a branch of the US-based Bank of Boston. The bomb smashed windows, destroyed an ATM, and caused minor damage to two adjacent stores. Police found a pamphlet at the site that said "death to the empire," which they took as a reference to the United States. No one claimed responsibility.

28 March — Afghanistan

In Tirin Kot, armed terrorists killed an El Salvadorian Red Cross worker while he was traveling with Afghan colleagues to check on water supplies, according to press reports. Although no one has claimed responsibility, the attack involved a group of 60 armed men, and the leader was instructed via telephone to kill only the Westerner in the captured group.

Italy

In Rome, unknown radicals firebombed a Ford-Jaguar dealership—the two brands taken as symbols of the US-UK Coalition that is fighting in Iraq. Approximately a dozen Fords were burned and another 10 damaged. A five-pointed star—a symbol of the Red Brigades, a group not known to plan firebomb attacks—was found at the site. No one has claimed responsibility.

29 March — Greece

In Athens, an unknown assailant threw a hand grenade at a McDonald's restaurant, causing significant material damage. Police stated that it was a British "mills" hand grenade. No one has claimed responsibility.

30 March — Bosnia and Herzegovina

In Sarajevo, Islamic terrorists placed a hand grenade with an anti-US message near a local Coca-Cola company. No one claimed responsibility.

India

In Punch, Kashmir, a bomb exploded in a field where a cricket match was being played, killing one person and injuring two others, according to press reports. No one claimed responsibility.

31 March — Cuba

In Havana, a man armed with two hand grenades hijacked a domestic airliner with 46 passengers and crew onboard in an attempt to reach the United States. After an emergency landing at Havana airport due to insufficient fuel, the plane remained on the runway all night. On 1 April, more than 20 passengers left the aircraft apparently unharmed. With at least 25 passengers on board, the hijacked plane departed Havana airport and safely landed in Key West, Florida.

Italy

In Bologna, IBM employees found an explosive device in a large bag and notified the police. The bomb squad found a "dangerous, though rudimentary" bomb. Antiterrorism investigators established a link between the modus operandi of this incident and an earlier bombing incident that took place in July 2001 in Bologna. An investigation is currently under way. No one has claimed responsibility.

Cyprus

In Nicosia, a 26-year-old man hurled a Molotov cocktail against the outside wall of the US Embassy. No damages were reported. Police arrested the man.

2 April — Philippines

In Davao, a bomb exploded on a crowded passenger wharf, killing 16 persons and injuring 55 others, according to press reports. The attack may have been carried out by two Indonesian members of Jemaah Islamiya (JI), a regional terrorist group with links to al-Qaida. Two individuals were arrested for this attack: Ismael Acmad (a.k.a. Toto), the alleged planner, and an accomplice, Tahome Urong (a.k.a. Sermin Tohami)—members of the MILF. They told investigators they also were involved in the Davao Airport bombing, and JI provided funds. The ammonium nitrate explosive used in the wharf attack is similar to that purchased by JI operative, Father Rohman Ghozi, and seized by police in January 2002 shortly after Ghozi's arrest by Philippine police. Several Indonesian members of JI have been spotted in terrorist training camps on the southern island of Mindanao.

3 April — Turkey

In Istanbul, a "high pressure resonance bomb" detonated near a United Parcel Service (UPS) building, smashing the windows of a nearby pharmacy and olive-seller's shop. The explosion caused minor damage to the wall surrounding the UPS building, as well as a transformer near the wall. No one claimed responsibility.

Turkey

In Istanbul, a bomb exploded at the British Consulate General causing considerable damage to the consulate and also blowing out windows of an adjacent hotel, leaving one Turkish hotel guest with minor cuts. Turkish police believe the bomb was a resonant device (sound bomb) of relatively crude construction. The terrorist group Marxist-Leninist Communist Party (MLK-P) is suspected although no one has claimed responsibility.

Algeria

In the Sahara Desert, eight Austrian tourists were kidnapped by terrorists while traveling in that region, according to press reports. The GSPC is probably responsible for the abduction. (See entry for 22 February for additional details.)

4 April — Algeria

In the Sahara Desert, terrorists kidnapped 11 German tourists traveling in small groups without guides, bringing the total number of Germans abducted (up to this point) to 15. GSPC is believed responsible. (See entry for 22 February for additional details.)

5 April — Lebanon

In Dowra, TNT placed in the trash receptacle of a McDonald's restaurant men's room exploded, wounding 10 persons and causing considerable damage to the restaurant, which is located 7 to 10 kilometers south of the US Embassy. Five to 10 seconds later, there was a minor explosion in a car adjacent to the restaurant building. The explosions were a partial detonation of a three-stage improvised explosive device of TNT, an unidentified quantity of C-4, and three gas-filled containers. No one claimed responsibility.

8 April   **Algeria**

In the Sahara Desert, one Swede and one Dutch citizen were kidnapped, according to press reports. The GSPC is responsible. (See entry for 22 February for additional details.)

Jordan

In Amman, a US official with the diplomatic corps was slightly wounded when terrorists fired at him, according to press reports. The official had exited his hotel to use his cell phone when a car carrying three persons fired a shot barely missing the official, leaving only a superficial wound. No one claimed responsibility.

8 April   **Turkey**

In Izmir, concussion hand grenades placed before the Bornova Court, Citibank, and the British Consulate exploded, causing material damage. No one was hurt in these attacks. The MLK-P was probably responsible for the attacks.

10 April   **India**

In Kashmir, a bomb exploded in the famous Mughal Garden causing no damage, according to press reports. No one claimed responsibility.

Germany

In Hamburg, unknown perpetrators set fire to a party bus for children in the parking lot of a McDonald's restaurant and then set fire to a McDonald's billboard. At both sites, fliers of a leftwing extremist group were found. The extent of material damage is not known. An investigation is under way.

11 April   **Algeria**

In the Sahara Desert, two mountaineers disappeared, according to the Austrian Foreign Ministry. Approximately 30 individuals were abducted or disappeared in the same general area during a three-month period. The GSPC was believed responsible. Subsequently, everyone was released unharmed after a ransom was paid.

12 April   **Venezuela**

In Caracas, a bomb made of C-4 exploded in the Organization of American States office. No one was injured, although the basement was significantly damaged. No one has claimed responsibility.

India

In Kulgam, terrorists threw a hand grenade at a police patrol and missed, injuring two private citizens standing near by, according to press reports. No one claimed responsibility.

India

In Qazigund, terrorists threw a hand grenade at an army patrol, injuring two soldiers and 21 private citizens standing near by, according to press reports. No one claimed responsibility.

India

In Qazigund-Anantnag, Kashmir, terrorists threw a hand grenade into a bus station, killing one person and injuring 20 others, according to press reports. No one claimed responsibility.

13 April   **Philippines**

In Siasi, armed terrorists kidnapped a Filipino-Chinese businesswoman on her way to the local mosque, according to press reports. She was last seen being taken to the island of Jolo, a stronghold of the Abu Sayyaf Group (ASG).

Pakistan

Near Charman, armed terrorists shot and killed two relatives of the governor of Kandahar, Afghanistan, and wounded one other as they were traveling by car to a local bazaar, according to press reports. The attacker was later caught by authorities and identified as a member of Fazlur Rahman's JuI (Jamiat Ulema-e Islami).

14 April   **Afghanistan**

In Yakatut, a missile fired at the US Embassy landed four kilometers away, failing to explode and causing no damage or injures, according to press reports. No one claimed responsibility.

France

In Sergy, terrorists set fire to a car parked outside the rear entrance of a McDonald's restaurant. The resulting fire partially destroyed the restaurant. No one has claimed responsibility.

15 April   **Turkey**

In Istanbul, terrorists bombed two McDonald's restaurants, partially collapsing a wall that injured a pedestrian. The Revolutionary People's Liberation Front (DHKP-C) later claimed responsibility.

16 April   **Afghanistan**

In Jalalabad, a bomb destroyed the UNICEF building, according to press reports. No one claimed responsibility.

22 April   **India**

In Gulshanpora Batagund, Kashmir, a bomb exploded in a dairy yard, killing six persons, injuring 12 others, and killing several cows, according to press reports. No one claimed responsibility.

Argentina

In Avellaneda, a homemade bomb exploded in front of a McDonald's restaurant on Mitre Avenue and Berutti Street. Security officials found an iron tank about 30 centimeters long, as well as evidence of gunpowder. The explosion shattered the windows but did no interior damage. No injuries were reported, and no one claimed responsibility.

24 April   **Israel**

In Kefar Saba, a security guard—a dual Israeli-Russan citizen—was killed and 11 others wounded when a lone suicide bomber blew himself up at the entrance to a busy train station, according to press reports. The al-Aqsa Martyrs Brigade claimed responsibility.

Chronology of Significant Terrorist Incidents 1961–2005

25 April — India
In Patan, Kashmir, a bomb exploded on the lawn of a courthouse, killing three persons and injuring 34 others, according to press reports. No one claimed responsibility.

26 April — India
In Kashmir, a landmine exploded near a site being inspected by the Finance Minister, injuring 11 persons, according to press reports. The Finance Minister was not injured. No one claimed responsibility.

30 April — Israel
In Tel Aviv, two suicide bombers approached the entrance to a pub, Mike's Place. One bomber successfully activated his bomb, killing three Israeli citizens and injuring 64 others—including one US citizen—according to press reports. The second bomber fled, unable to activate his bomb. His body was later found washed up on a Tel Aviv beach. The pub is located a few hundred yards from the US Embassy and is popular with foreigners. Al-Aqsa Martyrs Brigade claimed responsibility.

4 May — Turkey
During the night in Adana, a series of five sound bombs exploded, resulting in minor material damage, but no casualties. A UPS office, Tommy Hilfiger store, local Turkish bank, the US Consulate, and the Nationalist Turkish Political Party headquarters were all targeted. No one claimed responsibility.

5 May — India
In Duderhama, Kashmir, terrorists threw a hand grenade at a National Conference leader's car, injuring the leader, according to press reports. No one claimed responsibility.

India
In Doda, Kashmir, a bomb exploded at a bus stand, killing one person and injuring 25 others, according to press reports. No one claimed responsibility.

5 May — Colombia
German national Heiner Hansen was freed by his kidnappers—presumed to be FARC terrorists—according to press reports. Mr. Hansen was kidnapped near Buenaventura on 31 December 2002.

12 May — Algeria
In the Sahara Desert, terrorists kidnapped a German tourist—16 Germans have been abducted recently—according to press reports. The kidnapping possibly took place in April or early May. The GSPC is probably responsible for the abduction. (See entry for 22 February for additional details.)

Saudi Arabia
In Riyadh, suicide bombers driving cars boobytrapped with explosives drove into the guarded Vinnell housing complex, killing eight US citizens and one Saudi, according to press reports. Al-Qaida is probably responsible.

Saudi Arabia
In Riyadh, suicide bombers driving cars boobytrapped with explosives drove into the Al-Hamra complex, killing one US citizen, two Jordanians, four Saudis, two Filipinos, one Lebanese, and one Swiss, and injuring 194 others, according to press reports. Al-Qaida is probably responsible.

Saudi Arabia
In Riyadh, suicide bombers driving cars boobytrapped with explosives drove into the guarded Jedawal compound housing international workers, killing two Saudis, according to press reports. Al-Qaida is probably responsible.

15 May — Pakistan
In Karachi, 19 small bombs exploded at Shell stations; an Anglo-Dutch–owned company; and at two Caltex petrol stations, a subsidiary of US giant Caltex, injuring seven persons, according to press reports. The small bombs—firecrackers fitted with timing devices—were packed into boxes placed in garbage bins and appeared aimed to scare. The group Muslim United Army claimed responsibility in a faxed letter to the newspaper, *Dawn*.

16 May — Morocco
In Casablanca, one of five near-simultaneous bombs exploded in the street outside the Belgium Consulate and next to a Jewish-owned restaurant, killing two police officers and injuring another, according to press reports. The restaurant, Positano, could have been the target. A Positano employee said a colleague stopped three suspects as they entered the restaurant. One of the suspects fled, and the other two died in the blasts. Belgian security cameras showed the bombers tried but failed to enter the restaurant. Belgian officials, including Foreign Minister Louis Michel, said the restaurant was probably the target. According to press reports, about 14 persons (ages 18–22) took part in the five attacks, killing a total of 42 persons and injuring at least 100. Several of those arrested were cooperating with police. According to press reports, the group al-Sirat al Mustaqim—with possible links to al-Qaida—is responsible.

Morocco
In Casablanca, one of five near-simultaneous bombs exploded at the Casa De Espana restaurant nightclub, killing approximately 42 persons, including three Spaniards and one Italian, according to press reports. (See above entry for details.)

19 May — India
In Rajauri, Kashmir, armed terrorists fired into a private residence, killing six persons, according to press reports. No group claimed responsibility.

India
In Srinagar, Kashmir, two bombs exploded at Kashmir's busiest bus terminal, injuring 14 persons, according to press reports. No group claimed responsibility.

Israel
In the French Hill Intersection, Northern Jerusalem, a suicide bomber dressed as an Orthodox Jew and wearing a prayer shawl boarded a commuter bus, detonated the bombs attached to himself and killed seven persons and injured 26 others according to press reports. One of those injured was a US citizen. Izz al-Din al-Qassam Brigades, the military wing of HAMAS, claimed responsibility.

24 May
Afghanistan
In Haska Meyna, three persons working for a nongovernmental organization (NGO) were injured when their vehicle hit a remote-controlled landmine, according to press reports. No group claimed responsibility.

27 May
Colombia
In Guamalito, military officials reported either ELN or FARC terrorists bombed a section of the Cano Limon-Covenas oil pipeline, spilling 7,000 barrels of crude oil into the Cimitarra creek, a major source of drinking water for more than 5,000 people and causing extensive environmental damage. The pipeline is owned by Colombian and US oil companies.

30 May
Colombia
In Guamalito, terrorists attacked a section of the Cano Limon-Covenas oil pipeline, spilling nearly 7,000 barrels of crude oil and leaving about 4,700 families without drinking water. This pipeline is jointly owned by Ecopetrol of Colombia and a consortium of US and West European companies. No group claimed responsibility, although both FARC and ELN terrorists have attacked this pipeline previously.

31 May
India
In Khudwani, Kashmir, a hand grenade exploded, injuring 11 persons and two police officers, according to press reports. No one claimed responsibility.

1 June
India
In Jammu, Kashmir, terrorists set fire to a private residence and exchanged gunfire with police while leaving the scene, killing four persons in the crossfire, according to press reports. The terrorists escaped. No one claimed responsibility.

Afghanistan
In Kandahar, a bomb exploded at a German NGO office, Deutsche Fuer Technische Zusammenarbeit, causing minor damage to the building, according to press reports. The building was closed on the weekend so there were no injuries. Al-Qaida possibly is responsible.

4 June
Belgium
In Brussels, letters containing the nerve agent adamsite were sent to the US, British, and Saudi Embassies; the government of Prime Minister Guy Verhofstadt; the Court of Brussels; a Belgian ministry; the Oostende airport; and the Antwerp port authority, according to press reports. After exposure to the substance, at least two postal workers and five policemen were hospitalized with skin irritation, eye irritation, and breathing difficulty. In Oostende, three persons exposed to the tainted letter were hospitalized. Belgium police suspected a 45-year-old Iraqi political refugee opposed to the US war in Iraq. On 5 June, police searched his residence and confiscated a document and a plastic bag containing some powder. The antiterrorism investigators also suffered skin irritation, eye irritation, and breathing difficulty. The Iraqi was charged with premeditated assault.

7 June
Afghanistan
In Kabul, a taxi rigged with explosives rammed into a bus carrying German peacekeepers of the International Security Assistance Force, killing five German peacekeepers and injuring 29 others, according to press reports. The US-funded police school located about 300 feet from the explosion lost 13 windows. No one claimed responsibility, but authorities blame al-Qaida.

8 June
Somalia
In Mogadishu, an armed militia group fired on a car carrying a US freelance journalist, his driver, and his interpreter, slightly wounding the journalist, according to press reports. No one claimed responsibility.

9 June
Peru
In Lima, approximately 60 Shining Path terrorists kidnapped 71 workers employed by Techint Group, an Argentine company building a natural gas pipeline in southeastern Peru. The kidnapped group consisted of 64 Peruvians, four Colombians, two Argentines, and a Chilean. A rescue operation freed all the hostages on 11 June, but the terrorists escaped.

11 June
Israel
Near Jerusalem, two US citizens were killed in a bus bombing near Klal Center on Jaffa Road.

Turkey
In Adana, 33-year-old Cumali Kizilgoca threw two hand grenades into the US Consulate garden and was detained. One of the hand grenades did not explode and was later detonated by the police. No one was injured. Kizilgoca attacked the consulate in retaliation for the recent assassination attempt by Israel on a HAMAS leader, according to press reports.

12 June
Greece
In Thessalonika, unidentified culprits entered the front lobby of the US-owned Citibank, doused the ATM in a flammable liquid, placed a gas canister in it, and set it on fire, according to press reports. The explosion destroyed the ATM and caused extensive damage to the lobby and office equipment.

17 June
Italy
In Rome, a bomb exploded in front of the Spanish school Cervantes, damaging the school and a few cars within a 20-meter radius. Authorities speculate that the device contained approximately 500 grams of chlorite- and nitrate-based explo-

sives. No one claimed responsibility, but investigators believe whoever placed the device was experienced with explosives and was probably connected to an Italian anarchist group aligned with Basque Fatherland and Liberty (ETA). Similar devices have been used in past attacks and have been linked to Italian anarchists supporting the ETA.

17 June   India
In Shopian, Kashmir, a bomb exploded outside a store selling chickens, injuring five persons, according to press reports. No one claimed responsibility.

India
In Kashmir, armed terrorists entered a private residence, killing the son of a Muslim politician, according to press reports. No one claimed responsibility.

18 June   France
In Yvelines, members of the Corsican National Liberation Front activated explosive charges during the early morning hours, seriously damaging two French villas and a British housing company, according to press reports. The houses were unoccupied, and nobody was injured.

20 June   West Bank
One US citizen was killed in a shooting attack near the settlement of Ofra.

India
In Srinagar, Kashmir, a bomb exploded at a crowded market, injuring 16 persons, according to press reports. No one claimed responsibility.

In Charar-i-Sharif, Kashmir, a hand grenade hurled at a police station injured two officers inside, according to press reports. No one claimed responsibility.

23 June   India
In Pulwama, Kashmir, a hand grenade thrown at a military vehicle missed its intended target, killing two persons and wounding 48 others standing near by, according to press reports. No one claimed responsibility.

27 June   Kenya
In Mandera, armed terrorists using hand grenades killed one person and seriously injured four others, including a doctor from the Netherlands working with "Doctors Without Frontiers," according to press reports. No one claimed responsibility.

28 June   Gaza Strip
In Bayt Lahiyah, several bombs exploded near a US Embassy car, according to press reports. The bombs were apparently aimed at a diplomatic-plated vehicle belonging to the US Consulate since the Israel Defense Forces (IDF) were not operating in the area.

30 June   Israel
In Yabed, Northern Israel, a Bulgarian construction worker was killed when his truck came under fire, according to press reports. The al-Aqsa Martyrs Brigade claimed responsibility.

3 July   Colombia
In Caldono, armed terrorists kidnapped five persons, including a Swiss citizen working for the NGO, Hands of Colombia Foundation, according to press reports. FARC claimed responsibility.

Iraq
In Baghdad, terrorists killed a British journalist outside the Iraq National Museum, according to press reports. No one claimed responsibility.

4 July   India
In Larnu, Kashmir, terrorists killed two persons—a school teacher and a private citizen—and wounded 20 others, including the rural development minister of Jammu-Kashmir, two government officials, two police officers, and 15 others when they opened fired and threw several hand grenades into a meeting between the minister and health officials, according to press reports. No one claimed responsibility.

8 July   Afghanistan
In Kabul, terrorists attacked the Pakistani Embassy, destroying computers and telephones, according to press reports. No one claimed responsibility.

9 July   India
In Aram Mohalla Shopian, Kashmir, terrorists threw a hand grenade toward a security patrol party. The hand grenade missed its intended target and exploded on the roadside, injuring three persons, according to press reports. No one claimed responsibility.

11 July   Greece
In Athens, authorities safely dismantled a bomb in an office building near a branch of the American Life Insurance Company, according to press reports. No one claimed responsibility, but the device was similar to others produced by the Revolutionary Nuclei and Revolutionary People's Struggle (ELA) terrorists groups.

13 July   Greece
In Athens, three Molotov cocktails were thrown at a branch office of the Eurobank, causing minor damage, according to US Embassy reporting. No one claimed responsibility.

14 July   Afghanistan
In Jalalabad, a bomb exploded near the offices of the United Nations Human Rights Commission (UNHRC), causing major damage to two buildings, according to press reports. No one claimed responsibility.

16 July   Colombia
In La Pesquera, military officials reported either ELN or FARC terrorists bombed a section of the Cano Limon-Covenas oil pipeline at the KM 07 and 02N intersection,

causing an unknown amount of damage. The pipeline is owned by US and Colombian oil companies.

Colombia

In La Pesquera, military officials reported either ELN or FARC terrorists bombed a section of the Cano Limon-Covenas oil pipeline at the KM 71 and 26 W intersection, causing an unknown amount of damage. The pipeline is owned by US and Colombian oil companies.

21 July **India**

In Jammu, Kashmir, two hand grenades exploded at a crowded community kitchen, killing seven persons and injuring 42 others, according to press reports. No one claimed responsibility.

23 July **Sri Lanka**

In Valachchenai, terrorists stoned a vehicle carrying two Scandinavians working as truce monitors, according to press reports. The truce monitors were not injured, but the car was damaged. No one claimed responsibility.

2 August **Iraq**

In Baghdad, a vehicle bomb exploded in front of the Jordanian Embassy, killing 19 persons, injuring 50 others, and damaging the outside facade of the embassy, according to press reports. No one claimed responsibility.

4 August **India**

In Mahore Tehsil, Kashmir, armed terrorists shot and killed an educator attending a marriage function, according to press reports. No one claimed responsibility

5 August **India**

In Dhar Galoon, Kashmir, two persons were injured by mortar shelling, according to press reports. No one claimed responsibility.

India

In Katjidhok, Kashmir, armed terrorists shot and killed one person, according to press reports. No one claimed responsibility.

Iraq

In Tikrit, a US contractor for Kellogg Brown and Root was killed when his car ran over an improvised explosive device, according to press reports. He was under military escort when the explosion occurred. No group claimed responsibility.

Indonesia

In Jakarta, a car bomb exploded in the front of the Marriott Hotel during lunchtime rush hour, killing 13 persons and injuring 149 others, according to press reports. The adjoining office block was set on fire, with several cars burning in the hotel's front driveway and hotel windows shattered up to the 21st floor. Al-Qaida claimed responsibility.

10 August **Eritrea**

In Adobha, armed terrorists attacked a vehicle carrying Eritrean passengers working for the US charity, Mercy Corps killing two persons and injuring three others, according to press reports. No one claimed responsibility.

13 August **India**

In Bandipora, Kashmir, a bomb attached to a bicycle exploded outside the State Bank of India, injuring 31 persons, according to press reports. No one claimed responsibility.

15 August **India**

In Pakherpora, Kashmir, a hand grenade thrown at a police patrol missed its target, landing in a crowd of bystanders and exploded, injuring 18 persons, according to press reports. No one claimed responsibility.

19 August **Iraq**

In Baghdad, a truck entered the driveway of the Marriott Hotel, the headquarters of the UNHCR, and was stopped by a security guard. The truck exploded, killing 23 persons—including the director of the UNHCR and three US citizens—injuring 100 others, and badly damaging several stories of the Marriott Hotel and other buildings almost a mile away, according to press reports. The arrested suspects admitted that the bomb was to have been detonated in the hotel lobby by a suicide bomber where a meeting of US officials was taking place. Al-Qaida is probably responsible.

Israel

In Jerusalem, a suicide bomber riding a bus detonated his explosives, killing 20 persons—five of whom were US citizens—and injuring 140 others, according to press reports. HAMAS claimed responsibility.

Serbia

In Bujanova, unidentified persons threw two hand grenades into the courtyard of a house belonging to Ramiz Ramizi—an ethnic Albanian—wounding his 8-year-old grandson and four other members of his family, according to press reports. No one claimed responsibility.

6 September **India**

In Srinagar, Kashmir, a bomb exploded in a busy marketplace, killing six persons and injuring 37 others, including an Indian army officer, according to press reports. Police believe the intended target of the blast was the army officer. No one claimed responsibility.

8 September **Afghanistan**

Near Moqor, armed terrorists killed four Danish members working for the NGO Danish Committee For Aid To Afghan Refugees assisting local Afghanis on an irrigation project, according to press reports. The Taliban is probably responsible.

9 September **Israel**

In Jerusalem, eight persons were killed—including two US citizens—and 30 others wounded when a suicide bomber blew himself up on the hitchhiking stop near the Asaf Harofe

Chronology of Significant Terrorist Incidents 1961–2005

Hospital, according to press reports. No one claimed responsibility.

India

In Sopat, Kashmir, armed terrorists shot and killed a former state forest minister, according to press reports. No one claimed responsibility.

Iran

In Tehran, armed terrorists fired three to four shots at the British Embassy, causing no damage or injuries, according to press reports. No one claimed responsibility.

11 September   **India**

In Srinagar, Kashmir, a hand grenade was thrown at a military bunker house, missing its target, killing one private citizen and injuring 14 others standing near by, according to press reports. No one claimed responsibility.

14 September   **Colombia**

In Tayrona National Park, armed terrorists attacked several cabins, kidnapping eight foreign nationals—four Israelis, two Britons, a German, and a Spaniard— according to press reports. On 25 September, one of the two Britons escaped safely from the kidnappers. ELN has claimed responsibility for this attack. On 24 November, the German and Spanish nationals were released.

15 September   **Iran**

In Tehran, shots were fired at the British Embassy, causing no injuries, according to press reports. No one claimed responsibility.

19 September   **Afghanistan**

In Ghazni, four rockets were fired at a facility housing Turkish road workers and equipment, causing no injuries or damage, according to press reports. The Taliban is probably responsible.

22 September   **Iraq**

In Baghdad, a vehicle bomb exploded near the UN Headquarters, killing a guard and injuring 18 others; the building was not damaged, according to press reports. No one claimed responsibility.

25 September   **Iraq**

In Baghdad, a bomb exploded at the news bureau of US broadcaster NBC, killing one person and injuring one other, according to press reports. No one claimed responsibility.

30 September   **India**

In Gagran, Kashmir, a hand grenade thrown at a police patrol exploded, injuring six police officers and 14 civilians, according to press reports. No one claimed responsibility.

2 October   **Malaysia**

In Sabah, armed terrorists kidnapped six persons—three Indonesians, two Filipinos, and a Malaysian—from a resort area; one escaped and five were found executed on 29 October in Languyan, Philippines, according to press reports. No one claimed responsibility. ASG is probably responsible.

5 October   **Afghanistan**

In Kabul, a bomb exploded next to the offices of the international aid agencies, Oxfam and Save the Children, causing no casualties, according to press reports. No one claimed responsibility.

Somalia

In Borama, armed terrorists shot and killed an Italian missionary in her private residence, according to press reports. No one claimed responsibility.

9 October   **Iraq**

In Baghdad, armed terrorists shot and killed a Spanish military attache at his private residence, according to press reports. No one claimed responsibility.

14 October   **Iraq**

In Baghdad, a suicide car bomb detonated near the Turkish Embassy, wounding one Turkish and one Iraqi employee, according to press reports. No one claimed responsibility.

15 October   **India**

In Lolab, Kashmir, a landmine triggered by rebels exploded in a forested area, injuring nine persons, according to press reports. No one claimed responsibility.

Gaza Strip

In Gaza Strip, a US Embassy Tel Aviv motorcade was struck by an apparent roadside charge on Saladin Street, according to press reports. The blast destroyed the second car in the convoy, killing three persons and wounding one, all US citizens and contractors providing security for the United States in Israel and the Middle East. The Palestinian Revolutionary Committee initially claimed responsibility but later recanted its statement.

20 October   **India**

In Doda, Kashmir, armed terrorists shot and killed two persons, according to press reports. No one claimed responsibility.

India

In Anantnag, Kashmir, a hand grenade thrown at a security patrol missed its target and exploded in a busy market, killing one person and injuring seven others, according to press reports. No one claimed responsibility.

26 October   **India**

In Gagal, Kashmir, armed terrorists dressed in army uniforms hijacked a car, killing two of the occupants and injuring four others, according to press reports. No one has claimed responsibility.

26   October   India
In Samba, Kashmir, a bomb exploded in the toilet of a coach car, causing no injuries but derailing five cars, according to press reports. No one claimed responsibility.

India
In Bijbehara, Kashmir, a hand grenade thrown at a military convoy missed its target and exploded on the road, injuring 12 persons, including one police officer and an individual who worked in the office of the Indo-Tibetan border police, according to press reports. No one claimed responsibility.

Iraq
In Baghdad, rockets were fired at the al-Rashid hotel housing the US and Coalition forces, killing one US citizen, injuring 15 persons, and damaging the hotel, according to press reports. No one claimed responsibility.

27   October   Afghanistan
In Shkin, two US Government contract workers were killed in an ambush by armed terrorists, according to press reports. No one claimed responsibility.

Iraq
In Baghdad, a car bomb exploded inside the compound of the International Committee of the Red Cross headquarters, killing 12 persons and injuring 22 others, according to press reports. No one claimed responsibility.

28   October   India
In Lal Chowk, Kashmir, a bomb exploded at the customer billing counter in a telegraph office building, injuring 36 persons, according to press reports. No one claimed responsibility.

29   October   India
In Anatnag, Kashmir, a hand grenade thrown at a police patrol missed its target and exploded in a busy market, injuring 13 persons, according to press reports. No one claimed responsibility.

11   November   Afganistan
In Kandahar, a vehicle bomb exploded outside the United Nations Assistance Mission in Afghanistan offices, killing one person, injuring one other, and causing major material damage to the building, according to press reports. The Taliban or al-Qaida may be responsible.

Greece
In Athens, authorities neutralized an explosive device detected outside Athens Citibank Branch. An unidentified person phoned the Athens newspaper and announced a bomb was going to explode at the bank, according to press reports. The Organization Khristos Kassimis is probably responsible.

2004

1   January   India
In Srinagar, Kashmir, India, a militant on a bicycle was carrying a bomb, which prematurely exploded, injuring six civilians. No group claimed responsibility.

2   January   Columbia
Between Puerto Colon and San Miguel, Colombia, 11 bombs exploded at different points along the Trans-Andean Pipeline, suspending Colombia's exports of petroleum. The bombs had been placed between the 20th and 29th kilometers of the pipeline. No group claimed responsibility, although local police blamed the Revolutionary Armed Forces of Colombia (FARC).

India
In Kashmir, India, two armed militants opened fire at a Jammu railway station, killing four Indian security personnel and wounding 17 civilians. This attack occurred one day before the Indian Prime Minister was due to make his first visit to Pakistan in four years. No group claimed responsibility.

India
In Bijbehara, Kashmir, India, militants threw a grenade at an army convoy, killing one soldier and one civilian and wounding eight other civilians. This attack occurred one day before the Indian Prime Minister was due to make his first visit to Pakistan in four years. No group claimed responsibility.

4   January   Iraq
In Mosul, Iraq, an improvised explosive device exploded inside a taxicab, killing two Iraqis and wounding one Jordanian. It is unknown if the blast was premature or if the taxicab and its occupants were the intended targets. No group claimed responsibility.

5   January   Bolivia
In Oruro, Bolivia, a bomb exploded at a building of the National Telecommunications Enterprise (Entel), a telecom company under the management of Italian Telecom, injuring two security guards and a civilian. The explosion also shattered almost all of the windows on the north side of the building and partially collapsed several walls. No group claimed responsibility.

Iraq
Near Falluja, Iraq, unknown attackers shot and killed two French nationals and wounded one other. The victims worked for a US company contracted to repair Iraqi infrastructure. No group claimed responsibility.

United Kingdom
In Manchester, England, anarchists sent a letter bomb to the office of Gary Titley, leader of the Labor Party's members of the European Parliament. The device burst into flames when Titley's secretary opened the package, and a fire spread throughout the office. There were no reported injuries. This

was the sixth bomb sent from Italy to European Union officials throughout Western Europe. A group calling itself the Informal Anarchic Federation claimed responsibility.

5 January   **India**

In Shopian, Kashmir, India, Islamic militants opened fire at a police patrol, killing one shopkeeper. This incident occurred as India and Pakistan resumed diplomatic talks. No group claimed responsibility.

9 January   **India**

In Srinagar, Kashmir, India, an Islamic militant threw a grenade at a crowded mosque during prayers, missing the intended target and hitting the roof of a shop, killing two civilians and injuring 18 others. The attack occurred after India and Pakistan agreed to resume bilateral talks, and Islamabad pledged it would not allow its soil to be used for terrorism. No group claimed responsibility, but police blamed the United Jihad Council.

India

In the Kupwara District, Kashmir, India, armed militants beheaded a police officer. The attack occurred after India and Pakistan agreed to resume bilateral talks, and Islamabad pledged it would not allow its soil to be used for terrorism. No group claimed responsibility.

10 January   **India**

In Baramulla District, Kashmir, India, Islamic militants shot and killed a Muslim couple in their home and then beheaded the husband's body. No group claimed responsibility, but police blamed the United Jihad Council.

India

In Kupwara District, Kashmir, India, Islamic militants beheaded a police official. No group claimed responsibility, but police blamed the United Jihad Council.

11 January   **India**

In Chanapora Village, Pulwama District, Kashmir, India, Islamic militants threw a grenade into a home, killing one villager and injuring one other. No group claimed responsibility, but police blamed the United Jihad Council.

12 January   **India**

In the southern district of Anantnag, Kashmir, India, Islamic militants threw a grenade at a police patrol, killing one officer and a Muslim woman and wounding eight police officers and five civilians. No group claimed responsibility.

13 January   **India**

In the Poonch District, Kashmir, India, armed militants shot and killed a Muslim village chief. No group claimed responsibility.

India

At Gagra Village, in the Gool area of the Udhampur District of Kashmir, India, armed militants opened fire on a police patrol, killing one police officer and injuring one other. No group claimed responsibility.

West Bank

Near the Jewish settlement of Talmon, outside Ramallah, West Bank, a Palestinian gunman opened fire on a car, killing one Israeli and injuring two others. The al-Aqsa Martyrs Brigade claimed responsibility.

14 January   **Gaza Strip**

In the Gaza Strip, a female Palestinian suicide bomber blew herself up at a major border crossing point between Israel and the Gaza Strip, killing four Israelis and wounding 10 others. HAMAS and the al-Aqsa Martyrs Brigade claimed joint responsibility.

Iraq

Near Tikrit, Iraq, unidentified armed men attacked a contractor convoy, killing three contractors (1 US; 2 unknown) working for the United States and wounding one US soldier. No group claimed responsibility.

15 January   **India**

In the Hyderpora suburb of Srinagar, Kashmir, India, armed militants detonated a car bomb as a paramilitary convoy passed, wounding seven soldiers. The Hizbul-Mujahedin and Al-Mansurian claimed joint responsibility.

India

In Tral, Kashmir, India, armed militants fired upon a police patrol, killing one officer. No group claimed responsibility.

17 January   **India**

In Narwal-Lajoora, Pulwama, Kashmir, India, armed militants attacked a police patrol, killing two officers. Police forces returned fire, killing two of the attackers. No group claimed responsibility, but it is widely believed that Hizbul-Mujahedin was responsible.

West Bank

In Kiryat Arba, near Hebron, West Bank, gunmen entered the settlement, knocked on the door of a Jewish residence, and opened fire on the occupants, killing one Israeli and wounding two others. HAMAS claimed responsibility.

18 January   **Colombia**

Near Arauquita, Colombia, attackers dynamited the Cano Limon-Covenas Pipeline in several spots near the Venezuela border. No group claimed responsibility, although oil company officials blamed the Revolutionary Armed Forces of Colombia (FARC).

20 January   **India**

In the Udhamput District, Kashmir, India, a land mine exploded, killing one police officer and wounding two others. No group claimed responsibility.

India

In Arnia, Kashmir, India, a bomb exploded, injuring seven civilians. No group claimed responsibility.

21   January   France

In Ghisonaccia, Corsica, France, militants detonated an explosive device outside a vacation home owned by a German national, destroying the home. On 28 January 2004, the National Front for the Liberation of Corsica (FLNC) claimed responsibility for this attack and seven other attacks against vacation homes between 29 November 2003 and 28 January 2004.

23   January   India

In the Doda District, Kashmir, India, assailants threw a grenade at a security bunker near a bus stand, injuring five civilians and damaging nearby buses and a hotel. No group claimed responsibility.

24   January   India

In Anantnag District, Kashmir, India, armed militants shot and killed a woman. The killing was one of several during the run-up to India's independence celebration. No group claimed responsibility.

India

In Hyderpora, Srinagar, Kashmir, India, armed militants shot and killed a Border Security Force officer. The killing was one of several during the run-up to India's independence celebration. No group claimed responsibility.

India

In Poonch District, Kashmir, India, armed militants shot and killed a teenage student. The killing was one of several during the run-up to India's independence celebration. No group claimed responsibility.

25   January   Iraq

In Ramadi, Iraq, unidentified militants shot and killed a Jordanian truck driver. No group claimed responsibility.

27   January   India

In Shopian District, Kashmir, India, armed militants shot and killed a teenager. The killing was one of several that followed India's independence celebration. No group claimed responsibility.

India

In Kupwara District, Kashmir, India, armed militants invaded a home and began shooting killing one Muslim civilian and wounding another. The attack was one of several that followed India's independence celebration. No group claimed responsibility.

India

In Baramulla District, Kashmir, India, armed militants killed a Muslim woman. The killing was one of several that followed India's independence celebration. No group claimed responsibility.

India

In Doda District, Kashmir, India, armed militants killed a civilian. The killing was one of several that followed India's independence celebration. No group claimed responsibility.

28   January   Iraq

In Baghdad, Iraq, a car bomb exploded, killing four civilians including one South African, and wounding 17 others, including four South Africans. The blast also caused damage to the Shahine Hotel and destroyed a police station. No group claimed responsibility.

29   January   Israel

In Jerusalem, Israel, a suicide bomber destroyed a bus near the Prime Minister's residence, killing 11 civilians, including one Ethiopian, and injuring 30 civilians. The al-Aqsa Martyrs Brigade and HAMAS claimed joint responsibility.

30   January   Iraq

In Baghdad, Iraq, attackers fired two rocket-propelled grenades at the Dutch Embassy, causing a small fire, completely destroying one room, and badly damaging the rest of the building. No group claimed responsibility.

1   Febuary   India

In Magam, Budgam District, Kashmir, India, Islamic militants threw a grenade at a crowded bus stand, injuring 11 people. No group claimed responsibility.

Iraq

In Irbil, Iraq, suicide bombers launched simultaneous attacks on the offices of the Kurdistan Democratic Party and the Patriotic Union of Kurdistan, killing 109 people and wounding 200 others. Among the dead were the region's Deputy Prime Minister and a Turkish businessman. Ansar al-Sunna claimed responsibility.

2   February   India

In Srinagar, Kashmir, India, Islamic militants shot at a deputy inspector general of police as he was leaving a mosque, killing him and wounding a civilian. The militants fired from close range with pistols fitted with silencers. The deputy inspector general was in charge of crime and railways in Kashmir. The Save Kashmir Movement claimed responsibility.

India

In Shopian, Pulwama District, Kashmir, India, armed militants threw a grenade at a border police patrol, wounding two officers. No group claimed responsibility.

4   February   India

In Chewdara Village, Budgam District, Kashmir, India, armed militants invaded a home and shot and killed a Muslim couple and their neighbor. No group claimed responsibility.

5   February   India

In Sakars, Anantnag District, Kashmir, India, Islamic militants detonated a bomb as an army vehicle passed, killing

Chronology of Significant Terrorist Incidents 1961–2005 819

four soldiers and wounding three others. No group claimed responsibility.

6 February   **Russia**
In Moscow, Russia, a suicide bomber attacked a subway car that had just departed Avtozavodskaya Station, killing 41 people (2 Armenian; 1 Moldovan) and injuring 230 others. No group claimed responsibility, but it is widely believed that the Karachayev Djamaat was responsible.

7 February   **India**
In Shopian, Kashmir, India, Islamic militants threw a grenade into a crowd and began shooting, killing two civilians and wounding 25 civilians and three soldiers. No group claimed responsibility.

9 February   **Iraq**
In Baghdad, Iraq, a mortar attack killed a former Fijian soldier employed by the London-based security company, Global Risk Strategies. This was the second former-Fijian soldier killed in Iraq. No group claimed responsibility.

14 February   **Iraq**
Between Babil and Baghdad, Iraq, unidentified gunmen opened fire on a taxi, killing a Baptist minister from Rhode Island and wounding three other Baptist ministers from Connecticut, Massachusetts, and New York. No group claimed responsibility.

15 February   **India**
In Qazigund, Anantnag, Kashmir, India, Islamic militants detonated a bomb in a market, injuring 14 soldiers and three civilians. The bomb was concealed in a handcart and exploded when an army convoy entered the area. Hizbul-Mujahedin claimed responsibility.

                                                         India
In Kawoosa, Budgam, Kashmir, India, Islamic militants shot and killed two men, including a Kashmir political party worker. No group claimed responsibility.

16 February   **India**
In Srinagar, Kashmir, India, Islamic militants ambushed a political leader, killing him and a nearby police officer, and wounding another officer. The Save Kashmir Movement claimed responsibility.

                                                         India
In Goshabugh Village, Baramulla District, Kashmir, India Islamic militants attempted to storm a police station, killing one police officer. No group claimed responsibility, although it is widely believed that Hizbul-Mujahedin was responsible.

                                                         Iraq
In Baghdad, Iraq, unknown gunmen shot and killed an American Service Center employee in his driveway. No group claimed responsibility.

17 February   **India**
In Aripanthan, Budgam, Kashmir, India, Islamic militants invaded the home of a political leader, killing him. No group claimed responsibility.

                                                         India
In Srinagar, Kashmir, India, militants detonated a bomb, hidden inside a scooter parked along the Srinagar-Jammu national highway, damaging several vehicles. The Chief Minister of Kashmir, who was nearby, was not harmed. No group claimed responsibility.

20 February   **Greece**
In Thessaloniki, Greece, a gas canister bomb exploded under a British diplomatic vehicle, causing a small fire that damaged the vehicle and another car parked nearby. A group calling itself the Indomitable Marxists claimed responsibility.

22 February   **Afghanistan**
In Panjwai, Kandahar Province, Afghanistan, assailants opened fire on a helicopter belonging to Louis Berger Group Incorporated killing the Australian pilot and wounding three others (1 American; 1 British; 1 Afghan). The victims had been inspecting the construction of a health clinic in the town. The Taliban claimed responsibility.

                                                     Germany
In Hamburg, Germany, an unknown attacker threw a hand grenade backstage during a concert at Audimax Hall at Hamburg University, injuring two university security guards. Police indicated that the target of the attack was probably a Turkish-Kurdish singer performing at the concert. No group claimed responsibility.

                                                    India
In Bugdam, Kashmir, India, armed militants shot and killed a political candidate. Al-Mansurian claimed responsibility.

                                                    Israel
In Jerusalem, Israel, two Palestinian suicide bombers blew themselves up on a crowded bus, killing eight people and wounding 62 others. The al-Aqsa Martyrs Brigade claimed responsibility.

23 February   **India**
In Tral, Kashmir, India, a bomb exploded, killing one Muslim teenager and wounding four others. No group claimed responsibility.

                                                     Iraq
In Iskandariya, Iraq, an improvised explosive device exploded as a US civilian vehicle passed, killing one US contractor and wounding three others. No group claimed responsibility.

27 February   **India**
In Budgam, Kashmir, India, armed militants threw two grenades at a public official during a speech, killing a Muslim

girl and injuring one police officer and three civilians. Jamiat ul-Mujahedin claimed responsibility.

India

In Manshward, Rajpora area Pulwama District, Kashmir, India, armed militants shot and killed the wife of a former counter-insurgent. No group claimed responsibility.

West Bank

In Eshkolot, West Bank, unknown gunmen attacked and killed an Israeli man and woman in their car. The al-Aqsa Martyrs Brigade and the Popular Front for the Liberation of Palestine (PFLP) claimed joint responsibility.

28 February   India

In Bijbehara, Kashmir, India, Islamic militants threw a grenade at a military convoy, injuring five soldiers and eight civilians. No group claimed responsibility.

29 February   India

In Srinagar, Kashmir, India, armed militants fired four grenades at a security camp, missing their target and injuring eight civilians in a residential area. No group claimed responsibility.

India

In Pulwama District, Kashmir, India, armed militants shot and killed two People's Democratic Party's workers. No group claimed responsibility.

1 March   India

In Srinagar, Kashmir, India, armed militants threw a grenade at a police patrol, missing their target and injuring 14 civilians at a nearby intersection. Al-Mansurian claimed responsibility.

2 March   India

In Gund Village, Kashmir, India, armed militants invaded a home and shot and killed an army cadet who had been on leave. No group claimed responsibility.

India

In Parraypora, Srinagar, Kashmir, India, a bomb hidden inside a scooter exploded as a military convoy passed, injuring one soldier. No group claimed responsibility.

Iraq

In Karbala, Iraq, suicide bombers set off explosives as Shia Muslims were celebrating the Shia religious holiday, Ashura, killing 106 civilians, including 49 Iranians, and wounding 233 others. No group claimed responsibility, although Iraqi officials believe al-Qaida terrorists were responsible for this attack and a near-simultaneous bombing in Baghdad. US officials, however, point to Abu Mus'ab al-Zarqawi's Jama'at al-Tawhid wa'al-Jihad group.

Iraq

In Baghdad, Iraq, three suicide bombers set off explosives at a shrine as Shia Muslims celebrated the Shia religious holiday, Ashura, killing 65 worshipers and wounding 320 others. No group claimed responsibility, although Iraqi officials believe al-Qaida terrorists were responsible for this attack and a near-simultaneous bombing in Karbala. US officials, however, point to Abu Mus'ab al-Zarqawi's Jama'at al-Tawhid wa'al-Jihad group.

5 March   Afghanistan

Near Shah Joy, Zabol Province, Afghanistan, assailants attacked a vehicle carrying subcontractors working for a US construction firm, killing two (1 Turkish; 1 Afghan) and kidnapping two (1 Turkish; 1 Afghan). On 26 June 2004, assailants released the Turkish and afghan captives. No group claimed responsibility, but it is widely believed that the Taliban was responsible.

9 March   India

In Sringar, Kashmir, India, armed militants attacked a government information center building with grenades and small arms, wounding five soldiers. Al-Mansurian claimed responsibility.

India

In Budgam, Kashmir, India, a militant threw a grenade into a group of people trying to stop him from abducting a local person, killing five civilians and injuring 42 others. No group claimed responsibility.

Iraq

In Hillah, Iraq, unidentified gunmen disguised as Iraqi policemen shot and killed two US civilian employees and an Iraqi interpreter at a fake checkpoint. The attackers took the vehicle but were later captured by Polish troops who discovered the bodies of the victims in the car. No group claimed responsibility.

11 March   India

In Khrew, Pulwama district, Kashmir, India, armed militants attacked an Indian army anti-insurgency training camp, killing two soldiers and two civilians, and wounding five other civilians. Jaish-e-Mohammed claimed responsibility

Spain

During the morning, in Madrid, Spain, 10 bombs exploded on the city's commuter transit system killing 191 people and wounding approximately 1,900 others. The bombs, hidden in backpacks, were placed in stations and on strains along a single rail line. By the end of March, Spanish authorities arrested over 20 people in connection with the attacks. On 3 April 2004, a key figure in the attacks blew himself up along with six other suspects, in his apartment after the police surrounded the building. The Abu Hafs al-Masri Brigades, on behalf of al-Qaida, and several other groups claimed responsibility, but Spanish authorities are investigating an al-Qaida affiliated network with transnational ties to Pakistan, Spain, Morocco, Algeria, Tunisia, and Syria, and possible links to September 11, 2001 attacks in the United States.

14 March   **Israel**
In Ashdod Port, Israel, two suicide bombers launched near-simultaneous attacks inside a workshop and outside the port, killing 10 and wounding 18 others. HAMAS and the al-Aqsa Martyrs Brigade claimed joint responsibility.

15 March   **India**
In the Sopore area of Baramula District, Kashmir, India, armed militants shot and killed a retired police officer. No group claimed responsibility

Iraq
In Mosul, Iraq, attackers launched a machine-gun attack, killing four US citizens and wounding one other. The victims were missionaries associated with the Southern Baptist International Mission Board. No group claimed responsibility.

16 March   **Iraq**
Near Karbala, Iraq, gunmen attacked a vehicle, killing four German hydraulic engineers and two Iraqis, and wounding two other German engineers. The engineers worked for a company contracted by the Iraqi Ministry of Irrigation for projects in the Karbala area. No group claimed responsibility.

Iraq
Near Hilla, Iraq, unidentified gunmen shot and killed two European engineers (1 German; 1 Danish) and two Iraqi nationals. No group claimed responsibility.

17 March   **Iraq**
In Baghdad, Iraq, a car bomb exploded at the Mount Lebanon Hotel (Jabal Libnan Hotel), killing seven civilians, including one Briton, and wounding 35 others. The attack also caused significant damage to the hotel and surrounding homes, offices, shops, and cars. Although the hotel was known to be frequented by westerners, US officials believe that the hotel may not have been the target of the attack. No group claimed responsibility, although it is widely believed that either Abu Mus'ab al-Zarqawi's Jama'at al Tawid wa'al-Jihad, al-Qaida, or Ansar al-lslam was responsible for the attack.

18 March   **India**
In Srinagar, Kashmir, India, Islamic militants invaded the home of a political party activist, forced him out of the house, and shot and killed him. No group claimed responsibility.

19 March   **Israel**
In Jerusalem, Israel, gunmen shot and killed an Israeli student. The al-Aqsa Martyrs Brigade claimed responsibility.

22 March   **Iraq**
In Baghdad, Iraq, unidentified gunmen shot and killed two Finnish businessmen on their way to a meeting with the Ministry of Electricity. One victim worked in the electrical and power networks field, and the other victim specialized in constructing railways. No group claimed responsibility.

Israel
In Jaffa, Israel, an Arab youth on a bus attacked and wounded three Israelis with a knife. Israeli police attributed this incident to retaliation for the death of HAMAS leader Ahmed Yassin. No group claimed responsibility.

Israel
Outside an army base near Tel Aviv, Israel, a Palestinian attacked and wounded three people with an axe. Israeli police attributed this incident to retaliation for the death of HAMAS leader Ahmed Yassin. No group claimed responsibility.

23 March   **Serbia**
Near the village of Shakovica, in Podujevo, Kosovo, a region administered by the UN, gunmen attacked a police patrol, killing a Ghanaian police officer from the United Nations Interim Mission in Kosovo (UNMIK) and a Kosovo Police Service (SHPK) officer, and wounding a language interpreter. No group claimed responsibility, but authorities believe Albanian nationalists were responsible.

27 March   **India**
In Udhampur District, Kashmir, India, armed militants shot and killed a special police officer. No group claimed responsibility.

India
In Hasgmat Village, Doda District, Kashmir, India, armed militants invaded a home and shot to death the resident. No group claimed responsibility.

India
At Khooni Nallah, in Poonch District, Kashmir, India, armed militants attacked a security patrol, killing one civilian and injuring two security personnel. No group claimed responsibility.

Thailand
In Sunhai Kolok District, Narathiwat Province, Thailand, a bomb hidden on a motorcycle exploded outside the "TopTen 2004" karaoke bar and Marina Hotel, injuring 28 people, including 8 Malaysians. No group claimed responsibility, but authorities believe the attackers were Islamic militants.

28 March   **India**
In the Anantang District, Kashmir, India, Islamic militants shot and killed a police officer as he waited for a bus. No group claimed responsibility.

Iraq
In Mosul, Iraq, unidentified gunmen attacked a convoy, enroute to a power station in Mosul, killing two private security guards (1 British; 1 Canadian). Three other British engineers traveling in the same convoy escaped unharmed. No group claimed responsibility.

31 March   **Iraq**
In Fallujah, Iraq, unidentified assailants ambushed a contractor convoy, killing four US civilian contractors and setting

them ablaze. The burned bodies of the four Americans were mutilated and dragged through the streets, and at least two bodies were hanged from a bridge over the Euphrates River. The contractors, employed by Blackwater Security Consulting of North Carolina, were providing security for food-delivery trucks headed to a US military base at the time of the attack. The Brigades of Martyr Ahmed Yassim claimed responsibility.

1   April   Iraq

In Fallujah, Iraq, unknown assailants attacked a convoy and detained two German security guards. According to Germany's Foreign Ministry, one of the guards was found dead on 1 May 2004. As of 29 March 2005, the disposition of the second victim was unknown. No group claimed responsibility

2   April   Somalia

Near Berbera, Somalia, militants attacked aid workers from the German Agency for Technical Assistance, killing a Kenyan and injuring a German aid worker. No group claimed responsibility, but it is widely believed that al-Qaida was responsible.

3   April   West Bank

In the Avnei Hafetz and Enav settlements, West Bank, gunmen attacked two neighboring Israeli settlements, killing one Israeli and wounding a child. HAMAS and Palestine Islamic Jihad claimed joint responsibility

5   April   India

In Doda, Kashmir, India, Islamic militants began shooting at a police post, killing one police officer. No group claimed responsibility.

Iraq

In Nasiriyah, Iraq, militants abducted a British citizen as he traveled from a US base. The abductors later released him on 11 April 2004. No group claimed responsibility.

Nepal

Near the Indian border, in Kailali District, Nepal, attackers set nine empty Indian tanker trucks on fire. No group claimed responsibility, although it is widely believed that the Communist Party of Nepal (Maoist)/United People's Front was responsible.

6   April   India

In Rajpora Chowk, Pulwama District, Kashmir, India, armed militants threw a grenade at a Border Security Force vehicle, but missing the intended target and hitting a crowded marketplace, wounding three police officers and 61 civilians, including two children. India was preparing for national elections (20 April to 13 May) when the attack occurred. No group claimed responsibility.

India

In Pattan, Kashmir, India, armed militants shot and killed a former militant. India was preparing for national elections (20 April to 13 May) when the attack occurred. No group claimed responsibility.

Iraq

In Nasiriyah, Iraq, unknown assailants opened fire on a convoy of trucks, killing a Bulgarian driver. No group claimed responsibility.

7   April   India

In Parigam Village, Anantang District, Kashmir, India, armed militants invaded a home and shot and killed a young girl. India was preparing for national elections (20 April to 13 May) when the attack occurred. No group claimed responsibility.

India

In Payar, Pulwama District, Kashmir, India, armed militants invaded a house, and shot and killed the occupant. India was preparing for national elections (20 April to 13 May) when the attack occurred. No group claimed responsibility.

India

In Dadarhama Village, Pulwama, Kashmir, India, armed militants shot and killed a man. India was preparing for national elections (20 April to 13 May) when the attack occurred. No group claimed responsibility.

Iraq

In Kut, Iraq, unknown assailants entered a home and attacked the occupants, killing one South African contractor. No group claimed responsibility.

Iraq

Near Baghdad, Iraq, unknown assailants used a rocket-propelled grenade to attack a diplomatic convoy from Amman, Jordan, killing a South African contractor. The convoy had been carrying Iraqi diplomats and Jordanian ministers. No group claimed responsibility.

Malaysia

In Kuala Lumpur, Malaysia, four Rohingya Burmese Muslims armed with an axe, knives, and iron rods climbed over the walls of the Myanmar Embassy, doused it with gasoline, and set fire to the building, destroying 70 percent of the embassy. The attackers also seriously wounded the embassy's minister-counselor and an embassy staff member. The four assailants were arrested and charged with attempted murder and the destruction of property. No group claimed responsibility.

8   April   India

In Uri, Kashmir, India, a bomb exploded at an election rally, killing nine civilians and wounding 50 others, including two elected officials. India was preparing for national elections (20 April to 13 May) when the attack occurred. The Save Kashmir Movement claimed responsibility.

Iraq

In Baghdad, Iraq, unknown assailants kidnapped an Israeli employee of USAID and a Syrian-born Canadian employee of the International Relief Committee. Both victims were freed in April 2004. Ansar al-Din claimed responsibility.

Iraq

In Iraq, unidentified assailants kidnapped a Canadian citizen, who had been carrying out repair work at the Abu Ghraib prison. As of the end of 2004, the disposition of the victim was unknown. No group claimed responsibility.

Iraq

Near Baghdad, Iraq, unknown assailants attacked a US civilian vehicle, killing one US contractor. No group claimed responsibility.

Iraq

In Iraq, unknown assailants kidnapped three Japanese civilians. The attackers later released a video, threatening the victims with guns and knives, and saying they would burn the victims alive if Japan did not withdraw its 550 troops within three days. On 15 April 2004, the three Japanese civilians were released. The Mujahideen Brigades (Saraya al-Mujaheddin) claimed responsibility.

9 April   Iraq

In Baghdad, Iraq, Militants kidnapped and later killed a US businessman. An Islamist website broadcast a video, which showed the victim's decapitation and ended with an appearance of Abu Musab Al-Zarqawi's signature and the date 11 May 2004. Abu Mus'ab al-Zarqawi's Jama'at al-Tawhid wa'al-Jihad claimed responsibility.

Iraq

In Hit, Iraq, unknown assailants opened fire on a group of security officers guarding electrical contractors, killing one British security guard. No group claimed responsibility.

Iraq

Near Baghdad, Iraq, unknown assailants attacked a civilian vehicle, and eight US contractors were kidnapped. Five of the abducted contractors were found dead in April 2004. The sixth contractor was found dead on 5 January 2005. On 2 May 2004, in Tikrit, Iraq, the seventh contractor escaped from his captors unharmed. As of 18 March 2005, the eighth contractor was still missing. No group claimed responsibility.

Iraq

In northern Iraq, a civilian vehicle drove over a landmine killing the two Nepalese occupants. No group claimed responsibility.

10 April   Iraq

In Mosul, Iraq, unknown militants shot and killed a Red Crescent official and his wife. No group claimed responsibility.

Iraq

In Fallujah, Iraq, unknown assailants kidnapped seven Japanese civilians. By 12 April 2004, all victims had been released. The unknown captors were possibly trying to derail a planned visit by US vice president Dick Cheney. No group claimed responsibility.

11 April   India

In the Anantnag District, Kashmir, India, armed militants shot and killed a member of the ruling People's Democratic Party. India was preparing for national elections (20 April to 13 May) when the attack occurred. No group claimed responsibility.

Iraq

In Taji, Iraq, unknown assailants abducted and killed a Danish citizen. The body of the victim was found on 12 April 2004. No group claimed responsibility.

Iraq

In Baghdad, Iraq, unknown assailants opened fire on a security convoy, killing a Romanian civilian working for a security company and injuring one other. No group claimed responsibility.

Iraq

In Baghdad, Iraq, unidentified assailants kidnapped three Czech journalists as they prepared to journey from Baghdad to Amman. The journalists were released on 16 April 2004. No group claimed responsibility.

Philippines

Near Lingkian Island, off the coast of Sabah, between the Philippines and Malaysia, armed men boarded a barge and kidnapped two Malaysians and one Indonesian. The victims were taken to the Cagayan de Tawi-Tawi Islands near Malaysia. On 23 November 2004, on Baguan Island, Tawi-Tawi, Philippines, the Armed Forces of the Philippines recovered skeletal remains, believed to be the bodies of the three kidnapped men. The Abu Sayyaf Group claimed responsibility.

12 April   Iraq

In Basra, Iraq, assailants wearing police uniforms kidnapped one Jordanian from his hotel. As of the end of 2004, the disposition of the Jordanian was unknown. No group claimed responsibility.

Iraq

In Baghdad, Iraq, masked gunmen kidnapped eight employees (3 Russian; 5 Ukrainian) of a Russian energy company. The captors released the victims unharmed less than 24 hours later. No group claimed responsibility.

Iraq

Near Baghdad, Iraq, militants abducted four Italians working for a US security firm. The militants executed one of the hostages after the Italian government refused to remove its troops from Iraq. On 8 June, the remaining hostages were rescued, along with a Polish construction worker who had been kidnapped on 1 June 2004. A group calling itself "the Green Battalion" claimed responsibility.

Iraq
In Iraq, unknown attackers kidnapped a Jordanian citizen. As of 29 March 2005, the disposition of the victim was unknown. No group claimed responsibility.

13 April — Iraq
In Baghdad, Iraq, unidentified assailants kidnapped a French television journalist and his cameraman as they filmed a US military convoy. The cameraman was released the same day, and the journalist was freed on 14 April 2004. No group claimed responsibility.

14 April — India
In Banihal, Kashmir, India, armed militants threw a grenade at an election rally, wounding seven people. An elected official, who was speaking at the time of the blast, was not harmed. India was preparing for national elections (20 April to 13 May) when the attack occurred. No group claimed responsibility.

India
In Baramulla India, Islamic Militants set off a bomb missing their intended target, an enemy convoy, and injuring six civilians. India was preparing for national elections (20 April to 13 May) when the attack occurred. No group claimed responsibility.

15 April — Iraq
In Baghdad, Iraq, gunmen assassinated an Iranian diplomat as he drove out of the Iranian Embassy. No group claimed responsibility.

17 April — Gaza Strip
At a main border crossing between Gaza and Israel, a Palestinian suicide bomber killed an Israeli border police officer and injured three Israeli soldiers. HAMAS and the al-Aqsa Martyrs Brigade claimed joint responsibility.

19 April — Gaza Strip
In Nitzanit, Gaza Strip, a Qassam rocket struck a house in a Jewish settlement injuring one person. No group claimed responsibility.

India
In Rafiabad Village, Kashmir, India, armed militants shot and killed a police officer at a polling station. The officer was on guard duty at the polling station at the time of the shooting. India was preparing for national elections (20 April to 13 May) when the attack occurred. No group claimed responsibility.

India
In Barmula, Kashmir, India, Islamic militants detonated a bomb at a polling station injuring two civilians, two poll workers, and four police officers. India was preparing for national elections (20 April to 13 May) when the attack occurred. No group claimed responsibility.

India
In Sopore, Kashmir, India, Islamic militants threw a grenade near a polling station injuring five policemen and two civilians. India was preparing for national elections (20 April to 13 May) when the attack occurred. No group claimed responsibility.

Venezuela
In Bolivar, Venezuela, armed individuals hijacked a state police helicopter and forced the pilot to fly out of the area. The pilot was later released. No group claimed responsibility, although the governor of Bolivar State claimed that the hijackers were guerrillas from the Revolutionary Armed Forces of Columbia (FARC).

20 April — Gaza Strip
In Nitzanit, Gaza Strip, a rocket struck the house of a Jewish settler, injuring three people and causing significant damage to the house. No group claimed responsibility.

India
In Bandipura, Kashmir, India, Islamic militants detonated a remote-controlled landmine near a polling station, injuring three civilians and a policeman. India was in the midst of national elections (20 April to 13 May) when the attack occurred. No group claimed responsibility.

21 April — India
In the Pulwama District, Kashmir, India, armed militants threw a grenade at a campaign vehicle, missing the target and injuring 11 civilians on the roadside. India was in the midst of national elections (20 April to 13 May) when the attack occurred. No group claimed responsibility.

Saudi Arabia
In Riyadh, Saudi Arabia, a car bomb exploded at the Public Security Department, killing 5 people, including one Syrian child and wounding 148 other civilians. No group claimed responsibility, although it is widely believed that al-Qaida was responsible.

22 April — India
In Srinagar, Kashmir, India, a truck bomb exploded, killing two people and wounding one other. India was in the midst of national elections (20 April to 13 May) when the attack occurred. No group claimed responsibility.

India
In Srinagar, Kashmir, India, a bomb exploded, killing two laborers and injuring six others. India was in the midst of national elections (20 April to 13 May) when the attack occurred. No group claimed responsibility.

Iraq
In the Adhamiyah neighborhood, Baghdad, Iraq, a gunman killed a Spanish civilian and seriously wounded his Iraqi translator. No group claimed responsibility.

Iraq

In Baghdad, Iraq, unknown gunmen shot and killed a South African security guard and injured his translator. No group claimed responsibility.

23 April   **India**

In Srinagar, Kashmir, India, armed militants attacked the offices of a political party with guns and grenades, wounding three soldiers and two journalists. India was in the midst of national elections (20 April to 13 May) when the attack occurred. No group claimed responsibility.

Japan

In Osaka, Japan, a Japanese man rammed a bus into the front gate of the Chinese Consulate General, causing no injuries, but setting fire to the vehicle and damaging the gate. The perpetrator attacked the Consulate in protest against China's claim of possession of the Senkaku Islands. No group claimed responsibility.

24 April   **Angola**

Near Massabi, in Cabinda, Angola, unknown attackers opened fire with machine guns and mortars, killing six (3 Angolan; 3 Congolese) and wounding 10 others. No group claimed responsibility.

Bosnia

In Pale, Bosnia-Herzegovina, a bomb exploded next to the police station on Srpskih Ratnika Street, blowing out the building's windows, destroying the car of the ex-police chief, and damaging a European Union Police Mission vehicle. No group claimed responsibility.

25 April   **India**

In the Kulgam District, Kashmir, India, Islamic militants threw grenades and fired shots at the motorcade of the People's Democratic Party president, killing four people and wounding 45 others. The political party president escaped unharmed. India was in the midst of national elections (20 April to 13 May) when the attack occurred. No group claimed responsibility.

India

In Srinagar, Kashmir, India, Islamic militants launched a grenade at a police station, wounding 13 police officers. India was in the midst of national elections (20 April to 13 May) when the attack occurred. No group claimed responsibility.

India

In Khool-Noorabad Village, Kashmir, India, a grenade exploded at a political rally, killing one civilian and wounding nine others. India was in the midst of national elections (20 April to 13 May) when the attack occurred. No group claimed responsibility.

Iraq

Near Bayji, Iraq, a roadside bomb exploded as a convoy of private security contractors passed, killing one US contractor and wounding two others, who later died from their wounds. No group claimed responsibility.

West Bank

In Idna near Hebron, West Bank, gunmen attacked a car carrying three Israelis, wounding all three of the passengers. No group claimed responsibility.

26 April   **India**

In Srinagar, Kashmir, India, Islamic militants threw a grenade at a government building, wounding five people. India was in the midst of national elections (20 April to 13 May) when the attack occurred. No group claimed responsibility.

India

In Kupwara District, Kashmir, India, armed militants shot and killed a civilian outside his home. India was preparing for national elections (20 April to 13 May) when the attack occurred. No group claimed responsibility.

27 April   **India**

During the night, in Kashmir, India, Islamic militants kidnapped a political party worker. India was in the midst of a national election (20 April to 13 May) when the attack occurred. As of the end of 2004, the disposition of the victim was unknown. No group claimed responsibility.

28 April   **India**

In the Rajouri District, Kashmir, India, Islamic militants attacked an army camp with grenades and small arms, killing one soldier and wounding three others. The soldiers returned fire, killing three militants. India was in the midst of an election (20 April to 10 May) when the attack occurred. No group claimed responsibility, although authorities identified the attackers as members of Lashkar-e-Tayyiba.

India

In the Doda District, Kashmir, India, a bomb exploded at an election rally, killing three civilians and injuring 49 others. A former elected official was about to speak at the rally when the explosion occurred, but he was not harmed by the blast. India was in the midst of an election (20 April to 13 May) when the attack occurred. No group claimed responsibility.

India

In Shopian, Anantnag District, Kashmir, India, armed militants threw a grenade at a politician's motorcade, injuring two policemen and eight civilians. The political official at the center of the motorcade was not harmed. India was preparing for national elections (20 April to 13 May) when the attack occurred. No group claimed responsibility.

India

In Handwara, Kashmir, India, armed militants attacked a police station with a grenade, wounding seven policemen and seven civilians. India was in the midst of an election (20 April to 13 May) when the attack occurred. No group claimed responsibility.

29 April   **Iraq**

In Basra, Iraq, unknown gunmen killed a South African civilian in a drive-by shooting. No group claimed responsibility.

30 April   **Iraq**

In Fallujah, Iraq, unknown assailants attacked and killed a South African civilian. No group claimed responsibility.

Iraq

In southern Iraq, unknown gunmen opened fire at a convoy of vans, killing three civilians (1 Filipino; 2 Ukrainian). No group claimed responsibility.

Iraq

In Tikrit, Iraq, unknown attackers fired rocket-propelled grenades at a US convoy, killing one US contractor. No group claimed responsibility.

1 May   **Saudi Arabia**

In Yanbu, Saudi Arabia, four gunmen attacked the offices of ABB Lummus, killing six civilians (2 American; 2 British; 1 Australian; 1 Italian) and wounding 19 Saudi policemen. The gunmen then attacked a Holiday Inn, a McDonald's restaurant, and various shops before throwing a pipe bomb at the International School in Yanbu. Al-Qaida claimed responsibility.

2 May   **Gaza Strip**

On the road between Israel and Gush Katif, Gaza Strip, gunmen ambushed a car and shot to death the occupants, a pregnant Jewish settler and her four children. The Popular Resistance Committee and the al-Aqsa Martyrs Brigade claimed joint responsibility.

Iraq

In Mosul, Iraq, a bomb exploded, killing two Fijian security guards and injuring two others. The British private security firm, Global Risk Strategies, employed all four people. No group claimed responsibility.

3 May   **India**

In Srinagar, Kashmir, India, Islamic militants threw a grenade at the residence of a People's Democratic Party candidate, injuring eight people. India was preparing for national elections (20 April to 13 May) when the attack occurred. No group claimed responsibility.

Iraq

In Baghdad, Iraq, unknown assailants kidnapped a US citizen. As of 18 March 2005, the American was still being held hostage. A group calling itself the Islamic Rage Brigade claimed responsibility.

Nepal

In Parbat, Nepal, assailants kidnapped and hanged a former Indian Army Officer. No group claimed responsibility, although it is widely believed the Communist Party of Nepal (Maoism)/United People's Front was responsible.

Pakistan

In Gwadar, Baluchistan Province, Pakistan, a car bomb exploded, killing three Chinese engineers and wounding 11 other people. No group claimed responsibility.

4 May   **India**

In Anantnag, Kashmir, India, Islamic militants fired a grenade at a police camp outside a polling station, injuring six people, including two poll workers. India was preparing for national elections (20 April to 13 May) when the attack occurred. No group claimed responsibility.

India

In Bijbehara, Kashmir, India, Islamic militants fired a grenade at an election polling station, injuring one police officer. India was in the midst of national elections (20 April to 13 May) when the attack occurred. No group claimed responsibility.

5 May   **Afghanistan**

In Mandol, Laghman Province, Afghanistan, militants killed two British contractors working for the London-based company Global Risk Strategies and their Afghan translator. The victims were working to register Afghan citizens for the forthcoming elections. The Taliban claimed responsibility.

India

In the Anantnag District, Kashmir, India, armed militants fired a grenade at a general election polling facility, missing their target and killing one civilian and wounding three others. India was in the midst of national elections (20 April to 13 May) when the attack occurred. No group claimed responsibility.

India

In Bijbehara, Kashmir, India, Islamic militants threw a grenade near a polling station, injuring five policemen and ten civilians. India was in the midst of national elections (20 April to 13 May) when the attack occurred. No group claimed responsibility.

7 May   **Iraq**

In Latafiya, Iraq, unidentified gunmen attacked a crew working for Poland's TVP television, killing a Polish war correspondent, his producer and wounding their cameraman. No group claimed responsibility.

8 May   **Afghanistan**

Near the village of Grabawa, in the Nangarhar Province, Afghanistan, an improvised explosive device exploded, injuring one Afghan UN election worker. No group claimed responsibility.

9 May   **India**

In Doda, Kashmir, India, Islamic militants threw a hand grenade and began shooting at a polling station, injuring three police officers and three civilians. India was in the midst of national elections (20 April to 13 May) when the attack occurred. Hizbul-Mujahedin claimed responsibility.

India
In the Doda District, Kashmir, India, Islamic militants threw a grenade at a motorcade, killing one government official and wounding four police officers and 17 civilians. India was in the midst of national elections (20 April to 13 May) when the attack occurred. No group claimed responsibility, although it is widely believed that Hizbul-Mujahedin was responsible.

Iraq
In Baghdad, Iraq, an improvised explosive device exploded behind the Four Seasons Hotel (Al-Fossul Al-Arabaa Hotel), injuring six security guards (2 British; 2 Nepalese; 2 Iraqi). The blast also damaged the hotel's ceiling and spread debris through the dining room. No group claimed responsibility.

10 May — Iraq
In Kirkuk, Iraq, unidentified gunmen killed a New Zealand engineer, a South African engineer, and an Iraqi driver as they worked on a reconstruction project. No group claimed responsibility.

Iraq
In Musayyib, Iraq, unknown militants attacked a vehicle, killing one Russian, injuring an Iraqi, and abducting two other Russians. The two abducted Russians were released on 17 May 2004. No group claimed responsibility.

11 May — Iraq
Near Rutba, Iraq, unknown gunmen attacked a civilian convoy traveling from Syria to Baghdad, injuring four drivers, destroying seven trucks, and seizing eight other trucks. The 20-vehicle convoy belonged to a Turkish subcontractor affiliated with US contracting company Kellogg, Brown & Root. Despite initial reports of kidnappings, all 20 drivers reached Baghdad in the surviving 5 vehicles. No group claimed responsibility.

Iraq
In Mosul, Iraq, unknown gunmen attacked employees of Yuksel Insaat, a Turkish construction firm, killing a Turkish worker and his Turkish driver. No group claimed responsibility.

14 May — Iraq
In Baghdad, Iraq, unknown gunmen entered the residence of a British contractor and killed him. Although no group claimed responsibility, a witness indicated that the attackers were members of the Baghdad police force.

15 May — Nepal
In the Palpa District, Nepal, assailants set fire to three Indian tour buses, destroying the vehicles. No group claimed responsibility, although it is widely believed the Communist Party of Nepal Maoism/United People's Front was responsible.

17 May — India
In the Kupwara District, Kashmir, India, armed militants invaded a home and opened fire, killing two civilians and injuring one other. No group claimed responsibility.

18 May — India
In Kashmir, India, militants lobbed a hand grenade at a police patrol, missing their target and hitting a crowded bus stop, wounding three children, three civilians, and one police officer. No group claimed responsibility.

Iraq
In Mosul, Iraq, masked militants in a car attacked two civilian vehicles, killing one British security contractor working for ArmorGroup, a London-based company. The vehicles were believed to be carrying foreign reconstruction contractors. No group claimed responsibility.

20 May — India
In Baramula, Kashmir, India, armed militants abducted two people from their home and killed them. Both victims were sons of a retired security officer. No group claimed responsibility.

India
In Bandh Village, Pulwama, Kashmir, India, armed militants captured a polling agent for the People's Democratic Party, tortured him outside the village, and then abandoned him. The attackers also shot five passing villagers in their legs. No group claimed responsibility.

Turkey
In the Acibadem District of Istanbul, Turkey, a bomb exploded in the parking lot of a McDonald's restaurant, breaking windows, destroying one car, and damaging several other vehicles. No group claimed responsibility.

21 May — Bangladesh
In Sylhet, Chittagong Division, Bangladesh, a bomb exploded at the Hazrat Shahjalal shrine, killing three people and injuring 100 others, including the British High Commissioner to Bangladesh. No group claimed responsibility.

India
In Chadoura, Budgam District, Kashmir, India, Islamic militants detonated a bomb near a security post killing two children and one adult and wounding 24 others. No group claimed responsibility, but authorities considered Hizbul-Mujahedin responsible.

22 April — Iraq
In Baghdad, Iraq, a Syrian suicide bomber attempted to assassinate the Iraqi deputy interior minister. The blast injured the minister and 12 others, and killed four police officers and an unidentified woman. Abu Mus'ab al Zarqawi's Jama'at al-Tawhid wa'al Jihad claimed responsibility

Saudi Arabia
In Riyadh, Saudi Arabia, unknown gunmen shot and killed a German national. No group claimed responsibility.

West Bank
In the West Bank, a suicide bomber detonated his explosive device at an army checkpoint injuring an Israeli soldier and four civilians. No group claimed responsibility.

23 May — India
Near Lowermunda, Kashmir, India, Islamic militants detonated a bomb under a bus killing three children six women and 19 police officers, and wounding two civilians and 13 police officers. Hizbul Mujahedin claimed responsibility.

Mexixo
In Juitepec, Mexico, bombs exploded at three banks throughout the city, causing property damage at the Bencomer, Banamex, and Santander Serfin facilities. No casualties reported. The Comodo Jaramillista Morelense 23 de Mayo group claimed responsibility.

24 May — Iraq
In Baghdad, Iraq, a bomb exploded near the entrance of the green zone, killing two Britons and wounding two others as they passed in an armored vehicle. No group claimed responsibility,

25 May — West Bank
In Hebron, West Bank, unknown attackers threw an explosive device at a vehicle, wounding an Israeli civilian. No group claimed responsibility.

26 May — Iraq
In Baghdad, Iraq, unidentified gunman fired on a bus carrying employees of Interenergoservis, a Russian energy firm, killing three Russian specialists and injuring four others. As a result of the incident and pervious attacks on Interenergoservis staff, the company ordered its 234 remaining employees to leave Iraq. No group claimed responsibility.

27 May — India
In Pulwama District, Kashmir, India, armed militants shot and killed a former Special Police Officer in his home. No group claimed responsibility.

Iraq
South of Baghdad, Iraq, unidentified gunmen fired on a civilian vehicle, killing two Japanese journalists and one Iraqi translator, and injuring their Iraqi driver. No group claimed responsibility.

Iraq
In Baghdad, Iraq, unidentified attackers killed a Turkish truck driver. No group claimed responsibility.

Nepal
Near Tilkapur, Nawalparasi District, Nepal, assailants set fire to an Indian jeep and passenger bus on the Mahendra Highway. No group claimed responsibility, although it is widely believed the Communist Party of Nepal (Maoism)/United People's Front was responsible.

28 May — Greece
In Thessaloniki, Greece, unknown assailants detonated a bomb under a car belonging to a Turkish Black Sea Bank employee. The blast, which occurred at the employee's apartment building, destroyed the car and damaged two other vehicles. No injuries were reported. No group claimed responsibility.

29 May — Democratic Republic of the Congo
Near Bukavu, Democratic Republic of the Congo, unidentified armed men attacked and killed a military observer from the UN Mission in the Democratic Republic of the Congo (MONUC) and slightly wounded another. No group claimed responsibility.

30 May — Iraq
In Baghdad, Iraq, unknown gunmen opened fire on a convoy traveling to Baghdad International Airport, killing an American contractor. No group claimed responsibility.

Saudi Arabia
In Al-Khobar, Saudi Arabia, militants attacked two oil industry compounds, housing offices, and employee apartments, killing 22 civilians ([including] 1 American; 8 Indian; 3 Filipino; 2 Sri Lankan; 1 Swedish; 1 Italian; 1 British; 1 Egyptian; 1 South African) and wounding 25 Saudi civilians. Al-Qaida claimed responsibility.

1 June — Iraq
In Baghdad, Iraq, unknown assailants kidnapped two Polish construction workers, three Kurdish security guards, and two Iraqi female employees. Between 2 June 2004 and 7 June 2004, one of the Polish victims escaped from his captors. On 8 June 2004, coalition forces rescued the second Polish captive. As of 29 March 2005, the disposition of the Iraqi and Kurdish victims was unknown. No group claimed responsibility.

2 June — Afghanistan
In Qades, Badghis Province, Afghanistan, assailants attacked a vehicle belonging to the Doctors Without Borders aid group, killing five aid workers (1 Belgian; 1 Norwegian; 1 Dutch; 2 Afghan). No group claimed responsibility.

India
In Anantnag, Kashmir, India, armed militants shot and killed a People's Democratic Party member outside his home. No group claimed responsibility.

Iraq
In southern Iraq, an improvised explosive device exploded as a vehicle passed, killing an American contractor. No group claimed responsibility.

3 June — India
In Doda, Kashmir, India, armed militants threw a grenade at a police patrol, missing their target and wounding seven civilians. No group claimed responsibility.

4 June — Russia

In Samara, Russia, a bomb exploded at a busy section of a market near a rail line, killing at least 11 civilians ([including] 2 Armenians; 3 Vietnamese), and injuring 71 others. No group claimed responsibility, but officials detained Chechen separatists from Kazakhstan on 10 June 2004 in connection with the incident.

5 June — Iraq

In Baghdad, Iraq, militants attacked and killed four security contractors (2 American; 2 Polish) and injured one other Polish contractor. The US-based security company, Blackwater, employed the four contractors. Abu Mus'ab al-Zarqawi's Jama'at al-Tawhid wa'al-Jihad claimed responsibility.

Iraq

In Al Asad, Iraq, a vehicle struck a landmine, killing an American contractor and destroying the vehicle. No group claimed responsibility.

Iraq

Near Baghdad, Iraq, attackers kidnapped a Kuwaiti truck driver who was delivering supplies to the US military. As of the end of 2004, the disposition of the Kuwaiti hostage was unknown. A group calling itself the Waqas Islamic Brigade claimed responsibility.

Sudan

In Darfur Region, Sudan, militants kidnapped 16 aid workers, including three unidentified foreigners and 13 Sudanese. The militants claimed the detention of the aid workers had been for their protection, since the aid workers were in militant territory, and released them on 6 June 2004. The Sudanese Liberation Army claimed responsibility.

6 June — Iraq

In Mosul, Iraq, gunmen attacked a civilian convoy, killing a British contractor and wounding three others. No group claimed responsibility.

Saudi Arabia

In Riyadh, Saudi Arabia, an unknown gunman fired at two BBC journalists, both British, killing one and injuring the other. No group claimed responsibility, although it is widely believed that al-Qaida was responsible.

7 June — Iraq

In Fallujah, Iraq, unknown assailants abducted two Turkish businessmen, working for the Serka Insaat construction firm. One of the victims was released on 8 June 2004, and the other victim was released by 4 December 2004. No group claimed responsibility.

8 June — Chile

In Santiago, Chile, a group of hooded individuals hurled bombs at a McDonald's restaurant, completely destroying the restaurant. The attack came during a demonstration calling for the release of prisoners who had been behind bars for more than 10 years on terrorism charges. This was one of several attacks in a three-day period, all seemingly related to an anti-terror legislation bill. No group claimed responsibility.

Saudi Arabia

At a villa in northeast Riyadh, Saudi Arabia, five unknown gunmen in a car shot and killed an American citizen working for the Vinnell Corporation, which had been contracted by the US Army to train the Saudi National Guard. Al-Qaida claimed responsibility.

9 June — Iraq

In Fallujah, Iraq, gunmen kidnapped two Turkish contractors. On 6 July 2004, the two contractors were released when their company agreed to stop supplying the US military with air conditioning units. Abu Mus'ab al-Zarqawi's Jama'at al-Tawhid wa'al-Jihad claimed responsibility.

Nepal

In Chobhar, on the outskirts of Kathmandu, Nepal, Several timed improvised explosive devices exploded at the Modern Indian School grounds, destroying one school bus and damaging six others. No group claimed responsibility, although it is widely believed the communist party of Nepal(Maoism)/ United People's Front was responsible.

10 June — Afghanistan

In Kunduz province, Afghanistan, assailants fired upon a road construction site, killing 11 Chinese engineers and wounding five others, including four Chinese. No group claimed responsibility, but in October 2004 four men were arrested and convicted of the attack.

Iraq

In Iraq, militants abducted seven Turkish citizens. The victims were released on 12 June 2004. A group calling itself the Jihad Squadrons claimed responsibility.

Iraq

In Iraq, unidentified attackers kidnapped a Lebanese citizen. The victim was released on 17 June, 2004. A group calling itself the Islamic Anger Brigades claimed responsibility.

12 June — India

In Kashmir, India, Islamic militants threw a grenade into a crowded hotel killing one child and three adults, and wounding six other children and 18 other adults. Al-Nasreen claimed responsibility

India

In Handwara, Kashmir, India, armed militants threw a grenade at a security patrol, missing their target and wounding 23 civilians. No group claimed responsibility.

Iraq

In Fallujah, Iraq, unknown assailants kidnapped a Lebanese citizen, and then shot and killed him. No group claimed responsibility,

Saudi Arabia

In Riyadh, Saudi Arabia, three militants shot and killed an American citizen, working for Advanced Electronics Company, as he parked his car in front of his villa. Al-Qaida claimed responsibility

Saudi Arabia

In Riyadh, Saudi Arabia, attackers abducted an American contractor. On 19 June 2004, an Islamic website posted pictures of the victim's decapitated body which was later found on a street in eastern Riyadh. The al-Qaida Organization in the Arabian Peninsula claimed responsibility.

13 June   India

In Khowai, West Tripura, India, militants kidnapped five Bangladeshi traders. As of 29 March 2005, the disposition of the victims were unknown. No group claimed responsibility, but it is widely believed that the All Tripura Tiger Force was responsible.

14 June   India

In Rirum, Baramulla, Kashmir, India, armed militants threw a grenade at a home, killing two civilians and injuring one other. No group claimed responsibility.

India

Near Kuri Village, Tripura, India, militants abducted 37 people (24 Bangladeshi; 13 Indian) on a remote road in the state. On 15 June 2005, the assailants released the Indian captives. As of 29 March 2005, the disposition of the 24 Bangladeshi captives was unknown. The National Liberation Front of Tripura claimed responsibility.

India

Near Kunzer Village, Kashmir, India, armed militants attacked and killed a government worker. No group claimed responsibility.

Iraq

In Al-Tahrir Square, near Al-Sa'dun Street, Baghdad, Iraq, a suicide car bomber detonated his explosives next to a convoy of General Electric contractors, killing 13 people ([including] 2 British; 1 French; 1 American; 1 Filipino) and wounding 60 others, including two Sudanese. The blast also destroyed eight vehicles and nearby buildings. Abu Mus'ab al-Zarqawi's Jama'at al-Tawhid wa'al-Jihad claimed responsibility.

Iraq

In Iraq, unknown assailants kidnapped a US contractor. On 21 June 2004, the victim was found dead in a Baghdad morgue. No group claimed responsibility.

15 June   India

In Kulgam, Kashmir, India, Islamic militants threw a grenade at a security patrol, wounding 10 Muslim students. No group claimed responsibility.

India

In Dangerpora area, Kashmir, India, Islamic militants killed the brother of a Kashmiri politician. No group claimed responsibility.

India

In the Dangerpora area, Sopore, Kashmir, India, armed militants invaded the home of a Kashmiri lawmaker from the Congress Party and attacked the occupants, killing the lawmaker's brother and wounding his cousin. No group claimed responsibility.

Iraq

In Baghdad, Iraq, militants attacked and killed one Iraqi national and wounded two foreign contractors as they passed beneath an overpass. No group claimed responsibility.

Iraq

In Iraq, militants took two Lebanese construction workers hostage. Both victims were released on 19 June 2004. No group claimed responsibility.

16 June   Afghanistan

Near Kunduz City, Kunduz Province, Afghanistan, an improvised explosive device exploded near a vehicle belonging to the German-run Provincial Reconstruction Team, killing four Afghans and wounding one other. No group claimed responsibility, but it is widely believed that al-Qaida was responsible.

Iraq

In Ramadi, Iraq, unidentified assailants detonated a car bomb, killing four Iraqi policemen and wounding a foreigner. The blast also destroyed an Iraqi police car and one other vehicle. No group claimed responsibility.

17 June   India

In Sopore, Kashmir, India, Islamic militants attacked a security patrol with a grenade, killing one guard and wounding four others and 12 civilians. No group claimed responsibility.

Iraq

In Iraq, unidentified assailants kidnapped a South Korean contractor and beheaded him on 22 June 2004. Abu Mus'ab al-Zarqawi's Jama'at al-Tawhid wa'al-Jihad claimed responsibility.

Iraq

At an unspecified location in Iraq, a landmine exploded as a convoy passed, killing a US contractor. No group claimed responsibility.

19 June   Iraq

Near Basra, Iraq, a remote-control improvised explosive device exploded, killing a Portuguese national, an Iraqi police officer, and an Iraqi oil worker. No group claimed responsibility.

20 June   **Pakistan**

In Chaman, Baluchistan Province, Pakistan, assailants destroyed an oil tanker belonging to Shell Pakistan Limited, a majority-owned subsidiary of Royal Dutch Shell, wounding three civilians and destroying two other tanker trucks parked in the area. The Taliban claimed responsibility.

21 June   **Afghanistan**

In Kandahar Province, Afghanistan, unknown assailants attacked a vehicle of the United Nations Assistance Mission in Afghanistan, killing one Afghan guard, wounding two others, and completely destroying the vehicle. No group claimed responsibility.

22 June   **Gaza Strip**

In Kfar Darom, Gaza Strip, unknown attackers fired small arms, mortars, and anti-tank missiles into an Israeli settlement, killing a Thai worker. The Izz al-Din al-Qassam Brigades (HAMAS) claimed responsibility.

23 June   **India**

In Bejibehara, Anantnag, Kashmir, India, Islamic militants threw a grenade at a police post, missing their target and wounding 19 civilians. No group claimed responsibility.

India

In Charsoo, Kashmir, India, militants kidnapped an Indian railway construction engineer and his brother. On 25 June 2004, in the morning, in Sugan Village, the victims' bodies were found with their throats slit. No group claimed responsibility.

24 June   **Turkey**

In Ankara, Turkey, a bomb exploded near a Hilton Hotel, injuring two police officers and a civilian. The police officers, based on an anonymous tip, were inspecting a package when it exploded near the hotel entrance. President Bush was expected to stay at the Ankara Hilton Hotel two days later, just before a NATO summit. A small leftwing Marxist group, commonly known as the MLKP-FESK, claimed responsibility.

25 June   **India**

In Tiali Kathamara Village, Kashmir, India, armed militants stormed a village and opened fire, killing twelve civilians, including one child and injuring twelve other civilians. No group claimed responsibility.

India

In Bejibehara, Kashmir, India, militants shot and killed a police officer. No group claimed responsibility.

26 June   **India**

In Surankot, Poonch District, Kashmir, India, armed militants entered a village, broke into homes, and began shooting at people as they slept, killing five children and seven men, and wounding 10 others. All of the victims were Muslim. No group claimed responsibility.

India

In Bejibehara, Kashmir, India, armed militants shot and killed a police officer. No group claimed responsibility.

Iraq

In Mosul, Iraq, militants kidnapped three Turkish workers and threatened to kill them in 72 hours if Turkey did not stop working with US forces. On 30 June 2004, the militants released the three men, unharmed. Abu Mus'ab al-Zarqawi's Jama'at al-Tawhid wa'al-Jihad claimed responsibility.

28 June   **Israel**

In S'derot, Israel, attackers fired rockets into a neighborhood, killing two Israelis and wounding 15 others. One rocket landed near a kindergarten in a residential area. HAMAS claimed responsibility.

29 June   **India**

In Srinagar, Kashmir, India, Islamic militants threw a bomb at a security post, missing their target and wounding five civilians and four police officers. No group claimed responsibility.

Israel

In S'derot, Israel, attackers fired a rocket into a neighborhood, impacting near a kindergarten and killing two Israelis, including one child, and wounding at least 10 others. HAMAS claimed responsibility.

1 July   **Iraq**

In Balad, Iraq, a roadside bomb exploded when a civilian vehicle drove over it, killing a US contractor. No group claimed responsibility.

2 July   **India**

In Srinagar, Doda District, Kashmir, India, Islamic militants detonated a remote-controlled improvised explosive device as a security convoy drove past a political rally, killing six police officers and wounding five officers and four civilians. No group claimed responsibility.

3 July   **India**

In the Dalgate area, Srinagar, Kashmir, India, Islamic militants detonated an explosive-laden hand cart near a tourist attraction on a road used by government officials, killing two people and wounding 29 others, including two children and five students. No group claimed responsibility.

India

In the Dalgate area, Srinagar, Kashmir, India, armed militants detonated a bomb, killing one civilian and injuring 13 others, including two children. No group claimed responsibility.

India

In Anantnag District, Kashmir, India, armed militants threw a grenade at a military convoy near a marketplace, injuring four soldiers and 25 civilians. No group claimed responsibility.

4 July   Iraq
In Iraq, unidentified assailants kidnapped a Filipino truck driver. The victim was later released on 22 July 2004, when President Gloria Arroyo started to pull Filipino troops out of Iraq. The Khaled Ibn al-Walid Brigade claimed responsibility.

West Bank
In Mevo Dotan, West Bank, gunmen ambushed a car, killing one Israeli settler and wounding one other. The al-Aqsa Martyrs Brigade claimed responsibility.

5 July   Gaza Strip
In N'vei Dekalim, Gaza Strip, unknown attackers fired two mortar rounds into a Jewish settlement, injuring an Israeli soldier. No group claimed responsibility.

6 July   Iraq
In Iraq, unidentified assailants kidnapped an Egyptian truck driver. The victim was released on or about 19 July 2004. A group calling itself the Iraqi Legitimate Resistance claimed responsibility.

7 July   Gaza Strip
In Netzer Hazani, Gaza Strip, attackers fired two rockets into an Israeli settlement, killing two Israeli settlers. HAMAS claimed responsibility.

8 July   Afghanistan
In Khogyani, Nangarhar Province, Afghanistan, a landmine exploded underneath a UN vehicle, killing one UN worker and injuring three others, one seriously. The Taliban claimed responsibility.

Iraq
In Iraq, unidentified assailants kidnapped two Bulgarian truck drivers and later beheaded them. On 29 July 2004, authorities found the victims' bodies in the Tigris River. Abu Mus'ab al-Zarqawi's Jama'at al-Tawhid wa'al-Jihad claimed responsibility.

9 July   Iraq
In Samarra, Iraq, unknown gunmen fired at a tanker truck as it passed, causing the vehicle to crash and killing the Turkish driver and his passenger. No group claimed responsibility.

10 July   India
In the Anantnag District, Kashmir, India, Islamic militants threw a grenade at a police car, missing their target and hitting a crowd at a bus stop, injuring 34 people. No group claimed responsibility.

11 July   Israel
In Tel Aviv, Israel, a Palestinian suicide bomber detonated his explosives at a bus stop, killing one Israeli soldier and wounding 20 civilians. The al-Aqsa Martyrs Brigade claimed responsibility.

12 July   India
In Hderpora, Kashmir, India, Islamic militants attacked a convoy, injuring three soldiers, four students, and two civilians. No group claimed responsibility.

India
In the afternoon, in Kupwara District, Kashmir, India, Islamic militants threw a grenade at soldiers, missing their target and killing a student and injuring 21 others (19 civilians; 2 police officers). No group claimed responsibility.

13 July   India
In Kashmir, India, Islamic militants fired a grenade at a motorcade, missing their target and injuring three policemen and a child. The motorcade had been escorting the Deputy Chief Minister of Kashmir, India. No group claimed responsibility.

India
In Srinagar, Kashmir, India, Islamic militants detonated a bomb near the Mughal-built Nishat Garden, killing one civilian and injuring 12 others. No group claimed responsibility.

15 July   India
In the Poonch District, Mendhar area, Kashmir, India, Islamic militants threw two grenades at a police station, killing one civilian and one police officer, and wounding three other police officers. No group claimed responsibility.

17 July   Gaza Strip
In Khan Younis, Gaza Strip, gunmen kidnapped five French aid workers at a restaurant, taking them to the local Red Crescent headquarters and ordering the building to be emptied. The hostages were released unharmed after several hours. The Abu al-Rish Brigades claimed responsibility.

Iraq
Near Ramadi, Iraq, unidentified militants shot and killed a Jordanian truck driver who had been transporting supplies from Amman to Baghdad. No group claimed responsibility.

Iraq
In Mosul, Iraq, unidentified assailants attacked a convoy, killing one Turk and abducting a Turkish driver, who was released on 31 July 2004. No group claimed responsibility.

18 July   India
In Shopian, Kashmir, India, armed militants threw a grenade into the home of a senior Congress leader, killing him and his wife, and seriously injuring their daughter. No group claimed responsibility.

19 July   India
In Srinagar, Kashmir, India, Islamic militants threw a grenade into the middle of a political rally, killing five civilians and injuring 50 others. The attack was intended to assassinate the Deputy Chief Minister of Indian Kashmir, but the official escaped unharmed. No group claimed responsibility.

Iraq

In Mosul, Iraq, unidentified gunmen fired on a car, killing a local Turkmen leader and a Turkmen broadcaster and injuring two other people. No group claimed responsibility.

Israel

In Tel Aviv, Israel, gunmen shot and killed an Israeli judge outside his home. The al-Aqsa Martyrs Brigade claimed responsibility.

20 July — India

In Gurdan Village, Rajouri District, Kashmir, India, armed militants shot and killed a former police constable and four members of his family. No group claimed responsibility, but it is widely believed that Lashkar-e-Tayyiba was responsible.

India

In Koti Village, Doda District, Kashmir, India, Islamic militants shot and killed four police officers and injured one other. No group claimed responsibility, although it is widely believed Lashkar-e-Tayyiba was responsible.

21 July — India

In Anantnag District, Kashmir, India, armed militants shot and killed a People's Democratic Party member. No group claimed responsibility.

Iraq

In Iraq, unidentified assailants kidnapped seven foreign-national truck drivers (3 Indian; 3 Kenyan; 1 Egyptian). The kidnappers released the hostages on 1 September 2004. A group calling itself the Black Banners Division of the Islamic Secret Army claimed responsibility.

23 July — Iraq

Near Baghdad, Iraq, unidentified assailants kidnapped two Pakistani contractors and an Iraqi driver. On 28 July 2004, the militants released a videotape showing the lifeless bodies of the two contractors. The Iraqi driver was subsequently released. The Islamic Army in Iraq claimed responsibility.

Iraq

In Iraq, unidentified assailants kidnapped an Egyptian diplomat as he returned from evening prayer. The victim was released on 26 July 2004. A group calling itself the Usd Allah (Lions of God/Lions of Allah) claimed responsibility.

24 July — India

In Anantnag, Kashmir, India, Islamic militants killed two police officers and wounded two civilians during a shootout. No group claimed responsibility.

India

In Tarana Village, Balnoi area, Mendhar, Kashmir, India, an improvised explosive device exploded, injuring one civilian. No group claimed responsibility.

25 July — Gaza Strip

In N'vei Dekalim, Gaza Strip, attackers fired an anti-tank rocket into a gathering of Jewish settlers, wounding six Israeli children. HAMAS claimed responsibility.

India

In Kashmir, India, armed militants beheaded a man, his son, and his daughter. His wife was also wounded in the attack. No group claimed responsibility.

India

In Baramulla District, Kashmir, India, armed militants threw a grenade at a house, injuring a seven-year-old child. No group claimed responsibility.

Iraq

In Mosul, Iraq, unknown attackers killed a Jordanian businessman who had been accused of working as a translator for the Coalition and who had allegedly been warned to leave the country. No group claimed responsibility.

26 July — India

In Baramulla Town, Kashmir, India, Islamic militants threw a grenade at a hospital where Border Security Forces had been admitted for treatment, killing one person and injuring 30 others. No group claimed responsibility.

India

In Kishtwar Town, Doda District, Kashmir, India, an improvised explosive device exploded in a hardware store belonging to a politician, injuring a Bharatiya Janata Party leader and two of his bodyguards. No group claimed responsibility.

Iraq

In Iraq, unidentified assailants kidnapped two Jordanian truck drivers. Both drivers worked for Daoud and Partners, a Jordanian company assisting the US military with construction and food services. The victims were released on 9 August 2004. A group calling itself the Mujahedeen Corps in Iraq claimed responsibility.

27 July — India

In Srinagar, Kashmir, India, two Islamic militants shot at a hotel, killing five soldiers and wounding five others. Nearby soldiers killed the two militants during an ensuing gunfight. Al-Mansurian claimed responsibility.

Iraq

In Iraq, unidentified assailants kidnapped three Jordanian drivers and a businessman. A local tribal chief, Sheik Haj Ibrahim Jassam, located the hostages, organized a raid, and freed all four hostages on 4 August 2004. A group calling itself the Mujahedeen of Iraq, the Group of Death claimed responsibility.

28 July — Afghanistan

In Ghazni Province, Afghanistan, unknown attackers detonated a bomb at a mosque, killing two UN election workers and four Afghan civilians, seriously wounding two other UN elections workers, and destroying the mosque. No group claimed responsibility.

29 July — India

In Tral, Kashmir, India, militants beheaded a woman. No group claimed responsibility.

Iraq

In Iraq, unidentified assailants kidnapped a Somali truck driver working for a Kuwaiti company. The assailants freed the victim on 2 August 2004, after his Kuwaiti company agreed to leave Iraq. Abu Mus'ab al-Zarqawi's Jama'at al-Tawhid wa'al-Jihad claimed responsibility.

Iraq

In Baghdad, Iraq, unidentified militants invaded the apartment of a Jordanian businessman, killing one Jordanian and abducting one other. The abducted victim was subsequently released by 5 August 2004. No group claimed responsibility.

30 July — Iraq

In Baghdad, Iraq, unidentified gunmen kidnapped a Lebanese dairy farmer. On or about 10 August 2004, the captors released him. No group claimed responsibility.

Uzbekistan

In Tashkent, Uzbekistan, a suicide bomber detonated his explosives at the Israeli embassy killing two Uzbek guards. A simultaneous suicide bomber attack struck the U.S. embassy; no one was hurt in that incident. The Islamic Jihad Group of Uzbekistan claimed responsibility for the bombings.

A third explosion occurred the same afternoon at the prosecutor general's office, killing one person and wounding five others. The incidents occurred a few days after Uzbek prosecutors began their case against 15 suspects accused of aiding and/or conducting a series of bomb attacks and shootings in late March.

31 July — India

In Lohara Thawa, Bhaderwah Tehsil, Doda District, Kashmir, India, militants invaded a home and attacked the people inside, killing two men and injuring two others. No group claimed responsibility.

India

In the Kanipora Village, Anantnag District, Kashmir, India, armed militants killed two members of the Ikhwan, an Indian counter-insurgency group. No group claimed responsibility.

Iraq

In Baghdad, Iraq, a Lebanese director of Lara Construction Company was kidnapped. The disposition of the victim was unknown as of the end of 2004. No group claimed responsibility.

1 August — Iraq

In Bayji, Iraq, an improvised explosive device exploded as a convoy carrying construction supplies passed, killing an American military contractor and two Iraqi civilians and wounding two other American contractors. No group claimed responsibility,

West Bank

In Nablus, West Bank, four Palestinian gunmen kidnapped three foreign church volunteers (1 American; 1 British 1 Irish) as the victims traveled home from work. The gunmen released the volunteers unharmed shortly after being surrounded by Palestinian police at the Balata refugee camp. Al-Aqsa Martyrs Brigade claimed responsibility.

2 August — Gaza Strip

In Dohoul, Gaza Strip, attackers fired a rocket into an Israeli settlement, heavily damaging the impacted area. The Izz al-Din al-Qassam Brigades (HAMAS) claimed responsibility.

India

In Lasana, Jammu, India, militants slit the throat of a Muslim woman. Militants had previously occupied the woman's home before they were discovered and killed by police. The woman was subsequently suspected of turning in the militants. No group claimed responsibility.

Iraq

In Iraq, unidentified assailants kidnapped three Turkish truck drivers and later released footage of one being shot and killed. The other two Turkish truck drivers had been released by 4 August 2004 when their employers agreed to stop shipping goods into Iraq for the US military. Abu Mus'ab al-Zarqawi's Jama'at al-Tawhid wa'al-Jihad claimed responsibility.

Iraq

In Filfayl, Iraq, unidentified attackers shot and killed a Turkish truck driver. No group claimed responsibility.

Iraq

In Baghdad, Iraq, unidentified gunmen opened fire on a truck, killing a Turkish truck driver. No group claimed responsibility.

3 August — India

In Dhara Baghia, Rajouri, Kashmir, India, armed militants entered a home and attacked the occupants, killing two Muslim civilians. No group claimed responsibility.

Saudi Arabia

In eastern Riyadh, Saudi Arabia, unknown attackers shot and killed an Irish civil engineer in his office. No group claimed responsibility, although it is widely believed that al-Qaida was responsible.

Venezuela

In La Fria, Venezuela, unknown assailants kidnapped and later killed two men for distributing identification cards to

Colombian citizens working in the Venezuelan border area. Colombian paramilitary forces claimed responsibility.

4 August — India

In Srinagar, Kashmir, India, armed militants attacked an army camp, killing nine soldiers and wounding nine others. The attack came hours before India and Pakistan met for peace talks. Al-Mansurian claimed responsibility.

India

In Raj Bagh, Srinagar, Kashmir, India, armed militants attacked a police camp, killing three policemen and wounding six others. Al-Mansurian claimed responsibility.

Iraq

In Karbala, Iraq, militants kidnapped the Iranian Consul in Karbala. He was released on 27 September 2004. A group calling itself the Islamic Army of Iraq claimed responsibility.

5 August — India

In Assam, India, militants abducted a Royal Bhutan Army soldier. On 26 August 2004, the soldier's body was found in the Dhansiri River. No group claimed responsibility, although it is widely believed that either the United Liberation Front of Assam or National Democratic Front of Bodoland was responsible.

Iraq

In Baghdad, Iraq, unknown attackers kidnapped three international civilians (2 Lebanese; 1 Syrian). On 16 August 2004, the three kidnapped men were released. No group claimed responsibility.

6 August — India

In Arigoripora, Kashmir, India, armed militants attacked a village, killing two soldiers and one civilian, and wounding two soldiers and one civilian. No group claimed responsibility.

7 August — India

In Jogma Kalan Khour, Kashmir, India, a landmine exploded, injuring three civilians. No group claimed responsibility.

8 August — India

In Pulwama District, Kashmir, India, Islamic militants detonated a roadside bomb as a convoy passed, killing one soldier. No group claimed responsibility.

India

In Kashmir, India, a landmine exploded, killing one soldier and wounding 10 others. No group claimed responsibility.

10 August — Iraq

In Iraq, unknown assailants kidnapped and decapitated an Egyptian national. Abu Mus'ab al-Zarqawi's Jama'at al-Tawhid wa'al-Jihad claimed responsibility.

Turkey

In Istanbul, Turkey, two bombs exploded simultaneously at two tourist hotels, killing two people, including one Iranian and wounding 11 others ([including] 1 Ukrainian; 2 Chinese; 4 Spanish; 2 Dutch). The Freedom Falcons of Kurdistan (aligned with the Kongra-Gel/PKK) and the Abu Hafs al-Masri Brigades both claimed responsibility, although local authorities suspected the Kongra-Gel.

11 August — Iraq

In Iraq, an improvised explosive device exploded as a convoy delivering supplies and equipment to US troops passed, killing an American truck driver. No group claimed responsibility.

Israel

In Jerusalem, Israel, a car bomb exploded on the road between two Israeli army checkpoints, killing two Palestinians and wounding seven Israelis and eight Palestinians. The al-Aqsa Martyrs Brigade claimed responsibility.

12 August — Iraq

In Baghdad, Iraq, an improvised explosive device exploded, killing an Indian contractor and wounding three others. No group claimed responsibility.

13 August — Iraq

In Basra, Iraq, 20 masked gunmen abducted a British journalist and released him the same day. A group calling itself Abu al-Abbas claimed responsibility.

Iraq

In Nasiriyah, Iraq, two armed men kidnapped a US journalist and his Iraqi translator. On 22 August 2004, the journalist and translator were released. A group calling itself the Mahdi Army claimed responsibility.

West Bank

In Itamar, West Bank, unknown attackers opened fire on a group of Israeli settlers, killing one Jewish settler and wounding one other. The Al-Aqsa Martyrs Brigade claimed responsibility.

14 August — Iraq

In Mosul, Iraq, armed assailants kidnapped two Turkish truck drivers. Police later discovered the bodies of the two victims and one unidentified man. Abu Mus'ab al-Zarqawi's Jama'at al-Tawhid wa'al-Jihad claimed responsibility.

16 August — Iraq

In Mosul, Iraq, unidentified assailants attacked a civilian convoy, killing a South African security contractor. No group claimed responsibility.

18 August — Gaza Strip

In N'vei Dekalim, Gaza Strip, unknown attackers fired two mortar rounds into an Israeli settlement, injuring two settlers. No group claimed responsibility.

India

In Malachamlan, Udhampur District, Kashmir, India armed militants broke into a home, killing a man and his three children No group claimed responsibility, but it is widely believed that Lashkar-e-Tawiba was responsible.

19 August   **Iraq**

South of Baghdad, Iraq, unknown assailants kidnapped two French journalists as they traveled to Najaf. On 28 August 2004, the captors released a video of the French journalists. On 21 December 2004, the journalists were released. No group claimed responsibility.

20 August   **Iraq**

Between Baghdad and Najaf, Iraq, militants attacked a vehicle carrying an Italian journalist, kidnapping him and killing his driver. On 26 August 2004, the journalist was executed. A group calling itself the Islamic Army in Iraq, the 1920 Brigade claimed responsibility.

Iraq

In Iraq, militants abducted 12 Nepalese employees of a Jordanian firm in Iraq. The hostages were killed on 31 August 2004. Ansar al-Sunna claimed responsibility.

Ukraine

In Kiev, Ukraine, two bombs hidden in trash cans at the Troyeshchyna Market exploded within three minutes of each other, killing one woman and injuring 13 others, including five Vietnamese and an unspecified number of Bangladeshis and Pakistanis. No group claimed responsibility, but police arrested five suspects, two of whom had membership cards from the nationalist Ukrainian People's Party (PUP). The PUP, however, denied involvement and claimed the membership cards were fake.

21 August   **India**

In Kupwara District, Kashmir, India, Islamic militants shot and killed two Indian soldiers in an ambush. No group claimed responsibility.

Spain

In San Xenxo, Spain, a small bomb in a glass-recycling container exploded near a resort, injuring four people, including two Portuguese citizens. This was one of two attacks reported in northern Spain on this day, although this was the only attack to impact international assets. The Basque Fatherland and Liberty (ETA) claimed responsibility.

22 August   **Gaza Strip**

In Morag, Gaza Strip, attackers fired three mortar rounds into a settlement, injuring nine Israelis. The Izz al-Din al-Qassam Brigades (HAMAS) claimed responsibility.

Iraq

In Mosul, Iraq, unidentified gunmen shot and killed an Indonesian engineer. No group claimed responsibility.

23 August   **India**

In Safarwaw Gund, Kashmir, India, armed militants shot and killed two Muslims believed to be police informants. No group claimed responsibility.

India

In the Budgam District, Kashmir, India, armed militants shot and killed two Muslims believed to be police informants. No group claimed responsibility.

India

In Sopore, Kashmir, India, Islamic militants killed a policeman and injured a civilian at a bus stop. No group claimed responsibility.

Iraq

In Bayji, Iraq, an unknown gunman shot and killed a Turkish oil engineer and two Iraqis as they left the Bayji oil refinery. No group claimed responsibility.

24 August   **Russia**

A suicide bomber aboard a Sibir Airlines Tu-134 airplane traveling from Domodedovo airport Moscow to Volgograd, detonated an explosive device in the lavatory, causing the plane to crash in the Tula Region, near the village of Buchaiki, Russia, killing 44 people, including one Israeli civilian. The Islambouli Brigades and the Riyad us-Saliheyn Martyrs' Brigade both claimed responsibility.

25 August   **India**

In Khara, Doda District, Kashmir, India, armed militants threw a grenade at a Central Reserve Police Force bunker, missing their target and killing two children and injuring their parents. No group claimed responsibility.

26 August   **India**

In Satipara Village, Goalpara District, Kashmir, India, a bomb exploded on a bus, killing two soldiers and a child and wounding six civilians. No group claimed responsibility, but it is widely believed that the United Liberation Front of Assam was responsible.

India

In Tangia Township, Darrang District, Kashmir, India, a grenade exploded in a crowded market, injuring seven civilians. No group claimed responsibility, but it is widely believed that the United Liberation Front of Assam was responsible.

Sudan

A group of 15 Eritreans being repatriated from Libya hijacked the Libyan military transport carrying them, slightly injuring a member of the crew and taking 69 other Eritrean passengers hostage. The hijackers, who had illegally entered Libya, forced the plane to land in Khartoum, Sudan, and demanded asylum for unspecified political reasons. The hijackers, lacking fuel for the aircraft, were then forced to surrender to Sudanese authorities. They were later sentenced to five years in prison and deported to an undisclosed location.

27 August   Iraq
In Bayji, Iraq, unknown attackers killed one Egyptian worker and abducted one other. On 5 September 2004, in Bayji, Iraq, the dead body of the abducted Egyptian was found by a roadside. No group claimed responsibility.

Iraq
In Bayji, Iraq, unidentified attackers shot and killed two civilians, including one Turk. No group claimed responsibility.

28 August   India
In Kulgam, Kashmir, India, a bomb hidden in front of a residence exploded, killing two children and injuring one other. No group claimed responsibility.

India
In Doda District, Kashmir, India, armed militants shot and killed a 56-year-old Muslim man. This attack came as India and Pakistan agreed to hold talks on Kashmir. No group claimed responsibility.

Nepal
In Basamadi, Makwanpur District, Nepal, 15 assailants detonated three bombs inside the Indian-owned Nepal Lever Public Limited Company building, causing significant damage to heavy equipment in the factory. No group claimed responsibility, although it is widely believed the Communist Party of Nepal (Maoist)/United People's Front was responsible.

Sudan
In Darfur, Sudan, unidentified armed men kidnapped eight aid workers. The victims, all Sudanese nationals, worked for the Red Crescent and the World Food Program in the militant-held area. The aid workers were later released unharmed on 1 September 2004. No group claimed responsibility, but the Government of Sudan blamed the Sudan Liberation Army (SLA).

29 August   Afghanistan
In the Shari-i-Naw area of Kabul, Afghanistan, an improvised explosive device exploded in front of a DynCorp facility, killing ten people (3 American; 3 Nepalese; 4 Afghan) and wounding 22 others (1 American; 2 Nepalese; 19 Afghan). The blast also destroyed several vehicles in the surrounding area and caused unspecified damage to the building. The Taliban claimed responsibility.

31 August   India
In Srinagar, Kashmir, India, Islamic militants threw a grenade at a bus, killing one teacher and injuring 20 civilians; including four police officers. No group claimed responsibility.

Israel
In Beersheba, Israel, two suicide bombers simultaneously blew up two Israeli buses, killing 16 people and injuring 85 others. HAMAS claimed responsibility.

Russia
In Moscow, Russia, a female suicide bomber blew herself up at the Rizhskaya subway stop, killing nine civilians and wounding more than fifty others, including a Georgian citizen. The Islambouli Brigades claimed responsibility.

1 September   India
In the Badgam District, Kashmir, India, armed militants shot and killed a senior official of the People's Democratic Party. No group claimed responsibility.

India
In Anantnag District, Kashmir, India, militants shot at two counter-insurgents, killing one and seriously wounding the other. No group claimed responsibility.

Russia
In North Ossetia, Beslan, Russia, 32 armed men and women seized School Number 1 on the first day of school, taking over 1,300 people hostage for two days with little or no food or water. On 3 September 2004, an explosion inside the gymnasium where hostages were held sparked a fierce gun battle between the hostage takers and security forces. According to official figures, 331 people were killed, 172 of them children, though many believe the actual number of deaths was higher. More than 600 others were injured. On 17 May 2005, a surviving hostage-taker will stand trial. The Riyad us-Saliheyn Martyrs' Brigade claimed responsibility.

2 September   India
In Nishbat Bagh, Srinagar, Kashmir, India, Islamic militants threw a grenade at a police station, wounding six policemen and two civilians. No group claimed responsibility.

India
Early in the day, in the Rajouri District, Kashmir, India, militants shot at a family, killing a teenage boy and injuring his mother and sister. This attack came as India and Pakistan agreed to hold talks on Kashmir. No group claimed responsibility.

Iraq
North of Baghdad, Iraq, the bodies of three Turkish truck drivers were found shot to death. No group claimed responsibility.

3 September   Afghanistan
In Jalalabad, Nangarhar Province, Afghanistan, unknown assailants fired four rockets, hitting the property of a Swedish aid agency and injuring an Afghan woman and child. No group claimed responsibility.

Afghanistan
In Kandahar, Afghanistan, a bomb exploded near a UN vehicle, killing an Afghan civilian and wounding five others, including a US liaison officer. No group claimed responsibility.

India

In Sheendara, near Poonch, Kashmir, India, Islamic militants shot and killed an Indian soldier and took two civilians hostage inside a mosque. The two civilians were rescued two hours later, but the militants escaped. No group claimed responsibility.

4   September   Iraq

In Iraq, unidentified assailants kidnapped a Turkish driver. On 6 September 2004, the kidnappers released the driver. A group calling itself the Islamic Resistance Movement, Nu'man Brigades claimed responsibility.

Iraq

In Taji, Iraq, unknown attackers fired on a vehicle returning from Camp Anaconda, killing a US contractor and critically wounding one of his bodyguards. No group claimed responsibility.

5   September   Iraq

In Fallujah, Iraq, unknown assailants kidnapped four truck drivers (3 Jordanian; 1 Sudanese). On 6 September 2004, the victims were released. A group calling itself the Fallujah Mujahideen claimed responsibility.

7   September   India

In Udhampur District, Kashmir, India, armed militants shot and killed two civilians. No group claimed responsibility.

Iraq

In Baghdad, Iraq, armed gunmen stormed a villa occupied by the Italian humanitarian aid group Bridge to Iraq, taking four hostages, including two Italians. The kidnappers released the hostages on 28 September 2004. No group claimed responsibility.

Iraq

Near Samarra, Iraq, armed men using anti-tank weapons, rocket propelled grenades, and rifles attacked a truck convoy, killing a Turkish driver and destroying his truck. No groups claimed responsibility.

8   September   India

In the village of Maria Doria, Rajouri Region, Kashmir, India, armed militants stormed a village and beheaded three Muslim civilians. No groups claimed responsibility

Nepal

In Dolpa District, Nepal, assailants kidnapped members of a medical team (1 American, 1 British, 1 Nepalese). Assailants assaulted the US citizen and robbed the team of medical supplies and equipment. The victims were ultimately released. No groups claimed responsibility, although it is widely believed that the Communist part of Nepal (Maoist)/United People's Front was responsible.

9   September   India

In the town of Doda, Kashmir, India, Islamic militants detonated a bomb under a bus carrying military personnel, killing two soldiers. Hizbul-Mujahedin claimed responsibility.

India

In Pul Doda Morh, Doda district, Kashmir, India, a bomb exploded on the road, killing three police officers and injuring four others. Hizbul-Mujahedin claimed responsibility.

India

In Kashmir, India, Islamic militants killed two civilians and injured three others during a shootout with Indian soldiers. No group claimed responsibility

Indonesia

In Jakarta, Indonesia, armed militants detonated a car bomb outside the Australian embassy, killing 10 people including nine Indonesians and wounding 182 others (4 Chinese, 1 Australian child). The car was packed with nearly 200 kilograms of explosives and caused significant damage to the embassy and nearby buildings. On 5 November 2004, Indonesian authorities captured four Jemaah Isamiya (JI) members in connected with the attack. JI claimed responsibility.

10   September   India

In Budgam District, Kashmir, India, armed militants opened fire at a military checkpoint, killing two soldiers and wounding two others. No group claimed responsibility.

Iraq

In Baghdad, Iraq, unknown gunmen disguised as Iraqi police officers attacked a house, killing three Lebanese occupants and wounding one other. No group claimed responsibility.

Iraq

In Baghdad, Iraq, unidentified gunmen opened fire on a civilian vehicle, killing one US civilian. No group claimed responsibility.

11   September   India

In Kulgam, Anantnag District, Kashmir, India, armed militants threw a grenade at the home of a Communist Party activist, killing one of the occupants and wounding one other. No group claimed responsibility.

India

In the afternoon, in Kupwara, Kashmir, India, Islamic militants threw a grenade into a crowded marketplace, killing one civilian and wounding four police officers and 16 civilians. No group claimed responsibility.

India

In Srinagar, Kashmir, India, Islamic militants fired a grenade at the York Hotel, injuring three soldiers. No group claimed responsibility.

India
In Kashmir, India, assailants attacked the Central Reserve Police Force, killing three Indian soldiers. Indian authorities associated this attack with hardliners' resistance to India-Pakistan peace talks. No group claimed responsibility.

Iraq
In Basra, Iraq, unknown attackers detonated a bomb outside a US consular office, killing one civilian and injuring two others. No group claimed responsibility.

12 September — India
In Srinagar, Kashmir, India, three armed militants launched a suicide attack on an army camp, killing three soldiers and wounding five others. One militant fled after soldiers killed two of his companions. Al-Mansurian claimed responsibility.

India
In Khanetar Top, Poonch District, Kashmir, India, Islamic militants detonated a bomb, killing one civilian and wounding one other. No group claimed responsibility.

India
In Poonch District, Kashmir, India, armed militants invaded a home and opened fire at the occupants, killing three members of a family. No group claimed responsibility, but it is widely believed that Lashkar-e-Tayyiba was responsible.

13 September — Iraq
In Iraq, armed men loyal to Abu Mus'ab al-Zarqawi abducted and beheaded a Turkish truck driver. The video of his death was broadcast on Abu Mus'ab al-Zarqawi's Jama'at al-Tawhid wa'al-Jihad group's website.

14 September — Iraq
Near Tikrit, Iraq, unknown assailants abducted two Turkish truck drivers en route to Kirkuk. As of 29 March 2005, the disposition of the victims was unknown. No group claimed responsibility.

Iraq
In Baghdad, Iraq, unknown assailants abducted a Jordanian truck driver. The kidnappers released the hostage on 16 September 2004. A group calling itself the Brigades of Al Tawhid Lions claimed responsibility.

Iraq
In Balad, Iraq, unidentified attackers fired a rocket-propelled grenade into a civilian vehicle, killing one US contractor and wounding two others. No group claimed responsibility.

Iraq
In Baghdad, Iraq, a vehicle-borne improvised explosive device exploded, killing two Canadian civilians. No group claimed responsibility.

15 September — India
In Srinagar, Kashmir, India, armed militants shot and killed an aide of a Kashmiri politician. No group claimed responsibility.

Saudi Arabia
In Riyadh, Saudi Arabia, two gunmen shot and killed a British contractor, who had been working for the Marconi Communications firm, in a shopping center parking lot. The al-Qaida Organization in the Arabian Peninsula claimed responsibility.

16 September — India
In Chirpora Village, Kashmir, India, armed militants shot and killed a 17-year-old student, believed by the attackers to be a police informer. No group claimed responsibility.

Iraq
In Mansour District, Baghdad, Iraq, unknown assailants abducted two Americans and one British citizen. On 20 September 2004, the hostage takers beheaded one American. On 22 September 2004, the assailants beheaded the other American. The Briton was killed on 7 October 2004. Abu Mus'ab al-Zarqawi's Jama'at al-Tawhid wa'al-Jihad claimed responsibility.

17 September — India
In Prem Nagar, Kashmir, India, Islamic militants detonated a bomb hidden in a fruit basket, killing one civilian and wounding one other. No group claimed responsibility.

Iraq
Between Baghdad and Fallujah, Iraq, unknown assailants abducted three Lebanese citizens and their Iraqi driver as they traveled between Baghdad and Fallujah. The three Lebanese citizens had been released by 14 October 2004. As of the end of 2004, the disposition of the Iraqi driver was unknown. No group claimed responsibility.

Venezuela
In Apure State, Venezuela, unidentified armed militants launched an attack along the Venezuela-Colombia border, killing five soldiers and one state-oil-company employee and wounding one soldier and one civilian. No group claimed responsibility, but Venezuelan authorities suspect either Colombian left-wing guerrillas or the United Self-Defense Forces of Colombia (AUC).

18 September — India
In Poonch District, India, armed militants invaded a home and beheaded a man. No group claimed responsibility.

India
In Rajouri District, India, armed militants invaded a home and shot and killed two occupants. No group claimed responsibility.

Iraq

In Iraq, unknown assailants abducted a Turkish truck driver employed by the US Army. On 21 September 2004, near Mosul, Iraq, the victim's body was discovered. No group claimed responsibility.

Iraq

In Yusufiye, Iraq, unknown assailants kidnapped 10 Turkish construction employees from Visnan. In September 2004, the company began freezing operations in hope of saving the workers. On 10 October, the assailants released the 10 Turkish hostages. The Salafist Brigades of Abu Bakr al-Siddiq claimed responsibility.

| 19 | September | India |

In Pulwama, Kashmir, India, armed militants shot and killed a politician. No group claimed responsibility.

Venezuela

In Maracaibo, Venezuela, unidentified attackers threw grenades into an office building owned by the Royal Dutch Shell Oil Company, wounding a security guard and causing minor damage to the building. No group claimed responsibility.

| 20 | September | Afghanistan |

In the province of Zabul, Afghanistan, a group of men that included two Pakistanis and an Arab beheaded three Afghan soldiers, who had been traveling out of uniform from the Naubahar District to the provincial capital of Qalat. The Taliban Jaish-e-Muslimeen claimed responsibility.

| 21 | September | India |

In Surankote, Poonch District, Kashmir, India, Islamic militants threw a grenade at a hospital, wounding two civilians. No group claimed responsibility.

India

In Ranjana Thathri Village, Doda District, Kashmir, India, militants threw a grenade at a police station, hitting the home of a 70-year-old woman, wounding her. No group claimed responsibility.

| 22 | September | India |

In Anantnag District, Kashmir, India, armed militants fired grenades at a political party office, wounding six policemen. Jamiat ul-Mujahedin claimed responsibility.

Iraq

In Baghdad, Iraq, unknown attackers abducted two Egyptian businessmen working for a mobile telephone company from their office. On 20 October 2004, Both hostages were released. Abu Mus'ab al-Zarqawi's Jama'at al-Tawhid wa'al-Jihad claimed responsibility.

Iraq

In Al-Qaim, Iraq, unknown assailants abducted four Egyptian and two Iraqi telecommunications workers. The victims had been installing telecommunications towers near Fallujah and Al-Qaim. On 27 September, the assailants released one Egyptian hostage and the two Iraqi hostages. On 28 September, assailants released the remaining three Egyptian hostages. No group claimed responsibility.

Israel

In Jerusalem, Israel, a female suicide bomber blew herself up as she approached a bus stop, killing two Israeli police officers and wounding 16 civilians. The al-Aqsa Martyrs Brigade claimed responsibility.

| 24 | September | Gaza Strip |

In the Gaza Strip, attackers fired two mortar rounds into a Jewish settlement, striking an Israeli residence and killing an American-Israeli citizen and wounding an Israeli citizen. HAMAS claimed responsibility.

| 26 | September | India |

In Astop, Qazigund, Anantang District, Kashmir, India, armed militants detonated a bomb, wounding three soldiers. Hizbul-Mujahedin claimed responsibility.

Saudi Arabia

In Jeddah, Saudi Arabia, gunmen shot and killed a French defense electronics worker as he sat in his car near a supermarket. No group claimed responsibility, although it is widely believed that al-Qaida was responsible.

| 27 | September | Gaza Strip |

In Gaza City, Gaza Strip, armed Palestinians stopped a car carrying a CNN producer and another passenger. The gunmen kidnapped the producer and left the other passenger unharmed. The producer was released unharmed on 28 September 2004. The al-Aqsa Martyrs Brigade claimed responsibility.

Iraq

Near Mosul, Iraq, unknown perpetrators attacked a truck carrying construction material, killing a Turkish driver. No group claimed responsibility.

| 28 | September | India |

In Achhad, Poonch District, Kashmir, India, armed militants attacked a police patrol, killing one police officer and wounding one other. No group claimed responsibility, although it was widely believed that Hizbul-Mujahedin was responsible.

Iraq

In Iraq, an improvised explosive device exploded near a US convoy, killing one US contractor. No group claimed responsibility.

Peru

In Cuzco, Peru, local coca growers stormed an Inca temple and took 19 tourists (17 French; 2 German) hostage. The hostages were rescued by Peruvian Special Forces. No injuries were reported. No group claimed responsibility.

29 September   **India**
In Chini Chowk near Ziyarat Reshi Mohalia, Kashmir, India, two armed militants attacked the vehicle of the General Secretary of Congress for Islamabad District, killing him and his bodyguard. No group claimed responsibility.

Israel
On 29 September 2004, in S'derot, Israel, unknown attackers fired rockets at a residential block, killing two children and injuring 13 other civilians. No group claimed responsibility.

West Bank
Near Hebron, West Bank, five attackers assaulted five international volunteers who had been escorting Palestinian children to school, seriously wounding all five of the volunteers ([including] 2 American; 1 Italian). No group claimed responsibility, although the civilians claimed their attackers were Jewish settlers.

30 September   **India**
In Srinagar, Kashmir, India, two gunmen shot and killed the leader of the People's Liberation League at his home. No group claimed responsibility.

India
In Kanishpora, Baramula District, Kashmir, India, armed militants detonated a bomb, killing three civilians and wounding five others. No group claimed responsibility.

Iraq
In Iraq, unidentified assailants kidnapped 10 civilians (2 Indonesian women; 6 Iraqi; 2 Lebanese). The two Indonesian women were released on 4 October 2004. At the end of 2004, the disposition of the other hostages was unknown. A group calling itself the Islamic Army in Iraq claimed responsibility.

2 October   **Iraq**
In Iraq, assailants released footage showing the executions of one Turkish and one Iraqi civilian. A group calling itself the Salafist Brigades of Abu Bakr al-Siddiq claimed responsibility.

Iraq
In Iraq, unknown gunmen shot and killed an Italian civilian and a Turkish civilian. No group claimed responsibility.

3 October   **India**
In Sopore, Baramula District, Kashmir, India, armed militants threw a grenade, killing one civilian and wounding three others. No group claimed responsibility.

5 October   **Afghanistan**
Near Jaji Maidan District, Khost Province, Afghanistan, unknown assailants fired shots at a UN vehicle, injuring three Afghan election officials. No group claimed responsibility, but it is widely believed that the Taliban was responsible.

India
In Lawaypora, Kashmir, India, armed militants fired on a group of Indian military personnel, killing three soldiers. No group claimed responsibility.

India
In Hanjiveera Pattan, Varmul District, Kashmir, India, an improvised explosive device exploded, damaging a security vehicle and injuring an Indian soldier. No group claimed responsibility, but it is widely believed that Lashkar-e-Tayyiba was responsible.

7 October   **Egypt**
At the Moon Island and Baddiyah campsites, Ras al-Shitan, near Nuweiba, Egypt, two car bombs exploded, killing two Israelis and wounding 12 other people, including seven Egyptians. This incident was part of a series of attacks that occurred on this day. Egyptian security service officials claimed that two Egyptians carried out the attacks and were still at large. Authorities arrested five other Egyptian citizens on 26 October 2004 in connection with the attacks. The Battalions of the Martyr Abdullah Azzam, al-Qaida in the Levant and Egypt claimed responsibility.

Egypt
In Taba, Egypt, Islamic assailants drove a car bomb into the lobby of the Hilton Hotel, detonating the explosives and killing 34 people ([including] 13 Israeli; 10 Egyptian; 2 Italian; 1 Russian; 1 American) and wounding 159 others (8 Russian; 2 Briton; 2 American). The hotel sustained major damage, including 10 collapsed floors. This incident was part of a series of attacks that occurred on this day. Egyptian authorities identified two militants, a Palestinian and an Egyptian, as the two perpetrators. On 26 October, authorities arrested five other Egyptian citizens in connection with the attacks. Tawhid Islamic Brigades; Jamaah al-Islamiya organization (JI); and the Battalions of the Martyr Abdullah Azzam, al-Qaida in the Levant and Egypt all claimed responsibility.

India
In Kashmir, India, armed militants shot and killed a political party worker. Harakat ul Mujahidin claimed responsibility.

India
In Kupwara District, Kashmir, India, armed militants shot and killed an off-duty soldier in his home. No group claimed responsibility.

8 October   **France**
In Paris, France, a bomb exploded at the Indonesian Embassy, injuring 10 people and shattering windows in the embassy and nearby buildings. A group calling itself the French Armed Islamic Front claimed responsibility.

India
In Gojwara, Kashmir, India, militants threw a grenade at a military bunker, missing their target and injuring a civilian.

No group claimed responsibility, but it is widely believed that Jaish-e-Mohammed was responsible.

Iraq
Near Bayji, Iraq, unknown assailants attacked a civilian fuel convoy with rocket-propelled grenades and automatic firearms, injuring one Turkish driver and destroying a fuel tanker. The attackers also kidnapped one other Turkish driver, who was later beheaded on 11 October 2004. Ansar al-Sunna claimed responsibility.

9 October — India
On the Srinagar-Baramulla Highway, Kashmir, India, a militant drove a car into a bus, killing four soldiers and one civilian and injuring 15 soldiers and 20 civilians. Six civilian vehicles and the bus were also damaged in the attack. Jaish-e-Mohammed claimed responsibility.

India
In the Broh Village, Kalakote Tehsil, Rajouri District, Kashmir, India, armed militants invaded a home and attacked the occupants, killing one and wounding one other. No group claimed responsibility.

Pakistan
In Chagmalai, South Waziristan, Pakistan, unknown assailants kidnapped two Chinese engineers working on Pakistan's Gomal Zam Dam project for China's state-owned Sino Hydro Corporation. The hostage takers demanded the release of two Uzbek extremists in exchange for the Chinese captives. On 14 October 2004, Pakistani authorities conducted an operation to find the captives, rescuing one and finding the other to be dead. No group claimed responsibility.

10 October — Haiti
In Gonvaives, Haiti, unidentified armed men shot and injured a UN peacekeeper from the Argentine Marine contingent. The UN peacekeepers and the Haitian police were conducting a joint operation when the attack occurred. No group claimed responsibility.

Haiti
In Port-au-Prince, Haiti, unidentified armed men attacked and injured a member of the Brazilian UN contingent during a gun battle in the Bel Air neighborhood. No group claimed responsibility.

Iraq
In Baghdad, Iraq, unidentified assailants kidnapped a US freelance photographer for World Picture News. The victim was released on 13 October 2004. No group claimed responsibility.

12 October — Iraq
In Iraq, unidentified kidnappers abducted a Jordanian businessman. The kidnappers released the victim on 26 October 2004. No group claimed responsibility.

Iraq
In Iraq, unknown assailants attacked two South African civilians, killing them both. No group claimed responsibility.

13 October — India
In Phislan area, Pahalgam District, Kashmir, India, a landmine exploded, injuring three poll officers, three security guards, and one driver. No group claimed responsibility.

14 October — India
In the Shalimar area, Kashmir, India, armed militants entered the home of a land broker and slit his throat. Al-Mansurian claimed responsibility.

India
In Lard Mahore, Udhampur District, Kashmir, India, armed militants invaded a home and attacked the occupants, killing a man and injuring a girl. No group claimed responsibility.

Iraq
In Samarra, Iraq, unidentified gunmen attacked a civilian supply convoy, kidnapping two Turkish drivers. As of the end of 2004, the disposition of the victims was unknown. No group claimed responsibility.

Iraq
In Baghdad, Iraq, two bombs exploded at an outdoor shopping area and in a cafe in the Green Zone, killing four US citizens and wounding 18 other people. Abu Mus'ab al-Zarqawi's Jama'at al-Tawhid wa'al-Jihad claimed responsibility.

Iraq
In Iraq, unidentified assailants kidnapped a Turkish truck driver. On 14 October 2004, a video was found showing the beheading of a Turkish truck driver, presumed to be the kidnapped victim. Ansar al-Sunna claimed responsibility.

15 October — India
In New Theed, Harwan area, Kashmir, India, four armed militants invaded a home and attacked the occupants, killing a political official and his son. No group claimed responsibility.

India
In the Pattan area, Baramula District, Kashmir, India, armed militants shot and injured a People's Democratic Party activist. No group claimed responsibility.

16 October — Iraq
In Baghdad, Iraq, unidentified kidnappers abducted an Australian journalist. The journalist was released on 17 October 2004. No group claimed responsibility.

18 October — India
In Khog, Billawar, Kashmir, India, militants hurled a grenade at members of a Village Defense Committee, killing one and wounding 14 others. Although no group claimed responsibility, it is widely believed that Lashkar-e-Tayyiba was responsible.

19 October — Iraq

Unknown assailants kidnapped a humanitarian worker. The Arabic satellite station Al-Jazeera reported on 16 November 2004 that it had a tape of the victim's murder, and the British Foreign Office indicated that the woman executed on the tape is the humanitarian worker previously kidnapped. A body of a western woman was found in Fallujah, but was determined to be a different, unidentified victim. No group claimed responsibility.

20 October — India

In the Narbal Village, Kashmir, India, armed militants invaded a home and attacked the occupants, killing two civilians. No group claimed responsibility.

21 October — India

In Sarnal Village, near Anantnag, Kashmir, India, Islamic militants shot and killed the former Jammu-Kashmir State Minister and seriously injured his security guard. No group claimed responsibility.

22 October — Gaza Strip

In N'vei Dekalim, Gaza Strip, attackers fired fifteen mortars into an Israeli settlement, damaging several homes. HAMAS claimed responsibility.

23 October — Afghanistan

In Kabul, Afghanistan, an assailant detonated a bomb on Chicken Street, a shopping area for tourists, killing two civilians (1 American; 1 Afghan) and wounding three Icelandic soldiers and five Afghan civilians. The Taliban claimed responsibility.

India

In Kashmir, India, militants beheaded a woman. No group claimed responsibility.

Iraq

In Balidiyat, Iraq, unidentified gunmen fired on a group of truck drivers, killing two drivers (1 Turkish; 1 Croatian) and wounding two others. No group claimed responsibility.

24 October — India

In Kashmir, India, armed militants detonated a remote-controlled improvised explosive device at a funeral, killing one civilian and wounding six others. The leader of the National Conference Party, who was in attendance at the funeral, was not harmed. No group claimed responsibility.

India

In Chanapore, Srinagar, Kashmir, India, armed militants fired shots through a house window, killing a former militant. No group claimed responsibility.

India

In Salbala, Gool, Udhampur District, Kashmir, India, armed militants invaded a home and opened fire on the occupants, killing two people and wounding two others. One resident was kidnapped, and his body was later found by police. No group claimed responsibility.

India

In the Ramsoo area, Doda District, Kashmir, India, armed militants invaded a home and attacked the occupants, killing a teenage girl and injuring her brother. No group claimed responsibility.

Iraq

In Baghdad, Iraq, unknown assailants kidnapped a Japanese civilian. Authorities found the victim's beheaded body on 31 October 2004. Abu Mus'ab al-Zarqawi's Tanzim Qaidat al-Jihad fi Bilad al-Rafidayn (QJBR) (al-Qaida in Iraq) claimed responsibility.

Iraq

In Bayji, Iraq, assailants shot and killed a Turkish truck driver. No group claimed responsibility.

Turkey

In Trabzon, Turkey, a bomb exploded at a McDonald's restaurant, injuring six people. No group claimed responsibility.

25 October — India

Near Zainapora, Shopian, Kashmir, India, militants fired at the motorcade of the Divisional Commissioner for the Muslim-Majority Kashmir Valley, injuring one security guard. The Commissioner was not harmed. Jaish-e-Mohammed and Harakat ul Mujahidin claimed joint responsibility.

26 October — France

In Olmeto, Corsica, France, a bomb exploded outside a vacation home owned by an Italian family, causing significant damage to the home. This attack was one of several attacks during the month of October, although it is the only one affecting international assets. No group claimed responsibility.

27 October — Iraq

In Baghdad, Iraq, assailants abducted a Polish national with Iraqi citizenship. The victim was released on 24 November 2004. A group calling itself the Abu Bakr al-Siddiq Fundamentalist Brigades claimed responsibility.

Iraq

In Baghdad, Iraq, an improvised explosive device exploded near a civilian vehicle, killing one US contractor. No group claimed responsibility.

28 October — Afghanistan

In Kabul, Afghanistan, assailants kidnapped three UN election workers (1 Filipino; 1 Kosovar Albanian; 1 Irish) as they traveled in a UN vehicle. On 23 November 2004, the captors released the three kidnapped UN election workers unharmed. The Taliban Jaish-e-Muslimeen claimed responsibility.

India

In Budgam District, Kashmir, India, armed militants fired at Indian military personnel, killing one soldier and one civilian and injuring one other. One other civilian was also killed in the crossfire. No group claimed responsibility.

India

In the Numtahaal Village, Kashmir, India, armed militants posing as villagers, attacked a military camp with grenades and small arms, killing one soldier and one civilian and injuring four soldiers and one civilian. No group claimed responsibility.

Iraq

Near a US base in Fallujah, unknown assailants kidnapped one Bangladeshi and one Sri Lankan. As of the end of 2004, the disposition of the two victims was unknown. The Islamic Army in Iraq claimed responsibility.

Pakistan

In Islamabad, Pakistan, a bomb exploded at the Marriott Hotel, injuring eight people (1 American diplomat; 3 Italian; 4 Pakistani). The hotel lobby also suffered minor damage from the blast. Al-Qaida claimed responsibility.

Thailand

In Sungai Kolok, Narathiwat Province, Thailand, two unidentified perpetrators on a motorcycle approached a bar and deposited a package containing a remote-controlled bomb, which exploded moments later, killing two, including one Malaysian, and injuring 20 others, including one Malaysian. No group claimed responsibility.

29 October   **India**

In the Sanat Nagar suburb, Srinagar, Kashmir, India, an improvised explosive device strapped to a bicycle exploded, killing one police officer and injuring two civilians. No group claimed responsibility.

India

In the Qazibagh area, Anantnag District, Srinagar, Kashmir, India, Islamic militants lobbed grenades at a police unit, killing one policeman and injuring one other. A civilian was also injured in the crossfire. Hizbul-Mujahedin claimed responsibility.

India

In Qazibagh, Srinagar, Kashmir, India, militants hurled a grenade at Indian troops, injuring two soldiers. No group claimed responsibility.

India

In the Mahore area, Udhampur District, Kashmir, India, armed militants attacked the home of a member of India's ruling Congress Party, killing him and his son. His wife was also seriously injured in the attack. No group claimed responsibility.

Iraq

In Ramadi, Iraq, attackers kidnapped a Sudanese civilian working for a US contractor. The victim was released on 6 November 2004. A group calling itself the Islamic Army in Iraq, the 1920 Revolution Brigades claimed responsibility.

Iraq

In Yarmuk Square, Mosul, Iraq, unidentified gunmen ambushed a convoy carrying bottled water, killing one Turkish truck driver and destroying a truck. No group claimed responsibility.

30 October   **Iraq**

In Baghdad, Iraq, unidentified attackers detonated a car bomb outside of the Dubai-based al-Arabiya television station, killing five civilians, wounding 14 others, and collapsing the first floor of the building. A group calling itself the Islamic Army in Iraq, the 1920 Revolution Brigades claimed responsibility.

Iraq

In Baghdad, Iraq, attackers kidnapped a Sudanese man who had been working as an interpreter for a US contractor. On 6 November 2004, the interpreter was released unharmed. A group calling itself the Islamic Army in Iraq, the 1920 Revolution Brigades claimed responsibility.

31 October   **India**

In Srinagar, Kashmir, India, a Muslim militant fired at a crowded marketplace, injuring a policeman and a civilian before being subdued by police. No group claimed responsibility.

1 November   **India**

In Shopian, Kashmir, India, militants threw a grenade into a crowded marketplace near a police bunker, injuring 21 civilians. No group claimed responsibility.

India

In the Rajouri District, Kashmir, India, militants beheaded a civilian. No group claimed responsibility.

India

In the Poonch District, Kashmir, India, Islamic militants beheaded a civilian. No group claimed responsibility.

India

In the Surankote area, Poonch District, Kashmir, India, armed militants attempted to abduct a Special Police Officer, shooting and wounding him when he resisted. No group claimed responsibility.

Iraq

In Baghdad, Iraq, unknown assailants kidnapped six workers (1 American; 1 Filipino; 1 Nepalese) from their office in the Mansour District. On 2 November 2004, the captors released the three Iraqi hostages. On 5 November 2004, they released the Nepalese captive. As of the end of 2004, the disposition of the US and Filipino hostages was unknown. No group claimed responsibility.

Israel

At the Carmel Market in Tel Aviv, Israel, a suicide bomber detonated an explosive device, killing three civilians and injuring 30 others. The Popular Front for Liberation of Palestine (PFLP) claimed responsibility.

2 November — **India**

In Sopore, Kashmir, India, armed militants threw a grenade at Border Security Forces, injuring one soldier. No group claimed responsibility.

India

In Gund Kangan, Kashmir, India, armed militants kidnapped a retired police officer. He was later found dead from gunshot wounds. No group claimed responsibility.

India

In the Village of Litter, Pulwama District, Kashmir, India, armed militants shot and killed a police officer in his home. No group claimed responsibility.

India

In the Kanagan area, Srinagar, Kashmir, India, armed militants shot and killed a People's Democratic Party member in his home. No group claimed responsibility.

Iraq

In Baghdad, Iraq, unknown assailants abducted a Lebanese-American from his office in the Mansour District. As of 29 March 2005, the disposition of the victim was unknown. No group claimed responsibility.

Iraq

In Rutba, Iraq, unidentified assailants attacked a group of Jordanian truck drivers, killing one and kidnapping three others. The three drivers were released on 11 November 2004. No group claimed responsibility.

Iraq

In Baghdad, Iraq, unidentified gunmen shot and killed a US contractor paramedic. No group claimed responsibility.

3 November — **India**

In the Kupwara District, Kashmir, India, armed militants shot and killed a man suspected by the attackers of being a police informer. No group claimed responsibility.

6 November — **India**

In Sopore, Srinagar, Kashmir, India, Islamic militants attacked a Border Security Force camp with grenades and small arms, killing one soldier and wounding four others. No group claimed responsibility.

India

In Kashmir, India, Islamic militants threw a grenade at soldiers in a shopping area, killing two soldiers and injuring one soldier and one civilian. No group claimed responsibility.

India

In Budgam, Kashmir, India, armed militants attacked the home of an Indian Congress Party member, killing a civilian and a guard. The politician was not harmed in the attack. No group claimed responsibility.

Iraq

Near Mosul, Iraq, a bomb exploded, killing a Turkish truck driver, destroying two Turkish transport vehicles, and damaging a US military vehicle. No group claimed responsibility.

7 November — **Iraq**

In Basra, Iraq, unidentified assailants detonated an improvised explosive device under an armored vehicle carrying employees of Olive Security, a London-based security firm, killing one British and one South African bodyguard. No group claimed responsibility.

Iraq

Near Samarra, Iraq, unidentified attackers shot and killed a Turkish truck driver. No group claimed responsibility.

West Bank

In Shomron, West Bank, gunmen attacked a crowd on a street, killing one Israeli and wounding two others. The al-Aqsa Martyrs Brigade claimed responsibility.

8 November — **India**

In the Sundervani Village, Kashmir, India, a suicide bomber blew himself up in front of a military camp, injuring four soldiers, three critically. The blast also damaged the entrance to the camp. No group claimed responsibility.

India

In Kashmir, India, armed militants shot at a house belonging to an Indian Congress Party leader, killing one civilian and one police officer. The politician was not at home during the attack. No group claimed responsibility.

Iraq

In Baghdad, Iraq, an unidentified suicide bomber attempted to assassinate a US weapons inspector, killing two members of the security detail. No group claimed responsibility.

Iraq

In Al-Zubayr, outside Basra, Iraq, unidentified assailants detonated an improvised explosive device as a convoy of vehicles passed, killing at least two private contractors, including one Briton, and injuring one other contractor. No group claimed responsibility.

9 November — **Iraq**

In Mosul, Iraq, unidentified gunmen shot and killed a Turkish truck driver. No group claimed responsibility.

Philippines

In Kauswagan, Lanao del Norte Province, Philippines, four masked gunmen kidnapped the project director for the Italian relief organization Movimondo and two Filipino civilians.

The three victims were released unharmed. No group claimed responsibility, although authorities believe that a Muslim separatist group, possibly the Abu Sayyaf Group, was responsible.

Serbia

In Urosevac, Kosovo, Serbia and Montenegro, a car bomb exploded at the Ben-af shopping mall as police and US peacekeepers inspected the vehicle for explosives, injuring one US soldier and one civilian. No group claimed responsibility.

10   November   Iraq

In Balad, Iraq, an improvised explosive device exploded, killing an American DynCorp employee, who had been in Iraq to train policemen. No group claimed responsibility.

Iraq

Near Jebel Makhul, Iraq, unidentified attackers killed a Turkish truck driver and burned his vehicle. No group claimed responsibility.

Iraq

In Tikrit, Iraq, a roadside bomb exploded as a US convoy passed, killing a US contractor. No group claimed responsibility.

11   November   Iraq

In Baghdad, Iraq, unidentified assailants kidnapped a US citizen from his home in the Mansour District. As of the end of 2004, the disposition of the victim was unknown. A group calling itself the Islamic Army in Iraq, 1920 Revolution Brigades claimed responsibility.

12   November   Iraq

In Balad, Iraq, unidentified attackers shot and killed a Turkish driver. Authorities noted that the victim had been previously kidnapped and released after agreeing to not work for the US military. No group claimed responsibility.

13   November   India

At Nadimarg, in the Pulwama District, Kashmir, India, militants attacked a police post, killing three policemen. Although no group claimed responsibility, it is widely believed that both Jaish-e-Mohammed and Lashkar-e-Tayyiba were responsible.

14   November   Iraq

In Baghdad, Iraq, unknown assailants shot and killed a US contractor. No group claimed responsibility.

15   November   India

In the Magam area of the Badgam District, Kashmir, India, militants invaded a house and attacked the occupants, killing six people. Although no group claimed responsibility, it is widely believed that Hizbul-Mujahedin was responsible.

India

In the Magam area, Badgam District, Kashmir, India, militants shot and killed the widow of a counter-insurgent. Although no group claimed responsibility, it is widely believed that the Hizbul-Mujahedin was responsible.

Thailand

In Krong Pinang District, Thailand, unknown attackers entered a home and opened fire on the occupants, killing a retired Thai police officer and a Burmese teenager. No group claimed responsibility, although authorities believe Islamic separatists were responsible.

16   November   India

In Kachdora, in the Pulwama District, Kashmir, India, armed militants attacked military personnel guarding a bank on Shopian-Kulgam Road, killing one soldier and injuring two others. No group claimed responsibility.

17   November   Argentina

In Buenos Aires, Argentina, near-simultaneous bombs exploded at three bank locations in the city, killing one security guard, injuring one police officer, and causing minor damage to the exteriors of the banks. The first two bombs exploded at two US-owned Citibank branch locations. The third explosion occurred at a branch of Banco Galicia. No group claimed responsibility.

India

In Doda District, Kashmir, India, Islamic militants detonated a bomb during a funeral ceremony, killing one civilian and injuring four others. No group claimed responsibility.

India

In Kupwara District, Kashmir, India, armed militants shot and killed a policeman. No group claimed responsibility.

India

In Anantnag District, Kashmir, India, armed militants shot and injured a People's Democratic Party worker. No group claimed responsibility.

Iraq

In Baghdad, Iraq, unknown attackers fired rocket-propelled grenades at a civilian convoy, killing three Turkish truck drivers. No group claimed responsibility.

18   November   India

In Kulangam, Kupwara District, Kashmir, India, armed militants invaded the house of a former Hizbul-Mujahedin member, killing him and his teenage daughter. No group claimed responsibility.

India

In Shahdhra Sharief Village, Rajouri District, Kashmir, India, armed militants abducted the village chief from his home. The victim's body was found on 24 November 2004. No group claimed responsibility.

19 November   **India**
In the Bahramgali area, Poonch District, Kashmir, India, an army convoy drove over a landmine, killing three soldiers and wounding four others. No group claimed responsibility.

India
In Baramulla District, Kashmir, India, Islamic militants engaged Indian soldiers, killing a bystander during the gunfight. No group claimed responsibility.

India
At Shalagund, near Lalpora, in Kupwara District, Kashmir, India, armed militants invaded a home and kidnapped the occupant. As of 29 March 2005, the disposition of the victim was unknown. No group claimed responsibility.

21 November   **Gaza Strip**
On the Kissufim Road, Gaza Strip gunmen ambushed a group of cars carrying Jewish settlers, wounding nine of the settlers. Islamic Jihad Jerusalem and the Popular Front for the Liberation of Palestine (PFLP) claimed joint responsibility.

22 November   **India**
In the Dangiwachi Village, Baramulla District, Kashmir, India, Islamic militants shot at a police post, killing one police officer and seriously injuring two others. No group claimed responsibility.

23 November   **India**
In Anantnag District, Kashmir, India, armed militants shot and killed an Indian soldier in his home. No group claimed responsibility.

India
In Kunzer Village, in northern Baramula District, Kashmir, India, Islamic militants shot and killed a former militant and his brother-in-law outside their home. No group claimed responsibility.

Iraq
In Kirkuk, Iraq, unknown assailants invaded the home of a Turkish contractor working for US forces in Iraq, abducting the contractor and injuring two of his family members. As of the end of 2004, the disposition of the victim was unknown. No group claimed responsibility.

24 November   **India**
In Baramula District, Kashmir, India, militants threw a grenade at a military bunker, missing their target and killing three nearby civilians. No group claimed responsibility.

India
In Indira Chowk, Kashmir, India, armed militants threw a grenade into a shopping area, injuring 17 civilians. No group claimed responsibility.

Iraq
In Baghdad, Iraq, gunmen shot and killed a US diplomat who had been serving as senior consultant to the Iraqi Ministers of Education and Higher Education. Abu Mus'ab al-Zarqawi's Tanzim Qaidat al Jihad fi Bilad al-Rafidayn (QJBR) (al-Qaida in Iraq) claimed responsibility.

25 November   **India**
In Anchidora, Anantnag District, Kashmir, India, Islamic militants attacked a police patrol, killing two officers and injuring one other. No group claimed responsibility.

India
Near Anantnag District, Kashmir, India, Islamic militants shot at police officers, killing two and wounding two others. No group claimed responsibility.

India
In Doda District, Kashmir, India, Islamic militants shot and killed two members of the local Village Defense Committee. No group claimed responsibility.

India
In the Baramulla District, Kashmir, India, armed militants dragged a high school student out of his home and shot him to death. No group claimed responsibility.

Iraq
In Baghdad, Iraq, unknown assailants fired mortars into the Green Zone, killing four British contractors and wounding 15 other civilians. Ansar al-Sunna claimed responsibility.

26 November   **India**
In the town of Sopore, Kashmir, India, a bomb, tied to a dog, exploded inside a shopping area, wounding four civilians. No group claimed responsibility.

India
In the Anantnag District, Kashmir, India, armed militants ambushed a military vehicle, killing two soldiers and injuring two others. No group claimed responsibility.

India
In the Dachan area, Doda District, Kashmir, India, unknown gunmen shot and killed two Special Police Officers. No group claimed responsibility.

27 November   **India**
In Shudaan Village, Doda District, Kashmir, India, militants shot and injured two police officers on Bharath Road. Although no group claimed responsibility, it is widely believed that Lashkar-e-Tayyiba was responsible.

India
In Budgam District, Kashmir, India, armed militants shot and killed a former militant. No group claimed responsibility.

India
In Baramulla District, Kashmir, India, armed militants shot and killed a former militant. No group claimed responsibility.

28 November   **India**
In Anantnag District, Kashmir, India, armed militants shot and killed a former militant outside his home. No group claimed responsibility.

India
In Anantnag District, Kashmir, India, armed militants killed a former commander of Ikhwan, an Indian counterinsurgency group, outside his home. No group claimed responsibility.

29 November   **India**
In Srinagar, Kashmir, India, armed militants threw a grenade at a Central Reserve Police Force bunker, missing their target and injuring four civilians and two police officers in the nearby Lal Chowk marketplace. Al Khandaq claimed responsibility.

30 November   **India**
In Jehangir Chowk, Srinagar, Kashmir, India, armed militants threw two grenades at a police patrol, injuring two police officers and four civilians. No group claimed responsibility.

3 December   **India**
In the Sopore area, Baramula District Kashmir, India, two militants attacked a police camp with small arms, killing five officers and injuring seven others. Al-Mansurian claimed responsibility.

4 December   **Iraq**
In Bayji, Iraq, an improvised explosive device exploded, killing an unidentified truck driver, reported to be a third-country national. No group claimed responsibility.

5 December   **Democratic Republic of the Congo**
In Bunia, Democratic Republic of the Congo, unidentified armed men attacked troops from the UN Mission in the Democratic Republic of the Congo (MONUC), wounding two peacekeepers and one civilian. No group claimed responsibility.

India
In Wachi Village, Pulwama District, Kashmir, India, a landmine exploded under a jeep, killing 10 soldiers and a civilian and destroying the jeep. Hizbul-Mujahedin claimed responsibility.

6 December   **Saudi Arabia**
In Jeddah, Saudi Arabia, five attackers broke through the gate of the US Consulate, threw explosives, and fired automatic weapons, killing five people (1 Filipino; 1 Sudanese; 1 Yemeni; 1 Indian; 1 Sri Lankan) and injuring nine others, including two Saudi Arabian National Guardsmen at the gate. The al-Qaida Organization in the Arabian Peninsula claimed responsibility.

7 December   **India**
In Utigam Village, Beerwah area, Budgam District, Kashmir, India, unknown gunmen shot and injured a member of the Central Reserve Police Force. No group claimed responsibility.

8 December   **India**
In Anantnag District, Kashmir, India, Islamic militants threw a grenade near a police patrol and crowded marketplace, injuring 35 civilians and one police officer. No group claimed responsibility.

Iraq
In Baghdad, Iraq, unidentified attackers ambushed a two-vehicle convoy transporting contractors from Taji to Baghdad, killing two US contractors and one Iraqi national. A group calling itself the Jihad Brigades claimed responsibility.

9 December   **India**
In Imam Sahib Village, near Shopian Township, Kashmir, India, Islamic militants attacked a police camp with small arms, killing two officers and injuring five others. Hizbul-Mujahedin claimed responsibility.

10 December   **Gaza Strip**
In N'vei Dekalim, Gaza Strip, attackers fired five mortar rounds into an Israeli settlement, injuring four Israelis. HAMAS claimed responsibility.

India
In the village of Magani, Southern Kathua District, Kashmir, India, militants attacked a police post, killing four officers. Hizbul-Mujahedin claimed responsibility.

India
In Poonch District, Kashmir, India, militants first locked in sleeping occupants and then set fire to a house, killing one civilian. No group claimed responsibility.

Sudan
In Rejaf, near Juba, Sudan, unidentified armed men brutally attacked and killed seven people and wounded eight others. The victims, primarily women and children, were reportedly hacked to death with machetes. The perpetrators likely crossed the border into Sudan from Uganda to execute the attack. Although no group claimed responsibility, authorities blamed the Ugandan-based Lord's Resistance Army (LRA).

12 December   **Gaza Strip**
Near Rafah, on the Gaza-Egypt border, attackers detonated half a ton of explosives in a tunnel under an Israeli checkpoint, killing five Israeli Defense Forces troops and wounding another six. The Fatah Hawks and HAMAS claimed joint responsibility.

Gaza Strip
In Nisanit, Gaza Strip, unknown attackers fired four mortar rounds into an Israeli settlement, causing heavy damage to parts of the settlement. The Izz al-Din al-Qassam Brigades (HAMAS) claimed responsibility.

Sri Lanka
In Colombo, Western Province, Sri Lanka, a grenade exploded in the audience attending the "Temptation 2004" show, hosted at the Colombo Race Course grounds, killing one Sri Lankan journalist and one other civilian and wounding one Indian and 18 Sri Lankan civilians. No group claimed responsibility.

Sudan
Between Nyala and Al-Fashir, in Darfur, Sudan, unidentified gunmen attacked and killed two humanitarian workers from the Save the Children relief organization. The assailants also wounded another worker during the attack and seized two vehicles, which had been transporting medicine and other aid. No group claimed responsibility.

13 November — Gaza Strip
In Ganei Tal, Gaza Strip, unknown attackers fired several mortar rounds at an Israeli settlement, seriously wounding a Thai worker and slightly wounding two others. No group claimed responsibility.

India
In the Gambhir area, Rajouri District, Kashmir, India, a landmine exploded, injuring an army captain. No group claimed responsibility.

India
In Rajouri District, Kashmir, India, militants hanged one Muslim civilian. No group claimed responsibility.

14 December — Afghanistan
Near Asadabad, Konar Province, Afghanistan, assailants kidnapped a Turkish engineer who had been working on a road project, along with his Afghan driver and interpreter. On 15 December 2004, the captors killed the Turkish engineer, but released the two Afghan hostages. No group claimed responsibility.

Gaza Strip
In N'vei Dekalim, Gaza Strip, attackers fired several mortar rounds at an Israeli settlement, injuring four people (3 Israeli; 1 Belgian). HAMAS claimed responsibility.

Gaza Strip
In Khan Yunis, southern Gaza Strip, attackers fired several mortar rounds into an Israeli settlement, killing a Thai worker. The Izz al-Din al-Qassam Brigades (HAMAS) claimed responsibility.

India
In Panzigam, Bandipora area, Kashmir, India, armed militants shot and killed a former Special Police Officer in her home. No group claimed responsibility.

15 December — Gaza Strip
At the Kissufim Crossing Site, Gaza Strip, gunmen opened fire on an Israeli Defense Forces (IDF) checkpoint, wounding four IDF troops and an Israeli civilian. The al-Aqsa Martyrs Brigade and Palestine Islamic Jihad claimed joint responsibility.

Gaza Strip
On the Kissufim Road, Gaza Strip, a gunman shot at passing vehicles, wounding a civilian and an Israeli Defense Forces (IDF) soldier and slightly wounding three other IDF personnel. Palestine Islamic Jihad and the al-Aqsa Martyrs Brigade claimed joint responsibility.

India
In the Handwara Forest area of Kupwara District, Kashmir, India, militants shot and killed a civilian and his daughter. No group claimed responsibility, although it is widely believed Hizbul-Mujahedin was responsible.

India
At Thana Mandi, in Rajouri District, Kashmir, India, militants killed an Indian soldier. No group claimed responsibility.

India
In Sopore, in the Baramula District, Kashmir, India, militants threw grenades at a Border Security Force camp, injuring three police officers. No group claimed responsibility, although it is widely believed Lashkar-e-Tayyiba was responsible.

Iraq
In Balad, Iraq, unidentified assailants attacked a truck, killing two Turkish drivers and burning their vehicle. No group claimed responsibility.

Nepal
In Kailali District, Nepal, assailants kidnapped a Swiss International Development Agency employee and three Nepalese colleagues as they were traveling to the Dadeldhura District. The victims were released unharmed on 16 December 2004. Although no group claimed responsibility, it is widely believed the Communist Party of Nepal (Maoist)/United People's Front was responsible.

16 December — Gaza Strip
In Kissufim Crossing Site, Gaza Strip, attackers fired two rockets into a Jewish settlement, injuring six settlers. HAMAS claimed responsibility.

India
In Srinagar, Kashmir, India, Islamic militants threw a grenade at the Khanyar Police Station, injuring seven police officers. No group claimed responsibility.

India
In Qazigund, Kashmir, India, armed militants threw a grenade at an office building, injuring a civilian. No group claimed responsibility.

Iraq
In Ramadi, Iraq, unidentified gunmen shot and killed an Italian aid worker at a roadblock. A group calling itself the Islamic Movement of Iraqi Mujahidin claimed responsibility.

17 December   **India**
In Pulwama District, Kashmir, India, Muslim militants hanged a shopkeeper. No group claimed responsibility.

Iraq
In Bayji, Iraq, unidentified assailants detonated an improvised explosive device, wounding four US security contractors. No group claimed responsibility.

Iraq
In Mosul, Iraq, unidentified gunmen fired on a Turkish diplomatic convoy, killing five Turkish security officers and two Iraqi drivers and wounding the Turkish defense attache. No group claimed responsibility.

18 December   **India**
In Anantnag District, Kashmir, India, armed militants shot and killed a member of the People's Democratic Party. No group claimed responsibility.

20 December   **India**
In Udhampur District, Kashmir, India, armed militants invaded a home, abducted a Muslim woman and killed her. No group claimed responsibility.

Iraq
In Tikrit, Iraq, unidentified attackers detonated an explosive device as a US convoy passed, killing one Turkish truck driver. No group claimed responsibility.

Iraq
Near Mosul, Iraq, unidentified assailants attacked a truck, killing one Turkish driver and burning his vehicle. No group claimed responsibility.

21 December   **Gaza Strip**
In Netzarim, Gaza Strip, unknown attackers fired a rocket at a synagogue, severely damaging the building and causing eight civilians to be treated for shock. No group claimed responsibility.

India
In Ganjoot Village, Mahore area of Udhampur District, Kashmir, India, Islamic militants threw grenades at Indian military forces, injuring two soldiers. Although no group claimed responsibility, it is widely believed that Lashkar-e-Tayyiba was responsible.

22 November   **India**
In Sangam, Anantnag District, Kashmir, India, armed militants threw a grenade at a security bunker, killing one civilian and injuring five police officers and nine civilians. No group claimed responsibility.

India
In Srinagar, Kashmir, India, armed militants engaged Indian troops, killing a civilian in the crossfire. No group claimed responsibility.

West Bank
West of Hebron, West Bank, unknown gunmen shot and killed an Israeli man near a barrier being built close to the border between Israel and the West Bank. The al-Aqsa Martyrs Brigade claimed responsibility.

24 December   **India**
In Pakherpora Township, Budgam District, Kashmir, India, Islamic militants threw a grenade at security forces, missing their target and killing two civilians and injuring 26 civilians and two police officers. No group claimed responsibility.

27 December   **Iraq**
In Bayji, Iraq, unidentified gunmen shot and killed a Turkish truck driver. No group claimed responsibility.

29 December   **India**
In Srinagar, Kashmir, India, armed militants shot and killed a senior leader of the National Conference Party. No group claimed responsibility.

India
Near Tral, Srinagar, Kashmir, India, militants engaged Indian troops, killing one soldier and three civilians. No group claimed responsibility.

India
In Sopore, Kashmir, India, militants shot and killed a soldier at a bus stop. Hizbul-Mujahedin claimed responsibility.

Iraq
In Baghdad, Iraq, unidentified gunmen kidnapped two Lebanese businessmen. The kidnappers released the hostages on 16 February 2005. Musa'b Bin-Umayr-The Islamic Jihad claimed responsibility.

Iraq
In Samarra, Iraq, unidentified gunmen shot and killed a Turkish truck driver. No group claimed responsibility.

30 December   **India**
In Pulwama District, Kashmir, India, Islamic militants opened fire on a bus, killing three civilians and injuring four others. No group claimed responsibility.

India
At Wagoora, in the Budgam District, Srinagar, Kashmir, India, armed militants invaded the home of a former militant, killing him and one civilian, and wounding one other. No group claimed responsibility.

2005

1–4 January   **Peru**
In Peru a group of some 150 heavily armed ultra-nationalist army reservists in the town of Andahuaylas took over a police station. They killed four police and held ten hostage. One rebel was also killed. President Toledo placed a 30-day state of emergency on the region and sent in federal troops. After

a 4-day siege, the rebels surrendered. Major Antauro Humala, the ringleader opposed to foreign interests in Peru, faces charges of kidnapping and murder.

3   January   Pakistan
In Pakistan, opposition politician Manzoor Hussain Shah, his driver and two bodyguards were shot dead in an ambush, possibly politically motivated, on January 3.

8   January   Pakistan
Ten people were killed in Shia/Sunni sectarian violence in Gilgit.

9   January   Philippines
Philippine troops and separatists of the Moro Islamic Liberation Front (MILF) engaged in the worst fighting since the July 2003 ceasefire on the night of January 9, ahead of peace talks planned for next month. The fighting broke out when more than 100 MILF guerillas attacked a military post, killing at least six soldiers.

11–15 January   Pakistan
Pakistan troops are guarding Baluchistan gas fields after several days of clashes with tribal militants killed at least eight people. Hostages held by the militants were freed.

16 January   India
In Indian-administered Kashmir a daylong siege ended with the death of two militants and two soldiers.

18 January   Spain
Spanish separatist group ETA set off a car bomb near Bilbao, injuring a police officer, amid rumors of a possible ceasefire.

Gaza Strip
In the Gaza Strip, a weekend of violence culminated in a suicide bombing on Tuesday, shortly before newly elected President Abbas arrived for ceasefire talks. The attacker killed himself and a security agent and injured six Israelis. HAMMAS claimed responsibility and Israel banned all contacts with Abbas. On 19 January there were a number of militant attacks against Israeli troops including one exchange of fire that killed two militants. To pave the way for truce talks, Israel lifted the ban on contacts with Abbas and agreed that Palestinian security would be allowed to guard the Gaza border. This police deployment is a crucial test for the Palestinian Authority and has, so far, been effective. Abbas believes a ceasefire will be in place very soon.

India
In Indian-administered Kashmir, a gun battle with security forces killed two militants; the bodies of two soldiers were found in a burnt-out building. Indian authorities report shooting four suspected militants across the Line of Control and also say that mortar shells were fired across the boundary. Pakistan denies the charge. Both parties are discussing the alleged raids. The World Bank is considering Pakistan's request to mediate a dispute over a dam planned in an Indian-administered section of a river, in alleged breach of a shared-water treaty.

20 January   Afghanistan
Afghanistan has called for more funding for alternative crops to help eliminate the economic dependency on opium. This strategy has gained ground over short-term plans for aerial spraying to eradicate crops. Renowned Afghan warlord General Abdul Rashid Dostam escaped an attempted assassination by a suicide bomber. He was unhurt, but 25 people were injured, three critically. The Taliban claimed credit for the bombing.

Nepal
Nepal's Maoist rebels killed at least 24 security forces. Six rebels were also killed.

24 January   India
In the Indian state of Andhra Pradesh senior opposition party leader Paritala Ravi and a colleague were killed in a bomb attack. Protestors with Ravi's party, the Telugu Desam Party, called a strike to protest the killing. The area was closed down and there were a number of violent incidents, including arson against some 400 buses.

26 January   India
Suspected separatists in Assam state in India exploded five bombs on Republic Day. Two people were killed by the bombings, and eight died when Indian troops fired to disperse an angry mob.

27 January   Bangladesh
Bangladeshi police are questioning 64 people accused of belonging to the banned militant Islamic group the Jagrata Muslim Janata that is blamed for clashes with security forces earlier in the week. Another grenade attack, directed against the opposition Awami League party, killed five people including former Finance Minister Shah AMS Kibria. Riots following the attack led to 50 injuries and 40 arrests and a 3-day general strike.

1   February   Colombia
Colombian rebels of the Revolutionary Armed Forces of Colombia (FARC) attacked a military post, killing at least 14 marines and injuring 25. This attack was followed two days later with another, in which FARC rebels set off mines on a bridge as a patrol crossed, killing 15.

Georgia
Outside a Georgian police station in Gori, a car bomb killed three policemen and injured at least ten. Gori is the regional capital of an area including the breakaway region of South Ossetia.

3   February   India
In India, suspected Maoist rebels are blamed for election violence in the Indian states of Jharkhand, Bihar and Haryana. At least 20 people were killed in several incidents.

5 February — Gaza Strip
In Gaza, HAMAS has begun taking control of the towns it won in the recent elections. The fragile ceasefire was threatened after a 10-year-old Palestinian girl was shot dead in the school playground and sparked a series of mortar attacks. The source of the shooting is under investigation.

7 February — Iraq
25 people have been killed in two separate insurgent bombing attacks in Iraq targeting the police force.

8 February — Pakistan
In Balochistan province of Pakistan attacks against government installations continued, focusing on power sources and distribution. Suspected militants used four bombs to destroy a key rail line. In south Waziristan province there have been attacks against journalists, with two shot dead.

Sri Lanka
Sri Lankan Tamil Tiger leader E Kausalyan and five associates were ambushed and shot dead. Following an angry protest by Tamil members, parliament was suspended. The government has denied responsibility but suspicion has fallen on paramilitaries. Kausalyan, a political leader, was the most senior Tiger killed since the February 2002 ceasefire and his murder raises fears of a return to civil war.

9 February — Spain
In Madrid, Spain, Basque separatist group ETA claimed responsibility for a car bomb that injured 43 people.

Iraq
Nine people have been killed in another day of violence in Iraq, including a correspondent for a US-funded Arabic TV station.

10 February — Colombia
Colombian rebels of the Revolutionary Armed Forces of Colombia (FARC) ambushed troops in the northwest jungle, killing 20 soldiers.

Iraq
Eight Iraqi police were killed and more than 60 wounded when rebels attacked a police station south of Baghdad.

11 February — India
In the Indian state of Karnataka suspected Maoist rebels attacked police, killing six.

14 February — Philippines
The southern Philippines entered the second week of clashes between government forces and Muslim rebels of the Abu Sayyaf, as well as some members of the Moro National Liberation Front (MNLF) who object to their peace accord with the government. In addition to fierce gun battles at army and rebel camps, there were bombings in three major cities, killing dozens and injuring hundreds. Abu Sayyaf said that coordinated attacks on the 14th were a "Valentine's Day gift" for President Arroyo, who has promised to wipe out the rebels.

Lebanon
Former Lebanese Prime Minister Rafik Hariri was killed in a massive car bomb explosion. Some 600 pounds of explosives opened up a 15-foot crater and sent a car to the third floor of a nearby hotel. In addition to Hariri, 14 others died and more than 135 were injured. It was the largest bombing in Lebanon since the end of the civil war more than 15 years ago. A previously unknown group called Victory and Jihad claimed responsibility, but there have been many other suspects, including Syria. Hariri's funeral turned into a protest against Syria's presence in Lebanon. The UN is sending a team of experts to investigate the attack.

17 February — Russia
In the southern Russian region of Dagestan a car bomb near the Chechen border killed three and injured five. The attack was blamed on Chechen rebels.

Thailand
Thai investigators examining the Sungei Golok bombing of February 17 report the explosion, which killed six and injured 40, was both the largest bomb in the region and also the first car bombing, marking a significant escalation in violence. Warned of further inflaming tensions in the south, Thai Prime Minister Thaksin has reversed his plan to cut funding to pro-militant villages.

19 February — Pakistan
Pakistan's southwestern city of Quetta was the scene of raids in which 27 Sunni militants of the banned Lashkar-e-Jhangvi (LeJ) were detained following a suicide attack in which two militants were planning to attack a Shia religious procession. Six LeJ suspects were also arrested in Balochistan. Tribal fighting in North Waziristan killed two foreign nationals, possibly because of militant infighting.

24 February — Iraq
A car bomb at police headquarters in Tikrit killed 15 and injured 22.

India
In Indian-administered Kashmir, two militants stormed the main government offices. They killed three police and two civilians and forced the evacuation of more than 200 people before they were killed. The militant group Al Mansurian claimed responsibility.

1 March — India
Maoist rebels of the Communist Party India-Maoist (a merger of the People's War Group and the Maoist Communist Center) in Andhra Pradesh state killed eight people and abducted 50.

Nepal
Nepal's Maoist rebels called off a national transport strike and travel has returned to normal. Government forces claim

they killed 46 rebels in a gun battle in the southwest district of Bardiya. Four security force members were also killed, and [authorities] continue to search for rebels who fled. Political leaders in Nepal have had their house arrest extended by two months. Independent media coverage has been banned.

19 March   Pakistan
In Balochistan Province tensions remain high, with troops besieged by tribesmen and repeated clashes with security forces. The death toll from the March 19 Quetta (Balochistan's capital) bombing has risen to 46. Tensions in Balochistan have led to warnings of civil war.

20 March   Qatar
In Qatar, a suicide car bombing killed a British man and injured twelve. This is the first such attack in Qatar and came on the second anniversary of the start of the Iraq war.

21 March   Sri Lanka
Sri Lanka's Tamil Tiger rebels report two men killed and three injured in fighting between rival factions.

27 March   Thailand
Suspected Islamic rebels ambushed a train, injuring 19, when two bombs caused the train to turn over.

28 March   Sri Lanka
Sri Lanka's Tamil Tiger's political office in the north suffered a grenade attack that injured three. The attack was attributed to a Tiger splinter group.

1 April   India
Indian state Andhra Pradesh saw two policemen killed by suspected Maoist rebels. Separatist rebels of the United Liberation Front of Assam are being targeted in police operations underway in Assam.

Pakistan
Pakistani scholar Allama Ghulam Hussain Najafi was shot dead in a sectarian attack in Lahore. His daughter and her friend were injured. In North Waziristan a hand grenade missed the army convoy it targeted and landed on a private vehicle, injuring at least 15 civilians.

2 April   Afghanistan
In Afghanistan, the end of winter has led to an increase in Taliban attacks. Last week a roadside bomb remotely detonated when a Canadian diplomatic vehicle drove by, injuring four, There was also an attack in Helmand that killed three police and injured four, and gunmen ambushed a military convoy near the Pakistani border, killing three drivers.

4 April   Thailand
Thailand increased security at transportation centers after a series of bombs last weekend, but attacks continued. On April 4 a police station and government were targeted and on the 6th a bomb blast injured two police officers when the arrived at a restaurant to inspect the device, which was found in a flower pot.

6 April   Brazil
A Brazilian death squad, possibly of rogue police, killed at least 30 people in two districts of Rio de Janeiro. Brazil's indigenous population is the subject of a new Amnesty International report, "Foreigners in Our Own Country" that cites land rights as the most critical issue and says that without long-promised reservations, their very existence is threatened.

Kashmir
After 60 years of separation, the first bus service crossing Indian- and Pakistani-controlled sectors opened. Two days before the service opened a bomb blast on the route injured seven, while two other land mines were defused. The day before, militants attacked and caused a massive fire in which the buildings were destroyed. Both militants were shot dead and the passengers were successfully evacuated, with up to 40 treated for injuries. Militant groups Al-Nasirin, Al-Arifin, Farzandan-e-Millat, and the Save Kashmir Movement all claimed responsibility.

7 April   Egypt
In Egypt a bomb thrown from a motorbike went off in a major shopping bazaar in Cairo, killing four people and injuring 18. The dead included the attacker, two French and one American tourist. The attack, claimed by an unknown Islamic group, raised speculation that it could be the start of a campaign against foreign tourism.

9 April   India
In the state of Andhra Pradesh, suspected Maoist rebels have shot dead Congress party politician Ramdev Reddy.

15 April   Haiti
In Haiti, a weekend operation between peacekeepers and police led to the death of gang leaders Renee Jean Anthony (aka Grenn Sonnen) and Ravix Remissainthe as well as five of their followers. As UN Security Council and the Ad Hoc Consultative Group on Haiti arrived for an economic assessment, one of the peacekeepers was shot dead.

Nepal
Nepal's Maoist rebels continued threats against private schools, forcing a number of them to shut down. A bomb left by suspected rebels exploded in a village, killing five children and wounding three more as they played with the device. The Nepalese army claims it lost three personnel and killed 22 rebels in clashes in the western Rukum district.

21 April   Sri Lanka
Sri Lanka's Tamil Tiger rebels continued internecine fighting in which a breakaway group attacked a camp, killing five and injuring seven.

25 April   Nepal
In Nepal, bomb threats from Maoist rebels have closed a number of private schools. In a punishment attack, rebels killed ten villagers and injured seven for not supporting the cause. King Gyanendra says he will hold municipal elections

by April 2006 and decided to allow UN staff in to stop human rights abuses.

26 April   **Kashmir**
In Indian-administered Kashmir, clashes with troops killed six suspected militants.

27 April   **Colombia**
Colombian rebels of the Revolutionary Armed Forces of Colombia (FARC) have stepped up attacks in the southwest, leading to a new government plan to improve military cooperation with regional joint commands. Four top army generals disagreed with the changes and have been dismissed.

29 April   **Russia**
A shootout in the North Caucasus killed four gunmen believed associated with the Islamic militant group Yarmuk, and one policeman.

Afghanistan
Afghan police, on alert after last Sunday's car bombing in Kabul, stopped an explosives-laden car at a Herat checkpoint and arrested the driver, believed to be planning a suicide attack. A Taliban attack in Kandahar killed four attackers, targeting the mayor's office, and two police. In Uruzgan province a US soldier on patrol was killed in a Taliban ambush, and a US air strike killed three civilians and four militants. In Helmand province, four police were killed in a Taliban ambush, and clashes between Afghan troops and police killed six. Despite the outbreak of violence coinciding with the spring thaw, voter registration has opened for parliamentary and local elections scheduled for September.

Sri Lanka
Sri Lankan journalist Sharmaretnam Sivaram, a supporter of the Tamil Tiger rebels, has been kidnapped and shot dead in the capital, Colombo. The Tigers blame Sri Lankan military intelligence and rival Tiger paramilitaries, but responsibility for the attack is unknown.

2 May   **West Bank**
In the West Bank, a shootout killed one Israeli soldier and an Islamic Jihad member on May 2. On the 5th, a 14-year-old and a 15-year-old boy were both shot dead by Israeli soldiers. The two boys were among a group of stone-throwers. The Israeli commander of the operation has been suspended for unreasonable conduct.

5 May   **Haiti**
In Haiti, two foreign businessmen—an Indian and a Russian—have been kidnapped in two separate incidents, becoming the first foreign hostages since President Aristide's exile in February 2004.

United States
In New York City, two explosives went off outside the British consulate, causing minor property damage. The devices were novelty grenades packed with gunpowder and apparently detonated by hand. A suspect is being questioned. The UN and other international organizations stepped up security measures as a precaution.

7 May   **Burma**
Burma's capital, Rangoon, suffered three nearly simultaneous bombings in a shopping area. Eleven people were killed and 150 injured. The ruling military junta blamed ethnic and pro-democracy opponents, which have denied involvement.

10 May   **Afghanistan**
Afghanistan's insurgency has continued its spring expansion, with clashes against US-led forces, attacks against government security personnel, suicide and other attacks in areas frequented by foreigners, etc. More than a hundred militants were reported killed, as well as scores of security forces and foreigners. Taliban leader Mullah Mohammed Omar said that if the Afghan government does offer an amnesty program, he would refuse it, being in no need of safety guarantees.

Pakistan
In Pakistan's Balochistan province anti-government bombings and rocket attacks continued. One person was killed and one injured as they planted a roadside bomb. Fifty-eight leading Islamic scholars issued a decree against suicide attacks.

11 May   **Kashmir**
In Indian-administered Kashmir, an explosion in Srinagar killed one and injured 34. A car bomb or landmines caused the blast, and militant group Al-Nasarin claimed responsibility. Also in Srinigar, a grenade exploded near a school, killing two women and injuring more than 40, mostly schoolboys and girls. Nearby, a parcel bomb exploded, killing three members of a family. The motive and responsibility are unknown.

14 May   **India**
In the northeast state of Manipur, [there was] fighting last weekend between rival rebels of the Zomi Revolutionary Army (ZRA) and the United National Liberation Front (UNLF). The number killed has not been verified but is thought to be at least five.

15 May   **Spain**
In Spain last weekend, small bombs went off at two chemical plants and two factories. The four attacks have been attributed to Basque separatist group ETA. To popular approval, the Spanish parliament has given permission for the government to begin peace talks if ETA abandons violence.

18 May   **Israel**
Violence between Israelis and Palestinians had declined but recent weeks have shown a slow increase, including rocket attacks and military operations. In Gaza, near the Egyptian border, Israeli forces shot dead HAMAS member Ahmad Barhoum, [and] missiles fired at a Jewish settlement led to retaliatory fire in which one militant was killed and two escaped. There were also a number of Israeli operations targeting wanted Palestinians in the West Bank, with one Palestinian shot dead at a checkpoint.

Chronology of Significant Terrorist Incidents 1961–2005

19 May — Afghanistan

In Afghanistan suspected Taleban militants ambushed and killed anti-drug workers in Helmand and Zabul, killing at least eleven people. Zabul was also the scene of a bomb attack in which one US soldier died and three were injured.

20 May — Kashmir

Indian troops operating in Kashmir were ambushed by suspected separatist militants and four were killed.

27 May — Pakistan

In Karachi, Pakistan, a suicide attack against a Shia mosque killed five people and injured 20. Riots followed, and a Kentucky Fried Chicken was set on fire. Six people were killed in the blaze. More unrest followed, and many shops and business closed in protest at the government's failure to prevent the sectarian violence.

28 May — Indonesia

On the Indonesian island of Sulawesi, two bombs exploded on May 28, killing at least 22 and injuring 40. The two bombs in a crowded market went off within minutes of each other. The island has been the scene of ongoing Muslim-Christian violence despite a 2001 peace agreement, and it was suggested that the bombings could have been designed to incite further violence.

1 June — Afghanistan

A suicide bomb attack occurred at a mosque in Kandahar. 20 people were killed as they mourned the death of Fayaz. In Afghanistan, attacks against a mosque are extremely rare. Responsibility is unknown, but the governor suggests al Qaeda Arabs were involved.

India

India's northeast state of Manipur was the scene of two attacks blamed on separatists in which three people were killed.

2 June — Lebanon

Lebanese journalist Samir Qasir was killed by a bomb outside his home. This is the most prominent assassination since former Prime Minister Hariri's death, and has led to anti-Syrian protests and calls for pro-Syrian President Lahoud to resign. Qasir was opposed to Syria's presence in Lebanon. Suspicion for the attack has fallen on Syria, which denies any involvement.

6 June — Mauritania

A Mauritanian army base was attacked by five members of the Salafist Group for Preaching and Combat (GSPC) who killed 15 soldiers and injured 17. The government organized anti-terrorism marches in which tens of thousands of people protested the attack.

7 June — Nepal

Nepal's Maoist rebels are blamed for a landmine that blew up a passenger bus, killing at least 38 and injuring more than 70. This was the bloodiest attack since the Maoist insurgency began fighting in 1996 and they have admitted it is a serious mistake, and that government soldiers had been the intended target. A group of rebels carrying bombs took shelter in a civilian house, when one of the bombs went off, destroying the house, killing five rebels, and injuring five residents.

9 June — Algeria

Algerian militants, possibly with the Salafist Group for Preaching and Combat (GSPC), have been blamed for an explosion in the north that killed 13 government guards who were part of an operation directed against Islamist militants.

10 June — Spain

Spain's Basque separatist group ETA set off a mortar attack near Zaragoza airport. Given prior warning, the terminal was evacuated and there were no casualties.

12 June — Russia

A Russian train returning from Chechnya was derailed by an explosion attributed to separatists, which injured at least 12. Earlier in the week, Chechen separatists ambushed Russian police officers, leaving seven dead.

13 June — Kashmir

A car bomb in Indian-administered Kashmir outside a high school killed 14 and injured more than 100, including many students. A strike was called to protest the attack. Responsibility is unknown, but has been blamed on both separatists and Indian agencies.

15 June — Iraq

Bombers hit Iraqi security forces in and around Baghdad, killing at least 33 people in two separate attacks. At least 25 Iraqi soldiers were killed in the first blast, by a suicide bomber wearing an Iraqi army uniform.

17 June — Nigeria

Nigeria's capital, Lagos, received security threats that led to the temporary closure of the British, German, Italian, Russian, and US diplomatic missions. In the oil-rich Delta, a group of gunmen kidnapped six Shell oil workers, who were later freed after talks and without conditions. The kidnappers were angry because Shell's promises to support Nigerian development had not been met.

19 June — Afghanistan

A suicide bomber killed himself and at least 16 people in a restaurant in Baghdad.

20 June — India

In the Indian state of Assam clashes killed four separatist rebels and one soldier, while more than 30 suspected associates of the United Liberation Front of Assam have been arrested. Maoist rebels in Bihar state clashed with police, leaving 16 rebels, two police, and two civilians dead after a rebel attack against state offices. In Punjab, state police say that an operation to counter Sikh militants has been successful, including some 24 arrests.

Nepal

Nepal's Maoist rebels attacked a prison in the east, freeing more than 60 inmates, while leaving five police and two rebels dead. There were more clashes in the east during the week, with unknown casualties, and 12 security personnel were kidnapped. At the end of the week five rebels and a soldiers were killed when rebels attacked a security checkpoint in the western district of Bardiya.

22 June   Thailand

In southern Thailand, the head of a Buddhist man was found with a note saying his murder was in response to the arrest of a prominent Muslim student leader the previous week. Such sectarian violence in the Muslim majority south has claimed more than 700 lives since January 2004.

Thailand

In southern Thailand, suspected Muslim militants shot then decapitated a man in a teashop. There have been five beheadings in the past two weeks, taking revenge against repressive government measures, but this is the first to be so publicly undertaken.

23 June   Afghanistan

18 people were killed and 46 others were wounded in three car bomb attacks in a Shia district of Baghdad. Hours earlier, in the same district, gunmen shot dead a prominent Sunni Muslim lawyer and his 15-year-old son.

24 June   Kashmir

In Indian-administered Kashmir, a bomb blast remotely detonated as an army convoy drove past killed four Indian soldiers and injured several others. Hizbul Mujahideen claimed responsibility.

India

20 people were killed in a fierce gun battle between Maoist rebels and police in the Indian state of Bihar.

26 June   Colombia

Colombian rebels of the Revolutionary Armed Forces of Colombia (FARC) ambushed government troops in Putamayo province near the border with Ecuador, killing 19 soldiers. FARC also battled troops for control of a road near the Venezuelan border, killing six. More than a dozen soldiers are missing and may have been taken hostage. Rebel casualties are unknown.

28 June   Democratic Republic of Congo

In Democratic Republic of Congo UN peacekeeping troops engaged in dismantling a militia camp in the eastern province of Ituri came under sustained attack with mortars, grenades, and machine guns by a rebel National Liberation Front (FNL) force of more than 1,000. The rebels also used women and children as human shields. Most of the 4,000 residents of the village fled. Casualties from that incident are not yet known, but at least seven people were killed in and around the capital Kinshasa during protests against a delay of at least six months in holding parliamentary elections.

30 June   Iraq

Iraq's oldest member of parliament, Dhari al-Fayadh, has become its second to die since the government was installed in April. His son and three bodyguards were also killed in the same suicide car bombing.

Afghanistan

In Afghanistan, a rocket-propelled grenade brought down a US helicopter, killing the 16 soldiers on board. It is believed that troops on the ground were alive, but they are missing. US fighter planes bombed a suspected Taliban hideout in the same area, killing 25 people, and have now acknowledged that number may include civilians who also lived inside the residential compounds. Ahead of parliamentary elections due in September the violence has been increasing, but the UN-backed disarmament, demobilization and reintegration program marked a milestone with the completion of the first two phases. The final phase of reintegration will take another year.

Haiti

Haiti's armed gangs were the target of UN peacekeeping operations. Troops stormed a shantytown and engaged in a gun battle that killed at least two men, possibly including the powerful gang leader Emmanuel Wilmey ("Dread Wilmey").

7 July   England

In London, England, three time bombs detonated almost simultaneously in three separate underground trains, at approximately 8:50 a.m. At 9:47 another bomb exploded on a bus. The attacks killed at least 49 people and injured more than 700. Britons are remembering those who died in this most recent bombing while also commemorating the 60th anniversary marking the end of World War II. July 10 is the designated national remembrance day.

8 July   Iraq

Egyptian ambassador Ihab al-Sherif was abducted and held by Abu Musab al-Zarqawi's group, al Qaeda in Iraq. He was later killed, although details of his assassination remain unclear. Shortly after Sherif's kidnapping, Pakistan's envoy escaped an attack uninjured, but Bahrain's ambassador, Hassan Malallah al-Ansari, was shot and wounded. Other violence during the week included large suicide bombings, mortar attacks, as well as roadside and car bombs. Italy will begin withdrawing troops within two months. Coca-Cola has returned to Iraq 37 years after it withdrew, competing there with Pepsi.

10 July   Sri Lanka

In Sri Lanka, a grenade attack on a Tamil Tiger office killed two rebel officials and two civilians.

11 July   Afghanistan

In Afghanistan, attacks associated with Taliban guerillas have continued, including the assassination of a pro-government cleric. US troops found the body of a missing soldier, one of the group in which only one of four was rescued last week. Four "dangerous enemy combatants" escaped from Bagram prison and are being hunted. Despite such operations, more than 200 local commanders have been disarmed, and Australia has agreed to send 150 special forces to help counter increasing attacks ahead of September's parliamentary elections.

12 July   Kenya
In northeast Kenya, ethnic Borana crossed the border from Ethiopia into the ethnic Gabra village of Turbi, where they surrounded a school and nearby houses and opened fire, killing 76 people, including 22 children. Ten of the attackers were killed. Those who fled, with stolen livestock, apparently returned to Ethiopia. The raids also displaced at least 6,000 people. Armed forces are arriving in the remote territory to prevent further attacks.

Spain
Spain's Basque separatist group ETA has been blamed for four explosion that struck a power station. There were no casualties. A policeman was injured as a homemade bomb outside the Italian Cultural Institute in Barcelona exploded. Responsibility in unknown, but graffiti indicated an anarchist connection.

Israel
At the Israeli coastal town of Netanya a suicide bomber killed himself and five others at a mall entrance. At least 30 people were injured. Islamic Jihad was responsible for the attack and now faces relentless retaliation. Israeli security forces have arrested at least five militants and are continuing operations, including the reoccupation of the West Bank town of Tulkarm. A raid on Nablus has killed one member of al Aqsa Martyr's Brigades.

14 July   England
Londoners faced a mirror attack, one week after 7/7. Explosives were set off in three underground stations and one bus. This time, the triggers went off but the explosives did not detonate, and only one person was injured. Indications are that the same technique was used but that the homemade explosive had deteriorated. Much more forensic information was left behind, and a massive manhunt continues. A casualty of these incidents was Brazilian Jean Charles de Menezes, who was shot dead by police in South London, although he was innocent and had no connection with the attacks. An inquiry will be held into the shooting.

16 July   Turkey
In Turkey, an explosion on July 16 in the Aegean resort of Kusadasi, killed five, and injured 13, including several foreign tourists. Kurdish PKK militants are blamed for the attack. On July 24 in Istanbul, an explosion in a restaurant injured two people. The cause is under investigation.

23 July   Egypt
In the Egyptian resort of Sharm el-Sheikh three bomb attacks have killed at least 64 people and injured more than 200. Two car bombs were detonated at 1:15 a.m., one at a hotel and the second two miles away at the Old Market. A third, hidden in a sack, went off near a beach walkway. Most of the dead were Egyptians, but foreigners were also killed. The attack prompted immediate condemnation by international governments. The Abdullah Azzam Brigades, al Qaeda in Syria in Egypt, claimed responsibility, as they had for an April bombing in Cairo, in a web posting. The previously unknown Holy Warriors of Egypt also claimed responsibility, faxing a statement to newspapers that listed names of five attackers. Neither claim has been verified.

Nepal
Nepal's Maoist rebels have reinstated Baburam Bhattarai, who had been suspended because of disagreements with the leader, Prachanda. Rebels killed seven security personnel in the west. Following that ambush, security forces killed two rebels.

25 July   India
In Indian-administered Kashmir, three soldiers and a civilian were killed when a suicide bomber drove an explosive-packed car into an army vehicle in Srinagar. Hizbul Mujahideen claimed responsibility. In another incident, six male members of a Muslim family were shot dead by suspected militants in a village house in Udhampur. A gun battle between militants and soldiers left three suspected militants, believed belonging to Hizbul Mujahideen, dead. There were a number of other incidents. Late on the night of the 24th, four Kashmiri youths were shot dead by Indian troops who mistook them for rebels. Hundreds of protestors demonstrated against the shooting.

Ethiopia
In Ethiopia's Somali region five people were killed and more than 30 injured in a series of grenade attacks across six locations. The simultaneous attacks at a nightclub and official residences are believed designed to interfere with August 21 elections. The attacks were attributed to Ogaden National Liberation Front (ONLF) rebels. Somali is the last region in which elections are to be held. Official results so far indicate that the ruling coalition is nearing a majority, a result rejected as fraudulent by opposition leaders.

27 July   Colombia
Colombian rebels of the Revolutionary Armed Forces of Colombia (FARC) have closed off the southern province of Putumayo, cutting off electricity and blockading roads. The government has had to airlift basic supplies. FARC have been blamed for a deadly roadside bombing in the northern Sierra Nevada region that killed at least 14 police officers. FARC have refused to enter into hostage-release talks until government forces leave two mountain areas in the western province of Valle del Cauca and ensure that two commanders, Ricardo Palmero and Nayibe Rojas are part of the return deal. Both

men have been extradited to the US on drug trafficking charges. About 2,000 members of the right-wing paramilitary United Self-Defense Forces of Colombia (AUC) have begun disarming and demobilization.

29 July — Kashmir

In Indian-administered Kashmir, five Hindus were murdered when suspected Muslim militants raided a village and cut their throats. An investigation is underway. Heavy fighting has entered its second day in Srinagar. The fighting began the evening of 29 July when militants of the Al-Mansurin and Jamiat-ul Mujahhideen attacked a police vehicle then entered a hotel complex. When security forces stormed a building and killed a militant hiding there, a gunbattle broke out. There are a number of casualties.

1 August — Kashmir

In Indian-administered Kashmir, three separate clashes between militants and security forces led to the death of six suspected militants.

8 August — India

In the Indian state of Assam, suspected separatists with the United Liberation Front of Assam (ULFA) set off an explosion that caused a huge fire and badly damaged an oil pipeline. Naga tribesmen have been blockading a major highway for two weeks, forcing the Indian military to begin airlifting essential goods to the area.

12 August — India

Suspected Maoist rebels were blamed for an attack at a police station in Bihar state. Two policemen were killed and four injured.

Nepal

Nepal's Maoist rebels claim that 159 soldiers were killed and 50 taken prisoner in an attack in the northwest Kalikot district that also killed 26 rebels. The government denies this, saying that around 40 soldiers were killed, but more than 100 are missing, and the military is searching for them. Further clashes later in the week killed 12 rebels and one soldier.

Sri Lanka

Sri Lanka has been placed under a state of emergency following the assassination of Foreign Minister Lakshman Kadirgamar. Tamil Tigers are suspected, and a massive investigation is underway.

17 August — India

India's Andhra Pradesh state imposed a ban on the rebel Communist Party of India-Maoist and several front organizations following an attack in which a Congress Party legislator and nine other people were shot dead, and eight others injured. This was believed to be the first CPI-M attack at a public gathering.

PART 5

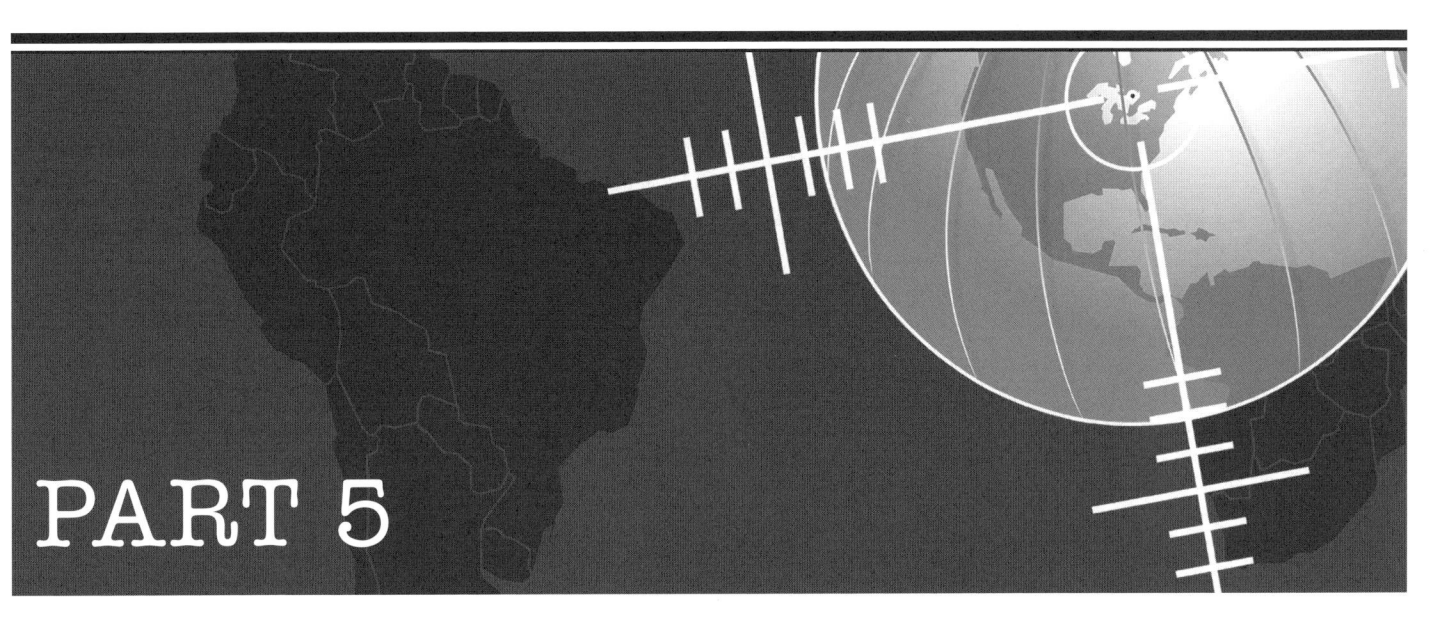

TERRORIST INCIDENTS BY COUNTRY AND GROUP

Overview of Terrorist Incidents by Country, 1985–2004

Anna Sabasteanski

This section uses tables to present the annual number of incidents by country from 1985 to 2004. This data was used to build the maps that follow the tables, and was gathered from the National Counterterrorism Center (NCTC) Worldwide Incidents Tracking System (WITS) and the MIPT Terrorism Knowledge Base that integrates data from the RAND Terrorism Chronology and RAND-MIPT Terrorism Incident databases. WITS was launched in July 2005, and its methodology is described in Part 6, "Trends over Time: Graphs on Terrorism"

Data in these tables has not been normalized to account for name changes over time; it is merely reproduced as it was entered into the database. For example, in 1985 there were both the Federal Republic of Germany (West Germany) and the German Democratic Republic (East Germany), and the Soviet Union was still intact. Transkei, the first of the nominally independent black homelands within apartheid South Africa, was the scene of two incidents in 1985. Transkei is now part of the Eastern Cape province of South Africa. Today, WITS separately records the occupied territories as the Gaza Strip and West Bank.

New countries have also been added. When the United Nations began in 1945, it had fifty-one member states. Decolonization increased membership to 126 by 1970. In 2005, largely driven by the breakup of the Soviet Union and Yugoslavia, there are 191 member states. In addition to officially recognized countries, there are a number of regions and areas of interest specified in the database. For example, the final status of several areas in the former Yugoslavia has not been determined. Incidents in Kosovo, Montenegro, and Serbia are documented separately. Chechnya was not allowed to separate from Russia as the Soviet Union broke apart. Although part of the Russian Federation, the area suffers high levels of terrorism and political violence and is also tracked separately. Kashmir, an historic princely state, was divided into two regions, one administered by India and one by Pakistan. With one of the highest levels of terrorist attacks, it is tracked separately. Note that in both Chechnya and Kashmir, most of the violence has been domestic. Domestic incidents were only added to the database in 1998, so the earlier years do not reflect the actual level of attacks.

Areas listed in the database include Afghanistan, Albania, Algeria, American Samoa, Andorra, Angola, Anguilla, Antigua and Barbuda, Argentina, Armenia, Aruba, Ashmore and Cartier Islands, Australia, Austria, Azerbaijan, Azores, Bahamas, Bahrain, Baker Island, Bangladesh, Barbados, Bassas da India, Belarus, Belgium, Belize, Benin, Benin (Dahomey), Bermuda, Bhutan, Bolivia, Bosnia, Bosnia and Herzegovina, Bosnia-Herzegovina, Botswana, Bouvet Island, Brazil, British Honduras, British Virgin Islands, Brunei, Bulgaria, Burkina Faso, Burma (Myanmar), Burundi, Cambodia, Cameroon, Canada, Canary Islands, Cape Verde, Cayman Islands, Central African Republic, Chad, Chechnya, Chile, China, China (Republic of [Taiwan]), Christmas Island, Clipperton Island, Cocos (Keeling) Islands, Colombia, Comoros, Congo (Brazzaville), Congo (Democratic Republic), Congo (Democratic Republic of the), Congo (Republic of), Congo (Republic of the), Cook Islands, Coral Sea Islands, Corsica, Costa Rica, Cote d'Ivoire, Croatia, Cuba, Cyprus, Czech Republic, Czechoslovakia, Denmark, Djibouti, Dominica, Dominican Republic, East Timor, Ecuador, Egypt, El Salvador, Equatorial Guinea, Eritrea, Estonia, Ethiopia, Europa Island, Falkland Islands (Islas Malvinas), Faroe Islands, Federal Republic of Germany, Fiji, Finland, France, French Guiana, French Polynesia, FRY, FRY (Kosovo), FRY (Montenegro), FRY (Serbia), FRY (Southern Serbia), Gabon, Gambia, Gaza Strip, Georgia, German Democratic Republic, Germany, Ghana, Gibraltar, Glorioso Islands, Golan Heights, Greece, Greenland, Grenada, Guadeloupe, Guam, Guatemala, Guernsey, Guinea, Guinea-Bissau, Guyana, Haiti, Holy See (Vatican City), Honduras, Hong Kong, Howland Island, Hungary, Iceland, India, Indonesia, Iran, Iraq, Ireland, Israel, Italy, Ivory Coast, Jamaica, Jan Mayen, Japan, Jarvis Island, Jersey, Johnston Atoll, Jordan, Juan de Nova Island, Kashmir, Kazakhstan, Kenya, Kingman Reef, Kiribati, Korea, North, Korea, South, Kuwait, Kyrgyzstan, Laos, Latvia, Lebanon, Lesotho, Liberia, Libya, Liechtenstein, Lithuania, Luxembourg, Macau, Macedonia, Macedonia (Republic of), Madagascar, Malawi, Malaysia, Maldives, Mali, Malta, Man (Isle of), Marshall Islands, Martinique, Mauritania, Mauritius, Mayotte, Mexico, Micronesia (Federated States of), Midway Islands, Moldova, Monaco, Mongolia, Montserrat, Morocco, Mozambique, Namibia, Namibia SWAf, Nauru, Navassa Island, Nepal, Netherlands, Netherlands Antilles, New Caledonia, New Zealand, Nicaragua, Niger, Nigeria, Niue, Norfolk Island, North Korea, Northern Ireland (UK), Northern Mariana Islands, Norway, Occupied Territories, Oman, Pakistan, Palau, Palestine Inter Arab, Palmyra Atoll, Panama, Papua New Guinea, Paracel Islands, Paraguay, Persian Gulf, Peru, Philippines, Pitcairn Islands, Poland, Portugal, Puerto Rico, Qatar, Reunion, Romania, Russia, Rwanda,

Saint Kitts and Nevis, Saint Lucia, Saint Pierre and Miquelon, Saint Vincent and the Grenadines, Samoa, San Marino, Sao Tome and Principe, Saudi Arabia, Senegal, Serbia, Serbia and Montenegro, Seychelles, Sierra Leone, Singapore, Slovakia, Slovenia, Solomon Islands, Somalia, South Africa, South Georgia and the Islands, South Korea, Spain, Spanish Sahara, Spratly Islands, Sri Lanka (Ceylon), Sudan, Suriname, Svalbard, Swaziland, Sweden, Switzerland, Syria, Taiwan, Tajikistan, Tanzania, Thailand, Togo, Tokelau, Tonga, Transkei, Trinidad and Tobago, Tromelin Island, Trucial Oman States, Tunisia, Turkey, Turkmenistan, Turks and Caicos Islands, Tuvalu, Uganda, Ukraine, United Arab Emirates, United Kingdom, United States, Uruguay, USSR, Uzbekistan, Vanuatu, Vatican City, Venezuela, Viet Nam, South, Vietnam, Virgin Islands, Wake Island, Wallis and Futuna, West Berlin, Western Sahara, Yemen, Yugoslavia, Zaire (Belgian Congo), Zambia, Zimbabwe, Zimbabwe (Rhodesia),

Only a minority of these countries is subjected to terrorist attacks in the course of a year, and even fewer ever show up in *Patterns of Global Terrorism*. The table below documents the number of countries affected by terrorist incidents in the course of each year:

Only fourteen are listed in every year: Colombia, France, Germany, Israel, Lebanon, Occupied Territories (Gaza Strip and West Bank), Pakistan, Peru, Spain, Turkey, the United Kingdom, the United States, and Venezuela. Italy was listed in every year except 1995, and India every year except 1986.

Statistical analysis of attacks can be found in Part 6, "Trends over Time: Graphs on Terrorism."

Year	Number of Countries Affected
1985	63
1986	57
1987	57
1988	60
1989	67
1990	61
1991	67
1992	60
1993	60
1994	70
1995	61
1996	56
1997	62
1998	88
1999	67
2000	57
2001	81
2002	81
2003	70
2004	78

1985

Country	Incidents	Country	Incidents
Afghanistan	1	Lebanon	82
Algeria	1	Libya	1
Angola	3	Luxembourg	1
Argentina	3	Malta	1
Australia	2	Morocco	5
Austria	3	Mozambique	6
Belgium	10	Netherlands	2
Bolivia	3	New Zealand	1
Botswana	1	Nicaragua	4
Canada	2	Norway	1
Chad	1	Occupied Territories	7
Chile	24	Pakistan	4
Colombia	18	Peru	15
Cyprus	11	Philippines	3
Denmark	8	Portugal	12
Egypt	5	Romania	1
El Salvador	1	Saudi Arabia	3
Ethiopia	1	Singapore	1
Federal Republic of Germany	24	South Africa	2
France	19	Spain	17
German Democratic Republic	1	Sweden	1
Greece	26	Switzerland	5
Guadeloupe	1	Thailand	1
Guatemala	4	Transkei	1
Honduras	1	Tunisia	2
India	3	Turkey	4
Iraq	4	United Arab Emirates	1
Israel	45	United Kingdom	3
Italy	13	United States	3
Japan	2	USSR	1
Jordan	2	Zimbabwe (Rhodesia)	1
Kuwait	6		

1986

Country	Incidents	Country	Incidents
Afghanistan	2	Italy	6
Angola	2	Japan	3
Argentina	1	Korea, South	2
Australia	1	Kuwait	2
Austria	3	Lebanon	62
Bahrain	1	Mexico	2
Belgium	2	Morocco	5
Bolivia	2	Mozambique	3
Brazil	1	Netherlands	1
Canada	1	Nicaragua	3
Chile	14	Pakistan	12
Colombia	29	Peru	44
Costa Rica	2	Philippines	3
Cyprus	2	Portugal	3
Denmark	1	Spain	31
Egypt	6	Sri Lanka (Ceylon)	4
El Salvador	1	Sudan	4
Ethiopia	2	Sweden	4
Federal Republic of Germany	13	Syria	2
France	26	Thailand	2
German Democratic Republic	1	Tunisia	1
Greece	10	Turkey	5
Guatemala	5	United Arab Emirates	1
Haiti	1	United Kingdom	5
Indonesia	3	United States	3
Iran	2	Venezuela	2
Iraq	1	Yemen	1
Israel	27		

1987

Country	Incidents	Country	Incidents
Afghanistan	2	Lebanon	41
Angola	1	Luxembourg	1
Argentina	1	Malta	4
Austria	4	Mauritania	1
Belgium	1	Mexico	2
Bolivia	5	Morocco	1
Chad	1	Mozambique	3
Chile	13	Nicaragua	1
Colombia	13	Norway	1
Congo (Brazzaville)	1	Pakistan	26
Costa Rica	1	Panama	1
Cyprus	4	Peru	38
Djibouti	1	Philippines	19
Dominican Republic	3	Saudi Arabia	1
Egypt	2	Singapore	2
Ethiopia	3	Somalia	1
Federal Republic of Germany	12	Spain	27
Fiji	1	Sri Lanka (Ceylon)	2
France	15	Sudan	2
Greece	11	Swaziland	1
Honduras	5	Switzerland	2
India	1	Thailand	1
Iran	4	Tunisia	4
Iraq	5	Turkey	6
Israel	32	United Kingdom	6
Italy	4	United States	7
Jamaica	2	Venezuela	3
Jordan	1	Zambia	1
Kuwait	5		

1988

Country	Incidents	Country	Incidents
Afghanistan	6	Korea, South	15
Argentina	3	Kuwait	3
Australia	3	Lebanon	33
Bangladesh	1	Morocco	1
Belgium	3	Mozambique	1
Bolivia	5	Namibia	1
Botswana	1	Netherlands	2
Canada	1	Nicaragua	2
Chile	8	Nigeria	1
China, Republic of (Taiwan)	1	Pakistan	34
Colombia	26	Peru	15
Costa Rica	3	Philippines	16
Cyprus	5	Portugal	2
Dominican Republic	2	Romania	1
Ecuador	1	Singapore	1
Egypt	6	South Africa	3
El Salvador	14	Spain	28
Ethiopia	2	Sri Lanka (Ceylon)	3
Federal Republic of Germany	13	Sudan	4
France	10	Sweden	1
Gibraltar	1	Switzerland	2
Greece	13	Thailand	1
Guatemala	3	Turkey	12
Honduras	6	Uganda	1
India	4	United Kingdom	3
Iran	1	United States	3
Israel	31	Venezuela	1
Italy	2	Yemen	1
Japan	4	Zambia	2
Jordan	2	Zimbabwe (Rhodesia)	1

1989

Country	Incidents	Country	Incidents
Afghanistan	2	Japan	1
Angola	3	Kenya	1
Austria	1	Korea, South	6
Bangladesh	1	Laos	2
Belgium	7	Lebanon	18
Bolivia	4	Libya	1
Brazil	1	Malaysia	1
Burma (Myanmar)	1	Mexico	1
Canada	1	Morocco	1
Chad	1	Mozambique	3
Chile	25	Namibia, SWAf	1
Colombia	22	Netherlands	5
Costa Rica	1	Nicaragua	1
Cote d'Ivoire	1	Pakistan	15
Cyprus	2	Panama	1
Czechoslovakia	1	Peru	29
Denmark	1	Philippines	9
Dominican Republic	8	Saudi Arabia	3
Ecuador	6	South Africa	3
Egypt	2	Spain	17
El Salvador	13	Sri Lanka (Ceylon)	6
Federal Republic of Germany	12	Sudan	1
Fiji	1	Suriname	1
France	9	Switzerland	2
Greece	6	Syria	1
Guatemala	9	Tanzania	1
Haiti	1	Thailand	1
Honduras	9	Turkey	12
Hungary	1	United Arab Emirates	1
India	1	United Kingdom	13
Iran	1	United States	9
Iraq	2	Venezuela	2
Israel	27	Zambia	1
Italy	8		

1990

Country	Incidents	Country	Incidents
Afghanistan	2	Lebanon	8
Albania	1	Liberia	1
Angola	3	Libya	1
Argentina	9	Mexico	1
Austria	1	Morocco	1
Belgium	2	Netherlands	5
Bolivia	4	Nicaragua	1
Brazil	1	Northern Ireland (UK)	2
Bulgaria	1	Occupied Territories	3
Chile	22	Pakistan	4
Colombia	8	Panama	5
Congo (Brazzaville)	1	Papua New Guinea	4
Costa Rica	1	Peru	26
Cote d'Ivoire	1	Philippines	36
Cyprus	1	Poland	4
Djibouti	1	Somalia	3
Egypt	4	South Africa	2
El Salvador	1	Spain	11
Federal Republic of Germany	4	Sudan	1
France	7	Suriname	2
German Democratic Republic	1	Sweden	6
Greece	18	Switzerland	1
Guatemala	4	Thailand	4
Honduras	2	Turkey	8
India	1	Uganda	1
Israel	23	United Kingdom	2
Italy	1	United States	2
Japan	3	Uruguay	1
Jordan	4	Venezuela	3
Korea, South	3	Zimbabwe (Rhodesia)	1
Laos	1		

1991

Country	Incidents	Country	Incidents
Afghanistan	1	Korea, South	2
Albania	1	Kuwait	1
Algeria	2	Latvia	1
Argentina	4	Lebanon	33
Australia	3	Malaysia	3
Austria	2	Mexico	5
Belgium	2	Mozambique	1
Bolivia	2	Netherlands	2
Brazil	4	Northern Ireland (UK)	2
Bulgaria	1	Norway	1
Chile	33	Occupied Territories	2
China	1	Pakistan	11
Colombia	3	Panama	4
Costa Rica	2	Peru	44
Cuba	1	Philippines	3
Cyprus	4	Romania	1
Ecuador	7	Saudi Arabia	1
Egypt	1	Somalia	3
El Salvador	3	Spain	7
Federal Republic of Germany	31	Sri Lanka (Ceylon)	2
Finland	1	Sudan	1
France	14	Sweden	2
Greece	33	Tunisia	2
Guatemala	4	Turkey	30
Honduras	2	Uganda	1
Hungary	2	United Arab Emirates	1
India	13	United Kingdom	3
Indonesia	1	United States	4
Iran	4	Uruguay	1
Iraq	1	USSR	4
Israel	15	Venezuela	3
Italy	23	Yemen	5
Japan	3	Zimbabwe (Rhodesia)	2
Jordan	9		

1992

Country	Incidents	Country	Incidents
Afghanistan	2	Japan	2
Algeria	6	Jordan	2
Angola	5	Kuwait	6
Argentina	3	Lebanon	3
Austria	1	Liberia	3
Bolivia	3	Netherlands	3
Brazil	1	Nicaragua	1
British Honduras	1	Nigeria	1
Cambodia	6	Pakistan	2
Canada	1	Panama	5
Chile	23	Peru	14
Colombia	21	Philippines	5
Costa Rica	1	Poland	1
Cuba	1	Rwanda	1
Czechoslovakia	1	Sierra Leone	2
Egypt	6	Somalia	3
El Salvador	2	South Africa	1
Estonia	1	Spain	5
Ethiopia	2	Sudan	1
Federal Republic of Germany	35	Sweden	3
France	7	Thailand	1
Ghana	1	Turkey	19
Greece	2	United Kingdom	6
Guatemala	3	United States	1
Hungary	1	USSR	2
India	1	Venezuela	3
Iran	4	Vietnam	1
Iraq	10	Yemen	4
Israel	11	Yugoslavia	1
Italy	8	Zambia	1

1993

Country	Incidents	Country	Incidents
Afghanistan	4	Jordan	1
Algeria	9	Korea, South	1
Angola	6	Kuwait	1
Argentina	1	Lebanon	14
Austria	2	Mozambique	1
Bolivia	2	Nigeria	1
Brazil	1	Norway	1
Burma (Myanmar)	1	Occupied Territories	1
Cambodia	13	Pakistan	1
Canada	1	Panama	1
Chile	11	Peru	17
China	1	Philippines	3
Colombia	9	Poland	1
Costa Rica	1	Sierra Leone	1
Czechoslovakia	1	Somalia	20
Denmark	1	Spain	2
Ecuador	1	Sweden	3
Egypt	15	Switzerland	4
El Salvador	1	Tajikistan	1
Estonia	1	Tanzania	1
Federal Republic of Germany	18	Thailand	1
France	15	Tunisia	1
Hungary	1	Turkey	19
India	3	Uganda	2
Iran	2	United Kingdom	5
Iraq	3	United States	2
Ireland	1	USSR	2
Israel	15	Venezuela	2
Italy	3	Yemen	9
Japan	4	Yugoslavia	1

1994

Country	Incidents	Country	Incidents
Afghanistan	1	Jordan	2
Albania	1	Kenya	1
Algeria	31	Lebanon	9
Angola	4	Mali	1
Argentina	3	Mexico	1
Australia	2	Morocco	1
Azerbaijan	1	Mozambique	2
Belgium	1	Netherlands	1
Benin, Dahomey	1	Nicaragua	2
Bolivia	1	Norway	1
Bosnia	11	Occupied Territories	5
Bulgaria	1	Pakistan	1
Burundi	1	Panama	1
Cambodia	3	Peru	2
Chile	4	Philippines	7
Colombia	33	Romania	1
Croatia	2	Russia	2
Cuba	1	Rwanda	4
Cyprus	1	Saudi Arabia	1
Denmark	1	Sierra Leone	3
Ecuador	1	Somalia	13
Egypt	16	South Africa	3
El Salvador	1	Spain	3
Estonia	1	Sri Lanka (Ceylon)	1
Ethiopia	1	Sweden	1
Federal Republic of Germany	6	Thailand	2
France	3	Tunisia	1
Greece	18	Turkey	15
Guatemala	4	United Kingdom	6
India	5	United States	3
Iran	3	Uruguay	1
Iraq	8	Venezuela	2
Ireland	5	Yemen	6
Israel	24	Yugoslavia	1
Italy	4	Zaire (Belgian Congo)	1

1995

Country	Incidents	Country	Incidents
Afghanistan	2	Lebanon	3
Algeria	12	Liberia	1
Angola	2	Malta	1
Argentina	2	Morocco	1
Austria	5	Netherlands	7
Bahrain	1	Nicaragua	1
Belgium	1	Occupied Territories	5
Bosnia	2	Pakistan	9
Bulgaria	1	Papua New Guinea	1
Burundi	7	Peru	2
Cambodia	1	Philippines	2
Chad	1	Russia	3
Colombia	10	Saudi Arabia	3
Croatia	1	Senegal	1
Denmark	1	Serbia	1
Egypt	5	Sierra Leone	7
El Salvador	1	Somalia	4
Ethiopia	3	Spain	2
Federal Republic of Germany	72	Sri Lanka (Ceylon)	1
France	15	Sudan	2
Georgia	3	Sweden	1
Greece	3	Switzerland	5
Guatemala	3	Tajikistan	4
Haiti	1	Tunisia	1
Honduras	1	Turkey	8
India	4	Ukraine	1
Iraq	7	United Kingdom	5
Israel	11	United States	1
Japan	2	Venezuela	1
Jordan	1	Zimbabwe (Rhodesia)	1
Kashmir	1		

1996

Country	Incidents	Country	Incidents
Afghanistan	3	Korea, South	2
Algeria	4	Lebanon	5
Angola	1	Liberia	2
Austria	1	Mauritania	1
Bahrain	10	Mexico	2
Bangladesh	2	Nicaragua	3
Bosnia	4	Occupied Territories	3
Burundi	3	Pakistan	8
Cambodia	5	Panama	1
Chile	1	Peru	2
China	1	Philippines	5
Colombia	22	Poland	1
Cyprus	2	Russia	7
Egypt	5	Saudi Arabia	1
Eritrea	1	Somalia	6
Ethiopia	3	Spain	7
Federal Republic of Germany	20	Sri Lanka (Ceylon)	5
France	15	Sudan	6
German Democratic Republic	1	Switzerland	3
Greece	8	Syria	1
Haiti	2	Tajikistan	4
Honduras	1	Turkey	8
India	4	Uganda	5
Indonesia	3	United Kingdom	1
Iraq	4	United States	1
Israel	10	Venezuela	6
Italy	1	Yemen	2
Jordan	1	Zaire (Belgian Congo)	1

1997

Country	Incidents	Country	Incidents
Albania	2	Korea, South	1
Algeria	2	Lebanon	2
Angola	1	Lithuania	1
Bahrain	1	Mali	1
Belgium	1	Malta	1
Bosnia	3	Netherlands	3
Bosnia and Herzegovina	2	Niger	1
Bulgaria	1	Nigeria	2
Burma (Myanmar)	1	Northern Ireland (UK)	4
Cambodia	3	Occupied Territories	1
Central African Republic	1	Pakistan	5
China	2	Peru	3
Colombia	12	Philippines	7
Croatia	2	Poland	1
Cuba	13	Russia	7
Ecuador	1	Saudi Arabia	2
Egypt	2	Somalia	1
Ethiopia	2	South Africa	1
Federal Republic of Germany	2	Spain	1
France	4	Sri Lanka (Ceylon)	6
Georgia	2	Sweden	1
Greece	2	Tajikistan	6
Guatemala	1	Thailand	3
Haiti	1	Turkey	2
Honduras	5	Uganda	2
India	3	Ukraine	1
Iraq	1	United Kingdom	4
Ireland	2	United States	14
Israel	6	Uruguay	1
Italy	1	Venezuela	3
Jordan	2	Yemen	10

1998

Country	Incidents	Country	Incidents
Afghanistan	4	Japan	7
Albania	28	Jordan	7
Algeria	81	Kashmir	20
Angola	4	Kenya	1
Armenia	3	Kyrgyzstan	2
Austria	3	Latvia	6
Azerbaijan	2	Lebanon	11
Bahrain	1	Libya	1
Belarus	1	Lithuania	4
Belgium	5	Macedonia, The Republic of	10
Bosnia and Herzegovina	43	Mexico	3
Brazil	3	Moldova	2
Bulgaria	2	Morocco	1
Burma (Myanmar)	1	Nicaragua	1
Cambodia	6	Nigeria	2
Chechnya	4	Northern Ireland (UK)	63
Chile	1	Norway	1
China	1	Occupied Territories	31
Colombia	136	Pakistan	48
Croatia	6	Paraguay	1
Cyprus	3	Peru	10
Czech Republic	1	Philippines	14
East Timor	2	Poland	4
Ecuador	3	Puerto Rico	3
Egypt	2	Russia	85
France	38	Sierra Leone	1
FRY (Kosovo)	63	Slovakia	4
FRY (Montenegro)	7	Somalia	1
FRY (Serbia)	5	South Africa	2
Georgia	21	Spain	109
Germany	1	Sri Lanka	16
Greece	42	Sudan	2
Guatemala	4	Swaziland	2
Guyana	4	Switzerland	2
Haiti	1	Tajikistan	10
Honduras	1	Tanzania	1
Hungary	2	Thailand	3
India	34	Turkey	86
Indonesia	5	Uganda	6
Iran	7	Ukraine	9
Iraq	4	United Kingdom	3
Ireland	3	United States	6
Israel	20	Venezuela	15
Italy	11	Yemen	38

1999

Country	Incidents	Country	Incidents
Albania	2	Latvia	2
Algeria	14	Lebanon	5
Angola	7	Liberia	1
Armenia	3	Macedonia, The Republic of	2
Austria	1	Nepal	4
Bangladesh	4	Netherlands	2
Bolivia	1	Nigeria	1
Bosnia and Herzegovina	7	Northern Ireland (UK)	62
Burma (Myanmar)	2	Occupied Territories	10
Burundi	1	Pakistan	30
Cambodia	1	Paraguay	1
Chechnya	8	Peru	3
Chile	4	Philippines	8
Colombia	94	Russia	41
Croatia	1	Sierra Leone	6
Denmark	2	Slovakia	2
East Timor	5	Somalia	1
Ecuador	2	South Africa	8
Ethiopia	2	Spain	172
France	108	Sri Lanka	18
FRY (Kosovo)	9	Sudan	1
FRY (Serbia)	2	Sweden	1
Georgia	5	Switzerland	1
Germany	3	Tanzania	1
Greece	55	Thailand	2
Guatemala	1	Turkey	304
Haiti	1	Uganda	9
Hungary	1	Ukraine	1
India	22	United Arab Emirates	1
Indonesia	14	United States	8
Iraq	4	Venezuela	6
Israel	14	Yemen	12
Italy	26	Zambia	1
Kashmir	6		

2000

Country	Incidents	Country	Incidents
Algeria	8	Kashmir	11
Angola	1	Lebanon	1
Azerbaijan	1	Malaysia	1
Bosnia and Herzegovina	1	Mexico	2
Burma (Myanmar)	2	Nigeria	1
Cambodia	2	Northern Ireland (UK)	41
Chechnya	4	Norway	1
Chile	3	Occupied Territories	167
Colombia	192	Pakistan	32
Denmark	1	Paraguay	2
East Timor	1	Peru	4
Ecuador	6	Philippines	41
Estonia	1	Russia	14
Ethiopia	2	Saudi Arabia	4
France	44	South Africa	11
FRY (Kosovo)	2	Spain	210
FRY (Serbia)	1	Sri Lanka	24
Georgia	2	Sweden	2
Germany	4	Switzerland	2
Greece	49	Tanzania	1
Guinea	1	Thailand	1
Haiti	7	Turkey	110
India	26	Uganda	3
Indonesia	27	Ukraine	1
Iraq	4	United Kingdom	6
Ireland	1	United States	9
Israel	19	Venezuela	9
Italy	11	Yemen	3
Jordan	1		

2001

Country	Incidents	Country	Incidents
Afghanistan	3	Ireland	1
Albania	3	Israel	85
Algeria	4	Italy	23
Angola	5	Japan	4
Argentina	1	Jordan	1
Australia	1	Kashmir	38
Azerbaijan	2	Kyrgyzstan	3
Bangladesh	15	Lebanon	7
Belarus	1	Macedonia, The Republic of	16
Bolivia	5	Madagascar	2
Bosnia and Herzegovina	8	Malaysia	1
Brazil	4	Mexico	2
Bulgaria	1	Moldova	1
Burma (Myanmar)	1	Nepal	7
Cambodia	5	Nicaragua	1
Chechnya	25	Nigeria	6
Chile	1	Northern Ireland (UK)	185
China	6	Occupied Territories	328
Colombia	126	Pakistan	47
Congo, Democratic Republic of the	2	Peru	5
Costa Rica	1	Philippines	43
Croatia	4	Russia	25
Cyprus	2	Saudi Arabia	5
East Timor	1	Somalia	1
Ecuador	4	South Africa	2
El Salvador	1	Spain	236
France	72	Sri Lanka	11
FRY	2	Sudan	2
FRY (Kosovo)	9	Switzerland	1
FRY (Serbia)	1	Tajikistan	9
FRY (Southern Serbia)	1	Thailand	17
Georgia	3	Turkey	64
Germany	1	Uganda	3
Greece	23	Ukraine	2
Guatemala	1	United Kingdom	6
Haiti	3	United States	39
Honduras	1	Uzbekistan	1
India	57	Venezuela	7
Indonesia	70	Vietnam	1
Iran	3	Yemen	12
Iraq	3		

2002

Country	Incidents	Country	Incidents
Afghanistan	65	Italy	22
Albania	3	Japan	4
Algeria	5	Jordan	3
Angola	1	Kashmir	485
Argentina	1	Kazakhstan	1
Armenia	2	Kenya	4
Bangladesh	10	Korea, South	1
Belgium	1	Kuwait	2
Bolivia	1	Kyrgyzstan	3
Bosnia and Herzegovina	18	Laos	1
Brazil	3	Lebanon	21
Bulgaria	2	Macedonia, The Republic of	25
Burma (Myanmar)	3	Nepal	92
Cambodia	3	Netherlands	3
Chad	1	New Zealand	1
Chechnya	57	Nigeria	1
Chile	1	Northern Ireland (UK)	93
China	1	Occupied Territories	432
Colombia	432	Pakistan	80
Croatia	4	Peru	6
Czech Republic	2	Philippines	43
Ecuador	11	Portugal	1
Egypt	1	Russia	47
Estonia	1	Saudi Arabia	6
Ethiopia	3	Slovenia	1
France	72	South Africa	9
FRY	7	Spain	114
FRY (Kosovo)	16	Sudan	2
FRY (Montenegro)	5	Sweden	1
FRY (Serbia)	4	Tajikistan	1
FRY (Southern Serbia)	5	Thailand	25
Georgia	8	Tunisia	1
Germany	2	Turkey	35
Greece	29	Turkmenistan	1
Honduras	2	Uganda	1
Hungary	1	Ukraine	7
India	76	United Kingdom	3
Indonesia	48	United States	16
Iraq	14	Venezuela	20
Ireland	1	Yemen	5
Israel	109		

2003

Country	Incidents	Country	Incidents
Afghanistan	150	Japan	10
Albania	1	Jordan	1
Algeria	7	Kashmir	238
Argentina	3	Kenya	1
Bangladesh	17	Kuwait	3
Belgium	9	Kyrgyzstan	2
Bolivia	2	Lebanon	9
Bosnia and Herzegovina	3	Macedonia, The Republic of	7
Brazil	3	Malaysia	1
Burma (Myanmar)	3	Mexico	1
Burundi	1	Morocco	6
Chechnya	40	Nepal	36
Chile	4	Netherlands	2
Colombia	147	New Zealand	1
Cote d'Ivoire	1	Northern Ireland (UK)	98
Cyprus	2	Occupied Territories	164
Czech Republic	1	Pakistan	69
Ecuador	9	Peru	3
El Salvador	1	Philippines	19
Eritrea	1	Russia	42
Estonia	1	Saudi Arabia	12
Ethiopia	4	Somalia	2
France	117	South Africa	1
FRY (Kosovo)	11	Spain	46
FRY (Serbia)	4	Sri Lanka	4
Georgia	15	Switzerland	2
Germany	7	Tajikistan	1
Greece	55	Thailand	1
India	95	Togo	2
Indonesia	9	Turkey	78
Iran	4	Uganda	3
Iraq	147	United Kingdom	1
Ireland	2	United States	18
Israel	75	Venezuela	26
Italy	34	Yemen	2

2004

Country	Incidents	Country	Incidents
Afghanistan	146	Kyrgyzstan	1
Albania	1	Laos	7
Algeria	12	Lebanon	3
Argentina	3	Macedonia, The Republic of	3
Bangladesh	24	Madagascar	3
Belgium	2	Mauritania	1
Bolivia	2	Mexico	3
Bosnia and Herzegovina	4	Moldova	1
Burma (Myanmar)	3	Nepal	111
Chechnya	67	Netherlands	2
Chile	2	Nigeria	1
China	2	Northern Ireland (UK)	75
Colombia	74	Occupied Territories	349
Cyprus	6	Pakistan	84
Denmark	1	Paraguay	1
Djibouti	1	Peru	2
Ecuador	3	Philippines	21
Egypt	3	Qatar	1
Eritrea	2	Russia	62
Estonia	1	Saudi Arabia	13
Ethiopia	3	Serbia	1
France	71	Slovakia	2
FRY (Kosovo)	9	Somalia	1
FRY (Montenegro)	1	Spain	51
FRY (Serbia)	1	Sri Lanka	6
Georgia	12	Sweden	1
Germany	1	Switzerland	1
Greece	42	Syria	1
Guatemala	1	Taiwan	1
Honduras	2	Tanzania	2
India	38	Thailand	169
Indonesia	23	Turkey	105
Iraq	789	Uganda	7
Israel	25	Ukraine	2
Italy	19	United Kingdom	1
Japan	1	United States	6
Kashmir	51	Uzbekistan	8
Kazakhstan	2	Venezuela	9
Kuwait	1	Yemen	2

Maps of Terrorist Incidents by Country 1985–2004

Overview of Maps of Terrorist Incidents by Country 1985–2004

Anna Sabasteanski

This section illustrates the geographic distribution of terrorist incidents that occurred between 1985 and 2004. The data used to build these maps can be found in "Overview of Terrorist Incidents by Country," at the beginning of Part 5. The overview to that section also describes the methodology used in collecting and presenting the data, and lists the annual number of countries affected by terrorist incidents. Please note that 1995–1997 data covers only international incidents while 1998–present includes domestic incidents as well.

In these maps, black marks the locations of higher numbers of incidents—those countries experiencing more than 40 attacks per year. This corresponds with the divisions used in *Patterns,* but does not take into account increasing levels of violence in the last decade. Year-by-year comparisons are very informative, but numbers of incidents are only one measure of terrorism. Had we drawn maps based on casualties, the picture would be rather different.

Colombia and Spain were the first countries in which more than a hundred incidents were recorded in the course of a single year. In 1998, Colombia experienced 136 incidents, the vast majority internal and directed against government or utility targets. Also in 1998 there were 109 attacks in Spain that were directed against a range of targets including government, police, business and transportation.

In 1999, incidents in Colombia had fallen to 94, while attacks in Spain rose to 172. France joined the 100+ club with 108 incidents, most connected to Breton or Corsican separatist groups opposed to the central government. Turkey, however, set a new record with 304 incidents, most associated with Kurdish separatism and directed against a broad range of targets, including significant numbers of private citizens and property.

A year later, Spain took the lead with 210 incidents primarily against government or police targets and businesses. The beginning of the second intifada (Palestinian uprising) in 2000 was responsible for the Occupied Territories joining this list, with 167 incidents, the majority against private citizens and property in Israeli settlements. (There were 19 incidents in Israel.) There were 110 incidents in Turkey and 192 in Colombia.

In 2001 the Occupied Territories had 328 attacks, predominantly against private citizens and property in Israeli settlements. (There were 85 attacks inside Israel.) In Northern Ireland an outbreak of loyalist violence directed mostly against private citizens and property generated 185 incidents. These spilled over into the British mainland with six Real IRA attacks, and one by an unknown group. Spain suffered 236 attacks, and Colombia 126.

Kashmir had the largest number of attacks in 2002, with 485, connected with separatist militants attacking government, private citizens and property, and a range of other targets. Colombia and the Occupied Territories tied with 432 attacks each, maintaining the same general attack profile. 2002 marked the first time that Israel suffered more than a hundred attacks. While most involved private citizens and property, a significant number were against transportation and government or police targets. There were 114 attacks in Spain.

Again in 2003 Kashmir had the largest number of attacks, with 238. Attacks also fell in the Occupied Territories, to 164. (In Israel, attacks fell to 75.) Afghanistan and Iraq went over 100 for the first time. In Afghanistan, Taliban and other militants were responsible for 150 attacks against a wide range of targets. In Iraq, militants launched 147 attacks. Also in 2003, Colombia suffered 147 incidents and France 117.

The number of incidents, primarily militant attacks, in Iraq grew dramatically, to 789 in 2004. The Occupied Territories experienced 349 attacks (Israel 25), and Afghanistan 146. There were 105 attacks in Turkey. Two new additions were Nepal and Thailand. Thailand's 169 incidents were driven by unrest in the south, predominantly Islamic area, against targets associated with Christianity or the government, including police and educational institutions. Nepal's Maoists reacted to the King's dissolution of parliament and assumption of control with 111 incidents, most against government targets and individuals or entities associated with the government.

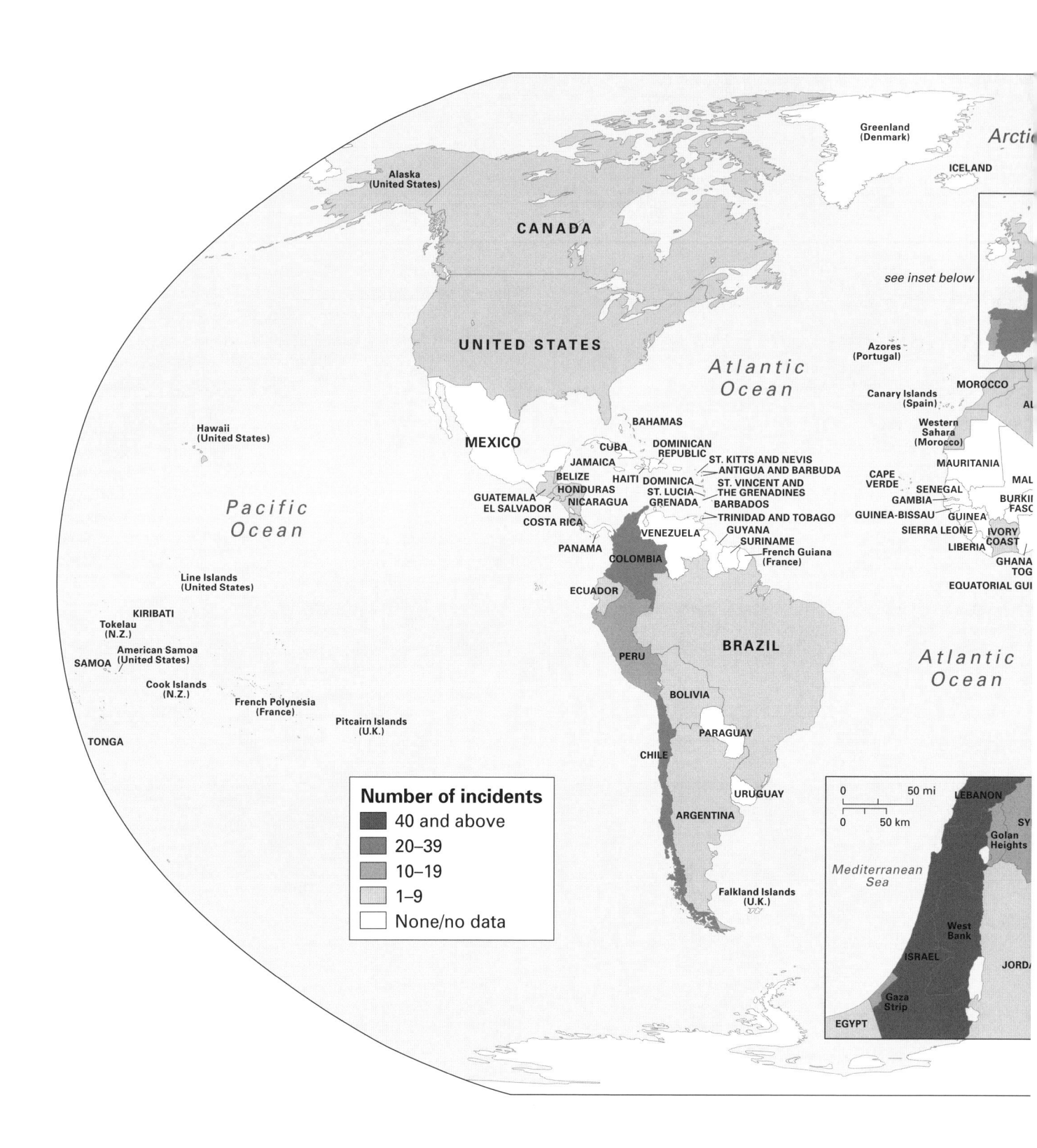

Number of incidents
- 40 and above
- 20–39
- 10–19
- 1–9
- None/no data

International Terrorist Incidents, 1985

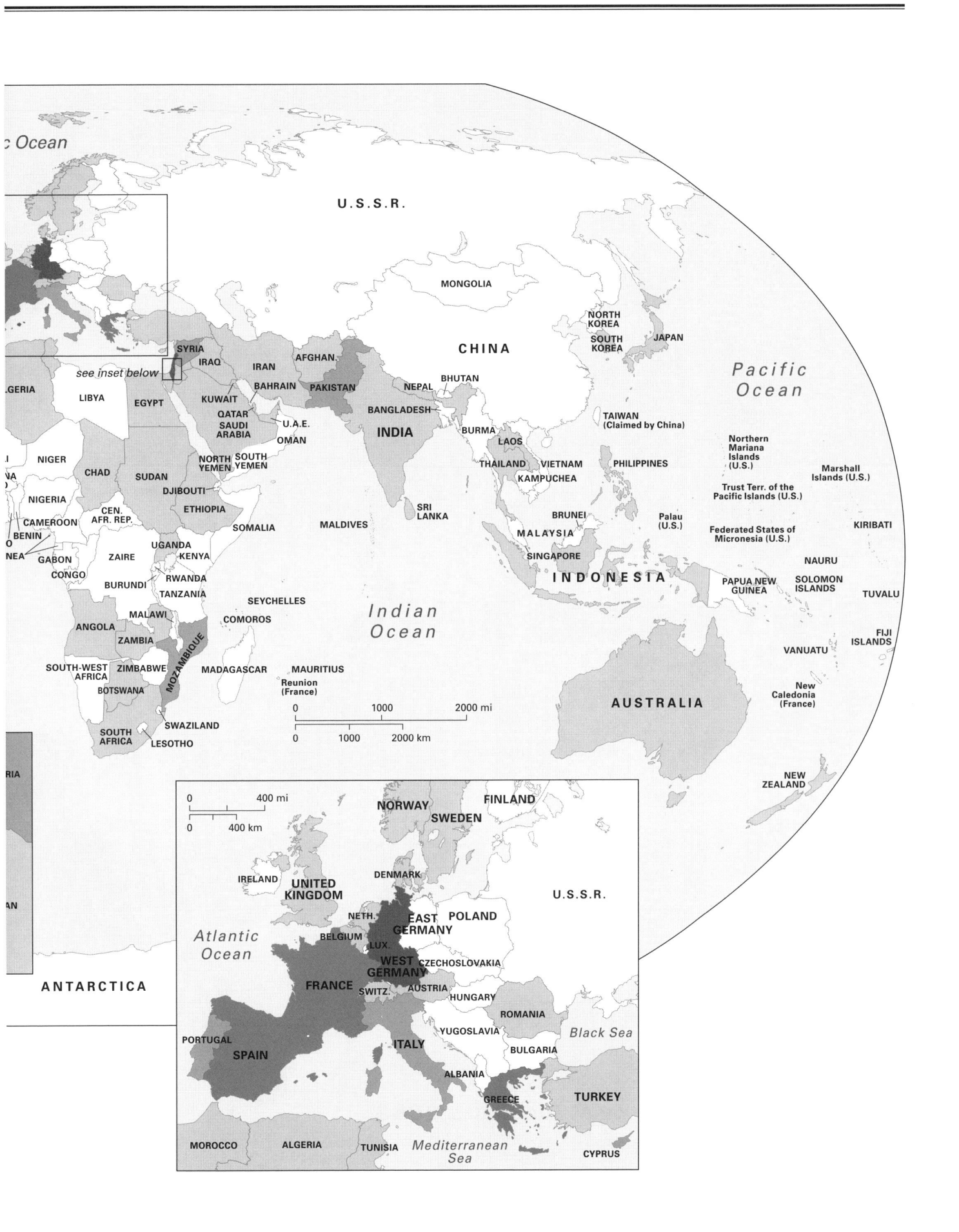

Maps of Terrorist Incidents by Country 1985–2004 **885**

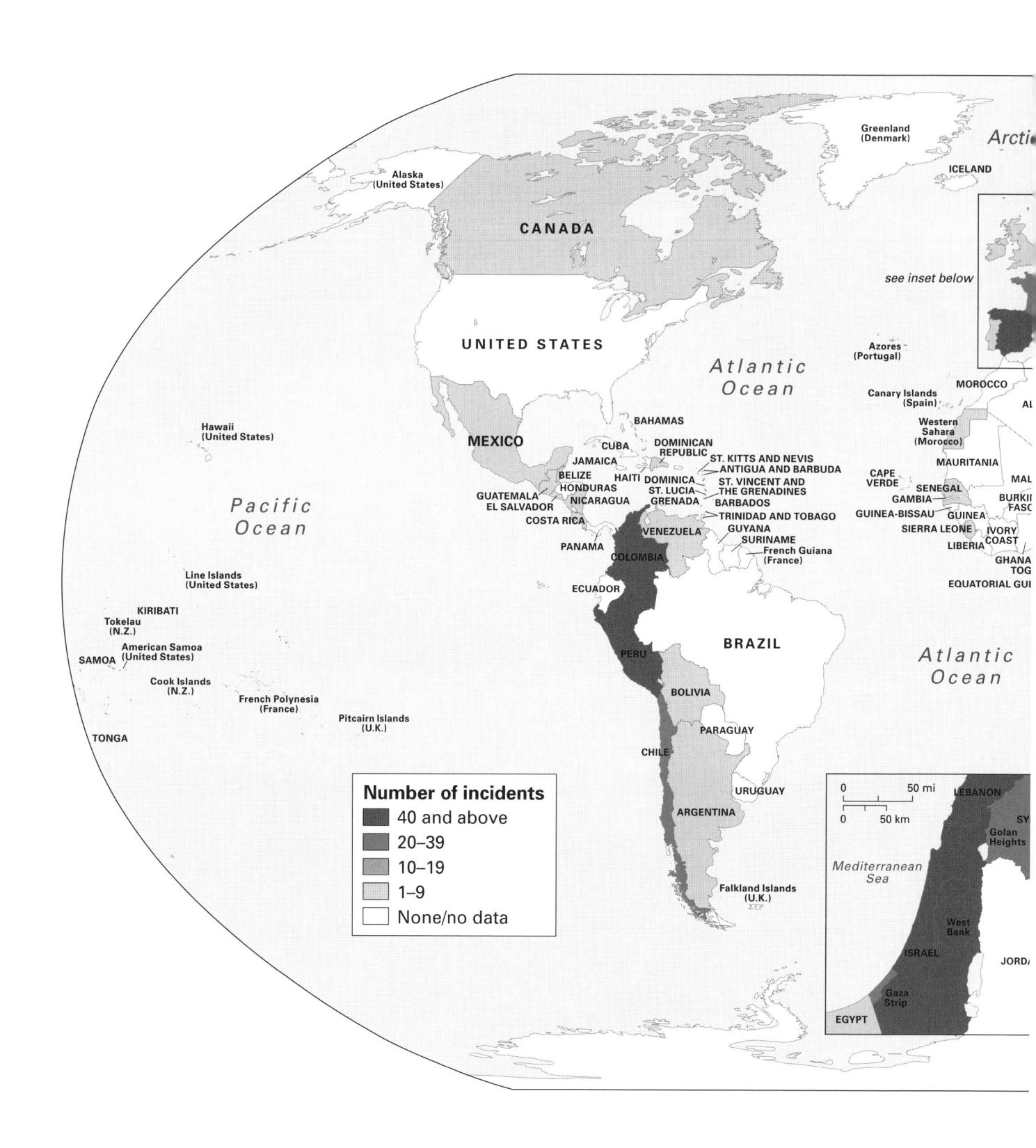

Number of incidents
- 40 and above
- 20–39
- 10–19
- 1–9
- None/no data

International Terrorist Incidents, 1986

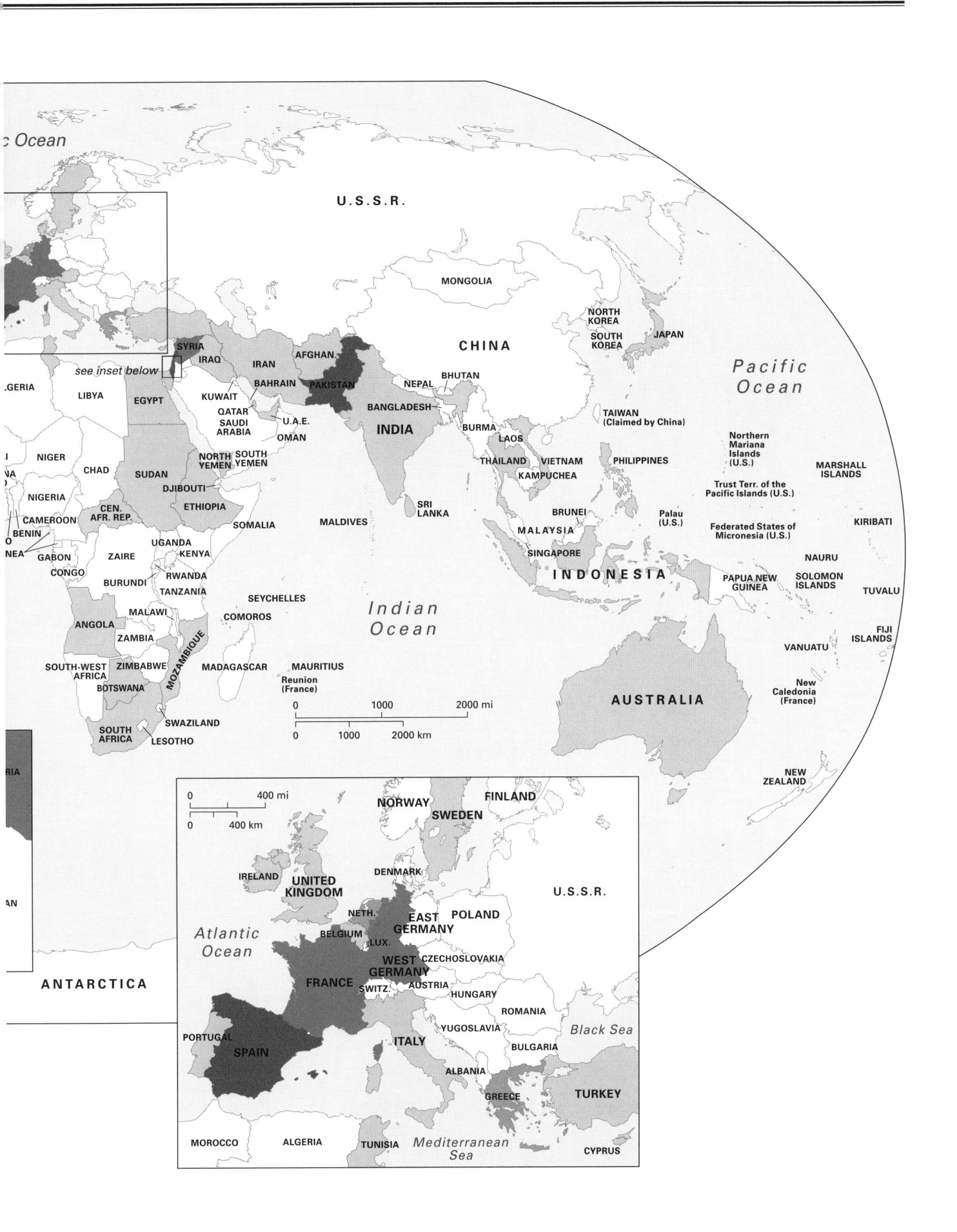

Maps of Terrorist Incidents by Country 1985–2004   **887**

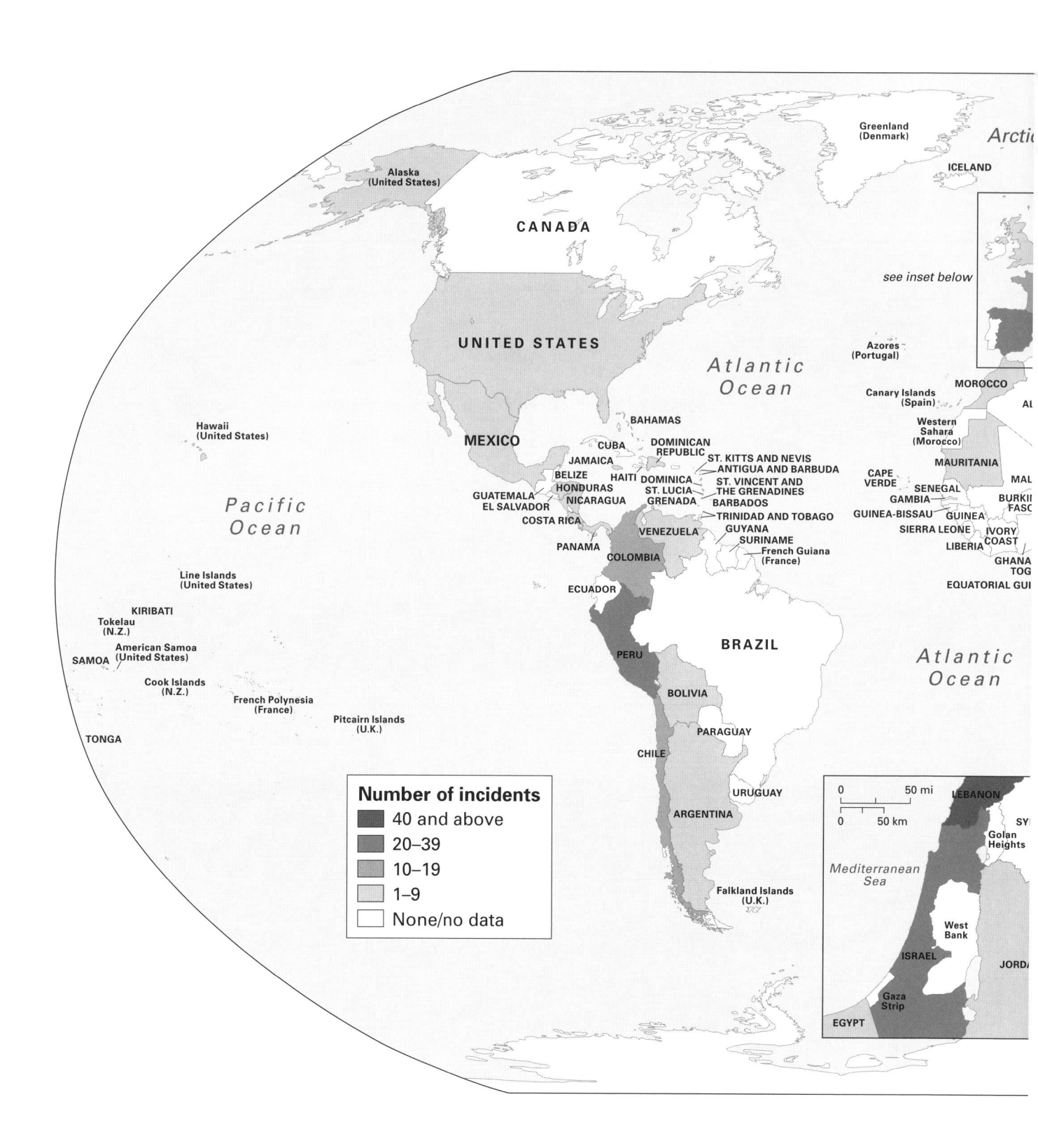

888 Patterns of Global Terrorism

Number of incidents
- 40 and above
- 20–39
- 10–19
- 1–9
- None/no data

International Terrorist Incidents, 1987

Maps of Terrorist Incidents by Country 1985–2004

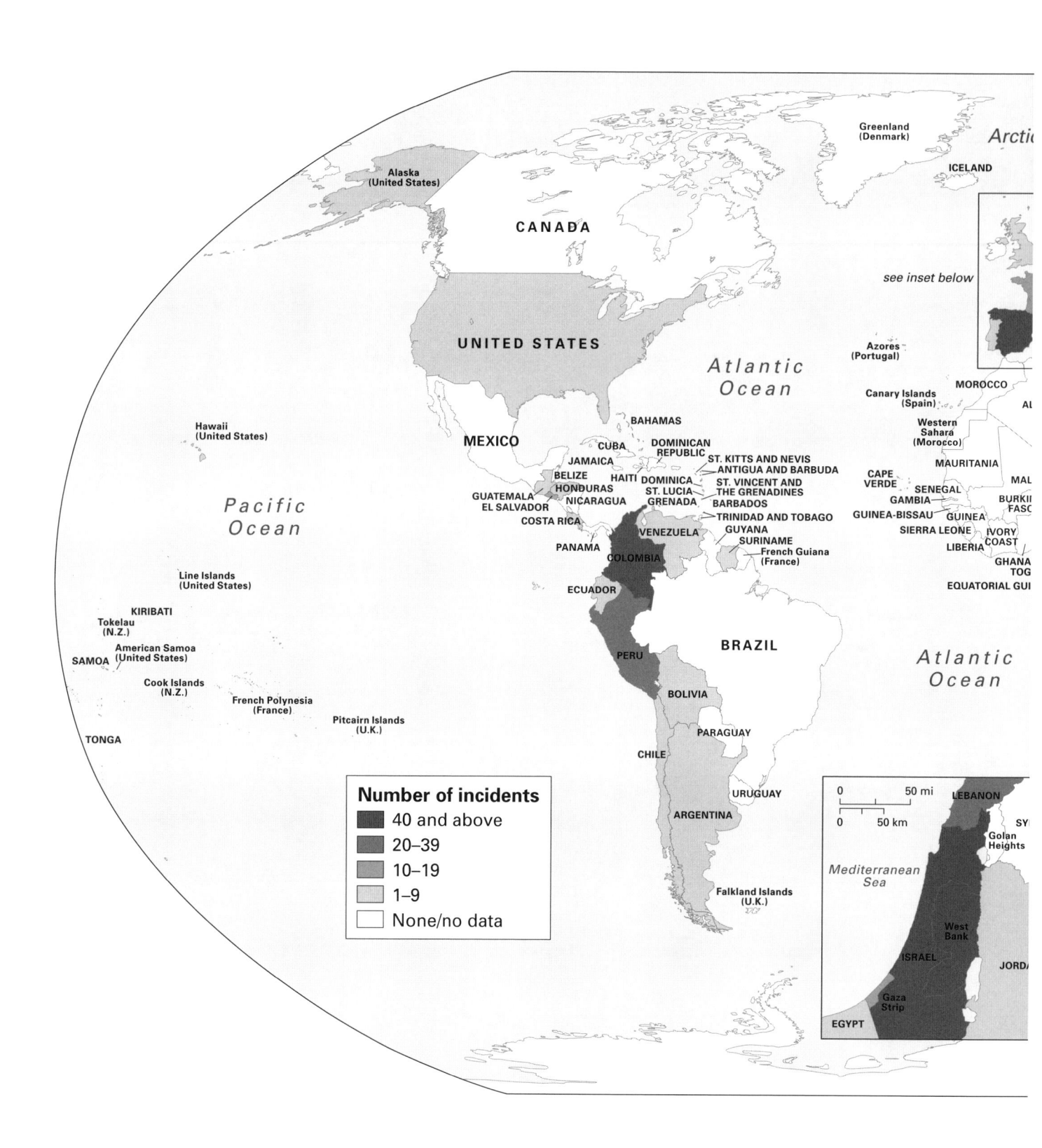

Number of incidents
- 40 and above
- 20–39
- 10–19
- 1–9
- None/no data

International Terrorist Incidents, 1988

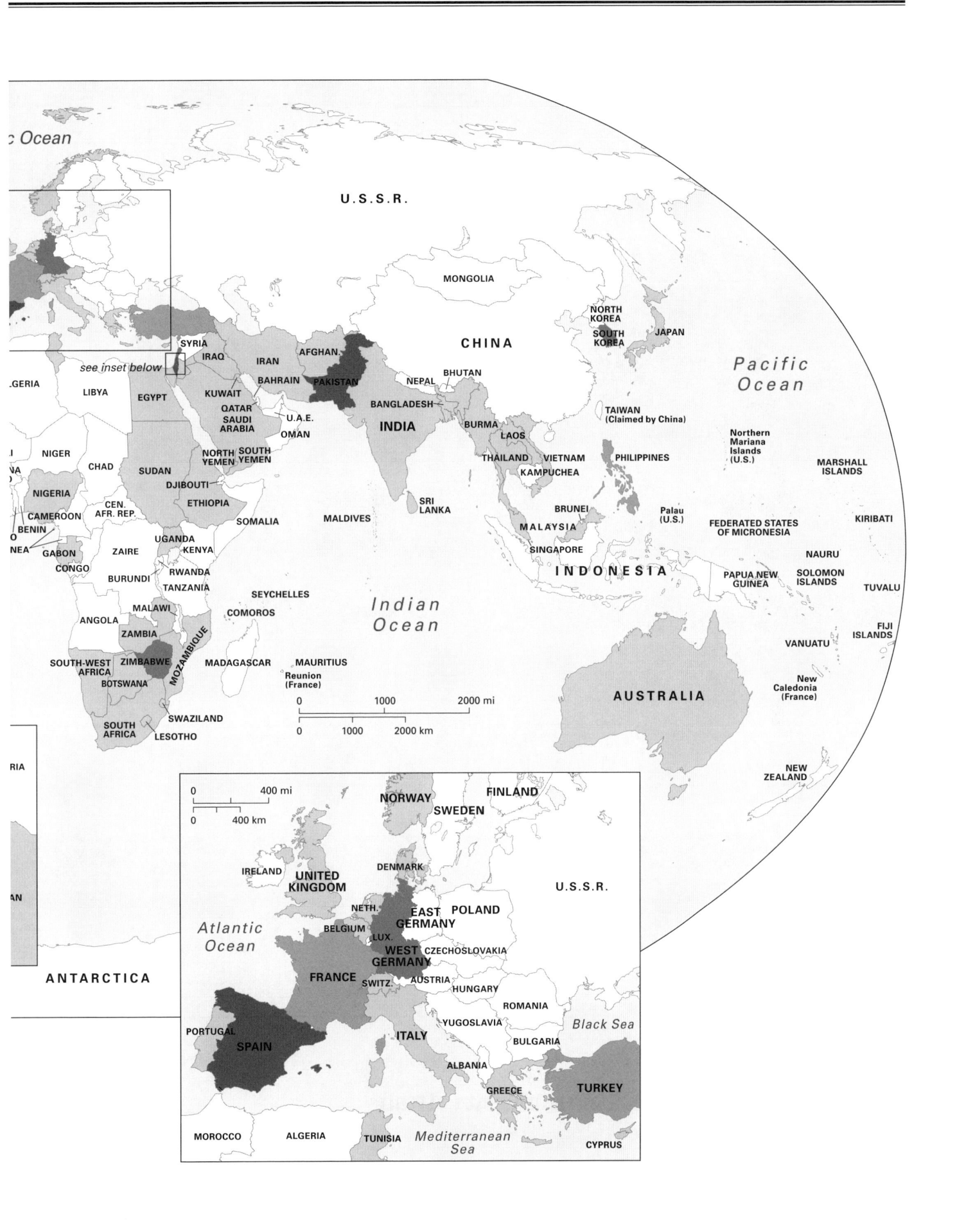

Maps of Terrorist Incidents by Country 1985–2004

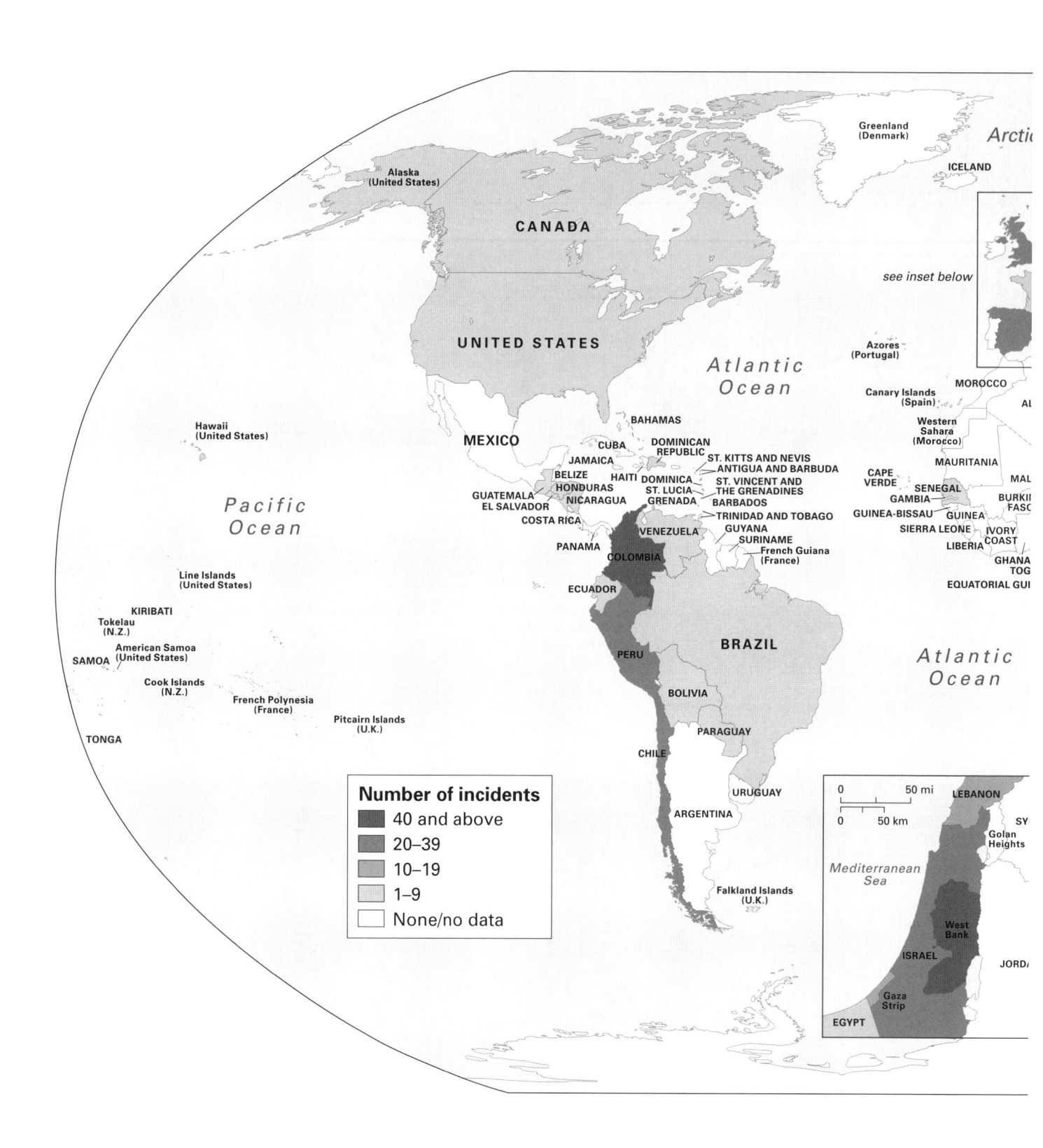

Patterns of Global Terrorism

Number of incidents
- 40 and above
- 20–39
- 10–19
- 1–9
- None/no data

International Terrorist Incidents, 1989

Maps of Terrorist Incidents by Country 1985–2004

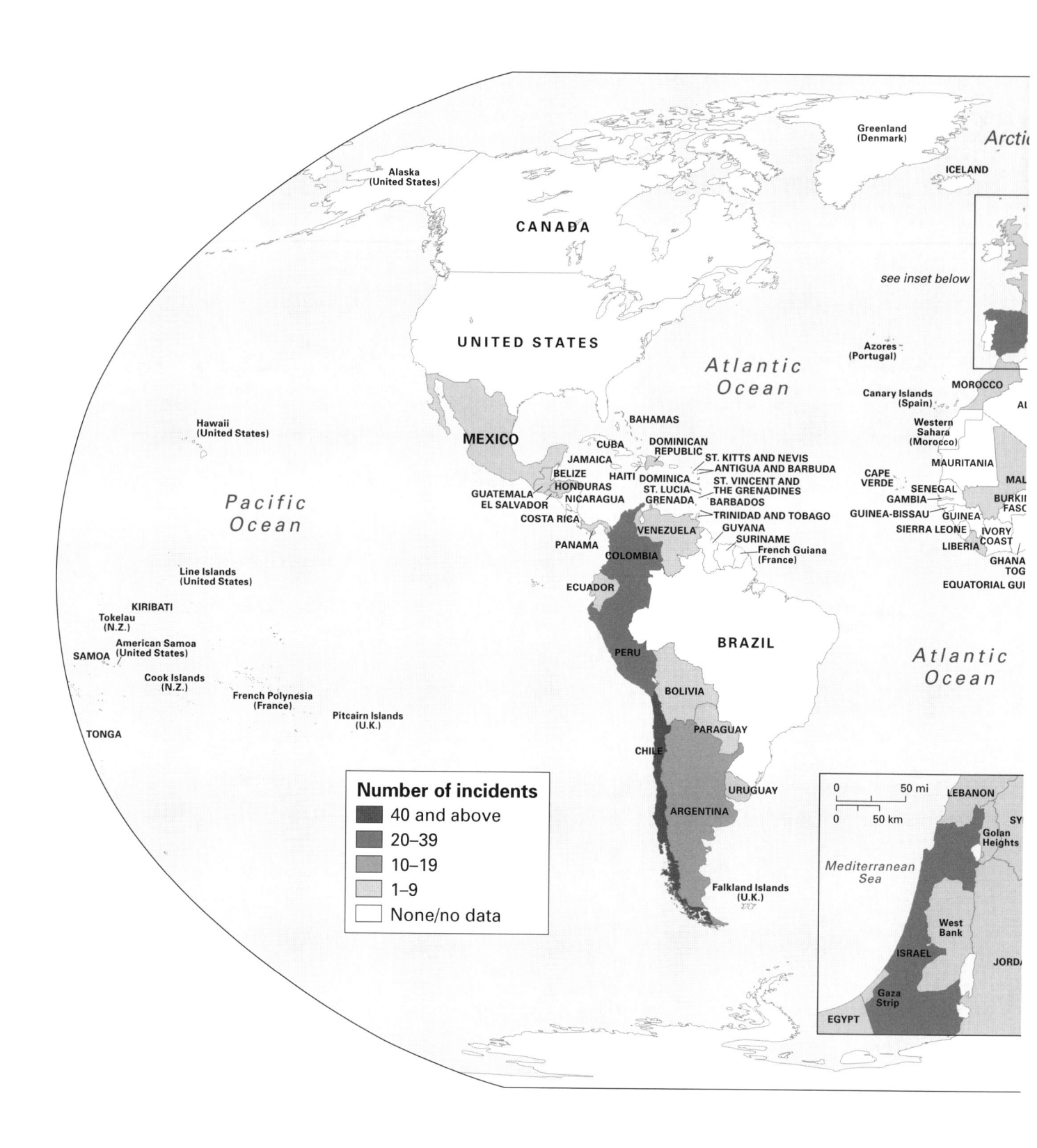

894 Patterns of Global Terrorism

International Terrorist Incidents, 1990

Number of incidents:
- 40 and above
- 20–39
- 10–19
- 1–9
- None/no data

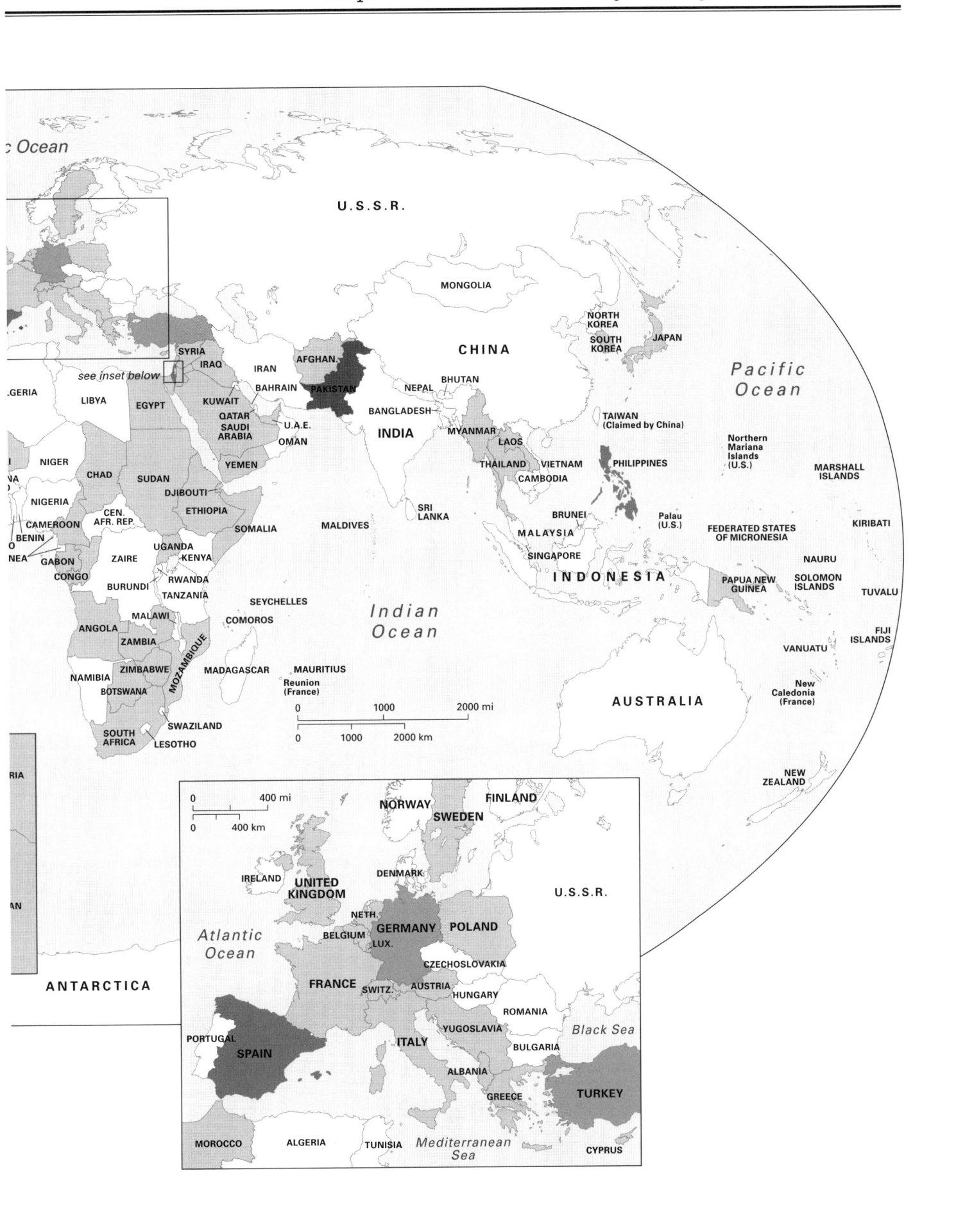

Maps of Terrorist Incidents by Country 1985–2004

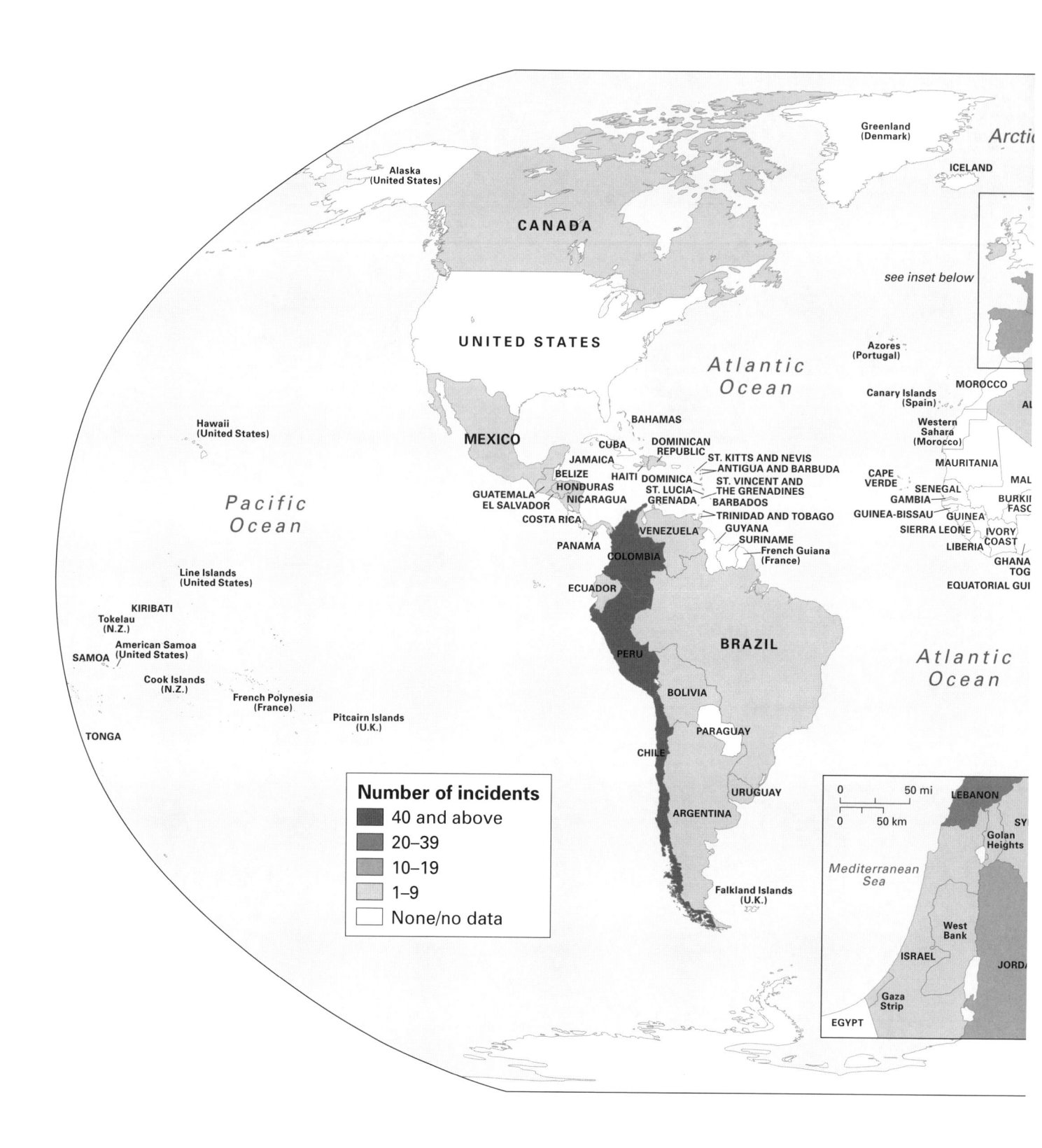

Number of incidents
- 40 and above
- 20–39
- 10–19
- 1–9
- None/no data

International Terrorist Incidents, 1991

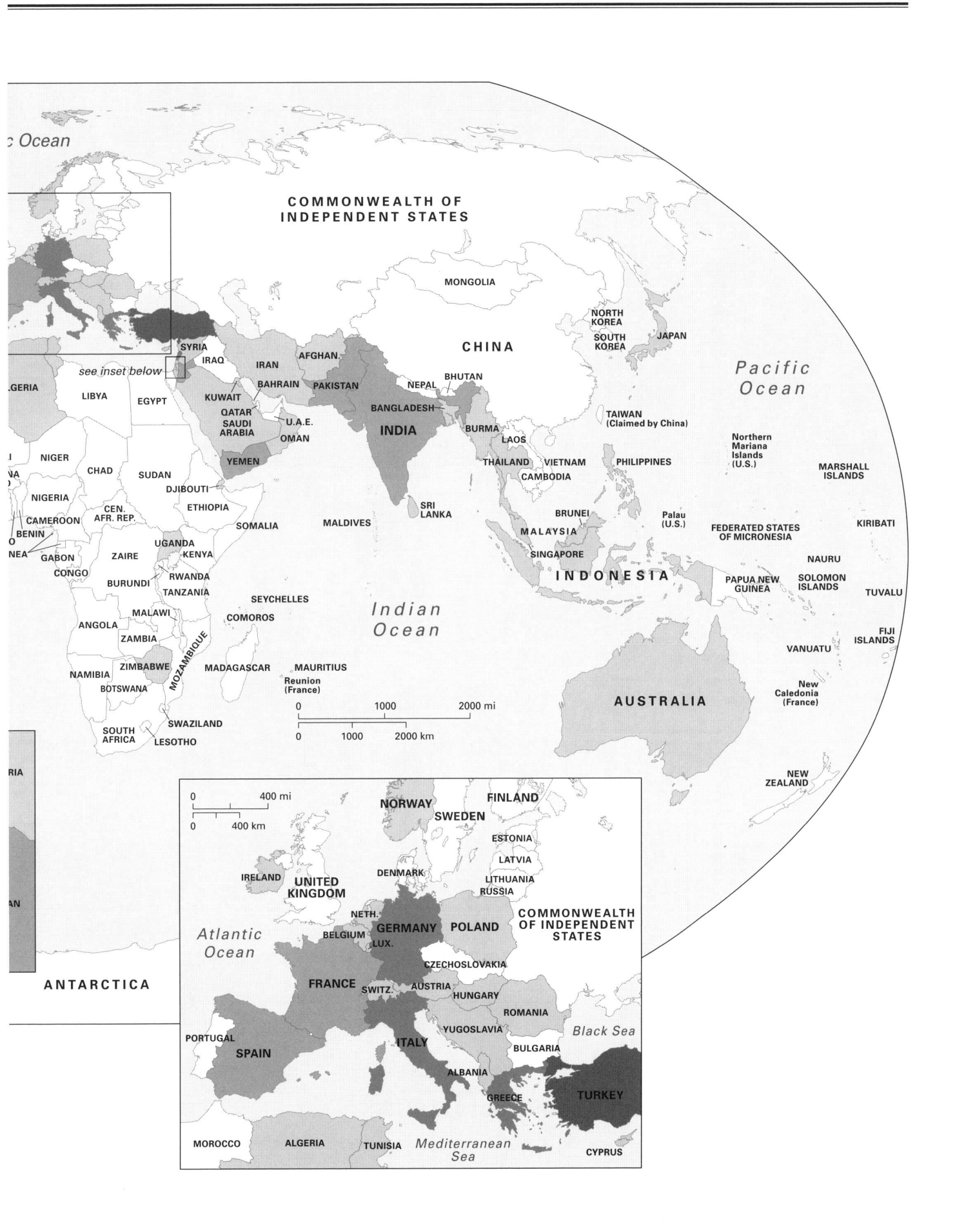

Maps of Terrorist Incidents by Country 1985–2004   **897**

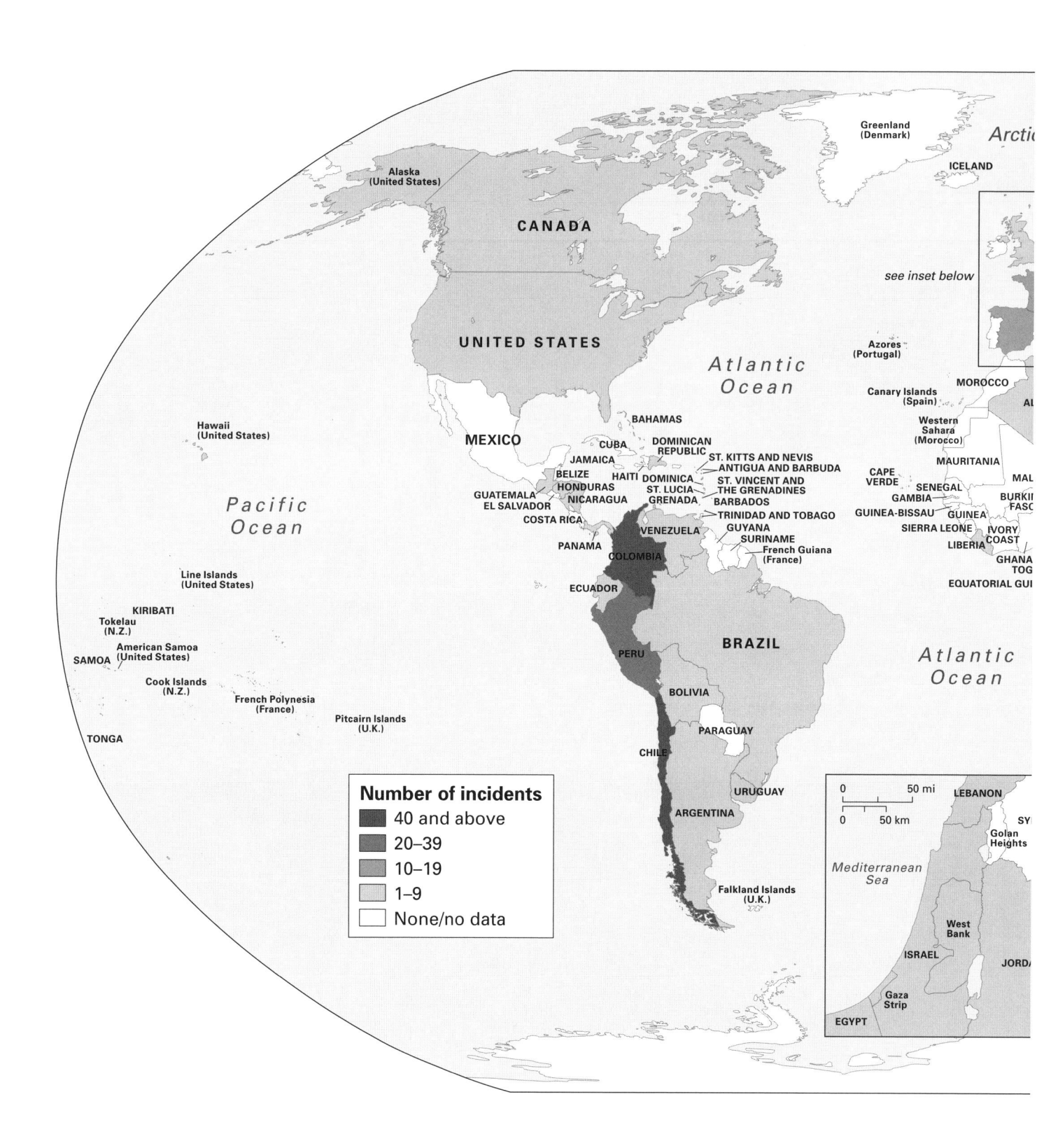

Patterns of Global Terrorism

Number of incidents
- 40 and above
- 20–39
- 10–19
- 1–9
- None/no data

International Terrorist Incidents, 1992

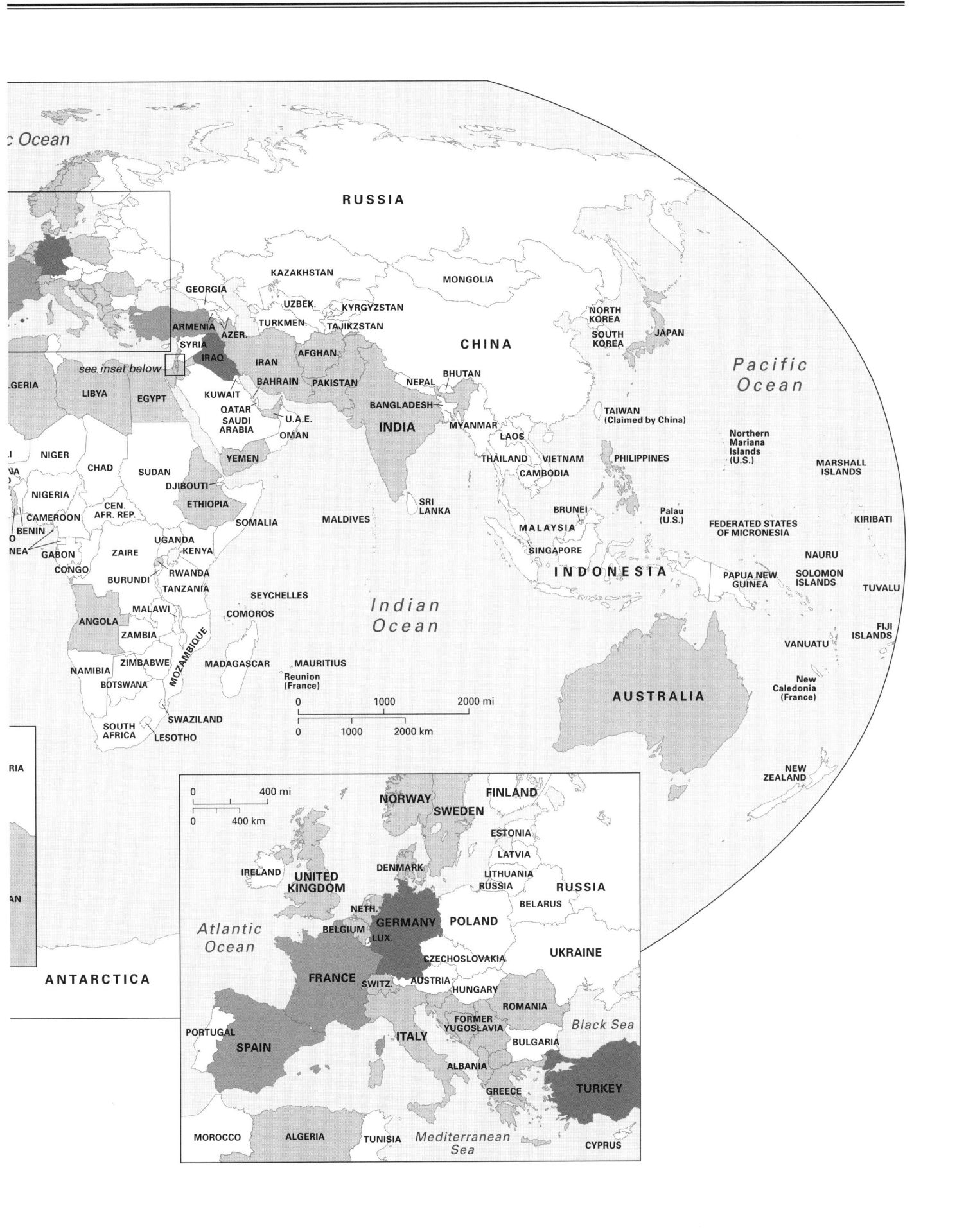

Maps of Terrorist Incidents by Country 1985–2004   **899**

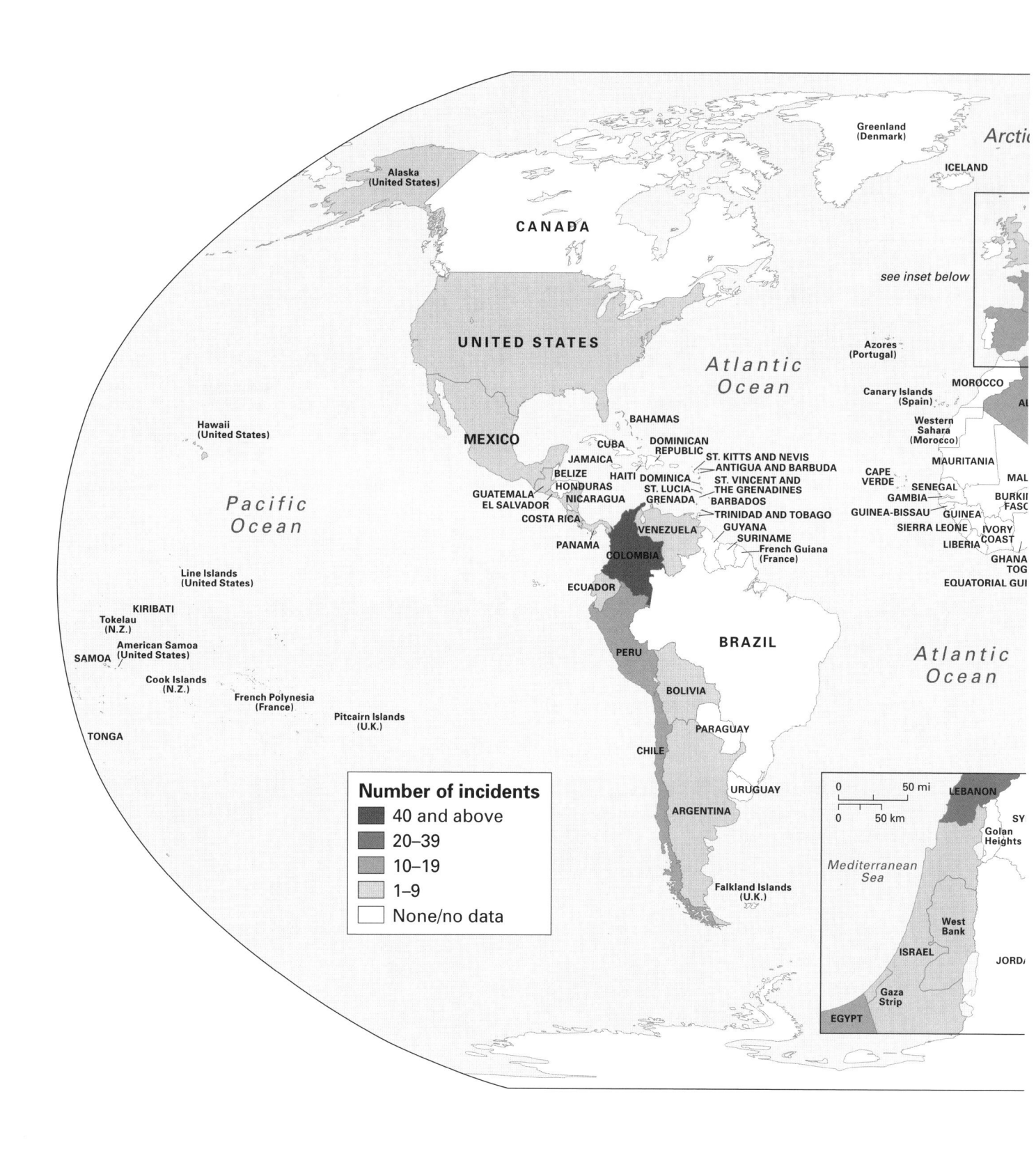

International Terrorist Incidents, 1993

Number of incidents
- 40 and above
- 20–39
- 10–19
- 1–9
- None/no data

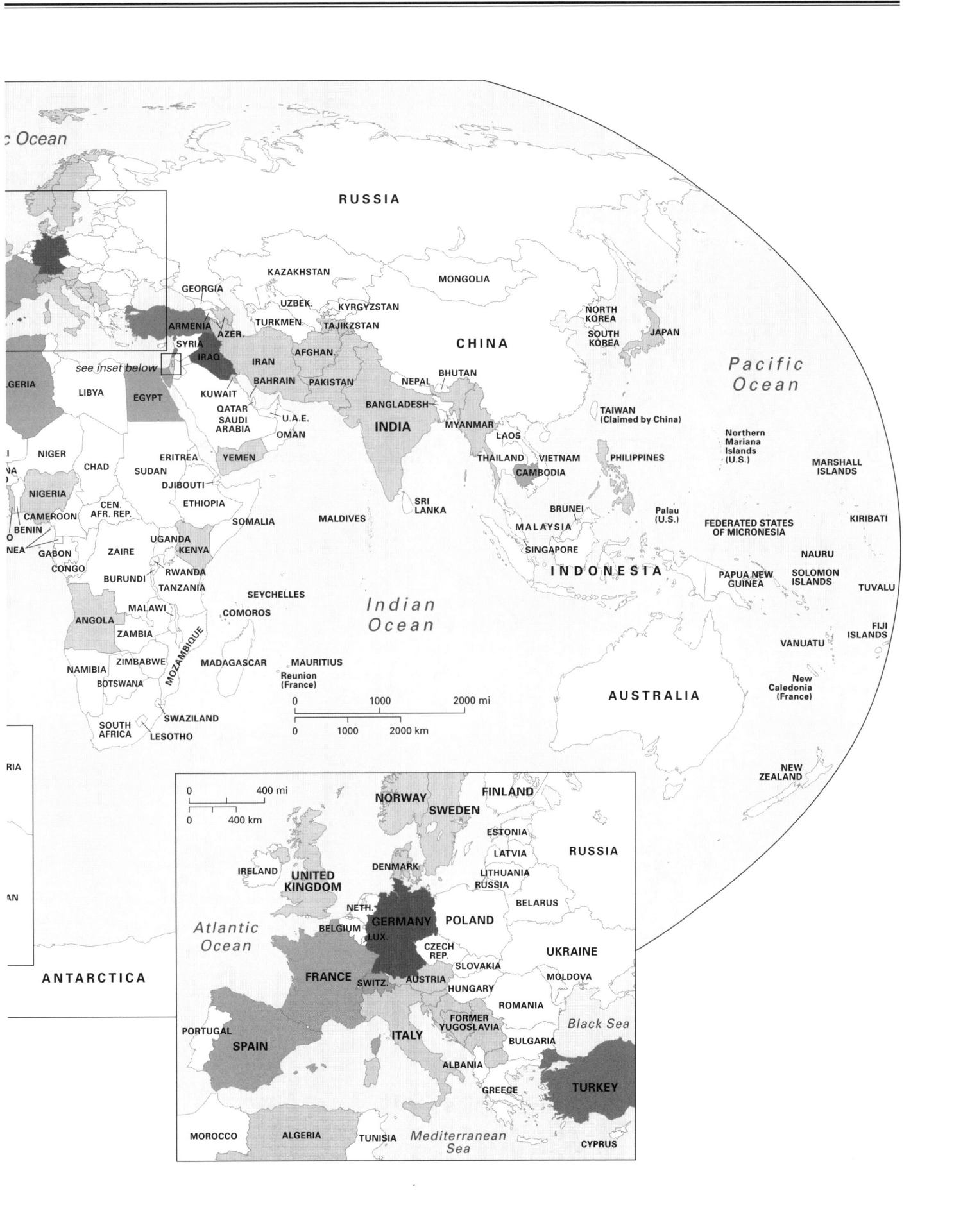

Maps of Terrorist Incidents by Country 1985–2004

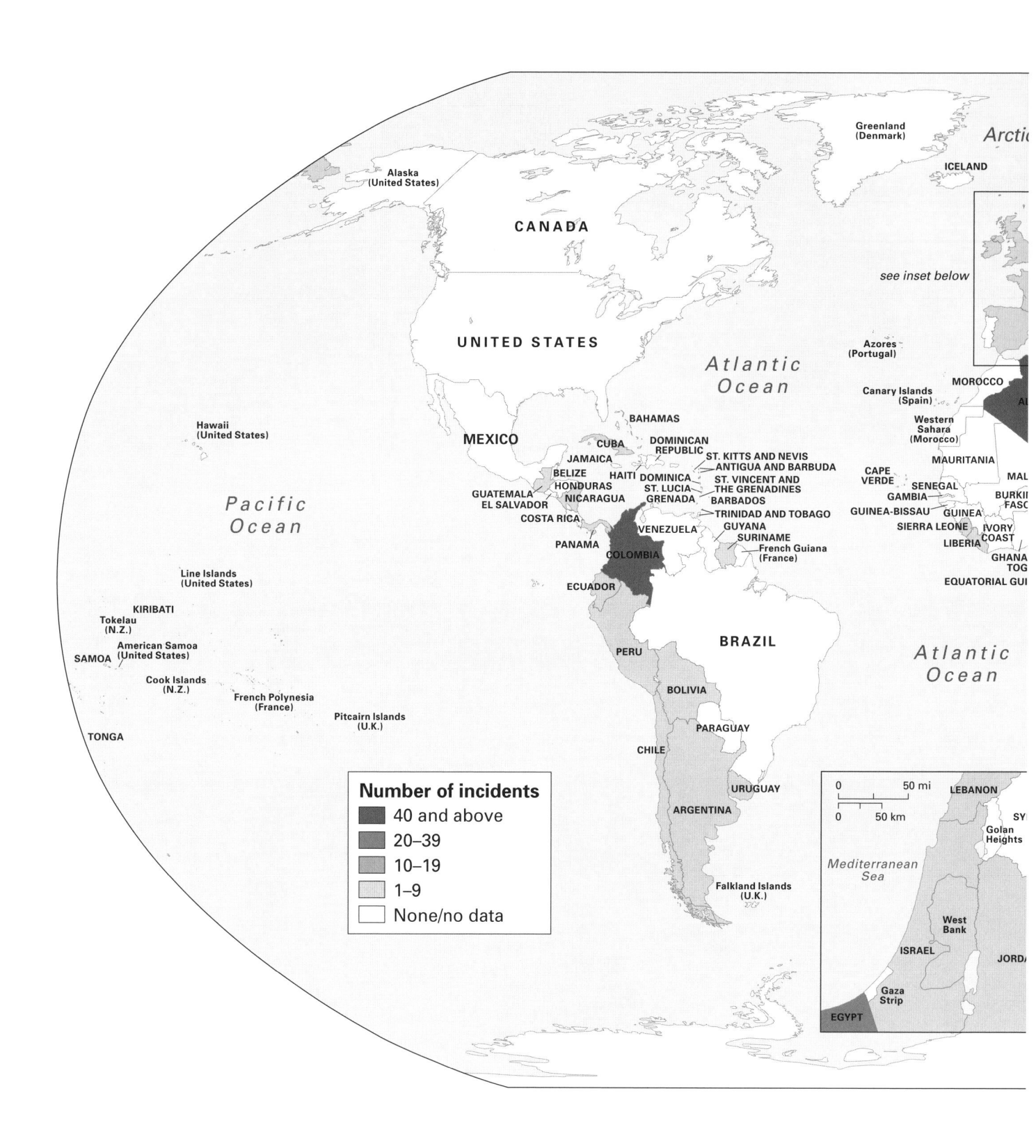

International Terrorist Incidents, 1994

Number of incidents
- 40 and above
- 20–39
- 10–19
- 1–9
- None/no data

Maps of Terrorist Incidents by Country 1985–2004

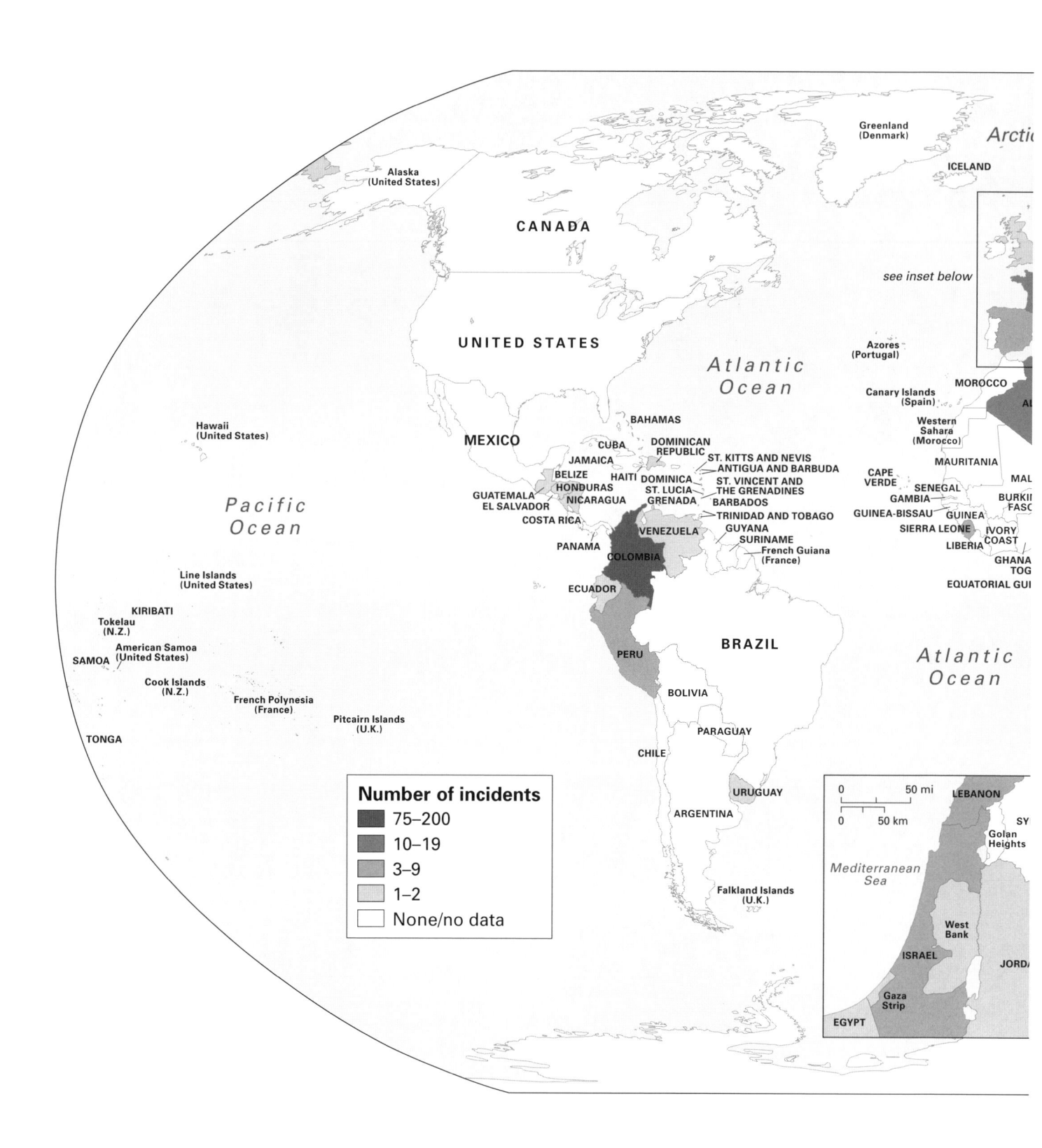

Number of incidents
- 75–200
- 10–19
- 3–9
- 1–2
- None/no data

International Terrorist Incidents, 1995

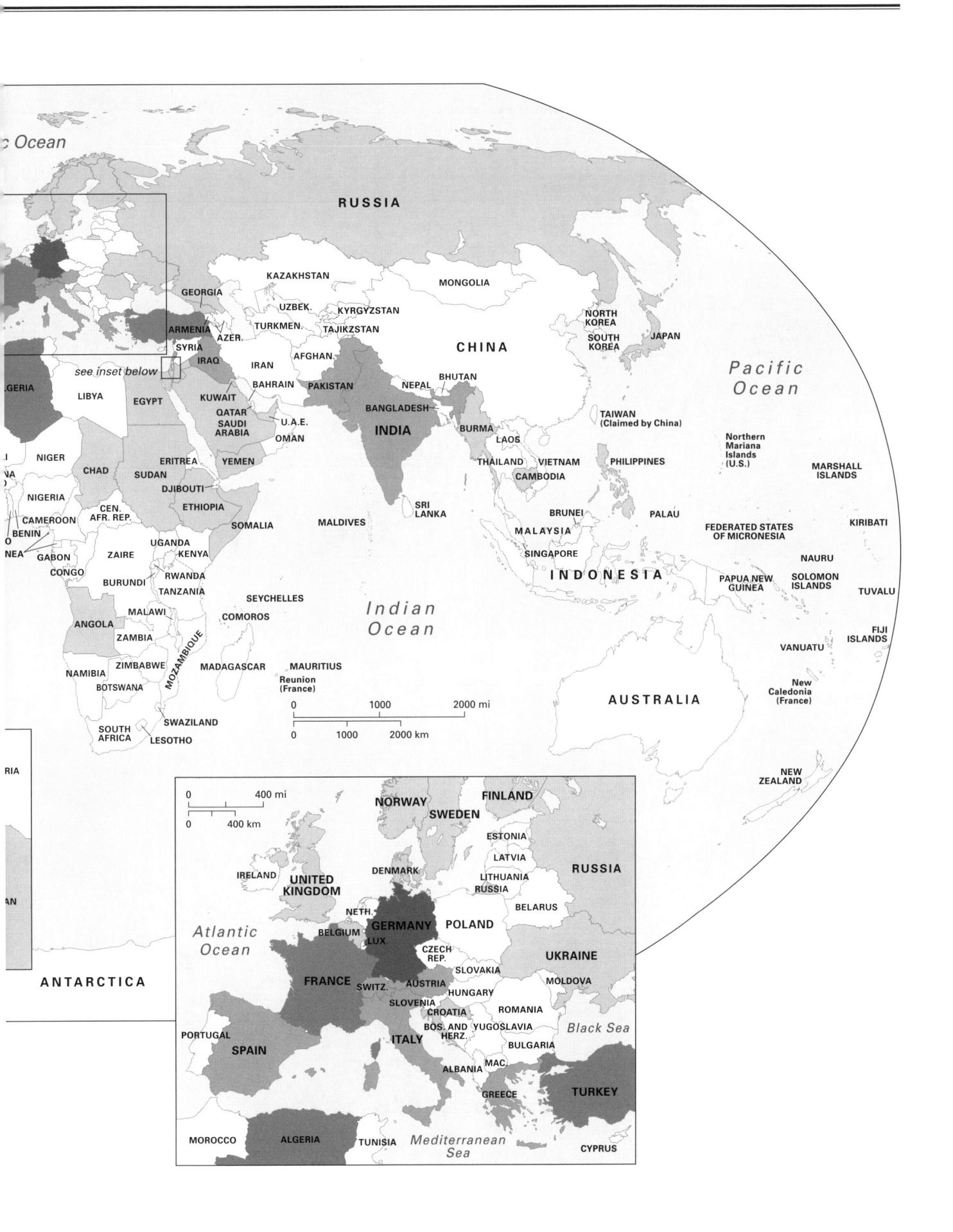

Maps of Terrorist Incidents by Country 1985–2004

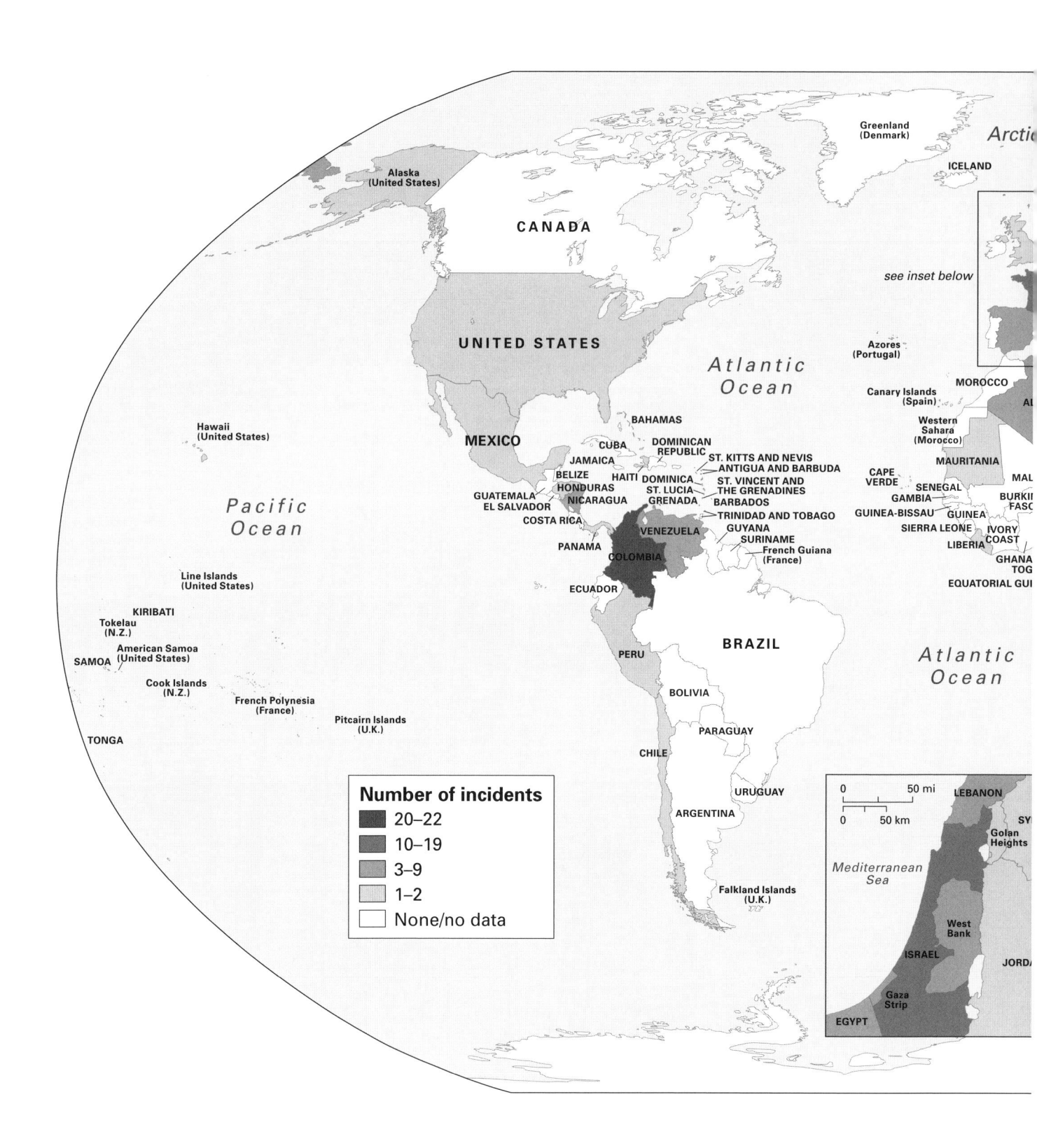

International Terrorist Incidents, 1996

Number of incidents:
- 20–22
- 10–19
- 3–9
- 1–2
- None/no data

Maps of Terrorist Incidents by Country 1985–2004

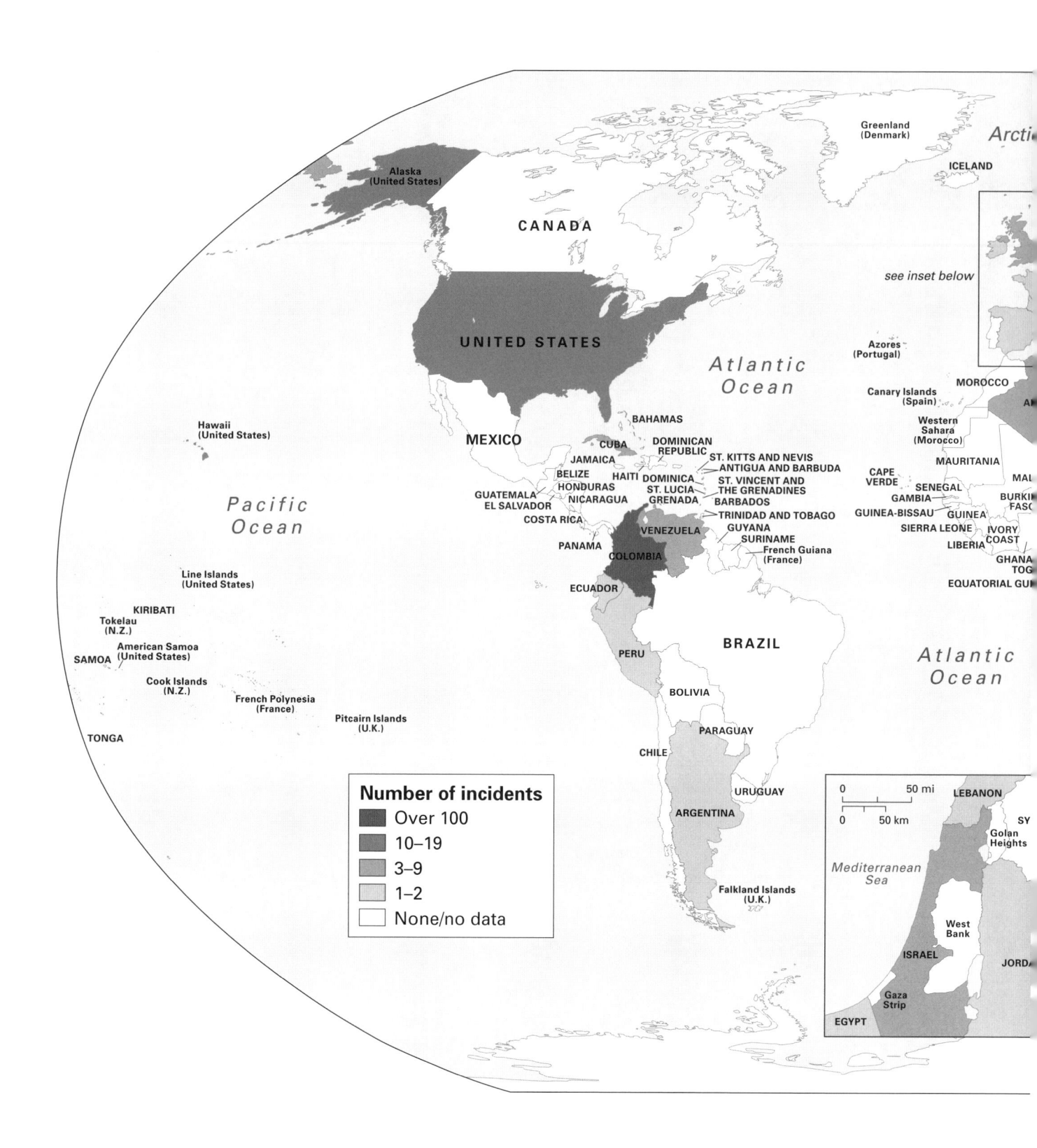

Number of incidents
- Over 100
- 10–19
- 3–9
- 1–2
- None/no data

International Terrorist Incidents, 1997

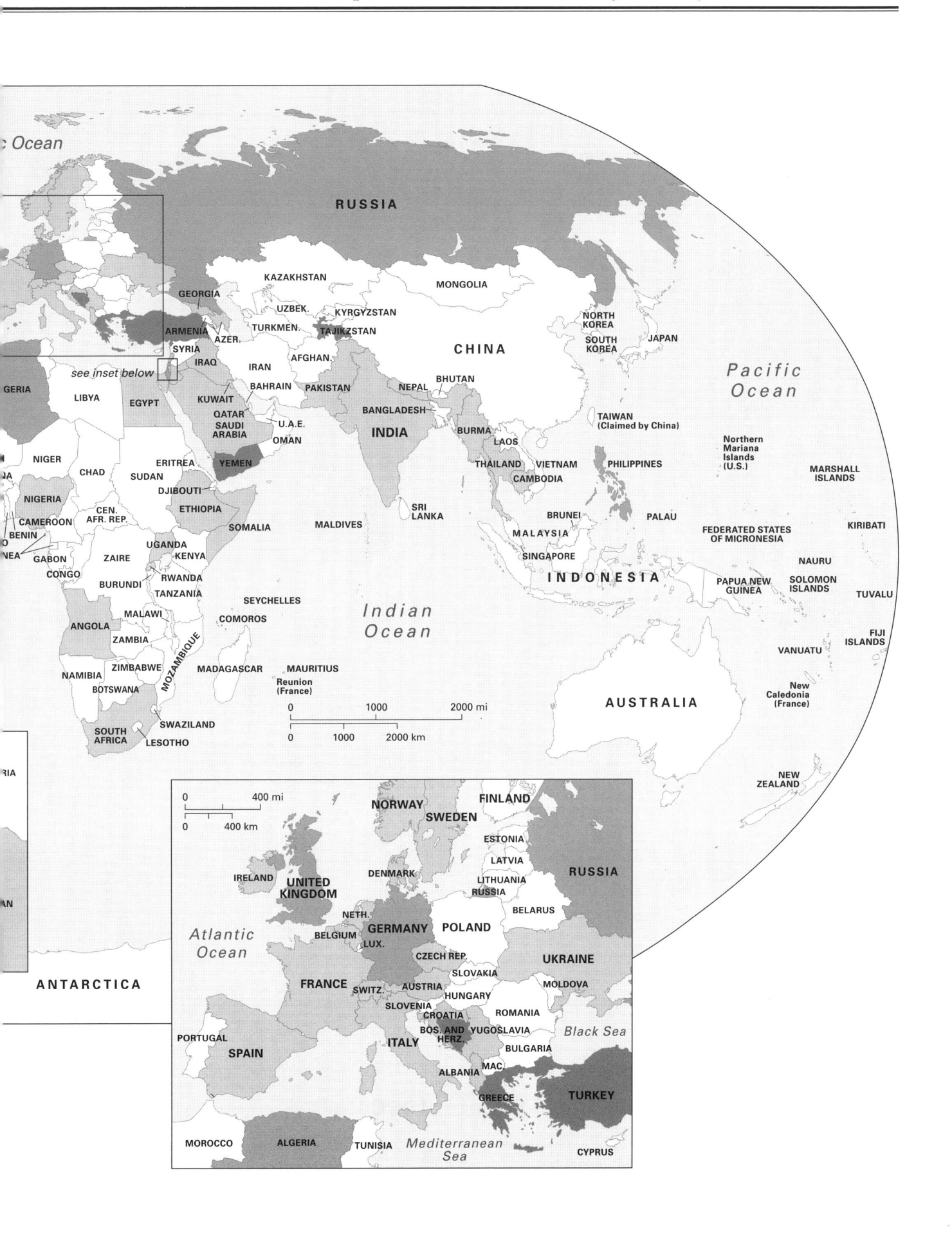

Maps of Terrorist Incidents by Country 1985–2004

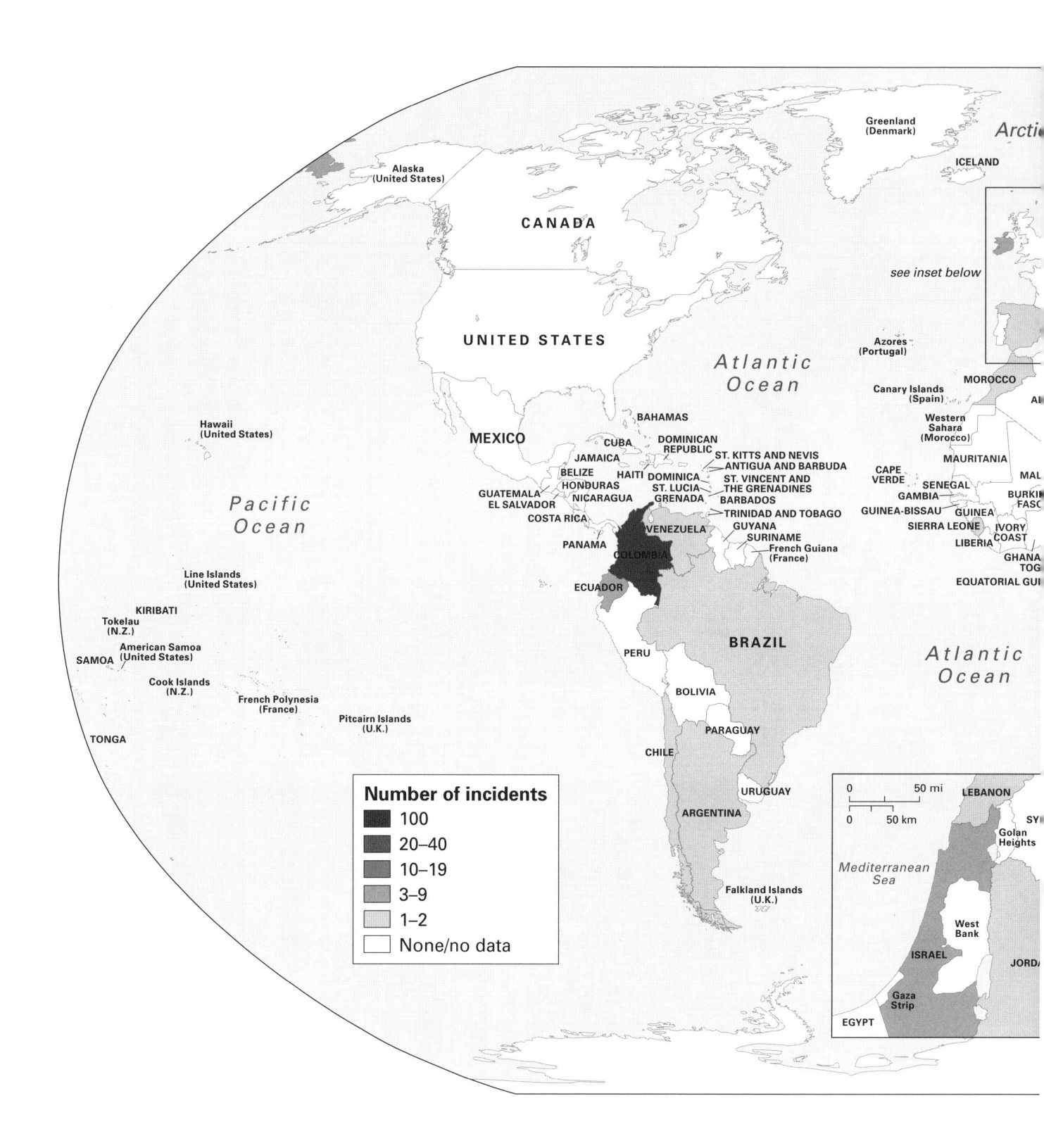

Number of incidents
- 100
- 20–40
- 10–19
- 3–9
- 1–2
- None/no data

International Terrorist Incidents, 1998

Maps of Terrorist Incidents by Country 1985–2004

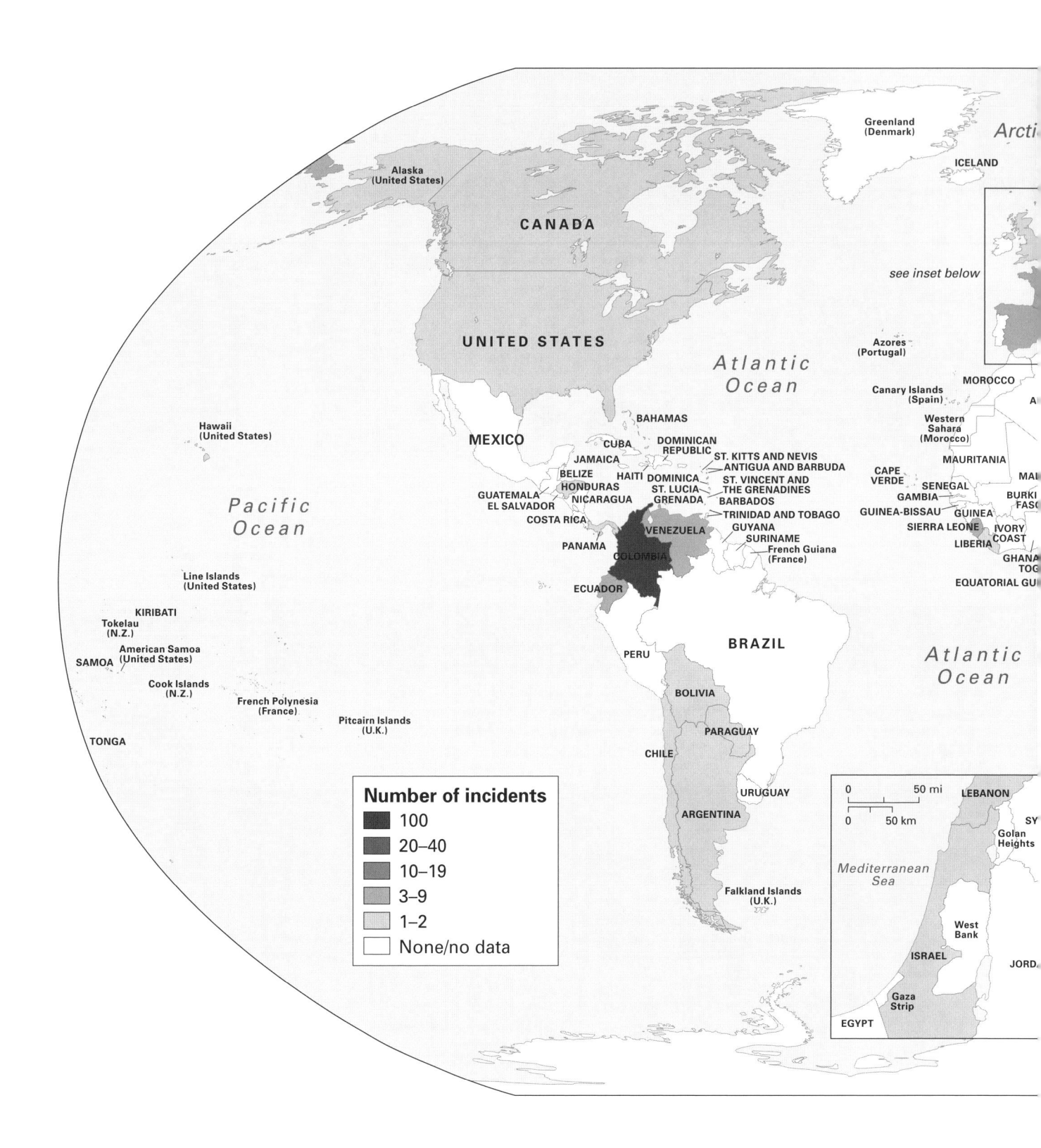

Patterns of Global Terrorism

Number of incidents
- 100
- 20–40
- 10–19
- 3–9
- 1–2
- None/no data

International Terrorist Incidents, 1999

Maps of Terrorist Incidents by Country 1985–2004

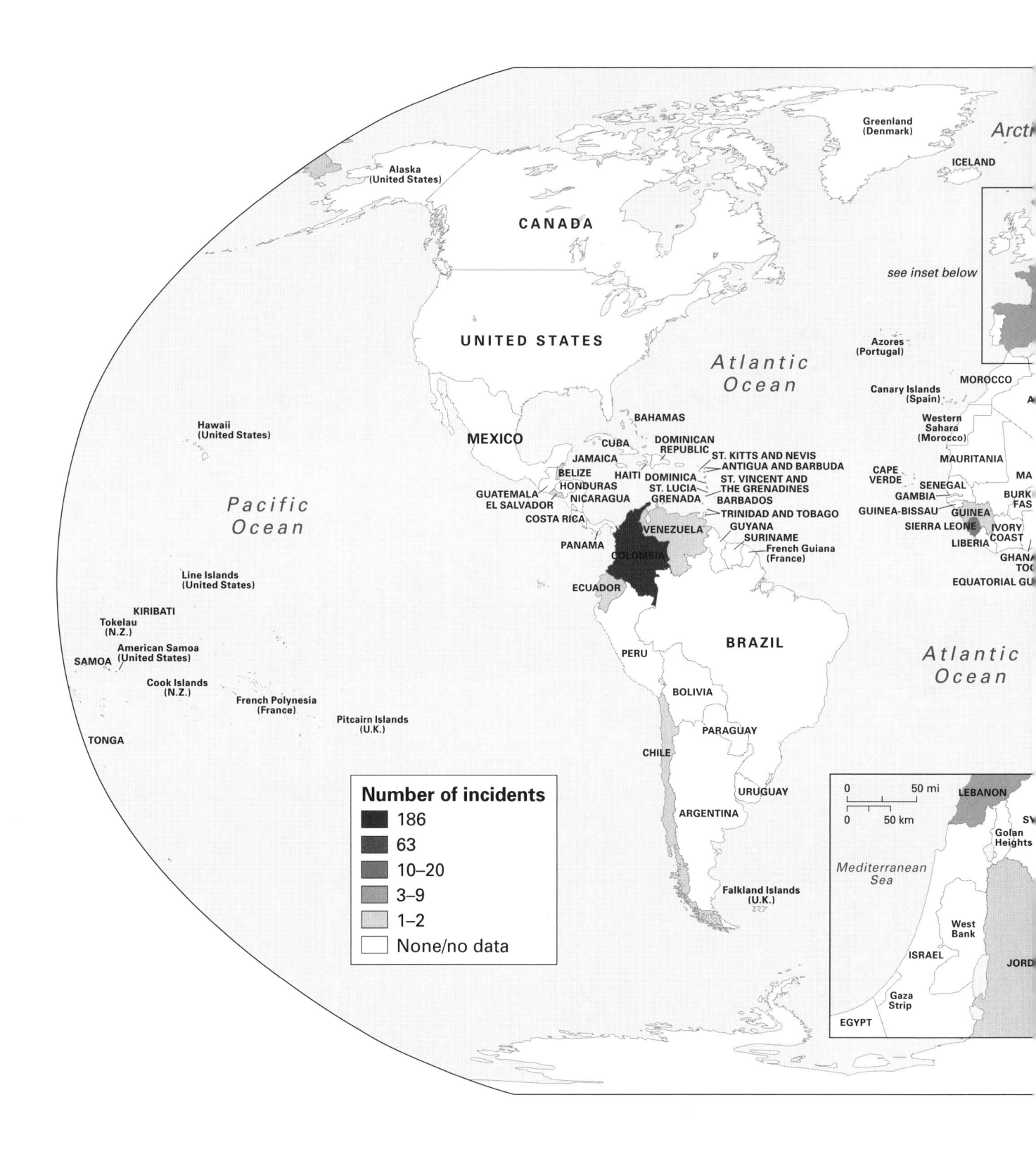

Patterns of Global Terrorism

Number of incidents
- 186
- 63
- 10–20
- 3–9
- 1–2
- None/no data

International Terrorist Incidents, 2000

Maps of Terrorist Incidents by Country 1985–2004

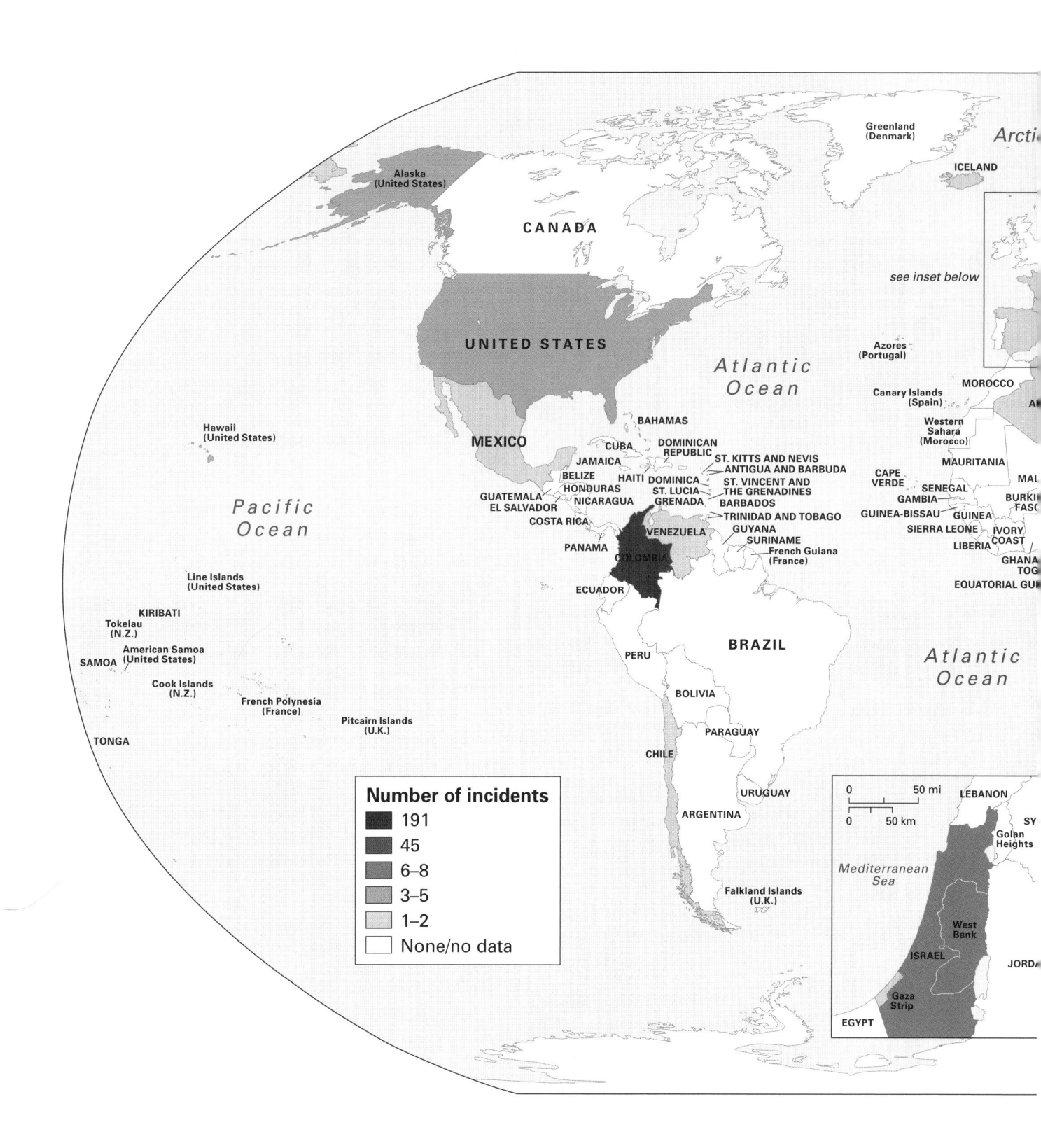

Patterns of Global Terrorism

Number of incidents
- 191
- 45
- 6–8
- 3–5
- 1–2
- None/no data

International Terrorist Incidents, 2001

Maps of Terrorist Incidents by Country 1985–2004

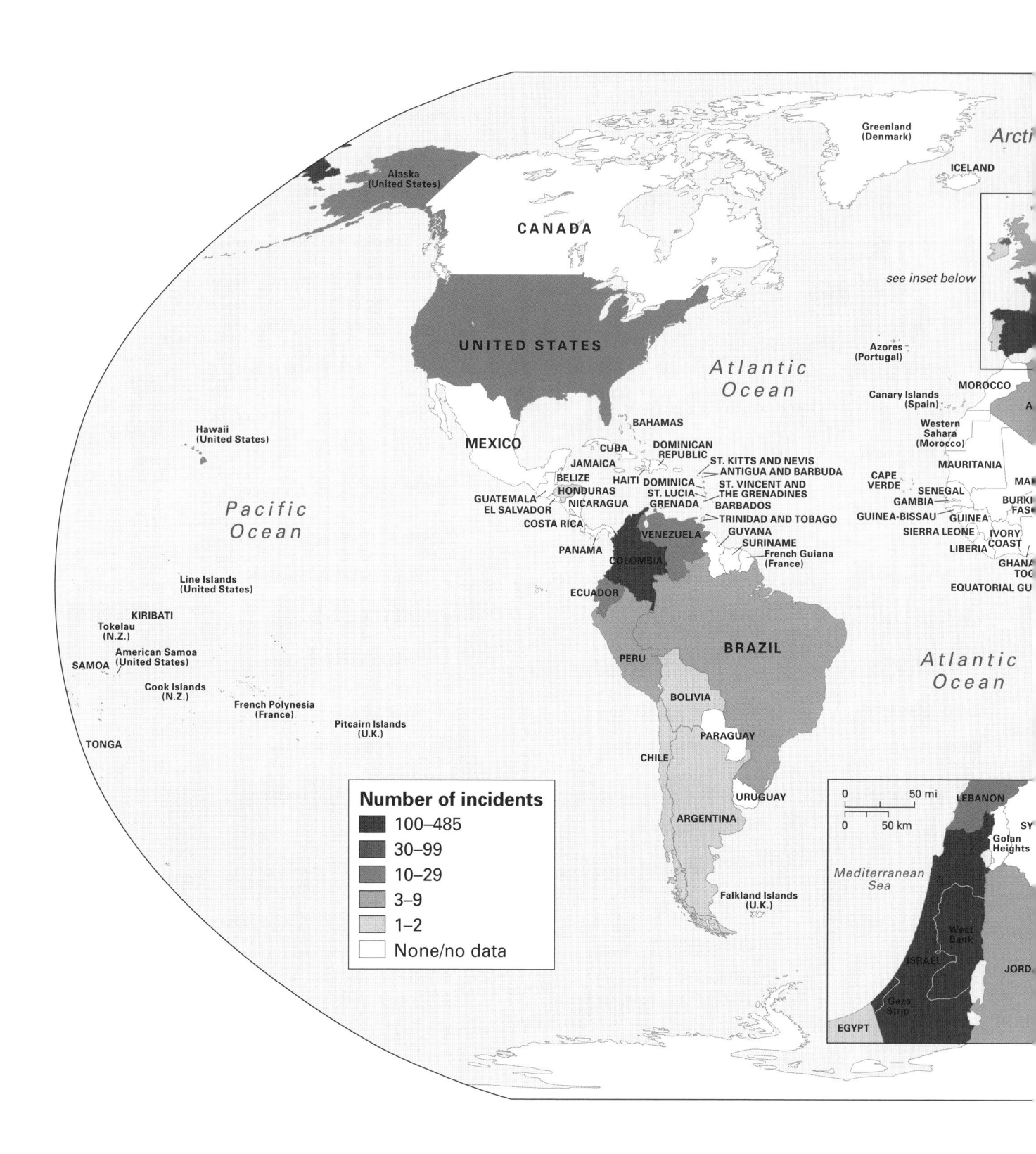

International Terrorist Incidents, 2002

Number of incidents
- 100–485
- 30–99
- 10–29
- 3–9
- 1–2
- None/no data

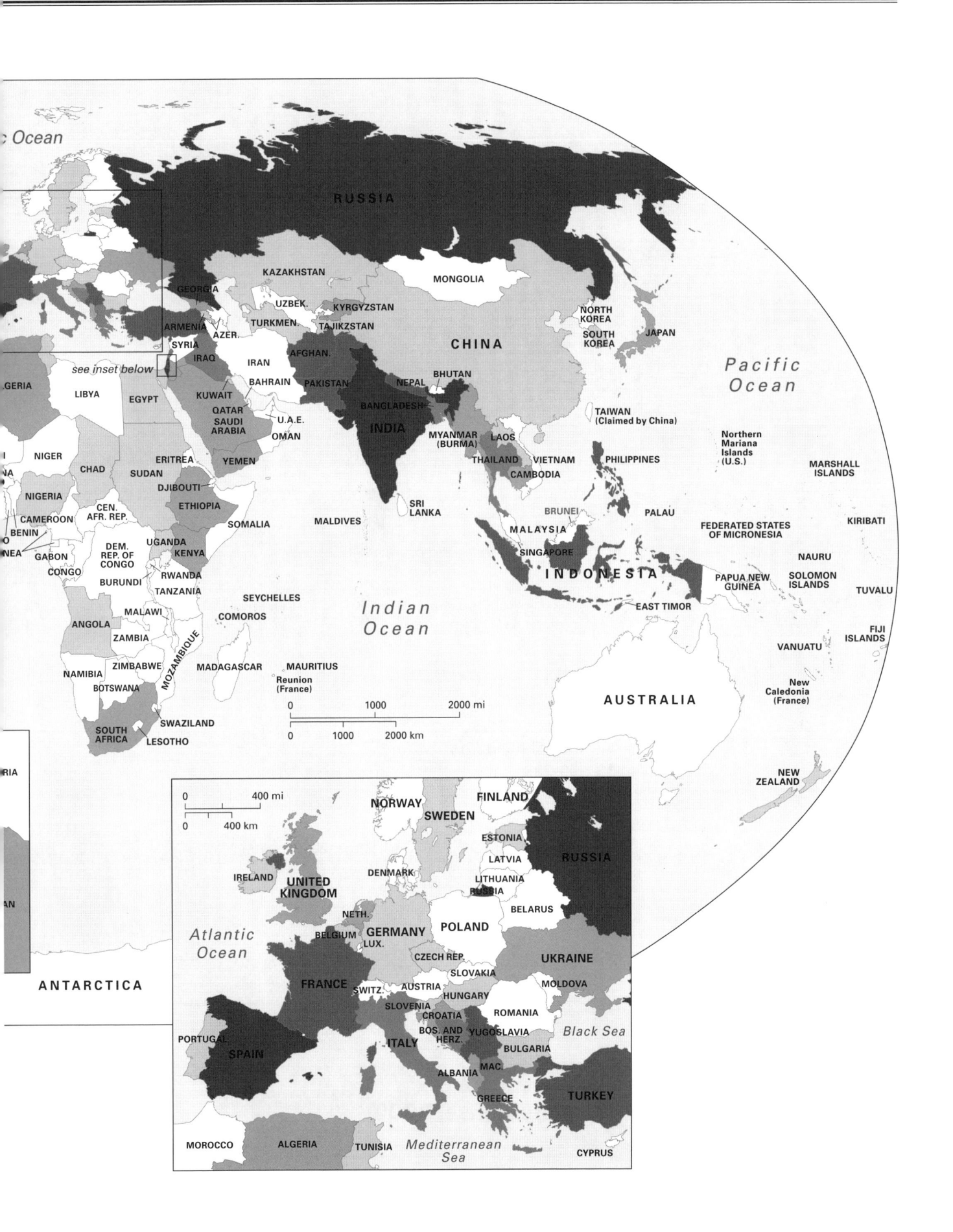

Maps of Terrorist Incidents by Country 1985–2004   **919**

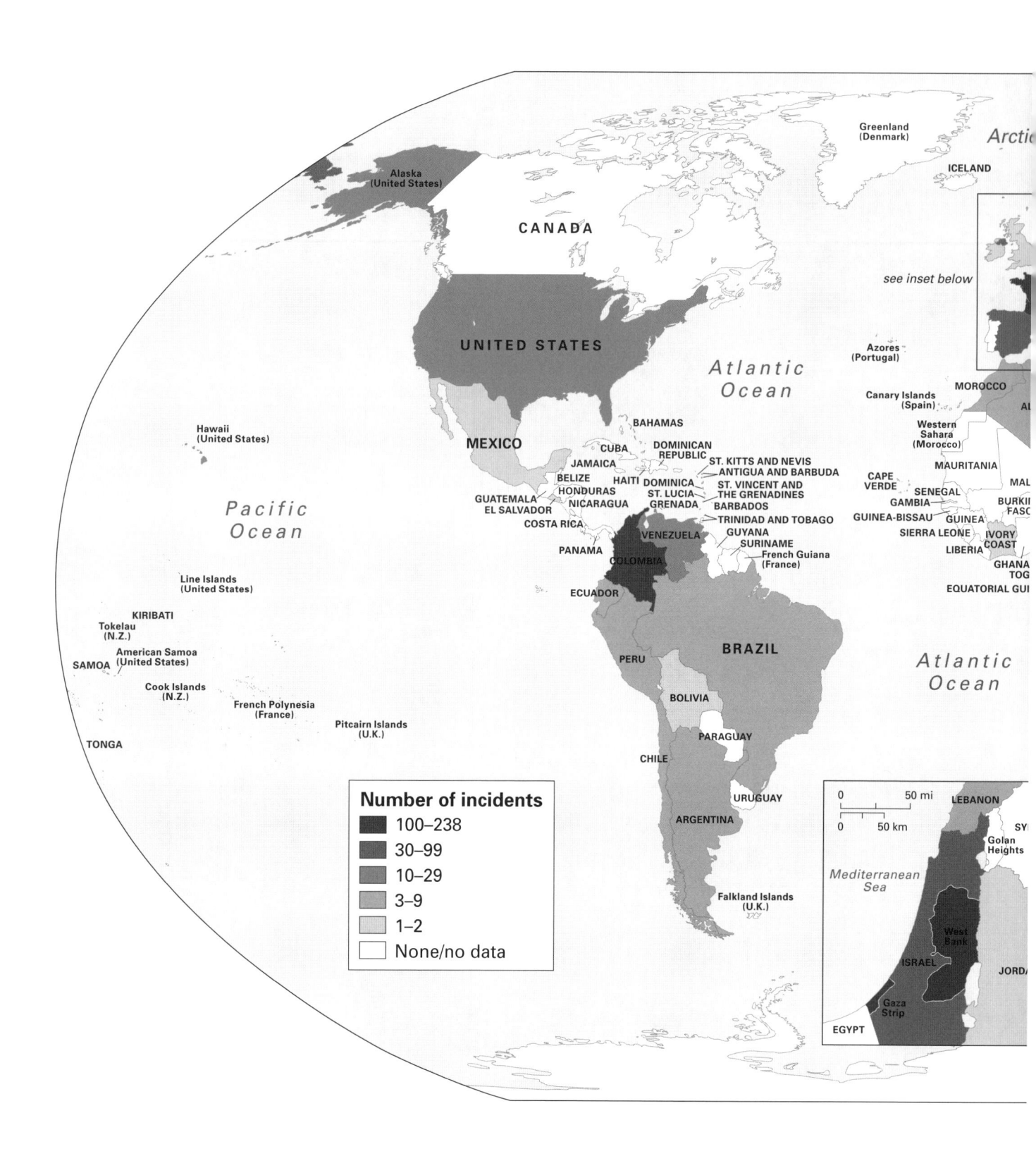

Number of incidents
- 100–238
- 30–99
- 10–29
- 3–9
- 1–2
- None/no data

International Terrorist Incidents, 2003

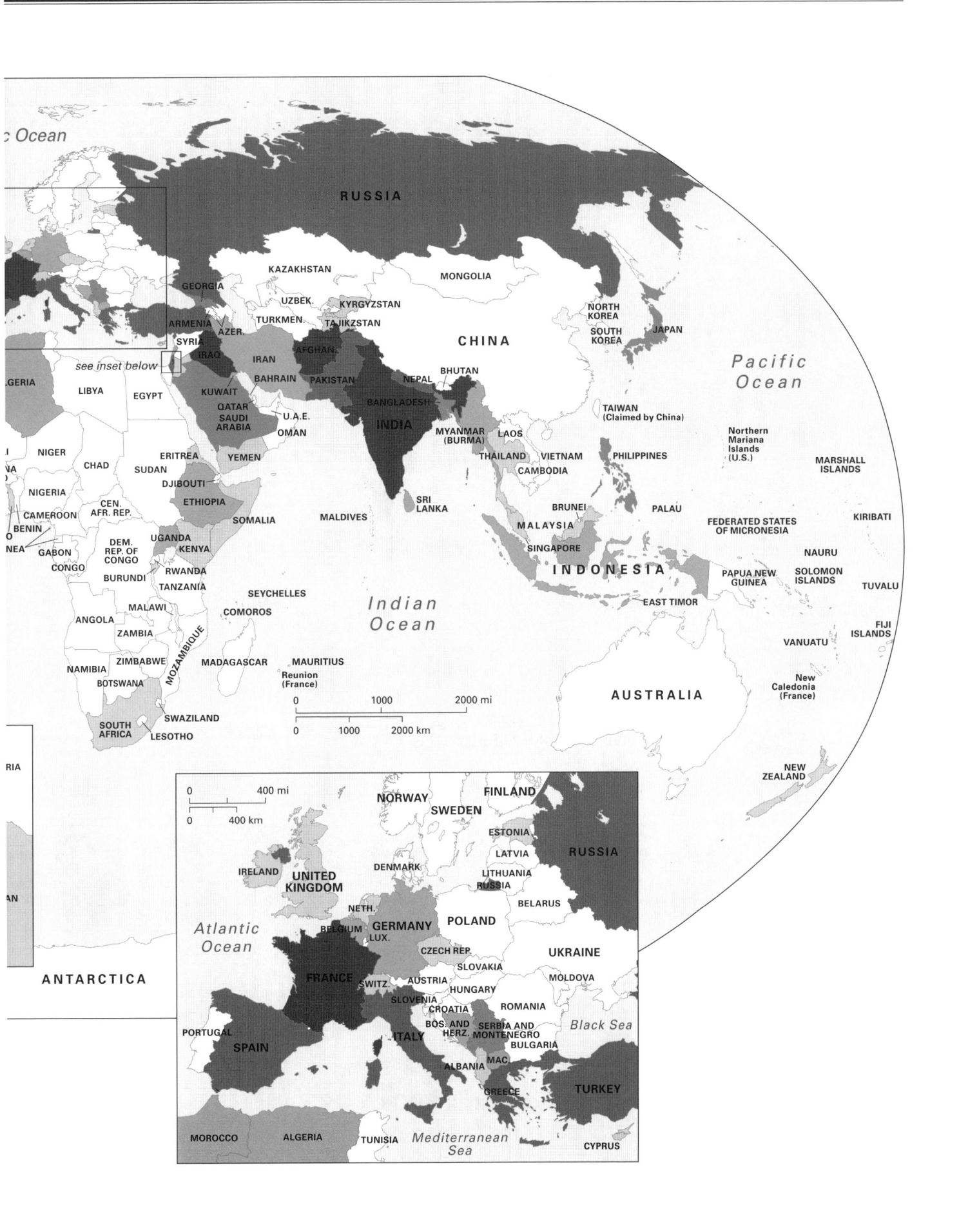

Maps of Terrorist Incidents by Country 1985–2004

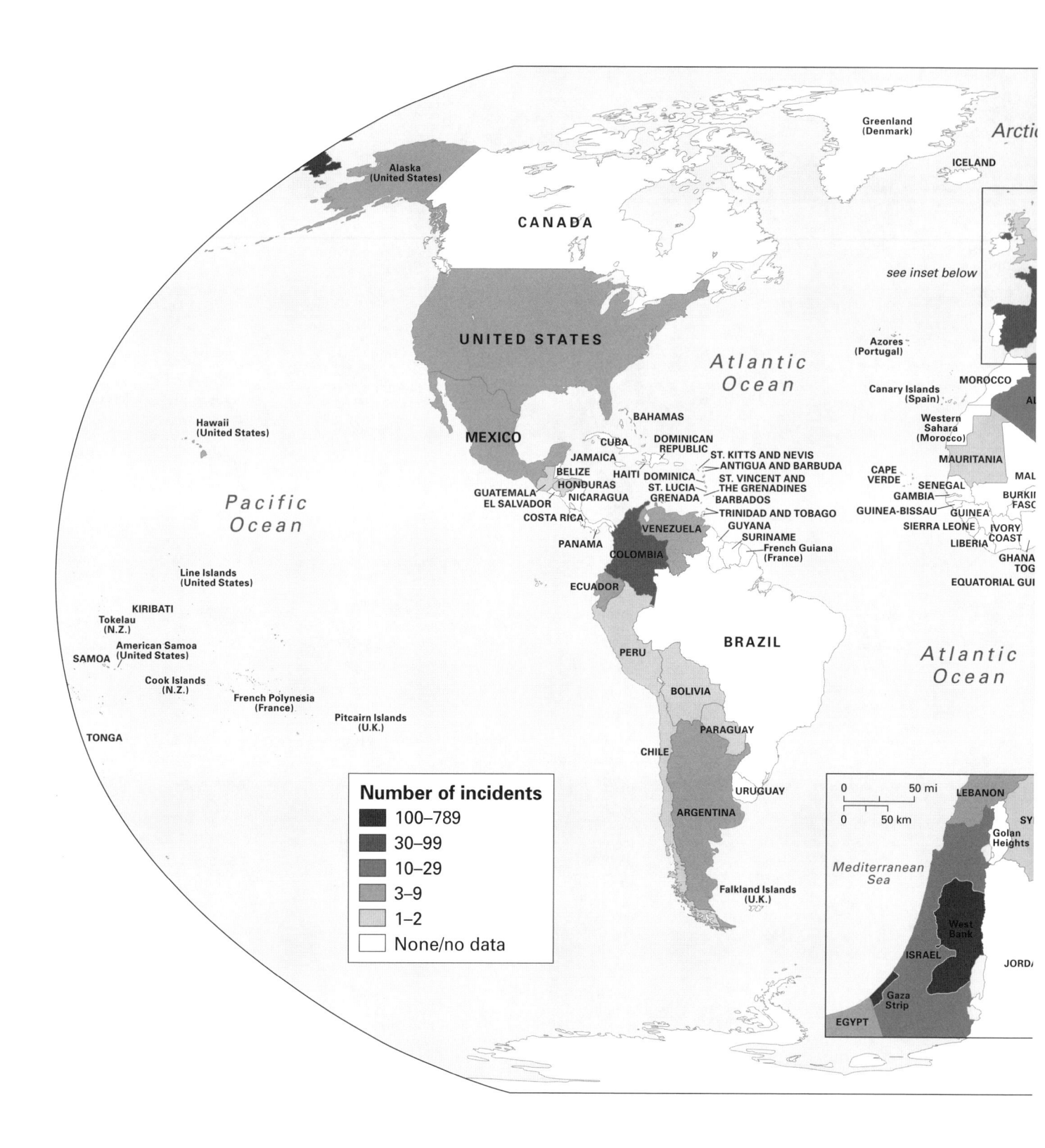

International Terrorist Incidents, 2004

Number of incidents
- 100–789
- 30–99
- 10–29
- 3–9
- 1–2
- None/no data

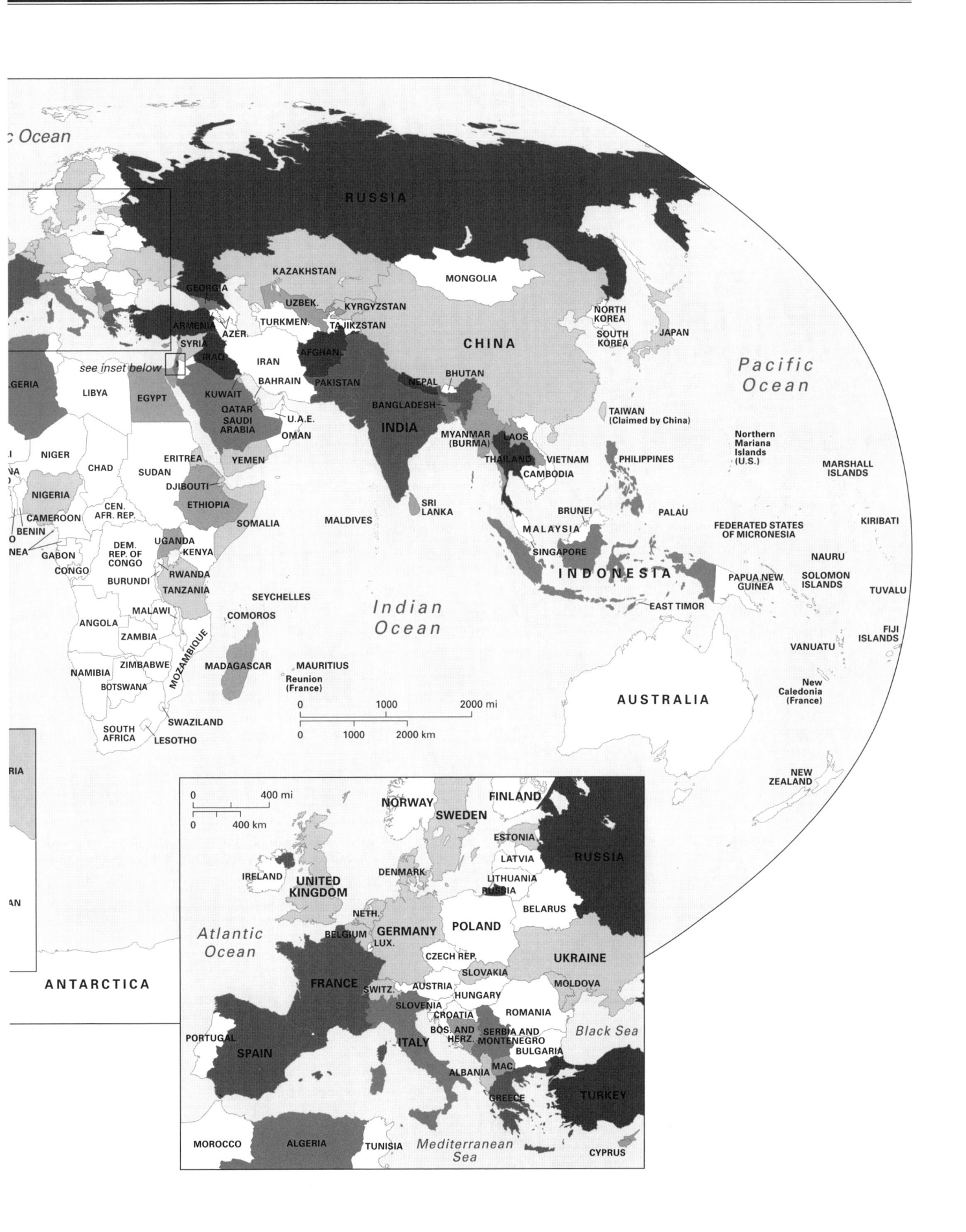

Maps of Terrorist Incidents by Country 1985–2004

Tables of Terrorist Incidents by Group 1985–2005

Overview of Tables of Terrorist Incidents by Group 1985–2005

Anna Sabasteanski

This group of tables sets out numbers of incidents, injuries and fatalities associated with terrorist groups 1985–2004, plus data for January–July 2005.

In the twenty-seven years from 1968 to 1994, 366 named groups and others unknown were responsible for 7,441 attacks, causing 18,164 injuries and 6,965 fatalities. Five groups were responsible in more than a hundred incidents each: Anti-Castro Cubans (200), Basque Fatherland and Freedom (200), Hizballah (152), Shining Path (119), and Tupac Amaru Revolutionary Movement (101). Fifty-eight groups were responsible for between 10 and 92 incidents. The ten deadliest groups during this period (with number of fatalities listed in parenthesis) were: Hizballah (771 fatalities); Front for the Liberation of Lebanon from Foreigners (221); Abu Nidal Organization (210); Popular Front for the Liberation of Palestine–General Command (163); Liberation Tigers of Tamil Eelam (161); Fatah (142); Popular Front for the Liberation of Palestine (130); Ansar Allah (117); Shining Path (89); and Anti-Castro Cubans (85).

Events picked up significantly in the mid-1990s. From 1995 to 2004, 447 named groups and others unknown were responsible for 13,105 attacks, 54,131 injuries, and 19,786 fatalities. Responsible for more than 100 attacks were the Revolutionary Armed Forces of Colombia with 403, HAMAS (337), Communist Party of Nepal–Maoist (227), National Liberation Army (194), Basque Fatherland and Freedom (179), al-Fatah (110), and the Taliban (104). More than forty other groups listed in the table were each responsible for 11–94 incidents.

The ten deadliest groups during this period were: al-Qaeda (3,512 fatalities); Riyad us-Saliheyn Martyrs' Brigade (514); HAMAS (494); Lord's Resistance Army (464); Armed Islamic Group (445); Revolutionary Armed Forces of Colombia (434); Liberation Tigers of Tamil Eelam (353); UNITA (297); al-Fatah (266); and Dagestan Liberation Army (248).

From January to July 2005 there have been 2,852 attacks causing 8,777 injuries and 4,388 fatalities. Only HAMAS with 171 and Qa'idat al-Jihad fi Bilad al-Rafidayn (al-Qaeda in Iraq) with 144 were responsible for more than 100 incidents. Palestinian Islamic Jihad was responsible for 33 attacks, al-Fatah and Popular Front for the Liberation of Palestine (PFLP) for 15 each, and Popular Resistance Committees 16. In Iraq Ansar al-Sunnah Army undertook 31 attacks. Maoist groups in Nepal and India accounted for 52 and 27, respectively. The Taleban was responsible for 51 attacks in Afghanistan. Other groups undertaking ten or more attacks include the Baloch Liberation Army (14), Basque Fatherland and Freedom (11), Fronte di Liberazione Naziunale di a Corsica (14), Liberation Tigers of Tamil Eelam (16), Revolutionary Armed Forces of Colombia (10), and United Liberation Front of Assam (11). The eighty-two other named groups were responsible for one to nine incidents.

The ten deadliest groups were: Tanzim Qa'idat al-Jihad fi Bilad al-Rafidayn (785 casualties); Ansar al-Sunnah Army (277); Taliban (114); Secret Organization of al-Qaeda in Europe (56); Soldiers of the Prophet's Companions (53); Communist Party of India-Maoist (48); Arbav Martyrs of Khuzestan (40); Lord's Resistance Army (LRA) (39); Communist Party of Nepal-Maoists (CPN-M) (25); Revolutionary Armed Forces of Colombia (22); and Islamic Army in Iraq (22).

The data for these tables was retrieved from the National Counterterrorism Center's (NCTC) Worldwide Incidents Tracking System (WITS) and the MIPT Terrorism Knowledge Base that integrates data from the RAND Terrorism Chronology and RAND-MIPT Terrorism Incident databases, in July–August, 2005. NCTC's methodology is described in more detail in "Overview of Trends over Time," in Part 6.

1985

Group	Incidents	Injuries	Fatalities	Total Casualties
15 May Organization for the Liberation of Palestine	1	14	1	15
Abu Nidal Organization (ANO)	13	265	93	358
Action Directe	1	0	0	0
African National Congress (South Africa)	3	0	0	0
al-Borkan Liberation Organization	1	0	1	1
al-Fatah	8	0	10	10
al-Saiqa	1	0	0	0
Amal	14	2	10	12
Anti-Terrorist Liberation Group	5	4	3	7
Arab Unionist Nationalist Organization	1	0	1	1
Armenian Revolutionary Army	1	1	1	2
Armenian Revolutionary Federation (ARF)	2	0	2	2
Armenian Secret Army for the Liberation of Armenia (ASALA)	2	0	0	0
Basque Fatherland and Freedom	13	4	3	7
Black Brigade	1	0	0	0
Black September	10	25	2	27
Chukakuha	1	0	0	0
Civilian Home Defense Forces (CHDF)	1	0	1	1
Communist Combatant Cells	6	3	0	3
Democratic Front for the Liberation of Palestine (DFLP)	2	1	0	1
Egypt's Revolution	1	2	1	3
Farabundo Marti National Liberation Front	1	0	13	13
Federation of Armenian Revolutionaries	1	0	1	1
Guerrilla Army of the Poor	1	0	2	2
Hizballah	29	171	43	214
Islamic Liberation Organization	1	0	1	1
Jewish Defense League (JDL)	1	0	0	0
Khaibar Brigades	2	0	0	0
Khristos Kasimis Revolutionary Group for International Solidarity	4	0	0	0
Lebanese Armed Revolutionary Faction	1	0	0	0
Lebanese National Resistance Front	2	1	7	8
Manuel Rodriguez Patriotic Front	15	7	1	8
Moraza Nist Front for the Liberation of Honduras (FMLH)	1	0	0	0
Movement of April 19	2	0	1	1
Mozambique National Resistance Movement	6	1	5	6
National Front (Greece)	1	78	0	78
National Liberation Army (Colombia)	3	0	0	0
New People's Army (NPA)	1	0	0	0
Norwegian National-Socialist (Nazi) Front	1	1	0	1
Other Group	90	109	383	492
Palestine Liberation Front	3	25	1	26

1985 *(continued)*

Group	Incidents	Injuries	Fatalities	Total Casualties
Palestine Liberation Organization (PLO)	17	13	1	14
Palestinian Revolution Forces General Command	2	1	0	1
Pan-Turkish Organization	1	0	0	0
Patriotic Union of Kurdistan (PUK)	2	0	0	0
Peace Conquerors	1	42	3	45
Polisario Front	4	2	4	6
Popular Forces of April 25	9	1	0	1
Popular Front for the Liberation of Palestine–General Command (PFLP-GC)	1	0	0	0
Proletarian Action Group	1	0	0	0
Red Army Faction	9	20	3	23
Regional Intendancy of the Sixth Region	1	0	0	0
Revolutionary Armed Forces of Colombia	4	0	1	1
Revolutionary Autonomous Group	1	0	0	0
Revolutionary Front for Proletarian Action	3	2	0	2
Revolutionary Nuclei	3	0	0	0
Revolutionary Organization of Socialist Muslims	4	93	1	94
Revolutionary People's Struggle	1	0	0	0
Shining Path	2	0	0	0
Syrian Social Nationalist Party	3	3	25	28
Tigray Peoples Liberation Front (TPLF)	1	0	0	0
Tupac Amaru Revolutionary Movement	11	0	1	1
Ukrainian Reactionary Force	1	0	1	1
UNITA	3	0	0	0
Unknown Group	102	277	109	386
TOTAL	**441**	**1168**	**736**	**1904**

1986

Group	Incidents	Injuries	Fatalities	Total Casualties
Abu Nidal Organization (ANO)	16	144	51	195
Action Directe	3	1	0	1
al-Fatah	9	28	4	32
Amal	5	3	4	7
Angry Brigade	1	1	0	1
Anti-American Arab Liberation Front	1	196	3	199
Arab Fedayeen Cells	3	1	0	1
Arab Liberation Front (ALF)	1	0	0	0
Arab Revolutionary Front	1	1	0	1
Armenian Secret Army for the Liberation of Armenia (ASALA)	1	0	1	1
Basque Fatherland and Freedom	27	34	1	35
Black September	1	1	0	1
Chukakuha	1	0	0	0
Commando Internacionalista Simon Bolivar	1	0	0	0
Committee of Solidarity with Arab and Middle East Political Prisoners (CSPPA)	12	161	6	167
Egypt's Revolution	1	3	1	4
Eritrean Liberation Front (ELF)	1	1	1	2
Ethiopian People's Revolutionary Army	1	0	0	0
Farabundo Marti National Liberation Front	1	0	1	1
Front of Justice and Revenge	1	0	1	1
Greek Bulgarian Armenian Front	1	0	1	1
Green Brigades	1	0	0	0
Hizballah	14	57	79	136
Islamic Society	1	0	0	0
Japanese Red Army (JRA)	3	0	0	0
Jewish Defense League (JDL)	3	21	0	21
Khristos Kasimis Revolutionary Group for International Solidarity	1	0	0	0
Lebanese Armed Revolutionary Faction	1	0	0	0
Liberation Tigers of Tamil Eelam (LTTE)	3	40	23	63
Manuel Rodriguez Patriotic Front	2	0	0	0
Movement of April 19	6	0	0	0
Mozambique National Resistance Movement	3	0	0	0
National Liberation Army (Colombia)	18	0	1	1
National Revolutionary Command (Omar al-Mukhtar)	4	0	0	0
New People's Army (NPA)	1	3	0	3
Other Group	56	267	107	374
Palestine Liberation Organization (PLO)	1	65	1	66
Palestinian Revolution Forces General Command	4	6	2	8
Pattani United Liberation Organization (PULO)	1	0	0	0
Pedro Leon Arboleda Movement	3	1	0	1
People's Command	1	0	0	0

1986 *(continued)*

Group	Incidents	Injuries	Fatalities	Total Casualties
Polisario Front	3	2	3	5
Popular Forces of April 25	2	0	0	0
Popular Front for the Liberation of Palestine (PFLP)	2	18	2	20
Rebel Armed Forces	2	0	0	0
Red Army Faction	2	0	0	0
Revolutionary Eelam Organization (EROS)	1	0	0	0
Revolutionary People's Struggle	2	0	0	0
Shining Path	16	49	13	62
Sudan People's Liberation Army	2	0	0	0
Tigray Peoples Liberation Front (TPLF)	1	0	2	2
Tupac Amaru Revolutionary Movement	22	1	1	2
UNITA	2	0	0	0
United Arab Revolution	1	1	0	1
United Popular Action Movement	1	0	0	0
Unknown Group	103	130	42	172
TOTAL	**378**	**1236**	**351**	**1587**

1987

Group	Incidents	Injuries	Fatalities	Total Casualties
17 November Revolutionary Organization (RO-N17)	2	31	0	31
Abu Nidal Organization (ANO)	3	2	2	4
al-Fatah	6	3	9	12
Alejo Calatayu	1	0	0	0
Amal	10	3	0	3
Anti-Castro Cubans	1	0	0	0
Anti-Imperialist International Brigade	5	0	0	0
Armenian Secret Army for the Liberation of Armenia (ASALA)	1	1	2	3
Autonomous Cells	1	0	0	0
Basque Fatherland and Freedom	18	2	2	4
Brother Julian	1	14	0	14
Chadian People's Revolutionary Movement	1	0	0	0
Commando Internacionalista Simon Bolivar	1	0	0	0
Egypt's Revolution	1	2	0	2
Ethiopian People's Liberation Front	1	0	0	0
Ethiopian People's Revolutionary Army	1	0	0	0
Fedayeen Khalq (People's Commandos)	1	3	0	3
Green Cells	1	0	0	0
HAMAS	1	15	0	15
Hizballah	22	18	4	22
Irish Republican Army (IRA)	2	31	0	31
Japanese Red Army (JRA)	1	0	0	0
Jewish Defense League (JDL)	1	0	0	0
Jihad Brigades	1	0	0	0
June 16 Organization	3	0	0	0
Kurdistan National Union	2	0	0	0
Lautaro Youth Movement	3	0	0	0
Lebanese Liberation Front	2	21	1	22
Liberation Battalion	1	0	2	2
Liberation Tigers of Tamil Eelam (LTTE)	1	150	25	175
Manuel Rodriguez Patriotic Front	2	0	0	0
Maximiliano Gomez Revolutionary Brigade	3	0	0	0
Moro National Liberation Front (MNLF)	1	1	1	2
Movement of the Revolutionary Left	1	0	0	0
Mozambique National Resistance Movement	4	7	7	14
Mujahedin-e-Khalq (MeK)	1	2	0	2
National Liberation Army (Colombia)	7	0	0	0
New People's Army (NPA)	14	14	4	18
Other Group	82	511	212	723
Palestine Liberation Organization (PLO)	1	0	1	1
Palestinian Revolution Forces General Command	7	4	2	6

1987 *(continued)*

Group	Incidents	Injuries	Fatalities	Total Casualties
Partisans of Holy War	1	0	0	0
Patriotic Union of Kurdistan (PUK)	1	0	0	0
People's Liberation Front (JVP)	1	0	0	0
Polisario Front	2	0	0	0
Popular Front for the Liberation of Palestine (PFLP)	2	8	7	15
Popular Front for the Liberation of Palestine–General Command (PFLP-GC)	1	0	0	0
Popular Revolutionary Resistance Organization	1	0	3	3
Revolutionary Armed Forces of Colombia	2	0	0	0
Revolutionary People's Struggle	2	0	0	0
Revolutionary Popular Resistance Organization	1	5	0	5
Shining Path	7	5	3	8
Simon Bolivar Guerilla Coordinating Board (CGSB)	1	0	0	0
Sinhalese Janatha Vimukthi Peramuna (JVP)	1	0	0	0
Sudan People's Liberation Army	2	0	0	0
Syrian Mujahideen	1	0	1	1
Terra Lilure (TL)	3	8	0	8
Tigray Peoples Liberation Front (TPLF)	1	0	0	0
Tupac Amaru Revolutionary Movement	17	7	0	7
UNITA	1	0	1	1
United Nasirite Organizaiton	1	2	0	2
Unknown Group	95	295	86	381
TOTAL	**363**	**1165**	**375**	**1540**

1988

Group	Incidents	Injuries	Fatalities	Total Casualties
17 November Revolutionary Organization (RO-N17)	6	0	1	1
Abu Nidal Organization (ANO)	12	164	23	187
African National Congress (South Africa)	3	0	0	0
al-Fatah	6	2	14	16
al-Sadr Brigades	1	0	0	0
Amal	8	38	5	43
Anti-Imperialist International Brigade	3	0	0	0
Armenian Secret Army for the Liberation of Armenia (ASALA)	1	0	1	1
Basque Fatherland and Freedom	19	2	0	2
Black Friday	1	0	0	0
Black September	2	2	0	2
Che Guevara Brigade	2	0	0	0
Christians for Peace and National Salvation	1	0	0	0
Chukakuha	2	0	0	0
Democratic Front for the Liberation of Palestine (DFLP)	7	2	4	6
Ethiopian People's Revolutionary Army	1	0	0	0
Farabundo Marti National Liberation Front	8	0	0	0
Hizballah	10	2	11	13
Hotaru (Firefly)	1	0	0	0
Irish Republican Army (IRA)	7	16	7	23
Japanese Red Army (JRA)	2	17	5	22
Kach	1	0	0	0
Liberation Tigers of Tamil Eelam (LTTE)	3	1	11	12
Mano Blanca	1	0	0	0
Manuel Rodriguez Patriotic Front	4	0	0	0
Masada, Action and Defense Movement	2	16	1	17
Morazanist Patriotic Front (FPM)	2	0	1	1
Moro National Liberation Front (MNLF)	2	1	2	3
Movement of April 19	9	0	0	0
National Front for the Liberation of Egypt	1	0	0	0
National Front for the Liberation of Kurdistan	1	0	1	1
National Liberation Army (Colombia)	14	18	1	19
New People's Army (NPA)	6	0	4	4
Other Group	102	1389	508	1897
Palestine Liberation Front	1	1	0	1
Polisario Front	1	0	8	8
Popular Front for the Liberation of Palestine (PFLP)	1	2	0	2
Popular Front for the Liberation of Palestine–General Command (PFLP-GC)	1	1	0	1
Red Army Faction	2	0	0	0
Revolutionary People's Struggle	1	13	0	13
Shining Path	4	9	9	18

1988 *(continued)*

Group	Incidents	Injuries	Fatalities	Total Casualties
Simon Bolivar Guerilla Coordinating Board (CGSB)	2	0	0	0
Socialist-Nationalist Front (SNF)	1	5	0	5
South-West Africa People's Organization (SWAPO)	1	31	14	45
Terra Lilure (TL)	1	0	0	0
Tigray Peoples Liberation Front (TPLF)	1	0	0	0
Tupac Amaru Revolutionary Movement	7	2	0	2
Unknown Group	100	98	74	172
Venceremos	1	0	0	0
Workers' Revolutionary Party	1	0	1	1
TOTAL	**377**	**1832**	**706**	**2538**

1989

Group	Incidents	Injuries	Fatalities	Total Casualties
Abu Nidal Organization (ANO)	2	0	1	1
African National Congress (South Africa)	3	0	0	0
al-Fatah	3	1	1	2
Amal	5	0	5	5
Anti-Castro Cubans	2	0	0	0
Arabian Peninsula Freemen	1	0	1	1
Arnoldo Camu Command	1	0	0	0
Autonomia Sinistra Ante Parlamentare	2	0	0	0
Basque Fatherland and Freedom	21	5	0	5
Continuing Struggle	1	0	0	0
Farabundo Marti National Liberation Front	6	1	0	1
Fronte di Liberazione Naziunale di a Corsica (FLNC)	1	0	0	0
Generation of Arab Fury	2	16	1	17
Guatemalan National Revolutionary Unity (URNG)	2	0	0	0
HAMAS	1	3	2	5
Hizballah	12	16	179	195
Irish Republican Army (IRA)	10	8	4	12
June 16 Organization	1	0	0	0
Kurdistan Workers' Party	1	0	0	0
Lautaro Youth Movement	3	0	0	0
Lebanese Liberation Front	1	0	0	0
Liberation Tigers of Tamil Eelam (LTTE)	3	0	31	31
Manuel Rodriguez Patriotic Front	7	1	0	1
Morazanist Patriotic Front (FPM)	3	7	0	7
Moro National Liberation Front (MNLF)	1	3	2	5
Mozambique National Resistance Movement	3	0	4	4
Mujahideen of the People	1	0	0	0
National Liberation Army (Colombia)	7	0	0	0
National Liberation Union	1	0	0	0
National Resistance Front (Chile)	1	0	0	0
New People's Army (NPA)	7	1	4	5
Other Group	87	133	59	192
Palestinian Islamic Jihad (PIJ)	1	0	0	0
Palestinian Popular Struggle Front (PSF)	1	0	0	0
Popular Front for the Liberation of Palestine (PFLP)	3	3	1	4
Popular Front for the Liberation of Palestine–General Command (PFLP-GC)	1	0	0	0
Popular Liberation Army	2	3	0	3
Revolutionary Army of the People	2	0	0	0
Revolutionary People's Liberation Party/Front (DHKP-C)	6	0	0	0
Revolutionary People's Struggle	5	4	0	4
Revolutionary United Front Movement	1	5	0	5

1989 *(continued)*

Group	Incidents	Injuries	Fatalities	Total Casualties
Shining Path	14	42	8	50
Terra Lilure (TL)	1	0	0	0
The Extraditables	1	0	0	0
Tupac Amaru Revolutionary Movement	10	0	0	0
UNITA	3	1	0	1
United Organization of Halabjah Martyrs	1	25	0	25
Unknown Group	103	190	43	233
Zarate Willka Armed Liberation Forces	4	0	2	2
TOTAL	**361**	**468**	**348**	**816**

1990

Group	Incidents	Injuries	Fatalities	Total Casualties
Abu Nidal Organization (ANO)	2	1	1	2
al-Fatah	1	1	3	4
Amal	2	1	2	3
Arab Communist Revolutionary Party	1	0	0	0
Basque Fatherland and Freedom	13	3	0	3
Che Guevara Brigade	2	0	0	0
Chilean Committee for Disarmament and Denuclearization	1	8	0	8
Chukakuha	2	0	0	0
Comando Alejo Calatayud	1	0	0	0
Eva Peron Organization	3	0	0	0
Farabundo Marti National Liberation Front	1	0	0	0
First of October Antifascist Resistance Group (GRAPO)	1	0	0	0
Free Papua Movement (OPM)	1	0	0	0
Front for the Liberation of the Cabinda Enclave	3	0	0	0
Fronte di Liberazione Naziunale di a Corsica (FLNC)	1	0	0	0
Gracchus Babeuf	2	0	0	0
Guatemalan National Revolutionary Unity (URNG)	1	0	0	0
Hizballah	3	19	13	32
Irish Republican Army (IRA)	9	5	3	8
Islamic Front for the Liberation of Palestine (IFLP)	1	0	0	0
Lautaro Youth Movement	6	0	0	0
Lebanese National Resistance Front	1	0	1	1
Liberation Tigers of Tamil Eelam (LTTE)	1	0	13	13
Manuel Rodriguez Patriotic Front	6	2	0	2
Morazanist Patriotic Front (FPM)	1	7	0	7
Movement of April 19	1	0	0	0
National Front for the Liberation of Angola (FNLA)	1	0	0	0
National Liberation Army (Colombia)	6	0	0	0
Nestor Paz Zamora Commission	1	1	1	2
New People's Army (NPA)	12	0	10	10
Omar Torrijos Commando for Latin American Dignity	1	0	0	0
Other Group	50	155	36	191
Palestine Liberation Front	1	0	0	0
Palestine Liberation Organization (PLO)	2	3	1	4
Palestinian Islamic Jihad (PIJ)	6	54	7	61
Patriotic Resistance Army (ERP)	1	3	0	3
Popular Front for the Liberation of Palestine–General Command (PFLP-GC)	1	0	0	0
Revolutionary Action Organization of the Arab Resistance Front	1	2	0	2
Revolutionary Armed Forces of Colombia	1	0	0	0
Revolutionary Organization 17 November (RO-N17)	3	3	0	3
Sekihotai	1	0	0	0

1990 *(continued)*

Group	Incidents	Injuries	Fatalities	Total Casualties
Shining Path	6	1	9	10
Social Resistance	12	0	0	0
The Extraditables	1	0	1	1
Tupac Amaru Revolutionary Movement	15	4	0	4
Unknown Group	97	47	21	68
TOTAL	**286**	**320**	**122**	**442**

1991

Group	Incidents	Injuries	Fatalities	Total Casualties
17 November Revolutionary Organization (RO-N17)	15	4	2	6
Abu Nidal Organization (ANO)	2	0	3	3
al-Fatah	1	0	1	1
Anti-Castro Cubans	1	0	0	0
Arab Communist Revolutionary Party	1	0	0	0
Armenian Secret Army for the Liberation of Armenia (ASALA)	1	0	0	0
Basque Fatherland and Freedom	22	7	0	7
Chukakuha	1	0	0	0
December 20 Torrijist Patriotic Vanguard (VPT-20)	1	0	0	0
Eritrean Liberation Front (ELF)	1	0	0	0
Farabundo Marti National Liberation Front	2	0	12	12
Fronte di Liberazione Naziunale di a Corsica (FLNC)	3	0	0	0
Gracchus Babeuf	1	0	0	0
HAMAS	1	3	6	9
Heroes of Palestine	1	0	0	0
Hizballah	8	1	2	3
Irish Republican Army (IRA)	2	0	0	0
Islamic Brotherhood	1	0	0	0
Jihad Brigades	1	0	0	0
Kach	1	0	0	0
Lautaro Youth Movement	1	0	0	0
Lebanese Armed Revolutionary Faction	1	0	0	0
Liberation Tigers of Tamil Eelam (LTTE)	2	9	27	36
Manuel Rodriguez Patriotic Front	5	2	0	2
Morazanist Patriotic Front (FPM)	1	0	0	0
Mozambique National Resistance Movement	1	0	0	0
National Liberation Army (Colombia)	1	0	0	0
Nestor Paz Zamora Commission	1	0	0	0
Other Group	70	67	35	102
Popular Army of National Liberation	1	0	0	0
Popular Front for the Liberation of Palestine (PFLP)	1	0	0	0
Red Army Faction	2	0	0	0
Revolutionary Armed Forces of Colombia	2	9	4	13
Revolutionary People's Liberation Party/Front (DHKP-C)	24	2	3	5
Revolutionary People's Struggle	7	0	0	0
Revolutionary Worker Clandestine Union of the People Party	3	0	0	0
Shining Path	20	22	29	51
Tontons Macoutes	2	0	2	2
Tupac Amaru Revolutionary Movement	9	4	1	5
Turkish Islamic Jihad	2	2	1	3
Turkish People's Liberation Front (TPLF) (THKP-C)	3	1	0	1

1991 *(continued)*

Group	Incidents	Injuries	Fatalities	Total Casualties
United Popular Action Movement	1	0	0	0
Unknown Group	193	103	64	167
Venceremos	1	0	0	0
TOTAL	**421**	**236**	**192**	**428**

1992

Group	Incidents	Injuries	Fatalities	Total Casualties
17 November Revolutionary Organization (RO-N17)	3	0	0	0
Abu Nidal Organization (ANO)	2	0	5	5
Actiefront Nationistisch Nederland	1	0	0	0
al-Gama'at al-Islamiyya (GAI)	3	15	1	16
Amal	1	1	0	1
Anti-Castro Cubans	1	0	0	0
Basque Fatherland and Freedom	13	9	0	9
Chilean Committee of Support for the Peruvian Revolution	1	0	0	0
Cinchoneros Popular Liberation Movement	2	0	0	0
Democratic Front for the Liberation of Palestine (DFLP)	1	0	0	0
Front for the Liberation of the Cabinda Enclave	3	0	0	0
HAMAS	3	1	2	3
Hizballah	2	250	29	279
Irish National Liberation Army (INLA)	1	0	1	1
Irish Republican Army (IRA)	3	29	0	29
Islamic Golden Army	1	0	0	0
Islamic Salvation Front	3	0	0	0
Jewish Defense League (JDL)	1	0	0	0
Khmer Rouge	4	1	0	1
Kurdistan Workers' Party	5	1	3	4
Lautaro Youth Movement	7	0	0	0
Manuel Rodriguez Patriotic Front	4	3	0	3
Mujahedin-e-Khalq (MeK)	3	0	0	0
National Liberation Army (Colombia)	6	0	5	5
National Patriotic Front of Liberia (NPFL)	2	0	10	10
New People's Army (NPA)	3	1	2	3
Other Group	62	60	37	97
People's Revolutionary Organization	2	0	0	0
Popular Front for the Liberation of Palestine (PFLP)	1	0	0	0
Red Army Faction	1	0	0	0
Revolutionary Armed Forces of Colombia	12	4	2	6
Revolutionary People's Liberation Party/Front (DHKP-C)	8	0	1	1
Revolutionary United Front (RUF)	1	0	8	8
Shahin (Falcon)	1	0	0	0
Shining Path	8	10	4	14
Simon Bolivar Guerilla Coordinating Board (CGSB)	2	0	0	0
Sovereign Panama Front (FPS)	1	2	0	2
Sudan People's Liberation Army	1	0	2	2
Tupac Amaru Revolutionary Movement	4	3	0	3
Tupac Katari Guerrilla Army (EGTK)	3	0	0	0
Union of Young Kurdish Revolutionaries	1	0	0	0

1992 *(continued)*

Group	Incidents	Injuries	Fatalities	Total Casualties
UNITA	1	0	0	0
United Popular Action Movement	1	0	0	0
Unknown Group	84	166	34	200
TOTAL	**273**	**556**	**146**	**702**

1993

Group	Incidents	Injuries	Fatalities	Total Casualties
Abu Nidal Organization (ANO)	1	0	1	1
Abu Sayyaf Group (ASG)	1	0	0	0
al-Fatah	1	11	0	11
al-Gama'at al-Islamiyya (GAI)	7	34	1	35
All Burma Students' Democratic Front (ABSDF)	1	0	0	0
Armed Islamic Group	8	1	7	8
Basque Fatherland and Freedom	4	3	0	3
December 20 Torrijist Patriotic Vanguard (VPT-20)	1	0	1	1
Egyptian Islamic Jihad	1	20	4	24
Front for the Liberation of the Cabinda Enclave	1	0	0	0
Group of the Martyrs Mostafa Sadeki and Ali Zadeh	1	0	0	0
HAMAS	5	0	5	5
Hizballah	6	13	14	27
Irish Republican Army (IRA)	3	0	0	0
Kahane Chai	1	0	0	0
Kakurokyo	3	0	0	0
Khmer Rouge	10	35	12	47
Kurdistan Workers' Party	23	26	0	26
Liberation Army Fifth Battalion	1	1042	6	1048
Manuel Rodriguez Patriotic Front	3	0	0	0
Moro National Liberation Front (MNLF)	1	0	0	0
Movement of the Revolutionary Left	2	4	0	4
National Liberation Army (Colombia)	2	0	0	0
Other Group	84	1313	369	1682
Palestinian Islamic Jihad (PIJ)	2	5	3	8
Pattani United Liberation Organization (PULO)	1	0	0	0
Popular Front for the Liberation of Palestine (PFLP)	1	0	1	1
Popular Front for the Liberation of Palestine–General Command (PFLP-GC)	2	3	3	6
Popular Liberation Army	1	0	1	1
Red Brigades	1	0	0	0
Revolutionary Armed Forces of Colombia	1	0	0	0
Revolutionary Outburst Movement	1	0	0	0
Revolutionary People's Liberation Party/Front (DHKP-C)	1	0	1	1
Revolutionary United Front (RUF)	1	1	2	3
Shining Path	9	61	8	69
Tupac Amaru Revolutionary Movement	3	0	0	0
Tupac Katari Guerrilla Army (EGTK)	2	0	0	0
Uganda Democratic Christian Army (UDCA)	2	0	2	2
Ulster Volunteer Force (UVF)	1	2	0	2
Unified Unit of Jihad	1	2	2	4
UNITA	4	0	4	4
Unknown Group	67	101	24	125
TOTAL	**272**	**2677**	**471**	**3148**

1994

Group	Incidents	Injuries	Fatalities	Total Casualties
17 November Revolutionary Organization (RO-N17)	6	0	2	2
Abu Nidal Organization (ANO)	1	0	1	1
Abu Sayyaf Group (ASG)	2	11	1	12
al-Gama'at al-Islamiyya (GAI)	14	20	7	27
al-Hadid	3	0	0	0
Alex Boncayao Brigade (ABB)	3	2	0	2
Ansar Allah	2	236	117	353
Anti-Castro Cubans	1	0	1	1
Armed Islamic Group	24	24	54	78
Basque Fatherland and Freedom	1	0	0	0
de Fes	1	2	2	4
Democratic Front for the Liberation of Palestine (DFLP)	1	0	1	1
Front for the Liberation of the Cabinda Enclave	2	1	0	1
HAMAS	13	176	61	237
Harkat-ul-Ansar	1	0	0	0
Hizballah	2	0	0	0
Irish Republican Army (IRA)	3	0	0	0
Islamic Great Eastern Raiders Front	2	0	0	0
Islamic Party of Egypt	1	4	0	4
Kach	1	250	40	290
Khmer Rouge	3	0	13	13
Kurdish Patriotic Union	3	31	1	32
Kurdistan National Liberation Front (ERNK)	1	0	0	0
Kurdistan Workers' Party	5	27	2	29
Liberation Tigers of Tamil Eelam (LTTE)	1	0	0	0
Manuel Rodriguez Patriotic Front	1	0	0	0
Moro National Liberation Front (MNLF)	1	0	0	0
Mozambique National Resistance Movement	2	0	0	0
Mujahedin-e-Khalq (MeK)	2	70	25	95
National Liberation Army (Colombia)	1	0	0	0
Nuclei Communist Combatants	1	0	0	0
Other Group	76	91	48	139
Palestinian Islamic Jihad (PIJ)	1	0	1	1
Pattani United Liberation Organization (PULO)	1	7	0	7
Popular Front for the Liberation of Palestine (PFLP)	1	0	1	1
Revolutionary Armed Forces of Colombia	19	2	2	4
Revolutionary Bolivariano Movement 200	1	0	0	0
Revolutionary Nuclei	1	0	0	0
Revolutionary People's Struggle	4	0	0	0
Shining Path	1	0	0	0
Simon Bolivar Guerilla Coordinating Board (CGSB)	3	0	0	0

1994 *(continued)*

Group	Incidents	Injuries	Fatalities	Total Casualties
Southern California IRA	1	0	0	0
Turkish National Intelligence Organization	1	0	1	1
Ulster Volunteer Force (UVF)	5	1	1	2
Union of Peaceful Citizens of Algeria	1	0	0	0
UNITA	1	0	0	0
Unknown Group	90	127	53	180
TOTAL	**312**	**1082**	**435**	**1517**

1995

Group	Incidents	Injuries	Fatalities	Total Casualties
Abu Sayyaf Group (ASG)	1	0	0	0
al-Faran	2	0	1	1
al-Gama'at al-Islamiyya (GAI)	8	113	23	136
al-Qaeda	1	60	7	67
Alex Boncayao Brigade (ABB)	1	0	0	0
Anti-Establishment Nucleus	2	0	0	0
Anti-Imperialist Cell (AIZ)	1	0	0	0
Anti-Imperialist Group Liberty for Mumia Abu Jamal	1	0	0	0
Armed Islamic Group	19	174	33	207
Armenian Resistance Group	2	0	0	0
Aum Shinri Kyo	1	5000	12	5012
Basque Fatherland and Freedom	3	8	1	9
Cell for Internationalism	2	0	0	0
Chukakuha	1	0	0	0
Dukhta-ran-e-Millat	1	1	1	2
Ey Al (Fighting Jewish Organization)	1	0	1	1
Free Papua Movement (OPM)	1	0	0	0
HAMAS	6	181	23	204
Hizballah	6	25	4	29
International Justice Group (Gama'a al-Adela al-Alamiya)	1	0	1	1
Islamic Renewal Movement	1	1	0	1
Jammu and Kashmir Islamic Front	1	30	0	30
Kahane Chai	1	1	0	1
Khmer Rouge	1	1	2	3
Kurdish Islamic Unity Party	1	30	2	32
Kurdistan Workers' Party	25	46	10	56
Liberation Tigers of Tamil Eelam (LTTE)	2	0	0	0
Morazanist Patriotic Front (FPM)	1	0	0	0
Movement for Democracy and Development (MDD)	1	0	0	0
National Liberation Army (Colombia)	3	0	4	4
Other Group	81	728	250	978
Palestinian Islamic Jihad (PIJ)	1	62	21	83
Popular Front for the Liberation of Palestine (PFLP)	2	1	2	3
Popular Liberation Army	1	0	0	0
Recontra 380	1	0	0	0
Red Daughters of Rage	1	0	0	0
Revolutionary Armed Forces of Colombia	2	0	0	0
Revolutionary People's Liberation Party/Front (DHKP-C)	8	0	0	0
Revolutionary United Front (RUF)	6	0	10	10
Shining Path	1	0	1	1
Southern Sudan Independence Movement (SSIM)	1	0	0	0

1995 *(continued)*

Group	Incidents	Injuries	Fatalities	Total Casualties
Taliban	2	0	0	0
UNITA	2	0	27	27
Unknown Group	60	45	24	69
TOTAL	**267**	**6507**	**460**	**6967**

1996

Group	Incidents	Injuries	Fatalities	Total Casualties
Abu Sayyaf Group (ASG)	1	4	0	4
al-Gama'at al-Islamiyya (GAI)	2	15	18	33
al-Ittihad al-Islami (AIAI)	2	20	6	26
Armed Islamic Group	4	29	9	38
Bani Hilal Tribe	1	0	0	0
Basque Fatherland and Freedom	7	54	0	54
Free Papua Movement (OPM)	1	0	2	2
Front for the Liberation of the Cabinda Enclave	1	0	0	0
Fronte di Liberazione Naziunale di a Corsica (FLNC)	1	0	0	0
HAMAS	5	258	60	318
Hizballah	6	542	33	575
Irish Republican Army (IRA)	1	0	0	0
Islamic Movement for Change	1	42	11	53
Jammu and Kashmir Islamic Front	1	50	25	75
Khmer Rouge	3	0	1	1
Kurdistan Workers' Party	2	0	0	0
Liberation Tigers of Tamil Eelam (LTTE)	5	1409	96	1505
Liberia Peace Council	1	0	0	0
Lord's Resistance Army (LRA)	2	0	6	6
Movement of April 19	1	0	0	0
Mujahedin-e-Khalq (MeK)	1	0	2	2
National Liberation Army (Colombia)	8	6	4	10
New People's Army (NPA)	1	0	1	1
Nihilists Faction	1	0	0	0
November 25 Anarchist Group	1	0	0	0
Other Group	67	138	175	313
Popular Front for the Liberation of Palestine (PFLP)	1	0	2	2
Popular Liberation Army	1	0	4	4
Revolutionary Armed Forces of Colombia	12	0	1	1
Revolutionary Front for Communism	1	0	0	0
Revolutionary Nuclei	1	0	0	0
Revolutionary People's Liberation Party/Front (DHKP-C)	1	0	0	0
Revolutionary Struggle	1	0	0	0
Shining Path	1	10	0	10
Sudan People's Liberation Army	5	0	0	0
Taliban	2	2	0	2
Territorial Anti-Imperialist Nuclei	1	0	0	0
Tupac Amaru Revolutionary Movement	1	0	17	17
Turkish Communist Party/Marxist (TKP-ML)	1	0	0	0
Turkish Islamic Jihad	1	40	17	57
Unknown Group	77	315	67	382
West Nile Bank Front (WNBF)	3	23	10	33
TOTAL	**237**	**2957**	**567**	**3524**

1997

Group	Incidents	Injuries	Fatalities	Total Casualties
Abu Sayyaf Group (ASG)	2	0	0	0
al-Gama'at al-Islamiyya (GAI)	2	32	84	116
Anti-Castro Cubans	13	3	1	4
Armed Islamic Group	2	0	2	2
Armenian Secret Army for the Liberation of Armenia (ASALA)	1	0	0	0
Basque Fatherland and Freedom	1	0	0	0
Boere Aanvals Troepe (BAT)	1	2	0	2
Front for the Liberation of the Cabinda Enclave	1	0	0	0
HAMAS	4	428	26	454
Hizballah	1	1	3	4
International Revolutionary Struggle	1	0	0	0
Internet Black Tigers (Tamils)	1	0	0	0
Irish National Liberation Army (INLA)	1	0	1	1
Jordanian Islamic Resistance	1	0	2	2
Khmer Rouge	2	16	12	28
Kurdistan Workers' Party	2	1	1	2
Lashkar-e-Jhangvi (LeJ)	1	0	7	7
Liberation Tigers of Tamil Eelam (LTTE)	5	100	14	114
Loyalist Volunteer Force (LVF)	2	8	2	10
Moro National Liberation Front (MNLF)	4	0	0	0
National Liberation Army (Colombia)	8	0	2	2
Other Group	51	129	51	180
Pattani United Liberation Organization (PULO)	3	24	6	30
Revolutionary Armed Forces of Colombia	2	0	6	6
Shining Path	2	0	0	0
Simon Bolivar Guerilla Coordinating Board (CGSB)	1	0	0	0
Tupac Amaru Revolutionary Movement	1	0	0	0
Ulster Volunteer Force (UVF)	2	0	0	0
Unknown Group	64	189	39	228
TOTAL	**182**	**933**	**259**	**1192**

1998

Group	Incidents	Injuries	Fatalities	Total Casualties
15 May Organization for the Liberation of Palestine	1	0	0	0
17 November Revolutionary Organization (RO-N17)	4	0	0	0
Abu Sayyaf Group (ASG)	4	11	4	15
Aden Abyan Islamic Army (AAIA)	1	2	7	9
al-Qaeda	2	5077	301	5378
Alex Boncayao Brigade (ABB)	3	0	0	0
Amal	1	5	1	6
Anarchist Street Patrol	1	0	0	0
Armed Forces Revolutionary Council (AFRC)	1	0	0	0
Armed Islamic Group	5	1	401	402
Army of God	1	1	1	2
Autonomous Cells of Rebel Action	1	0	0	0
Autonomous Revolutionary Activity	1	0	0	0
Bagramyan Battalion	1	0	0	0
Basque Fatherland and Freedom	9	1	6	7
Breton Revolutionary Army (ARB)	3	0	0	0
Chukakuha	1	0	0	0
Committee for the Security of the Highways	2	0	0	0
Conscientious Arsonists (CA)	8	0	0	0
Continuity Irish Republican Army (CIRA)	4	0	0	0
Earth Liberation Front (ELF)	2	0	0	0
Egyptian Islamic Jihad	1	0	1	1
Fighting Guerillas of May	1	0	0	0
First of October Antifascist Resistance Group (GRAPO)	8	2	0	2
Francs Tireurs (Mavericks)	1	0	0	0
Fronte di Liberazione Naziunale di a Corsica (FLNC)	11	2	0	2
HAMAS	3	65	3	68
Harakat al-Shuhada'a al-Islamiyah	1	1	4	5
Hizballah	5	16	7	23
Indian Intelligence Research and Analysis Wing (RAW)	2	36	23	59
Irish National Liberation Army (INLA)	4	5	2	7
Irish Republican Army (IRA)	4	0	1	1
Islamic Defense Force	1	4	0	4
Islamic Great Eastern Raiders Front	1	12	0	12
Islamic Jihad Jerusalem	1	25	2	27
Jaime Bateman Cayon Group (JBC)	1	4	0	4
Jammaa Islamiya (JI)	1	13	4	17
Jihad Committee	1	0	0	0
Justice Army of Defenseless People (EJPI)	1	3	0	3
Kach	2	0	0	0
Kakurokyo	1	1	0	1

1998 *(continued)*

Group	Incidents	Injuries	Fatalities	Total Casualties
Kosovo Liberation Army (KLA)	10	2	1	3
Kurdish Democratic Party	1	2	0	2
Kurdistan Workers' Party	2	23	1	24
Lashkar-e-Jhangvi (LeJ)	1	25	23	48
Leftist Nucleus	1	0	0	0
Liberation Tigers of Tamil Eelam (LTTE)	11	296	74	370
Lord's Resistance Army (LRA)	1	17	16	33
Loyalist Volunteer Force (LVF)	7	1	3	4
Macheteros	1	0	0	0
May-98	2	0	0	0
Melting Nuclei	1	0	0	0
Mohajir Qami Movement	1	10	8	18
Moro Islamic Liberation Front (MILF)	1	0	0	0
Movement of April 19	1	0	0	0
Movement of the Fifth Republic (MVR)	1	1	0	1
Mujahedin-e-Khalq (MeK)	7	2	9	11
Muslims Against Global Oppression (MAGO)	1	27	1	28
National Army for the Liberation of Uganda (NALU)	1	6	30	36
National Liberation Army (Colombia)	28	38	71	109
National Liberation Front of Tripura (NLFT)	1	0	3	3
Night Avengers	1	0	1	1
November's Children	1	0	0	0
Orange Volunteers (OV)	1	0	0	0
Other Group	2	0	0	0
Padanian Armed Separatist Phalanx	1	1	0	1
Palestinian Islamic Jihad (PIJ)	2	24	2	26
Pattani United Liberation Organization (PULO)	1	1	1	2
People's National Congress (PNC)	2	1	0	1
Popular Liberation Army	3	0	2	2
Popular Revolutionary Army	1	0	4	4
Real Irish Republican Army (RIRA)	4	59	29	88
Red Hand Defenders (RHD)	1	0	1	1
Revolutionary Armed Forces of Colombia	35	15	10	25
Revolutionary Nuclei	4	1	0	1
Revolutionary People's Army (ERP)	1	0	0	0
Revolutionary People's Liberation Party/Front (DHKP-C)	2	4	0	4
Revolutionary Subversive Faction-Commando Unibomber	1	0	0	0
Revolutionary United Front (RUF)	1	0	0	0
Russian National Bolshevist Party	1	0	0	0
Russian National Unity	1	3	0	3
Shining Path	6	4	5	9

1998 *(continued)*

Group	Incidents	Injuries	Fatalities	Total Casualties
Sword of Islam	1	0	0	0
Taliban	1	0	10	10
Tigers	2	10	1	11
Tupac Amaru Revolutionary Movement	1	0	0	0
Turkish Communist Party/Marxist (TKP-ML)	1	2	0	2
Ulster Defence Association/Ulster Freedom Fighters	3	1	2	3
Ulster Volunteer Force (UVF)	1	0	0	0
UNITA	1	12	8	20
United Liberation Front of Assam (ULFA)	2	20	3	23
United Revolutionary Front	2	1	0	1
Unknown Group	993	2281	1113	3394
World Islamic Jihad Group	1	0	0	0
Zomi Revolutionary Army (ZRA)	1	0	7	7
TOTAL	**1273**	**8185**	**2244**	**10384**

1999

Group	Incidents	Injuries	Fatalities	Total Casualties
Abdurajak Janjalani Brigade (AJB)	1	0	0	0
Abu Sayyaf Group (ASG)	3	86	10	96
Action Committee of Winegrowers	1	0	0	0
Action Directe	1	0	0	0
Ahmadiya Muslim Mission	1	12	2	14
al-Nawaz	1	9	2	11
Alex Boncayao Brigade (ABB)	2	0	0	0
All Tripura Tiger Force (ATTF)	1	12	17	29
Anarchist Faction	1	0	0	0
Angry Brigade	2	0	0	0
Animal Liberation Front (ALF)	3	0	0	0
Anti-Power Struggle	1	0	0	0
Anti-Racist Guerrilla Nuclei	1	0	0	0
Anti-State Action	3	0	0	0
Anti-Zionist Movement	1	0	0	0
Apo's Revenge Hawks	2	0	0	0
Apo's Youth Revenge Brigades	1	0	0	0
Armata Corsa	2	0	0	0
Armed Forces Revolutionary Council (AFRC)	4	0	0	0
Autonomous Decorators	1	0	0	0
Basque Fatherland and Freedom	2	0	0	0
Black Star	2	0	0	0
Breton Revolutionary Army (ARB)	8	1	0	1
Clandestini Corsi	1	8	0	8
Communist Party of Nepal-Maoists (CPN-M)	3	0	0	0
Communist Revolutionaries in Europe	1	0	0	0
Corsican Patriotic Front (FPC)	5	0	0	0
Dagestan Liberation Army	4	453	248	701
Earth Liberation Front (ELF)	2	0	0	0
First of October Antifascist Resistance Group (GRAPO)	1	0	0	0
Free Papua Movement (OPM)	1	0	0	0
Freedom for Mumia Abu-Jamal	1	0	0	0
Friendship Society	2	0	0	0
Front for the Liberation of the Cabinda Enclave	1	0	0	0
Fronte di Liberazione Naziunale di a Corsica (FLNC)	23	0	0	0
Gazteriak	1	0	0	0
HAMAS	1	2	0	2
Hawks of Thrace	1	1	0	1
Indian Intelligence Research and Analysis Wing (RAW)	4	23	2	25
Irish Republican Army (IRA)	1	0	1	1
Islamic Great Eastern Raiders Front	8	1	1	2

1999 *(continued)*

Group	Incidents	Injuries	Fatalities	Total Casualties
Israeli Arab Islamic Movement	1	1	3	4
Kayin National Union (KNU)	2	0	20	20
Kosovo Liberation Army (KLA)	1	7	0	7
Kurdistan Workers' Party	11	79	13	92
Liberation Tigers of Tamil Eelam (LTTE)	5	30	24	54
Loyalist Volunteer Force (LVF)	1	1	0	1
Macedonia Dawn	1	0	0	0
Moro Islamic Liberation Front (MILF)	1	0	0	0
National Kurdish Revenge Teams	1	8	1	9
National Liberation Army (Colombia)	28	1	0	1
Nationalist Kurdish Revenge Teams	1	0	0	0
New Revolutionary Alternative	1	2	0	2
November's Children	2	1	0	1
Nusantara Islamic Jihad Forces (AMIN)	1	0	0	0
Odua Peoples' Congress	1	1	0	1
Ogaden National Liberation Front (ONLF)	1	0	0	0
Orange Volunteers (OV)	7	4	0	4
Other Group	4	104	63	167
Pattani United Liberation Organization (PULO)	1	0	0	0
People's Liberation Army of Kurdistan (ARGK)	6	14	11	25
People's Liberation Forces (El Salvador)	1	0	0	0
Popular Liberation Army	4	0	3	3
Popular Revolutionary Front (LEM)	1	0	0	0
Red Brigades	1	0	1	1
Red Hand Defenders (RHD)	6	0	1	1
Red Line	3	0	0	0
Revolutionary Nuclei	3	1	1	2
Revolutionary People's Liberation Party/Front (DHKP-C)	6	28	2	30
Revolutionary United Front (RUF)	1	0	0	0
Rigas Fereos	1	0	0	0
Shining Path	1	0	8	8
Sudan People's Liberation Army	1	0	4	4
Supporters of Horst Ludwig Meyer	1	0	0	0
Sword of Islam	1	0	0	0
Taliban	1	0	1	1
Tupamaro Revolutionary Movement–January 23	1	0	0	0
Turkish Communist Laborer's Party/Lenist (TKEP/L)	1	0	0	0
Turkish Communist Party/Marxist (TKP-ML)	5	0	1	1
Turkish People's Liberation Front (TPLF) (THKP-C)	1	0	0	0
Turkish Worker's and Peasant's Liberation (TIKKO)	3	8	6	14
Ulster Defence Association/Ulster Freedom Fighters	1	0	0	0

1999 *(continued)*

Group	Incidents	Injuries	Fatalities	Total Casualties
Ummah Liberation Army	1	0	0	0
UNITA	3	0	5	5
United Liberation Front of Assam (ULFA)	3	0	0	0
United Self-Defense Forces of Colombia (AUC)	10	0	24	24
Unknown Group	895	1435	366	1801
Vigorous Burmese Student Warriors	1	0	0	0
Vitalunismo	1	0	0	0
TOTAL	**1159**	**2333**	**849**	**3174**

2000

Group	Incidents	Injuries	Fatalities	Total Casualties
17 November Revolutionary Organization (RO-N17)	1	0	1	1
Abu Sayyaf Group (ASG)	13	22	1	23
al-Fatah	3	0	3	3
al-Nawaz	1	4	0	4
al-Qaeda	1	39	17	56
Alex Boncayao Brigade (ABB)	2	0	0	0
Anarchist Faction	2	0	0	0
Anarchist Faction for Subversion	1	0	0	0
Anarchist Struggle	1	0	0	0
Anarchists' Attack Group	1	0	0	0
Animal Liberation Front (ALF)	2	0	0	0
Anti-Authority Erotic Cells	1	0	0	0
Anti-Communist Command	1	0	0	0
Anti-Mainstream Self Determination Faction	1	0	0	0
Anti-Power Struggle	1	0	0	0
Anti-State Nuclei	1	0	0	0
Basque Fatherland and Freedom	36	104	20	124
Black Star	6	0	0	0
Breton Revolutionary Army (ARB)	6	0	1	1
Construction of the Fighting Communist Party (NTA-PCC)	1	0	0	0
Continuity Irish Republican Army (CIRA)	3	0	0	0
Earth Liberation Front (ELF)	7	0	0	0
First of October Antifascist Resistance Group (GRAPO)	7	0	1	1
Free Aceh Movement (GAM)	1	20	6	26
Free Papua Movement (OPM)	1	0	0	0
Front for Defenders of Islam	1	0	0	0
Front for the Liberation of the Cabinda Enclave	1	0	0	0
Fronte di Liberazione Naziunale di a Corsica (FLNC)	5	0	0	0
God's Army	1	0	10	10
Group of Popular Combatants (GPC)	2	0	0	0
Guevarista Revolutionary Army (ERG)	1	0	0	0
Hindu Sena Rashtriya Sangh Party	1	90	19	109
Hizbul Mujahedin (HM)	1	0	0	0
International Solidarity	2	0	0	0
Irish Republican Army (IRA)	3	2	0	2
Islamic Great Eastern Raiders Front	3	0	0	0
Lashkar-e-Tayyiba (LeT)	1	0	3	3
Liberation Tigers of Tamil Eelam (LTTE)	12	337	109	446
Lord's Resistance Army (LRA)	3	60	10	70
Mohammed's Army	1	0	0	0
Moro Islamic Liberation Front (MILF)	11	96	27	123

2000 *(continued)*

Group	Incidents	Injuries	Fatalities	Total Casualties
Movement for the Struggle of the Jordanian Islamic Resistance	1	1	0	1
Mujahideen Division Khandaq	1	21	2	23
National Liberation Army (Colombia)	45	14	1	15
New People's Army (NPA)	2	15	9	24
November's Children	1	0	0	0
Oromo Liberation Front (OLF)	1	1	14	15
Other Group	3	1	0	1
Overthrown Anarchist Faction	1	0	0	0
People Against Gansterism And Drugs (PAGAD)	1	0	0	0
People's Revolutionary Army (Colombia)	1	1	1	2
People's War Group (PWG)	1	0	2	2
Popular Liberation Army	6	0	2	2
Popular Revolutionary Front (LEM)	1	0	0	0
Real Irish Republican Army (RIRA)	2	0	0	0
Red Brigades	1	1	0	1
Red Hand Defenders (RHD)	2	0	0	0
Revolutionary Armed Forces of Colombia	41	38	39	77
Revolutionary Armed Forces of the People (FARP)	1	3	0	3
Revolutionary Leninist Brigades	1	3	0	3
Revolutionary Nuclei	7	0	0	0
Revolutionary People's Liberation Party/Front (DHKP-C)	3	0	0	0
Revolutionary Perspective	1	0	0	0
Revolutionary Proletarian Nucleus	1	0	0	0
Revolutionary Socialists	1	0	0	0
Revolutionary Struggle	1	0	0	0
Revolutionary United Front (RUF)	1	0	0	0
Salafist Group for Call and Combat (GSPC)	1	0	0	0
Self-Defense Groups of Cordoba and Uraba (ACCU)	2	0	2	2
Turkish Communist Laborer's Party/Lenist (TKEP/L)	1	3	1	4
Turkish Communist Party/Marxist (TKP-ML)	4	12	4	16
Ulster Defence Association/Ulster Freedom Fighters	1	0	0	0
Ummah Liberation Army	1	2	0	2
United Liberation Front of Assam (ULFA)	3	17	16	33
United People's Democratic Solidarity (UPDS)	1	0	8	8
United Self-Defense Forces of Colombia (AUC)	18	1	69	70
Unknown Group	826	1620	375	1995
TOTAL	**1138**	**2536**	**777**	**3301**

2001

Group	Incidents	Injuries	Fatalities	Total Casualties
Abu Sayyaf Group (ASG)	10	61	31	92
al-Ali bin Falah	1	0	0	0
al-Fatah	14	57	8	65
al-Qaeda	3	2337	2982	5319
Anarchist Liberation Brigade	1	0	0	0
Andres Castro United Front (FUAC)	1	13	1	14
Animal Liberation Front (ALF)	3	0	0	0
Anti-Power Struggle	1	0	0	0
Anticapitalist Attack Nuclei (NAA)	2	0	0	0
Armed Islamic Group	2	30	0	30
Badr Forces	1	0	1	1
Basque Fatherland and Freedom	57	160	17	177
Bersatu	3	47	1	48
Cambodian Freedom Fighters (CFF)	1	0	0	0
Catholic Reaction Force (CRF)	3	0	0	0
Chukakuha	1	0	0	0
Coalition to Save the Preserves (CSP)	2	0	0	0
Committee for the Security of the Highways	2	7	3	10
Communist Party of Nepal-Maoists (CPN-M)	3	15	8	23
Continuity Irish Republican Army (CIRA)	2	0	1	1
Cooperative of Hand-Made Fire & Related Items	3	2	0	2
Earth Liberation Front (ELF)	13	0	0	0
Ecuadorian Rebel Force	1	0	0	0
Enraged Proletarians	1	0	0	0
Fighters for Freedom	1	0	0	0
For a Revolutionary Perspective	1	0	0	0
Free Aceh Movement (GAM)	17	9	41	50
Free Papua Movement (OPM)	1	0	0	0
Free Vietnam Revolutionary Group	1	0	0	0
Front for Defenders of Islam	1	0	0	0
Front for the Liberation of the Cabinda Enclave	3	6	0	6
Fronte di Liberazione Naziunale di a Corsica (FLNC)	5	0	0	0
Group of Carlo Giuliani	1	0	0	0
Group of Guerilla Combatants of Jose Maria Morelos y Pavon (CGNJMMP)	1	0	0	0
Guevarista Revolutionary Army (ERG)	1	0	0	0
HAMAS	20	539	75	614
Hizballah	1	0	0	0
Hisba	1	0	0	0
Hizbul Mujahedin (HM)	2	0	0	0
Independent Kashmir	1	8	0	8
Indian Intelligence	1	0	0	0

2001 (continued)

Group	Incidents	Injuries	Fatalities	Total Casualties
Islam Chhatra Shibir (ICS)	1	110	21	131
Islamic Great Eastern Raiders Front	2	0	0	0
Islamic Jihad Jerusalem	1	8	2	10
Islamic Movement of Uzbekistan (IMU)	1	2	0	2
Jaish-e-Mohammad (JeM)	1	60	38	98
Janashakti	1	0	0	0
Lashkar-e-Jhangvi (LeJ)	1	6	0	6
Lashkar-e-Tayyiba (LeT)	2	18	14	32
Lashkar-I-Omar	1	5	18	23
Latin American Patriotic Army (EPLA)	1	1	0	1
Liberation Tigers of Tamil Eelam (LTTE)	9	25	24	49
Macedonian Revolutionary Organization (VMRO)	1	0	0	0
Maoist Communist Center (MCC)	4	8	13	21
Moro Islamic Liberation Front (MILF)	4	8	12	20
Moro National Liberation Front (MNLF)	1	0	0	0
Movement Against State Arbitrariness	3	0	0	0
Mujahedin-e-Khalq (MeK)	2	3	0	3
Mujahideen Kompak	1	0	0	0
Muttahida Qami Movement (MQM)	5	8	4	12
National Democratic Front of Bodoland (NDFB)	5	120	23	143
National Liberation Army (Colombia)	25	29	12	41
National Liberation Front of Tripura (NLFT)	3	0	9	9
New People's Army (NPA)	7	1	9	10
November's Children	1	0	0	0
Other Group	37	164	59	223
Palestinian Islamic Jihad (PIJ)	17	246	24	270
People's War Group (PWG)	14	12	6	18
Popular Self-Defense Forces (FAP)	1	0	0	0
Protesting Miners	1	0	0	0
Real Irish Republican Army (RIRA)	13	9	0	9
Red Hand Defenders (RHD)	14	1	3	4
Revolutionary Armed Corps (CAR)	1	0	0	0
Revolutionary Armed Forces of Colombia	25	26	54	80
Revolutionary Armed Forces of the People (FARP)	1	1	0	1
Revolutionary Army	1	0	0	0
Revolutionary Front for Communism	1	0	0	0
Revolutionary People's Liberation Party/Front (DHKP-C)	3	22	8	30
Revolutionary Proletarian Initiative Nuclei	1	0	0	0
Revolutionary Violence Group (RVG)	1	0	0	0
Shining Path	3	6	16	22
Sri Nakharo	1	0	2	2
Students Islamic Movement of India (SIMI)	1	1	0	1

2001 *(continued)*

Group	Incidents	Injuries	Fatalities	Total Casualties
Sudan People's Liberation Army	2	0	0	0
Taliban	1	0	0	0
Tibetan independence forces	1	3	0	3
Totally Anti-War Group (ATAG)	1	0	0	0
Tupac Amaru Revolutionary Movement	1	0	0	0
Ulster Defence Association/Ulster Freedom Fighters	13	4	0	4
UNITA	2	165	255	420
United Liberation Front of Assam (ULFA)	2	0	0	0
United People's Democratic Solidarity (UPDS)	1	0	8	8
United Self-Defense Forces of Colombia (AUC)	16	6	111	117
United Tajik Opposition (UTO)	1	0	1	1
Unknown Group	1275	2004	630	2634
Uygur Holy War Organization	2	1	2	3
TOTAL	**1732**	**6374**	**4555**	**10921**

2002

Group	Incidents	Injuries	Fatalities	Total Casualties
17 November Revolutionary Organization (RO-N17)	1	1	0	1
Abu Sayyaf Group (ASG)	8	175	21	196
Accolta Nazinuale Corsa	1	0	0	0
Achik National Volunteer Council (ANVC)	1	0	0	0
Aden Abyan Islamic Army (AAIA)	1	12	1	13
al-Aarifeen	2	0	1	1
al-Badr	1	0	0	0
al-Fatah	58	597	193	790
al-Intiqami al-Pakistani	1	3	6	9
al-Madina	3	0	0	0
al-Nasireen	2	4	0	4
al-Qaeda	3	100	28	128
al-Qanoon	1	45	11	56
al-Umar Mujahideen	1	0	0	0
Albanian National Army (ANA)	1	0	0	0
Anarkhiki Omadha 20 Iouli	1	0	0	0
Animal Liberation Front (ALF)	1	0	0	0
Ansar al-Islam	2	4	0	4
Armata di Liberazione Naziunale	1	0	0	0
Bangladesh Nationalist Party (BNP)	1	0	0	0
Basque Fatherland and Freedom	21	56	7	63
Black Star	1	0	0	0
Burning Path	1	0	0	0
Carapaica Revolutionary Movement	1	5	0	5
Chaotic Attack Front	1	0	0	0
Combatant Proletarian Nucleus	1	0	0	0
Communist Party of Nepal-Maoists (CPN-M)	87	78	16	94
Communist Workers Movement	1	0	0	0
Continuity Irish Republican Army (CIRA)	5	0	0	0
Democratic Front for the Liberation of Palestine (DFLP)	2	8	6	14
Democratic Karen Buddhist Army (DKBA)	1	4	0	4
Earth Liberation Front (ELF)	11	0	0	0
East Turkistan Liberation Organization	1	0	2	2
Five C's	1	0	0	0
Free Aceh Movement (GAM)	10	23	7	30
Fronte di Liberazione Naziunale di a Corsica (FLNC)	15	0	0	0
Gora Euskadi Askatata	1	0	0	0
Group of People's Fighters (GCP)	1	0	0	0
Group of Popular Combatants (GPC)	1	0	0	0
Guevarista Revolutionary Army (ERG)	1	0	0	0
HAMAS	33	609	181	790

2002 (continued)

Group	Incidents	Injuries	Fatalities	Total Casualties
Harkat ul-Jehad (HUGI)	1	20	5	25
Harkat ul-Mujahedin	1	0	3	3
Hizbul Mujahedin (HM)	2	4	2	6
Hizbul Mujahedin's (HM)/Billal Group	1	0	5	5
Indigenous People's Federal Army (IPFA)	6	0	0	0
Irish Republican Army (IRA)	2	0	0	0
Islamic Shashantantra Andolon (ISA)	2	125	3	128
Jaish-e-Mohammad (JeM)	1	0	1	1
Jemaah Islamiya (JI)	1	300	202	502
July 20th Brigade	1	0	0	0
Kach	1	0	0	0
Kanglei Yawol Kanna Lup (KYKL)	1	10	0	10
Karen National Union	1	30	7	37
Kayin National Union (KNU)	1	0	0	0
Laiki Antistasi	1	0	0	0
Lashkar-e-Jhangvi (LeJ)	4	19	7	26
Lashkar-e-Tayyiba (LeT)	8	102	63	165
Laskar Jihad (LJ)	1	10	14	24
Lord's Resistance Army (LRA)	2	0	60	60
Loyalist Volunteer Force (LVF)	2	1	1	2
Maoist Communist Center (MCC)	7	6	5	11
Moro Islamic Liberation Front (MILF)	4	35	22	57
Movement for Democracy and Justice in Chad (MDJT)	1	0	1	1
Movsar Baryayev Gang	2	657	162	819
Mujahideen al-Mansooran	1	0	0	0
National Democratic Front of Bodoland (NDFB)	8	29	52	81
National Liberation Army (Colombia)	37	8	6	14
National Liberation Front of Tripura (NLFT)	4	5	14	19
New People's Army (NPA)	8	5	8	13
Oromo Liberation Front (OLF)	2	0	0	0
Other Group	8	5	19	24
Palestinian Islamic Jihad (PIJ)	14	200	64	264
People's Revolutionary Army (Colombia)	4	0	0	0
People's Revolutionary Militias	2	3	0	3
People's War Group (PWG)	24	103	54	157
Popular Front for the Liberation of Palestine (PFLP)	6	85	13	98
Popular Liberation Army	3	1	2	3
Popular Resistance	2	0	0	0
Proletarian Reprisals	1	0	0	0
Pueblo Reagrupado	1	0	0	0
Real Irish Republican Army (RIRA)	4	1	1	2

2002 *(continued)*

Group	Incidents	Injuries	Fatalities	Total Casualties
Red Brigades	1	0	1	1
Red Guerrillas	1	0	0	0
Red Hand Defenders (RHD)	3	2	1	3
Revenge of Hebrew Babies	1	10	0	10
Revolutionary Armed Forces of Colombia	189	507	164	671
Revolutionary Army	2	0	0	0
Revolutionary Brigades	1	0	0	0
Revolutionary Front for Communism	2	0	0	0
Riyad us-Saliheyn Martyrs' Brigade	1	280	72	352
Sardinian Autonomy Movement (MAS)	1	0	0	0
Save Kashmir Movement	1	0	1	1
Shining Path	2	34	10	44
Shurafa al-Urdun	1	0	1	1
Solidarity for Political Prisoners	1	0	0	0
South Maluku Republic (RMS)	1	63	4	67
Turkish Communist Party/Marxist (TKP-ML)	1	0	1	1
Ulster Defence Association/Ulster Freedom Fighters	4	4	0	4
Uncontrolled Rage	1	0	0	0
UNITA	1	0	2	2
United Kuki Liberation Front (UKLF)	1	0	0	0
United Liberation Front of Assam (ULFA)	1	20	2	22
United Self-Defense Forces of Colombia (AUC)	17	1	27	28
United Self-Defense Forces of Venezuela (AUV)	2	0	7	7
Unknown Group	1935	2932	1189	4121
Young Liberators of Pattani	1	0	0	0
TOTAL	**2650**	**7344**	**2759**	**10099**

2003

Group	Incidents	Injuries	Fatalities	Total Casualties
21-Jun	1	0	0	0
313	1	8	6	14
Abu Sayyaf Group (ASG)	1	0	0	0
al-Faruq Brigades	1	1	7	8
al-Fatah	19	145	37	182
al-Haramayn Brigades	1	0	0	0
al-Mansoorain	1	50	11	61
al-Nasireen	1	2	1	3
al-Qaeda	11	1159	152	1311
Albanian National Army (ANA)	2	0	2	2
All Tripura Tiger Force (ATTF)	7	17	42	59
Anarchist Attack Teams	1	0	0	0
Anarchist Struggle	1	0	0	0
Animal Liberation Front (ALF)	2	0	0	0
Ansar al-Islam	2	20	11	31
Ansar al-Sunnah Army	1	37	2	39
Ansar Allah	1	0	0	0
Anti-State Defense	1	0	0	0
Baloch Liberation Army (BLA)	1	0	0	0
Basque Fatherland and Freedom	16	16	2	18
Birsa Commando Force (BCF)	1	0	0	0
Black Widows	2	179	52	231
Bodo Liberation Tigers (BLT)	1	0	1	1
Bolivarian Guerilla Movement (MGB)	1	0	0	0
Bolivarian Liberation Forces (FBL)	1	5	0	5
Borok National Council of Tripura (BNCT)	3	0	2	2
Caucasian Front for the Liberation of Abu Achikob	1	0	0	0
Children of Fire	2	0	0	0
Commando Anarchist Group	1	0	0	0
Communist Party of Nepal-Maoists (CPN-M)	34	16	10	26
Communist Workers Movement	1	0	0	0
Consciously Enraged	1	0	0	0
Continuity Irish Republican Army (CIRA)	7	6	0	6
Earth Liberation Front (ELF)	11	0	0	0
Eritrean Islamic Jihad Movement (ELJM)	1	1	2	3
Fighting Ecologist Activism	1	0	0	0
Free Aceh Movement (GAM)	3	11	0	11
Free People of Galillee	1	0	0	0
Fronte di Liberazione Naziunale di a Corsica (FLNC)	18	19	0	19
Group of Popular Combatants (GPC)	2	0	0	0
Group Revolutionary Reconstruction	1	0	0	0

2003 *(continued)*

Group	Incidents	Injuries	Fatalities	Total Casualties
HAMAS	59	285	59	344
Hizballah	3	8	3	11
Hizbul Mujahedin (HM)	1	0	1	1
Immediate Action	1	0	0	0
Informal Anarchist Federation	1	0	0	0
Islamic Jihad Jerusalem	2	130	42	172
Jaish-e-Mohammad (JeM)	1	70	10	80
Jamiat ul-Mujahedin (JuM)	3	25	6	31
Jenin Martyrs' Brigade	1	40	17	57
Kenkoku Giyugun Chosen Seibatsutai	4	0	0	0
Kenkokugiyudan Betsudotai Kokuzokseibatsutai	1	0	0	0
Knights of the Torched Bank	1	0	0	0
Kuki Liberation Arm (KLA)	1	0	0	0
Kurdistan Workers' Party	4	5	6	11
Lashkar-e-Tayyiba (LeT)	2	150	53	203
Liberation Party	1	3	0	3
Liberation Tigers of Tamil Eelam (LTTE)	3	4	5	9
Lord's Resistance Army (LRA)	3	20	56	76
Loyalist Volunteer Force (LVF)	1	0	0	0
Maoist Communist Center (MCC)	6	6	5	11
Moro Islamic Liberation Front (MILF)	6	172	42	214
Mujahideen Message	1	0	0	0
Muslim United Army	1	7	0	7
National Democratic Front of Bodoland (NDFB)	2	0	2	2
National Liberation Army (Colombia)	10	78	14	92
National Liberation Front of Tripura (NLFT)	14	21	28	49
Other Group	16	60	49	109
People's Revolutionary Militias	3	4	0	4
People's War Group (PWG)	34	7	23	30
Popular Front for the Liberation of Palestine (PFLP)	3	26	6	32
Popular Justice	1	0	0	0
Popular Revolutionary Action	1	0	0	0
Proletarian Nuclei for Communism	1	0	0	0
Proletarian Resistance	2	0	0	0
Proletarian Solidarity	1	0	0	0
Purbo Banglar Communist Party (PBCP)	6	1	13	14
Real Irish Republican Army (RIRA)	7	0	0	0
Red Brigades	1	0	0	0
Resistenza Corsa	3	0	0	0
Revolutionary Armed Forces of Colombia	54	252	91	343
Revolutionary Cells Animal Liberation Brigade	1	0	0	0

2003 *(continued)*

Group	Incidents	Injuries	Fatalities	Total Casualties
Revolutionary Front for Communism	1	0	0	0
Revolutionary Liberation Action	1	0	0	0
Revolutionary Memory	1	0	0	0
Revolutionary Nuclei	1	0	0	0
Revolutionary Offensive Cells	1	0	0	0
Revolutionary People's Liberation Party/Front (DHKP-C)	6	7	1	8
Revolutionary People's Front	1	15	6	21
Revolutionary Solidarity	5	0	0	0
Revolutionary Struggle	1	1	0	1
Revolutionary Youth of Ecuador	1	1	0	1
Riyad us-Saliheyn Martyrs' Brigade	1	72	52	124
Saif-ul-Muslimeen	1	0	0	0
Salafia Jihadia	1	0	1	1
Salafist Group for Call and Combat (GSPC)	1	0	1	1
Sihala Urumaya	1	4	0	4
Societa Editoriale Sarda	1	0	0	0
Solidarity Gas Canisters	1	0	0	0
Solidarity with 17N	1	0	0	0
Taliban	22	29	25	54
Tanzim	1	0	0	0
Tawhid and Jihad	7	7	83	90
Territorial Anti-Imperialist Nuclei	1	0	0	0
The Inevitables	1	0	0	0
Torrid Winter	1	0	0	0
Turkish Communist Party/Marxist (TKP-ML)	2	0	0	0
Ulster Defence Association/Ulster Freedom Fighters	3	3	0	3
United Liberation Front of Assam (ULFA)	3	8	0	8
United People's Democratic Solidarity (UPDS)	2	4	9	13
United Self-Defense Forces of Colombia (AUC)	10	4	11	15
Unknown Group	1372	2844	1280	4124
White Legion	1	0	0	0
TOTAL	**1897**	**6153**	**2347**	**8405**

2004

Group	Incidents	Injuries	Fatalities	Total Casualties
Abu al-Abbas	1	1	0	1
Abu Bakr al-Siddiq Fundamentalist Brigades	1	0	1	1
Abu Hafs al-Masri Brigade	5	606	193	799
Abu Nayaf al-Afgani	1	0	0	0
Abu Sayyaf Group (ASG)	2	9	119	128
al-Fatah	16	126	25	151
al-Islambouli Brigades of al-Qaeda	1	50	8	58
al-Mansoorain	1	2	5	7
al-Nasireen	1	24	4	28
al-Qaeda	6	35	25	60
al-Qaeda in the Arabian Penninsula (AQAP)	3	25	10	35
al-Quds Brigades	1	0	0	0
Ansar al-Din	1	0	0	0
Ansar al-Jihad	1	0	0	0
Ansar al-Sunnah Army	9	275	166	441
Anti-Olympic Flame	2	0	0	0
Armed Revolutionary Left	2	1	0	1
Army of the Corsican People	2	3	0	3
Army of the Followers of Sunni Islam	1	0	3	3
Baloch Liberation Army (BLA)	8	0	0	0
Basque Fatherland and Freedom	27	15	0	15
Battalion of the Martyr Abdullah Azzam, Al-Qaeda in the Levant and Egypt	1	12	2	14
Black and Red Brigades	1	0	0	0
Bolivarian Liberation Forces (FBL)	1	0	0	0
Brigades for the Defense of Holy Shrines	1	0	0	0
Brigades of Martyr Ahmed Yassim	1	0	4	4
Brigades of the Mujahideen in Iraq	1	0	0	0
Brigades of the Victorious Lion of God	1	0	0	0
Clandestini Corsi	5	0	0	0
Comando Jaramillista Morelense 23 de Mayo	1	0	0	0
Communist Party of Nepal-Maoists (CPN-M)	100	116	67	183
Corsican People's Army	2	0	0	0
Corsican Revolutionary Armed Forces	1	0	0	0
Council of Organizations for the Development of People (CODEP)	1	0	0	0
Cypriot Nationalist Organization (OKE)	1	0	0	0
Dario Santillan Command	2	0	0	0
Democratic Front for the Liberation of Palestine (DFLP)	3	0	1	1
Divine Wrath Brigades	2	0	0	0
Earth Liberation Front (ELF)	4	0	0	0
EPA (Ejercito del Pueblo en Armas)	1	0	0	0
Fallujah Mujahideen	1	0	0	0

2004 (continued)

Group	Incidents	Injuries	Fatalities	Total Casualties
Fires of Hell	1	0	0	0
Free Aceh Movement (GAM)	3	1	4	5
Fronte di Liberazione Naziunale di a Corsica (FLNC)	16	0	0	0
Global Intifada	1	0	0	0
Group for Social Resistance to the State Mechanism	1	0	0	0
HAMAS	206	210	67	277
Harkat ul-Mujahedin	2	29	4	33
Hikmatul Zihad	1	300	19	319
Hizballah	1	0	0	0
Hizb-I-Islami	1	4	10	14
Hizbul Mujahedin (HM)	2	22	1	23
Iduwini Youths	1	0	0	0
Indomitable Marxists	1	0	0	0
Informal Anarchist Federation	1	0	0	0
Iraqi Legitimate Resistance	1	0	0	0
Islamic Army in Iraq	12	0	7	7
Islamic Jihad Jerusalem	11	9	0	9
Islamic Movement of Holy Warriors	1	0	0	0
Islamic Movement of Iraqi Mujahideen	1	0	2	2
Islamic Movement of Uzbekistan (IMU)	3	6	7	13
Islamic Resistance Brigades	1	0	0	0
Jaish al-Mujahedeen	1	0	0	0
Jaish-e-Mohammad (JeM)	1	1	0	1
Jaish-ul-Muslimin	1	0	4	4
Jamiat ul-Mujahedin (JuM)	1	4	1	5
Jemaah Islamiya (JI)	2	240	25	265
Kongra Gel (PKK)	21	25	9	34
Kurdistan Freedom Hawks	9	24	5	29
Lashkar-e-Jhangvi (LeJ)	3	180	70	250
Liberation Tigers of Tamil Eelam (LTTE)	3	11	7	18
Lord's Resistance Army (LRA)	7	129	316	445
Mahdi Army	4	0	0	0
Maoist Communist Center (MCC)	1	4	1	5
Maras Salvatruchas	1	12	28	40
Midnight Saboteurs	1	0	0	0
Movement of the Revolutionary Left	1	0	0	0
Mujahideen Army	2	0	8	8
Mujahideen in Iraq	1	0	0	0
National Democratic Front of Bodoland (NDFB)	4	51	40	91
National Liberation Army (Colombia)	2	8	3	11
New People's Army (NPA)	8	7	10	17

2004 *(continued)*

Group	Incidents	Injuries	Fatalities	Total Casualties
Nuclei for Promoting Total Catastrophe	1	0	0	0
Oromo Liberation Front (OLF)	2	3	1	4
Other Group	43	108	89	197
Palestinian Islamic Jihad (PIJ)	6	0	3	3
Pattani United Liberation Organization (PULO)	1	0	0	0
People's Defense Forces (HPG)	2	1	2	3
People's Revolutionary Army (Colombia)	1	0	0	0
People's War Group (PWG)	1	0	26	26
Popular Front for the Liberation of Palestine (PFLP)	9	32	5	37
Popular Resistance Committees	4	2	0	2
Popular Revolutionary Action	2	0	0	0
Proletarian Combatant Groups	1	0	0	0
Proletarian Nuclei for Communism	2	0	0	0
Real Irish Republican Army (RIRA)	1	0	0	0
Revolution of the 1920s Brigade	1	0	0	0
Revolutionary Armed Forces of Colombia	27	123	61	184
Revolutionary People's Liberation Party/Front (DHKP-C)	1	15	4	19
Revolutionary Struggle	3	0	0	0
Revolutionary Torch-Bearing Run	1	0	0	0
Riyad us-Saliheyn Martyrs' Brigade	9	784	390	1174
Salafist Group for Call and Combat (GSPC)	4	12	2	14
Saraya al-Shuhuada al-jihadiyah fi al-Iraq	2	19	7	26
Saraya Usud al-Tawhid	1	0	0	0
Save Kashmir Movement	1	50	9	59
Taliban	75	137	152	289
Tanzim	2	0	0	0
Tanzim Qa'idat al-Jihad fi Bilad al-Rafidayn	10	224	120	344
Tawhid and Jihad	17	212	108	320
Tawhid Islamic Brigades	1	159	34	193
The Committee for Promotion of Intransigence	1	0	0	0
The Holders of the Black Banners	1	0	0	0
Turkish Communist Party/Marxist (TKP-ML)	2	1	0	1
Ulster Defence Association/Ulster Freedom Fighters	2	1	0	1
Underground Government of the Free Democratic People of Laos	1	0	0	0
United Liberation Front of Assam (ULFA)	27	194	29	223
United Self-Defense Forces of Colombia (AUC)	3	0	1	1
Unknown Group	1732	6146	2643	8789
Usd Allah	1	0	0	0
Vigorous Burmese Student Warriors	1	1	0	1
TOTAL	**2571**	**10807**	**4969**	**15768**

2005

Group	Incidents	Injuries	Fatalities	Total Casualties
Abu Sayyaf Group (ASG)	4	112	10	122
Action Group Extreme Beate	1	0	0	0
Akhil Krantikari	1	0	0	0
al-Aarifeen	1	1	4	5
al-Ahwal Brigades	1	0	0	0
al-Bara bin Malek Brigades	2	4	4	8
al-Fatah	15	30	12	42
al-Islah	1	0	1	1
al-Jihad	1	0	0	0
al-Jihad Brigades	1	0	7	7
al-Mansoorain	1	5	6	11
al-Nasirin	2	0	3	3
al-Qaeda	1	52	21	73
Albanian National Army (ANA)	1	2	0	2
Ali Bin Abu Talib Jihad Organization	1	0	0	0
Ansar al-Islam	1	0	6	6
Ansar al-Sunnah Army	31	525	277	802
Arbav Martyrs of Khuzestan	4	75	9	84
Army of the Levant	1	16	1	17
Babbar Khalsa International	1	49	1	50
Baloch Liberation Army (BLA)	14	14	0	14
Basque Fatherland and Freedom	11	47	0	47
Brigades of Imam al-Hassan al-Basri	1	1	2	3
Communist Party of India-Maoist	26	113	48	161
Communist Party of Nepal-Maoists (CPN-M)	50	36	24	60
Communists Liberation Faction	2	0	0	0
Continuity Irish Republican Army (CIRA)	2	2	0	2
Democratic Front for the Liberation of Palestine (DFLP)	3	1	0	1
Doku Umarov	1	0	0	0
Ethnocacerista	1	5	6	11
Fronte di Liberazione Naziunale di a Corsica (FLNC)	14	2	0	2
Global Intifada	2	0	0	0
HAMAS	171	51	7	58
Harkat ul-Mujahedin	1	0	1	1
Hizballah	1	0	0	0
Hizbul Mujahedin (HM)	2	4	0	4
Hizbul Mujahedin's (HM)/Billal Group	1	100	16	116
Indian Intelligence Research and Analysis Wing (RAW)	1	100	19	119
Informal Anarchist Federation	8	2	0	2
Iraqi Revenge Brigades	1	0	0	0
Islamic Army in Iraq	6	14	22	36

2005 *(continued)*

Group	Incidents	Injuries	Fatalities	Total Casualties
Islamic Glory Brigades in the Land of the Nile	1	18	4	22
Islamic Jihad Jerusalem	8	0	0	0
Islamic Resistance Brigades	1	0	0	0
Jagrata Muslim Janata Bangladesh	1	1	0	1
Jamatul Mujahedin	2	55	1	56
Jund al-Sahabah fi Al-Iraq	1	1	0	1
Jund Allah Organization for the Sunni Mujahideen in Iran	1	0	1	1
Kach	1	6	1	7
Kangleipak Communist Party	1	0	0	0
Karen National Union	1	15	8	23
Karenni National Progressive Party	1	0	0	0
Kata'ib al-Junayd al-Jihadiyah	1	0	0	0
Kurdistan Freedom Hawks	5	59	6	65
Kurdistan Workers' Party	2	0	1	1
Lashkar-e-Tayyiba (LeT)	2	0	10	10
Liberating Communist Faction	1	0	0	0
Liberation Tigers of Tamil Eelam (LTTE)	16	18	7	25
Lord's Resistance Army (LRA)	8	65	25	90
Mariano Moreno National Liberation Commando	1	0	0	0
Martyr Abu-Ali Mustafa Brigades	1	0	0	0
Moro Islamic Liberation Front (MILF)	1	0	1	1
Muadh Ibn Jabal Brigade	2	0	0	0
Mujahideen in Iraq	1	0	0	0
Mujahideen Without Borders	1	1	1	2
National Socialist Council of Nagaland-Isak-Muivah	1	0	4	4
New People's Army (NPA)	6	1	6	7
Other Group	12	61	3	64
People's Defense Forces (HPG)	4	0	0	0
People's Liberation Army (PLA)	1	7	3	10
Kongra Gel (PKK)	1	0	0	0
Popular Front for the Liberation of Palestine (PFLP)	15	0	3	3
Popular Resistance Committees	16	3	0	3
Popular Revolutionary Action	1	0	0	0
Protectors of Islam Brigade	1	0	0	0
Purbo Banglar Communist Party (PBCP)	1	0	1	1
Rappani Khalilov	1	0	0	0
Rasul Makasharipov	1	0	0	0
Rebolusyonaryong Hukbong Bayan (RHB)	1	0	2	2
Revolutionary Armed Forces of Colombia	10	42	22	64
Revolutionary People's Liberation Party/Front (DHKP-C)	1	0	1	1
Revolutionary Struggle	1	0	0	0

2005 *(continued)*

Group	Incidents	Injuries	Fatalities	Total Casualties
Salafist Group for Call and Combat (GSPC)	1	1	1	2
Salah al-Din Battalions	1	0	0	0
Secret Organization of al-Qaeda in Europe	4	220	56	276
Shura Council of the Mujahideen of Iraq	2	0	0	0
Soldiers of the Prophet's Companions	1	100	53	153
Strugglers for the Unity and Freedom of Greater Syria	1	1	1	2
Support and Jihad in Syria and Lebanon	1	120	20	140
Takfir wa Hijra	1	0	12	12
Taliban	47	52	107	159
Tanzim Qa'idat al-Jihad fi Bilad al-Rafidayn	144	1709	785	2494
The Aguarunas	1	0	0	0
The National Anti-Corruption Front	1	0	0	0
United Liberation Front of Assam (ULFA)	11	18	3	21
United National Liberation Front (UNLF)	1	2	0	2
United Self-Defense Forces of Colombia (AUC)	2	0	1	1
Unknown Group	2027	4496	2642	7138
Yunadi Turchayev	1	0	0	0
TOTAL	**2807**	**8534**	**4320**	**12734**

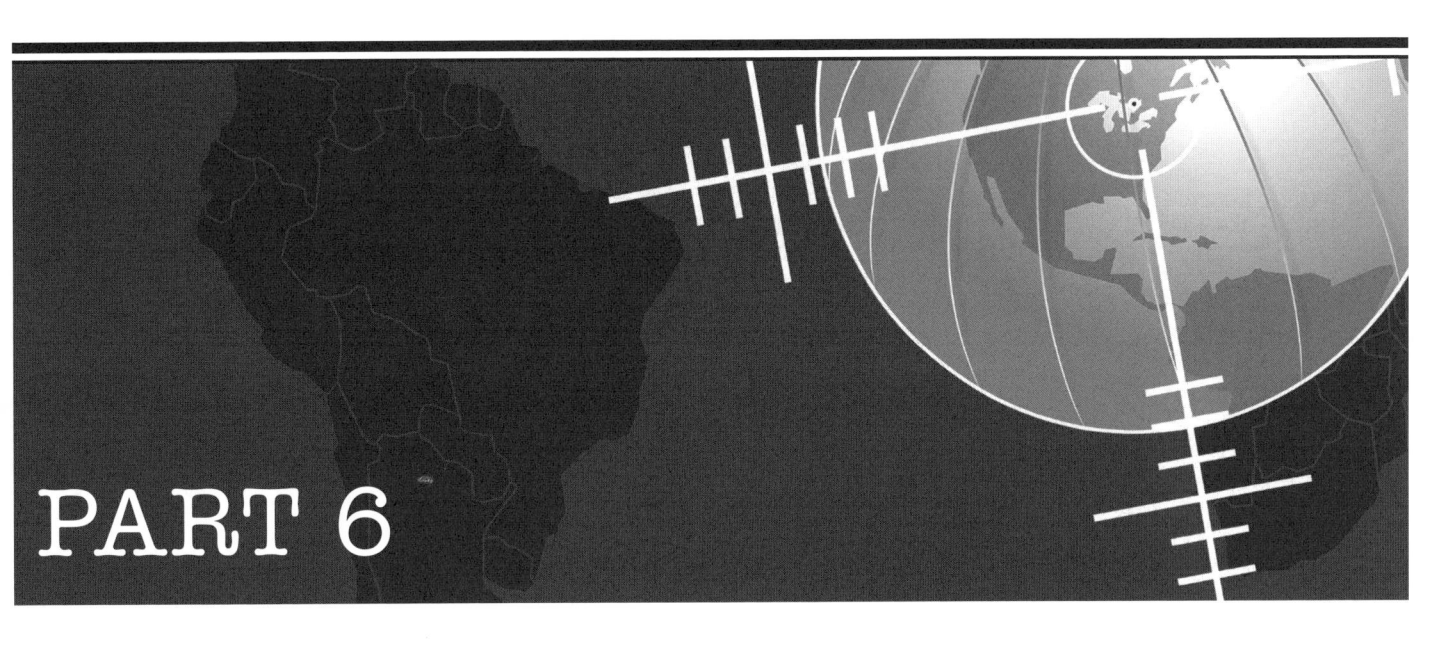

PART 6
TRENDS OVER TIME: GRAPHS ON TERRORISM

Overview of Trends over Time: Graphs on Terrorism

Anna Sabasteanski

Although the U.S. Department of State has overall responsibility for producing an annual terrorism report, other government offices provide data and analysis that contribute to various portions of the report. The Central Intelligence Agency's Counterterrorism Center (CTC), the successor Terrorist Threat Integration Center (TTIC), and the new National Counterterrorism Center (NCTC) have played a critical role in collecting and analyzing international incidents, and in providing the Department of State with the data used in the charts and graphs included in the annual reports. These statistics are only one measure for analyzing terrorism, and should never be the only measure used.

Terrorism analysis spreads far and wide, using a broad range of sources that range from local news sources to data intercepts. While news of mass casualties reaches the international press, local incidents and those that fail often fall below this radar screen. Detailed terrorism analysis incorporates attempted incidents, and uses data obtained from even the smallest events to help understand current and emerging threats. However, the annual reports focus only on those considered significant. This definition is something of a moving target, and in practice it has come down to a consensus evaluation among the terrorism analysts, department officials, and the Department of State's Independent Review Panel (IDP).

To develop the graphs in this section, we used data provided in *Patterns of Global Terrorism*, the MIPT Terrorism Knowledge Base, which integrates data from the RAND Terrorism Chronology and RAND-MIPT Terrorism Incident databases, and the NCTC's Worldwide Incidents Tracking System (WITS). From this data, we designed a set of graphs that chart incidents, casualties, targets, and tactics. The sources for each category are cited in their respective overviews.

The WITS database was launched in July 2005, as a major initiative of the new organization and in connection with the Department of State's shift to *Country Reports on Terrorism*, with NCTC providing the Chronology and Graphs separately. On its website (http://www.tkb.org/NCTCMethodology.jsp), NCTC describes its methodology. Describing terrorist attacks as "incidents in which subnational or clandestine groups or individuals deliberately or recklessly attacked civilians or noncombatants," they offer an important caveat that such determination "can be more art than science" due to incomplete information and details that emerge over time.

To help limit subjectivity, they use counting rules such as eliminating failed or foiled attacks, hoaxes, spontaneous hate crimes, and genocide. They categorize "event type," but warn that incidents, particularly multiple attacks, can be hard to categorize. The examples of distinguishing between terrorism, crime, sectarian and other violence in Iraq and Afghanistan is particularly difficult. NCTC also attempts to include "defining characteristics" to provide more detail about motive, victim, and so on.

The data specified numbers killed, wounded, and kidnapped. According to NCTC, "Kidnapped victims who were later killed are counted as killed, and kidnapped victims either liberated or still in captivity are counted as kidnapped." In addition, information regarding damage estimates is given: "Light ($1 to $500 thousand), Moderate ($500 thousand to $20 million), or Heavy (over $20 million)." This type of data, though difficult to assess, helps give an overall sense for trends in attacks.

Incidents

Overview of Incidents

Anna Sabasteanski

This set of graphs includes the following illustrations, based on the numbers of attacks that the Department of State has designated as significant:

- international incidents by region (1981–2004)
- anti-U.S. attacks compared to attacks (1981–2004) in total
- anti-U.S. attacks compared to attacks (1981–2004) as relative percentages
- anti-U.S. attacks by region (1985, 1990–2004).

As demonstrated in these graphs, in the past two decades, terrorism spread from Europe through the Middle East and increased around the globe. The number of incidents has increased in every region, including large numbers in the Middle East and recent sharp spikes in Asia.

These numbers have grown even more rapidly in 2005. Determination of which attacks are considered "significant" has not been concluded, but comparing the total number of international attacks is instructive. In 2004, there were a total of 2,571 attacks, of which 651 were deemed "significant" and included in the NCTC report that supplemented the Department of State's *Country Reports on Terrorism*. The first eight months of 2005 has already significantly exceeded last year's record total.

The overall percentage of attacks directed against U.S. interests remains a relatively small part of the whole, although it too is increasing.

Anti-U.S. data was taken from annual *Patterns of Global Terrorism*. Specific detail is not available for all years. Please note that 1968–1997 data covers only international incidents while 1998–present includes domestic incidents as well.

The general trends are discussed in the annual regional overviews and country reports.

The international data is retrieved from the National Counterterrorism Center's (NCTC) Worldwide Incidents Tracking System (WITS) and the MIPT Terrorism Knowledge Base that integrates data from the RAND Terrorism Chronology and RAND-MIPT Terrorism Incident databases.

International Incidents, 1 January 2005–31 August 2005

Region	Incidents
Africa	22
Americas	34
Asia	658
Europe	244
Middle East	1857
Total	2815

Table developed in part from data retrieved from the MIPT Terrorism Knowledge Base in September 2005.

We have grouped this data into five standard regions: Africa, Americas, Asia, Europe, and Middle East. In both *Patterns* and in WITS, regional designations may vary. For example, Egypt is variously considered Middle East and North Africa. We did not normalize this data. Americas includes North America, Central America, South America, and the Caribbean. Europe used to be divided between East and West. For this analysis, Eastern Europe and the Soviet Union joined Western Europe. The independent states east of the Caucasus that were created after the collapse of the Soviet Union (Central Asia) are included in Asia, while the Caucasus states and those to the west, including the Russian Federation, are included in Europe. In addition to Central Asia, South Asia, East Asia, Southeast Asia, and Oceania are incorporated in the general regional category of Asia.

NCTC's methodology is explained in full on its website (http://www.tkb.org/NCTCMethodology.jsp). In the database, it includes "incidents in which subnational or clandestine groups or individuals deliberately or recklessly attacked civilians or noncombatants." To be included, the attack must have been initiated and executed. Failed or foiled attacks, hoaxes, and spontaneous hate crimes without intent to cause mass casualties are excluded "to the greatest extent practicable." Genocide is excluded, "in part because of the inherent difficulty in counting such events and because the inevitable undercount does not do justice to the scope and depth of such atrocities."

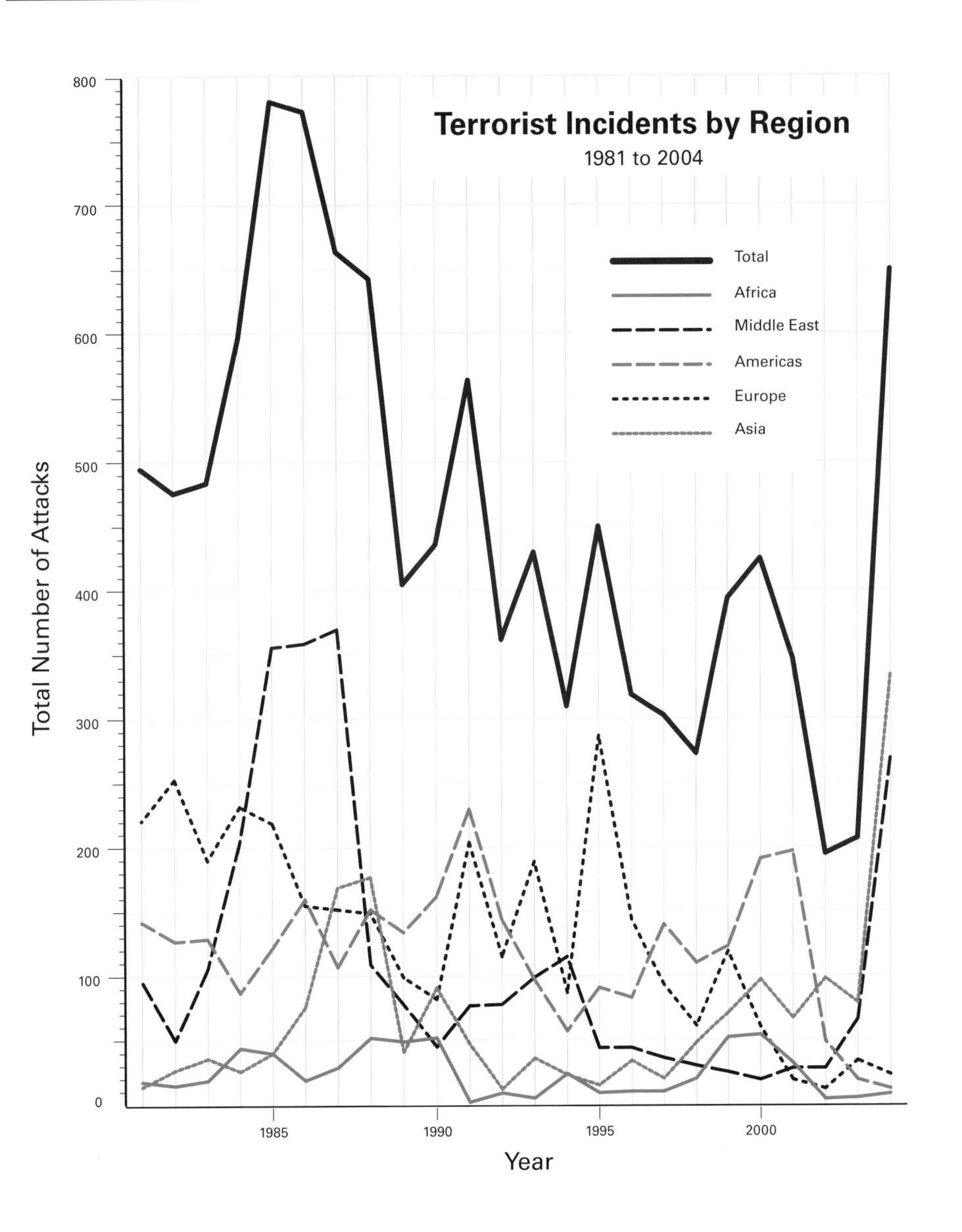

Terrorist Incidents by Region
1981 to 2004

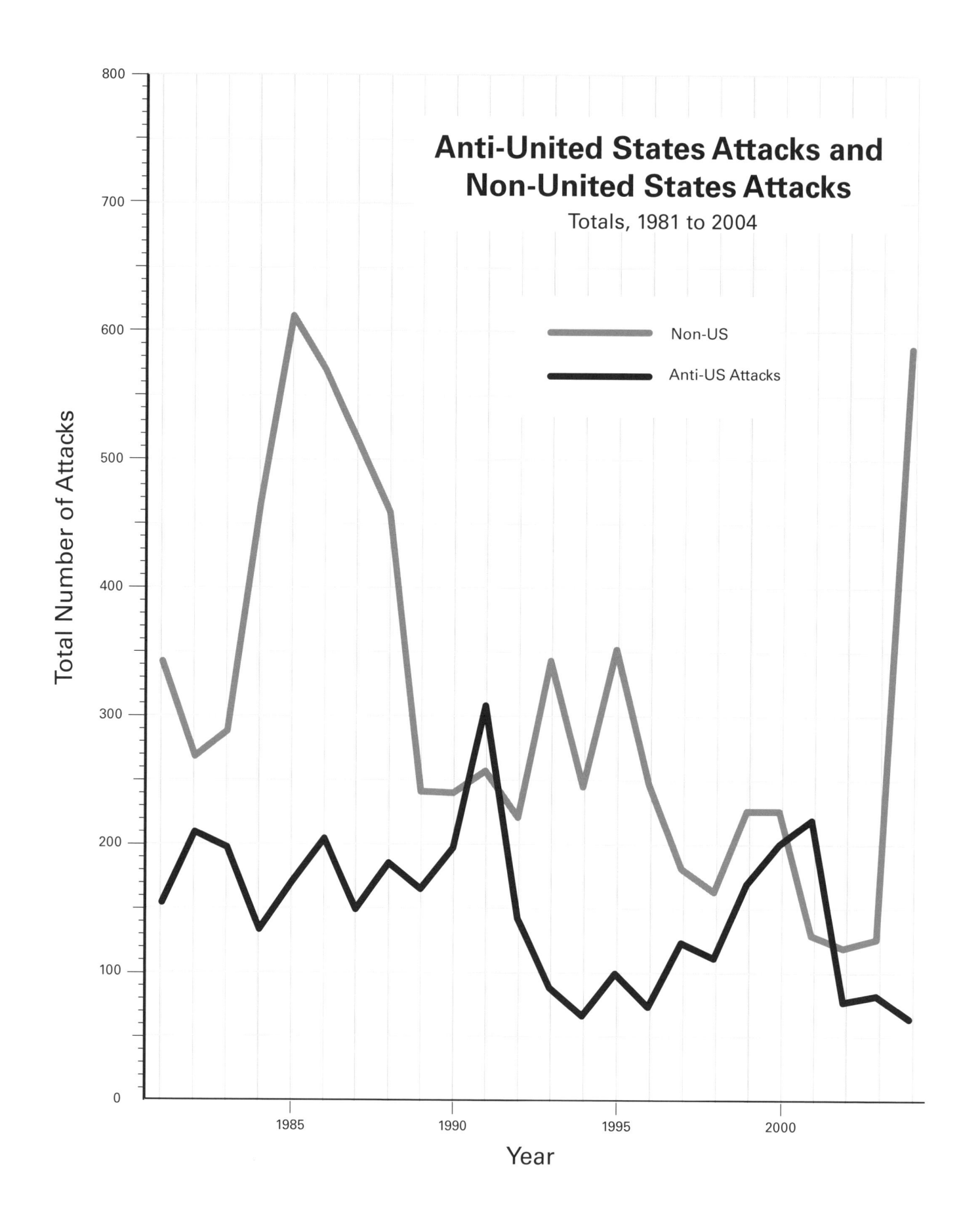

Anti-United States Attacks and Non-United States Attacks
Totals, 1981 to 2004

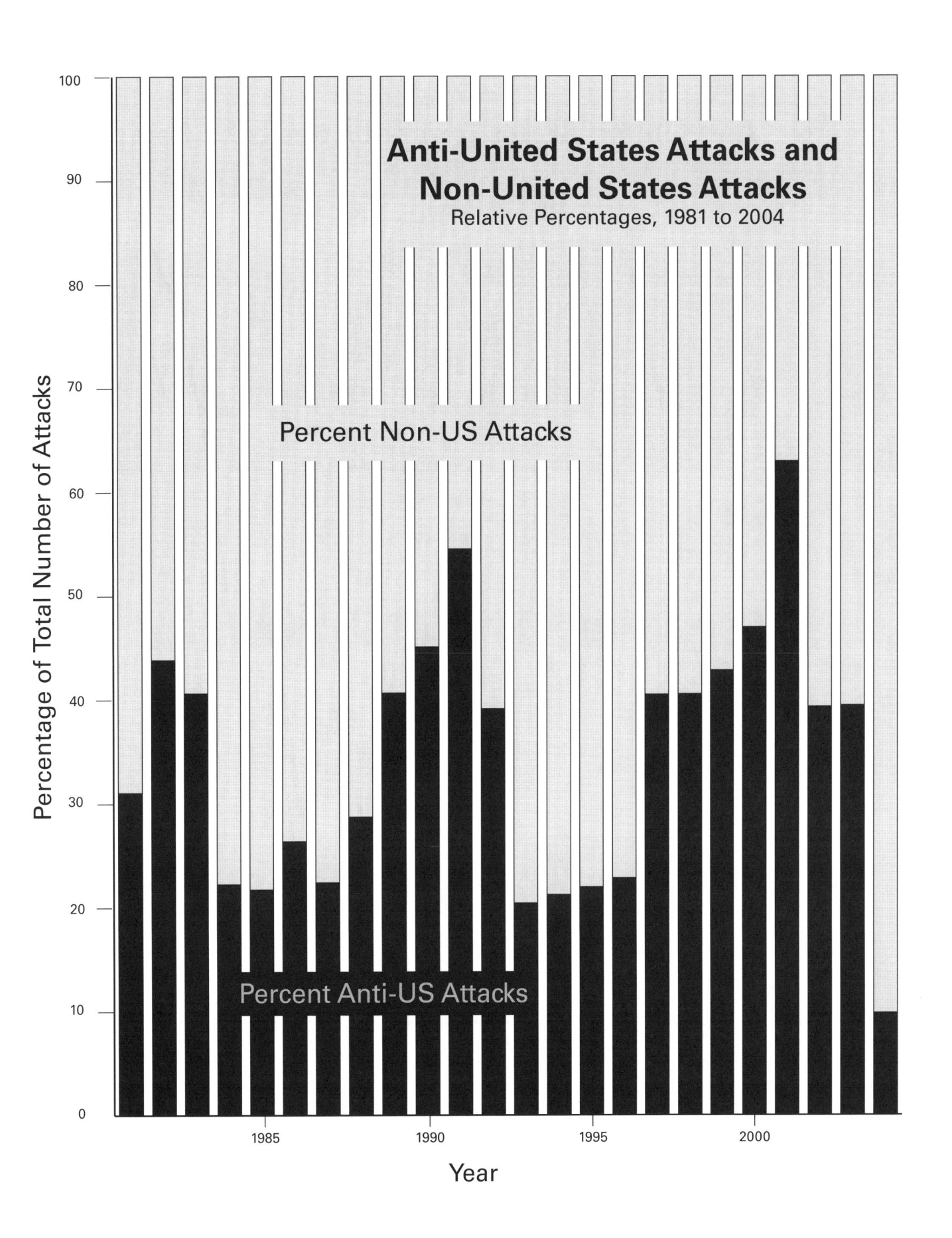

Anti-United States Attacks and Non-United States Attacks
Relative Percentages, 1981 to 2004

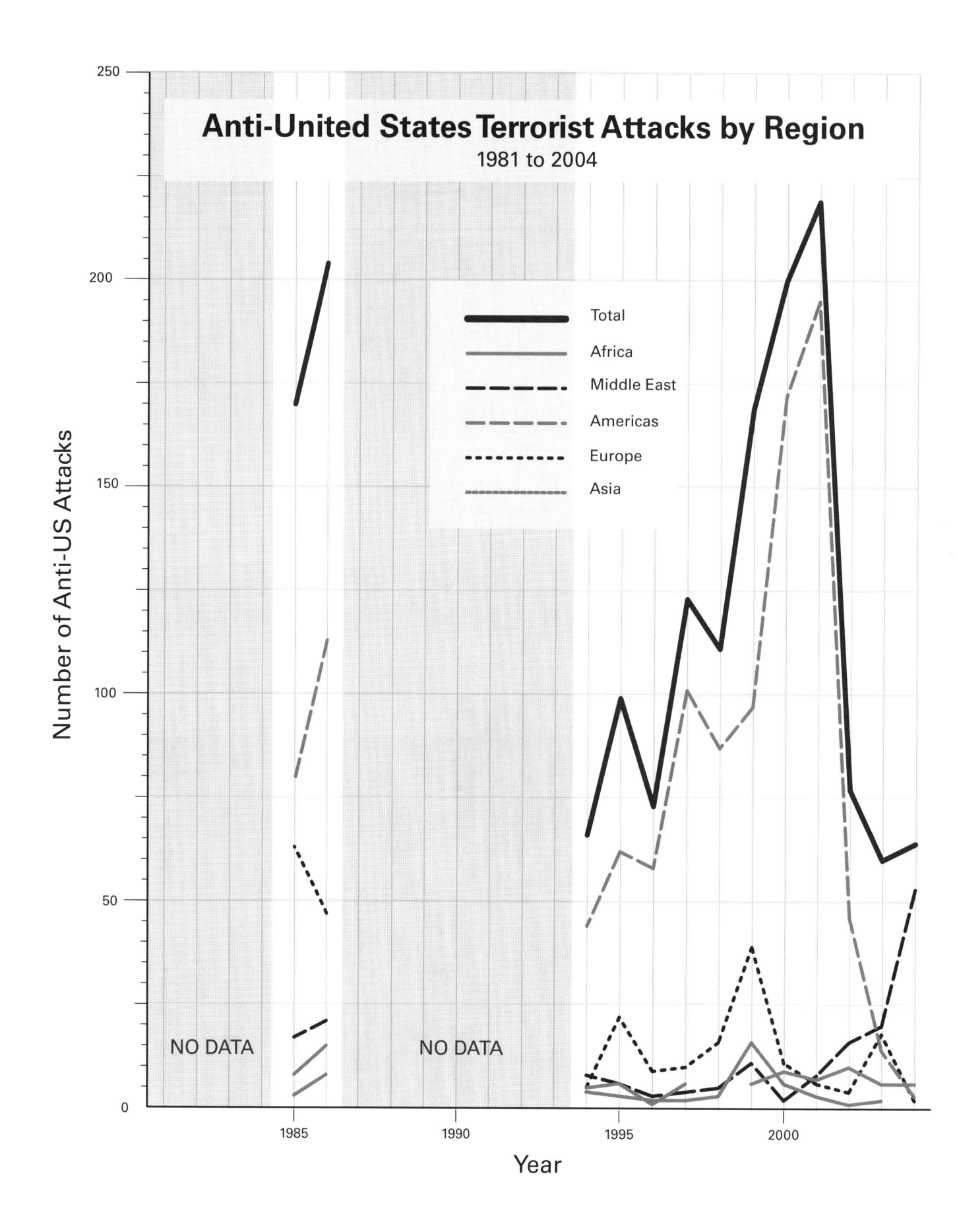

Anti-United States Terrorist Attacks by Region
1981 to 2004

Casualties

Overview of Casualties

Anna Sabasteanski

This set of graphs includes the following illustrations: total number of deaths and injuries by region (1968–2004); number of deaths by region (1968–2004); number of injuries by region (1968–2004); international casualties by region (1988–2004); anti-U.S. casualties (1988–2004); and percentage of anti-U.S. casualties compared to the total (1988–2004).

In line with the rapid increase in the number of incidents, casualty numbers have been on the rise across the globe. Peaks in the numbers are tied to specific attacks. For example:

- In 1979, Mecca's Grand Mosque attack killed 158 and injured 560.
- The 1985 Air India bombing by Sikh extremists killed 329 people.
- In 1988, the Pan Am 103 "Lockerbie" bombing killed 270 and injured 12.
- In 1998, al-Qaeda bombed U.S. Embassies in Africa, killing 303 people and injuring more than 5,000.
- The 2001 al-Qaeda attacks against the United States killed 2,749 and injured 2,261.
- The October 2002 Jemaah Islamiah bombings in Bali killed 202 and injured 300 (mostly tourists).
- In 2004, the Madrid bombings by al-Qaeda killed 191 and injured 600.
- The Chechen separatist siege of the Beslan school in Russia left 331 people dead, mostly children, and 727 injured.

Apart from the extraordinary toll of the 2001 attacks against the United States, U.S. casualties constitute a relatively small part of the whole, although they are increasing. (Military casualties are not included in these reports.)

Anti-U.S. data was taken from annual *Patterns of Global Terrorism*. Specific detail is not available for all years, although the general trends are discussed in the annual regional overviews and country reports. (The 1968–1997 data covers only international incidents while 1998–present includes domestic incidents.).

The international data is retrieved from the National Counterterrorism Center's (NCTC) Worldwide Incidents Tracking System (WITS) and the MIPT Terrorism Knowledge Base that integrates data from the RAND Terrorism Chronology and RAND-MIPT Terrorism Incident databases.

We have grouped this data into five standard regions: Africa, Americas, Asia, Europe, and Middle East. In both *Patterns* and in WITS, regional designations may vary. For example, Egypt is variously considered Middle East and North Africa. We did not normalize this data. Americas includes North America, Central America, South America, and the Caribbean. Europe used to be divided between East and West. For this analysis, Eastern Europe and the Soviet Union joined Western Europe. The independent states east of the Caucasus that were created after the collapse of the Soviet Union (Central Asia) are included in Asia, while the Caucasus states and those to the west, including the Russian Federation, are included in Europe. In addition to Central Asia, South Asia, East Asia, Southeast Asia, and Oceania are incorporated in the general regional category of Asia.

NCTC's methodology is described in full at the NCTC website, http://www.tkb.org/NCTCMethodology.jsp, including how casualties are treated. It points out particular difficulties in Iraq and Afghanistan, where comprehensive information is hard to find and it is difficult to "distinguish terrorism from the numerous other forms of violence, including crime and sectarian violence." In Iraq, citizens "participate in both the Abu Musab al-Zarqawi terrorist network as well as the Baathist, former-regime-elements insurgency, targeting both civilians and combatants and often affecting both populaces. Therefore, some combatants may be included as victims in some incidents, when their presence was incidental to an attack intended for noncombatants."

International Casualties, 1 January 2005– 31 August 2005

Region	Injuries	Fatalities	Total
Africa	152	61	213
Americas	66	39	105
Asia	1938	636	2574
Europe	384	80	464
Middle East	6001	3504	9505
Total	8541	4320	12861

Table developed in part from data retrieved from the MIPT Terrorism Knowledge Base in September 2005.

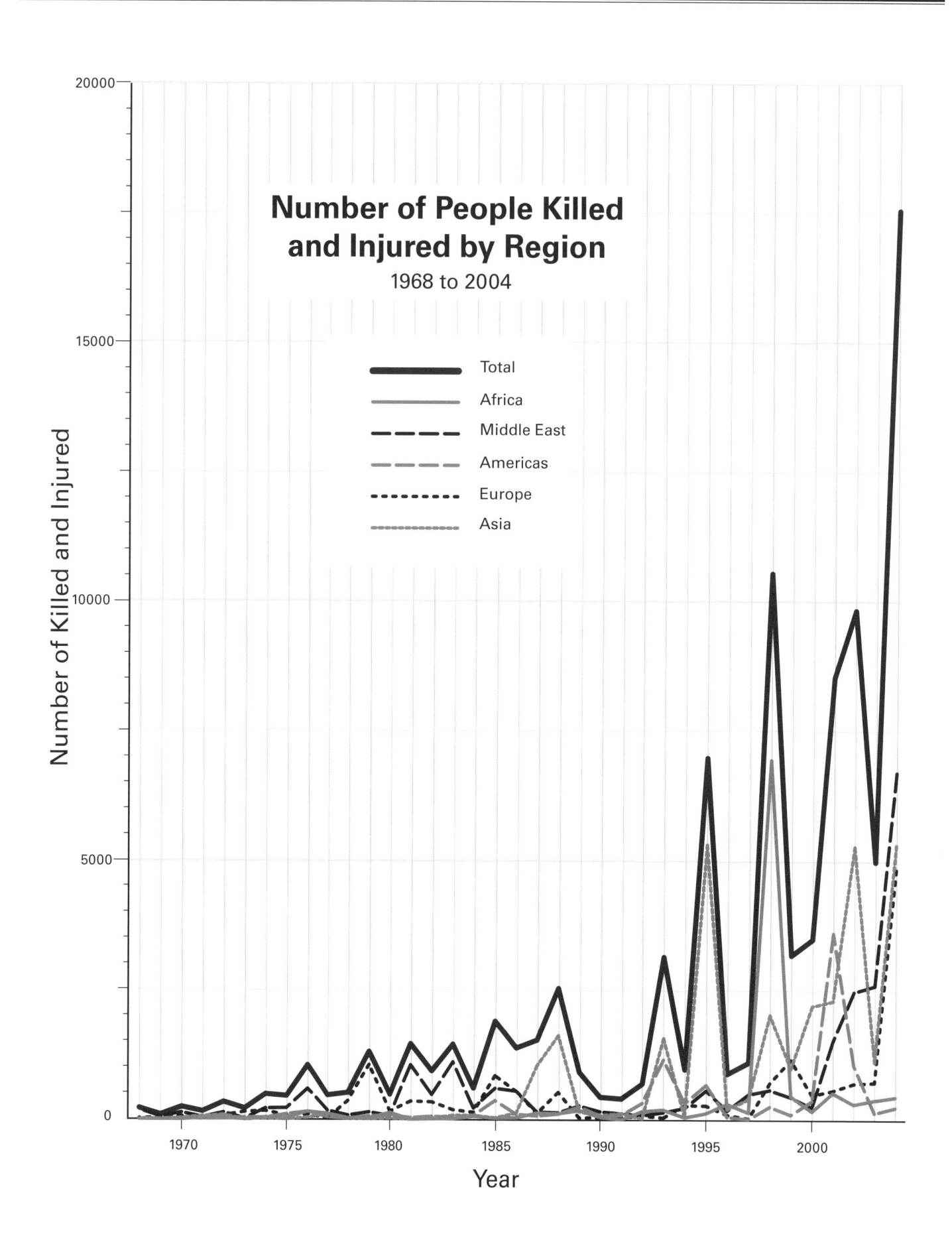

Number of People Killed and Injured by Region
1968 to 2004

Number of Deaths by Region
1968 to 2004

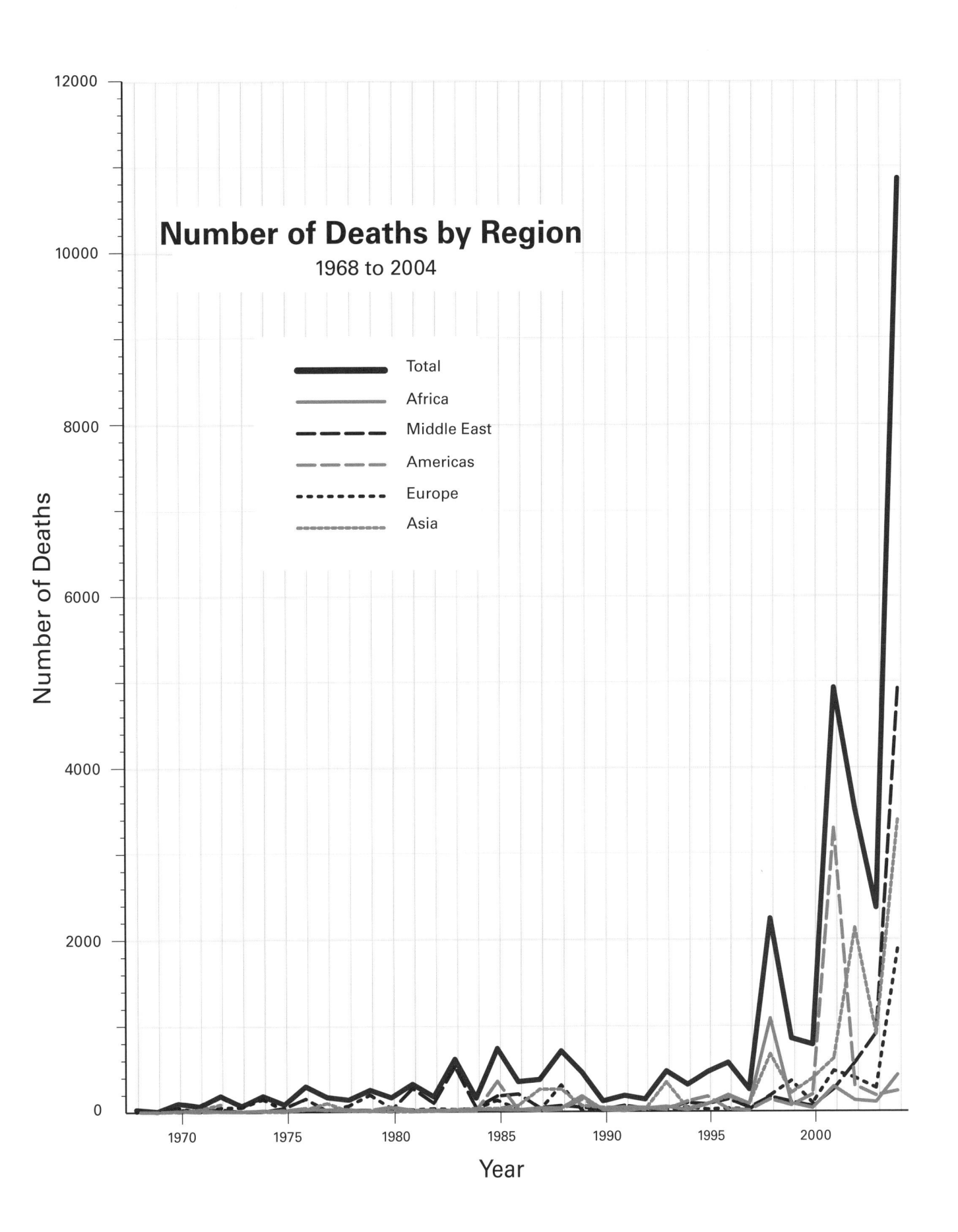

Number of Injuries by Region
1968 to 2004

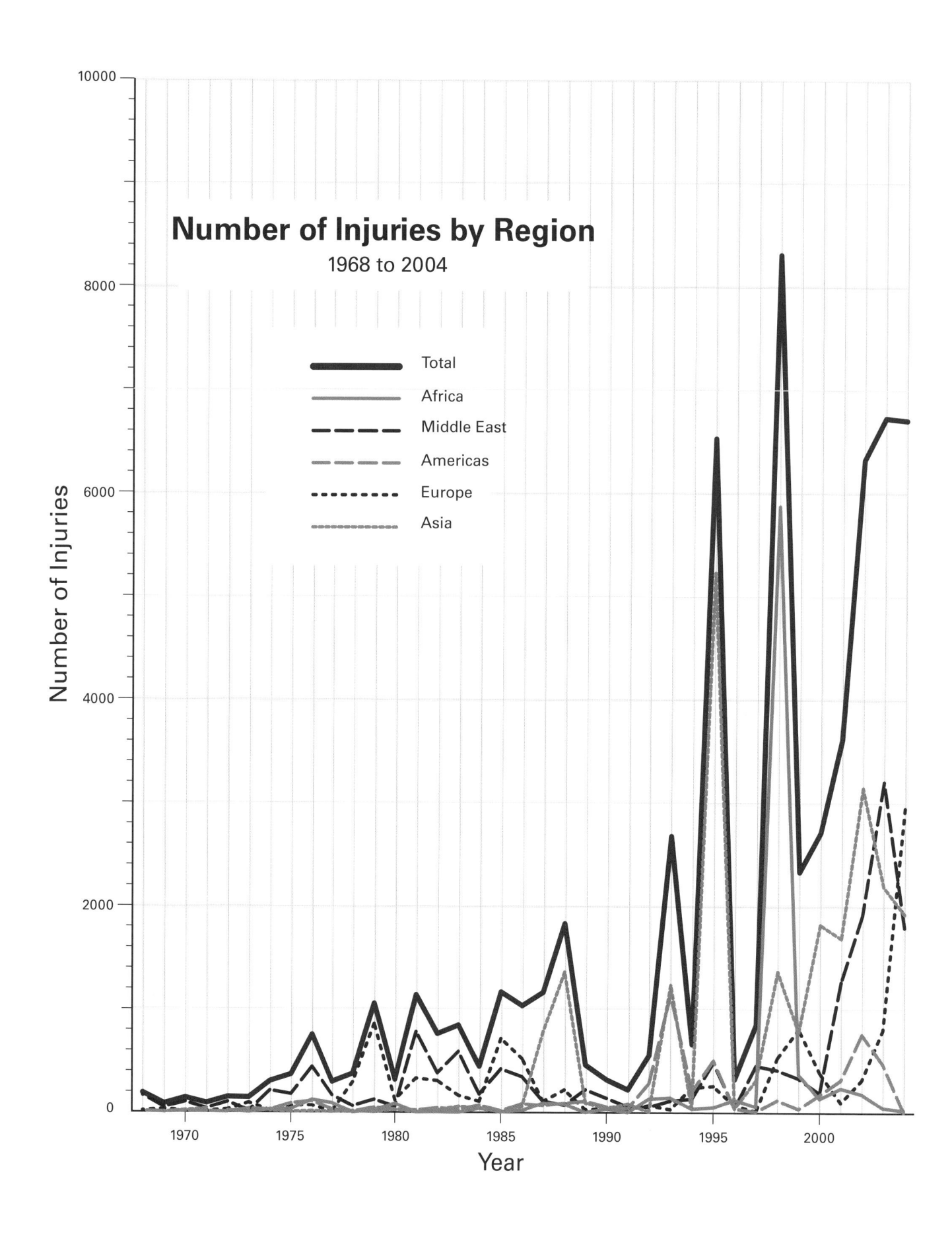

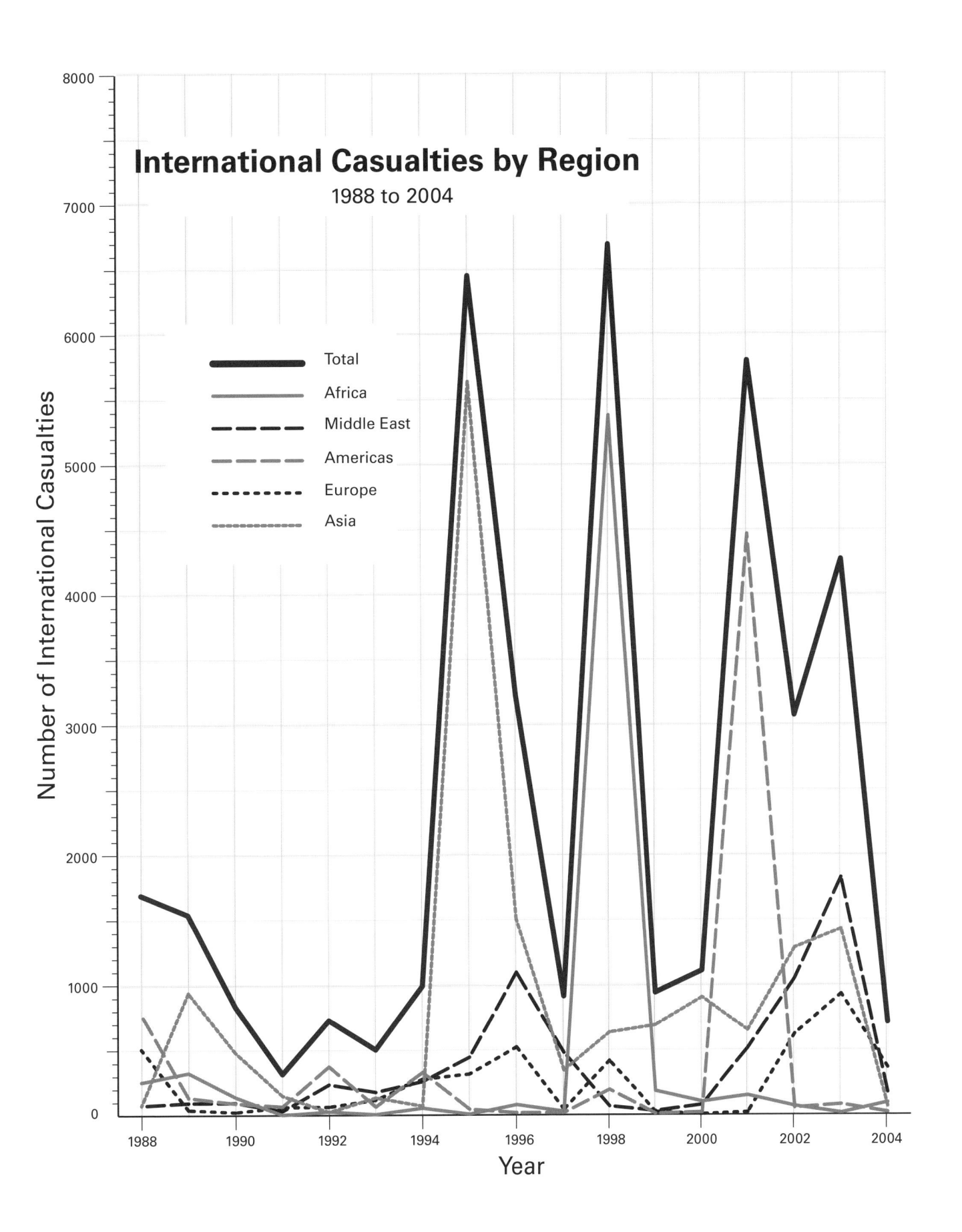

International Casualties by Region
1988 to 2004

Anti-United States Casualties
1988 to 2004

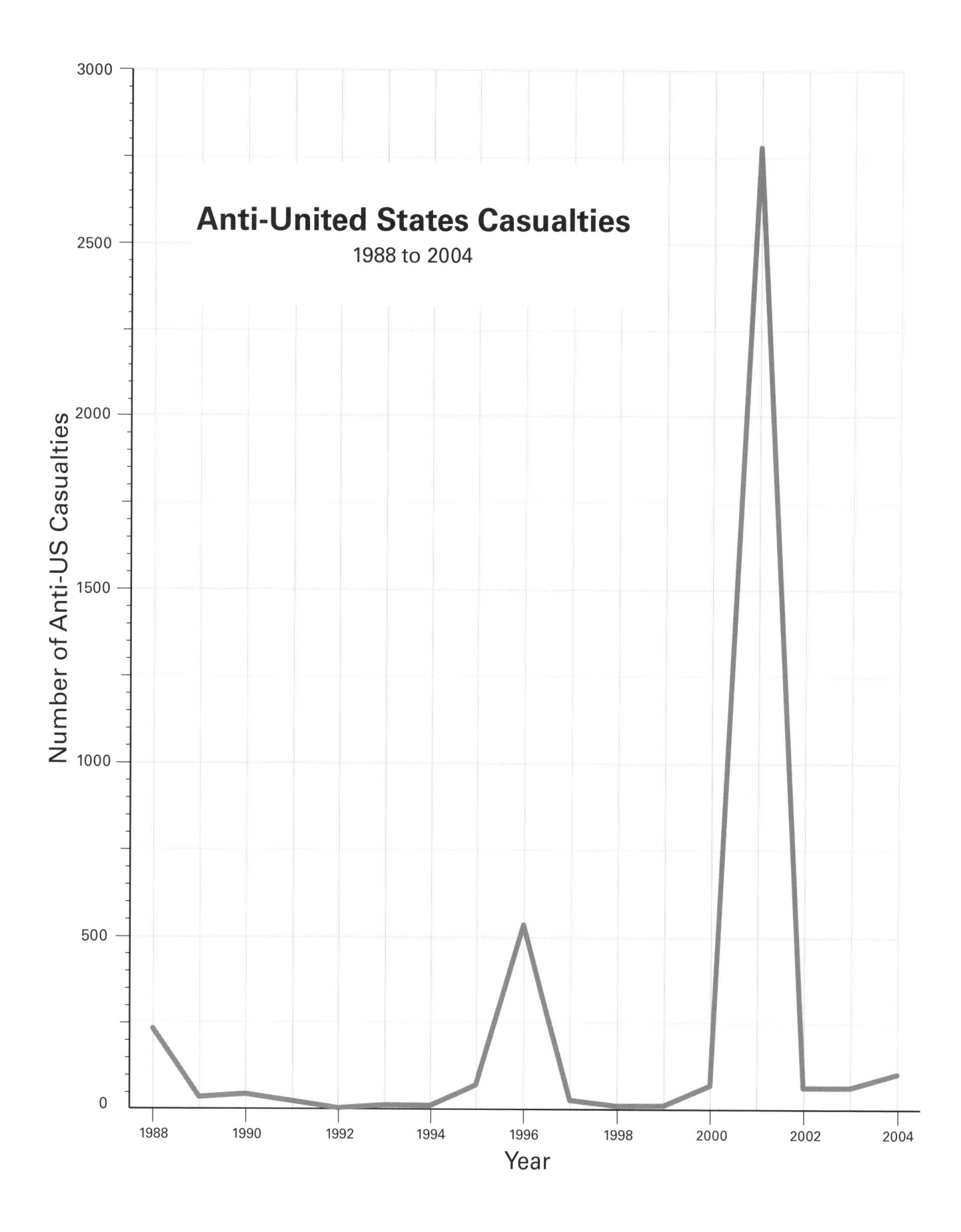

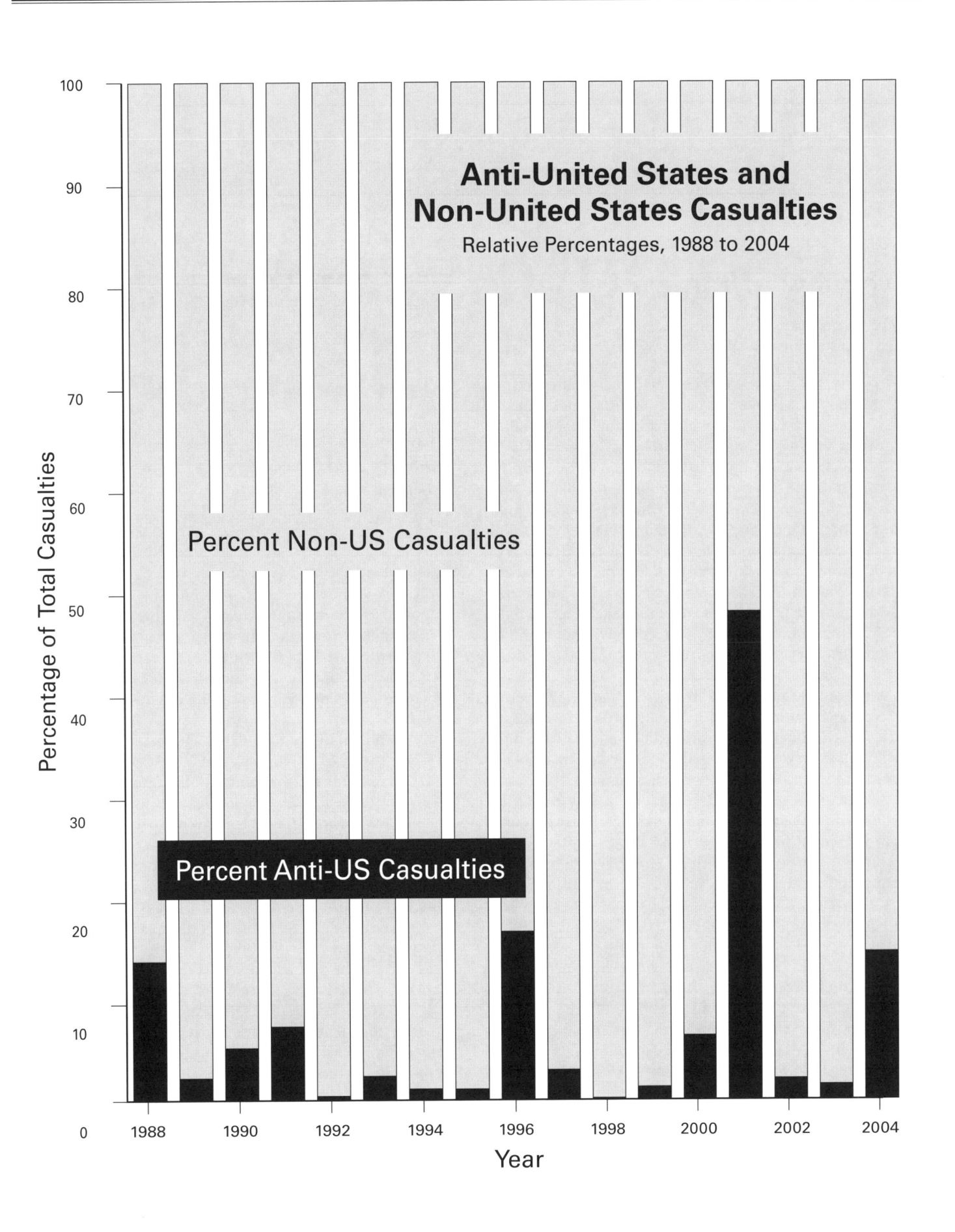

Anti-United States and Non-United States Casualties
Relative Percentages, 1988 to 2004

Targets

Overview of Targets

Anna Sabasteanski

This set of graphs illustrates incidents, injuries and fatalities for the following types of targets, for the years 1968–2004, plus data for January–July 2005: Abortion-related; Airports and Airlines; Business; Diplomatic; Educational Institutions; Food and Water Supply; Government; Journalists and Media; Maritime; Military; Non-Governmental Organizations; Other Targets; Police-Related; Private Citizens and Property; Religious Figures or Institutions; Telecommunications; Terrorists; Tourists; Transportation; Unknown; and Utilities. In addition, a comparison graph illustrates the relative numbers of attacks against business, diplomatic, government, military, and other facilities from 1989–2003. (The 1968–1997 data covers only international incidents while 1998–present includes domestic incidents as well.)

Although the military is still targeted, particularly during times of war, terrorists from 1968 to the present have turned increasingly to softer targets. Airlines and airports were high-profile targets in the 1970s and 1980s, when incidents of mass casualties raised the profile of, in particular, Palestinian and Sikh nationalist groups. International security measures greatly reduced their impact until the dramatic use of planes as weapons in the 9/11 attacks. From 1968 to 2004, 796 attacks involved airports and airlines, and 847 involved other transportation targets. These caused 4,581 and 13,436 casualties, respectively. The highest level of casualties was the 1995 Aum Shrinrikyo sarin nerve gas attack on the Tokyo subway system (12 deaths, 5,000 injuries).

Attacks against private citizens and properties remained at low levels until the late 1990s. In the 27 years from 1968 to 1994, there were 225 incidents causing 2,090 injuries and 490 deaths (an average of 8 incidents causing 96 casualties per year). In the ten years from 1995 to 2004, there were 3,289 incidents (one a day) causing 10,882 injuries and killing 4,789. Between January and July of 2005, there have been 527 attacks causing 1,140 injuries and killing 509—the largest group targeted.

Businesses face the second most frequent number of attacks. Between 1968 and 2004 they were targeted 3,145 times, incurring 14,696 casualties. In the 27 years from 1968–1994, there were 1575 incidents causing 3,908 injuries and 703 deaths (an average of 58 incidents and about 170 casualties per year). In the ten years from 1996 to 2004, there were 1,570 incidents (an average of 157 per year) causing 7,643 injuries and killing 4,118 (an average of 1,176 casualties per year). From January to August of 2005 there have been 169 attacks, injuring 684 and killing 234.

Governments were targeted 2,844 times between 1968 and 2004, with 6,380 injuries and 2,901 fatalities while the 2,602 attacks directed against diplomatic targets injured 8,290 and killed 1,237. Attacks against other soft targets emerged in the early 1990s, and have grown rapidly since the U.S.-led invasion of Iraq in 2003.

Comparative facility data was taken from annual *Patterns of Global Terrorism*. Specific detail is not available for earlier years, although the general trends are discussed in the annual regional overviews and country reports. Specific category data is retrieved from the National Counterterrorism Center's (NCTC) Worldwide Incidents Tracking System (WITS) and the MIPT Terrorism Knowledge Base that integrates data from the RAND Terrorism Chronology and RAND-MIPT Terrorism Incident databases. NCTC's methodology is described in full at its website: http://www.tkb.org/NCTC Methodology.jsp.

Selected Targets, 1 January 2005–31 August 2005

Target	Incidents	Casualties
Business	169	918
Diplomatic, Government, Military	682	2498
Police	684	4628
Private Citizens and Property	530	1649
Religious Figures/Institutions	120	1298
Transportation, including all Air	86	637

Table developed in part from data retrieved from the MIPT Terrorism Knowledge Base in September 2005.

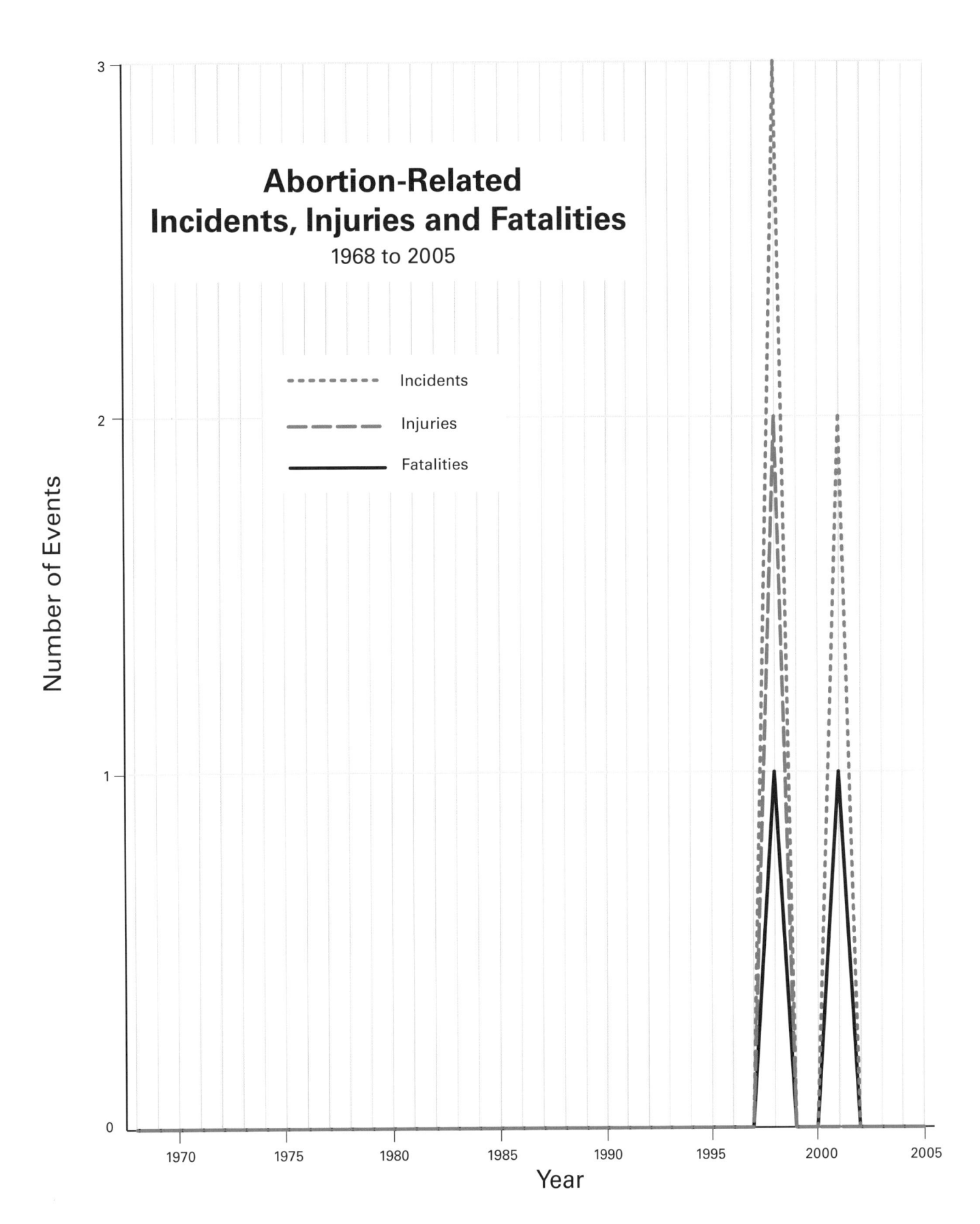

Abortion-Related Incidents, Injuries and Fatalities
1968 to 2005

- .... Incidents
- — — — Injuries
- ——— Fatalities

Number of Events

Year

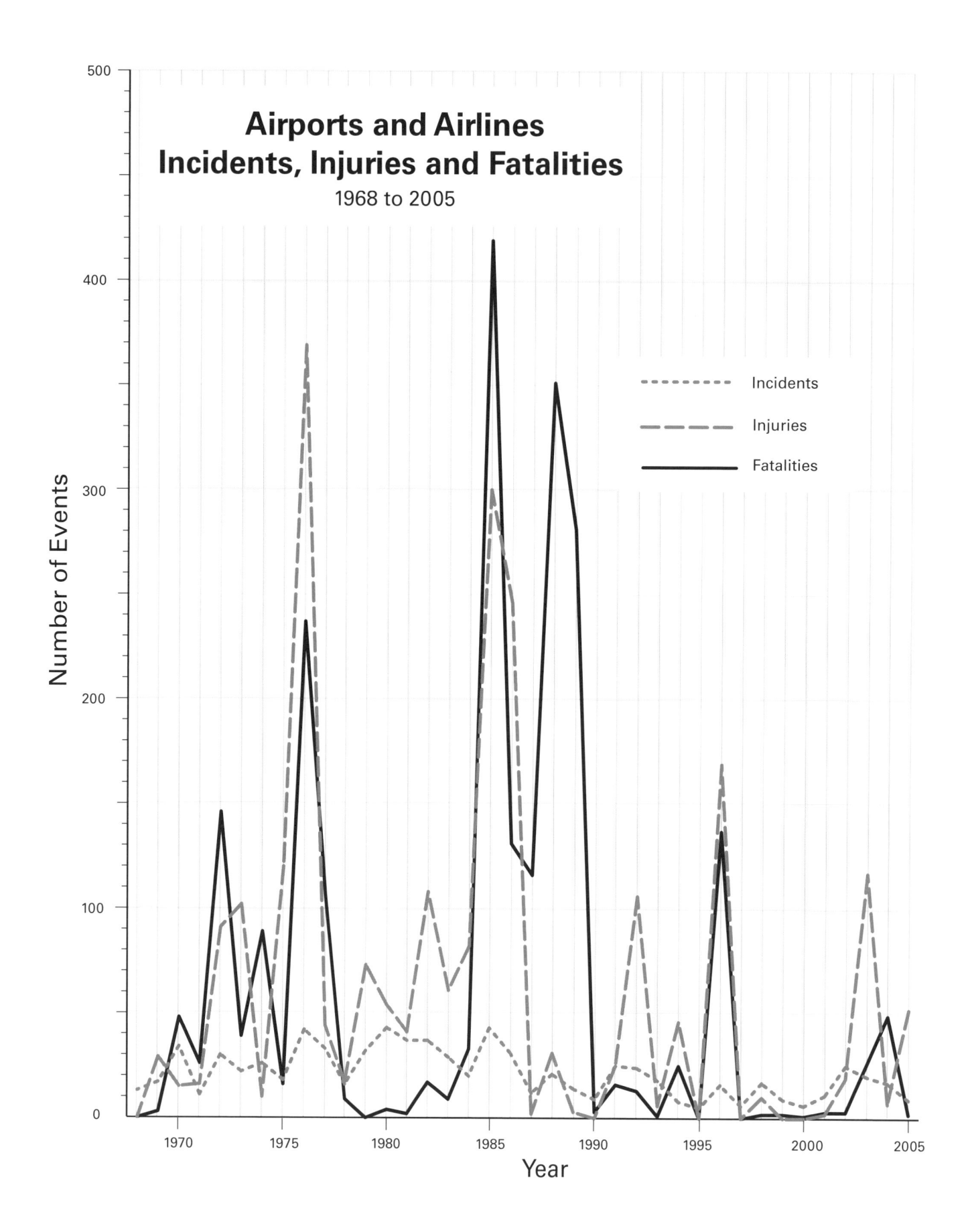

Airports and Airlines Incidents, Injuries and Fatalities
1968 to 2005

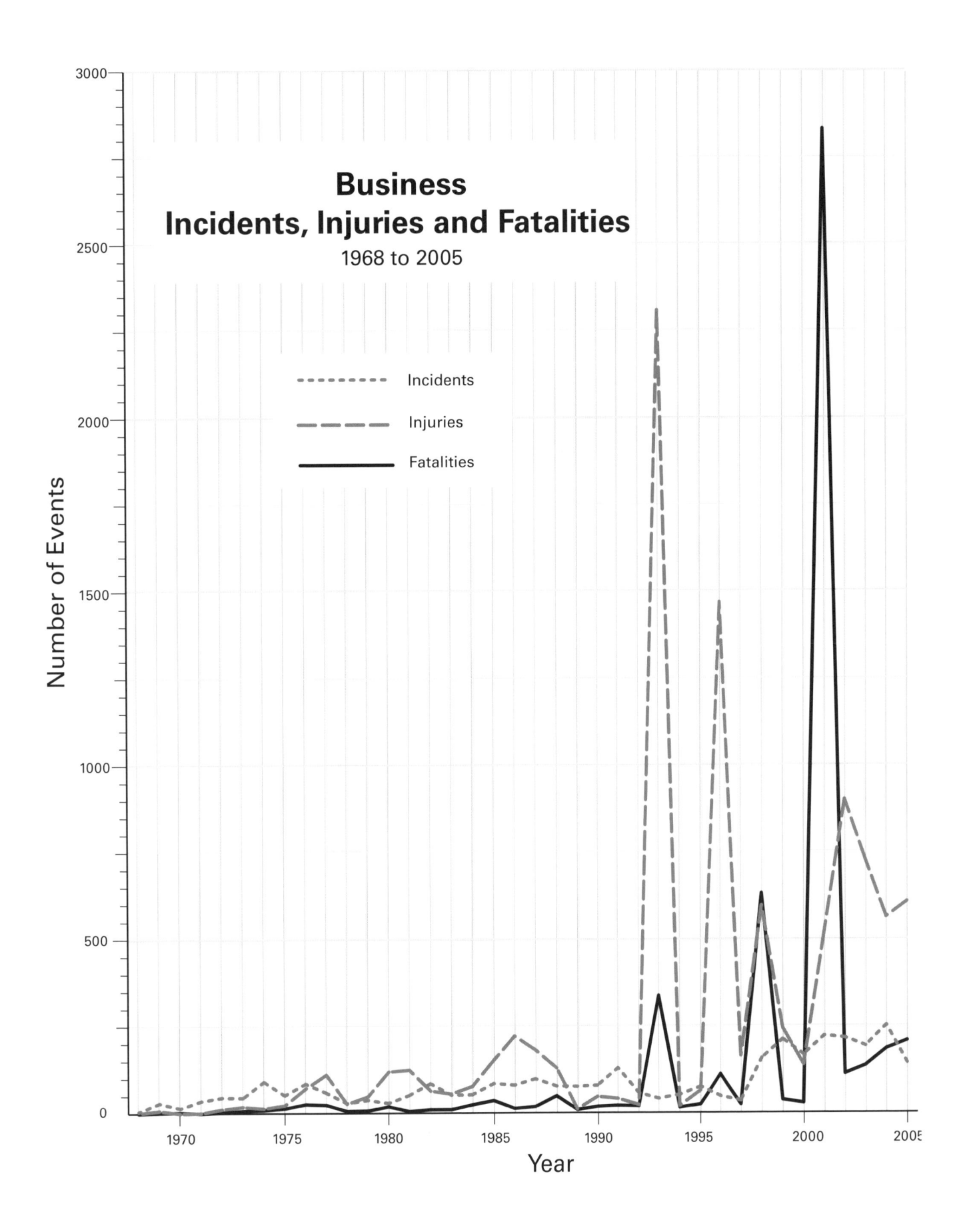

Business
Incidents, Injuries and Fatalities
1968 to 2005

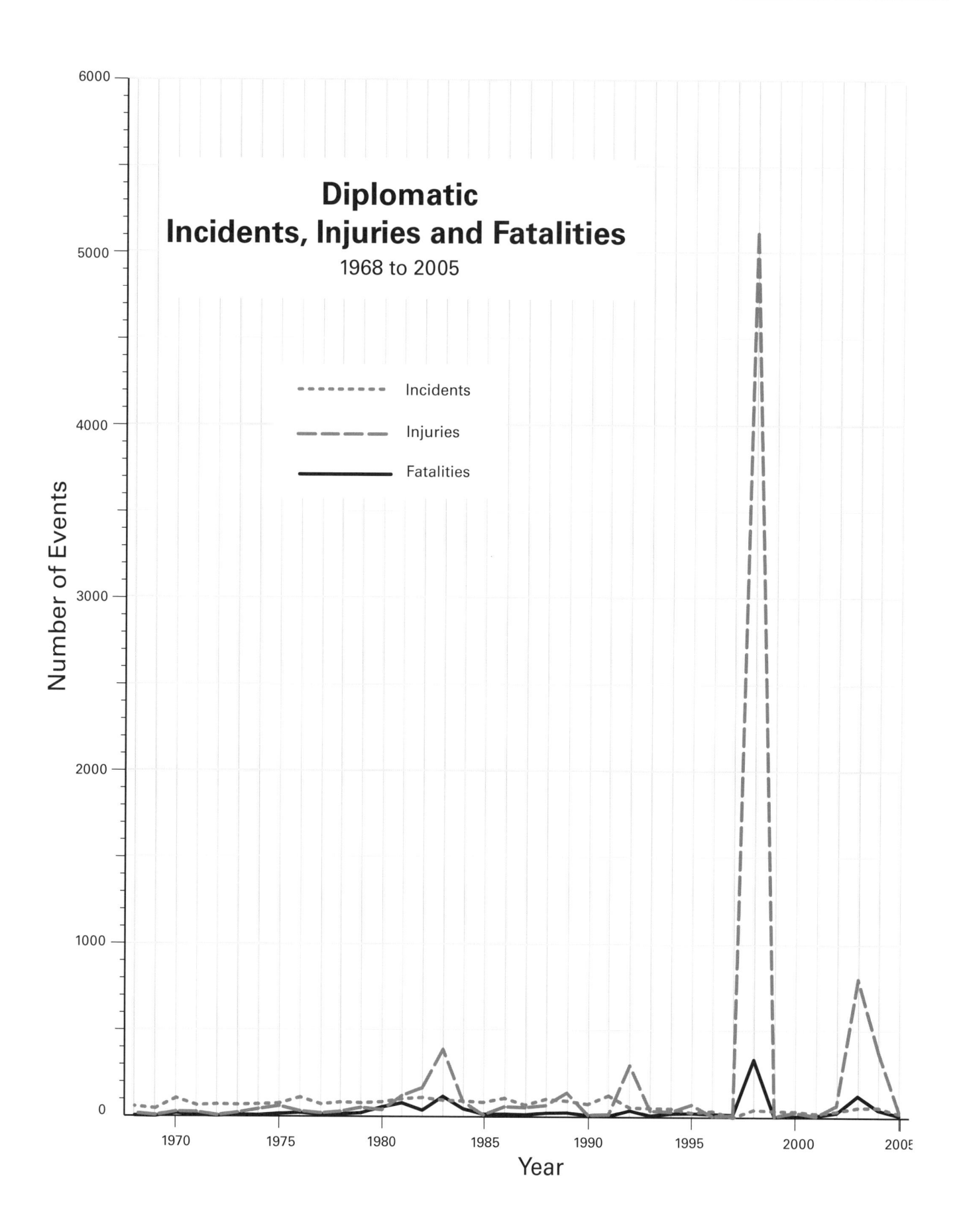

Diplomatic Incidents, Injuries and Fatalities
1968 to 2005

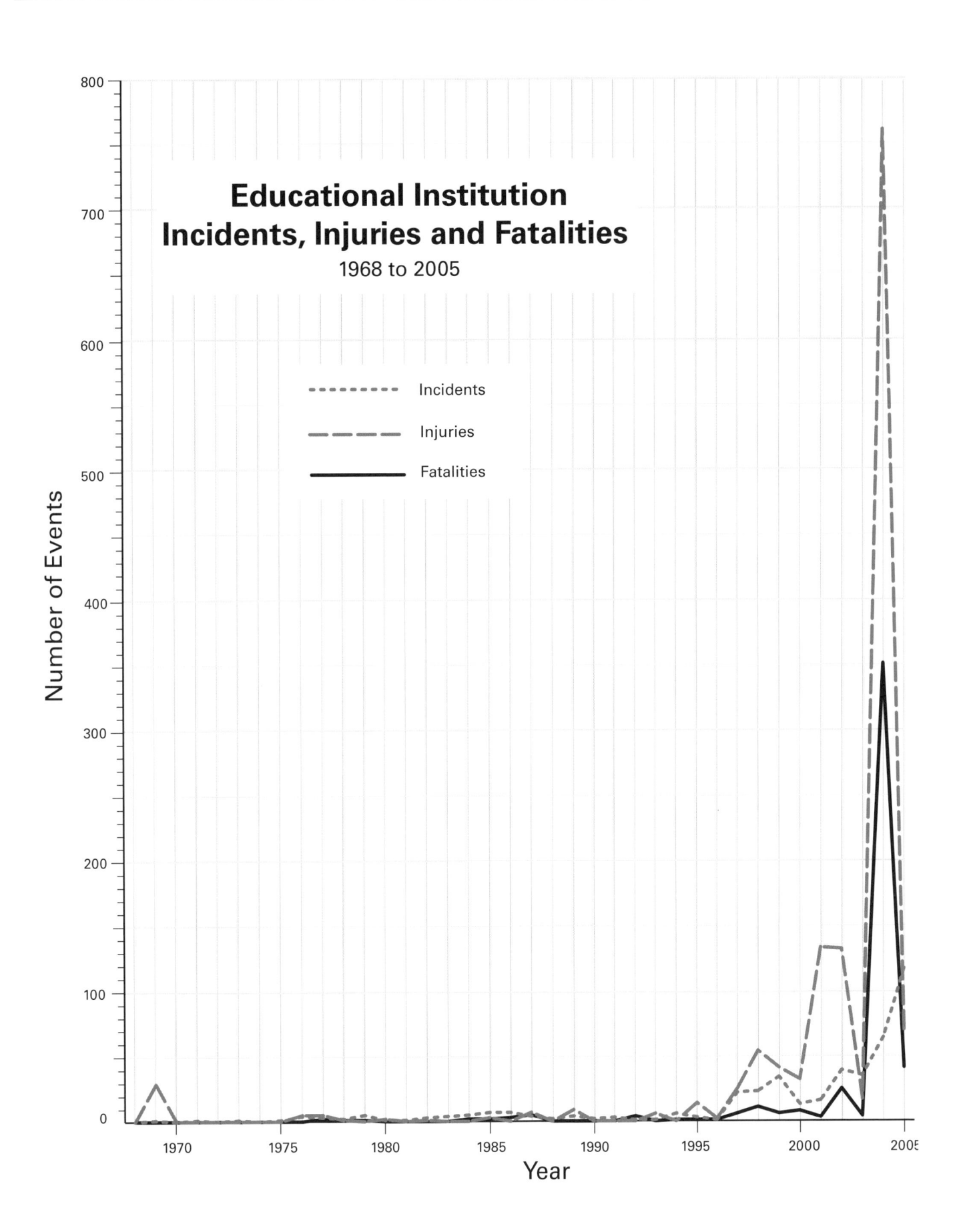

Educational Institution Incidents, Injuries and Fatalities
1968 to 2005

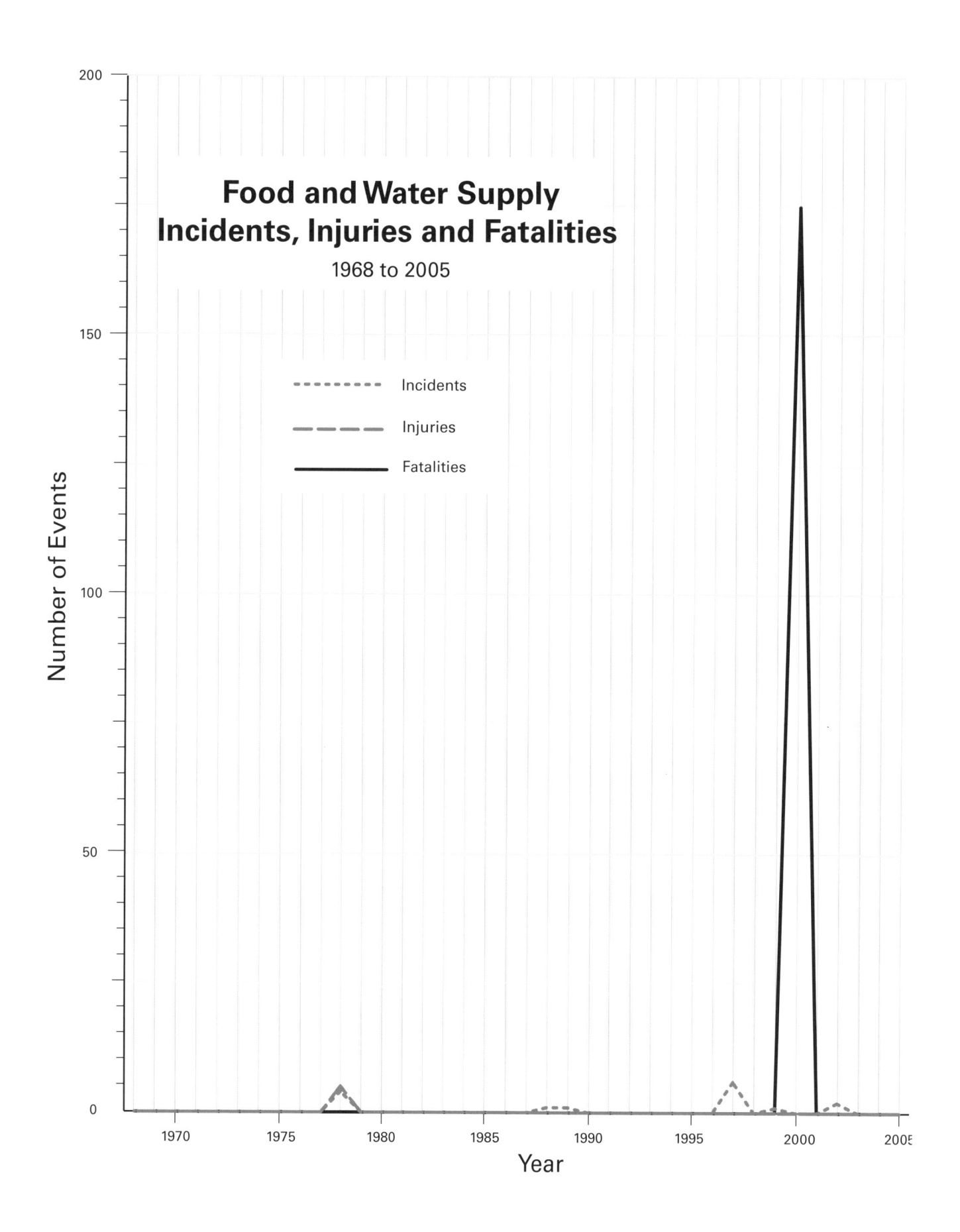

Food and Water Supply Incidents, Injuries and Fatalities
1968 to 2005

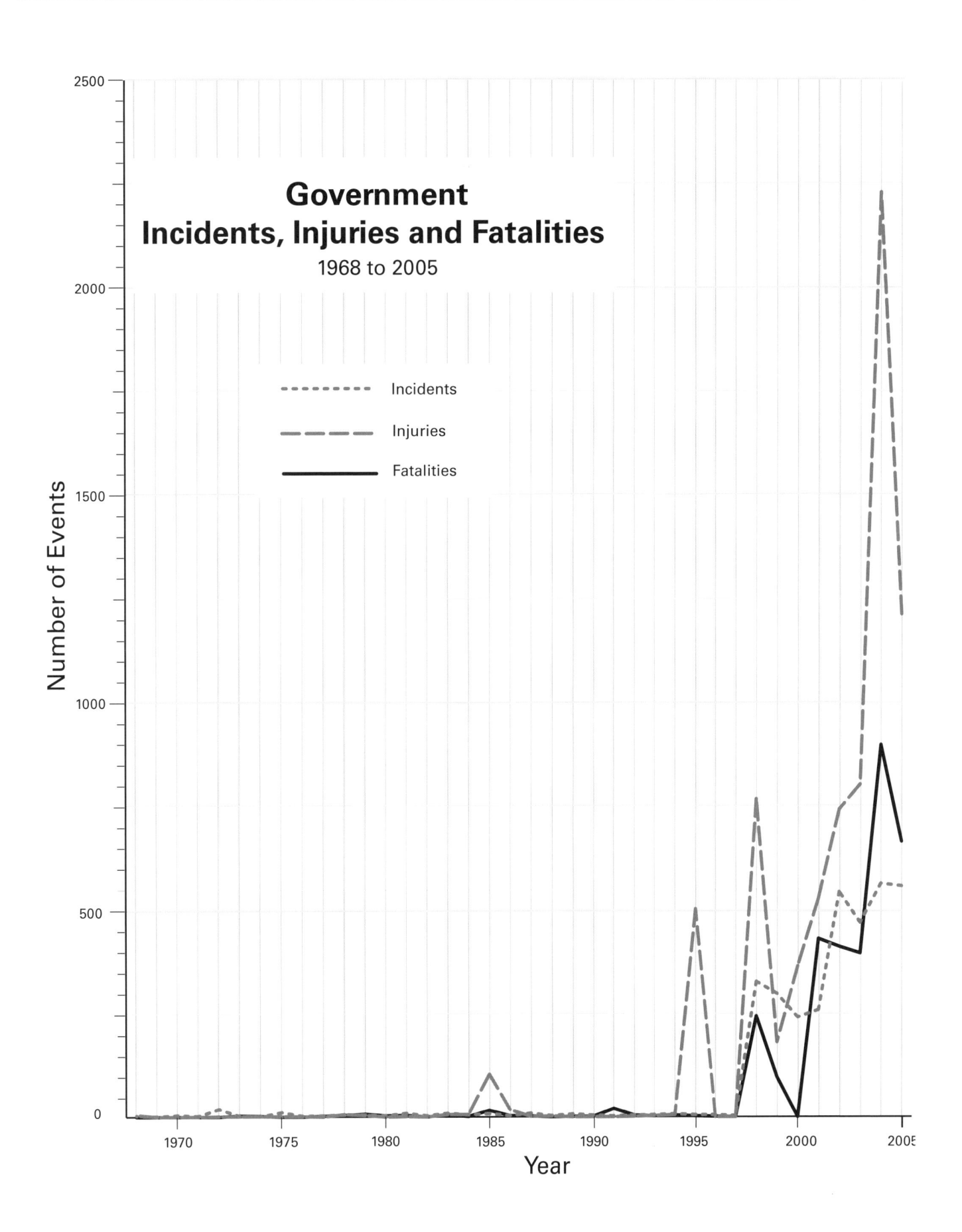

Government
Incidents, Injuries and Fatalities
1968 to 2005

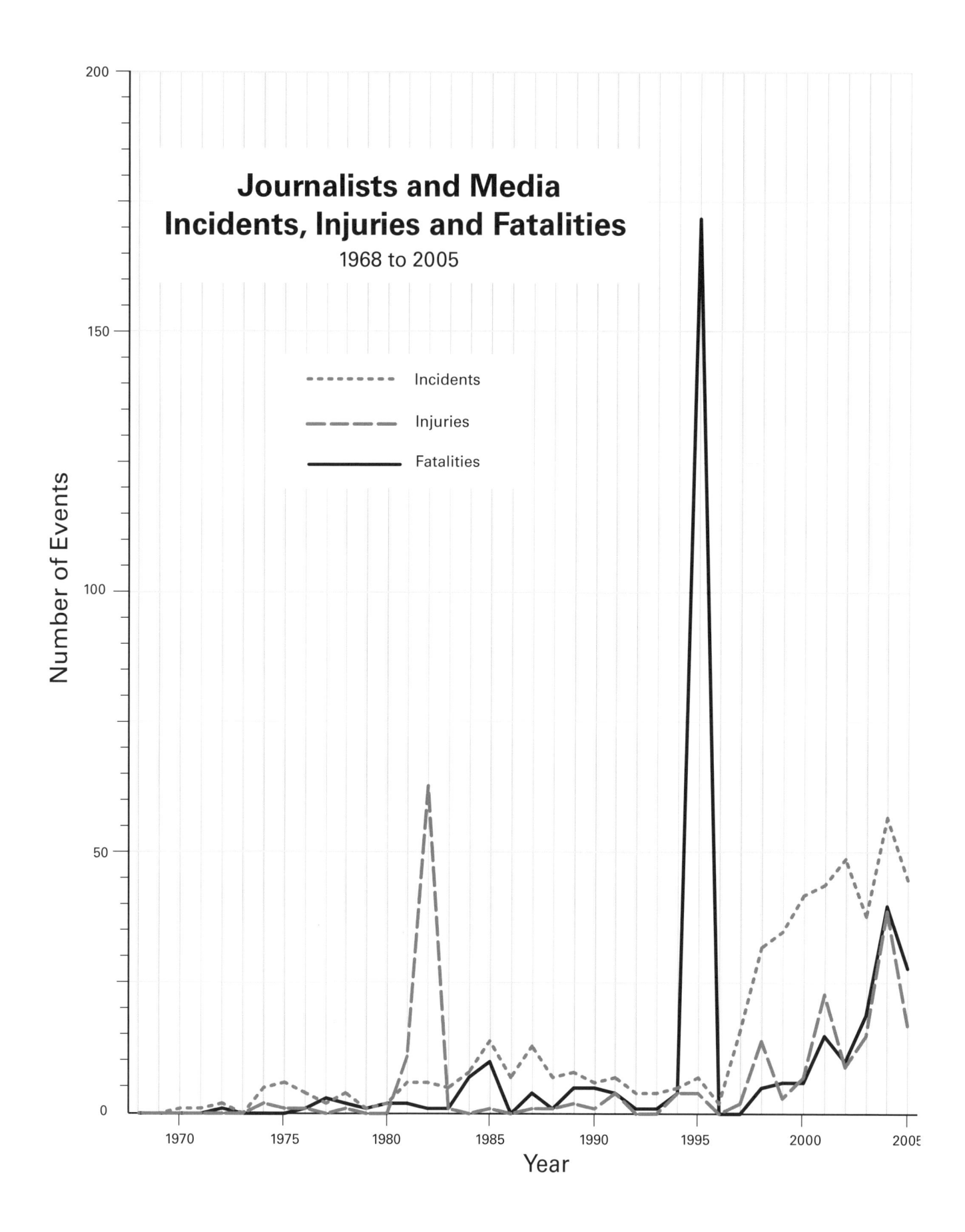

Journalists and Media Incidents, Injuries and Fatalities
1968 to 2005

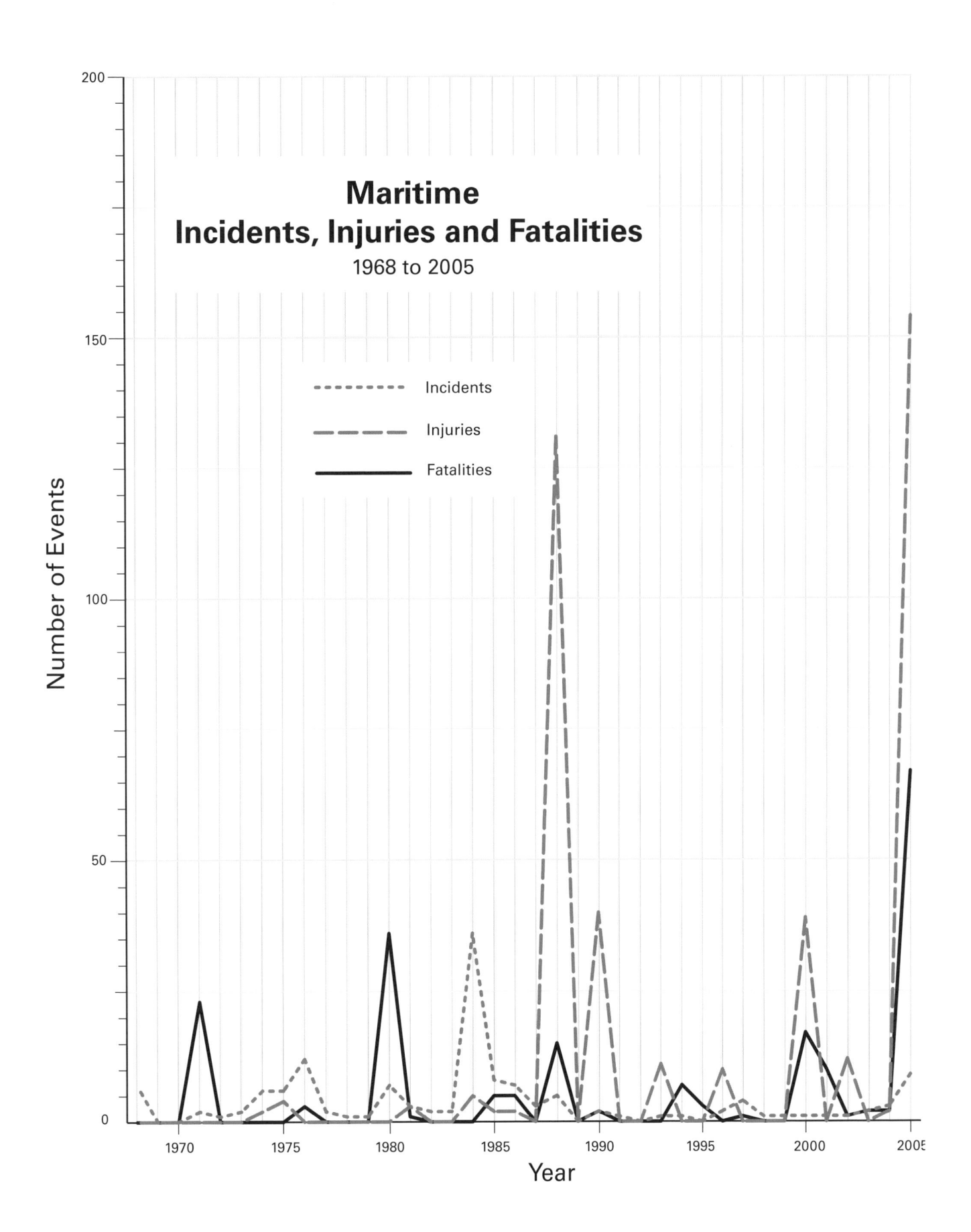

Maritime
Incidents, Injuries and Fatalities
1968 to 2005

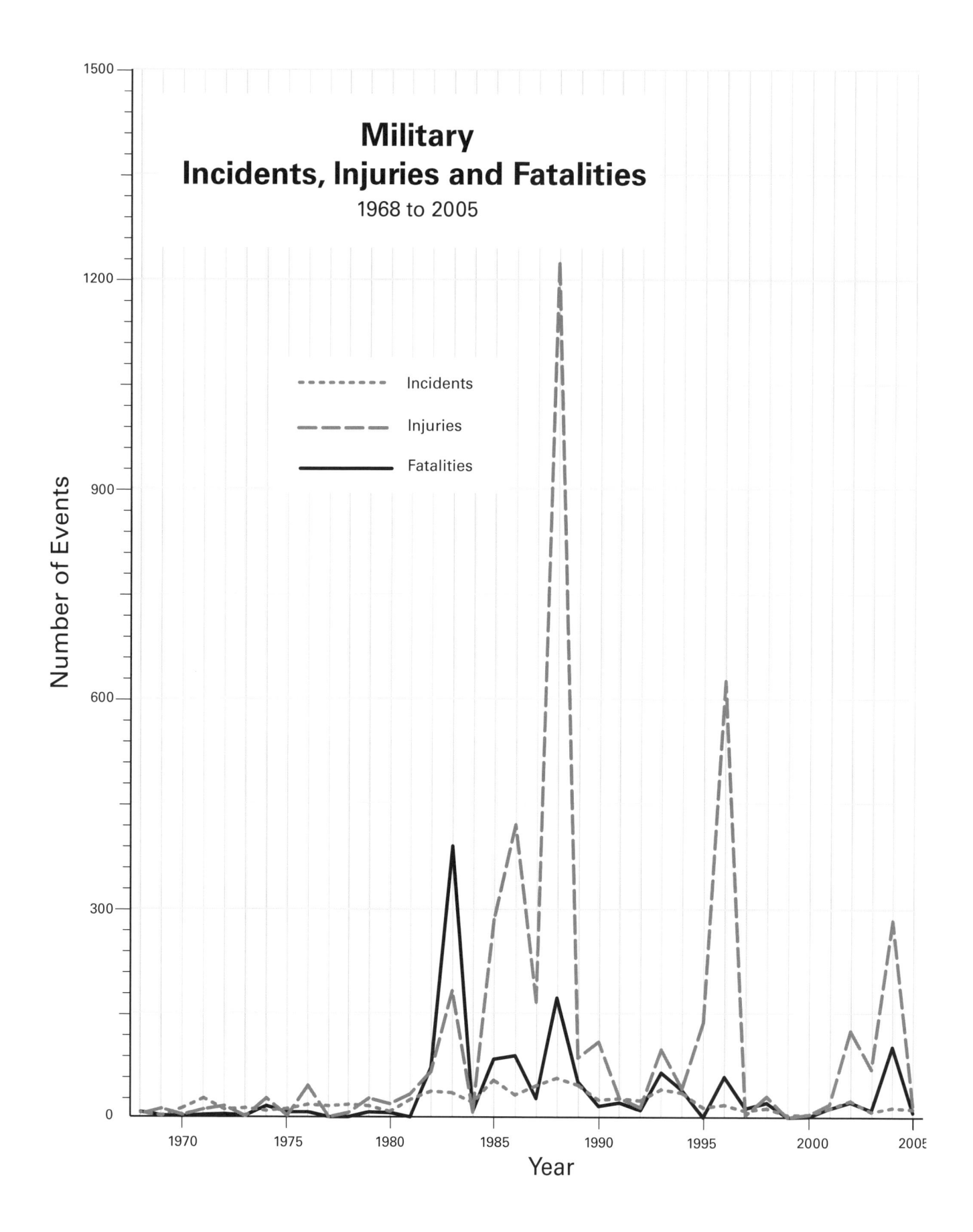

Military
Incidents, Injuries and Fatalities
1968 to 2005

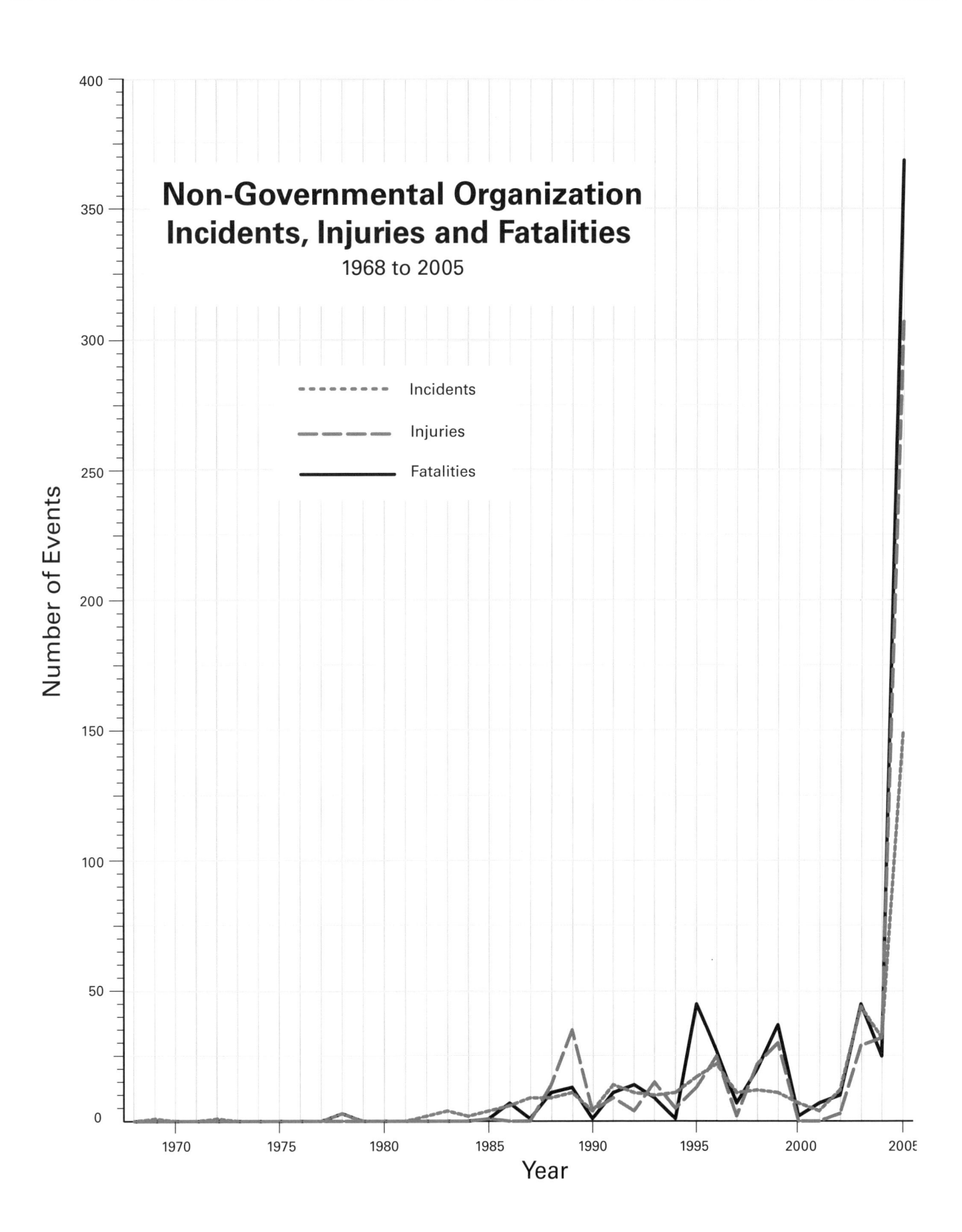

Non-Governmental Organization Incidents, Injuries and Fatalities
1968 to 2005

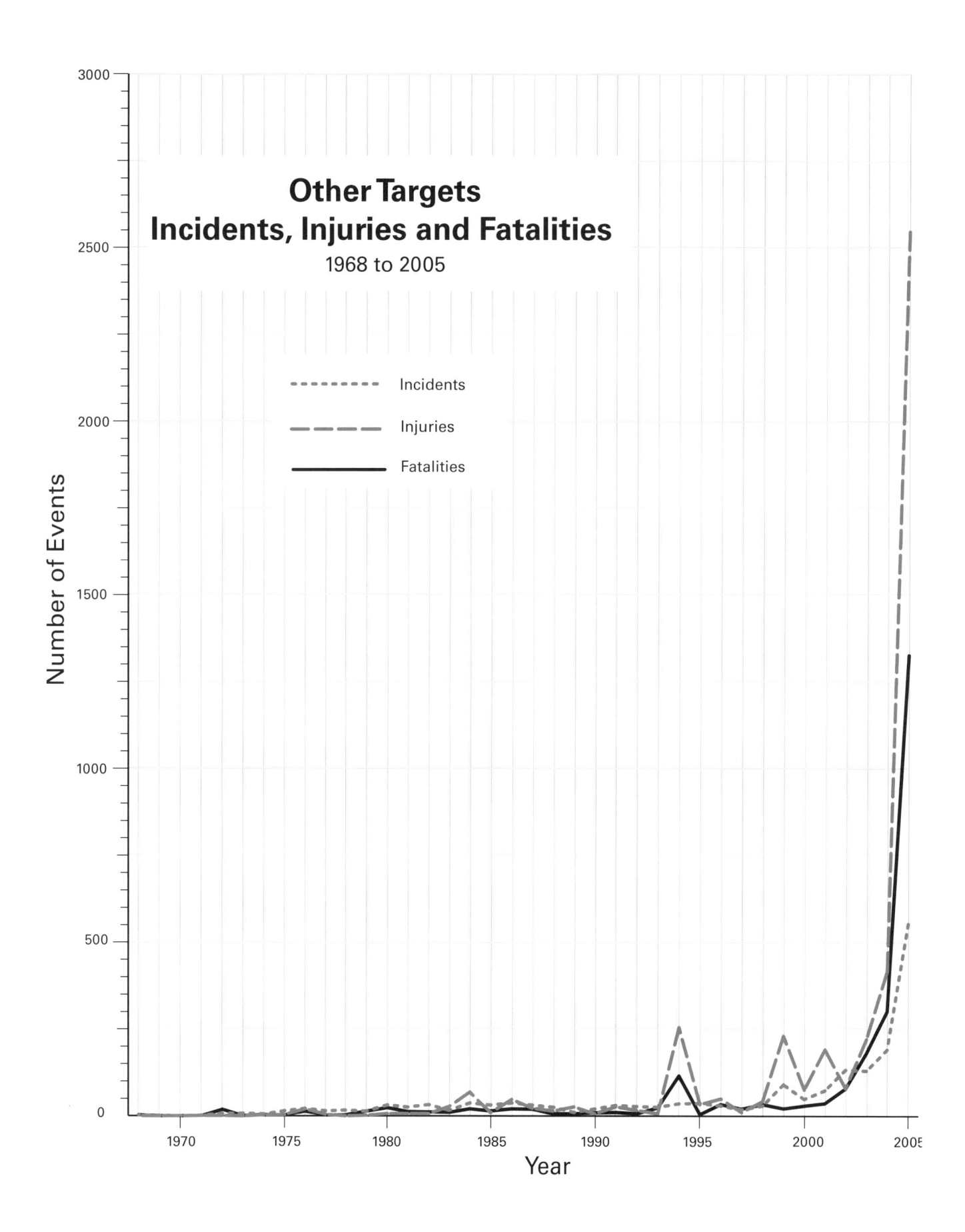

Other Targets
Incidents, Injuries and Fatalities
1968 to 2005

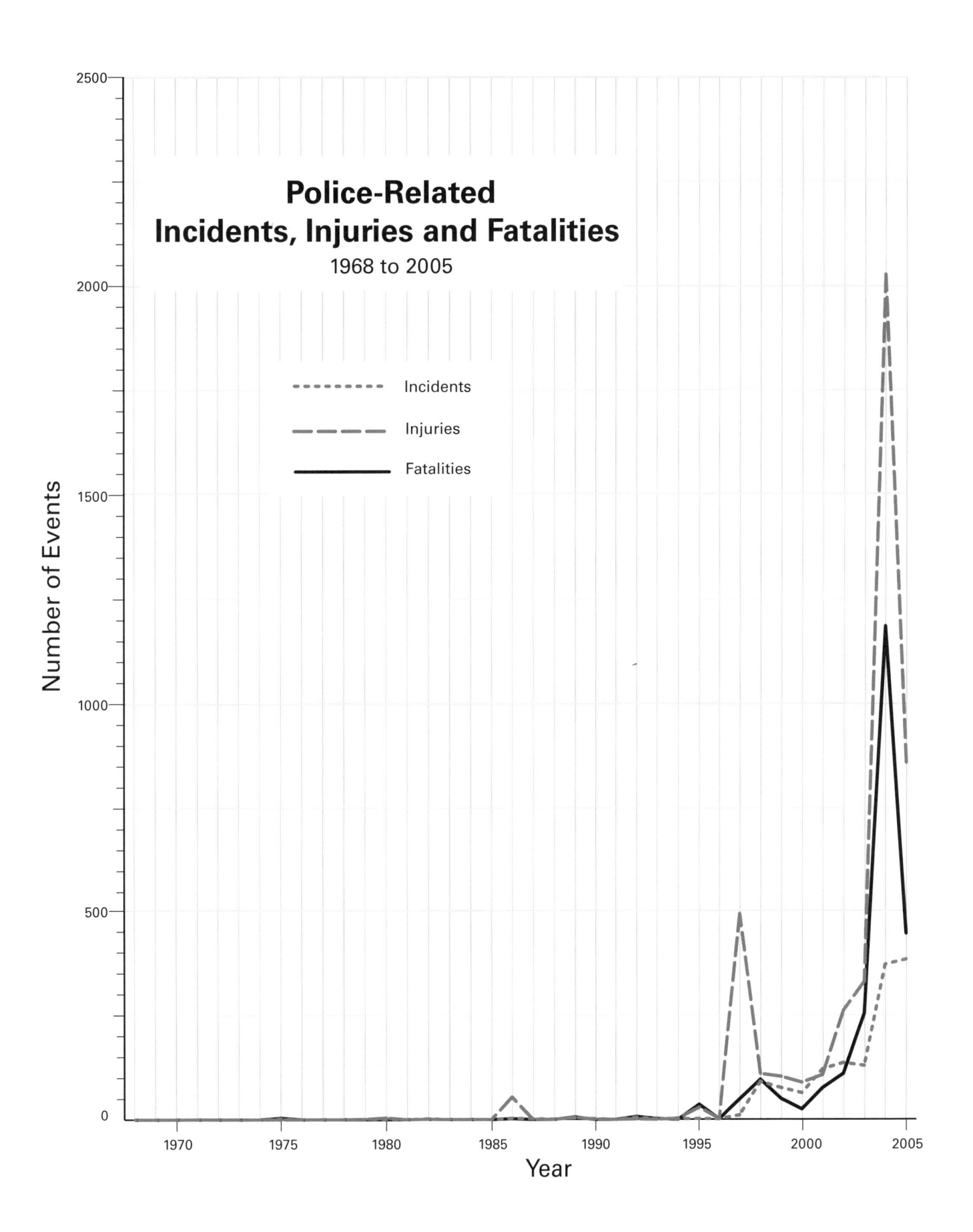

Police-Related Incidents, Injuries and Fatalities
1968 to 2005

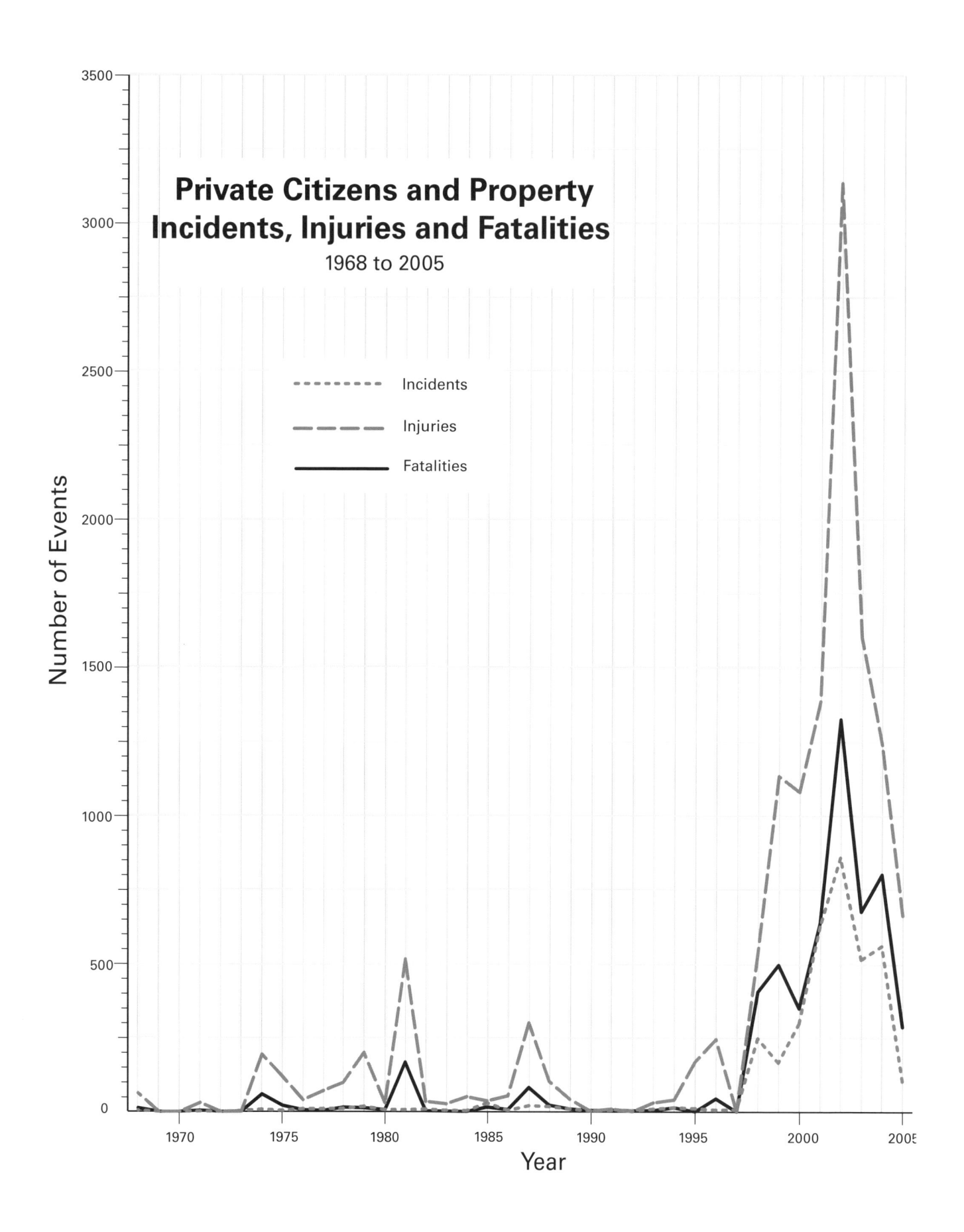

Private Citizens and Property Incidents, Injuries and Fatalities
1968 to 2005

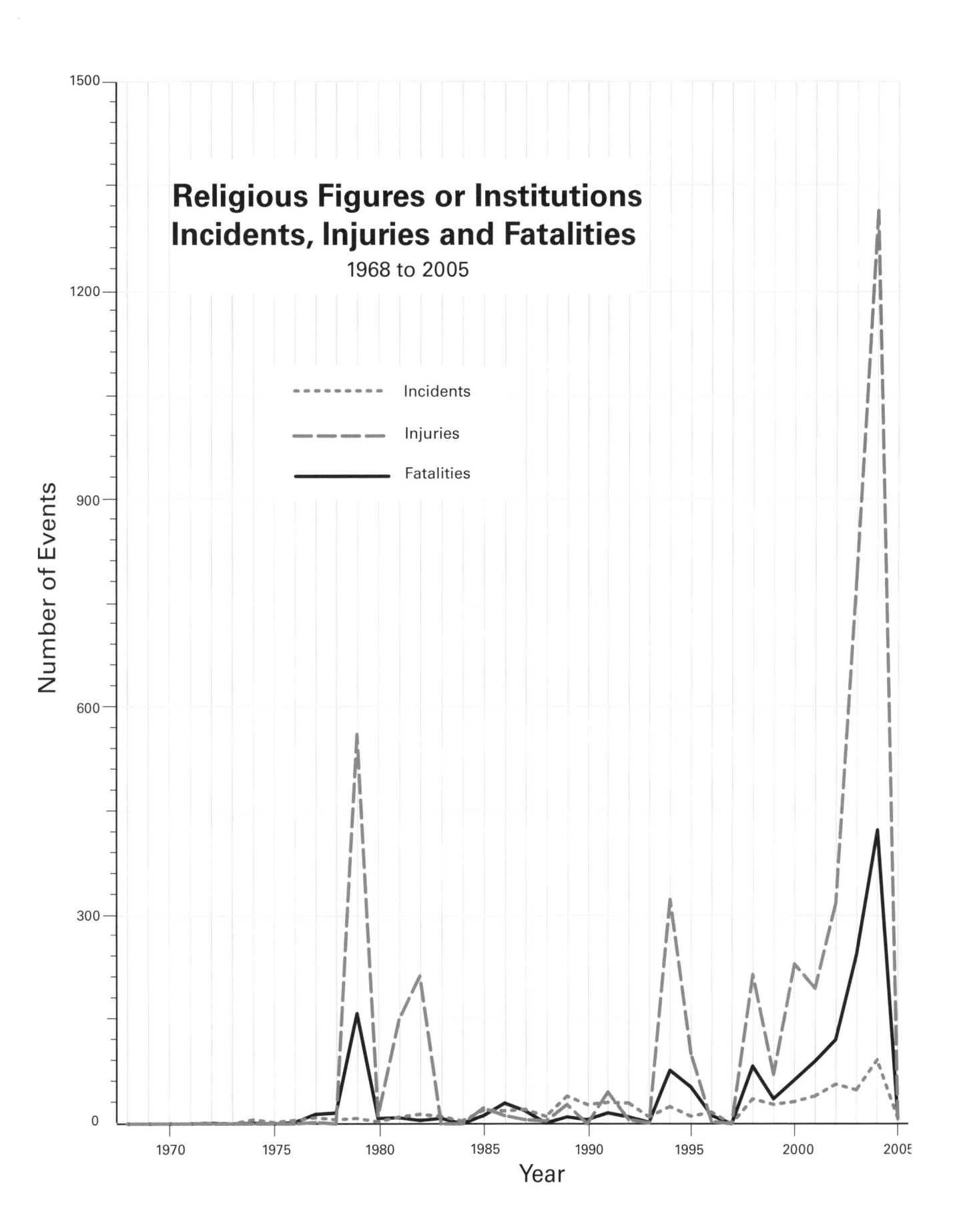

Religious Figures or Institutions
Incidents, Injuries and Fatalities
1968 to 2005

- - - - - - - Incidents
- - - - - Injuries
——— Fatalities

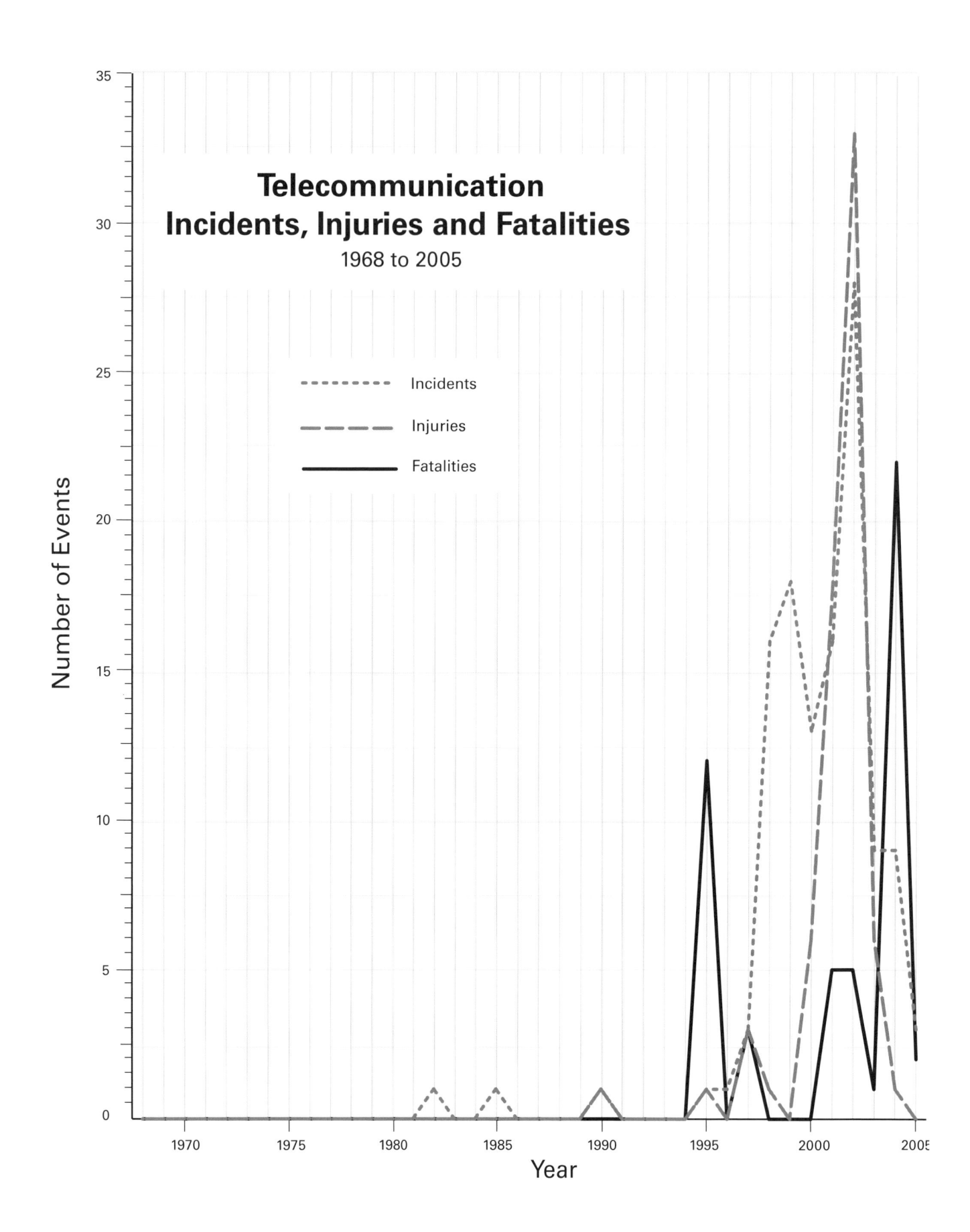

Telecommunication Incidents, Injuries and Fatalities
1968 to 2005

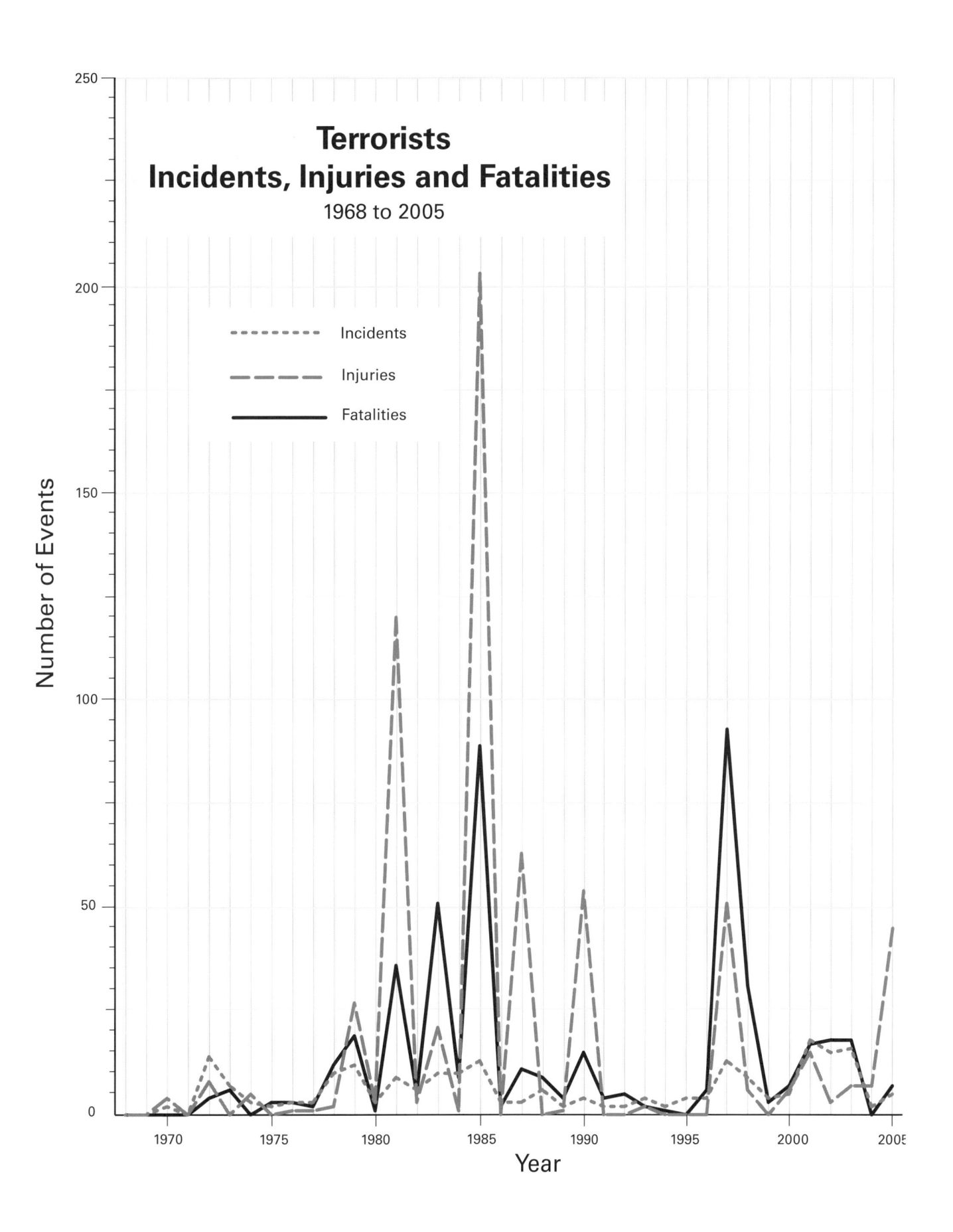

Terrorists
Incidents, Injuries and Fatalities
1968 to 2005

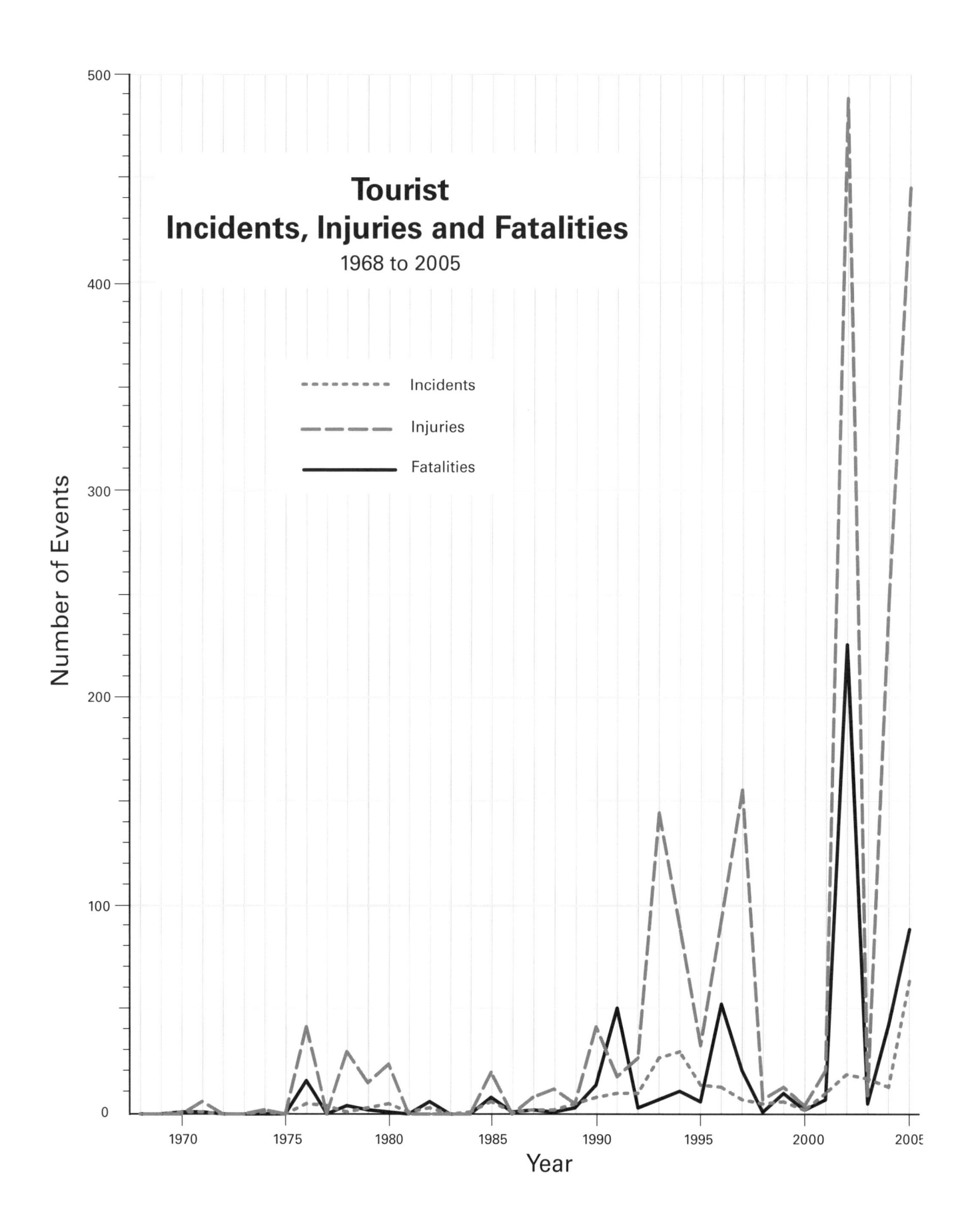

Tourist Incidents, Injuries and Fatalities
1968 to 2005

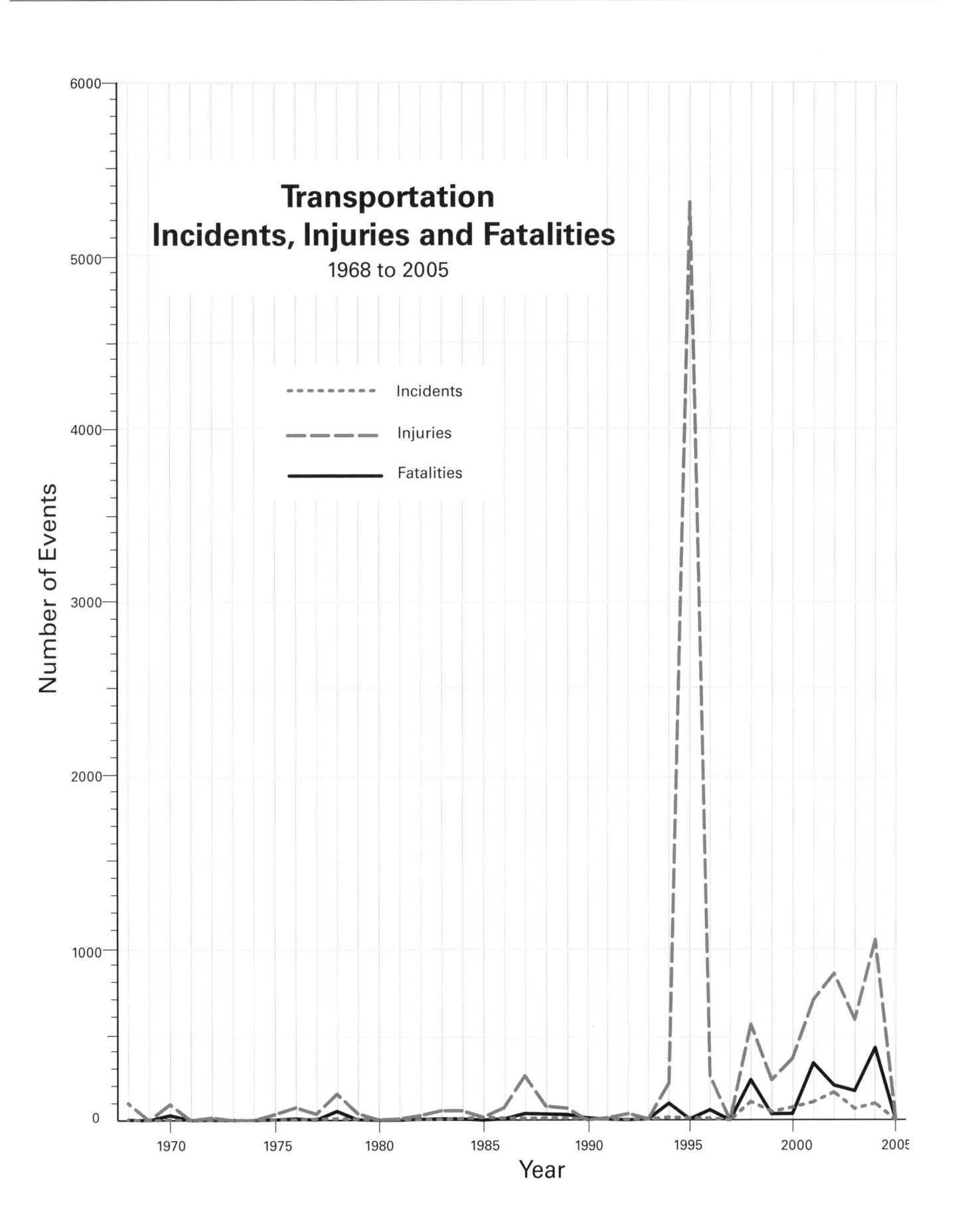

Transportation
Incidents, Injuries and Fatalities
1968 to 2005

- - - - - - Incidents
— — — Injuries
——— Fatalities

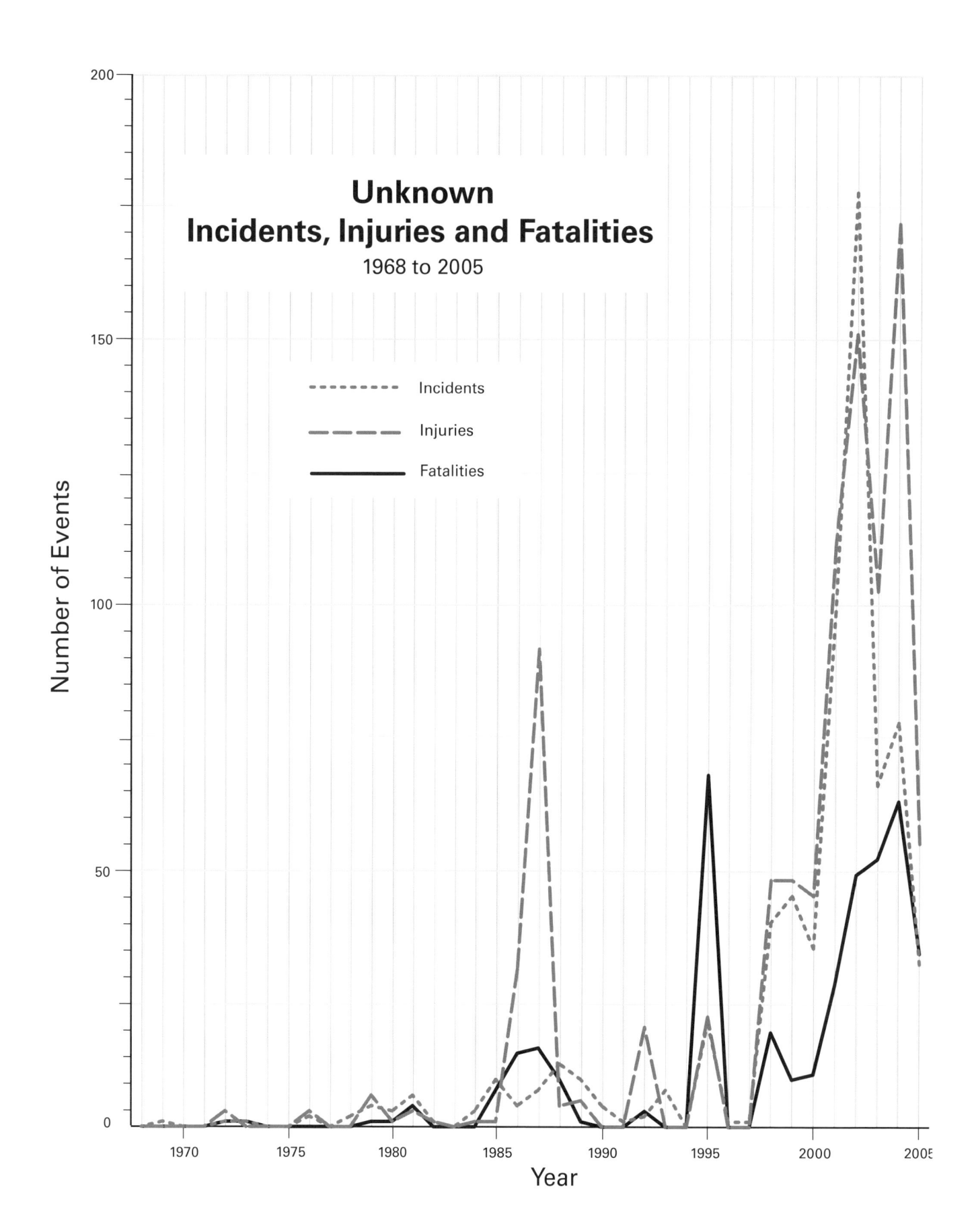

1006 Patterns of Global Terrorism

**Unknown
Incidents, Injuries and Fatalities**
1968 to 2005

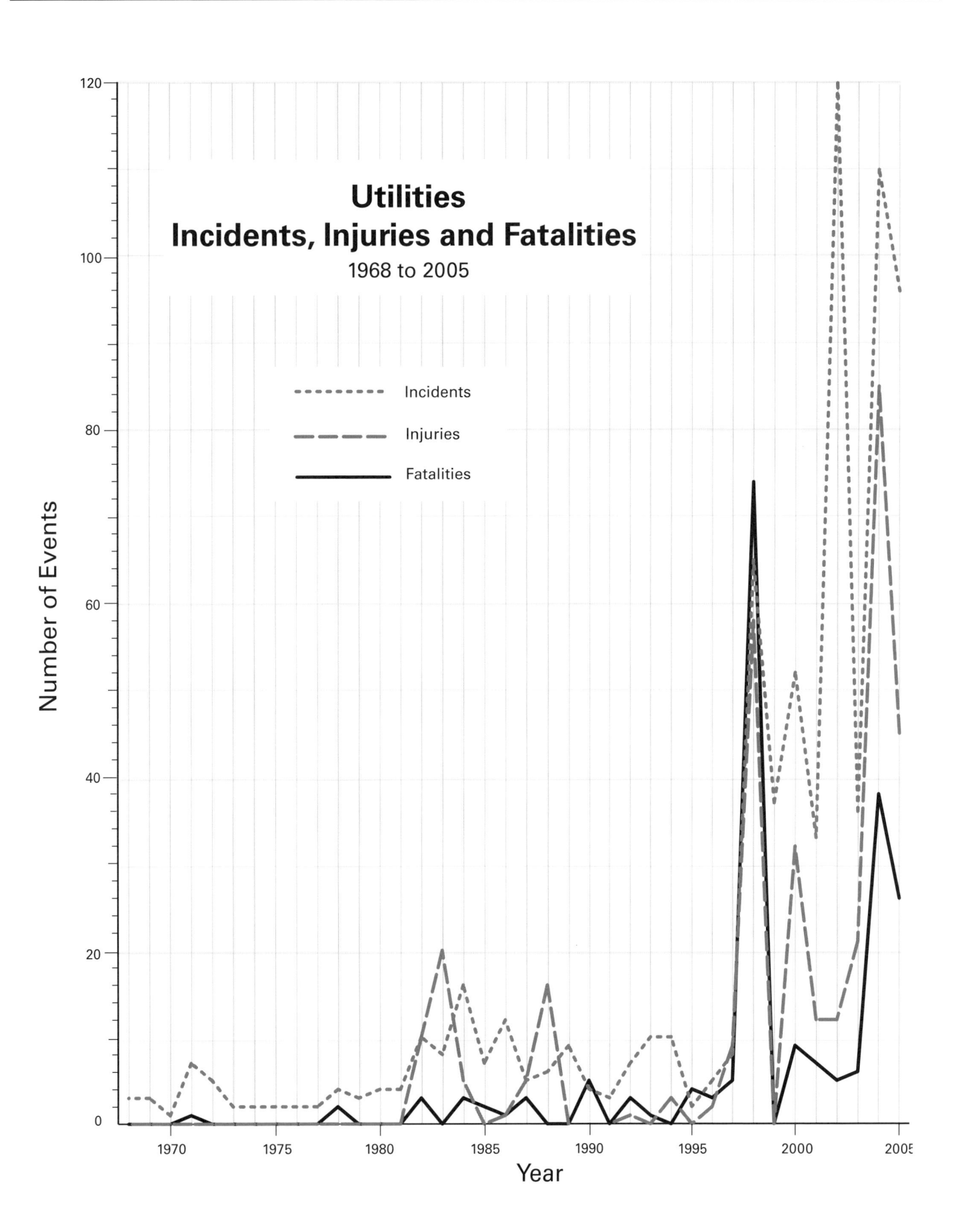

Utilities
Incidents, Injuries and Fatalities
1968 to 2005

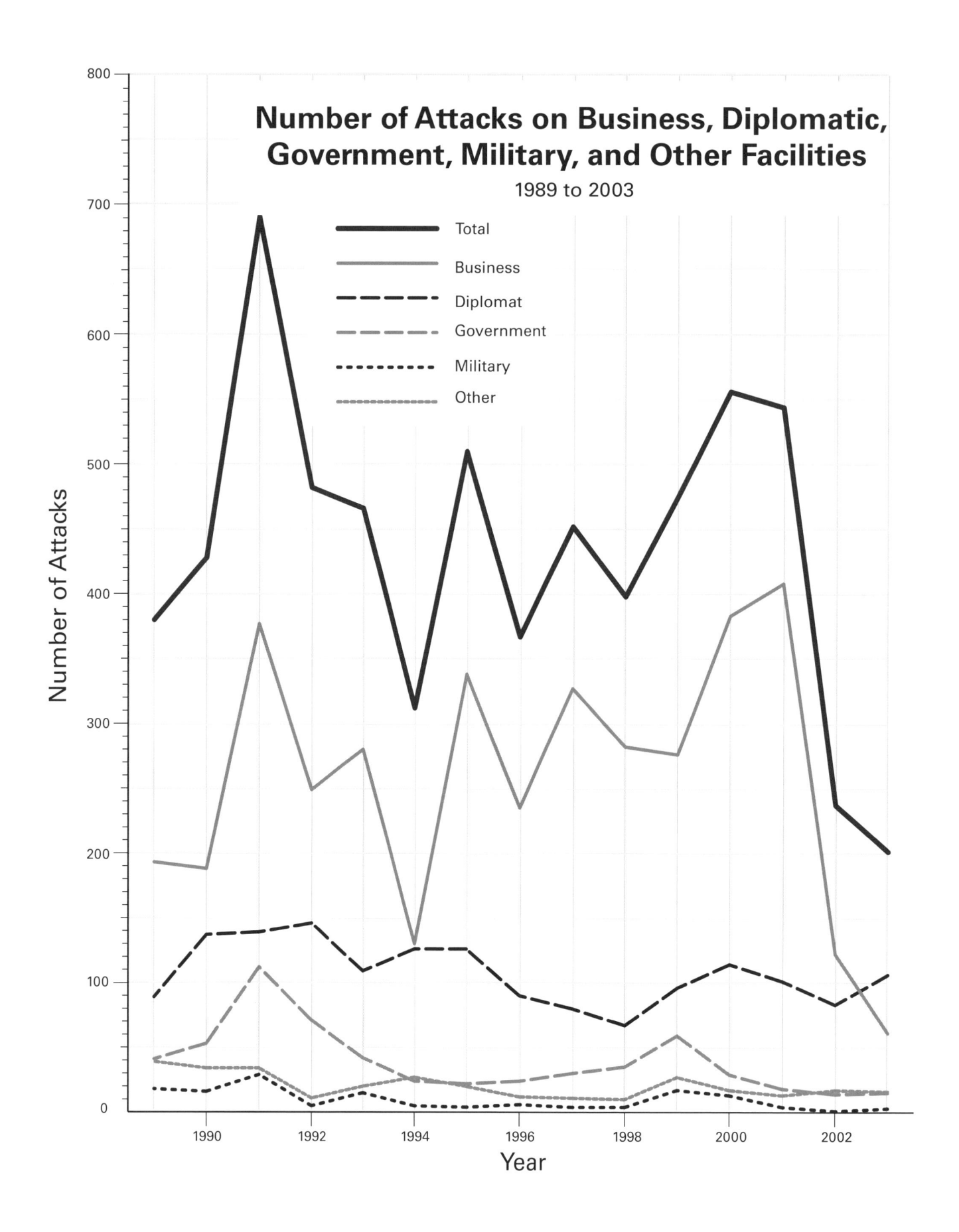

Number of Attacks on Business, Diplomatic, Government, Military, and Other Facilities
1989 to 2003

Tactics

Overview of Tactics

Anna Sabasteanski

This set of graphs illustrates incidents, injuries and fatalities for the following tactics, for the years 1968-2004, plus data for January–July 2005: Armed attacks; Arson; Assassination; Barricade/Hostage; Bombing; Hijacking; Kidnapping; Other; Unconventional; and Unknown.

In the 1970s and 1980s, publicity generated by high-profile hijackings, often carried out by Palestinian groups, pushed this tactic to the forefront. Between 1968–2004 there were 233 hijackings, associated with 858 casualties. High levels of casualties were associated with only four incidents: A Malaysian jet in 1977; attacks by Abu Nidal and Hizballah in 1986, and an Ethiopian airline in 1996.

At this time, there were low levels of bomb attacks, but their number increased in the mid-1980s and grew rapidly from the mid-1990s, to become the preferred tactic and the leading source of death and injury. In the 27 years from 1968–1994, there were 4,503 incidents causing 15,031 injuries and 4,434 deaths (an average of 166 incidents per year, annually causing about 721 casualties). In the ten years from 1995 to 2004, there were 7,603 incidents (an average of 760 per year—more than two a day) causing 40,356 injuries and killing 9,087 (an average of nearly 5,000 casualties per year). Between January and August of 2005, there have been 1,622 attacks causing 7,570 injuries and killing 2,577. This dramatic increase in the level of violence is unprecedented.

Armed attacks are the second most lethal terrorist tactic. Between 1968 and 1994 1,021 incidents resulted in 2,692 casualties. In the following decade the numbers nearly doubled, with 2,110 armed attacks, causing 12,076 casualties. Armed attacks are not associated with mass casualties, with the dramatic exception of the 1995 Aum Shrinrikyo sarin nerve gas attack on the Tokyo subway system that killed 12 and injured 5,000.

Assassination comes third in the number of casualties it causes. From 1968 to 1994, 640 incidents resulted in 801 casualties. In the ten years from 1995 to 2004, 2,027 incidents caused 3,568 casualties. The peak year for assassinations was 2002, primarily involving South Asian government targets.

Until 2001 only one incident of barricade/hostage-taking —the siege of the Grand Mosque in Mecca—was associated

Tactics: 1 January 2005–31 August 2005

Tactic	Incidents	Injuries	Fatalities
Armed Attack	819	879	1345
Arson	75	15	6
Assassination	71	17	75
Barricade/Hostage	4	8	56
Bombing	1622	7570	2577
Kidnapping	150	15	171
Other	28	31	24
Unknown	46	6	66
Total	2815	8541	4320

with major casualties.. Since 2001 there have been numerous incidents, of which the most serious were two in Russia: the 2002 sieges of the Moscow and the Beslan schools.

Casualties associated with kidnapping remained low until 2002 when they began to spiked due to incidents in Colombia and Kashmir. Between 1968 and 1994, 701 incidents resulted in 45 injuries and 149 fatalities. From 1995 to 2004, the number of incidents rose to 851, involving 54 injuries and 476 fatalities. Arson is associated with fewer than 100 incidents per year. Only the Lord's Resistance Army attack against refugees in 2004 resulted in mass casualties. Miscellaneous tactics include assaults, involvement of biological or chemical agents, crime, hoaxes, rioting, theft, and so forth. These are unusual and have produced few casualties, with the exception of 9/11 when airplanes were used as weapons.

The data for these graphs was retrieved from the National Counterterrorism Center's (NCTC) Worldwide Incidents Tracking System (WITS) and the MIPT Terrorism Knowledge Base that integrates data from the RAND Terrorism Chronology and RAND-MIPT Terrorism Incident databases. NCTC's methodology is described in full on the NCTC website, http://www.tkb.org/NCTCMethodology.jsp, which explains that most incidents can be coded with their taxonomy but "other kinds of attacks are more difficult to define. Incidents that involve multiple types of attack are especially problematic. Incidents involving mortars, rocket propelled grenades, and missiles generally fall under armed attack, although improvised explosive devices fall under bombing."

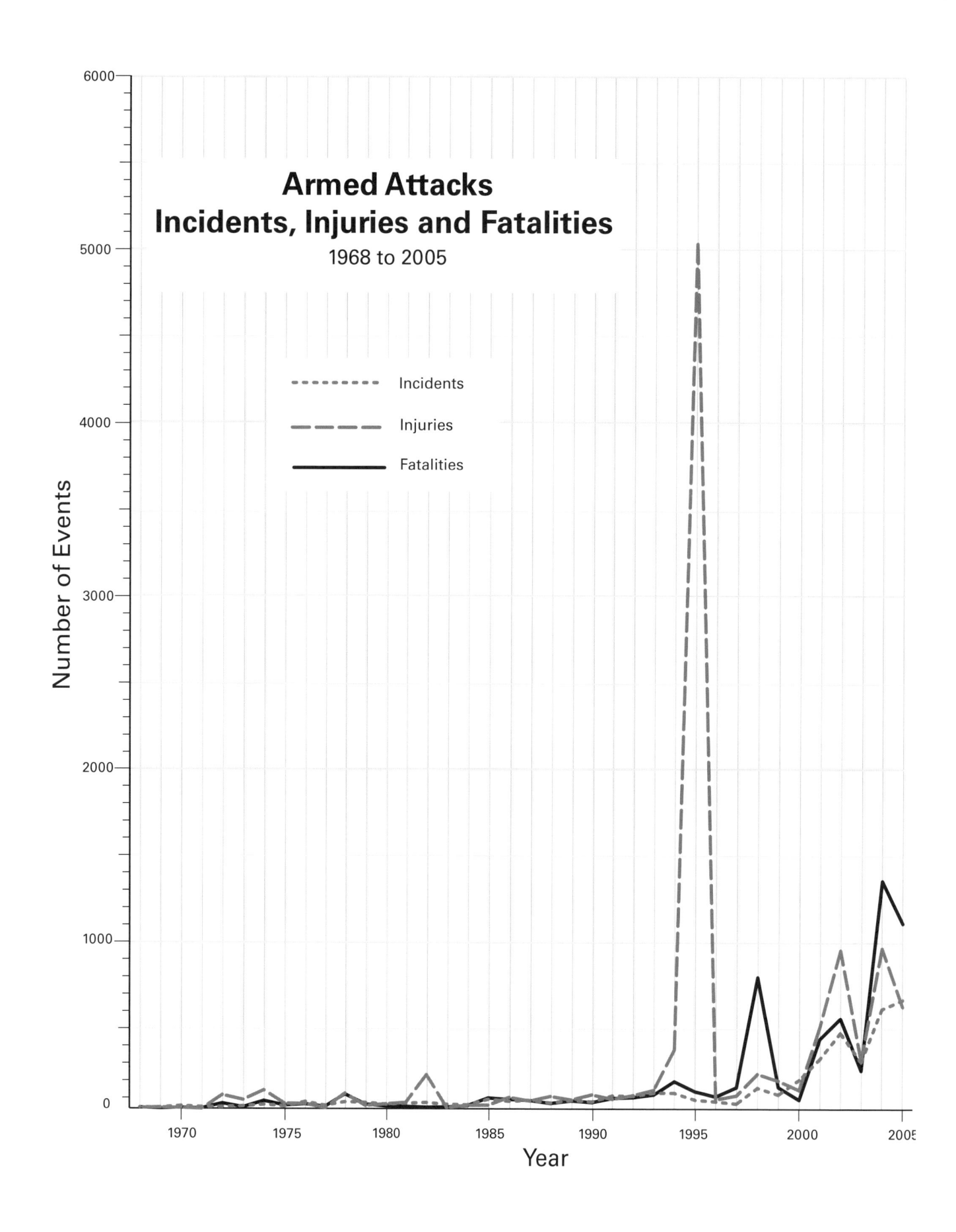

**Armed Attacks
Incidents, Injuries and Fatalities**
1968 to 2005

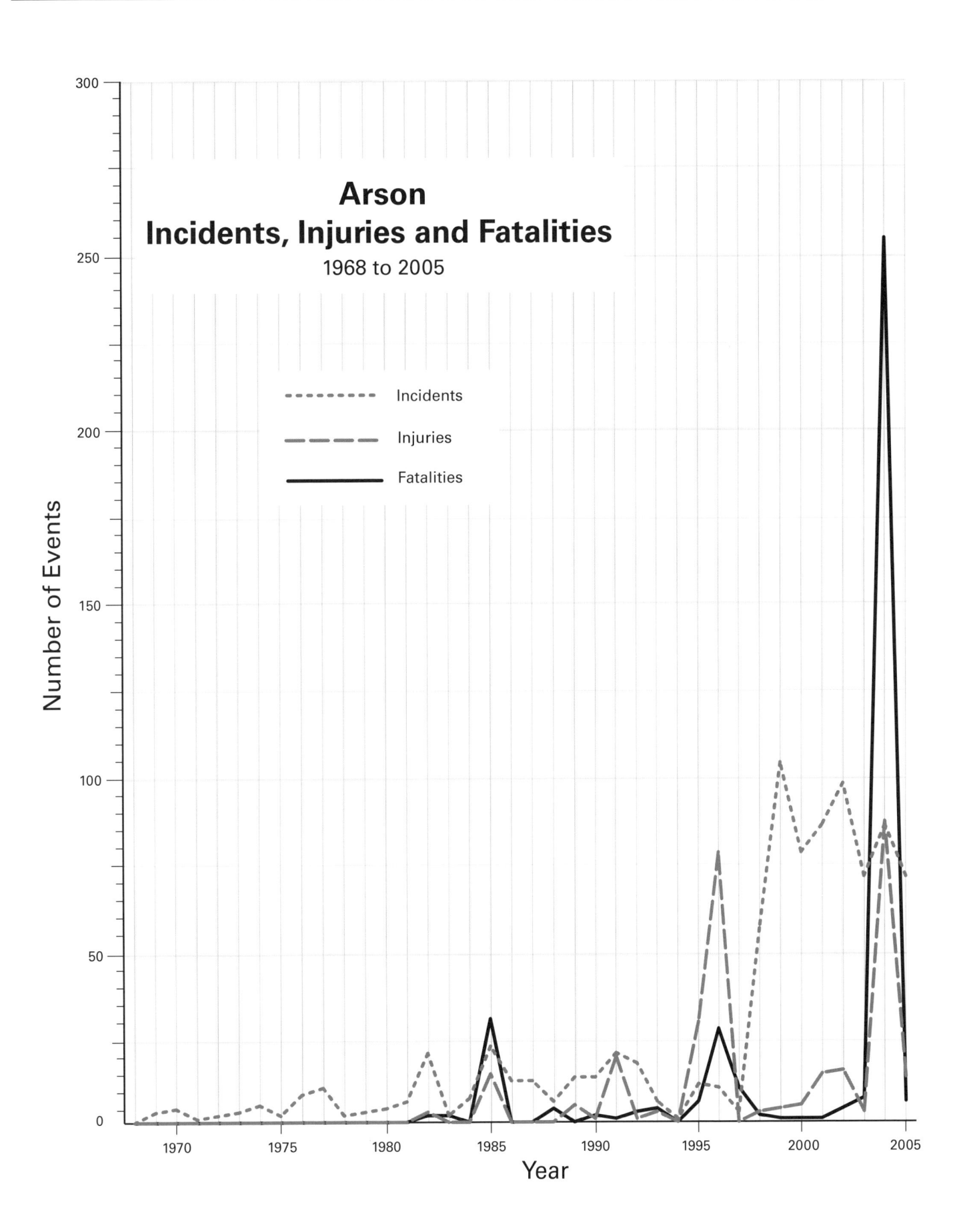

Arson
Incidents, Injuries and Fatalities
1968 to 2005

- .... Incidents
- – – – – Injuries
- ——— Fatalities

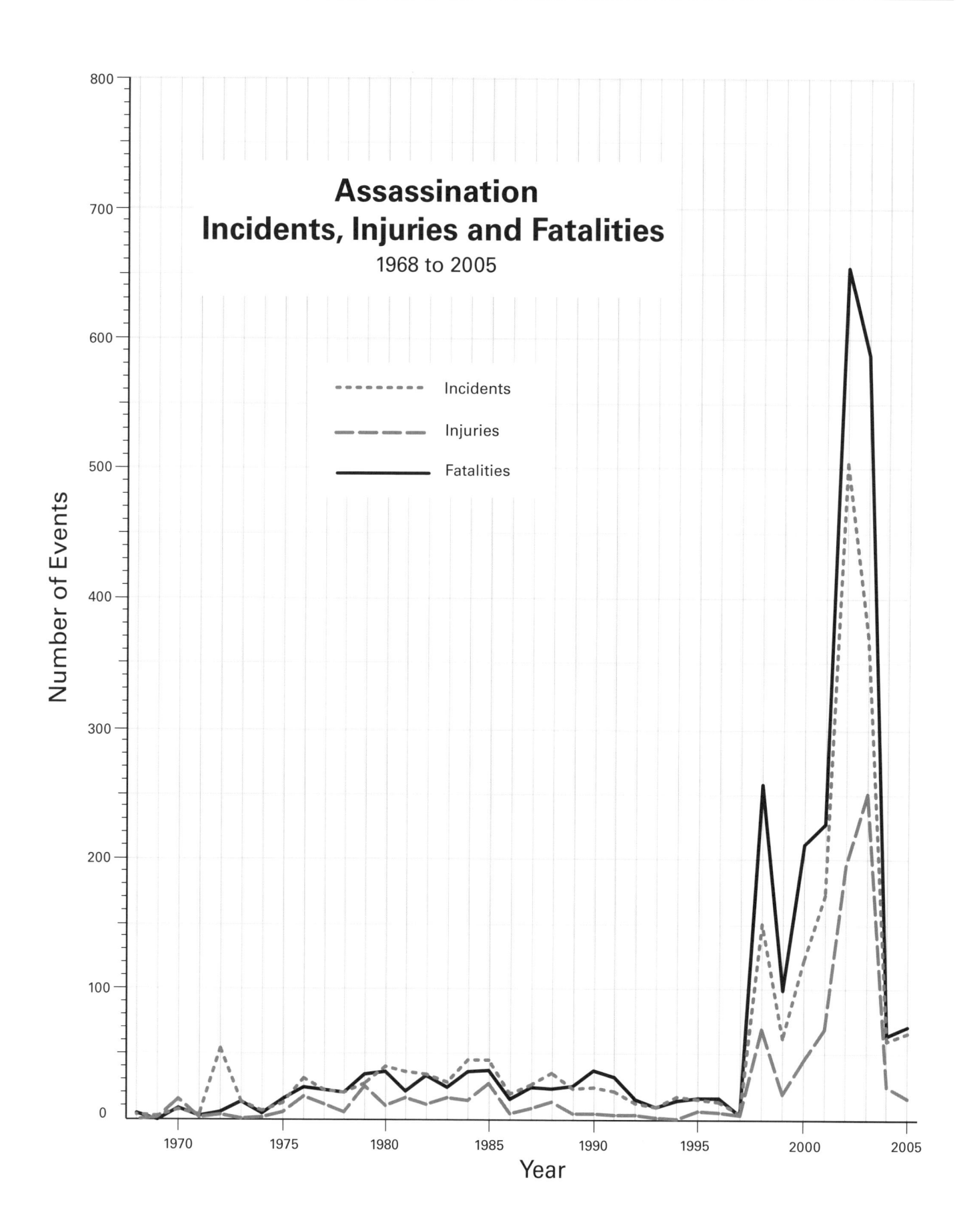

Assassination
Incidents, Injuries and Fatalities
1968 to 2005

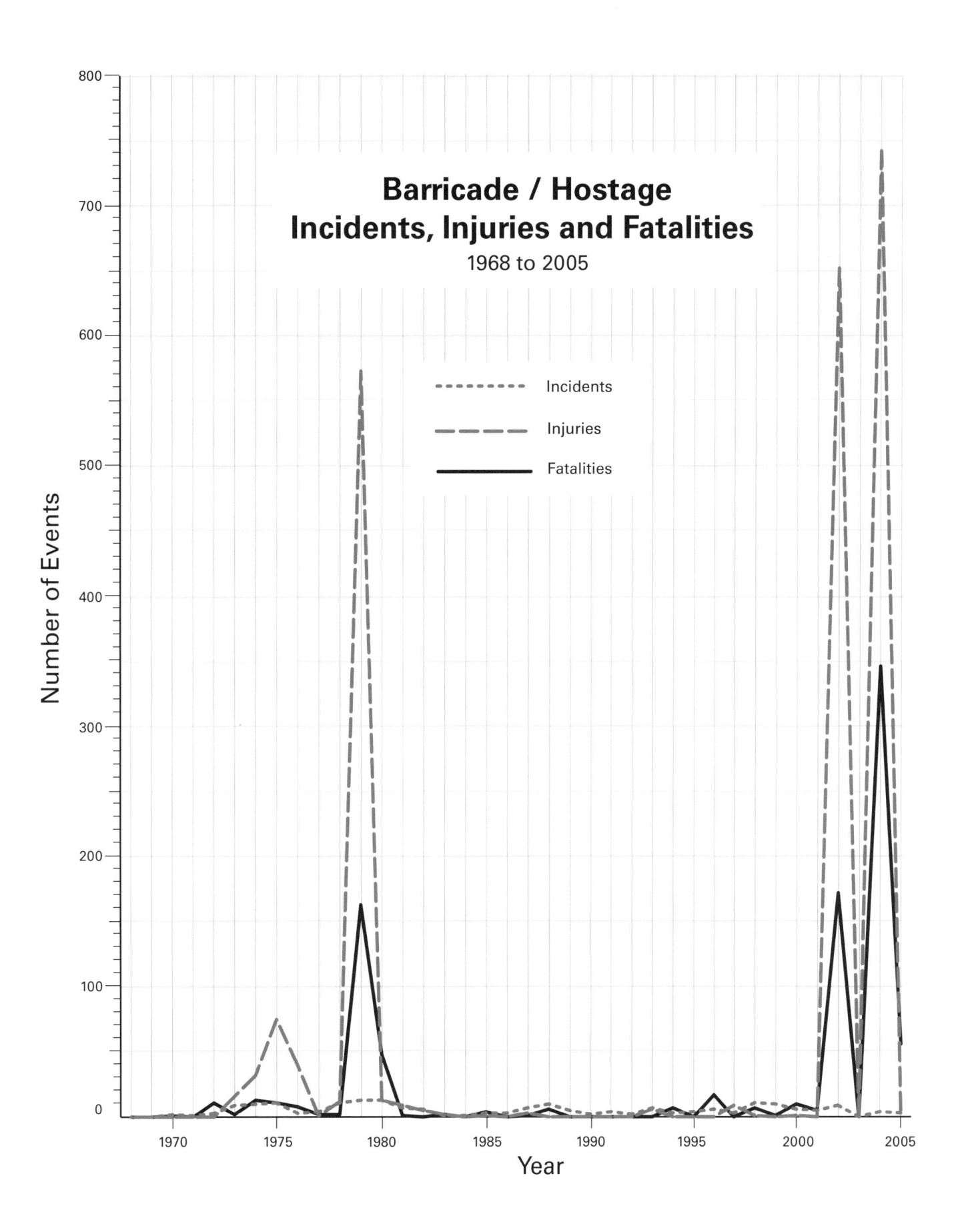

Barricade / Hostage Incidents, Injuries and Fatalities
1968 to 2005

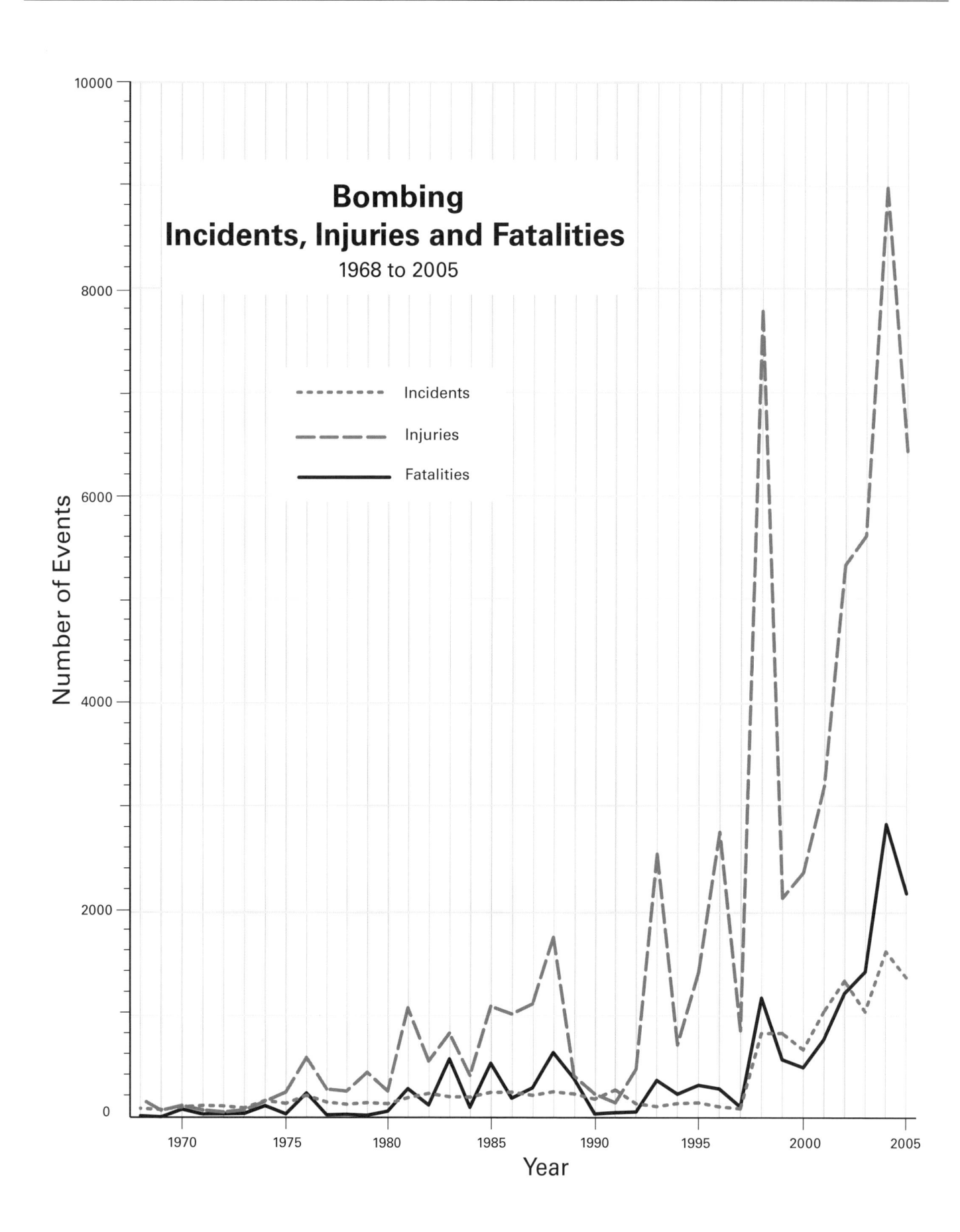

Bombing
Incidents, Injuries and Fatalities
1968 to 2005

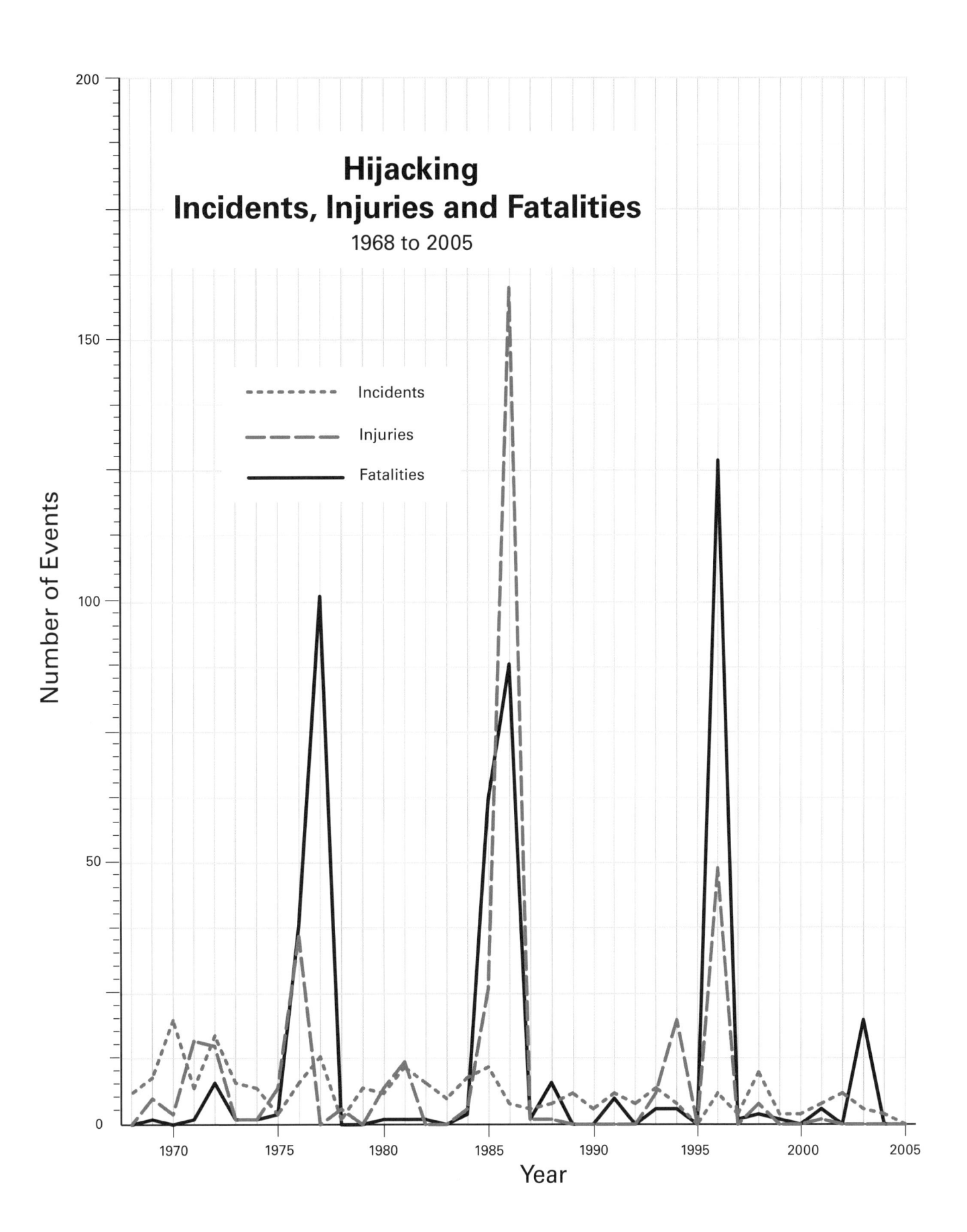

Hijacking
Incidents, Injuries and Fatalities
1968 to 2005

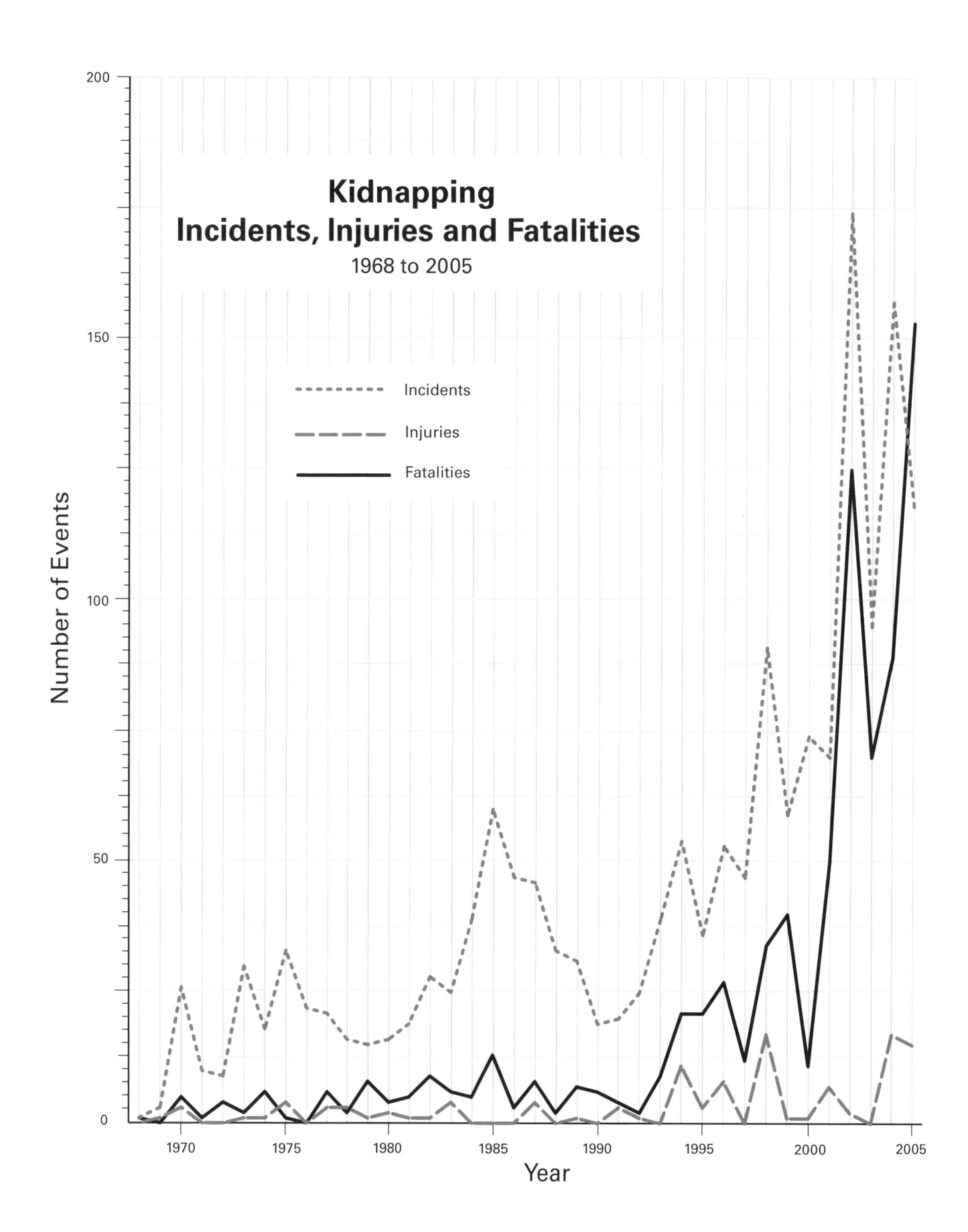

Kidnapping
Incidents, Injuries and Fatalities
1968 to 2005

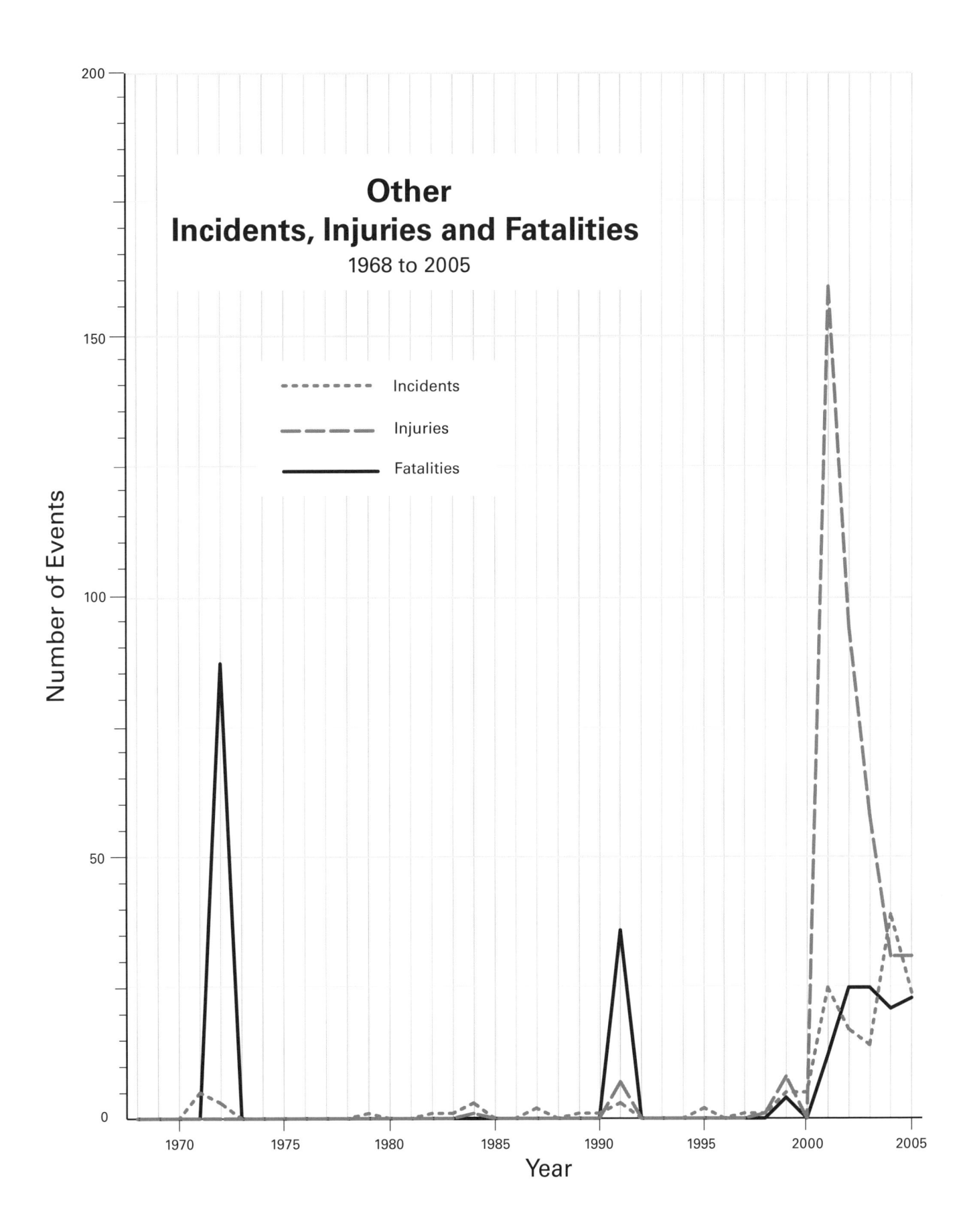

Other
Incidents, Injuries and Fatalities
1968 to 2005

- ·········· Incidents
- ─ ─ ─ ─ Injuries
- ───── Fatalities

Number of Events

Year

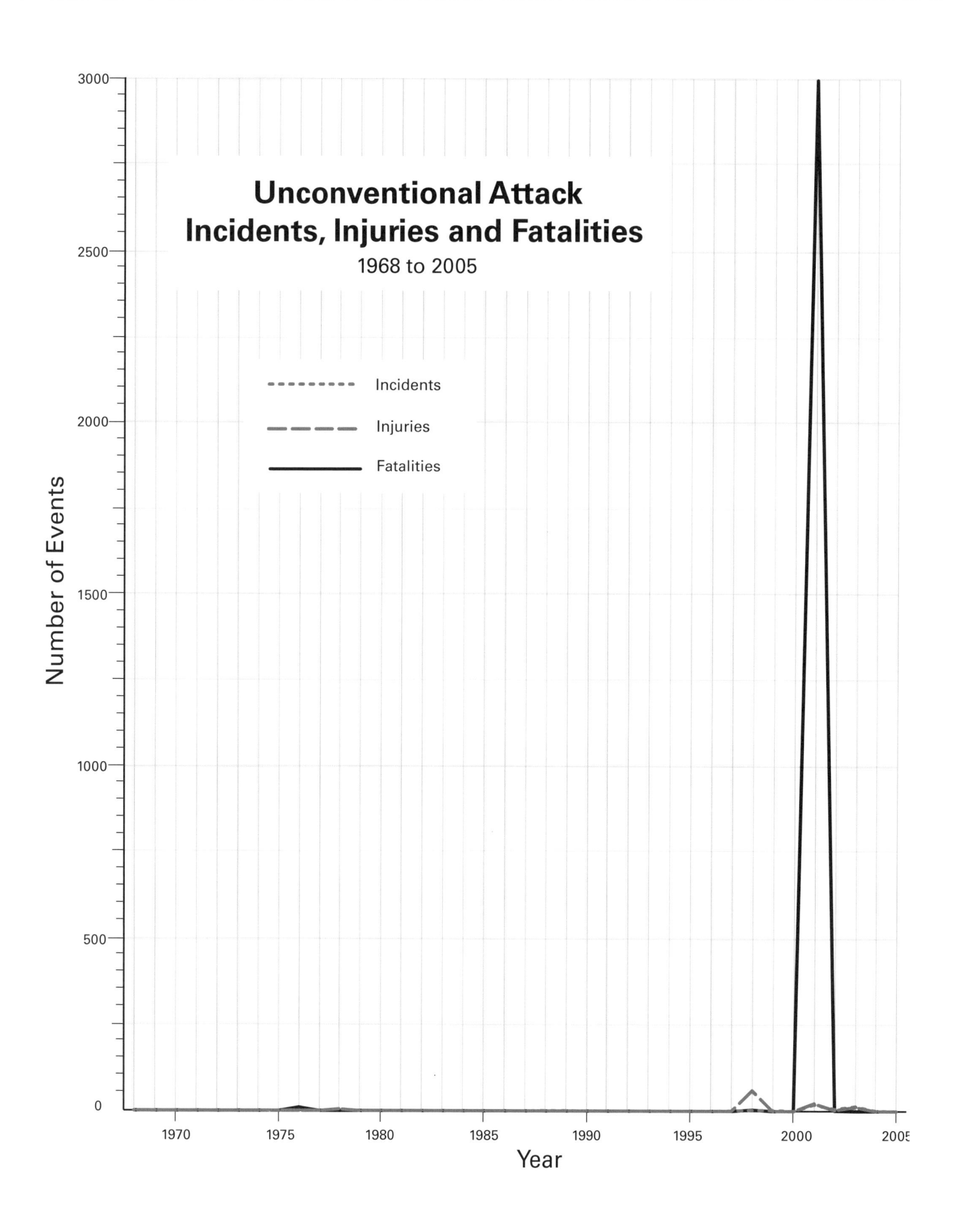

Unconventional Attack Incidents, Injuries and Fatalities
1968 to 2005

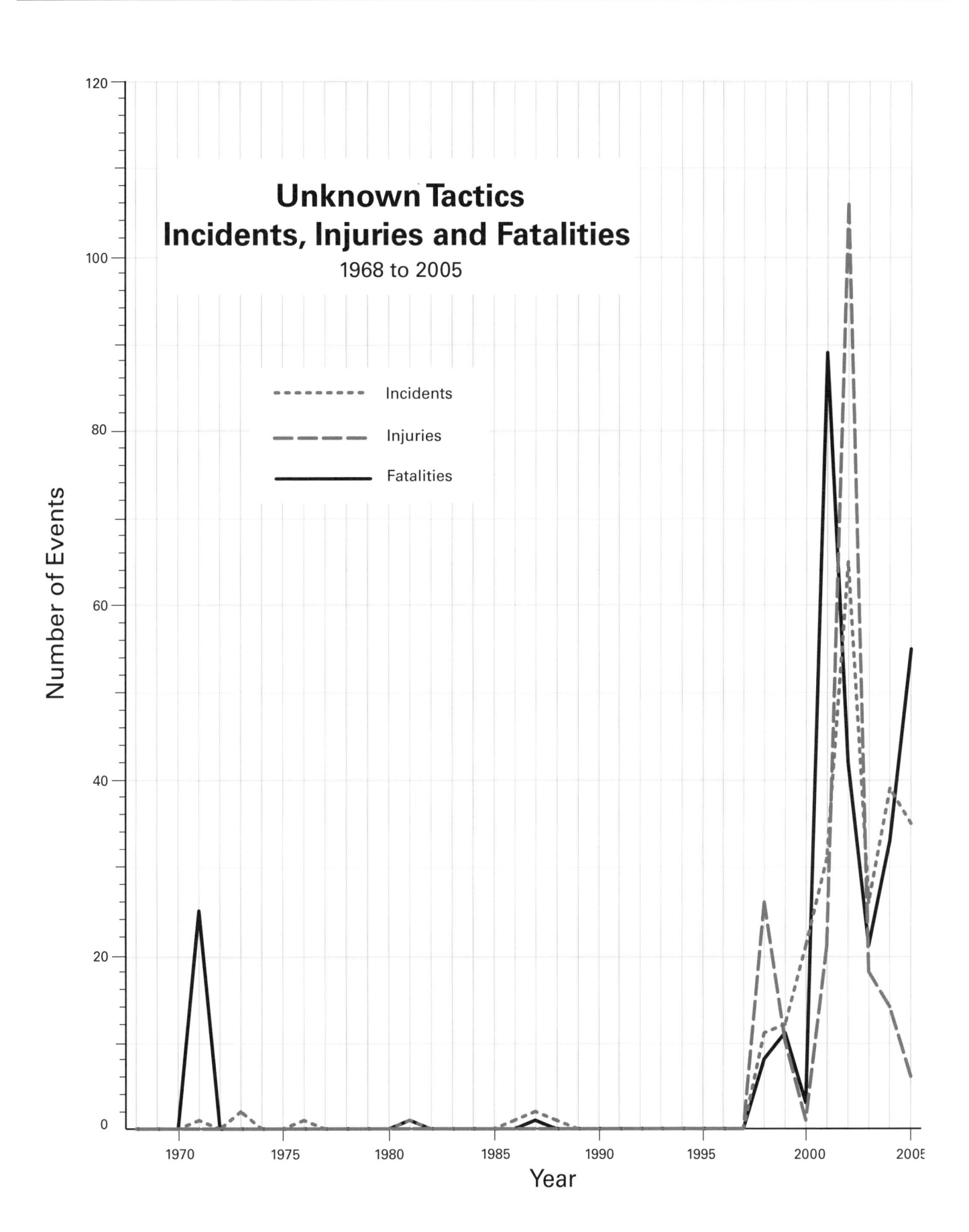

Unknown Tactics
Incidents, Injuries and Fatalities
1968 to 2005

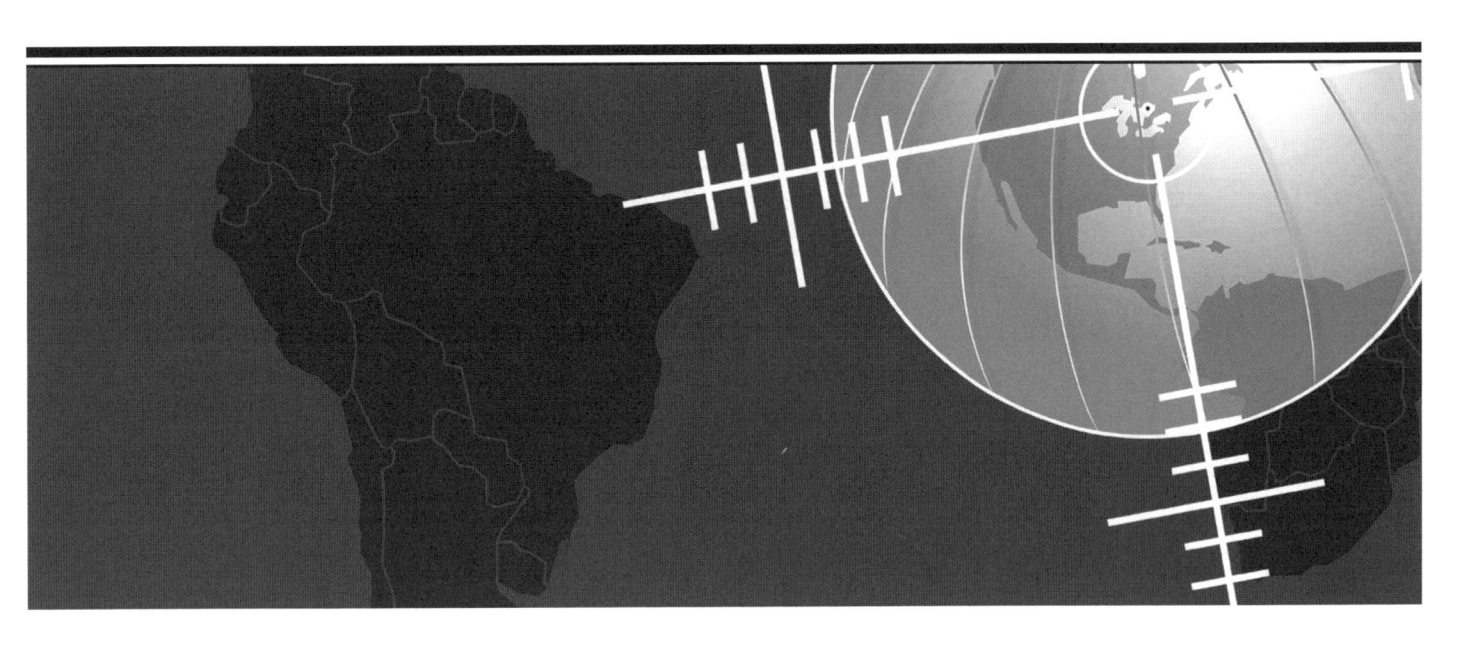

INDEX

Index

Note: Pages 1 to 535 can be found in volume 1; pages 536 to 1019 are in volume 2.

1 May organization, 285, 305, 323, 738
11 September Command, 227, 235
15 May Organization
    Iraq and, 73, 74, 78
    profile of, 160
    TWA flight bombing, 223, 733
16 June Organization, 288
17 November Revolutionary Organization
    chronology of incidents (1985–1989), 730, 736, 738
    chronology of incidents (1990–1996), 741–744, 751, 758
    in Greece (*See* Greece, country reports on)
    profile of, 160
19th of April Movement. *See* M-19 (Movement of 19 April)
32-County Sovereignty Committee. *See* Real Irish Republican Army (RIRA)

A

AAIA. *See* Islamic Army of Aden
ABB. *See* Alex Boncayao Brigade
Abbas, Hiram, 308
Abbas, Mahmoud, 677–678
Abbas, Mohammad Abu
    conviction of, 223
    death of, 189
    PLF and, 73, 76, 189
    Yugoslavia and, 97
Abd-al-Nabi, Khalid, 576
Abd al-Rahman, Shaykh Umar
    cease fire and, 445
    conviction of, 370–371
    Gama'a al-Islamiyya and, 173
    Islamic Group and, 367
    World Trade Center bombing and, 347, 355
Abd al-Rahman, Umar, 767
Abdallah, Georges Ibrahim
    calls for release of, 223
    Lebanese Armed Revolutionary Faction and, 184
    prosecution and conviction of, 29, 232, 240
Abdel Nasser, Khalid (Khaled Abdel Naser), 265–266, 314
Abdelaziz, Abbi, 196
Abdic, Fikret, 387
Abdollahi, Hashem, 68
Abdul Aziz, Nik Adli Nik, 182
Abdul Rahman, Habib (Ibn al-Khattab), 178, 421, 437
Abdullah, Abdullah Ahmed, 32
Abdullah, Crown Prince, 19
Abdullah, Obaidah Yusuf, 536
Abdullah Azzam Brigades, al Qaeda in Syria and Egypt, 857. *See also* Battalions of the Martyr Abdullah Azzam
Abdurrahman, Omar, 343
Aberkan, Abelhouaid, 663
Abo Ghaith, Sulaiman Jassem Sulaiman, 112–113
Abouhalima, Mohammad, 31, 415
Absandze, Guram, 420
Abu al-Abbas, 835
Abu al-Rish Brigades, 832
Abu Bakr al-Siddiq Fundamentalist Brigades, 843. *See also* Salafist Brigades of Abu Bakr al-Siddiq
Abu Hafs al-Masri Brigades, 820, 835
Abu Musa Fatah rebels
    chronology of incidents (1986), 734
    in Europe, 222
    in Israel, 225, 356
    prosecution of members of, 30, 232
    in Spain, 239
    See also Fatah Rebels (Fatah-the-Intifada)
Abu Nidal Organization (ANO)
    in Austria, 242
    in Belgium, 302, 321

1024 Index

Abu Nidal Organization *(continued)*
  chronology of incidents (1980s), 733, 735, 737, 738
  chronology of incidents (1994), 750
  conviction of members of, 232–233
  in Cyprus, 258
  in Greece, 260
  hijacking by, 83, 268
  in India, 266
  in Iraq, 73–79
  in Israel, 213, 224
  in Italy, 242, 261, 286
  in Jordan, 214, 251, 369
  in Kuwait, 213
  in Lebanon, 234, 252
  in Libya, 81, 84–90, 222
  in Pakistan, 244
  in Peru, 256–257, 280
  in Philippines, 246
  profile of, 160–161
  prosecution of members of, 29, 30
  in South Yemen, 97
  in Soviet bloc, 97, 98
  in Sudan, 99–101, 271, 295
  in Syria, 103–107
  in Turkey, 263
  Western Europe attacks, 211, 222
  in Yemen, 397
  See also Arab Revolutionary Brigades; Black September; Revolutionary Organization of Socialist Muslims
Abu Sayyaf Group (ASG)
  chronology of incidents (1993–1995), 749, 752, 757
  chronology of incidents (2000–2005), 786, 788, 795–796, 801, 810, 823, 845–846, 852
  hostages of, 137
  Libya and, 90
  in Malaysia (2000–2004), 455
  in Philippines (1990–1994), 349
  in Philippines (1995–1999), 374, 386, 402–403, 419, 435
  in Philippines (2000–2004), 455, 476, 508–509, 549, 659, 699
  profile of, 161
Abulgassem Musbah, Eter, 407

Note: Pages 1 to 535 can be found in volume 1; pages 536 to 1019 are in volume 2.

ACC (Arnoldo Camu Command), 739
ACHA (Chilean Anti-Communist Action Group), 235
Achraf, Mohamed (Mikael Etienne Christian Lefevre), 670
Acmad, Ismael (aka Toto), 809
Action Directe (AD)
  chronology of incidents (1985–1987), 732, 735
  in France (1985–1989), 214, 227–228, 239, 259
  in Germany (1985–1989), 265
  profile of, 161–162
Action Organization for the Liberation of Palestine, 728
AD. *See* Action Directe
Adel, Saif Al, 32
Aden-Abyan Islamic Army (AAIA). *See* Islamic Army of Aden
ADF. *See* Allied Democratic Forces; Anti-War Democratic Front
Afghan Ministry of State Security. *See* WAD
Afghanistan
  9/11 Commission on, 637
  beginnings of military operation in, 9, 18
  chronology of incidents (1970s), 729
  chronology of incidents (1991–1992), 742, 744
  chronology of incidents (1992), 745
  chronology of incidents (2000–2002), 788, 795, 803
  chronology of incidents (2003), 806, 809, 810, 812–816
  chronology of incidents (2004), 819, 820, 826, 828–834, 837–838, 840, 843, 849
  chronology of incidents (2005), 851, 853–857
  civilian casualties in, 24
  country reports on (1985–1989), 290
  country reports on (1990–1994), 299, 318–319, 336, 348, 359–360
  country reports on (1995–1999), 372, 385, 401, 418, 432
  country reports on (2000–2004), 452, 471–472, 502, 540, 683
  Iran and, 72
  Operation Enduring Freedom and ISAF, 137–138, 468–469, 540 (*See also specific countries participating*)
  Powell on, 5
  sanctions against, 35–36, 47
  as state sponsor of terrorism, 53–55
  terrorism financing and, 125
  Transitional State of Afghanistan (TISA), 137

U.S. military campaigns in, 4, 135–138
See also Taliban
AFRC (Armed Forces Revolutionary Council), 431, 774, 775, 781–782
Africa
    regional patterns (1990–1994), 297, 318, 335, 347–348, 358–359
    regional patterns (1995–1999), 371, 384, 399, 415, 430
    regional patterns (2000–2004), 450–451, 469, 499–500, 537, 653
    Sub-Saharan regional patterns (1985–1989), 210, 219, 230–231, 246, 269–270, 293
    See also Middle East and North Africa; *specific countries*
African National Congress (ANC)
    attacks on, 247
    in Europe (1985–1989), 257
    in France (1985–1989), 259
    Libya and, 85
    in Mozambique (1985–1989), 270
    profile of, 162
    in South Africa (1985–1989), 219, 231, 248, 270–271, 294–295
    in South Africa (1990–1994), 299
    in Tanzania (1985–1989), 295
    terrorist designation, 153
    in Zambia (1985–1989), 271, 295
    in Zimbabwe (1985–1989), 271
African Union (AU), 499, 674. *See also* Organization of African Unity (OAU)
Afrikaner Resistance Movement (AWB), 359
Agiza, Hussein, 675
Aguirre Lete, Juan "Isuntza," 388
Ahdal, Abdullah al-, 321
Ahdal, Muhammad Hamdi al- (aka Abu Asim al-Makki), 576
Ahmad, Abu. *See* Zarqawi, Abu Mus'ab al-
Ahmad, Mahmoud El Abed, 233
Ahmad al-Daqamisah Group, 791
Ahmed, Babar, 672
Ahmed, Rabei Osman Sayed, 666
AIAI. *See* Al-Ittihad al-Islami (AIAI or Islamic Union)
AIG. *See* Armed Islamic Group
AIIB. *See* Anti-Imperialist International Brigade
Aimal Khufia Action Committee, 402, 767
AIS (Islamic Salvation Army), 394, 411, 426
AIZ (Anti-Imperialist Cells), 375, 388–389, 439, 757
AJ. *See* Al-Jihad (AJ) or Egyptian Islamic Jihad (EIJ)

Akhtar, Qari Saifullah, 174
Al-Aqsa Foundation, 665, 668
Al-Aqsa Martyrs Brigade
    chronology of incidents (2001), 796
    chronology of incidents (2002), 799, 800, 802, 803
    chronology of incidents (2003), 806, 810, 811, 813
    chronology of incidents (2004), 817–821, 824, 826, 832–835, 840, 845, 849, 850
    in Israel (2000–2004), 494, 525–526, 572, 677
    profile of, 162
    terrorist designation, 157
Al-Arifeen, 804, 853
Al-Asifa (Al-Fatah), 163
Al-Aslam, 758
Al Badhr Mujaheddin, 162
Al-Barakaat network, 7
Al-Faran, 755
Al Fatah (Kashmir), 744
Al-Fatah (Palestine), 163, 319
Al-Furqan, 113
Al-Gama'at al-Islamiyya (Islamic Group or IG)
    bin Laden and, 54
    chronology of incidents (1993), 747, 749–750
    chronology of incidents (1994), 750, 752
    chronology of incidents (1995), 753, 754, 756, 757
    chronology of incidents (1996), 759
    in Croatia (1995–1999), 375
    in Egypt (1990–1994), 343, 355, 367–368
    in Egypt (1995–1999), 380–381, 395, 412, 427, 445
    in Egypt (2000–2004), 464–465, 493, 525, 571, 675
    in Ethiopia (1995–1999), 371
    in Italy (1995–1999), 376
    Luxor attacks by, 69
    nonviolence policy, conversion to, 571
    profile of, 173
    Sudan and, 99–101
    in Uruguay (2000–2004), 492
Al-Haramain & al-Masjed al-Aqsa Charity Foundation, 113, 668, 681
Al-Haramain Islamic Foundation, 113
Al-Intigami al-Pakistani, 802
Al-Ittihad al-Islami (AIAI or Islamic Union)
    chronology of incidents (1996–1998), 757, 760, 771

Al-Ittihad al-Islami *(continued)*
  in Ethiopia, 384, 416, 500, 538, 653
  profile of, 163
  in Somalia, 470, 501, 539, 654
Al-Jabhah al-Islamiyyah al-'Alamiyyah li-Qital al-Yahud wal-Salibiyyin. *See* al-Qaeda (al-Qaida)
Al-Jama'a al-Islamiyyah al-Muqatilah bi-Libya. *See* Libyan Islamic Fighting Group (LIFG)
Al-Jamaa wal Sunnah, 528
Al-Jihad (AJ) or Egyptian Islamic Jihad (EIJ)
  in Albania, 421
  in Egypt, 427, 445, 493
  profile of, 163–164
  Sudan and, 101, 102
Al Khandaq, 848
Al-Mansurian
  chronology of incidents (2002), 801
  chronology of incidents (2004), 817, 819, 820, 833, 835, 839, 842, 848
  chronology of incidents (2005), 852, 857
  See also Lashkar-i-Tayyiba (LT)
Al-Ma'unah, 455, 476
Al-Nasirin, 853, 854
Al-Qaeda (al-Qaida)
  9/11 attacks and, 143, 798
  in Afghanistan, 9, 135–137, 471, 502, 540
  African embassy bombings (1998) and, 4, 7, 135, 416, 417
  Al-Jihad and, 163–164
  Ambassador Black on, 585, 587, 588, 590
  chronology of incidents (2002), 804, 805
  chronology of incidents (2003), 811, 812, 814
  chronology of incidents (2004), 820, 822, 824, 826, 829, 830, 834, 840, 844
  founding of, 54
  funding of, 21, 22, 111, 118, 120, 123–125
  in Germany, 561, 562
  global jihadist movement and, 696–697
  interdiction of cells of, 32–33
  Iran and, 72–73
  Iraq and, 79, 138–140, 676
  in Italy, 520, 564
  in Jordan (1995–1999), 446
  in Kenya, 500
  in Lebanon, 467
  Libyan statement on, 90
  in Pakistan, 503, 685
  in Philippines, 21
  profile of, 164–165
  progress against, 140–141
  in Saudi Arabia, 680
  in Southeast Asian region, 542
  in Spain, 567
  successes against, 33, 34
  in Sudan, 101, 102
  Syria and, 109, 110
  terrorist designation, 153, 157
  war on terrorism and, 18–19
  WMD and, 21
  in Yemen, 529, 576, 682
  Zarqawi Network and, 198
Al-Qaeda in Iraq. *See* Tanzim Qa'idat al-Jihad fi Bilad al-Rafidayn (QJBR)
Al-Qaeda in Syria and Egypt (Abdullah Azzam Brigades), 857. *See also* Battalions of the Martyr Abdullah Azzam
Al-Qaeda in the Levant and Egypt, 841
Al-Qaeda Organization in the Arabian Peninsula, 830, 839, 848
Al-Sirat al Mustaqim, 811
Al-Takfir wa Al-Hijrah, 102, 571
Al-Taqwa network, 7
Al-Tawhid, 519, 562
Al Ummah, 165
Al-Wa'ad ("The Promise"), 493, 525
Al-Zarqawi Network. *See* Tanzim Qa'idat al-Jihad fi Bilad al-Rafidayn (QJBR)
Al-Zufikar, 218
Albania
  9/11 response, 482
  country reports on (1990–1994), 361
  country reports on (1995–1999), 421, 438
  country reports on (2000–2004), 482, 516–517, 559, 662–663
Albright, Madeleine, 30–31
Alcides Cruz, Luis, 578
Aldasoro, Ramon, 423
Alex Boncayao Brigade (ABB)
  in Philippines (1995–1999), 374, 386, 435
  in Philippines (2000–2004), 455, 476
  profile of, 162
ALF (Animal Liberation Front), 773, 775
ALF (Arab Liberation Front), 73, 75–79, 138
Alfaro Vive, Carajo! (AVC), 92–93, 217. *See also* Ecuador, country reports on

Note: Pages 1 to 535 can be found in volume 1; pages 536 to 1019 are in volume 2.

Alfi, Hassan al-, 163
Algeria
　9/11 response, 492
　chronology of incidents (1992–1994), 746, 748–752
　chronology of incidents (1995–1997), 753–758, 760, 761, 765, 768
　chronology of incidents (2001–2003), 792, 793, 799, 802, 807, 809–811
　chronology of incidents (2005), 855
　country reports on (1985–1989), 274
　country reports on (1990–1994), 314, 331, 343, 355, 367
　country reports on (1995–1999), 380, 394–395, 411–412, 426–427, 445
　country reports on (2000–2004), 464, 492–493, 524, 570, 674
　Sudan and, 102
Algeti Wolves, 375
Ali, Mohamed Hamed, 32
Ali, Siddig Ibrahim Siddig, 31, 430
Ali Mohammed, 31, 430
Aliganga, Jesse N., 414
Alikhadzhiyeva, Zulikhan, 556
Alimonti, Giovanni, 259
ALIR (Army for the Liberation of Rwanda), 33, 171, 501, 539. *See also* Democratic Forces for the Liberation of Rwanda (FDLR)
Aliyev, Abdulla, 669
All Tripura Tiger Force, 830
Allah Tigers, 300
Allah's Martyrs, 517
'Allawi, Iyad (Ayad), 77, 78, 665
Allied Democratic Forces (ADF)
　chronology of incidents (1999), 777
　profile of, 164
　in Uganda, 431, 452, 471, 502, 540
Almoudi, Abdulrahman, 92
ALNC (Corsican National Liberation Army), 303, 518, 813
American Battalion, 217
American National Standards Institute (ANSI), 639
AMIA (Argentine-Israel Mutual Association), 67, 68, 364, 491, 582, 751
Amin, Yousef, 69
Amini, Osman Muhammed, 67, 68
Amn Araissi. *See* Hawari Group
An-Nahda, 198, 346, 397, 429
Anarchic Attack Groups, 794

Anarchist Black Cross, 798
Anarchist Faction, 460
Anarchists Attack Team, 792
ANC. *See* African National Congress
Andaman Sea, 737
Andang, Ghalib, 549, 660
Anderson, Danilo, 695
Anderson, Terry, 61, 233, 252, 731, 745
Andrade, David, 578, 687
Andres Castro United Front (FUAC), 783
Androulidakis, Kostas, 738
Angola
　9/11 response, 469–470
　chronology of incidents (1994–1997), 752, 756, 763
　chronology of incidents (1998), 769, 770, 774, 775
　chronology of incidents (1999), 775, 776, 778–781
　chronology of incidents (2000), 785, 787, 789–790
　chronology of incidents (2001), 793, 795, 796
　chronology of incidents (2004), 825
　country reports on (1985–1989), 220
　country reports on (1990–1994), 297–298, 335, 348, 359
　country reports on (1995–1999), 371, 399, 415, 430–431
　country reports on (2000–2004), 451, 469–470, 500, 537
　sanctions against, 47
Animal Liberation Front (ALF), 773, 775
Annan, Kofi, 146
ANO. *See* Abu Nidal Organization
Ansar al-Din, 822
Ansar al-Islam, 79–80, 138, 165, 564
Ansar al-Sunna
　chronology of incidents (2004), 818, 836, 842, 847
　in Iraq (2000–2004), 676
Ansar Allah (Followers of God), 364, 365
ANSI (American National Standards Institute), 639
Anthony, Renee Jean (aka Grenn Sonnen), 853
Anti-Imperialist Cells (AIZ), 375, 388–389, 439, 757
Anti-Imperialist Freedom Connection for Benjamin, 376
Anti-Imperialist International Brigade (AIIB)
　chronology of incidents (1986–1987), 734, 736
　in Indonesia (1985–1989), 230

Anti-Imperialist International Brigade *(continued)*
   in Italy (1985–1989), 242
   JRA and, 245
   in Spain (1985–1989), 239, 262
   See also Japanese Red Army (JRA)
Anti-Imperialist Territorial Nuclei (NTA), 165–166, 808
Anti-Regime Nuclei (ARN), 755
Anti-War Democratic Front (ADF), 267
Antiterrorist Liberation Group (GAL), 214, 215, 286
Antza, Mikel, 671
Aoun, Michael, 282
APEC (Asia-Pacific Economic Cooperation), 514, 551
APF (Azeri Popular Front), 744
"Appel gang," 282
Applebaum, David, 537
Applebaum, Naava, 537
Arab Liberation Front (ALF), 73, 75–79, 138
Arab Nationalist Movement, 190
Arab Revolutionary Brigades, 732, 733. *See also* Abu Nidal Organization (ANO)
Arab Revolutionary Organization, 731
Arafat, Yasser (Yassir)
   Al-Fatah and, 163
   counterterrorist efforts, 368
   death of, 677
   Force 17 and, 173
   France visit, 749
   PLO and, 189–190
   Security Council Resolutions, acceptance of, 250
   and terrorist activity, 19
Araqi, Abdullah al-, 140
ARB (Breton Revolutionary Alliance), 284, 459, 786
ARC (Caribbean Revolutionary Alliance), 284
Argentina
   9/11 response, 491
   chronology of incidents (1992–1994), 745, 751
   chronology of incidents (2003–2004), 810, 846
   country reports on (1990–1994), 340, 364
   country reports on (1995–1999), 377–378, 392, 410, 424–425, 443, 444
   country reports on (2000–2004), 463–464, 491, 533–534, 581–583, 693–694
   Iran-sponsored terrorism in, 65, 67, 68
Argentine-Israel Mutual Association (AMIA), 67, 68, 364, 491, 582, 751

Note: Pages 1 to 535 can be found in volume 1; pages 536 to 1019 are in volume 2.

Arian, Sami Al-, 33
Arizjuren Ruiz, Javier (aka Kantauri), 458
Armed Forces of National Resistance (FARN), 172
Armed Forces of Rwanda (FAR), 171
Armed Forces Revolutionary Council (AFRC), 431, 774, 775, 781–782
Armed Islamic Group (GIA or AIG)
   in Algeria (1990–1994), 355, 367
   in Algeria (1995–1999), 380, 394, 411, 426, 445
   in Algeria (2000–2004), 464, 493
   in Bosnia, 483
   chronology of incidents (1993–1994), 749, 751, 752
   chronology of incidents (1995–1996), 753–758
   European sting against (1998), 422
   in France (1990–1994), 362
   in Italy (1995–1999), 407
   profile of, 166
   Salafist Group for Call and Combat and, 196
   in Spain (1995–1999), 390
   in Tunisia (1995–1999), 383
Armed Liberation Forces (FAL). *See* Zarate Willka Armed Liberation Forces (FAL)
Armenia, 420, 436, 552–553, 663
Armenian Revolutionary Army, 181, 233
Armenian Secret Army for the Liberation of Armenia. *See* ASALA
Armitage, Richard, 513, 555, 597
Armstrong, Jack, 198
Army for the Liberation of Rwanda (ALIR), 33, 171, 501, 539. *See also* Democratic Forces for the Liberation of Rwanda (FDLR)
Army of Palestine, 805
Army of the Pure and Righteous. *See* Lashkar-i-Tayyiba (LT)
ARN (Anti-Regime Nuclei), 755
Arnaout, Enaam, 560
Arnoldo Camu Command (ACC), 739
Artemio (aka Ala Macario), 196
Asad, Bashar al-, 109
Asahara, Shoko, 167, 373, 385, 402
ASALA (Armenian Secret Army for the Liberation of Armenia)
   in Belgium (1995–1999), 404
   chronology of incidents (1985), 733
   chronology of incidents (1991), 745
   in Europe, 223, 327
   in Lebanon, 233, 234

Libya and, 83
profile of, 166–167
Syria and, 103–106
Asbat al-Ansar (League of the Followers)
in Lebanon, 447, 467, 495, 527
profile of, 167
terrorist designation, 157
Ascensios, Evorcio ("Camarada Canale"), 196
ASEAN (Association of Southeast Asian Nations)
9/11 response, 144–145, 473–474
Australia and, 545
Cambodia and, 546
Joint Declaration for Cooperation on Counterterrorism, 507
Philippines and, 549
Asemblia Izquierda Tudelana, 262
ASG. See Abu Sayyaf Group
Ashcroft, John, 32
Ashker, Bassam Al, 324
Asia
regional patterns (1985–1989), 210, 217, 229, 244, 266, 290
regional patterns (1990–1994), 299, 318, 335, 348, 359
regional patterns (1995–1998), 371–372, 384, 400–401, 417–418
regional patterns after 1998 (See East Asia; South Asia)
See also Eurasia; specific countries
Asia-Pacific Economic Cooperation (APEC), 514, 551
Asif Raza Commandoes, 799
Aslan, Amir, 197
Aspin, Les, 630
Assad, Hafez, 103–105
Assad'ad, Ahmad al-, 382
Assadi, Ali Mohammed, 67
Association of Southeast Asian Nations. See ASEAN
Atef, Muhammad, 31, 140
Athulathmudali, Lalith, 350
Atiya, Abu, 139
Atlantic Ocean, 732
Ato, Usman (Hasan Ali), 797
Atris, Muhammad, 69
Atwa, Ali, 175
Atwah, Muhsin Musa Matwalli, 32
AU (African Union), 499, 674. See also Organization of African Unity (OAU)
AUC. See United Self-Defense Forces of Columbia

Audran, Rene, 730
Aum Shinrikyo (aleph)
in Japan (1995–1999), 373, 385, 402, 418, 434–435
in Japan (2000–2004), 454, 547–548, 658
profile of, 167–168
Sarin gas attack, 21, 385
Auque, Roger, 233
AUSTRAC, 544
Australia
9/11 response, 473
country reports on (1985–1989), 230, 246, 266, 290–291
country reports on (2000–2004), 505, 544–545, 656–657
prosecutions in, 30
Austria
chronology of incidents (1985), 730, 733
chronology of incidents (1989), 739
chronology of incidents (1995–1996), 756, 757, 760
chronology of incidents (1999), 777
country reports on (1985–1989), 242, 257, 281
country reports on (1995–1999), 374–375, 404, 438
country reports on (2000–2004), 458, 663
prosecutions in, 29
Austrian Relief Committee, 745
AVC (Alfaro Vive, Carajo!), 92–93, 217. See also Ecuador, country reports on
AWB (Afrikaner Resistance Movement), 359
Awkil, Nabil, 465
Ayad, Aatollah, 69
'Ayn al-Hilwah refugee camp (Lebanon), 167
Azadfer, Behram, 748
Azaouaj, Ibrahim, 438
Azerbaijan
9/11 response, 478
chronology of incidents (1991–1997), 744, 750, 763
country reports on (1990–1994), 361
country reports on (1995–1999), 436
country reports on (2000–2004), 456, 478–479, 511, 553, 663
sanctions against, 47
Azeri Popular Front (APF), 744
Azhar, Masood, 175, 179, 432
Aziz, Abdul (aka Imam Samudra), 506, 547
Aziz, Tariq, 74

Azraq, Abu. *See* Zarqawi, Abu Mus'ab al-
Azzam, Abdullah, 292

B

Baader-Meinhof Gang, 192, 729
Ba'asyir, Abu Bakar, 140, 180, 182, 658
Babbar Khalsa International, 112, 197, 373
Babeuf, Gracchus, 303
Badawi, Jamal al-, 682
Baghdad, Rajeh Heshan Mohamed, 375
Bahonar, Mohammad-Javad, 187
Bahrain
    chronology of incidents (1995–1997), 753, 758, 761, 762, 765
    country reports on (1985–1989), 225, 234
    country reports on (1995–1999), 395, 412, 427
    country reports on (2000–2004), 493, 524, 570, 674–675
    Iran-sponsored terrorism in, 69
    terrorism financing and, 124
Bahraini Hizballa, 411
Bajuwarian Liberation Front (Bavarian Liberation Army), 374, 404, 757
Bakhtiar, Shapur, 64, 65, 321, 744
Bakoyiannis, Pavlos, 285, 740
Balafas, Georgios, 351, 376
Bali, bombing in
    Australia and, 505
    Bashir and, 547
    Indonesian response to, 506, 546
    joint investigation into, 545
Baltics, 361–362. *See also* Estonia; Latvia; Lithuania
Balzarani, Barbara, 215, 228
Banbangida, Ibrahim, 348
Bangladesh
    chronology of incidents (1999–2005), 776, 793, 827, 851
    country reports on (2000–2004), 683–684
    terrorism financing and, 126
Bani-Hamed, Fayiz, 497
Bani Sadr, Abolhassn, 388
Banna, Sabri Al- (Abu Nidal)
    ANO and, 160, 161
    conviction in absentia, 242, 261
    in Iraq, 77
    Libya and, 84, 85

Note: Pages 1 to 535 can be found in volume 1; pages 536 to 1019 are in volume 2.

Baragiola-Lojacano, Aluaro, 308
Barakat, Assad Ahmad
    arrested in Argentina, 534
    Chilean investigation into, 531–532
    conviction of, 694
    designated as terrorist, 113
    extradition of, 582, 583
    investigation into, 489
    in Triborder region, 491
Barakat, Hatem, 694
Barakat Yarkas, Imad Eddin, 671
Barayev, Mosvar, 804
Barayev, Shamil, 513
Barco, Virgilio, 117
Bargishev, Shadid, 420
Barhoum, Ahmad, 854
Barisan Revolusi Nasional (BRN), 456
Barnes, Michael, 337, 745
Bartley, Julian L., Jr., 414
Bartley, Julian L., Sr., 414
Barumand, Abdal Rahman, 65
Bary, Adel Mohammed Abdul Almagid, 31, 672
Basayev, Shamil, 437, 480, 555
Basha, S. A., 165
Bashir, Abu Bakar, 506, 547
Bashir, Umar al-, 99, 100, 102
Basque Communist Party (Iraultza), 215, 228, 239, 262, 287
Basque Fatherland and Liberty (ETA)
    in Algeria (1985–1989), 274
    in Belgium (2000–2004), 458
    chronology of incidents (1985), 732
    chronology of incidents (1989), 738, 739
    chronology of incidents (1991), 743
    chronology of incidents (1995), 755, 757
    chronology of incidents (2000), 785
    chronology of incidents (2004), 836
    chronology of incidents (2005), 851, 852, 854, 855, 857
    Cuba and, 57–60
    in Dominican Republic (1985–1989), 278
    in France (*See* France, country reports on)
    in Italy (1990–1994), 323
    in Mexico (2000–2004), 585
    in Netherlands (1985–1989), 286
    Nicaragua and, 92–93
    profile of, 168
    in Spain (*See* Spain, country reports on)
Basque Nationalist Party (PNV), 461

Basyev, Shamil, 178
Batasuna, 521–522, 567
Battalions of the Martyr Abdullah Azzam, 841.
    See also Abdullah Azzam Brigades
Batterjee, Adel Abdul Jalil, 113
Bavarian Liberation Army (Bajuwarian Liberation
    Front), 374, 404, 757
BBC (British Broadcasting Corporation), 755, 756
BCG (US-Canada Bilateral Consultative Group on
    Counterterrorism Cooperation), 498, 535,
    583, 688
Beahan, Charles, 295
Beckurts, Karl-Heinz, 734
Beer, Alan, 536
Beghal, Djamel, 483, 561, 664
Beheshti, Ayatollah Mohammad, 187
Bekaa Valley. *See* Lebanon
Belgium
    9/11 response, 482
    chronology of incidents (1985), 730
    chronology of incidents (1989), 739, 740
    chronology of incidents (1998), 773
    chronology of incidents (2003), 812
    country reports on (1985–1989), 215, 228, 240,
        257–258, 281
    country reports on (1990–1994), 302, 321
    country reports on (1995–1999), 404, 422, 438
    country reports on (2000–2004), 458, 482–483,
        517, 559, 663
Belhadj, Ali, 367
Belkeziz, Abdelouahed, 143
Ben Hassine, Saifallah, 198
Ben Henin, Lased, 484
Ben Khemais, Essid Sami, 485
Benevolence International Foundation (BIF), 517–
    518, 553, 560
Benevolence International Nederland (BIN), 668
Bengal Liberation Army, 244
Benin, 84, 270
Bennett, Lansing H., 30, 399
Bennett, Marla, 499
Bentley, Jason Eric, 536
Berenson, Lori, 490, 692–693
Berg, Nicholas, 198
Berlin, 733–734
Bernardo, Reynaldo, 301
Bertelsman, Clarence William, 360–361
Besse, Georges, 239, 735
Bhattarai, Baburam, 856

Bhinderanwala Tiger Force, 197
Bhutto, Benazir, 360
Bhutto, Shaheed, 386
Bhutto, Shahnawaz, 218
Biagi, Marco, 188, 520
Bianco, Enrico, 406, 422
Bidart, Phillipe, 259
Biden, Joseph R, Jr., 613–614
BIF (Benevolence International Foundation), 517–
    518, 553, 560
BIN (Benevolence International Nederland), 668
Bin Ali, Arifin, 550
Bin Attash, Walid, 541
Bin Isomoddin, Nurjaman Riduan (aka Hambali),
    180, 182, 542, 550
Bin Laden, Osama (Usama)
    9/11 attacks and, 798
    added to terrorist list, 4, 416
    in Afghanistan, 385, 401, 432, 471, 502
    Benevolence International Foundation and, 560
    bounty on, 24, 31
    on Chechnya, 513
    embassy bombings and, 772
    fatwah issued by, 20
    funds of, 22, 23, 35
    history and goals of, 54–55
    Hizb-I-Islami Gulbudin and, 176
    indictment on embassy bombings, 31
    Iraq and, 139, 140
    Saudi Arabia, threats against, 414, 428, 467
    in Sudan, 99–101
    Taliban and, 9, 35
    on Ten Most Wanted list, 430
    U.S. military campaign in Afghanistan and, 136
    WMD procurement by, 21
    See also al-Qaeda (al-Qaida); World Islamic Front
        for Jihad Against the Jews and Crusaders
Bin Nurhasyim, Amrozi, 547
Black, Cofer, 585–601, 686
Black Banners Division of the Islamic Secret Army,
    833
Black Liberation Army, 56
Black September, 728, 731, 732, 790. *See also* Abu
    Nidal Organization (ANO)
Black Star (Mavro Asteri), 460, 485
Black War, 228, 259
Blair, Todd Michael, 536
Blaustein, Sara, 469
Blutstein, Benjamin, 499

Boaz, Avi, 499
Bodo Security Force (BSF), 336
Boere Aanvals Troepe, 400, 762
Boland, Edward, 628
Bolivia
   9/11 response, 488
   chronology of incidents (1988–1990), 738–742
   chronology of incidents (2004), 816
   country reports on (1985–1989), 253–254, 277
   country reports on (1990–1994), 310, 328, 340
   country reports on (2000–2004), 488, 531, 578, 687
Boren, David, 630
Borujerdi, Ayatollah Morteza, 77
Bosnia and Herzegovina
   9/11 response, 483
   chronology of incidents (1996–1997), 759, 760, 762, 764
   chronology of incidents (1999–2000), 779, 790
   chronology of incidents (2003–2004), 809, 825
   country reports on (1990–1994), 352
   country reports on (1995–1999), 387, 405
   country reports on (2000–2004), 483, 517–518, 559–560, 664
   sanctions against, 47
   war in, 352, 364
   See also Yugoslavia
Botswana, 247–248
Bouakaze, Amar, 459
Boucher, Richard, 80–81
Boudiaf, Nouredine, 674
Bouteflika, Abdelaziz, 445
BR. *See* Red Brigades
BR-CCP (Red Brigades–Communist Combatant Party), 564, 667
BR-PCC. *See* Red Brigades–Fighting Communist Party
BR-UCC (Red Brigades–Union of Communist Combatants), 192, 241–242, 284, 736
Branchizio, John, 537
Brazil
   9/11 response, 491
   chronology of incidents (1969), 728
   chronology of incidents (2005), 853
   country reports on (1995–1999), 444

   country reports on (2000–2004), 463–464, 491, 533–534, 581–583, 693–694
Brennan, John
   in hearing on Annual Terrorism Report, 709–710
   press conference on 2004 country report, 697–707
   remarks on revised 2003 report, 592, 593–594, 599–601
Breton Revolutionary Alliance (ARB), 284, 459, 786
Briceno, Jorge ("Mono Jojoy"), 193
Brigades of Al Tawhid Lions, 839
Brigades of the Martyr Abdallah al-Hudhaifi, 397
Brigades of the Martyr Ahmed Yassim, 821–822
Britain. *See* United Kingdom (UK)
British Broadcasting Corporation (BBC), 755, 756
BRN (Barisan Revolusi Nasional), 456
Brown, Harold, 630
Bruce, David, 620–621
Bruguiere, Jean-Louis, 64
Bryant, Fred, 536
BSF (Bodo Security Force), 336
Buckley, William
   abduction of, 212, 213, 730
   assassination of, 333
   burial of, 745
Buehring, Charles H., 537
Bulgaria
   country reports on (1985–1989), 290
   country reports on (1990–1994), 327
   country reports on (2000–2004), 560, 664
   as state sponsor of terrorism, 97, 98
Bureau of Administration (State Dept.), 13
Bureau of Consular Affairs (State Dept.), 13, 14
Bureau of Democracy, Human Rights and Labor (State Dept.), 205
Bureau of Diplomatic Security (State Dept.), 13, 14–15
Bureau of Industry and Security (BIS) (Commerce Dept.), 36
Bureau of Intelligence and Research (State Dept.), 15, 26
Bureau of International Organization Affairs (State Dept.), 14
Bureau of Overseas Buildings Operations (State Dept.), 13
Bureau of Political-Military Affairs (State Dept.), 14, 15, 36
Bureau of Public Affairs (State Dept.), 205
Burke, Arleigh, 621

Note: Pages 1 to 535 can be found in volume 1; pages 536 to 1019 are in volume 2.

Burma (Myanmar)
  chronology of incidents (1980–1984), 729
  chronology of incidents (1987), 737
  chronology of incidents (2005), 854
  country reports on (1995–1999), 401
  country reports on (2000–2004), 454, 474, 505, 545
  sanctions against, 47
Burnham, Gracia, 161, 499, 508
Burnham, Martin, 161, 508, 801
Burundi, 781, 783, 791, 793–797
Bush, George H. W., 75, 76, 357
Bush, George W.
  and Coalition partners, 6
  economic measures by, 7, 22
  FBI Academy speech (7/05), 9–10
  on freedom, 9
  sanctions imposed by, 23
  State of the Union addresses, 18
  on war against terrorism, 6, 468
Buthe, Suliman al-, 113

C

Cabardo, Antonio, 301
Cabinda Liberation Front–Cabinda Armed Forces (FLEC-FAC), 399, 415, 763, 769
CAC (Continuity Army Council), 391, 408–409. *See also* Continuity Irish Republican Army (CIRA)
Caliphate State, 519
Camarena Salazar, Enrique, 212
Cambodia
  chronology of incidents (1994–1995), 752, 753
  chronology of incidents (1996–1998), 758, 759, 761, 764, 770
  country reports on (1990–1994), 360
  country reports on (1995–1999), 372, 385, 401, 418, 434
  country reports on (2000–2004), 545–546, 657
  sanctions against, 47
Cambodian Freedom Fighters (CFF), 168–169, 545, 657
Cameroon, 82
Canada
  9/11 response, 498
  chronology of incidents (1985), 731
  country reports on (1985–1989), 238, 258, 281–282
  country reports on (1995–1999), 448

  country reports on (2000–2004), 498, 535–536, 584–585, 687–688
  prosecutions in, 29
Cape Town, South Africa, 190
Cardenas, Elizabeth (Comrade Aurora), 394
Caribbean Revolutionary Alliance, 731
Caribbean Revolutionary Alliance (ARC), 284
Carlos "the Jackal" (aka Ilyich Ramirez Sanchez)
  conviction of, 405
  extradition of, 362
  interrogation of, 404
  Sudan and, 99
  Syria and, 106
Carlson, Wilson, 537
Carpenter, James Lee, II, 536
Carter, Diane Leslie, 499
Carter, Jimmy, 629
Carton, Marcel, 252
Casamance Movement of Democrative Forces, 800
Casner, Karri, 499
Castro, Fidel, 55–58
Catalan Red Liberation Army (ERCA), 192, 239, 262, 737
Catalonia, 192, 198, 239. *See also* Spain
CCB (Civil Cooperation Bureau), 299
CCC. *See* Communist Combatant Cells
CDC (Centers for Disease Control), 641
CEF (Cuban Expeditionary Force), 621
Cell for Internationalism, 375
CENTCOM (U.S. Central Command), 135
Centers for Disease Control (CDC), 641
Central African Republic, 247, 416, 736
Central American Revolutionary Worker's Party (PRTC)
  FMLN and, 172
  Mardoqueo Cruz Urban Commando Detachment, 169, 216, 731
  Nicaragua and, 92
  profile of, 169
Central Intelligence Agency (CIA)
  9/11 Commission on, 645
  Counterterrorist Center (CTC) of, 607
  Intelligence Committee recommendations on, 638
  intelligence reorganization proposals and, 615–622, 624–631, 634–635
CERF (Clara Elizabeth Ramirez Front), 169, 227
Cerpa Cartolini, Nestor, 411
Cetiner, Ali, 304

CFF (Cambodian Freedom Fighters), 168–169, 545, 657
CGSB. *See* Simon Bolivar Guerilla Coordinator
Chad
    chronology of incidents (1998), 768, 769
    country reports on (1985–1989), 220, 246–247, 294
    country reports on (1995–1999), 371, 416
    country reports on (2000–2004), 653
    Libyan activities in, 84
Chae Do-sung, 733
Chavez, Hugo, 690
Chechnya
    Brennan on, 700
    chronology of incidents (*See under* Russia)
    country reports on (*See under* Russia)
    Georgia, spillover into, 479
    See also Russia
Cheney, Dick, 823
Chesimard, Joanne, 56, 59, 60
Chico, Raymond Matthew, 347, 747
Chile
    9/11 response, 489
    arms caches found (1986), 60
    chronology of incidents (1986–1989), 735, 739
    chronology of incidents (1990–1994), 741–743, 747, 748, 752
    chronology of incidents (2000–2004), 791, 798, 808, 829
    country reports on (1985–1989), 217, 226–227, 235, 254, 277–278
    country reports on (1990–1994), 310, 328, 340, 353, 364–365
    country reports on (1995–1999), 410, 425
    country reports on (2000–2004), 489, 531–532, 578–579, 688
    Cuba and, 56, 58–59
    sanctions against, 48
Chilean Anti-Communist Action Group (ACHA), 235
China, People's Republic of
    9/11 response, 474
    country reports on (1995–1999), 401
    country reports on (2000–2004), 474–475, 505–506, 546, 657–658
    East Turkistan Islamic Movement in, 475
    sanctions against, 50
    trade status of, 41
China, Republic of. *See* Taiwan
Chochiyev, Sergei, 555
Chosen Soren, 245
Chukaku-Ha (Middle Core Faction, or Nucleus Faction)
    chronology of incidents (1985–1988), 730, 733, 734, 737, 738
    chronology of incidents (1991–1993), 743, 748
    in Japan (*See* Japan, country reports on)
    profile of, 169
Church, Frank, 616, 625
CIA. *See* Central Intelligence Agency
Cicippio, Joseph
    abduction of, 61, 105, 735
    death threats against, 276
    release of, 745
CICTE (Inter-American Committee Against Terrorism), 530, 577
CIRA (Continuity Irish Republican Army), 113, 171, 177, 673. *See also* Continuity Army Council (CAC)
CIS (Commonwealth of Independent States), 150, 477
Civil Cooperation Bureau (CCB), 299
CJTF—HOA (Combined Joint Task Force—Horn of Africa), 538
Clandestine Worker's Revolutionary Party, Union of the Poor (PROCUP), 330
Clara Elizabeth Ramirez Front (CERF), 169, 227
Clark, Mark W., 619
Clifford, Clark, 628
Cline, Ray, 628
Clinton, Bill, 4, 135, 440
Clodfelter, Kenneth Eugene, 450
CNG (National Guerilla Coordinator), 226
CNPZ. *See* Nestor Paz Zamora Commission
Cochetel, Vincent, 421
Collective Security Treaty Organization (CSTO), 554
Collett, Alec, 82, 734
Colombia
    9/11 response, 490
    Ambassador Black on, 591
    chronology of incidents (1980–1984), 729
    chronology of incidents (1985–1988), 732–735, 737
    chronology of incidents (1992–1995), 745–747, 750–756

Note: Pages 1 to 535 can be found in volume 1; pages 536 to 1019 are in volume 2.

chronology of incidents (1996), 758, 760–762
chronology of incidents (1997), 763–768
chronology of incidents (1998), 769–775
chronology of incidents (1999), 776–782, 784, 785
chronology of incidents (2000), 785–790
chronology of incidents (2001), 793, 794, 796–798
chronology of incidents (2002), 799–802
chronology of incidents (2003), 806, 807, 811–815
chronology of incidents (2004), 816, 817
chronology of incidents (2005), 851, 852, 854, 856, 857–858
country reports on (1985–1989), 216–217, 226, 236, 254–255, 278
country reports on (1990–1994), 310–311, 329, 340–341, 353, 365
country reports on (1995–1999), 378, 392–393, 410, 425, 443
country reports on (2000–2004), 462–463, 489–490, 532, 579–580, 688–690
Cuba and, 55–60
narcoterrorism in, 117, 254–255
See also FARC (Revolutionary Armed Forces of Colombia)
Colombian Communist Party, 193
Colombian Communist Party/Marxist-Leninist, 190
Combatant Communist Nuclei (NCC), 363, 750
Combined Joint Task Force–Horn of Africa (CJTF-HOA), 538
Combined Military Loyalist Command, 364
Commercial Bank of Syria, 125
Committee for Solidarity With Arab and Middle Eastern Political Prisoners (CSPPA), 223
Commonwealth of Independent States (CIS), 150, 477
Communist Combatant Cells (CCC)
  in Belgium (1985–1989), 215, 228, 240, 258
  profile of, 169
Communist Combatant Party (New Red Brigades), 188, 192
Communist Party of Chile (PCCH), 328
Communist Party of El Salvador's Armed Forces of Liberation (FAL), 172
Communist Party of India (Maoist), 169–170, 852, 857

Communist Party of Nepal (Maoist)/United People's Front
  chronology of incidents (2004), 822, 826–829, 837, 838, 849
  profile of, 170
Communist Party of Spain, 172
Communist Party of the Philippines/New People's Army (CPP/NPA)
  Alex Boncayao Brigade and, 162
  chronology of incidents (1987), 736
  chronology of incidents (1989), 739, 740
  chronology of incidents (1990), 741
  Libya and, 85, 86
  in Netherlands (1985–1989), 286
  North Korea and, 94
  in Philippines (*See* Philippines, country reports on)
  profile of, 170–171
  terrorist designation, 33, 112, 157
Comodo Jaramillista Morelense 23 de Mayo, 828
Congo, Democratic Republic of (former Zaire)
  chronology of incidents (1998), 773
  chronology of incidents (2000–2001), 788, 794, 795
  chronology of incidents (2004–2005), 828, 848, 856
  country reports on (1995–1999), 416
  sanctions against, 48
  See also Zaire
Congo, People's Republic of, 82, 294
Congressional Research Service (CRS), 711
Connolly, Niall, 58
Consultation of Ministers of Foreign Affairs, 143–144
Continuity Army Council (CAC), 391, 408–409. *See also* Continuity Irish Republican Army (CIRA)
Continuity Irish Republican Army (CIRA), 113, 171, 177, 673. *See also* Continuity Army Council (CAC)
Contreras, Manuel, 353
Cools, Jan, 281
Coordinator for Counterterrorism, State Dept. (S/CT), 607–613
Coorea, Matthias, 618
Corach, Carlos, 410
Cordes, Rudolf, 63, 252, 265
Cordesman, Tony, 709
Corsican National Liberation Army (ALNC), 303, 518, 813
Corsican National Liberation Front (FLNC)
  chronology of incidents (1985), 731

Corsican National Liberation Front *(continued)*
    chronology of incidents (2004), 818
    in France (1985–1989), 214–215, 240, 259, 284
    in France (1990–1994), 303, 322
    in France (1995–1999), 405
Cortes, Francisco, 578
Costa Rica, 84, 85, 737, 747
Costelow, Richard, 450
Coulter, Janis Ruth, 499
Counter Terrorism Committee, 22
Counterterrorism Action Group (CTAG)
    creation of, 18
    FATF and, 121
    and multilateralism, 11
    U.N. Counterterrorism Committee and, 117
    U.S.-EU Declaration and, 114
Counterterrorism Finance Unit, 111
Counterterrorism Security Group, 25
Counterterrorist Center (CTC) of the CIA, 607
Courtailler, David, 439
CPP. *See* Communist Party of the Philippines/New People's Army (CPP/NPA)
"Crazy Gas Cannisters" (organization), 792
Croatia, 352, 375, 387, 756. *See also* Yugoslavia and Former Yugoslavia
CRS (Congressional Research Service), 711
CSPPA (Committee for Solidarity With Arab and Middle Eastern Political Prisoners), 223
CSTO (Collective Security Treaty Organization), 554
CTAG. *See* Counterterrorism Action Group
CTC (Counterterrorist Center of the CIA), 607
CTC (U.N. Counterterrorism Committee), 117, 146
Cuba
    Bay of Pigs (Operation Zapata), 621–622
    bombings in, 58
    Chilean arms caches and, 60
    chronology of incidents (1997), 765, 766
    chronology of incidents (2003), 809
    country reports on (2000–2004), 604
    sanctions against, 40, 41, 42, 48
    as state sponsor of terrorism, 19, 55–60
    UN counterterrorism conventions signed by, 58
    Zelikow on, 703–704
Cuban Expeditionary Force (CEF), 621
Cubas, Cecilia, 694
Curcio, Renato, 324, 351

Note: Pages 1 to 535 can be found in volume 1; pages 536 to 1019 are in volume 2.

Cyprus
    chronology of incidents (1970s), 729
    chronology of incidents (1985–1986), 731, 735
    chronology of incidents (1988–1989), 738, 739
    chronology of incidents (2003), 809
    country reports on (1985–1989), 243, 258, 282
    country reports on (1990–1994), 302
    Libyan activity in, 83
Czech Republic, 77–79, 481, 560, 664
Czechoslovakia
    country reports on, 290, 302, 327
    as state sponsor of terrorism, 97, 98

D

Dadesho, Sargon, 76
Dagestan Liberation Army, 437
Dahoumane, Abdelmajid, 492–493
Dahroug, Ali Nizar, 534, 583, 694
Dahroug, Muhammad Dahroug, 534
Dal Khalsa, 197
Dalizu, Jean Rose, 415
Dalkamoni, Hafiz, 283, 304, 322
Danish Committee for Aid to Afghan Refugees, 814
D'Antona, Massimo, 188, 440, 460
Daoudi, Kamel, 561
Dar al-Islam Western Front, 397
Darabi, Kazem, 69
Darkanzali, Mamoun, 665
Darwish, Sulayman Kahlid, 119
Daschle, Tom, 613–614
Dastgiri, Hossein, 403, 419
Davies, Rodger P., 729
Dawa Party, 333
Dawson, Earnest, 317, 329
Dayf, Muhammad al-, 466
De Luca, Antonio, 305
December 13 Independence Group, 302
Deek, Khalil al-, 446, 466
Defense Intelligence Agency (DIA), 626
Dekkushev, Adam, 512
Demirchian, Karen, 552
Democratic Forces for the Liberation of Rwanda (FDLR), 171, 539, 654. *See also* Army for the Liberation of Rwanda (ALIR)
Democratic Front for the Liberation of Palestine (DFLP)
    in Israel (1985–1989), 213, 224
    in Israel (1990–1994), 331, 344, 368

in Jordan (1995–1999), 446
in Lebanon (1990–1994), 333
profile of, 171–172
South Yemen and, 97
Syria and, 105
Democratic Iraqi Opposition, 803
Dempsey, Joan A., 633
Denmark, 282–283, 405, 560–561, 732
Dermichyan, Karen, 436
Deuba, Sher Bahadur, 472
Deutch, John, 633
Dev Sol
    chronology of incidents (1990–1991), 742–744
    in Lebanon's Bekaa Valley, 106
    profile of, 194
    in Turkey (1985–1989), 288
    in Turkey (1990–1994), 308, 325, 351, 363
    See also Revolutionary People's Liberation Party/Front (DHKP/C)
Dev Yol, 288
DFLP. See Democratic Front for the Liberation of Palestine
DHHS (U.S. Department of Health and Human Services), 642, 643
DHKP/C. See Revolutionary People's Liberation Party/Front
DHS. See U.S. Department of Homeland Security
DIA (Defense Intelligence Agency), 626
Diaz, Herman, 536
Diaz Quezada, Delfin, 353
Din, Hasan Izz al-, 175
Diodato, Marco Marino, 687
Djibouti
    9/11 response, 470
    chronology of incidents (1987), 735–736
    chronology of incidents (1990), 742
    country reports on (1985–1989), 246, 270, 294
    country reports on (1990–1994), 298
    country reports on (2000–2004), 470, 500, 537–538, 653
Djibouti Youth Movement, 742
Djiboutian Youth Movement, 298
Doctors Without Borders (Medecins Sans Frontieres), 555, 784, 792, 794
Doha, Abu, 672
Dominican Republic, 237, 278, 739
Doolittle, James H., 615, 620
Dostam, Abdul Rashid, 851
Douglas, Leigh, 733, 734

Dozier, James, 193
Dragseth, Raymond, 365
Drown, Arvey, 320
Duarte Duran, Inez, 216, 732
Dubs, Adolph, 729
Dukhtaran-e-Milat, 756
Dulles, Allen W., 618, 621
Dulles, John Foster, 621
Dunlayiei, Faisal (aka Kani Yilmaz, Kani), 377, 406
Durell, Gary C., 370

E

EAG (Eurasian Group), 121, 668, 669
East and Southern Africa Anti-Money Laundering Group (ESAAMLG), 655
East Asia
    regional patterns before 1999 (See Asia)
    regional patterns (1999–2001), 433–434, 453–454, 473–474
    regional patterns (2002–2004), 504–505, 542–544, 655–656
    See also specific countries
East Germany (German Democratic Republic), 98, 290, 303. See also Germany
East Turkestan Islamic Party (ETIP), 475
East Turkestan Liberation Organization (SHAT), 475
East Turkistan Islamic Movement (ETIM), 172, 512
Eastern Europe, regional patterns in, 302, 327, 350. See also Europe; Soviet Union and Soviet bloc; specific countries
Eberstadt, Ferdinand, 617
ECOMOG (Economic Community of West African States Cease-Fire Monitoring Group), 776
Economic Community of West African States (ECOWAS), 298, 499–500, 654
Economic Community of West African States Cease-Fire Monitoring Group (ECOMOG), 776
ECOWAS (Economic Community of West African States), 298, 499–500, 654
ECTK (Thomas Katari Communal Army), 328
Ecuador
    9/11 response, 490
    chronology of incidents (1995–1999), 757, 763, 772–774, 783
    chronology of incidents (2000–2003), 790, 803, 808
    country reports on (1985–1989), 217, 227, 236, 278
    country reports on (1990–1994), 329, 353, 365

Ecuador *(continued)*
  country reports on (2000–2004), 463, 490, 532, 580, 690–691
Egmont Group of Financial Intelligence Units, 11, 126
EGP (Guerilla Army of the Poor). *See* Guatemalan National Revolutionary Unit (URNG)
EGTK (Tupac Katari Guerilla Army), 199, 328, 340
Egypt
  chronology of incidents (1980–1984), 729
  chronology of incidents (1985–1986), 732, 733
  chronology of incidents (1990–1993), 740, 742, 746–750
  chronology of incidents (1994–1996), 750, 752, 753, 756, 759
  chronology of incidents (1997), 766, 767
  chronology of incidents (2004–2005), 840, 853, 857
  country reports on (1985–1989), 234, 250–251, 274
  country reports on (1990–1994), 314, 331, 343–344, 355, 367–368
  country reports on (1995–1999), 380–381, 395, 412, 427, 445
  country reports on (2000–2004), 464–465, 493, 524–525, 570–571, 675
  Libyan activities in, 82, 84
  Sudan and, 99–101
Egyptian Islamic Jihad/Vanguards of Conquest, 412
Egyptian Islamic Jihad. *See* Al-Jihad (AJ) or Egyptian Islamic Jihad (EIJ)
Egyptian Revolution, 732
Egypt's Revolution
  chronology of incidents (1986), 733
  in Egypt (1985–1989), 234, 250, 274
  in Egypt (1990–1994), 314
  Libya and, 84
  Nasser (Khalid Abdel) and, 265–266
Eidarous, Ibrahim Hussein Abdelhadi, 31, 672
EIJ. *See* Al-Jihad (AJ) or Egyptian Islamic Jihad (EIJ)
Eisenhower, Dwight D., 619–621
Ejupi, Florim, 667
El Mocho (aka Victor Hugo Navarro), 689
El Salvador
  chronology of incidents (1980–1984), 729
  chronology of incidents (1985), 731, 732
  chronology of incidents (1988), 738
  chronology of incidents (1991), 742
  chronology of incidents (2000), 786
  country reports on (1985–1989), 216, 227, 237, 255, 278–279
  country reports on (1990–1994), 311, 329
  Cuba and, 56, 57
  Declaration of San Salvador Against Terrorism, 530
ELA. *See* Revolutionary People's Struggle
Elbrick, Charles Burke, 728
Elhag, Mahamed Salim, 257
Ellalan Force. *See* Liberation Tigers of Tamil Eelam (LTTE)
Ellis, Desmond, 327
ELN (National Liberation Army)
  in Bolivia, 340, 578, 687
  chronology of incidents (1986), 734, 735
  chronology of incidents (1992–1994), 745, 747, 750
  chronology of incidents (1995–1996), 753, 754, 758–760
  chronology of incidents (1997), 764, 765, 767, 768
  chronology of incidents (1998), 769, 771, 774, 775
  chronology of incidents (1999), 776, 778–780, 785
  chronology of incidents (2000–2003), 788, 790, 794, 806
  in Colombia (*See* Colombia, country reports on)
  Cuba and, 55–60
  in Peru, 692
  profile of, 187–188
  in Venezuela, 492, 583, 695
Emgann ("Combat"), 459
England. *See* United Kingdom (UK)
"Enough is Enough in the Niger River" (organization), 781
EPL. *See* People's Liberation Army
EPR (Popular Revolutionary Army), 393
ERCA (Catalan Red Liberation Army), 192, 239, 262, 737
Erdal, Fehriye, 438, 458
Erignac, Claude, 561
Eritrea, 101, 762, 814
ERNK (National Liberation Front of Kurdistan), 422, 438
ERP (People's Revolutionary Army), 172

Note: Pages 1 to 535 can be found in volume 1; pages 536 to 1019 are in volume 2.

ESAAMLG (East and Southern Africa Anti-Money Laundering Group), 655
Esber, Jacqueline, 303
Escobar, Pablo, 329, 340–341, 353
Escrigas Estrada, Fausto, 732
Esebua, Gocha, 420
Espinoza, Pedro, 353
Estonia, 561
ETA and ETA-M. *See* Basque Fatherland and Liberty
Ethiopia
   9/11 response, 470
   chronology of incidents (1995–1996), 754, 757, 760, 761
   chronology of incidents (1997–1998), 763, 764, 769, 771
   chronology of incidents (1999), 779, 782
   chronology of incidents (2001), 795
   chronology of incidents (2005), 857
   country reports on (1990–1994), 298
   country reports on (1995–1999), 371, 384, 399–400, 416, 431
   country reports on (2000–2004), 470, 500, 538, 653
   Sudan and, 99–102
ETIM (East Turkistan Islamic Movement), 172, 512
ETIP (East Turkestan Islamic Party), 475
Eurasia
   regional patterns (1995–1999), 374, 386–387, 404, 419–420, 435–436
   regional patterns (2000–2004), 456, 477–478, 510–511, 551–552, 661–662
   See also Soviet Union and Soviet bloc
Eurasian Group (EAG), 121, 668, 669
Eurojust, 115
Europe
   regional patterns before 1992 (*See under* Eastern Europe; Western Europe)
   regional patterns (1992–1994), 337–338, 350, 361
   regional patterns (1995–1999), 374, 386–387, 404, 421, 438
   regional patterns (2000–2004), 457–458, 481–482, 516, 558–559, 661–662
European Commission, 116, 117
European Relief Organization, 750
European Union (EU)
   9/11 response, 481
   asset blocking by, 8
   Dutch presidency, 668
   OSCE and, 511
   regional patterns (2000–2004), 516, 558, 661
   U.S.-EU Declaration, 114–117
Europol, 115
Ewaywi, Abbas Othman, 466
Export-Import Bank, 42–45, 47, 49–51
EYAL (Fighting Jewish Organization), 381
EZLN (Zapatista National Liberation Army), 393

F

Fadhil, Mustafa Mohammed, 31
Fadhli, 'Ayyad al-, 119
Fadlallah, Muhammad Husayn, 730–731
FAF (Fighting Guerrilla Formation), 406, 768
Fahd, Nasir al-, 575
Fahima, Al-Amin Kalifa, 32, 85, 89, 90, 462
Faisal, Shaykh Abdullah Ibrahim el-, 522, 568
FAL. *See* Zarate Willka Armed Liberation Forces
FAL (Communist Party of El Salvador's Armed Forces of Liberation), 172
Fallahian, Ali, 69
FAO (U.N. Food and Agriculture Organization), 78
Faour, Daher, 323
Faqih, Saad Rashed Mahammad al-, 113
FAR (Armed Forces of Rwanda), 171
FAR (Revolutionary Armed Forces). *See* Guatemalan National Revolutionary Unit (URNG)
Farabundo Marti Liberation Movement. *See* FMLN
Farabundo Marti Popular Liberation Forces (FPL), 172
FARC (Revolutionary Armed Forces of Colombia)
   in Brazil (2000–2004), 582
   chronology of incidents (1983), 729
   chronology of incidents (1992–1994), 745–747, 751, 752
   chronology of incidents (1995–1996), 755, 757, 758, 761
   chronology of incidents (1997–1998), 763, 764, 767, 769–772, 775
   chronology of incidents (1999), 777–779, 781–784
   chronology of incidents (2000–2002), 790, 793, 799, 802
   chronology of incidents (2003–2004), 807, 813, 816, 817, 824
   chronology of incidents (2005), 851, 852, 854, 856, 857
   in Colombia (*See* Colombia, country reports on)
   Cuba and, 57–60

FARC *(continued)*
   in Ecuador, 580, 690–691
   funding of, 21
   IRA and, 193–194, 487, 488
   narcoterrorism and, 117
   in Paraguay, 694
   in Peru, 463, 692
   profile of, 193–194
   in Venezuela, 19, 492, 535, 583, 695
Faris, Iyman, 33
FARN (Armed Forces of National Resistance), 172
Farooqui, Amjad, 140, 685
Farroukh, Tawfiz Muhammad, 527, 573, 679
Farzandan-e-Millat, 853
Fatah Hawks, 848
Fatah Rebels (Fatah-the-Intifada)
   in Israel, 213, 224, 344
     Syria and, 103–105, 108, 109
     Tanzim of, 494
Fatah Revolutionary Council. *See* Abu Nidal Organization (ANO)
Fatah Special Operations Group. *See* Hawari Group
FATF. *See* Financial Action Task Force on Money Laundering
Faught, Edward, 745
Fawwaz, Khalid Al-, 31, 424, 672
Fayad, Sobhi, 583, 694
FBI. *See* Federal Bureau of Investigation (FBI)
FDIP (Indigenous Defense Front for Pastaza Province), 772
FDLR (Democratic Forces for the Liberation of Rwanda), 171, 539, 654. *See also* Army for the Liberation of Rwanda (ALIR)
FDR (Revolutionary Democratic Front), 237, 256
Federal Bureau of Investigation (FBI)
   counterterrorism efforts, 6–7, 32
     Intelligence Committee recommendations on, 638, 644
     Russian Federal Security Service and, 555
Federation of Latin American Banking Associations (FELA-BAN), 114–115
FELA-BAN (Federation of Latin American Banking Associations), 114–115
Feliciano (aka Oscar Alberto Ramirez Durand), 444
Fhimah, Lamen Khalifa, 327

Note: Pages 1 to 535 can be found in volume 1; pages 536 to 1019 are in volume 2.

Fifteen Khordad Foundation, 69
Fighting Guerrilla Formation (FAF or MAS), 406, 768
Fighting Islamic Group. *See* Libyan Islamic Fighting Group (LIFG)
Fighting Jewish Organization (EYAL), 381
Fighting Revolutionary Cells, 733
Filipino Antiterrorism Task Force, 140
Financial Action Task Force on Money Laundering (FATF)
   India and, 125
   in Middle East and North Africa (MENA FATF), 121, 124–125, 674, 681
   and multilateralism, 11
   overview of, 131–134
   Philippines and, 508, 550
   role of, 118, 121–122, 129
   Russia and, 514
   Special Recommendations of, 114, 121, 132, 133
   Ukraine and, 515
FinCEN (Financial Crimes Enforcement Network), 114, 566, 580
Finland, 561, 664
FIS. *See* Islamic Salvation Front
FIT (Tunisian Islamic Front), 383
Flag of Freedom Organization, 742
Flatow, Alisa, 70, 381
FLEC. *See* Front for the Liberation of the Enclave of Cabinda
FLEC-FAC (Cabinda Liberation Front–Cabinda Armed Forces), 399, 415, 763, 769
FLEC-Renewed (Front for the Liberation of the Enclave of Cabinda–Renewed), 793
FLNC. *See* Corsican National Liberation Front
FMLN (Farabundo Marti Liberation Movement)
   chronology of incidents (1983), 729
   chronology of incidents (1988), 738
   chronology of incidents (1991), 742
   Cuba and, 56
   in El Salvador (*See* El Salvador, country reports on)
   in Honduras, 279, 312
   in Mexico, 237, 256
   in Nicaragua, 92–93, 312
   in Panama, 236
   profile of, 172
   PRTC and, 169
FNC (Nationalist Combat Front), 235
FNL (National Liberation Front), 856

FNTR (National Front for the Renewal of Chad), 416, 769
Foda, Fara, 343
Foley, Laurence, 139, 198, 499, 526, 570, 572
Folini, Maurizio, 261, 305–306
Fontaine, Marcel, 252
Force 17 organization, 173, 213, 253. *See also* PLO (Palestinian Liberation Authority)
Former Soviet Union, country reports on (1990–1994), 324–325, 339, 352, 361. *See also specific countries*
FP-25. *See* Popular Forces of 25 April
FPL (Farabundo Marti Popular Liberation Forces), 172
FPM. *See* Morazanist Patriotic Front
FPMR. *See* Manuel Rodriguez Patriotic Front
France
  9/11 response, 483
  chronology of incidents (1985–1987), 730, 731, 733, 735, 736
  chronology of incidents (1989–1991), 738, 739, 742–744
  chronology of incidents (1993), 749
  chronology of incidents (1995–1996), 755, 757, 759–762
  chronology of incidents (1999–2000), 777, 786
  chronology of incidents (2002–2004), 799, 810, 813, 818, 840, 843
  country reports on (1985–1989), 214–215, 227–228, 239–240, 258–260, 283–285
  country reports on (1990–1994), 302–303, 321–322, 350, 362
  country reports on (1995–1999), 375, 387–388, 405, 422, 439
  country reports on (2000–2004), 458–459, 483–484, 518, 561–562, 664–665
  Iranian attacks in, 64, 66, 68
  Libyan attacks on, 83, 85–92
  prosecutions in, 29, 67
Francis, Lakeina Monique, 450
Franks, Tommy, 135
FRAP (Front for Proletarian Action), 215, 258
Fraszczak, Augustine, 337
Fraxia Midheniston (Nihilist Faction), 759
Free Aceh Movement (GAM), 434, 454, 788
Free Democratic People's Government of Laos, 548, 659
Free Papua Movement (OPM)
  chronology of incidents (1996), 757
  chronology of incidents (2001), 792
  in Indonesia, 402, 434
  in Papua New Guinea, 300
Freedom and Democracy Congress of Kurdistan. *See* PKK (Kurdish Workers' Party or KADEK)
Freedom Falcons of Kurdistan, 835
Freedom Strugglers, 345–346
Frei, Eduardo, 410
Freitas, Terrence, 430
French Armed Islamic Front, 841
French Guiana, 83
Froehlich, Margo, 376
Front for Proletarian Action (FRAP), 215, 258
Front for the Liberation of the Enclave of Cabinda (FLEC)
  in Angola (1990–1994), 297–298, 335, 348, 359
  in Angola (2000–2004), 451
Front for the Liberation of the Enclave of Cabinda–Renewed (FLEC-Renewed), 793
Front Pembela Islam (Islamic Defenders Front), 475
Fronte Nazionale (National Front), 460
FRP-LZ (Popular Revolutionary Forces–Lorenzo Zelaya), 191, 237, 279, 280
FUAC (Andres Castro United Front), 783
Fujimori, Alberto, 330, 341

G

G-8 (Group of 8), 481, 485. *See also* Counterterrorism Action Group (CTAG)
Gakayev, Magomed, 555
GAL (Antiterrorist Liberation Group), 214, 215, 286
GAM (Free Aceh Movement), 434, 454, 788
Gamaskhurdia, Zviad, 201
Ganczarski, Christian, 561, 562, 664, 665
Gandhi, Indira, 266, 730
Gandhi, Rajiv, 218, 230, 743
Gandy, John, 317, 325
Ganic, Ejup, 352
Garcia, Alan, 217
Gariety, Kathleen, 499
Garnoui, Ishan, 665
Gates, Robert, 623
Gauna, Timothy Lee, 450
Gaviria, Cesar, 341
Gaviria, Juan Carlos, 392
Gay, Lahe'ena'e, 430
Gaza. *See* Israel and occupied territories
GCC (Gulf Cooperation Council), 493
GCP (Popular Combatants Group), 690

Gemayel, Bashir, 729
Georgia, Republic of
 9/11 response, 479
 chronology of incidents (1995), 753–754
 chronology of incidents (1997–1998), 763, 766, 768–769, 773
 chronology of incidents (1999–2000), 781, 783–784, 788, 789
 chronology of incidents (2002), 799
 chronology of incidents (2005), 851
 country reports on (1995–1999), 375, 405, 420, 436
 country reports on (2000–2004), 456–457, 479, 511–512, 553, 665
 U.S. military training in, 137
German-Arab Friendship Association, 733
Germany
 9/11 response, 484
 chronology of incidents (1970s), 728
 chronology of incidents (1981), 729
 chronology of incidents (1985–1989), 730–734, 736, 738–740
 chronology of incidents (1990–1994), 741, 743, 746, 747
 chronology of incidents (1995–1999), 755–757, 760, 761, 764, 777, 781
 chronology of incidents (2000–2004), 789, 803, 810, 819
 country reports on (1985–1989), 214, 227, 240–241, 264–265, 283, 290
 country reports on (1990–1994), 303–304, 322–323, 338, 350, 362
 country reports on (1995–1999), 375–376, 388–389, 405–406, 422, 439
 country reports on (2000–2004), 459, 484, 518–519, 562–563, 665–666
 Iranian attacks and abductions in, 63, 65, 66, 69
 Libyan activity in, 85, 86, 89, 90, 92
 merger of East and West, 303
 prosecutions in, 30, 69
 state sponsorship of terrorism (East Germany), 98
 Syria and, 103, 104
Ghailani, Ahmed Khalfan, 31, 140, 655, 685
Ghana, 348
Ghandafar, Abdel Fattah, 322
Ghannouchi, Rachid, 346

Note: Pages 1 to 535 can be found in volume 1; pages 536 to 1019 are in volume 2.

Gharavi, Ayatollah Ali, 77
Ghawsha, Ibrahim, 382, 413, 495
Ghiringhelli, Marcello, 441
Ghoni, Abdul (aka Mukhlas or Ali Ghufron), 506, 547
Ghosheh, Samir, 191
Ghozi, Fathur Rahman Al- (aka Abu Saad or Sammi Sali Jamin), 508, 549–550, 809
Ghufron, Ali (aka Mukhlas or Abdul Ghoni), 506, 547
Ghuraybi, Shaikh Nureddin, 70
GIA. *See* Armed Islamic Group
Gibraltar, 264
GICM (Moroccan Islamic Combatant Group), 186, 664, 670, 679–680
Gilani, Shayhk Mubarik Ali, 179
Giorgieri, Licio, 241, 736
Glaser, Daniel, 124
Glass, Charles, 61, 104, 233
Global Relief Foundation, 488
Gluck, Kenneth, 480, 555
GN 95 organization, 389
Gnecco, Jose Eduardo, 689
Gogh, Theo van, 668, 710
Goldstein, Baruch, 181, 368
Goldstein, Craig, 536
Gomez Hurtado, Alvaro, 256, 378
Gonsalves, Marc D., 536, 807
Gonzalez, Pedro Miguel, 379, 410, 425
Gonzalez-Penalva, Belen, 439, 441
Gorbachev, Mikhail, 98
Gorriaran Merlo, Enrique, 378
Goss, Porter, 17
Gourken Yanikian Military Unite, 404
Government of Universal Palestine in Exile, 805
Gow, Ian, 742
GPML (U.N. Global Programme Against Money Laundering), 117
Grams, Wolfgang, 350
Granda Escobar, Rodrigo, 689, 695
GRAPO (October 1st Antifascist Resistance Group), 172–173, 459, 731. *See also* Spain, country reports on
Greece
 9/11 response, 484
 17 November organization attacks on, 160
 chronology of incidents (1985–1989), 730–733, 736–740
 chronology of incidents (1990–1991), 741–744

chronology of incidents (1994–1996), 750, 751, 753, 755, 758, 759
chronology of incidents (1998–1999), 768, 774, 776, 779, 780
chronology of incidents (2000–2001), 788, 790, 792, 794
chronology of incidents (2003), 808, 809, 812, 813, 816
chronology of incidents (2004), 819, 828
country reports on (1985–1989), 215–216, 228, 242–243, 260–261, 285
country reports on (1990–1994), 304–305, 323, 338, 351, 362
country reports on (1995–1999), 376, 389, 406, 422, 439–440
country reports on (2000–2004), 459–460, 484–485, 519–520, 563, 666
Green, Barbara, 499
Green Battalion, 823
Greenbaum, Judith, 469, 797
Gregg, Herbert, 420
Gritz, David, 499
Group for the Preservation of Holy Sites. *See* al-Qaeda (al-Qaida)
GSPC. *See* Salafist Group for Call and Combat
Guadaloupe, Mexico, 731
Guardia, Lenin, 489, 531
Guatemala
    chronology of incidents (1968), 728
    country reports on (1985–1989), 279
    country reports on (1990–1994), 311–312, 329, 365
    country reports on (1995–1999), 378–379, 393
    Cuba and, 56, 57
    sanctions against, 48
Guatemalan National Revolutionary Unit (URNG), 329, 365, 378–379, 393
Guatemalan Workers' Party. *See* Guatemalan National Revolutionary Unit (URNG)
Guerilla Army of the Poor (EGP). *See* Guatemalan National Revolutionary Unit (URNG)
Guevara, Che, 187–188
Guevarista Revolutionary Army, 765
Guinea, 451, 790
Gulf Cooperation Council (GCC), 493
Guly, Jaffar Hasso, 388
Gunawan, Rusman "Gun Gun," 658
Gund Allah (Soldiers of God), 571
Gunn, Cherone Louis, 450

Guven, Ihsan, 178
Guzman, Abimael
    peace letters by, 353–354, 365–366
    retrial of, 692
    Shining Path and, 196, 341–342
Guzman, Jaime, 328

H

Habash (Habbash), George, 78–79, 190
Habibi, Hassan, 68
Hachani, Abdelkader, 445
Hadden, Susan Ginsburg, 372
Hadouti, Tabdelkrim El, 482
Hadri, Enver, 321
Haeusler, Andrea, 389, 406
Hage, Wadih El, 31
Hagopian, Hagop, 97, 166, 738
Haig, Alexander, 375
Haiter, Mouloud, 663
Haiti
    chronology of incidents (2004–2005), 842, 853, 854, 856
    country reports on (1985–1989), 237
    sanctions against, 48
Haitian Liberation Organization (OLH), 237
Hajj, Khalid Ali al-, 140
Hakim, Abdel Aziz al-, 676
Hakim, Mahdi Al-, 271
Halbi, Shaykh Nizar al-, 382
Halima, Mahmoud Abu, 33
Hamadei, Abbas, 241
Hamadei, Mohammed, 233, 241
HAMAS (Islamic Resistance Movement)
    chronology of incidents (1994–1996), 752, 758
    chronology of incidents (2001), 798
    chronology of incidents (2002), 800, 802, 803, 805
    chronology of incidents (2003), 808, 814
    chronology of incidents (2004), 817, 818, 821, 822, 824, 831–833, 840, 843, 848, 849
    chronology of incidents (2005), 851, 852
    extradition of members of, 34
    funding of, 119, 128
    Hizballah and, 176
    Iran and, 65–66, 68
    Iraq and, 79, 139–140
    in Israel (1990–1994), 344, 356, 368
    in Israel (1995–1999), 381, 396, 412–413, 427, 445

HAMAS *(continued)*
   in Israel (2000–2004), 465–466, 493–494, 525, 572, 677
   in Jordan (1995–1999), 382, 396, 413, 428, 446
   in Jordan (2000–2004), 495
   in Lebanon (2000–2004), 495–496
   Libya and, 87
   profile of, 173–174
   in Saudi Arabia (1990–1994), 346
   in South America, 491, 533
   Sudan and, 99–103
   Syria and, 107–109
   in Yemen (2000–2004), 682
   See also Izz al-Din al-Qassam Brigades
Hambali (aka Nurjaman Riduan bin Isomoddin), 180, 182, 542, 550
Hamdan, Muhammad, 261
Hamilton, Lee, 39
Hammadi, Abbas Ali, 265, 338, 350
Hammadi, Muhammad Ali, 265, 283, 338, 350, 739
Hamza, Abu, 672
Hamza, Khidir Abd al-Abbas, 753
Hamza, Mustafa, 173
Handicap International, 750
Hani, Chris, 94
Hanratty, Gerard, 304
Hansen, Heiner, 811
Haq, Abdul, 779
Harakat-ul-Ansar (HUA)
   in India, 372
   Masood Azhar and, 179
   in Pakistan, 373, 402, 418
Harakat ul-Jihad-I-Islami (HUJI), 174, 776, 799
Harakat ul-Jihad-I-Islami/Bangladesh (HUJI-B), 174
Harakat ul-Mujahidin (HUM)
   chronology of incidents (1999–2000), 776, 783, 786
   chronology of incidents (2004), 841
   in Pakistan, 418, 432, 453, 685
   profile of, 174–175
Hardy, Molly Huckaby, 415
Hargrove, Thomas, 752
Hariri, Hussein Ali Muhammad, 263
Hariri, Rafik, 852
Hashmona'im organization, 344
Hasina, Sheikh, 174

Note: Pages 1 to 535 can be found in volume 1; pages 536 to 1019 are in volume 2.

Hattab, Hassan, 426–427, 464
Haubner, Robert, 430
Haule-Frimpong, Eva, 265
Hawari, Colonel, 175, 259
Hawari Group, 175. *See also* PLO (Palestinian Liberation Authority)
Hawatmah, Nayif, 171
Hawillo, Omar, 258
Hazama-ha, 229
Heffernan, Megan, 499
Heihachiro, Togo, 291
Hekmatyar, Gulbuddin, 385
Helton, Arthur, 536
Hemed, Rashid Sweleh, 655
Hensley, Jack, 198
Hepp, Odfried, 30
Hernandez, Owell, 341
Hernandez, Zak, 365, 379, 410
Hernandez Norambuena, Mauricio, 353, 534, 579
Herrera Iles, Gerardo, 580
Herrhausen, Alfred, 283, 740
Hezbollah. *See* Hizballah
HIG. *See* Hizb-I-Islami Gulbudin
Higgins, William
   abduction of, 63, 252, 737
   assassination of, 276, 333
   burial of, 745
   release of, 105
Hijazi, Ra'id, 466, 495, 678
Hikmatyar, Gulbuddin, 359–360
Hilal, Mohammed, 397
Himatyar, Gulbuddin, 176
Hindawi, Nizar, 103
Hiyari, Bilal Mansur al-, 119, 678
Hizb al-Tahrir al-Islami (Islamic Liberation Party), 525, 675
Hizb-I-Islami Gulbudin (HIG)
   in Afghanistan, 336, 540
   Al Badhr Mujaheddin and, 162
   chronology of incidents (1991), 742
   Hizbul-Mujahedin and, 176
   profile of, 176
Hizb ut-Tahrir
   in Azerbaijan, 478, 511
   in Germany, 562, 665–666
   in Kazakhstan, 479, 667
   in Kyrgyzstan, 512–513, 667–668
   in Tajikistan, 480
   in Uzbekistan, 481, 515

Hizballah
- abductions by, 65
- Ambassador Black on, 288–289
- in Bahrain, 69
- in Central African Republic, 247
- chronology of incidents (1986–1989), 735–737, 739
- chronology of incidents (1991–1995), 744, 745, 749, 754
- in Cyprus, 282
- in France, 259
- Iran-sponsored terrorism by, 61–68, 71
- in Israel, 332, 356, 572, 677
- in Kuwait (1985–1989), 250
- narcoterrorism and, 118
- profile of, 175–176
- in Saudi Arabia, 235
- in South America, 489, 491, 533
- in Spain, 287
- Sudan and, 99–101
- Syria and, 105–110
- in Turkey, 66
- See also Bahraini Hizballa; Kuwaiti Hizballah; Palestinian Hizballah; Saudi Hizballah; Turkish Hizballah

Hizballah al-Khalij, 397
Hizballah of the Hijaz, 253
Hizballain Lebanon. See Lebanon, country reports on
Hizbul-Mujahedin (HM)
- Al Badhr Mujaheddin and, 162
- chronology of incidents (1998–2002), 775, 783, 788, 803
- chronology of incidents (2004), 817, 819, 826–828, 838, 840, 844, 846, 848–850
- chronology of incidents (2005), 856, 857
- profile of, 176

HM. See Hizbul-Mujahedin
Hobson, Kenneth Ray, II, 415
Hofmann, Sieglinde, 375
Hogefeld, Birgit, 350, 362, 388
Holy Land Foundation for Relief and Development, 7, 128
Holy Warriors of Ahmad Daqamseh, 466, 495
Holy Warriors of Egypt, 857
Homeland Security Department. See U.S. Department of Homeland Security
Honduras
- chronology of incidents (1987–1989), 736, 738–739
- chronology of incidents (1990–1995), 741, 743, 753
- country reports on (1985–1989), 236–237, 255–256, 279–280
- country reports on (1990–1994), 312
- Cuba and, 56

Hooper, Richard, 536
Hoover, Herbert, 617
Hopkins, Adrian, 323
Horowitz, Debra Ruth, 536
Horowitz, Elnatan Eli, 536
Hosseini, Sendar, 68
Howes, Christopher, 401
Howes, Thomas R., 536, 807
HPG (People's Defense Force), 182
HUA. See Harakat-ul-Ansar
Hubayshi, Muhammad, 494
Huddleston, Walter, 628
HUJI (Harakat ul-Jihad-I-Islami), 174, 776, 799
HUJI-B (Harakat ul-Jihad-I-Islami/Bangladesh), 174
Hul, Abu, 160–161
HUM. See Harakat ul-Mujahidin
Humala, Antauro, 851
Humary, Haysayn, 303
Hungary
- 9/11 response, 481
- chronology of incidents (1991), 745
- country reports on (1990–1994), 302, 327
- country reports on (2000–2004), 520, 563, 666

Hunt, Leamon, 193, 241
Hussein, Azahari, 658
Hussein, King, 107, 356
Hussein (Husayn), Saddam
- call for terrorism by, 74
- capture of, 137
- Dawa Party vs., 61
- hostage taking and, 74
- and Iraq War, 18
- Powell on, 138–140
- suicide bombing payments by, 79

Husseini, Faisal, 344
Hyde, William, 536

I

IAA. See Islamic Army of Aden
IAEA (International Atomic Energy Agency), 146
IARA (Islamic African Relief Agency), 103, 113
IBDA-C (Islamic Great East Raiders–Front), 178, 408
Ibrahim, Abu, 73–78, 160, 274, 284–285

1046 Index

IBT (Internet Black Tigers), 403
ICAO (International Civil Aviation Council), 258
Iceland, 563–564
ICRC. *See* International Red Cross
ICS (Intelligence Community Staff), 623
IDF (Israeli Defense Force), 795
Idris, Abdulmukim "Mukim," 549–550
IFLB (Islamic Front for the Liberation of Bahrain), 225, 234, 758
IG. *See* al-Gama'at al-Islamiyya (Islamic Group or IG)
IGAD (Inter-Governmental Authority on Development), 103
IIPB (Islamic International Peacekeeping Brigade), 178
IIS (Iraqi Intelligence Service), 78, 79
IJG (Islamic Jihad Group), 178, 667
IK (Iparretarrak), 259, 284, 321
IMF (International Monetary Fund), 47, 129, 132
IMRO (Internal Macedonia Revolutionary Organization), 309
IMU. *See* Islamic Movement of Uzbekistan
INC (Iraq National Congress), 76–77
Incident Review Panel (IRP), 607, 609
Independent National Patriotic Front of Liberia (INPFL), 298
India
    9/11 response, 472
    chronology of incidents (1980–1984), 730
    chronology of incidents (1985–1989), 731, 737, 738
    chronology of incidents (1991–1992), 743–745
    chronology of incidents (1995–1997), 755–757, 759, 766
    chronology of incidents (1998), 768, 770–775
    chronology of incidents (1999), 775–780, 782–784
    chronology of incidents (2000), 785–792
    chronology of incidents (2001), 793–799
    chronology of incidents (2002), 799–806
    chronology of incidents (2003), 806–816
    chronology of incidents (2004), 816–850
    chronology of incidents (2005), 851–858
    country reports on (1985–1989), 230, 244–245, 266, 291
    country reports on (1990–1994), 299–300, 319, 336, 348–349, 360
    country reports on (1995–1999), 372–373, 385, 401–402, 418, 432
    country reports on (2000–2004), 452, 472, 502–503, 540–541, 684
    Sikh violence in, 218
    terrorism financing and, 125
Indian Peace Keeping Force (IPKF), 269
Indigenous Defense Front for Pastaza Province (FDIP), 772
Indonesia
    bombing of U.S. embassy in, 30
    chronology of incidents (1986), 734
    chronology of incidents (1991), 742
    chronology of incidents (1996), 757
    chronology of incidents (1999), 781
    chronology of incidents (2000–2001), 788, 790, 792, 793, 796
    chronology of incidents (2002–2005), 804, 805, 814, 838, 855
    country reports on (1985–1989), 219, 229–230
    country reports on (1995–1999), 402, 434
    country reports on (2000–2004), 454, 475, 506, 546–547, 658
    sanctions against, 48–49
Informal Anarchic Federation, 816–817
INLA. *See* Irish National Liberation Army
INPFL (Independent National Patriotic Front of Liberia), 298
Intelligence Community Staff (ICS), 623
Intelligence Resources Advisory Committee (IRAC), 623
Inter-American Committee Against Terrorism (CICTE), 530, 577
Inter-Governmental Authority on Development (IGAD), 103
Internal Macedonia Revolutionary Organization (IMRO), 309
International Atomic Energy Agency (IAEA), 146
International Civil Aviation (ICAO) Council, 258
International Criminal Tribunal for former Yugoslavia, 44
International Criminal Tribunal for Rwanda, 44
International Front Against Imperialism, 239
International Islamic Front for Jihad Against Jews and Crusaders. *See* al-Qaeda (al-Qaida)
International Justice Group, 756, 757
International Monetary Fund (IMF), 47, 129, 132
International Police Task Force (IPTF), 387

Note: Pages 1 to 535 can be found in volume 1; pages 536 to 1019 are in volume 2.

International Red Cross (ICRC)
  attacks on (1985-1989), 287
  attacks on (1990-1994), 307-308, 318, 336, 745
  attacks on (1994-1999), 761, 762, 771, 780, 784
  attacks on (1995-1999), 389-390, 407, 416
  attacks on (2000-2005), 795
International Rescue Committee, 745
International Sikh Youth Federation, 197
Internet Black Tigers (IBT), 403
Iparragirre, Soledad, 671
Iparretarrak (IK), 259, 284, 321
IPKF (Indian Peace Keeping Force), 269
IPLO (Irish People's Liberation Organization), 288
IPTF (International Police Task Force), 387
Iqbal, Muhammad (aka Abu Jibril), 548
IRA. *See* Irish Republican Army
IRAC (Intelligence Resources Advisory Committee), 623
Iran
  Afghanistan and, 72
  African activities of (1990-1994), 347
  Bremer Commission on, 637
  chronology of incidents (1970s), 729
  chronology of incidents (1991-1994), 743, 749, 750
  chronology of incidents (1999-2000), 780, 782, 787
  chronology of incidents (2003), 815
  cooperation with U.S., 72
  country reports on (1985-1989), 212, 222, 224, 248-249
  country reports on (1990-1994), 331, 342, 354
  country reports on (2000-2004), 603
  Iran-Contra investigation and, 629-630
  Pakistan and, 244, 292
  sanctions against, 49
  as state sponsor of terrorism, 19, 60-73
  Sudan and, 99
  and weapons of mass destruction, 17, 18, 21, 22, 49
IRAP (Irish Republican Socialist Party), 176
Iraq
  Ambassador Black on, 586, 589, 598
  bombing of (1993), 24
  Brennan on, 699-700
  chronology of incidents (1985), 731
  chronology of incidents (1992-1994), 745-751
  chronology of incidents (1996-1999), 757, 761, 762-763, 770, 771, 780
  chronology of incidents (2003), 808, 813-816
  chronology of incidents (2004), 816-840, 842-850
  chronology of incidents (2005), 852, 856
  country reports on (1985-1989), 274-275
  country reports on (1990-1994), 313, 342, 354
  country reports on (2000-2004), 603-604, 675-676
  FTO list, removal from, 156
  Iran-sponsored terrorism and activity in, 61, 69, 70, 72, 73
  Kuwait invasion and Gulf War, 74-75, 317, 330
  Operation Iraqi Freedom, 137, 569 (*See also specific countries participating*)
  sanctions against, 49
  as state sponsor of terrorism, 19, 53, 73-81, 138-140, 586
  war against, 18
  WMD in, 21, 49
Iraq National Congress (INC), 76-77
Iraqi Communist Party, 78
Iraqi Intelligence Service (IIS), 78, 79
Iraqi Legitimate Resistance, 832
Iraqi National Accord, 77
Iraultza, 215, 228, 239, 262, 287
Ireland, Republic of
  chronology of incidents (1994), 750
  country reports on (1985-1989), 261, 285
  country reports on (1990-1994), 305, 323
  See also Northern Ireland
IRGC (Islamic Revolutionary Guard Corps), 66, 67, 105
Irish Continuity Army. *See* Continuity Irish Republican Army (CIRA)
Irish National Liberation Army (INLA)
  feud within, 238
  in Ireland (1985-1989), 261
  in Northern Ireland (1995-1999), 377
  profile of, 176-177
  in UK (1985-1989), 288
  in UK (1995-1999), 408-409
Irish People's Liberation Organization (IPLO), 288
Irish Republican Army (IRA)
  chronology of incidents (1972), 728
  chronology of incidents (1996), 758, 759
  Cuba and, 59
  FARC and, 193-194, 487, 488, 689-690
  in France, 322
  profile of, 177

Irish Republican Army *(continued)*
  in UK (1995–1999), 391, 408–409, 424
  in UK (2000–2004), 487
  See also Continuity Irish Republican Army (CIRA); Official IRA (OIRA); Provisional Irish Republican Army (PIRA); Real Irish Republican Army (RIRA); Sinn Fein
Irish Republican Socialist Party (IRAP), 176
IRP (Incident Review Panel), 607, 609
Islami Inqilabi Mahaz, 402, 767
Islamic Action (Islamic Movement Organization), 66–67
Islamic African Relief Agency (IARA), 103, 113
Islamic Anger Brigades, 829
Islamic Army for the Liberation of Holy Places, 416, 800. *See also* al-Qaeda (al-Qaida)
Islamic Army in Iraq, 833, 835, 841, 844
Islamic Army in Iraq, the 1920 Brigade, 836, 844, 846
Islamic Army of Aden (IAA) or Aden-Abyan Islamic Army (AAIA)
  profile of, 177
  USS Cole bombing and, 468
  in Yemen (1995–1999), 429, 447
  in Yemen (2000–2004), 576
Islamic Awakening Youths, 446
Islamic Deterrence Force, 468
Islamic Front, 800
Islamic Front for the Liberation of Bahrain (IFLB), 225, 234, 758
Islamic Front for the Liberation of Palestine, 224
Islamic Great East Raiders–Front (IBDA-C), 178, 408
Islamic Group. *See* al-Gama'at al-Islamiyya (Islamic Group or IG)
Islamic International Brigade, 555
Islamic International Peacekeeping Brigade (IIPB), 178
Islamic Jihad
  in Argentina (1990–1994), 340, 364
  assassinations by, 63
  chronology of incidents (1983–1986), 729–730, 733, 735
  chronology of incidents (1989–1992), 740, 743, 745
  chronology of incidents (2002), 802

Note: Pages 1 to 535 can be found in volume 1; pages 536 to 1019 are in volume 2.

  in Turkey (1985–1989), 243
  See also Hizballah
Islamic Jihad Group (IJG), 178, 667
Islamic Jihad Group of Uzbekistan, 834
Islamic Liberation Organization, 732
Islamic Liberation Party (Hizb al-Tahrir al-Islami), 525, 675
Islamic Movement for Change, 397, 756
Islamic Movement of Iraqi Mujahidin, 849
Islamic Movement of Uzbekistan (IMU)
  chronology of incidents (2000), 790
  in Kyrgyzstan (1995–1999), 436
  in Kyrgyzstan (2000–2004), 457, 479, 554
  profile of, 179
  in Tajikistan (1995–1999), 437
  in Tajikistan (2000–2004), 515
  terrorist designation, 157
  in Uzbekistan (1995–1999), 437–438
  in Uzbekistan (2000–2004), 457, 480–481, 557–558
Islamic Movement Organization (Islamic Action), 66–67
Islamic Rage Brigade, 826
Islamic Renewal and Reform Organization, 467
Islamic Resistance Movement. *See* HAMAS
Islamic Resistance Movement, Nu'-man Brigades, 838
Islamic Revolutionary Guard Corps (IRGC), 66, 67, 105
Islamic Sal. *See* al-Qaeda (al-Qaida)
Islamic Salvation Army (AIS), 394, 411, 426
Islamic Salvation Front (FIS)
  in Algeria, 343, 355, 367, 411
  chronology of incidents (1995), 755
  in France, 422
  Sudan and, 100
  See also Islamic Salvation Army (AIS)
Islamic Unification Movement, 213
Islamic Union. *See* Al-Ittihad al-Islami (AIAI or Islamic Union)
Ismail, Mustafa Osman, 102
Israel and occupied territories
  9/11 response, 493
  chronology of incidents (1986), 735
  chronology of incidents (1990–1994), 741, 744, 749, 752
  chronology of incidents (1995–1998), 753–756, 758, 759, 765–768
  chronology of incidents (2001), 794, 796–798

chronology of incidents (2002), 799–803, 805
chronology of incidents (2003), 806, 808, 810–815
chronology of incidents (2004), 817–822, 824–826, 828, 831–837, 840, 843, 845, 847–850
chronology of incidents (2005), 851, 852, 854, 857
country reports on (1985–1989), 213, 224–225, 233, 251, 275
country reports on (1990–1994), 314–315, 331–332, 344, 355–356, 368
country reports on (1995–1999), 381, 395–396, 412–413, 427, 445–446
country reports on (2000–2004), 465–466, 493–494, 525–526, 571–572, 676–678
Iran vs., 71–73
Syria and, 110
Israeli Defense Force (IDF), 795
Israel's Islamic Movement, 467
Issuikai (One Water Society), 336
Italy
  9/11 response, 485
  chronology of incidents (1970s), 728–729
  chronology of incidents (1985–1989), 731–733, 736, 737, 739
  chronology of incidents (1991–1994), 744, 747, 748, 750
  chronology of incidents (1998–1999), 775, 777
  chronology of incidents (2003), 808, 809, 812–813
  country reports on (1985–1989), 215, 228, 241–242, 261–262, 285–286
  country reports on (1990–1994), 305–306, 323–324, 351, 363
  country reports on (1995–1999), 376, 389, 406–407, 422–423, 440–441
  country reports on (2000–2004), 460, 485, 520, 564, 666–667
  prosecutions in, 29, 30
Ivory Coast, 270
Iyad, Abu, 160–161
Izz al-Din al-Qassam Brigades
  chronology of incidents (1995–1997), 755, 758, 765, 766
  chronology of incidents (2001–2004), 794, 812, 831, 834, 836, 848
  in Israel (1990–1994), 356, 368
  See also HAMAS (Islamic Resistance Movement)

J

Jabbar, Abdul, 179
Jabril, Ahmad, 64, 191
Jackson, Alex, 536
Jackson, William, 618
Jacobsen, David, 731, 735
Jaghbir, Muammar al-, 678
Jaime Bateman Cayon Front, 755
Jaish-e-Mohammed (JEM)
  chronology of incidents (2000–2001), 789, 791, 792, 798–799
  chronology of incidents (2004), 820, 842, 843, 846
  in India, 541, 684
  in Pakistan, 473
  profile of, 179
  in Southeast Asian region, 542
  terrorist designation, 157
Ja'ja, Samir, 369, 382
Jakarta Center for Law Enforcement Cooperation (JCLEC), 657, 658
Jakobsmeier, Ingrid, 362
Jalandoni, Luis, 170
JAM (Jamaat Al Muslimeen), 313
Jama'a Combattante Tunisienne, 198
Jamaat Al Muslimeen (JAM), 313
Jama'at al-Tawhid wa'al-Jihad (JTJ)
  chronology of incidents (2004), 820, 823, 827, 829–832, 834, 835, 839, 840, 842
  in Iraq, 676
  See also Tanzim Qa'idat al-Jihad fi Bilad al-Rafidayn
Jamaat-E-Islami, 786
Jamaat ul-Fuqra, 179–180
Jamal, Mumia Abu, 376, 755
James, Michael, 745
Jamiat ul-Ansar (JUA), 473. *See also* Harakat ul-Mujahidin (HUM)
Jamiat ul-Mujahedin (JUM)
  chronology of incidents (2000–2002), 792, 801, 803
  chronology of incidents (2004–2005), 820, 857
  profile of, 180
Jamiat Ulema-i-Islam, Fazlur Rehman faction (JUI-F), 174, 179
Jamiat Ulema-I-Islami (JUI), 473, 810
Jamin, Sammi Sali (aka Fathur Rahman Al-Ghozi or Abu Saad), 508, 549–550, 809
Jammu and Kashmir. *See* India

Jammu and Kashmir Islamic Front (JKIF), 386, 757, 803
Jammu and Kashmir Liberation Front (JKLF), 291, 299–300
Janatha Vimukht Peramuna (JVP), 245, 269, 293, 301
Janis, Thomas, 536, 578
Janjalani, Khadafi Abubaker, 113, 161, 660
Jannati, Ayatollah Ahmad, 72
Japan
 chronology of incidents (1969), 728
 chronology of incidents (1985–1988), 730, 732–734, 737, 738
 chronology of incidents (1991–1995), 743, 744, 748, 756–757
 chronology of incidents (2004), 825
 country reports on (1985–1989), 218, 229, 245, 266–267, 291–292
 country reports on (1990–1994), 300, 336, 349
 country reports on (1995–1999), 373, 385, 402, 418, 434–435
 country reports on (2000–2004), 454–455, 475, 506–507, 547–548, 658
 North Korea and, 94–96
Japanese Red Army (JRA) or Japanese Communist League—Red Army Faction
 Anti-Imperialist International Brigade and, 242
 chronology of incidents (1986), 734
 chronology of incidents (1988), 737
 in Indonesia (1985–1989), 229–230
 in Japan (See Japan, country reports on)
 in Lebanon, 413, 467
 Libya and, 84
 North Korea and, 93–96
 in Philippines, 246
 profile of, 180
 prosecution of member of, 30
 Syria and, 104–107
 See also Anti-Imperialist International Brigade (AIIB)
Jarah, Ziad, 527
Jarallah, Ali Ahmed Mohamed, 576, 682
Jawary, Khalid Duhan al-, 324
Jayshulla, 456, 553
JCAG (Justice Commandos of the Armenian Genocide), 181, 233

Note: Pages 1 to 535 can be found in volume 1; pages 536 to 1019 are in volume 2.

JCLEC (Jakarta Center for Law Enforcement Cooperation), 657, 658
Jehanzeb, Mohammed, 779
JEM. *See* Jaish-e-Mohammed
Jemaah Islamiya Group (JI)
 al-Qaeda ideology and, 697
 attacks by, 140
 in Cambodia, 545, 657
 chronology of incidents (2003–2004), 809, 838, 841
 designation as terrorist organization, 33, 112
 in Indonesia, 506, 546–547, 658
 Kumpulan Mujahidin Malaysia and, 182
 in Malaysia, 476, 507
 in Philippines, 508, 549
 profile of, 180–181
 in Singapore, 476, 509, 548–550, 660
Jenco, Lawrence, 730, 734
Jerusalem Warriors, 462
JI. *See* Jemaah Islamiya Group (JI)
Jibril, Abu (aka Muhammad Iqbal), 548
Jihad, Abu (Khalil al Wazir), 251, 253, 737
Jihad Brigades, 848
Jihad Group, 749, 757
Jihad Squadrons, 829
JKIF (Jammu and Kashmir Islamic Front), 386, 757, 803
JKLF (Jammu and Kashmir Liberation Front), 291, 299–300
John Paul II, Pope, 405, 764
Johnson, Larry C., 713–716
Joint Terrorism Analysis Center (JTAC), 568
Jordan
 9/11 response, 494
 chronology of incidents (1992–1997), 746, 753, 766
 chronology of incidents (2000–2003), 791, 799, 805, 810
 country reports on (1985–1989), 214, 251
 country reports on (1990–1994), 315, 332–333, 344–345, 356, 369
 country reports on (1995–1999), 381–382, 396, 413, 427–428, 446–447
 country reports on (2000–2004), 466–467, 494–495, 526, 572, 678
 Iraqi attacks in, 77
 Syria and, 103, 107, 108
 terrorism financing and, 125
Jordanian Islamic Resistance, 766, 791

Joyu, Fumihiro, 167, 435
JRA. *See* Japanese Red Army (JRA) or Japanese Communist League—Red Army Faction
JTAC (Joint Terrorism Analysis Center), 568
JTJ. *See* Jama'at al-Tawhid wa'al-Jihad
JUA (Jamiat ul-Ansar), 473. *See also* Harakat ul-Mujahidin (HUM)
Juan Carlos (King of Spain), 376, 458
JUI (Jamiat Ulema-I-Islami), 473, 810
JUI-F (Jamiat Ulema-i-Islam, Fazlur Rehman faction), 174, 179
JUM. *See* Jamiat ul-Mujahedin
Justice Commandos of the Armenian Genocide (JCAG), 181, 233
Justice Department, U.S., 25, 119, 155, 157–158
JVP (Janatha Vimukht Peramuna), 245, 269, 293, 301

K

Kach. *See* Kahane Chai (Kach)
KADEK (Kurdistan Freedom and Democracy Congress). *See* PKK (Kurdish Workers' Party or KADEK)
Kadirgamar, Lakshman, 857
Kadyrov, Akhmad, 556, 670
Kahane, Binyamin, 181, 465
Kahane, Meir, 181
Kahane Chai (Kach)
    chronology of incidents (1993), 749
    FTO listing combined, 157
    in Israel, 356, 368
    profile of, 181
Kahlistan Liberation Front, 319
Kakurokyo (Revolutionary Workers Association), 291, 300
Kamal, Majid, 99
Kamel, Abed Abdulrazak al-, 576, 682
Kamel, Fateh, 483
Kandahar, Afghanistan, 136
Kandiah Perinbanathan, 388
Kansai Revolutionary Army, 169
Kansi, Mir Amal
    arrest and conviction of, 24, 30, 399, 402, 767
    extradition of, 33
Kantauri (aka Javier Arizjuren Ruiz), 458
Kaplan, Metin, 459, 665
Karachayev Djamaat, 819
Karadzic, Radovan, 352
Karatas, Dursun, 362

Karen National Union, 545
Karimov, Azizbek, 558
Karimov, Islom, 437
Karkar, Saleh, 350
Karoma, John Paul, 782
Karzai, Hamid
    inauguration of, 137, 683
    progress of, 138
    visit to Washington, 136
Kashmir
    Brennan on, 699, 707
    chronology of incidents (*See under* India; Pakistan)
    country reports on (*See under* India; Pakistan)
    Johnson (Larry C.) on, 714
Kashmiri, Farooqi, 174
Kassem, Tala'at Fuad, 375, 756
Kastari, Mas Selamat, 550
Katayev, Ayyub, 555
Kauffman, Jean-Paul, 252
Kausalyan, E., 852
Kavaler, Prabhi, 415
Kayyaly, Mohammed Atef Al, 536
Kazakhstan
    9/11 response, 479
    country reports on (1995–1999), 420
    country reports on (2000–2004), 457, 479, 512, 553–554, 667
Kazue, Yoshimura, 394
KDPI (Kurdish Democratic Party of Iran), 65, 67, 69, 406
Kean, Thomas, 127, 634
Keenan, Brian, 734
Kelkal, Khaled, 375
Kemptner, Thomas, 333–334, 338
Kennedy, John F., 621–622
Kennedy, Robert, 621
Kenya
    9/11 response, 470
    chronology of incidents (1998), 772
    chronology of incidents (2002–2005), 805, 813, 857
    country reports on (1995–1999), 416
    country reports on (2000–2004), 470, 500–501, 538, 653–654
    embassy bombings in, 4, 7, 31, 32, 55, 135, 414–416, 772
Kerrey, Robert, 633
Kessler, Arthur, 746
KGB, 53, 54

KGK (Kongra-Gel). *See* PKK (Kurdish Workers' Party or KADEK)
Khaderi, Mohammad, 748
Khalaylah, Ahmad Fadhil Nazzal. *See* Zarqawi, Abu Mus'ab al-
Khaldykhoroyeva, Lidiya, 556
Khaled, Abdelrahim (Abdul Rahim), 323, 324, 389
Khaled Ibn al-Walid Brigade, 832
Khalfaoui, Slimane, 518
Khalidi, Ahmed al-, 575
Khalil, Fazlur Rehman, 174
Khalistan Liberation Front (KLF), 744
Khalistan Liberation Tiger Force, 757
Khamenei, Ayatollah, 23, 65, 69, 71–73
Khan, Abdul Qadeer, 53
Khan, Naeem Noor, 140, 685
Kharrazi, Kamal, 69
Khatami. Mohammad, 71
Khattab, Ibn al- (Habib Abdul Rahman), 178, 421, 437
Khieu Samphan, 418
KHK (Kurdistan People's Congress). *See* PKK (Kurdish Workers' Party or KADEK)
Khmer Rouge
  in Cambodia (*See* Cambodia, country reports on)
  chronology of incidents (1994–1995), 752, 753
  chronology of incidents (1996–1997), 759, 764
  profile of, 181
Khodjiev, Juma (aka Juma Namangani), 457
Khodr, Bashir, 242
Khomeini, Ayatollah, 61, 63, 175
Khristos Kassimis, 816
Khudayr, Shaykh Ali bin Ali al-, 575
Khuddam ul-Islam (KUI), 179
Khudoberdiev, Mahmud, 515
Kidwani, Farid, 445
Kikhia, Mansur, 87, 88–89, 750
Kikumura, Yu, 180, 263, 266–267
Kilburn, Peter, 82, 212, 223, 734
Killian, James, 620
Kim Hyon Hui, 268–269, 301
Kim Jong Il, 96, 301
Kintanar, Romulo, 268, 337
Kirca, Coskum, 731
Kirk, Arlene, 415
Kirkpatrick, Lyman B., Jr., 622

Note: Pages 1 to 535 can be found in volume 1; pages 536 to 1019 are in volume 2.

Kissinger, Henry A., 623
Kizilgoca, Cumali, 812
KLA (Kosovo Liberation Army), 458
Klein, Hans-Joachim, 459
KLF (Khalistan Liberation Front), 744
Klinghoffer, Leon, 189, 212, 390
Klump, Andrea, 438, 439, 459
KMM (Kumpulan Mujahidin Malaysia), 182, 476, 507
Knox, Quincy Lee, 536
Koehn, William, 499
Koizumi, Junichiro, 96
Kokabi, Mehrdad, 309
Kongra-Gel (KGK). *See* PKK (Kurdish Workers' Party or KADEK)
Kony, Joseph, 185
Korea. *See* North Korea (Democratic People's Republic of Korea); South Korea (Republic of Korea)
Koromah, Johnny Paul, 431
Kosovo
  chronology of incidents (2004), 821
  country reports on (1990–1994), 309
  country reports on (2000–2004), 458, 487–488, 667
Kosovo Liberation Army (KLA), 458
Krekar, Mullah, 521, 668, 678
Krymshamkhalov, Yusef, 512
KUI (Khuddam ul-Islam), 179
Kumaratunga, Chandrika, 433
Kumpulan Mujahidin Malaysia (KMM), 182, 476, 507
Kurdish Democratic Party of Iran (KDPI), 65, 67, 69, 406
Kurdish Independence Party, 307
Kurdish Workers' Party. *See* PKK (Kurdish Workers' Party or KADEK)
Kurdistan Freedom and Democracy Congress. *See* PKK (Kurdish Workers' Party or KADEK)
Kurdistan Liberation Hawks (TAK), 671
Kurdistan People's Congress. *See* PKK (Kurdish Workers' Party or KADEK)
Kurdistan People's Congress (KHK). *See* PKK (Kurdish Workers' Party or KADEK)
Kuwait
  Bush assassination attempt in, 75, 76
  chronology of incidents (1985), 730–732
  chronology of incidents (1988), 737
  chronology of incidents (1992–1993), 746, 747

chronology of incidents (2002–2003), 804–806
country reports on (1985–1989), 213–214, 225, 234, 251–252, 275–276
country reports on (1990–1994), 315–316, 333, 345, 357
country reports on (1995–1999), 396
country reports on (2000–2004), 467, 495, 526–527, 572–573, 678–679
Iranian-backed terrorism in, 61, 62
Iraq invasion of, 74
prosecutions in, 29
terrorism financing and, 124
Kuwait Fund for the Sick, 553
Kuwait Society for the Revival of the Islamic Heritage, 478
Kuwaiti HAMAS movement, 572
Kuwaiti Hizballah, 396
Kyrgyzstan (Kyrgyz Republic)
chronology of incidents (1999–2000), 782, 790
country reports on (1995–1999), 420, 436–437
country reports on (2000–2004), 457, 479, 512–513, 554, 667–668

L

Lagos, Ricardo, 578
Lahijani, Seyeed Ahmad Sadr, 751
Lahkani, Hermant, 555
Laidouni, Ahmed, 439
Lajevardi, Asadollah, 70
Laos, 455, 475, 507, 548, 659
LARF (Lebanese Armed Revolutionary Faction), 29, 184, 223, 261
Lashkar i Jhangvi (LJ)
chronology of incidents (2005), 852
designation as terrorist organization, 33
in Pakistan (1995–1999), 402
profile of, 183
terrorist designation, 112
Lashkar-i-Tayyiba (LT)
chronology of incidents (1998), 770
chronology of incidents (2000–2002), 786, 798–799, 802, 803, 805
chronology of incidents (2004), 825, 833, 836, 839, 841, 842, 846, 847, 849, 850
in India, 452, 503, 541, 684
in Pakistan, 473
profile of, 182–183
terrorist designation, 157
U.S., threats against, 418

Laskar Jihad, 475
Laskar Jundullah, 805
Latin America
regional patterns (1985–1989), 209–210, 216, 235, 253, 277
regional patterns (1990–1994), 309–310, 327–328, 339–340, 352, 364
regional patterns (1995–1999), 377, 391–392, 409–410, 424, 442–443
regional patterns (2000–2004), 462, 488, 530–531, 577–578, 686–687
See also specific countries
Latvia, 361–362, 423, 564
Lautaro Popular Rebel Forces, 277
Lautaro Youth Movement (MJL)
in Chile (1985–1989), 277
in Chile (1990–1994), 310, 328, 340, 353, 742
profile of, 183
Lawrence, Brian, 734
Lawson, Clifford J., 536
League of Arab States, 150
Leahy, Patrick, 613–614
Lebanese Armed Revolutionary Faction (LARF), 29, 184, 223, 261
Lebanese Hizballah. *See* Hizballah
Lebanese Liberation Front, 281–282
Lebanon
9/11 response, 495
Ambassador Black on, 590
chronology of incidents (1980–1984), 729, 730
chronology of incidents (1985–1989), 730–737, 739, 740
chronology of incidents (1990–1994), 448, 741, 744, 745, 750, 751
chronology of incidents (1998), 771
chronology of incidents (2002–2003), 801, 805, 809
chronology of incidents (2005), 852, 855
country reports on (1985–1989), 212–213, 224, 233–234, 252, 276
country reports on (1990–1994), 316, 333–334, 345–346, 357, 369
country reports on (1995–1999), 382, 396–397, 413, 428, 447
country reports on (2000–2004), 467, 495–496, 527, 573–574, 679
Iranian terrorism in, 61–65
Iraqi attacks in, 75, 76

Lebanon *(continued)*
  state sponsors of terror list and, 53
  Syria and, 103–110
Lefevre, Mikael Etienne Christian (Mohamed Achraf), 670
Leftist Revolutionary Armed Commandos for Peace, 774
Leon, Alfredo de, 337
Leonhardy, Terrence, 728
Lesotho, 270
Lesotho Liberation Army (LLA), 270
Lesperoglou, Avraam, 440, 460, 484–485
Letelier, Orlando, 254, 278, 729
Levin, Carl, 613–614
Levin, Jeremy, 212
Levinger, Moshe, 332
Libbi, Abu Farraj Al, 125
Liberation Army of Presevo, Madvedja, and Bujanovac (PMBLA), 458, 482
Liberation Army of Veneration, 447
Liberation Tigers of Tamil Eelam (LTTE) or Tamil Tigers
  chronology of incidents (1991), 743
  chronology of incidents (1996–1998), 758, 760, 765, 773
  chronology of incidents (2001), 797
  chronology of incidents (2005), 853, 856
  in France, 388
  in India, 319
  law suit over FTO listing, 159
  profile of, 184
  in Sri Lanka (*See* Sri Lanka, country reports on)
  in Thailand, 456
Liberia
  chronology of incidents (1999), 780, 782
  country reports on (1990–1994), 298
  country reports on (1995–1999), 431
  sanctions against, 49
Liberty for Mumia Abu Jamal, 376
Liby, Anas Al, 32
Libya
  air strikes against, 24, 135
  airplane bombings and, 85–92
  Ambassador Black on, 586, 587
  Benin, activity in, 270

Note: Pages 1 to 535 can be found in volume 1; pages 536 to 1019 are in volume 2.

  country reports on (1985–1989), 222, 230–232, 246, 249
  country reports on (1990–1994), 342, 347, 354
  country reports on (2000–2004), 604
  Cuba and, 57
  sanctions against, 49–50, 91
  Soviet Union and, 97
  as state sponsor of terrorism, 19, 53, 81–92
  U.S. airstrikes against (1986), 83, 84
  and War on Terrorism, 19
  weapons of mass destruction in, 18, 21, 22, 50
Libyan Islamic Fighting Group (LIFG), 92, 184
Libyan People's Bureau (LPB)
  activities of, 82–84
  in Australia, 246
  in Austria, 257
  in Panama, 256
  in West Africa, 230–231
Libyan Revolutionary Committees, 84
Lieberman, Joseph, 722
LIFG (Libyan Islamic Fighting Group), 92, 184
Limbong, Alhamzer, 660
Linde, John Martin, Jr., 537
Lioce, Desdemona, 667
Lions of God (Usd Allah), 833
Lithuania, 362, 520–521, 564–565
Litle, Abigail Elizabeth, 536
LJ. *See* Lashkar i Jhangvi
LLA (Lesotho Liberation Army), 270
Lonsdale, Jorge, 310
Lopez, Humberto, 531
Lopez, Jose, 341
Lopez Candia, Humbero, 489
Lord's Resistance Army (LRA)
  chronology of incidents (1994), 751
  chronology of incidents (1998), 775
  chronology of incidents (2000), 790
  chronology of incidents (2004), 848
  profile of, 185
  in Sudan, 103, 537
  in Uganda (1990–1994), 359, 655
  in Uganda (1995–1999), 417
  in Uganda (2000–2004), 452, 471, 502, 540
Lounici, Djamel, 422
Lovett, Robert, 620–621
Loyalist Volunteer Force (LVF)
  profile of, 185
  Red Hand Defenders and, 185, 193

in UK (1995–1999), 408–409
weapons surrendered by, 424
LPB. *See* Libyan People's Bureau
LRA. *See* Lord's Resistance Army
LT. *See* Lashkar-i-Tayyiba
LTTE. *See* Liberation Tigers of Tamil Eelam (LTTE) or Tamil Tigers
Lubowski, Anton, 295
Ludwig-Mayer, Horst, 438
Lugar, Richard, 38, 39
Luxembourg, 216
LVF. *See* Loyalist Volunteer Force

M

M-19 (Movement of 19 April)
    chronology of incidents (1985), 732, 733
    chronology of incidents (1988), 737
    chronology of incidents (1995), 755
    chronology of incidents (2001), 796
    in Colombia (1985–1989), 216–217, 226, 254, 278
    Cuba and, 55
    Libya and, 81–82, 84
    narcoterrorism and, 117
    Nicaragua and, 92–93
    in Panama (1985–1989), 256
    profile of, 186
M-20 organization, 312, 341
Maamar, Habib, 303
Maaroufi, Tarek
    arrest and investigation of, 482–483, 517
    conviction of, 559, 663
    Tunisian Combatant Group and, 198
Macapagal-Arroyo, Gloria, 476
Macario, Ala (aka Artemio), 196
Macedonia
    chronology of incidents, 779, 803
    country reports on (2000–2004), 458, 482
    IMRO in, 309
MAD (Movement for the Advancement of Democracy), 348
Madani, Abassi, 367
Madrid, Spain, 140
MAGO (Muslims Against Global Oppression), 416, 773
Maguire, Donna, 302
Mahdi Army, 835
Mahgoub, Rifat al, 314

Major, John, 743
Makhsum, Hassan, 172
Makki, Abu Asim al- (aka Muhammad Hamdi al-Ahdal), 576
Makki, Bassam, 283, 304
Maktab al-Khidamat. *See* al-Qaeda (al-Qaida)
Malaek, Seyed Mohammad Hossein, 241, 263
Malaysia
    chronology of incidents (2000–2004), 786, 815, 822
    country reports on (2000–2004), 455, 475–476, 507, 548–549, 659
Mali, 501, 538, 653
Malian, Antonio, 807–808
Malik, Fu'ad, 382
Malta, 242, 262, 286, 733
Mandell, Yaakov Nathan, 469
Mankins, David, 747
Mann, Jack, 744
Mann, Jackie, 327
Mansour, May, 223
Manuel Rodriguez Patriotic Front (FPMR)
    arms caches of, 60
    in Chile (*See* Chile, country reports on)
    chronology of incidents (1986), 735
    chronology of incidents (1990–1991), 741–743
    chronology of incidents (1994), 752
    Cuba and, 56, 57–58
    profile of, 185
Maoist Communist Center of India, 169, 852. *See also* Communist Party of India (Maoist)
Maoist Peruvian Communist Party. *See* Shining Path
Marcial, Felipe, 337
Mardoqueo Cruz Urban Commando Detachment, 169, 216, 731
Markaz-ud-Dawa-wal-Irshad (MDI), 182–183
Markov, Georgi, 327
Martin, Mary Louise, 415
Martin, Michael Jerrald, Jr., 469, 798
Martyrs of al-Aqsa, 465
Martyrs of tal Al Za'atar. *See* Hawari Group
Marulanda, Manuel (aka Tirofijo), 193
Maruoka, Osamu, 245, 267, 349
Marvick, Victor D., 317, 326, 462
Marxist-Leninist Armed Propaganda Unit (MLAPU), 288
MAS (Fighting Guerrilla Formation), 406, 768
Maskhadov, Aslan, 420

Masri, Abu Muhammad al-, 167
Massoud, Ahmad Shah, 198, 385, 521, 559
Matsuki, Kaoru, 96
Mauritania, 50, 653, 855
Mauro Hoyos, Carlos, 255
MAVI (Northern Epirus Liberation Front), 361
Mavro Asteri (Black Star), 460, 485
Maximilio Gomez Revolutionary Brigade, 237
Mayahi, Walid al-, 79
Maziotis, Nikos, 485
Mazlouman, Reza, 68, 387
Mazombite, Ruller ("Camarada Cayo"), 196
McCarthy, Andrew C., 709
McCarthy, John, 65, 327, 333, 734, 744
McCloy, Mark, 370
McCone, John, 622
McCormick, Robert, 499
McCurdy, Dave, 630
McDaniels, James Rodrick, 450
McGeough, Gerard, 304
McKevitt, Michael "Mickey," 192, 569
McNally, Peter, 321
MDI (Markaz-ud-Dawa-wal-Irshad), 182–183
Mecca, Saudi Arabia, 62, 63. *See also* Saudi Arabia
Medecins Sans Frontieres (Doctors Without Borders), 555, 784, 792, 794
Mediterranean Sea, 732–733
Megrahi, Abdel Basset al-
  conviction of, 8, 32, 89, 90
  extradition of, 89
  indictment of, 85, 327
Mehdi, Karim, 561, 562, 664
Mehri, Ali Khalil, 463
Mein, John Gordon, 728
MEK. *See* Mujahedin-e Khalq
Meliani, Group, 562
Melouk, Farid, 438
Meloy, Francis, 369, 382, 527
Memon, Yaqub, 360
MENA FATF (Middle East and North African Financial Task Force), 121, 124–125, 674
Mendoza, Gavino, 692
Menezes, Jean Charles de, 856
Mexico
  9/11 response, 498
  anti-U.S. violence in (1985–1989), 212

Note: Pages 1 to 535 can be found in volume 1; pages 536 to 1019 are in volume 2.

  chronology of incidents (1970s), 728
  chronology of incidents (1985), 731
  chronology of incidents (2004), 828
  country reports on (1985–1989), 237, 256
  country reports on (1990–1994), 329–330
  country reports on (1995–1999), 393
  country reports on (2000–2004), 498, 536, 585, 691
Meyer, A. H., 728
Middle Core Faction. *See* Chukaku-Ha
Middle East and North Africa
  regional patterns (1985–1989), 212, 224, 232–233, 250, 273–274
  regional patterns (1990–1994), 313–314, 330–331, 342–343, 354–355, 366–367
  regional patterns (1995–1999), 379–380, 394, 411, 426, 444
  regional patterns (2000–2004), 464, 492, 523–524, 569–570, 673–674
  spillover into Western Europe (1985–1989), 210–211, 222–223
  See also specific countries
Middle East and North African Financial Task Force (MENA FATF), 121, 124–125, 674
Midhar, Zein al-Abidine al-, 447
MILF. *See* Moro Islamic Liberation Front
Military Liberation Union, 765
Millat-i-Islami Pakistan (Sipah-i-Sahaba Pakistan), 183, 197, 755
Miller, Susan, 430
Milligan, George "Joe," 499
MIR (Movement of the Revolutionary Left), 186, 227, 748
Miret Prieto, Pedro, 57
Misri, Imad al-, 483
Misuari, Nur, 507, 508
Mitchell, George, 408, 442
Mitrione, Dan, 728
Mitterand, Francois, 746
Mizoshita, 266
MJF (Muslim Janbaz Force), 319, 743
MJL. *See* Lautaro Youth Movement (MJL)
MLAPU (Marxist-Leninist Armed Propaganda Unit), 288
MLKP-FESK, 831
MNLF. *See* Moro National Liberation Front
Moeller, Irmgard, 362
Moffitt, Ronni, 278
Mohajir Quami Movement (MQM), 386

Mohamed, Khalfan Khamis, 31, 33, 430
Mohammadi, Mahmud, 69–70
Mohammed, Fazul Abdullah, 31
Mohammed, Khalid Sheikh, 575
Mohammed, Mahmoud Mohammed Issa, 258, 282
Mohammed VI, King, 679
Mokhles, al-Said Hassan, 492, 535, 583
Molqi, Majed Yousef al-, 390
Montenegro. *See* Serbia and Montenegro
Monteneros Patria Libre (MPL), 278
Morales, William, 56, 256
Morazanist Patriotic Front (FPM)
    chronology of incidents (1989–1991), 738–739, 741, 743
    chronology of incidents (1995), 753
    in Honduras (1990–1994), 312
    profile of, 186
Morgan, Calvin R., 399
Moro, Aldo, 193, 261, 729
Moro Islamic Liberation Front (MILF)
    chronology of incidents (1994–1997), 752, 767
    chronology of incidents (2001–2005), 794, 806, 808, 851
    in Philippines (1995–1999), 386, 402, 419, 435
    in Philippines (2000–2004), 455, 508, 549
    in Singapore (2000–2004), 660
Moro National Liberation Front (MNLF)
    Abu Sayyaf Group and, 161
    chronology of incidents (1990), 740
    chronology of incidents (2001), 797
    chronology of incidents (2005), 852
    in Malaysia (2000–2004), 507
    in Philippines (1985–1989), 218, 230, 292
    in Philippines (1990–1994), 337, 361
    in Philippines (1995–1999), 373, 386, 402–403
Moroccan Islamic Combatant Group (GICM), 186, 664, 670, 679–680
Morocco
    9/11 response, 496
    chronology of incidents (1998), 769
    chronology of incidents (2003), 811
    country reports on (1985–1989), 276
    country reports on (1990–1994), 369–370
    country reports on (1995–1999), 382–383, 397, 413
    country reports on (2000–2004), 496, 527, 574, 679–680
Morote, Osman, 256, 280, 313, 692
Mostafavi, Mehdi Ahari, 241

Motassadeq, Mounir el, 519, 562, 665
Moussaoui, Zacarias, 518, 519
Moutassadeq, Mounir El, 484
Movement for the Advancement of Democracy (MAD), 348
Movement for the Liberation of the Canary Islands, 239
Movement for the Struggle of the Jordanian Islamic Resistance, 466, 791
Movement of 19 April. *See* M-19
Movement of the Revolutionary Left (MIR), 186, 227, 748
Movement Towards Socialism, 578
Mozambican National Resistance (RENAMO)
    chronology of incidents (1985), 732
    profile of, 186–187
    in southern Africa (1985–1989), 219, 231, 247, 270, 271, 294, 295
    in southern Africa (1990–1994), 298
Mozambique
    chronology of incidents (1985), 732
    country reports on (1985–1989), 219, 231, 247, 270, 294
    country reports on (1990–1994), 298
Mozelle, Bobbie Eugene, 317, 325
MPL (Monteneros Patria Libre), 278
MPL-Cinchoneros (Popular Liberation Movement–Cinchoneros), 255, 279, 280
MQM (Mohajir Quami Movement), 386
MRP (People's Revolutionary Militias), 808
MRTA (Tupac Amaru Revolutionary Movement)
    in Bolivia (2000–2004), 687
    chronology of incidents (1988), 737, 738
    chronology of incidents (1990–1991), 740–742
    chronology of incidents (1996), 761
    in Italy, 406
    Libya and, 84, 85
    Nicaragua and, 92–93
    in Peru (*See* Peru, country reports on)
    profile of, 199
Msalam, Fahid Mohammed Ally, 31
Mubarak, Hosni
    assassination attempt in Ethiopia (1995), 54, 99–101, 173, 371, 754
    assassination attempt in Port Said (1999), 445
    Libyan targeting of, 82
Mueller, Christopher Glenn, 537
Mughniyah, Fuad, 397, 443, 527
Mughniyah, 'Imad, 175, 250, 252

Mugniyah, Imad, 679
Muhadjer, Mohammed, 259
Muhammad, Khalid Shaykh, 541
Muhammad VI, King, 574
Muhammad's Army, 332, 333, 468
Mujahedeen Corps in Iraq, 833
Mujahedeen Jamaat (Islamic Jihad Group), 178, 667
Mujahedeen of Iraq, the Group of Death, 833
Mujahedin (Afghanistan), 54, 267
Mujahedin-e Khalq (MEK)
    chronology of incidents (1996), 758
    chronology of incidents (2000), 787
    Iran vs., 65–71
    Iraq and, 73–80, 676
    law suit over FTO listing, 159
    profile of, 187
Mujahideen Brigades (Saraya al-Mujaheddin), 823
Mujahidin Kashmir, 300
Mujhin, Abu, 167
Mukhlas (aka Abdul Ghoni or Ali Ghufron), 506, 547
Mumcu, Ugur, 747
Mundus, Khair, 659–660
Muqrin, Abdulaziz al-, 140
Murad, Abdul Hakim, 30, 31, 33, 373, 415
Murphy, Robert D., 624
Musa, Abu. *See* Abu Musa Fatah Rebels
Musa, Rifa'i Ahmad Taha, 445, 493
Musa, Solomon, 774
Musalayeva, Larisa, 556
Musavi-Ardabili, Ayatollah, 65
Musawi, Abbas, 340, 344, 345
Museveni, Yoweri, 471
Musharraf, Pervez, 471
Muslim Brotherhood, 173
Muslim Janbaz Force (MJF), 319, 743
Muslims Against Global Oppression (MAGO), 416, 773
Mustapha, Abu Ibrahim (aka Nabil Sahraoui), 196, 570, 674
Mutayri, Sami al-, 806
Muzhikhoyeva, Zarema, 555, 556, 669
Muzlokandov's Gang, 759
Myanmar. *See* Burma
Myers, Martha, 499
Myers, Richard, 137
Mzoudi, Abdelghani, 519, 562, 665

Note: Pages 1 to 535 can be found in volume 1; pages 536 to 1019 are in volume 2.

N

Naccache, Anis, 303
Nadeem, Allama Shoaib, 70
Nagore Mugica, Maria, 388
Naidu, Chandrababu, 541
Najafi, Allama Ghulam Hussain, 853
Najim, Eyad Mahmoud Ismail, 30, 31, 33, 399, 415
NALU (National Army for the Liberation of Uganda), 164
Namangani, Juma (aka Juma Khodjiev), 457
Namibia
    chronology of incidents (2000), 785, 788, 789, 791
    chronology of incidents (2001), 793–795
    country reports on (1985–1989), 220, 248
    country reports on (2000–2004), 451
Nashiri, Abd al-Rahim al- (Abdul Rahemm Al-), 529, 682
Nasrallah, Hasan, 175
Nathansen, Tehilla, 537
National Army for the Liberation of Uganda (NALU), 164
National Combat Force, 227
National Counterterrorism Center (NCTC)
    9/11 Commission on, 639
    chronology of incidents and, 727–728
    Country Reports on Terrorism by, 205
    CRS report on, 717–724
    establishment of, 18, 25, 717
    Gilmore Commission on, 645
    hearing on Annual Report on Terrorism, 707–716
    Johnson (Larry C.) on, 714
    press conference with State Dept., 698–706
National Democratic Front (NDF), 170, 509
National Front (Cypriot), 730
National Front for the Renewal of Chad (FNTR), 416, 769
National Front for the Salvation of Libya, 84
National Guerilla Coordinator (CNG), 226
National Homeland Security Agency (NHSA), 645
National Intelligence Tasking Center (NTIC), 629
National Islamic Front (NIF), 99, 100, 318, 335
National Liberation Army. *See* ELN
National Liberation Army (NLA or UCK), 482
National Liberation Front (FNL), 856
National Liberation Front of Kurdistan (ERNK), 422, 438
National Liberation Front of Tripura, 830
National Patriotic Front of Liberia (NPFL), 298

National Rifles, 300
National Security Agency (NSA), 626, 649
National Security Council (NSC)
    Church Committee on, 626
    Congressional recommendations on, 638
    Hart-Rudman Commission on, 645
    Pike Committee on, 627
    role of, 25
    working groups of, 15
National Union for the Total Independence of Angola. *See* UNITA
National Volunteer Group, 291
Nationalist Combat Front (FNC), 235
NATO (North Atlantic Treaty Organization)
    9/11 response, 142–143, 481, 483
    Communist Combatant Cells and, 169
    discussions with EU on crisis management, 116
    Operation Active Endeavor, 565, 662, 670
    terrorist opposition to, 153, 214, 215
    Washington Treaty invoked, 8
Navarro, Victor Hugo (aka El Mocho), 689
Naxalites, 169
NCC (Combatant Communist Nuclei), 363, 750
NCTC. *See* National Counterterrorism Center
NDF (National Democratic Front), 170, 509
Negroponte, John, 17
Nelson, Rosemary, 442
Nepal
    chronology of incidents (1985), 731–732
    chronology of incidents (1999), 785
    chronology of incidents (2004), 822, 826–829, 837, 838, 849
    chronology of incidents (2005), 851–858
    country reports on (1985–1989), 219
    country reports on (2000–2004), 472, 503, 541, 684–685
Nestor Paz Zamora Commission (CNPZ)
    in Bolivia (1990–1994), 328, 340
    chronology of incidents (1990), 741, 742
    profile of, 187–188
    See also ELN (National Liberation Army)
Netherlands
    chronology of incidents (1988–1990), 738, 740, 741
    chronology of incidents (1995–1999), 754, 764, 777
    country reports on (1985–1989), 229, 262, 286
    country reports on (1990–1994), 306, 324
    country reports on (2000–2004), 521, 565, 668

Neusel, Hans, 741
New Caledonia, 218–219
New Jewish Underground, 677
New Jihad, 355
New Partnership for African Development, 654
New Pattani United Liberation Organization, 419, 435, 456
New People's Army. *See* Communist Party of the Philippines/New People's Army
New Red Brigades. *See* Red Brigades–Fighting Communist Party (BR-PCC)
New Tribes Mission (NTM), 353
New York City
    1995 bombings, Sudan's role in, 100
    September 11 attacks, 468, 798
    World Trade Center bombing (1993), 347, 415, 747
New Zealand, 473, 508, 549, 659
NHSA (National Homeland Security Agency), 645
Nicaragua
    Chilean arms caches and, 60
    chronology of incidents (1995–1996), 754, 759
    chronology of incidents (1999), 783
    country reports on (1985–1989), 280
    country reports on (1990–1994), 312
    country reports on (2000–2004), 530
    Cuba and, 56
    Iran-Contra investigation and, 629–630
    sanctions against, 50
    as state sponsor of terrorism, 92–93
Nidal, Abu. *See* Abu Nidal Organization (ANO); Banna, Sabri Al- (Abu Nidal)
Nieto, Mark Ian, 450
NIF (National Islamic Front), 99, 100, 318, 335
Niger, 294, 451, 653, 739
Nigeria
    chronology of incidents (1993), 749
    chronology of incidents (1997), 764, 768
    chronology of incidents (1999–2000), 776–778, 780–784, 786, 788, 789
    chronology of incidents (2001–2002), 793, 796, 797, 800
    chronology of incidents (2005), 855
    country reports on (1990–1994), 348
    country reports on (1995–1999), 400, 416, 431
    country reports on (2000–2004), 451, 470, 501, 538, 654
    economic sanctions and, 41
Nimr, Halimeh, 458

NIPR (Revolutionary Proletarian Initiative Nuclei), 195, 485
Nishikawa, Jun, 402
Nixon, Richard M., 623
Niyazov, Saparmurat, 557
NLA (National Liberation Army or UCK), 482
Noel, Cleo A., 728
Nordeen, William, 260
Noriega, Manuel, 236, 256, 280
North Africa. *See* Middle East and North Africa
North America
　regional patterns (1985–1989), 237–238, 257, 281
　regional patterns (2000–2004), 498, 530–531, 577–578, 686–687
　See also specific countries
North Atlantic Council, 142–143
North Atlantic Treaty Organization. *See* NATO
North Korea (Democratic People's Republic of Korea)
　Ambassador Black on, 587, 589
　country reports on (2000–2004), 603
　Japan's condemnation of, 245
　sanctions against, 42, 50
　Soviet bloc and, 98
　as state sponsor of terrorism, 19, 93–96
　Turkey and, 244
　and weapons of mass destruction, 17, 19, 95
North Yemen (Yemen Arab Republic), 97, 316, 734. *See also* Yemen
Northern Alliance (Afghanistan), 136
Northern Epirus Liberation Front (MAVI), 361
Northern Ireland
　chronology of incidents (1970s), 728
　chronology of incidents (1985–1987), 730, 736–737
　chronology of incidents (1990), 742
　chronology of incidents (1998), 772, 773
　country reports on (1985–1989), 216, 228, 264, 288–289
　country reports on (1990–1994), 308–309, 326–327, 339, 351–352, 363–364
　country reports on (1995–1999), 377, 391, 408–409, 424, 442
　country reports on (2000–2004), 462, 487, 673
Norway, 565, 668, 748, 808

Note: Pages 1 to 535 can be found in volume 1; pages 536 to 1019 are in volume 2.

November 17–Theofilos Georgiadis Commandos, 751. *See also* 17 November Revolutionary Organization
NPA. *See* Communist Party of the Philippines/New People's Army (CPP/NPA)
NPFL (National Patriotic Front of Liberia), 298
NSA (National Security Agency), 626, 649
NSC. *See* National Security Council
NTA (Anti-Imperialist Territorial Nuclei), 165–166, 808
NTIC (National Intelligence Tasking Center), 629
NTM (New Tribes Mission), 353
Nuon Chea, 418

O

OAS. *See* Organization of American States
OAU (Organization of African Unity), 100, 145–146, 150. *See also* African Union (AU)
Obasanjo, Olusegun, 654
Obeid, Sheik Abdul Karim, 275, 276
Ocalan, Abdullah
　arrest of, 438, 441–442
　deportations of, 422–423, 440
　Germany and, 388, 390–391, 405–406, 422, 439
　Greece and, 406, 422, 440
　PKK and, 181–182, 748
　sentence of, 522
　Syria and, 107, 108
　Turkey and, 408
Ocalan, Ahmed, 106
Ocalan, Osman, 71
O'Connor, Michelle, 415
October 1st Antifascist Resistance Group (GRAPO), 172–173, 459, 731. *See also* Spain, country reports on
Odeh, Mohammed Sadeek, 31, 33
OECD (Organization for Economic Cooperation and Development), 131
OFDA (Office of Foreign Disaster Assistance), 15
Office of Foreign Assets Control (OFAC) (Treasury Dept.), 36–37, 115
Office of Foreign Disaster Assistance (OFDA), 15
Office of Homeland Security, 25. *See also* U.S. Department of Homeland Security (DHS)
Office of Management and Budget (OMB), 623
Office of the Coordinator for Counterterrorism (State Dept.), 13, 15, 111, 609–613
Office of the Inspector General (OIG), 607–608

Office of the Legal Advisor (State Dept.), 14
Office on Drugs and Crime (UNODC), 114
Official IRA (OIRA), 176
Ogaden National Liberation Front (ONLF)
   chronology of incidents (1998–1999), 769, 779
   chronology of incidents (2005), 857
   in Ethiopia, 416, 431
O'Grady, John, 261
O'Hara, Patrick, 730
O'Hare, Dessie, 261
OIC (Organization of the Islamic Conference), 143, 150, 496
OIG (Office of the Inspector General), 607–608
OIRA (Official IRA), 176
Okamoto, Kozo, 180, 218, 454
Okudaira, Junzo, 336
Olaechea, Adolfo Hector, 581
Olarra, Juan Antonio, 521
Olds, Sherry Lynn, 415
OLF (Oromo Liberation Front), 500
OLH (Haitian Liberation Organization), 237
Oman
   country reports on (2000–2004), 496, 528, 574, 680
   terrorism financing and, 124
Omar, Jarala, 806
Omar, Mullah, 136
Omar, Mullah Mohammed, 854
Omar al-Mukhtar Group, 83
OMB (Office of Management and Budget), 623
ONLF. *See* Ogaden National Liberation Front
OPEC (Organization of Petroleum Exporting Countries), 46
OPM. *See* Free Papua Movement
OPS (Santamaria Patriotic Organization), 85
Orange Volunteers (OV), 188
Order of the Boer People, 299
Organization for Economic Cooperation and Development (OECD), 131
Organization for Security and Cooperation in Europe (OSCE)
   attacks on (1994–1999), 760
   attacks on (1995–1999), 387
   Counterterrorism Conference (2002), 510
   Georgia and, 457
   Kyrgyzstan and, 479
Organization for the Defense of Free People, 736
Organization of African Unity (OAU), 100, 145–146, 150. *See also* African Union (AU)
Organization of American States (OAS)
   9/11 response, 144, 488, 489, 498
   attacks on, in El Salvador (1988), 255
   attacks on, in Venezuela (2003), 810
   convention on terrorism, 150
   Cuba and, 48
   Inter-American Committee Against Terrorism, 530, 577, 688
   International Convention Against Terrorism, 530
   Rio Treaty invoked, 8
Organization of Arab Fedayeen Cells, 266
Organization of Jihad Brigades, 261, 737. *See also* Japanese Red Army (JRA)
Organization of Petroleum Exporting Countries (OPEC), 46
Organization of the Islamic Conference (OIC), 143, 150, 496
Organization of the Oppressed, 732
Organization of the Oppressed on Earth, 737
Orjuela, Jorge Alberto, 499
Oromo Liberation Front (OLF), 500
ORPA (Revolutionary Organization of the People in Arms). *See* Guatemalan National Revolutionary Unit (URNG)
Orsoni, Jean-Andre, 259
Ortega Ortega, Laureano, 338
Ortiz, Ramierez, 728
Ortiz Montenegro, Patricio, 185, 410, 425
OSCE. *See* Organization for Security and Cooperation in Europe
Osman, Shauqat, 174
Ossandon, Guillermo, 365
OV (Orange Volunteers), 188
Owens, Ronald Scott, 450
Owhali, Mohamed Rashed Daoud al-, 31, 33

P

PA. *See* Palestinian Authority
Pablo Zarate Wilca National Indigenous Force, 253
Padfield, Philip, 733, 734
PAGAD. *See* People Against Gangsterism and Drugs
Pakistan
   9/11 Commission on, 637
   9/11 response, 472–473
   Afghanistan and, 53–54
   al-Qaeda in, 140
   chronology of incidents (1986–1987), 735, 736

Pakistan *(continued)*
    chronology of incidents (1990–1992), 741, 745, 746
    chronology of incidents (1995), 753–755, 757
    chronology of incidents (1997), 763, 767, 768
    chronology of incidents (1998), 769, 771, 774
    chronology of incidents (1999), 776, 779, 781, 782, 784
    chronology of incidents (2000–2001), 786, 795
    chronology of incidents (2002), 799, 801, 802, 805, 806
    chronology of incidents (2003), 806, 810, 811
    chronology of incidents (2004), 826, 831, 842, 844
    chronology of incidents (2005), 851–855
    country reports on (1985–1989), 218, 229, 244, 292
    country reports on (1990–1994), 319–320, 336–337, 349, 360
    country reports on (1995–1999), 373, 386, 402, 418, 432–433
    country reports on (2000–2004), 452–453, 472–473, 503–504, 541, 604, 685
    Johnson (Larry C.) on, 714
    sanctions against, 50
    as state sponsor of terrorism, 53
    Taliban and, 138
    terrorism financing and, 125
Pakistani People's Party (PPP), 320, 743
Palestine
    country reports on (1985–1989), 213, 224–225
    country reports on (1990–1994), 314–315, 331–332, 344, 355–356, 368
    country reports on (1995–1999), 395–396, 412–413, 427, 445–446
    country reports on (2000–2004), 465–466, 493–494
    Rafsanjani on, 63
    See also Israel and occupied territories; *specific terrorist groups*
Palestine Liberation Front (PLF)
    chronology of incidents (1985), 733
    chronology of incidents (1990), 741
    conviction of members of, 232
    in Europe (1985–1986), 223
    Iraq and, 73, 75, 76, 78, 79, 138
    in Israel (1990), 314
    Libya and, 85
    See also PLO (Palestinian Liberation Authority)
Palestinian Authority (PA)
    al-Aqsa and, 526
    assessment of, 19
    efforts against violence, 381, 413, 427, 445–446, 494, 526, 572
    See also Palestine
Palestinian Hizballah, 465, 795
Palestinian Islamic Jihad (PIJ)
    chronology of incidents (1990–1991), 740, 744
    chronology of incidents (1996), 758
    chronology of incidents (2002–2004), 800, 822, 849
    in Egypt (1990–1994), 314
    indictment of leader of, 33
    Iran and, 65, 71
    Iraq and, 79, 140
    in Israel (1990–1994), 315, 331–332, 344, 368
    in Israel (1995–1999), 427, 445
    in Israel (2000–2004), 465, 494, 525, 572
    in Jordan (1990–1994), 315, 333
    Libya and, 87–90
    profile of, 189
    Sudan and, 99–102
    Syria and, 106–110
    U.S. court decision against, 70
    in Yemen (2000–2004), 682
Palestinian Islamic Jihad–Shaqaqi Faction (PIJ–Shaqaqi Faction), 381, 753
Palestinian Liberation Authority. *See* PLO
Palestinian National Salvation Front, 191
Palestinian Revolutionary Committee, 815
Palme, Olaf, 229, 733
Palmer, Lakiba Nicole, 450
Palmera, Juvenal Ovidio Ricardo (aka Simon Trinidad), 193, 689, 691
Palmero, Ricardo, 856–857
Panama
    chronology of incidents (1990–1994), 741, 746, 747, 752
    chronology of incidents (1996–1999), 760, 784
    country reports on (1985–1989), 236, 256, 280
    country reports on (1990–1994), 312–313, 341, 365

Note: Pages 1 to 535 can be found in volume 1; pages 536 to 1019 are in volume 2.

country reports on (1995–1999), 379, 393, 410–411, 425
country reports on (2000–2004), 691–692
Nicaragua, 56
sanctions against, 50
Papineau, Jill, 347, 747
Papua New Guinea, 300
Para, Abderrazak al- (aka Amari Saifi), 92, 196, 653, 674
Paraguay
9/11 response, 491
country reports on (1995–1999), 444
country reports on (2000–2004), 463–464, 491, 533–534, 581–583, 693–694
"The paramilitaries." *See* United Self-Defense Forces of Columbia (AUC)
Parlett, Joshua Langdon, 450
Parot, Henri, 306–307, 325
Parson, Mark T., 537
Party for the Liberation of Rwanda, 171
Pasdaran-I-Inquilab-e-Islam, 319
Patriotic Morazanista Liberation Front, 255–256. *See also* Morazanist Patriotic Front (FPM)
Patriotic Union of Kurdistan (PUK), 760
Pattani United Liberation Organization (PULO), 230, 337, 419
PCC (Policy Coordination Committee), 119
PCCH (Communist Party of Chile), 328
PDBTS (Policy Dialogue on Border and Transport Security), 116
Peace Conquerors, 731
Peace Corps, 300
Pearl, Daniel, 112, 136, 140, 175, 183, 499, 503
Pedro Pablo Castillo Command, 216, 732
Pembgul, Binbir, 308
Pentagon Gang, 796
People Against Gangsterism and Drugs (PAGAD)
chronology of incidents (1998), 773
profile of, 190
in South Africa (1995–1999), 416, 431
in South Africa (2000–2004), 452, 501
People in Action for the Liberation of Rwanda, 416, 773
People's Defense Force (HPG), 182
People's Democratic Republic of Yemen (South Yemen), 96–97, 156, 316. *See also* Yemen
People's Liberation Army (EPL)
chronology of incidents (1985–1986), 733, 735

chronology of incidents (1995–1998), 753, 759, 774
in Colombia (1985–1989), 216, 226
profile of, 190
People's Liberation Organization of Tamil Eelam (PLOTE), 433
People's Mujahedin, 240
People's Republic of China. *See* China, People's Republic of
People's Revolutionary Armed Forces, 728
People's Revolutionary Army (ERP), 172
People's Revolutionary Militias (MRP), 808
People's War, 169
People's War Group, 541, 852. *See also* Communist Party of India (Maoist)
Peratikos, Constantine, 406
Perl, Raphael F., 711–713
Peru
chronology of incidents (1986–1989), 734, 738–740
chronology of incidents (1990–1994), 740–750
chronology of incidents (1995–1997), 753, 754, 759, 762, 766
chronology of incidents (2002–2005), 799–800, 812, 840, 850–851
country reports on (1985–1989), 217, 226, 236, 256–257, 280
country reports on (1990–1994), 313, 330, 341–342, 353–354, 365–366
country reports on (1995–1999), 379, 393–394, 411, 425–426, 443–444
country reports on (2000–2004), 490, 532–533, 580–581, 692–693
narcoterrorism in, 117
Peruvian Communist Party (Patria Roja), 692
Petsos, George, 285, 739
PFLP. *See* Popular Front for the Liberation of Palestine
PFLP-GC. *See* Popular Front for the Liberation of Palestine–General Command
PFLP-SC (Popular Front for the Liberation of Palestine–Special Command), 96–97, 191
PFLP-SOG (Popular Front for the Liberation of Palestine–Special Operations Group), 160, 191
PFLP-SSNP (Popular Front for the Liberation of Palestine–Syrian Socialist National Party), 224

Philippines
   al-Qaeda in, 21
   chronology of incidents (1986–1989), 734, 736, 739, 740
   chronology of incidents (1990–1994), 740–742, 744, 745, 749, 752
   chronology of incidents (1995–1999), 757, 766–767, 773, 780
   chronology of incidents (2000–2002), 788, 792, 794–799, 806
   chronology of incidents (2003–2005), 808–810, 823, 845–846, 851, 852
   country reports on (1985–1989), 218, 230, 246, 268, 292–293
   country reports on (1990–1994), 300–301, 320, 337, 349–350, 360–361
   country reports on (1995–1999), 373–374, 386, 402–403, 419, 435
   country reports on (2000–2004), 455, 476, 508–509, 549–550, 659–660
   Filipino Antiterrorism Task Force, 140
   Iraqi bombing attempt in, 74
   Libyan activity in, 85
   North Korea and, 94
   U.S. military training in, 137
Pickett, David, 317, 329, 742
PIJ. *See* Palestinian Islamic Jihad
PIJ–Shaqaqi Faction (Palestinian Islamic Jihad–Shaqaqi Faction), 381, 753
Pike, Otis G., 616, 625, 627
Pimental, Edward, 212
Pinochet, Augusto, 735
PIRA. *See* Provisional Irish Republican Army
Pirzadi, Reza, 70
Pizarro, Carlos, 186
PKK (Kurdish Workers' Party or KADEK)
   Ambassador Black on, 588
   chronology of incidents (1991–1994), 748, 749, 751, 752
   chronology of incidents (1995–1998), 755, 763, 766, 769, 771
   chronology of incidents (2005), 857
   in Cyprus, 302
   in France, 350
   in Germany (1985–1989), 240, 283, 405–406

Note: Pages 1 to 535 can be found in volume 1; pages 536 to 1019 are in volume 2.

   in Germany (1990–1994), 322
   in Germany (1995–1999), 375–376, 388
   in Greece, 376, 422
   Iran and, 64, 66–71
   in Iraq, 74, 75, 77, 78, 80, 274, 676
   law suit over FTO listing, 159
   in Netherlands, 286
   Ocalan arrest and, 438, 441
   profile of, 181–182
   Syria and, 103–109
   in Turkey (*See* Turkey, country reports on)
   Turkish Hizballah and, 199
PLF. *See* Palestine Liberation Front
PLO (Palestinian Liberation Authority)
   Al-Fatah and, 163
   attack on, in Cyprus (1988), 258
   Egypt's influence on, 250–251
   Force 17 and, 173, 253
   in Iraq, 73
   in Israel (*See* Israel, country reports on)
   in Lebanon (1985–1989), 276
   profile of, 189–190
   sanctions against, 47
   in Saudi Arabia (1990–1994), 346
   terrorism renounced by, 250
   in Tunisia, 235
PLOTE (People's Liberation Organization of Tamil Eelam), 433
PMBLA (Liberation Army of Presevo, Madvedja, and Bujanovac), 458, 482
PNV (Basque Nationalist Party), 461
Pol Pot, 418
Poland
   ANO and, 98
   chronology of incidents (1996), 759
   country reports on (1990–1994), 302, 327
   country reports on (1995–1999), 389
   country reports on (2000–2004), 485, 565–566, 668
Polay, Victor, 313, 692
Polhill, Robert, 64, 105
Policy Coordination Committee (PCC), 119
Policy Dialogue on Border and Transport Security (PDBTS), 116
Popular Combatants Group (GCP), 690
Popular Democratic Front for the Liberation of Palestine, 728
Popular Forces of 25 April (FP-25)
   chronology of incidents (1985), 730

in Portugal, 215, 228, 286
profile of, 190
Popular Forces of Liberation, 216
Popular Front for the Liberation of Palestine (PFLP)
chronology of incidents (1976), 729
chronology of incidents (1991–1995), 744, 756
chronology of incidents (2002–2004), 799, 820, 845, 847
Democratic Front for the Liberation of Palestine and, 171
in Denmark (1985–1989), 282
Iraq and, 78–79
in Israel (1985–1989), 225
in Israel (1990–1994), 331–332, 344
in Israel (1995–1999), 396
in Israel (2000–2004), 494, 677
in Jordan (1990–1994), 345
PFLP-GC and, 191
PLO and, 189
profile of, 190–191
Syria and, 103, 104, 108–110
Popular Front for the Liberation of Palestine–General Command (PFLP-GC)
chronology of incidents (1988), 738
in Germany, 265, 283, 322–323
Iran and, 64, 65
Iraq and, 79
in Israel, 494
Libya and, 85, 88–90
PLF and, 189
profile of, 161
Syria and, 104–110
Yugoslavia and, 265
Popular Front for the Liberation of Palestine–Special Command (PFLP-SC), 96–97, 191
Popular Front for the Liberation of Palestine–Special Operations Group (PFLP-SOG), 160, 191
Popular Front for the Liberation of Palestine–Syrian Socialist National Party (PFLP-SSNP), 224
Popular Liberation Movement–Cinchoneros (MPL-Cinchoneros), 255, 279, 280
Popular Resistance Committee (PRC), 571, 677, 826
Popular Revolutionary Army (EPR), 393
Popular Revolutionary Forces–Lorenzo Zelaya (FRP-LZ), 191, 237, 279, 280
Popular Struggle Front (PSF)
in Djibouti, 246
in Italy, 286
Libya and, 83

profile of, 191
South Yemen and, 97
in Sweden, 307
Syria and, 104, 105
Portland Six, 546
Portugal
chronology of incidents (1985–1986), 730, 733
country reports on (1985–1989), 215, 228, 286
country reports on (2000–2004), 668–669
Potros, Santi, 259
Pouliot, Michael Rene, 536
Powell, Colin L.
Afghanistan campaign and, 136
on Iraq, 138–140
on post-9/11 policy, 5
on Sudan, 102
terrorist organizations designated by, 7, 32
Powell, Nancy, 118
PPP (Pakistani People's Party), 320, 743
PRC (Popular Resistance Committee), 571, 677, 826
Premadasa, Ranasinghe, 350
Prima Linea, 92
PROCUP (Clandestine Worker's Revolutionary Party, Union of the Poor), 330
Progressive Unionist Party, 200
Prophet Mohammed's Forces in Kuwait–Revolutionary Organization, 234
Provisional Irish Republican Army (PIRA)
in Belgium (1990–1994), 302, 321
chronology of incidents (1985–1989), 730, 736–740
chronology of incidents (1990–1994), 741–743, 750
in France (1985–1989), 240, 284
in Germany (1985–1989), 240, 258, 265, 283
in Germany (1990–1994), 304, 322
in Ireland (1985–1989), 261
in Ireland (1990–1994), 305
Libya and, 84, 87
in Malta, 242
in Netherlands (1985–1989), 262
in Netherlands (1990–1994), 306, 324
in Northern Ireland (*See* Northern Ireland, country reports on)
Soviet bloc and, 98
PRTC. *See* Central American Revolutionary Worker's Party
PSF. *See* Popular Struggle Front
Public Designations Unit (State Dept.), 111

PUK (Patriotic Union of Kurdistan), 760
Puka Inti (Red Sun), 191, 353, 365
PULO (Pattani United Liberation Organization), 230, 337, 419
Punjab, India, 244, 266
PUP (Ukrainian People's Party), 836

Q

Qadhafi, Muammar, 19, 81–92, 458–459
Qadir, Abdul, 137
Qadir, Haji, 779
Qai'idat al-Jihad. *See* al-Qaeda (al-Qaida)
Qasir, Samir, 855
Qatar
   9/11 response, 496
   chronology of incidents (2005), 853
   country reports on (2000–2004), 496, 528, 574, 680
   terrorism financing and, 124
Qatar Humanitarian Organization, 553
Qattamash, Ahmad, 344
Qibla, 190, 416, 431
Qital, Mohammad, 658
Quayle, Dan, 292
Quso, Fahad al-, 682

R

Rabbani, Amin, 174
Rabbani, Burhanuddin, 372
Rabin, Yitzak, 381
Radio Free Europe/Radio Liberty, 77–79
Radjavi, Kazem, 307
RAF. *See* Red Army Faction
Rafiqdust, Mohsen, 70
Rafsanjani, Ali Akbar Hashemi
   indictment and conviction in Germany, 69
   on Palestine, 63
   Rushdie death threat and, 63
   views and politics of, 64–65, 67, 68
Rahman, Fazlur, 810
Rainsy, Sam, 398, 764
Rajaei, Mohammad-Ali, 187
Rajavi, Kazem, 65, 66
RAM (Reform the Armed Forces Movement), 293
Ramirez Durand, Oscar Alberto (aka Feliciano), 444
Ramirez Sanchez, Ilyich. *See* Carlos "the Jackal"

Ramizi, Ramiz, 814
Ramos-Vega, Benjamin, 376
Rantisi, Abdul Aziz, 167
RARA (Revolutionary Anti-Racist Action Group), 262, 286, 324
Rashid, Mohammed
   15 May Organization and, 160
   conviction of, 75, 323
   extradition and indictment of, 31, 33, 260–261, 285, 415
   release of, 389
   Yugoslavia and, 265
Raul, Jaime, 499
Rayel, Abbas, 69
Rayyis, Ibrahim bin Muhammad bin Abdallah al-, 575
Real Irish Republican Army (RIRA)
   chronology of incidents (1998), 772, 773
   IRA and, 177
   in Northern Ireland and UK (1995–1999), 424
   in Northern Ireland and UK (2000–2004), 462, 487, 523, 569, 673
   profile of, 191–192
   terrorist designation, 157
Red Army Faction (RAF)
   chronology of incidents (1981), 729
   chronology of incidents (1985–1986), 730–732, 734
   chronology of incidents (1988–1991), 738, 740, 741, 743
   in Germany (*See* Germany, country reports on)
   profile of, 192
   in Spain, 262
Red Brigades (BR)
   chronology of incidents (1978), 729
   chronology of incidents (1985), 731
   chronology of incidents (1988–1989), 737, 739
   chronology of incidents (1993–1994), 748, 750
   in Italy (*See* Italy, country reports on)
   Nicaragua and, 92–93
   profile of, 192–193
   Revolutionary Proletarian Initiative Nuclei and, 195
   in Spain, 239
   in Switzerland, 288
Red Brigades–Communist Combatant Party (BR-CCP), 564, 667
Red Brigades–Fighting Communist Party (BR-PCC)
   chronology of incidents (1989), 739

Note: Pages 1 to 535 can be found in volume 1; pages 536 to 1019 are in volume 2.

in France, 284
in Italy, 241, 261, 460, 520
profile of, 192
Red Brigades–Union of Communist Combatants (BR-UCC), 192, 241–242, 284, 736
Red Cross. *See* International Red Cross (ICRC)
Red Daughters of Rage, 374–375
Red Hand Defenders (RHD), 193. *See also* Loyalist Volunteer Force (LVF)
Red Scorpion Group (RSG), 337, 745
Red Sun. *See* Puka Inti
Red Zorra, 362
Reddy, Ramdev, 853
Reed, Frank, 61, 64, 105, 735
Refke, Taufek, 549
Reform and Defiance Movement, 427–428, 446
Reform the Armed Forces Movement (RAM), 293
Reid, Harry, 613–614
Reid, Richard Colvin, 165, 518
Reinitz, Mordechai, 537
Remissainthe, Ravix, 853
RENAMO. *See* Mozambican National Resistance
Reno, Janet, 4, 135
Republican Sinn Fein, 113, 171
Ressam, Ahmed, 448
Reunion Island, 561–562
Revolutionary Action, 406
Revolutionary Action Organization, 741
Revolutionary Anti-Racist Action Group (RARA), 262, 286, 324
Revolutionary Armed Forces (FAR). *See* Guatemalan National Revolutionary Unit (URNG)
Revolutionary Armed Forces of Colombia. *See* FARC
Revolutionary Armed Forces of Ecuador, 803
Revolutionary Army of the People, 278
Revolutionary Democratic Front (FDR), 237, 256
Revolutionary Justice Organization, 61, 735
Revolutionary Nuclei (Revolutionary Cells)
in Germany, 241, 265, 362, 563
in Greece, 440, 460
profile of, 194
Revolutionary Organization 17 November. *See* 17 November Revolutionary Organization
Revolutionary Organization of Socialist Muslims, 732, 734. *See also* Abu Nidal Organization (ANO)
Revolutionary Organization of the People in Arms (ORPA). *See* Guatemalan National Revolutionary Unit (URNG)
Revolutionary People's Liberation Party/Front (DHKP/C)
in Belgium, 438
chronology of incidents (2003), 810
profile of, 194
in Turkey (1995–1999), 377, 391, 408, 442
in Turkey (2000–2004), 461, 486, 522, 568, 671
See also Dev Sol
Revolutionary People's Solidarity, 260
Revolutionary People's Struggle (ELA)
chronology of incidents (1994), 750, 751
in Greece (*See* Greece, country reports on)
profile of, 195
Revolutionary Nuclei and, 194
Revolutionary Perspective, 792
Revolutionary Popular Struggle, 740
Revolutionary Proletarian Army (RPA), 162
Revolutionary Proletarian Initiative Nuclei (NIPR), 195, 485
Revolutionary Proletarian Nucleus, 460
Revolutionary Solidarity, 741
Revolutionary Struggle (RS), 195, 666
Revolutionary United Front (RUF)
chronology of incidents (1995), 753, 754
chronology of incidents (1999), 776–777, 784
chronology of incidents (2000), 787, 789
in Guinea (2000–2004), 451
profile of, 195
in Sierra Leone (1990–1994), 359
in Sierra Leone (1995–1999), 371, 416
in Sierra Leone (2000–2004), 451, 539
Revolutionary Violence Group, 485
Revolutionary Workers Association (Kakurokyo), 291, 300
Rey-Domecq, Alberto, 561
Rezaq, Omar Mohammad Ali
conviction of, 30, 262, 286, 384
extradition of, 33, 348
Rezgui, Farid, 390
RHD (Red Hand Defenders), 193. *See also* Loyalist Volunteer Force (LVF)
Ricardo Franco Front, 217
Rice, Condoleeza, 17
Rich, Mark, 747
Ridge, Tom, 639
Rincon, Miguel, 379, 394
RIRA. *See* Real Irish Republican Army
Riyad us-Saliheyn Martyrs' Brigade, 837

Riyadus-Salikhin Reconnaissance and Sabotage Battalion of Chechen Martyrs (RSRSBCM), 195–196, 513, 555
Riyati, Ahmad al-, 678
Rockefeller, John D., IV, 613–614
Rockefeller, Nelson A., 625
Rodriguez, Manuel. *See* Manuel Rodriguez Patriotic Front (FPMR)
Rogen, Hannah, 499
Rogencamp, Scarlett, 212
Rohwedder, Detlev, 322, 743
Rojas Cabrera, Nayibe (aka Sonia), 689, 856–857
Romania, 98, 566, 669, 744
Rome, Italy, 728–729
Roth, Malka, 469, 797
Rowe, James, 162, 292, 293, 739
Roy, Patrick Howard, 450
Royal Dutch Shell Group, 759
Royce, Ed, 707–708
RPA (Revolutionary Proletarian Army), 162
RS (Revolutionary Struggle), 195, 666
RSG (Red Scorpion Group), 337, 745
RSRSBCM (Riyadus-Salikhin Reconnaissance and Sabotage Battalion of Chechen Martyrs), 195–196, 513, 555
Rudolph, Piet "Skiet," 299
RUF. *See* Revolutionary United Front
Ruffilli, Roberto, 261, 737
Rushdie, Salman
    fatwah of death against, 63–65, 67–71
    in hiding, 327
Russia
    9/11 response, 479
    chronology of incidents (1995–1997), 756, 761–764
    chronology of incidents (1998–1999), 768, 773, 780, 782
    chronology of incidents (2001–2002), 792, 801, 804, 806
    chronology of incidents (2004), 819, 829, 836, 837
    chronology of incidents (2005), 852, 854, 855
    country reports on (1990–1994), 363
    country reports on (1995–1999), 376, 389–390, 407, 420–421, 437

Note: Pages 1 to 535 can be found in volume 1; pages 536 to 1019 are in volume 2.

country reports on (2000–2004), 457, 479–480, 513–514, 554–556, 669–670
    sanctions against, 50–51
Russian Federal Security Service, 555
Russian National Bolshevist Party, 423
Rux, Kevin Shawn, 450
Rwanda
    chronology of incidents (1992), 746
    chronology of incidents (1997), 762, 763
    country reports on (1995–1999), 400
    country reports on (2000–2004), 501, 538–539, 654
Ryan, Patrick, 261, 285

S

S/CT (Coordinator for Counterterrorism, State Dept.), 607–613
Saad, Abu (aka Fathur Rahman Al-Ghozi or Sammi Sali Jamin), 508, 549–550, 809
Sa'ad, al-Sharif Hassan, 483
SAARC (South Asian Association for Regional Cooperation), 150
Sabnani, Fajiumar Narainda, 534
Sabotage and Military Surveillance Group of the 'Riyadh al-Salikhin Martyrs, 195–196, 513, 555
Sachs, Albie, 270
Sadat, Anwar, 163, 729
Sa'di, Mahir al-, 167
Sadr, Abolhassan Bani, 69, 70
Sadr, Muqtada al-, 73
Saeed, Hafiz Muhammad, 183
Safarini, Zayd Hassan Abd al-Latif Masud al-, 8, 33
Sagristano, Fernando, 750
Saheed Khalsa Force, 197
Sahraoui, Abdelbaki, 375, 380
Sahraoui, Nabil (aka Abu Ibrahim Mustapha), 196, 570, 674
Said, Haitham, 103
Saifi, Amari (aka Abderrazak al-Para), 92, 196, 653, 674
Saiqa, 104, 105
Salaf Tabliq group, 164
Salafist Brigades of Abu Bakr al-Siddiq, 840, 841. *See also* Abu Bakr al-Siddiq Fundamentalist Brigades
Salafist Group for Call and Combat (GSPC)
    al-Qaeda affiliation, 140
    in Algeria (1995–1999), 426–427, 445

in Algeria (2000–2004), 464, 493, 524, 537, 570, 674
chronology of incidents (2003), 807, 809–811
chronology of incidents (2005), 855
in Italy, 520
Libya and, 92
in Mali, 538
profile of, 196
in Sahel region, 653
terrorist designation, 157
Salafiya Jihadiya, 574, 679–680, 697
Salah, Shaykh Ra'id, 467
Salah al-Din Battalions, 465
Salamat, Hashim, 435
Salehi, Haj Hassan, 70
Salim, Abu, 191
Salim, Mamdouh Mahmud, 31, 33
Samper, Ernesto, 365
Samudra, Imam (aka Abdul Aziz), 506, 547
Sandanistas, 92–93. *See also* Nicaragua
Sander, Ronald, 469, 490
Sands, Bernadette, 408
Sanei, Ayatollah Hassan, 67
Sanginov, Rahom "Hitler," 407
Sankoh, Foday, 195
Santamaria Patriotic Organization (OPS), 85
Santiago, Ronchester Mananga, 450
Santoni, Francois, 484
Sanusi, Muhammad al-, 88
Sanussi, Abdullah, 85
Saraiva de Carvalho, Otelo, 286
Saraya al-Mujaheddin (Mujahideen Brigades), 823
Sargsian (Sarkisyan), Vazgen, 436, 552
Sarmiento Hidalgo, Hector, 328
Satterfield, David, 167
Saudi Arabia
    9/11 Commission on, 637
    9/11 response, 496
    Ambassador Black on, 591
    assessments of, 19
    chronology of incidents (1970s), 729
    chronology of incidents (1986–1989), 735, 739
    chronology of incidents (1991), 742, 743
    chronology of incidents (1995–1997), 756, 759
    chronology of incidents (2001), 795, 798
    chronology of incidents (2003), 807, 811
    chronology of incidents (2004), 824, 826–830, 834, 839, 840, 848
    country reports on (1985–1989), 234–235, 253, 276–277
    country reports on (1990–1994), 316, 334, 346, 357
    country reports on (1995–1999), 383, 397, 413–414, 428–429, 447
    country reports on (2000–2004), 467–468, 496–497, 528, 574–575, 604, 680–681
    Iranian terrorism against, 62, 63
    terrorism financing and, 123–124, 129
Saudi Higher Authority for Religion and Charity Work, 527
Saudi Hizballah, 414
Saunders, Stephen, 459–460, 788
Saunders, Timothy Lamont, 450
Save Kashmir Movement
    chronology of incidents (2004–2005), 818, 819, 822, 853
    Jaish-e-Mohammed and, 179
    Lashkar e-Tayyiba and, 179
Sayegh, Hani al-, 31, 414, 428–430, 447
Sayyaf, Abdul Rasul, 359–360, 372, 373, 385
Schaufelberger, Albert, 216
Schleicher, Regis, 29
Schlesinger, James R., 623
Schray, Ralph, 63
Schultz, George, 310, 738
SCIRI (Supreme Council for the Islamic Revolution in Iraq), 676
SCO (Shanghai Cooperation Organization), 478, 546, 554, 557, 673
Scotland, 31, 89–92, 738
Scott, Daniel, 317, 329, 742
SEARCCT (Southeast Asian Regional Center for Counterterrorism), 548, 659
SECI (Southeast European Cooperation Initiative), 662
Sedky, Atef, 163
Seikijuku (Righteous Spiritual School), 300
Sendero Luminoso. *See* Shining Path or Sendero Luminoso (SL)
Senegal
    9/11 response, 470
    chronology of incidents (1988), 737
    chronology of incidents (2002), 800
    country reports on (1985–1989), 270
    country reports on (2000–2004), 470
Senki-ha, 229

Sensui, Hiroshi, 267, 268, 336
Senzani, Giovanni, 228
September, Dulcie, 271
September 11 Command, 227, 235
Serbia and Montenegro
    chronology of incidents (1993), 747
    chronology of incidents (1999), 779, 780
    chronology of incidents (2003–2004), 814, 821, 846
    country reports on (1990–1994), 352
    country reports on (2000–2004), 458, 482
    sanctions against, 51
    See also Yugoslavia
Seselj, Vojislav, 352
Shabab al-Nafer al-Islami, 344–345
Sha'ban, Muhammad Salah, 772
Shah, Manzoor Hussain, 851
Shah, Thomas, 415
Shah, Wail Khan Amin, 30, 33, 384
Shahid, Ibn al-, 167
Shai-i-Kot valley, Afghanistan, 136
Shanghai Cooperation Organization (SCO), 478, 546, 554, 557, 673
Shaqaqi, Fathi, 87, 381, 465
Shara', Farouk al-, 106
Sharif, Nawaz, 183
Sharif, Safwat, 747
Sharif, Shabaz, 183
Sharki Turkestan Azatlik Tahkilati, 475
SHAT (East Turkestan Liberation Organization), 475
Shatsky, Keren, 499
Shaykh, Shaykh Abd al-Aziz Al al-, 680–681
Sheik, Ahmed Omar, 175
Sheikhattar, Hussein, 321
Shelby, Richard, 633, 634
Shevardnadze, Eduard
    assassination attempts on, 375, 405, 420
    Zviadists and, 201, 420, 768–769
Shibata, Yasuhiro, 93, 267
Shigenobu, Fusako, 180, 336, 454
Shihi, Marwan Al-, 497
Shikhattar, Hussein, 64
Shingenobu, Fusako, 105
Shining Path or Sendero Luminoso (SL)
    in Bolivia, 687
    chronology of incidents (1988–1989), 738, 739
    chronology of incidents (1990–1993), 740, 742–746, 748
    chronology of incidents (1994–1997), 750, 754, 759, 766
    in Colombia, 254, 310
    narcoterrorism and, 117
    in Peru (*See* Peru, country reports on)
    profile of, 196–197
Shirazi, Ali Sayyad, 78
Shirosaki, Tsutomu
    extradition, trial, and conviction of, 30, 33, 399, 402
    in Indonesia, 230
    Japanese Red Army and, 180
Shuli, Mahmud al-, 466
Siddiqui, Maulana Habibur Rehman, 70
Sierra Leone
    chronology of incidents (1995), 753, 754
    chronology of incidents (1998–1999), 774–777, 781–782, 784
    chronology of incidents (2000), 787–789
    country reports on (1990–1994), 359
    country reports on (1995–1999), 371, 416, 431
    country reports on (2000–2004), 451, 539
Sikh Terrorism (organization), 197
Sikh Youth Federation, 217–218
Simon, James, 633
Simon Bolivar Guerilla Coordinator (CGSB)
    chronology of incidents (1992), 746
    chronology of incidents (1997), 764
    in Colombia (1985–1989), 236, 253–254
    in Colombia (1990–1994), 329, 340
Simon Bolivar Guerrilla Commando, 738
Singapore
    9/11 response, 476
    chronology of incidents (1991), 743
    country reports on (1985–1989), 219
    country reports on (1990–1994), 320
    country reports on (2000–2004), 476–477, 509, 550–551, 660
Singh, Manjit, 336
Singh, Mithileshwar, 252
Singh Bagga, Harkirat, 258
Singh Longowal, Harchand, 218
Sinn Fein
    Cuba and, 58
    peace talks and, 408–409, 424
    Red Hand Defenders and, 193
    RIRA and, 192

Note: Pages 1 to 535 can be found in volume 1; pages 536 to 1019 are in volume 2.

UVF attack on, 750
    See also Irish Republican Army (IRA); Republican Sinn Fein
Sipah-i-Sahaba Pakistan (SSP), 183, 197, 755
Sipahioglu, Omer, 751
Sison, Jose Maria, 112, 170, 286, 509
Sisulu, Walter, 294
Sivaram, Sharmaretnam, 854
SL. *See* Shining Path
SLA (South Lebanon Army), 333, 345
SLA (Sudan Liberation Army), 829, 837
Sledd, Antonio J., 499
Slovakia, 566
Slovenia, 566–567, 670
Smith, Brian Thomas, 499
Smith, Walter Bedell, 619
Snodgrass, Deborah Lea, 499
Sobero, Guillermo, 161, 469, 476
Social Resistance (organization), 260
Socialist-Nationalist Front, 263
Sodirov, Bahrom, 407, 762, 763, 767
Sodirov, Rezvon, 407, 763
Sohl, Edward, 223, 735
Soldiers of the Right, 281, 740
Soliman, Mohammed Ali Aboul-Ezz al-Mahdi Ibrahim, 534
Somali Islamic Union, 99
Somali National Alliance, 99
Somalia
    chronology of incidents (1995–1998), 754, 760, 768, 769
    chronology of incidents (2001–2004), 794, 797, 812, 815, 822
    country reports on (1990–1994), 298
    country reports on (1995–1999), 371, 400, 417
    country reports on (2000–2004), 451, 470–471, 501, 539, 654
    Sudan and, 99
Sonnen, Grenn (aka Renee Jean Anthony), 853
Sontag, Camille, 734
Sota, Larua, 754
Soto Vargas, Justino, 463
South Africa
    9/11 response, 471
    chronology of incidents (1994), 751
    chronology of incidents (1997–2000), 762, 773, 775, 791
    country reports on (1985–1989), 219, 231, 247, 248, 270–271, 294–295

    country reports on (1990–1994), 299, 359
    country reports on (1995–1999), 416, 431
    country reports on (2000–2004), 452, 471, 501, 539, 654–655
    regional patterns (1995–1999), 400
    RENAMO and, 247, 248
    sanctions against, 41
South African Native National Congress, 162
South Asia
    regional patterns before 1999 (*See* Asia)
    regional patterns (1999–2001), 432, 452, 471
    regional patterns (2002–2004), 502, 540, 682–683
    See also Asia; *specific countries*
South Asian Association for Regional Cooperation (SAARC), 150
South Korea (Republic of Korea)
    9/11 response, 474
    chronology of incidents (1986), 735
    country reports on (1985–1989), 230, 245, 293
    country reports on (1990–1994), 301
    North Korea and, 93, 94–95
South Lebanon Army (SLA), 333, 345
South Pacific Forum, 266
South-West Africa People's Organization (SWAPO), 220, 248, 299
South Yemen (People's Democratic Republic of Yemen), 96–97, 156, 316. *See also* Yemen
Southeast Asia. *See* East Asia
Southeast Asian Regional Center for Counterterrorism (SEARCCT), 548, 659
Southeast European Cooperation Initiative (SECI), 662
Southeast European Cooperative Initiative, 566
Soviet Union and Soviet bloc
    Afghanistan and, 53–54
    attacks on diplomats in Lebanon (1985), 213
    Cold War and, 52
    country reports on (1990–1994), 306, 324–325
    hijackings in, 98
    regional patterns (1985–1989), 289–290
    sanctions against, 51
    as state sponsor of terrorism, 97–98
    See also Former Soviet Union; Russia
Spain
    9/11 response, 485–486
    chronology of incidents (1980–1984), 730
    chronology of incidents (1985–1989), 731, 732, 734, 737, 739

Spain *(continued)*
    chronology of incidents (1991–1992), 743, 746
    chronology of incidents (1995–1996), 755, 757, 760
    chronology of incidents (1999–2000), 780, 785, 792
    chronology of incidents (2001–2002), 797, 798, 802
    chronology of incidents (2004), 820, 836
    chronology of incidents (2005), 852, 854, 855, 857
    country reports on (1985–1989), 215, 228, 238–239, 262–263, 286–287
    country reports on (1990–1994), 306–307, 325, 338, 351, 363
    country reports on (1995–1999), 376, 390, 407, 423, 441
    country reports on (2000–2004), 460–461, 485–486, 521–522, 567, 670–671
    prosecutions in, 29, 30
    train bombings in, 140
Special Purpose Islamic Regiment (SPIR), 197, 513, 555
SPIR (Special Purpose Islamic Regiment), 197, 513, 555
SPLA. *See* Sudanese People's Liberation Army
Squads of the New Disciples of Martyr Rahya Ayyash, 758
SRG (Strategic Resources Group), 622
Sri Lanka
    9/11 response, 473
    chronology of incidents (1986), 734
    chronology of incidents (1991–1994), 743, 751
    chronology of incidents (1996–1998), 758, 760, 765–766, 773
    chronology of incidents (2000–2001), 791, 797
    chronology of incidents (2003–2005), 814, 849, 852–854, 856, 858
    country reports on (1985–1989), 218, 229, 245, 269, 293
    country reports on (1990–1994), 301, 320, 337, 350, 361
    country reports on (1995–1999), 374, 386, 403, 419, 433
    country reports on (2000–2004), 453, 473, 504, 542, 685–686

Note: Pages 1 to 535 can be found in volume 1; pages 536 to 1019 are in volume 2.

SSNP (Syrian Social Nationalist Party), 104, 105
SSP (Sipah-i-Sahaba Pakistan), 183, 197, 755
Stacey, Bradley Richard, 295
Stansell, Keith, 536, 807
Starger, Colin Patrick, 748
Starovoytova, Galina, 420
Starr, Nicholas, 30, 399
State Department. *See* U.S. Department of State
Steen, Alann, 745
Stethem, Robert, 265, 283, 739
Stewart, Michael, 732
Stewart, Ronald Odell, 317, 743
Strategic Resources Group (SRG), 622
Struebig, Heinrich, 333–334, 338
Students of Yahya Ayyash, 758
Sudan
    air strike against pharmaceutical plant, 135
    bin Laden and, 55
    chronology of incidents (1970s), 728
    chronology of incidents (1986–1988), 734, 738
    chronology of incidents (1996–1999), 760, 761, 770, 778
    chronology of incidents (2000–2001), 785, 793
    chronology of incidents (2004), 829, 836, 837, 848, 849
    counterterrorism conference in, 103
    country reports on (1985–1989), 295
    country reports on (1990–1994), 299, 318, 335
    country reports on (2000–2004), 604
    Iran and, 66, 67
    Libya and, 82, 83
    military strikes against (1998), 4
    sanctions against, 51, 100, 102
    as state sponsor of terrorism, 19, 98–103
Sudan Liberation Army (SLA), 829, 837
Sudanese People's Liberation Army (SPLA)
    chronology of incidents (1996), 760
    chronology of incidents (1996–1998), 760, 770
    chronology of incidents (1999–2000), 778, 785
    Libya and, 82
Sudanese Revolutionary Committee, 82, 83
Sufaat, Yazid, 548
Suhayl, Shaykh Talib Ali al-, 751
Suleiman, Ibrahim Ahmad, 31, 415
Supreme Council for the Islamic Revolution in Iraq (SCIRI), 676
Sutherland, Thomas, 61, 233, 252, 731, 745
SWAPO (South-West Africa People's Organization), 220, 248, 299

Swedan, Sheikh Ahmed Salim, 31
Sweden
  chronology of incidents (1986–1989), 733, 740
  country reports on (1985–1989), 229, 287
  country reports on (1990–1994), 307, 325
  country reports on (1995–1999), 407
  country reports on (2000–2004), 567
Swenchonis, Gary Graham, 450
Switzerland
  chronology of incidents (1987), 736
  chronology of incidents (1990), 741
  chronology of incidents (1995), 756
  chronology of incidents (1999), 777
  chronology of incidents (2001), 792
  country reports on (1985–1989), 241, 263, 287–288
  country reports on (1990–1994), 307–308
  country reports on (1995–1999), 441
Syria
  Bremer Commission on, 637
  chronology of incidents (1986), 733
  country reports on (1985–1989), 214, 222, 225, 232
  country reports on (1990–1994), 342
  country reports on (2000–2004), 523, 604
  criticisms of, 17
  Iraq and, 73
  money laundering in, 125
  sanctions against, 23, 51
  as state sponsor of terrorism, 19, 103–110
Syrian Social Nationalist Party (SSNP), 104, 105

T

Ta Mok, 181, 434
Tagle, Carmen, 739
Taha Musa, Rifa'i, 173
Taibah International (Bosnia), 113
Taiwan
  9/11 response, 477
  country reports on (1985–1989), 269
  country reports on (2000–2004), 477, 509–510, 551, 660–661
Tajikistan
  9/11 response, 480
  chronology of incidents (1996), 759, 760, 762
  chronology of incidents (1997), 762, 763, 765, 767
  chronology of incidents (1998), 772
  chronology of incidents (2000–2001), 787, 790, 796
  country reports on (1995–1999), 390, 407, 421, 437
  country reports on (2000–2004), 457, 480, 514–515, 556, 671
TAK (Kurdistan Liberation Hawks), 671
Takfir wa al-Hijra, 446, 467, 729
Taliban
  in Afghanistan (1995–1999), 372, 401, 418, 432, 471
  in Afghanistan (2000–2004), 452, 471, 502, 540
  assets frozen against, 483
  chronology of incidents (2004), 819, 832, 837, 841, 843
  chronology of incidents (2005), 854
  Lashkar i Jhangvi and, 183
  in Pakistan, 503, 685
  Pakistan and, 138, 432
  Powell on, 5
  sanctions against, 35–36
  U.S. military attack on, 9, 18, 135–138
Taliban Jaish-e-Muslimeen, 840, 843
Talkhigov, Zaurbek, 555
Taloh-Meyaw, Saarli, 456
Tamil Eelam Army, 229
Tamil Tigers. *See* Liberation Tigers of Tamil Eelam (LTTE) or Tamil Tigers
Tanaka, Yoshimi, 94–95, 454
Tanzania
  chronology of incidents (1998), 772
  chronology of incidents (2001), 793
  country reports on (1985–1989), 295
  country reports on (1995–1999), 417
  country reports on (2000–2004), 502, 539, 655
  embassy bombings in, 4, 7, 31, 32, 55, 135, 414–415, 772
  Libya and, 82
Tanzim Qa'idat al-Jihad fi Bilad al-Rafidayn (QJBR) (Al-Zarqawi Network or al-Qaeda in Iraq)
  chronology of incidents (2004), 843, 847
  in Iraq, 137, 138–140
  profile of, 198
  terrorist designation, 113
  See also Jama'at al-Tawhid wa'al-Jihad (JTJ)
Tarantelli, Enzo, 215, 731
Tarasouleas, Panaylotis, 738
Tawhid Islamic Brigades, 841
Taylor, Charles, 195

Taylor, Francis X., 5-9, 143
Taylor, Maxwell, 621-622
TCG (Tunisian Combatant Group), 198-199
Teas, Martha, 536
Technical Support Working Group (TSWG), 26
Tehrik-i-Jihad, 784
Teleldin, Carlos, 378, 392
Tenenoff, Rick, 747
Tenet, George, 633
Ternera, Josu (Jose Urruticoechea), 284, 303
Terre Lilure (TL), 198, 262, 287, 737
Terrorism Prevention Branch of UNODC (TPB), 114
Terrorist Finance Working Group (TFWG), 122
Terrorist Threat Integration Center (TTIC)
    Ambassador Black on, 594-596
    Brennan on, 593-594, 709-710
    creation of, 719
    Gilmore Commission on, 645
    Johnson (Larry C.) on, 714
    responsibilities and methods, 602, 607-613
TFWG (Terrorist Finance Working Group), 122
Thailand
    9/11 response, 477
    chronology of incidents (1990), 740
    chronology of incidents (1999-2002), 783, 792, 801
    chronology of incidents (2004), 821, 844, 846
    chronology of incidents (2005), 852, 853, 856
    country reports on (1985-1989), 230, 269
    country reports on (1990-1994), 337, 361
    country reports on (1995-1999), 403-404, 419, 435
    country reports on (2000-2004), 456, 477, 510, 551, 661
Thaler, Rachel Donna, 499
Thatcher, Margaret, 261
Thomas Katari Communal Army (ECTK), 328
Tietmeyer, Hans, 265, 283
TIKKO (Turkish Workers and Peasants Liberation Army), 288, 326
Tilao, Aldam (aka Abu Sabaya), 508, 509
Tilao, Satrap, 659-660
Tirofijo (aka Manuel Marulanda), 193
Tiruchelvam, Neelan, 433
TISA (Traditional Islamic State of Afghanistan), 502

Note: Pages 1 to 535 can be found in volume 1; pages 536 to 1019 are in volume 2.

TISA (Transitional State of Afghanistan), 137
Tita, Bertin Joseph, 536
Titley, Gary, 816
TKEP/L (Turkish Communist Laborers' Party/Leninist), 408
TL (Terre Lilure), 198, 262, 287, 737
Tlays, Hussein, 397
TNCC (Transnational Crime Center), 657
The TOGETHER Center, 566
Togo, 359
Tohami, Sermin (aka Tahome Urong), 809
Tokcan, Muhammed, 486
Top, Noording Mohammad, 658
Tora Bora, Afghanistan, 136
Toto (aka Ismael Acmad), 809
Tower, John, 629
Townsend, Frances, 123
TPB (Terrorism Prevention Branch of UNODC), 114
Trabelsi, Nizar, 482, 517, 559, 663
Tracy, Edward, 61, 276, 735, 744
Traditional Islamic State of Afghanistan (TISA), 502
Transitional State of Afghanistan (TISA), 137
Transnational Crime Center (TNCC), 657
Transport Security Cooperation Group (TSCG), 116
Transportation Security Administration (TSA), 639
Treasury, U.S. *See* U.S. Department of the Treasury
Treasury Dept. (Office of Foreign Assets Control (OFAC)), 36-37, 115
Trevi Group, 261, 284
Trinidad, Simon (aka Juvenal Ovidio Ricardo Palmera), 193, 689, 691
Trinidad and Tobago, 85, 313
Triplett, Andrew, 450
Trubnikov, Vyacheslav, 513, 555
True IRA. *See* Real Irish Republican Army (RIRA)
Truman, Harry S., 616
TSA (Transportation Security Administration), 639
TSCG (Transport Security Cooperation Group), 116
TSWG (Technical Support Working Group), 26
TTIC. *See* Terrorist Threat Integration Center
Tunisia
    9/11 response, 497
    chronology of incidents (1988), 737
    chronology of incidents (2002), 800
    country reports on (1985-1989), 235, 253
    country reports on (1990-1994), 346
    country reports on (1995-1999), 383, 397, 414, 429

country reports on (2000–2004), 497, 528–529, 575–576, 681
Tunisian Combatant Group (TCG), 198–199
Tunisian Islamic Front (FIT), 383
Tupac Amaru Revolutionary Movement. *See* MRTA
Tupac Katari Guerilla Army (EGTK), 199, 328, 340
Tupamaro Revolutionary Movement, 782
Tupamaros, 728
Turabi, Hassan, 99
Turkey
   anti-Rushdie movement in, 66
   Brennan on, 700
   chronology of incidents (1986), 734, 735
   chronology of incidents (1989), 740
   chronology of incidents (1990–1994), 742–748, 750–752
   chronology of incidents (1995–1996), 754–758, 761
   chronology of incidents (1997–1998), 766, 768, 769, 771
   chronology of incidents (2001), 793–794, 798
   chronology of incidents (2002), 801, 805
   chronology of incidents (2003), 807, 809–812
   chronology of incidents (2004), 827, 831, 835, 843
   chronology of incidents (2005), 857
   country reports on (1985–1989), 228, 243, 263–264, 288
   country reports on (1990–1994), 308, 325–326, 339, 351, 363
   country reports on (1995–1999), 376–377, 390–391, 408, 423–424, 441–442
   country reports on (2000–2004), 461–462, 486–487, 522, 567–568, 671–672
   Iran-sponsored terrorism in, 65–69
   sanctions against, 51
   Syria and, 104–108
Turki, Hassan Abdullah Hersi al-, 113
Turkish Communist Laborers' Party/Leninist (TKEP/L), 408
Turkish Communist Party, 264
Turkish Communist Party/Marxist Leninist, 461
Turkish Hizballah, 199–200, 461–462, 486
Turkish Islamic Jihad, 65, 744, 760
Turkish Workers and Peasants Liberation Army (TIKKO), 288, 326
Turkmenistan, 556–557, 672
Turner, Jesse, 744

U

UAE. *See* United Arab Emirates
UCK (National Liberation Army or NLA), 482
UDA (Ulster Defense Association), 193, 200, 289, 673
UDF (Union of Democratic Forces), 416, 768
UFF (Ulster Freedom Fighters), 193, 200
Uganda
   9/11 response, 471
   chronology of incidents (1970s), 729
   chronology of incidents (1994–1997), 751, 761, 767
   chronology of incidents (1998–1999), 769, 771, 775, 777–779
   chronology of incidents (2000–2002), 786, 790, 797, 800
   country reports on (1990–1994), 359
   country reports on (1995–1999), 384, 400, 417, 431
   country reports on (2000–2004), 452, 471, 502, 539–540, 655
   Sudan and, 103
Uganda National Rescue Front II, 417
UK. *See* United Kingdom
Ukraine
   chronology of incidents (2004), 836
   country reports on (1995–1999), 377
   country reports on (2000–2004), 515, 557, 672
   sanctions against, 51
Ukrainian People's Party (PUP), 836
ULFA. *See* United Liberation Front of Assam
ULIMO-K and ULIMO-J, 780
Ulster Defense Association (UDA), 193, 200, 289, 673
Ulster Freedom Fighters (UFF), 193, 200
Ulster Volunteer Force (UVF), 185, 200, 673, 750
Umar al-Mukhtar Forces, 465
Umari, Muhammad al-. *See* Ibrahim, Abu
Umm al-Qura, 545, 657
U.N. Counterterrorism Committee (CTC), 117, 146
U.N. Food and Agriculture Organization (FAO), 78
U.N. Global Programme Against Money Laundering (GPML), 117
U.N. Office of Drug Control, 117
U.N. Security Council
   9/11 response (resolutions 1368 and 1373), 146–148
   counterterrorism resolution, 6

U.N. Security Council *(continued)*
  on freezing of assets, 22
  Iraq resolutions, 75, 76
  Libya resolutions, 86–88, 90
  resolutions on terrorism (1989–2005), 149–150
  on self-defense, 8
  Sudan resolutions, 100, 101
  U.S.-EU Declaration and resolutions of, 114
  Wayne testimony on role of, 120
UNAVEM (United Nations Angola Verification Mission), 371
UNESCO, 87
Unified Nasserite Organizations, 83
UNIFIL (U.N. Interim Force in Lebanon), 61
Union of Democratic Forces (UDF), 416, 768
UNITA (National Union for the Total Independence of Angola)
  in Angola (1985–1989), 220, 298
  in Angola (1990–1994), 335
  in Angola (1995–1999), 415, 430–431
  in Angola (2000–2004), 451, 470, 500
  chronology of incidents (1994–1995), 752, 756
  chronology of incidents (1998), 770, 774, 775
  chronology of incidents (1999), 775, 776, 780
  chronology of incidents (2000), 785, 789–790
  chronology of incidents (2001), 793, 795
  in Namibia (2000–2004), 451
United Arab Emirates (UAE)
  chronology of incidents (1989), 739
  country reports on (2000–2004), 497, 529, 576, 681–682
  terrorism financing and, 124
United Jihad Council, 817
United Kingdom (UK)
  9/11 response, 487
  al-Qaeda arrests in, 140
  chronology of incidents (1986–1989), 734, 738, 739
  chronology of incidents (1990–1994), 742, 743, 750, 752
  chronology of incidents (1995–1999), 753, 758, 759, 777, 780
  chronology of incidents (2002–2005), 801, 807, 816–817, 856, 857
  country reports on (1985–1989), 238, 264, 288–289

Note: Pages 1 to 535 can be found in volume 1; pages 536 to 1019 are in volume 2.

  country reports on (1990–1994), 308–309, 326–327, 339, 351–352, 363–364
  country reports on (1995–1999), 377, 391, 408–409, 424, 442
  country reports on (2000–2004), 462, 487, 522–523, 568–569, 672–673
  Libyan attacks on, 83, 84
  Syrian attacks, 103, 104
  See also Northern Ireland; Scotland
United Liberation Front of Assam (ULFA)
  chronology of incidents (1991), 743
  chronology of incidents (1999), 780
  chronology of incidents (2004), 836
  chronology of incidents (2005), 853, 855, 857
  in India (1990–1994), 300, 319, 336
  profile of, 200–201
United Liberation Movement for Democracy, 431
United National Liberation Front (UNLF), 854
United Nations (U.N.)
  9/11 response, 146–148
  attacks on, in Africa, 775, 787, 789
  attacks on, in Asia, 781
  attacks on, in Iraq, 75, 76
  conventions on terrorism, 148–149
  See also entries beginning with U.N.
United Organization of the Halabjah Martyrs, 274
United People's Front. *See* Communist Party of Nepal (Maoist)/United People's Front
United Popular Action Movement, 747
United Self-Defense Forces of Columbia (AUC)
  chronology of incidents (2005), 857
  in Colombia, 489, 532, 579, 689–690
  in Nicaragua, 530
  profile of, 201
  terrorist designation, 157, 489
  in Venezuela, 695
United Services Organization (USO), 737
United States
  chronology of incidents (1961), 728
  chronology of incidents (1970s), 729
  chronology of incidents (1993), 747
  chronology of incidents (1997), 762, 764
  chronology of incidents (2005), 854
  in country reports (1985–1989), 210, 211–212, 223–224, 231–232, 249, 272
  country reports on (1985–1989), 281–282
  in country reports (1990–1994), 317–318, 334, 347, 358

Index **1077**

in country reports (1995–1999), 370, 383–384, 398, 399, 414–415, 429–430
country reports on (1995–1999), 448
in country reports (2000–2004), 450, 469, 499, 536–537
September 11 attacks, 468–469, 798
UNLF (United National Liberation Front), 854
UNODC (U.N. Office on Drugs and Crime), 114
UNSCOM (United Nations Special Commission), 77
Urduni, Abu Hafs al-, 178
Uribe, Alvaro, 532
URNG (Guatemalan National Revolutionary Unit), 329, 365, 378–379, 393
Urong, Tahome (aka Sermin Tohami), 809
Urruticoechea, Jose (aka Josu Ternera), 284, 303
Uruguay
   9/11 response, 491–492
   chronology of incidents (1970s), 728
   country reports on (1990–1994), 366
   country reports on (2000–2004), 491–492, 534–535, 583, 694–695
U.S. Central Command (CENTCOM), 135
U.S. Department of Health and Human Services (DHHS), 642, 643
U.S. Department of Homeland Security (DHS)
   9/11 Commission on, 638–639
   Container Security Initiative, 660–661
   creation of, 24–25
   FTO list and, 155, 157
   Gilmore Commission on, 641, 642, 645
   Intelligence Committee recommendations on, 643–644
   See also Office of Homeland Security
U.S. Department of State
   coordination of international efforts by, 12
   Coordinator for Counterterrorism (S/CT), 607–613
   counterterrorism programs, 12–16, 25–26
   country reports by, 205–206
   Fifth Counterterrorism Conference for Eurasian States (2003), 552
   FTO list, 154–159
   hearing on Annual Report on Terrorism, 707–716
   Intelligence Committee recommendations on, 638
   and international Coalition, 6
   Pan-Sahel Initiative (PSI), 653
   press conference with NCTC (2005), 697–707
   rewards program, 23–24
   role of, 25
   on sanctions, 41
   Saudi Arabia and, 123
   terrorist financing and, 111, 119, 126
U.S. Department of the Treasury
   FTO list and, 155, 157
   Office of Foreign Assets (OFAC), 115
   terrorist financing and, 7, 119
U.S.-EU Troika, 115
US-Canada Bilateral Consultative Group on Counterterrorism Cooperation (BCG), 498, 535, 583, 688
USAID (U.S. Agency for International Development)
   attacks on, in Latin America, 255, 256, 759, 800–801
   attacks on, in Middle East, 805
   role of, 15, 16
Usama Kassass Organization, 382
Usd Allah (Lions of God), 833
Usmanov, Alisher, 669
USO (United Services Organization), 737
UVF (Ulster Volunteer Force), 185, 200, 673, 750
Uzbekistan
   9/11 response, 480
   Brennan on, 700
   chronology of incidents (2004), 834
   country reports on (1995–1999), 437–438
   country reports on (2000–2004), 457, 480–481, 515–516, 557–558, 673

V

Vacek, Elizabeth, 750
Vacek, Russell, 750
Vaezi, Mahmoud, 68
Valbuena, Humberto (aka Yerbas), 689
Van Dyke, Elizabeth, 730
Van Dyke, Timothy, 370, 392
Van Landingham, Jacqueline Keys, 370
Vargas Rueda, Nelson, 580
Vasat, 408
Venezuela
   Ambassador Black on, 591–592
   assessment of, 19
   chronology of incidents (1996), 758, 759, 761
   chronology of incidents (1997–1998), 763–766, 770, 771
   chronology of incidents (1999), 776, 778, 779, 781, 782
   chronology of incidents (2002–2003), 799, 807–808, 810

Venezuela *(continued)*
    chronology of incidents (2004), 824, 834–835, 839, 840
    country reports on (1985–1989), 257
    country reports on (2000–2004), 492, 535, 583–584, 695–696
Vernardos, Anastasios, 738
Vieira de Mello, Sergio, 198, 536
Vietnam, Social Republic of, 51, 60, 404
Vilnius Group, 481
Von Bories, Monica, 687

W

Wachsman, Nachshon, 358, 368
WAD (Afghan Ministry of State Security)
    in Afghanistan (1985–1989), 290
    in Afghanistan (1990–1994), 299
    chronology of incidents (1987), 736
    in Pakistan (1985–1989), 244, 267, 292
    terrorist sponsorship and, 53–54
Wade, Abdoulaye, 470
Waite, Terry, 233, 327, 745
Waldo (aka Jose Zabaleta-Elosegui), 302–303
Walid, Abu al-, 178
Walker, John, 212
Walton, Charles, 349
Waqas Islamic Brigade, 829
Waring, Robert, 369, 382
Warriors of the Boer Nation, 501
Washinawatok, Ingrid, 430
Watson, Charles M., 749
Wayne, E. Anthony, 118–126
Wazir, Khalil al (Abu Jihad), 251, 253, 737
Weather Underground, 729
Webster, David, 295, 299
Webster, Steven, 499
Weinberger, Caspar, 230
Weinrich, Johannes, 375
Weir, Benjamin, 212
Welsh, Steve, 370, 392
West Bank. *See* Israel and occupied territories
West Berlin, 733–734
West Germany. *See* Germany
Western Europe
    chronology of incidents (1993), 748, 749
    Middle Eastern spillover into (1985-1989), 207–211, 222–223, 231–233, 249–250, 257, 273, 281
    regional patterns (1985–1989), 214, 227, 237–238, 257, 281
    regional patterns (1990–1991), 301–302, 320–321
    regional patterns after 1991 (*See under* Europe)
    See also Europe; *specific countries*
Western Hemisphere overviews (2000–2004), 530–531, 577–578, 686–687. *See also* Latin America; North America
Western Nongovernmental Organization, 349
White Legion, 763
White Liberation Army, 299
Wibberley, Craig Bryan, 450
Wijeratne, Ranjan, 320
Willem Onde Group, 792
Williams, Stephen E., 30, 399
Winer, Jonathan, 128
Witherall, Denise, 499
Wolfowitz, Paul D., 537
Woolsey, James, 22
Working Group on Counterterrorism, 555
Working Group on Counterterrorism and Law-Enforcement Cooperation, 541
World Bank, 129
World Food Program (WFP)
    chronology of incidents (1998), 770, 771, 775
    chronology of incidents (1999), 781
    chronology of incidents (2001), 794, 796
World Health Organization, 77
World Islamic Front for Jihad Against the Jews and Crusaders, 55, 164, 427
Worldwide Fund for Nature, 757
Wormsley, Kristen, 499
WPF. *See* World Food Program
Wright, Billy "King Rat," 409
Wybran, Joseph, 281, 321

X

Xinjiang Province, China, 172

Y

Yandarbiyev, Zelimkhan, 555
Yap, Debora, 161, 508
Yarmuk, 854
Yashai, Shoshana Ben, 469, 798
Yassin, Ahmad, 332, 821

Note: Pages 1 to 535 can be found in volume 1; pages 536 to 1019 are in volume 2.

Yassin, Ali Mohamed Osman, 102
Yassin, Sheik Ahmed, 167
Yassine, Salah Abdul Karim, 463
Yazdi, Ayatollah, 71
Yazidi, Khalid al-Nabi al-, 177
Yemen
   9/11 response, 497
   chronology of incidents (1991–1992), 742, 746
   chronology of incidents (1996–1997), 758, 761, 764–768
   chronology of incidents (1998), 768–772, 774–775
   chronology of incidents (1999), 776, 781–784
   chronology of incidents (2000), 785, 786, 788, 790, 791
   chronology of incidents (2001), 792, 796, 797
   chronology of incidents (2002), 804, 806
   country reports on (1990–1994), 316–317, 334, 346–347, 357–358
   country reports on (1995–1999), 397–398, 414, 429, 447–448
   country reports on (2000–2004), 468, 497–498, 529–530, 576–577, 682
   Sudan and, 102
   terrorism financing and, 124
   USS Cole bombing, 450, 468
   See also North Yemen (Yemen Arab Republic); South Yemen (People's Democratic Republic of Yemen)
Yemeni Islamic Jihad, 358
Yerbas (aka Humberto Valbuena), 689
Yilmaz, Kani (aka Faisal Dunlayiei), 377, 406
Yodo-go, 94–95
Yokota, Megumi, 96
Yoldashev, Tohir, 179
Young, Jacob, 499
Younis, Bahij, 375
Yousef, Ramzi Ahmed
   arrest of, 11, 24, 370
   conviction of, 30, 31, 384, 399
   extradition of, 33, 370, 373
   and terrorist organizations, 21
Yugoslavia and Former Yugoslavia
   9/11 response, 487–488
   chronology of incidents (1993), 747
   chronology of incidents (2000), 785, 786, 788
   country reports on (1985–1989), 243–244, 265–266, 289
   country reports on (1990–1994), 309, 327, 339, 352, 364
   country reports on (2000–2004), 458, 487–488
   sanctions against, 40, 41
   as state sponsor of terrorism, 97
   See also Bosnia and Herzegovina; Croatia; Macedonia; Serbia and Montenegro; Slovenia
Yuldashev, Tohir, 457
Yunos, Saifullah (aka Muklis Yunos), 549

Z

Zabaleta-Elosegui, Jose (aka Waldo), 302–303
Zaire, 82. *See also* Congo, Democratic Republic of (former Zaire)
Zambia, 247, 295, 431, 778
Zapatista National Liberation Army (EZLN), 393
Zarate Willka Armed Liberation Forces (FAL)
   in Bolivia, 277, 328, 340
   chronology of incidents (1989), 739
   profile of, 166
   See also Pablo Zarate Wilca National Indigenous Force
Zarkowsky, Eli, 537
Zarkowsky, Goldy, 537
Zarqawi, Abu Mus'ab al-
   activities of, 79
   al-Qaeda and, 164
   Ambassador Black on, 590
   bin Laden and, 140
   decapitation incident and, 823
   Iraq and, 676
   Jordan and, 678
   See also Jama'at al-Tawhid wa'al-Jihad (JTJ); Tanzim Qa'idat al-Jihad fi Bilad al-Rafidayn (QJBR)
Zawahiri, Ayman al-, 24, 163
Zelikov, Philip, 697–709
Zimbabwe, 247, 295, 318, 737
Zimmerman, Ernst, 730
Zindani, Shayk 'Abd al-Majid al-, 113, 682
Zomar, Abdel Osama al-, 260, 261
Zomi Revolutionary Army (ZRA), 854
Zouabri, Antar, 426–427, 464, 493
ZRA (Zomi Revolutionary Army), 854
Zubaydah, Abu, 21, 179, 483
Zukhurov, Saidamir, 763
Zurate, Juan, 128
Zviadists, 201, 420
Zyazikov, Murat, 670